POP

D0512535

Philippa had been beguiled by the romance of France and Francis Balfour. How could she have been so foolish as to have fallen in love with a man who only saw her as a means to an end . . .?

Books you will enjoy
by JACQUELINE GILBERT

A HOUSE CALLED BELLEVIGNE

Just at the right moment, Troy Maitland's grandmother had left her a house in France—but when she went to Bellevigne to take over she received an unpleasant surprise—for her grandmother, it seemed, had got things wrong, and the house in question belonged not to her but to Lucien Charon, and Troy had no claim at all. So what did she do now?

THE CHEQUERED SILENCE

Five years ago, for what she had considered the best of reasons, Leah had broken off her relationship with Max Calvert, without ever explaining. Not unnaturally he had been bitterly resentful. Now they had met up again, in very different circumstances. Would Leah be able to pick up the threads again, or was Max lost to her forever?

CAPRICORN MAN

Nicola had always fought with her stepcousin, Michael, as a child. But she was twenty-eight now, and she found that living with him brought a deeper dimension to their relationship . . .

POPPY GIRL

BY

JACQUELINE GILBERT

MILLS & BOON LIMITED
15–16 BROOK'S MEWS
LONDON W1A 1DR

All the characters in this book have no existence outside the imagination of the Author, and have no relation whatsoever to anyone bearing the same name or names. They are not even distantly inspired by any individual known or unknown to the Author, and all the incidents are pure invention.

The text of this publication or any part thereof may not be reproduced or transmitted in any form or by any means, electronic or mechanical, including photocopying, recording, storage in an information retrieval system, or otherwise, without the written permission of the publisher.

This book is sold subject to the condition that it shall not, by way of trade or otherwise, be lent, resold, hired out or otherwise circulated without the prior consent of the publisher in any form of binding or cover other than that in which it is published and without a similar condition including this condition being imposed on the subsequent purchaser.

First published in Great Britain 1986
by Mills & Boon Limited

© Jacqueline Gilbert 1986

Australian copyright 1986
Philippine copyright 1986
This edition 1986

ISBN 0 263 75381 6

Set in Monophoto Times 11 on 11 pt.
01-0686 – 49614

Printed and bound in Great Britain by
Collins, Glasgow

For
Pat and Peter
fellow francophiles
and adopted Cumbrians

CHAPTER ONE

ON an afternoon in early May the city of Orange, in that region of France known as Provence, was enjoying blue skies and a blazing sun. The open-air Roman theatre, always a focal point for visitors, had just re-opened after lunch and a small group of English tourists were gathered round the talking-guide machine, digging into their pockets and handbags in search of the required coins—two francs—to make the machine work.

Philippa Ingram, sitting half-way back in the auditorium, looked down on them, her attention caught by their raised voices. Elbows resting on the stone step behind her, bare legs and sandalled feet outstretched for coolness, she listened to the frustrated voices and then tried to block them out. It was a lovely day and the sun was making her feel lazy. She could feel it burning her bare arms and legs and she wafted the pages of the guide book she was reading back and forth to create a breeze.

As Philippa looked round the theatre, her interest quickening, it was easy to allow a sense of history to take over. For the huge, austere stonework backing the stage was incredibly awe-inspiring, and the size of the whole place made her feel extremely small and insignificant.

Unfortunately, history was being upstaged by her fellow-countrymen. The francs needed to work the machine, which provided a short history of the theatre available in four languages, were proving elusive. Philippa's eyes returned unwillingly to the group. Really, she thought in mild exasperation, among six people, surely they could come up with a couple of francs! Almost on the thought, one was found and as the search continued Philippa burrowed into her canvas shoulder bag, deciding she was not going to have any peace and quiet until the other was produced. She began to climb down the steep steps that made up the seating arrangements of the theatre, her coming noticed, faces turning expectantly. One of the group, a man wearing a bright check shirt, had already shown an interest in Philippa's solitary state and how darted towards her. Before he could say anything, she held out the coin and to avoid encouragement adopted a cool, practical manner, saying,

'I have a franc here, if it helps.'

Check shirt beamed up at her. 'That's kind of you. Would you like to join us? It should be interesting.'

Philippa dropped the coin into his open palm. 'Thanks, but I'm getting all I need from this,' and she held up the guide book still in her hand. She smiled to the group in general and made her way back up the steps, very conscious of his eyes still on her. Resuming her seat, she shielded her own from the sun and peered up at the imposing statue of the Emperor Augustus who had originally built the theatre in 14 B.C. Holding his general's baton, the stone figure dominated the huge interior stage wall from his arched cavity high up, centre stage.

There must have been jubilation when the archaeologists found him and pieced him together again, Philippa mused, and sensitive to atmosphere, she imagined the massive auditorium filled with ten thousand conquering Romans. Only seven thousand spectators could be accommodated now. She grinned. *Only* seven? Dear, dear!

The acoustics were supposed to be excellent, and proof was now given as audible words of disappointment began to float upwards. The guide machine, it seemed, was out of order. Philippa groaned a laugh. She could imagine the thoughts flying through Check Shirt's head at this moment, no doubt remembering her guide book. Well, he could borrow it with pleasure, she decided with mischievous amusement, but she hoped he could read French. Assistance came from an unexpected quarter.

'Can I help?' The question, coming from below, immediately arrested Philippa's attention. It came from a man who had been studying Augustus's statue and who now walked with an easy stride to the group. His voice, pleasantly friendly, held a hint of diffidence, allowing his offer to be declined without embarrassment should it not be taken up.

No fear of that, observed Philippa with amusement, as the two women in the group fought over who should explain the faulty machine. Saved by a Good Samaritan—and rather an intriguing one. She had noticed him earlier, could not help noticing him, for he was in front of her in the queue for the entrance tickets, talking in French to his companion, an attractive brunette. Her curiosity now grew as she listened to his excellent, idiomatic English.

Languages being her own line of business, Philippa was intrigued. It was not uncommon for a Frenchman to be able to speak English, but for him to be so comfortable in the language was interesting, and he certainly knew his history. He dealt briefly with the Roman occupation and was now saying, his voice a low drawl as if he found some amusement in the role he was taking, 'Plays and concerts are held here, which is good, don't you think? A pity to waste such a magnificent setting.' He bent his head towards a questioner and nodded. 'Yes, incredible, isn't it?' and all eyes turned to the interior stage wall. 'Orange is the only Roman theatre in existence with the *frons scenae* miraculously intact.' There were murmurs of appreciation from his listeners. 'The acoustics,' and here he swung round and allowed his gaze to sweep the curved auditorium, lingering momentarily on Philippa in her solitary spot half-way up, before coming back to the group, '... are excellent. You can try them out if you're feeling energetic. About forty rows to the top, I believe, but don't forget to leave one of you down here on the stage, to say something, will you?' There was a teasing note in his voice which produced chuckles from his listeners.

Philippa closed the guide book and searched the sky. There was not a cloud in sight and the blue heavens made a magnificent ceiling to the theatre. It might not be a bad idea to take her photographs now, before the peace began to fill up, she decided, and collecting her things together, she stood up. How many steps had he said? Forty? Then she had about twenty to go. Not stopping to take a breather, she arrived at the top, panting slightly, and leaned on the back stonework, arms folded on the shoulder-high retaining wall. The scene that greeted her was one of roof-tops in reds and blues and, beyond the city, distant green hills shimmered in the heat. There was a slight breeze up here and Philippa closed her eyes and lifted her face to it.

It was a vulnerable face she turned to the sky,

one which she did not often allow the world to see. A face not at first glance any way remarkable, being rather too strong on character for some who only saw the obstinate chin, the disconcerting level stare from large brown eyes, and a mobile mouth that could pull down in an uncompromising grimace of disagreement. Only her closest friends knew of her wicked sense of humour, her loyalty to those she held dear, her refreshing honesty. Philippa Ingram had led an unconventional early life and had learned in her youth to adapt to circumstances, covering up her inner feelings. She had been the practical member of her family, the job forced upon her, and she had come to believe that that was what she was, sensible and practical. It had brought some measure of personal success and an orderly existence, but a restlessness had been growing within her of late, she could not pin its cause, and no doubt there was no single reason. Perhaps she was becoming fed up with being practical and sensible.

Two things were bothering her today. The first was the date; it was the anniversary of her father's death. The second was the envelope lying in her bag. Doubts and indecisions brought their own form of vulnerability. It had been a startling and unnerving experience to receive word from Cumbria. Her thoughts over the past weeks had been turning more and more towards her father's relations and Copperthwaite in Cumbria, his birthplace. Why she should suddenly have this curiosity about the Ingrams in England after so many years studiously ignoring them, she did not know, except it was part of the restlessness. Receiving word from them, right out of the blue, was weird.

Not a letter, but an invitation . . . to the eighty-fifth birthday celebrations of Philip Ingram, her grandfather. As if it were the most natural thing in the world for a loving granddaughter to be in attendance, when that same granddaughter and grandfather had never met. And why had they never met? Because Philip Ingram, her grandfather, had told Robert Ingram, her father, never to darken his door again, or words to that effect.

Philippa grimaced a smile, wryly amused at the dramatic turn of phrase. She came back from an imagined house called Copperthwaite stuck on some bleak fells in Cumbria and felt the sun warm on her body. She loved France, but it was here that she felt the loss of her parents the most, especially her father, for her mother, Rose, had died when she was a child. Even after seven years she missed him fiercely, missed his easy, light-hearted banter, missed organising him into some semblance of reasonable day-to-day living. If he were with her now he would be sketching, the blank page coming to life with a few swift strokes—the roof-tops, the church steeple, the pigeons perched on the nearby chimney stack . . .

'Is something the matter?'

The quiet, restrained question broke into her thoughts and Philippa stiffened, giving a quick startled glance over her shoulder before glaring balefully at the roof-tops once more. He had a light tread, this fair man. How long had he been there? Had he seen the wretched tears? She blinked furiously and said dismissively, 'No. Thank you,' showing plainly by the tone of her voice that any further comment would be unwelcome, and willing him to go, the roof-tops still blurred.

There was a slight pause. 'This, I believe, is yours.'

Damn him, why didn't he go? Philippa took a deep breath and steeled herself to turn, saying brusquely, 'What did you say?' She had an impression of tanned arms above rolled-up sleeves, piercing cornflower blue eyes and a head of corn-coloured hair.

'This franc. I'm told it's yours.' The voice was patient and controlled. The fair head nodded towards the English group now clicking cameras down below. 'They didn't want to be accused of stealing and as I was on my way up . . .' He held out a long, narrow hand and as Philippa's came up to meet it he dropped the coin carefully into her palm.

At least he had the gumption not to look at her, she thought furiously, knowing her face was bright red with embarrassment. Her anger, directed less at him and more at herself for being such a sentimental idiot, helped her to gain control.

He went on, 'They didn't need it, the franc. The machine was out of order.' He must have known the explanation was unnecessary, but she was glad of the breathing space.

He was around the six foot mark, and slim, with eyes that didn't miss much. An interesting face with a touch of arrogance in the sweep of brow, the droop of eyelid, the set of the mouth. He was, she guessed, the type to take over in an emergency and then back off. He made her feel—she struggled to analyse just what she did feel, and came up with something that gave her a jolt. This man made her aware of herself, of being a woman, and it was unnerving, for his own manner could not be criticised. He was extremely polite and the cool blue gaze was completely impersonal.

That gaze was upon her now, and thoroughly

off-balance, she glanced down at the coin in her hand and, for something to say, said, 'Hardly worth the effort of the climb.' Too late she saw the words as an invitation to a compliment and clamped her jaw with annoyance and waited for the inevitable, ready to squash him and it when it came.

She underestimated him. Lashes flickered over limpid eyes and a brow twitched, but he did not say the obvious. Instead, he observed, 'You read French,' as his eyes fell to the guide book.

'François, *viens! Nous devons partir, n'est-ce pas?*' The plaintive request to leave floated upwards. The brunette was bored and showed it.

'*J'arrive tout de suite*, Lisette,' was his answer. Lisette swept Philippa a suspicious look, shrugged an eloquent shlulder and was silent.

'I'm afraid Roman ruins do not interest my friend,' he confided with a wry smile, as if apologising for Lisette's rudeness. He had retained his French and went on, 'So if there is nothing more I can do for you . . .' His brows rose slightly, and Philippa had the feeling he would have said more under different circumstances.

'Thank you, no. It was kind of you to take the trouble.' Her own French was excellent, but she was aware that he gave no hint of surprise. Perversely, this niggled.

'In that case, I'll say goodbye,' and he gave her a nod and dropped lightly and unhurriedly down the steps.

Philippa watched them leave, the fair head bent close to the dark one. François. Francis. The name suited him—sleek, spare and silky.

She gave herself an impatient reprimand. So his name was Francis and he spoke English and

French like a native. What did it matter? She would not see him again and he would be remembered only for intruding on a stupid, silly emotional moment. She dismissed him from her mind and took upher camera, and for the next ten minutes circled the auditorium in the hope of fitting the theatre into her view-finder. When she was done she left, collecting the Metro from a side street and following the signs south to Avignon, to take tea with Sylvie.

'My dear Phippy, sightseeing in all this heat? How energetic of you!' Sylvie Rousard languidly poured the tea from an elegant Limoges pot into delicate china cups as she sat cool and composed beneath the shade of a tree. 'Was it worth it?'

'Yes, it was, as you should know.' Philippa lay on a rug on the grass, enjoying the privacy and beauty of the Rousards' walled garden. Angélique, her goddaughter, shared the rug and watched as Philippa built her a tower of coloured bricks.

Sylvie yawned daintily. 'I'm much too lazy these days to chase the ghosts of Romans.' She eyed the sprawling figure of her friend. 'Did Augustus fall off his pedestal at the sight of those legs of yours?' Sylvie was a diminutive five-two and envied her friend's extra four inches.

Philippa grinned. 'Shorts are definitely the most practical garment for climbing steep steps,' she claimed, and gave eight-month-old Angélique a succession of growling kisses on her tummy, making the baby chuckle out loud before observing, 'She's the image of Fabien, isn't she?'

'She is,' agreed her mother, 'but perhaps she will grow out of it, poor cherub. Of course, the likeness pleases my dear *Belle-mère*, which is something. She dared to voice her disappointment in Fabien's hearing that Angélique was not a boy and pouf! how she was put in her place!'

Philippa chuckled at the satisfaction in Sylvie's voice. Her mother-in-law sounded a daunting personage.

'Politely, you understand,' Sylvie went on, 'for that is Fabien's way, but she has never said it again, and secretly I believe she has come to adore the *bébé*.'

'How can she resist?' declared Philippa, allowing Angélique to pull a coloured bangle from her wrist.

'Oh, how nice it is to talk together like this!' Sylvie's dark eyes brightened. 'Remember how we talked after lights-out? And read Georgette Heyer under the covers by torchlight?'

'And cried over *Beau Geste*?'

The two friends exchanged reminiscent smiles. Sylvie pouted and heaved a sigh. 'I wish you would settle in France, Phippy.' She eyed the other girl speculatively as Philippa lay back and stared up at the sky through the branches of the tree. 'I understand why you could not return when your father died,' Sylvie went on, 'you were still studying, but Phippy, I always thought you would live in France.' There was a plaintive note in Sylvie's voice as she said this.

Philippa wrinkled up her nose thoughtfully. 'So did I, but somehow things contrived to keep me in England. The flat in Grace's house became vacant and I got my first translating job, and so I just stayed on.'

'Don't you find it constricting, living with your aunt?'

Philippa laughed and shook her head. 'I don't think of Grace as being an aunt, she's more like a sister, or a close friend, and the house is divided into two completely separate flats, with their own entrance.' She cast an amused glance at her friend. 'I can have anyone I like to stay over without any difficulty and without upsetting Grace. She's a liberated woman and respects my privacy as I do hers.'

'That's all very well,' retorted Sylvie with asperity, 'but do you? Have anyone stay over, I mean?' She scowled. 'No, no—I have no right to ask such a question. I just want you to be happy with the right man, Phippy!'

Philippa's eyes twinkled at Sylvie's anguished expression. 'It's been known to happen, Sylvie, the house guest, but not often, I have to admit—they all seem to turn out to have feet of clay.'

'For someone who was brought up a Bohemian and allowed to run wild for the first ten years you are very conservative in your love life.' Sylvie's tone was one of rueful, laughing disgust.

'That's why, Sylvie dear, that's why. I have conflicting streaks in my character, I'm afraid, and no illusions.'

'Have you ever fallen in love, really and truly, so that you're no longer sensible?'

Amusement tinged Philippa's, 'No.'

Sylvie sighed deeply. 'I might have guessed! One day, Phippy, you are going to fall in love like a . . . like a . . .'

'Ton of bricks?'

'That will serve perfectly. A ton of bricks is heavy enough.' Sylvie ran exasperated fingers through her short dark curls. 'You turn those discerning brown eyes of yours on every man you meet and find him wanting. No man is perfect!' and catching the raised brows of her friend she added, laughing, 'No, not even Fabien is perfect! Somewhere there must be someone able to stab your soul with Cupid's arrow and make you lose your head, and when that happens, hooray! I shall be a most interested spectator.' She frowned. 'I cannot believe that there's been no one to stop your heart from its regular beat.' She looked encouragingly. 'No one to make your pulse race faster.'

Philippa grinned. 'Oh, there's no shortage of interesting men,' she offered, lazily biting at a piece of grass. 'The trouble is after a while they turn out to be the most complete bore. Rather deflating!'

'You might meet someone while you're here,' mused Sylvie, keeping her voice casual and gleefully brooding on one name from her guest list for that evening.

'There was the most ravishing man at the theatre this afternoon.'

Sylvie sat up. 'Really? Ravishing? Tell me more!'

'Fair, slim and aristocratic-looking,' replied Philippa dreamily, 'like a superior Afghan hound—you know the sort I mean—long and silky, looking down a slender nose rather disdainfully. Sleek and beautifully made and ready to go like the wind if let loose. Not brown eyes, but bright blue, and before you begin to get excited he was already on a leash. His owner was a brunette—sulky and very sexy.'

'What a pity,' sympathised Sylvie, dismissing the ravishing man and thinking about Jules Morin. She had been delighted to learn that he was back home and was enjoying the anticipation of introducing her best friend to one of Fabien's oldest friends, already seeing them, in her mind's eye, walking together hand in hand towards marital bliss.

During this companionable silence while Sylvie dreamed of matchmaking, Philippa was remembering Orange and the bright blue eyes, the crisp fair hair and the way his mouth curved at the corners . . .

She banished her thoughts abruptly and gave herself a mental shake. Had it come to this—mooning over a man she had met once, briefly? Changing the subject, she announced, 'I had an invitation today.'

Sylvie perked up. 'An invitation to what?'

'To my grandfather's eighty-fifth birthday. Ouch, Angel, that's my hair you're tugging, *ma petite*!' Philippa half sat up, leaning on one elbow.

Puzzled, Sylvie queried, 'Your grandfather? I thought, surely, that your grandparents were no longer living?'

Struggling with a small plump hand that had a strong hold on a fistful of hair, Philippa answered, 'You're thinking of my mother's side, the Stanhopes. No, this is my Ingram grandfather.'

'Oh, *him*—but I thought you didn't have anything to do with that side of the family?'

'I don't. He washed his hands of us all.'

'Will you go?'

'I don't know.' Philippa frowned. 'Part of me is madly curious to learn something of these relatives I've never met, and then I remember nothing came from the Ingrams when Mother died and I feel I can never forgive them for ignoring us all these years.'

'He's very wealthy, isn't he?' pondered Sylvie thoughtfully, and gave a knowing smile. 'Think of all that lovely money, Phippy!'

Philippa laughed. 'He's hardly likely to leave it to me, now is he? Dad had a sister, so there must be a few more likely candidates, and anyway, I don't want his money. I haven't even decided to go.' As she said it, Philippa suddenly realised that she would go.

Sylvie looked at her watch and gave a hurried exclamation. '*Hélas!* You must hurry or you will be late for this evening. Fabien will call for you at eight o'clock.'

'That isn't necessary,' protested Philippa. Fabien Rousard was a doctor, a paediatrician, and a busy man. 'I have my own car.'

Sylvie fluttered her hands dismissively. 'Fabien will not permit it. You must be fetched and taken home. He could not be happy otherwise.'

'Who is coming?' Philippa swung Angélique into the air, making the baby chuckle.

'Tch! Who is not coming! I thought, at first, to have a small dinner party, but the guest list has escalated so much that it is now no longer an intimate affair.' Sylvie hesitated. 'There is a friend of Fabien's I want you to meet—his name is Jules Morin, and he is very, very charming.' Before Philippa could comment she glanced at her watch again, exclaiming, 'Come, Angel, to Maman . . . Auntie Phippy must go now.' Sylvie took her daughter from Philippa and beamed a smile. 'How nice to practise my English—I so rarely get the chance, but tonight, Phippy, you can be wholly French, I promise.'

At ten minutes to eight Philippa was ready, a quick dash of perfume being all that was necessary to complete her toilette, and this she now applied. Fabien was usually prompt and she did not want to keep him waiting. She collected a silk-fringed shawl from a drawer and made for the sitting-room, hesitating at the wardrobe mirror.

She saw a young woman of medium height in a dusky pink dress of fine fabric which fitted at the waist and fell in soft folds to mid-calf. With thin straps and a low back it showed off a slim but curved figure and its simple lines suited her. Brown hair, streaked red and gold by the sun and washed barely an hour ago, was springing into slightly unmanageable waves and tamed by two strands, either side, being taken to the back and caught up with a mother-of-pearl slide. She pushed her feet into matching pink shoes and passed into the main room.

It was a pleasant flat, above a craft shop in the town of Villeneuve-lès-Avignon, which was situated on the opposite bank of the Rhône and linked to Avignon by a bridge. Fabien had found the place for her and Philippa had already lost her heart to Villeneuve, loving its narrow streets and old, quaint buildings. This house was one of a row, climbing steeply, all joined together as if for support, the front door leading directly out on to the narrow cobbled street. Opposite, the ground fell dramatically, the houses built on a lower level affording an amazing, uninterrupted view of the city of Avignon, with its crenellated walls and Popes' Palace glowing golden in the sunlight.

The view was well worth having to climb the hill. Every morning Philippa would walk down to the Place Jean Jaurés, take her place in the queue at the bakery in the square and bring back her breakfast, a warm croissant—a roll in the shape of a crescent—and bread for the day—a long stick called a *baguette*. The smell from the bakery was mouthwatering.

The door bell interrupted her thoughts and Philippa turned from the view at the window, collected clutch bag and shawl and went to answer it. She locked the door at the top of the stairs and ran down to open the outer door.

Afterwards she tried to recapture how she felt at that moment, but there were too many conflicting emotions. All she knew for certain was that colour flooded her face and with her heart pumping faster, she stammered, 'Oh! it's you . . .! I mean . . .' She took a breath and said lamely, 'Hello.'

'Hello.' He smiled, the cool, cornflower blue eyes resting thoughtfully on her face. 'You are Sylvie's friend Philippa, aren't you?' and when she nodded, still dazed by his unexpected appearance, he went on, 'It's a small world, isn't it? When Sylvie described you to me, she little realised we'd already met.' He waited a moment, giving her a chance to comment, and when she didn't, added, 'Fabien was late from hospital and so I was asked to pick you up.'

'Oh—yes, I see.' Philippa pulled herself together—he must think her dim-witted!

'I'm an old friend of Fabien's. He has, perhaps, mentioned the Morins to you?'

Morin? The name rang a bell. She said, 'I think Sylvie spoke of you this afternoon as being one of her guests.'

'Ah, that would be my cousin, Jules. This afternoon Sylvie did not know I was back in town.' He pulled a droll face. 'It is always to be my fate, this confusion between me and Jules. Such an audacious fellow! When we were boys he got me into the most fearful scrapes and we became known for evermore as the terrible twins.' He had been speaking in English, taking his cue from her startled exclamation as she opened the door, but now he switched to French, saying gently, 'The Roussards have a superb cook. It would be a pity for him to hand in his notice because we are late.' He frowned. 'You would, perhaps like to telephone—to check I'm genuine? My name is Francis . . .'

'Oh, no, that won't be necessary,' Philippa said hurriedly, a wave of embarrassment sweeping over her. Had she been staring? His presence on her doorstep was enough to make anyone think they were dreaming! 'Yes, of course, let's go.'

'If you will allow me?' Francis Morin pulled the door on to its catch and putting a light impersonal hand beneath her elbow, led her across the cobbles to where his car was parked a few yards further on.

CHAPTER TWO

THE car was a white Alfa Romeo Spider, sleek and powerful. Philippa waited while Francis Morin opened the passenger door and noticed that it was a right-hand drive—was he, then, English?

As she drew in her legs, the skirt of her dress caught the sill and they both reached at the same moment to tuck it in out of harm's way. Their hands touched. An insignificant thing, but Philippa pulled hers away quickly. His touch had sent a shiver through her. She told herself furiously to grow up, that she was imagining this peculiar sensitivity between herself and this man, but she knew she was fooling herself. It had never happened before, this instant attraction to a man she knew nothing about, and it was unnerving and the sooner she pulled herself together the better.

By the time Francis joined her she had regained some measure of serenity, outwardly, at least, but it was difficult to ignore him totally, good manners alone demanded that she should make some form of conversation, and the close confines of the car did not help. And if she were truthful she did not wish to ignore him, only to disguise the effect he had on her. Everything he did seemed spare of unnecessary energy. She remembered how he had lightly dropped from step to step at the theatre that afternoon, in command of his body. She thought suddenly that that seemed to sum him up. He was a man in total command of himself, and it annoyed her that he had managed to ruffle her own self-possession.

A wide gold watch encircled a slim wrist, she noticed, as he reached for the ignition key. His head turned to her and those incredible blue eyes engulfed her as he asked, 'Ready?' and she nodded.

They drove past the Fort of Saint André which dominated the top of the hill and wound their way through the labyrinth of narrow streets to join the main road, traffic lights at the entrance to the Daladier Bridge halting their progress. Francis began to talk of the theatre at Orange, asking if she had been to Arles or Nîmes, and she replied, his easy, relaxed manner helping, but she was still incredibly flustered, and very much aware of him.

The casual clothes of the afternoon were gone and in their place was a cream suit, superbly cut, the jacket of which was lying across the back seat. His shirt was dark blue with a fine white stripe and was teamed with a cream silk tie. Philippa guessed the cream leather shoes were handmade Italian.

I'm not attracted to fair men, she said to herself.

The faint tang of aftershave mingled elusively with *Arpège* and body oil—it seemed that every sense was sharpened, and then she suddenly realised that Francis was waiting for her to speak. She said hurriedly, 'I'm sorry—what did you say?'

'Don't you think it's like a cut-out in a fairy book?' he repeated, indicating the view ahead. They were now travelling across the bridge, and this was exactly what the ramparts and the Palace of the Popes looked like, and Philippa murmured her agreement. Her conversation so far had hardly been impressive. Her eyes caught the four remaining arches of the St-Bénézet Bridge, stretching from the Avignon bank to mid-stream.

'I remember being so disappointed when I first saw that,' she said, and Francis, following the direction of her gaze, began to hum *Sur le Pont d'Avignon* breaking off to say,

'Probably the first bit of French that English children learn. Did you know that they couldn't have danced on the bridge? It's only wide enough to walk across and it's now thought that they danced under it, where it crossed the island in the middle of the river.' He glanced her way, smiling wryly. 'Nothing is sacred, is it? Not even a nursery rhyme.' Swinging the car round the Place Crillon, taking the road parallel to the river, he went on, 'How do you know the Rousards?'

Here was a question that needed little thought. 'I met Sylvie at school in Grenoble,' Philippa explained. 'I've only known Fabien since their marriage.'

'And what was an English girl doing at school in Grenoble?'

'My parents moved to France and settled in the south, my mother's health was not good and it was hoped that a warmer climate might suit her better.' She paused, wondering if she should go on, but he had seemed interested. 'She died when I was eight and I was sent to boarding school when I was ten.'

'Did you like it, the school?'

She laughed softly. 'I hated it at first, only Sylvie made it bearable. If it had been left to my father I wouldn't have had to go, but my mother's parents descended on us and found me running wild—at least, that's how they put it.' She laughed again, remembering. 'Oh, dear! They were good people but terribly conventional. My father was a painter and we lived a free and easy life, one in their eyes not at all ideal for a ten-year-old girl, but it suited Father and me. In the summer I virtually lived on the beach and in the sea. We rented a small house on the coast near Cap Camarat, the headland just south of St Tropez—do you know it?'

'I know St Tropez and know what the coast is like along there.'

'Our house was off the beaten track and there was a stiff climb down to the beach, which put most people off, so we were very private. Anyway, Robert, my father, didn't see anything wrong in me going with him to the local bar while he and his cronies set the world to rights, but my poor Stanhope grandparents were horrified. They were caring people and were afraid for my health because of my mother—she had lung trouble—but it was obvious I was a little toughie, so they attacked on the question of my education.' She pulled a rueful face. 'Which was unorthodox, I admit. I only went to school when I felt like it, but I could recite the histories of all the famous painters, writers and philosophers; could speak English, French, Italian and Spanish—the artist community along the coast was truly cosmopolitan so we kids were a mixed bag—and I could cook the basics, but much else was negligible. So it was either boarding school in France or back to England with them. Luckily, my father hit a good period at that time and sold a few paintings, or I could have ended up in Northamptonshire, which to me, at that time, was on another planet.' She stopped suddenly and searched his face anxiously for boredom. 'I haven't spoken about myself like this for years. What a dangerous man you are!'

He smiled slightly, his eyes turning her way briefly. 'No, no, merely a good listener. I'm interested. Tell me about your father.' She remained silent and he prompted, 'You say he was a painter?'

She nodded. 'He wasn't bothered much about anything but painting, and he didn't ask a great deal from life. He was popular, generous—he'd help anyone and spend his last franc doing it—easygoing, irresponsible and fun to be with.'

'You, I gather, kept him in order.'

Philippa chuckled. 'I tried to. He died seven years ago.' She gave a small shrug. 'He had a fall. It was a stupid thing to happen. I stayed at Grenoble until I was eighteen—I'd begun to like learning by that time and found I had an aptitude for languages. Robert decided I should get to know England and I was keen, so feelers were put out for me to finish my education there. I went to university and read languages, and during my second year, when I was twenty, Robert had this fall.'

'How old was he?'

'Forty-eight, and he was fit. Like all accidents, it shouldn't have happened. There'd been unusually heavy rain and high winds along the coast—it was February, and Robert knew the cliff path to our home well, we both did, even in the dark—you could only reach the cottage on foot from the nearest village. Anyway, he'd had a few glasses of wine with his friends, nothing in excess, they told me, but he wasn't as careful as he should have been and because of the storms the cliff had collapsed at one point and he didn't know of it, didn't see it on his walk back. He wasn't found until the next day. They sent for me, but he died before I could get there.'

Francis said gently, 'I'm sorry. It must have been an unhappy time for you.' He waited a moment and then asked, 'Was he a good painter?'

Philippa considered the question thoughtfully. 'He was good at what he did best, portraits, but there was a limited call in that line, so his bread and butter was provided by the pictures he did of the harbour at Cannes or the old back streets of Nice. You know the kind I mean, pictures the tourists take back home to remind them of a happy holiday.' She went on a little defensively, 'No good turning your nose up at the bread and butter when it can provide the cake. Those sales paid for the oils and canvas for his portraits. Yes, he was a good painter, but he had very little ambition, and you need that to get your name known. I have some paintings in store, with the rest of his things, but I haven't looked at them since he died.' She turned to her companion. 'Enough about me. Tell me, I'm having a hard time working out whether you're English or French—your accent gives me no clue. I think I'll go for English, because your car has a right-hand drive.'

Francis Morin turned a mock-horrified face her way and tut-tutted reproachfully. 'I'll not answer to being English! I'm half French and half Scottish. My mother is French and lives mostly in Paris since my father died ten years ago.' He slowed the car and swung the wheel over, driving through the open-gated entrance, saying, 'And here we are at the Rousards'.'

How annoying that they had arrived, thought Philippa, wanting to know more. Talking freely about herself had been relaxing. Now there was silence between them again and she was once more conscious of a slight nervousness tinged with excitement rising up in her.

The Spider slid behind two cars already parked. Beyond the courtyard, through a stone arch, was the walled garden where that afternoon Philippa had taken tea with Sylvie. To the right was the house, typically French, with its square blue roofs and rounded turrets.

In the silence after the engine died, Philippa could hear the monotonous chirping of the cicadas and she turned her head and found Francis watching her. He was in no hurry to move and beneath his regard she found her hard-won composure beginning to disintegrate.

'Why were you crying this afternoon, Philippa?'

Whatever she had expected it certainly was not this. She turned and stared out front. 'I wasn't crying.'

'There were tears on your lashes.'

She managed a laugh. 'I was indulging in self-pity. You caught me out.'

'Not something, I'm sure, that you do often.'

'No.' She looked at him then.

'You were annoyed that I caught you at such a vulnerable moment.'

There was a heady fascination being the subject of his concern. Philippa gave a rueful laugh. 'Yes, I was.'

'Do you need help?'

'No, really, it's just a decision I have to make.'

'But perhaps there's a faithful swain back in England who should be asking you that question—ready to share your ups and downs?'

The silence seemed heavy with unspoken words. She lifted her head and looked at him. 'No,' she said simply. And then, 'Does Lisette share yours?'

There was a glimmer of a smile in his eyes. 'You're mixing me up with Jules—it happens all the time.' He gave a wicked smile and she found herself smiling back.

When he opened the passenger door for her to alight a curious feeling swept over her, as if the step she was about to take was far bigger than merely lifting her feet from the car to the paving stones. Giving herself a mental shake, Philippa accepted his steadying hand, wondering if he was as sensitive to her touch as she was to his. Long after contact was broken she could still feel the imprint and thrust her hand into her skirt pocket out of harm's way. Walking towards the house they did not speak.

Fabien came to meet them, a smile of greeting on his face. A small man with wispy brown hair and intelligent eyes behind rimless glasses, he had a quiet gentle manner and a sweet smile. He took her hands, saying warmly,

'Philippa, my dear, how charming you look.' His eyes went beyond her. 'Thank you, Francis, for being a taxi service. There was a crisis at the hospital which delayed me.'

The drawling voice behind her said, 'It was no hardship, Fabien,' and Fabien laughed, replying, 'No, I don't suppose it was. No need to put the jacket on,' he added, as Francis began to do so, 'it's much too warm and we're informal tonight among our friends.' He waited while his guests went before him up the steps to the terrace. 'We're sitting outside as it's such a lovely evening. I have a new wine I want you to try, Francis, it has an interesting flavour,' and to Philippa, 'Sylvie will be down in a moment. She's settling Angélique, who seems to know that we're having friends in and wishes to join us.' His voice was lovingly indulgent.

The terrace was shaded from one end by a bamboo blind, and as the threesome approached, the hum of conversation from the guests already there died down and faces turned their way.

'You all know Francis,' announced Fabien.

'Once seen never forgotten,' quipped a dark-haired man, and everyone laughed.

'So he needs no introduction,' Fabien continued, 'but you don't know Philippa Ingram, an old friend of Sylvie's who is here on holiday from England.' Introductions were set in motion. There were ten guests present, but only two names made any impression on Philippa. The first was Jules Morin, the dark-haired man who had just spoken, and the woman, Lisette, last seen leaving the Orange theatre with Francis Morin.

It was obvious that Lisette recognised Philippa. She gave the English girl a languid greeting in contrast to the sudden narrowing of her dark, thickly lashed eyes. She was dressed in a figure-hugging black dress and close to was even more beautiful than Philippa remembered.

Jules put a drink into Philippa's hand and found her a chair, and even as she responded to the talk around her she was aware that Francis had slowly made his way to the corner of the terrace and was now leaning against the wooden railing. She had to make a conscious effort not to look at him.

Sylvie breezed in, trailing pale green chiffon, her dark curls bouncing as she turned this way and that smiling and greeting her guests. She spied her friend and exclaimed, 'Oh, good, you've arrived, Phippy.' She turned to Francis. 'Thank you, Francis, you were a dear to fetch her for us.'

Francis inclined his head, accepting the thanks, an amused gleam in his eyes. Philippa, attuned to her friend, gave her a closer look. Although in total command of herself, underneath Sylvie was flustered, Philippa could tell. What, she thought, is going on?

Jules appeared at Philippa's side. He was as dark as his cousin was fair and had a much more flamboyant personality. 'May I congratulate you on your command of our language?' He gave her glass a refill.

'Phippy is a language genius,' asserted Sylvie proudly, slipping an arm around her friend's shoulder as she perched on the arm of the chair. 'I could hardly cope with my mother tongue, but Phippy romped away with all the language prizes in the school!'

'Sylvie is exaggerating, as usual,' broke in Philippa. Jules asked, 'Do you use your languages in your job?'

Philippa nodded. She could see the sulky Lisette looking their way.

'She translates books, and goes to conferences and has done *French for Beginners* on television, and made an Italian tape . . .'

Philippa laughingly interrupted her friend. 'Sylvie would make a good agent!'

'How many languages do you have?' asked Jules, and Philippa wondered why he was taking the trouble to get to know her.

'French, Italian and Spanish well enough to use in my job, enough German to get by and a little Dutch.' She smiled, giving a small shrug. 'It's easy if you're that way inclined.'

Fortunately the conversation swun away from her as Lisette called Jules to her side to satisfy some point under discussion from that end of the terrace. Jules excused himself and Philippa sat back, sipping her wine and listening to what was going on around her. Eventually her eyes wandered to the corner.

A shaft of dying sunlight splintered through the blind, catching the pale wheaten hair and turning it to gold. There was unconscious artistic line in the way his body was set against the railing, a wine glass held delicately between long fingers. Robert Ingram had, through his paintings, taught his daughter to appreciate body line, and she wished she had the skill to transpose what she could see on to paper. François ... Francis ... A shiver snaked its way down her spine. It was a long, long time since she had been so attracted to someone with such instant intensity. There—it was voiced! Francis Morin attracted her physically and mentally, and this attraction was not one-sided, she knew that too.

His expression at the moment was a little austere as he gazed down at his wine, and then Fabien approached to refill the glass and stayed to talk, and a smile appeared, softening his features as he listened to his friend.

The time to run—if that's what you want to do—is now, Philippa told herself calmly, before it's too late to turn back. Provide a blinding headache and get Fabien to take you home, if you don't fancy playing with fire.

Sylvie gave a little clap of the hands and called, 'Food is ready, so do, please, go through into the house.'

Her guests obeyed and began to wander inside, still talking to each other, and by dint of manoeuvring tactics Sylvie managed to pull Philippa to one side, whispering urgently,

'He's the wrong one, Phippy!'

Philippa, puzzled, whispered back, 'Who is?'

'Francis! I asked Jules here for you tonight, not Francis!'

'That's very kind of you, Sylvie, but I think Lisette would quarrel with you over that little scheme,' advised Philippa, amused.

'I know that *now*,' responded Sylvie crossly. 'Jules rang Fabien to say that Francis had just arrived from London and could he bring him along, with this Lisette person, and of course Fabien said yes, naturally—we like Francis, he's an asset to any party.'

'Well?' queried Philippa.

'Not well at all,' answered Sylvie, crosser than ever. 'If this Lisette is with Jules then you are automatically partnered with Francis, and he is not husband material, whereas Jules . . .'

'He's married already?' Philippa felt her heart stupidly plummet. Oh God, not another married man on the lookout for a few cheap thrills on the side!

'No, no—but he has a reputation.' Sylvie frowned and bit her lip. 'Damn—if I say that, you'll only be more intrigued. He's wildly attractive, but not what I wish for you, Phippy darling,' and her voice ended on a subdued wail.

'Oh, I don't know,' murmured Philippa mischievously. 'I wouldn't mind him being gift-wrapped and addressed to me.'

'Yes, yes, as an affair of the heart he is well enough, and no stranger to such a thing—naturally, he is a man after all, and discreet.' Sylvie broke off as Fabien turned back to see what was keeping them, his face enquiring. 'Yes, Fabien darling, we are coming,' Sylvie called, and as they began to walk through the house she went on hurriedly, 'Francis is terribly successful in everything he does and his name has been coupled many times with various women, but never has there been someone permanent in his life.' They were nearly at the dining-room entrance and Sylvie stopped in her tracks, saying dramatically, 'He watches you, Phippy, I've noticed—he is attracted to you, I can tell. He's a terrible heartbreaker, though I don't think it's his fault, for he never makes any promises—but I've put him next to you at table!'

'He's hardly going to break my heart over dinner, Sylvie love,' soothed Philippa. 'I promise to be very careful and not to let him seduce me between courses.'

Sylvie reluctantly laughed and heaved a sigh. 'Very well, I've warned you.'

I need no warning, reflected Philippa as she followed her friend into the dining-room, where the glitter of silver, the blood red candles and their flickering flames and the highly polished table set the tone for the rest of the evening. It was one that Philippa was to remember.

Extension leaves had been added to the dining-table and folding doors opened up so that the table actually took over two rooms. The women were already seated and the men were standing, waiting for their hostess to arrive. Fabien held the chair at one end of the table for his wife, and Philippa made for the other vacant place between the Morin cousins.

Jules pulled back her chair with a flourish and she shot him a quick smile of thanks. When seated she took a deep, steadying breath and turned to Francis, to find amusement gleaming in those shrewd blue eyes, almost as if he knew of Sylvie's warnings.

Oh dear, oh dear, thought Philippa, her resolve to be cool rapidly disintegrating as he smiled and offered her wine.

The cousins were a formidable duo. By half-way through the evening Philippa's ribs ached with laughing. The one was a perfect foil for the other, and it was as if they had set their stall out to entertain her. Jules was the lighthearted comic, Francis the droll cynic, and they slipped into their double act with the ease of many years' practice.

The general conversation was stimulating and not averse to becoming slightly heated, but only in the way that is possible among close friends. Politics both sides of the Channel were given punishing blows, music was discussed, art and books argued over. Philippa had not enjoyed herself like this in a long time, and the *sotto voce* remarks either side of her at pertinent moments threatened her composure more than once.

Over some delicious local cheeses and while cutting a stem of lush green grapes for Philippa from the fruit platter, Jules asked,

'Do you find you have a dual personality when you come over here? I understand you spent your formative years in France. Do you have difficulty relating to which country you belong?' He dropped the cluster of grapes on to her plate. 'Francis says it is not difficult, that he slips easily into being what is expected of him. In Provence no one thinks of him as being any other than French. How do you find it?'

Philippa thought for a moment. A serious Jules was not to be brushed lightly aside and the question interested her. She said slowly,

'When I first went to England I felt a little strange, but not for long, as I remember. You see,

I spoke without an accent—we always talked together in English, my parents and I, and I have an English name, so people there just accepted me. Oxford is a world of its own anyway. As for France . . .' She frowned. 'I think we were always considered foreigners, looking back, even though we spoke French and lived the life of the locals. There was such a cosmopolitan community around us too. As a child I liked to think myself as being French because I didn't want to be different. As an adult I feel very English with special French roots.'

'I'm glad you like our country.' Jules smiled at her, his dark eyes approving. Philippa wondered what Lisette, on the other side of Francis, was thinking of the seating arrangements.

'I love it,' she answered enthusiastically. 'I'm not here as much as I like to be, that's why I've made a great effort to come this time and stay longer than I usually do.' She held out her glass for a refill and Jules obliged. 'I've brought work with me, so unfortunately it's not all holiday.'

'Francis visits us regularly, but always for brief spells. This time he, too, has a little longer than usual. He's been working too hard and needs to forget his responsibilities. It would be a great kindness if you could look after him during his stay.'

'My dear Jules, I wish you would mind your own business,' came the drawling request from her other side. 'I am quite capable of arranging my own life, thank you,' and Francis turned a bland face to his cousin.

'Indeed he is,' came in Philippa smoothly. 'I think you will find that he is being looked after perfectly adequately. Perhaps you should ask your cousin how he enjoyed his visit to the Roman theatre at Orange this afternoon.' She directed this suggestion to Jules who, with quickening interest, repeated, 'Roman theatre?' with amused anticipation. Philippa, enjoying herself, turned to Francis, finding him selecting cheese with due seriousness.

'Roman theatre?' interrupted Sylvie sharply, catching the words in a lull and sending a piercing look across the table. 'At Orange?'

'Why, yes, Sylvie, at Orange,' agreed Francis calmly.

'*You* were there this afternoon?' demanded Sylvie, her eyes going quickly to her friend. Philippa gave a rueful grimace and Sylvie caught her breath, her mind racing over the conversation with Philippa that afternoon. Ravishing man—fair, slim, aristocratic, bright blue eyes! Oh dear, oh dear! She said, 'I didn't know they allowed dogs in the theatre.'

'Dogs?' echoed Jules, alive to something going on and determined to know what it was.

'Yes,' answered Sylvie, with wide-eyed innocence. 'Francis, did you see an Afghan hound there? On a chain, wasn't he, Phippy? Let me see, how did you describe him? Aristocratic, sleek and silky, a bit superior, fair with bright blue eyes, I think that was it. He sounds very dangerous.'

'Blue eyes? Dogs don't have blue eyes!' This came from Lisette who had, at first, been talking to the guest on her other side, but whose ears had pricked up at the mention of Orange. 'I did not see any dog there, did you, Francis?' Her manner was slightly scornful and she shot Philippa an irritable look.

Philippa, a pang of dismay shooting through

her, suddenly remembered that Lisette was Jules' girl-friend and she swung her head round anxiously to see his reaction. Her worries disappeared as she met the laughter dancing in his eyes.

'You took *Lisette* to the Roman theatre at Orange, Francis?' Jules asked, allowing just the hint of surprise to touch his voice. 'I'm sure she was fascinated by it.'

'It was very interesting,' muttered Lisette, and tossed her dark curls and studiously turned her back on him.

'Lisette wished to drive the Spider and offered to accompany me,' put in Francis mildly, dropping his voice for his cousin alone, although with Philippa sitting between them she was bound to hear, 'and she wanted a shoulder to cry on.' He lifted a brow. 'I do wish your love-life was not so volcanic, Jules, it makes things complicated.'

Jules grinned unrepentantly and conversation resumed round the table, and after a suitable interval an amused voice on Philippa's right said,

'So you liken me to an Afghan hound, do you?'

Philippa turned her head and met his gaze. 'You should be flattered.'

A laugh trembled on his voice. 'Oh, my dear, I am. I've been called many things in my time. Such a beautiful animal, with a prestigious pedigree, makes a change. I admit to being a little concerned about the superior bit, but really . . .! On a chain?' and he regarded her reproachfully.

'I see now I was mistaken,' Philippa replied kindly, 'although the role of Dutch uncle is not one I can easily see you in.'

'And what role do you see me in?' The question

was lazily put, but the blue eyes narrowed thoughtfully.

Philippa gave a small laugh and shook her head. 'Oh, no! I won't commit myself on such a short acquaintance.' Her eyes slid past him and rested momentarily upon Lisette. 'She is very attractive.'

'Yes, she is, isn't she?' agreed Francis, 'but not really interested in Roman remains—or Shakespeare.' His mouth curved and try as she might Philippa could not stop her own from trembling in answer. She caught her bottom lip between her teeth, fought a losing battle, and asked resignedly,

'What has Shakespeare got to do with it?'

'They are performing *A Midsummer Night's Dream* there next week. I went to buy two tickets. It's rather a good setting for fairies and magic, enchantment and romance, don't you think?' He speared some cheese with his knife and then turned his eyes her way. 'Will you come with me?'

A nerve fluttered in her throat and Philippa looked away, almost immediately returning to find his regard still upon her.

'Yes, please,' she said, burning her boats. His response was a quick smile and a quiet, 'Good,' and then they were drawn into other talk.

It was arranged that Fabien would take her home. No doubt Sylvie's doing—she had been eyeing them all evening, and if Sylvie was surprised that Francis made no move to offer himself in Fabien's place she did not show it.

Philippa was content. She needed to catch her breath. Was it only that afternoon that she had confessed to never having fallen so much in love that she lost all sense? Fate must have laughed out loud! Not that she had fallen in love—good heavens, that was much too over-dramatic, but she had a strong presentiment that she was heading into some emotional involvement. There was something about this slim, fair man that pulled at her senses, and the suddenness was alarming. It seemed to her that everyone in the room had become more animated, more interesting and attractive because of his presence. That was what was so panicky. That she could think such romantic twaddle—she who was usually so pragmatic. After all, she was not a silly young thing to be swept off her feet by a pair of smiling blue eyes and a drawling voice. She was a sensible woman of twenty-seven who was independent and answerable to no one. So it was unnerving, to say the least, to find herself flapping around exactly like a silly young thing.

Before leaving, she looked in on Angélique. The light from the landing shone faintly across the curve of a glowing cheek, eyelashes that trembled slightly and sweetly shaped, out-thrust bottom lip. As Philippa stood gazing down on to the sleeping child a shadow joined her, causing her to put a finger to her lips, and for a moment they stood together, sharing the intimate occasion, then they made their way quietly from the room.

'Your shawl was downstairs. It had dropped to the floor.' Francis held up the lost shawl as evidence and inclined his head towards the nursery. 'She's aptly named at the moment.'

Philippa chuckled and they began to descend the stairs. 'Angélique? Yes, she is, isn't she? My knowledge of small babies is very nearly nil—Angel is the only one I come into real contact with, and she's my goddaughter. And you?'

'The Morin family is large,' he admitted,

smiling. He dropped the shawl round her shoulders, taking care not to touch her. 'Have you anything planned for tomorrow?'

Philippa shook her head. Do not, she told herself sternly, look too pleased.

'Have you done any canoeing?'

She found herself smiling. Canoeing was hardly soft lights and sweet music and seduction! 'In my childhood,' she admitted. 'Why do you ask?'

'We'll canoe down the Ardèche. It's quite impressive. I'll call for you at nine-thirty.'

Two arms encircled her from behind and a growly voice asked, 'Would you like a chaperone, Philippa? I could always take the day off.'

'You can paddle your own canoe, cousin,' said Francis, and Jules grinned and kissed her on both cheeks as he said good night.

Francis neither kissed her, nor took her hand.

CHAPTER THREE

THE drive back to Villeneuve-lès-Avignon seemed a perfect opportunity to pump Fabien for some information.

Fabien was innocently forthcoming. 'Francis? I've known him ever since I can remember—he's part of my boyhood, along with Jules and a handful of others. The Morins are an extraordinary family and Francis is no exception . . . nothing seems to daunt him, he'll try his hand at anything in his quiet way, and usually succeeds. He keeps success and failure close to his chest and he's a good man to have around. He's one of the few people I could go to if I were ever in real trouble—he'd help and ask no questions.'

'What does he do?' asked Philippa curiously, and Fabien laughed a little.

'Difficult question. He read science at university which led him into electronics. You should get him to tell you how today's high technology will transform our lives—amazing stuff! Do you realise that by the turn of the century, lasers could replace the silicone chip altogether? That's because light travels much faster than electrons.' He laughed, adding, 'Or so Francis was telling me tonight.'

'But he's involved in more than that?' prompted Philippa, her interest and respect growing.

Fabien gave a little nod of the head. 'I believe he inherited shares from his father, something to do with the wool industry, and, of course, the family firm which makes glass, and he's on the board of directors of a couple of firms here in Provence to my knowledge, and probably in England too. He's always dashing off to some place or another, but he doesn't talk about himself much. Jules reckons the secret of his success is that he has the right amount of nerve to take a gamble when it's necessary. In a funny sort of way, his father made Francis what he is today.'

'How do you mean?'

'From what I can gather, he and his father were different as chalk and cheese. Francis has a keen brain and likes to use it. His father sat back and expected the family business to take care of itself, speculating badly on the Stock Exchange, and his marriage wasn't working. Hélène Morin didn't transplant easily to your northern shores—Jules says family opinion was that they should never have married—but Hélène isn't the kind of woman to give in without trying. After her husband's death . . .'

'How was that?'

'Broke his neck on the hunting field, if I remember right, and afterwards Hélène made Paris her permanent home. She rarely goes to England now and runs a very successful antique business. Luckily Francis inherited her energy and intelligence and has brought the family business into prominence again.'

'I wonder why he isn't married?' Philippa murmured.

'I asked him that myself recently and he said he hadn't time! That's nonsense, of course, and he didn't expect to be taken seriously. I don't suppose his parents' unhappiness has helped, one's not so quick to tie oneself down with such a background, and his work has something to do with it too, he's a busy man.' He laughed. 'His lady friends are slotted into his life to suit Francis.'

'And there's no shortage,' broke in Philippa drily, and Fabien shrugged eloquently.

Philippa wondered if she was prepared to be slotted into Francis Morin's life. Fabien was silent as they re-crossed the Daladier Bridge, the lights of Villeneuve twinkling ahead of them.

'It has just occurred to me,' he announced suddenly, sounding pleased with himself, 'you should get Francis to take you around, Philippa, show you the sights. You've never stayed long enough to explore much, have you, and Francis is on holiday and knows Provence well.'

Philippa hid a smile. 'That's quite an idea, Fabien.' Ye gods! she thought, how Sylvie would scream if she could hear her husband at this minute! Dear, sweet Fabien . . .

Francis Morin arrived on the dot of nine-thirty, as Philippa suspected he would, and had given her cotton top and matching shorts with their cover-up skirt an approving glance. He was not to know that it was the third set of clothing she had put on since getting up. He looked even more approving when she told him she was wearing a swim-suit underneath, adding, 'Just in case I take a ducking.'

'Oh, I shall take better care of you than that, I hope,' he replied, smiling lazily. 'And a woman who can be ready on time! How promising!' They stood for a moment, eyeing each other over the Spider's roof, and the same challenging sparks began to flow between them.

'That's a typical male observation,' said Philippa, and the smile broadened.

'Yes, isn't it? Shall we go?'

The Ardèche Gorge was impressive. To get to the starting point for their journey down river it was necessary to drive through the mountain pass, with the occasional glimpses of the river twisting its way far below. Every now and then, Francis would stop the car at a vantage point and he and Philippa would get out and walk to the edge. The views were breathtaking and a little frightening.

At the Pont d'Arc, a massive natural archway hewn out of rock by the force of the river and elements, Francis arranged for the Spider to be driven back to await them at the end of their journey down river. Money changed hands and they climbed down the steep path to the river's edge. There was a small launching beach and soon they were afloat.

'We needn't be energetic,' Francis told her, paddle laid across the bows as he turned to speak to her. 'The river is going the same way as we are.' He gave a lopsided grin. 'If we capsize, first rescue priority is lunch,' and he indicated a canvas grip he had placed neatly in the centre of the canoe.

The Ardèche wound its way between the giant towering cliffs, sometimes in sunshine, sometimes in shade. After an hour's paddling, Francis pointed to an inlet similar to one of the many they had already passed and they steered their way towards it. Having stripped off his slacks at the start, revealing dark navy swim trunks, and with canvas shoes on his feet, Francis now jumped into the shallow water and angled the canoe between the jagged rocks until Philippa could gain the beach without a wetting. They pulled the canoe out of the water and stood, breathing a little heavily, and exchanged smiles of satisfaction.

'Well done, First Officer. Shall we swim before lunch?'

'Aye, aye, Skipper.'

All very juvenile, but fun. Francis did not look at all juvenile, however, when he stripped off his sports shirt and stood waiting for Philippa to rid herself of her own clothes. As she did so she was very much aware of the slim, compact frame and lots of bare, tanned flesh only a few feet away. Now down to her coral bathing suit, a one-piece, beautifully cut and boasting a horrendous price tag, she was determined not to feel self-conscious. Tossing away the shorts, aiming them to drop neatly on to the already discarded skirt and top, she straightened and met his eyes, her expression slightly on the defensive.

Francis said easily, 'Beware hidden rocks,' and strolled down to the river's edge. Relieved, she followed and waded in, stepping carefully. The water was cold. Philippa's breath left her on first contact, but she had always accepted any reasonable challenge and set out with a clean stroke, making for the other side of the river. Francis kept up with her, stroke for stroke, although she guessed he could have overtaken her. As the water became more shallow they made for a rock and hauled themselves on to it to take a breather. When Philippa began to shiver, Francis said, 'Time to go back. Make for that rock a little higher up from our beach—see it? The current might take you further down if you're not aware of what's happening. I'll keep down river of you. Ready?'

Philippa nodded, took a breath and slid in. She

could see what he meant. The pull was quite strong now that they were going slightly against the flow. She was not sorry when she found she could put her feet to the bottom.

Taking her hand and pulling her up the sand, Francis smiled and said, 'Good girl!' and she felt a ridiculous pleasure sweep over her.

'What would you have done if I couldn't have made it?' she asked curiously.

He threw her a towel and took another from the grip and began to briskly dry himself. 'We would have drifted with the river and landed further down, then climbed back over the rocks.' He straightened and gave his hair a quick rub, then added, 'I always try to be one step ahead,' and regarded her thoughtfully for a second before smiling.

Philippa caught her breath. That smile just wasn't fair! 'Is that a threat or a promise?' she asked, and found herself returning the smile.

'I hope,' said Francis, stepping forward and dabbing the towel across her shoulders, where she had missed drying herself, 'that it's a promise. Let's eat.'

The grip produced a baguette, pâté, goat's cheese, large juicy tomatoes and wine in a flask to keep cool.

'How marvellously domesticated you are!' exclaimed Philippa with teasing admiration. It was a useful protection against the expanse of freckled chest and even browner length of arms and legs only a touch away. His hair had a tendency to wave when wet.

'I like the simple things in life,' he admitted with the drawl she was coming to expect. As he poured the wine into one of the flask's tops, he added casually, 'Do you suppose Sylvie is up above, eyeing us through binoculars?' His brows rose exaggeratedly and Philippa burst out laughing.

'No, no, Sylvie can't stand heights,' she assured him soothingly, her eyes brimming with amusement.

'And I thought Sylvie was my friend,' he complained, full of hurt.

'You have a reputation.' Philippa bit into the crusty bread, waiting for his reply, enjoying herself.

'Really? She thinks you need to be protected from me?' The idea obviously pleased him.

Pausing before taking a drink, Philippa asked, 'Isn't she right?' then allowed the cool, sparkling liquid to trickle down her throat. It was a provocative pose, but one she could not help. Everything she did seemed to be provocative, so aware was she of her body when she was in his company. Eyes closed, the sun beating on to her bare flesh, she could see in her mind's eye the mass of damp, springing waves of her hair, red-gold where the sun had kissed it, spilling down her back. Could see the tilted profile—the curve of throat, the drying swim-suit with grains of sand clinging to the shiny material, the swell of her breasts, the curve of her hips, her legs, one outstretched, the other arched at the knee.

And if she were completely truthful, deep down in her heart of hearts, she wanted Francis to like what he could see.

She heard him say calmly, 'Of course Sylvie's right. The point is, do you want to be protected?'

She opened her eyes and put down the drink. Francis was sitting with his arms round updrawn knees, hands loosely clasped, eyes resting pensively upon her. He seemed to be very relaxed. Philippa envied him his self-control.

With the pulse throbbing in her neck and warmth rising to her face, she said, 'No, I don't,' and after a moment, heightened by a frisson of expectancy charging the air between them, Francis said softly, 'Good,' and leaned forward and touched his lips to hers, very, very gently.

As he drew back he murmured, 'You taste of wine—delicious! Can I tempt you with an orange? I'll peel it for you,' and the moment, brief and exquisite, was put aside.

'Tell me about your family,' demanded Francis lightly, stretching out on his back, hands behind his head.

'Not much to tell,' replied Philippa, offering an orange segment. 'I don't know the Ingrams, and the only Stanhope I have anything to do with is my mother's sister, Grace. She has a house in Wimbledon which is divided into two flats and I live in the upstairs one.'

'What do you mean, you don't know the Ingrams?'

'Just that. I've never met them. They live in Cumbria.' She shrugged. 'I've not missed them. My father left home and never returned after a row with his father.'

'Aren't you curious about them?' asked Francis.

Philippa reached for the towel and wiped her hands free of orange juice. 'To my surprise I find I am.'

'Why surprise?'

'Well, you see . . .' She stopped and pulled a face. 'I don't want to bore you with my family history . . .'

'I'm quite capable of changing the subject,'

drawled Francis, and Philippa considered this statement and said cheerfully,

'You've been warned.' She hugged her knees and gazed thoughtfully across the river. 'It's the old, old story of a father trying to impose his will on to his son—my grandfather wanted my father to go into the family business. The Ingrams founded Copperthwaite Mills years ago and make cloth, rather good stuff actually. The idea of Robert in a factory situation is mind-boggling, but he left school and dutifully went to the Mills to learn the trade from the bottom up and hated it, because all he wanted to do was paint. My grandfather was an obstinate man, from all accounts. He had already lost one son, Father's elder brother, in a drowning accident, and all his hopes were on Father. I can understand that, but you can't live your children's lives for them, can you?'

Francis said, 'No, of course you can't.'

'And then, to complicate things further, Father met Mother. She was, according to my aunt, beautiful. I can only remember her when she was ill, but at nineteen, when Father met her, she was lovely. To a painter, and one whose interest was in portraiture, she was perfection—lovely bones, transparent skin, pale green eyes and dark brown hair the colour of a matured conker. How could Father resist her?'

'I gather he didn't.' Francis eyed her. 'Are you like your mother?'

Philippa laughed. 'Unfortunately no. I have her bone structure, but not her constitution, for which I'm grateful, and her mop of hair, but not the colour, which is infuriating. The rest is pure Ingram, including, according to Grace, the Ingram stubbornness.' She wrinkled her nose speculatively. 'Dad told my grandfather that he wasn't interested in wool, that he was going to paint, and that he was going to marry Rose—my mother. There was an almighty row and that was that.' She allowed sand to trickle through her fingers and went on slowly, 'My grandfather was a fool. He should have realised that, for all his easy ways, Dad was as stubborn as himself, but he didn't, and it's stupid to issue ultimatums. They always backfire.'

Francis leaned up on one elbow, saying, 'He probably would agree with you.'

'I think Mother could have put things right eventually, given the chance. She was so sweet-natured and kind, but they moved to France for her health just after I was born and never returned to England.'

Francis sat up and began to brush the sand from his back. 'Shall you eventually satisfy your curiosity about the Ingrams, do you think?'

'The opportunity does seem to have offered itself,' Philippa admitted, and told him about the birthday invitation. 'The need to know one's roots seems to grow as the years pass.'

'So you'll go.'

She looked at him and gave a little laugh. 'Yes, I'll go.' She tilted her head. 'You sure have a knack of making me talk! What about your family?'

'Very thin over in England, extremely prolific over here.' He grinned. 'What I lack in siblings I gain in cousins, although Jules is more like a brother.' He twisted round and peered upwards, assessing the position of the sun. 'We're going to be blocked out in a minute and the time's getting on anyway, so my family will have to wait.'

They packed up the picnic things and pulled clothing over their by now dry swimsuits. It was incredible, thought Philippa, how the time had flown, and even more so how happy she was. So far there had been no discordant note in their relationship, no rushing of fences, and she liked that. And they had talked, arguing amicably over some things, during the car journey. It was a relief to find a man who did not want to dominate her with his opinions. It was a delightful experience knowing she was being drawn more and more under his spell and not resisting.

As they set off down river she feasted her eyes on him with no fear of discovery. The cotton shirt straining at the seams as he drove the paddle deep into the water showed the strength across his shoulders. There were droplets of water clinging to his arms and the ruffled buttermilk hair drew colour from the sun.

How amazing when I'm not usually attracted to fair men, she thought, smiling to herself.

When Francis threw back the occasional glance or remark, she allowed her happiness to show on her face and didn't give a damn. The small, sly voice inside her head that still insisted she was playing with dynamite, she drowned in the waters of the Ardèche without scruple.

At St Martin the gorge widened, and it was here that they handed in the canoe and collected the Spider.

'Tired?' asked Francis, turning to her as they drove off, and she answered, 'Mmm . . . pleasantly so.'

'What would you like to do now?' Francis looked at the dash clock and went on, 'I know an inn, off the main road south of Bagnols, which has a good chef and a pianist who sings the best jazz and blues in the district.'

'Sounds just right—so long as there's the means to wash and brush up. I hope it's not too grand? I feel a mess.'

'It's a very casual place, but you need have no fears, you look——' he gave her a brief glance, paused slightly, and went on,'——delightful.'

'That wasn't the word you were going to use,' accused Philippa, laughing, lifting up a strand of hair. 'Could it have been windswept that first came to mind?'

'I was going to say adorable,' Francis replied tranquilly.

Philippa shot him a swift look, faint pink colouring her cheeks. She let out a feeble 'Oh.'

'*I* am quite happy with adorable, but it may be too soon for you. I have to keep reminding myself that we only met yesterday . . . so I'll settle for delightful.'

There seemed to be no answer to that, and Philippa hugged adorable to herself in secret.

As it was fairly early the inn was only sparsely scattered with diners. Francis was greeted with enthusiasm by the *patron* and they were shown to a table by the window which overlooked a pretty courtyard.

'Speciality of the house today is rabbit—*Sauté de Lapin aux Pruneaux*—have you a liking for rabbit with prunes?' Francis asked, lifting his eyes from the menu, eyes teasing.

'I'll let you know,' promised Philippa loftily, and he raised his brows and drawled,

'She's on time, she's delightfully adorable and ready to try *lapin aux pruneaux*! The gods are laughing! Or you could have fish, duck or . . .'

'Rabbit,' broke in Philippa firmly. 'Never let it be said I was a quitter!'

The dish was delicious. The chef came to speak with them and informed Philippa that it was a country dish from Picardy, where he himself had been born. He begged to be allowed to bring Mademoiselle a crêpe which he would create in her honour. He beamed a smile when she accepted his offer and a few moments later the chafing dish and table burner were brought forward and with considerable interest from the rest of the diners Crêpe Philippa was created. Invited to take a taste, Philippa gave her wholehearted approval and the chef, satisfied, bustled back to his kitchen.

Francis, who had refused dessert, sat back in his chair watching her, occasionally sipping his claret.

'A healthy appetite too,' he murmured, adding to his list, and Philippa, spoon poised, said indignantly,

'So I should think! Canoeing is strenuous work, you know!' She finished the last mouthful and groaned, 'Absolutely gorgeous . . . I couldn't eat another thing. How grand to have a pudding named after oneself!'

'Crêpe Suzette was inspired by a *petite amie* of Edward VII when he was Prince of Wales,' offered Francis, eyes gleaming.

Philippa widened her own. 'Really? What snippets of information you do have!' She dropped the bantering and said quietly, 'Thank you, Francis, for today . . . it has been lovely.'

'I'm glad. Perhaps you'll allow me to be your guide tomorrow?' He saw hesitation cross her face and said quickly, 'But you have something else planned. Never mind, another day . . .?'

'No, I have nothing planned,' she said, and

raised her eyes to his, and they contemplated each other for a second or two that had no hurry and she said simply, 'Where shall we go?'

When the following day's itinerary had been discussed Francis said casually, 'I have to fly to Bonn on Friday on business.'

'I thought Jules said you were on holiday?' Damn! Had she shown too much disappointment?

'I am, but Bonn is something I can't put off. I'll be there four days, but I'll be back in time to take you to see the play,' promised Francis, very content to hear the disappointment.

Provence, in the days that followed, became touched with magic. They explored its treasures, driving the Spider up into the hills to seek out tiny villages perched upon craggy cliffs. They discovered gaily coloured harbours full of fishing boats, wide graceful avenues, churches and village squares. They watched *pétanque*, the game of bowls played with deadly seriousness by men young and old, gave their considered opinion on several wines and when Francis had to leave for Bonn, Philippa resigned herself to the work she should have been doing anyway. She found it difficult to concentrate and more often than not ended up calling on Sylvie.

On the fourth day of his absence Sylvie remarked drily, 'It seems that the ton of bricks has fallen.'

Philippa, who was gazing absently out of the window, gave a short laugh. 'It has.'

'I hope you know what you're doing, Phippy,' Sylvie said with some anxiety, and Philippa returned ruefully,

'I'm not doing anything, as yet.'

'Which proves he has patience,' declared Sylvie,

adding quickly, 'Sorry, sorry—I hereby resign from being mother hen!'

Philippa flapped a forgiving hand. 'You don't say anything I haven't said to myself, Sylvie. I've held back, really I have, but it's no good. These four days have seemed like four months. I can't believe it's happening to me! I can't describe what it's like being with him and I feel only half alive when he's away.' Philippa gave a groaning laugh. 'Hell, how banal I sound! He's a rag-bag of information, he makes me laugh, he knows when to talk and when to listen—I've talked more about myself to him than to any other living soul apart from you—his intellect appeals to me and . . .' She stopped short.

'He's physically attractive to you,' finished Sylvie. 'You could be in love.'

'You do like him, don't you, Sylvie?' asked Philippa a little urgently, unable to look at her friend as she asked.

'I've always liked him, Phippy, he's an old friend of Fabien's. I just don't want you to be hurt, that's all.'

'Why should I be?' demanded Philippa, and frowned. 'I might be,' she conceded, 'who can tell? Anyway, I don't care.'

Sylvie sighed. 'Yes, you're in love.'

Francis returned. There was no ignoring the implosion of pleasure she felt when she opened the door to him. She was careful not to show how much she had missed him but, if anything, the four days' absence seemed to strengthen their rapport. They went to Orange and watched Shakespeare's lighthearted play about fairies and crossed lovers, and to Philippa, she and Francis seemed to be living in a similar enchantment. She knew there was no turning back, and that he held her happiness in his hands.

The next morning found them speeding south towards the Camargue, the district where the River Rhône empties out into the sea. There was a festival held every year at a town on the coast called Les Saintes Maries de la Mer, which Francis thought Philippa would enjoy.

'The place is named after the three Marys from the gospel,' he told her as he drove. 'Marie Jacobé—she was the sister of the Virgin Mary; Marie Salomé—the mother of James and John; and Mary Magdalene. There's a story attached to them,' he added, and glanced her way.

'Tell me,' urged Philippa lightly. They had greeted each other that morning with the slight wariness of people about to set off on an escapade the outcome of which could turn out to be a mite dangerous. A story could ease things.

'Well,' said Francis, 'all three were at the Crucifixion and according to legend they left Palestine, with Lazarus and Martha and some others, together with a black servant called Sara, in a boat without oars or sails.'

'Without . . .?' You mean they just drifted with the tides and winds right across the Mediterranean?' exclaimed Philippa.

'That's what is said. They landed safely on the coast—miraculously, I suppose, would be the right word, and Marie Jacobé and Marie Salomé stayed, with Sara, and built a small chapel on the site of pagan temple. Later, a church was built on the same spot and later still, when the gipsies began to arrive in Provence in the fifteenth century, they adopted Sara as their patron saint.'

'Do you think it's true?'

'The whole of Provence is a pot-pourri of myth and history, and steeped in so many different religions and races how can legend and history be disentangled?' Francis drew her attention outside. 'See how flat the land is becoming? We're into the delta of the Rhône now.'

Philippa looked out of the window. Miles and miles of marshland spread before her as far as the horizon, the flatness broken only by the occasional clump of trees or church spire. A flock of birds emerged from the long grass and flew low across the marsh, settling into obscurity further away. Glimpses of water could be seen, reflecting the sun, and Francis, following the flight of birds with a quick glance, remarked,

'The authorities have made the marsh into a zoological and botanical nature reserve with stringent rules for protection of the wild life here. The best way to see the Camargue is on horseback. We're staying with my cousin and her husband, who own one of the many ranches dotted around the area.'

Philippa said teasingly, 'Wherever we go there seems to be a Morin cousin!'

Jean and Colette made them welcome, greeting Francis enthusiastically and Philippa with smiling friendliness and an underlying interest, confirmed by Colette's words as she showed Philippa to her bedroom.

'We were delighted to learn that Francis was bringing someone with him.' She walked round the bedroom, on the lookout for anything not quite right. Satisfied, she turned to Philippa, adding, 'He usually comes alone,' and on that piece of information, she left.

Thoughtfully, Philippa unpacked the small case she had brought and changed into a pair of jodhpurs and boots she had borrowed, then wandered over to the window, tucking in her blouse at the waist as she looked out on to the stable yard below. A string of Camargue horses—white to the uninitiated, grey to equestrians—were returning from taking their riders out on an exploration trail of the marshes. Their voices floated upwards, cheerful, with the odd laugh, as they entered the ranch house for refreshment.

A knock on the door and Francis calling her name caused Philippa to hurry. Joining him, she found he was holding two riding hats.

'I want you to put this on,' he said. 'I make it a rule never to ride without one, in case of accidents. It's a bind, especially when it's hot, but I've known too many people either killed or injured for life to ignore the dangers.' He watched critically as Philippa adjusted the chin-strap and then put on his own as he led the way to the stables. The horses were waiting for them, already saddled, and again Francis took time to check the girths and made sure he was completely satisfied before they set off.

He rode behind for a while, obviously assessing Philippa's capability, and then moved up to join her. She looked at him and smiled, saying,

'It's like riding a bike, you never forget, but I reckon I'm going to pay for it tomorrow!'

'There's always payment for everything in some form or another,' Francis responded, throwing her a slightly sardonic smile.

They followed the track for a little under two miles, Francis naming the birds they flushed and reining in his mount brought their leisurely ride to a halt, staring out across the marsh.

'I was here two years ago when the pink flamingoes came through on their way from North America. Ten thousand of them—it was an incredible sight, one I'll never forget. I can't provide flamingoes at the moment, but . . .' He stood in the stirrups and put up binoculars. After a moment he handed them over, '. . . to the right and beyond that clump of bushes. They blend into the landscape, but you can just make them out. A herd of bulls, and a little further on, about thirty wild horses.' He waited while Philippa got them into focus and added, 'There's a *corride* tonight. Shall we go?'

'A bullfight?' Philippa lowered the glasses and turned to him consideringly. 'They don't kill the bull here, do they, so I'll say yes.' She handed back the binoculars and as his hand closed over hers he said teasingly,

'Softhearted Pippa!'

He so rarely touched her that when there was contact it was like an electric shock. Her eyes flew up to his and heat flooded her face.

'You called me Pippa.' She said the first thing that came into her head.

The horses moved impatiently, jostling closer.

'I'm sorry.' Francis frowned and looked down at her hand, still retained in his. 'Would you rather I didn't?'

'No . . . my father was . . . he called me Pippa,' she offered lamely, and then, 'You may—if you wish.'

He smiled and as the animals moved abruptly the smile took a comical downward turn at the corners and he was forced to let go her hand as his horse side-stepped away. Checking it, he said ruefully, 'This isn't the most practical of places to whisper sweet nothings, is it?'

Philippa burst out laughing and raised her brows, asking lightly, 'Francis Morin, are you making love to me?'

Francis said slowly, 'Balfour, not Morin.' His eyes searched her face as they began to move forward again, seeing the puzzlement she was feeling.

'What do you mean?' she asked.

'You forget that my mother is the Morin. My father was Duncan Balfour, a Scot. My name is Francis Morin Balfour.' He paused. 'I did tell you, I think, that I was half Scot, half French.'

Feeling oddly disconcerted, Philippa replied, 'Yes, I remember you did, but . . .'

'Nothing's changed. I'm still the same person.'

'But I've always thought of you as Francis Morin,' she protested, 'and now I'm going to have to get used to you as Francis Balfour!'

'I don't care how you think of me, so long as you do.' He gave her an amused side-glance. 'If it's any consolation I doubt whether anyone ever thinks of me as Balfour in France. I spent so much time with my cousins that I'm considered to be a Morin.' He checked his watch. 'We've been out long enough, I think. If we take this track we can go back by another route.'

They trotted into the yard some time later and Philippa groaned as Francis walked over to help her dismount.

'I don't think I can get off! Canoeing, swimming and now this. I suspect you're putting me through some sort of secret endurance test!'

Francis threw back his head and roared with

laughter. 'Poor girl, is that what it feels like?' He held up his hands and clasped her waist and she slipped off the saddle. As her feet touched the ground he remained holding her and with a quizzical look on his face he said, 'The answer to your question is yes.'

Trying to remember their earlier conversation, Philippa asked, puzzled, 'What question?'

'Yes, I am making love to you.'

Philippa's mount moved abruptly and bumped her sharply against his chest and his arms went round her. With a gasp of surprise she asked, 'Did you train him to do that?' laughing a little, her senses quickening.

'To get what I want, nothing is beyond me,' drawled Francis smugly, then his face changed and his mouth came down on hers.

The blood pounded in Philippa's ears and every nerve ending burst into a whoosh of happiness. She could feel his heart beating as fast and as hard as her own and her body moulded to his with incredible perfection.

'Adorable beautiful Pippa!' His voice was quietly exultant, his breath warm against her face. 'I knew this could happen the moment I set eyes on you.'

They walked to the house, arms around each other, and brought in with them an aura of romance, endorsing Colette's hopes as she watched them.

That evening they drove into Les Saintes Maries and wandered through the town, mingling with the festive crowd. Gipsies, Camargue cowboys, the fifes and tambours of the musicians, all added to the noise and gaiety of the dancing and sideshows.

'The gipsies come from all over,' explained

Francis, holding her close so that they could not become separated in the crowd. 'Tonight they'll keep a vigil in the crypt of the church, tomorrow there's a special service in the Saints' honour and a procession carries the statues of the Saints in a model boat down to the shore. The boat will be carried into the waves and the Bishop will bless the sea. The real festivities begin then—Provençal dances, feats of horsemanship, wrestling with the bulls, sideshows—in fact, all the fun of the fair.' He stopped. 'I don't believe you've heard a word I've been saying!'

'Yes, I have,' Philippa protested truthfully, but she had been watching him, as well as listening. The crisp blue shirt accentuated the blue of his eyes. His fair head always drew attention wherever they went, especially female, and tonight was no exception. Philippa was merely enjoying the fact that it was she who was walking in the shelter of his arm and not someone else.

At the *corride* they cheered with the rest of the spectators as competitors tried to secure the red cockade hanging between the horns of the bull with the multi-pronged hook used especially for the purpose. Quite late, they returned to the ranch, and Francis kissed her outside her bedroom door and pushed her gently through. She had known instinctively that he would not come to her while they stayed there.

Colette's approval blossomed and she was very happy to talk about Francis to Philippa in the odd moments they were alone together. Philippa learned that it was Francis who had loaned his cousin the initial down-payment on the ranch and was in no hurry for it to be repaid, preferring to be a partner in the venture.

'So you see, I am prejudiced about him,' admitted Colette, smiling, 'but you know his worth. Francis is loyal to his family and friends. I am so glad he has at last found someone to make him happy. Ah, you blush, but he has never brought anyone with him before,' she said firmly, 'and he is happy. I can tell.'

In the face of such certainty Philippa did not argue and went away to build a few dreams.

The festival over, they left the ranch with the afternoon nearly gone. For some miles there was silence between them and then Francis asked, a trifle abruptly, 'Do you have to return to Villeneuve today?' He glanced briefly her way and when Philippa murmured, 'No,' he turned at the next fork in the road, saying, 'Then I shall take you to Les Baux.'

The terrain was changing. The flat delta was left behind and they began to climb. The road wound its way upwards through a range of arid, craggy hills. On the lower slopes were olive and almond trees, higher up the trees gave way to scrub and coarse grass. The summits of the hills were bare rock.

Les Alpilles. This mountain range had a wild, peculiar haunting quality which appealed to Philippa, and the village of Les Baux remained invisible almost to the last turn of the road. As Francis swung the Spider to a halt she thought the place looked as though it was hewn out of the rock it stood upon.

'You'll understand why we have to leave the car here when you see how narrow the streets are—some of them are even stepped.' He tucked her arm through his as they entered the village through an archway and Philippa looked round her with quickening curiosity. The street they were slowly climbing was extremely narrow and on either side the buildings clung to each other, all built of the same rough grey stone. Tiny windows showed their wares—craft-work, pottery and paintings.

'How old is it?' asked Philippa.

Francies replied, 'Oh, Les Baux goes back to the Iron Age, but it was in the Middle Ages that it came into its own. Stuck up on this peak it's a natural fortress and was owned by one of the most powerful families in southern France—the *seigneurs* of Baux. It was once a notorious bandits' nest.'

'You know such picturesque bits of history,' praised Philippa.

'That's not the reason I've brought you here.'

'No? You have another quaint story for me?'

'If you think troubadours quaint, then yes. It was here that they found their inspiration in what was called the Courts of Love.' Francis was smiling, but she sensed a purpose behind the banter.

'Ah!' she breathed, playing the game. 'The poets with their lutes and lyres, singing songs of gallantry, courtship and chivalry!'

'With the winner receiving a crown of peacocks' feathers and a kiss from the most beautiful lady present.'

They were now standing outside an open doorway, the entrance dropping downwards to accommodate the slope of the mountain.

Philippa's eyes sparkled. 'Why, Francis! Do you feel in good voice? I'm not too sure of the peacocks' feathers, but I've seen a couple of pigeons!' She peered into the dark interior and could just make out a reception desk. 'I wonder if they could provide the lute?' She straightened and turned to face him, and her heart began to beat faster at the look on his face.

Francis said, 'Shall we go in and find out?' and Philippa replied gravely, 'I thought you'd never ask.'

The room was delightful—the furniture old and the double bed canopied. The view from the window scanned the steep slope of the mountain and Francis, withdrawing his head, announced, 'I'm glad I don't have to climb up that to sing you a love song.'

'I'll let down my hair,' promised Philippa.

They went for a walk after their evening meal, finally ending up on the edge of a wide, rock-strewn promontory.

'To watch the sun rise over the southern plain from here is said to be one of the wonders of the world.' Francis narrowed his eyes, peering into the distance. 'On a clear day you can see as far as the coast.' He glanced down at her, his arm tightening, drawing her closer. 'Not cold, are you?'

Philippa shook her head and dug her hands deeper into her jacket pockets. 'No, not really. We're awfully high up here, aren't we? I think it must be the ghosts that are prowling. It's a bit desolate, isn't it?' She looked back over her shoulder to the ruined fortifications, dark grey and sombre in the fading light. 'The whole village is so full of history it positively bristles with ghosts.' She laughed ruefully. 'It probably looks better in sunshine. I'm not usually so sensitive to atmosphere.'

'You have every right to be sensitive just here. It's said,' Francis informed her whimsically, 'that the Vicomte de Baux used to hurl hostages who couldn't pay their ransom money over this very edge to die a nasty death.'

Philippa peered ghoulishly down to the depths below. 'Did he? I trust he came to a horrible end?'

Amused, Francis replied, 'He did. He drowned in the Rhône trying to escape his pursuers.'

'I'm very pleased to hear it.' Philippa gave another shiver. 'Let's go in. We've seen the sun set, we'll take its rise for granted, shall we?' She raised herself on tiptoes and brushed her lips against his.

Francis held her look for a long moment, his face oddly austere, then he let out a breath and replied, 'Yes, let's. I can think of other warmer, more comfortable places to be.'

'And I've never slept under a canopy before,' said Philippa.

CHAPTER FOUR

FABIEN poured out the Châteauneuf du Pape and exclaimed with quiet satisfaction, 'Well, this is extremely agreeable.'

Sylvie looked at her husband with fond exasperation, caught Philippa's eye across the table and they exchanged a smile.

'Fabien, my sweet, it is much more than that,' Sylvie stated imperially. 'Today is a day to remember!' She eyed Jules and Lisette across the table benignly. 'Who would have thought we would be celebrating an engagement?'

Jules grinned and Lisette gazed adoringly at him. Francis sought Philippa's eye and raised his glass in a silent toast. She returned the gesture, hugging her own personal happiness to her. She was happy, happy, happy, and wanted the world to know, and if not the world, then the friends gathered round the table today.

It was a beautiful late May day. The sun was shining and nature still had a freshness about her despite the warmth of the preceding month. Their table was set on the immaculately trimmed lawn of the hotel where they were dining and their party was the sole occupant, having outstayed the rest of the diners.

'Our ladies are a credit to us,' declared Fabien, his eyes going round the table. 'How beautiful they are. Gentlemen! We are lucky fellows!'

Sylvie, eyes brimming with laughter, broke in, 'I

think we should order coffee now, Fabien. We shall be thrown out if we're not careful.'

'Nonsense,' declared her husband confidently. 'This is a special occasion,' and his smile embraced them all. 'Nevertheless, perhaps we should come down to earth. Coffee would be a good idea, Sylvie.'

The waiter was summoned and coffee ordered. Sylvie, her eyes on Lisette, murmured to Philippa,

'Lisette improves with time, doesn't she?' She shot her friend a sly glance. 'I'm not much good as a matchmaker, am I?' and she gazed reflectively on Francis who was talking to Fabien. She gave a rueful sigh. 'I did so want you to marry a Frenchman so that you'd live in France,' she paused and gave Philippa a teasing look, 'But a half-Frenchman . . .' and she took a sip of wine, her eyes dancing above the rim.

'So you're finishing your holiday on the coast,' Fabien was observing to Francis, the slight hint of a question in his voice.

'We're going to lay a ghost,' admitted Francis quietly. 'Philippa has never been back to Gigaro since her father was killed.'

'Ah, I see. Yes, Sylvie mentioned that. Robert Ingram had an accident, did he not? A fall?'

Francis nodded. 'We're not staying on the coast—the Riviera in June will be crowded. No, we shall stay in the mountains and visit Gigaro from there.' He looked at his watch and turned to Philippa. 'I think we should make a move as soon as we've finished coffee,' and Philippa agreed, glancing back to the hotel and murmuring,

'We've just about overstayed our welcome, I think,' and then her eyes returned to his face.

'Have I told you how beautiful you are

recently?' asked Francis, his voice a lazy caress, the message in his eyes bringing a faint pink to her cheeks.

'Not for at least three hours,' reproached Philippa, her heart singing.

Coffee over, the three couples rose to their feet and amidst much laughter and kissing they departed, each making for their car, calling exuberant farewells. Doors slammed and engines sprang to life, and one by one the cars drew away and went their separate ways.

'Are we mad, do you think?' Philippa asked suddenly, when they had driven in companionable silence for a few miles.

'More than likely,' replied Francis with a drawl, 'and if you keep on looking at me like that I shall have to stop and kiss you. The prospect is not unattractive, but we have a few miles ahead of us.'

'I'll try to behave,' promised Philippa demurely.

La Garde-Freinet, a spacious village dominated by its ruined Saracen castle, lay fourteen kilometres north-west of St Tropez in the mountains known as the Massif des Maures. It was an idyllic setting and Philippa fell in love with it right away. They put up at an inn, small and cosy, with an excellent cuisine, and Philippa, as the days passed, had not thought that such happiness could exist. She kept warning herself that this was not normal living, with the stress and strains of day-to-day problems, but even this sensible attitude did nothing to diminish the magic surrounding them. They made love in the quaint, sloping-ceilinged room, with doves from a nearby cote fluttering and cooing on the roof of the dormer window. Philippa searched for their discarded feathers and made a crown which she presented to Francis with a kiss, saying solemnly,

'Peacocks are in short supply, darling, but here's your crown of feathers,' and she placed it on his head with mock ceremony while Francis took her face in his hands and replied whimsically,

'This troubadour thanks the beautiful lady and swears undying love,' and his mouth covered hers, gently at first, and then whimsy was left behind as their emotions took over, singing their own special poetry.

With three lazy halcyon days behind them they eventually made for Gigaro where the Spider was left parked by an old drinking trough and they took to the cliff path. There was a light breeze off the sea which lifted Philippa's hair, throwing it across her face so that she needed a hand to secure it. Francis tucked her other hand through his arm, still retaining a hold, and they walked without talking. When Philippa slowed to a halt, Francis stared down at the cruel rocks below, frowning, and asked,

'Is this the place?'

She nodded. After a moment, her eyes raking sea and land, she remarked, 'It's very beautiful, isn't it? I'd forgotten how beautiful it is.' She drew him on. 'Let's find the cottage. It's just beyond the next bay, behind those forlorn-looking trees.'

The gate was half off its hinges and the path overgrown. Panes of glass were broken in the windows and weeds were staking a claim across the front door. It was obviously empty.

Philippa turned to Francis who was watching her and explained, 'There's no running water, but the well water is delicious—at least, it was—cold and clear. No electricity or gas.' Her gaze swept the terrain. 'The whole of this cliff top is covered in poppies in the summer—it's a fantastic sight. Splashes of red on green. Dad painted a picture of me once sitting in the grass surrounded by them . . . I wonder where that went to?' She turned back to the house. 'The door was painted bright poppy red and—yes, see here? you can just make out Poppy Cottage on the name-plate.' She contemplated the faded peeling paint and pulled a rueful face. 'Ah, well, I shall have to remember it the way it was.'

'Does it distress you?'

Philippa shook her head, leading the way down the path, placing her feet carefully on the uneven stones. 'No. I feel sorry for the place, it deserves better than this, but Poppy Cottage belongs to a happy childhood and it would be silly to forget that, wouldn't it?'

Francis took her hand. 'What a sensible person you are—most of the time,' he added, smiling.

'Stop bragging! It's quite apparent that where you're concerned I have no sense at all.' Philippa flicked him a probing look, half laughing, half serious. 'Do you often make snap decisions, Francis?'

'What a sweeping question! No, I can't say I do.' He bent his head and brushed her lips with his. 'But if I do, there's a good reason.' He pulled her against him and smiled down into her eyes. 'I can just see you as a child here—I bet you were a tomboy, and a bossy-boots.'

Philippa grinned. 'How did you guess?' Her face sobered and she put her arms round his neck. 'Thank you for helping me to lay the ghosts.' She glanced back. 'They're friendly ones.' She broke away and tugged his hand, making him run.

Philippa awoke the next morning early. The sun slanted through the unshuttered window, foretelling another lovely day. She could hear the muted early morning sounds coming from the inn and the doves were awake, their gentle cooing soothing.

She moved her head carefully on the pillow and contentedly lay watching Francis. It was something she liked doing. Their relationship was so new that she was frightened of showing him how much he meant to her. It was a sort of rearguard action which she scorned and yet felt powerless to alter. It still amazed her that they had met at all, let alone fallen in love. So these few moments before he woke were precious ones, for she saw a Francis usually hidden—unaware and defenceless—and she could allow her eyes to wander over him as freely as she liked.

He was lying on his front, his head turned towards her. The arm nearest her was lying heavily across her hip and she was close enough to the rounded curve of his shoulder to put her lips against his skin. She did this, very stealthily, and then ran her tongue over them, tasting him. She could see a smattering of freckles over the sweeping dip to his backbone, bronzed flesh brushed with the fairest of body hair. Her eyes went back to his face. His breathing was quiet. What beautifully shaped lips he had—not full, not thin, but just right, with curved laughter lines faintly visible. His chin was bristly with golden stubble and she resisted the urge to smooth back the front of his hair that was tumbling over his forehead. She wondered lazily how many different colours there were in it and loved the way it sprang, thick and crisp. Her hands itched to press against the, at the moment, untamed thatch of it, but again she resisted the temptation, for that would certainly wake him, and she wanted to hang on to these moments for as long as she could.

Soon, just looking wasn't enough. Fractionally, with great stealth, she eased forward, inching her way so that they touched more completely and her lips curved in anticipation, wondering how long it would be before his body told him and woke him.

She might have known he would take her by surprise. In a single action she was drawn to him by a quick moving arm, his body shifting to accommodate her more thoroughly, and a leg wound itself confidently over her, making her a prisoner. The bristly stubble scrubbed her chin as those beautiful lips claimed hers, first with exuberant enjoyment and then gentling, moving away, wandering down her throat, tasting, exploring with supreme mastery.

Philippa gathered back her breath and demanded, 'How long have you been awake, you wretch?' her colour deepening as his head came up and those incredibly blue eyes enveloped her.

'Long enough,' came the lazy reply. 'I've decided you're a shameful hussy.'

Her lips curved. 'A cat can look at a king . . . you'll be late,' she murmured feebly, shivering, as the exquisite drift of his hands travelled sensuously down her back, sliding comfortably over the swell of her hips and coming to rest authoritatively at full stretch, cupping her to him.

She gave in and spread her fingers through his hair and laughed low in her throat, softly. 'I take it,' she managed, her body quivering to the insidious prowess of his tongue, 'that you're not awfully interested in *petit déjeuner*?' and then amusement vanished and she was away on the crest of emotions that left her bereft of any thought that was not coupled with the two of them, in that room, at that moment in time.

Afterwards they lay, their bodies entwined, not saying anything, their breathing gradually returning to normal. The church clock struck the hour.

Francis gave a soft, 'Damn!' and leaned up on one elbow, gazing down at her. He smoothed the hair from her face and said quietly, 'I have to go.'

'Yes, I know.' Philippa lifted a hand and rubbed a finger across the roughness of his chin.

'I'm sorry business has intruded. If I could've put it off I would have done so.' He searched her face and was reassured by her clear gaze.

'The outside world is edging its way in whether we like it or not,' she murmured, giving a small smile.

'But I didn't want it to, not until the holiday was over.'

'Who's being the impractical romantic now?' teased Philippa, her eyes smiling up at him. 'If you hurry you'll have time for coffee.'

'I'll be here for dinner. If anything happens to detain me, I'll ring you.' Francis buried his face in the curve of her neck and shoulder, savouring the moment, before lifting himself off the bed and making for the bathroom.

Philippa listened to the shower running. She knew he had cancelled a number of meetings he had intended to make while in Europe so that they could spend these days together. Now his thoughts would be on what lay ahead, in another world, a world she wasn't part of.

Francis came back, his face already wearing the

look she was beginning to recognise, one of complete absorption in what he was doing. She smiled to herself. Did he realise how he changed and how she was beginning to read him? She watched him get dressed with his usual economy of energy and movement. Here was the Francis emerging she did not know, this stranger in the light grey suit and the purposeful look about him. He could not have risen so highly in the business world without being resourceful and firm. Ruthless? Yes, even ruthless. Francis, on being questioned by her once, had merely said that success was knowing a bit of information at the right time with the right person, but it must be more than that, she mused, her eyes following him as he moved round the room, collecting together his things.

'What will you do while I'm away?' Francis paused to ask, glancing at her before collecting the loose change and car keys from the bedside table.

'I shall work.' Philippa put her hands behind her head and continued mockingly, 'You're not the only one who earns a living. I did have an existence before I met you.'

Francis crossed to the bed and bent down to kiss her, his eyes flickering over her. With his mouth poised above her, he murmured, 'If you don't behave, neither of us will earn a penny piece.' His lips pressed against hers, firmly and briefly. He straightened, saying, 'Take care. I'll see you this evening.' He crossed to the door, hesitated and turned his head her way, his gaze resting pensively on her. 'Pippa . . .'

Philippa sat up and wrapped the sheet round her. 'Go,' she ordered, her voice mock-stern. 'Anything else you have to tell me can wait. You'll be late.'

Francis smiled. 'You sound like a nagging wife! I'm going.'

Philippa looked at the closed door and turned over on to her stomach. How ridiculous she was to feel so forlorn. He was only going to be away a few hours. She had very nearly said drive carefully, which sounded even more wifely! Heaven forbid! She had just stopped herself in time, but she couldn't stop herself thinking it. Was this what love was like then? Worrying? Things must, she thought, get into perspective eventually. She had always been a fatalist, and worrying about Francis driving along the autoroute to Cannes wasn't going to make him drive more carefully, or anyone else, for that matter. There was a bit more to this loving lark than met the eye, that much was evident, she concluded, and drifted into sleep.

Philippa eased her conscience later in the morning by sitting in the sun, adding a few pages to the story she was translating—a children's book from the French into English. At midday she closed her books and returned to their room to lose them in the bottom of her suitcase. Lunch, with an aperitif, beckoned.

A pile of Michelin maps, a couple of magazines and a newspaper had been tidied by the maid and placed on the bedside table. They must have fallen to the floor. Philippa recognised the English paper as the one Francis had bought the day before in St Tropez. He'll be annoyed, she thought, picking it up, remembering him looking for it that morning and murmuring to himself that it must be in the car. She was seized with the sudden urge to find out what was happening in the outside world and took it down with her to read.

She ordered a half-bottle of Pouilly Fuissé and

began to read, enjoying catching up with the news, even though it was already out of date.

There was no reason why she should have read the business pages, except that she had been without a newspaper for so long that now she had one it seemed the thing to do, to digest it from cover to cover. And Francis would have read this section, which was a silly enough reason for reading it, but one that fitted a woman in love. All the incomprehensible information contained in it—stocks and shares, business take-overs, directors kicked out—all would have meant something to Francis.

She nearly missed it. With her interest rapidly dwindling, it was only her own name that caught her eye as she was about to discard the paper. Curious, she began to scan the column.

Shares in Ingrams were gaining strength, owing to an expanding export market. Ingrams, trademark Copperthwaite Wool, were becoming popular abroad—due, no doubt, to the influence of Francis Balfour, one of the directors of Ingrams. Francis Balfour of Balfour Data Products, a firm rising steadily in its own right.

As the chill spread through her, Philippa read on, hoping against hope that it was a mistake. Francis Balfour, the article said, the man who had joined the board of directors five years ago, had expanded interest in the company first of all in France, but interest was growing further afield. Philip Ingram, semi-retired from the company, would make no comment when asked whether his nephew Ross Fairley or Francis Balfour would succeed him as chairman.

Philippa sat, stunned, her whole being weighted down by what she had just learned. Francis

Balfour had just made love to Philip Ingram's granddaughter! The words screamed round in her head, mocking her, tantalising her with a welter of insinuations.

The innkeeper was surprised when Philippa asked him to order her a taxi—surprised, but too polite to show it. Monsieur, he was told, would be arriving back this evening and would settle everything. The car in thirty minutes, please. Madame was charming but firm, and her orders were not to be questioned.

All emotion held firmly in check, Philippa packed quickly and methodically, and when she was done she drew a circle in red pen around the Ingram article and left it lying in the centre of the bed—an ironic place. About to leave, she saw the crown of doves' feathers perched jauntily on the bedpost. She pulled it bitterly to pieces and scattered the feathers over the paper.

The taxi took her to Le Cannet where she hired a Renault and was soon on the autoroute heading west. St Maximin, Aix-en-Provence, Salon, Cavaillon were passed by with Philippa hardly aware of their existence. She knew she needed all the self-control she could summon to do what she had to do, and blocking everything out but the sign to Avignon, she followed the N7 with unswerving concentration.

She paid the toll dues at the Avignon turn-off and made quickly for the car-hire offices where she left the Renault. She went to the bank and cashed a cheque, then took a taxi to Villeneuve. She packed the rest of her belongings, dumped them in the Metro, and returned back across the river, her eyes stonily ignoring the Palace of the Popes, refusing to hear the oh-so-familiar voice declaring that it looked like a fairy cut-out, and not succeeding.

Sylvie, luckily, was in. She opened the door and exclaimed in surprise, 'Phippy! What are you doing here? You're a day early, surely? Is Francis with you?' and peered beyond her friend expectantly, and then took another look at her face. 'Something's wrong, Phippy!' and she drew Philippa with her into the house.

'Sylvie, I haven't much time. Here's the key to the apartment. Will you ask Fabien what I owe him and I'll send a cheque from England.'

'What's the matter? Oh, Phippy dear, what is it?'

'I want to get back home. I've been such a fool—at least, I think I have.'

'You're not making sense.'

'I know—I'm sorry. Francis will come here, looking for me, and I want to get started before he catches up with me.'

Thoroughly alarmed, Sylvie said hurriedly, 'You can't go like this, you'll have an accident! Really, Phippy, you look dreadful. Let me pack you up some food—have you eaten today?'

'Just a croissant and coffee at breakfast.' It seemed easier to give in, and she told Sylvie about the newspaper article while home-made bacon and egg pie, cheese and fruit were hastily packed into a bag. Sylvie listened intently and when Philippa came to an end, she said,

'But why are you running away, Phippy? This isn't like you.'

'I haven't been like myself since meeting Francis, have I?' Philippa came back bitingly.

'Wouldn't it be better to have it out with him? Ask him why he didn't tell you he knew your grandfather?'

'That's what he would prefer. He knows I would find it difficult to believe anything bad about him once he—oh, once he was given the chance to get round me. I need time, Sylvie.'

Sylvie gave a deep sigh. 'It does look bad, but might not the explanation be a simple one?'

'Then why didn't he tell me earlier? He's had so many chances to drop that snippet of information it can't be simple. You said yourself that Grandfather is wealthy. Money and power—two deadly serious things, Sylvie, to some people, and the little I know about Francis is that he doesn't do anything, *anything* on the spur of the moment. Not even falling in love.'

'You don't know that, Phippy,' exclaimed Sylvie miserably. 'None of us have ever seen him like he is with you.'

'Oh, I attract him physically, no doubt about that, which must have been a bonus. Sylvie, I didn't even know his name was Balfour until the Camargue trip—surely that must have been because he wasn't sure how much I knew—whether I was aware that there was a Balfour connected with Copperthwaite?' Philippa gave a distraught laugh. 'God, I went down like a love-starved adolescent right on cue! I took the bait and he hauled me in. Well, I've managed to get off the hook and I have no intention of being eaten alive for dinner.' She stood up and looked wildly around, collecting together her belongings. 'I'm going, Sylvie. I shall cross from Cherbourg, he won't expect me to do that.'

'You think he'll come?'

'He'll come. You might just give him this, and this,' and Philippa struggled with the jewellery Francis had given her over the past few weeks, tossing it down on to the counter top, 'with my compliments.'

Sylvie trailed her worriedly to the door. 'I wish Fabien were here. He'd know what to do,' she observed tearfully, taking Philippa into her arms in a fierce hug.

Philippa managed a good imitation of a laugh. 'You always said I'd be in trouble if ever I fell in love. I wish you hadn't been so right. Damn him! What a gullible fool I've been!' She broke from her friend and stalked down the steps to the Metro.

'Do take care, Phippy,' called Sylvie, 'and ring me. Promise!'

'I will. Sorry to land you in all this.' Philippa backed the car and drove through the gateway, leaving Sylvie standing despondently on the steps, watching her go.

Motorway driving is monotonous and tiring. Philippa intended keeping on the autoroute for as long as she dared, working out the earliest possible time Francis could arrive in Avignon if he returned from Cannes as planned. The Spider was faster than the Metro, but she had some hours' start. Always supposing his plans had not changed—the meeting at Cannes might have finished earlier than expected. Always supposing he came after her. She thought he would. His pride would make him.

It was eight o'clock by the time she reached Lyons and she came off the autoroute and stopped at the first hotel she came to. She left at six o'clock the next morning, driving cross-country to Tours, and then headed north to Cherbourg. She arrived there at seven in the evening, exhausted and numb. She booked a place on the next ferry and managed to get a cabin, then took her place in the car park queue, dozing until a ship's siren told her that the ferry had arrived in from Portsmouth. It would unload its passengers and then she and her fellow travellers could embark. The queue behind her was growing, and all the time she wondered if she would see the Spider come round the corner and nose its way into line. It was an outside chance and she grew cross with herself as her eyes kept flicking nervously to the mirror, but she was not convinced that Francis had not the power to read her mind. She found herself thinking, hurry, hurry! as the cars and lorries disembarked, and had to forcibly make herself relax. It was stupid. If Francis walked up to her now there was nothing she could do about it.

Activity began on the quayside and with a wave of an arm Philippa was directed up the gangplank. She left the Metro in the car bay and made her way to the deck. The ferry was an English-owned vessel and she felt a curious lessening of tension as she heard the crew's voices. She was on a bit of England, or so it seemed, and nearly home.

For three-quarters of an hour she stood by the rail, the darkness closing in around her, and when there had been no vehicle arrive for a third of that time, she began to feel she could relax. She was joined at the rail by a woman passenger, and Philippa, out of politeness, made conversation. During their talk they found they were sharing the same cabin.

When the white Alfa Romeo came slowly round the corner, the lights from the quay picking out the number plate, Philippa hardly noticed it, and then, as it came nearer, it registered. She must have made some exclamation, because the woman looked at her, then turned her attention down to the car.

'Someone you know?' she asked, and Philippa nodded, feeling sick with disappointment. Making her excuses, she went to find the cabin.

She sat on the bunk, her head in her hands. She had felt all the time that she was not going to make it. The whys and wherefores did not matter. What did was that Francis would be on the ship and he would try and contact her.

The door opened and the woman from the deck came in. She looked at the two sets of double bunks and settled herself on the bottom of the other one.

'The purser reckons there'll be just us in here. Some people don't think the crossing's long enough to warrant a berth, but if there's one going I always take it. I'm Joan, by the way, Joan Markham.'

Philippa returned her own name. It was a relief, in a way, to have to make talk. It stopped her thinking about Francis. Mrs Markham, her husband and son had been camping, so she told Philippa, in Brittany. After a while, Mrs Markham said,

'You look tired. Better get some sleep.'

Philippa nodded. She ached with fatigue and her head was beginning to pound.

'Is your car a red Metro?' Mrs Markham asked casually, and startled, Philippa said,

'Yes—how did you know?'

'Are you in trouble? I don't want to pry, but I've a daughter of my own and if she was in difficulty I wouldn't like to think no one would help her.'

'You're very kind,' began Philippa helplessly, and then, 'Not in trouble, exactly.'

'Something to do with the white Italian car, isn't it? You went so pale when you saw it I thought you were going to faint. Is he following you, the driver?'

'Yes.' Philippa felt too ill to prevaricate and it was obvious her companion knew something. What did it matter anyway? Francis had caught up with her, and she so wanted a breathing space, time to distance herself from him and find a sense of proportion again. At the moment she couldn't even think straight.

'I waited for him to come up,' Mrs Markham was saying, 'not intentionally, you understand, I was looking for Jimmy, my son—fourteen and an absolute terror for disappearing when you want him. I went to look for him in the car bay, knowing how crazy he is about engines, and the engine room leads off from the bay, you see. He was there, right enough, chatting to some of the crew. I saw the white car being directed into line and the driver got out—a good-looking fellow, with fair hair. I thought he'd come up the steps, but he didn't, he wandered down the rows of cars until he came to the red Metro. Then he came up. Passed me with a nice smile, though his face had been a bit grim.' She paused. 'Nothing is as bad as it seems, my dear. Have you had a tiff?'

Philippa was lost in thought. She swung round and gave the other woman all her attention, saying urgently, 'Does your Jimmy know about tyres? Enough to let one down?'

Mrs Markham laughed, 'I shouldn't be at all surprised!' The ship shuddered and the engine noise increased. 'We're away.'

Her story had to be good enough to warrant action on Jimmy's part, Philippa decided, her mind racing. She had always had a good imagination. 'The fair man . . . he's . . . my husband, and I came home earlier than expected—we live in France, he's half-French—and found him with someone else. I . . . I caught them together, you see.' Would this explanation do? Mrs Markham gave a sympathetic murmur, and encouraged, Philippa went on, 'I just turned tail and ran. I thought he'd miss the boat, but as you saw, he didn't. I want to have a breathing space to think things over. If Jimmy could let down a tyre for me I'd have the chance to give him the slip.'

'Men! Just wait here—I'll have a word with Jimmy. You wouldn't like more than one tyre?'

Philippa choked a laugh and shook her head. 'Just one will do. Tell Jimmy to be careful, I shouldn't like him to get into trouble, and,' she got out her purse, 'give him this and tell him to treat himself.'

'Bribery and corruption work wonders,' agreed Jimmy's mother, and she took the money and went out. Twenty minutes later she was back. 'It's done. Don't worry, my dear, you'll be off and away when we arrive at Portsmouth. Now try and get some sleep. I'll do the same,' and she lay down on the bunk opposite and gave a chuckle. 'Quite an experience for Jimmy, being encouraged to commit a crime! It'll take some getting over.'

To her surprise, Philippa slept deeply. The shuddering of the engines in reverse woke her. Sitting up quickly, she opened her eyes and decided she felt awful, lying back with a groan. Her berth companion entered, carrying a cup.

'I've brought you this. I took the chance you were a coffee drinker.' She handed over the cup, sitting down herself to give the younger girl a thoughtful look. 'Your husband's in the restaurant, brooding over his.'

Philippa's hand jerked, nearly spilling the coffee. It was a shock to hear Francis called her husband.

'Now you listen to me, my dear. Think hard about what you're going to do. You've got to stop running some time and when you do, make sure you know what you really want. Maybe you'll see things differently in a day or two, but don't do anything in a rush. I'm not condoning your husband, but men don't see such things quite the same way as women do. If you love him, think what it will be like without him, eh?'

Philippa gave a wan smile. 'It's a bit more complicated than that, Mrs Markham.'

'Maybe, but most things come down to the basics in the end. And you be careful—he doesn't look the sort to cross.' Mrs Markham stood up and collected her things. 'Take care now,' and with an encouraging smile she left.

Philippa bestirred herself and went to the washroom. Feeling a little better, she gathered together her belongings just as the tannoy issued its orders for car passengers to go to their cars.

The passageway was crowded with people and she eased her way into the general exodus. Some yards along her wrist was grasped strongly and she was pulled urgently out of the queue, the well-known drawling voice saying, 'Sorry—excuse me—thanks,' to those who had to give way, which they did with no interest in the fair man with the set, resolute face and cold blue eyes or the girl who allowed it to happen because she did not want to cause an embarrassing scene.

'Let me go, Francis,' said Philippa, when she was clear, not raising her voice, but glaring at him with angry eyes. She pulled ineffectually at his grasp, which did not lessen.

'Pippa, we must talk.'

'Don't you dare call me that—don't you *ever* dare to call me that again!' She wrenched her wrist once more. '*Will* you please let me go—I can't bear you to touch me!' She ground the words out with deep loathing.

'Won't you let me explain?'

Philippa gave a bitter laugh. 'Oh, I'm sure you could sweet-talk your way into some semblance of explanation.' She took a deep breath. 'I loathe and despise you, and I never want to see you again!'

Remote, the pale patrician face as expressionless as marble, Francis relaxed his grip and released her. Eyes hooded, a small tight smile appeared on his lips and he drawled, 'Forgive me for delaying you,' and stepped aside with obnoxious politeness.

A crewman coaxing along a few remaining stragglers called, 'Everyone to their cars. Hurry along, please!'

Rubbing her wrist, Philippa resisted the temptation to strike that cold smile from Francis' face, and swinging away, she stalked after the crewman. Francis let her go.

In the car bay the noise of the car engines, the exhaust fumes and the lorries revving battered Philippa's senses. She flung herself into the Metro and started it, glaring stonily ahead.

Damn him—damn him! She was unaware of the tears streaming down her face as she followed the lorries up the ramp and off the ferry. She was waved through Customs without being stopped and headed for London.

She imagined the scene she was leaving

behind—all the cars leaving and Francis pumping up the flat tyre.

Serve him right!

It did not help knowing that if he had said, I love you, she would have gone into his arms.

With gritted teeth and knuckles white on the steering wheel, Philippa told herself grimly, 'Then it's a good job he didn't say it, isn't it?'

CHAPTER FIVE

'You have had a busy holiday, haven't you, darling?' said Grace Stanhope to her niece. She was sitting behind her desk, glasses removed, books piled high all round, a half-filled sheet of typing, an article she was writing for a magazine, set before her in the typewriter. She put a finger in the open page of one of the books to keep the place and waited patiently. She did not allow any of the surprise she felt at the news just imparted to show on her face or appear in her voice.

Grace's matter-of-fact understatement, so typical of her attitude to life in general, was a welcome relief to Philippa's own twisted, shredded emotions. Even the telling seemed to help, and she gave a reluctant laugh and said wryly,

'You can't be thinking me any bigger a fool than I think myself.'

'Falling in love isn't foolish. It's how it can cloud one's judgment, even making the simplest of decisions. For instance, you didn't consider waiting to ask him for an explanation, this Francis of yours?'

'I did think about it, yes,' replied Philippa a little defensively, 'but I knew if I let him . . . that he would . . .'

'Persuade you by soft voice and gentle touch—now who said that?—no matter. I quite understand what you're trying to say. I'm not in my dotage yet.'

'Yes, well, I wasn't thinking too much of explanations. It was not telling me he knew the

Ingrams, was involved in the family business, that was such a shock, such a hurt. How could he have not told me that? There must be a reason.'

'Perhaps he intended to eventually and left it too late.'

'There's nothing indecisive about Francis, Grace. You'd know that if you met him. It was sheer bad luck for him that I read that newspaper. No, he has too much control over his life—and why are you making excuses for him? Whose side are you on anyway?'

Grace raised her brows at the outburst. 'You know I like to see every point of view—and he doesn't appear to have controlled things too well at the moment, does he?'

'He hasn't done too badly,' muttered Philippa grimly.

'What are you going to do now?'

'Catch up on work and forget him.'

'Be sensible, darling!'

Philippa gave an impatient laugh. 'Oh, very well—short term, I shall work, long term, I shall go to Cumbria and introduce myself to my grandfather.'

Approval showed on her aunt's face. 'I think that's a good idea. When will you go?'

'I'll wait for the birthday celebration in September.'

'And if your Francis comes here?'

'I shan't see him.' It came out defiantly, but as her aunt's countenance did not alter from one of calm interest, Philippa said less aggressively, 'I don't think he'll come, Grace, but if he does, or if he phones, I shan't speak to him. My guess is that he'll wait until September, because I'm positive he'll be there, at Grandfather's.'

'He sounds an extraordinary young man. There can't be many who could have such patience.'

'Francis has,' retorted Philippa, remembering acutely the delicate patience of his wooing.

'I look forward to meeting him,' Grace acknowledged. 'Any man who can sweep you off your feet must be special.' Her eye caught a word on the open page. 'Ah, just the word I was looking for.' She looked up, satisfied, and carried on. 'I was beginning to think you were too much like me.'

Philippa smiled reluctantly. 'What's that supposed to mean?'

'It means, my dear Philippa, that I like my own way too much. I've been on the verge of saying "yes" to marriage a couple of times in my forty-odd years, and each time the thought of spending the rest of my life having to consider another person before I can do what I want to do held me back. However, what suits me doesn't suit everyone, and I suspected not you. I'm glad to hear I'm right. I must remember to thank your Francis.'

'I can't see anything to be glad about,' muttered Philippa crossly, 'and I wish you wouldn't keep on calling him *my* Francis.'

Ignoring the exasperated interruption, Grace went on, 'I've never said this to you before, Philippa, but I strongly disagreed with Robert keeping you away from the Ingrams.'

Philippa stared, indignation rising. 'They didn't want to know us! My precious grandfather didn't even send an acknowledgment when Mother died! I know he was told, because I wrote to him!'

Startled, Grace echoed, 'You wrote?'

'Yes, I sent him a letter. He didn't answer it.'

'But, my dear, you were only . . .' Grace frowned, working it out, '. . . eight at the time. Did Robert know?'

'No. I did it all by myself, except for addressing the envelope. I got one of the barmen to do that, and I posted it myself.'

There was silence while Grace digested this piece of news. She said at last, 'I'm not saying your grandfather was right in all this, Philippa, I'm merely looking at it with regard to yourself. Robert should have made some attempt to heal the breach, but he only lived for the present. If he had money to buy canvas and paint . . .'

'He loved me. He looked after me.'

'Darling, of course he did, but if he'd been a different type of man he would have considered your future. It isn't right to wipe out half of one's family. Who have you, beside me?'

'I've never needed anyone other than you. I didn't know you felt like this. You've never said.' Philippa looked at her aunt, puzzled.

'The question didn't arise. Now it has. You should go to Cumbria, meet your family, and make up your own mind about them. I realise that it's already made up, in one respect. No one likes to be ignored for twenty-seven years, but now you have an invitation to visit.'

Philippa considered her aunt thoughtfully. Grace had never been one to thrust her opinions on anyone. She was there when needed, but was not obtrusive. Philippa knew she owed a lot to Grace's sensible view of life. She said slowly,

'You told me once that I was my grandfather's heir.'

Grace lifted her head from her books. 'Yes, that's right.'

'I suspect that's why Francis . . .' Philippa broke off, a mixture of bitterness and anger welling up.

'Darling, that's a bit Gothic, isn't it? And not very subtle—making up to the heir in the hopes of a fat legacy! Your grandfather does have other relations.'

'Exactly! I don't want his wretched money!'

Grace ignored this outburst and went on musingly, 'There's your father's older sister—that's your aunt Harriet, she must be in her early sixties and to my knowledge has never married. The other brother was drowned as a child, so yes, you must be the direct heir.'

'I've been thinking a lot about them, just lately—Mum and Dad, I mean,' Philippa smiled. 'Not many people can boast that their parents ran away to get married.'

Grace gave an impatient snort. 'They were a couple of romantics, both of them. Infants! Rose would have lived anywhere with Robert and because Robert was happy, Rose was.'

'Did you like him?' asked Philippa suddenly.

'Who, Robert?' Grace smiled. 'Of course I liked him—he was an extremely likeable person. I didn't always approve of him, but he made Rose happy and he loved you, when he remembered you.' She paused and went on musingly, 'I've always wondered why he never married again after Rose died. He didn't seem the sort to live alone.'

Philippa grinned. 'He didn't, there was always his latest model. They were nice women, and kind to me. Besotted with Father, every last one of them, and he was always so offhand, but I suppose that was part of his charm.'

'He did have charm, Robert, and he was selfish, as all true artists are.' Grace shut her books with a bang. 'Let's go and eat. I pushed a chicken in the oven when you rang and it should be cooked by now.' She rose. 'If Francis Balfour comes knocking at my door I ought to be able to recognise him. Describe him to me, Philippa.'

Her niece rubbed a finger across her forehead. For a few minutes she had forgotten Francis, but he was not going to be wiped out that easily. 'He's about six foot, slim, fair and blue-eyed.' She stopped and gave an impatient sigh. 'Wait, I have a photograph of him somewhere,' and she rummaged in her bag and took from it a snapshot which she handed to Grace. She waited, almost nervously, for comment, remembering the day she had taken it, and the zany, mad mood they were in.

Grace studied it for a moment and observed drily, 'I can quite see why you fell, darling, and you say he has brains as well? What a bonus! I doubt he'll let you go without a struggle, there's a possessive look in those eyes of his.' She handed the photograph back. 'I don't need to tell you not to cut off your nose to spite your face, do I?'

'I suppose you think I'm being silly.'

'No, no—you're feeling vulnerable . . . love's like that, and you want to find out if your Francis loves you or Philip Ingram's granddaughter. Come along, let's eat. And then you'd better go to bed. Making a fool of oneself can be very tiring.'

Grace's astringency was like a tonic. Philippa found herself laughing and followed her aunt into the kitchen, smelt the chicken casserole and found she was hungry.

Philippa settled into everyday living. At first, each time the telephone or doorbell rang she tensed before answering. Then, as Francis made no move to contact her, she was afflicted with a mass of contradictory feelings, depending on her mood of the moment. Unhappiness lay like a heavy weight inside her and she was beset with doubts and fears. Had she been too hard—too condemning? These were brushed aside by flashes of anger. She came to accept the moodiness fairly philosophically. She had told Francis on the ferry that she did not want to see him again and he had accepted that—which was an admission of guilt if ever there was one! She was left with her pride and her work, neither good bedfellows. She was learning that the clock could not be put back. Those golden days in Provence could never be recaptured, but the memories clung like a limpet. She was a different person because of them. Not completely whole, as yet, but time, so they said, was a great healer.

Work took her to Brussels and Geneva. She finished the children's stories and started on a travel book on Italy. One day she returned home to find that a huge basket of poppies had been delivered. Grace had taken them in, questioned the delivery girl, who knew nothing of the order.

Seeing the splash of colour, the fragile petals, Philippa was immediately transported to the cliff top with the breeze blowing off the Mediterranean and Francis standing with her close to him as she told him about the poppies that grew there in the summer months. She shut the image from her mind. It still hurt like hell. There was no message on the card, but none was necessary.

Grace said, 'They don't last, poppies, once they've been cut.'

'How symbolic,' replied Philippa stiffly, and Grace made no further comment, only making a mild request for their removal because of her hay fever. Philippa could not bring herself to throw them away and took them to an old people's home nearby, after taking one perfectly formed bloom and pressing it between two books. It would be a sardonic reminder not to be such a fool again.

The telephone rang one evening mid-week and it was not until a stranger's voice answered that Philippa realised how much she had wanted it to be Francis. She would, naturally, have put the phone down, but . . .

'Philippa Ingram?' The man's voice was pleasant and warm. 'My name is Ross Fairley. That probably means nothing to you, but we're cousins.'

'Are we?' replied Philippa cautiously, adding, 'How nice of you to call.'

He must have picked up a nuance of uncertainty in her voice, for he laughed and said, 'Look, we really are related. Your grandfather, Philip Ingram, is my great-uncle. My grandmother was his sister. Now, that's not too confusing, is it?' His voice had a smile in it, a teasing quality that Philippa found disarming, and she laughed.

'I think I can about grasp that.'

'Good. We're all delighted to learn that you're coming to Uncle's birthday celebrations, and as my sister Lucy and I are in London at the moment we wondered if you'd like to meet up with us and we can introduce ourselves so that when you finally come to Copperthwaite you'll at least know us.'

Touched by this consideration, Philippa exclaimed, 'Why, thank you, I'd like that. When do you suggest?'

'Tomorrow evening? Is that too short notice?'

Philippa hastily glanced at her engagement pad and answered, 'Yes, that's fine.'

'Excellent—I'll pick you up, say, around eight?'

Ross Fairley turned out to be in his early thirties, with light brown hair, grey eyes and pleasant features. Smiling, he took Philippa's hand in his and said warmly,

'So! I meet the long-lost granddaughter at last!'

'I haven't really been lost,' replied Philippa wryly, and his smile turned downwards as he responded quickly,

'No, of course you haven't—I'm sorry, that was a thoughtless remark, but my pleasure at meeting you is genuine, I assure you. Lucy and I have wondered about you for years.' He studied her face, his own serious. 'I do hope you can forgive Uncle Philip. He's an old man now and . . .' He ran fingers through his hair and gave a likeable grimace coupled with an expressive shrug of the shoulders. 'You're coming to Copperthwaite and that's all that matters.'

Feeling sorry for the awkwardness, Philippa smiled and said, 'I'm looking forward to it, but have to admit I'm a bit nervous. Meeting you and your sister tonight will be a great help.' She peered beyond him. 'Isn't Lucy with you?'

'No.' Ross followed her into the hallway. 'She'll be at the restaurant waiting for us—I hope!' He grinned. 'Lucy is notorious for being late, but I read her the riot act before I left. You're obviously not like her—a punctual lady is a bonus I hadn't expected!'

Philippa had not expected his words to trigger off the memory of Francis saying almost the same thing. These spasmodic yet nerve-racking memories came like blinding flashes out of nowhere and as usual left her feeling shaken.

As they drove into the centre of the city Ross, in an obvious endeavour to put her at her ease, talked.

'Did you know that Lucy and I live at Copperthwaite?' His side-glance took in Philippa's negative shake of the head. 'The reason is that we're orphans, our parents were killed when I was six and Lucy only a baby. They were experienced climbers, so I've been told, who went to another climber's aid during appalling, unexpected weather conditions on a weekend climb in Scotland. To be truthful I can barely remember them and Lucy not at all. Great-Uncle took us in and made himself responsible for us, and Harriet—that's your Aunt Harriet—helped bring us up. I work at the Copperthwaite Mills and call your grandfather Uncle Philip outside their walls and Sir inside them. Lucy calls him Nunkie, but she can get away with anything.'

'How old is Lucy?' asked Philippa, and he smiled indulgently.

'She's twenty-five, beautiful and terribly spoiled. She has a share in a Keswick boutique. I'm thirty, intelligent, kind to animals and the elderly, and like taking extremely attractive new cousins out for dinner.'

Ross's lighthearted conversation was pleasant and Philippa's spirits lifted. If Lucy was as nice as her brother then Copperthwaite wouldn't be so daunting. She drew her jacket round her shoulders while she waited for Ross to park the car and they walked the rest of the way to the restaurant, arms linked, finding out that they both loved London and exchanging favourite places.

Subdued lights, a bustle of waiters serving food and an agreeable murmur of conversation greeted them as they entered the restaurant. The manager glided forward and accepted Ross's name with a welcoming smile. A flick of the fingers brought the head waiter to their side and he led the way down the room to their table. Ross turned a grinning face over his shoulder to exclaim, 'Wonders will never cease—Lucy's here before us!'

The table was blocked from view, but as the waiter stepped aside Ross drew Philippa forward eagerly, introducing her with much enthusiasm to his sister.

Lucy was indeed a very lovely girl, with a clear pale skin and fine straight hair, parted in the middle, which fell way beyond her shoulders, the almost white blondeness a startling contrast to the ruby red dress she was wearing. She had her brother's grey eyes but not his spontaneous friendliness. There was a slightly bored, indolent air about her that Philippa suspected covered up a wariness, maybe a resentment over this meeting. After all, if Lucy Fairley had been living at Copperthwaite all her life, why should she welcome Philippa with open arms?

Ross was now saying, as he took a step sideways, 'We hope you don't mind, Philippa, but to even up the numbers we've invited an old friend of ours to join us.'

Philippa found she was staring straight into the cool, offensively amused blue eyes of Francis, and she was unable to conceal the sharp intake of breath as she drowned helplessly in their depths.

The smile that had automatically been forming on her lips froze. Her hand was taken in his and she found herself saying, 'How do you do?' and he was saying, 'I've been looking forward to this meeting,' which unleashed the flood of anger within her and her eyes flashed the reply—I bet you have!

With great politeness Francis pulled out a chair for her and she sat down. As Lucy and Ross exchanged words she turned to him and demanded in a furious undertone,

'What the hell are you doing here?'

'Like the proverbial bad penny, you'll find that I always turn up,' he replied, matching his tone to hers, and then, 'What do you fancy to eat?'

'My appetite has strangely disappeared. What I'd really like to do is get up and walk out, but you know damn well I can't do that.'

'It would provoke some awkward questions,' agreed Francis smoothly, his eyes on the menu, 'which you evidently are not prepared to answer.' He turned his head, one brow raised, eyes challenging.

'You're right, I'm not,' replied Philippa emphatically, returning his look with equal intent and then regarding the menu, although it could have been in Chinese for all she could take the words in.

When their orders had been given Lucy monopolised the conversation for a while, talking about a fashion exhibition she had been to see, also dropping in the fact that she and Francis had been to see a West End hit musical the night before together.

Philippa smiled, and conversed, and ate her food, which was tasteless ... and tried to stop herself hating Lucy. It was difficult to ignore the fact that Lucy and Francis had known each other for some years, and the thought came whirling into her head that they had been lovers. At this idea a wave of jealousy swept through her, its intensity leaving her feeling sick. If you don't want him, it can't matter, can it? she told herself angrily, and hardened her resolve to armour herself against any more hurt. She knew now that her instinct to keep right out of his way had been sound. He still had the power, if she let him, to reduce her to a senseless idiot.

In any other circumstances this meeting with her new cousins would have been highly enjoyable, but even if she disregarded Francis sitting next to her, she couldn't blot him out completely. She thought he looked singularly well—when he should have been looking haggard and drawn. As always he seemed to outshine every man in the room, and he certainly made a great effort to keep the evening rolling along, she would grant him that. She only hoped her own performance was as good.

She might have known he would engineer things to his advantage. Before she was aware of what was happening it was decided that Francis was taking her home. It seemed logical that brother and sister should return together to their hotel, and although Philippa began to make some babbling attempt to say she could take a taxi, this was naturally overruled. As Ross and Lucy bade her goodbye with the promise of her visit to Cumbria ahead, Philippa found herself walking towards the Spider, parked in a side street, Francis' hand firmly beneath her elbow. As they turned the corner, out of sight of the Fairleys, she whirled round, wrenching her arm away, saying vehemently,

'I thought I told you I didn't want to see you again!'

Francis bent to unlock the door and opened it. He said calmly, 'I know what you said, Philippa, but even you have to admit the request is unreasonable and unrealistic. Get in and I'll take you home . . . or aren't you strong enough to be alone in my company for the time that takes?' He watched her with bleak amusement as she struggled with the implications of that taunt. Philippa knew there was too much truth involved for her not to pick up the challenge.

Without another word she slid into the car and Francis closed the door, his countenance quite impassive, carefully not allowing any hint of satisfaction to show. In a few moments they were drawing away and Philippa said, 'Where are you taking me?'

Francis rattled off her address, adding, 'That's where you want to go, isn't it? If not, I'm more than willing to take you back to my flat.' His voice was insufferably expressionless.

Philippa threw him a cold look and they spoke no more until they neared Wimbledon, when Francis asked for more detailed directions which Philippa gave as briefly as possible. As the Spider slowed to a halt she said swiftly,

'Thank you for the lift,' and made a move to leave. Francis' hand clamped down on her wrist, fingers and thumb encircling with a grip that brooked no nonsense. Philippa's head swung round and with her chin up she sustained his long, steady look.

'You're not going to get rid of me easily, Pippa,' he said softly. She answered numbly, 'Thanks for the warning,' and looked pointedly down at her wrist.

Francis lifted the wrist and placed his lips gently on the jumping pulse, and a small tremor went through her. Mutely, he let her go, widening his fingers to allow her to pull away.

As she walked up the path to the front door she knew he was watching her gain entry. When she stepped inside she heard the Spider accelerate off.

How dared he waltz back into her life with such brazen coolness! And no word of explanation! Philippa glared at her reflection in the mirror as she cleaned her teeth. Would you have listened? she asked herself, and scowled. She went to bed, tossed and turned, and wondered how someone so organised and sensible as herself could land in such a quagmire.

In late August she received a letter from her aunt Harriet.

'They would like me to go up the week before Grandfather's birthday,' she told Grace. She read the address at the top of the page and murmured, 'Copperthwaite, Caldbeck, Cumbria—it has a lovely sound to it, doesn't it?'

Grace said, 'Cumbria has Norse origins. Thwaite, I think, is a clearing in a forest. Will you go earlier?'

'One part of me thinks yes, the other holds back,' admitted Philippa. 'I think I must still have my childhood hang-up about the Ingrams. I really worked up a hatred of them, Grace . . . blew them up out of all proportion, of course. I do realise nothing can be totally one-sided and Father must have hurt them too.'

'Well, you've already met your Fairley cousins, so that's a help, but going up earlier would mean meeting the rest by degrees, instead of having the whole lot thrust on you in one go. Your presence is bound to create an interest, isn't it?'

'Long-lost granddaughter,' Philippa added wryly, and Grace gave a philosophic shrug.

Philippa had told her aunt about her meal out with the Fairleys, and that Francis had been present also—just the bare details, and Grace had not questioned her further.

'It's a pleasant letter,' Grace said, and Philippa nodded. Her aunt Harriet sounded nice and she remembered her father speaking of her with affection.

'I think I shall go earlier,' she decided suddenly. 'I think I can organise my work around those dates.'

As motorways go, the M6 was surprisingly attractive. The distance from London to Penrith was not far short of three hundred miles and the last seventy before Penrith were truly beautiful. Philippa hardly knew what to expect, but the distant peaks excited her and seemed to draw her on. She came off the motorway at junction 40 and took the Keswick road, turning north for Caldbeck and following the National Park boundary all the way.

Caldbeck looked a real working village, not yet taken over completely by the tourist trade. It had a traditional village green, a duckpond, a twelfth-century church and the fame of John Peel, the huntsman with the grey coat and the hounds, lying buried in the churchyard.

Philippa parked the car and found a café where she ordered a pot of tea and took out the latest letter from her aunt which enclosed a pencil drawing of the route to Copperthwaite from Caldbeck. The letter was short but welcoming. Philippa thought her aunt Harriet might be an ally—for she had to admit that she could find no filial feelings for Philip Ingram, her grandfather, only strong curiosity.

Deciding she was only putting off the evil hour, Philippa drank up and made herself clean and tidy in the ladies' room, paid her bill and strolled back to the car. It was a pleasant day, but she was glad of the trouser suit she was wearing, for the breeze was fresh. She spread out the Ordnance Survey map across the passenger seat and took stock. Her eyes picked up names like Willy Knott, High Pike and Little Cockup, teasing her interest in the land of her forebears. Aunt Harriet had suggested she brought stout walking shoes with her, for the best way to see Cumbria was on foot. Philippa liked walking and was happy to do as her aunt suggested, and the map whetted her appetite.

Memorising the route which took her off the main road, she drove out of Caldbeck and a mile or so out of the village came to the turn-off and crossed the cattle grid. The road now wound over the fells, unfenced, crossing a small bridge straddling a quick-flowing beck. The sign Philippa was looking for, to Copperthwaite, directed her along a road to the right which, although having a good surface, was narrow and bordered either side with a ditch. For a while the road climbed, and then she saw Copperthwaite for the first time. The house was in a dip and rose starkly out of the landscape. Not by any stretch of the imagination could Copperthwaite be called beautiful, although there was, perhaps, a kind of beauty in the weathered brickwork matching the starkness of the fells rising above it, making the house impressive, even imposing in a solid way.

Philippa wondered what it would be like in winter, for the winds would sweep across the fells from the sea and there was very little protection for the house. A line of copper beeches was standing tall along the west boundary and hedges and bushes formed some kind of perimeter along the three other sides. There was a well kept kitchen garden in the southern corner and a few ornamental tubs with brightly coloured annuals still showing bravely. The fells seemed to come right up to the house.

Philippa drew up before the front and switched off the engine. She sat for a moment, unwilling to make a move, when a figure appeared at the door. A woman hurried down the stone steps and crunched across the gravel.

'Philippa? Yes, I thought it must be you. How lovely! Have you had a good journey? You must be tired, such a long way for you to drive—but then you modern girls do everything, don't you? Lucy tells me I'm sadly out of date, and she's right, of course. Will you put the car round by the side of the house, dear? I'll send someone for your luggage . . .'

'Oh, no, that won't be necessary, I can carry it. Er—it is Aunt Harriet, isn't it?'

Her aunt gave a laugh. 'Yes, how silly of me!' Her hands fluttered in the way Philippa was to recognise as a gesture peculiarly her own, and she embraced her niece, murmuring, 'It's been too long. Really, Robert was very naughty, but you've come at last and we shall get to know you. I shall go and tell Father you've arrived. You shall see him at dinner.'

Philippa found she was smiling as she parked the Metro. Her aunt's absentminded air was belied by the straightforward instructions in her letters. She could not see anything of her father in Harriet—brother and sister were not alike physically. Harriet had grey eyes, Robert's had been brown, and Harriet was tiny and dumpy whereas Robert had been tall and thin, but there was something in the smile that was reminiscent of her father, Philippa thought, as she dragged the case from the rear of the car.

'Can I take that for you, Miss Philippa?'

Philippa turned and saw a man coming towards her, dressed in a dark suit, the jacket of which he was still putting on, as if he had been disturbed.

'Thank you,' replied Philippa, smiling, 'although it's not heavy.'

He returned the smile. He looked to be in his early forties, strongly built and with the soft burr of the south-west county accent.

'I'm Ainsley, miss—I look after your grandfather.' As he said this he began to walk towards the house, and Philippa followed, asking,

'How is my grandfather?'

'As well as can be expected. He's been looking forward to your coming.'

They had now entered the house and were climbing the stairs, a long landing leading off. They passed three doors and the fourth Ainsley opened, indicating Philippa to precede him.

'This is your room, miss.' He put the case on a chair just inside the door. 'Dinner's at seven, and it's a formal affair—Mr Ingram likes to keep the old customs. There's hot water in the bathroom two doors further on, and if you go to the end there,' he pointed along the landing, 'you'll find the main stairs. The drawing-room's on the left, the dining-room on the right.' He gave the room a quick appraisal and then said quietly, 'Welcome home, Miss Philippa. If you need anything, just ask,' and then he was walking briskly back down the landing.

Welcome home! Thoughtfully Philippa closed the door.

She crossed to the window. The room faced north with a sweeping view of the fells. They were in sunshine at the moment, soft greens and browns, but as the clouds passed briefly over the sun there was an indication of a much harsher picture, although one still demanding admiration. She stood, frowning pensively. Somehow she just could not imagine her father living out his life in this rugged part of the world. He fitted in much better in the hot, easygoing atmosphere of southern France.

A pang of homesickness tinged with panic swept over her. She was back in Provence with the sun burning her skin and Francis was smoothing oil over her body as they lay on the rocks of a small bay, made private by a particularly steep descent to which only the nimble and determined applied themselves. She could feel his hands still, as they worked their way along her arms and shoulders and down her back, and a wave of physical longing to be able to turn the clock back enveloped her with such intensity that she felt dizzy. Taking a deep breath, she turned from the window and made herself concentrate on the room. The walls were papered in a delicate rosebud pattern and the curtains and carpet echoed the deep rose pink. The furniture was old and well cared for and the whole was pleasing to the eye.

Philippa bathed and dressed for dinner, choosing a black dress which she considered would see her through the first meeting with her grandfather. It had long sleeves and was draped from one shoulder and caught in at the waist, the folds following through the line of the skirt. She took particular care with her face—she looked rather pale, but that was probably nerves—and her hair, and with nothing more to keep her she ventured out and sought the main stairs. When she was halfway down, the door on the left of the hall opened and Ross came striding out, pausing on seeing her.

'Hello, Philippa! You've arrived safely, I see. I was just coming to find you.' He held out welcoming hands and Philippa ran down the remaining stairs and returned his smile.

'Oh, Ross, you can't imagine how good it is to see a face I know!' she exclaimed, laughing ruefully.

'Are you nervous? No need to be.' He looked at her admiringly. 'Uncle's had a couple of bad days, but he's a little better today and you'll do his old heart good when he sees you—you're an Ingram right enough. As you see,' and he indicated his evening suit, 'your grandfather is a stickler for the old rules. Come along and let me get you a drink, you probably need one. What would you like?' He stood aside as he opened the door and as Philippa entered the room she was relieved to find her grandfather was not present. Lucy was sprawled in graceful ease in a nearby armchair, turning the pages of a magazine in a desultory manner, and Harriet was sitting on a sofa. Both greeted Philippa, Lucy with a half-wave of the hand and Harriet with a beaming smile, and as Philippa murmured, 'Sherry, please,' to Ross's question, he went to pour out the drink.

'What do you think of Copperthwaite, now you're here?' he asked, as he handed her the glass.

'It's much bigger than I expected,' admitted Philippa, adding, 'Where are the Copperthwaite Mills?'

Lucy looked up in surprise. 'Goodness, you really don't know anything, do you? They're in Carlisle.'

'We scan four generations,' Harriet added, 'and the Copperthwaite Wool Mark is known the whole world over.' She glanced at the carriage clock on the mantel and frowned. 'I think we'd better go in, children. Father is such a stickler for punctuality at mealtimes.'

Lucy tossed down the magazine and rose, walking languidly to the door. She was looking lovely in a cream silk-knit dress and made no effort to include Philippa as they crossed the hall to the dining-room.

'Chin up,' whispered Ross, his eyes signalling encouragement. 'Uncle's bark is worse than his bite!'

'Good evening, Father,' said Harriet, a little flustered. 'Here is Philippa.'

'So I see.' Philip Ingram nodded at Ross, lifted his cheek for Lucy to kiss, his eyes all the time upon Philippa, who was thinking with shocked surprise—why, he's in a wheelchair!

She walked forward and said coolly, 'Good evening, Grandfather,' and held out her hand.

Steel grey eyes enveloped her. His handshake was brief and he gestured to the empty chair on his right, next to Ross, and waited until she was seated before saying abruptly,

'You look like your grandmother.'

'You can see it too, Father? I thought the very same thing the moment I saw her. Mother's brown eyes and the way her hair grows to a peak,' broke in Harriet eagerly.

Lucy asked, 'Who else is coming, Nunkie darling?' eyeing the empty chair beside her, and before her uncle could reply, the door opened and a voice said,

'Sorry, Philip, I hope I haven't held things up? It was an important call I couldn't possibly put off.'

Philippa froze. She knew she would have to meet him again, but on her first evening here—oh, it was too much!

Francis surveyed the occupants of the room with a swift, searching glance, betraying nothing as it passed over Philippa to rest on Lucy, who, showing animation for the first time that evening, cried,

'Oh, good, it's Francis!' and lifted her cheek for a kiss.

The two younger men exchanged greetings and Francis then crossed the room to bend to kiss Harriet, saying, 'Sorry, Harriet, I don't like mixing business with pleasure, but it happens occasionally.' He straightened and looked very definitely across at Philippa.

Philippa met his gaze steadily, a faint warmth colouring her cheeks. Mixing business with pleasure indeed! What else had Provence been? she wondered grimly. If only he didn't look so darned attractive! In evening suit with fancy white shirt and black tie he looked in full control of both himself and the situation. Lucy's delighted welcome was like turning the knife in the wound. She schooled her features to show nothing of her thoughts and lifted her chin defiantly.

Philip Ingram said, 'Francis, I understand you know my granddaughter Philippa?'

At these words Philippa's eyes widened and she glared up at Francis, who answered smoothly,

'That's right, Philip—we met in London.'

Philippa allowed a relieved sigh to escape from parted lips. Her grandfather turned to her.

'Philippa, Francis is the grandson of an old friend of mine, dead these many years.'

Francis touched the old man's shoulder lightly in passing and stood before Philippa. She was obliged to raise her eyes and found nothing but polite, good-mannered interest in his expression. Had he, at last, accepted that she wanted nothing more to do with him? Her heart gave a stupid lurch.

'It's good to see you here at Copperthwaite, Philippa.'

'Thank you.' She waited until Francis gained his seat and went on, 'I have such a lot to learn about you all—tell me, please, are you also involved in the family business, Mr Balfour?'

There was a slight pause before Francis replied evenly, 'Yes, I am—and won't you call me Francis? As you hear, I'm much too old a friend of the family for us to be so formal.'

There had been nothing formal about their lovemaking. The thought shot into Philippa's head and was as quickly banished.

'A *sleeping* partner?' She saw the shot had gone home by a slight tightening of his jaw and she savoured the intoxicating delight of a small triumph.

'Indeed not,' put in Philip Ingram, smiling. 'Francis is on the board of directors and plays an important part in all aspects of Copperthwaite Mills, as does Ross.' The warmth in the grey eyes was now directed to his great-nephew. 'I'm extremely lucky in my two youngest directors.'

And one of them, Grandfather, is extraordinarily ambitious, thought Philippa bitterly.

CHAPTER SIX

After dinner, Philip Ingram was wheeled into his suite of rooms on the ground floor, saying he would see Philippa there in half an hour.

'You mustn't let Father bully you, Philippa, my dear,' Harriet told her anxiously as they retired to the drawing-room for coffee.

'Philippa doesn't look the kind of girl to be bullied by anyone,' observed Francis, pouring out his coffee. Philippa could see he was very much at home at Copperthwaite, and a sharp stab of jealousy hit her each time Lucy made him smile. She tried to tell herself that Lucy could have him and welcome, but she knew she was fooling herself. If anything, his treachery seemed even greater now he was here, surrounded by Ingrams, and yet her heart still raced when she heard his voice, her eyes were still drawn to him whenever she was unobserved. Her own weakness fuelled the fire of her anger.

'Can't we go into Penrith or somewhere to do something?' asked Lucy plaintively, and Ross answered briskly,

'Don't look to me, sister dear. I have to be up at the crack of dawn to catch the London train—some people have to work for their living. And Philippa is about to receive the Royal Summons.' He glanced enquiringly at Francis, who turned to Lucy, asking,

'Does it have to be Penrith? Friends have just opened a pub at Bewaldeth. We could go there.'

'Lovely!' Lucy's face brightened. 'I'll go and fetch a coat,' and she ran out of the room. Philippa glanced up and found Francis watching her, a small cynical smile shaping his lips . . . as if to say, if you don't want anything to do with me there are others who are happy to oblige. With eyes locked, she demanded silently, go and enjoy yourself and see if I care! unaware of how white she had gone.

The door opened and Lucy popped her head round. 'I'm ready, Francis. 'Bye, everyone.'

Francis put down his cup and gave an indulgent laugh. 'Everything has to be instant with Lucy! Good night, Harriet. Thank you for an excellent dinner, as always. I'll see Philip before I go. Good night, Ross.' He moved towards the door, pausing by Philippa's chair. 'Are you staying on after your grandfather's birthday celebration?'

Philippa stared down at her cup. 'I don't know. It depends on my work load.'

'See as much of Cumbria as you can, it's beautiful country.'

'Why don't you come with us on Tuesday, Francis?' broke in Ross. 'We thought we'd take Philippa up Skiddaw—it's an easy mountain to climb first. Uncle has given me permission to play hookey and Lucy has fixed it with the shop.' He waited expectantly as Francis hesitated.

'Oh yes, do, Francis,' urged Lucy prettily, returning to hear the request. 'We're going to go the long way round by Dash Falls.'

'Don't you think it would be better to go from Keswick?' suggested Francis, frowning slightly, and Lucy pouted. 'Boring,' she moaned, and Philippa broke in quickly,

'The route Ross has planned suits me fine . . .

and perhaps Mr Balfour has too many commitments—I wouldn't wish him to put himself out on my behalf.'

'Tuesday will suit me perfectly,' Francis answered smoothly, and taking Lucy's arm he gave a general 'good night' and they left.

'Tuesday it is,' murmured Ross, picking up the newspaper, 'that is if the weather holds. I apologise for my sister, Philippa. She should have stayed in on your first night here, but just lately she can't sit still for a minute. I don't know what's the matter with her.'

'Lucy has always been one for doing things,' claimed Harriet placidly, picking up her knitting, 'and I'm sure Philippa doesn't want to be treated like a guest. She's one of the family.' The needles stopped. 'Ross—do you think Lucy and Francis . . .?' She left the question hanging in the air and looked at Ross eagerly.

Ross smiled and turned to Philippa. 'Harriet has been trying to marry Lucy and me off for the past five years.'

'I want to see young children running about at Copperthwaite,' said Harriet, 'there's nothing strange in that, is there? I'm sure Father would like to see you both settled.' The needles began again, but slowly, as she went on thoughtfully, 'Francis would be most suitable. I've wondered about them before—he's always so attentive to her.'

Lucy and Francis! The idea was unpalatable.

There was silence while Harriet brooded over her idea, Ross read the paper and Philippa drank her coffee, her mind made purposefully blank. When she rose to place her cup on the table, she asked hesitantly,

'Why is Grandfather in a wheelchair?'

Harriet sighed and dropped the knitting to her lap. 'About three years ago—it is three, isn't it, Ross? Yes, it must be—your grandfather had a fall—not a bad one, or so we thought, but it damaged the nerves in his spine. He was such a vigorous man, so fit and healthy, never a day's illness—the doctors were very concerned after the fall, but he made a remarkable recovery. He keeps surprisingly well for his age.'

'We couldn't cope without Ainsley,' said Ross, referring to the man who had come for her grandfather after dinner, Philippa realised. 'Ainsley doesn't say much,' Ross went on, 'but he's extremely able and gets on well with Uncle, which is the main thing, as his temper couldn't be said to have mellowed with the years, eh, Harriet?'

'He has much to contend with,' scolded Harriet. 'Father's perfectly reasonable if he gets his own way,' and when her two companions burst out laughing she joined in with them. 'Oh, dear—we all are, aren't we?'

'Does Grandfather still go to the Mills?' asked Philippa, and Ross snorted a laugh.

'You bet he does—not one to hand over the reins, is Uncle Philip.' This was said with fond amusement.

At that moment Ainsley came to summon Philippa to her grandfather. Outwardly composed but with her pulse racing a little, Philippa followed his dark-suited figure through the hall and down a corridor, where he stopped at the first door and tapped lightly upon it. At a command from within Ainsley opened the door and entered, saying, 'Miss Philippa, sir,' and then she was standing before her grandfather.

Philip Ingram was sitting in a winged armchair in front of the fire. He was in a dressing-gown and a plaid rug was thrown over his legs. He gestured a thin hand, and Ainsley pulled another chair forward and Philippa sat down. After bringing a silver tray with decanters and glasses to the small table within easy reach of his employer, Ainsley ascertained that there was nothing more he could do and left the room.

'Would you like a drink?' Philip Ingram began to pour one for himself. 'There seems to be a selection here. I'm having a brandy.'

'Thank you,' replied Philippa as he poised the decanter over a glass, and when the drink was passed to her she said spontaneously, 'What a beautiful glass!'

'It's Balfour—distinctive, isn't it? Francis has some good designers these days. The Balfour glass works is based in Carlisle, very near to Copperthwaite Mills.' He raised his glass. 'To a better understanding of each other.'

That was something she could drink to, and Philippa joined him. There was silence for a while as Philip Ingram stared down into his glass, the flames from the fire turning the liquid into a deep russet. 'Tell me why you've come,' he said at last, speaking carefully, as if to reassure her that the answer she gave would be accepted for consideration without bias.

Philippa said, 'I came because I was asked.'

His lips pursed a little. 'There were no other reasons?' He had a long, thin face, deeply lined, and grey hair cut close to the scalp. He must have been a tall man in his prime, thought Philippa, and he still sat upright, his grey eyes shrewd and penetrating. She sorted out her words.

'Curiosity too. As I've grown older I have felt

curious. I think, had the invitation not come, I should have sought you out eventually.'

'Always supposing I was here,' Philip Ingram observed drily. He frowned and compressed his lips. 'I didn't expect to outlive my son.' He gestured impatiently with his free hand. 'Your father and I didn't get on. We said hurtful things to each other before he left. I didn't think his going would be so final.' He shot her a look. 'At least he called you after me.'

'That was my mother's doing,' explained Philippa matter-of-factly. 'She was a gentle person who didn't like hurting people. She thought you might like the idea.'

'Hum . . . you were brought up to hate me.'

'On the contrary, whenever your name was mentioned, which I have to admit wasn't often, Dad spoke as if he'd had a happy childhood. Mother made excuses for you both.' She paused. 'I hated you without any help from my parents.'

His eyebrows met. 'You did, eh?'

'Of course. You didn't expect me to love grandparents who wanted nothing to do with me, did you? And when you didn't reply to my letter . . .' She shrugged eloquently.

His head came up. 'What letter?'

Philippa stared at him thoughtfully, then explained, 'I wrote to you after Mother died, when I was eight.' She waited a moment and went on calmly. 'You're now going to tell me that you didn't receive it, aren't you?'

'Yes, I am,' Philip Ingram replied abruptly, frowning into the fire.

She took a sip of brandy. 'Well, it's nearly twenty years ago, and there's nothing we can do about it now. Would you have replied?'

His head came round. 'Yes, I would have replied.' His eyes narrowed slightly. 'So—how long did this hatred last?'

Philippa pursed her lips pensively. 'Until my late teens, I think, and then I came to England to study and matured, I suppose. Students spend endless hours talking, you know, and my rejection was discussed along with everyone else's hang-ups.' She noticed him wince at that, and couldn't help feeling a tiny bit of satisfaction. 'I came to the conclusion that there was a case for both sides. It's quite clear that stubbornness and pride are Ingram failings. I have them myself.'

He barked a laugh. 'Got a bit of spirit, I'm glad to see! So you think I'm stubborn, do you, eh?'

'Foolish, too,' claimed Philippa calmly. 'It's never wise to issue ultimatums unless you're prepared to have them carried out.' Very clever at doling out platitudes, but you might take heed of them yourself, Philippa was telling herself sarcastically.

His eyes were, by now, mere slits. 'Stubborn, proud and foolish—that's your opinion, is it?' He grunted a laugh. 'No one can say you're buttering up to me.' He thrust forward his chin. 'Now you're here, perhaps you're wondering if I'll leave you my money?' His eyes challenged her and Philippa took her time answering.

'Surely I don't have to point out that if that's my ambition I'd have come years ago?' she said at last. '*I* know I'm not interested in your money and that's all that matters to me, but you may think what you please. I shall be quite happy to keep in touch with you, Grandfather, and I'm glad I've met my aunt and cousins, and seen the house where my father was born, but if I walked out tomorrow and never came back, my life would go on just as it has been doing. I don't need you or your money. Do you want me to go tomorrow?'

He grinned wolfishly, his face suddenly looking much younger. 'Putting all your cards on the table, aren't you? No, I don't want you to go tomorrow, dammit, and you know it. I have no intention of altering my will, but I'd like to get to know my granddaughter, even if I've only a week to do it in. This tomfool party is all Harriet's affair and I'm letting her get on with it, but I'll admit to being glad if it's made you come. Tell me about yourself,' he commanded, 'what are you doing with your life?'

'I'd better start at the beginning,' offered Philippa, laughing a little at the enormity of the question and she talked and he listened, asking a few questions now and again. When the clock struck the hour the door opened and Ainsley entered.

Philip Ingram said testily, 'Yes, what is it?'

'You asked me to come back at this time, sir.'

Philippa rose, saying, 'Goodness, is it so late? I'll come and talk tomorrow evening, if I may? Good night, Grandfather.' She crossed the hearth and stooped to kiss his forehead, catching a look of approval from Ainsley. She took with her the image of an old man, face immobile, sitting proudly in his chair, the firelight playing on the planes of his face.

Harriet met her in the hall, her hands fluttering nervously. 'How . . . I mean, did Father . . .?'

When the question failed to materialise, Philippa said, 'It's all right, Aunt Harriet. He tried to bully me a bit, but as Francis says, I'm not easily bullied. It was all very civilised.'

'Your father hurt him dreadfully, leaving as he did.' Harriet's voice trembled. 'I shouldn't like Father to be hurt again.'

'I promise he'll not come to any hurt through me. Do you mind if I go to bed now? I'm rather tired.'

'No, no, of course I don't mind. Off you go. Are you sure you don't want anything? A hot drink, perhaps?'

Philippa shook her head, murmured, 'Nothing, thanks,' and began to climb the stairs. At the turn she glanced back to find her aunt still there, looking up with an odd, uncertain expression on her face, rather like a small worried chipmunk, Philippa thought, and gave her a reassuring smile before she passed out of sight.

Progress with Philip Ingram was encouraging, each of them feeling their way carefully. Philippa visited his room every evening, shared a drink and talked—not specifically of the past, but of things relating to their lives and beliefs. Philippa knew her grandfather often made controversial statements to test her reaction and she had to keep her wits about her, but she spoke her mind and enjoyed the sparring. There began to grow between them a grudging respect.

Tuesday, the day planned for Skiddaw, dawned bright and Ross, scanning the sky, claimed that the day would be perfect. He turned and gave Philippa the once-over, nodding as if satisfied as he remarked, 'No matter what the weather is like when you set out you can guarantee it'll change, so it's best to be prepared.' He held out a hand. 'I'll have that waterproof in my haversack,' and his eyes again took in the chunky sweater, cord trousers and walking shoes. 'Wool socks too—

good girl!' He looked at his watch. 'I'll go and hurry up Lucy—Francis should be here in a minute.' He glanced over his shoulder and added with a grin, 'Talk of the devil!' then disappeared inside, and Philippa could hear him shouting his sister.

A metallic grey Rover was coming over the brow of the hill and Philippa waited as it swung into the drive, her thoughts and composure held in check. Francis got out and strolled towards the house, hands in pockets, eyes lazily regarding her. He was wearing an Arran sweater that looked very much like the twin to the one Harriet was knitting at the moment, and he too was carrying a small haversack on his back.

He saw the direction of her eyes and said softly, 'Not chilled wine, French bread, pâté and goat's cheese this time—or have you wiped out all the memories?'

Philippa was saved replying by the arrival of Lucy and Ross. Lucy made a fuss of Francis and automatically took her place next to him in the Rover. Philippa joined Ross in the back. They saw few people on the drive across Uldale Fell and they parked the car just past Mirkholme and set off at an easy pace with Cockup on their right and Dash Beck over on the left. There was no need for Philippa to make sure that she and Ross walked together, Lucy commandeered Francis from the start and he made no objection.

The northern fells do not attract the crowds, Ross had told Philippa, and indeed, they did not see another soul until they had passed Dash Falls, and that was a shepherd in the distance. At midday they sat and ate sandwiches and fruit with Whit Beck babbling cold and clear within their hearing. Before they set off again Francis came over to Philippa and asked,

'Are you feeling fit?'

Philippa replied, 'Yes, thank you,' and when he held out a hand to help her up from her rock seat she pretended she had not seen it and stood up by herself, brushing crumbs from her lap. Francis dropped his hand and his voice remained even. 'Say, if you're not. You've done very well, even this far. If you're feeling tired someone can go with you into Keswick and you can wait to be picked up.'

'I've said I'm all right,' she replied, ignoring a slight soreness on one of her heels. She was damned if she was going to give up!

Francis eyes her coolly for a minute, nodded, and went back to Lucy. Ross, who had been washing his hands in the beck, returned and they all set off again.

The view, looking back over their shoulders at Keswick and Derwentwater, was splendid, with visibility clear, and had Philippa been on her own with Ross she would have completely enjoyed the outing. As it was, she was always aware of Lucy and Francis, either visually ahead or verbally behind, constantly intruding. They made it to the top and Ross brought out a camera and took some photographs. It was cool now, with a strong breeze, and Philippa was glad of the windproof anorak. Both heels were hurting by this time, but she was on the last stretch home and thought she could make it without complaining.

How it came about she could not tell, but after one of their short rest spells—mainly, she suspected, for her benefit—Philippa found herself walking by the side of Francis, brother and sister some yards ahead. She was not walking so easily now, but luckily Francis made no comment, merely pointing out some landmarks, making general conversation.

'Did you know that the Lake District National Park is the biggest Park in England?'

Taking her cue from him, Philippa shook her head. 'You have to have permission to build or alter, don't you?'

'Yes . . . there's a special Planning Board which doles out permission and it protects footpaths and listed buildings.'

Francis had always been a good talker and before she was aware of it they had reached the road. It was decided that Ross and the two girls would walk into High Side, and Francis would go for the Rover. So—he did notice I was limping, thought Philippa, watching him go.

Back at Copperthwaite she went straight to her room and peeled off her socks and shoes. Two ugly blisters were on each heel and as she sat, wondering what to do for the best, a light tap sounded on the door and when she hobbled over and opened it, Francis walked in, carrying a bowl and cotton wool.

'I thought you could do with this,' he announced, taking over when he saw the blisters. 'Why the hell didn't you say something earlier, Philippa?' he demanded. 'I had plasters on me that would have saved the darned things from bursting. Now it'll sting like mad. Sit down.'

'I can manage perfectly well . . .'

'Sit down.'

It wasn't worth arguing. She sat down and allowed him to bathe the blisters, gritting her teeth as the antiseptic stung. She looked down at the ruffled fair hair, so easily accessible, and pushed her hands in her pockets, out of harm's way.

Plastered and freshly socked, Philippa stood up, saying coolly, 'Thank you, that feels much better.'

Francis' look, as he threw down the towel with which he had been drying his hands, was shrewd and ironic. 'Don't act the ice-maiden, Pippa, because it won't work,' and he pulled her to him.

Off guard, Philippa had no time to protest and her mouth was caught, soft and mobile against his, as one hand went to the back of her head, his fingers thrust through her hair, and the other to the base of her spine, bringing her firmly against him.

As she came up for air, Philippa managed, 'Francis! Let me . . .' but the outraged 'go' was silenced.

When he finally put her away from him, Francis gazed at the flushed cheeks and bright eyes sparkling with anger and said with energy, 'That's something you can remember during the long, lonely nights!' before swinging on his heel and leaving the room.

Philippa glared at the closed door and with a forceful, 'Damn!' turned her back on it. Here she came up against her reflection in the mirror and for a moment she stared, glowering back at herself. Was it anger that had brought the flush to her cheeks and the light to her eyes? she demanded silently. Keep away from him, you fool!

As the week progressed Philippa learned more about the Copperthwaite household. Harriet was an odd mixture of capability and fussiness. She ran the house with the help of a small staff, the whole geared round the welfare and happiness of her father. As she had never married, he was the reason for Harriet's being, and when Lucy and Ross were taken in, some of this devotion had been shared out to them. Lucy took advantage of her cousin indiscriminately, as if it was her due. Ross had more conscience, but, as he explained to Philippa, 'If it makes Harriet happy to fuss over us, then who are we to deny her?'

Ross was out of the house early each morning, driving into Carlisle to the Mills. He had, he told Philippa, worked his way up from the age of eighteen, through all the departments, and was now in control of their sales, home and abroad.

Lucy was not so easy to understand. She was friendly, but not to the extent of putting herself to any trouble on Philippa's account, but gradually Philippa realised that behind Lucy's lazy manner there was a brain and a talent and a good deal of ambition.

Copperthwaite inside belied its bleak exterior, having an old-world charm and simplicity about it. Its furnishings and brasses were lovingly cared for by Harriet and her small band of helpers, and her aunt was always ready to sit and talk about the past.

'The farm bailiff's cottage was the original house,' Harriet told Philippa during a mid-morning coffee break. 'The first wool was spun and woven there—it was only a cottage industry then, but it was the beginning of the Copperthwaite Wool Mark.' There was undisguised pride in Harriet's voice. 'As business grew our ancestors decided to build a larger house, and its basic structure hasn't been altered.'

'It's full of character,' agreed Philippa, her eyes wandering over the low ceilings, the copper warming pan and kettle and the blazing log fire.

'If you like Copperthwaite you should see Inglewood,' Lucy said carelessly, having just joined them. 'Francis Balfour's place.'

'Red sandstone, Lucy dear,' protested Harriet, 'from a different quarry altogether.'

'Yes, I know, but still old and beautiful,' insisted Lucy, and Philippa suffered the usual feeling of resentment that Lucy Fairley knew Francis better than she did herself. Silly and unreasonable, but it was there just the same.

Philippa said casually, 'I thought Francis was a Scot? Balfour is a Scottish name.'

'So it is,' agreed Harriet, 'but like many families the Balfours intermarried south of the border and settled in Cumbria.'

'Is that his home, Inglewood?' Philippa knew he had a flat in London, but he had kept Inglewood from her. Situated in Cumbria, it would have caused too many awkward questions and given his game away. Was that what Provence had been? A game?

'He's all over the place,' offered Lucy airily, 'but I guess you could call Inglewood his real home. He has business offices in Carlisle and London—a flat in London too . . . which is done out in superb taste.' She gave a small, secret smile. 'I would say that, of course, as I helped him do it.'

Harriet put down her knitting and gazed fondly at her young relation, turning to Philippa to say, 'Lucy chose the colour scheme for your room—she has a way with colours.'

Philippa murmured something appropriate and disliked the sound of the London flat sight unseen.

Philip Ingram's birthday celebrations were being held in Carlisle, in the ballroom of a hotel. The Ingrams were staying there overnight and Ainsley drove them into Carlisle in the Daimler limousine, a glorious relic of the past, in which Philip Ingram was transported for his weekly visit to the Mills.

Philippa was aware of a great deal of interest in herself as she stood with the family by the side of her grandfather's chair, welcoming his guests. She felt confident enough in her appearance—she and Grace had searched London for a dress suitable for this occasion and had agreed upon a bronze silk dress in a nineteen-thirties style with a sequinned motif across one shoulder, and she had put her hair up, it seemed to fit the period.

She was introduced to friends of her father and at intervals found her eyes roaming, seeking the one person she knew had been invited whose fair head she had not yet seen.

'Looking for me?' a drawling voice asked behind her, and she swung round, saying with raised brows,

'Whatever gave you that idea?'

Francis gave a tight smile and his eyes travelled insolently over her. 'Very nice—but I don't suppose I'm the first to tell you that. I've been sent to fetch you. Your grandfather wants you to wheel him in to dinner. You'll be delighted to know I'm sitting on your other side.'

'I'm already trembling with eager anticipation,' returned Philippa shortly.

It was a grand affair. The women sparkled with colour and jewels, and the men looked smart in their evening suits, the Ingram men no exception. Harriet, whose hair was normally escaping from her bun and who had no interest in clothes, had been taken over by Lucy and Philippa. She was looking remarkably splendid in a deep burgundy velvet dress. Lucy, too, was a credit to the family, turning many heads her way as she weaved in and out of the guests, a vivid splash of emerald green.

Francis allowed the meal to reach the main course, taking advantage of the fact that Philippa was a captive audience, before asking,

'When are you going to end this farce, Pippa?'

How coolly he put the question! Philippa shot him a sparkling glare. 'I thought I asked you not to call me that?'

'I can't resist it. Anger is preferable to stony silence. But to keep the peace I'll try and remember not to call you Pippa.' He leaned back in his chair, his eyes resting upon her, and her cheeks grew warm beneath his look. 'But it's difficult, because that's how I always think of you. Memories can't be wiped out to order.'

Philippa stared down at her plate. No, memories couldn't be dismissed easily, and sitting so close, when by the turn of her head she could command instant knowledge of him, that was not easy either.

Francis gave a heavy sigh. 'I apologise for not telling you I knew Philip. I should have done. It was an error of judgment.'

'You mean you gambled and lost?' retorted Philippa. 'If I hadn't come across that newspaper article when would you have told me?'

'What happened between us has nothing whatsoever to do with your grandfather,' Francis intervened quietly.

'When?' demanded Philippa in an undertone.

Francis took a sip of his wine, considered her question, and replied, 'I would have chosen my moment carefully, I admit.'

'In bed, do you mean?' she suggested scornfully. 'Like putty in your hands?' she added, goaded by the flicker of amusement that fanned his face.

'Ah, come on now, Pippa—I can never think of you as putty!'

'It's not a joke!' Philippa ground out, the words harsh in her throat. '*You* might think so, but I don't!'

'You must agree it has its comical overtones,' he urged casually, 'and if I allowed myself to become too serious I doubt I could control my temper.' His eyes were no longer amused, but ice-blue and hard. 'I have a certain amount of patience which I'm prepared to hang on to, Philippa, but don't test it too much, will you?' Only when he was sure that she had received his message did Francis turn away and begin to talk to Harriet.

Philippa toyed with her food, her thoughts racing, and her grandfather had to say her name twice before he had her attention.

'Sorry, Grandfather, what did you say?' She collected her wits and gave him a quick smile.

'I asked if you were enjoying yourself, child, because this is for you—you know, all this. I wanted everyone to meet my granddaughter.' There was a smile in his eyes, shrewd and steady.

'You're an old fraud! You'd have had the party even if I hadn't come,' she teased. 'The place is full of owed business lunches!'

The smile moved to his lips and he waited while their plates were cleared and then asked,

'You seemed to be having a long chat with Francis. Do you like him, Philippa?'

'I hardly know him,' she answered lightly.

'I'm prejudiced, of course. Francis' grandfather was an old and close friend of mine, his father was my godson. So you see I've known him all his life. He inherited shares from his father in Copperthwaite and has shown his worth to the

Company. Then there's Ross—not quite so canny, but a worker and reliable. It's time they were both married. I married early and never regretted it, and I don't think your grandmother did either.' He took a sip of wine and wiped his mouth delicately on his napkin. 'You couldn't do better than cast your eyes over them. They're a good catch for any girl.'

'And Ross and Francis, what do they get out of it, Grandfather?' enquired Philippa mildly.

He gave a cynical smile. 'Don't denigrate yourself, child—and you're old Ingram's granddaughter . . . that's something, surely?'

'You've already pointed out that you aren't going to change your will,' offered Philippa. He was enjoying himself, she could tell by the glint in his eye. It was like playing chess with a master-player.

'So I did. Well now, an old man could change his mind, given sufficient reason, couldn't he? Think on it.'

'You're playing puppetmaster, Grandfather, and I refuse to dance to your tune,' Philippa told him severely, and changed the subject.

After the meal there was dancing to a small band. Philippa did not lack for partners—Ross claimed her more than most. She refused to count the number of times Lucy and Francis took to the floor, their fair heads close, and it did not help to see Harriet watching them too, a smile of satisfaction on her face.

Eventually word was sent to Philippa that her grandfather had gone to his room and wanted to see her. She made her way to the second floor of the hotel and Ainsley answered her knock at the door. Philip Ingram was waiting for her and she felt a swift pang, knowing she could never love him as she would wish to love him had the past been different, but she had grown to admire and respect him in many ways, and knew she should have come to Cumbria sooner.

'You wanted to see me, Grandfather?' She sat on the chair set already by his side.

Philip Ingram reached for her hand. 'Ainsley has been opening some of the presents I've received. Didn't want any, at my age I've got all I want, but nobody took any notice.' He pulled an irritated grimace, which softened as his eyes returned to her. 'But yours was special. Thank you, Philippa.'

Philippa said a little awkwardly, 'I'm glad it pleases you.'

'It's as if your grandmother is looking out of your eyes,' he remarked quietly, and glancing beyond Philippa, added, 'Can you see the likeness, Francis?'

Philippa gave a start. From out of her line of vision Francis walked forward and stood behind them, looking over their shoulders.

He said, 'Yes, Philip, I can.'

'She never reproached me, Philippa, but I knew, deep down, that it broke your grandmother's heart when your father went away.' Philip Ingram handed the photograph to Francis. 'Put it by the bed, please. No use regretting the past, doesn't get you anywhere. Off you go, child, and enjoy yourself. Francis, see her down.'

Philippa rose, bending to kiss his cheek. 'Good night, Grandfather, sleep well.'

At the door, Philip Ingram stopped them with an afterthought, calling, 'Francis—what you were asking, I give you leave, as you think best.'

Francis seemed to know what the conversation was about and nodded, without making a reply. He was silent on the way to the lift, and fortunately they were not alone as it descended, and when another guest buttonholed Francis when they reached the ballroom, Philippa made her escape.

Later, in search of fresh air, she slipped through the french windows and out on to the terrace, taking a deep breath and feeling her head clear as she did so. She leaned against the stone parapet and looked out over the moonlit gardens, wondering if her life would ever settle down to some semblance of normality. Everything seemed so complicated, and a long-drawn-out sigh escaped her lips. As she stood there, deep in thought, the music started up again inside the ballroom. It was a polka, an infectious little tune, which sent the toe of her foot tapping as she wrestled with unanswerable questions.

She gave a shiver. It was too cool to stay out long, but the freshness and the heady perfume of a late honeysuckle stayed her going.

Light spilled across the paving and the music swelled as a figure stepped from the ballroom through the same french window that she had used.

'So this is where you are. I've been looking for you.' Francis closed the window and stood barring her way.

She said pointedly, 'I was just about to go back in.'

'Running away again, Pippa?' The question was a challenging drawl.

'I'm going to find Ross—I've promised him the last waltz.'

'Ross is under the impression you've gone to bed.'

She stared at him, anger rising, colour flooding her cheeks. 'Your doing, I suppose?'

'He's soothing his hurt feelings in the arms of a pretty redhead, and enjoying himself, by the look of it.' There was grim satisfaction in his voice.

'Well, really, Francis!' exploded Philippa furiously.

'Well, really, Philippa!' mimicked Francis, and then, 'I think Ross has had too much of my *wife's* attention this evening,' and he pulled her into his arms, bringing his mouth ruthlessly down on hers.

CHAPTER SEVEN

SHE lay in his arms, a mass of confusion, the bitter-sweet, taunting word of *wife* echoing inside her head, and slowly opened her eyes to meet the triumphant searching regard of those blue eyes. Sanity returned. She thrust the palms of her hands, already spread across his chest, hard against him, crying, 'This solves nothing, Francis, nothing!' and he released her momentarily, his hands coming up to clasp her upper arms, warm through the silk of her dress. His lips twisted into a smile.

'Maybe not,' he conceded, 'but it proves plenty.'

He was, she noted, breathing heavily, and at least his damned cool had been shattered, if only briefly, which gladdened her heart.

'Do you think passion is enough?' she retorted scornfully. 'For a while, maybe, but I have to respect the man I give myself to!'

Absolute silence greeted her words. Francis lifted his hands carefully away from her and took a step back. His face was white. Philippa caught her breath on a sob. The sound of the waltz in the background was a mocking dream.

'Ah—respect!' Voice expressionless, Francis went on, 'I see. Forgive me, I've been more than a little obtuse. I'm accused of something more than knowing your grandfather.'

'You knew where to find me. It was no accident that you were at Avignon.' Philippa heard the words tumbling from her lips, challengingly, hating saying them, needing to say them.

He studied her carefully for a moment. 'Yes, I knew where to find you.'

Although she had expected it, his answer smote her cruelly. Through dry lips she asked, almost inaudibly, 'How?'

'Through Jules. I've known for some time of your friendship with Sylvie.' He saw her shiver and added abruptly, 'Let's go in, you're cold.'

'No!' Philippa backed off a pace and looked at him stonily. Francis took off his jacket and walked to her, draping it round her shoulders as he said,

'I gather I'm accused of making love to you for some specific reason. If we discount true love then it must be for gain, and if it's gain, then it must be Copperthwaite.' His voice, which had become more cynical with each observation, now became soft with conjecture. 'You believe that as you're your grandfather's heir, I'm after your inheritance.'

'I don't want to think that,' broke in Philippa angrily, 'but what other explanation is there?'

'It has, I suppose, crossed your mind that you might not be in his will?'

'Of course it has, and bad luck to you, because I'm not!'

'It might, I suppose, have crossed my mind too?'

'Francis, stop playing with me!' burst out Philippa furiously.

'My dear girl, I have no intention of playing with you.' His voice was the soft drawl, infuriating her further. 'I'm merely trying to the best of my ability to fathom the workings of your mind. You must also have realised that your grandfather hasn't long to live. To have you here under his roof at last will allow him to die in peace when the time comes. If I were a gambling man, and sometimes I am, I would lay high odds that Philip Ingram is having second thoughts. If you're not in his will I think he will reinstate you.' He smiled unpleasantly. 'It's obvious to all who see you together that he's besotted with you. It is, of course, an added bonus that you resemble his wife.'

'Don't!' whispered Philippa.

Francis gave a quick, exasperated exclamation. 'You want the truth, but don't like it when it's put to you.' He swung away and went to the window. 'I really do think you should go in. It would be a little too dramatic if I had to carry you in.' He opened the window with a flourish. Philippa made no movement. The music was coming to a finish and the curtains fluttered in the breeze.

'Have you told Grandfather about us?' she demanded, and Francis shook his head, eyeing her with watchful aloofness.

'What were you and he talking about before I came in tonight?'

There was a pause. 'Why don't you ask him?' suggested Francis smoothly.

Tightening her lips, not knowing whether to throw herself into his arms or wipe the cynical smile from his face with her hand, Philippa dragged the coat from her shoulders, flung it at him, and swept into the ballroom.

'Did you know,' said Ross, as he negotiated Carlisle's one-way system, heading for home, 'that the Scottish Border wasn't always north of the city?'

'You mean Carlisle was part of Scotland?' questioned Philippa. 'No, I have to admit that's news to me.'

'And that it boasts the only cathedral in Cumbria?'

'No, to that too—but I do know that Mary Queen of Scots fled from Scotland and took refuge in Carlisle Castle,' declared Philippa gleefully, adding, 'and if I drive through on my own I think I'd better bring a map!'

'It can be tricky,' agreed Ross, edging into an outside lane. As they waited for the lights to change he asked lightly, 'And now you've seen them, what do you think of the Copperthwaite Mills?'

'Fascinating!' declared Philippa with quick enthusiasm. 'The cloth is beautiful, and so exciting—full marks to your designers.'

'The designs are good, aren't they?' Ross spoke jauntily, and as the lights turned to green he drove on. 'We've recently acquired a new girl—Marion Parks—and she's making the buyers sit up and take notice.'

'The pretty redhead?' asked Philippa. 'I recognised her from last night—it was her at Grandfather's do, wasn't it?' She gave her cousin a quick side-glance, brows raised, and smiled inwardly as Ross nodded with admirable nonchalance. 'Is this design one of hers?' and she lifted the brown paper of the parcel on her lap and ran her fingers across the cloth inside—a mixture of browns and russets with a fine mustard line, which Philippa had chosen at Ross's insistence. 'I should hang on to Miss Parks if I were you,' she advised demurely, and Ross, giving her a quick, sharp look, replied, 'I have every intention of doing so.'

They were now out on the open road and traffic was easier, more ideal for bringing up a subject that had been on Philippa's mind for some days. She took a breath and said, 'Ross, can I ask you something, and will you answer me as honestly as you can?'

Amused, Ross answered, 'Go ahead.'

'Do you resent me coming to Cumbria?' She watched him choose his words.

'Resent? I have no right to resent you, Philippa. Lucy and I are the children of your grandfather's favourite niece, and I know he's fond of us, but we're not his grandchildren. He's done us proud all our lives and we've probably taken it rather too much for granted. In some ways your coming has made us both sit up and take stock. I'm glad for the old man's sake that you've come. He doesn't say much, but I can tell it means a lot to him, you being here.' He paused, frowning slightly. 'So no, resentment isn't what I'm feeling, but I wouldn't be human if I didn't admit to speculation as to what's going to happen now.'

'Nothing's going to happen,' Philippa told him crossly. 'I shall go back to London in a couple of days' time and get on with my life. I'll come back to Copperthwaite if I'm asked.'

'Some things happen without our knowledge or our control,' said Ross drily, and Philippa said quickly and earnestly,

'You're thinking about the business and, I suppose, the house, and I don't blame you. Do you honestly think Grandfather would cast you off just because I've arrived on the scene? For heaven's sake, Ross! What do *I* know about the wool trade?'

Ross shrugged. 'One part of me thinks, no, he wouldn't, the other part takes one look at you, the image of your grandmother, and I'm not so sure.

Uncle has a guilt complex about your father which he could ease through you.'

'Not to the extent of hurting you and Lucy, Ross. I've been talking to him and I've made it quite plain that I'm not interested in anything but getting to know you all. I've told him I won't live at Copperthwaite, that I have my own life and intend to go on just the way I always have. Grandfather has too much of a sense of duty to do anything silly, and he's too passionately involved with the mills to put them in jeopardy.' She paused. 'And in any event, you and Francis have some power in the Company, haven't you?'

'We would both follow the Old 'Un's wishes.'

Philippa allowed him to take a tricky corner and then said mildly, 'I'll tell you this, Ross—I have no intention of marrying you.'

Ross turned a startled face her way and burst into laughter. 'Oh, lord, has the Old 'Un been on to you too?'

'He has. You can't blame him, it would solve everything, wouldn't it? I could grow very fond of you, Ross, as a cousin . . .'

Ross grinned. 'But not as a husband, eh? There's someone else, isn't there?'

'Yes, but it's complicated. And you?'

Ross pursed his lips. 'Yes, but it's early days yet.' He flicked her a teasing glance. 'Not that I couldn't take you on—given encouragement.' His voice went evilly dramatic. 'Especially if I knew you were going to inherit Copperthwaite, my dear!'

'Thank you very much,' responded Philippa, laughing indignantly. She paused and went on hesitantly, 'Could you do that, Ross? Marry for money?'

Ross checked to see she was serious, and shrugged. 'We all marry for gain in some form or another. Perhaps you're not aware of it at the time . . . companionship, security, possessiveness, even gratitude. Pecuniary gain is always looked down on, but if it's purely incidental and real feelings are involved, then it doesn't matter, does it?'

Philippa lapsed into silence which Ross did not interrupt. Incidental! But Francis had admitted to her that it was no accident that they had met, that he had planned it! He need not have admitted it. He could have lied to her and she would not have found out, for Jules would never have betrayed his cousin. So why had Francis admitted it? Her head was beginning to ache and she couldn't think straight any more. She was glad when Ross began to make small talk, and she was obliged to answer. It stopped all the whys and wherefores buzzing around in her head.

Ross said, 'The birthday went off well last night, I thought. Perhaps Harriet can relax now. She's been a mass of nerves this past week. I think your coming steamed her up too.'

'She's very fond of you and Lucy,' observed Philippa, and he nodded. They were approaching Caldbeck and he slowed for a pedestrian crossing. Schoolchildren were waiting and Ross signalled them to cross. How much easier, thought Philippa, if I'd fallen in love with Ross. How nice and tidy.

'We're the children Harriet never had,' Ross went on, as he gathered speed.

'Has she never had the chance to marry?' asked Philippa curiously.

'Not to my knowledge. It seems she was never the same after the other brother died. You knew about that?'

'Yes, but no details.'

'I know only that he was drowned in a tarn out on Caldbeck Fell. There's hundreds of pools not big enough to be on a map but big enough for a nine-year-old to drown in. Harriet took his death badly ... his name was Philip, after your grandfather ... and she was ill for a time. It's not talked about.' He peered through the windscreen towards the house which had just come into view. 'That looks like Francis' Spider!' He frowned. 'And Dr Bell's Ford. I wonder what's up?'

Francis met them in the hall to say that Philip Ingram had been taken ill. 'He wasn't feeling well when we left Carlisle this morning, but insisted on coming home. I followed Ainsley in case it was needed to chase off for a doctor en route.'

'What's the matter with him?' asked Philippa, beating Ross to the question by a few seconds.

Francis lifted his hands and dropped them again, his face troubled. 'Exhaustion? Excitement? He's kept going for so long and now his body is forcing him to realise his limitations.' He ran fingers through his hair and rubbed the back of his neck. 'He's as clear as ever in his mind.' He shook his head wonderingly, grimacing a smile. 'When I suggested we took him to hospital, he insisted he was going to die in his own bed.'

Philippa suddenly realised how close Francis was to her grandfather. He really loved the old man!

'Is Doc with him now?' asked Ross, striding to the door, and Francis called after him, 'I think he's with Harriet. She needed attention.'

With Ross's going, silence fell between them. Francis walked to the window and stared out.

After a moment, Philippa asked quietly, 'Will he die?' and he replied without turning,

'No, but he hasn't long.' He glanced over his shoulder. 'A few weeks, perhaps.'

Philippa sank into a chair and leaned her head back, closing her eyes. She said heavily, 'I'm sorry. You're fond of him.'

'Yes, I am.' The reply was almost curt.

How her head ached! It was her own fault. All she had to do was to get up and walk over to him and go into his arms. She would lay her head on his chest and he would fold his arms round her . . . and they would find again the magic they had lost. She wanted to share his grief, wanted to be included in everything he felt and did. Wanted to catch his eye in a crowd and pass those secret messages known only to lovers. She wanted to share his bed and comfort him when he needed comforting, and laugh with him and talk with him and bear his child . . .

She ached to go over and could not. After what had been said last night, she could not go to him. There was something in his face that daunted her, and with a heavy heart she realised that she might even have left it too late.

'You go tomorrow.' His voice was expressionless as he turned from the window, and opening her eyes she found indifference on his face.

'Yes, unless Grandfather worsens. I have some important jobs coming up which I shall cancel if I have to.'

Any more conversation between them was stopped by Ross entering the room, saying, 'Doc's just left. He's sedated Harriet and confined her to bed. Uncle's satisfactory, but Doc says we must remember he's an old man whose body is winding down.' He pushed his hands in his pockets, scowling down at the carpet. 'Bit of a shock, isn't it? He's never seemed old before, and now he does. He looks frighteningly frail. Are you staying, Francis? Cook wants to know.'

Francis shook his head. 'I must go, Ross. Will you keep me posted? I'll be at my London number until Thursday and then I fly to the States.' He paused in his walk to the door, adding, 'If Philip . . . if you need me, the office will be able to contact me.' The two men exchanged looks of shared grief and then Francis turned to Philippa, saying briefly, 'Goodbye—have a safe journey home,' and then he was gone.

Ainsley came to fetch Philippa, as usual, after dinner. She asked anxiously as they walked to her grandfather's room,

'Is he well enough to see me tonight, Ainsley?'

'Mr Ingram wishes to see you now, Miss Philippa. If you stay for a bit it can't do him any harm, and not seeing you might give him a restless night.' Ainsley smiled encouragingly as he ushered her into the bedroom.

Philip Ingram was propped up on pillows, and as she approached he opened his eyes and she sat on the chair next to the bed and took his hand in hers, saying gently,

'Hey, what's this? Trying to get attention?'

He gave a dry smile. 'I doubt I'll see the New Year in, child, but I'm ready. The spirit's willing but the flesh is weak.' He glared at her. 'So no damned-fool pussyfooting pretending, eh?'

'No pussyfooting, Grandfather,' consented Philippa softly.

'You're off to London tomorrow, I suppose? Don't know what you see in the place—ugh! Can't stand it. Too big, too crowded. Nobody knows anybody.' He stopped, taking a rest, and went on, 'Now up here you can breathe. Everyone knows their own business and yours too!' He gave a breathy laugh. 'Or thinks they do.' He looked at her keenly. 'Are you glad you came?'

'Yes, Grandfather.' Philippa hesitated. 'I want to say something, but I don't quite know how to go about it.'

'Straight out, that's the best way.'

Philippa looked him full in the face, her voice serious. 'I don't want to cause trouble—for Lucy and Ross.' She stared at him, willing him to understand. His face cleared and he closed his eyes.

'I shall do what I have to do.' He patted her hand. 'Don't worry, child.' He was silent for a while and Philippa wondered if he'd fallen asleep, and then he said, 'Harriet's the problem—always has been. But I can't worry about her now. Francis has promised to do his best.'

Philippa said suddenly, 'Grandfather, you remember when I came to say good night to you at the hotel and Francis was with you?'

'I remember.'

'You'd been talking together and before we left you granted Francis a request he had made to you before I'd arrived.'

'Well?' His eyes opened and he stared unblinkingly at her. 'Curious, are you?'

'Francis said I could ask you what you meant,' she explained lamely, the colour rising to her cheeks beneath his shrewd eyes.

'Huh! You'll have to ask him again.' Philip Ingram waved a dismissive hand. 'I'd made him promise something and released him from it, that's all. Damn fool things, promises. Especially deathbed ones.' His eyes glared. 'I shan't demand any. The most ordinary promises become extraordinary the minute they're given—remember that.' He lapsed into silence, once more saying firmly, 'There's two kinds of people, Philippa. The ones that keep 'em, and the ones that don't.'

'And Francis keeps them,' stated Philippa slowly. She sat for a moment, thinking. 'Perhaps he ought to give me a few lessons,' she murmured at last, remembering the promises she had made in the Town Hall at Avignon in front of the Mayor, with Sylvie and Jules as witnesses. Remembering the bright sunshine as they came out of the building into the Place de l'Horloge, and the celebratory meal they had with Sylvie and Fabien, and the newly engaged Lisette and Jules.

She lifted her grandfather's hand to her cheek and said softly, 'I want to tell you something, Grandfather, about Francis and me. Something you'll be pleased to learn.'

She spoke quickly, unburdening herself, and when she had finished her grandfather made no judgment, merely held her hand a little tighter, saying soothingly, 'Ask him to explain again, Philippa.'

Philippa went to bed, strangely happy for the first time in weeks.

'As I thought,' said Grace, twenty-four hours later when Philippa had brought her up to date. 'Just a foolish, stubborn old man.'

'Dad was just the same,' pointed out Philippa reasonably. 'They were too much alike—each wanting his own way.' She gave a small, exasperated sigh. 'If Dad hadn't had the bad luck to fall off that cliff he could have come to

Copperthwaite with me. I know I could have talked him round.'

'No good stubbing your toe against fate, my girl. All you'll end up with is a sore foot.'

Philippa smiled reluctantly and made herself more comfortable in the armchair. It had poured with rain all the way down the motorway and she was glad to be home.

'I can't say you look as though your week away has done you much good,' observed Grace, looking at her niece critically and noting the dark shadows beneath her eyes.

'I admit to not sleeping too well, but I had things on my mind.'

'I wonder if your husband would be gratified to learn that he's termed a "thing"?' Grace asked slyly, and Philippa pulled a face.

'Since telling Grandfather I feel much better,' admitted Philippa. She hesitated and went on slowly, 'Now all I have to do is ask Francis about this promise he made—if he'll let me.'

'Oh, he'll let you,' claimed Grace comfortingly, 'but he'll choose his own time and place, if I know anything.'

'I'm not so sure. You didn't see his face when I virtually accused him of marrying me for Copperthwaite,' responded Philippa, and sank into a depressed silence.

One day to catch up on correspondence—there was a long letter from Sylvie begging for news—and to sort out the telephone messages on the answering machine, and then Philippa started out the following day for the business premises of Dronfield & Farnsworth Incorporated, importers of wine from France, Italy and Spain. She had done work for them before, but had never sat in on a meeting, which was what she was to do that day.

Peter Farnsworth, with whom she had had previous contact, greeted her warmly, allowing an admiring glance to pass over her tweed Prince of Wales check suit and its accompanying red shirt. As she took off the matching red felt hat and ran fingers through her hair, he said,

'I wish more women wore hats. I love 'em.' He paused and his smile deepened. 'Hats, I mean. Better not admit to loving women or my wife will be after me!' He glanced at his watch and indicated for Philippa to walk with him. 'The boardroom is a gloomy place at the best of times and October seems to be foretelling a harsh winter, don't you think? Bitterly cold wind today.' Not really expecting an answer, he led the way and ushered Philippa into a room in which a highly polished oval table with chairs set round in perfect symmetry dominated. Past Presidents gazed sombrely down from the walls. A middle-aged woman was sitting at a side table and was introduced as the minutes secretary, and Philippa took her place, noting the glass of water within easy reach, together with blotter, paper and pen. This format was duplicated all round the table.

Peter Farnsworth excused himself and returned some seconds later with the rest of the meeting in tow. Philippa was introduced to them all, taking special note of two Frenchmen, the purpose of her being there, father and son, the Messieurs Bouviers, who were delighted to be able to talk in their own language.

'Ah, good, here he is now. We can begin.' Peter Farnsworth's exclamation filtered through. The empty chair at the table was now apparent as members had taken their places, and all heads turned to the latecomer. It was Francis who now walked into the room.

Philippa sat riveted to her chair, the breath knocked out of her, and realising that her mouth had dropped open she shut it quickly. She hardly knew what she was feeling as she watched him shake hands, finishing with the Bouviers, speaking to them in his fluent French. At last he turned to Philippa.

'Good morning,' Francis said calmly. 'If there's anything you don't understand, ask, won't you?'

'Thank you, I will.' The words came out somehow, and she felt her cheeks grow warm under his impersonal gaze. How could he stand there and look at her as if she were a stranger? Her heart gave a lurch and pain shot through her. She lowered her eyes, thankful when he moved away and took his seat.

The meeting began and for a few minutes Philippa found she was flustered by Francis' presence, but gradually she settled down, hoping her nervousness had not been apparent. She was acutely aware of him, all the time, sitting quietly—he had the capacity for stillness—thoughtfully considering the business put before them.

When a break for coffee came, Philippa was given the chance to feast her eyes on him as he stood talking on the other side of the room to the Bouviers. Grey suit, pink shirt, grey striped tie—he looked modern, immaculate and absolutely wonderful. He was sporting his listening expression, and Philippa suddenly realised that Francis was a good listener. He had let her talk during their time together in Provence. He must have known a little of what she had to tell, but he had been genuinely interested, she knew that now, and it had been therapeutic for her to spill it all out.

She lifted her eyes from the coffee cup again, allowing them to find him. He had a half-smile on his lips and his arms were folded across his chest, body relaxed. His gaze drifted away from the Frenchmen and met hers, fully, for the first time. Everything and everyone paled into insignificance and all Philippa could hear was the thumping of her heart in her ears. One brow rose as he studied her thoughtfully and her cheeks grew warm, but she held his look.

The secretary's voice intruded with, 'Another cup of coffee, Miss Ingram?'

Philippa refused with a quick smile and wondered what would happen if she said, Actually, my name is Balfour, Mrs Francis Balfour . . . That would shake his infuriating cool—or would it? With Francis you never could tell.

The meeting resumed. Philippa had always known Francis was clever, that he had an agile brain and a fluent command of facts and figures, but it was something else, seeing him in action. He controlled the meeting, allowing a point to be argued until it had reached saturation and then arbitrated, summing up until agreement was met. At the close, Philippa was commandeered by Monsieur Bouvier junior, who was trying to persuade her to join him for lunch, and when she looked round the room she realised that Francis was no longer present. Disappointment swept over her beyond all expectation. She could hardly be civil to poor Monsieur Bouvier and choked off his advances with unladylike shortness, excused herself and went in search of Peter Farnsworth.

'Has Francis . . . Mr Balfour gone?' she asked, already knowing the answer but deep down hoping against hope she would be proved wrong.

'Yes, I'm afraid he had to dash . . . he's due at Heathrow in an hour for his flight to America.' Peter Farnsworth looked at her with some curiosity. 'Francis asked me to look after you, take you to lunch. He apologises for not taking you himself, but that's my good fortune.' He waited a moment, nonplussed by her lack of response, and added carefully, 'You do know each other, don't you?'

Philippa pulled herself together and said hurriedly, 'Yes, yes, we do,' and fought down the impulse to shout: I'm his wife, you idiot! realising, with shock, that that was the second time within an hour that she had had to resist the temptation.

His face cleared and he smiled. 'I thought I was right. That's why I didn't introduce you both. After all, it was Francis who put us on to you in the first place.'

Philippa stared, eyes widening. '*Francis* did?' Her voice rose incredulously.

He clapped a palm against his forehead. 'Whoops! Didn't you know? Perhaps I've let the cat out of the bag!'

'But I've been doing work for you for three years,' protested Philippa, and he nodded, totally unaware that he had said anything fantastic.

'And very pleased we are with your work too. Now, how about lunch?'

'I'm sorry, but,' and Philippa looked vaguely round for her things, 'I'm already engaged, a business lunch with a publisher which I can't put off.' But I would have, for Francis, she was thinking. Three years? I can't believe it—Peter Farnsworth's got it wrong, he must have!

She asked abruptly, 'Are you sure? About Francis recommending me to you?'

Peter Farnsworth looked at her thoughtfully. 'Yes, Philippa, I'm sure. You see? *Philippa!* I always think of you as Philippa, not Miss Ingram, because that's what Francis has always called you. So you see . . .' His voice trailed and his eyes began to twinkle, taking in her rising colour. 'Never underestimate him, Philippa. He's a clever, devious devil at times.'

'Three years ago, Grace!' Philippa stood in the middle of her aunt's study, her face flushed, her hair wild where she had ran impatient fingers through it, bewilderment rising in her voice. 'How did he know what I was doing three years ago? Know me well enough to recommend me to Peter Farnsworth? We only met in May, for heaven's sake! Why didn't he tell me?'

'Why don't you ask him?' mimicked Grace drily.

Philippa ground her teeth. 'I would, only he's over the Atlantic right this minute. Oh!' and the exclamation exploded as a long-drawn-out groan of frustration.

'He's left a message,' Grace said casually, and Philippa spun round.

'Who?' She eyed her aunt with suspicion.

'Your Francis. In the kitchen. I think he's determined to play havoc with my allergies.'

'Not more poppies?' exclaimed Philippa incredulously. 'At this time of the year?'

'No, not more poppies. Why don't you go and have a look?' Grace sounded amused, and giving her an exasperated look Philippa swept in to the kitchen and Grace heard her cry,

'Oh, my goodness!' and then, laughter breaking through, 'Oh, my goodness!'

'Exactly,' said Grace, joining her. 'I hope your husband doesn't think I'll look after the thing while you're traipsing all over the world at his heels.'

'Oh, you beauty, you little beauty!' and Philippa sank to her knees, her eyes shining.

'Little? Well, he might be—yes, I've ascertained he's a he—he might be little at the moment, but they grow! Boy, do they grow!'

Philippa took the Afghan hound's head between her hands and they stared at each other solemnly, the pup's tail wagging tentatively at the tip.

'The man who delivered him said he had orders to come tomorrow to see if we're going to keep him. I gather we are. Correction—you are. Dogs make me sneeze, you know that.'

'You're beautiful,' crooned Philippa, turning a shining face upwards to demand, 'Grace, isn't he beautiful?'

'Yes, yes, we agree he's beautiful. He's also beautifully mannered for a pup. He watered the old rug and not the new one. Wasn't that clever of him?'

Philippa began to giggle. 'I wonder what his name is?'

'Wonder no more.' Grace rummaged in a box. 'His pedigree is here somewhere—ah, yes, let me see . . .' She beamed a smile and began to laugh. 'His name is Beau François of Inglewood, out of Paladin of Greystoke and Beautiful Star. Beau François! You can hardly call him Francis, can you? Very confusing, so it's got to be Beau, which suits him perfectly. The man left a list of instructions and a box of foodstuff. Highly organised, this Francis of yours.'

CHAPTER EIGHT

GRACE, grumbling goodnaturedly, agreed to have Beau while Philippa was in Italy.

The trip went as planned, without incident, and on the return journey as the aircraft circled the airport prior to landing, Philippa was already thinking ahead, planning how to contact Francis. Whenever she thought of him, which was often, she was filled with a mixture of excitement and apprehension.

Grace was waiting as she came out of Customs, and one look at her aunt's face caused Philippa to ask urgently,

'Grace, what's wrong? Francis . . .?'

'No, my dear, it's your grandfather.'

A feeling of relief, followed quickly by one of regret, swept over Philippa.

'He died two days ago,' Grace went on. 'There was no time to send for you, and Ross and I decided there was no point in bringing you home. The funeral is tomorrow.'

'I must go,' said Philippa.

Grace answered, 'Of course you must go, but by train, my dear, not by car. The weather forecast isn't good—they've had snow and blizzards in the north, and the prospect for the next few days is the same. Ross will meet you off the train if you'll let him know which one. There's one from Euston to Carlisle which gets in around eight. You can have a meal at home and then I'll run you to the station.'

Philippa left all the arrangements to Grace and found herself sitting in the railway carriage going north almost before she had time to catch her breath. She felt sad at the news of her grandfather's death. It seemed unfair, just when she was getting to know him. She wondered how Harriet was taking it. Badly, no doubt.

The thought suddenly struck her that Francis would be there, and she felt a lifting of tension and settled back and pondered what she would say to him when she saw him.

At Carlisle station she peered along the platform for a sign of Ross. She could not see him, and as she handed in her ticket she came to the conclusion that the weather must have worsened and he had been held up. She would telephone Copperthwaite and find out what was happening.

As she began to make her way towards the telephone kiosk a figure suddenly barred her way and she stopped in her tracks. He was wearing a tweed overcoat, collar upturned, snowflakes glistening on the shoulders, and the crown and brim of a felt hat which was pulled down over one brow.

'Francis!' His name escaped her lips on a breath, the blood rushed to her face and then left it just as quickly. He seemed to have grown taller and thinner, and he was pale—his usually enigmatic face hollowed and shadowed. She swayed slightly and his hands came out of the pockets of the coat and grabbed her by the arms. They stared into each other's eyes and then she was in his arms, crushed until the breath nearly left her and his mouth came down, fiercely, hungrily, and she was returning the kiss with all the pent-up longing and remorse spilling out.

As they broke away, Francis said, 'No more

play-acting, Pippa. I can't take any more.'

Philippa lifted her hands to his face, replying almost incoherently, 'Nor can I. Oh, Francis, hold me!' and she was gathered into his arms again, her face buried in the rough material of his coat. She gave a long-drawn-out sigh and murmured, 'Oh, you don't know how I've longed for this!'

'So have I, but not quite under these conditions, when there's very little I can do about it.' The wry amusement in his voice brought her head up and she began to laugh, aware suddenly of the hustle and bustle of the station around them and the occasional protracted glances of passers-by. She felt drunk with happiness and amazingly carefree.

'What do you suggest?' she asked him, her lips curving into a mischievous smile.

'That you come home, where you belong,' Francis replied challengingly, picking up her case and swinging her towards the exit, a proprietorial arm around her.

The Rover was parked awaiting, snow thick across the windscreen, and while Philippa settled herself Francis cleared all the windows and then took his seat, the thick coat hampering his movements. When the door was secure he turned to her and said grimly, 'I love you, Pippa, and whatever's in that damn will tomorrow matters not one jot—do you understand?' and he cupped a hand round her neck and pulled her to him, kissing her almost angrily. When their lips parted he searched her face, eyes intense, his breathing impaired. He released her abruptly and gripped the wheel, the knuckles showing white, grinding out between clenched teeth, 'I promised myself I'd be gentle, but you make it so bloody difficult!'

'I don't want you to be gentle.'

His head came round at that and brown and blue eyes locked. Without speaking, Francis started the engine. The wipers cleared the driving snow and as they gained the main road, Philippa asked,

'What happened to Ross?'

'Nothing happened to him.' Francis gave a tight smile. 'I didn't knock him down to take his place, if that's what you mean, although I would have done had it proved necessary. I reckon Ross guessed as much. Anyway, I told him that I'd pick you up and would he let me know what train you were arriving on. I also told him not to expect you at Copperthwaite until tomorrow afternoon.'

'What did he say to that?'

'Nothing.' Francis flicked her an unrepentant glance. 'I was not prepared to argue, and my manner gave some indication as to how serious I was.'

'You mean you were your normal arrogant, bossy self?' Philippa murmured, and he gave a short laugh.

'Possibly. Ross isn't stupid. He accepted the implications and we left it at that, without discussion. I shall apologise for my high-handedness when I'm in a calmer frame of mind.'

Exultation swept over Philippa. That infuriating self-control was shattered—he did love her! The cool, urbane Francis Balfour was gone and she was seeing raw, truthful emotion, nothing hidden or camouflaged. She hugged the knowledge to her, as incredulous joy spread through her.

'Where are you abducting me to, Francis?' she murmured.

'Home—Inglewood. It's been waiting for you long enough—and so have I.' He shot her another challenging look. 'I would have come for you in any event. My patience had come to an end even before I got your message.'

'What message was that?' she asked cautiously.

'Don't come the innocent, Pippa. I came back from the States and Philip sent for me. You'd told him all about us. I knew you'd never have told him if there was no chance for us—not even to make him happy. I made myself wait until I reached home and then rang you, only to find you were in Italy, and I had some more waiting to do.'

'You're quite good at it,' observed Philippa mildly, and Francis said with swift grimness,

'Not any more.' He peered ahead through the driving snow. 'Not far now. Nearly home.'

Home. Philippa wriggled with happiness. She sneaked a look at him. Every line and curve of his face she knew intimately, carried with her all these weeks of denial. It gave her exquisite pleasure to indulge herself now. Francis felt her eyes upon him and turned to her, and they exchanged looks, and he muttered,

'Damn this snow—just when I want to get you home!'

Outside, Philippa became aware that open country had changed to forest land, and then Francis turned into a gateway and a house loomed up out of the darkness in the beam of the headlamps. A light was burning in the porch, and Francis murmured with satisfaction,

'Good—Mrs Tulley has been in, bless her.' He pulled to a halt, explaining, 'The Tulleys farm down the road and keep an eye on the place while I'm away. Stay still until I get the front door open.'

Philippa watched him carry her case indoors, the headlamps left on to illuminate the path. Light from the hall spilled out and then Francis returned, ploughing his way back through the snow, opening the car door and helping her out. She was wearing low-heeled boots, but even so was glad of his support, for the snow was deep. The cold was intense, yet she was hardly aware of it. She seemed to be glowing from inside and the feel of his arm around her, steadying her, delighted her. At the porch Francis stopped and she looked at him questioningly, a gasp escaping her lips as she was swung up into his arms.

'Francis! What on earth . . .?'

'I'm carrying you over the threshold.' The snow was settling on them, like confetti.

'You idiot!' Philippa folded her arms round his neck and kissed him. 'You romantic idiot,' she repeated softly, resting her cheek against his.

'That's not the general image I like to put about,' Francis answered drily, carrying her through into the house and kicking the door shut with a foot, 'and I'd be grateful if you'd keep it to yourself.' He let her feet fall gently to the floor, retaining his hold of her. 'There's enough food in the house to feed an army and enough booze in the cellar to float a battleship, so don't worry about being marooned by the blizzard.'

'Who says I'm worried?' quipped Philippa.

'There should be a good fire going, through there. Go in and get warm while I put the car away.' Francis stood for a moment, looking at her before backing slowly away and then out through the front door. Philippa smiled and wandered into the room he had indicated. There was a good fire, but she did not need one. The blood was coursing through her veins and she put up a hand to her face, feeling the heat in her cheeks. Giving a choking laugh, she took off her coat and put it across the back of a chair, then looked around her with interest. It was a large room, beautifully furnished with what looked like genuine antique furniture, one wall completely covered in book-shelves. Wall-lights gave an intimate atmosphere, helped by floor-length curtains at each end in apricot velvet. Two huge sofas faced each other, either side of the stone fireplace, in a neutral material, and an Indian rug separated the two. Some pictures on the walls, to be inspected later at leisure, and some interesting sculptured pottery figures were all she had time to see before Francis returned, minus his outdoor things. He crossed to the fire, holding his hands forward for warmth. He was wearing a thick navy-blue sweater which hung round hips clad in matching cords. As he straightened Francis turned to look at her, and a strange awkwardness fell between them.

'Would you like a drink? Something to eat?' Francis lifted a hand in the direction of a corner cupboard.

A light sprang to Philippa's eyes and she wanted to shout out with happiness. Was this *Francis* who was incredibly unsure of himself?

'For someone who's too clever by half,' she said in a shaking voice, 'you're awfully dumb where my appetite's concerned, just at this particular moment.' She did not need to say any more. He was across the space between them and she was in his arms, and they were saying words that had been held in for too long, words that tumbled out, incoherent, breathless, until they fell silent at the same time, drawing away slightly to gaze into each other's eyes. The exultant laughter came then, delighting in each other.

Slowly, savouring every second, Francis went to

the light switch and the room was illuminated by the bright orange flames of the fire. They undressed each other, fingers dealing delicately with zips and buttons and their reunion was fierce, born of a separation which had, perhaps, been necessary to allow a coming to terms with their dependence upon each other.

The growth of feeling and blossoming love had, in Provence, been touched with a magic that by its very swiftness made them vulnerable.

'What a fool I've been,' murmured Philippa contentedly.

Francis gave a rueful laugh and caught her hand and brought it to his lips. 'I don't come out with much credit, Pippa love. Philip reckoned you must have bewitched me, and he wasn't far wrong.' He became serious, gazing intently into her eyes. 'I didn't intend to sweep you off your feet like I did, it just happened, and I didn't want to spoil anything with explanations. Stupid, I know, but I wanted you on my own terms, without any complications due to your family. So far as I was concerned, it was just you and me.'

'I think you could say it was that,' teased Philippa, smoothing her fingers across his shoulder, needing to touch him, feel him close, to make sure this was all real.

'You were mine, and I was damned if I was going to wait while I persuaded you that the Ingrams weren't the baddies you'd believed them to be all your life.'

'You've got an awful lot of explaining to do,' accused Philippa, 'and I'm hungry.' She felt him shake with laughter.

Francis raised himself on one elbow and looked down at her humorously. 'Here, wrap yourself in this while I go and get you a dressing-gown,' and he drew a tartan blanket from a chair and draped it round her. Struggling into a sweater that seemed to have everything inside-out, he grinned at her. 'As for being hungry, you have your priorities in perfect order. We shall have a bottle of claret—a Château Haut-Brion—which I've been saving for just such an occasion as this. It is, perhaps, a little grand for Mrs Tulley's excellent "tattie pot", a Cumbrian delicacy which I hope hasn't spoiled for the waiting. And then we shall talk.'

This promise was given halfway out of the room. A few minutes later he returned, carrying a striped black-and-tan towelling dressing-gown. He held out his hands and pulled Philippa to her feet. He helped her into it, and watching her tie the belt, said roughly, 'I suppose I shall get used to seeing you here. I've dreamed of it long enough.'

Philippa murmured, 'Oh, I'm real enough,' and wound her arms round his waist, snuggling close. A thought struck her. 'Francis, I haven't thanked you for Beau! He's a darling.'

Francis laughed. 'I thought he was rather appropriate as a reminder of me. Now! Time you started learning where everything is. I'll fetch the wine, you find glasses in that cabinet over there.'

They ate informally by the fire and then Philippa curled up on the sofa in the shelter of Francis' arms. She slipped a hand inside his sweater, spreading her palm over his heartbeat. The thud, thud was a most reassuring phenomenon, giving credence to the fact that he too was for real. She said thoughtfully, 'Francis?'

'Mmm?' Francis moved a few inches into a more comfortable position so that he could see her face easily.

'Why did you come to Provence? Did Grandfather ask you to?'

He shook his head. 'No, that was all my idea. I knew you'd been sent an invitation and suspected that Philip desperately wanted you to come, so I thought I'd do a spot of checking up. I certainly didn't realise what I was getting myself into.' He smiled into her upturned face. 'I need to go back a bit for you to understand wholly.' He frowned slightly, assembling his thoughts. 'I saw your grandfather the morning before he died. He sent for me. Harkness, the solicitor, was there . . .'

'Oh, Francis, I do hope he wasn't changing his will!' Philippa sat up in alarm and Francis gently pulled her back to him.

'My dear girl, your grandfather was entitled to do whatever he wished. And he wasn't changing it, he was merely adding a codicil. He knew he hadn't long to live. He made me go over again how we had met—he was enormously happy about us, Pippa—his granddaughter and the grandson of his closest friend.'

'I wish I could have had a bit longer knowing him,' Philippa murmured sadly.

'He felt the same, and told me it was difficult to look back and see any sense in what had happened between himself and your father. It was, of course, very different thirty years ago. The north of England is a harsh country and demands hard living, and painting in those days was not considered to be work, and certainly not a means to earn a living. I think Philip thought your father would soon find that out and return. He was angry and disappointed when Robert didn't, but he didn't cut Robert off completely. He traced you all eventually to France and kept a watching brief.'

'You mean Grandfather knew what was happening to us all the time?' The words came out slowly as Philippa took in the implications.

Francis lifted a hand and smoothed back the hair from her face, saying gently, 'There's more to come.'

Philippa looked into Francis' face as if searching for reassurance. 'I can hardly believe it,' she breathed. 'Did Dad know?'

'Not to my knowledge.'

A thought struck her and she demanded, 'Why didn't Grandfather answer my letter, then?'

'Ah, yes, your letter. Philip did ask me, if it were possible, that we keep this bit to ourselves. It seems that your letter did reach Copperthwaite, but not your grandfather.'

'Someone took it.' Philippa considered this and then said pensively, 'Aunt Harriet?'

'Yes, I'm afraid so,' confirmed Francis, frowning slightly. 'It made painful telling for Philip, but he wanted you to know that he hadn't refused your cry for help, which is what that letter was really all about, wasn't it?'

'Yes, I suppose it was, although I didn't ask for anything.' Philippa pulled a rueful face. 'If you only knew how I waited and waited for a reply!' She laid her head on his shoulder and urged, 'Go on.'

'I need to fill you in with some family history. You remember that your grandparents had a son, called Philip, who died? You can imagine what his arrival meant—the Ingram name and tradition could be carried on. Harriet was born two years later and became young Philip's adoring slave. As he grew up Philip showed an amazing interest in the mills, begging to be taken at every opportunity.

He was a bright boy, a bit of a dare-devil, and spoilt by everyone. Now we come to the tragedy which must have changed all their lives, your father's too. He was only a baby at the time, but the result affected him later. Philip and Harriet were not allowed out on the fells alone and they were forbidden to swim in the tarns even when accompanied—some are extremely deep and even when the sun is shining the water is cold. Philip was nine and Harriet seven and they set off by themselves for a picnic. They knew the fells well, of course, and often went out with the shepherds as your grandfather encouraged them to know the land and what went on in it. However, this time they went out without permission. It was hot and when they came to the tarn Philip said he was going to swim. He was a strong swimmer for his age and Harriet wouldn't have been able to stop him, not once he'd made up his mind. She was a law-abiding soul and only a weak swimmer anyway, so she sat and watched. We don't know for certain what happened, but it's supposed Philip got cramp. In any event, Harriet had to watch her adored brother drown.'

Philippa went cold at the thought and shivered, murmuring, 'Poor Aunt Harriet, how horrible for her!'

'It left an indelible mark on her. Somehow she felt guilty, felt she had let her parents down—which was, of course, ridiculous. Your grandparents were shattered, your grandmother was ill with grief for a long time. Harriet had help in her recovery in the form of her baby brother, your father, transferring all her passions to him.'

'Who was no substitute for his brother,' remarked Philippa with swift insight, and Francis quickly agreed.

'Robert was Philip's opposite in almost every way. He hated the mills and the weight of their inheritance hung heavy on him, even as a child. He was a popular boy, easygoing up to a point, and he did try to be what his father wanted him to be, but in the end he had to break away. Nowadays it's happening all the time, but then, for the only son to turn his back on a family business that had been going for years and years, you can imagine the outrage, can't you? Robert's going not only affected your grandparents, but Harriet as well. She had now "lost" two brothers who were her whole world. She was devastated. If she had married, things would have been different, but she stayed at home and devoted herself to her parents, and when your grandmother died, to her father.'

'And when Lucy and Ross came to Copperthwaite, she transferred some of that devotion to them,' observed Philippa pensively. 'My letter, when it arrived, posed a threat. I was the daughter of someone who had turned his back on Copperthwaite and I had no right to be part of it.' She moved restlessly, uncurled and slipped from the sofa to kneel in front of the fire. Francis watched her and sat forward, elbows on knees, his eyes never leaving her.

'I've always had a funny feeling about Harriet,' Philippa went on. 'She seemed welcoming and yet didn't do anything much to help me fit in, and I'd sometimes catch her looking at me with a peculiarly fixed expression on her face. I put it down to a slight resentment, which she had every right to feel—Ross and Lucy too—so I ignored it, hoping that as time went by they would realise I only wanted to be part of the family and hadn't come for gain.' She gave a sigh. 'Harriet would never have believed that, would she?' She frowned into the fire and then turned slightly to ask, 'How did Grandfather find out about the letter?'

'Harriet confessed, the day Philip collapsed after the party . . . do you remember she had to be sedated? She thought your grandfather was going to die, there and then, and became emotional. When he asked her outright if she'd destroyed your letter all those years ago she admitted she had—became quite hysterical.'

'It's not nice to be hated,' Philippa said sombrely, and Francis joined her on the hearthrug and folded his arms round her comfortingly.

'She's sick, Pippa, and needs help.' His voice became lighter purposefully. 'Something else too. Your grandfather periodically bought your father's paintings, so indirectly he was responsible for your education.'

'That's rather a nice thought.'

'Yes, isn't it? And there's a growing interest in Robert's painting. An art dealer is interested in putting on an exhibition of his work and I've promised Philip to organise it, so we'll have to look into what was packed up and sent on to you when your father died.'

Philippa's face brightened and she turned shining eyes to him, exclaiming, 'Now, that *is* great news! I've always considered his work to be undervalued.' She fell silent and after a few moments' thought asked a little uncertainly, 'Francis, does this mean that Grandfather has been keeping his eye on me all this time?' She swivelled round in his arms and searched his face intently, and Francis smiled.

'Yes, he has. First through my father, who was, if you remember, his godson and very close, and went frequently to Grenoble and spoke to the Head of your school, taking back reports of your wellbeing and achievements.' He paused and the smile twisted wryly. 'When my father died I took his place.'

Philippa stared at him.

He went on, 'I only went to Grenoble once, for the Leavers' Ceremony. I sat discreetly at the back of the hall and watched you walk up and receive your prizes.' He grinned. 'I have to admit that at the ripe old age of twenty-four, the eighteen-year-old Philippa Ingram was still, in my eyes, a school-kid.'

Philippa clapped a hand to her forehead and gasped, 'I can't believe it! Do you mean to say that you came . . . Oh, my goodness! It's as if a piece of a jigsaw from my life that was missing has been found, and yet I didn't know it was lost! You! No wonder you had no difficulty in recognising me at Orange.' She thought for a moment and then asked, her voice rising in wonderment, 'Francis, did you go to Oxford too?'

'I was at your graduation,' he admitted cheerfully, 'again sitting well out of the way at the back. My wretched hair doesn't help me to become part of a crowd.'

'Very difficult for you to become nondescript,' agreed Philippa teasingly, running her fingers through his mop of hair before giving an incredulous laugh. 'I still can scarcely believe all this, you know!' She smiled up into his face. 'It gives me a nice feeling to know you were there.'

'I'm glad,' replied Francis simply, and they fell silent for a moment, each thinking their own thoughts, and then Francis said pensively, 'By this time I was beginning to feel that I knew you rather well and hoped to be able to persuade Philip to get in touch with you, but he refused. He was very upset at your father's death . . .'

'I know he sent flowers,' put in Philippa. 'I had mixed feelings about that.'

'I think he was scared you'd openly show your contempt of him, a contempt which he considered was his due, but he was very proud of you, and the way you were coping with your life. He contented himself with keeping a peripheral watch on you just in case you ever needed his help.' He paused and added wryly, 'Which brings us to May of this year . . .'

'. . . and the Roman theatre at Orange,' finished Philippa slyly.

'Exactly. Philip guessed something had happened when I asked to be released from his promise not to tell you all this.' He frowned and fell silent again, continuing slowly, 'At the time, I honestly believed I went to Provence purely for Philip's sake. I know now that I must have been a little bit in love with you even then, without realising it. I had held my watching brief for ten years and was interested in meeting you. I thought I could find out your feelings on the subject of your grandfather and see if you intended to go to the party. If you were not, I was going to try and persuade you otherwise. I really did need a holiday, and Maman was making noises about not seeing me and I had some business to attend to in Europe, so when Jules told me you were visiting Sylvie it all seemed to fit together beautifully. I would go to Avignon and "accidentally" meet you, but I did more than that, didn't I? Poor fool, I came a complete cropper!' He gave a self-mocking laugh, and traced her profile lightly with a finger.

Philippa caught his hand and kissed it, saying

fiercely, 'So did I! Ah, Francis, so did I!'

'Jules watched it all happening with great delight, as you can imagine,' Francis told her drily, tucking her into the crook of his arm more comfortably. 'He did say that perhaps I should tell you of my involvement with your grandfather, but all that seemed totally unimportant. This was just me and you, and I wanted it to stay that way until I was forced to do otherwise. I realised how stupid that was when I returned earlier than I expected to the inn at La Garde-Freinet and found you gone.'

'I didn't know what to believe,' Philippa admitted softly against his chest. 'I panicked and ran away.'

'I have something for you,' said Francis, feeling in his pocket and bringing out a handkerchief which he unrolled into the palm of his hand. 'As instructed, Sylvie gave me these. Poor Sylvie! She kept saying how sorry she was, but that wasn't much consolation. She did, however, hint that you would cross by Cherbourg.'

'The wretch!' exclaimed Philippa comfortably.

'Time to put these on again, don't you think?'

'I've always wanted to be draped in diamonds and nothing but diamonds,' Philippa declared huskily, and in one fluid movement she slipped the dressing-gown from her shoulders and sat quietly while Francis fastened the necklace round her throat and slipped the wedding ring and solitaire on her finger.

With the firelight as a backcloth, he searched her face and she put her arms round his neck and whispered,

'I won't run away again, Francis, I promise,' and drew him tenderly to her.

* * *

Ross said, 'Hello, Philippa. I'm glad you came.' He took her hands in his and studied her for a moment. 'I'm only sorry your return visit is for a sad reason.' He kissed her cheek and held out a hand to Francis. 'Come into the library, there's a good fire going—and we need one, don't we? The graveside was so bleak, but at least the snow held off for a while.' He ushered them in and closed the door behind them, smiling at them. 'You're both looking very well,' he went on in a lighter vein, the smile lingering, and Francis answered,

'Thank you for keeping out of the way yesterday, Ross.'

Ross inclined his head, accepting the thanks, and Philippa looked from one to the other with pretty uncertainty. 'For keeping out of the way?' she echoed, and when Francis merely smiled without replying, Ross explained.

'I met the train, just in case. Don't get me wrong, Francis, I trust you implicitly, but Philippa might not have wanted to go with you. I just waited long enough to make sure.' He grinned, his eyes dancing. 'There was no doubt as to the warmth of your welcome.'

'Oh, Ross, how kind of you!' exclaimed Philippa, giving him a hug. 'You do care what happens to me!'

'Of course I do, stupid,' Ross asserted, going bright red. He addressed Francis. 'I thought you'd caught sight of me, but I was glad you telephoned.'

Seeing Philippa's bewildered face, Francis said, 'I rang Copperthwaite to say we'd arrived home safely, and to put Ross's mind at rest I told him about us.'

Philippa gave Ross an apologetic grimace. 'How

I shall be glad when everyone knows. The whole thing is too embarrassing for words, and the only way to get through it is to give absolutely no explanations!'

Ross laughed and put an arm round each of them, saying, 'Congratulations, Francis, I admire your choice,' and planting a kiss on Philippa's cheek added, 'and you, cousin, keep a good secret. I'm glad all your problems have worked out.' He glanced at his watch. 'We'd better go in. Mr Harkness said three o'clock. By the way, I should warn you that Harriet is in a bad way. She's cracked completely and is insisting on being present, although the doctor says she should be in bed. He's given her something to calm her down. Unfortunately, she's taken against you, Philippa, for some reason. I hope you'll bear with her.'

'Don't worry, Ross,' soothed Philippa, and slipped her hand into Francis' for comfort.

They followed Ross into the drawing-room where Mr Harkness, the family solicitor, had set out his papers. He came forward to greet them, face and voice subdued as warranted the occasion but his eyes bright and his handshake warm.

'May I congratulate you, Francis, on your good news?' He swung round to Philippa. 'I know your grandfather was delighted, Mrs Balfour,' and he retained Philippa's hand and led her to a chair.

Philippa murmured a reply, her cheeks reddening, heard Lucy give a gasp of surprise and sought out her aunt, who was sitting in an armchair in the corner. Harriet was extremely pale and seemed to have shrunk in stature. Ross crossed to the chair and knelt down by her side, taking her hand, saying,

'Harriet—Francis and Philippa are married.

Isn't that a pleasant surprise?'

Philippa smiled at her aunt and saw a look of anger pass over the blank features, and realised that Harriet had wanted Francis for Lucy—something else for her hatred to feed on.

'Married!' exclaimed Lucy, her eyes wide. 'You secretive pair!'

Mr Harkness cleared his throat and returned to the table. 'I think we should begin, don't you? Everyone in this room is a beneficiary.' He glanced over his spectacles and allowed his gaze to cover them all. 'This is the last Will and Testament of Philip Robert Ingram, of this address, dated . . .'

Philippa listened in surprise, for the will was dated seven years previously, just after her father was killed.

It was quite simple. Bequests were made to the servants for long and faithful service. Harriet was to be allowed to live her life out at Copperthwaite, if that was her wish, and was given an annuity. The house and contents, together with shares in Copperthwaite Mills, were left to Philippa. Ross and Lucy were left sums of money and shares in the Company. The number of shares that Francis held was increased and he was named as successor to the Board of Directors.

'A fair will, in my opinion,' expounded Mr Harkness, smiling all round. 'I share the duties of Executor with Francis Balfour, and we will let you know when all the formalities have been dealt with.'

Harriet said flatly, 'Father made the will seven years ago.' Her eyes swung round wildly to Philippa. 'Before he ever met you!' Her voice rose. 'I didn't want you to come here!'

'Yes, I know, Aunt,' soothed Philippa. Harriet burst out, 'I didn't want you to come,' and pulled her handkerchief between agitated fingers.

'Miss Ingram, I think you would be better in your room, lying down quietly.' Mr Harkness approached her and encouraged her to rise from the chair and take his arm.

'I'll get some tea brought up to you. You'd like that, wouldn't you?' coaxed Ross. 'Some bread and butter, and cake too?'

'He left you Copperthwaite!' accused Harriet venomously, stopping in front of Philippa and fixing her with a wild stare. Mr Harkness and Ross urged her on, but she acquired strength and resisted them. 'Robert doesn't deserve Copperthwaite! He left it! He left me! They've all left me!' This ended on a savage cry. The passion seeped away and with a curious lack of intonation which made the words more intense, she added, 'I'm not sorry about the letter,' which sent a shiver down Philippa's spine and she clutched for Francis' hand which grasped hers tightly.

Ross said quietly, 'Come, Harriet,' and he drew her to the door where she held back, her eyes seeking out Philippa, and when she finally left, the tension eased, and everyone seemed to let out a long-held-in breath.

Mr Harkness, well used to awkward situations, declined refreshment, saying that because of the weather he felt that he should be getting home. Francis went with him to see him off and when he returned Ross had rejoined them, the tea trolley hard at his heels.

'Are we allowed an explanation now?' demanded Lucy, her eyes darting between Francis and Philippa. 'What's this letter that Harriet says she's not sorry about?'

Francis raised a brow at Philippa and she pulled

a rueful face and murmured, 'You tell,' and he then recounted the main details—that Philip Ingram had been secretly monitoring his granddaughter all her life; that Harriet had held back a letter written by Philippa to her grandfather when she was a child; that he and Philippa had met in Provence earlier in the year and had married; and finally, that Philippa had decided to come to Cumbria to meet them all and acquaint herself with the family.

'But why didn't you come together? Why pretend you didn't know each other?' asked Lucy, puzzled, and Francis replied coolly,

'Because Philippa wasn't too sure of my motives.' He sent his wife a wicked look. 'She thought I was marrying her for her money.'

'But, Philippa,' exclaimed Lucy, turning an incredulous face to her cousin, 'Francis is awfully rich!'

'Don't be vulgar,' said Ross, tweaking her hair.

Everyone laughed, and the tea was poured and plates handed round. Lucy came and sat down beside Philippa, looking at her as though properly for the first time. She said, a little abruptly,

'You won't be bothered with me around here for much longer. I'm moving to London—we're negotiating for premises and going to hit the big city with our talents.' She pulled a face. 'Ross says I haven't been very welcoming towards you.' She gave a shrug. 'I suppose I did feel a bit resentful about you coming, but without realising it I probably took my cue from Harriet. I'm sorry.'

'I understand,' Philippa replied, and Lucy gave a laugh.

'Yes, I think you do.' Her eyes went to Francis, talking to her brother. 'As much as I'm capable, I've always loved him, but he thinks it's only a hangover from a schoolgirl crush—and perhaps it is. Anyway, he's never thought of me that way.'

'Thank you for telling me.'

'Don't say anything to him, will you?'

'No, I won't,' promised Philippa, and Lucy gave a little nod, said, 'Good luck,' and wandered off. Philippa took some pains to catch Ross by himself and assured him that nothing would change at Copperthwaite.

He sighed, frowning slightly. 'We'll take each day as it comes. Lucy tells me she's off to London, while I . . .' He hesitated, and Philippa teased,

'You'll be working on your new designer, persuading her that her future lies with the Copperthwaite Mills and Ross Fairley in particular!'

Ross laughed. 'You see too much, cousin.' He tucked her hand in his arm and they walked across the hall.

'Would you consider living here, Ross?'

'No. It's your birthright, Philippa. Do you hate the place?'

'Goodness, no—I can imagine it to be a happy house, with children growing up here.' She became excited by the thought. 'We shall have holidays together here—the Morin cousins and their children and yours and Lucy's . . .'

'What are you planning now?' asked Francis, joining them and putting his arm round his wife.

'. . . and ours, of course,' went on Philippa, warming to her theme. 'Holidays to remember.'

'A little precipitate,' drawled Francis, 'but a nice idea.'

On the drive back to Inglewood, Philippa found she was turning the plain gold band on her finger, still not used to it being there.

'Peter Farnsworth told me you'd recommended me to his company,' she said.

'Peter has a large mouth,' declared Francis drily.

'Have you been putting business my way, Francis?' She stared at him and caught a too innocent look in return. 'You have! What a devious man you are!'

Francis laughed and shook his head. 'I merely put your name forward, if ever the occasion arose. If you got the job then it was purely on merit!'

Philippa smiled and made no answer. After a moment she said soberly, 'I suppose Grandfather had to leave me the house.' It was not quite a question, but Francis answered it as such.

'Of course he did. Your father would have inherited it had he been alive, and you, as his only child, were next in line. One of the reasons Philip was delighted to learn of our marriage was that there was a chance of children growing up there again.'

'I thought I was pregnant when I came back to England,' offered Philippa, in a small voice, 'but it was a false alarm.'

'Yes, I know.' Francis held his breath and then gave a soft, 'Damn!'

Philippa, dreaming about Francis's baby, blond and blue-eyed, registered what he had said and swung her head round. 'You knew?' she asked, and gave a resigned sigh. 'Grace.'

'Not her fault, Pippa darling, I swear it. I telephoned—I had to know how you were. She was very strict, we didn't talk about anything other than your health. I think I could get to like Grace—there's a no-nonsense charm about her.' He grinned. 'I tell a lie. We did, once, talk about

Beau and she waxed eloquent on the subject.'

That evening, relaxing by the fire, Francis drew a letter from his pocket, saying, 'I've heard from Jules. He and Lisette have set the date for their wedding.' He handed it to Philippa, who scanned the pages quickly, looking up with a smile to say,

'A June date. It will be lovely to spend our first anniversary over there. I must write to Sylvie and tell her everything is right between us.' She paused. 'It is, isn't it, Francis?'

'Extremely right,' he confirmed, putting a finger beneath her chin and drawing her face round to his. 'I knew you were angry and hurt by my deception, but I didn't think it was totally that which sent you running. I had to make .myself have patience because I sensed you needed time to sort yourself out. Am I right?'

She nodded. 'I was all mixed up, about my identity, I suppose. And Copperthwaite and Grandfather must have been lying dormant for a long time. On an emotional level, your involvement there seemed incredibly right, but on a mental one, it appeared horribly sinister—and yet I never stopped loving you.'

'I'm very glad to hear it. Come along, I have something to show you.' Francis pulled her up from the sofa and led her through the hallway and into another room off. 'This is my study, for want of a better word,' he said, 'and I want you to see this,' and he put on a wall light and they stood looking at a picture.

It was a portrait of a young girl sitting with her arms full of poppies. Wild grasses, sprinkled with splashes of red, danced in the breeze against a backcloth of a Mediterranean blue sky.

'Girl with Poppies,' breathed Philippa, and

turned to Francis, her eyes wide. 'Where did you get this, Francis?'

He looked from her to the portrait and back again. 'I came across it two years ago. The supply of your father's pictures had, rather naturally, dried up, but this was unearthed in a gallery in Paris, one I frequent regularly. The owner is a friend of mine and I'd asked him if ever he came across a Robert Ingram could he put it on one side for me to look at. Where this one came from originally we don't know. He'd picked it up at a sale in Lyons.'

'You mean you've had it for two years?' Philippa gazed at the picture wonderingly and turned to find his eyes upon her, the look on his face bringing a confused warmth to her cheeks.

'So you see,' Francis said gravely, 'you've been part of me for all that time without knowing it.'

'I was about sixteen. It's good, isn't it?'

'Very good. I'll loan it to the Ingram exhibition, but it's not for sale,' claimed Francis firmly. 'I'm greedy—I want both the portrait and the original!' His lips brushed hers before he walked her to the desk at the far end of the room. 'I half-thought I'd give you the painting for a wedding present, but I found I couldn't part with my Poppy Girl, and then I had another idea. I hope you like it.' He leaned over and opened a drawer, taking out an envelope which he handed to her.

Philippa looked at the manila envelope thoughtfully and drew out the papers inside. She began to read them, registering that they were the title deeds to Poppy Cottage.

She lifted a glowing face. 'Francis, how good you are!'

'Rubbish!' The colour flooded his face.

'How did you know that I desperately wanted to rescue the cottage?'

'I just guessed.' He took back the envelope and dropped it into the drawer, then holding her close, 'We'll start putting the renovations in hand now—they have a leisurely work-pace, the French artisan! And in June, when we go for Jules' and Lisette's wedding, we'll see how things are progressing.'

Philippa smiled up at him. 'That sounds wonderful.' She tilted her head. 'There's someone else I shall visit, to pay my respects,' she said, purposely enigmatic, 'and to offer up my thanks.'

Francis eyed her for a moment and as understanding dawned he grinned and asked, 'May I come too?'

The sun was high in a blue, cloudless sky, its rays beating down on the statue of the Emperor Augustus as he stood regally in his arched niche overlooking the vast auditorium. The doors of the Roman theatre at Orange had just been re-opened after the midday break and a few tourists were coming in, forerunners of another busy afternoon in this second week of June.

A brown-eyed, long-limbed woman, glowing with good health and vitality, climbed steadily up the stone steps, taking one or two rests on the way, until she finally reached the top. She watched the fair-haired man leisurely following her, smiling down at him, and then allowed her gaze to envelop the whole theatre, finally remaining on the statue of the Emperor Augustus.

Reaching her, Francis followed the direction of her gaze and asked teasingly, 'Have you given thanks?'

Philippa threw out her arms, embracing everything before her. 'I've given thanks to whoever is out there listening,' she declared soberly, spinning round to look out over the roof-tops. 'Francis, I do believe that's the same pigeon strutting on that chimney—look, do you see him?' She gave a long, happy sigh and studied her husband thoughtfully. 'I've never asked, but did you know I'd be here, when we first met?'

Francis grinned. 'I wasn't as clever as that—no, how could I have known? That I should meet you at Sylvie's dinner party, yes, but our actual meeting was entirely accidental.'

'The gods were on our side then,' declared Philippa delightedly. 'Did you recognise me right away?'

Francis leaned back against the wall, his elbows resting on the ledge. 'Jules had mentioned you were driving a red Metro and I remembered the number. I saw it parked outside, and thought you might be in the theatre. I had genuinely gone for tickets for *The Dream*, hoping to entice you into coming with me, and I dragged Lisette inside—she thought I was crazy.'

'And I thought she was your *bonne amie*,' offered Philippa slyly.

'Good—that means you were showing some interest even then.'

She turned her head and laughed into his eyes and leaned back against him, her bare arm brushing his. 'You pack a powerful punch, *monsieur*. I couldn't understand why you should be having such an effect on me and it be so one-sided.'

'One-sided be damned!' scoffed Francis rudely. 'When you turned round and I found myself staring at the girl in my picture I was landed such a wallop, the whole place somersaulted! If I seemed cool and composed it was some good acting on my part.'

Philippa slipped her arm through his, laughter trembling her voice. 'You're just trying to get round me. I was sixteen when Dad painted that portrait, which happens to be over ten years ago.'

'You don't look more than ten days older,' declared Francis lovingly.

She glanced down at herself and then sought his eyes, her own dancing. 'There's a bit more of me.' She patted the bump under the baggy cotton dungarees she was wearing, adding softly, 'And I've offered up thanks for this too.'

Francis covered her hand with his and they both felt a kick.

'Wow—I reckon he's going to be a Rugby player!' gasped Philippa, laughing and Francis said teasingly, 'He could be a she.' He glanced at his watch. 'I think we'd better make tracks. You ought to have a rest before we go to Sylvie and Fabien's party.' They began to walk slowly down the steps, Francis giving Philippa a hand down. She gave a chuckle.

'Did you know Sylvie had Jules lined up for me?'

'The devil she had!'

'She reckons she knew that was a non-starter the minute she saw us together. You did stare rather,' and Philippa smiled complacently.

Francis stopped their descent and said softly, 'I couldn't believe you were real.'

'Excuse me, do you speak English?'

As one, they turned to the speaker. He was holding a ten-franc note.

'Oh, lord!' breathed Philippa, laughter bubbling up inside. 'This is where we came in!'

'It's for the . . .'

'Yes, yes, we know—and here,' Francis delved into his pocket, 'do have these, with our compliments.' He thrust the two coins into the surprised Englishman's hand, and with a beaming smile drew Philippa towards the exit and their laughter floated lightly in the air.

The Englishman watched them go, their laughter infectious and making him smile.

The Emperor Augustus looked on.

The burning secrets of a girl's first love.

She was young and rebellious, fighting the restrictions imposed by her South American convent.

He was a doctor, dedicated to the people of his war-torn country.

Drawn together by a sensual attraction. Nothing should have stood in their way.

Yet a tragic secret was to keep them apart ...

Following Hidden in the Flame's tremendous success last year here's another chance to read this passionate story.

WORLDWIDE

AVAILABLE FROM JUNE 1986. Price £2.50.

ROMANCE

Variety is the spice of romance

Each month, Mills & Boon publish new romances. New stories about people falling in love. A world of variety in romance — from the best writers in the romantic world. Choose from these titles in June.

AN ELUSIVE MISTRESS Lindsay Armstrong
ABODE OF PRINCES Jayne Bauling
POPPY GIRL Jacqueline Gilbert
TO SPEAK OF LOVE Claudia Jameson
A MAN POSSESSED Penny Jordan
VILLA IN THE SUN Marjorie Lewty
LAND OF THUNDER Annabel Murray
THE LAST BARRIER Edwina Shore
ONE LIFE AT A TIME Natalie Spark
SO NEAR, SO FAR Jessica Steele
***AT DAGGERS DRAWN** Margaret Mayo
***BOSS OF YARRAKINA** Valerie Parv

On sale where you buy paperbacks. If you require further information or have any difficulty obtaining them, write to: Mills & Boon Reader Service, PO Box 236, Thornton Road, Croydon, Surrey CR9 3RU, England.

*These two titles are available *only* from Mills & Boon Reader Service.

Mills & Boon

the rose of romance

ROMANCE

Next month's romances from Mills & Boon

Each month, you can choose from a world of variety in romance with Mills & Boon. These are the new titles to look out for next month.

A WILLING SURRENDER Robyn Donald
PRISONER Vanessa James
ESCAPE FROM THE HAREM Mary Lyons
CAPTURE A SHADOW Leigh Michaels
GLASS SLIPPERS AND UNICORNS Carole Mortimer
THE WAITING MAN Jeneth Murrey
THE LONELY SEASON Susan Napier
BODYCHECK Elizabeth Oldfield
WIN OR LOSE Kay Thorpe
SHADOW PRINCESS Sophie Weston
***SURRENDER, MY HEART** Lindsay Armstrong
***WILD FOR TO HOLD** Annabel Murray

Buy them from your usual paperback stockist, or write to: Mills & Boon Reader Service, P.O. Box 236, Thornton Rd, Croydon, Surrey CR9 3RU, England. Readers in South Africa-write to: Independent Book Services, Postbag X3010, Randburg, 2125, S. Africa.

*These two titles are available *only* from Mills & Boon Reader Service.

Mills & Boon
the rose of romance

Imagine marrying the man your sister rejected.

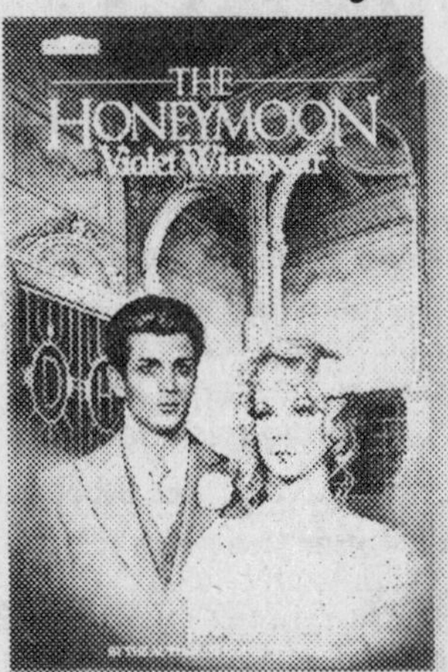

When Jorja's sister rejected Renzo, he turned his attentions to Jorja and demanded that she should marry him instead.

Whilst Renzo succeeded in unleashing all the hidden emotion which Jorja's sheltered upbringing had suppressed, the doubt still remained. Was it herself or merely her resemblance to her sister that stirred Renzo to such passion and desire?

Mills & Boon

FROM THE AUTHOR OF THE HOUSE OF STORMS.
THE HONEYMOON IS AVAILABLE FROM JULY, PRICE £2.25.

Take 4 Exciting Books Absolutely FREE

Love, romance, intrigue... all are captured for you by Mills & Boon's top-selling authors. By becoming a regular reader of Mills & Boon's Romances you can enjoy 6 superb new titles every month plus a whole range of special benefits: your very own personal membership card, a free monthly newsletter packed with recipes, competitions, exclusive book offers and a monthly guide to the stars, plus extra bargain offers and big cash savings.

AND an Introductory FREE GIFT for YOU.
Turn over the page for details.

As a special introduction we will send you four exciting Mills & Boon Romances Free and without obligation when you complete and return this coupon.

At the same time we will reserve a subscription to Mills & Boon Reader Service for you. Every month, you will receive 6 of the very latest novels by leading Romantic Fiction authors, delivered direct to your door. You don't pay extra for delivery — postage and packing is always completely Free. There is no obligation or commitment — you can cancel your subscription at any time.

You have nothing to lose and a whole world of romance to gain.

Just fill in and post the coupon today to MILLS & BOON READER SERVICE, FREEPOST, P.O. BOX 236, CROYDON, SURREY CR9 9EL.

Please Note:- READERS IN SOUTH AFRICA write to Independent Book Services P.T.Y., Postbag X3010, Randburg 2125, S. Africa

---

FREE BOOKS CERTIFICATE

To: Mills & Boon Reader Service, FREEPOST, P.O. Box 236, Croydon, Surrey CR9 9EL.

Please send me, free and without obligation, four Mills & Boon Romances, and reserve a Reader Service Subscription for me. If I decide to subscribe I shall, from the beginning of the month following my free parcel of books, receive six new books each month for £6.60, post and packing free. If I decide not to subscribe, I shall write to you within 10 days. The free books are mine to keep in any case. I understand that I may cancel my subscription at any time simply by writing to you. I am over 18 years of age.

Please write in BLOCK CAPITALS

Signature ____________________

Name ____________________

Address ____________________

____________________ Post code ____________________

SEND NO MONEY — TAKE NO RISKS.

Please don't forget to include your Postcode.

Remember, postcodes speed delivery. Offer applies in UK only and is not valid to present subscribers. Mills & Boon reserve the right to exercise discretion in granting membership. If price changes are necessary you will be notified.

EP86

6R

Offer expires July 31st 1986

102 049 934 6

UNLOCKING THE LAW

UNLOCKING CRIMINAL LAW

KT-445-800

Sheffield Hallam University
Learning and Information Services
Withdrawn From Stock

5th edition

Jacqueline Martin
Tony Storey

LONDON AND NEW YORK

Fifth edition published 2015
by Routledge
2 Park Square, Milton Park, Abingdon, Oxon OX14 4RN

and by Routledge
711 Third Avenue, New York, NY 10017

Routledge is an imprint of the Taylor & Francis Group, an informa business

© 2015 Jacqueline Martin and Tony Storey

The right of Jacqueline Martin and Tony Storey to be identified as authors of this work has been asserted by them in accordance with sections 77 and 78 of the Copyright, Designs and Patents Act 1988.

All rights reserved. No part of this book may be reprinted or reproduced or utilised in any form or by any electronic, mechanical, or other means, now known or hereafter invented, including photocopying and recording, or in any information storage or retrieval system, without permission in writing from the publishers.

Trademark notice: Product or corporate names may be trademarks or registered trademarks, and are used only for identification and explanation without intent to infringe.

First edition published by Hodder Education 2004
Fourth edition published by Routledge 2013

British Library Cataloguing in Publication Data
A catalogue record for this book is available from the British Library

Library of Congress Cataloging in Publication Data
A catalog record for this book has been requested

ISBN: 978-1-138-78093-4 (pbk)
ISBN: 978-1-315-77037-6 (ebk)

Typeset in Palatino
by Wearset Ltd, Boldon, Tyne and Wear

Printed by Bell and Bain Ltd, Glasgow

SHEFFIELD HALLAM UNIVERSITY
WL 345 MA
LEARNING CENTRE

Contents

15 FRAUD 513

16 CRIMINAL DAMAGE 537

Acknowledgements

The books in the Unlocking the Law series are a departure from traditional law texts and represent one view of a type of learning resource that the editors always felt is particularly useful to students. The success of the series and the fact that many of its features have been subsequently emulated in other publications must surely vindicate that view. The series editors would therefore like to thank the original publishers, Hodder Education, for their support in making the original project a successful reality. In particular we would like to thank Alexia Chan for showing great faith in the project and for her help in getting the series off the ground. We would also like to thank the current publisher Routledge for the warm enthusiasm it has shown in taking over the series. In this respect we must also thank Fiona Briden, Commissioning Editor for the series for her commitment and enthusiasm towards the series and for her support.

Guide to the book

Unlocking the Law books bring together all the essential elements for today's law students in a clearly defined and memorable way. Each book is enhanced with learning features to reinforce understanding of key topics and test your knowledge along the way. Follow this guide to make sure you get the most from reading this book.

AIMS AND OBJECTIVES

Defines what you will learn in each chapter.

SECTION

Highlights sections from Acts.

definition

Find key legal terminology at a glance

tutor tip

Provides key ideas from lecturers on how to get ahead

ARTICLE

Defines Articles of the EC Treaty or of the European Convention on Human Rights or other Treaty.

CLAUSE

Shows a Bill going through Parliament or a draft Bill proposed by the Law Commission.

REGULATION

Defines a provision in a statutory instrument.

CASE EXAMPLE

Illustrates the law in action.

JUDGMENT

Provides extracts from judgments on cases.

QUOTATION

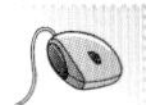

Indicates that you will be able to test yourself further on this topic using the Key Questions and Answers section of this book on www.unlockingthelaw.co.uk.

Encourages you to engage with primary sources.

KEY FACTS

Outlines important cases and principles.

ACTIVITY

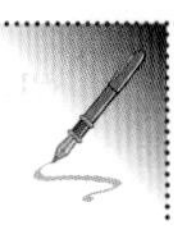

Enables you to test yourself as you progress through the chapter.

student mentor tip

Offers advice from law graduates on the best way to achieve the results you want

SAMPLE ESSAY QUESTIONS

Provide you with real-life sample essays and show you the best way to plan your answer.

SUMMARY

Concludes each chapter to reinforce learning.

Preface

The 'Unlocking the Law' series on its creation was hailed as an entirely new style of undergraduate law textbooks and many of its ground-breaking features have subsequently been emulated in other publications. However, many student texts are still very prose dense and have little in the way of interactive materials to help a student feel his or her way through the course of study on a given module.

The purpose of the series has always been to try to make learning each subject area more accessible by focusing on actual learning needs, and by providing a range of different supporting materials and features.

All topic areas are broken up into manageable sections with a logical progression and extensive use of headings and numerous sub-headings as well as an extensive contents list and index. Each book in the series also contains a variety of flow charts, diagrams, key facts charts and summaries to reinforce the information in the body of the text. Diagrams and flow charts are particularly useful because they can provide a quick and easy understanding of the key points, especially when revising for examinations. Key facts charts not only provide a quick visual guide through the subject but are also useful for revision.

Many cases are separated out for easy access and all cases have full citation in the text as well as the table of cases for easy reference. The emphasis of the series is on depth of understanding much more than breadth of detail. For this reason each text also includes key extracts from judgments where appropriate. Extracts from academic comment from journal articles and leading texts are also included to give some insight into the academic debate on complex or controversial areas. In both cases these are highlighted and removed from the body of the text.

Finally the books also include much formative 'self-testing', with a variety of activities ranging through subject specific comprehension, application of the law, and a range of other activities to help the student gain a good idea of his or her progress in the course. Appendices with guides on completing essay style questions and legal problem solving supplement and support this interactivity. Besides this a sample essay plan is added at the end of most chapters.

A feature of the most recent editions is the inclusion of some case extracts from the actual law reports which not only provide more detail on some of the important cases but also help to support students in their use of law reports by providing a simple commentary and also activities to cement understanding.

The first part of this book covers important concepts which underpin the criminal law. These include *actus reus*, *mens rea* and strict liability, participation in crime, capacity, inchoate offences and general defences. The second part covers the most important offences. These include fatal and non-fatal offences against the person, sexual offences, offences against property and the main offences against public order.

The book is designed to cover all of the main topics on undergraduate and professional criminal law syllabuses.

Note that all incidental references to 'he', 'him', 'his', etc., are intended to be gender neutral.

The law is stated as we believe it to be on 1 September 2014.

Jacqueline Martin
Tony Storey

List of figures

Table of cases

UNITED KINGDOM

INTERNATIONAL

Australia

Canada

European Court of Human Rights

New Zealand

South Africa

United States

Table of statutory instruments

Table of legislation

Table of European instruments

Part I

Concepts in criminal law

1

Introduction to criminal law

AIMS AND OBJECTIVES

After reading this chapter you should be able to:

- Understand the basic origins and purposes of criminal law
- Understand the definitions and classifications of criminal law
- Understand the basic workings of the criminal justice system
- Understand the basic concept of the elements of *actus reus* and *mens rea* in criminal law
- Understand the burden and standard of proof in criminal cases
- Understand how human rights law may have an effect on criminal law

This book deals with substantive criminal law. Substantive criminal law refers to the physical and mental element (if any) that has to be proved for each criminal offence. It also includes the general principles of intention and causation, the defences available and other general rules such as those on when participation in a crime makes the person criminally liable. Substantive criminal law does not include rules of procedure or evidence or sentencing theory and practice. However, these are equally important parts of the criminal justice system.

This chapter, therefore, gives some background information on criminal law. The purpose of the criminal law is considered, as well as how we know what is recognised as a crime, and the sources of criminal law. There are also brief sections explaining the courts in which criminal offences are tried, and the purposes of sentencing. The penultimate section of this chapter explains the burden and standard of proof in criminal cases. The final section looks at the effect of human rights law on criminal law.

1.1 Purpose of criminal law

The purpose of criminal law has never been written down by Parliament and, as the criminal law has developed over hundreds of years, it is difficult to state the aims in any precise way. However, there is general agreement that the main purposes are to:

- protect individuals and their property from harm;

- preserve order in society;
- punish those who deserve punishment.

However, on this last point, it should be noted that there are also other aims when a sentence is passed on an offender. These include incapacitation, deterrence, reformation and reparation.

In addition to the three main aims of the criminal law listed above, there are other points which have been put forward as purposes. These include:

- educating people about appropriate conduct and behaviour;
- enforcing moral values.

The use of the law in educating people about appropriate conduct can be seen in the drink-driving laws. The conduct of those whose level of alcohol in their blood or urine was above specified limits has only been criminalised since 1967. Prior to that, it had to be shown that a driver was unfit to drive as a result of drinking. Since 1967, there has been a change in the way that the public regard drink-driving. It is now much more unacceptable, and the main reason for this change is the increased awareness, through the use of television adverts, of people about the risks to innocent victims when a vehicle is driven by someone over the legal limit.

1.1.1 Should the law enforce moral values?

This is more controversial, and there has been considerable debate about whether the law should be used to enforce moral values. It can be argued that it is not the function of criminal law to interfere in the private lives of citizens unless it is necessary to try to impose certain standards of behaviour. The Wolfenden Committee reporting on homosexual offences and prostitution (1957) felt that intervention in private lives should only occur in order to:

- preserve public order and decency;
- protect the citizen from what is offensive or injurious;
- provide sufficient safeguards against exploitation and corruption of others, particularly those who are especially vulnerable.

Lord Devlin disagreed. He felt that 'there are acts so gross and outrageous that they must be prevented at any cost'. He set out how he thought it should be decided what type of behaviour be viewed as criminal by saying:

QUOTATION

> 'How are the moral judgments of society to be ascertained . . . It is surely not enough that they should be reached by the opinion of the majority; it would be too much to require the individual assent of every citizen. English law has evolved and regularly uses a standard which does not depend on the counting of heads. It is that of the reasonable man. He is not to be confused with the rational man. He is not to be expected to reason about anything and his judgment may be largely a matter of feeling . . . for my purpose I should like to call him the man in the jury box . . .
>
> It is not nearly enough that to say that a majority dislike a practice: there must be a real feeling of reprobation . . . I do not think one can ignore disgust if it is deeply felt and not manufactured. Its presence is a good indication that the bounds of toleration are being reached.'
>
> Lord Devlin, *The Enforcement of Morals* (Oxford University Press, 1965)

There are two major problems with this approach. First, the decision of what moral behaviour is criminally wrong is left to each jury to determine. This may lead to inconsistent results, as there is a different jury for each case. Second, Lord Devlin is content to rely on what may be termed 'gut reaction' to decide if the 'bounds of toleration are being reached'. This is certainly neither a legal method nor a reliable method of deciding what behaviour should be termed criminal. Another problem with Lord Devlin's approach is that society's view of certain behaviour changes over a period of time. Perhaps because of the lack of agreement on what should be termed 'criminal' and the difficulty of finding a satisfactory way of legally defining such behaviour, there is another problem in that the courts do not approach certain moral problems in a consistent way. This can be illustrated by conflicting cases on when the consent of the injured party can be a defence to a charge of assault. The first is the case of *Brown* [1993] 2 All ER 75.

CASE EXAMPLE

Brown [1993] 2 All ER 75

Several men in a group of consenting adult sado-masochists were convicted of assault causing actual bodily harm (s 47 Offences Against the Person Act 1861) and malicious wounding (s 20 Offences Against the Person Act 1861). They had carried out in private such acts as whipping and caning, branding, applying stinging nettles to the genital area and inserting map pins or fish hooks into the penises of each other. All of the men who took part consented to the acts against them. There was no permanent injury to any of the men involved and no evidence that any of them had needed any medical treatment. The House of Lords considered whether consent should be available as a defence in these circumstances. It took the view that it could not be a defence and upheld the convictions.

Lord Templeman said:

JUDGMENT

'The question whether the defence of consent should be extended to the consequences of sado-masochistic encounters can only be decided by consideration of policy and public interest ... Society is entitled and bound to protect itself against a cult of violence. Pleasure derived from the infliction of pain is an evil thing. Cruelty is uncivilised.'

Two of the judges dissented and would have allowed the appeals. One of these judges, Lord Slynn, expressed his view by saying:

JUDGMENT

'Adults can consent to acts done in private which do not result in serious bodily harm, so that such acts do not constitute criminal assaults for the purposes of the 1861 [Offences Against the Person] Act. In the end it is a matter of policy in an area where social and moral factors are extremely important and where attitudes could change. It is a matter of policy for the legislature to decide. It is not for the courts in the interests of paternalism or in order to protect people from themselves to introduce into existing statutory crimes relating to offences against the person, concepts which do not properly fit there.'

The second case is *Wilson* [1996] Crim LR 573, where a husband had used a heated butter knife to brand his initials on his wife's buttocks, at her request. The wife's burns had become infected and she needed medical treatment. He was convicted of assault causing actual bodily harm (s 47 Offences Against the Person Act 1861) but on appeal the Court of Appeal quashed the conviction. Russell LJ said:

JUDGMENT

'[W]e are firmly of the opinion that it is not in the public interest that activities such as the appellant's in this appeal should amount to a criminal behaviour. Consensual activity between husband and wife, in the privacy of the matrimonial home, is not, in our judgment, a proper matter for criminal investigation, let alone criminal prosecution ... In this field, in our judgment, the law should develop upon a case by case basis rather than upon general propositions to which, in the changing times we live, exceptions may arise from time to time not expressly covered by authority.'

The similarities in the two cases are that both activities were in private and the participants were adults. In *Brown* there were no lasting injuries and no evidence of the need for medical treatment, whereas in *Wilson* the injuries were severe enough for Mrs Wilson to seek medical attention (and for the doctor to report the matter to the police). The main distinction which the courts relied on was that in *Brown* the acts were for sexual gratification, whereas the motive in *Wilson* was of 'personal adornment'. Is this enough to label the behaviour in *Brown* as criminal? (See sections 8.6.3 and 8.6.4 for further discussion of the decision in *Brown* and also the decision of the European Court of Human Rights in the case.)

The reference in Russell LJ's judgment to changing times acknowledges that society's view of some behaviour can change. There can also be disagreement about what morals should be enforced. Abortion was legalised in 1967, yet some people still believe it is morally wrong. A limited form of euthanasia has been accepted as legal with the ruling in *Airedale NHS Trust v Bland* [1993] 1 All ER 821, where it was ruled that medical staff could withdraw life support systems from a patient, who could breathe unaided but was in a persistent vegetative state. This ruling meant that they could withdraw the feeding tubes of the patient, despite the fact that this would inevitably cause him to die. Many people believe that this is immoral, as it denies the sanctity of human life.

All these matters show the difficulty of agreeing that one of the purposes of criminal law should be to enforce moral standards.

1.1.2 Example of the changing nature of criminal law

As moral values will have an effect on the law, what conduct is criminal may, therefore, vary over time and from one country to another. The law is likely to change when there is a change in the values of government and society. A good example of how views on what is criminal behaviour change over time can be seen from the way the law on consensual homosexual acts has changed.

- The Criminal Law Amendment Act 1885 criminalised consensual homosexual acts between adults in private. It was under this law that the playwright Oscar Wilde was imprisoned in 1895.
- The Sexual Offences Act 1967 decriminalised such behaviour between those aged 21 and over.
- The Criminal Justice and Public Order Act 1994 decriminalised such behaviour for those aged 18 and over.

- In 2000 the government reduced the age of consent for homosexual acts to 16, though the Parliament Acts had to be used as the House of Lords voted against the change in the law.

We will now move on to consider where the criminal law comes from.

1.2 Sources of criminal law

The two main areas from which our criminal law is derived are case decisions (common law) and Acts of Parliament.

1.2.1 Common law offences

The courts have developed the criminal law in decisions over hundreds of years. In some instances offences have been entirely created by case law and precedents set by judges in those cases. An offence which is not defined in any Act of Parliament or delegated legislation is called a common law offence. Murder is such an offence. The classic definition of murder comes from the seventeenth-century jurist, Lord Coke. This definition has continually been refined by judges, including some important decisions during the 1980s and 1990s. Other common law offences include manslaughter and assault and battery. Equally, some defences have been entirely created by the decisions of judges. The defences of duress, duress of circumstances, automatism and intoxication all come into this category.

One problem with common law offences is that they can be very vague. This is illustrated by the common law offence of outraging public decency. This offence has arisen so rarely that there have even been debates about whether it actually exists, but it was used in two separate cases in the 1990s. The first case was *Gibson and another* [1991] 1 All ER 439.

CASE EXAMPLE

Gibson and another [1991] 1 All ER 439

In this the first defendant had created an exhibit of a model's head with earrings which were made out of freeze-dried real human foetuses. He intended to convey the message that women wear their abortions as lightly as they wear earrings. This model was put on public display in the second defendant's art gallery. Both men were convicted of outraging public decency and their convictions were upheld by the Court of Appeal.

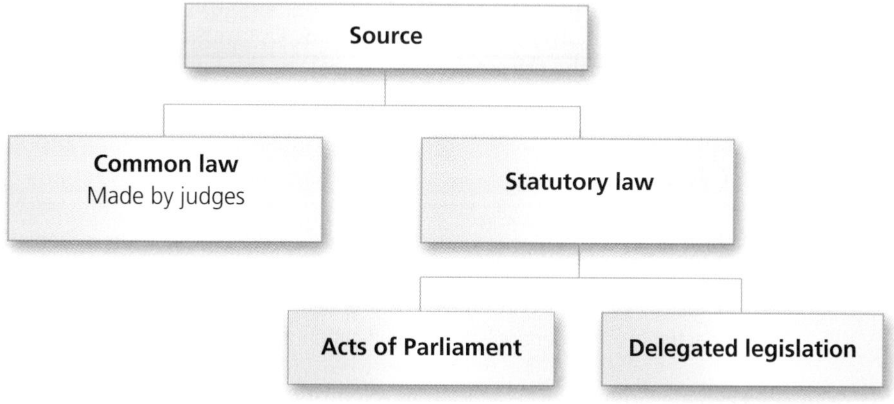

Figure 1.1 Sources of criminal law.

The second case was very different. This was *Walker* [1995] Crim LR 44, where the defendant had exposed his penis to two girls in the sitting room of his own house. The Court of Appeal allowed the defendant's appeal against his conviction, as the place where the act occurred was not open to the public. The prosecution's choice of charge seems odd, but presumably the fact that there had been very few cases made it difficult for them to know whether it was necessary to prove only that other people had been outraged or whether, as decided by the Court of Appeal, it had to be in a place where there was a real possibility that members of the general public might witness the act. In fact in *Walker* there were other more suitable offences with which the defendant could have been charged.

In some instances the courts will develop the law and then it will be absorbed into a statute. This happened with the defence of provocation (a defence to murder). It had been developed through case law but was then set out in the Homicide Act 1957. Even where there is a definition in an Act of Parliament, the courts may still have a role to play in interpreting that definition and drawing precise boundaries for the crime.

1.2.2 Statutory offences

Today the majority of offences are set out in an Act of Parliament or through delegated legislation. About 70 to 80 Acts of Parliament are passed each year. In addition there is a considerable amount of delegated legislation each year, including over 3,000 statutory instruments created by government ministers. Most offences today are statutory ones. Examples include theft, robbery and burglary, which are in the Theft Act 1968. Criminal damage is set out in the Criminal Damage Act 1971. The law on sexual offences is now largely contained in the Sexual Offences Act 2003. The various offences of fraud are set out in the Fraud Act 2006.

Note that, even when offences have been created by Acts of Parliament or delegated legislation, judges still play a role in interpretation. Different sources of law are shown in Figure 1.1.

1.2.3 Codification of the criminal law

One of the main problems in criminal law is that it has developed in a piecemeal way and it is difficult to find all the relevant law. Some of the most important concepts, such as the meaning of 'intention', still come from case law and have never been defined in an Act of Parliament. Other areas of the law rely on old Acts of Parliament, such as the Offences Against the Person Act which is nearly 150 years old. All these factors mean that the law is not always clear. In 1965 the government created a full-time law reform body called the Law Commission. The Law Commission has the duty to review all areas of law, not just the criminal law. By s 3(1) of the Law Commissions Act 1965 the Commission was established to:

SECTION

'take and keep under review all the law … with a view to its systematic development and reform, including in particular the codification of such law, the elimination of anomalies, the repeal of obsolete and unnecessary enactments, the reduction of the number of separate enactments and generally the simplification and modernisation of the law.'

The Law Commission decided to attempt the codification of the criminal law to include existing law and to introduce reforms to key areas. A first draft was produced in 1985, and this was followed by consultation which led to the publication of A Criminal Code for England and Wales (1989) (Law Com No 177). The two main purposes of the code were regarded as:

- bringing together in one place most of the important offences;
- establishing definitions of key fault terms such as 'intention' and 'recklessness'.

The second point would also have helped Parliament in the creation of any new offences as it would be presumed that, when using words defined by the code in a new offence, it intended the meanings given by the criminal code unless they specifically stated otherwise.

The Draft Criminal Code has never been made law. Parliament has not had either the time or the will for such a large-scale technical amendment to the law. Because of this the Law Commission has since 1989 tried what may be called a 'building-block' approach, under which it has produced reports and draft Bills on small areas of law in the hope that Parliament would at least deal with the areas most in need of reform. In its Tenth Programme in 2008 the Law Commission removed the codification of criminal law from its law reform programme. It stated that it continued to support the objective of codifying the law and would continue to codify where it could. However, it considered that it needs to redefine its approach and intends to simplify areas of the criminal law as a step towards codification.

Past Law Commission reports for reform of the criminal law have included:

- *Legislating the Criminal Code: Offences Against the Person and General Principles* (1993) Law Com No 218;
- *Legislating the Criminal Code: Intoxication and Criminal Liability* (1995) Law Com No 229;
- *Legislating the Criminal Code: Involuntary Manslaughter* (1996) Law Com No 237;
- *Fraud* (2002) Law Com No 276;
- *Inchoate Liability for Assisting and Encouraging Crime* (2006) Law Com No 300;
- *Murder, Manslaughter and Infanticide* (2006) Law Com No 304;
- *Participating in Crime* (2007) Law Com No 305;
- *Intoxication and Criminal Liability* (2009) Law Com No 314;
- *Conspiracy and Attempts* (2009) Law Com No 318.

These reports deal with areas of law in which cases have highlighted problems. Although these are areas of law where reform is clearly needed, Parliament has been slow to enact the Law Commission's reports on reform of specific areas of criminal law. For example there has been no reform of the law on offences against the person or on the defence of intoxication.

However, since 2006 there have been a number of reforms as the result of some of the Law Commission's reports. In 2006 Parliament passed the Fraud Act partially implementing the proposals on fraud. The Corporate Manslaughter and Corporate Homicide Act 2007 implemented proposals made in *Legislating the Criminal Code: Involuntary Manslaughter* (1996) Law Com No 237. The Serious Crime Act 2007 implemented the Law Commission's report *Inchoate Liability for Assisting and Encouraging Crime* (2006) Law Com No 300. The Bribery Act 2010 implemented the report *Reforming Bribery* (2008) Law Com No 313.

It is worth noting that most European countries have a criminal code. France's Code pénal was one of the earliest, being introduced by Napoleon in 1810, though there is now a new code, passed in 1992.

1.2.4 Reform of the law

Even if the law were codified, it would still be necessary to add to it from time to time. Modern technology can lead to the need for the creation of new offences. A recent example of this is that it is now a criminal offence to use a handheld mobile phone when driving. Pressure for new laws comes from a variety of sources. The main ones are:

- government policy
- EU law
- Law Commission reports
- reports by other commissions or committees
- pressure groups.

It is also necessary since the passing of the Human Rights Act 1998 to ensure that new laws are compatible with the European Convention on Human Rights.

1.3 Defining a crime

As seen in section 1.1.2, it is difficult to know what standard to use when judging whether an act or omission is criminal. The only way in which it is possible to define a crime is that it is conduct forbidden by the state and to which a punishment has been attached because the conduct is regarded by the state as being criminal. This is the only definition which covers all crimes.

As the criminal law is set down by the state, a breach of it can lead to a penalty, such as imprisonment or a fine, being imposed on the defendant in the name of the state. Therefore, bringing a prosecution for a criminal offence is usually seen as part of the role of the state. Indeed, the majority of criminal prosecutions are conducted by the Crown Prosecution Service (CPS), which is the main state agency for criminal prosecutions. There are other state agencies which bring prosecutions for certain types of offences. For example, the Serious Fraud Office brings cases relating to large-scale frauds, and the Environmental Agency handles breaches of law affecting the environment.

It is also possible for a private individual or business to start a prosecution. For example the RSPCA brings prosecutions on offences relating to animal welfare. However, it is unusual for an individual to bring a prosecution. Even where an individual brings a prosecution, the state still can control the case by the CPS taking over the prosecution and then making the decision on whether to continue with the prosecution or not. Alternatively the Attorney-General can stay (i.e. halt) the proceedings at any time by entering what is called a ***nolle prosequi*** without the consent of the prosecutor.

nolle prosequi
An order halting the prosecution of a case

1.3.1 Conduct criminalised by the judges

Some conduct is criminalised not by the state but by the courts. This occurs where the courts create new criminal offences through case law. In modern times this only happens on rare occasions, because nearly all law is made by Parliament. An example of conduct criminalised by the courts is the offence of conspiracy to corrupt public morals. This offence has never been enacted by Parliament. Its creation was recognised in *Shaw v DPP* [1962] AC 220. In this case the defendant had published a Ladies Directory, which advertised the names and addresses of prostitutes with their photographs and details of the 'services' they were prepared to offer. In the House of Lords, Viscount Simonds asserted that the offence of conspiracy to corrupt public morals was an offence known to the common law. He also claimed:

JUDGMENT

'[T]here is in [the] court a residual power, where no statute has yet intervened to supersede the common law, to superintend those offences which are prejudicial to the public welfare. Such occasions will be rare, for Parliament has not been slow to legislate when attention has been sufficiently aroused. But gaps remain and will always remain since no one can foresee every way in which the wickedness of man may disrupt the order of society.'

Another offence which has been recognised in modern times by the judges is marital rape. This was declared a crime in *R v R* [1991] 4 All ER 481 (see next section for details on this case).

1.3.2 Retroactive effect of case law

It is argued that it is wrong for the courts to make law. It is Parliament's role to make the law, and the courts' role is to apply the law. One of the arguments for this view is that Parliament is elected while courts are not, so that lawmaking by courts is undemocratic.

The other argument involves the fact that judge-made law is retrospective in effect. This means that when courts decide a case, they are applying the law to a situation which occurred before they ruled on the law. At the time of the trial or appeal they decide, as a new point of law, that the conduct of the defendant is criminal. That decision thus criminalises conduct which was not thought to be criminal when it was committed months earlier.

This point was considered in *R v R*, where a man was charged with raping his wife. The court in *R v R* had to decide whether, by being married, a woman automatically consented to sex with her husband. There had never been any statute law declaring that it was a crime for a man to have sexual intercourse with his wife without her consent. Old case law dating back as far as 1736 had taken the view that 'by their mutual matrimonial consent the wife hath given up herself in this to her husband, which she cannot retract'. In other words, once married, a woman was always assumed to consent and she could not go back on this. This view of the law had been confirmed as the law in *Miller* [1954] 2 QB 282, even though in that case the wife had already started divorce proceedings. In *R v R* the House of Lords ruled that it was a crime of rape when a man had sexual intercourse with his wife without her consent, pointing out that:

JUDGMENT

'The status of women and the status of a married woman in our law have changed quite dramatically. A husband and wife are now for all practical purposes equal partners in marriage.'

Following the House of Lords' decision, the case was taken to the European Court of Human Rights in *CR v United Kingdom* (Case no 48/1994/495/577 [1996] FLR 434) claiming that there was a breach of art 7 of the European Convention on Human Rights. The article states:

ARTICLE

'No one shall be held guilty of any criminal offence on account of any act or omission which did not constitute a criminal offence under national or international law at the time when it was committed.'

The European Court of Human Rights held that there had not been any breach, as the debasing character of rape was so obvious that to convict in these circumstances was not a variance with the object and purpose of art 7. In fact, abandoning the idea that a husband could not be prosecuted for the rape of his wife conformed with one of the fundamental objectives of the Convention, that of respect for human dignity. (See section 1.9 for further discussion on human rights and criminal law.)

1.4 Classification of offences

There are many ways of classifying offences depending on the purpose of the classification. They are:

- by source
- by police powers
- by type of offence
- by place of trial.

1.4.1 Classifying law by its source

As already explained in section 1.2, law comes from different sources. This distinction is important from an academic point of view. So law can be categorised as:

- common law (judge-made);
- statutory (defined in an Act of Parliament);
- regulatory (set out in delegated legislation).

1.4.2 Categories for purposes of police powers of detention

summary offence
An offence that can only be tried in a magistrates' court

indictable offence
An offence that can only be tried in the Crown Court

Police powers to detain a suspect who has been arrested depend on the category of offence. There are three categories:

- *summary offences*
- indictable offences
- terrorism offences.

Summary offences

Under s 24 Police and Criminal Evidence Act 1984 (PACE), as amended by s 110 of the Serious Organised Crime and Police Act 2005, a constable can make an arrest for any offence. However, an arresting officer can only arrest if he or she has reasonable grounds for believing that it is necessary to make the arrest for one of the following reasons:

- to enable the person's name or address to be ascertained;
- to prevent the person from:
    - causing physical injury to him or herself or any other person,
    - suffering physical injury,
    - causing loss of or damage to property,
    - committing an offence against public decency where members of the public cannot reasonably be expected to avoid the person in question,
    - causing an unlawful obstruction of the highway;

- to protect a child or other vulnerable person;
- to allow the prompt and effective investigation of the offence or of the conduct of the person;
- to prevent any prosecution for the offence from being hindered by the disappearance of the person in question.

Where the offence is *not* one of terrorism or an indictable offence, the police can only detain a person for a maximum of 24 hours. They must also allow someone to be informed of the arrest and for the suspect to have legal advice as soon as possible after arrest.

Indictable offences

For these the police have the power to detain any person who has been arrested for an initial period of 24 hours. This can then be extended to 36 hours by an officer of the rank of superintendent or above under s 42(1) of the Police and Criminal Evidence Act 1984 (PACE) (as amended). The police then have the right to apply to a magistrate for permission to detain the suspect for up to a maximum of 96 hours.

In addition there are restrictions on the rights of the suspected person. The right to have someone informed of their arrest may be delayed for up to 36 hours (s 56 Police and Criminal Evidence Act 1984). The right to legal advice may also be delayed for up to 36 hours (s 58 Police and Criminal Evidence Act 1984).

Terrorism offences

The Terrorism Act 2000 controls powers of detention for terrorism offences. Under s 8 of this Act, as amended by the Terrorism Act 2006, the police can detain a person arrested on suspicion of terrorism offences for 48 hours. After this they can apply to a judge to extend the period up to a maximum of 14 days. The PACE Code of Practice H applies to those detained for a terrorism offence.

1.4.3 Classifying by the type of harm caused by the crime

When studying criminal law it is usual to study offences according to the type of harm caused. The main categories here are:

- offences against the person
- offences against property
- offences against public order.

1.4.4 Classification by where a case will be tried

One of the most important ways of classifying offences is by the categories that affect where and how a case will be tried. For this purpose offences are classified as:

triable either way offence
An offence which can be tried in either the magistrates' courts or the Crown Court

1. *Indictable only offences*. These must be tried on indictment at the Crown Court (e.g. murder, manslaughter, rape).
2. *Triable either way offences*. These can be tried either on indictment at the Crown Court or summarily at a magistrates' court (e.g. theft, burglary, assault occasioning actual bodily harm).
3. *Summary offences*. These can be tried only at a magistrates' court (e.g. assaulting a policeman in the execution of his duty, common assault).

1.5 Criminal justice system

There are two types of courts which try criminal cases. These are:

- the magistrates' courts
- the Crown Court.

As already seen in the section on classification of offences (section 1.4.4), the decision as to where the trial will take place depends on whether the offence is summary, triable either way or indictable.

1.5.1 Trials in the magistrates' courts

Magistrates can try summary offences and any triable either way offences where they accept jurisdiction and the defendant elects for the case to be tried in a magistrates' court. Cases are tried by a panel of two or three lay justices or by a District Judge (magistrates' courts).

Lay justices have no legal qualifications, sit only part-time and are not paid a salary, although they are paid expenses. They are appointed from ordinary members of the community. The only qualifications they need are six key qualities:

- good character
- understanding and communication
- social awareness
- maturity and sound temperament
- sound judgment
- commitment and reliability.

Those appointed must be prepared to sit at least 26 half-days per year, although consideration is being given to making this 24 half-days, that is one day a month, in order to attract more people into the magistracy.

District judges (magistrates' court) are qualified barristers or solicitors of at least five years' standing. District judges may hear cases on their own or they may form a panel with one or two lay magistrates.

Both lay magistrates and district judges have dual roles. They hear the case and decide if the defendant is guilty or not guilty. Where the defendant is found guilty or has pleaded guilty, they pass sentence.

Magistrates' powers of sentencing are limited to a maximum of six months' imprisonment for one offence, or a total of 12 months' imprisonment for two or more offences. Magistrates' maximum fine used to be £5,000. In 2014 the government announced that it was increasing the maximum fine to £20,000. In addition it proposed that for some offences (usually committed by businesses) there would be no limit on the amount magistrates could fine.

1.5.2 Trials in the Crown Court

The offences which can be tried at the Crown Court are all indictable only offences and any triable either way offences where the magistrates have declined jurisdiction or the defendant has elected trial at the Crown Court.

Where the defendant pleads not guilty the case is heard by a judge and a jury of 12. The judge decides the law and sums up to the jury. The jury decide the facts and, accordingly, whether the defendant is guilty or not guilty. If the defendant is found guilty, it is then the role of the judge to pass sentence.

As the judge is the decider of law and the jury the decider of facts, the judge can decide at the end of the prosecution case that, as a matter of law, the prosecution has not proved the case, and he can direct that the defendant be acquitted. Statistics of trials in the Crown Court show that about 12 per cent are ended by a judge-directed acquittal.

Where the case continues, then, at the end of the whole case, the judge will direct the jury on any relevant points of law and they will then decide whether the defendant is guilty or not guilty. If they find the defendant not guilty, he is acquitted. Where they convict then the judge decides the appropriate sentence to impose on the defendant. If a defendant pleads guilty then the judge deals with the case on his own. There is no jury.

Use of juries

The use of a jury in the Crown Court is regarded as an important constitutional right and a way of protecting human rights. There have been several attempts to restrict the use of juries in criminal cases. In both 1999 and 2000, the government tried to get a Bill passed which would have removed from offenders charged with triable either way offences the right to choose jury trial. On both occasions the House of Lords voted against the Bill so that it was not made law.

In 2003 the Criminal Justice Bill included two clauses which would have affected the defendant's right to trial by jury. The first gave the defendant the right to choose to be tried by a judge alone without a jury. The House of Lords defeated this clause. The other clause provided for the prosecution to apply for trial by a judge alone in complex fraud cases. The House of Lords voted against this, but eventually a compromise was reached so that the section was passed as part of the Criminal Justice Act 2003. However, it was subject to an affirmative resolution which meant that it could not become law unless both the House of Commons and the House of Lords in the future vote in favour of this. In 2012 this provision was repeated without ever having come into effect. In 2006 there was another attempt to restrict the use of juries in fraud trials, but again the Bill was defeated.

There are, however, some limited situations in which a defendant can be tried by a judge alone. Section 44 of the Criminal Justice Act 2003 allows the prosecution to make an application for a trial without a jury where there is evidence of a real and present danger that jury tampering would take place. The first occasion this was used successfully was in *R v T and others* [2009] EWCA Crim 1035 when earlier trials had collapsed because of interference with the jury. The Court of Appeal gave permission for the case to go ahead without a jury.

The other situation is under the Domestic Violence, Crime and Victims Act 2004 where the defendant is charged with a large number of similar offences. In order to simplify the case, the prosecution may choose to have the defendant tried on a small number of sample counts. This trial will be with a jury. If the defendant is found guilty, then he can be tried for the rest of the offences by a judge alone.

1.5.3 Appeals from a magistrates' court

There are two different appeal routes, as shown in Figure 1.2.

Case stated appeal to the Queen's Bench Divisional Court

This is used where the appeal is on a point of law. The magistrates are asked to state a case (finding of facts). This route is available for both the prosecution and the defence. The Divisional Court can quash the decision, confirm it or remit the case to a magistrates' court for a rehearing. Where reference is made to judgments of the Divisional Court or Queen's Bench Divisional Court (QBD) in any textbook on criminal law, then the case must have originally been tried in a magistrates' court.

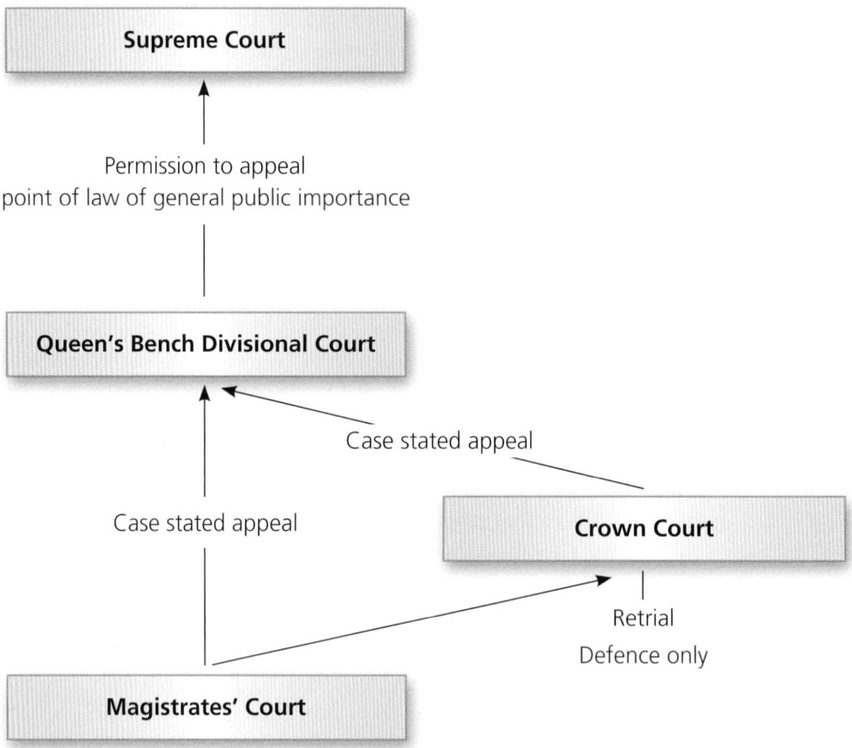

Figure 1.2 Appeal routes from a magistrates' court.

A further appeal is possible to the Supreme Court. This must be on a point of law of general public importance, and the Supreme Court (or QBD) must give permission to appeal. Very few cases reach the Supreme Court by this route: only about two or three per year.

Appeal to the Crown Court

This route is only available to the defendant. The appeal can be against sentence or conviction or both. The whole case is reheard at the Crown Court by a judge and two lay magistrates. They decide whether the defendant is guilty or not guilty and, if guilty, can pass any appropriate sentence. There is no further appeal from the Crown Court, unless a point of law is involved in which case the appeal then goes to the QBD and Supreme Court as above.

1.5.4 Appeals from trials in the Crown Court

Appeals by the defendant

The defendant has the possibility of appealing against conviction and/or sentence to the Court of Appeal (Criminal Division). The rules on appeals are set out in the Criminal Appeal Act 1995 and in all cases the defendant must obtain leave to appeal from the Court of Appeal, or a certificate that the case is fit for appeal from the trial judge. On the hearing of an appeal the Court of Appeal can allow a defendant's appeal and quash the conviction. Alternatively it can vary the conviction to that of a lesser offence of which the jury could have convicted the defendant. So far as sentence is concerned, the court can decrease it, but cannot increase it on the defendant's appeal. Finally, the court can dismiss the appeal.

Appeals by the prosecution

Originally the prosecution had no right to appeal against either the verdict or sentence passed in the Crown Court. Gradually, however, some limited rights of appeal have been given to it by Parliament. With one small exception, the prosecution cannot appeal against a finding of not guilty by a jury. The exception is for cases where the acquittal was the result of the jury being 'nobbled', that is where some jurors are bribed or threatened by associates of the defendant. In these circumstances, provided there has been an actual conviction for 'jury nobbling', the Criminal Procedure and Investigations Act 1996 allows the prosecution to appeal and the High Court can order a retrial.

However, the prosecution has a special referral right in cases where the defendant is acquitted. This is under s 36 of the Criminal Justice Act 1972, which allows the Attorney-General to refer a point of law to the Court of Appeal in order to get a ruling on the law. The decision by the Court of Appeal on that point of law does not affect the acquittal, but it creates a precedent for any future case involving the same point of law. When this has occurred, the reported case is cited in the form of *Attorney-General's Reference (No x of 2004)*.

Under the Criminal Justice Act 2003 it is also possible for a defendant who has been acquitted of certain serious offences to be tried a second time. This can only happen where the Court of Appeal decides that there is new and compelling evidence which justifies a second trial.

Appeals to the Supreme Court

Both the prosecution and the defence may appeal from the Court of Appeal to the Supreme Court, but it is necessary to have the case certified as involving a point of law of general public importance and to get leave to appeal, either from the Supreme Court or from the Court of Appeal. Very few criminal appeals are heard by the Supreme Court. Figure 1.3 shows the appeal route from the Crown Court.

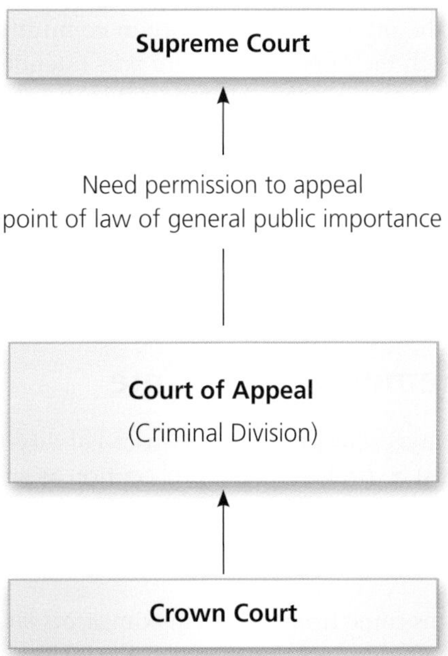

Figure 1.3 Appeals from the Crown Court.

1.5.5 The hierarchy of the courts

This hierarchy of the appeal courts is important for judicial precedent. Decisions by the Supreme Court (formerly the House of Lords) on points of law are binding on all the other courts in England and Wales. The only exception to this is where there has been a decision by the European Court of Justice when lower courts should follow this and not a Supreme Court decision. Also, all courts have to take account of judgments of the European Court of Human Rights and may choose to follow such a decision. However, decisions of this court do not have to be followed.

The lower courts must also follow decisions of the Court of Appeal where there is no decision by the Supreme Court. However, decisions made by the Court of Appeal can be overruled by the Supreme Court. The Divisional Court is below the Court of Appeal in the hierarchy for the purposes of precedent, but lower courts are bound to follow any decisions made by the Divisional Court if there is no decision by either the Court of Appeal or the Supreme Court.

1.6 Sentencing

1.6.1 Purposes of sentencing

It is recognised that sentencing can be aimed at different purposes, but for the first time the government has set down the key aims in a statutory context. The Criminal Justice Act 2003 sets out the purposes of sentencing for those aged 18 and over, saying that a court must have regard to:

- the punishment of offenders;
- the reduction of crime (including its reduction by deterrence and by the reform and rehabilitation of offenders);
- the protection of the public;
- the making of reparation by offenders to persons affected by their offences.

The Act also states that 'in considering the seriousness of any offence, the court must consider the offender's culpability in committing the offence and the harm, or risk of harm, which the offence caused or was intended to cause'. Previous convictions are an aggravating factor if the court considers this so in view of the relevance to the present offence and the time which has elapsed since the previous conviction. Racially or religiously aggravated offences are viewed seriously and the Act allows for an increase in sentence in these situations. There can be a reduction in sentence for a guilty plea, particularly where made early in the proceedings.

The Sentencing Guidelines Council issues guidelines on the level of sentence appropriate in certain types of cases.

actus reus
The physical element of an offence (see Chapter 2 for full discussion)

1.7 Elements of a crime

For all crimes, except crimes of strict liability (see Chapter 4), there are two elements which must be proved by the prosecution as shown in Figure 1.4. These are:

- *actus reus*
- *mens rea*.

mens rea
The mental or fault element of an offence (see Chapter 3 for full discussion)

These terms come from a Latin maxim, *actus non facit reum nisi mens sit rea*, which means 'the act itself does not constitute guilt unless done with a guilty mind'. Both an act (or omission) and a guilty mind must be proved for most criminal offences.

ACTUS REUS	+	*MENS REA*	=	OFFENCE

Figure 1.4 Elements of an offence.

tutor tip

'*Actus reus* and *mens rea* are essential topics in criminal law: make sure you study these topics in detail in the next two chapters.'

Actus reus has a wider meaning than an 'act', as it can cover omissions or a state of affairs. The term has been criticised as misleading. Lord Diplock in *Miller* [1983] 1 All ER 978 preferred the term 'prohibited conduct', while the Law Commission in the Draft Criminal Code (1989) used the term 'external element'. *Actus reus* as a concept is considered fully in Chapter 2.

Mens rea translates as 'guilty mind', but this also is misleading. The Law Commission in the Draft Criminal Code (1989) used the term 'fault element'. The levels of 'guilty mind' required for different offences vary from the highest level, which is specific intention for some crimes, to much lower levels such as negligence or knowledge of a certain fact for less serious offences. The levels of *mens rea* are explained in detail in Chapter 3.

The *actus reus* and *mens rea* will be different for different crimes. For example, in murder the *actus reus* is the killing of a human being and the *mens rea* is causing the death with 'malice aforethought'. For theft the *actus reus* is the appropriation of property belonging to another, while the *mens rea* is doing this dishonestly and with the intention permanently to deprive the other of the property. The *actus reus* and the *mens rea* must be present together, but if there is an ongoing act, then the existence of the necessary *mens rea* at any point during that act is sufficient. This is explained fully in Chapter 3. Even where the *actus reus* and *mens rea* are present, the defendant may be not guilty if he has a defence.

There are some crimes which are an exception to the general rule that there must be both *actus reus* and *mens rea*. These are crimes of strict liability, where the prosecution need only prove the *actus reus*; no mental element is needed for guilt. (See Chapter 4 for strict liability.)

1.8 Burden and standard of proof

1.8.1 Presumption of innocence

An accused person is presumed innocent until proven guilty. The burden is on the prosecution to prove the case. This means that it must prove both the required *actus reus* and the required *mens rea*. The prosecution may also have to disprove a defence which the defendant raises. This was confirmed in the case of *Woolmington v DPP* [1935] AC 462.

CASE EXAMPLE

Woolmington v DPP [1935] AC 462

D's wife had left him and gone to live with her mother. D wanted her to return to him. He went to the mother's house and shot his wife dead. He claimed that he had decided to ask his wife to come back to him and, if she refused, to commit suicide. So he took with him a loaded sawn-off shotgun. He attached a piece of wire flex to the gun so he could put the flex over his shoulder and carry the gun underneath his coat. When his wife indicated that she would not return to him, he threatened to shoot himself and brought the gun out to show her he meant it. As he brought it across his waist it somehow went off, killing his wife. He claimed this was a pure accident.

The judge at the trial told the jury that the prosecution had to prove beyond reasonable doubt that the defendant killed his wife. He then went on to tell them that, if the prosecution satisfied them of that, the defendant had to show that there were circumstances which made that killing pure accident. This put the burden of proof on the defendant to prove the defence. In the House of Lords it was held that this was a misdirection.

Lord Sankey stated that:

JUDGMENT

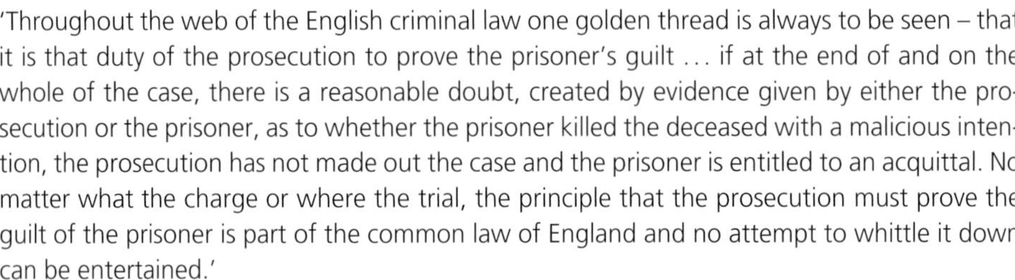

'Throughout the web of the English criminal law one golden thread is always to be seen – that it is that duty of the prosecution to prove the prisoner's guilt ... if at the end of and on the whole of the case, there is a reasonable doubt, created by evidence given by either the prosecution or the prisoner, as to whether the prisoner killed the deceased with a malicious intention, the prosecution has not made out the case and the prisoner is entitled to an acquittal. No matter what the charge or where the trial, the principle that the prosecution must prove the guilt of the prisoner is part of the common law of England and no attempt to whittle it down can be entertained.'

This judgment makes several important points which the House of Lords regards as fixed matters on English law. These are:

- The prosecution must prove the case.
- This rule applies to all criminal cases.
- The rule must be applied in any court where there is a criminal trial (currently the magistrates' courts and Crown Court).
- Guilt must be proved beyond reasonable doubt.
- A reasonable doubt can be raised by evidence from either the prosecution or the defence.

1.8.2 Raising a defence

If the defendant raises a defence then it is for the prosecution to negate that defence. In *Woolmington* the defendant stated that the gun had gone off accidentally, thus raising the defence of accident. The prosecution was obliged to disprove this if the defendant was to be found guilty.

For all common law defences, except insanity, the defendant only has to raise some evidence of the key points of the defence. This can be from evidence given by the defence or by the prosecution. If evidence of a defence is given at the trial, then even where the defendant has not specifically raised the defence, the prosecution must disprove at least one element of that defence. The trial judge must direct the jury to acquit unless they are satisfied that the defence has been disproved by the prosecution.

Reverse onus

For certain defences, the burden of proof is on the defendant. For example, if the defendant claims that he was insane at the time of the crime, the burden of proving this is on the defendant. This shifting of the burden of proof to the defendant is known as the 'reverse onus'. As well as the common law defence of insanity, it applies to exceptions which have been created by statute. One of these is the defence of diminished responsibility in the Homicide Act 1957, where s 2(2) states:

SECTION

> '2(2) On a charge of murder, it shall be for the defence to prove that the person charged is by virtue of this section not liable to be convicted of murder.'

Where a statute places the burden of proof on the defendant to prove a defence, the standard is the civil one of balance of probabilities. This was decided in *Carr-Briant* [1943] 2 All ER 156, where the defendant was charged under the Prevention of Corruption Act 1916. Section 2 of the Act states that any money or other gift given by someone trying to get a contract with a government department or other public body to the holder of a public office 'shall be deemed to have been paid or given and received corruptly as such inducement or reward ... unless the contrary is proved'.

The trial judge had directed the jury that this meant the defendant had to prove his innocence beyond reasonable doubt. On appeal the conviction was quashed on another ground, but the court went on to state that this direction was wrong:

JUDGMENT

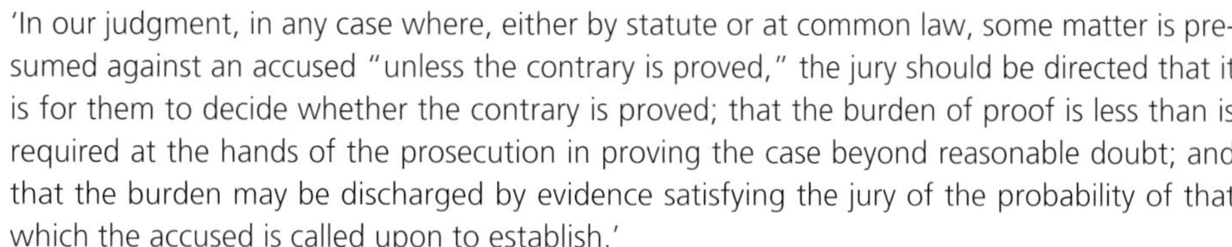

> 'In our judgment, in any case where, either by statute or at common law, some matter is presumed against an accused "unless the contrary is proved," the jury should be directed that it is for them to decide whether the contrary is proved; that the burden of proof is less than is required at the hands of the prosecution in proving the case beyond reasonable doubt; and that the burden may be discharged by evidence satisfying the jury of the probability of that which the accused is called upon to establish.'

There may be a breach of human rights when the defence has to prove a defence. (See section 1.9 for a full discussion of this.)

1.8.3 Standard of proof

The standard of proof in order for a defendant to be found guilty is 'beyond reasonable doubt'. This is usually explained by the judge telling the jury that they should only convict if they are satisfied that they are sure of the defendant's guilt.

1.9 Criminal law and human rights

The Human Rights Act 1998 incorporated the European Convention on Human Rights into our law. Under s 3 of the Act all Articles of the Convention have to be taken into consideration by English courts. Much of the effect of the Convention is on evidence and procedure but it has also had an effect on substantive criminal law.

In criminal law the most relevant rights under the Convention are:

- the right to liberty (art 5);
- the right to a fair trial (art 6(1));
- the presumption of innocence (art 6(2));
- that there should be no punishment without law (art 7(1)).

However, challenges to our substantive criminal law have been made under other Articles. These include:

- the right not to be subjected to inhuman or degrading treatment (art 3(1));

- the right of respect for a person's private life (art 8);
- that, in the application of the Convention rights and freedoms, there should be no discrimination on the grounds of sex, race, religion or political opinion (art 14).

1.9.1 The right to a fair trial

This right is contained in art 6(1) of the European Convention.

ARTICLE

> '6(1) Everyone is entitled to a fair trial and public hearing within a reasonable time by an independent and impartial tribunal established by law.'

In *G* [2008] UKHL 37, it was held that the fact that the offence was one of strict liability did not render the trial unfair. See section 4.4.5 for more details.

The House of Lords upheld D's conviction unanimously. They held that a strict liability offence was not a breach of art 6(1) or art 6(2). Lord Hoffmann stated in his judgment:

JUDGMENT

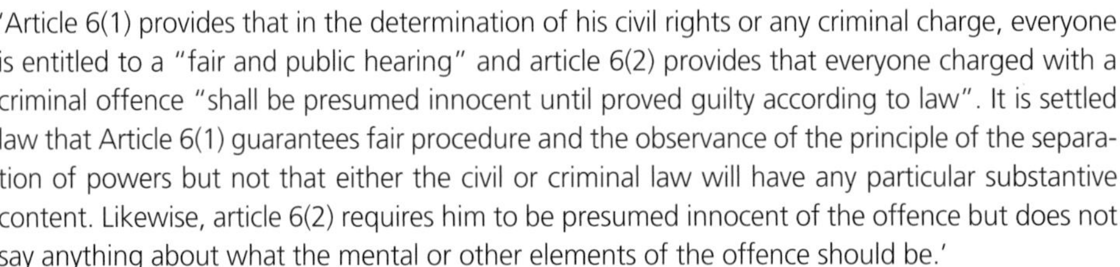

> 'Article 6(1) provides that in the determination of his civil rights or any criminal charge, everyone is entitled to a "fair and public hearing" and article 6(2) provides that everyone charged with a criminal offence "shall be presumed innocent until proved guilty according to law". It is settled law that Article 6(1) guarantees fair procedure and the observance of the principle of the separation of powers but not that either the civil or criminal law will have any particular substantive content. Likewise, article 6(2) requires him to be presumed innocent of the offence but does not say anything about what the mental or other elements of the offence should be.'

G applied for the case to be heard by the European Court of Human Rights (ECHR), but the application was ruled inadmissible (*G v United Kingdom (Admissibility) (37334/08)* [2012] Crim LR 46).

The ECHR did not consider that Parliament's decision not to make available a defence based on reasonable belief that the complainant was aged 13 or over could give rise to any issue under art 6. They also pointed out that it is not the ECHR's role under either art 6(1) or 6(2) to dictate the content of domestic criminal law. This includes issues of whether there should be a particular defence available to the accused and whether or not a blameworthy state of mind should be one of the elements of an offence.

1.9.2 Burden of proof

Article 6(2) states that 'Everyone charged with a criminal offence shall be presumed innocent until proven guilty.'

This places the burden of proof on the prosecution and effectively makes the same provision for the standard of proof in a criminal trial as already exists in our legal system. The only potential conflict with human rights is where the defendant has to prove a defence. Defences which place the burden of proving the defence on the defendant may be in breach of art 6(2).

In the conjoined appeals of *Attorney-General's Reference (No 4 of 2002)* and *Sheldrake v DPP* [2004] UKHL 43; [2005] 1 All ER 237, the House of Lords considered whether defences which require the defendant to prove them on the balance of probabilities were a breach of the presumption of innocence under art 6(2) of the European Convention on Human Rights. The Lords came to the conclusion that in many cases the wording of the Act could be interpreted so that it did not create a legal burden to prove the defence as was held in *Attorney-General's Reference (No 4 of 2002)*. However, they held that even if a section did breach art 6(2) it was permissible if it was 'justifiable, legitimate and proportionate'. This was the situation in the case of *Sheldrake v DPP*.

CASE EXAMPLE

Sheldrake v DPP [2004] UKHL 43; [(2005] 1 All ER 237

Sheldrake was convicted of being in charge of a motor car in a public place while over the drink-drive limit, contrary to s 5(1)(b) of the Road Traffic Act 1988. Section 5(2) of the Act allows a defence if D can prove that there was no likelihood of his driving while he was over the limit. He was convicted but the Divisional Court quashed the conviction. The prosecution then appealed to the House of Lords.

The defence argued that s 5(2) infringed the presumption of innocence guaranteed by art 6(2) as it imposed on the defendant a legal burden of proving innocence by proving a defence.

The House of Lords held that s 5(2) did impose a legal burden of proof on the defendant. However, they pointed out that there is an obvious risk that a person who is in charge of a car when unfit to drive may drive and so risk causing death or serious injury. As a result, the Lords allowed the prosecution's appeal and reinstated the conviction.

CASE EXAMPLE

Attorney-General's Reference (No 4 of 2002) [2004] UKHL 43; [2005] 1 All ER 237

This case concerned s 11 of the Terrorism Act 2000. The defendant had been charged with counts of (1) being a member of a proscribed organisation and (2) professing to be a member of a proscribed organisation, both contrary to s 11(1). The question was whether s 11(2) imposed a legal or evidential burden on the defendant.

Section 11(2) states:

SECTION

'11(2) It is a defence for a person charged with an offence under subsection 11(1) to prove:

a. that the organisation was not proscribed on the last (or only) occasion on which he became a member or began to profess to be a member, and
b. that he has not taken part in the activities of the organisation at any time while it was proscribed.'

At the trial the judge ruled that there was no case to answer on the two counts. The Attorney-General referred the point of law for the opinion of the Court of Appeal, who ruled in the Attorney-General's favour. The defence referred the matter to the House of Lords which ruled that s 11(2) could be read down as imposing an evidential instead of a legal burden.

Lord Bingham gave the leading speech in these conjoined cases. His judgment is particularly useful as he gave a review of reverse burden situations covering:

- the pre-Convention law of England and Wales;
- the Convention and the Strasbourg jurisprudence;
- the leading United Kingdom cases since the Human Rights Act 1998.

After considering cases decided by the European Court of Human Rights, Lord Bingham said:

JUDGMENT

'From this body of authority certain principles may be derived. The overriding concern is that a trial should be fair, and the presumption of innocence is a fundamental right directed to that end. The Convention does not outlaw presumptions of fact or law but requires that these should be kept within reasonable limits and should not be arbitrary' (para 21).

He went on to point out that:

JUDGMENT

'Relevant to any judgment on reasonableness or proportionality will be the opportunity given to the defendant to rebut the presumption, maintenance of the rights of the defendant, flexibility in application of the presumption, retention by the court of a power to assess the evidence, the importance of what is at stake and the difficulty which a prosecutor may face in the absence of a presumption' (para 21).

UK decisions since the Human Rights Act 1998

Lord Bingham reviewed several cases. The most important being:

- *R v DFF, ex p Kebilene* [2000] 2 AC 326 regarding the provisions of the Prevention of Terrorism (Temporary Provisions) Act 1989, in which the majority of the Lords held that the relevant provision could be read down as imposing an evidential and not a legal burden.
- *Lambert* [2001] UKHL 37; [2002] 1 All ER 2 which concerned s 28(2) of the Misuse of Drugs Act 1971. The appeal failed because a majority of the Lords held that the Human Rights Act 1998 was not retrospective. Although the appeal failed on this ground the Lords did consider the presumption of innocence and a majority held that if s 28(2) of the Misuse of Drugs Act 1971 was read as imposing a legal burden on the defendant to prove lack of knowledge, then this undermined the presumption of innocence to an impermissible extent. However, they thought it could be read down as imposing only an evidential burden.
- *Johnstone* [2003] UKHL 28 concerning s 92(5) of the Trade Marks Act 1994. The Law Lords held that the section did impose a legal burden on the defendant and so derogated from the presumption of innocence. However, this could be justified if it was necessary to maintain a balance between the public interest and the interests of the defendant.

Lord Bingham pointed out that the first question the House of Lords had to consider in each case was whether the provision in question did, unjustifiably, infringe the presumption of innocence. In order to do this it was necessary to consider the following:

- Did the provision make an inroad into art 6?

- If so, was an inroad justifiable, legitimate and proportionate?

If an inroad into art 6 was justifiable, legitimate and proportionate, then a legal burden was placed on the defendant. If an inroad was unjustified, then a further question arose – could and should the provision be 'read down' in accordance with the courts' interpretative obligation under s 3 of the Human Rights Act 1998 so as to impose an evidential and not a legal burden on the defendant? 'Reading down' in this context means the Act could be interpreted to mean the lower level of an evidential burden of proof.

In *Sheldrake* the Law Lords decided that there was an inroad into art 6 but that it was justifiable, legitimate and proportionate. In *Attorney-General's Reference (No 4 of 2002)* they decided that the provision could be read as imposing an evidential burden on the defendant.

Andrew Ashworth in his commentary on the cases of *Attorney-General's Reference (No 4 of 2002)* and *Sheldrake v DPP* criticises the decision of the House of Lords, pointing out:

QUOTATION

'The least satisfactory aspect of this decision is that it furnishes the courts with no clear guidance on how to interpret statutes that impose a burden of proof on the defendant. The only certainty is that courts should use s 3 of the Human Rights Act 1998 fully, and should not defer to Parliament's intention, least of all where there is no evidence that the legislature had the presumption of innocence in mind. Beyond that there seem to be three major factors to be taken into account – maximum penalty, the danger of convicting the innocent, and the ease of proof. All three factors remain problematical as a result of this decision.'

A. Ashworth, '*Attorney-General's Ref (No 4 of 2002), Sheldrake v DPP:* Case and Commentary' (2005) Crim LR 215

The issue has been considered in subsequent cases including *Webster* [2010] EWCA Crim 2819, *Williams* [2012] EWCA Crim 2162 and *Foye* [2013] EWCA Crim 475.

CASE EXAMPLE

Webster [2010] EWCA Crim 2819

The defendant was convicted of corruptly giving a gift under s 1(2) of the Prevention of Corruption Act 1889. He had a business which supplied educational aids to schools. About half of his business came from the local authority. The conviction related to a gift of £100 cash to an employee of the local council. The Court of Appeal quashed the conviction because the 1889 Act required the defendant to prove that the gift was not 'given . . . corruptly as . . . [an] inducement or reward'.

This placed a reverse burden of proof on the defendant and violated the presumption of innocence under Article 6(2) of the European Convention on Human Rights. The Court of Appeal stated that s 3 of the Human Rights Act 1998 could have been used to make the legislation comply with the presumption of innocence. Reading down the requirement on proof would have placed a burden on the defendant to raise in evidence the issue of whether the gift was corruptly made within the meaning of s 1 of the 1889 Act. Then the prosecution would have had to prove beyond reasonable doubt that it was corrupt.

CASE EXAMPLE

Williams [2012] EWCA Crim 2162

The defendant was convicted of possession of a firearm under the Firearms Act 1982. Section 1(5) of that Act provided a defence if the defendant could show that he did not know and had no reason to suspect that an imitation firearm was so constructed or adapted as to be readily converted into a useable firearm.

The Court of Appeal held that this subsection imposed a reverse burden of proof on the defendant. On the question of whether this violated art 6(2) of the European Convention on Human Rights, the Court of Appeal held that the reverse burden was justified as a 'necessary, reasonable and proportionate derogation' from the presumption of innocence. Firearm offences were a very serious problem and the need to protect the public was obvious. This included the need for protection in the case of readily convertible imitation firearms.

CASE EXAMPLE

Foye [2013] EWCA Crim 475

The defendant, who was already serving a life sentence for murder, killed a fellow prisoner. He was convicted of murder with the jury rejecting his defence of diminished responsibility. D appealed on the basis that s 2(2) of the Homicide Act 1975 (which sets out the defence of diminished responsibility) contravened art 6(2) of the European Convention on Human Rights as it imposed a reverse burden of proof.

The Court of Appeal dismissed the appeal. They pointed out that s 2(2) did not require the defendant to disprove an element of the offence to establish an exception or excuse, so the better view was that s 2(2) did not impinge on the presumption of innocence. Even if it did, the subsection was a justified modification of the presumption as it would be virtually impossible for the prosecution to disprove beyond reasonable doubt a defendant's assertion that he was suffering from diminished responsibility. The defendant was under no obligation to submit to a medical examination on behalf of the prosecution. He could also refuse, lawfully, to make available past medical records. These provided fundamental reasons why the reverse onus was essential to the working of the law of diminished responsibility.

1.9.3 No punishment without law

This is covered by art 7 which states:

ARTICLE

'7(1) No one shall be held guilty of any criminal offence on account of any act or omission which did not constitute a criminal offence under national or international law at the time when it was committed.

7(2) This article shall not prejudice the trial and punishment of any person for any act or omission which, at the time when it was committed, was criminal according to the general principles of law recognised by civilised nations.'

This Article was used to challenge the conviction in *CR v UK* (1995) 21 EHRR 363. D had been convicted of raping his wife. The argument was that such an offence did not exist until the conviction, so there was no law against it at the time of D's assault on his wife. The challenge was unsuccessful for two reasons. The first was that there had been earlier cases where such an offence was beginning to be recognised. The second was that the offence is one which supported fundamental objectives of the Convention. As a result it was not in breach of this Article.

Uncertainty

In other cases there have been challenges under art 7 on the basis that the offence is too uncertain or lacks clarity. This happened in *Misra; Srivastava* [2004] EWCA Crim 2375; [2005] 1 Cr App R 21, where the defendants were charged with gross negligence manslaughter. The defence argued that the elements of this offence were not certain. They relied on the Law Commission's paper *Legislating the Criminal Code: Involuntary Manslaughter* (Law Com No 237) in support of this argument. The paper had identified that the current test was circular and this circularity led to uncertainty. On this point the paper concluded:

QUOTATION

> 'It is possible that the law in this area failed to meet the standard of certainty required by the European Convention on Human Rights.'
>
> *Legislating the Criminal Code: Involuntary Manslaughter* (Law Com No 237)

The Court of Appeal rejected the argument. They held that the elements of the offence of gross negligence manslaughter were made clear in *Adomako* [1995] 1 AC 171. They were that:

- A duty of care was owed.
- That duty had been broken.
- The breach of the duty of care amounted to gross negligence.
- The negligence was a substantial cause of the death of the victim.

On the issue of risk it was clear from *Adomako* and subsequent cases that the risk must relate to death. It was not enough to show that there was risk of bodily injury or injury to health. (See section 10.4.2 for full details on gross negligence manslaughter.) As the elements of gross negligence manslaughter were clear, there was no breach of art 7.

Another unsuccessful challenge on the basis of lack of clarity was in the case of *Goldstein* [2005] UKHL 63; [2005] 3 WLR 982 where D was charged with public nuisance.

CASE EXAMPLE

Goldstein [2005] UKHL 63; [2005] 3 WLR 982

Goldstein had sent an envelope containing salt through the post as a joke relating to kosher food and also to a public scare in the United States over anthrax. The salt spilled out of the envelope in a sorting office causing the evacuation of the building due to fears that it was anthrax. D was charged with causing a public nuisance contrary to the common law. The defence argued that this offence lacked precision and clarity of definition, the certainty and the predictability necessary to meet the requirements of art 7.

The House of Lords held that the offence was defined by Sir James Stephens in *A Digest of Criminal Law* 1877 and subsequent cases so that it was clear, precise, adequately defined and based on a discernible rational principle. However, they allowed D's appeal as it had not been proved that he knew or ought to have known that the salt would escape from the envelope.

1.9.4 Other human rights

There have been challenges to the criminal law on the basis of other rights in the Convention. Article 3 states:

ARTICLE

'3 No one shall be subjected to torture or inhuman or degrading treatment or punishment.'

In *Altham* [2006] EWCA Crim 7, D argued that the refusal to allow him the defence of necessity in respect of his use of cannabis for extreme physical pain was a breach of art 3.

CASE EXAMPLE

Altham [2006] EWCA Crim 7

D had been seriously injured in an accident some 15 years earlier in which he dislocated both hips and suffered a fracture of his pelvis. He subsequently had surgery but this was not successful, so, in 1997, his entire left hip was removed. Since then he had had chronic pain in his legs. He claimed that cannabis gave him more relief from pain than any prescribed drug and it also had fewer side effects. He was charged with possession of a controlled drug. At the trial the judge ruled that the defence of necessity or duress of circumstances should not be left to the jury. Following this ruling D pleaded guilty and received an absolute discharge.

He appealed on the basis that art 3 prohibits 'inhuman or degrading treatment' and there were circumstances where severe medical symptoms can amount to 'inhuman or degrading treatment'. If the state provides that the only way to avoid those symptoms is to break the criminal law and risk punishment up to and including imprisonment, then the state is subjecting that person to 'inhuman or degrading treatment'. The Court of Appeal dismissed the appeal holding that the state had done nothing to subject D to inhuman or degrading treatment.

The Court of Appeal has also heard appeals in cases of breach of right to respect for private lives under art 8.

ARTICLE

'8(1) Everyone has the right to respect for his private and family life, his home and his correspondence.

8(2) There shall be no interference by a public authority with the exercise of this right except such as is in accordance with the law and is necessary in a democratic society in the interests of national security, public safety or the economic well-being of the country, for the prevention of disorder or crime, for the protection of health or morals, or for the protection of the rights and freedoms of others.'

In *Quayle* [2005] EWCA Crim 1415, the Court of Appeal heard appeals in five cases where the defendants claimed the defence of medical necessity for using cannabis. Ds argued that the refusal to allow them the defence of necessity in respect of use of cannabis for medical reasons was a breach of their right to respect for their private lives under art 8. This challenge failed.

In *E v DPP* [2005] EWHC 147 (Admin) D was a 15-year-old boy who was charged with unlawful sexual intercourse with a girl under the age of 16, contrary to s 6 of the Sexual Offences Act 1956 which has since been repealed. The girl was also aged 15 and was a willing participant. By prosecuting D, the state was criminalising his behaviour and treating the girl as the victim, when this was not, in fact, the situation. At the trial it was argued that this was contrary to art 6 (the right to a fair trial) and art 14 (the right not to be discriminated against on the ground of sex). At the appeal in the Divisional Court the defence added the argument that it was also contrary to art 8 (respect for D's private life).

The Divisional Court found there was no breach of art 8(1). They further pointed out that even if there had been a breach, the state could assert a legitimate aim under art 8(2), that of protection of health or morals. Since art 14 does not create a free-standing right, the fact that there was no breach of art 8 meant there could not be a breach of art 14. Even if there had been a breach of art 14, the court stated that there would have been justification for the different treatment of males and females. That justification was to be found in the fact that females needed protection from the risk of pregnancy.

In *G* [2008] UKHL 37, D was charged with rape of a child under 13 when he had had consensual sex with a 12-year-old girl, reasonably believing her to be 15 (see section 4.4.5 for fuller facts).

The defence argued that there was a breach of art 8. This was because D's right to respect for his private life had been violated because the prosecution did not substitute a charge under s 13 of the Sexual Offences Act 2003 for the one under s 5. This meant that D was convicted of an offence bearing the label 'rape'.

The judges in the House of Lords were divided on the point of whether there was a breach of art 8. Lord Hoffmann took the view that it was not engaged on the facts of D's case. Baroness Hale (and Lord Mance agreeing with her) was also of the view that it was not engaged but went on to point out that even if it were engaged, it was entirely justified. She pointed out:

JUDGMENT

'The concept of private life "covers the physical and moral integrity of the person, including his or her sexual life". This does not mean that every sexual relationship, however brief or unsymmetrical, is worthy of respect, nor is every sexual act which a person wishes to perform. It does mean that the physical and moral integrity of the complainant, vulnerable by reason of her age if nothing else, was worthy of respect. The state would have been open to criticism if it did not provide her with adequate protection. This it attempts to do by a clear rule that children under 13 are incapable of giving any sort of consent to sexual activity and treating penile penetration as a most serious form of such activity. This does not in my view amount to a lack of respect for the private life of the penetrating male.'

Lords Hope and Carswell dissented on this point. They thought that the use of s 5 was disproportionate and so a breach of art 8. Lord Hope stated that:

JUDGMENT

'I would hold that it was unlawful for the prosecutor to continue to prosecute the appellant under section 5 in view of his acceptance of the basis of the appellant's plea which was that the complainant consented to intercourse. This was incompatible with his article 8 Convention right, as the offence fell properly within the ambit of section 13 and not section 5.'

G then applied for a hearing by the European Court of Human Rights. This application was refused (*G v United Kingdom (Admissibility) (37334/08)* [2012] Crim LR 46). In its reasons for the refusal to hold a full hearing the court agreed that the sexual activity in the case of G did fall within the meaning of art 8(1).

It also stated that bringing criminal proceedings against him did constitute interference by a public authority into his right for private and family life. However, the interference was 'necessary in a democratic society' and was proportionate to the legitimate aim of protecting young and vulnerable children from premature sexual activity, exploitation and abuse.

Article 10

This gives the right to freedom of expression. Many laws restrict our freedom of expression but are justified on the basis that it is necessary for national security, or to prevent crime or disorder. In *Dehal v DPP* [2005] EWHC 2154 (Admin), it was held there was a breach of art 10 by bringing a criminal prosecution where it was more suitable to deal with the matter under civil law.

CASE EXAMPLE

Dehal v DPP [2005] EWHC 2154 (Admin)

D entered a temple and placed a notice stating that the preacher at the temple was 'a hypocrite'. D was convicted of an offence under s 4A of the Public Order Act 1986. D argued that his right to freedom of expression was infringed by being prosecuted for his action. The Divisional Court quashed his conviction. They held that the criminal law should not be invoked unless the conduct amounted to such a threat to public order that it required the use of the criminal law and not merely the civil law.

1.9.5 Human rights and criminal procedure

One of the main effects of human rights has been on the procedure for trying child defendants, where they are charged with a very serious offence. Such offences must be tried in the Crown Court. However, the procedure and formality of the Crown Court can mean that a child defendant is unable to understand what is happening. In *T v UK: V v UK* (1999) 7 EHRR 659 the European Court of Human Rights held there was a breach of art 6 (the right to a fair trial), as the defendants were unable to participate effectively in the trial. Following this decision by the European Court of Human Rights, special arrangements must be made whenever a child is tried at the Crown Court, to ensure that he or she understands what is happening.

KEY FACTS

Keys facts on human rights and the criminal law

Article	Right	Comment/case
3	Right not to be subjected to inhuman or degrading treatment or punishment	Refusal to allow defence of necessity to charge of possessing cannabis was not a breach (*Altham* (2006)).
5	Right to liberty	Important in law on arrests and detention.
6(1)	Right to a fair trial	Strict liability offences are not a breach (*G* (2008)).
6(2)	Presumption of innocence	Reverse burdens of proof can be a breach of this Article but may be justified (*Attorney-General's Reference (No 4 of 2002)* and *Sheldrake v DPP* (2004)).

7	Can only be convicted if the offence existed and was sufficiently certain	*CR v UK* (1996) *Misra; Srivastava* (2004) *Goldstein* (2005)
8	Right to respect for private life	No breach for failure to allow defence of necessity to charge of possessing cannabis (*Quayle* (2005)). Possible breach if consequences of offence are out of proportion (*G* (2008)).
9	Freedom of thought, conscience and religion	This could affect the law of blasphemy.
10	Freedom of expression	Criminal law should not be invoked unless the conduct amounted to such a threat to public order that it was required (*Oehal v DPP* (2005)).
11	Freedom of peaceful assembly	Restriction can be justified where it is necessary for national security, public safety or prevention of disorder or crime, such as regulations limiting demonstrations outside the Houses of Parliament. Also this freedom does not extend to purely social gatherings, e.g. a group hanging about in a shopping centre (*Anderson & others v UK* (1997) 25 EHRR CD 172).
14	Right not be discriminated against on basis of sex or race, religion, political or other opinion, property, birth or other status	Can only be invoked if there is an infringement of another right (*E v DPP* (2005)). As well as race, the Article includes that there should be no discrimination on the basis of colour, language, national origin or association with a national minority.

SUMMARY

The purpose of criminal law is to:

- protect individuals and their property from harm;
- preserve order in society;
- punish those who deserve punishment.

Also, but more debatable, criminal law can:

- educate about appropriate conduct;
- enforce moral values.

Sources of law are:

- common law (decisions of judges);
- statutory law (Acts of Parliament and delegated legislation).

The definition of a crime is conduct which is forbidden by the state and for which there is a punishment.

Criminal offences can be classified in different ways depending on the purpose of the classification. The main ways are:

- by source
- by police powers

- by type of offence
- by place of trial.

Criminal Justice System:
In the criminal justice system trials take place in either the magistrates' courts or the Crown Court.

- The elements of a crime are the *actus reus* and the *mens rea.*
- The burden of proving guilt is on the prosecution. The defendant is presumed innocent until proven guilty.
- The standard of proof is beyond reasonable doubt.
- The European Convention on Human Rights applies to criminal law in England and Wales. All statutory offences must be interpreted in such a way as to make them compatible with the Convention. Decisions of the European Court of Human Rights must be taken into account.

ACTIVITY

Self-test questions

1. What are the main purposes of criminal law?
2. How is it possible to define a crime?
3. What are the main sources of criminal law?
4. What is the burden of proof on the prosecution?
5. In the exceptional cases where the defence has to adduce evidence of a defence, what is the standard of proof on the defence?

Further reading

Books

Huxley-Binns, R and Martin, J, *Unlocking the English Legal System* (4th edn, Routledge, 2014), Chapter 5 'Criminal courts and procedure'.

Ormerod, D, *Smith and Hogan Criminal Law* (13th edn, Oxford University Press, 2011) Chapter 1 'Defining crime' and Chapter 2 'Sources of criminal law'.

Articles

Ashworth, A, 'Is the criminal law a lost cause?' (2000) 116 LQR 223.

Ashworth, A, 'The Human Rights Act and substantive law' (2000) Crim LR 564.

Ashworth, A, 'Attorney-General's Ref (No 4 of 2002), Sheldrake v DPP: case and commentary' (2005) Crim LR 215.

Devlin, Lord, 'The conscience of the jury' (1991) 107 LQR 398.

Madhloon, L, 'Corruption and a reverse burden of proof' (2011) 75 J Crim L 96.

Wells, C, 'Reversing the burden of proof' (2005) NLJ 183 (4 Feb).

Internet links

www.cjsonline.gov.uk for general information on the criminal justice system.

www.lawcom.gov.uk for the work of the Law Commission and its reports.

www.legislation.gov.uk for all Acts of Parliament from 1988 onwards and for all Statutory Instruments from 1987 onwards.

www.parliament.gov.uk for all draft Bills before Parliament and for all debates in Hansard.

2

Actus reus

AIMS AND OBJECTIVES

After reading this chapter you should be able to:

- Understand when liability can be imposed for a failure to act (an omission)
- Understand the rules on factual causation, the 'but for' test
- Understand the rules on legal causation
- Analyse critically the laws on omissions and causations
- Apply the law to factual situations to determine whether there is liability for a failure to act or whether there has been a break in the 'chain of causation'

This chapter examines the physical elements that are required to be proved for liability to be imposed. The Latin phrase '*actus reus*' is used as a convenient shorthand for describing all the physical elements that go to make up different criminal offences.

2.1 The physical element

The majority of criminal offences considered in this textbook require as a starting point some physical element on the part of the defendant (D). Precisely what that physical element is depends on the criminal offence. To give some examples:

- Murder and manslaughter require, in most cases, that D does an act which causes the death of the victim (V) (see Chapter 10).
- Battery requires that D applies unlawful force to the body of the victim. The crime of malicious wounding requires that D does some act which cuts the skin of the victim (see Chapter 11).
- Rape requires that D 'penetrates' the vagina, anus or mouth of the victim with his penis and without V's consent (see Chapter 12).
- Theft requires that D 'appropriates' 'property' which 'belongs to another' person (see Chapter 13).

2.1.1 Conduct and consequences

You will see that the physical element in murder actually subdivides into two elements: an act (conduct) and death (consequence). The act part could be, for example, aiming a gun at V and pulling the trigger; stabbing V with a knife; strangling V with a piece of cord; or pushing V from the top of a tall building (no doubt you can think of plenty of other examples). The consequence that must follow from D's act, namely the death of V, is also part of the physical element. In most cases death follows fairly swiftly after D's act but, in some cases, there may be a delay of minutes, hours, days or even longer. Has D caused V's death if he strangles her, leaving her in a coma as a result of hypoxia (loss of oxygen to the brain) from which she eventually dies six months later? It is impossible to give a definite answer to this question; it is a question of fact for a jury. However, there are a number of legal principles which exist to help a jury in such cases and these will be examined below.

With malicious wounding, the conduct and consequence could be regarded as inseparable: the act of stabbing or slashing at V with a knife, broken bottle, etc. (conduct) must cause V's skin to be cut (consequence). In battery, the physical element requires conduct (applying force to V's body) but there is no consequence requirement. Similarly, in rape there is a conduct requirement (penetration) but no consequence is required. Theft is another example: there is a conduct element (D must 'appropriate', which means to assume rights over, property) but there is no consequence requirement.

2.1.2 Circumstances

Some criminal offences require certain circumstances to exist in addition to the conduct/consequence elements. One of the physical elements required in rape is that V must not have consented. This is a circumstance that must exist at the time D penetrates V's vagina, anus or mouth, and without it there is no crime. Similarly, in theft, in addition to the conduct element of appropriating, there must be 'property' that 'belonged to another' at the time of the appropriation. D, a vagrant, might assume rights of ownership over an old, worn-out shoe that he finds lying in the street, but this would probably not be enough to satisfy all the physical elements in the crime of theft, as it is likely that the shoe has been abandoned and hence is ownerless.

2.1.3 The physical element alone is not a crime

Look again at the conduct elements of the crimes above. In none of the cases does it automatically follow that D has committed a crime. In most rape cases, the conduct element is penetration of V's vagina or anus by D's penis, which are, generally speaking, perfectly lawful activities (subject to V having attained the age of consent, which in England is 16 (Sexual Offences (Amendment) Act 2000)). In theft, the conduct element is 'appropriating' property, an act which does not imply any wrongdoing. If you are reading this book whilst sitting at a desk in a library, you are 'appropriating' the seat and the desk because you are assuming rights of ownership over them (albeit temporarily). What prevents this performance of the physical element from amounting to a criminal offence is, in some cases, the lack of other physical elements. Thus, for D to use his penis to penetrate V's vagina, anus or mouth is, generally speaking, not the crime of rape, because V consents. In other cases, all the physical elements (whether conduct, consequences or circumstances) may be present, but still the crime may not be committed because the mental element of the crime is missing. Thus, in order to commit theft, it is necessary that D has the 'intention to permanently deprive' the owner of their property and that D was 'dishonest'.

Someone sitting innocently at a library desk does not have either the requisite intent or the dishonesty. There are exceptions to this rule, however. Some criminal offences may be committed with no, or a very little, mental element. These crimes are known as 'absolute' or 'strict' liability offences and will be examined in Chapter 4.

2.1.4 Omissions

It was stated above that, in murder and manslaughter, 'in most cases' D must do some act which causes death. The exception is where D does nothing to prevent V's death. In certain circumstances, D may be under a duty to take positive steps to assist V and failing to take them can amount to the physical element of the crimes of murder and manslaughter. This topic will be examined below.

2.2 Voluntary conduct

In *Bratty v Attorney-General of Northern Ireland* [1963] AC 386, Lord Denning said that: 'The requirement that [the act of the accused] should be a voluntary act is essential ... in every criminal case. No act is punishable if it is done involuntarily.' An example of this might be if the defendant, D, were to push a bystander, E, so that E lost his balance and knocked a second bystander, V. If V loses his balance and falls to the ground, fracturing his leg, has E committed the *actus reus* of battery or even assault occasioning actual bodily harm? The *actus reus* of battery requires the unlawful application of physical force to the body of the victim; the *actus reus* of actual bodily harm is the same plus the infliction of some hurt or injury to the victim. The answer is that E is not guilty of any crime: although E was the immediate cause of V falling to the ground and hence his injuries, in no sense can E be said to have 'acted'. Moreover, even if E could be said to have performed an 'act' in the above scenario, it was clearly not 'voluntary' in the sense of being a deliberate or willed 'act' on his behalf. (These are the facts of *Mitchell* [1983] QB 741. V, aged 89, died of a pulmonary embolism caused by thrombosis, which in turn was caused by the fracture. In the event, D (and not E) was charged and convicted of her manslaughter.)

2.3 Omissions

Originally, the English criminal law only punished those who caused a prohibited result by a positive act. But it came to accept that it should also punish those who fail to act, when a duty to act could be implied, with the result that the prohibited result ensued. Nevertheless, on the whole, the position is still that there is no general duty to act. There may well be a *moral* obligation on someone to be a 'Good Samaritan', but there is not a *legal* one. There are two requirements:

- The crime has to be capable of being committed by omission (known as result crimes).
- D must be under a duty to act.

2.3.1 Commission by omission

Generally speaking, the crime must be capable of being committed by omission. Nearly all of the leading cases involve murder or gross negligence manslaughter. Other crimes capable of being committed by omission are arson (*Miller* [1983] 2 AC 161, which will be discussed below) and assault and battery. This was decided in *DPP v Santana-Bermudez* [2003] EWHC 2908.

CASE EXAMPLE

DPP v Santana-Bermudez [2003] EWHC 2908

V, a female police officer, asked D to turn out all his pockets, which he did. V asked him if he had removed everything; he replied 'Yes'. She then asked 'Are you sure that you do not have any needles or sharps on you?' D said 'No'. V commenced her search but when she put her hand into one pocket she pricked her finger on a hypodermic needle. V noticed that D was smirking. D was convicted of assault by magistrates, but appealed to the Crown Court, successfully arguing that it was legally impossible to commit an assault by omission. The prosecution appealed to the Divisional Court, which allowed the appeal.

Conversely, a crime that is incapable of being committed by omission is constructive manslaughter (a positive act is always required, according to *Lowe* [1973] QB 702; see Chapter 10). Sometimes the definition of the *actus reus* makes it clear that a positive act is required. For example, burglary (s 9 of the Theft Act 1968 requires D to 'enter' into a building; see Chapter 14) and making off without payment (s 3 of the Theft Act 1978 requires D to 'make off'; see also Chapter 14). The definition of rape in s 1(1) of the Sexual Offences Act 2003 makes clear that the offence is committed only when D 'penetrates the vagina, anus or mouth of another person with his penis'. Section 79(2) of the same Act states that 'penetration is a continuing act'. This would seem to rule out any possibility of committing rape by omission (although see the discussion of the cases of *Kaitamaki* [1984] 2 All ER 435 and *Cooper and Schaub* [1994] Crim LR 531 on this point in Chapter 12). Another example is the offence of 'throwing missiles' (s 2 Football Offences Act 1991). In *Ahmad* [1986] Crim LR 739, D, a landlord, was convicted of 'doing acts calculated to interfere with the peace and comfort of a residential occupier with intent to cause him to give up occupation of the premises', contrary to the Protection from Eviction Act 1977. The relevant acts had been done without the requisite intent; D had then deliberately refrained from rectifying the situation. The Court of Appeal quashed the conviction; D had not 'done acts' with the requisite intent.

One problem with the imposition of liability for failing to act in 'result' crimes, such as murder and gross negligence manslaughter, which the courts have not really acknowledged, is the requirement of causation. Suppose D, a professional lifeguard on duty, sees a small child fall into a pool, but simply stands and watches while she struggles and eventually drowns. No one else is present. There is little doubt that D is under a duty to save the girl (because of contractual responsibility; see below) and failure to do so could well be murder (if D intends death or serious injury) or gross negligence manslaughter. But did D 'cause' the girl to die? She would almost certainly have died in exactly the same way – the same 'result' would have occurred – had she been completely alone and D had not been there. The Law Commission tackles this when it provides in its Draft Criminal Code (1989), clause 17(1), that 'a person causes a result ... when ... (b) he omits to do an act which might prevent its occurrence and which he is under a duty to do according to the law relating to that offence'.

2.3.2 Imposition of a duty to act

The most important factor is that D must be under a duty, recognised by the law, to act or intervene in the circumstances. In *Khan and Khan* [1998] EWCA Crim 971; [1998] Crim LR 830, the Court of Appeal quashed manslaughter convictions of two drug dealers because the judge had made no ruling as to whether the facts were capable of giving rise to any relevant duty, nor had he directed the jury in relation to that issue.

CASE EXAMPLE

Khan and Khan [1998] EWCA Crim 971; [1998] Crim LR 830

D and E were drug dealers in Birmingham. V, a 15-year-old prostitute, went to a flat where they supplied her with heroin. She ingested a large amount, lapsed into a coma and was obviously in need of medical assistance. However, D and E left the flat, leaving V alone to die. They were charged with murder but were convicted of manslaughter. The Court of Appeal quashed their convictions. The Crown's case was that the appellants' omission to summon medical assistance formed the basis of their liability. However, the Court of Appeal decided that, in such circumstances, before they could convict, the jury had to be sure that D was criminally responsible, and this required that D be standing in such a relation to the victim that he is under a duty to act.

It should be noted that the above case does not decide that no duty was (or could be) owed on the facts; rather that it must be left to the jury to decide whether, on the facts, a duty was in fact owed. Such a duty may be owed in a variety of situations, as the following cases illustrate.

Duty arising out of contractual liability

Where failure to fulfil a contract is likely to endanger lives, the criminal law will impose a duty to act. The duty is owed to anyone who may be affected, not just the other parties to the contract. The leading cases are *Pittwood* (1902) 19 TLR 37 and *Adomako* [1995] 1 AC 171. In *Pittwood,* D was a signalman employed by the railway company to look after a level crossing and ensure the gate was shut when trains were due. D left the gate open and was away from his post, with the result that someone crossing the line was hit and killed. D was convicted of manslaughter. The court rejected D's argument that his duty was owed simply to the railway company: he was paid to look after the gate and protect the public. This duty will be held by members of the emergency services, lifeguards, etc. In *Adomako,* a duty to act was imposed on a hospital anaesthetist (see Chapter 10). In *Singh* [1999] EWCA Crim 460; [1999] Crim LR 582, a duty to act was imposed on a landlord. D, who helped his father run a lodging house, was convicted of manslaughter after carbon monoxide poisoning from a defective gas fire killed one of the tenants. On appeal he contended that no duty to act had arisen, whether as rent collector, maintenance man or anything else. However, the Court of Appeal decided that, as it was D's responsibility to maintain the flat, a duty to act was imposed on him to deal with any danger by calling in expert help.

Duty arising out of a relationship

Parents are under a duty to their children (*Gibbins and Proctor* (1918) 13 Cr App R 134) and spouses owe a duty to each other (*Smith* [1979] Crim LR 251; see *Hood* [2003] EWCA Crim 2772 below).

Duty arising from the assumption of care for another

A duty will be owed by anyone who voluntarily undertakes to care for another person, whether through age, infirmity, illness, etc. The duty may be express but is more likely to be implied from conduct. Thus in *Nicholls* (1874) 13 Cox CC 75, D, a grandmother who took her granddaughter into her home after the girl's mother died, was held to have undertaken an express duty to act. In *Instan* [1893] 1 QB 450, D moved in with her elderly aunt, who became ill and for the last 12 days of her life was unable to care for herself or summon help. D did not give her any food or seek medical assistance, but continued to live in the house and eat the aunt's food. Eventually the aunt died and D was convicted of manslaughter. In *Gibbins and Proctor*, the court found that the deliberate non-performance of a legal duty to act could result in liability for murder being imposed on D, who had voluntarily undertaken responsibility to care for a child.

CASE EXAMPLE

Gibbins and Proctor (1918) 13 Cr App R 134

G was the father of several children, including a seven-year-old daughter, Nelly. His wife had left him and he was living with a lover, P. They kept Nelly separate from the other children and deliberately starved her to death. Afterwards they concocted a story about how Nelly had 'gone away'; in fact G had buried her in the brickyard where he worked. Both adults were convicted of murder and the Court of Criminal Appeal upheld the convictions. G owed Nelly a duty as her father; P was held to have undertaken a duty.

The leading case is now *Stone and Dobinson* [1977] QB 354.

CASE EXAMPLE

Stone and Dobinson [1977] QB 354

S lived with his mistress, D. In 1972, S's sister, Fanny, aged 61, came to live with them. Fanny was suffering from anorexia nervosa and although initially capable of looking after herself, her condition deteriorated. Eventually, in 1975, she was confined to bed in the small front room where she remained until her death, refusing to eat anything other than biscuits. S was then 67, partially deaf, nearly blind and of low intelligence. D was 43 but was described as 'ineffectual' and 'somewhat inadequate'. Both were unable to use a telephone. They had tried to find Fanny's doctor but failed; eventually a local doctor was called, but by this point it was too late. Fanny had died, weighing less than five-and-a-half stone, in an excrement- and urine-soiled bed with two large, maggot-infested ulcers on her right hip and left knee, and bone clearly visible. The Court of Appeal upheld S and D's manslaughter convictions. They had assumed a duty of care to Fanny, and their pathetically feeble efforts to look after her amounted to gross negligence.

ACTIVITY

Self-test question

Would Stone and Dobinson have been better off simply ignoring Fanny after she became bedbound?

Duty arising from the creation of a dangerous situation

Where D inadvertently, and without the requisite *mens rea*, does an act which creates a dangerous situation then, on becoming aware of it, he is under a duty to take all such steps as lie within his power to prevent or minimise the harm. If he fails to take such steps with the appropriate *mens rea*, then he will be criminally liable. This situation arose in *Miller*.

CASE EXAMPLE

Miller [1983] 2 AC 161

D, a vagrant, was squatting in a house in Birmingham. He had fallen asleep one night but awoke to find that a cigarette he had been smoking had set fire to the mattress. He did nothing to extinguish the fire, but moved to another room and went back to sleep. The house caught fire, and £800 of damage was caused. The House of Lords upheld his conviction, on the basis that his inadvertent creation of a dangerous situation imposed a duty on him to take steps to minimise that danger as soon as he realised what he had done. What those steps are will depend on what is reasonable in the circumstances. At the least, D might have been expected to try to put out the fire or, if it was beyond control, call the fire brigade.

A number of subsequent cases have discussed the *Miller* principle.

- In *Matthews and Alleyne* [2003] EWCA Crim 192; [2003] Crim LR 553 (the full facts of which appear in the next chapter in the context of intention) the trial judge suggested that D and E could have been convicted of murder if, having pushed V into a river, they subsequently realised that he was unable to swim and (with intent that he should die or suffer serious injury) took no steps to rescue him. The appellants and V were strangers to each other prior to this event, so the basis on which D and E owed V a duty to act could be regarded as similar to that in *Miller*.
- In *Santana-Bermudez*, the facts of which were given above, the Divisional Court expressly applied *Miller* as the basis for finding D's duty to act. The court held that, when D gave V a dishonest assurance about the contents of his pockets, he exposed her to a reasonably foreseeable risk of injury. His subsequent failure to inform her of the presence of needles in his pockets constituted an evidential basis for a finding that the *actus reus* of assault occasioning actual bodily harm had occurred.

The most recent example of the *Miller* principle is the case of *Evans* [2009] EWCA Crim 650; [2009] 1 WLR 1999, in which the principle was applied to gross negligence manslaughter.

CASE EXAMPLE

Evans [2009] EWCA Crim 650; [2009] 1 WLR 1999

D lived with her 16-year-old half-sister, V, a heroin addict, and their mother. One day, D bought £20 of heroin and gave some to V, who self-injected. Later, it was obvious that V had overdosed but neither D nor their mother contacted the emergency services. Instead they put V to bed hoping that she would recover. Instead, she died during the night. Both D and her mother were convicted of gross negligence manslaughter. D appealed, but the Court of Appeal upheld the conviction on the basis that D owed V a duty of care based on the *Miller* principle.

Lord Judge CJ stated:

JUDGMENT

'The duty necessary to found gross negligence manslaughter is plainly not confined to cases of a familial or professional relationship between [D] and [V]. In our judgment, consistently with *Adomako* and the link between civil and criminal liability for negligence, for the purposes of gross negligence manslaughter, when a person has created or contributed to the creation of a state of affairs which he knows, or ought reasonably to know, has become life threatening, a consequent duty on him to act by taking reasonable steps to save the other's life will normally arise.'

The Draft Criminal Code (1989), clause 23, also endorses the *Miller* principle:

CLAUSE

'23 Where it is an offence to be at fault in causing a result, a person who lacks the fault required when he does an act that causes or may cause the result nevertheless commits the offence if –

a. he has become aware that he has done the act and that the result had occurred and may continue, or may occur; and
b. with the fault required, he fails to do what he can reasonably be expected to do that might prevent the result continuing or occurring; and
c. the result continues or occurs.'

Clause 31 of the Draft Criminal Law Bill (1993) is to similar effect.

Release from duty to act

One issue that has troubled the courts is whether D, having undertaken a duty or having had one imposed on him, may be released from it. In *Smith* (1979), D's wife had given birth to a stillborn child at home. She hated doctors and would not allow D to call one. When she finally gave D permission it was too late; she died and D was charged with manslaughter. The judge directed the jury 'to balance the weight that it is right to give to his wife's wish to avoid calling a doctor against her capacity to make rational decisions. If she does not appear too ill it may be reasonable to abide by her wishes. On the other hand, if she appeared desperately ill then whatever she may say it may be right to override.' The jury were unable to agree and D was discharged. The principle that, provided V is rational, she may release D from a duty to act was confirmed in *Re B (Consent to Treatment: Capacity)* [2002] EWHC 429 (Fam); [2002] 2 All ER 449. Here, the High Court held that, when a competent patient gives notice that they wish life-preserving treatment to be discontinued, anyone responsible up to that point for providing such treatment (in this case doctors) would be obliged to respect that notice.

Cessation of duty to act

In *Airedale NHS Trust v Bland* [1993] AC 789 (like *Re B*, a civil case), the House of Lords provided guidance on the issue of when a duty to act ceases. Bland, who had been suffocated during the Hillsborough Stadium tragedy in 1989, had been in a persistent vegetative state in hospital for over three years. When the hospital authorities applied for judicial authority to discontinue treatment in the form of artificial feeding and hydration, the House of Lords held that, on the facts, it was permissible to do so. Lord Goff, giving the leading judgment, stated that there was no absolute rule that a patient's life had to be prolonged regardless. The fundamental principle was the sanctity of life, but respect for human dignity demanded that the quality of life be considered. The principle of 'self-determination' meant that an adult patient of sound mind could refuse treatment. Doctors (or other persons responsible for the patient) would have to respect that. In *Bland*, the House of Lords was careful to characterise the withdrawal of life support as an omission (a failure to continue treatment). The case does not stand as an authority for the proposition that doctors may take positive steps to end a patient's life. Euthanasia, therefore, remains illegal in England and Wales.

The crime of assisting another's suicide is also unaffected by the *Bland* decision. This was demonstrated in *R (on the application of Pretty) v DPP* [2001] UKHL 61; [2002] 1 AC 800. P was suffering from motor neurone disease which she knew would eventually lead to her suffocating to death. She applied to the courts for a judicial declaration that, if her

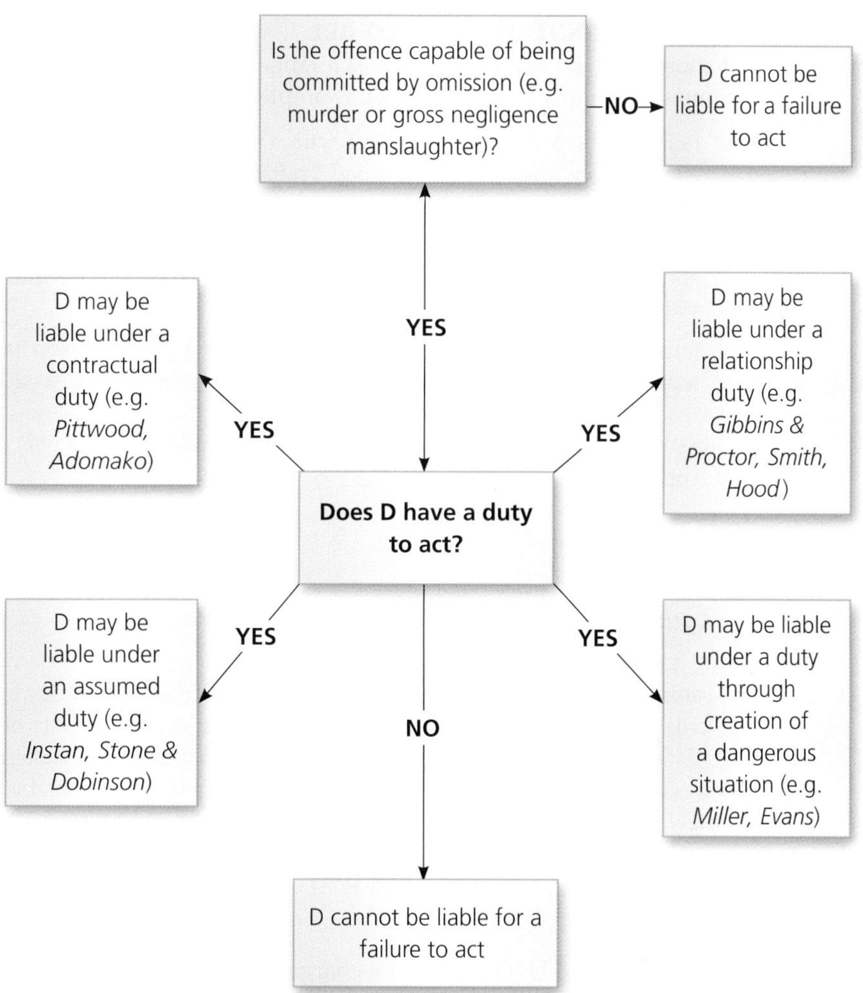

Figure 2.1 Does D have a duty to act?

husband assisted her to commit suicide, he would not be prosecuted (her physical condition having deteriorated to such an extent by this point that she was unable to take her own life unassisted). This request was denied by the High Court and confirmed by the Court of Appeal and House of Lords. Assisting another person to commit suicide seems, inevitably, to amount to a positive act. A final appeal to the European Court of Human Rights also failed, the Court in Strasbourg ruling that English law did not infringe P's human rights.

In *Re A (Children) (Conjoined Twins: Surgical Separation)* [2000] EWCA Civ 254; [2000] 4 All ER 961, the Court of Appeal (Civil Division) confirmed that a surgical procedure to separate two baby girls who were born joined together at the abdomen was a positive act and not an omission. Therefore, because the doctors knew that the procedure would inevitably lead to the death of one girl, the doctors had both the *actus reus* and *mens rea* of murder. However, the doctors were able to apply the defence of necessity (the twins shared one functioning heart which would eventually fail as they grew, therefore the operation was necessary to save one girl's life – not operating would lead to both girls' deaths) and the court held that the procedure was lawful (see Chapter 8 for further discussion of this case).

2.3.3 Breach of duty to act

It should also be noted that there is a range of crimes (mostly statutory) which can be committed simply by failing to act. Examples include the following:

- failing to provide a police officer with a specimen of breath when required to do so is an offence under s 6 of the Road Traffic Act (RTA) 1988;
- failing to stop and provide a name and address to any person reasonably requiring it when your vehicle has been involved in an accident where there has been injury to another person or damage to another vehicle is an offence under s 170 of the RTA 1988;
- failing to disclose to the police information that another person has committed certain terrorist offences is an offence under s 19 of the Terrorism Act 2000.

One such offence exists at common law and a conviction for it was upheld by the Court of Appeal in *Dytham* [1979] QB 722.

CASE EXAMPLE

Dytham [1979] QB 722

D, a police officer, was on duty near a nightclub at about 1 a.m. He was standing about 30 yards from the door when a bouncer ejected V from the club. A noisy fight ensued in which a large number of men participated. Three men eventually kicked V to death, all of which was clearly audible and visible to D. However, he took no steps to intervene and, when the incident was over, adjusted his helmet and drove off, telling two people nearby that he was going off duty. D was convicted of the common law offence of misconduct whilst acting as an officer of justice, in that he had wilfully omitted to take any steps to carry out his duty to preserve the Queen's Peace or to protect V or to arrest or otherwise bring to justice his assailants. The Court of Appeal upheld his conviction.

Interestingly, PC Dytham was not charged with manslaughter, a result crime, although it could well be argued that, on the facts, he owed a duty to act to V to intervene and assist him, this duty arising from D's contractual obligations. The reason that D was not charged with the more serious crime may be because of the difficulties in proving that he had actually made a causative contribution to V's death.

2.3.4 Reform

Advocates of reform of this area suggest that where rescue of the victim would not pose a danger to D, then liability should be imposed for failing to act, even where there was no pre-existing legal duty on D (A Ashworth, 'The scope of criminal liability for omissions' (1989) 105 LQR 424). There are, however, serious moral and practical objections:

- Definition of when it would be easy for D to attempt a rescue.
- Moral objection to forcing citizens to watch out for and protect each other, especially as most citizens already pay (through taxes) for highly trained and well-equipped professionals (police, fire brigade officers, lifeboat crew, paramedics, etc.) to do that job on our behalf.
- Possibility that D may (genuinely and/or reasonably) misjudge the situation and either fail to attempt a rescue when it was in fact easy (D thinking it would be dangerous) or attempt a dangerous rescue (D thinking it was actually easy). In the former scenario, D faces potential liability for homicide if V is killed. In the latter scenario,

D's own life is put at risk and genuine rescuers (police etc.) now have two people to rescue (D and V) instead of just V.

- Possible imposition of liability on large numbers of people. For example, when a train platform is crowded with commuters and all fail to come to the aid of V who has slipped and fallen on to the tracks and is lying unconscious, despite the fact that no train is due for several minutes, should all the commuters be held liable? Alternatively, what about all the sunbathers on a crowded beach who all choose to ignore V who is clearly drowning 20 yards from shore?

2.4 Causation

student mentor tip

'A good way to study causation and *actus reus* is to draw diagrams and label all the exceptions.' *Gayatri, University of Leicester.*

When D is charged with any result crime, the Crown must prove that his acts or omissions caused the prohibited consequence. For example, in murder or manslaughter (see Chapter 10), it is necessary to prove that D, by his or her acts or omissions, caused V's death. If V dies because of some other cause, then the offence has not been committed even though all the other elements of the offence, including the *mens rea*, are present. D may of course be liable for attempt instead (*White* [1910] 2 KB 124; see below and see Chapter 6 for discussion of attempts). Similarly, if D is charged with causing grievous bodily harm with intent, contrary to s 18 of the Offences Against the Person Act (OAPA) 1861, the Crown must prove that D's acts or omissions caused V to suffer serious injuries. The issue of causation is for the jury to decide. The judge should direct them as to the elements of causation, but it is for them to decide if the causal link between D's act and the prohibited consequence has been established. Usually it will be sufficient to direct the jury (*per* Robert Goff LJ in *Pagett* [1983] Crim LR 393): 'simply that in law the accused's act need not be the sole cause, or even the main cause, of the victim's death, it being enough that his act contributed significantly to that result'. When a problem arises, as occasionally happens, then it is for the judge to direct the jury in accordance with the legal principles which they have to apply. There are two main principles:

- The jury must be satisfied that D's conduct was a factual cause of V's death or injuries.
- The jury must also be satisfied that D's conduct was a legal cause of V's death or injuries.

2.4.1 Factual causation

This is determined using the 'but for' test; that is, it must be established that the consequence would not have occurred as and when it did *but for* D's conduct. If the consequence would have happened anyway, there is no liability. The leading example of this is *White* [1910] 2 KB 124.

CASE EXAMPLE

White [1910] 2 KB 124

D put potassium cyanide into his mother's drink. He had direct intent to kill, in order to gain under her will. Later V was found dead, sitting on the sofa at her home. Although she had drunk as much as a quarter of the poisoned drink, medical evidence established that she had died of a heart attack, not poisoning. In any event D had not used enough cyanide for a fatal dose. D was acquitted of murder: he had not caused her death. (He was, however, convicted of attempted murder.)

Factual causation on its own is insufficient for liability. As the Supreme Court explained in *Hughes* [2013] UKSC 56; [2013] 1 WLR 2461:

JUDGMENT

'The law has frequently to confront the distinction between "cause" in the sense of a *sine qua non* without which the consequence would not have occurred, and "cause" in the sense of something which was a legally effective cause of that consequence. The former, which is often conveniently referred to as a "but for" event, is not necessarily enough to be a legally effective cause. If it were, the woman who asked her neighbour to go to the station in his car to collect her husband would be held to have caused her husband's death if he perished in a fatal road accident on the way home.'

2.4.2 Legal causation

Factual causation alone, therefore, is not enough for criminal liability. It is essential that legal causation is established as well. This is again a question for the jury: the question is whether the consequence (death, serious injury, as the case may be) can fairly be said to be D's fault. In an early case, *Dalloway* (1847) 2 Cox CC 273, D was acquitted because, although V's death would not have occurred but for D driving a horse and cart over him, the jury were not convinced that D was to blame.

CASE EXAMPLE

Dalloway (1847) 2 Cox CC 273

D was driving a horse and cart without holding the reins, which were lying loose on the horse's back. A child, V, ran in front of the cart, was struck by one of the wheels and killed. D was charged with manslaughter but the jury acquitted. It appeared from the evidence that, even if D had been holding the reins, he could not have stopped the cart in time. Hence the death was not D's fault.

This principle was seen in *Marchant and Muntz* [2003] EWCA Crim 2099; [2004] 1 WLR 442, a case of causing death by dangerous driving. V, a motorcyclist, impaled himself on a metre-long spike (called a tine) attached to the front of an agricultural vehicle being driven on a public road. There was no suggestion that D's driving was dangerous; rather, the allegation was that simply having the vehicle on the road at all was dangerous. Although D was convicted, the Court of Appeal quashed the conviction. Expert evidence at trial indicated that the spike could have been 'covered by some sort of guard', but Grigson J concluded that 'even had such a guard been in place, it would not have prevented the collision. The consequences to anyone striking a tine *or the guard* at speed would have been very severe, if not fatal' (emphasis added). In other words, D had not caused V's death.

In *Hughes* (2013), the Supreme Court confirmed that legal causation, as a pre requisite in any result crime, implied proof of some level of fault. The case involved the offence of causing death by driving whilst uninsured and/or unlicensed to drive, contrary to s 3ZB of the Road Traffic Act 1988. The Crown case was that an accused charged under s 3ZB was guilty if death occurred as a result of taking a vehicle on to the road when the driver was uninsured or unlicensed to drive, irrespective of the blameworthiness of the driving itself. The Supreme Court rejected this on the basis that it would be unacceptably harsh to impose liability for a homicide offence on motorists whose actual driving was entirely blameless. The Court used a number of hypothetical examples to illustrate: where V committed suicide by stepping out in front of D's car; where V was killed after ramming their car into D's car in a deliberate attempt to kill or injure an occupant of D's car; where

V stumbled, drunk, from the pavement directly in front of D's car and was run over and killed; where V was killed playing 'chicken' by running out in front of oncoming vehicles; where D's car was struck by another motorist and the impact of the collision shunted D's car on to the pavement where a child was run over and killed. The Supreme Court rejected the notion that V's death in all of those examples had been 'caused' by D.

Instead, the Court held that it must be proved 'that there was something which [D] did or omitted to do by way of driving which contributed in a more than minimal way to the death'. As to what that 'something' was, the Court held that the expression 'causes ... death' in the RTA 1988 implied that 'there is *something properly to be criticised* in the driving of [D], which contributed in some more than minimal way to the death ... Juries should be directed that there must be *something open to proper criticism* in the driving of the defendant, beyond the mere presence of the vehicle on the road, and which contributed in some more than minimal way to the death' (emphasis added).

CASE EXAMPLE

Hughes [2013] UKSC 56; [2013] 1 WLR 2461

On a late Sunday afternoon, V was driving along the A69, heading west from Newcastle. He was on the return leg of a 400-mile round trip from his place of work on the west coast of Scotland and was over-tired. He was also under the influence of heroin, and had been driving erratically for some time, narrowly missing colliding with other vehicles. He rounded a bend on the wrong side of the road and crashed head-on into a camper van being driven in the opposite direction by D. V was fatally injured. It was accepted that D's driving had been faultless and that, on a 'common sense' view, V was entirely responsible for his own death. D was, however, uninsured at the time, and driving under a provisional licence. He was therefore charged with causing V's death by driving whilst uninsured and/or unlicensed to drive, contrary to s 3ZB of the RTA 1988. The trial judge accepted the defence argument that D had not caused V's death. The Crown appealed to the Court of Appeal, which held that D *had* caused the death, on the basis that the offence did not require that there be anything wrong with the defendant's driving. D appealed to the Supreme Court, where the trial judge's decision was reinstated. The Supreme Court disagreed with the appeal court and held that there *did* have to be something wrong with the defendant's driving. In the present case, D had not caused V's death. Admittedly, by driving along the A69 that afternoon, D had 'created the opportunity' for his camper van to be run into by V's car, but it was 'a matter of the merest chance' that it was D's vehicle that V hit. He might 'just as easily have gone off the road and hit a tree', but in that scenario no one would have said that V's death had been caused by the planting of the tree.

Minimal causes may be discounted

If D's act or omission provides only a minimal contribution to V's death or injuries, then it may be discounted under the *de minimis* principle (the law ignores trivialities). R N Perkins and R N Boyce in *Criminal Law* (3rd edn, Foundation Press, 1982) give the following example, where V has suffered two stab wounds from different defendants:

QUOTATION

'Suppose one wound severed the jugular vein whereas the other barely broke the skin of the hand, and as the life blood gushed from the victim's neck one drop oozed from the bruise on his finger ... metaphysicians will conclude that the extra drop of blood hastened the end by the infinitesimal fraction of a second. But the law ... will conclude that death be imputed only to the severe injury in such an extreme case as this.'

It is sometimes said that D's act must be a 'substantial' cause of death; this probably states the case too favourably for D. What is required is that D's act provides a more than minimal contribution. Thus, in *Kimsey* [1996] Crim LR 35, a case of causing death by dangerous driving, the trial judge told the jury that they did not have to be sure that D's driving 'was the principal, or a substantial cause of the death, as long as you are sure that it was a cause and that there was something more than a slight or trifling link'. On appeal, it was argued that it was wrong to say that D's driving did not have to be a 'substantial cause'. The Court of Appeal dismissed the appeal; reference to 'substantial cause' was not necessary and moreover might encourage the jury to attach too much importance to D's driving. Reference to 'more than a slight or trifling link' was permissible and a useful way of avoiding the term *'de minimis'*.

More recently, in *Hughes* (2013), the Supreme Court explained the minimum threshold requirement for legal causation as follows:

JUDGMENT

'Where there are multiple legally effective causes, it suffices if the act or omission under consideration is a significant (or substantial) cause, in the sense that it is not *de minimis* or minimal. It need not be the only or the principal cause. It must, however, be a cause which is more than *de minimis*, more than minimal.'

Multiple causes

D's act or omission need not, therefore, be the sole or even the main cause of V's death or injuries. It is sufficient that D's act or omission provides a more than minimal cause. Other contributory causes may be the acts of others, or even of V themselves.

Actions of third parties

The early case of *Benge* (1865) 4 F & F 504 provides a good example. D, the foreman of a track-laying crew, misread the railway timetable, so that the track was up at the time the train was due. He realised his error and placed a signalman with a flag 540 yards up the line, although statutory regulations specified a distance of at least 1,000 yards. However, the train driver was not keeping a proper lookout and failed to stop. Several deaths were caused. Thus, the deaths were a combination of:

- D misreading the train timetable;
- the signalman's failure to stand 460 yards further up the line;
- the train driver's failure to keep a proper lookout.

Nevertheless, the jury were directed to convict D if they were satisfied that his conduct mainly or substantially caused the deaths (they were so satisfied, and D was convicted).

A slightly different approach is required in cases where D's act or omission triggers some further act by a third party, and it is the latter act or omission which is the immediate cause of death. D is clearly a factual cause of death, but to what extent can D also be regarded as the legal cause? The leading case is *Pagett*, where Goff LJ said that, where the third party's act is a reasonable response to D's initial act, the chain will not be broken. D did not escape liability where a third party, forced into reasonable self-defence by D, inadvertently caused V's death.

CASE EXAMPLE

Pagett [1983] Crim LR 393

Several police officers were trying to arrest D for various serious offences. He was hiding in his first-floor flat with his 16-year-old girlfriend, V, who was pregnant by him. D armed himself with a shotgun and, against her will, used V's body as a shield. He fired at two officers, who returned fire; three bullets fired by the officers hit V. She died from the wounds. D was convicted of manslaughter; his appeal was dismissed.

It is crucial that the question of causation is left to the jury to decide. If it is not, convictions may be quashed. A good example is *Watson* [1989] 2 All ER 865 (examined in detail in Chapter 10). D was convicted of manslaughter on the basis that his act of burgling V's home had triggered a fatal heart attack 90 minutes later. However, D's conviction was quashed on the ground of causation: the heart attack may have been caused by the arrival of the police or council workmen to board up the window. There is now a considerable body of case law on the application of these principles to cases where the third parties are medical personnel dealing with injuries inflicted by D. These cases raise special considerations of public policy and will be dealt with separately below.

Actions of the victim: deliberate acts

Over the years, the appeal courts have heard a series of cases involving similar facts. D, a drug dealer, provides V, a drug addict, with a syringe containing a mixture of heroin and water. The heroin is then injected into V, but V accidentally overdoses and dies. The question is: has D caused V's death? The answer is: it depends on whether it was D who injected the heroin into V, or whether D handed the syringe to V, who self-injected.

- Where D injects the heroin into V, who overdoses and dies, then D has caused V's death and faces liability for constructive manslaughter (see Chapter 10). This, essentially, was the situation in *Cato* [1976] 1 All ER 260.
- Where D hands the syringe to V, who self-injects, overdoses and dies, the chain of causation is broken. V's deliberate, voluntary act is deemed to have broken the chain and therefore D is not liable for V's death. This was the situation in *Dalby* [1982] 1 All ER 916 and *Dias* [2002] 2 Cr App R 96. This principle has now been confirmed by the House of Lords in *Kennedy* [2007] UKHL 38; [2008] 1 AC 269.

CASE EXAMPLE

Kennedy [2007] UKHL 38; [2008] 1 AC 269

D and V both lived in a hostel. One night, at V's request, D prepared a dose of heroin and gave V a syringe ready for injection. V injected himself but later died, the cause of death being the inhalation of gastric contents while acutely intoxicated by heroin and alcohol. D was duly convicted of manslaughter, based on the unlawful act of administering a noxious substance. He appealed, unsuccessfully, to the Court of Appeal (twice) although on the second occasion the Court of Appeal certified the following question for the opinion of the House of Lords: 'When is it appropriate to find someone guilty of manslaughter where that person has been involved in the supply of a class A controlled drug, which is then freely and voluntarily self-administered by the person to whom it was supplied, and the administration of the drug then causes his death?' The Law Lords allowed the appeal and quashed the conviction. Lord Bingham said that the answer to the certified question was: 'In the case of a fully-informed and responsible adult, never.'

Lord Bingham, giving a single speech on behalf of the whole House in *Kennedy*, said:

JUDGMENT

'The criminal law generally assumes the existence of free will ... Thus [D] is not to be treated as causing [V] to act in a certain way if [V] makes a voluntary and informed decision to act in that way rather than another ... The finding that [V] freely and voluntarily administered the injection to himself, knowing what it was, is fatal to any contention that [D] caused the heroin to be administered to [V] or taken by him.'

There is an interesting contrast here between English and Scottish law. In *MacAngus and Kane v HM Advocate* [2009] HCJAC 8, the High Court of Justiciary in Edinburgh decided – on very similar facts to *Kennedy* – that V's self-injection of drugs supplied by D does not necessarily break the chain of causation:

JUDGMENT

'The adult status and the deliberate conduct of a person to whom a controlled drug is ... supplied by another will be important, in some cases crucial, factors in determining whether that other's act was or was not, for the purposes of criminal responsibility, a cause of any death which follows upon ingestion of the drug. But a deliberate decision by the victim of the reckless conduct to ingest the drug will not necessarily break the chain of causation.'

Actions of the victim: fright or flight

In some cases, V brings about his own death or injuries through attempting to escape from a threat (whether real or imagined) posed by D. However, D may remain responsible for those outcomes. The courts have devised a test which involves establishing a 'chain of causation' between D's original act or omission and V's ultimate death or injury. If V's actions in trying to escape from a threat posed by D are regarded by the jury as 'daft' (or 'unexpected' or 'unreasonable') then the 'chain' is broken and D escapes liability. If V's actions are not regarded as 'daft' then D remains liable. The question of 'daftness', which is one for the jury to answer, is particularly important in cases where D contends that V has misinterpreted his act or omission and (possibly in a state of confusion and/or panic) has overreacted. *Marjoram* [2000] Crim LR 372 provides a recent example.

CASE EXAMPLE

Marjoram [2000] Crim LR 372

D, who had been shouting abuse and kicking V's hostel room door, forced open the door, at which point V fell, or possibly jumped, from the window. V sustained serious injury in the fall. D maintained that he had broken down the door because he had heard the window being opened and had intended to rescue V from what he thought was a suicide bid. Nevertheless, D was convicted of inflicting grievous bodily harm, contrary to s 20 OAPA 1861. The Court of Appeal dismissed D's appeal. The jury were entitled to find that V's reaction to having D forcing open their door was not daft.

Similarly, in *Corbett* [1996] Crim LR 594, the Court of Appeal rejected D's appeal that V had overreacted and upheld his manslaughter conviction. D had punched and head-butted V, who had run off, tripped and fallen into the path of a passing car. D argued on appeal that it should have to be proved that what happened was the natural consequence of D's act. The Court of Appeal, however, confirmed that the jury had been properly directed that only a 'daft' reaction by V was capable of breaking the chain. The criterion of V's reaction being 'daft' stems from *Roberts* [1972] Crim LR 242, in which D was convicted of assault occasioning actual bodily harm (contrary to s 47 OAPA 1861) after the girl passenger in his car jumped out after he allegedly had tried to remove her coat. He appealed on the ground that causation had not been established. The Court of Appeal dismissed the appeal. Stephenson LJ said:

JUDGMENT

'The test is: was [V's reaction] the natural result of what [D] said and did, in the sense that it was something that could reasonably have been foreseen as the consequence of what [D] was saying or doing? ... If of course [V] does something so "daft" ... or so unexpected ... that no reasonable man could be expected to foresee it, then it is only in a very remote and unreal sense a consequence of [D's] assault, it is really occasioned by a voluntary act on the part of [V] which could not reasonably be foreseen and which breaks the chain of causation between the assault and harm or injury.'

novus actus interveniens

A new intervening act – something which breaks the chain of causation

If the jury agree that V's reaction was 'daft' and the chain of causation broken, it is common to refer to this reaction using the Latin term '*novus actus interveniens*', literally 'new intervening act'. Thus, in the words of Stuart-Smith LJ in *Williams and Davis* [1992] 2 All ER 183:

JUDGMENT

'V's conduct [must] be something that a reasonable and responsible man in D's shoes would have foreseen ... The nature of the threat is of importance in considering ... the question whether V's conduct was proportionate to the threat, that is to say that it was within the ambit of reasonableness and not so daft as to make it his own voluntary act which amounted to a *novus actus interveniens* and consequently broke the chain of causation.'

CASE EXAMPLE

Williams and Davis [1992] 2 All ER 183

D and E had given a lift to a hitchhiker, V. After some five miles, V opened a rear door and jumped out to his death. The Crown alleged that V had leaped out to escape being robbed. The defendants were convicted of robbery and manslaughter. The Court of Appeal quashed the latter convictions because of a lack of any direction on the question of causation. The jury should have been asked whether V's reaction in jumping from the moving car was 'within the range of responses' which might be expected from a victim placed in the situation in which V was. The jury should also have been told to bear in mind the fact that 'in the agony of the moment he may act without thought and deliberation'.

The accused must take the victim as they find them

D cannot complain if V is particularly susceptible to physical injury, e.g. haemophilia causing death, or brittle bones leading to worse injuries. In *Martin* (1832) 5 C & P 128, Parke J said: 'It is said that [V] was in a bad state of health; but that is perfectly immaterial, as, if [D] was so unfortunate as to accelerate her death, he must answer for it.' It was accepted in

Towers (1874) 12 Cox CC 692 that, because children are particularly susceptible to fright and shock, D may frighten a child to death. D violently assaulted a young girl who was holding V, a four-month-old baby, in her arms. The girl screamed, frightening V so much that it cried until its face turned black. V died a month later and D was convicted of manslaughter. The implication of this ruling was that it would not be possible to frighten an adult to death. However, this implication was rejected in *Hayward* (1908) 21 Cox CC 692.

CASE EXAMPLE

Hayward (1908) 21 Cox CC 692

D, in a state of 'violent excitement', was heard to say that he was going to give 'his wife something' when she returned home. When she did so, an argument ensued and D chased her from the house using violent threats. She collapsed in the road and died. Medical evidence was such that she was suffering from an abnormal condition that might be exacerbated by any combination of physical exertion with strong emotion or fright. The trial judge directed the jury that proof of death from fright alone, caused by some illegal conduct such as the threats of violence, would suffice.

The principle that D must take their victim as they find them is not confined to pre-existing physical or physiological conditions. In *Blaue* [1975] 3 All ER 446, it was extended to religious beliefs. Lawton LJ said:

JUDGMENT

'It has long been the policy of the law that those who use violence on other people must take their victim as they find them. This in our judgment means the whole man, not just the physical man. It does not lie in the mouth of the assailant to say that the victim's religious beliefs which inhibited him from accepting certain kinds of treatment were unreasonable. The question for decision is what caused her death. The answer is the stab wound. The fact that the victim refused to stop this end coming about did not break the causal connection between the act and death.'

CASE EXAMPLE

Blaue [1975] 3 All ER 446

D had approached his female victim, V, and asked for sex. When she refused he produced a knife and stabbed her four times, one wound penetrating a lung. She was admitted to hospital and told that a blood transfusion was necessary to save her life. As she was a Jehovah's Witness (by whom blood transfusions are regarded as contrary to the teachings of the Bible), she refused and died within a few hours of internal bleeding. Medical evidence indicated she would have survived had she accepted the transfusion. D was charged with murder, but was convicted of manslaughter (the jury having accepted his plea of diminished responsibility: see Chapter 10). On appeal against that conviction, he argued that her refusal was unreasonable and broke the chain of causation. This was rejected.

Question

Suppose V had been stabbed in a remote place and had died before medical assistance could reach her. Then D's liability would certainly have been manslaughter. Why should D be allowed to escape a manslaughter conviction on the ground that V declined medical assistance?

Actions of the victim: self-neglect

If V mistreats or neglects to treat his injuries, this will not break the chain of causation. In a very early case, *Wall* (1802) 28 State Tr 51, D, the governor of a British colony, was convicted of the murder of V, a soldier whom he had sentenced to an illegal flogging of 800 lashes, even though V had aggravated the injuries by drinking spirits in hospital. MacDonald LCB said that D was 'not at liberty to put another into such perilous circumstances as these, and to make it depend upon [V's] own prudence, knowledge, skill or experience', whether he escaped liability or not. In a slightly later example, *Holland* (1841) 2 Mood & R 351, D cut V on the finger with a piece of metal. The wound became infected, but V ignored medical advice that he should have the finger amputated or risk death. The wound caused lockjaw, and although the finger was then amputated, V died. The trial judge directed the jury that it made no difference whether the wound was instantly mortal, or became so by reason of V not seeking medical help. The jury convicted. Although medical science has advanced hugely since the early nineteenth century, it is still no answer to a homicide charge that V refuses treatment. D must accept that V may be irrational, stupid or afraid of hospitals. *Holland* was in fact followed in *Blaue* in the 1970s and the principles can be seen in use in a more recent case, *Dear* [1996] Crim LR 595.

CASE EXAMPLE

Dear [1996] Crim LR 595

D had slashed at V several times with a Stanley knife, severing an artery. V died from blood loss two days later. At his trial for murder, D pleaded provocation, claiming that he had only just discovered that V had been sexually interfering with his (D's) 12-year-old daughter. (See Chapter 10 for discussion of provocation as a defence to murder.) An alternative defence was that the chain of causation had been broken in that V had committed suicide by either (a) deliberately reopening the wounds, or (b) the wounds having reopened themselves, from failing to take steps to staunch the blood flow. The judge directed the jury that they were entitled to find D guilty of murder if V's wounds remained an 'operating' and 'substantial' cause of death. The jury convicted.

Medical treatment

A number of cases have arisen where doctors have been accused of causing death. The cases divide into two types:

- Where doctors are treating patients with naturally occurring diseases, and administer drugs to alleviate pain (palliative care). If a side effect of this treatment is to accelerate death, should the doctor face liability for homicide (murder or manslaughter, depending on the doctor's *mens rea*)?
- Where doctors are treating patients who have been rushed in for emergency surgery having (typically) been stabbed or shot by D. The treatment is imperfect and the patient dies. Should the doctor face liability for the death? Should the doctor's mistreatment relieve D of liability for the death?

Where doctors are providing patients with palliative care

Adams [1957] Crim LR 365 was a case involving a doctor who, in treating a terminally ill patient, may have contributed to her death through the administration of drugs. On trial for murder, the trial judge directed the jury that it did not matter that the victim's death was inevitable, nor that her days were numbered. He said, 'If her life were cut short by weeks or months it was just as much murder as if it was cut short by years.' However, he went on to say:

JUDGMENT

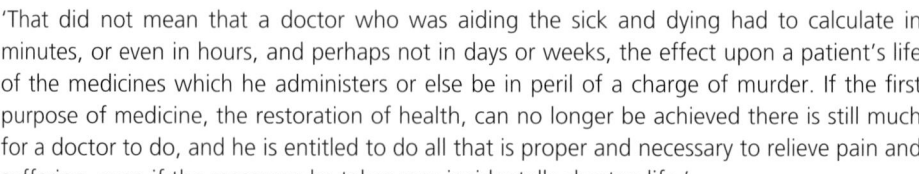

'That did not mean that a doctor who was aiding the sick and dying had to calculate in minutes, or even in hours, and perhaps not in days or weeks, the effect upon a patient's life of the medicines which he administers or else be in peril of a charge of murder. If the first purpose of medicine, the restoration of health, can no longer be achieved there is still much for a doctor to do, and he is entitled to do all that is proper and necessary to relieve pain and suffering, even if the measures he takes may incidentally shorten life.'

Where doctors provide medical mistreatment

Two questions were posed above. The first question, whether doctors who inadvertently (as opposed to deliberately) mistreat patients during surgery resulting in death may themselves face liability for homicide, will be dealt with in Chapter 10, specifically the section on gross negligence manslaughter (see in particular the case of *Adomako*). The answer to the second question, whether medical mistreatment provided to the victims of gunshots or stab wounds may relieve the original perpetrator of liability, is, generally speaking, no. In *Smith* (*Thomas*) [1959] 2 QB 35, Lord Parker CJ said:

JUDGMENT

'If at the time of death the original wound is still an operating cause and a substantial cause, then the death can properly be said to be the result of the wound, albeit that some other cause of death is also operating. Only if it can be said that the original wounding is merely the setting in which another cause operates can it be said that the death did not result from the wound. Putting it another way, only if the second cause is so overwhelming as to make the original wound merely part of the history can it be said that the death does not flow from the wound.'

CASE EXAMPLE

Smith (Thomas) [1959] 2 QB 35

D was a British soldier. During the course of a barrack-room fight he stabbed V, another soldier, twice with a bayonet. One of the wounds had pierced a lung. V eventually died of a haemorrhage (internal bleeding) but, before his death, the following had occurred: (a) another soldier carried V to the medical station and dropped him – twice; (b) the medics, who were under pressure, failed to realise that V had suffered serious injuries because D had been stabbed in the back; (c) the medics gave him treatment which, in light of this, was described as 'thoroughly bad and might well have affected [V's] chances of recovery'. D was convicted of murder at a court-martial, and the Court-Martial Appeal Court dismissed his appeal.

In *Cheshire* [1991] 3 All ER 670, Beldam LJ proposed a new test, asking not whether the wound was still 'operating' but rather whether D's act or omission could still be said to have 'contributed significantly' to V's death. Approaching the same question from the opposite direction, he indicated that only if the medical treatment could be classed as 'independent' of D's original act, would D escape liability. This new test is very important as it allows the jury to impose liability on D even in cases where V survives, perhaps on a life-support machine, for a long enough time after the original assault such that the gunshot wounds or stab wounds have healed. Beldam LJ said:

JUDGMENT

'[D] need not be the sole cause or even the main cause of death, it being sufficient that his acts contributed significantly to that result. Even though negligence in the treatment of [V] was the immediate cause of his death, the jury should not regard it as excluding the responsibility of [D] unless the negligent treatment was so independent of [D's] acts, and in itself so potent in causing death, that they regard the contribution made by [D's] acts as insignificant.'

Beldam LJ also suggested that it was only in the most extraordinary and unusual case that medical treatment would break the chain of causation. He said that 'Treatment which falls short of the standard expected of the competent medical practitioner is unfortunately only too frequent in human experience for it to be considered abnormal in the sense of extraordinary.'

CASE EXAMPLE

Cheshire [1991] 3 All ER 670

On 9 December, D and V got into an argument which culminated in D shooting V twice with a handgun, in the thigh and stomach. The second wound was the more serious and required an extensive bowel resection in hospital. Respiratory problems then ensued, necessitating a tracheotomy. By 8 February, however, V was recovering, although he began to complain of breathing difficulties. Various doctors who saw him around this time thought that his respiratory problems were caused by 'anxiety'. In fact his condition deteriorated rapidly on the night of 14 February and he died of cardio-respiratory arrest, as a result of his windpipe becoming narrow and eventually obstructed, a rare but not unknown side effect of the tracheotomy. By this time, the gunshot injuries had healed to the point where they were no longer life-threatening. D was convicted of murder, and the Court of Appeal upheld the conviction.

Beldam LJ's test in *Cheshire* has been followed since. In *Mellor* [1996] 2 Cr App R 245, V, a 71-year-old man, was attacked by a gang including D. V was taken to hospital suffering facial bruising and complaining of chest pain and a pain in his right shoulder. He died in hospital two days later. D tried to avoid liability by claiming the hospital failed to give V sufficient oxygen in time, as a result of which V had developed bronchopneumonia (the medical cause of death). However, the Court of Appeal upheld D's conviction of manslaughter. Schiemann LJ noted that, where the victim of a violent assault does not die immediately, 'supervening events' are quite likely to occur which may have some causative effect leading to the victim's death. He listed some examples: a delay in the arrival of the ambulance; a delay in resuscitation; V's reaction to medical or surgical treatment; and the quality of medical, surgical and nursing care. In all cases, however, Schiemann LJ said that it was a question for the jury to decide, bearing in mind the gravity of the 'supervening event', whether the injuries inflicted by the defendant remained a 'significant' cause of death. The 'operating' and 'substantial' factor test, first devised in *Smith* in the 1950s, has never been overruled, so it would not be a misdirection for a judge in an appropriate case to refer to it. Indeed in *Malcherek, Steel* [1981] 2 All ER 422, the Court of Appeal used the same words. However, it seems that, following the more recent *Cheshire* and *Mellor*, trial judges today are more likely to ask juries to consider whether the original injuries inflicted by D have made a 'significant' contribution to V's death. Finally, 'significant' means 'more than minimal' (Hughes (2013)).

The cases above all emphasise that it is ultimately a question for the jury to decide. They allow for the possibility that medical mistreatment could be so extreme as to relieve D from liability for V's death. In *Jordan* (1956) 40 Cr App R 152, this possibility duly occurred. The case remains unique, but that is not to imply that it is wrongly decided. Every rule has an exception and, if the rule is that generally speaking hospital mistreatment does not absolve D of liability, this is the exception to it. Indeed, in *Blaue*, Lawton LJ distinguished *Jordan* on the ground that it was 'a case decided on its own special facts' and in *Malcherek, Steel*, which will be discussed below, the Court of Appeal described *Jordan* as 'a very exceptional case'. You will note that neither court stated that *Jordan* was wrongly decided.

CASE EXAMPLE

Jordan (1956) 40 Cr App R 152

D had stabbed V with a knife, the wound penetrating the intestine in two places. V was rushed to hospital where the wound was stitched. Eight days later, however, he died, and D was convicted of murder. On appeal, fresh evidence was adduced which showed that, at the time of V's death, the wound had mainly healed. Doctors had given V a drug called terramycin to prevent infection, but he had shown intolerance to a previous injection. Defence experts described this treatment as 'palpably wrong'. Furthermore, large quantities of liquid had been administered intravenously, which had caused V's lungs to become waterlogged. This was also described as 'wrong' by the defence doctors. As a result of the waterlogging, V developed pulmonary oedema which led inevitably to bronchopneumonia, which was the medical cause of death. The Court of Criminal Appeal quashed D's conviction: if the jury had heard this evidence, they 'would have felt precluded from saying that they were satisfied that death was caused by the stab wound'.

Life-support machines

A particular problem concerns victims of violence who have been placed on life-support machines. If there is no prospect of recovery, and the doctors switch off the machinery, how (if at all) does this affect D's responsibility? In *Malcherek, Steel*, it was argued on appeal that in just such a case it was the doctors who had caused death. The Court of Appeal rejected the argument, describing it as 'bizarre'. Lord Lane CJ said:

JUDGMENT

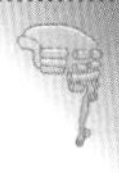

'Where a medical practitioner adopting methods which are generally accepted comes *bona fide* to the conclusion that the patient is for practical purposes dead, and that such vital functions as exist – for example, circulation – are being maintained solely by mechanical means, and therefore discontinues treatment, that does not prevent the person who inflicted the initial injury from being responsible.'

CASE EXAMPLE

Malcherek [1981] 2 All ER 422

On 26 March, Malcherek stabbed his estranged wife, C, nine times. She was admitted to hospital, where over one-and-a-half litres of blood were removed from her abdominal cavity. She seemed to be recovering, but on 1 April she suffered a pulmonary embolism. Her condition deteriorated, and her heart stopped. During open-heart surgery a massive blood clot was removed, at which point her heart restarted. However, 30 minutes had elapsed and severe brain damage had been caused, from which she never recovered. The doctors carried out five of the six tests recommended by the Royal College for establishing brain death (omitting the 'gag reflex' test), and on the strength of this switched off the life support. She was certified dead on 5 April.

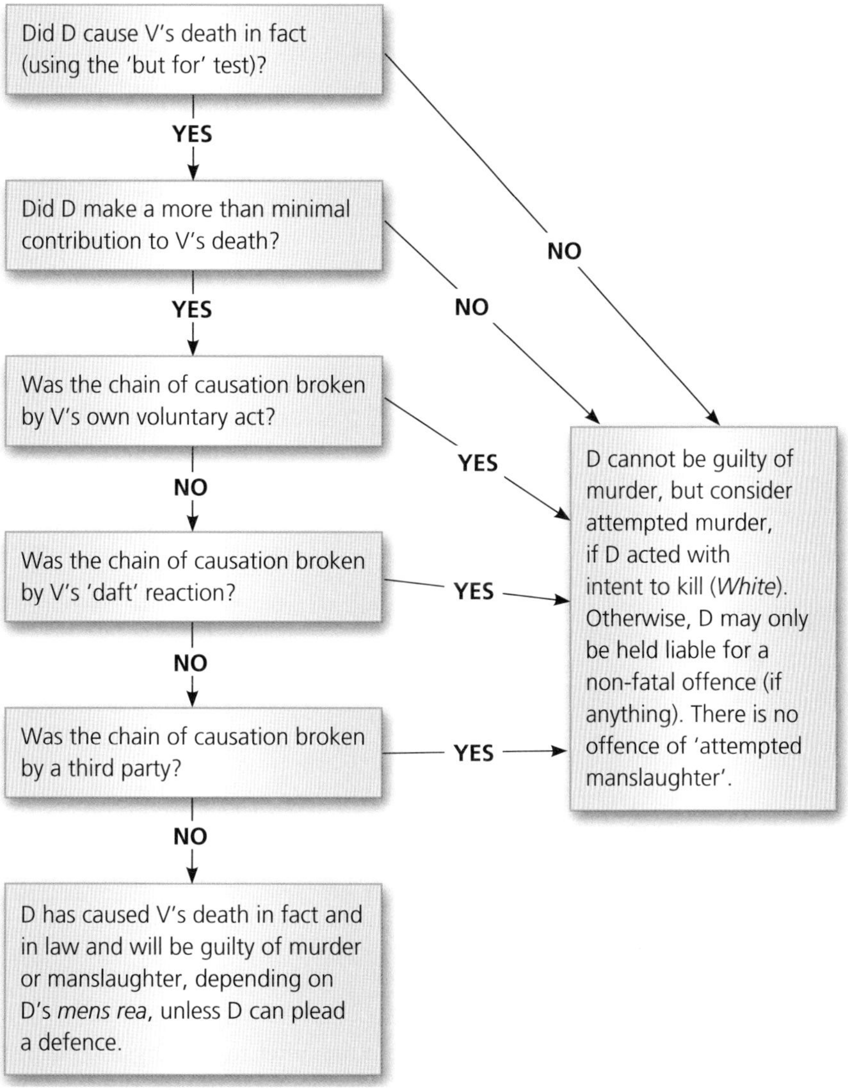

Did D cause V's death in fact (using the 'but for' test)?

YES ↓ / NO → D cannot be guilty of murder...

Did D make a more than minimal contribution to V's death?

YES ↓ / NO → D cannot be guilty of murder...

Was the chain of causation broken by V's own voluntary act?

NO ↓ / YES → D cannot be guilty of murder...

Was the chain of causation broken by V's 'daft' reaction?

NO ↓ / YES → D cannot be guilty of murder...

Was the chain of causation broken by a third party?

NO ↓ / YES → D cannot be guilty of murder...

D has caused V's death in fact and in law and will be guilty of murder or manslaughter, depending on D's *mens rea*, unless D can plead a defence.

D cannot be guilty of murder, but consider attempted murder, if D acted with intent to kill (*White*). Otherwise, D may only be held liable for a non-fatal offence (if anything). There is no offence of 'attempted manslaughter'.

Figure 2.2 Causation.

CASE EXAMPLE

Steel [1981] 2 All ER 422

On 10 October, Steel attacked W, a random stranger, in the street. He battered her about the head with a large stone, causing severe head injuries, and left her for dead. She was rushed to hospital and placed on life support immediately. However, she never recovered consciousness, and the system was withdrawn two days later after four of the six Royal College tests proved negative (the 'corneal reflex', where the eyeball is touched with cotton wool, and the 'vestibulo-ocular', where ice-cold water is dripped into the ear, tests were omitted). She was certified dead on 12 October.

Thus, both victims had life-support equipment switched off after some, but not all, of the Royal College tests indicated brain death. With the equipment switched off, the victims ceased breathing, their hearts stopped and 'conventional' death, that is, cessation of heartbeat, occurred. Malcherek and Steel were both convicted of murder, at Winchester and Leeds Crown Courts respectively. The Court of Appeal, which heard both cases together, rejected both appeals. The same principles apply if V is not brain dead but is in a persistent vegetative state (PVS). In *Airedale NHS Trust v Bland* (1993) (discussed above), Lord Goff said that in discontinuing treatment a doctor was 'simply allowing the patient to die in the sense that he [is] desisting from taking a step which might prevent his patient from dying as a result of his pre-existing condition'.

ACTIVITY

1. Consider whether the 'chain of causation' would be broken in the following example: V had been taken to hospital having been poisoned by D, his wife. At the hospital V is treated by Dr Young, an inexperienced doctor who is also very tired having spent the previous 36 hours on duty. Dr Young prescribes an antidote for the poison but, in his tired and confused state, tells the nurse to administer a dose ten times stronger than required. V suffers a massive heart attack and dies.
2. Consider the liability of D in this scenario:

   D, a middle-aged man, has been prescribed powerful painkillers in tablet form for chronic back pain. One day he discovers his teenage daughter, V, and her friend, W, slumped, unconscious, on V's bedroom floor. It is obvious that the girls have taken D's tablets from the medicine cabinet in the bathroom as the bottle is lying on the bedroom floor, empty. D panics because his doctor had warned him to keep the tablets out of the reach of any children in the house. He goes to the living room to fix himself a large drink to calm his nerves. Eventually he calls for an ambulance but by the time it arrives V has lapsed further into unconscious and dies in the ambulance. W survives but is left severely brain-damaged. D has now been charged with the manslaughter of V and with causing grievous bodily harm to W. The prosecution's case is that both girls might have survived and made full recoveries had D acted immediately on discovering them in the bedroom.

SUMMARY

- The *actus reus* elements of a crime refer to the physical elements: conduct, circumstances and consequences. These elements usually differ from one crime to another: the *actus reus* of murder is very different from the *actus reus* of theft. But some different crimes have the same *actus reus* – for example, murder and involuntary manslaughter. What distinguishes these crimes is their different *mens rea* elements (see Chapter 3).
- In some situations the conduct element can be satisfied by D's failure to act, an omission. This usually requires evidence that D was under a duty to act. There is no general duty to act in English law (although some commentators argue that there should be). Instead, there are specific duty situations, including duties imposed by contract (*Pittwood*), through a relationship (*Gibbins and Proctor*), through the voluntary assumption of a duty (*Stone and Dobinson*) and through the creation of a dangerous situation (the *Miller* principle). There are also a number of statutory offences of failing to act, plus one common law offence (*Dytham*).
- In 'result' crimes, a consequence must be proven. Thus, in murder and manslaughter it must be proven that D 'caused' V's death. D must be both the factual and legal cause; factual causation alone is not enough for liability (*Hughes*). Factual causation is satisfied using the 'but for' test (*White*). Legal causation looks for an

unbroken 'chain of causation'. In law, D need not be the sole, or even the main, cause of death provided he makes a more than minimal contribution to the result (*Pagett*, *Hughes*). Generally speaking, medical negligence does not break the chain provided D's acts were still the 'operating' cause (*Smith*). Certain events can break the chain of causation, however, including V's own voluntary act (*Kennedy*), and medical negligence which is both 'independent' and 'potent' (*Cheshire*, *Mellor*). Reasonably foreseeable events, either by V or a third party, will not break the chain. Only a 'daft' reaction by V in trying to escape from D will break the chain (*Roberts*).

SAMPLE ESSAY QUESTION

Critically consider the extent to which omitting to act can lead to liability for a criminal offence.

Give a brief outline of the law:

- General position is that criminal liability requires a positive act
- Note that some offences cannot be committed by omission (*Ahmad* (1987))
- Imposition of liability for failing to act is the exception to the general rule, but there are some statutory offences that can be committed by omission
- There is also one common law offence – misconduct of an officer of justice (*Dytham* (1979))
- Otherwise a duty to act must be established

Identify examples of statutory offences, e.g.

- Failing to provide a breath test (Road Traffic Act 1988)
- Failing to report terrorist activity (Terrorism Act 2000)
- Allowing the death of a child or vulnerable adult (Domestic Violence Crimes and Victims Act 2004)

Discuss situations when a 'duty to act' might exist, e.g.

- Contract (e.g. *Pittwood* (1902))
- Relationship (e.g. *Gibbins & Proctor* (1919); *Smith* (1979))
- Doctors (e.g. *Adomako* (1993); *Misra* (2004))
- Assumption of responsibility (e.g. *Instan* (1893); *Stone and Dobinson* (1977))
- Creation of danger (e.g. *Miller* (1983); *Evans* (2009))

Discuss areas of doubt/uncertainty, e.g.

- Who owes a relationship duty – parents and spouses only?
- When does parental duty cease?
- How/when can an assumed duty be discharged?

Discuss whether there should be a 'general' duty to act:

- Such a duty does exist in, e.g. France
- Might encourage people to help other people
- Problems if someone underestimates or overestimates the danger involved in a rescue
- Argument that rescues should be left to trained professionals
- Problem in identifying a defendant if dozens of people fail to act
- Problems in limiting the scope of liability – minimum/ maximum age limits, exemptions for physical disability, etc.

Conclude

SAMPLE ESSAY QUESTION

Consider whether the legal principles relating to whether the chain of causation has been broken are satisfactory.

Give a brief outline of the role of causation:

- Essential element in 'result' crimes – those requiring proof of a consequence, such as murder, manslaughter, some non-fatals
- Causation comes in two forms: factual and legal
- Both must be established for defendant to be held liable (*Hughes* (2013))
- Legal causation requires an unbroken 'chain of causation'

Explain factual causation:

- Defendant must have caused consequence in fact – tested using the 'but for' test
- Leading case is *White* (1910)

Explain principles of legal causation:

- Defendant must take victim as he finds her (the thin skull rule) (*Blaue* (1975))
- Defendant need not be the sole, or even the main cause, provided he makes a significant contribution (*Pagett* (1984))
- Defendant will be liable if he was the 'operating' and 'substantial' cause even if other causes are also operating (*Smith* (1959))
- Medical negligence will only break the chain if it is 'independent' and 'potent' (*Cheshire* (1991))
- Victim's escape attempt will only break the chain if it is so 'daft' as to be unforeseeable (*Roberts* (1972); *Marjoram* (2000))

Give examples of situations of breaks in the chain:

- Victim's own voluntary act (*Kennedy* (2007))
- 'Palpably wrong' medical treatment (*Jordan* (1956))

Analyse the above principles/cases, e.g.

- The courts' reluctance to allow defendants to escape liability in cases like *Roberts*, *Blaue*, *Pagett* and *Cheshire* is based on a policy of protecting the public from violent crime
- Compare/contrast the outcome in *Kennedy* with that in *Cato* (1976) and the Scottish case of *MacAngus* and *Kane* (2009)

Conclude

Further reading

Books

Ormerod, D, *Smith and Hogan Criminal Law* (13th edn, Oxford University Press, 2011), Chapter 4.

Articles

Beynon, H, 'Causation, omissions and complicity' [1987] Crim LR 539.

Cherkassky, L, '*Kennedy* and unlawful act manslaughter: an unorthodox application of the doctrine of causation' (2008) 72 JoCL 387.

Elliott, D W, 'Frightening a person into injuring himself' [1974] Crim LR 15.

Norrie, A, 'A critique of criminal causation' (1991) 54 MLR 685.

Tur, R, 'legislative technique and human rights: the sad case of assisted suicide' [2003] Crim LR 3.

Williams, G, 'Criminal omissions: the conventional view' (1991) 107 LQR 86.

Williams, G, 'Finis for *novus actus*?' (1989) 48 CLJ 391.

3

Mens rea

AIMS AND OBJECTIVES

After reading this chapter you should be able to:

- Understand the law of intention, both direct and oblique
- Understand the law of recklessness
- Understand the principles of transferred malice and coincidence
- Analyse critically the law on intention and recklessness

3.1 The mental element

It was noted at the start of the previous chapter that the physical element alone is, generally speaking, not enough to constitute criminal liability. The presence of some mental element is usually required. This allows the courts to impose punishment on those who acted with, at least, some awareness of what they were doing. As a general rule, courts in England are reluctant to apportion blame and impose punishment on those who acted inadvertently, that is, without awareness of the conduct, circumstances and consequence elements that make up the *actus reus*. As with the physical elements discussed in Chapter 2, a different mental element is required for each crime. Some criminal offences require one mental element, some require two, either in addition to each other or as alternative states. Some examples are as follows.

- In murder the *mens rea* is intention only (see Chapter 10).
- In theft one mental element is intention; however, there is an additional element of dishonesty.
- In criminal damage and most non-fatal offences against the person, such as assault and battery, the *mens rea* is intention or recklessness (see Chapters 11 and 16).
- In one form of manslaughter, the mental element is recklessness only, while in a different form of manslaughter, the mental element is 'gross negligence' (see Chapter 10).

3.2 Intention

As noted above, in many offences, the *mens rea* required is an 'intention'. However, intention does not exist as an abstract concept: there must be proof of an intention to cause a particular result. The following examples illustrate this.

- Murder requires as its mental element intention to kill or cause grievous bodily harm (see Chapter 10).
- The criminal offence found in s 18 of the Offences Against the Person Act (OAPA) 1861 requires as its mental element an intention to cause grievous bodily harm (see Chapter 11).
- In theft, the mental element is an intention permanently to deprive another person of their property, plus dishonesty (see Chapter 13).

direct intent
Mental or fault element involving aim, purpose or desire

oblique intent
Where D has foreseen a consequence as virtually certain

However, whichever crime is charged, the meaning of 'intent' is the same. In criminal law, there are two types of intent:

- **Direct intent** – this refers to someone's aim, purpose or desire.
- Indirect or **oblique intent** – this is much harder to define. The question whether D intends a consequence of his actions when he believes that it is *virtually certain*, or *very probable*, is one that has greatly troubled English courts for the last 30 years. The House of Lords has dealt with the problem on five occasions, all murder cases, the most recent in 1998.

3.2.1 Direct intention

As indicated above, **direct intention** refers to the situation when D desires an outcome. For example:

- D is a hired professional killer (an example is *Calhaem* [1985] 1 QB 808; see Chapter 5) who aims a loaded gun at V's heart and pulls the trigger. Clearly D has direct intent to kill. The fact that D's desire is motivated by cash is irrelevant: D still wanted to kill V.
- D is a sadistic psychopath who enjoys torturing and killing people. He strangles V to death and then cuts up the body (as in *Byrne* [1960] 2 QB 396; see Chapter 10). Clearly D again has direct intent to kill. The fact that D's desire is motivated by his abnormal mental condition is irrelevant to the question of intent: D still wanted to kill V.

An example of a situation where D does not desire a consequence but may still be said to have intended it might be where D sees a child trapped in a locked car, towards which a runaway lorry is heading at speed. D grabs a brick and smashes the windscreen to rescue the child. D's desire here was to save the child but in doing so he had to cause criminal damage to the car (see Chapter 16). If D were prosecuted for the offence of intentional criminal damage to the windscreen, it seems that the prosecution could establish the elements of the offence. (It is extremely unlikely that the Crown Prosecution Service would prosecute on these facts; even if they did, D would almost certainly be found not guilty by pleading duress of circumstances, see Chapter 8.)

3.2.2 Oblique intention

As indicated above, indirect or oblique intention occurs where D does not necessarily desire an outcome but realises that it is almost (but not quite) inevitable. However, this scenario invites problems. What *degree of probability* is required before an undesired consequence, but one which D has foreseen, can be said to have been intended? Some would argue none – that once one steps away from foresight of something as *100 per cent certain to happen*, then one is dealing with *risk*, and that means *recklessness*, not intent. Others would argue that very high probability would suffice. A good place to start an examination of 'intent' is the Criminal Justice Act 1967, which states that:

SECTION

'8 A court or jury in determining whether a person has committed an offence (a) shall not be bound in law to infer that he intended or foresaw a result of his actions by reason only of its being a natural and probable consequence of those actions; but (b) shall decide whether he did intend or foresee that result by reference to all the evidence, drawing such inferences from the facts as appear proper in the circumstances.'

This provision was passed in order to reverse the decision of the House of Lords in *DPP v Smith* [1961] AC 290. The Law Lords had declared that there was an irrebuttable presumption of law that a person foresaw and intended the 'natural consequences' of his acts. Proof that D did an act, the natural consequence of which was death, was proof that D intended to kill. Further, the test of what was a natural consequence was purely objective: 'not what [D] contemplated, but what the ordinary reasonable man would in all the circumstances of the case have contemplated as the natural and probable result'. None of this is now good law. The leading case is now that of *Woollin* [1998] UKHL 28; [1998] 3 WLR 382. Lord Steyn (with whom the other members of the House of Lords agreed) laid down a model direction for trial judges to use in cases where D's intention is unclear as follows:

JUDGMENT

'Where the charge is murder . . . the jury should be directed that they are not entitled [to find] the necessary intention, unless they feel sure that death or serious bodily harm was a virtual certainty (barring some unforeseen intervention) as a result of [D]'s actions and that [D] appreciated that such was the case.'

CASE EXAMPLE

Woollin [1998] UKHL 28; [1998] 3 WLR 382

D had killed his three-month-old son by throwing him against a wall, fracturing his skull. D did not deny doing this, but claimed that it was not intended. He claimed that he had picked the child up after he began to choke and shaken him. Then, in a fit of rage or frustration, he had thrown him with some considerable force towards a pram four or five feet away. The trial judge directed the jury that they might infer intention if satisfied that when D threw the child, he had appreciated that there was a 'substantial risk' that he would cause serious harm to the child. D was convicted of murder and appealed on the basis that the phrase 'substantial risk' was a test of recklessness, not of intent, and that the judge should have used 'virtual certainty'. The Court of Appeal dismissed the appeal but the House of Lords unanimously reversed that court's decision, quashed D's murder conviction and substituted one of manslaughter.

You will note that in the 1967 Act there is a verb, 'to infer'. This word was faithfully used by trial judges and the appeal courts until *Woollin*. But in that case the Law Lords agreed that juries would more easily understand the verb 'to find'. It appears that the Law

Lords simply intended to substitute one word for another, although academics argue that the words have slightly different meanings. Prior to *Woollin*, the most oft-quoted statement of the law of intent was found in *Nedrick* [1986] 3 All ER 1. This was a Court of Appeal case, in which Lord Lane CJ attempted to, as he put it, 'crystallise' the various speeches made in the House of Lords in two cases from the 1980s: *Moloney* [1985] AC 905 and *Hancock and Shankland* [1986] AC 455. Lord Lane stated:

JUDGMENT

'It may be advisable first of all to explain to the jury that a man may intend to achieve a certain result whilst at the same time not desiring it to come about . . . if the jury are satisfied that at the material time [D] recognised that death or serious harm would be virtually certain (barring some unforeseen intervention) to result from his voluntary act, then that is a fact from which they may find it easy to infer that he intended to kill or do serious bodily harm, even though he may not have had any desire to achieve that result. Where a man realises that it is for all practical purposes inevitable that his actions will result in death or serious harm, the inference may be irresistible that he intended that result, however little he may have desired or wished it to happen. The decision is one for the jury to be reached on a consideration of all the evidence.'

Directions on intention not always necessary

Most of the cases mentioned above reached the appeal courts because the trial judge unnecessarily confused the issue by raising indirect intent in the first place. When this happens it invites an appeal on the basis that the jury have been unnecessarily confused. As Lord Bridge put it in *Moloney*:

JUDGMENT

'The golden rule should be that . . . the judge should avoid any elaboration or paraphrase of what is meant by intent, and leave it to the jury's good sense to decide whether the accused acted with the necessary intent, unless the judge is convinced that, on the facts and having regard to the way that case has been presented . . . some further explanation or elaboration is strictly necessary to avoid misunderstanding.'

The case of *Fallon* [1994] Crim LR 519 provides a perfect example. D was charged with attempted murder (this requires proof of an intent to kill). He had shot a police officer in the leg. The prosecution alleged that he intended to kill; D argued that the gun had gone off accidentally when the officer tried to grab the gun, which D was trying to hand over. The trial judge directed the jury on intent, referring to *Moloney* and *Nedrick* and introducing the concept of virtual certainty. Unsurprisingly, the jury asked for clarification, and the judge gave them further direction, also based on *Nedrick*. After the jury convicted D of murder, the Court of Appeal allowed his appeal (although they instead substituted a conviction under s 18 OAPA 1861, of causing grievous bodily harm with intent to resist arrest). The prosecution accepted that the judge's directions were unnecessary and confusing; he had ignored Lord Bridge's 'golden rule'. The jury simply had to decide whether they believed the prosecution or the defence version of events. If they were sure the prosecution's version was correct, then they should convict (D had direct intent); if they thought the defence might be correct, then acquit (the shooting was an accident, D did not intend to do the officer any harm at all).

In *Wright* [2000] EWCA Crim 28; [2000] Crim LR 928, the Court of Appeal rejected D's appeal against a murder conviction based on the ground that the judge had not directed the jury according to *Nedrick* and *Woollin*. At the time of the killing, D and V were sharing a prison cell (D was on remand). One morning V was found lying on the cell floor, unconscious and with a piece of bed sheet tied round his neck. He died a week later. D denied murder, claiming that, while he (D) was asleep, V had hanged himself. Upholding the murder conviction, Beldam LJ said that in simply giving 'the straightforward direction on intention' – that is, by just directing the jury to consider direct intent – the judge was 'directing the jury to the real question they had to determine and steering them away from the chameleon-like concepts of purpose, foresight of consequence and awareness of risk'. This must be correct. The prosecution case was that D wanted to kill V – that is, he had direct intent; the defence case was that D had nothing to do with V's death at all. There was no need for any direction based on oblique intent; indeed, had the jury been directed to consider D's foresight of consequences it would only have served to have distracted them from the key question: did they believe the prosecution's version of the facts, or the defence's version?

Foresight is not intention but evidence of intention

All the courts agree on one thing: foresight of a consequence, even of a virtually certain consequence, is not intent, but is simply evidence from which intention may be found. It will therefore be a misdirection for the judge to equate foresight with intention. The jury must be left to 'find' intent from foresight. For example, in *Scalley* [1995] Crim LR 504, D was convicted of murder but on appeal his conviction was reduced to manslaughter. The problem was that the judge had directed the jury that if they found that D had foreseen death or serious injury as virtually certain, then he had intended it. However, this is somewhat confusing. If the jury are agreed that D foresaw a consequence as virtually certain, then they are entitled to 'find' that D intended that consequence. Equally, they are not compelled to do so. So when should a jury 'find' intention based on evidence that D foresaw a virtually certain consequence (and convict D), and when should they not (and acquit D)? The courts have failed to give any clues as to when, or how, juries are to take this step. It has been said that there is a 'logical gap' between foresight and intention (G Williams, 'Oblique intention' (1987) 46 CLJ 417).

Nevertheless, the proposition that foresight of a consequence is not intention but evidence of it was confirmed in *Matthews and Alleyne* [2003] EWCA Crim 192; [2003] 2 Cr App R 461.

CASE EXAMPLE

Matthews and Alleyne [2003] EWCA Crim 192; [2003] 2 Cr App R 461

D and E had pushed V from a bridge over the River Ouse (despite the fact he had told them he could not swim) where he fell about 25 feet and drowned. D and E were convicted of murder (among other offences including robbery and kidnapping) after the trial judge told the jury that if 'drowning was a virtual certainty and [D and E] appreciated that . . . they must have had the intention of killing him'. D and E appealed on the basis that this direction went beyond what was permitted by *Nedrick/Woollin* and equated foresight with intention. The Court of Appeal rejected the appeal. Although the judge had gone further than he was permitted (and had equated foresight with intention), the court thought that, on the particular facts of the case, if the jury were sure that D and E had appreciated the virtual certainty of V's death when they threw him into the river, it was 'impossible' to see how they could not have drawn the inference that D and E intended V's death.

student mentor tip

'Make sure you know the *actus reus* and *mens rea* inside out as this will always come up in an essay question.'
Adil, Queen Mary University

Criticism

Some academics take the view that intention should be limited to direct intention (desire, aim or purpose). As Finnis has pointed out ('Intention and side-effects' (1993) 109 LQR 329), in ordinary English we would not say that 'someone who hangs curtains knowing that the sunlight will make them fade' intends that they will fade – and yet according to the House of Lords, a jury would be entitled to 'find' that they did intend exactly that. Finnis described the definition of indirect or oblique intent as the 'Pseudo-Masochistic Theory of Intention – for it holds that those who foresee that their actions will have painful effects upon themselves intend those effects.'

Applying the law

Tony celebrates his birthday by drinking five glasses of red wine. He knows from previous, bitter experience that drinking anything more than two or three glasses of red wine will give him a terrible hangover in the morning. According to the *Nedrick/Woollin* definition, does Tony intend to have a terrible hangover?

The *Nedrick/Woollin* test fails to provide a clear distinction between intention and recklessness. How is it possible to distinguish a consequence foreseen as 'virtually certain' (which might be evidence of intent) from one foreseen as 'highly probable' (which would be evidence of recklessness)? There is no obvious cut-off point, and yet this is the dividing line between murder and manslaughter. There are also strong moral justifications for distinguishing D who acts in order to achieve V's death because that is what he wants to happen, and D who has one goal but foresees that V's death is certain to happen, although he desperately hopes it will not.

Reform proposals

In 2006, the Law Commission published a Report entitled *Murder, Manslaughter and Infanticide*, in which it was recommended that the *Woollin* direction on oblique intent should be codified, and that 'intention' should be defined – in full – as follows:

1. A person should be taken to intend a result if he or she acts in order to bring it about.
2. In cases where the judge believes that justice may not be done unless an expanded understanding of intention is given, the jury should be directed as follows: an intention to bring about a result may be found if it is shown that the defendant thought that the result was a virtually certain consequence of his or her action.

The government's response to the Report, published in July 2008, gives no indication that it intends to do anything about this recommendation. It is therefore safe to assume that, for the time being at least, the meaning of oblique intention (or the 'expanded understanding' of it) remains as set out in *Woollin*.

Another option would be to limit intention to D's aim or purpose, i.e. direct intention. This would have the advantage of making the legal definition fit with the word's everyday dictionary meaning. In *Steane* [1947] KB 997, D was charged with doing acts likely to assist the enemy with intent to assist the enemy, contrary to the Defence (General) Regulations 1939. He was a British film actor resident in Germany prior to the Second World War who had been arrested when the war broke out and forced, extremely reluctantly, to broadcast propaganda on German radio. Threats had been made to place his wife and children in a concentration camp if he did not comply. The Court of Criminal Appeal, quashing his conviction on the grounds of lack of intent, adopted a narrow interpretation of that concept, effectively limiting it to aim or purpose.

The American Law Institute's Model Penal Code takes a narrower approach. According to the Code, a person acts intentionally when it is his 'conscious object to engage in conduct of that nature or to cause such a result'. As to the mental state of foresight of virtual certainty, under the Code this forms a special category of *mens rea*, between intention and recklessness, namely knowledge. The Code states that: 'A person acts knowingly with respect to a material element of an offense when ... (ii) if the element involves a result of his conduct, he is aware that it is practically certain that his conduct will cause such a result.'

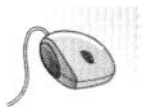

3.3 Recklessness

recklessness
Foresight by D of an unjustifiable risk

Recklessness generally involves D taking an unjustifiable risk of a particular consequence occurring, with awareness of that risk. Recklessness is the *mens rea* state sufficient for many crimes, some very serious, including manslaughter, malicious wounding, inflicting grievous bodily harm and assault occasioning actual bodily harm. The question that has troubled the appeal courts for over 30 years is whether recklessness should be assessed 'subjectively' – that is, by looking at the case from the defendant's perspective – or 'objectively' – that is, looking at the case from the perspective of the reasonable man. It will be seen that the courts have gone on a long, circular journey. After starting with a subjective test, in 1981 an objective test was introduced. For a short time in the early 1980s it seemed that the objective test would replace the subjective test, but the original test began a comeback in the mid-1980s and continued to reassert itself throughout the 1990s. Finally, in 2003, the objective test was banished to the pages of history.

3.3.1 The *Cunningham* test

maliciously
Mental or fault element meaning either intentionally or recklessly

The original case on the definition of recklessness is *Cunningham* [1957] 2 QB 396. Here the court gave us the classic, subjective test for recklessness. The question for the Court of Criminal Appeal was actually what was meant by the word 'maliciously' (in s 23 OAPA 1861; see Chapter 11). The judge had directed the jury that it meant 'wickedly'. The Court of Criminal Appeal did not agree. In quashing the conviction, the court approved a definition given by Professor Kenny in 1902:

QUOTATION

'In any statutory definition of a crime, "malice" must be taken not in the old vague sense of wickedness in general but as requiring either (i) an actual intention to do the particular kind of harm that in fact was done or (ii) recklessness as to whether such harm should occur or not (i.e. the accused has foreseen that the particular kind of harm might be done, and yet has gone on to take the risk of it).'

CASE EXAMPLE

Cunningham [1957] 2 QB 396

D ripped a gas meter from the cellar wall of a house in Bradford, in order to steal the money inside. He left a ruptured pipe, leaking gas, which seeped through into the neighbouring house, where V (actually the mother of D's fiancee) inhaled it. He was charged with maliciously administering a noxious substance so as to endanger life, contrary to s 23 OAPA 1861, and convicted. The crux of the matter was whether D had foreseen the risk, in this case, of someone inhaling the gas.

This definition was subsequently applied throughout the OAPA 1861 (for example *Venna* [1976] QB 421, a case of assault occasioning actual bodily harm contrary to s 47) and to other statutes, such as the Malicious Damage Act 1861 (MDA), whenever the word 'malicious' was used. In 1969, the Law Commission was working on proposals to reform the law of property damage. In its final *Report on Criminal Damage*, it recommended the replacement of the MDA with what became the Criminal Damage Act 1971 (CDA). The Law Commission considered that the mental element, as stated in *Cunningham*, was properly defined, but that for simplicity and clarity the word 'maliciously' should be replaced with 'intentionally or recklessly'. Unfortunately, the Act does not define 'reckless' anywhere; it is left to the courts to interpret. However, after 1971 the courts continued to define 'recklessness' by referring to D's awareness of the consequences of his actions. In *Stephenson* [1979] QB 695, for example, Lane LJ said:

JUDGMENT

'A man is reckless when he carries out the deliberate act appreciating that there is a risk that damage to property may result from his act ... We wish to make it clear that the test remains subjective, that the knowledge or appreciation of risk of some damage must have entered the defendant's mind even though he may have suppressed it or driven it out.'

CASE EXAMPLE

Stephenson [1979] QB 695

D was a schizophrenic; he was also homeless. One November night he had decided to shelter in a hollowed-out haystack in a field. He was still cold, and so lit a small fire of twigs and straw in order to keep warm. However, the stack caught fire and was damaged, along with various pieces of farming equipment. D was charged under s 1(1) of the CDA. Evidence was given that schizophrenia could have the effect of depriving D of the ability of a normal person to foresee or appreciate the risk of damage. The judge directed the jury that D was reckless if he closed his mind to the obvious fact of risk, and that schizophrenia could be the reason for D closing his mind. The Court of Appeal quashed his conviction. What mattered was whether D himself had foreseen the risk.

3.3.2 The *Caldwell* years: 1981–2003

In 1981, the House of Lords in *Metropolitan Police Commissioner v Caldwell* [1982] AC 341, a criminal damage case, introduced an objective form of recklessness. That is, recklessness was to be determined according to what the 'ordinary, prudent individual' would have foreseen, as opposed to the *Cunningham* test of what the defendant actually did foresee. Lord Diplock, with whom Lords Keith and Roskill concurred, said:

JUDGMENT

'A person charged with an offence under s 1(1) of the Criminal Damage Act 1971 is "reckless as to whether or not any such property be destroyed or damaged" if (1) he does an act which in fact creates an obvious risk that property will be destroyed or damaged and (2) when he does the act he either has not given any thought to the possibility of their being any such risk or has recognised that there was some risk involved and has nonetheless gone on to do it. That would be a proper direction to the jury.'

Because *Caldwell* was a criminal damage case it meant that, while *Stephenson* would be overruled, other areas of law were still subject to the *Cunningham* definition. However, in *Lawrence* [1982] AC 510, the House of Lords gave an objective definition to 'recklessness' in the context of the crime of causing death by reckless driving. A year later, in

Seymour [1983] 2 AC 493, a reckless manslaughter case, the House of Lords applied the objective test here too. Their Lordships also indicated that the *Caldwell/Lawrence* definition of 'recklessness' was 'comprehensive'. Lord Roskill said that 'Reckless should today be given the same meaning in relation to all offences which involve "recklessness" as one of the elements unless Parliament has otherwise ordained.'

This marked the high-water point for the *Caldwell/Lawrence* objective test. During the late 1980s and continuing into the 1990s the courts began a gradual movement to reject *Caldwell* and return to the *Cunningham* subjective test. In *DPP v K (a minor)* [1990] 1 All ER 331, the Divisional Court had applied *Caldwell* to s 47 OAPA 1861 (assault occasioning actual bodily harm), but almost immediately the Court of Appeal in *Spratt* [1991] 2 All ER 210 declared that *DPP v K* was wrongly decided. D had been convicted of the s 47 offence after firing his air pistol through the open window of his flat, apparently unaware that children were playing outside. One was hit and injured. At his trial, D pleaded guilty (on the basis that he had been reckless in that he had failed to give thought to the possibility of a risk that he might cause harm) and appealed. The Court of Appeal quashed his conviction. McCowan LJ pointed out that Lord Roskill's dictum in *Seymour* was clearly *obiter* and could not have been intended to overrule *Cunningham*. McCowan LJ added:

JUDGMENT

'The history of the interpretation of [the OAPA 1861] shows that, whether or not the word "maliciously" appears in the section in question, the courts have consistently held that the *mens rea* of every type of offence against the person covers both intent and recklessness, in the sense of taking the risk of harm ensuing with foresight that it might happen.'

Shortly afterwards the House of Lords dealt with a joint appeal involving both s 47 and s 20 OAPA 1861. In *Savage, DPP v Parmenter* [1992] AC 699, Lord Ackner, giving the unanimous decision of the House of Lords, said that 'in order to establish an offence under s 20 the prosecution must prove either that [D] intended or that he actually foresaw that his act would cause harm'. *Seymour* was effectively overruled by the House of Lords in *Adomako* [1995] 1 AC 171. Lord Mackay pointed out that, to the extent that *Seymour* was concerned with the statutory offence of causing death by reckless driving, it was no longer relevant as that offence had been replaced with a new statutory crime of causing death by dangerous driving (see Chapter 10). As far as manslaughter was concerned, Lord Mackay decided that objective recklessness set too low a threshold of liability for such a serious crime and restored the test based on gross negligence (see below).

3.3.3 Back to *Cunningham*: *G and another*

In October 2003, the House of Lords completed the circle begun 22 years earlier by overruling *Caldwell*. In *G and another* [2003] UKHL 50; [2003] 3 WLR 1060, their Lordships unanimously declared that the objective test for recklessness was wrong and restored the *Cunningham* subjective test for criminal damage. The case itself involved arson, as had *Caldwell*. The certified question from the Court of Appeal was:

JUDGMENT

'Can a defendant properly be convicted under s 1 of the CDA 1971 on the basis that he was reckless as to whether property would be destroyed or damaged when he gave no thought to the risk, but by reason of his age and/or personal characteristics the risk would not have been obvious to him, even if he had thought about it?'

In a number of earlier cases, this question had been answered 'yes': see *Elliott v C (a minor)* [1983] 1 WLR 939, *R (Stephen Malcolm)* (1984) 79 Cr App R 334 and *Coles* [1995] 1 Cr App R 157. All of those cases involved teenagers committing arson and being convicted because, under the *Caldwell* test, it was irrelevant that they had failed to appreciate the risk of property damage created by starting fires, because the risk would have been obvious to the ordinary prudent adult. However, in *G and another* the House of Lords held that the certified question should be answered 'no'. According to Lord Bingham the question was simply one of statutory interpretation, namely, what did Parliament mean when it used the word 'reckless' in s 1 of the 1971 Act? He concluded that Parliament had not intended to change the meaning of the word from its *Cunningham* definition. The majority of the Law Lords in *Caldwell*, specifically Lord Diplock, had 'misconstrued' the 1971 Act. There were four reasons for restoring the subjective test:

1. As a matter of principle, conviction of a serious crime should depend on proof that D had a culpable state of mind. While it was 'clearly blameworthy' to take an obvious risk, it was not clearly blameworthy to do something involving a risk of injury (or property damage) if D genuinely did not perceive that risk. While such a person might 'fairly be accused of stupidity or a lack of imagination', that was insufficient for culpability.
2. The *Caldwell* test was capable of leading to 'obvious unfairness'. It was neither 'moral nor just' to convict any defendant, but least of all a child, on the strength of what someone else would have appreciated.
3. There was significant judicial and academic criticism of *Caldwell* and the cases that had followed it. In particular, Lords Wilberforce and Edmund Davies had dissented in *Caldwell* itself and Goff LJ in *Elliott v C* had followed *Caldwell* only because he felt compelled to do so because of the rules of judicial precedent. That could not be ignored.
4. The decision in *Caldwell* was a misinterpretation of Parliament's intention. Although the courts could leave it to Parliament to correct that misinterpretation, because it was one that was 'offensive to principle and was apt to cause injustice', the need for the courts to correct it was 'compelling'.

Lord Bingham also observed that there were no compelling public policy reasons for persisting with the *Caldwell* test. The law prior to 1981 revealed no miscarriages of justice with guilty defendants being acquitted.

CASE EXAMPLE

G and another [2003] UKHL 50; [2003] 3 WLR 1060

One night in August 2000 the two defendants, G and R, then aged 11 and 12, entered the back yard of a shop. There they found bundles of newspapers, some of which they set alight using a lighter they had brought with them. They threw the burning paper under a large, plastic wheelie bin and left the yard. Meanwhile, the fire had set fire to the wheelie bin. It then spread to another wheelie bin, then to the shop and its adjoining buildings. Damage estimated at approximately £1 million was caused. G and R were charged with arson (that is, damaging or destroying property by fire, being reckless as to whether such property would be destroyed or damaged). At trial, they said that they genuinely thought the burning newspapers would extinguish themselves on the concrete floor of the yard. Hence, looking at the case *subjectively*, neither of them appreciated a risk that the wheelie bins, let alone the shop and its adjoining buildings, would be destroyed or damaged by fire. The judge, however, directed the jury according to the *Caldwell* test. The jury, looking at the case *objectively*, were satisfied that the ordinary prudent adult would have appreciated that risk, and therefore convicted the two boys. The Court of Appeal dismissed their appeal but certified the question for appeal to the House of Lords.

The Court of Appeal has confirmed the development in *G and another* on two occasions, in *Cooper* (2004) and *Castle* (2004), both aggravated arson cases. These cases will be examined in Chapter 16 on criminal damage (see section 16.2.4). There is a supreme irony to all this: on the facts of the *Caldwell* case itself, D would have been found guilty without any need for the objective test. D had been very drunk when he started a fire in a hotel. When charged with reckless arson, he argued that his extreme intoxication prevented him from foreseeing the consequences of his actions, and that he was therefore not guilty. However, the House of Lords had dealt with this very problem and very similar arguments only four years earlier. In *DPP v Majewski* [1977] AC 443, Lord Elwyn-Jones LC stated that when D is intoxicated and carries out the *actus reus* of a crime for which the *mens rea* state is recklessness, then his very intoxication:

JUDGMENT

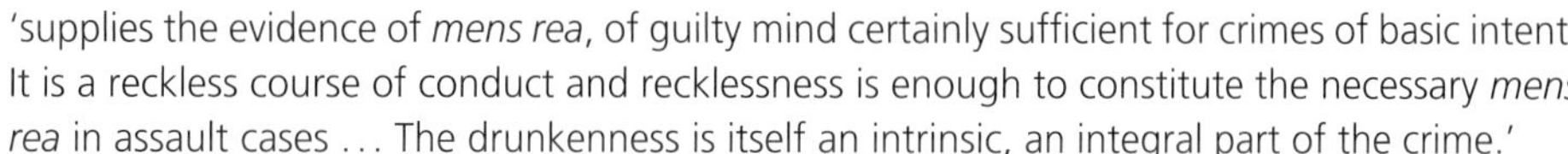

'supplies the evidence of *mens rea*, of guilty mind certainly sufficient for crimes of basic intent. It is a reckless course of conduct and recklessness is enough to constitute the necessary *mens rea* in assault cases ... The drunkenness is itself an intrinsic, an integral part of the crime.'

This case and the public policy arguments underpinning it will be looked at in detail in Chapter 9. Returning to *G and another*, it is worth noting that the House of Lords did give consideration to arguments from the Crown that the *Caldwell* definition could be modified. There were two possibilities, both of which were rejected.

1. That *Caldwell* be adapted for cases involving children and mentally disordered adults. Thus, according to the Crown, a teenage defendant could be convicted if he had failed to give any thought to a risk which would have been obvious to a child of the same age. The House of Lords rejected this, on the basis that it was just as offensive to the above principles. It would also 'open the door' to 'difficult and contentious arguments concerning the qualities and characteristics to be taken into account for the purposes of comparison'.
2. That *Caldwell* be adapted so that D would be reckless if he had failed to give thought to an obvious risk which, had he bothered to think about it at all, would have been equally obvious to him. This argument was rejected because it had the potential to over-complicate the jury's task. It was inherently speculative to ask a jury to consider whether D would have regarded a risk as obvious, had he thought about it. Lord Bingham thought that the simpler the jury's task, the more reliable its verdict would be.

It should finally be noted that, in addition to *Caldwell*, a significant number of Court of Appeal cases following *Caldwell* have, by necessity, been overruled too. As well as the cases cited above – *Elliott v C; R (Stephen Malcolm)* and *Coles* – the following have also been overruled: *Chief Constable of Avon v Shimmen* [1986] Cr App R 7 and *Merrick* [1995] Crim LR 802. It is safe to assume that the Law Commission will welcome the House of Lords' decision in *G and another*. In both the Draft Criminal Code (1989) and the Draft Criminal Law Bill (1993) the Commission defined 'recklessness' in a subjective sense. Professor Sir John Smith would also have welcomed the House of Lords' ruling. A well-known objector to *Caldwell*, he commented in the *Criminal Law Review* of the Court of Appeal's decision to refer the *G and another* case to the House of Lords that 'the law would be better without all the unnecessary complexity [*Caldwell*] introduced' ((2002) Crim LR at 928).

3.4 Negligence

Negligence is the mental element that must be proved in order to impose liability on defendants in some forms of civil litigation. In that context, it typically means that D is liable if he or she fails to appreciate circumstances or consequences that would have been appreciated by the reasonable man. This mental element is rarely found in mainstream criminal law, with two exceptions, because it is seen as too low a threshold to justify imposing punishment on the defendant. (In civil litigation, if liability is imposed on D, he or she is required to compensate the victim but is not otherwise punished.) One exception is a form of manslaughter – however, it should be noted that the mental element is 'gross' negligence. The leading case now is *Adomako*, but the position is perfectly summed up by Lord Atkin in the early House of Lords case of *Andrews v DPP* [1937] AC 576, who said:

JUDGMENT

'Simple lack of care as will constitute civil liability is not enough. For purposes of the criminal law there are degrees of negligence, and a very high degree of negligence is required to be proved before the [crime] is established.'

Gross negligence manslaughter will be considered in depth in Chapter 10.

The second exception is rape and some of the other offences in the Sexual Offences Act 2003. Section 1(1) of the Sexual Offences Act 2003 provides that D has the *mens rea* of rape if he intends to penetrate V and 'does not reasonably believe' that V consents to sex (see Chapter 12 for a full definition of the offence). Clearly, if D *realises* that V is not consenting (because she is struggling or screaming, for example) he cannot 'reasonably believe' that she is consenting and so D will have this element of the *mens rea*. However, there may well be other situations in which D *should have realised* that V is not consenting, and therefore if D intentionally penetrates V without her consent in circumstances when he should have realised that she was not consenting, D may be convicted of rape. The same *mens rea* state is also used in ss 2, 3 and 4 SOA 2003.

3.5 Dishonesty

This form of *mens rea* is used in the Theft Act 1968 and the Fraud Act 2006, although it is not defined in either statute. The meaning of 'dishonesty' has therefore been determined by the courts. For a period of time in the 1970s there was judicial disagreement about whether it should be tested subjectively (by reference to D's own standards) or objectively (by reference to the standards of reasonable and honest people). The leading case is now *Ghosh* [1982] 2 All ER 689, where the Court of Appeal adopted a hybrid test combining both a subjective and an objective element. This case is examined in Chapter 13.

transferred malice
Situation where the mental or fault element for an offence is transferred from one victim to another

3.6 Transferred malice

If D, with the *mens rea* of a particular crime, does an act that causes the *actus reus* of that crime, then he faces liability. It is no excuse to say that the way in which the *actus reus* was carried out was not exactly as D intended it. Suppose that D, intending to punch V, swings his fist in the direction of V who ducks so that D's fist connects with W who is standing immediately behind V. Should D be allowed to plead not guilty to the battery on W, on the basis that he had intended to punch V? The answer is no. This scenario is an example of the doctrine of **transferred malice**. Something very similar to those facts occurred in one of the leading cases, *Latimer* (1886) 17 QBD 359.

CASE EXAMPLE

Latimer (1886) 17 QBD 359

D was involved in a disagreement with V. He took off his belt and swung it at V. The belt glanced off V, and W, who was nearby, received virtually the full impact of the blow. She was badly wounded and D was charged with malicious wounding under s 20 OAPA 1861. At trial, the jury found that the injuries to W were 'purely accidental' and could not reasonably have been expected. However, the doctrine of transferred malice rendered this irrelevant, and D was convicted.

Latimer was followed and applied in *Mitchell* [1983] QB 741, the facts of which were given in Chapter 2. You may recall that D pushed E, who lost his balance and knocked V to the ground, where she broke her leg and eventually died of her injuries. D was convicted of V's manslaughter. In *Attorney-General's Reference (No 3 of 1994)* [1997] 3 WLR 421, Lord Mustill explained the transferred malice doctrine as follows:

JUDGMENT

'The effect of transferred malice . . . is that the intended victim and the actual victim are treated as if they were one, so that what was intended to happen to the first person (but did not happen) is added to what actually did happen to the second person (but was not intended to happen), with the result that what was intended and what happened are married to make a notionally intended and actually consummated crime.'

CASE EXAMPLE

Attorney-General's Reference (No 3 of 1994) [1997] 3 WLR 421

D had stabbed his girlfriend, V, who was between five and six months pregnant. She subsequently recovered from the wound but, some seven weeks later, gave birth prematurely. Subsequently, the child, W, died some four months after birth. It was clear the stab wound had penetrated W whilst in the womb and this was the cause of death. D was charged with W's murder, but was formally acquitted after the judge held that the facts did not disclose a homicide against the child. The case was referred to the Court of Appeal, which held the trial judge was wrong and that, applying the doctrine of transferred malice, a murder conviction was possible. Unusually, a further reference was made to the House of Lords, where it was decided that, at most, manslaughter was possible. The Law Lords took exception to the Court of Appeal's use of the transferred malice doctrine, holding that the 'transferee' had to be in existence at the time that D was proven to have formed the mental element. Lord Mustill said that it would 'overstrain the idea of transferred malice by trying to make it fit the present case'.

A more recent example of transferred malice is *Gnango* [2011] UKSC 59; [2012] 1 AC 827, a decision of the Supreme Court which will be examined in more detail in Chapter 5. Briefly, the case involved two men, Armel Gnango and a man known only as 'Bandana Man', who were engaged in a gun battle in a car park in southeast London. A young woman, Magda Pniewska, was caught in the crossfire and killed – shot once in the head by Bandana Man. In the course of his judgment, Lord Phillips said that 'It was common ground that Bandana Man had been guilty of the murder of Miss Pniewska, applying the principle of transferred malice in that he had plainly been attempting to kill or cause serious bodily harm to [Armel Gnango] ... Bandana Man accidentally shot Miss Pniewska. Under the doctrine of transferred malice he was liable for her murder.'

Meanwhile, if D, with the *mens rea* of one crime, does an act which causes the *actus reus* of *some different* crime, he cannot, generally speaking, be convicted of either crime. This is illustrated by the facts of *Pembliton* [1874] LR 2 CCR 119.

CASE EXAMPLE

Pembliton [1874] LR 2 CCR 119

D was involved in a fight involving 40–50 people, outside a pub in Wolverhampton. D separated himself from the group, picked up a large stone and threw it in the direction of the others. The stone missed them and smashed a large window. D was convicted of malicious damage but his conviction was quashed on appeal. The jury had found that he intended to throw the stone at the people but did not intend to break the window.

The *Pembliton* principle is not an absolute rule, however. In certain circumstances, transferred malice can be invoked where D intended one crime against V1 but actually caused a different crime to V2. This occurred recently in *Grant & others* [2014] EWCA Crim 143. Here, D (along with two accomplices) shot and seriously injured two people in a south London shop. D had actually fired two shots at another person, V1, with intent to kill, but had missed him. At his subsequent trial, the jury convicted D of one count of attempting to murder V1 and two counts of causing GBH with intent to do GBH, contrary to s 18 OAPA 1861, to V2 and V3. The latter convictions required application of transferred malice. D appealed to the Court of Appeal, contending that it was wrong to transfer his intent in this case, because he had one intent vis-à-vis V1 (intent to kill), and a different intent vis-à-vis V2 and V3 (intent to do GBH). This was rejected, on the basis that the intent required to convict D of attempting to murder V1 included the intent required to convict him of causing GBH with intent to V2 and V3. Rafferty LJ said:

JUDGMENT

'Proof of the *mens rea* for attempted murder by definition involves proof of the *mens rea* for causing GBH with intent ... A finding of intention to kill leads inevitably to a finding of intention to cause GBH – the consequence of the hierarchy of intent, with intention to kill at the top. It is impossible to kill without causing really serious harm.'

CASE EXAMPLE

Grant & others [2014] EWCA Crim 143

Nathaniel Grant, Kazeem Kolawole and Tony McCalla were all charged with attempted murder and two counts of causing GBH with intent. The Crown's case was that the three defendants were members of or associated with the Grind and Stack gang or Organised Crime/One Chance gang. One evening, the three defendants, on bicycles, had pulled up outside the Stockwell Food & Wine shop directly after Roshaun Bryan had run inside. Bryan was or was suspected to be a member of a rival gang, the All 'Bout Money gang. Grant produced a gun and fired two shots into the shop. One bullet hit and paralysed a five-year-old girl whose uncle owned the shop; the other hit, and remains in the head of, a customer. Bryan was unhurt. During his trial, D contended that the charges of attempted murder and causing GBH with intent were mutually inconsistent, as they involved different *mens rea*. However, the trial judge ruled that if D shot with the intention of killing, he intended to cause at least really serious bodily harm; the lesser intent may be subsumed in the greater. The jury convicted on all counts and the Court of Appeal upheld the convictions.

Criticism

Although a useful, practical device for obtaining convictions, the transferred malice doctrine has not gone uncriticised. Professor Williams argued that the doctrine is a 'rather arbitrary exception to normal principles' ('Convictions and fair labelling' (1983) CLJ 85). Considering the situation where D intends to kill V but misses and instead kills W, Professor Williams commented that because the indictment would actually charge D with killing W, strictly speaking it should be necessary to prove that D intended to kill (or seriously injure) W. However, this view has not attracted support from the courts.

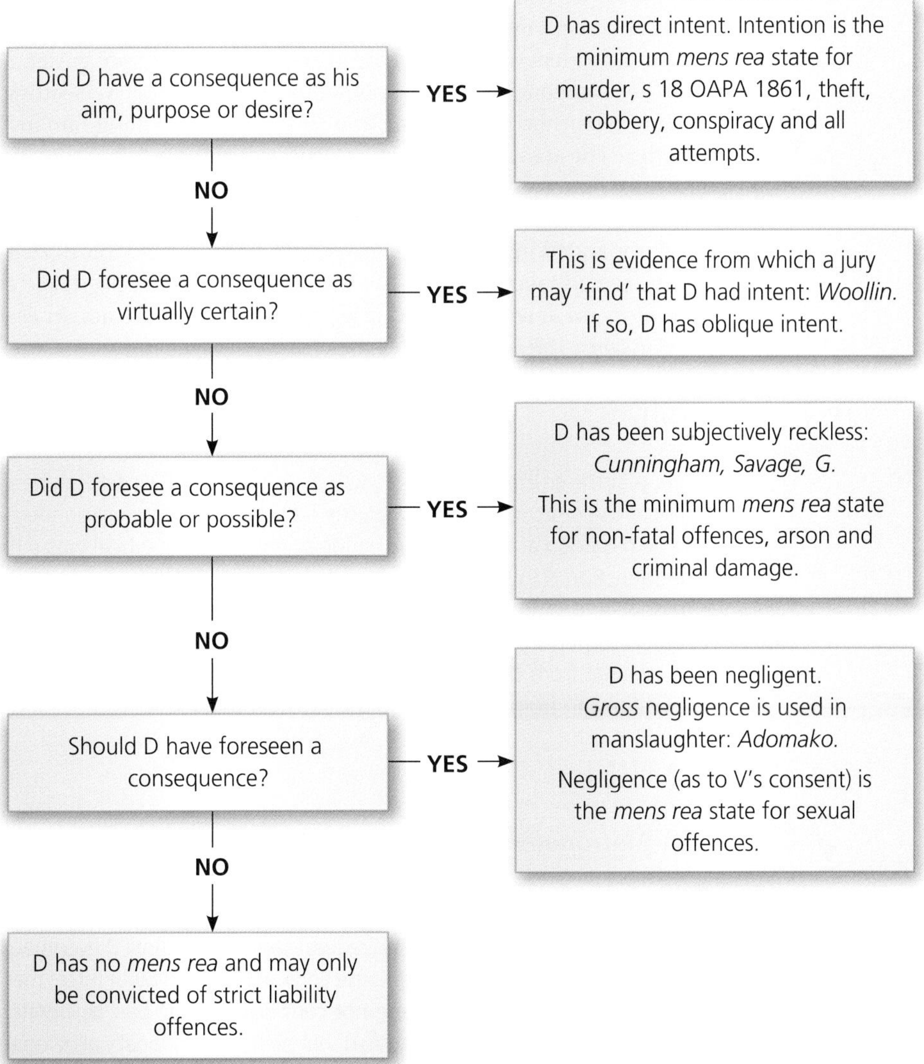

Figure 3.1 *Mens rea.*

Reform

The Law Commission, in both the Draft Criminal Code (1989) and the Draft Criminal Law Bill (1993), accepted the need to preserve the transferred malice doctrine. Clause 32(1) of the 1993 Bill provides as follows:

CLAUSE

'32(1) In determining whether a person is guilty of an offence, his intention to cause, or his awareness of a risk that he will cause, a result in relation to a person or thing capable of being the victim or subject-matter of the offence shall be treated as an intention to cause or, as the case may, an awareness of a risk that he will cause, that result in relation to any other person or thing affected by his conduct.'

coincidence
Principle that the *actus reus* and *mens rea* elements of an offence must occur at the same time

3.7 Coincidence of *actus reus* and *mens rea*

Suppose that D, the victim of domestic violence, forms a vague intention to kill her husband, V, at some convenient moment in the future if it should present itself, perhaps by pushing him off a set of ladders while he is cleaning leaves from the roof gutter. Ten minutes later, D reverses her car from the garage, oblivious of the fact that V is sitting in the driveway attempting to repair the lawnmower, and runs him over, killing him instantly. Is D guilty of V's murder? The answer would be 'no', because of the requirement that the *actus reus* of any crime must be accompanied at that precise moment in time by the *mens rea* of the same crime. Although D did cause death, and had formed an intention to do so, the various elements were separated in time. There are certain exceptions to this doctrine, however: first, where the *actus reus* takes the form of a continuing act, it has been held that it is sufficient if D forms *mens rea* at some point during the duration of the act. In *Fagan v Metropolitan Police Commissioner* [1969] 1 QB 439, James J said:

JUDGMENT

'We think that the crucial question is whether, in this case, [D's act] can be said to be complete and spent at the moment of time when the car wheel came to rest on the foot, or whether his act is to be regarded as a continuing act operating until the wheel was removed. In our judgment, a distinction is to be drawn between acts which are complete, though results may continue to flow, and those acts which are continuing ... There was an act constituting a battery which at its inception was not criminal because there was no element of intention, but which became criminal from the moment the intention was formed to produce the apprehension which was flowing from the continuing act.'

CASE EXAMPLE

Fagan v Metropolitan Police Commissioner [1969] 1 QB 439

D was being directed to park his car by a police officer. D accidentally drove his car on to the officer's foot, who shouted at D to move the car. At this point, D refused and even switched off the engine. The officer had to repeat his request several times until D eventually acquiesced. D was charged with battery (physical element: the application of unlawful force; mental element: intent or recklessness). The magistrates were not convinced that D had deliberately driven on to the officer's foot; however, they were satisfied that he had intentionally allowed the wheel to remain there afterwards. D was therefore convicted on the basis that allowing the wheel to remain on the officer's foot constituted a continuing act, and the Divisional Court dismissed D's appeal.

The second exception is where the *actus reus* is itself part of some larger sequence of events, it may be sufficient that D forms *mens rea* at some point during that sequence. The leading case is the Privy Council decision (hearing an appeal from South Africa) in *Thabo Meli and others* [1954] 1 All ER 373.

CASE EXAMPLE

Thabo Meli and others [1954] 1 All ER 373

The appellants, in accordance with a prearranged plan, took V to a hut where they beat him over the head. Believing him to be dead, they rolled his body over a low cliff, attempting to make it look like an accidental fall. In fact, V was still alive at this point in time but eventually died from exposure. The appellants were convicted of murder and the Privy Council dismissed their appeals, which had been based on an argument that the *actus reus* (death from exposure) was separated in time from the *mens rea* (present during the attack in the hut but not later, because they thought V was dead).

Lord Reid stated that it was:

JUDGMENT

'impossible to divide up what was really one series of acts in this way. There is no doubt that the accused set out to do all these acts in order to achieve their plan, and as part of their plan; and it is much too refined a ground of judgment to say that, because they were at a misapprehension at one stage and thought that their guilty purpose was achieved before it was achieved, therefore they are to escape the penalties of the law.'

This dictum appears to suggest that the judgment might have been different if the acts were not part of a prearranged plan. *Thabo Meli* was, indeed, distinguished on this ground in New Zealand (*Ramsay* [1967] NZLR 1005) and, at first, in South Africa (*Chiswibo* [1960] (2) SA 714). However, the Court of Appeal in England has followed *Thabo Meli*, in two cases where there was no antecedent plan. In *Church* [1965] 2 All ER 72, D got into a fight with a woman and knocked her unconscious. After trying unsuccessfully for 30 minutes to wake her, he concluded she was dead, panicked and threw her body into a nearby river. V drowned. The jury convicted D of manslaughter, after a direction that they could do so 'if they regarded [D]'s behaviour from the moment he first struck her to the moment when he threw her into the river as a series of acts designed to cause death or GBH'. D's conviction was upheld. A more recent case is *Le Brun* [1991] 4 All ER 673, where the Court of Appeal dismissed an appeal based on the significant time lapse that had occurred between the original assault (when D had *mens rea*) and V's eventual death (when he did not). Lord Lane CJ said:

JUDGMENT

'Where the unlawful application of force and the eventual act causing death are parts of the same sequence of events, the same transaction, the fact that there is an appreciable interval of time between the two does not serve to exonerate [D] from liability. That is certainly so where [D's] subsequent actions which caused death, after the initial unlawful blow, are designed to conceal his commission of the original unlawful assault.'

CASE EXAMPLE

Le Brun [1991] 4 All ER 673

D had a row with his wife as they made their way home late one night. Eventually he punched her on the chin and knocked her unconscious. While attempting to drag away what he thought was her dead body he dropped her, so that she hit her head on the kerb and died. The jury were told that they could convict of murder or manslaughter (depending on the mental element present when the punch was thrown), if D accidentally dropped V while (i) attempting to move her against her wishes and/or (ii) attempting to dispose of her 'body' or otherwise cover up the assault. He was convicted of manslaughter. The Court of Appeal upheld the conviction.

Fagan v Metropolitan Police Commissioner

D accidentally parks his car on V's foot. This is the *actus reus* of battery – the application of unlawful force. D has no *mens rea* at this point in time.

D later forms the *mens rea,* when he realises what he's done and refuses to move his car – he intends to apply unlawful force to V's foot.

D is guilty of battery using the 'continuing act' theory.

Thabo Meli and others

D attacks V with intent to kill. D has the *mens rea* of murder at this point in time, but not the *actus reus*, because V does not die. D thinks that V is dead and dumps the 'body' in bushes.

V later dies from exposure. This is the *actus reus* of murder, but D no longer has the *mens rea.*

D is guilty of murder using the 'transaction' theory.

Le Brun

D intentionally punches V in the face. This is enough *mens rea* for constructive manslaughter. However, V does not die, and so there is no *actus reus* of manslaughter at this point in time.

V hits her head on the pavement as D tries to move her, and she later dies from head injuries. This is the *actus reus* of manslaughter, but D no longer has the *mens rea.*

D is guilty of manslaughter using the 'transaction' theory.

Figure 3.2 Coincidence.

SUMMARY

Different crimes have different *mens rea* states. In this book the most common *mens rea* states are intention, recklessness, 'malice' (which means either intention or recklessness), negligence and dishonesty, although there are others such as 'belief' (used in the Serious Crime Act 2007).

Intention is the highest form of *mens rea* state and is an essential element of crimes such as murder, wounding or causing GBH with intent, robbery and theft. Intention may be direct, where a consequence is D's aim, purpose or desire, or oblique, where a consequence is not desired but is foreseen by D as 'virtually certain' (*Woollin*). Foresight is not the same thing as intention but is evidence from which a jury may 'find' intention. The Law Commission has proposed placing the case law definition of intention into statutory form.

Recklessness is the form of *mens rea* used in most non-fatal offences against the person, one form of manslaughter and criminal damage. It requires proof that D took an unjustifiable risk with awareness of that risk – this is referred to as 'subjective' recklessness as it refers to D's foresight of the consequences (*Cunningham*). In 1981 an 'objective' test for recklessness was introduced by *Caldwell*, according to which D was reckless if he failed to appreciate a risk which would have been obvious to an 'ordinary prudent individual'. *Caldwell* was overruled in *R v G* in 2003 on the basis that it is unfair to convict D of an offence based on what someone else would have foreseen.

Negligence is used as a *mens rea* state in rape and certain other sexual offences (D must have a 'reasonable belief' in V's consent) while 'gross' negligence is the *mens rea* state for one form of manslaughter.

The principle of 'transferred malice' means that if D fulfils the *actus reus* and *mens rea* elements of an offence, then D is liable even if the *actus reus* was carried out in an unexpected way. Thus, D is guilty of murder if he deliberately fires a gun and shoots V dead, even if D was aiming the gun at W. The fact that V's death was in one sense 'accidental' is no excuse as D's *mens rea* with respect to W is 'transferred' to V (*Latimer, Mitchell, Gnango, Grant and others*).

All the elements of the *actus reus* and *mens rea* must coincide at the same point in time. The courts are prepared to be flexible with this requirement and have adopted a variety of solutions such as finding that elements of the *actus reus* can be 'continuing' (*Fagan*) and that apparently separate acts can be classed as part of the same 'transaction' (*Thabo Meli, Le Brun*).

SAMPLE ESSAY QUESTION

Consider how successful the courts have been in defining the concept of intention.

Explain the role of intention:

- It is a *mens rea* state, associated with more serious offences such as murder
- It is tested purely subjectively (s 8, Criminal Justice Act 1967)
- It is essential in many offences, especially murder and attempts

Explain the difference between different forms of intention:

- Direct intention = D's aim, purpose or desire (e.g. *Steane* (1947))
- Oblique intent = D's foresight of a consequence may be used as evidence by a jury to 'find' that D intended it

Explain the cases on oblique intent:

- *Moloney* (1985) – foresight of a 'natural' consequence allows jury to infer intention. Lord Bridge's golden rule = directions on oblique intent should be used sparingly to avoid confusion
- *Hancock* (1986) – *Moloney* guidelines misleading – they omitted any reference to probability
- *Nedrick* (1986) – D's foresight should be of a 'virtually certain' consequence before jury may 'easily' infer intent
- *Woollin* (1998) – *Nedrick* approved except 'infer' changed to 'find'
- *Matthew & Alleyne* (2003) – suggests that foresight of a consequence may equal intention rather than just evidence of it

Evaluate the cases/principles:

- Discuss the argument that intent should mean direct intent only
- Discuss whether oblique intent overlaps with recklessness and blurs distinction between murder and manslaughter
- Discuss whether or not the verbs 'to infer' and 'to find' have different meanings
- Discuss whether foresight of a consequence should be intention or just evidence of it
- Refer to the Law Commission's proposals for a statutory definition of intention

Conclude

Further reading

Books

Ormerod, D, *Smith and Hogan Criminal Law: Cases and Materials* (14th edn, Oxford University Press, 2014), Chapter 5.

Articles

Duff, R A, 'The obscure intentions of the House of Lords' [1986] Crim LR 771.
Goff, Lord, 'The mental element in the crime of murder' (1988) 104 LQR 30.
Horder, I, 'Transferred malice and the remoteness of unexpected outcomes from intentions' [2006] Crim LR 383.
Lacey, N, 'A clear concept of intention: elusive or illusory?' (1993) 56 MLR 621.
Norrie, A, 'After Woollin' [1999] Crim LR 532.
Pedain, A, 'Intention and the terrorist example' [2003] Crim LR 579.
Simester, A P, 'Murder, *mens rea* and the House of Lords: again' (1999) 115 LQR 17.
Sullivan, G R, 'Contemporaneity of *actus reus* and *mens rea*' (1993) 52 CLJ 487.
Williams, G, 'Oblique intention' (1987) 46 CLJ 417.
Williams, G, 'The *mens rea* for murder: leave it alone' (1989) 105 LQR 387.
Wilson, W, 'Doctrinal rationality after *Woollin*' (1999) 62 MLR 448.

4

Strict liability

AIMS AND OBJECTIVES

After reading this chapter you should be able to:

- Understand the basic concept of strict liability in criminal law
- Understand the tests the courts use to decide whether an offence is one of strict liability
- Apply the tests to factual situations to determine the existence of strict liability
- Understand the role of policy in the creation of strict liability offences
- Analyse critically the concept of strict liability

The previous chapter explained the different types of *mens rea*. This chapter considers those offences where *mens rea* is not required in respect of at least one aspect of the *actus reus*. Such offences are known as strict liability offences. The 'modern' type of strict liability offence was first created in the mid-nineteenth century. The first known case on strict liability is thought to be *Woodrow* (1846) 15 M & W 404. In that case the defendant was convicted of having in his possession adulterated tobacco, even though he did not know that it was adulterated. The judge, Parke B, ruled that he was guilty even if a 'nice chemical analysis' was needed to discover that the tobacco was adulterated.

The concept of strict liability appears to contradict the basis of criminal law. Normally criminal law is thought to be based on the culpability of the accused. In strict liability offences there may be no blameworthiness on the part of the defendant. The defendant, as in *Woodrow*, is guilty simply because he has done a prohibited act.

A more modern example demonstrating this is *Pharmaceutical Society of Great Britain v Storkwain Ltd* [1986] 2 All ER 635.

CASE EXAMPLE

Pharmaceutical Society of Great Britain v Storkwain Ltd [1986] 2 All ER 635

This case involved s 58(2) of the Medicines Act 1968, which provides that no person shall supply specified medicinal products except in accordance with a prescription given by an appropriate medical practitioner. D had supplied drugs on prescriptions which were later found to be forged. There was no finding that D had acted dishonestly, improperly or even negligently. The forgery was sufficient to deceive the pharmacists. Despite this the House of Lords held that the Divisional Court was right to direct the magistrates to convict D. The pharmacists had supplied the drugs without a genuine prescription, and this was enough to make them guilty of the offence.

For nearly all strict liability offences it must be proved that the defendant did the relevant *actus reus*. In *Woodrow* this meant proving that he was in possession of the adulterated tobacco. For *Storkwain* this meant proving that they had supplied specified medicinal products not in accordance with a prescription given by an appropriate medical practitioner. In these cases it also had to be proved that the doing of the *actus reus* was voluntary. However, there are a few rare cases where the defendant has been found guilty even though they did not do the *actus reus* voluntarily. These are known as crimes of absolute liability.

4.1 Absolute liability

absolute liability
An offence where no *mens rea* is required and where *actus reus* need not be voluntary – very rare

Absolute liability means that no *mens rea* at all is required for the offence. It involves status offences; that is, offences where the *actus reus* is a state of affairs. The defendant is liable because they have 'been found' in a certain situation. Such offences are very rare. To be an absolute liability offence, the following conditions must apply:

- The offence does not require any *mens rea*.
- There is no need to prove that the defendant's *actus reus* was voluntary.

The following two cases demonstrate this. The first is *Larsonneur* (1933) 24 Cr App R 74.

CASE EXAMPLE

Larsonneur (1933) 24 Cr App R 74

The defendant, who was an alien, had been ordered to leave the United Kingdom. She decided to go to Eire, but the Irish police deported her and took her in police custody back to the United Kingdom, where she was put in a cell in Holyhead police station. She did not want to return to the United Kingdom. She had no *mens rea*; her act in returning was not voluntary. Despite this she was found guilty under the Aliens Order 1920 of 'being an alien to whom leave to land in the United Kingdom has been refused' who was 'found in the United Kingdom'.

The other case is *Winzar v Chief Constable of Kent*, *The Times*, 28 March 1983; Co/1111/82 (Lexis), QBD.

CASE EXAMPLE

Winzar v Chief Constable of Kent, The Times, 28 March 1983

D was taken to hospital on a stretcher, but when doctors examined him they found that he was not ill but was drunk. D was told to leave the hospital but was later found slumped on a seat in a corridor. The police were called and they took D to the roadway outside the hospital. They formed the opinion he was drunk so they put him in the police car, drove him to the police station and charged him with being found drunk in a highway contrary to s 12 of the Licensing Act 1872. The Divisional Court upheld his conviction.

As in *Larsonneur*, the defendant had not acted voluntarily. The police had taken him to the highway. In the Divisional Court Goff LJ justified the conviction:

JUDGMENT

'[L]ooking at the purpose of this particular offence, it is designed ... to deal with the nuisance which can be caused by persons who are drunk in a public place. This kind of offence is caused quite simply when a person is found drunk in a public place or highway ... . [A]n example ... illustrates how sensible that conclusion is. Suppose a person was found drunk in a restaurant and was asked to leave. If he was asked to leave, he would walk out of the door of the restaurant and would be in a public place or in a highway of his own volition. He would be there of his own volition because he had responded to a request. However, if a man in a restaurant made a thorough nuisance of himself, was asked to leave, objected and was ejected, in those circumstances he would not be in a public place of his own volition because he would have been put there ... It would be nonsense if one were to say that the man who responded to the plea to leave could be said to be found drunk in a public place or in a highway, whereas the man who had been compelled to leave could not.

This leads me to the conclusion that a person is "found to be drunk or in a public place or in a highway", within the meaning of those words as used in the section, when he is perceived to be drunk in a public place. It is enough for the commission of the offence if (1) a person is in a public place or a highway, (2) he is drunk, and (3) in those circumstances he is perceived to be there and to be drunk.'

It is not known how Winzar came to be taken to the hospital on a stretcher, but commentators on this case point out that there may be an element of fault in Winzar's conduct. He had become drunk, and in order to have been taken to hospital must have either been in a public place when the ambulance collected him and took him to hospital, or he must have summoned medical assistance when he was not ill but only drunk.

4.2 Strict liability

For all offences, there is a presumption that *mens rea* is required. The courts will always start with this presumption, but if they decide that the offence does not require *mens rea* for at least part of the *actus reus*, then the offence is one of strict liability. This idea of not requiring *mens rea* for part of the offence is illustrated by two cases, *Prince* (1875) LR 2 CCR 154 and *Hibbert* (1869) LR 1 CCR 184. In both these cases the charge against the defendant was that he had taken an unmarried girl under the age of 16 out of the possession of her father against his will, contrary to s 55 of the Offences Against the Person Act 1861.

OFFENCE

Taking an unmarried girl under the age of 16 out of the possession of her father

Contrary to s 55 Offences Against the Person Act 1861

***Prince* (1875)**	***Hibbert* (1869)**
Knew girl was in the possession of her father, but thought she was over 16 *GUILTY*	Did not know girl was in possession of her father *NOT GUILTY*
Because the offence was one of strict liability in respect to age	Because he had no intention to take the girl out of the possession of her father
D could not rely on mistake about age	*Mens rea* was required in respect of this aspect of the offence

Figure 4.1 Contrasting the cases of *Prince* and *Hibbert*.

Prince knew that the girl he took was in the possession of her father but believed, on reasonable grounds, that she was aged 18. He was convicted, as he had the intention to remove the girl from the possession of her father. *Mens rea* was required for this part of the *actus reus*, and he had the necessary intention. However, the court held that knowledge of her age was not required. On this aspect of the offence there was strict liability. In *Hibbert* the defendant met a girl aged 14 on the street. He took her to another place where they had sexual intercourse. He was acquitted of the offence as it was not proved that he knew the girl was in the custody of her father. Even though the age aspect of the offence was one of strict liability, *mens rea* was required for the removal aspect, and in this case, the necessary intention was not proved.

As already stated, the *actus reus* must be proved and the defendant's conduct in doing the *actus reus* must be voluntary. However, a defendant can be convicted if his voluntary act inadvertently caused a prohibited consequence. This is so even though the defendant was totally blameless in respect of the consequence, as was seen in *Callow v Tillstone* (1900) 83 LT 411.

CASE EXAMPLE

Callow v Tillstone (1900) 83 LT 411

A butcher asked a vet to examine a carcass to see if it was fit for human consumption. The vet assured him that it was all right to eat, and so the butcher offered it for sale. In fact it was unfit and the butcher was convicted of the offence of exposing unsound meat for sale. It was a strict liability offence, and even though the butcher had taken reasonable care not to commit the offence, he was still guilty.

4.2.1 No due diligence defence

due diligence
Where D has taken all possible care not to do the forbidden act or omission.

For some offences, the statute creating the offence provides a defence of **due diligence**. This means that the defendant will not be liable if he can adduce evidence that he did all that was within his power not to commit the offence. There does not seem, however, to be any sensible pattern for when Parliament decides to include a due diligence defence and when it does not. It can be argued that such a defence should always be available for strict liability offences. If it was, then the butcher in *Callow v Tillstone* above would not have been guilty. By asking a vet to check the meat he had clearly done all that he could not to commit the offence.

Another example where the defendants took all reasonable steps to prevent the offence but were still guilty, as there was no due diligence defence available, is *Harrow LBC v Shah and Shah* [1999] 3 All ER 302.

CASE EXAMPLE

Harrow LBC v Shah and Shah [1999] 3 All ER 302

The defendants owned a newsagent's business where lottery tickets were sold. They had told their staff not to sell tickets to anyone under 16 years. They also told their staff that if there was any doubt about a customer's age, the staff should ask for proof of age, and if still in doubt should refer the matter to the defendants. In addition there were clear notices up in the shop about the rules, and staff were frequently reminded that they must not sell lottery tickets to underage customers. One of their staff sold a lottery ticket to a 13-year-old boy without asking for proof of age. The salesman mistakenly believed the boy was over 16 years. D1 was in a back room of the premises at the time; D2 was not on the premises.

D1 and D2 were charged with selling a lottery ticket to a person under 16, contrary to s 13(1)(c) of the National Lottery etc. Act 1993 and the relevant Regulations. Section 13(1)(c) provides that 'Any other person who was a party to the contravention shall be guilty of an offence.' This subsection does not have any provision for a due diligence defence, although s 13(1)(a), which makes the promoter of the lottery guilty, does contain a due diligence defence. Both these offences carry the same maximum sentence (two years' imprisonment, a fine or both) for conviction after trial on indictment. The magistrates dismissed the charges. The prosecution appealed by way of case stated to the Queen's Bench Divisional Court.

The Divisional Court held the offence to be one of strict liability. They allowed the appeal and remitted the case to the magistrates to continue the hearing. The Divisional Court held that the offence did not require any *mens rea*. The act of selling the ticket to someone who was actually under 16 was enough to make the defendants guilty, even though they had done their best to prevent this happening in their shop.

Mens rea

For new statutory offences, a 'due diligence' defence is more often provided. However, it is argued that due diligence should be a general defence, as it is in Australia and Canada. The Draft Criminal Code of 1989 included provision for a general defence of due diligence, but the Code has never been enacted. (See section 1.2.3.)

4.2.2 No defence of mistake

Another feature of strict liability offences is that the defence of mistake is not available. This is important as, if the defence of mistake is available, the defendant will be acquitted when he made an honest mistake. Two cases which illustrate the difference in liability are *Cundy v Le Cocq* (1884) 13 QBD 207 and *Sherras v De Rutzen* [1895] 1 QB 918. Both of these involve contraventions of the Licensing Act 1872.

In *Cundy* the defendant was charged with selling intoxicating liquor to a drunken person, contrary to s 13 of the Act. This section enacts:

SECTION

'13 If any licensed person permits drunkenness or any violent quarrelsome or riotous conduct to take place on his premises, or sells any intoxicating liquor to any drunken person, he shall be liable to a penalty.'

The magistrate trying the case found as a fact that the defendant and his employees had not noticed that the person was drunk. The magistrate also found that while the person was on the licensed premises he had been 'quiet in his demeanour and had done nothing to indicate insobriety; and that there were no apparent indications of intoxication'. However, the magistrate held that the offence was complete on proof that a sale had taken place and that the person served was drunk and convicted the defendant. The defendant appealed against this, but the Divisional Court upheld the conviction. Stephen J said:

JUDGMENT

'I am of the opinion that the words of the section amount to an absolute prohibition of the sale of liquor to a drunken person, and that the existence of a bona fide mistake as to the condition of the person served is not an answer to the charge, but is a matter only for mitigation of the penalties that may be imposed.'

So s 13 of the Licensing Act 1872 was held to be a strict liability offence as the defendant could not rely on the defence of mistake. In contrast it was held in *Sherras v De Rutzen* that s 16 of the Licensing Act 1872 did not impose strict liability. In that case the defendant was able to rely on the defence of mistake.

CASE EXAMPLE

Sherras v De Rutzen [1895] 1 QB 918

In *Sherras* the defendant was convicted by a magistrate of an offence under s 16(2) of the Licensing Act 1872. This section makes it an offence for a licensed person to 'supply any liquor or refreshment' to any constable on duty. There were no words in the section requiring the defendant to have knowledge that a constable was off duty. The facts were that local police when on duty wore an armband on their uniform. An on-duty police officer removed his armband before entering the defendant's public house. He was served by the defendant's daughter in the presence of the defendant. Neither the defendant or his daughter made any enquiry as to whether the policeman was on duty. The defendant thought that the constable was off duty because he was not wearing his armband. The Divisional Court quashed the conviction. They held that the offence was not one of strict liability, and accordingly a genuine mistake provided the defendant with a defence.

When giving judgment in the case Day J stated:

JUDGMENT

> 'This police constable comes into the appellant's house without his armlet, and with every appearance of being off duty. The house was in the immediate neighbourhood of the police station, and the appellant believed, and had very natural grounds for believing, that the constable was off duty. In that belief he accordingly served him with liquor. As a matter of fact, the constable was on duty; but does that fact make the innocent act of the appellant an offence? I do not think it does. He had no intention to do a wrongful act; he acted in the *bona fide* belief that the constable was off duty. It seems to me that the contention that he committed an offence is utterly erroneous.'

It is difficult to reconcile this decision with the decision in *Cundy*. In both cases the sections in the Licensing Act 1872 were expressed in similar words. In *Cundy* the offence was 'sells any intoxicating liquor to any drunken person', while in *Sherras* the offence was 'supplies any liquor ... to any constable on duty'. In each case the publican made a genuine mistake. Day J justified his decision in *Sherras* by pointing to the fact that although s 16(2) did not include the word 'knowingly', s 16(1) did, for the offence of 'knowingly harbours or knowingly suffers to remain on his premises any constable during any part of the time appointed for such constable being on duty'. Day J held this only had the effect of shifting the burden of proof. For s 16(1) the prosecution had to prove that the defendant knew the constable was on duty, while for s 16(2) the prosecution did not have to prove knowledge, but it was open to the defendant to prove that he did not know.

The other judge in the case of *Sherras*, Wright J, pointed out that if the offence was to be made one of strict liability, then there was nothing the publican could do to prevent the commission of the crime. No care on the part of the publican could save him from a conviction under s 16(2), since it would be as easy for the constable to deny that he was on duty when asked as to remove his armlet before entering the public house. It is more possible to reconcile the two cases on this basis as in most cases the fact of a person being drunk would be an observable fact, so the publican should be put on alert and could avoid committing the offence.

4.2.3 Summary of strict liability

So where an offence is held to be one of strict liability, the following points apply:

- The defendant must be proved to have done the *actus reus*.
- This must be a voluntary act on his part.
- There is no need to prove *mens rea* for at least part of the *actus reus*.
- No due diligence defence will be available.
- The defence of mistake is not available.

These factors are well established. The problem lies in deciding which offences are ones of strict liability. For this the courts will start with presuming that *mens rea* should apply. This is so for both common law and statutory offences.

4.3 Common law strict liability offences

Nearly all strict liability offences have been created by statute. Strict liability is very rare in common law offences. Only three common law offences have been held to be ones of strict liability. These are

- public nuisance

- some forms of criminal libel
- outraging public decency.

Public nuisance and forms of criminal libel such as seditious libel probably do not require *mens rea*, but there are no modern cases. In *Lemon and Whitehouse v Gay News* [1979] 1 All ER 898, the offence of blasphemous libel was held to be one of strict liability. In that case a poem had been published in *Gay News* describing homosexual acts done to the body of Christ after his crucifixion and also describing his alleged homosexual practices during his lifetime. The editor and publishers were convicted of blasphemy. On their appeal to the House of Lords, the Law Lords held that it was not necessary to prove that the defendants intended to blaspheme. Lord Russell said:

JUDGMENT

'Why then should the House, faced with a deliberate publication of that which a jury with every justification has held to be a blasphemous libel, consider that it should be for the prosecution to prove, presumably beyond reasonable doubt, that the accused recognised and intended it to be such. The reason why the law considers that the publication of a blasphemous libel is an offence is that the law considers that such publications should not take place. And if it takes place, and the publication is deliberate, I see no justification for holding that there is no offence when the publisher is incapable, for some reason particular to himself, of agreeing with a jury on the true nature of the publication.'

Note that blasphemous libel has now been abolished by the Criminal Justice and Immigration Act 2008.

Outraging public decency was held to be an offence of strict liability in *Gibson and Sylveire* [1991] 1 All ER 439 since it does not have to be proved that the defendant intended to or was reckless that his conduct would have the effect of outraging public decency.

Criminal contempt of court used to be a strict liability offence at common law. It is now a statutory offence, and Parliament has continued it as a strict liability offence.

Note that the Law Commission consulted in 2010 on possible reform of the offences of public nuisance and outraging public decency. A report is due out but had not been published at the time of writing the text.

4.4 Statutory strict liability offences

The surprising fact is that about half of all statutory offences are strict liability. This amounts to over 5,000 offences. Most strict liability offences are regulatory in nature. This may involve such matters as regulating the sale of food and alcohol and gaming tickets, the prevention of pollution and the safe use of vehicles.

In order to decide whether an offence is one of strict liability, the courts start by assuming that *mens rea* is required, but they are prepared to interpret the offence as one of strict liability if Parliament has expressly or by implication indicated this in the relevant statute. The judges often have difficulty in deciding whether an offence is one of strict liability. The first rule is that where an Act of Parliament includes words indicating *mens rea* (e.g. 'knowingly', 'intentionally', 'maliciously' or 'permitting'), the offence requires *mens rea* and is not one of strict liability. However, if an Act of Parliament makes it clear that *mens rea* is not required, the offence will be one of strict liability. An example of this is the Contempt of Court Act 1981 where s 1 sets out the 'strict liability rule'. It states:

SECTION

'In this Act "the strict liability rule" means the rule of law whereby conduct may be treated as a contempt of court as tending to interfere with the course of justice in particular legal proceedings regardless of intent to do so.'

contempt of court
Interfering with the course of justice especially in relation to court proceedings

Throughout the Act it then states whether the 'the strict liability rule' applies to the various offences of **contempt of court**.

However, in many instances a section in an Act of Parliament is silent about the need for *mens rea*. Parliament is criticised for this. If they made clear in all sections which create a criminal offence whether *mens rea* was required, then there would be no problem. As it is, where there are no express words indicating *mens rea* or strict liability, the courts have to decide which offences are ones of strict liability.

4.4.1 The presumption of *mens rea*

Where an Act of Parliament does not include any words indicating *mens rea*, the judges will start by presuming that all criminal offences require *mens rea*. This was made clear in the case of *Sweet v Parsley* [1969] 1 All ER 347.

CASE EXAMPLE

Sweet v Parsley [1969] 1 All ER 347

D rented a farmhouse and let it out to students. The police found cannabis at the farmhouse, and the defendant was charged with 'being concerned in the management of premises used for the purpose of smoking cannabis resin'. The defendant did not know that cannabis was being smoked there. It was decided that she was not guilty as the court presumed that the offence required *mens rea*.

The key part of the judgment was when Lord Reid said:

JUDGMENT

'there has for centuries been a presumption that Parliament did not intend to make criminals of persons who were in no way blameworthy in what they did. That means that, whenever a section is silent as to *mens rea*, there is a presumption that, in order to give effect to the will of Parliament, we must read in words appropriate to require *mens rea* it is firmly established by a host of authorities that *mens rea* is an ingredient of every offence unless some reason can be found for holding that it is not necessary.'

This principle has been affirmed by the House of Lords in *B (a minor) v DPP* [2000] 1 All ER 833 where the House of Lords reviewed the law on strict liability. The Law Lords quoted with approval what Lord Reid had said in *Sweet v Parsley* (see section 4.4.8 for full details of *B v DPP*).

Although the courts start with the presumption that *mens rea* is required, they look at a variety of points to decide whether the presumption should stand or if it can be displaced and the offence made one of strict liability.

4.4.2 The *Gammon* criteria

In *Gammon (Hong Kong) Ltd v Attorney-General of Hong Kong* [1984] 2 All ER 503, the appellants had been charged with deviating from building work in a material way from the approved plan, contrary to the Hong Kong Building Ordinances. It was necessary to decide if it had to be proved that they knew that their deviation was material or whether the offence was one of strict liability on this point. The Privy Council started with the presumption that *mens rea* is required before a person can be held guilty of a criminal offence but went on to give four other factors to be considered. These were stated by Lord Scarman to be:

- The presumption in favour of *mens rea* being required before D can be convicted applies to statutory offences and can be displaced only if this is clearly or by necessary implication the effect of the statute.
- The presumption is particularly strong where the offence is 'truly criminal' in character.
- The only situation in which the presumption can be displaced is where the statute is concerned with an issue of social concern; public safety is such an issue.
- Even where the statute is concerned with such an issue, the presumption of *mens rea* stands unless it can be shown that the creation of strict liability will be effective to promote the objects of the statute by encouraging greater vigilance to prevent the commission of the prohibited act.

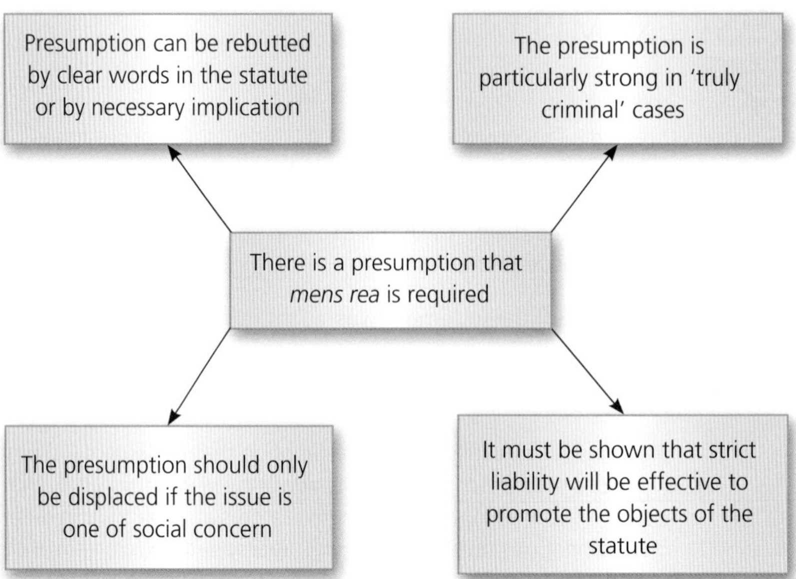

Figure 4.2 The *Gammon* criteria.

4.4.3 Looking at the wording of an Act

As already stated, where words indicating *mens rea* are used, the offence is not one of strict liability. If the particular section is silent on the point, then the courts will look at other sections in the Act. Where the particular offence has no words of intention, but other sections in the Act do, then it is likely that this offence is a strict liability offence. In *Pharmaceutical Society of Great Britain v Storkwain* the relevant section, s 58(2) of the Medicines Act 1968, was silent on *mens rea*. The court looked at other sections in the Act and decided that, as there were express provisions for *mens rea* in other sections, Parliament had intended s 58(2) to be one of strict liability.

However, the fact that other sections specifically require *mens rea* does not mean that the courts will automatically make the offence without express words of *mens rea* one of strict liability. In *Sherras*, even though s 16(1) of the Licensing Act 1872 had express words requiring knowledge, it was held that *mens rea* was still required for s 16(2), which did not include the word 'knowingly'. This point was reinforced in *Sweet*, when Lord Reid stated:

JUDGMENT

'It is also firmly established that the fact that other sections of the Act expressly require *mens rea*, for example because they contain the word "knowingly", is not of itself sufficient to justify a decision that a section which is silent as to *mens rea* creates an absolute offence. In the absence of a clear intention in the Act that an offence is intended to be an absolute offence, it is necessary to go outside the Act and examine all relevant circumstances in order to establish that this must have been the intention of Parliament.'

Where other sections allow for a defence of no negligence but another section does not, then this is another possible indicator from within the statute that the offence is meant to be one of strict liability. In *Harrow LBC v Shah and Shah* the defendants were charged under s 13(1)(c) of the National Lottery etc. Act 1993. The whole of s 13 reads:

SECTION

'13(1) If any requirement or restriction imposed by regulations made under section 12 is contravened in relation to the promotion of a lottery that forms part of the National Lottery,

(a) the promoter of the lottery shall be guilty of an offence, except if the contravention occurred without the consent or connivance of the promoter and the promoter exercised all due diligence to prevent such a contravention,

(b) any director, manager, secretary or other similar officer of the promoter, or any person purporting to act in such a capacity, shall be guilty of an offence if he consented to or connived at the contravention or if the contravention was attributable to any neglect on his part, and

(c) any other person who was a party to the contravention shall be guilty of an offence.

(2) A person guilty of an offence under this section shall be liable

(a) on summary conviction, to a fine not exceeding the statutory maximum;

(b) on conviction on indictment, to imprisonment not exceeding two years, to a fine or to both.'

The subsection under which the defendants were charged, (1)(c), contains no words indicating either that *mens rea* is required or that it is not, nor does it contain any provision for a defence of due diligence. However, subsection (1)(a) clearly allows a defence of due diligence. In addition it contains an element of *mens rea* as it provides for the defendant to be not guilty if the contravention was not done with his consent or connivance. Subsection (1)(b) clearly requires *mens rea*, as it only makes the accused guilty if he 'consented to or connived at the contravention or if the contravention was attributable to any neglect on his part'. The inclusion of a due diligence defence in part of s 13 but not in the section under which the defendants were charged was an important point in the Divisional Court coming to the decision that s 13(1)(c) was an offence of strict liability. Mitchell J said:

JUDGMENT

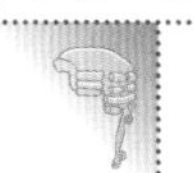

> 'Section 13 has two important features. First, whereas in subsection (1) paragraphs (a) and (b) the liability of the promoter and the promoter's directors, managers and the like is tempered by the provision of a statutory defence. In subsection (1)(c) the liability of "any other person" who was a party to the contravention of the regulations is not expressed to be subject to a statutory defence.'

In fact this statement by Mitchell J that in both paragraphs (1)(a) and (1)(b) liability is tempered by the provision of a statutory defence is not accurate. Only s 13(1)(a) has such a provision. But despite this, the case illustrates how the courts will look at the wording of other relevant provisions in the statute in deciding whether to impose strict liability.

In *Muhamad* [2002] EWCA Crim 1856, D was charged with 'materially contributing to the extent of insolvency by gambling' contrary to s 362(1)(a) of the Insolvency Act 1986. The Court of Appeal pointed out that the wording of the majority of offences in the Act clearly had an express requirement of a mental element. However, s 362(1)(a) was one of the few that did not specify any mental intention. This fact was one of the reasons why the Court of Appeal found that this was an offence of strict liability.

4.4.4 Quasi-criminal offences

In *Gammon* the Privy Council stated that the presumption that *mens rea* is required is particularly strong where the offence is 'truly criminal' in character. Offences which are regulatory in nature are not thought of as being truly criminal matters and are, therefore, more likely to be interpreted as being of strict liability. This idea of offences which are 'not criminal in any real sense, but are acts which in the public interest are prohibited under penalty' was a category mentioned by Wright J in *Sherras* as being an exception to the presumption of *mens rea* where the courts would hold that the offence was one of strict liability. Regulatory offences are usually classed as being 'not truly criminal'. In *Wings Ltd v Ellis* [1984] 3 All ER 584, the House of Lords was considering the Trade Descriptions Act 1968, which creates offences aimed at consumer protection. Lord Scarman pointed out that this Act was 'not a truly criminal statute. Its purpose is not the enforcement of the criminal law but the maintenance of trading standards.'

Regulatory offences are also referred to as 'quasi-crimes'. They affect large areas of everyday life. They include offences such as breaches of regulations in a variety of fields, such as

- selling food, as in *Callow*;
- the selling of alcohol, as in *Cundy*;
- building regulations, as occurred in *Gammon*;
- sales of lottery tickets to an underage child, as in *Harrow LBC*;
- the prevention of pollution, as in *Alphacell Ltd v Woodward* [1972] 2 All ER 475.

In the *Alphacell* case the company was charged with causing polluted matter to enter a river, contrary to s 2(1)(a) of the Rivers (Prevention of Pollution) Act 1951, when pumps which it had installed failed, and polluted effluent overflowed into a river. There was no evidence either that the company knew of the pollution or that it had been negligent. The offence was held by the House of Lords to be one of strict liability and the company found guilty. Lord Salmon stated:

JUDGMENT

'It is of the utmost public importance that rivers should not be polluted. The risk of pollution . . . is very great. The offences created by the Act of 1951 seem to me to be prototypes of offences which are "not criminal in any real sense, but are acts which in the public interest are prohibited under penalty" . . . I can see no valid reason for reading the word "intentionally", "knowingly" or "negligently" into section 2(1)(a) . . . this may be regarded as a not unfair hazard of carrying on a business which may cause pollution on the banks of a river.'

Penalty of imprisonment

Where an offence carries a penalty of imprisonment, it is more likely to be considered 'truly criminal' and so less likely to be interpreted as an offence of strict liability. In *B v DPP* the offence was the commission of gross indecency with or towards a child under 14 which, at the time the offence was committed, carried a maximum penalty of two years' imprisonment. Lord Nicholls pointed out that this was a serious offence, and this was important since 'the more serious the offence, the greater was the weight to be attached to the presumption [of *mens rea*], because the more severe was the punishment and the graver the stigma that accompanied a conviction'.

However, some offences carrying imprisonment have been made strict liability offences. In *Gammon* the offence carried a penalty of HK$250,000 and imprisonment for three years. The Privy Council admitted that this penalty was a 'formidable argument' against strict liability but went on to hold that there was nothing inconsistent with the purpose of the Ordinance in imposing severe penalties for offences of strict liability. It said 'the legislature could reasonably have intended severity to be a significant deterrent, bearing in mind the risks to public safety arising from some contraventions of the ordinance'. Similarly, in *Storkwain* the offence carried a maximum sentence of two years' imprisonment, but this fact did not persuade the House of Lords not to impose strict liability for the offence.

In both these cases the defendant was a corporation; hence, there was no question of a penalty of imprisonment actually being used. However, in *Howells* [1977] QB 614 the defendant was charged with possession of a firearm without a firearm certificate, contrary to s 1(1)(a) of the Firearms Act 1968. The maximum penalty for this offence was five years' imprisonment. Despite this the Court of Appeal held that the offence was one of strict liability. It thought that the wording of the Act and the danger to the public from the unauthorised possession of firearms outweighed the fact of the severity of the maximum sentence in deciding whether to impose strict liability.

More recently, in *Muhamad* [2002] EWCA Crim 186S, the Court of Appeal held that the offence of materially contributing to insolvency by gambling contrary to s 362(1)(a) of the Insolvency Act 1986 was one of strict liability even though it carried a maximum penalty of two years' imprisonment. They stated that it was open to doubt whether it would be regarded as 'truly criminal'. One of the reasons they reached this conclusion was because other offences under the same Act carried a maximum penalty of ten years' imprisonment.

It appears unjust that an individual should be liable to imprisonment even though the offence does not require proof of some fault on the behalf of the defendant. Some writers take the view that it is wrong to impose any penalty on a person where they are not blameworthy. Peter Brett, writing in 1963, put this view forward:

QUOTATION

'Let us now consider what ought to be the future of the doctrine of strict liability. There are those who believe that there is no great objection to it, and even that it serves a useful and proper social purpose. Sayre's general conclusion ("Public Welfare Offences", 33 Col L Rev 55 (1933)) was that the doctrine was applicable only to the minor public welfare offences, despite his recognition of its applicability in some other fields, which he attempted to distinguish on special grounds. In his view there is no objection to applying strict liability so long as only a light penalty is involved; but it ought not to be applied to "true crimes". This seems rather like saying that it is all right to be unjust so long as you are not too unjust. My own position is that any doctrine which permits the infliction of punishment on a morally innocent man is reprehensible.'

P Brett, *An Inquiry into Criminal Guilt* (Sweet & Maxwell, 1963), p. 114

4.4.5 Strict liability and human rights

Where a defendant is at risk of being sentenced to imprisonment, the question of whether this is a breach of human rights is also raised. In Canada, s 7 of their Charter of Human Rights states that 'everyone has the right to life, liberty and security of the person and the right not to be deprived thereof except in accordance with the fundamental principles of justice'. In 1986 the Supreme Court of Canada held that the fundamental principles of justice precluded strict liability where the offence was one which carried a penalty of imprisonment. They said that the 'combination of imprisonment and absolute liability violates s 7 irrespective of the nature of the offence'.

In England and Wales the Human Rights Act 1998 incorporated the European Convention on Human Rights into our law from October 2000. The right to liberty is contained in art 5 of the Convention, and the right to a fair trial in art 6. These are not as broadly worded as the Canadian Charter of Human Rights. They state:

ARTICLE

'5(1) Everyone has the right to liberty and security of person. No one shall be deprived of his liberty save as in the following cases and in accordance with a procedure prescribed by law:

(a) the lawful detention of a person after conviction by a competent court …

6(2) Everyone charged with a criminal offence shall be presumed innocent until proved guilty according to law.'

Unlike the Canadian Charter, this wording does not make any reference to 'fundamental principles of justice'. Instead, art 5 focuses on the procedure being 'prescribed by law', and provided the procedure is lawful and carried out by a competent court, then there is no breach of the Convention. With art 6 the focus is on a fair trial, though art 6(2) maintains the need for the prosecution to prove guilt. However, guilt can be established by proving that the defendant did the prohibited act.

In *K* [2001] 3 All ER 897 the Court of Appeal had to consider whether a genuine mistake was a defence to s 14 of the Sexual Offences Act 1956. It held that the offence was one of strict liability but that this was not incompatible with art 6(2). The Court of Appeal's ruling that the offence was one of strict liability was overruled by the House of Lords (see section 4.4.6); hence, the human rights implication was not a necessary part of the House of Lords' judgment. The Court of Appeal relied on a decision of the European Court of Human Rights in *Salabiaku v France* (1988) 13 EHRR 379, in which it had been said:

JUDGMENT

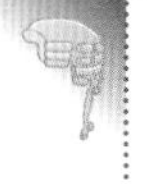

'Article 6(2) does not therefore regard the presumptions of fact or of law provided for in the criminal law with indifference. It requires states to confine them within reasonable limits which take into account the importance of what is at stake and maintain the rights of the defence.'

The House of Lords considered the effect of art 6 in *DPP, ex parte Kebilene* (1999) 4 All ER 801, and Lord Hope said of the provisions of the Convention: 'As a matter of general principle therefore a fair balance must be struck between the demands of the general interest of the community and the protection of the fundamental rights of the individual.'

The question of whether a strict liability offence may be a breach of the right to a fair trial was considered again in *G* [2008] UKHL 37.

CASE EXAMPLE

G [2008] UKHL 37

D was a boy aged 15 who had had sexual intercourse with a girl aged 12. He was charged under s 5 of the Sexual Offences Act 2003 (SOA) with rape of a child under 13. The girl was actually 12, but D believed on reasonable grounds that she was 15. She had told him so on an earlier occasion. D was held to be guilty as the offence is one of strict liability and may be committed irrespective of

- consent
- reasonable belief in consent
- a reasonable belief as to age.

The House of Lords upheld the Court of Appeal's decision that the fact that s 5 was an offence of strict liability did not breach human rights.

The House of Lords was unanimous in stating that strict liability did not breach art 6 of the European Convention on Human Rights. Lord Hoffmann said:

JUDGMENT

'It is settled law that Article 6(1) guarantees fair procedure and the observance of the principle of the separation of powers but not that either the civil or criminal law will have any particular substantive content . . . Likewise, article 6(2) requires him to be presumed innocent of the offence but does not say anything about what the mental or other elements of the offence should be.'

The judges in the Lords were very dismissive of the case of *Salabiaku* stating that no one had yet discovered what the paragraph from the judgment (see previous page) meant. They also pointed out that the European Court of Human Rights itself had ignored the *Salabiaku* in later cases.

G then applied for a hearing by the European Court of Human Rights. The court refused this application. In its reasons for refusal, the court noted that the s 5 offence was created to protect children from sexual abuse and that the prosecution was required to prove all elements of the offence beyond reasonable doubt. The court did not consider that Parliament's decision not to make a defence available where D had a reasonable belief that V was aged 13 or over could give rise to any issue under art 6.

They pointed out that it is not the court's role under art 6(1) or (2) to dictate the contents of domestic criminal law. This included whether an offence should require a blameworthy state of mind. It also included whether or not there should be any particular defence available to the accused.

So it now seems settled that the concept of strict liability does not breach human rights law.

4.4.6 Issues of social concern

The type of crime and whether it is 'truly criminal' is linked to another condition laid down by the case of *Gammon*; that is the question of whether the crime involves an issue of social concern. The Privy Council ruled that the only situation in which the presumption of *mens rea* can be displaced is where the statute is concerned with an issue of social concern. This echoed what had been said in *Sweet*, when Lord Diplock stated:

JUDGMENT

'Where the subject-matter of a statute is the regulation of a particular activity involving potential danger to public health, safety or morals, in which citizens have a choice whether they participate or not, the court may feel driven to infer an intention of Parliament to impose, by penal sanctions, a higher duty of care on those who choose to participate and to place on them an obligation to take whatever measure may be necessary to prevent the prohibited act, without regard to those considerations of cost or business practicability which play a part in the determination of what would be required of them to fulfil the ordinary common law duty of care.'

This allows strict liability to be justified in a wide range of offences as issues of social concern can be seen to cover any activity which is a 'potential danger to public health, safety or morals'. Regulations covering health and safety matters in relation to food, drink, pollution, building and road use are obviously within the range, but other issues such as possession of guns are also regarded as matters of public safety. It is recognised that even sexual offences may come within its ambit where the law is aimed at protecting children or other vulnerable people.

Even transmitting an unlicensed broadcast has been held to be a matter of social concern. This was in *Blake* [1997] 1 All ER 963, where the defendant was a disc jockey who was convicted of using a station for wireless telegraphy without a licence, contrary to s 1(1) of the Wireless Telegraphy Act 1949. His defence was that he believed he was making a demonstration tape and did not know he was transmitting. He was convicted on the basis that the offence was one of strict liability. He appealed to the Court of Appeal, but his appeal was dismissed. Hirst J said:

JUDGMENT

'[S]ince throughout the history of s 1(1), an offender has potentially been subject to a term of imprisonment, the offence is "truly criminal" in character, and … the presumption in favour of *mens rea* is particularly strong. However, it seems to us manifest that the purpose behind making the unlicensed transmissions a serious criminal offence must have been one of social concern in the interests of public safety … since undoubtedly the emergency services and air traffic controllers were using radio communications in 1949, albeit in a much more rudimentary form than nowadays … Clearly, interference with transmissions by these vital public services poses a grave risk to wide sections of the public … [T]he imposition of an absolute offence must surely encourage greater vigilance on the part of those establishing or using a station, or installing or using the apparatus, to avoid committing the offence, eg in the case of users by carefully establishing whether they are on air; it must also operate as a deterrent … In these circumstances we are satisfied that s 1(1) does create an absolute offence.'

KEY FACTS

Key facts on the factors affecting strict liability

Law	Comment	Case
The presumption is that the offence has a *mens rea* requirement.	This is an important presumption at common law and also applies to statutory offences.	*Sweet v Parsley* (1969) *B v OPP* (2000)
The presumption can only be displaced if this is clearly or by necessary implication the effect of the statute.	This can occur if there are clear words stating that no *mens rea* is required. If the Act is silent on *mens rea*, then the courts will look at words in other relevant sections.	*Gammon (Hong Kong) Ltd v Attorney-General of Hong Kong* (1984) *Pharmaceutical Society v Storkwain* (1986): strict liability as other sections had express provision for *mens rea* *R v K* (2001): no strict liability as sections were not part of a 'coherent legislative scheme'
The presumption is particularly strong where the offence is 'truly criminal'.	The graver the offence the less likely strict liability will be imposed. Where the potential penalty is a long term of imprisonment, the offence is unlikely to be one of strict liability. Some imprisonable offences are strict liability.	*B v DPP* (2000) *Sweet v Parsley* (1969) *Howells* (1977)
The only time strict liability should be imposed is where the issue is one of social concern.	These are issues where there is a potential danger to public health, safety or morals.	*Sweet v Parsley* (1969) *Blake* (1997): unauthorised radio transmission posed 'a grave risk'
The court should also be sure that strict liability will be effective in promoting the law.	If strict liability does not do this then it should not be imposed.	*Lim Chin Aik v The Queen* (1963) *Muhamad* (2002)

4.4.7 Promoting enforcement of the law

In *Gammon*, the final point in considering whether strict liability should be imposed, even where the statute is concerned with an issue of social concern, was whether it would be effective to promote the objects of the statute by encouraging greater vigilance to prevent the commission of the prohibited act. If the imposition of strict liability will not make the law more effective, then there is no reason to make the offence one of strict liability.

In *Lim Chin Aik v The Queen* [1963] AC 160, the appellant had been convicted under s 6(2) of the Immigration Ordinance of Singapore of remaining (having entered) in Singapore when he had been prohibited from entering by an order made by the Minister under s 9 of the same Ordinance. The Ordinance was aimed at preventing illegal immigration. However, the appellant had no knowledge of the prohibition, and there was no evidence that the authorities had even tried to bring it to his attention. The Privy Council thought that it was not enough to be sure that the statute dealt with a grave social evil in order to infer strict liability. It was also important to consider whether the imposition of strict liability would assist in the enforcement of the regulations. Lord Evershed said:

JUDGMENT

'It is pertinent also to inquire whether putting the defendant under strict liability will assist in the enforcement of the regulations. That means there must be something he can do, directly or indirectly, by supervision or inspection, by improvement of his business methods or by exhorting those whom he may be expected to influence or control, which will promote the observance of the regulations. Unless this is so, there is no reason in penalising him, and it cannot be inferred that the legislature imposed strict liability merely in order to find a luckless victim …

Where it can be shown that the imposition of strict liability would result in the prosecution and conviction of a class of persons whose conduct could not in any way affect the observance of the law, their Lordships consider that, even where the statute is dealing with a grave social evil, strict liability is not likely to be intended.'

bankruptcy
A declaration by a court that a person's liabilities exceed his assets

However, in *Muhamad* [2002] EWCA Crim 1865, the Court of Appeal thought that making the offence of 'materially contributing to insolvency by gambling' one of strict liability would 'encourage greater vigilance to prevent gambling which will or may materially contribute to insolvency'. The offence is committed by gambling in the two years prior to a petition for **bankruptcy** being made by D's creditors. Given this, it seems unlikely that awareness of strict liability would, in reality, persuade gamblers to desist from gambling.

4.4.8 Twenty-first century cases

In 2000 and 2001 the House of Lords considered the principles of strict liability in two important cases. These were *B v DPP* and *K*. In both they continued the trend, which started with *Sweet*, against the imposition of strict liability. In *B v DPP* the Lords reviewed the law on strict liability.

CASE EXAMPLE

B v DPP [2000] 1 All ER 833

B was a boy aged 15. He sat next to a 13-year-old girl on a bus and asked her to give him a 'shiner', meaning by that to have oral sex with him. He believed she was over the age of 14. He was charged with inciting a child under the age of 14 to commit an act of gross indecency. This is an offence under s 1(1) of the Indecency with Children Act 1960. This states: 'Any person who commits an act of gross indecency with or towards a child under 14 [subsequently raised to 16] or who incites a child under that age to such an act with him or another … is guilty of an offence.'

The question for the House of Lords was whether B's mistake about the girl's age gave him a defence to the charge. If the offence was one of strict liability, then he could not use the defence of mistake. Lord Nicholls gave the leading judgment. He started by pointing out that the section says nothing about the mental element required for the offence. In particular, it says nothing about what the position should be if the person who commits or incites the act of gross indecency honestly but mistakenly believed that the child was 14 or over.

He then reviewed the major elements which have to be considered in deciding whether the offence is one of strict liability. These were

- the presumption of *mens rea*;
- the lack of words of intention;
- whether that presumption was negatived by necessary implication;
- the severity of the punishment;
- the purpose of the section;
- evidential problems;
- effectiveness of strict liability.

What was said on each of these points will now be briefly examined.

Presumption of mens rea

Lord Nicholls said that the starting point was the presumption that *mens rea* was intended and he approved what Lord Reid had said in *Sweet* (see section 4.4.1) that it was firmly established that *mens rea* is an essential ingredient of every offence unless some reason can be found for holding that it is not necessary.

Lack of words of intention

The section had no words referring to the need for *mens rea*. Nor had Parliament expressly stated that there was no need for a mental element in the offence. This meant that the court had to consider whether the need for a mental element was negatived by necessary implication.

Necessary implication

Looking at the factors to be examined in considering whether Parliament's intention was to impose strict liability by 'necessary implication', Lord Nicholls pointed out that, in view of the presumption of *mens rea*, any necessary implication could only be satisfied by an implication that was 'compellingly clear'. He said that such an implication may be found in 'the language used, the nature of the offence, the mischief sought to be prevented and other circumstances that might assist in determining what intention was properly to be attributed to Parliament'. In this case he thought that the position was relatively straightforward. The section had created an entirely new offence which was set out in simple and straightforward language. A major feature was the penalty it attracted.

Severity of punishment

Lord Nicholls felt that these factors reinforced the application of the presumption of *mens rea*. The offence carried a severe penalty and also the stigma of being a sex offender.

Purpose of the section

Even though the purpose of s 1(1) of the 1960 Act was to protect children, this factor did not, of itself, lead to the conclusion that liability was intended to be strict so far as the age element was concerned.

Evidential problems

The fact that it might sometimes be difficult for the prosecution to prove that the defendant had not known that the child was under 14 or that the defendant had been recklessly indifferent about the child's age was not enough to make the offence one of strict liability. Lord Nicholls quoted from an Australian case, *Thomas v R* (1937) 44 ALR 37 on this point:

JUDGMENT

'[A] lack of confidence in the ability of a tribunal to estimate evidence of states of mind and the like can never be sufficient ground for excluding from inquiry the most fundamental element in a rational and humane code.'

Effectiveness of strict liability

On whether strict liability would promote the purpose of s 1(1) more effectively than if *mens rea* were required, Lord Nicholls simply pointed out that there was no general agreement that strict liability was necessary to the enforcement of the law protecting children in sexual matters. In fact the Draft Criminal Code proposed by the Law Commission in 1989 included a defence of belief that the child was over 16 on similar offences.

Effect of Prince

The final point considered was whether the decision in *Prince*, where it had been held that the defendant could not use a genuine belief that a girl was over 16 for an offence of removing her from her father's custody, should be followed. The prosecution submitted that the law had been settled since the case of *Prince* (1875) (i.e. that a mistaken belief about age was no defence) and that as the Sexual Offences Act 1956 had not been intended to change this, so the same was true of the 1960 Act. In addition, the prosecution argued that when Parliament intended belief as to age to be a defence, this was stated expressly. He cited s 6(3) of the 1956 Act as an example, where a belief that a girl was 16 or over was a defence to a defendant under 24 on a charge of unlawful sexual intercourse with a girl under 16. Lord Nicholls rejected these arguments for the following reasons:

- The reasoning in *Prince* has been subjected to sustained criticism.
- The offences gathered into the Sexual Offences Act 1956 displayed no overall consistent pattern, and therefore the compelling guidance that another statute would have to give to the present one under consideration was simply not there.

Conclusion

The Law Lords reached the conclusion that there was nothing to displace the common law presumption that *mens rea* was required. This is the modern approach which reinforces the need for *mens rea* and shows the courts' reluctance to declare an offence which is 'truly criminal' to be one of strict liability. However, it should be noted that the House of Lords did not specifically overrule the decision in *Prince* as it pointed out that the case concerned a different offence.

Commentators disagreed on the importance of this decision in *B v DPP*. Professor Sir John Smith, in a commentary on the case in (2000) Criminal Law Review 404, suggested it would have far-reaching consequences, whereas the editors of Archbold thought that this was 'significantly overstating its significance because it is far from clear what it decides other than in relation to the particular offence'. John Beaumont also highlighted the fact that it did not necessarily lay down general principles:

QUOTATION

'[T]he case does not really make any progress to solve the general problem of when strict liability should be imposed. The various considerations that are said by the House to be relevant in this context amount to no more than a restatement of the principles set out in earlier cases, such as *Sweet v Parsley*. They suffer from the same defect as all such attempts, in that they leave the law in this area in an uncertain state.'

John Beaumont, 'Mistake and strict liability' (2000) New Law Journal 382 and 433

Law reform

Finally, the case also highlighted the need for reform of the law and a consistent approach by Parliament on whether offences required *mens rea*. Lord Hutton said it was to be regretted that Parliament had not taken account of the expert advice that it had received over the years from bodies such as the Law Commission and the Criminal Law Reform Committee regarding the need to state clearly in all criminal offences whether or not *mens rea* is required.

Case of K

One year after *B v DPP* the use of strict liability offences was again considered by the House of Lords, in *K*. In this case it had to consider whether s 14(1) of the Sexual Offences Act 1956 was a strict liability offence. The defendant was a 26-year-old man who had taken part in consensual sexual activity with a 14-year-old girl. He honestly believed that she was aged 16 or over, and the point in the case was whether this could be a defence to s 14(1). The whole section provides

SECTION

'14(1) It is an offence, subject to the exception mentioned in subsection (3) of the section, for a person to make an indecent assault on a woman.

(2) A girl under the age of 16 cannot in law give any consent which would prevent an act being an assault for the purposes of this section.

(3) Where a marriage is invalid under section two of the Age of Marriage Act 1929 (the wife being a girl under the age of 16), the invalidity does not make the husband guilty of any offence under this section by reason of her incapacity to consent while under that age, if he believes her to be his wife and has reasonable cause for the belief.

(4) A woman who is a defective cannot in law give any consent which would prevent an act being an assault for the purposes of this section, but a person is only to be treated as guilty of an indecent assault on a defective by reason of that incapacity to consent, if that person knew or had reason to suspect her to be a defective.'

As in *B v DPP*, there are no words at all referring to *mens rea* contained in subs (1). However, there is a difference, in that there are two situations in which a mistake as to a fact (of a valid marriage or of being a defective) can provide a defence. At the trial, a preliminary issue was raised as to whether the prosecution had to prove that at the time of the incident K did not honestly believe that the girl was 16 or over. The trial judge ruled that the prosecution did have to prove that the defendant had an absence of genuine belief on this point. The prosecution appealed against this ruling and the Court of Appeal allowed the appeal holding that an absence of belief did not have to be proved. The Court of Appeal certified the following point of law of general public importance for the consideration of the House of Lords:

JUDGMENT

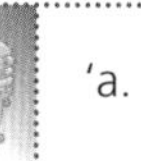

'a. Is a defendant entitled to be acquitted of the offence of indecent assault on a complainant under the age of 16 years, contrary to s 14(1) of the Sexual Offences Act 1956, if he may hold an honest belief that the complainant in question was aged 16 years or over?

b. If yes, must the belief be held on reasonable grounds?'

The House of Lords reversed the decision of the Court of Appeal and held that an honest belief was a defence to the charge. It considered the language of the section and concluded that they could not place any reliance on the structure of s 14. It said it was not part of a 'single coherent legislative scheme', but rather of a 'rag-bag nature'. In fact it had been a consolidation Act with offences being brought together from several earlier Acts. Lord Bingham pointed out that, within s 14, each subsection had its origins in different Acts.

- Section 14(1) derived from s 52 of the Offences Against the Person Act 1861.
- Section 14(2) had its origins in the Criminal Law Amendment Act 1880 when the age was 13 and this had been changed by the Criminal Law Amendment Act 1922 to the age of 16.
- Section 14(3) had its origins in the Age of Marriage Act 1929.
- Section 14(4) derives from s 56(3) of the Mental Deficiency Act 1913.

It could not, therefore, be said from looking at the structure of the section that Parliament had intended s 14(1) and s 14(2) to impose strict liability in relation to a situation where the defendant had made an honest mistake about the girl's age. They relied on the fact that there was no express exclusion of the need to prove an absence of genuine belief on the part of the defendant as to the age of an underage victim.

The Law Lords also thought that it was right to look at the Act involved in *B v DPP*, the Indecency with Children Act 1960, as the Lords in that case had been invited to treat the Acts as part of a single code. As absence of genuine belief as to the age of an underage victim had to be proved against a defendant under s 1 of the 1960 Act, it would create a 'glaring anomaly' if the same rule was not to be applied to s 14 of the 1956 Act. There was also a persistent and unacceptable anomaly within the 1956 Act, by which a defendant could plead the 'young man's defence' to a charge under s 6 of sexual intercourse with a girl under age 16, but could not rely on any similar argument in respect of a charge of indecent assault arising out of that sexual intercourse.

The Lords concluded that the presumption of *mens rea* had been underlined in *Sweet v Parsley* and again recently in *B v DPP*. In a statutory offence the presumption of *mens rea* could only be excluded by express words or by necessary implication. In s 14 there were no express words, and the 'rag-bag' nature of the Act, together with the anomaly arising from the young man's defence, made it impossible to find the necessary implication.

Although, as with *B v DPP*, this case does not expressly overrule *Prince*, the Lords in *R v K* referred to it as being 'discredited', and it appears to have been impliedly overruled.

The case of Kumar

The decisions in *B v DPP* and *K* were followed in *Kumar* [2004] EWCA Crim 3207 where the Court of Appeal held that buggery of a boy under the age of 16 (an offence under s 12 of the Sexual Offences Act 1956, now repealed) was not one of strict liability.

CASE EXAMPLE

Kumar [2004] EWCA Crim 3207

D, aged 34, picked up V, a 14-year-old boy at a recognised gay club. The club had a policy of admitting only those aged 18 or over. The evidence was that V looked about 17. V willingly went to D's flat and consensual sexual activity took place, including penetration of V's anus by D. The trial judge ruled that the offence was one of strict liability in regard to the age of V. D then pleaded guilty. He appealed on the ground that the judge was wrong in holding that the offence was one of strict liability and that an honest belief as to the age of V should be allowed as a defence. The Court of Appeal allowed the appeal.

In this case the Court of Appeal relied on the judgment in *B v DPP* [2000] Cr App R 65. They referred to several passages in it starting with Lord Nicholls when he said:

JUDGMENT

'As habitually happens with statutory offences, when enacting this offence Parliament defined the prohibited conduct solely in terms of the prescribed physical acts . . .

In these circumstances the starting point for a court is the established common law presumption that a mental element, traditionally labelled *mens rea*, is an essential ingredient unless Parliament has indicated a contrary intention either expressly or by necessary implication. The common law presumes that, unless Parliament indicated otherwise, the appropriate mental element is an unexpressed ingredient of every statutory offence.'

They also considered the judgment of another judge in *B v DPP*, Lord Steyn, who explained the principle in a slightly different way:

JUDGMENT

'The language is general and nothing on the face of s 1(1) [of the Indecency with Children Act 1960] indicates one way or the other whether s 1(1) creates an offence of strict liability. In enacting such a provision Parliament does not write on a blank sheet. The sovereignty of Parliament is the paramount principle of our constitution. But Parliament legislates against the background of the principle of legality.'

To explain the point of the principle of legality, Lord Steyn quoted from the judgment of Lord Hoffmann in *R v Secretary of State for the Home Department, ex p Simms* [1999] 3 WLR 328 where he said:

JUDGMENT

'But the principle of legality means that Parliament must squarely confront what it is doing and accept the political cost. Fundamental rights cannot be overridden by general or ambiguous words. This is because there is too great a risk that the full implications of their unqualified meaning may have passed unnoticed in the democratic process. In the absence of express language or necessary implication to the contrary, the courts therefore presume that even the most general words were intended to be subject to the basic rights of the individual.'

student mentor tip

'The best way to study criminal law is to read the cases in full. This will not only ensure you remember the principles but the facts are usually easy to remember and will help you recall the judgments too.'
Gayatri, University of Leicester

The Court of Appeal concluded that very similar considerations to those in *B v DPP* and *K* applied in *Kumar*. The mental element had not been excluded from s 12 of the Sexual Offences Act 1956 by necessary implication. Consequently an honest belief that V was over 16 was a defence.

Cases where strict liability has been found

Although the above cases demonstrate an unwillingness to declare an offence one of strict liability, there have been other recent cases where the courts have been prepared to rule that the offence was one of strict liability. For example in *Muhamad* [2002] EWCA Crim 1865, the Court of Appeal held that the offence of materially contributing to insolvency by gambling under s 362(1)(a) of the Insolvency Act 1986 was an offence of strict liability even though it carried a maximum sentence of two years' imprisonment. They held that it was not necessary to prove that D knew or was reckless as to whether his act of gambling would materially contribute to his insolvency. The Sexual Offences Act

2003 (SOA) has created several offences of strict liability in respect of belief in the age of a willing participant in sexual activity. In *G* [2006] EWCA Crim 821, the defence accepted that s 5 of the SOA 2003 (rape of a child under 13) created a strict liability offence, even where the defendant honestly and reasonably believed that the child was over 13, and the child was a willing participant. The defence accepted this as other sections in the Act have express references to reasonable belief that a child is over 16, whereas s 5 has no allowance for a reasonable belief as to age. Despite the fact that this offence is one of strict liability, it carries a maximum penalty of imprisonment for life.

The Firearms Act 1968 also has a number of sections which impose strict liability. In *Deyemi (Danny)* [2007] EWCA Crim 2060, D was stopped and searched, and an electrical stun gun was found. D was charged with possessing a prohibited weapon contrary to s 5(1)(b) of the Firearms Act 1968. D's evidence was that he did not know it was a stun gun; he thought it was a torch. The trial judge held that the offence was one of strict liability. So D then pleaded guilty, but appealed to the Court of Appeal. They held that physical possession of the gun was sufficient to make D guilty. The fact that he was ignorant of its nature was not relevant.

Another case of strict liability under the Firearms Act 1968 is *Zahid (Nasir)* [2010] EWCA Crim 2158 which involved possession of ammunition contrary to s 5(1A)(f). D had two bullets in his pocket and a brown paper package containing 38 more bullets in his house. His defence was that he had found the package outside his front door and believed it to contain bolts or screws left by workmen working at his house. He had put it into his pocket to take indoors and was unaware that anything had fallen into his pocket.

The reasoning in *Deyemi* was applied and the Court of Appeal held that the offence was one of strict liability. A genuine belief the article was something other than bullets was not a defence.

ACTIVITY

Applying the law

Read the following sections of the Food Safety Act 1990 and apply them to the situations below to decide whether an offence has been committed.

'14. Selling food not of the nature or substance or quality demanded

1. Any person who sells to the purchaser's prejudice any food which is not of the nature or substance or quality demanded by the purchaser shall be guilty of an offence.
2. In subsection (1) above the reference to sale shall be construed as a reference to sale for human consumption; and in proceedings under that subsection it shall not be a defence that the purchaser was not prejudiced because he bought for analysis or examination.'

'21. Defence of due diligence

1. In any proceedings for an offence under any of the preceding provisions of this Part, it shall ... be a defence for the person charged to prove that he took all reasonable precautions and exercised all due diligence to avoid the commission of the offence by himself or by a person under his control.
2. Without prejudice to the generality of subsection (1) above, a person charged with an offence under section 8, 14 or 15 above who neither:
   (a) prepared the food in respect of which the offence is alleged to have been committed; nor
   (b) imported it into Great Britain, shall be taken to have established the defence provided by that subsection if he satisfies the requirements of subsection (3) or (4) below.

3. A person satisfies the requirements of this subsection if he proves:

   (a) that the commission of the offence was due to an act or default of another person who was not under his control, or to reliance on information supplied by such a person;
   (b) that he carried out all such checks of the food in question as were reasonable in all the circumstances, or that it was reasonable in all the circumstances for him to rely on checks carried out by the person who supplied the food to him; and
   (c) that he did not know and had no reason to suspect at the time of commission of the alleged offence that his act or omission would amount to an offence under the relevant provision.'

Situations

1. Grant owns a pizza parlour. He buys toppings to put on pizzas from Home Foodies Ltd. When he bought the latest batch, he told the sales representative of Home Foodies that he did not want any of the toppings to contain nuts. The sales rep assured him that all their products were 'nut-free'. Halouma bought a pizza and suffered a severe allergic reaction, which was found to be because the topping contained traces of nuts.
2. Tanya owns a sandwich bar. Unknown to her, Wesley, one of the sandwich makers, used Edam cheese to make sandwiches described as 'cheddar cheese and chutney'. These sandwiches were sold in the sandwich bar.
3. Kylie, who is a trained nutritionist, owns a restaurant. On the menu certain meals are described as 'low-calorie'. Kylie has given the chefs a list of suitable ingredients to be used in these meals. This includes using low-fat yogurt instead of cream in making sauces. One evening a chef uses cream instead of the yogurt in a 'low-calorie' dish served to one of the diners.

4.5 Justification for strict liability

The main justification is that given in *Sweet*, that strict liability offences help protect society by regulation of activities 'involving potential danger to public health, safety or morals'. The imposition of strict liability promotes greater care over these matters by encouraging higher standards in such matters as hygiene in processing and selling food or in obeying building or transport regulations. It makes sure that businesses are run properly. This reason for justifying the use of strict liability was put by Kenny:

QUOTATION

'The application of strict liability can be justified in special cases: particularly with regard to the conduct of a business. In such a case, even a strict liability statute makes an appeal to the practical reasoning of the citizens: in this case, when the decision is taken whether to enter the business the strictness of the liability is a cost to be weighed. Strict liability is most in place when it is brought to bear on corporations. In such cases there may not be, in advance, any individual on whom an obligation of care rests which would ground a charge of negligence for the causing of the harm which the statute wishes to prevent: the effect of the legislation may be to lead corporations to take the decision to appoint a person with the task of finding out how to prevent the harm in question.'

A Kenny, *Free Will and Responsibility* (Routledge, 1978), p. 93

As failure to comply with high standards may cause risk to the life and health of large numbers of the general public, there is good reason to support this point of view. However, some opponents of strict liability argue that there is no evidence that strict liability leads to business taking a higher standard of care. Some even argue that strict liability may be counterproductive. If people realise that they could be prosecuted even though they have taken every possible care, they may be tempted not to take any precautions.

Other justifications for the imposition of strict liability include the following:

- It is easier to enforce, as there is no need to prove *mens rea*.
- It saves court time, as people are more likely to plead guilty.
- Parliament can provide a no negligence defence where this is thought appropriate.
- Lack of blameworthiness can be taken into account when sentencing.

As there is no need to prove *mens rea*, it is clear that enforcement of the law is more straightforward. In addition, rather than prosecute for minor regulatory breaches, the Health and Safety Executive and local trading standards officers are more likely to serve improvement notices or prohibition notices in the first instance. This can help ensure that the law is complied with, without the need for a court hearing. When a case is taken to court, the fact that only the act has to be proved saves time and also leads to many guilty pleas.

The use of due diligence defence (or a no negligence defence) can temper the law on strict liability. In many instances Parliament provides such a defence in the statute creating the offence. If the inclusion of such defences was done in a consistent way, then many of the objectors to the imposition of strict liability would be satisfied. However, the use of due diligence clauses in Acts often seems haphazard. For example in *Harrow LBC v Shah and Shah*, the relevant section allowed a due diligence defence for promoters of the lottery but not for those managing a business in which lottery tickets were sold (see section 4.2.1).

The final justification for strict liability is that allowances for levels of blameworthiness can be made in sentencing. Baroness Wootton wrote:

QUOTATION

> 'Traditionally, the requirement of the guilty mind is written into the actual definition of a crime. No guilty intention, no crime, is the rule. Obviously this makes sense if the law's concern is with wickedness: where there is no guilty intention, there can be no wickedness. But it is equally obvious, on the other hand, that an action does not become innocuous merely because whoever performed it meant no harm. If the object of the criminal law is to prevent the occurrence of socially damaging actions, it would be absurd to turn a blind eye to those which were due to carelessness, negligence or even accident. The question of motivation is in the first instance irrelevant. But only in the first instance. At a later stage, that is to say, after what is now known as a conviction, the presence or absence of guilty intention is all-important for its effect on the appropriate measures to be taken to prevent a recurrence of the forbidden act.'
>
> Baroness Wootton, *Crime and the Criminal Law* (2nd edn, Stevens, 1981)

4.5.1 Arguments against strict liability

Although there are sound justifications for imposing strict liability, there are also equally persuasive arguments against its use. The main argument against strict liability is that it imposes guilt on people who are not blameworthy in any way. Even those who have taken all possible care will be found guilty and can be punished. This happened in the case of *Harrow LBC v Shah and Shah*, where they had done their best to prevent sales of lottery tickets to anyone under the age of 16. Another case where all possible care had been taken was *Callow*. In this case even the use of an expert (a vet) was insufficient to avoid liability.

Although an important reason for imposition of strict liability is the maintenance of high standards so that health and safety are not put in jeopardy, there is, as already mentioned earlier, no evidence that it improves standards. With some of the offences it is difficult to see how strict liability would persuade other people not to commit the offence. A clear example is *Muhamad* where it was held that there was strict liability for materially contributing to insolvency by gambling. For this offence the conduct complained of could take place at any time in the two years before any petition for bankruptcy was filed against D. It, therefore, seems highly unlikely that any gambler would address their mind to potential creditors and a future risk of insolvency.

Finally, the imposition of strict liability where an offence is punishable by imprisonment is contrary to the principles of human rights.

4.6 Proposals for reform

The surest way to be certain whether a statutory offence is meant to be one of strict liability is for Parliament always to state expressly whether or not it is. The example of the Contempt of Court Act 1981 shows that this can be done. However, it seems unlikely that Parliament will take this route for every Act that creates criminal offences.

Another method which would avoid the worst effects of strict liability is that recommended by the Law Commission in its report *The Mental Element in Crime* (1978) (Law Com No 89). Its proposal was that all strict liability offences should be treated as crimes of negligence. This would mean the prosecution would have to prove that D had been negligent. So any defendant who had taken all possible care and not been negligent would not be guilty. Under this principle the pharmacist in *Storkwain* would not have been guilty, nor would the defendants in *Shah and Shah* have been guilty of selling a lottery ticket to an underage person.

A move towards making more strict liability offences ones of negligence would be for Parliament to include 'due diligence' or 'no negligence' defences more often when enacting criminal offences. This is already done in a number of regulatory Acts such as the Food Act 1984 or the Tobacco Advertising and Promotion Act 2002.

An alternative way of avoiding some of the problems of strict liability would be to take regulatory offences out of the criminal justice system and deal with them through the civil justice system instead. There has been a move towards this with the Regulatory, Enforcement and Sanctions Act 2008. Part 3 of the Act provides a number of civil sanctions by which regulators can be given power to impose for breaches of regulatory law. These include fixed monetary penalties. There are also discretionary powers including

- a variable monetary penalty, the amount being decided by the regulator;
- a requirement that certain steps be taken to ensure that the offence does not occur again;
- a restoration order requiring that the position be restored to what it would have been if the offence had not occurred;
- a stop notice which prohibits the person from carrying on an activity specified in the notice until they have taken the steps specified in the notice.

This method is suitable to deal with regulatory offences in such areas as selling food or alcohol or other items such as lottery tickets, but it obviously cannot be used for other offences such as drugs, firearms or sex offences. These have to remain in the criminal justice system.

SUMMARY

Absolute liability is where no *mens rea* is needed at all. In addition, it is not necessary to prove that the defendant's *actus reus* was voluntary. Absolute offences are very rare.

A **strict liability offence** is one where *mens rea* is not required for at least one part of the *actus reus*.

For strict liability offences there is no defence of due diligence. Also, the defence of mistake is not available.

The only strict liability offences in common law are public nuisance, criminal libel and outraging public decency.

More than half of all statutory offences are ones of strict liability. To decide whether an offence is one of strict liability the wording is considered. If it is clear that no *mens rea* is required, then the offence is one of strict liability. If the wording is not clear then the *Gammon* tests are used to decide. These are as follows:

1. There is a presumption that *mens rea* is required.
2. The presumption is particularly strong where the offence is 'truly criminal'.
3. The presumption applied can be displaced only if this is clearly or by necessary implication the effect of the statute.
4. The presumption can only be displaced where the statute involves an issue of social concern.
5. The creation of strict liability must be effective to promote the objects of the statute by encouraging greater vigilance to prevent the commission of the prohibited act.

Strict liability is justified because:

- It protects society.
- It is easier to enforce as there is no need to prove *mens rea*.
- It saves court time as people are more likely to plead guilty.
- Parliament can provide a no negligence defence where this is thought appropriate.
- Lack of blameworthiness can be taken into account when sentencing.

Arguments against strict liability are:

- Liability should not be imposed on people who are not blameworthy.
- Those who have taken all possible care should not be penalised.
- There is no evidence that it improves standards.
- It is contrary to the principles of human rights.

SAMPLE ESSAY QUESTION

Critically discuss the factors the courts take into account when considering whether a statutory offence is one of strict liability or not.

Define strict liability:

- Explain the presumption of *mens rea*
- State the *Gammon* criteria
- Could also state the elements reviewed in *B v DPP* (2000)
- Then expand each of the *Gammon* criteria using cases – see below

Presumption displaced only if this is clearly or by necessary implication the effect of the statute:

- Are there express words?
- If not, can look at other sections in the Act, but does this really indicate Parliament's intention?
- Courts not always consistent in applying this e.g. *Sherras v de Rutzen*

Presumption is particularly strong where the offence is 'truly criminal':

- Is there stigma attached to the offence?
- Is it punishable with imprisonment?
- Discuss cases e.g. *G* (2008), *B v DPP* (2000), *Howells* (1977), *Muhamad* (2002)
- Are the courts consistent?

Does offence involve an issue of social concern?

- What are matters of social concern?
- Obvious ones of public health and safety, pollution, etc.
- But what about other areas? e.g. gambling *Muhamad*, wireless transmissions *Blake* (1997)
- Do these involve social concern?

Will strict liability be effective to promote the objects of the statute?

- Does strict liability encourage greater vigilance to prevent offences?
- Compare courts' approach in *Gammon* (1984) and *Lim Chin Aik* (1963)
- Discuss other cases e.g. sex offences involving defendants under 16 – *B v DPPG*
- Discuss other areas of law e.g. gambling *Muhamad*

General points:

- Are the courts consistent in their approach?
- Courts may stress one of the criteria more than others

Conclude

ACTIVITY

Self-test questions

1. Explain what is meant by 'absolute liability'. How does this differ from 'strict liability'?
2. Explain with examples which defence is not available to a defendant charged with a strict liability offence.
3. What are the *Gammon* tests for deciding when a statutory offence will be construed as an offence of strict liability?
4. Give examples of matters which are considered to be of 'social concern' and, therefore, more likely to be construed as strict liability offences.
5. Explain the arguments for and against strict liability.

Further reading

Books

Clarkson, C M V and Keating, H, *Criminal Law: Text and Materials* (7th edn, Sweet & Maxwell, 2010), Chapter 3, Part I.

Articles

Beaumont, J, 'Mistake and strict liability' (2000) NLJ 382 and 433.

Horder, J, 'Strict liability, statutory construction and the spirit of liberty' (2002) 118 LQR 458.

Reed, A, 'Case comment: strict liability and the reasonable excuse defence' (2012) J Crim L 293.

Stanton-Ife, J, 'Strict liability: stigma and regret' (2003) 27 OJLS 151.

Smith, J C, 'Commentary on the case of B v DPP' (2000) Crim LR 404.

5

Parties to a crime

AIMS AND OBJECTIVES

After reading this chapter you should be able to:

- Understand the law of secondary liability – aiding, abetting, counselling or procuring
- Understand the law of joint enterprise
- Understand when secondary liability can be avoided by withdrawing
- Analyse critically the rules on secondary liability and joint enterprise
- Apply the law to factual situations to determine whether there is liability either as an accessory or for a joint enterprise

5.1 Principal offenders

The person who directly and immediately causes the *actus reus* of the offence is the 'perpetrator' or 'principal', while those who assist or contribute to the *actus reus* are 'secondary parties', or 'accessories'. Just because two (or more) parties are involved in the commission of a criminal offence, it does not mean that one of them must be the principal and the other their accessory. They may be both (or all) principals, provided that each has *mens rea* and together they carry out the *actus reus* (see below). If D and E plant a bomb, which explodes killing V, then they are both liable as principals for homicide. This often happens where D and E carry out a robbery or burglary together, which is referred to as a 'joint enterprise', although it is possible to conceive of a situation whereby D and E, for example, independently attack V and the combined effect is serious injury or death. Each would be guilty of assault as principal offenders.

5.1.1 Difficulties in identifying the principal

In some cases it may be obvious that a crime has been committed by one or both of two people but it may not be clear either who is the principal or whether the other was an accessory. In such a case, both may escape liability. There was a particular problem when a child died whilst being looked after by two parents or carers. In *Lane and Lane* (1986) 82 Cr App R 5, evidence showed that the Lanes' child was killed between 12 noon and 8.30 p.m. Each parent had been present for some of this time and absent for some of this time. It could not be proved that one was the principal, nor could it be proved that the other must have been an accessory. Both had to be acquitted of manslaughter.

This problem has now been addressed by Parliament. Section 5(1) of the Domestic Violence, Crime and Victims Act 2004, which is discussed more fully in Chapter 10, created a new offence of causing or allowing the death of a child or vulnerable adult. In *Ikram and Parveen* [2008] EWCA Crim 586; [2008] 4 All ER 253, which is factually very similar to *Lane and Lane*, the father of a one-year-old boy and the father's partner were convicted under s 5 after the child suffered a non-accidental broken leg, which caused a fat embolism (when fat enters the bloodstream) with fatal consequences. No one else had had any contact with the child on the fateful day, so one or other of the defendants must have been responsible. However, both defendants claimed not to know how the child's leg was broken and with no other evidence it would have been extremely difficult to convict either defendant of murder or manslaughter. Instead, they were both convicted under s 5 of the 2004 Act.

Meanwhile, if it can be proved that D, being one of two or more parties to a crime, must have been guilty as either principal or accessory, then he may be convicted. In *Giannetto* [1997] 1 Cr App R 1, D was convicted of the murder of his wife, V. According to the prosecution's case, V was murdered either by D or by a hired killer on his behalf. D appealed on the ground that, if the prosecution could not prove whether he had murdered V himself or someone else had done it, he was entitled to an acquittal. The Court of Appeal dismissed the appeal. Provided, in either case, that D had the requisite *actus reus* and *mens rea* (as principal, this is causing death with intent to kill or cause really serious injury; for secondary parties, see below), then it did not matter whether he had killed her himself or encouraged another to do so.

5.2 Innocent agents

Where the perpetrator of the *actus reus* of a crime is an 'innocent agent', someone without *mens rea*, or not guilty because of a defence such as infancy or insanity, then the person most closely connected with the agent is the principal. So if D, an adult, employs his eight-year-old son to break into houses and steal, the child is an innocent agent, and the father liable as principal. A well-known example of an 'innocent agent' acting without *mens rea* would be a postman unknowingly delivering a letter bomb. An example comes from the case of *Cogan and Leak* [1976] QB 217. L terrorised his wife into having sex with another man, C. C's conviction for rape was quashed because his plea that he honestly believed L's wife was consenting had not been left to the jury. L's rape conviction was upheld on the basis that he had procured (caused) the crime to happen (see below). The Court of Appeal also considered, *obiter*, that L may alternatively have committed the offence as principal through the doctrine of an innocent agency. Lawton LJ said that, 'had [L] been indicted as a principal offender, the case against him would have been clear beyond argument'.

5.3 Secondary parties

5.3.1 *Actus reus* of secondary parties: aiding, abetting, counselling or procuring

The law for indictable offences is set out in s 8 of the Accessories and Abettors Act 1861 (s 44 of the Magistrates' Courts Act 1980 provides the same for summary offences): 'Whosoever shall aid, abet, counsel or procure the commission of any indictable offence

aiding and abetting
Providing help or encouragement to another person to commit a crime

counselling
Advising or persuading another person to commit a crime

… is liable to be tried, indicted and punished as a principal offender.' This is a very wide definition. It should also be noted that it is possible for a secondary party to be held liable for committing an offence which they could not commit as principal. For example, a woman may commit rape as an accessory, although women cannot commit rape as principal offender (*DPP v K & C* [1997] Crim LR 121; see Chapter 12). A secondary party will be charged with '**aiding, abetting, counselling** or **procuring**' the particular offence (murder, robbery, theft, etc.) and is liable to be convicted provided that it can be proved that he participated in at least one of the four ways. The Court of Appeal has held that the words should simply bear their ordinary meaning. In *Attorney-General's Reference (No 1 of 1975)* [1975] 2 All ER 684, Lord Widgery CJ said:

JUDGMENT

'We approach s 8 of the 1861 Act on the basis that the words should be given their ordinary meaning, if possible. We approach the section on the basis also that if four ordinary words are employed here – aid, abet, counsel or procure – the probability is that there is a difference between each of those four words and the other three, because, if there were no such difference, then Parliament would be wasting time in using four words where two or three would do.'

procuring
Taking steps to cause another person to commit a crime

There is considerable overlap between the four words, and it is quite possible for D to participate in more than one way.

KEY FACTS

Aiding	Helping or assisting the principal, whether prior to, or at the time of, the commission of the *actus reus* by the principal. Typical examples: supplying information or equipment; keeping watch; acting as driver.
Abetting	Encouraging the principal at the time of the offence. An example might involve a crowd of onlookers shouting encouragement to the perpetrators of an assault or rape.
Counselling	Encouraging the principal prior to the commission of the *actus reus*. Also advising, suggesting or instigating an offence. The best-known English case involves hiring a 'hitman' to carry out a murder.
Procuring	Used to mean 'to produce by endeavour'. More modern cases indicate that it is enough for D to make some causal contribution to the performance by the principal of the *actus reus*.

'Aiding'

As indicated above, this means to provide some assistance before or during the commission of a crime by the principal. The scope of aiding is demonstrated by the case of *Robinson* [2011] UKPC 3, in which D was convicted of aiding a murder committed by E by acting as a lookout/backup. E had killed two men (who were twin brothers) with a baseball bat, while D guarded the door to the room where the attack took place. The brothers' decomposing bodies were found a month later down a cliff. D appealed, unsuccessfully, to the Privy Council. The Court stated that aiding 'imports a positive act of assistance' but added that:

JUDGMENT

'Of course, that positive act of assistance may sometimes be constituted by D2 being present, and communicating to D1 not merely that he concurs in what D1 is doing, but that he is ready and willing to help in any way required. The commission of most criminal offences, and certainly most offences of violence, may be assisted by the forbidding presence of another as back-up and support.'

'Abetting'

The threshold of involvement is very low. The Court of Appeal in *Giannetto* [1996] Crim LR 722 stated that 'any involvement from mere encouragement upwards would suffice' for a conviction of abetting. In turn, 'encouragement' could be 'as little as patting on the back, nodding, saying "Oh goody"'. Although it is not essential for D to be present at the scene of the crime if charged with aiding, it seems that it is essential for abetting.

A remarkable example of abetting is provided by the recent Supreme Court case of *Gnango* (2011).

CASE EXAMPLE

Gnango [2011] UKSC 59; [2012] 1 AC 827

One evening, Armel Gnango and a man known only as 'Bandana Man' engaged in a gun battle in southeast London. A young woman, Magda Pniewska, was caught in the crossfire and killed – shot once in the head by Bandana Man. Gnango was subsequently convicted of the attempted murder of Bandana Man and the murder of Magda, on the basis of joint enterprise. He successfully appealed against his murder conviction to the Court of Appeal, but the prosecution appealed to the Supreme Court. That court, sitting with seven judges, allowed the appeal, and reinstated the murder conviction – not on the basis of joint enterprise, but on the basis of secondary liability. Lord Phillips, Lord Judge CJ, Lord Dyson and Lord Wilson held that Gnango, by firing shots at Bandana Man, was simultaneously attempting to murder Bandana Man and, at the same time, aiding and abetting the attempted murder *of himself*. Bandana Man, meanwhile, was attempting to murder Gnango, but inadvertently shot Magda. Through the application of transferred malice, this would have made Bandana Man guilty of her murder. Finally, because of Gnango's participation in the attempted murder of himself, and a second application of transferred malice, that made Gnango guilty of Magda's murder. Lord Phillips explained his reasoning as follows:

JUDGMENT

'(i) Bandana Man attempted to kill [Gnango]. (ii) By agreeing to the shoot-out, [Gnango] aided and abetted Bandana Man in this attempted murder. (iii) Bandana Man accidentally killed Miss Pniewska instead of [Gnango]. Under the doctrine of transferred malice he was guilty of her murder. (iv) The doctrine of transferred malice applied equally to [Gnango] as aider and abetter of Bandana Man's attempted murder. He also was guilty of Miss Pniewska's murder.'

A number of cases have raised the issue whether mere presence at the scene of the crime (as opposed to presence combined with some actions: shouting, gesticulating, etc.) will suffice for the *actus reus* of abetting. In *Coney and others* (1882) 8 QBD 534, three onlookers at an illegal bare-knuckle fight were convicted of abetting assault. The Court of Criminal Appeal quashed their convictions following misdirections to the jury. The court held that, although presence alone may suffice for the *actus reus*, it must be combined with the culpable mental element for it to amount to the offence of abetting. Hawkins J said:

JUDGMENT

'A man may unwittingly encourage another in fact by his presence, by misinterpreted words, or gestures, or by his silence ... or he may encourage intentionally by expressions, gestures or actions intended to signify approval. In the latter case he aids and abets, in the former he does not. It is no criminal offence to stand by, a mere passive spectator of a crime ... But the fact that a person was voluntarily and purposely present witnessing the commission of a crime and offered no opposition to it ... or at least to express his dissent might under some circumstances afford cogent evidence upon which a jury would be justified in finding that he wilfully encouraged and so aided and abetted.'

There have been a number of cases since. The law now is that D may be guilty of abetting via presence alone if:

- His presence provided encouragement in fact.
- He intended to provide encouragement through his presence.

In *Allan* [1965] 1 QB 130, there was no actual encouragement in fact. D was present at an affray. He was totally passive, though he had a secret intention to join in to help his 'side' if need be. The Court of Appeal quashed his conviction of abetting a public order offence. To hold otherwise would be tantamount to convicting D for his thoughts alone. Meanwhile, in *Clarkson and others* [1971] 1 WLR 1402, there was no evidence of an intention to encourage. The appellants were soldiers at a British Army barracks in Germany who had witnessed the gang rape by at least three soldiers of an 18-year-old girl. Other soldiers had clearly aided and abetted the rape by holding the girl down, but there was no evidence that two of the appellants did anything other than just watch. However, both elements were present in *Wilcox v Jeffrey* [1951] 1 All ER 464.

CASE EXAMPLE

Wilcox v Jeffrey [1951] 1 All ER 464

Coleman Hawkins, a famous American saxophonist, appeared at a concert in London, illegally (the terms of his entry into the UK being that he did not take up employment). D was the owner of a magazine, *Jazz Illustrated*, who had met Hawkins at the airport, attended the concert and then written a very positive review of the concert in the magazine. D's conviction for abetting Hawkins' illegal concert was upheld, based on his voluntary presence in the crowd.

Abetting by omission

If D has knowledge of the actions of the principal, plus the duty or right to control them, but deliberately chooses not to, then he may be guilty of aiding or abetting by omission. In *Du Cros v Lambourne* [1907] 1 KB 40 and *Rubie v Faulkner* [1940] 1 KB 571, the defendants were the owners of cars who had allowed the principal to drive their cars carelessly, while they sat in the passenger seat. Both defendants were convicted of abetting road traffic offences. Presence in the vehicle, combined with (at least) the right to tell the driver what to do, was sufficient for liability. The principle is not limited to road traffic cases, as *Tuck v Robson* [1970] 1 WLR 741 illustrates. D, a pub landlord, had failed to get late drinkers out of his pub after closing time. D was convicted of aiding and abetting three customers to consume intoxicating liquor out of licensed hours, contrary to the Licensing Act 1964. His presence in the pub combined with his failure to take steps to ensure the drinkers drank up and left on time was enough for liability.

Du Cros v Lambourne was confirmed in *Webster* [2006] EWCA Crim 415.

CASE EXAMPLE

Webster [2006] EWCA Crim 415

D was convicted of abetting his friend, E, in causing death by dangerous driving. E, who had been drinking all day, drove D's car erratically and at high speed before losing control, leaving the road and crashing in a field. V, a rear seat passenger, was thrown out of the car and killed. E pleaded guilty to the substantive offence and D, who had pleaded not guilty, was convicted of abetting him by allowing him to drive his car, when E was obviously drunk. The Court of Appeal held that the crucial issue was whether D had an opportunity to intervene once he realised (because of the speed at which he was going) that E was driving dangerously. (D's conviction was subsequently quashed because of a misdirection concerning *mens rea* – see section 5.3.2.)

In *Martin* [2010] EWCA Crim 1450, D was convicted of aiding and abetting a learner driver, E, to commit the offence of causing death by dangerous driving. E was driving his car under D's supervision when he lost control and crashed head-first into another vehicle. E and a passenger were killed. The prosecution's case was that D had failed to instruct E to slow down before the impact. D claimed that it had not occurred to him that E's driving just before the accident was such as to require him to give a warning. The Court of Appeal allowed D's appeal on the basis of the trial judge misdirecting the jury. The Court took the opportunity to clarify the law in such cases. To convict, a jury would have to be sure that E (the driver) had caused death by dangerous driving; D (the supervisor) knew that E was driving in a manner which D knew fell far below the standard of a competent and careful driver; D, knowing that he had an opportunity to stop E from driving in that manner, deliberately did not take that opportunity; by not taking that opportunity, D intended to assist or encourage E to drive in that manner; and D did in fact, by his presence and failure to intervene, encourage E to drive dangerously.

'Counselling'

In *Calhaem* [1985] 1 QB 808, Parker LJ said that, 'we should give to the word "counsel" its ordinary meaning, which is ... "advise", "solicit", or something of that sort'. Although this is a wide definition, the scope of 'counselling' is subject to some limitations. In *Calhaem*, Parker LJ added that 'there must clearly be, first, contact between the parties and, second, a connection between the counselling and the [offence committed]. Equally, the act done must ... be done within the scope of the authority or advice and not, for example, accidentally'. *Luffman* [2008] EWCA Crim 1739 provides a good example. D was convicted of counselling murder on the basis that she had asked E to murder her ex-husband, agreed to pay him £30,000 to do it, and then pestered him to carry out the killing as quickly as possible, until he eventually did so.

CASE EXAMPLE

Calhaem [1985] 1 QB 808

D wanted a woman, V, killed. She hired a hitman, Z, to murder V and paid a down payment of £5,000. Subsequently, Z changed his mind about the killing but nevertheless went to V's house armed with a hammer, knife and a loaded shotgun with the intention of pretending to kill V so that he would not forfeit his down payment. When V answered the door, Z apparently 'went berserk', hit V several times with the hammer and then stabbed her in the neck. Z pleaded guilty to murder and D was convicted of counselling. On appeal, she argued that the causal connection between her instigation of the crime and Z's killing was broken when Z decided to kill V of his own accord. This was rejected and her conviction was upheld.

'Procuring'

In *Attorney-General's Reference (No 1 of 1975)* (1975), Lord Widgery CJ said that 'to procure means to produce by endeavour. You procure a thing by setting out to see that it happens and taking the appropriate steps to produce that happening.' A good example is provided by the facts of *Cogan and Leak* (1976), above: L clearly procured the crime of rape by terrorising his wife into having sex with C. However, recent cases have suggested that all that seems to be required now is a causal connection between D's act and the principal's commission of the offence. This is not inconsistent with the *Attorney-General's Reference*, above, where Lord Widgery said that, 'you cannot procure an offence unless there is a causal link between what you do and the commission of the offence'. Hence procuring means 'causing'. In *Millward* [1994] Crim LR 527, D, a farmer, had given his employee, E, instructions to drive a tractor and trailer on a public road. The tractor was poorly maintained and the trailer became detached, hit a car and killed V, a passenger in the car. E was acquitted of causing death by reckless driving (there being no suggestion that his driving was to blame), but D was convicted of procuring the offence and the Court of Appeal upheld the conviction.

In *Marchant and Muntz* [2003] EWCA Crim 2099; [2004] 1 WLR 442, another farmer was convicted of procuring the offence of causing death by dangerous driving after instructing an employee, E, to take an agricultural vehicle on to a public road. A motorcyclist collided with the vehicle and was killed and it was alleged that simply driving the vehicle itself on a public road was dangerous. Here D's conviction was quashed: the vehicle was authorised for use on a public road and D had not caused the motorcyclist's death simply by sending E out on to the public road in the vehicle, which was properly maintained. (This case is discussed further in Chapter 10.) In the *Attorney-General's Reference* case, above, Lord Widgery CJ also said that 'It may ... be difficult to think of a case of aiding, abetting or counselling when the parties have not met and have not discussed in some respects the terms of the offence which they have in mind. But we do not see why a similar principle should apply to procuring.' This proposition is still correct. D may be found guilty of procuring an offence by going against the principal's wishes, as the facts of the *Attorney-General's Reference* illustrate.

CASE EXAMPLE

Attorney-General's Reference (No 1 of 1975) [1975] QB 773

D surreptitiously added alcohol to the principal's soft drink, apparently for a joke. When the latter drove home he was arrested and charged with driving under the influence of alcohol. D was charged with procuring the offence. D's addition of alcohol to the principal's drink was the direct cause of the offence, and would, the Court of Appeal thought, amount to procuring.

What if the principal lacks mens rea*, or has a defence?*

The accessory may be liable here: what is crucial is the performance of the *actus reus* by the principal. This was seen in *Cogan and Leak*, above. Lawton LJ said that C's act of having sex with L's wife without her consent 'was the *actus reus*; it had been procured by L who had the appropriate *mens rea*', namely an intention that C should have sex with her without her consent. The Court of Appeal upheld L's conviction on the basis that he had procured the *actus reus* of rape (C's lack of *mens rea* – he honestly thought L's wife was consenting – was irrelevant to the question of L's liability). The same principle was used in *Millward*, above. The hapless driver of the tractor trailer on the occasion of the fatality was not convicted (he lacked the *mens rea* of the offence), but the owner of the machinery was found guilty of procuring the offence of causing death by reckless driving. Similarly, where the principal has committed both the *actus reus* and the *mens rea* of the offence but has a defence,

D remains liable. In *Bourne* (1952) 36 Cr App R 125, D forced his wife on two occasions to commit buggery with a dog. His conviction of aiding and abetting the offence was upheld, even though the principal, his wife, could not be convicted (had she been prosecuted), because of his duress. The *actus reus* (and *mens rea*) of buggery had been carried out.

5.3.2 *Mens rea* of secondary parties

The accessory must:

- intend to assist, encourage, etc., the principal to commit the offence;
- have knowledge of the circumstances which constitute the offence.

Intention

D must have intended to participate in the commission of the offence. As was noted in Chapter 3, intention is a legal concept which includes desire; foresight of consequences as virtually certain to happen is strong evidence of intent. It is enough that D intends to, for example, supply the principal with a gun; it is no defence that D is utterly indifferent as to whether the principal commits the offence or not. In *National Coal Board v Gamble* [1959] 1 QB 11, an abetting case, Devlin J said:

JUDGMENT

'An indifference to the result of the crime does not of itself negative abetting. If one man deliberately sells to another man a gun to be used for murdering a third, he may be indifferent about whether the third man lives or dies and interested only in the cash profit to be made out of the sale, but he can still be an aider and abetter. To hold otherwise would be to negative the rule that *mens rea* is a matter of intent only and does not depend on desire or motive.'

This gives accessorial liability a very wide scope. The House of Lords discussed this issue in *Gillick v West Norfolk and Wisbech AHA* [1986] AC 112, a civil case.

CASE EXAMPLE

Gillick v West Norfolk and Wisbech AHA [1986] AC 112

G was seeking a declaration that it would be unlawful for a doctor to give contraceptive advice to a girl under 16, because this would amount to aiding and abetting the girl's boyfriend to commit the offence of unlawful sexual intercourse with a girl under 16. (This offence was found in s 6 of the Sexual Offences Act 1956, which has since been replaced by s 9 of the Sexual Offences Act 2003; see Chapter 12.) The House of Lords thought that the doctor would not be acting illegally, provided what he did was 'necessary' for the physical, mental and emotional health of the girl. Lord Scarman said that the '*bona fide* exercise by a doctor of his clinical judgment must be a complete negation of the guilty mind which is an essential ingredient of the criminal offence of aiding, abetting the commission of unlawful sexual intercourse'.

Subsequently, Lord Hutton approved this decision in *English* [1999] AC 1; [1997] 4 All ER 545; [1997] UKHL 45, saying that 'I consider that a doctor exercising his clinical judgment cannot be regarded as engaging in a joint criminal enterprise with the girl.'

Question

These *dicta* of Lords Scarman and Hutton suggest that motive can be relevant and that a 'good' motive provides a defence. Traditionally, however, motive is regarded as irrelevant to the imposition of criminal liability. Motive apart, what difference – in terms of liability for aiding and abetting – is there between the gun salesman interested only in cash and the doctor interested only in the girl's best interests?

Knowledge of the circumstances

D must have knowledge of the circumstances that constitute the offence. In *Johnson v Youden and others* [1950] 1 KB 544, Lord Goddard CJ said:

JUDGMENT

'Before a person can be convicted of aiding and abetting the commission of an offence he must at least know the essential matters which constitute that offence. He need not actually know that an offence has been committed, because he may not know that the facts constitute an offence and ignorance of the law is not a defence.'

Johnson v Youden was followed in *Webster* [2006] EWCA Crim 415, the facts of which were given above. The Court of Appeal allowed D's appeal because the judge had invited the jury to consider whether D knew *or ought to have realised* that E was drunk. The Court of Appeal decided that this posed an objective standard instead of a purely subjective standard for D's *mens rea*. The judge compounded this error by inviting the jury to consider whether D realised (or ought to have realised) that allowing E to drive was dangerous. This was not the correct question, which should have been whether D realised that E was likely to drive dangerously.

contemplation principle
Mental or fault element in joint enterprise cases

Suppose D supplies the principal with a gun – what else does D have to know before he can be held liable as an accessory to murder? The law has developed a **contemplation principle.** In *Bainbridge* [1960] 1 QB 129, Lord Parker CJ said that it was not necessary to prove that D had 'knowledge of the precise crime' or 'knowledge of the particular crime'. Conversely, it was insufficient for the prosecution to prove simply that D knew that 'some illegal venture' was intended. Rather, a middle ground test was devised, according to which D is liable if he had knowledge of 'the type of crime that was in fact committed'.

CASE EXAMPLE

Bainbridge [1960] 1 QB 129

D had acquired some oxygen-cutting equipment for the principal, E, who subsequently used it to carry out a break-in at a bank. The equipment was left behind and it was subsequently traced back to D. He was convicted of aiding and abetting burglary and the Court of Criminal Appeal upheld his conviction. So what 'knowledge' did D need to have?

- Not enough: if D was aware that S was to use the equipment in some illegal venture, D would not be guilty.
- More than enough: the prosecution would not need to prove that D knew the details of the crime (e.g. the date, time of the break-in, the address of the bank, etc.).
- Enough: liability would depend on the prosecution proving that D knew that a crime of the same 'type' as burglary was to be committed.

In *DPP of Northern Ireland v Maxwell* [1978] 1 WLR 1350, the House of Lords extended the *Bainbridge* principle. Lord Fraser said that the 'possible extent of [D's] guilt was limited to the range of crimes any of which he must have known were to be expected that night'. Lord Scarman said:

JUDGMENT

'A man will not be convicted of aiding and abetting any offence his principal may commit, but only one which is within his contemplation. He may have in contemplation only one offence, or several; and the several which he contemplates he may see as alternatives. An accessory who leaves it to his principal to choose is liable, provided always the choice is made from the range of offences from which the accessory contemplates the choice will be made.'

5.3.3 Joint enterprise

joint enterprise
Where two or more people commit an offence together

In *Stewart and Schofield* [1995] 3 All ER 159, the Court of Appeal drew a clear distinction between participation in a 'joint enterprise' and secondary participation. Hobhouse LJ said that **joint enterprise** entailed taking part 'in the execution of a crime'. Conversely, 'a person who is a mere aider or abettor, etc, is truly a secondary party to the commission of whatever crime it is that the principal has committed'. Joint enterprise typically involves two parties, D and E, together taking part in a crime (murder, burglary, robbery, etc.). They both attack V, or burgle V's house. They are acting 'jointly', as part of a team, as opposed to the secondary liability situation where D is helping or encouraging E but not otherwise taking part.

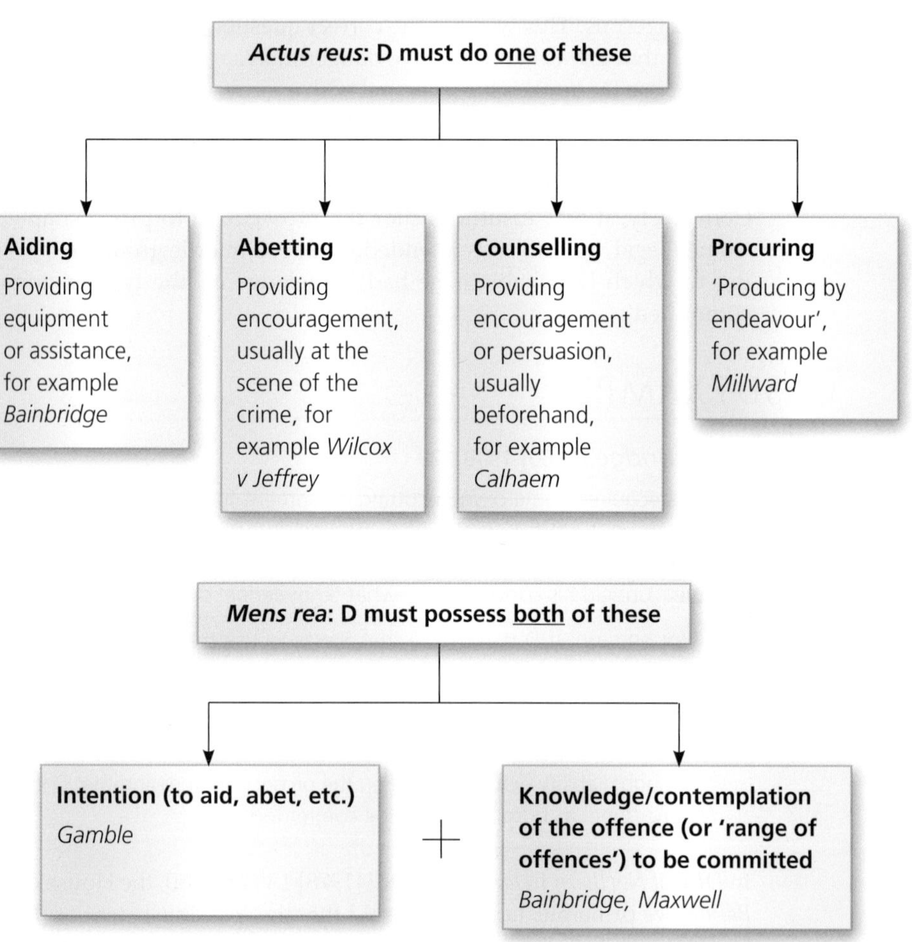

Figure 5.1 Secondary liability.

It should be noted that Lord Hobhouse LJ's proposition – that secondary participation and joint enterprise are separate concepts – is not one which is universally accepted. There is a school of thought which would prefer to say that the line between them is rather blurred. This was certainly the view of Laws LJ in a recent Court of Appeal case, *Jogee* [2013] EWCA Crim 1433, when he said:

JUDGMENT

'The distinction between [joint enterprise and secondary liability] is, to say the least, permeable. Encouragement is a form of participation; that is why it is enough to convict a secondary party. The *actus reus* of the secondary party's crime is lending support to the primary actor, whether by active participation or encouragement or both.'

However, for the purposes of this book they will be treated as separate concepts, albeit concepts raising very similar issues.

Mens rea *of joint enterprise*

The cases that have arisen before the appeal courts tend to involve the same issues. Typically, D and E have set out to commit burglary. They disturb the householder, V, and E produces a knife and stabs V to death. Is D liable for burglary and murder, or just burglary? The requirements for liability in this situation are as follows:

- D must have foresight (contemplation) that E may commit another crime.
- D must foresee (contemplate) that E will have the requisite *mens rea* at the time of committing it.
- The crime foreseen (contemplated) must be committed in the course of the enterprise.

D must have foreseen that E would commit a criminal offence; in other words, that E might perform the *actus reus* with the requisite *mens rea*. In the above burglary scenario, it would not be enough that D foresaw that E might stab V with a knife; D would only be liable for murder if he foresaw that E might stab V with the intent to kill or cause really serious harm. (The scenario is based on the Privy Council case of *Chan Wing-Siu and others* [1985] 1 AC 168, which will be considered below.) In one of the leading House of Lords cases, *English*, Lord Hutton, with whom the rest of the House of Lords agreed, said:

JUDGMENT

'There is a strong line of authority that where two parties embark on a joint enterprise to commit a crime and one party foresees that in the course of the enterprise the other party may commit, with the requisite *mens rea*, an act constituting another crime, the former is liable for that crime if committed by the latter in the course of the enterprise.'

English therefore establishes the proposition that, in joint enterprise cases involving murder, D must foresee that E might kill with malice aforethought. In *Rahman and others* [2008] UKHL 45; [2009] 1 AC 129, the House of Lords was asked whether D's foresight of what E might do had to be even more specific. It was suggested on appeal that if D foresaw that E might kill *with intent to do grievous bodily harm* (GBH), but in the event E killed *with intent to kill*, that this would therefore be an unforeseen killing, and hence D would not be liable. The House of Lords rejected that suggestion and D's conviction for murder was upheld.

CASE EXAMPLE

Rahman and others [2008] UKHL 45; [2009] 1 AC 129

The four appellants had all attacked a 16-year-old boy, Tyrone Clarke, in Beeston, near Leeds. They used a variety of blunt objects, including baseball bats and metal bars. However, Clarke was killed by two 'deep' knife wounds to the back, probably inflicted by someone else who escaped and was never apprehended. The four appellants denied knowledge of the knife but were convicted of murder. They appealed, without success, to the Court of Appeal, and again, to the House of Lords. There, it was asked whether, for D to face liability for murder in a joint enterprise case where V had been killed by one of the others (E), D had to have foreseen that E would kill with the intent to kill. The House of Lords unanimously answered that question 'no' and dismissed the appeals.

Lord Bingham said:

JUDGMENT

'Given the fluid, fast-moving course of events in incidents such as that which culminated in the killing of the deceased, incidents which are unhappily not rare, it must often be very hard for jurors to make a reliable assessment of what a particular defendant foresaw as likely or possible acts on the part of his associates. It would be even harder, and would border on speculation, to judge what a particular defendant foresaw as the intention with which his associates might perform such acts. It is safer to focus on the defendant's foresight of what an associate might do, an issue to which knowledge of the associate's possession of an obviously lethal weapon such as a gun or a knife would usually be very relevant.'

Despite Lord Bingham's attempt to clarify the law, his words – 'it is safer to focus on the defendant's foresight of what an associate might do' – are potentially ambiguous, as they could be taken to mean that, in cases of murder by joint enterprise, D could be convicted of murder if he foresaw simply that E might *kill* (whether intentionally or not). In *A and others* [2010] EWCA Crim 1622; [2011] QB 841, the Court of Appeal explained that the House of Lords in *Rahman* had not intended to change the law as decided in *English*. The Court of Appeal explained that what Lord Bingham had meant to say was that D could be convicted of murder if he participated in a joint enterprise and foresaw that in the course of it E might *commit murder*, i.e. kill with the intention to kill or do GBH.

D's knowledge that E is armed (and, if so, with what weapon)

It is often crucial in joint enterprise cases – typically when E produces a gun or knife and uses it to kill V during a burglary or robbery – to establish whether or not D knew in advance that E was armed (and, if so, with what weapon). If D did have this knowledge, it is much easier for the prosecution to prove that D foresaw the possibility that E might kill. It is this issue with which the House of Lords in *English* was primarily concerned.

CASE EXAMPLE

English [1997] UKHL 45; [1999] AC 1; [1997] 4 All ER 545

D and E took part in a joint enterprise to attack a police officer, V, with wooden posts. In the course of the attack, E produced a knife with which he killed V. There was a reasonable possibility that D did not know that E was armed with the knife. The trial judge nevertheless directed the jury to convict D of murder if they believed that D knew that E might cause really serious injury with the wooden post. He also directed them to convict if they believed that D had participated in the attack realising that there was a substantial risk that in the attack E might kill or cause serious injury. The Court of Appeal upheld E's conviction but, on further appeal, the House of Lords quashed D's conviction. Because D knew that E intended to attack V with one weapon but actually attacked him with another, the jury should have received further direction from the judge on this point.

On this point, Lord Hutton said:

JUDGMENT

'If the weapon used by the primary party is different to, but as dangerous as, the weapon which the secondary party contemplated he might use, the secondary party should not escape liability for murder because of the difference in the weapon, for example, if he foresaw that the primary party might use a gun to kill and the latter used a knife to kill, or *vice versa* ... There will be cases giving rise to a fine distinction as to whether or not the unforeseen use of a particular weapon or the manner in which a particular weapon is used will take a killing outside the scope of the joint venture, but this issue will be one of fact for the common sense of the jury to decide.'

English confirmed a long line of cases in both the Court of Appeal and Privy Council involving joint enterprise situations.

- *Chan Wing-Siu and others* [1985] 1 AC 168. D participated in an armed robbery during which one of his accomplices stabbed the householder to death. The trial judge directed the jury that D might be convicted of murder if, when he took part in the robbery, he contemplated that one of his accomplices might use a knife with the intention of inflicting serious injury. The jury convicted and the Privy Council rejected the appeal.
- *Hyde, Sussex and Collins* [1991] 1 QB 134. The three appellants kicked a man into unconsciousness in a pub car park. He later died, one kick to the forehead having been fatal. Although they denied joint enterprise, they were convicted of murder after the jury were directed that each man was guilty either because he delivered the fatal blow (with intent to cause at least serious injury) or he foresaw that one of the others might do so. The Court of Appeal upheld the convictions.
- *Hui Chi-Ming* [1992] 1 AC 34. Six men including D set off to attack V, who had upset the girlfriend of one of the six. V was struck over the head with a metal pipe and died. D was convicted of murder after the trial judge directed the jury to convict if satisfied that D had contemplated that, during the assault, one of the others might use the pipe with the intention of causing at least really serious bodily injury. The Privy Council upheld the conviction approving *Chan Wing-Siu* and *Hyde*.
- *Perman* [1996] 1 Cr App R 24. D and E were engaged on a joint enterprise to rob a newsagent's shop. E was carrying a loaded sawn-off shotgun, with which he shot V, a friend of the newsagent. D was convicted of robbery and manslaughter; he appealed against the latter conviction on the basis that, although he knew E had the gun, he did not know it was loaded and thought that it would be used only to frighten. The Court of Appeal quashed the manslaughter conviction because the jury had not been directed to consider the exact nature of D's contemplation of what E might do.

In all of these cases the appellants challenged murder convictions, although the facts giving rise to those convictions varied. Nevertheless, in *Roberts* [1993] 1 All ER 583, Lord Taylor CJ confirmed that the 'contemplation' principles were the same whether:

- the object of the enterprise was to cause physical injury or to do some other unlawful act, e.g. burglary or robbery;
- weapons were carried or not.

He added that it would 'be easier for the Crown to prove that [D] participated in the venture realising that [E] might wound with murderous intent if weapons are carried or if the object is to attack the victim or both. But that is purely an evidential difference, not a difference in principle.' The contemplation principle also represents the law in Australia (*McAuliffe* (1995) 183 CLR 108, High Court of Australia).

In *Uddin* [1998] EWCA Crim 999; [1998] 2 All ER 744, Beldam LJ attempted to encapsulate the law on joint enterprise where a death has occurred into seven principles:

- Where several persons join to attack V in circumstances which show that they intend to inflict serious harm and, as a result of the attack, the victim sustains fatal injury, they are jointly liable for murder but, if such injury inflicted with that intent is shown to have been caused solely by the actions of one participant of a type entirely different from actions which the others foresaw as part of the attack, only that participant is guilty of murder.
- In deciding whether the actions are of such a different type, the use by that party of a weapon is a significant factor. If the character of a weapon, e.g. its propensity to cause death, is different from any weapon used or contemplated by the others and if it is used with a specific intent to kill, the others are not responsible for the death unless it is proved that they knew or foresaw the likelihood of the use of such a weapon.
- If some or all of the others are using weapons which could be regarded as equally likely to inflict fatal injury, the mere fact that a different weapon was used is immaterial.
- If the jury conclude that the death of the victim was caused by the actions of one participant which can be said to be of a completely different type to those contemplated by the others, they are not to be regarded as parties to the death, whether it amounts to murder or manslaughter. They may nevertheless be guilty of offences of wounding or inflicting GBH with intent which they individually commit.
- If, in the course of the concerted attack, a weapon is produced by one of the participants and the others, knowing that he has it in circumstances where he may use it in the course of the attack, participate or continue to participate in the attack, they will be guilty of murder if the weapon is used to inflict a fatal wound.
- In a case in which, after a concerted attack, it is proved that the victim died as a result of a wound with a lethal weapon, e.g. a stab wound, but the evidence does not establish which of the participants used the weapon then, if its use was foreseen by the participants in the attack, they will be guilty of murder – notwithstanding that this particular participant who administered the fatal blow cannot be identified. If, however, the circumstances do not show that the participants foresaw the use of a weapon of this type, none of them will be guilty of murder though they may, individually, have committed offences in the course of the attack.
- The mere fact that, by attacking the victim together, each of them had the intention to inflict serious harm on the victim is insufficient to make them responsible for the death of the victim caused by the use of a lethal weapon used by one of the participants with the same or shared intention.

CASE EXAMPLE

Uddin [1998] EWCA Crim 999; [1998] 2 All ER 744

D was one of a group of at least six men who attacked and killed V. They beat him with parts of a snooker cue and he was also kicked. The medical evidence, however, was that death was caused by a single stab wound from a flick-knife to the base of the skull which penetrated the brain. The man who used the knife, E, was convicted of murder. D was also convicted of murder on the basis of joint enterprise in July 1996 (i.e. before the House of Lords gave judgment in *English*). D denied knowledge of E being armed. The Court of Appeal, hearing the case after *English*, quashed the conviction. The jury's attention had not been 'specifically focussed' on whether D was aware that E had a knife and also whether D foresaw that he might use it with intent to cause serious harm or death.

However, there was nevertheless evidence that a jury, directed in accordance with *English*, could have concluded that D was aware that one of the others had a knife and was prepared to use it and would thus be guilty of murder. Alternatively, it was open to the jury to say that the use of the knife was not so different from the concerted actions of hitting V with the snooker cue and kicking him that the actions of E went beyond what had been contemplated. The court, therefore, ordered a retrial. Other cases have explored this issue, including *Greatrex* [1999] 1 Cr App R 126 and *O'Flaherty and others* [2004] EWCA Crim 526; [2004] 2 Cr App R 20. In *Greatrex*, Beldam LJ stated that 'Foresight by the secondary party of the possible use of the fatal weapon is required in all cases of joint attack except those in which the use of a different but equally dangerous weapon is foreseen.' D had been convicted of murder having participated in an attack on V which primarily involved kicking. However, the fatal blow to V's head had been delivered by E using a blunt metal object (possibly a spanner). The Court of Appeal allowed D's appeal – the jury had not been invited to decide whether D had foreseen the use of the spanner or, if not, whether a spanner and a shod foot were 'equally dangerous' weapons.

In *O'Flaherty and others*, Mantell LJ emphasised that the principles set out in *Uddin* were 'matters of evidence', as opposed to 'principles of law'. He was keen to avoid 'the creation of a complex body of doctrine as to whether one weapon (for instance a knife) differs in character from another (for example a claw hammer) and which weapons are more likely to inflict fatal injury'. (This case will be examined in more detail below, in the context of withdrawal.) Lord Bingham also offered an observation on the *Uddin* principles in *Rahman and others* (2008). He stated:

JUDGMENT

'It is, with respect, clearly inappropriate to speak of a weapon's "propensity to cause death", since an inanimate object can have no propensity to do anything. But of course it is clear that some weapons are more dangerous than others and have the potential to cause more serious injury, as a sawn-off shotgun is more dangerous than a child's catapult.'

Justification of the contemplation principle

One of the grounds of appeal in *English* was that it was anomalous that a less culpable form of *mens rea* is required for a secondary party to a joint enterprise. Specifically, it is enough for D to be guilty of murder if he foresaw the possibility (albeit not a remote possibility) of the principal committing murder, whereas in the case of the principal the law insists on proof of intention to kill or cause really serious harm. Lord Steyn took a forthright view of the implied criticism of the contemplation principle:

JUDGMENT

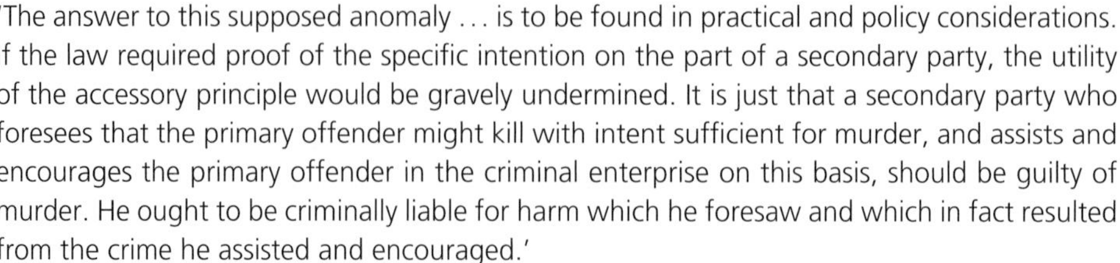

'The answer to this supposed anomaly . . . is to be found in practical and policy considerations. If the law required proof of the specific intention on the part of a secondary party, the utility of the accessory principle would be gravely undermined. It is just that a secondary party who foresees that the primary offender might kill with intent sufficient for murder, and assists and encourages the primary offender in the criminal enterprise on this basis, should be guilty of murder. He ought to be criminally liable for harm which he foresaw and which in fact resulted from the crime he assisted and encouraged.'

The reasons for this stance were twofold.

- First, the difficulty in proving that D had the requisite intention. Lord Steyn thought that it would 'almost invariably be impossible for a jury to say that the secondary party wanted death to be caused or that he regarded it as virtually certain'.
- Second, the desirability of controlling gangs: Lord Steyn said that 'The criminal justice system exists to control crime. A prime function of that system must be to deal justly but effectively with those who join with others in criminal enterprises. Experience has shown that joint criminal enterprises only too readily escalate into the commission of greater offences. In order to deal with this important social problem the accessory principle is needed and cannot be abolished or relaxed.'

In *Concannon* [2001] EWCA Crim 2607; [2002] Crim LR 213, D and E had embarked on a joint enterprise to commit robbery of V, a drug dealer, but when they reached the latter's home, E produced a knife and stabbed V to death. D was convicted of murder following a trial at which the judge had relied on *English*. D appealed, arguing that the principles of joint enterprise were in breach of art 6 of the European Convention on Human Rights, in that they denied him a 'fair trial'. The appeal was dismissed. Professor Sir John Smith, commenting in the Criminal Law Review, observed as follows:

QUOTATION

'Some lawyers would agree that the law of joint enterprise is unfair and many more would agree that mandatory penalties requiring the imposition of the same sentence on persons of widely varying culpability is unfair. But to allow the substantive law to be challenged on such grounds would throw the whole system into uncertainty and chaos.'

The 'fundamentally different' rule

Another way of looking at the liability of the members of a joint enterprise is to use the 'fundamentally' or 'radically' different rule. It involves asking whether E committed an act which was 'fundamentally' or 'radically' different from what D had contemplated in advance. If so, then D is not liable for that act. A good example of this rule is provided by *Rafferty* [2007] EWCA Crim 1846.

CASE EXAMPLE

Rafferty [2007] EWCA Crim 1846

D, E and F jointly attacked V on a beach in south Wales. While the attack continued, D left the scene with V's debit card and tried unsuccessfully to withdraw cash from his bank account. In D's absence, V was dragged across the beach by E and F, stripped naked, taken some distance into the sea and drowned. All three defendants were convicted of murder but, on appeal, D's conviction was quashed. D had participated in a joint enterprise involving the crimes of assault (by kicking and punching) and robbery. The deliberate drowning of V by E and F was of a 'fundamentally different' nature from those crimes and therefore D was not liable for it.

In *Mendez and Thompson* (2010), the Court of Appeal allowed the appellants' appeal against their murder convictions because the trial judge had failed to explain with sufficient clarity what was meant by the expression 'fundamentally different'.

CASE EXAMPLE

Mendez and Thompson [2010] EWCA Crim 516, [2011] QB 876

D1 and D2 went to a party in Sheffield. There, they got involved in a spontaneous group attack on V, during which he suffered numerous minor injuries from kicks and being hit by pieces of wood and metal bars. The cause of death was a stab wound to the heart, although it was unclear who actually used the knife. D1 and D2 were charged with murder on the basis of joint enterprise. The trial judge directed the jury that if they were sure that either defendant had joined an attack intending to cause really serious harm, or realising that others might do so, he was liable for murder unless another attacker (E) had produced a more lethal weapon of which he (the defendant) was unaware and which was more lethal than any contemplated by him so that the act of using that weapon was regarded as 'fundamentally different' from anything he had foreseen. D1 and D2 were convicted of murder and appealed. The Court of Appeal allowed their appeals (although a retrial for D2 was ordered), because the trial judge had failed to explain joint enterprise in a way that was sufficiently clear.

Toulson LJ said:

JUDGMENT

'It would not be just that D should be found guilty of the murder of V by E, if E's act was of a different kind from, and much more dangerous than, the sort of acts which D intended or foresaw as part of the joint enterprise. This is not a difficult idea to grasp and it is capable of being explained to a jury shortly and simply. It does not call for expert evidence or minute calibration … All that a jury can in most cases be expected to do is form a broad brush judgment about the sort of level of violence and associated risk of injury which they can safely conclude that D must have intended or foreseen. They then have to consider as a matter of common sense whether E's unforeseen act (if such it was) was of a nature likely to be altogether more life-threatening than acts of the nature which D foresaw or intended. It is a question of degree, but juries are used to dealing with questions of degree. There are bound to be borderline cases, but if the jury are left in real doubt they must acquit.'

Joint enterprise and murder: summary

This is, inevitably, quite a complex area of law, as it always involves two (or sometimes more) defendants, whose *mens rea* is often different. You may find helpful this summary of the various legal principles provided by Lord Brown in *Rahman and others* (2008):

JUDGMENT

'If D realises that E may kill or intentionally inflict serious injury, but nevertheless continues to participate with E in the venture, that will amount to a sufficient mental element for D to be guilty of murder if E, with the requisite intent, kills in the course of the venture unless (i) E suddenly produces and uses a weapon of which D knows nothing and which is more lethal than any weapon which D contemplates that E or any other participant may be carrying and (ii) for that reason E's act is to be regarded as fundamentally different from anything foreseen by D.'

Remoteness

You should note that, according to Lord Hutton in *English*, it is sufficient that the Crown proves that D foresaw that E 'may' commit murder. It is not necessary to prove that D foresaw that E would do so (a point made expressly by the Court of Appeal in *O'Brien* [1995] Crim LR 734). This begs the question, could D be held liable for any highly improbable crimes committed by his accomplices that he had, nevertheless, foreseen? This point was addressed by the Privy Council in *Chan Wing-Siu and others*. Sir Robin Cooke said that there was a remoteness principle:

JUDGMENT

'It is right to allow for a class of case in which the risk was so remote as not to make [D] guilty of a murder ... But if [D] knew that lethal weapons, such as a knife or a loaded gun, were to be carried on a criminal expedition, the defence should succeed only very rarely ... Various formulae have been suggested – including a substantial risk, a real risk, a risk that something might well happen ... What has to be brought home to the jury is that occasionally a risk may have occurred to an accused's mind but may genuinely have been dismissed by him as altogether negligible.'

Liability of principal and accessories/members of joint enterprise for different offences

In all of the above murder cases the accessory/member of the joint enterprise was either found guilty of murder along with the principal on the basis that he had foreseen that the principal might kill with intent to do at least serious harm (*Chan Wing-Siu; Hyde, Sussex and Collins; Hui Chi-Ming; Rahman and others*) or found not guilty of any offence, on the basis that the principal had unforeseeably departed from the agreed plan (*English; Uddin; Rafferty*). Other cases with a similar outcome to that in *English* are *Anderson and Morris* [1966] 2 QB 110 (During a joint enterprise to assault V, E produced a knife and killed V. D denied knowledge that E was armed, but was convicted of manslaughter. The Court of Appeal quashed the conviction.) and *Lovesey and Peterson* [1970] 1 QB 352 (During a joint enterprise to commit robbery, E unexpectedly used extensive force and killed V. D and E were convicted of murder. The Court of Appeal held that this went beyond the scope of the joint enterprise and thus D was not guilty of any homicide offence). This suggests that accessorial/joint enterprise liability is an 'all-or-nothing' situation. However, there is another line of case law, which holds that D might be liable for manslaughter even though the principal has been convicted of murder (*Betty* (1964) 48 Cr App R 6; *Reid* (1975) 62 Cr App R 109). In *Stewart and Schofield*, a joint enterprise case, Hobhouse LJ explained how this was possible:

JUDGMENT

'The question whether the relevant act was committed in the course of carrying out the joint enterprise in which [D] was a participant is a question of fact not law. If the act was not so committed then the joint enterprise ceases to provide a basis for a finding of guilt against [D]. He ceases to be responsible for the act. This is the fundamental point illustrated by *Anderson and Morris* and *Lovesey and Peterson*. But it does not follow that a variation in the intent of some of the participants at the time the critical act is done precludes the act from having been done in the course of carrying out the joint enterprise, as is illustrated by *Betty and Reid*.'

CASE EXAMPLE

Stewart and Schofield [1995] 3 All ER 159

D, E and a man called Lambert were engaged in a joint enterprise to rob a delicatessen. While D kept watch outside, E (who was armed with a knife) and Lambert (who was carrying a scaffolding pole) entered the shop. There, Lambert viciously beat the 60-year-old owner, V, with the pole, fatally injuring him. The three fled with £100. At their trial, Lambert pleaded guilty to robbery and murder. D and E pleaded guilty to robbery but not guilty to murder and were convicted of manslaughter after the judge directed the jury that they were guilty if they had realised or, if they had thought about it, must have realised, that Lambert 'might strike a blow intended to inflict some bodily injury'. They appealed, arguing that the vicious killing had gone beyond the scope of the joint enterprise. In particular, they claimed that Lambert was racially motivated (V was Pakistani). However, the Court of Appeal upheld their convictions.

In *Gilmour* [2000] 2 Cr App R 407, D drove E to a house in Ballymoney in the early hours of the morning. E threw a large petrol bomb (a one-and-three-quarter-litre whisky bottle containing petrol) into the house, starting a major fire which killed three of the six occupants, all young boys. Both D and E were convicted of murder but the Northern Ireland Court of Appeal quashed D's murder conviction and substituted a conviction of manslaughter. The court was satisfied that E, in throwing such a large bomb into a house in the middle of the night, intended to cause at least serious harm. With respect to D, however, the court decided that he did not have awareness of the size of the bomb and could not therefore be said to have appreciated that E intended to cause serious harm (most petrol bombs, apparently, do not cause death). Carswell LCJ said that 'It would be difficult to attribute to [D] an intention that the attack should result in more than a blaze which might do some damage, put the occupants in fear and intimidate them into moving from the house'. However, the court held that D was guilty of manslaughter. Carswell LCJ held that cases such as *Anderson and Morris, Lovesey and Peterson* and *English* were distinguishable. He said:

JUDGMENT

'The line of authority represented by such cases as *Anderson and Morris* deals with situations where the principal departs from the contemplated joint enterprise and perpetrates a more serious act of a different kind unforeseen by the accessory. In such cases it is established that the accessory is not liable at all for such unforeseen acts. It does not follow that the same result should follow where the principal carries out the very act contemplated by the accessory, though the latter does not realise that the principal intends a more serious consequence from the act. We do not consider that we are obliged by authority to hold that the accessory in such a case must be acquitted of manslaughter as well as murder … We do not … see any convincing policy reason why a person acting as an accessory to a principal who carries out the very deed contemplated by both should not be guilty of the degree of offence appropriate to the intent with which he so acted.'

The English Court of Appeal adopted similar principles in *Day, Day and Roberts* [2001] EWCA Crim 1594; [2001] Crim LR 984. D, E and F jointly attacked V and killed him. The cause of death was a brain haemorrhage caused by a kick to the side of the head. All three were charged with murder. However, the jury convicted D of manslaughter while E and F were convicted of murder. D appealed, arguing that if he was not guilty of murder then he should be acquitted altogether. The Court of Appeal dismissed D's appeal. Laws LJ said that there was 'a joint enterprise at least to inflict some harm' involving all three men, which was not negated by 'the larger intentions' of E and F to inflict serious harm. A P Simester and G R Sullivan in *Criminal Law Theory and Doctrine* (2nd edn, Hart Publishing, 2003) support this view: 'In principle it seems possible for [D] to be guilty of manslaughter in circumstances where [E] is guilty of murder.' The Court of Appeal tried to reconcile the various authorities in *Parsons* [2009] EWCA Crim 64. The Court held that it all depends on what exactly D had contemplated that E might do, and that in turn depended on what weapon D contemplated that E might use. Two situations presented themselves (assume in both cases that E killed V with malice aforethought and is convicted of murder, and that D was part of a joint enterprise with E):

- If V's death resulted from the use by E of a *blunt instrument* (such as a plank of wood or kicking with a boot) or even a *knife*, then it was a realistic possibility that D might not have realised that death or GBH might result and hence the jury might convict D of manslaughter, rather than murder. The killing of V was still within the scope of the joint enterprise provided that V was killed with the weapon that D contemplated that E would use, so D cannot escape all liability, but it does not automatically follow that D's liability has to be the same as E's.
- However, if V's death was caused by a *gun*, the discharge of which by E was envisaged as a possibility by D, and so the killing is within the scope of the joint enterprise, manslaughter is far less likely to be available as an alternative verdict. It would require a jury to accept that D foresaw the use of a gun to inflict only minor injuries, something a jury may find 'unrealistic'.

CASE EXAMPLE

Parsons [2009] EWCA Crim 64

D admitted driving E to V's house. When they got there, E got out of the car and shot V in the face with a 12-bore shotgun. E was subsequently convicted of murder and D was charged with the same offence. D claimed that it was only when E came back to the car that he saw the shotgun, and hence he had not contemplated its use beforehand. The trial judge directed the jury that (1) if they came to the conclusion that D knew about the shotgun in advance and contemplated its use then he would be guilty of murder; but (2) if they concluded that he genuinely did not know about the shotgun until afterwards, then he was not guilty of any offence. D was convicted of murder and appealed, arguing that a manslaughter verdict should have been left to the jury, relying on *Coutts* [2006] UKHL 39 (discussed in Chapter 10). This intermediate position would arise if the jury concluded that D had thought the gun might be used to 'pepper' or 'wing' V, causing him some (but not really serious) injury. The Court of Appeal rejected his appeal. For the judge to have been obliged to leave the possibility of a manslaughter verdict, the jury would have needed some evidence on which they could properly have found that D knew that E had a gun, foresaw that he might discharge it so that shooting was within the scope of the joint enterprise, but had not foreseen that that would cause death or serious harm to V. Without such evidence there was no basis for a manslaughter verdict.

In *Yemoh and others* (2009) and *Carpenter* (2011), the Court of Appeal confirmed that it was possible for a jury to convict some members of a joint enterprise of murder and others of manslaughter, because the verdict for each member depended on his or her *mens rea* at the time of the killing.

CASE EXAMPLE

Yemoh and others [2009] EWCA Crim 930; [2009] Crim LR 888

Several members of a gang, including the appellants, armed themselves with knives, bats and even a bull terrier dog before attacking V in a street in Hammersmith, west London. One of the gang stabbed V through the heart. The actual killer was never identified and the murder weapon was never found. However, several other members of the gang were arrested, and in due course two were convicted of murder while three others were convicted of manslaughter. The latter three appealed on the basis that it was inconsistent to convict them of manslaughter when the other two had been convicted of murder. The Court of Appeal dismissed the appeal. The appellants realised that the knifeman (whoever that was) intended to use the knife to cause some harm, which was enough to convict them of manslaughter. Moreover, the fact that the knifeman had in fact acted with an intention to kill or cause serious harm did not make the stabbing 'fundamentally different' from what the appellants had foreseen.

CASE EXAMPLE

Carpenter [2011] EWCA Crim 2568; [2012] 1 Cr App R 11

The Carpenter family and the Price family were both members of the travelling community. The two families had known each other for years and generally got on well. However, a feud developed between them, which the families decided to settle by their 19-year-old sons, Joe Carpenter and Shane Price, having a fight. The two families arranged to meet on a common. The Price family understood that it was meant to be a fistfight, but Joe turned up armed with a knife. In the ensuing fight, Joe fatally stabbed Shane. At trial, Joe admitted murdering Shane, and his parents were convicted of manslaughter on the basis of joint enterprise. Joe's mother Tracy appealed, arguing that it was inconsistent for the jury to convict her son of murder but her of manslaughter; it should have been 'murder or nothing'. The Court of Appeal dismissed the appeal, holding that there was a 'clear and well-established line of authority' – in particular *Day, Day & Roberts* and *Yemoh and others* – to the effect that one or more members of a joint enterprise might be guilty of manslaughter (based on their foresight of some harm) even though the killer in fact acted with malice aforethought and was therefore guilty of murder.

5.4 Withdrawal from participation

5.4.1 Pre-planned criminal activity

An accessory, or a member of a joint enterprise, may withdraw, and escape liability for the full offence. The principles appear to be identical in either case, as follows:

- Mere repentance without action is not enough.
- D must communicate his withdrawal to E in such a way as to 'serve unequivocal notice upon the other party to the common unlawful cause that if he proceeds upon it he does so without the further aid and assistance of those who withdraw' (according to Dunn LJ in *Whitefield* (1984) 79 Cr App R 36).

- D must take active steps to prevent the offence (this depends on how advanced the crime is). McDermott J in *Eldredge v United States* 62 F.2d 449 (1932) said: 'A declared intent to withdraw from a conspiracy to dynamite a building is not enough, if the fuse has been set; he must step on the fuse.'

These principles are demonstrated in *Becerra and Cooper* (1975) 62 Cr App R 212.

CASE EXAMPLE

Becerra and Cooper (1975) 62 Cr App R 212

D and E were engaged on a joint enterprise to commit burglary of a flat. They got into a confrontation with the householder and the commotion disturbed her neighbour upstairs, V, who came down to investigate. At this point D shouted 'Come on, let's go', climbed out of the window and ran off. E tried to escape but was prevented from doing so by V. There was a struggle and E, who had a knife, stabbed V to death. D and E were convicted of murder. D appealed on the ground that, by the time E stabbed V, he had withdrawn from the joint enterprise. The Court of Appeal upheld the convictions. Roskill LJ said that something 'vastly different and vastly more effective' was required from D before he could be said to have withdrawn.

The communication of withdrawal must be 'unequivocal'. Thus, simply failing to turn up on the day that the joint enterprise was due to take place does not constitute an effective withdrawal. This was demonstrated in *Rook* [1993] 2 All ER 955. A contract killing had been arranged and D was supposed to participate. However, on the appointed day, he simply failed to appear. His accomplices carried out the murder without him. D was convicted and the Court of Appeal rejected his appeal. Lloyd LJ said that D's absence 'could not possibly' amount to unequivocal communication of his withdrawal. Although D had made it quite clear 'to himself' that he did not want to be there, he did not make it clear to the others. Thus, the 'minimum necessary for withdrawal from the crime' was not established. This was confirmed in *Baker* [1994] Crim LR 444. Three men including D had taken V to some waste ground and stabbed him to death. D's own evidence was that he had reluctantly stabbed V three times before handing the knife to E, stating 'I'm not doing it', moving a short distance away and turning his back while the others finished the job (death was caused by 48 stab wounds). D was convicted of murder and appealed on the basis that he had withdrawn from the joint enterprise before the other 45 stab wounds were inflicted. The Court of Appeal dismissed his appeal – he had not unequivocally withdrawn from the joint enterprise. His words, 'I'm not doing it', were quite capable of meaning no more than 'I will not myself strike any more blows.'

5.4.2 Spontaneous criminal activity

In *Mitchell and King* [1998] EWCA Crim 2444; [1999] Crim LR 496, the Court of Appeal held that communication of withdrawal from a joint enterprise was only a necessary condition for disassociation from pre-planned violence. This was not the case where the violence is spontaneous. In such cases, it was possible to withdraw from the enterprise merely by walking away.

CASE EXAMPLE

Mitchell and King [1998] EWCA Crim 2444; [1999] Crim LR 496

D, E and F were together in an Indian take-away. There was a fight involving other customers, and damage was caused to the take-away. The three men then left, followed by some of the staff. Fighting broke out between all the men. Eventually D, E and F walked off, but F returned and inflicted fatal injuries on one of the staff who had been lying on the ground. F was subsequently convicted of murder. The prosecution case against D and E was that they were involved in a joint enterprise. There was a question as to whether D and E had withdrawn from the enterprise at the time when the fatal blows were struck. The judge told the jury that there had to be effective communication and, as there was no evidence of that, D and E were convicted of murder. However, their appeals were allowed.

Similar principles were used in *O'Flaherty and others* [2004] EWCA Crim 526; [2004] 2 Cr App R 20. D and two others were convicted using joint enterprise principles of the murder of V, who was stabbed to death by E after spontaneous violence broke out in the street following a performance by the garage act So Solid Crew. However, on appeal, the convictions of the two others were quashed. Although they had participated in the initial violence that broke out immediately outside the club, they had withdrawn from the enterprise by the time V was fatally wounded in a neighbouring street. D's conviction was upheld, however, as CCTV evidence showed that he had followed the disturbance into the neighbouring street and was actively participating in it at the time of the stabbing.

In *Mitchell* [2008] EWCA Crim 2552, spontaneous violence broke out between two rival groups outside a pub in Bradford, in which D was heavily involved. There was a temporary 'lull' in the violence, but after it resumed V was killed by E, one of D's group, who later pleaded guilty to murder. D, who was nearby at the time but no longer participating in the violence, was charged with murder based on joint enterprise. D claimed to have withdrawn but the trial judge told the jury that, where a person became party to a joint enterprise they were still, in law, taken to be participating in it unless they had demonstrably withdrawn. A mere change of heart was not sufficient. D was convicted and the Court of Appeal dismissed her appeal.

5.5 Assisting an offender

The above rules (whether on aiding, abetting, counselling and procuring or joint enterprise) only apply to assistance given to the principal offender either before or during the commission of a crime. However, a person may be held criminally liable for assisting an offender after the commission of an offence. Section 4(1) of the Criminal Law Act 1967 states:

SECTION

'4(1) Where a person has committed an arrestable offence, any other person who, knowing or believing him to be guilty of the offence or of some other arrestable offence, does without lawful authority or reasonable excuse any act with intent to impede his apprehension or prosecution shall be guilty of an offence.'

5.6 Reform

In May 2007, the Law Commission (LC) published a report, *Participation in Crime* (Law Com No 305) in which it made a number of proposals for reforming secondary liability and joint enterprise. The report includes the following proposals (amongst others):

- The abolition of the offences of aiding, abetting, counselling and procuring, under s 8 of the Accessories and Abettors Act 1861 and s 44 of the Magistrates' Courts Act 1980.

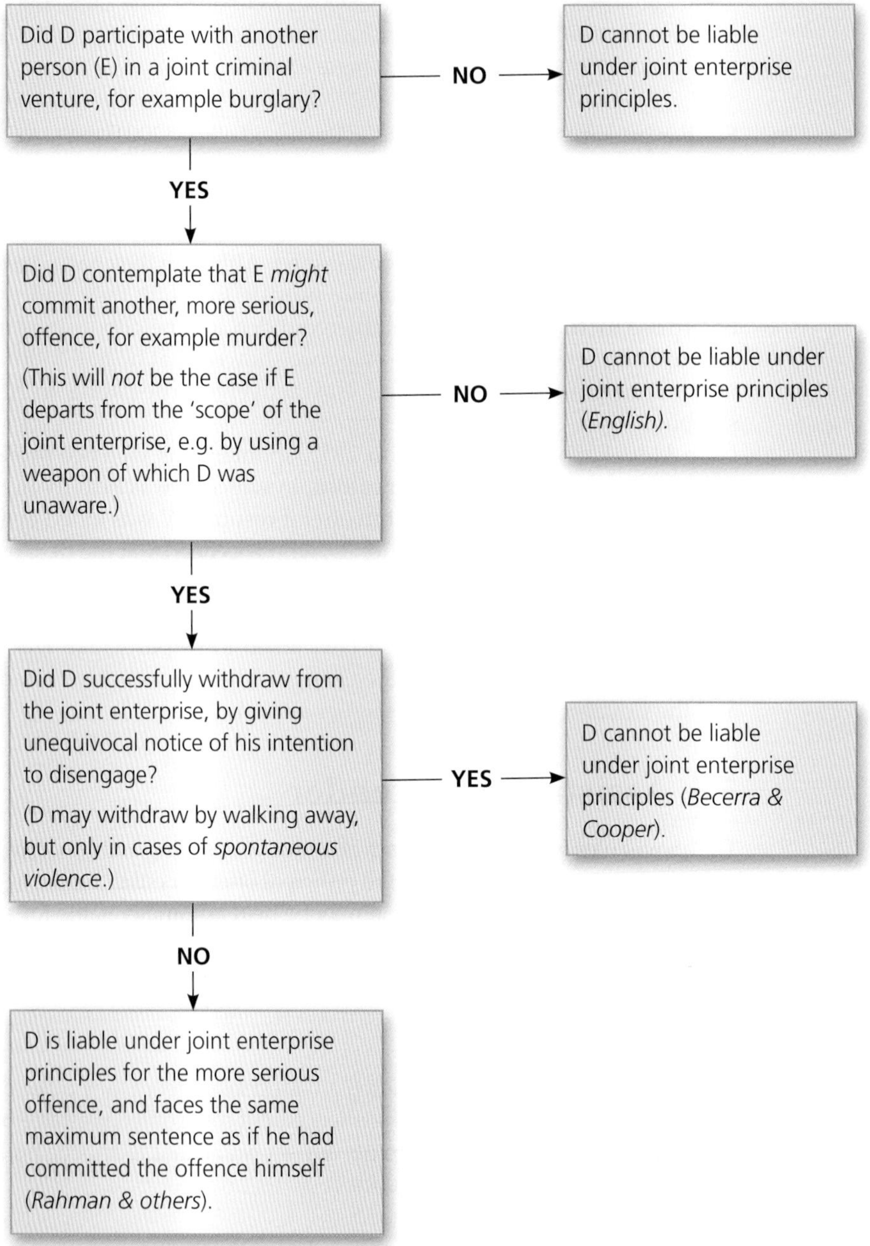

Figure 5.2 Joint enterprise.

- The creation of a new secondary liability offence of 'assisting or encouraging' the commission of an offence. 'Encouraging' would be defined as including (but not limited to) emboldening, threatening or pressurising someone else to commit an offence.
- The new offence could be committed by omission, if D failed to take 'reasonable steps' to discharge a duty.
- For liability under the new offence, D must intend that the 'conduct element' of the substantive offence be committed.
- The principle of 'innocent agency' should be retained.
- Joint enterprise should be retained, but the *mens rea* required should be modified.

The LC suggest that, for liability as part of a 'joint criminal venture', D should either intend that E should, or believe that E would or might, commit the 'conduct element' of the 'principal offence'. However, even if D had the required intent or belief, he would not be liable if E's conduct 'fell outside the scope of the joint venture'.

- D should be able to withdraw and therefore 'escape liability as a secondary party if he or she is able to demonstrate that he or she had negated the effect of his or her acts of assistance, encouragement or agreement before the principal offence was committed'.
- There should be a defence available if D acted for the purpose of 'preventing the commission' of an offence or 'to prevent or limit the occurrence of harm', provided in either case that it was 'reasonable' to act as D did in the circumstances.
- The exemption for victims (the *Tyrrell* principle) should be retained. This would apply where D assisted or encouraged an offence which existed in order to protect a 'particular category' of persons and D fell within that category.

In July 2008, the Ministry of Justice published a Consultation Paper entitled *Murder, Manslaughter and Infanticide: Proposals for Reform of the Law*. In the Paper the government made some proposals of its own for reform of secondary liability and joint enterprise – but only in the context of murder. The government proposed the creation of two new statutory offences:

1. assisting and encouraging murder;
2. assisting and encouraging manslaughter.

Both offences require E to kill V with assistance or encouragement from D, with D's intent being to assist or encourage E to kill or cause serious injury. The difference between the offences would be determined by E's liability. Offence (1) would apply if E actually committed murder whereas offence (2) would apply if E only committed (involuntary) manslaughter. The government also proposed placing the present law of joint enterprise involving murder on to a statutory basis. The government's proposed draft offence, 'murder in the context of a joint criminal venture', essentially codifies the principles set out in cases such as *English* (1999) and *Rahman and others* (2008), above. It would be committed if E committed murder in the context of a 'joint criminal venture', and D foresaw that either:

- a person *might* be killed by one of the other participants (not necessarily E) acting with intent to kill or cause serious injury; or
- serious injury *might* be caused to a person by one of the other participants (not necessarily E) acting with intent to cause such injury and E's criminal act was within the 'scope of the venture'.

E's criminal act would be within the 'scope of the venture' if it did not 'go far beyond' that which was planned, or agreed to, or foreseen, by D. Furthermore, D would not escape liability merely because at the time of the murder he was 'absent'. This is designed to place the decision in *Rook* (1993) on a statutory basis.

ACTIVITY

Applying the law

D and E have agreed a plan to burgle a house known to be the home of V, a well-known MP. D thinks that the house will be empty on the night they plan to burgle it. E, however, is aware that Parliament will not be sitting that day and that there is a strong possibility that the MP will be at home. E is fundamentally opposed to V's stance on a number of political issues and has often spoken to D of how he would like to 'finish off' V. D is unsure whether this means to kill V or just to destroy his political career. On the night of the burglary D sees E putting a sharp-looking knife into his pocket. D asks what this is for and E says it will only be used in an emergency to 'warn off anyone who comes snooping around'. D is satisfied with this explanation. When they reach the house at 2 a.m. it is in darkness. They break in through a rear window and start looking for a safe or any valuables. In fact, V is at home and is disturbed by the noise. He comes down to investigate. D hears footsteps coming down the stairs and shouts to E 'I'm off!' before climbing back out of the window. E waits behind and, when V enters the living room, stabs him in the neck, killing him. D and E are arrested soon after. At trial, E pleads guilty to aggravated burglary and murder. D pleads guilty to burglary but denies liability for murder.

Discuss D's liability for murder or manslaughter.

SUMMARY

Secondary liability refers to the imposition of liability on those who help, encourage or persuade another person to commit a crime or those who cause a crime to be committed by someone else.

Under s 8 of the Accessories and Abettors Act 1861, it is a crime to aid, abet, counsel or procure the commission of an offence by another person. The meaning of these four forms of secondary liability are now defined through case law (*Attorney-General's Reference (No 1 of 1975)*) but the Law Commission has proposed their abolition with the repeal of s 8 of the 1861 Act and its replacement with new offences of assisting or encouraging crime.

In addition to secondary liability are separate rules relating to joint enterprise, where D and E jointly commit a crime as part of a team. The main issue here is dealing with the situation where D and E set out together to commit one crime (say burglary), but E commits a more serious crime (typically murder). D's liability in this situation is governed by the 'contemplation' principle – D is liable only if he contemplated that E might kill with the *mens rea* for murder (*Chan Wing-Siu*; *English*; *Rahman and others*). D is also not liable for E's criminal conduct if it can be classed as 'fundamentally different' from that which D and E had expressly or impliedly agreed and which therefore falls outside the 'scope' of the joint enterprise (*Rafferty*).

It is possible for parties to withdraw from secondary liability and a joint enterprise. Where the criminal activity was pre-planned, unequivocal communication of withdrawal, as a minimum, is required (*Becerra and Cooper*). Where the criminal activity was spontaneous, then D can withdraw simply by walking away, but D must still demonstrate their withdrawal in some way.

The Law Commission has proposed certain reforms to the principles of joint enterprise, but the government has proposed more radical reform through the creation of two new offences, of assisting and encouraging murder and manslaughter, respectively.

SAMPLE ESSAY QUESTION

The 'contemplation' principle is too wide in that it is capable of imposing, for example, liability for murder on those who simply foresaw death or serious injury as a possible outcome of their involvement in a joint enterprise. Discuss.

Briefly explain the law of joint enterprise:

- Where D and E jointly commit an offence they can be held liable for each other's crimes if committed within the 'scope' of the enterprise
- D will be liable for all crimes committed by E provided they were 'contemplated' by D in advance
- D may withdraw from a joint enterprise

Explain the contemplation principle:

- Earlier cases referred to 'tacit agreement' (*Anderson and Morris* (1966))
- Explain the key cases developing the contemplation principle, e.g. *Chan Wing-Sui* (1986), *Hyde* (1991), *English* (1999), *Rahman and others* (2008)
- Discuss cases where D's liability depends on his knowledge/contemplation that E is armed and, if so, with what weapon, e.g. *Perman* (1996), *English*, *Greatrex* (1999), *Uddin* (1999)
- Explain the 'fundamentally different' rule and give examples, e.g. *Rafferty* (2007)

Discuss the principles regarding withdrawal, e.g.

- Withdrawal is possible, but in pre-planned criminal enterprises D must give unequivocal communication as a minimum (*Becerra & Cooper* (1976); *Rook* (1993); *Baker* (1994))
- Withdrawal in cases of spontaneous violence possible by walking away (*Mitchell & King* (1999)) but D must actually disengage from the violence (*O'Flaherty and others* (2004); *Mitchell* (2008))

Analyse the contemplation principle in murder cases:

- The principal (E) must have malice aforethought to be guilty of murder but D can be convicted of murder under joint enterprise based on foresight that E might kill (*English; Rahman and others*)
- This may be justified on the basis that D has agreed to participate in 'gang crime' often with knowledge that E is armed
- The contemplation principle is purely subjective so liability can be imposed only on the basis of D's actual knowledge/foresight
- D will avoid liability if E commits a 'fundamentally' different crime

Discuss reform proposals – refer to e.g.

1. Law Commission Report, *Participation in Crime*, Law Com No 305 (2007)
2. Ministry of Justice, *Murder, Manslaughter and Infanticide: Proposals for Reform of the Law*, Consultation Paper CP19/08 (2008)

Conclude

Further reading

Books

Ormerod, D, *Smith and Hogan Criminal Law* (13th edn, Oxford University Press, 2011), Chapter 8.

Articles

Buxton, R, 'Joint enterprise' [2009] Crim LR 233.

Simester, A P, 'The mental element in complicity' (2006) 122 LQR 578.

Smith, J C, 'Criminal liability of accessories: law and law reform' (1997) 113 LQR 453.

Smith, K J M, 'Withdrawal in complicity: a restatement of principles' [2001] Crim LR 769.

Sullivan, G R, 'Complicity for first degree murder and complicity in unlawful killing' [2006] Crim LR 502.

Sullivan, G R, 'Participating in crime: Law Com No. 305 – joint criminal ventures' [2008] Crim LR 19.

Taylor, R, 'Procuring, causation, innocent agency and the Law Commission' [2008] Crim LR 32.

Wilson, W, 'A rational scheme of liability for participating in crime' [2008] Crim LR 3.

Internet links

Law Commission, *Participation in Crime* (Law Com No 305) (2007), available at www.lawcom.gov.uk.

Ministry of Justice, *Murder, Manslaughter and Infanticide: Proposals for Reform of the Law* (Consultation Paper CP19/08) (2008), available at www.justice.gov.uk.

6

Inchoate offences

AIMS AND OBJECTIVES

After reading this chapter you should be able to:

- Understand the law on attempts
- Understand the law on conspiracy
- Understand the law on assisting or encouraging crime
- Understand the rules on impossibility
- Analyse critically the rules on inchoate liability
- Apply the law to factual situations to determine whether there is liability for an inchoate offence

6.1 Inchoate offences

attempt
Trying to commit an offence, with intent to do so

conspiracy
An agreement to commit a criminal offence

Inchoate offences refers to those offences where D has not actually committed a 'substantive' crime, such as murder, rape, theft or burglary, but D has done one of the following three things:

- made an **attempt** to do so (that is, D has tried to commit the crime but has failed, for some reason, to complete it);
- entered into a **conspiracy** with at least one other person to do so (that is, D has entered into an agreement that a criminal offence will be committed);
- **assisted** or **encouraged** someone else to commit a crime.

'Inchoate' literally means 'at an early stage'. Inchoate offences are designed to allow for liability to be imposed on those who have taken some steps towards the commission of an offence (whether the crime would have been committed by them personally or by someone else). It allows the police to intervene at an early stage and make arrests before a substantive crime has occurred, thus making a significant contribution towards public safety. Of course, where no substantive offence has been committed, obtaining sufficient evidence that an attempt or a conspiracy has actually occurred can be difficult. As we shall see, the point at which D can be regarded as having committed an attempt has troubled courts in England for many years (and the issue cannot be said to be completely settled even now). Moreover, in a modern democracy where freedom of expression is protected by law (art 10 of the European Convention on Human Rights, incorporated into English law by the Human Rights Act 1998), the criminal law has to strike the appropriate balance between the individual's right to free speech and society's interest in ensuring that those who make agreements with or encourage others to commit crimes are punished.

6.2 Attempt

The offence of attempt existed at common law but is now regulated by statute, the Criminal Attempts Act 1981.

SECTION

'1(1) If, with intent to commit an offence to which this section applies, a person does an act which is more than merely preparatory to the commission of the offence, he is guilty of attempting to commit the offence.'

6.2.1 *Actus reus* of attempt

The 1981 Act imposes liability on those who do 'an act which is more than merely preparatory to the commission of the offence'. Although the judge must decide whether there is evidence on which a jury could find that there has been such an act, the test of whether D's acts have gone beyond the merely preparatory stage is essentially a question of fact for the jury (s 4(3) of the 1981 Act). If the judge decides there is no such evidence, he must direct them to acquit; otherwise he must leave the question to the jury, even if he feels the only possible answer is guilty.

'More than merely preparatory'

What does this phrase mean? The first thing to note is that the test looks *forward* from the point of preparatory acts to see whether D's acts have gone beyond that stage. Prior to the 1981 Act there were a number of common law tests, one of which, the 'proximity' test, looked *backwards* from the complete substantive offence to see whether D's acts were so 'immediately connected' to the *actus reus* to justify the imposition of liability for an attempt. Thus, in *Eagleton* (1855) Dears 515, it was said that:

JUDGMENT

'Some act is required and we do not think that all acts towards committing a [criminal offence] are indictable. Acts remotely leading towards the commission of the offence are not to be considered as attempts to commit it, but acts immediately connected with it are.'

In the years immediately following the 1981 Act, the courts tended to refer back to some of the common law tests (which were not expressly excluded by the 1981 Act and so had persuasive value). Hence, in *Widdowson* (1986) 82 Cr App R 314, the Court of Appeal adopted Lord Diplock's 'Rubicon' test formulated in *DPP v Stonehouse* [1978] AC 55 as representing the law under the Act. Lord Diplock had said:

JUDGMENT

'Acts that are merely preparatory to the commission of the offence, such as, in the instant case, the taking out of insurance policies are not sufficiently proximate to constitute an attempt. They do not indicate a fixed irrevocable intention to go on to commit the complete offence unless involuntarily prevented from doing so. [D] must have crossed the Rubicon and burnt his boats.'

Shortly afterwards, in *Boyle and Boyle* [1987] Crim LR 111, the Court of Appeal referred to a test devised by Stephen known as the 'series of acts' test. According to this test, 'an attempt to commit a crime is an act done with intent to commit that crime, and forming part of a series of acts which would constitute its actual commission if it were not interrupted'. As a result the Court of Appeal upheld the appellants' convictions of attempted burglary (they had been found by a policeman standing near a door, the lock and one hinge of which were broken). However, in *Gullefer* [1990] 3 All ER 882, Lord Lane CJ tried to devise a new test that incorporated elements of the proximity, Rubicon and series of acts tests. According to this test D has committed an attempt when he has 'embarked on the crime proper'. Lord Lane said:

JUDGMENT

'The words of the Act seek to steer a midway course. They do not provide . . . that the *Eagleton* test is to be followed, or that, as Lord Diplock suggested, [D] must have reached a point from which it was impossible for him to retreat before the *actus reus* of an attempt is proved. On the other hand, the words give perhaps as clear a guidance as is possible in the circumstances on the point of time at which Stephen's "series of acts" begins. It begins when the merely preparatory acts have come to an end and [D] embarks upon the crime proper. When that is will depend of course upon the facts in any particular case.'

CASE EXAMPLE

Gullefer [1990] 3 All ER 882

D had placed an £18 bet on a greyhound race. Seeing that his dog was losing, he climbed on to the track in front of the dogs, waving his arms and attempting to distract them, in an effort to get the stewards to declare 'no race', in which case he would get his stake back. D was unsuccessful in this endeavour but he was prosecuted for attempted theft and convicted. The Court of Appeal quashed his conviction: D's act was merely preparatory. In order to have 'embarked on the crime proper' the Court thought that D would have to go to the bookmakers and demand his money back.

In *Jones* [1990] 3 All ER 886, Taylor LJ agreed with Lord Lane CJ in *Gullefer* (1990).

CASE EXAMPLE

Jones [1990] 3 All ER 886

D had been involved for some time in a relationship with a woman, X. When he discovered that she had started seeing another man, V, and that she no longer wanted to continue their relationship, D bought a shotgun and shortened the barrel. One morning, he went to confront V as the latter dropped his daughter off at school. D got into V's car, wearing overalls and a crash helmet with the visor down and carrying a bag. He took the sawn-off shotgun (which was loaded) from the bag and pointed it at V. He said, 'You are not going to like this.' At this point, V grabbed the end of the gun and pushed it sideways and upwards. There was a struggle during which V threw the gun out of the window. D was charged with attempted murder. He was convicted and the Court of Appeal upheld his conviction. Taylor LJ said that obtaining the gun, shortening the barrel, loading the gun and disguising himself were clearly preparatory acts. However, once D had got into V's car and pointed the loaded gun, then there was sufficient evidence to leave to the jury.

In the light of the expansive approach seen in *Gullefer* and *Jones*, the next Court of Appeal judgment, *Campbell* [1991] Crim LR 268, may be regarded as somewhat narrow. D had been arrested by police when, wearing a motorcycle crash helmet and armed with an imitation gun, he had approached to within a yard of a post office door. The Court of Appeal quashed his conviction for attempted robbery. Watkins LJ thought that there was no evidence on which a jury could 'properly and safely' have concluded that his acts were more than merely preparatory. Too many acts remained undone and those that had been performed – making his way from home, dismounting from his motorbike and walking towards the post office door – were clearly acts which were 'indicative of mere preparation'.

ACTIVITY

Applying the law

What should the police have done in order to ensure D's conviction for attempted robbery? Wait until D had entered the post office? Wait for him to approach the counter? Wait for him to make a demand for money?

The next case was *Attorney-General's Reference (No 1 of 1992)* [1993] 2 All ER 190. D had been charged with the attempted rape of a young woman, V, but had been acquitted after the trial judge directed the jury to acquit. The Court of Appeal, however, held that there was sufficient evidence on which the jury could have rightly convicted. Lord Taylor CJ stated:

JUDGMENT

'It is not, in our judgment, necessary, in order to raise a *prima facie* case of attempted rape, to prove that D ... had necessarily gone as far as to attempt physical penetration of the vagina. It is sufficient if ... there are proved acts which a jury could properly regard as more than merely preparatory to the commission of the offence. For example, and merely as an example, in the present case the evidence of V's distress, of the state of her clothing, and the position in which she was seen, together with D's acts of dragging her up the steps, lowering his trousers and interfering with her private parts, and his answers to the police, left it open to a jury to conclude that D had the necessary intent and had done acts which were more than merely preparatory. In short that he had embarked on committing the offence itself.'

In *Geddes* [1996] Crim LR 894, a case of attempted false imprisonment, the Court of Appeal offered another formulation for identifying the threshold, by postulating the following question: was D 'actually trying to commit the full offence?' Lord Bingham CJ stated:

JUDGMENT

'The line of demarcation between acts which are merely preparatory and acts which may amount to an attempt is not always clear or easy to recognise. There is no rule of thumb test. There must always be an exercise of judgment based on the particular facts of the case. It is, we think, an accurate paraphrase of the statutory test and not an illegitimate gloss upon it to ask whether the available evidence, if accepted, could show that [D] has done an act which shows that he has actually tried to commit the offence in question, or whether he has only got himself in a position or equipped himself to do so.'

CASE EXAMPLE

Geddes [1996] Crim LR 894

D was discovered by a member of staff in the boys' toilet of a school. He ran off, leaving behind a rucksack, in which was found various items including string, sealing tape and a knife. He was charged with attempted false imprisonment of a person unknown. The judge ruled that there was evidence of an attempt and the jury convicted. On appeal, the conviction was quashed. Although there was no doubt about D's intent, there was serious doubt that he had gone beyond the mere preparation stage. He had not even tried to make contact with any pupils.

More recent cases have continued to apply the test in *Geddes*. In *Tosti and White* [1997] EWCA Crim 222; [1997] Crim LR 746, D and E provided themselves with oxyacetylene equipment, drove to a barn which they planned to burgle, concealed the equipment in a hedge, approached the door and examined the padlock using a light, as it was nearly midnight. They then became aware that they were being watched and ran off. D claimed that they had gone to the barn to try to find water because their car engine was overheating; E admitted that they were on a reconnaissance mission with a future aim to burgle the barn. The Court of Appeal, applying *Geddes*, upheld their convictions of attempted burglary. There was evidence that D and E were trying to commit the offence. Beldam LJ said that the question was whether D and E 'had committed acts which were preparatory, but not merely so – so that it could be said the acts of preparation amounted to acts done in the commission of the offence. Essentially the question is one of degree: how close to, and necessary for, the commission of the offences were the acts which it was proved that they had done.'

In *Nash* [1998] EWCA Crim 2392; [1999] Crim LR 308, D left three letters addressed to 'Paper boy' in a street in Portsmouth. When opened, two were found to contain invitations to engage in mutual masturbation and/or oral sex with the author; the third, signed 'JJ', purported to offer work with a security company. At the instigation of the police a paper boy went to meet the writer of the third letter in a local park. There he met D, who asked him if he was looking for 'JJ'. D was arrested and convicted of three counts of attempting to procure an act of gross indecency. On appeal, it was argued that there was no case to answer with regard to the third letter, which was merely a preparatory act. The Court of Appeal confirmed the conviction with respect to the first two letters but allowed the appeal, following *Geddes* (1996), with respect to the third. Otton LJ said that the third letter 'was not sufficiently approximate to the act of procurement to amount to an attempt'. Otton LJ described *Geddes* as a 'helpful decision [that] illustrates where and how the line should be drawn'.

More than merely preparatory to what?

It is important to be clear exactly what it is that D needs to have gone beyond preparing for. This entails a clear understanding of the *actus reus* as opposed to the *mens rea* of the substantive offence. In *Toothill* [1998] Crim LR 876, D unsuccessfully appealed against his conviction of attempted burglary. V had seen D standing in her garden at approximately 11 p.m., apparently masturbating. She called the police and D was arrested. A knife and a glove were found in V's garden and a condom was found in D's pocket. D admitted knocking on V's door but claimed that he was lost and seeking directions. D was convicted and appealed on the ground that evidence of an attempt to enter V's home was insufficient; there had to be evidence of an attempt to commit rape as well. The Court of Appeal dismissed the appeal. The *actus reus* of burglary in s 9(1)(a) of the Theft Act 1968 is simply entering a building as a trespasser: there is no requirement in the *actus reus* that D actually rape anyone (indeed there is no requirement that anyone actually be in the building). The *actus reus* of attempted burglary was therefore doing an act which was more than merely preparatory to that entry. On the facts, there was evidence that D had gone beyond the preparatory stage, by actually knocking on V's door. (Note: the substantive offence of entering a building as a trespasser with intent to rape, contrary to s 9(1)(a) of the Theft Act 1968, was repealed by the Sexual Offences Act 2003. The facts in *Toothill* would now give rise to a charge of attempted trespass with intent to commit a sexual offence, contrary to s 63 of the SOA 2003.)

KEY FACTS

Key facts on 'more than merely preparatory'

Case	Offence attempted	Test proposed
Gullefer (1990)	Theft	'embarks upon the crime proper' – Lord Lane CJ
Jones (1990)	Murder	–
Campbell (1991)	Robbery	–
Att-Gen's Ref (No 1 of 1992) (1993)	Rape	'embarked on committing the offence itself' – Lord Taylor CJ
Geddes (1996)	False imprisonment	'actually tried to commit the offence in question' – Lord Bingham CJ
Tosti and White (1997)	Burglary	'had started upon the commission of the offence' – Beldam LJ
Nash (1999)	Procuring gross indecency	–

6.2.2 *Mens rea* of attempt

The essence of the *mens rea* in attempt cases is D's intention. In *Whybrow* (1951) 35 Cr App R 141, the Court of Appeal held that, although on a charge of murder, an intention to cause grievous bodily harm (GBH) would suffice, where attempted murder was alleged, nothing less than an intent to kill would do: 'the intent becomes the principal ingredient of the crime'. The *Nedrick* [1986] 3 All ER 1/*Woollin* [1998] 3 WLR 382 direction on when a jury may find that D intended a result based on D's foresight of virtually certain consequences has been applied to attempts by the Court of Appeal in *Walker and Hayles* [1990] Crim LR 44.

Conditional intent

Attempted theft and burglary cases have caused difficulties when it comes to framing the indictment. The problem is that most burglars, pickpockets, etc. are opportunists who do not have something particular in mind. The case of *Easom* [1971] 2 All ER 945 illustrates the problem. D had been observed rummaging in a handbag belonging to a plain-clothes policewoman. He did not take anything and was subsequently charged with the theft of the handbag and its contents (a purse, notebook, tissues, cosmetics and a pen). He was convicted, but the Court of Appeal quashed his conviction following a misdirection. The Court also declined to substitute a conviction of attempted theft of those articles: there was no evidence that D intended to steal those specific items. In *Attorney-General's Reference (Nos 1 and 2 of 1979)* [1979] 3 All ER 143, the Court of Appeal provided a solution to the problem: in such cases D should be charged with an attempt to steal 'some or all of the contents' of the handbag.

Relevance of recklessness

Where an attempt is charged, it may be possible to obtain a conviction even though D was reckless as to some of the elements of the *actus reus*. This is illustrated in *Attorney-General's Reference (No 3 of 1992)* [1994] 2 All ER 121.

CASE EXAMPLE

Attorney-General's Reference (No 3 of 1992) [1994] 2 All ER 121

A petrol bomb had been thrown from a moving car, narrowly missing a parked car in which four men were sitting and two other men standing nearby, and smashing into a wall. Those responsible for throwing the bomb were charged with attempted aggravated arson, the court alleging that, while the criminal damage was intentional, they had been reckless as to whether life would be endangered. At the end of the Crown case, the judge ruled no case to answer. He ruled that an attempted crime could not be committed without intent. It was impossible to intend to be reckless; therefore it had to be shown D both intended to damage property and to endanger life. The Court of Appeal held this was wrong: it was enough that D intended to damage property, being reckless as to whether life would be endangered.

In *Khan* [1990] 2 All ER 783, four men had been convicted of the attempted rape of a 16-year-old girl. All four had tried to have sex with her, unsuccessfully. Their convictions were upheld despite the trial judge's direction that, on a charge of attempted rape, it was only necessary for the Crown to prove that they had intended to have sex, knowing that the girl was not consenting, or not caring whether she consented or not. *Khan* was distinguished in a recent case, *Pace and Rogers* [2014] EWCA Crim 186, [2014] 1 Cr App R 34. Davis LJ rejected the notion that, in a case under the Criminal Attempts Act 1981, it was possible to intend some (but not necessarily all) of the elements of the substantive offence. He said that 'as a matter of ordinary language and in accordance with principle, an "intent to commit an offence" connotes an intent to commit *all* the elements of the offence. We can see no sufficient basis, whether linguistic or purposive, for construing it otherwise' (emphasis added).

CASE EXAMPLE

Pace and Rogers [2014] EWCA Crim 186

Martin Pace (P) worked at a scrap yard in Oxford owned by Simon Rogers (R) and his father. Local police undertook an investigation into scrap metal dealers, using undercover officers to test whether stolen items would be accepted. On several occasions, two officers visited the yard with scrap metal which they said was stolen. The metal, which was not in fact stolen, was purchased by the yard. P and R were charged with attempting to convert criminal property (the substantive offence found in s 327 of the Proceeds of Crime Act 2002). The Crown's case was that P and R suspected that the scrap metal was stolen, and that such *mens rea* was sufficient for attempts liability. P and R were convicted and appealed, successfully, to the Court of Appeal. The appeal court held that suspicion was too low a level of *mens rea* for attempted conversion. It was necessary to prove that P and R intended to convert stolen property, and that required proof that they believed (and not just suspected) that the property was stolen.

The decision in *Pace and Rogers* is controversial and almost immediately provoked divided opinion amongst commentators. On one hand, it is supported by J J Child and A Hunt, '*Pace and Rogers* and the *mens rea* of criminal attempt: *Khan* on the scrap heap?' (2014) 78 J Crim L 220. They contend that 'an intention/knowledge based approach is the only one which properly marries the wording of the Criminal Attempts Act 1981 with the achievement of a coherent model of attempts liability'. They predict that the case will be appealed to the Supreme Court and if/when that happens they argue that the Court of Appeal's decision should be upheld (and that *Khan* should be overruled).

On the other hand, *Pace and Rogers* is criticised by F Stark, 'The *mens rea* of a criminal attempt' (2014) 3 Arch Rev 7, who argues that it 'risks setting a dangerous precedent' and should not be followed. He points out that attempted rape will be 'virtually impossible to prosecute' if the Crown has to prove both (i) an intention to penetrate the victim and (ii) an intention that the victim not be consenting. He suggests that, if the case reaches the Supreme Court, the decision in *Khan* is the one that should be endorsed instead. *Pace and Rogers* is also criticised by M Dyson, 'Scrapping *Khan*' [2014] Crim LR 445. He acknowledges that the judgment in *Pace and Rogers* is 'more faithful to the literal meaning' of s 1 of the 1981 Act but contends that 'as a matter of policy [it] cannot be right', invoking the same attempted rape scenario as Stark.

6.2.3 Impossibility

If a crime is impossible, obviously no one can be convicted of actually committing it; but it does not follow that no one can be convicted of attempting to commit it. There may be an attempt where D fails to commit the substantive crime, because he makes a mistake or is ignorant as to certain facts. The crime may be:

- physically impossible (e.g. D attempts to pick V's pocket but, unknown to D, the pocket is in fact empty; D attempts to murder V by stabbing him with a dagger but, unknown to D, V died that morning of natural causes); or
- legally impossible (e.g. D handles goods, believing them to be stolen, when they are not in fact stolen).

There are also situations where the crime is physically and legally possible but, in the actual circumstances, because of the inadequate methods D plans to use, or does use, it is impossible to commit the substantive offence (e.g. D attempts to break into a three-inch-thick titanium steel safe using a plastic spoon). At common law, there was no liability for attempt if the crime attempted was physically or legally impossible; only if D used methods that were simply inadequate to commit the substantive offence could D be liable. This was seen in *White* [1910] 2 KB 124, where D was convicted of attempted murder after giving his mother an insufficient dose of poison. (Had he given her sugar instead, he would have been acquitted.) This rule was confirmed as recently as 1975 by the House of Lords in *Haughton v Smith* [1975] AC 476. However, s 1 of the Criminal Attempts Act 1981 was intended to make all three examples of impossibility capable of leading to liability:

SECTION

'(1) . . . (2) A person may be guilty of attempting to commit an offence to which this section applies even though the facts are such that the commission of the offence is impossible.

(3) In any case where –

(a) apart from this subsection a person's intention would not be regarded as having amounted to an intention to commit an offence; but

(b) if the facts of the case had been as he believed them to be, his intention would be so regarded,

then, for the purposes of subsection (1) . . . he shall be regarded as having had an intention to commit an offence.'

However, despite the new provisions above, in *Anderton v Ryan* [1985] AC 560 the House of Lords decided that the 1981 Act had not been intended to affect the situations of physical impossibility. Lord Roskill said that 'if the action is innocent and [D] does everything he intends to do, s 1(3) does not compel the conclusion that erroneous belief in the existence of facts which, if true, would have made his completed act a crime makes him guilty of an attempt to commit that crime'. This decision was overruled less than a year later. In *Shivpuri* [1987] AC 1, Lord Bridge said that:

JUDGMENT

'The concept of "objective innocence" is incapable of sensible application in relation to the law of criminal attempts. The reason for this is that any attempt to commit an offence which involves "an act which is more than merely preparatory to the commission of the offence" but which for any reason fails, so that in the event no offence is committed, must *ex hypothesi*, from the point of view of the criminal law be "objectively innocent". What turns what would otherwise ... be an innocent act into a crime is the intent of the actor to commit an offence.'

CASE EXAMPLE

Shivpuri [1987] AC 1

D was persuaded to act as a drugs courier. He was given instructions to receive drugs and transport them somewhere else. D duly collected a suitcase which he believed contained either heroin or cannabis. The suitcase contained several packages of white powder, one of which D took to the delivery point. There, he was arrested and was subsequently charged with attempting to be 'knowingly concerned in dealing in prohibited drugs'. This was despite the fact that the white powder was not drugs at all but perfectly legal snuff or some similar harmless vegetable matter. D was nevertheless convicted and the Court of Appeal and House of Lords upheld his conviction.

Shivpuri was followed in *Jones* [2007] EWCA Crim 1118; [2007] 3 WLR 907, in which D was convicted of attempting to incite a child under 13 to engage in sexual activity, contrary to s 8 of the Sexual Offences Act 2003. On the facts, the offence was impossible, as the 'child' whom he thought he was inciting was actually an undercover policewoman. The Court of Appeal, however, held that he had rightly been convicted of attempting to commit this impossible offence.

CASE EXAMPLE

Jones [2007] EWCA Crim 1118; [2007] 3 WLR 907

D wrote graffiti on the walls of train and station toilets seeking girls aged 8 to 13 for sex in return for payment and requesting contact via his mobile phone. A journalist saw one of the messages and contacted the police who began an operation using an undercover policewoman pretending to be a 12-year-old girl called 'Amy'. D sent several texts to 'Amy' in which he tried to persuade her to engage in sexual activity. Eventually, 'Amy' and D agreed to meet at a Burger King in Brighton, where he was arrested. At his trial, D pointed out that, as 'Amy' didn't exist, he had not intended to incite any actual person under the age of 13. The judge rejected the submission. D changed his plea to guilty and appealed, but the Court of Appeal upheld his conviction.

It has been argued that, in cases like *Shivpuri* and *Jones*, D is being punished solely for his criminal intention. However, this overlooks the fact that, for an attempt, there must be a 'more than merely preparatory' act. Furthermore, defendants like Shivpuri and Jones who intend to smuggle drugs or who intend to have sex with young girls (and are prepared to act on their intentions) are dangerous people; their prosecution and conviction is in the public interest. In many cases, the 'objectively innocent' nature of the acts means that the attempt will not come to light. But, in those cases where it does, D should not escape punishment.

6.2.4 Excluded offences

Section 1(4) of the 1981 Act excludes attempts to commit the following:

- conspiracy;
- aiding, abetting, counselling or procuring the commission of an offence (except where this amounts to a substantive offence, e.g. complicity in another's suicide contrary to s 2(1) Suicide Act 1961, as amended by s 53 of the Coroners and Justice Act 2009).

Moreover, there must be 'an act', so it is impossible to attempt to commit a crime which can only be committed by omission (e.g. failing to provide a breath test), or to attempt to commit a result crime by omitting to act when under a duty to act solely on that basis. However, in most cases there would presumably be some act to which liability could be attached.

Because intent is essential, where a crime cannot be committed intentionally, such as gross negligence manslaughter and reckless manslaughter (see Chapter 10), D cannot be liable for an attempt to commit it. There is therefore no offence in English law of 'attempted manslaughter'.

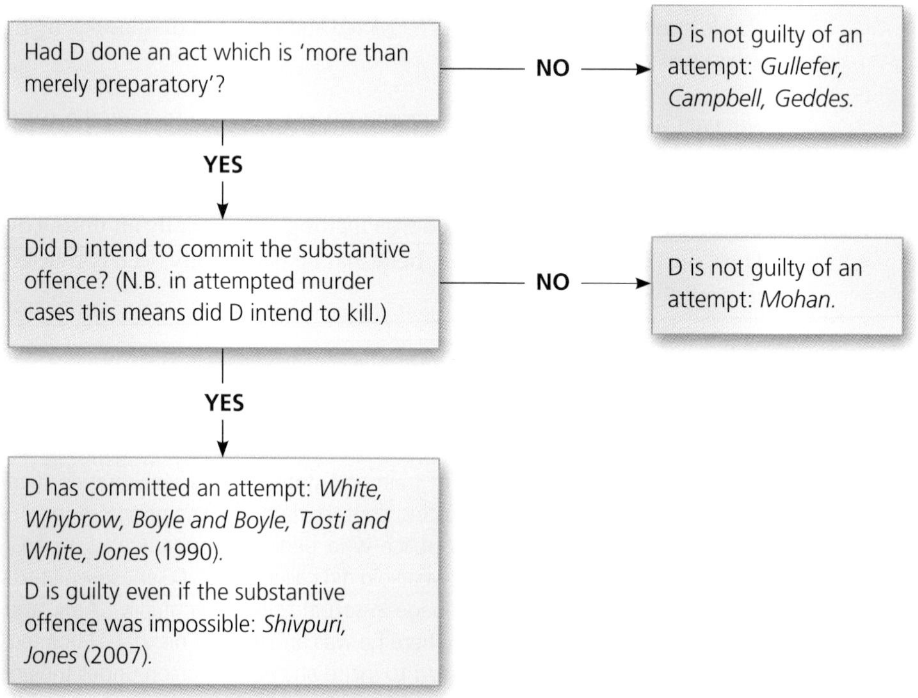

Figure 6.1 *Mens rea* of attempt.

6.2.5 Successful attempts

Is failure essential to successful conviction for attempt? A doctrine of 'merger' existed at common law, whereby an attempt blended in with the substantive crime, if committed. This was abolished, for indictable offences, by s 6(4) Criminal Law Act 1967. Now D may be convicted of an attempt, notwithstanding that he is also shown to be guilty of the completed offence.

6.2.6 Reform

In September 2007 the Law Commission (LC) published a Consultation Paper *Conspiracy and Attempts* (Paper No 183), in which it recommended the following (amongst other things):

- The present offence of attempt should be abolished and replaced with two new offences.
- First, a new attempt offence, limited to the situation where D reaches the last acts needed to commit the substantive offence.
- Second, a new offence of 'criminal preparation'.
- Both new offences would require proof of intention to commit the substantive offence (murder, robbery, etc.). Intention could, as at present, be either direct or oblique intent. Conditional intent would continue to suffice.
- Both new offences would carry the same (maximum) penalty as the substantive offence.
- It should be possible to commit either of the new offences by omission.

The LC is trying to resurrect the 'Last Act' test as set out in *Eagleton* (1855), which will significantly narrow the scope of the offence of attempt. It would not be possible, for example, to say that D in *Jones* (1990) would definitely be guilty of attempted murder under the proposed new attempt offence. In pointing the shotgun at V, he had gone beyond the 'merely preparatory' stage, but had he reached the 'last act' stage? However, if not, D could instead be convicted of 'preparing to commit murder'.

The LC describes the proposed new 'criminal preparation' offence as meaning acts which could be regarded (as attempt is at present) as part of the execution of D's intention to commit the substantive offence. Thus, D will still have to go beyond the 'merely preparatory' stage. The LC gives some examples of situations where D might incur liability for criminal preparation. One is the situation where D is caught examining or interfering with a door, window or lock. At present, such facts might support a conviction for attempted burglary (see *Boyle and Boyle* (1986) and *Tosti* (1997), above) but under the LC's proposals, this would become the offence of 'preparing to commit burglary'.

The primary motivation for the proposals is the need to address the reluctance of the Court of Appeal in some cases to accept that D has committed an 'attempt', as presently understood. The LC is confident that, in cases such as *Campbell* (1990) and *Geddes* (1996), discussed above, the courts would be more willing to convict the defendants of 'preparing to commit robbery' and 'preparing to commit false imprisonment', respectively, instead.

The proposal to allow for the new attempt/criminal preparation offences to be committed by omission is interesting and, it is submitted, welcome. For example, under the present law, it is possible to commit murder by omission (see *Gibbins and Proctor* (1918), discussed in Chapter 2), but it is not possible to commit attempted murder by omission. Yet if there is sufficient evidence that D is trying to kill V by starving them to death (but has not succeeded), surely D deserves to be punished for this?

6.3 Conspiracy

Where two or more people have agreed to commit a crime then there may be liability for a conspiracy. Gathering enough evidence to prove that the parties had agreed to commit a crime can present problems for the police but, where evidence is available, conspiracy is a valuable weapon for prosecuting those involved in large-scale organised crime. Typical cases involve prosecutions for conspiring to smuggle drugs (*Siracusa* (1989) 90 Cr App R 340) or conspiring to launder stolen money (*Saik* [2006] UKHL 18; [2007] 1 AC 18).

Until 1977, the law of conspiracy was a matter of common law. Since then, although certain conspiracies continue to exist as common law offences (agreements to defraud and, possibly, to corrupt public morals; see below), the law is regulated by the Criminal Law Act 1977. Section 1(1) provides that a person is guilty of conspiracy if he 'agrees with any other person or persons that a course of conduct shall be pursued which, if the agreement is carried out in accordance with their intentions … (a) will necessarily amount to or involve the commission of any offence or offences by one or more of the parties to the agreement'. Despite the statutory framework under the 1977 Act, judicial reference may be (and is) made to pre-1977 case law in order to help clarify the meaning and scope of the statutory provisions.

6.3.1 *Actus reus* of statutory conspiracy

'Agreement'

The offence of conspiracy is complete as soon as there is an 'agreement' to commit a criminal offence (*Saik* (2006)). This means that the parties must have reached agreement to commit the same offence. Sometimes this is not as straightforward as it appears. For example, in *Barnard* (1980) 70 Cr App R 28, D agreed to assist what he thought was a conspiracy to commit theft. In fact, the others had agreed to commit robbery. The Court of Appeal quashed D's conviction on the basis that an agreement to commit theft was not equivalent to an agreement to commit robbery (significantly, theft is less serious than robbery). This was also seen in *Taylor* [2002] Crim LR 205. The Court of Appeal decided that an agreement to import class B drugs was not equivalent to an agreement to import class A drugs (again, importing class B drugs is less serious than importing class A drugs). Conversely, because the greater includes the lesser, if D agrees to commit a more serious crime than his co-conspirators, he may be held liable. For example:

- D agrees to commit robbery while E and F have agreed to commit theft. D is guilty of conspiracy to commit theft.
- D agrees to import class A drugs (e.g. cocaine or heroin) while E and F have agreed to import class B drugs. D is liable for conspiracy to import class B drugs.

If the parties have reached general agreement to commit an offence, then the courts may be prepared to overlook disagreements as to the details. Thus, in *Broad* [1997] Crim LR 666, D and E were convicted of a conspiracy to produce a class A drug. The fact that D thought they had agreed to produce heroin while E thought they had agreed to produce cocaine was irrelevant. A conspiracy comes into existence as soon as there is an agreement between two or more conspirators, although the agreement continues until the substantive offence is either performed, abandoned or frustrated (*DPP v Doot* [1973] AC 807); this means that further parties may join a subsisting conspiracy at any time until then.

There is certainly no requirement that the substantive offence be committed (*Saik*). Indeed, the whole point of the offence of conspiracy is to allow for the prosecution and conviction of those who agree to commit a crime, even if they do not actually succeed in committing it.

'With any other person or persons'

Where more than two parties are involved, it is still a conspiracy even if all the conspirators never meet each other. This could happen in the following situations:

- A 'wheel' conspiracy exists where there is a coordinating party, D, who communicates separately with E and F, but E and F never meet.
- A 'chain' conspiracy exists where D communicates with E, E communicates with F and F communicates with G.

What is essential is that there is a common purpose or design, and that each alleged conspirator has communicated with at least one other (*Scott* (1979) 68 Cr App R 164). D must agree with someone, although no one need be identified (*Philips* (1987) 86 Cr App R 18). Certain parties are excluded by virtue of the 1977 Act. Section 2(1) provides that the 'intended victim' of an offence cannot be guilty of conspiring to commit it. For example, D, a 13-year-old girl, agrees to have sex with an E, an older man. D could not be convicted of conspiring to commit the offence of sexual activity with a child, contrary to s 9 of the Sexual Offences Act 2003 (see Chapter 12), because she would be the 'intended victim' of the offence. Section 2(2), as amended by the Civil Partnership Act 2004, provides there is also no conspiracy if D agrees with (a) his spouse or civil partner, (b) a person under the age of criminal responsibility or (c) the intended victim.

Spouse or civil partner (s 2(2)(a))

The exclusion of D's spouse was a pre-existing common law rule. Thus, in *Lovick* [1993] Crim LR 890, Mrs Lovick's conviction was quashed because it had not been established that anyone other than she and Mr Lovick were involved. However, if a third party is involved, spouses may face liability for conspiracy. This was seen in *Chrastny* [1992] 1 All ER 189. There was evidence that Mrs Chrastny had conspired with her husband (to supply cocaine) and that she knew he had conspired with others. The Civil Partnership Act 2004 amended the 1977 Act so that D cannot conspire with his or her civil partner.

A person under the age of criminal responsibility (s 2(2)(b))

This means that D cannot conspire with E if E is under ten years of age.

The intended victim (s 2(2)(c))

'Victim' is not defined in the Act. It may be restricted to victims of offences created specifically to protect that person, as in *Tyrrell* [1894] 1 QB 710. Here, D, a girl under 16 years old, had allowed E to have intercourse with her. D was subsequently convicted of aiding and abetting the offence of unlawful sexual intercourse contrary to s 5 of the Criminal Law Amendment Act 1885. On appeal, her conviction was quashed: the purpose of the statute was to protect 'women and young girls against themselves', according to Lord Coleridge, and the policy of the courts is that statutes should be construed so that they do not criminalise those they were designed to protect. It follows that, on the facts of *Tyrrell*, there was no conspiracy to commit unlawful sexual intercourse either, because D was the victim of the offence. However, the word 'victim' could be defined in a broader sense. If D, a sadist, agrees with V, a masochist, that D will whip V, is this a conspiracy to commit assault? If V is a 'victim', then the answer is 'no'.

The exclusion in s 2(2)(a) is controversial, because it means that, if Mr and Mrs X agree to kill their neighbour, no crime has been committed. But if the couple were unmarried and reached exactly the same agreement then this would be conspiracy to murder, a very serious offence. The exclusion in s 2(2)(c) is also controversial as it means that E (the older man in the above example) would also escape liability for conspiracy, even though he has agreed to have sex with a 13-year-old girl. The Law Commission has recently proposed abolition of both of these exclusions (see below).

6.3.2 *Mens rea* of statutory conspiracy

The parties must:

- agree ... that a course of conduct shall be pursued which,
- if the agreement is carried out in accordance with their intentions,
- will necessarily amount to or involve the commission of any offence or offences by one or more of the parties to the agreement.

'Course of conduct'

In *Siracusa* (1989) 90 Cr App R 340, the Court of Appeal decided that the *mens rea* sufficient to support the substantive offence would not necessarily be sufficient to support a charge of conspiracy. The offence charged was a conspiracy to import heroin, contrary to s 170(2) of the Customs and Excise Management Act 1979, which prohibits the importation of various classes of drugs, with various penalties attached. As far as the *mens rea* of the substantive offence is concerned, an intention to import any prohibited drug suffices. The question for the Court of Appeal was whether the same *mens rea* sufficed for the conspiracy. O'Connor LJ said that if the prosecution charged a conspiracy to import heroin, then the prosecution must prove that the agreed course of conduct was the importation of heroin. 'This is because the essence of the crime of conspiracy is the agreement and, in simple terms, you do not have an agreement to import heroin by proving an agreement to import cannabis.'

'In accordance with their intentions'

If D and E agree to commit a crime but D, secretly, has no intention of seeing it through, is there a conspiracy? Prior to the 1977 Act, the courts had held that D was not liable for conspiracy unless he intended that the agreement be seen through to its completion (*Thompson* [1965] Cr App R 1). However, in *Anderson* [1986] AC 27; [1985] 2 All ER 961, the House of Lords unanimously held that it was not necessary that D intend to see through the commission of the offence. Lord Bridge, giving judgment for the House, stated:

JUDGMENT

'I am clearly driven by consideration of the diversity of roles which parties may agree to play in criminal conspiracies to reject any construction of the statutory language which would require the prosecution to prove an intention on the part of each conspirator that the criminal offence or offences which will necessarily be committed by one or more of the conspirators if the agreed course of conduct is fully carried out should in fact be committed ... In these days of highly organised crime the most serious statutory conspiracies will frequently involve an elaborate and complex agreed course of conduct in which many will consent to play necessary but subordinate roles, not involving them in any direct participation in the commission of the offence or offences at the centre of the conspiracy. Parliament cannot have intended that such parties should escape conviction of conspiracy on the basis that it cannot be proved against them that they intended that the relevant offence or offences should be committed.'

CASE EXAMPLE

Anderson [1986] AC 27; [1985] 2 All ER 961

D agreed with E and F, for a fee of £20,000, to purchase and supply diamond wire (capable of cutting through prison bars) which would be used to enable F's brother, X, who was on remand in Lewes Prison awaiting trial on charges of serious drug offences, to escape. D was also to provide rope and a ladder, transport and safe accommodation where X could hide out.

D was charged with conspiracy to effect the escape of a prisoner, but argued that he had no intention of seeing the plan through to its conclusion. He claimed that he hoped to collect most of the £20,000 after supplying the diamond wire. He would then use the money to travel to Spain and would take no further part in the escape plan. Finally, he doubted that the escape plan would succeed. Therefore, he had no 'intention' to see X escape from prison. Despite all of this, D's conviction was upheld by the House of Lords.

The issue raises particular difficulty for police officers working undercover trying to infiltrate drug smuggling operations. It is perhaps inevitable that these officers will make agreements with criminals in order to lend credence to their undercover story. Do the officers intend to smuggle drugs? The Privy Council has dealt with such arguments on two occasions. In *Somchai Liangsiriprasert* [1991] AC 225, the Privy Council left open the question whether US drug enforcement officers were guilty of conspiracy when they infiltrated a plot to import drugs into the USA with the object of trapping the dealers. Then in *Yip Chiu-Cheung* [1995] 1 AC 111; [1994] 2 All ER 924, which involved a drug smuggling operation between Hong Kong and Australia, the Privy Council held that a conspiracy between D and E, an undercover agent working for the United States Drug Enforcement Administration, had been committed. A plan had been agreed upon, whereby E would fly from Australia to Hong Kong, collect the drugs from D and return to Australia with them. D was convicted of conspiracy and appealed, unsuccessfully. The Privy Council ruled that the fact that E would not be prosecuted did not mean that he did not intend to form an agreement with D to transport drugs.

Intention to take part?

In *Anderson* (1986) Lord Bridge also said, *obiter*, that 'beyond the mere fact of agreement, the necessary *mens rea* of the crime is, in my opinion, established if, and only if, it is shown that the accused, when he entered into the agreement, intended to play some part in the agreed course of conduct in furtherance of the criminal purpose which the agreed course of conduct was intended to achieve. Nothing less will suffice; nothing more is required.' This statement seems to suggest that it is necessary for the Crown to prove that any particular conspirators actually intended to play some physical part in the commission of the offence. If so, it would undermine what Lord Bridge said earlier in his speech (quoted above) when he explained that the policy of the 1977 Act was to allow for the prosecution of those with minor roles in the conspiracy, 'not involving them in any direct participation in the commission of the offence'. More seriously, it would prevent the prosecution for conspiracy of gang leaders or 'crime lords' who reach agreements with their subordinates but who deliberately distance themselves from physical participation in criminal activity.

This prompted the Court of Appeal in *Siracusa* (1989) (the facts of which were given above) to explain what Lord Bridge had, apparently, meant to say. The defendant in *Siracusa* (1989) had reached an agreement with others to smuggle drugs but it could not be proven that he intended to play any physical part in the operation. Nevertheless, the Court of Appeal upheld his conviction of conspiracy. O'Connor LJ said that D's 'intention to participate [was] established by his failure to stop the unlawful activity. Lord Bridge's *dictum* does not require anything more.'

'If the agreement is carried out': conditional intent

If D and E agree to rob a bank if it is quiet when they get there, have they agreed on a course of conduct, which will necessarily amount to the commission of an offence? The answer, according to *Reed* [1982] Crim LR 819, would be 'yes'.

CASE EXAMPLE

Reed [1982] Crim LR 819

D and E agreed that E would visit people contemplating suicide. He would then, depending on his assessment of the most appropriate course of action, either provide faith healing, consolation and comfort whilst discouraging suicide, or actively help them to commit suicide. They were both convicted of several counts of conspiracy to aid and abet suicide. On appeal it was argued that, if the agreement is capable of being successfully completed without a crime being committed, there is no conspiracy; moreover, in the present case, the agreement was capable of execution without the law being broken, and therefore they were wrongly convicted. The court rejected the argument and upheld the convictions.

In *Jackson* [1985] Crim LR 442, D and E agreed with V to shoot V in the leg if V, who was then on trial for burglary, was convicted (in order to encourage the judge to sentence him more leniently). They were convicted of conspiracy to pervert the course of justice. The Court of Appeal held that:

JUDGMENT

'Planning was taking place for a contingency and if that contingency occurred the conspiracy would necessarily involve the commission of an offence. "Necessarily" is not to be held to mean that there must inevitably be the carrying out of the offence; it means, if the agreement is carried out in accordance with the plan, there must be the commission of the offence referred to in the conspiracy count.'

In *Saik* (2006), Lord Nicholls gave another example of a 'conditional' agreement. A conspiracy 'to rob a bank tomorrow if the coast is clear when the conspirators reach the bank is not, by reason of this qualification, any less a conspiracy to rob'. In the same case, Lord Brown offered a different example: 'If two men agree to burgle a house but only if it is unoccupied or not alarmed they are clearly guilty of conspiracy to burgle.'

'Will necessarily amount to or involve the commission of any offence or offences'

A conspiracy may involve an agreement to commit one offence, or several offences. Thus, in *Roberts* [1998] 1 Cr App R 441, the prosecution alleged a single conspiracy against several defendants to commit both aggravated and simple criminal damage. This does not mean that the prosecution cannot allege more than one conspiracy deriving from the same agreement. In *Lavercombe* [1988] Crim LR 435, D and E were convicted of conspiracy to import cannabis into the UK from Thailand. The Court of Appeal upheld their convictions, despite the fact that they had already been convicted of conspiracy to possess cannabis by a court in Thailand.

Until quite recently, a conspiracy had to involve an agreement to commit an offence in England. However, the Criminal Justice (Terrorism and Conspiracy) Act 1998 inserted a new s 1A into the 1977 Act, allowing for conspiracies made in England to commit crimes in other jurisdictions to fall within the offence. Thus, for example, 'an agreement made in Birmingham to rob a bank in Brussels' is now a conspiracy contrary to English law and triable in English courts.

In *Kenning and others* [2008] EWCA Crim 1534; [2008] 3 WLR 1306, the Court of Appeal was asked whether the offence of conspiracy to aid, abet, counsel or procure the commission of an offence actually existed in English law. The court ruled not. D and E owned a shop selling hydroponic equipment, cannabis seeds and cannabis-related literature. They were convicted of conspiracy to aid and abet the production of cannabis, but their convictions were quashed on appeal. The Court emphasised that the 1977 Act requires that the conspirators' agreement will, if carried out, 'necessarily' involve the commission of an offence. That was not the case where the conspirators simply agreed to aid, abet or counsel someone else, because there was no guarantee that that other person would necessarily commit any offence.

Kenning and others was distinguished in a recent case with very similar facts. In *Dang and others* [2014] EWCA Crim 348, [2014] 2 Cr App R, the prosecution case was that the appellants had been engaged in a conspiracy to import and sell hydroponic equipment for other people to use in order to produce cannabis. However, rather than charging the appellants with conspiracy to aid and abet others to produce cannabis, the Crown charged them with conspiracy to be 'concerned in' the production of cannabis by others, contrary to s 4(2)(b) of the Misuse of Drugs Act 1971. The jury convicted and the Court of Appeal upheld the convictions, distinguishing *Kenning and others*. Pitchford LJ explained that, by framing the charge by reference to s 4(2)(b), no question of aiding and abetting arose. He added that, before the jury could convict of conspiracy on the basis of s 4(2)(b), the jury had to be sure that each defendant joined a conspiracy knowing that its objective was to provide equipment for the production of cannabis by another and that, when he joined it, the defendant shared that intention. A 'generalised awareness' that the equipment may be used for the unlawful purpose would not suffice.

Section 1(2)

Section 1(2) of the 1977 Act adds that 'Where liability for any offence may be incurred without knowledge on the part of the person committing it of any particular fact or circumstance necessary for the commission of the offence, a person shall nevertheless not be guilty of conspiracy to commit that offence ... unless he and at least one other party to the agreement *intend* or *know* that that fact or circumstance shall or will exist at the time when the conduct constituting the offence is to take place' (emphasis added). This provision has recently generated a large number of appeals in cases involving conspiracies to launder money (i.e. to convert money which is the proceeds of drug trafficking or some other criminal activity). The substantive offence of money laundering (now set out in the Proceeds of Crime Act 2002) can be committed if D *suspects* that the money is the proceeds of some criminal activity. But is suspicion enough for a conspiracy to launder money?

According to the House of Lords in *Saik* [2006] UKHL 18; [2007] 1 AC 18, the answer is 'no' – because s 1(2) requires that D must 'intend or know' that a fact or circumstance (such as whether money is the proceeds of drug trafficking or some other criminal activity) shall or will exist. Suspicion is not enough.

CASE EXAMPLE

Saik [2006] UKHL 18; [2007] 1 AC 18

D operated a bureau de change in Marble Arch, London. It was alleged that, in the course of his business, he had converted (from pounds into foreign currency) a substantial amount of cash which was the proceeds of drug trafficking or other criminal activity and he was charged with conspiracy to launder money. He admitted that he suspected the money may have been the proceeds of crime but appealed on the basis that he did not 'know' that it was. The Law Lords agreed that without proof that D knew the money was the proceeds of crime, there was no *mens rea* of conspiracy and quashed D's conviction.

Saik was followed in *Tree* [2008] EWCA Crim 261. D, a businessman who ran a firm called Performance Cars & Boats, was convicted of conspiracy to convert the proceeds of crime, specifically an Ebbtide Mystique speedboat, into cash. He had sold the speedboat for £14,000 in cash but did not record the transaction in his business accounts. D was convicted on the basis that he *suspected* the speedboat was criminal property (the Crown's case was that the boat's owner had bought it with money obtained through unlawful tax evasion). However, D's appeal was allowed. Following *Saik*, the Crown had to prove that D *knew* that the speedboat was criminal property – mere suspicion was not enough.

6.3.3 Common law conspiracy

The Criminal Law Act 1977 abolished the offence of conspiracy at common law, except for conspiracies:

- to corrupt public morals or to outrage public decency;
- to defraud.

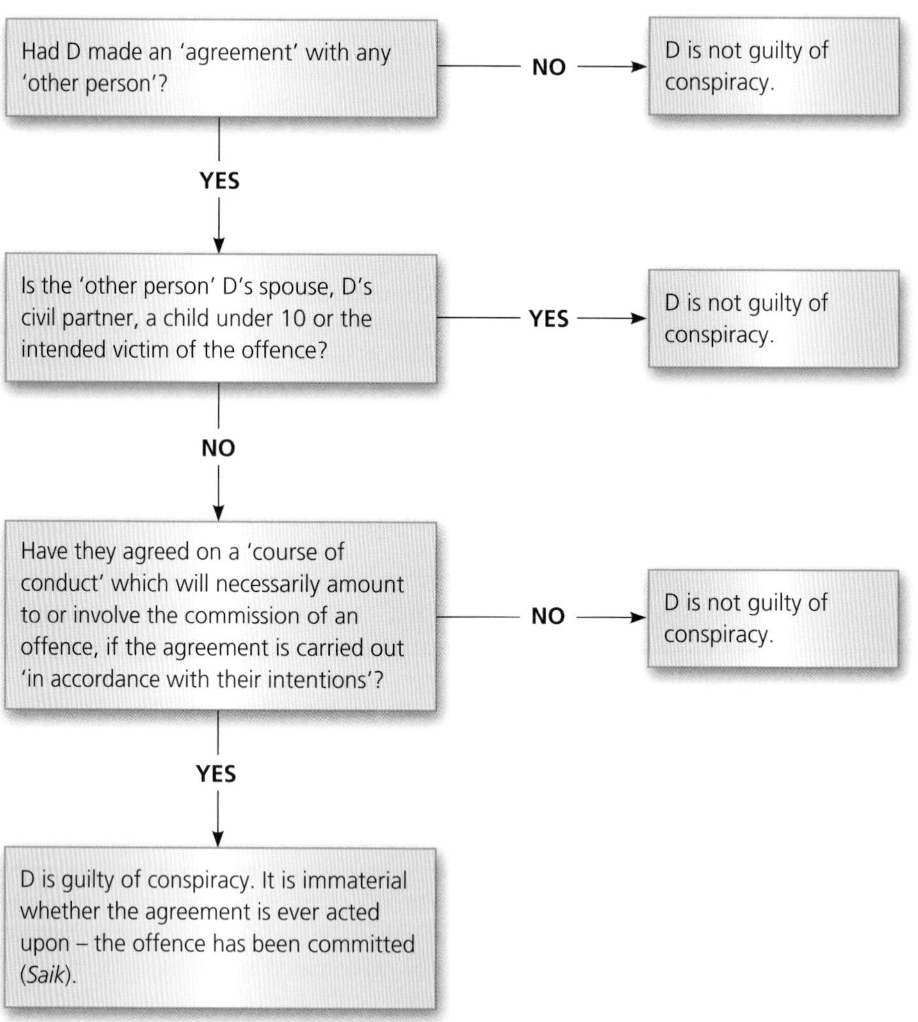

Figure 6.2 Conspiracy.

Conspiracy to corrupt public morals or outrage public decency

This is defined (by s 5(3) of the Criminal Law Act 1977, but preserving the common law nature of the offence) as an agreement 'to engage in conduct which (a) tends to corrupt public morals or outrages public decency; but (b) would not amount to or involve the commission of an offence if carried out by a single person otherwise than in pursuance of an agreement'. These types of common law conspiracy were retained because it was unclear at the time (1977) whether corrupting public morals or outraging public decency constituted substantive crimes. However, in *Gibson and another* [1990] 2 QB 619, the Court of Appeal held that outraging public decency was a substantive offence in its own right. Conspiracy to outrage public decency therefore now falls under the statutory offence, but conspiracy to corrupt public morals remains a common law offence. In *Shaw v DPP* [1962] AC 220, D had published a magazine entitled *Ladies Directory* containing the names and addresses of prostitutes and certain details of sexual perversions which they were willing to practise. The House of Lords upheld D's conviction for conspiracy to corrupt public morals.

In *Knuller (Publishing, Printing & Promotions) Ltd v DPP* [1973] AC 439, the House of Lords held that a finding that conduct was liable to corrupt public morals was not to be lightly reached. It was not enough that it is liable to 'lead morally astray'. Lord Simon said that the words 'corrupt public morals' suggested 'conduct which a jury might find to be destructive of the very fabric of society'.

Conspiracy to defraud

Actus reus

In *Scott v MPC* [1975] AC 818, Viscount Dilhorne said 'it is clearly the law that an agreement by two or more persons by dishonesty to deprive a person of something which is his or to which he is, or would be, entitled, and an agreement by two or more by dishonesty to injure some proprietary right of his, suffices to constitute the offence of conspiracy to defraud'.

Mens rea

There are two elements: D must intend to defraud, and must do so dishonestly.

Intention

In *Scott* (1975), Lord Diplock stated that the 'purpose of the conspirators must be to cause the victim economic loss'. However, it is doubtful whether many conspirators had as their purpose causing economic loss to anyone. Typically, defendants involved in fraud operations operate out of greed, not spite. D's purpose is almost inevitably to make profit for himself although, in many cases, he will recognise that it is an inevitable consequence that loss will be caused to V. This is illustrated in *Cooke* [1986] 2 All ER 985.

CASE EXAMPLE

Cooke [1986] 2 All ER 985

D, a British Rail steward, was charged, along with a number of his colleagues, with conspiracy to defraud British Rail. The allegation was that they had taken their own supplies of tea, coffee powder, cheese and beefburgers into the buffet car crew of a Penzance to Paddington train, intending to sell these to passengers as if they were BR's products and pocketing the proceeds. Although the others were acquitted, D was convicted and the House of Lords upheld the conviction. D's fraud involved fraudulent conduct going 'substantially' beyond cheating British Rail's passengers; the Crown was entitled to charge him with conspiracy to defraud.

Dishonesty

In *Ghosh* [1982] 2 All ER 689 the Court of Appeal held that the test was the same as in theft. The standard is that of ordinary decent people; if D knows he is acting contrary to that standard, he is dishonest (see Chapter 13).

6.3.4 Impossibility

At common law, impossibility was a defence to a charge of conspiracy except where it was down to D and E's choice of method being inadequate. This was seen in *DPP v Nock* [1978] AC 979.

CASE EXAMPLE

DPP v Nock [1978] AC 979

D and E resolved to extract cocaine from a powder, which they believed was a mixture of cocaine and lignocaine. In fact the powder was pure lignocaine hydrochloride, an anaesthetic used in dentistry, which contains no cocaine at all. Their convictions for conspiracy to produce a controlled drug were quashed: it was physically impossible to extract cocaine from the powder.

Now, however, s 1(1) of the Criminal Law Act 1977 (as amended by the Criminal Attempts Act 1981) provides that a person is guilty of statutory conspiracy even if it would be impossible for the agreement to be carried out as intended. You will recall that s 1(1)(a) of the Act states that a person is guilty of conspiracy if he agrees with at least one other person that a course of conduct shall be pursued which will necessarily amount to the commission of an offence. Section 1(1)(b) goes on to provide 'or would do so but for the existence of facts which render the commission of the offence or any of the offences impossible'.

Reform

In September 2007 the Law Commission (LC) published a Consultation Paper *Conspiracy and Attempts* (Paper No 183), in which it recommended the following (amongst other things):

- Abolition of the spousal immunity in s 2(2)(a) of the Criminal Law Act 1977, which the LC describes as 'anomalous and anachronistic'.
- Abolition of the exemptions in s 2(1) and s 2(2)(c) of the 1977 Act for the 'intended victim' and for those who conspire with the 'intended victim'. But the LC also recommend the creation of a specific statutory defence for victims charged with conspiracy based on their 'protected' status. However, the immunity for agreements between an adult and a child under the age of criminal responsibility in s 2(1)(b) would be retained, on the basis that in such a case there is no meeting of two 'criminal' minds.
- Repeal of s 1(2) of the 1977 Act. The LC recommends that where a substantive offence requires proof of a circumstance element, a person conspiring to commit that offence must be shown to have been reckless as to the possible existence of that element (unless a higher degree of fault, e.g. purpose, intention or knowledge, regarding that circumstance is required for the substantive offence, in which case it would be required for conspiracy as well). If s 1(2) is repealed, then defendants in cases like *Saik* (2006) and *Tree* (2008) would in the future be guilty of conspiracy.

6.4 Assisting or encouraging crime

6.4.1 Background

At common law it was an offence to 'incite' someone to commit any offence. This was committed if D encouraged or persuaded someone else to commit an offence, whether or not that offence actually took place. However, the general offence of incitement was abolished by s 59 of the Serious Crime Act 2007 and three new offences of encouraging or assisting crime have been created instead (see below). However, various specific incitement offences survive, including:

- Soliciting murder (s 4, Offences Against the Person Act 1861). In *Abu Hamza* [2006] EWCA Crim 2918; [2007] QB 659, D, the Imam of Finsbury Park mosque in north London, was convicted of six counts of this offence.
- Incitement to commit various offences involving the production, possession or supply of controlled drugs (s 19, Misuse of Drugs Act 1971).
- Incitement to commit certain sexual acts outside the United Kingdom, contrary to s 2 of the Sexual Offences (Conspiracy and Incitement) Act 1996.
- Inciting a child to engage in sexual activity (s 10, Sexual Offences Act 2003). In *Hinton-Smith* [2005] EWCA Crim 2575, D was convicted of this offence after he sent dozens of text messages to V, a 14-year-old girl, seeking to persuade her to perform acts of masturbation upon him or to engage in full sexual intercourse with him.
- Inciting a child under 13 to engage in sexual activity (s 8, SOA 2003). In *Jones* [2007] EWCA Crim 1118; [2007] 3 WLR 907, discussed above, D was convicted of attempting to commit this offence.
- Inciting a child family member to engage in sexual activity (s 26, SOA 2003).
- Inciting a person with a mental disorder to engage in sexual activity (s 31, SOA 2003).
- Inciting another person to become a child prostitute or to be involved in child pornography (s 48, SOA 2003).
- Inciting a person to become a prostitute (s 52, SOA 2003).
- Encouraging terrorism (s 1, Terrorism Act 2006).

6.4.2 Liability under the Serious Crime Act 2007

Sections 44–46 of the Serious Crime Act 2007 (SCA) create three new offences of doing an act 'capable of encouraging or assisting' crime. The new offences came into force in October 2008. The sections provide as follows:

SECTION

'44(1) A person commits an offence if –

(a) he does an act capable of encouraging or assisting the commission of an offence; and

(b) he intends to encourage or assist its commission.

(2) But he is not to be taken to have intended to encourage or assist the commission of an offence merely because such encouragement or assistance was a foreseeable consequence of his act.

45 A person commits an offence if –

(a) he does an act capable of encouraging or assisting the commission of an offence; and

(b) believes

(i) that the offence will be committed; and

(ii) that his act will encourage or assist its commission.

46(1) A person commits an offence if –

(a) he does an act capable of encouraging or assisting the commission of one or more of a number of offences; and

(b) he believes –

(i) that one or more of those offences will be committed (but has no belief as to which); and

(ii) that his act will encourage or assist the commission of one or more of them.

(2) It is immaterial for the purposes of subsection (1)(b)(ii) whether the person has any belief as to which offence will be encouraged or assisted.

(3) If a person is charged with an offence under subsection (1) –

(a) the indictment must specify the offences alleged to be the "number of offences" mentioned in paragraph (a) of that subsection; but

(b) nothing in paragraph (a) requires all the offences potentially comprised in that number to be specified.

(4) In relation to an offence under this section, reference in this Part to the offences specified in the indictment is to the offences specified by virtue of subsection (3)(a).'

In summary, the new offences require the doing of an act 'capable of encouraging or assisting' the commission of:

- an offence, *with intent* to encourage or assist (s 44);
- an offence, *believing* it will be committed and believing that the act will encourage or assist (s 45);
- one or more offences, believing that one or more of them will be committed and believing that the act will encourage or assist (s 46).

The first cases to reach the Court of Appeal involving the SCA were *Blackshaw; Sutcliffe* [2011] EWCA Crim 2312; [2012] 1 WLR 1126. Both cases occurred at the height of the riots in England in August 2011. The two defendants were sentenced to four years' imprisonment. They appealed, unsuccessfully, against sentence.

CASE EXAMPLE

Blackshaw; Sutcliffe [2011] EWCA Crim 2312; [2012] 1 WLR 1126

Blackshaw. On 8 August 2011, Jordan Blackshaw used Facebook to post a public event called 'Smash down in Northwich Town'. It called for participants to meet at the McDonalds in Northwich, Cheshire, at lunchtime the next day. The posting was aimed at his close associates, who he referred to as the 'Mob Hill Massive', and his friends, but he also opened it to public view. The post included a message: 'We'll need to get on this, kicking off all over.' Some members of the public alerted the police and the site was closed down, but not before nine people had confirmed their intention to attend. Blackshaw was arrested the next morning. He admitted to police that the effect of his actions was to encourage rioting and looting. In due course he pleaded guilty to encouraging or assisting riot, burglary and criminal damage, believing that one or more would be committed, contrary to s 46 SCA.

Sutcliffe. On 9 August 2011, Perry Sutcliffe created a Facebook page called 'The Warrington Riots'. He sent invitations to 400 contacts to meet at a Carvery in Warrington at 7 p.m. the next day. He also opened it to public view. Some members of the public alerted the police and the site was closed down, but not before 47 people had confirmed their intention to attend. Sutcliffe was arrested the next morning. In due course he pleaded guilty to encouraging or assisting riot, contrary to s 44 SCA.

After dismissing their appeals, the Court rejected any suggestion that these cases should be dealt with more leniently because the defendants had encouraged illegal activity via social media websites as opposed to face to face. Lord Judge CJ said:

JUDGMENT

'We are unimpressed with the suggestion that in each case the appellant did no more than make the appropriate entry in his Facebook. Neither went from door to door looking for friends or like-minded people to join up with him in the riot. All that is true. But modern technology has done away with the need for such direct personal communication. It can all be done through Facebook or other social media. In other words, the abuse of modern technology for criminal purposes extends to and includes incitement of very many people by a single step. Indeed it is a sinister feature of these cases that modern technology almost certainly assisted rioters in other places to organise the rapid movement and congregation of disorderly groups in new and unpoliced areas.

6.4.3 *Actus reus* elements

The *actus reus* of ss 44 and 45 is identical: they both require that D 'does an act capable of encouraging or assisting the commission of an offence'. The *actus reus* of s 46 is slightly broader; it requires that D 'does an act capable of encouraging or assisting the commission of one or more of a number of offences'.

'Doing an act'

All three of the new offences require that D 'does an act'. This does not mean, however, that the new offences cannot be committed by an omission to act, as s 65(2)(b) provides that 'doing an act' includes 'failing to take reasonable steps to discharge a duty'. An example of a situation where this might occur is provided by the facts of *Du Cros v Lambourne* [1907] 1 KB 40, examined in Chapter 5. D takes E, a learner driver, for a driving lesson in D's car. D notices that E is accelerating and the car's speed is approaching the speed limit for that stretch of road but D fails to do or say anything, intending that this failure (to discharge D's duty as the owner of the vehicle) will encourage or assist E to commit a driving offence. D would appear to be liable under s 44.

Another example might be a cleaner with the keys to an office block who deliberately fails to lock the back door to the building after she finishes her shift so that E can slip into the building to burgle it. D's liability (if any), under s 44, of intentionally 'failing to take reasonable steps to discharge a duty' in a way which is capable of assisting the commission of an offence (burglary) would depend on (i) whether the cleaner was under a duty to her employer and (ii) whether she had failed to take reasonable steps to discharge it. Whether or not a duty exists is normally a question of law for the judge. Whether or not D has failed to take reasonable steps would be a question of fact for the magistrates or jury. If D had failed to take reasonable steps to discharge a duty then she would be liable whether or not E actually committed the burglary (see s 49(1)).

Section 67 further provides that a 'reference to an act includes a reference to a course of conduct'. No further explanation is given and the meaning of this section remains somewhat opaque.

'Capable'

It is worth emphasising that D's act need only be 'capable' of encouraging or assisting E. Thus, if D shouts encouragement to E who is about to punch V, this is an act (shouting) which is obviously 'capable' of encouraging E to commit an offence (battery). It is entirely irrelevant whether or not E does then attack V, or even whether or not E hears D's shouts.

'Encouraging'

Section 65(1) provides that 'doing an act that is capable of encouraging the commission of an offence' includes (but is not limited to) 'doing so by threatening another person or otherwise putting pressure on another person to commit the offence'. This is a very broad definition of 'encouraging' but is consistent with cases under the old incitement offence (*Race Relations Board v Applin* [1973] 2 All ER 1190, a civil case, approved in *Invicta Plastics Ltd v Clare* [1976] RTR 251).

6.4.4 *Mens rea* elements

The *mens rea* requirements of ss 44 and 45 are different. Section 44(1) states that D must *intend* to encourage or assist commission of the offence, while s 44(2) adds that D is not to be taken to have the necessary intent 'merely because such encouragement or assistance was a foreseeable consequence of his act'. However, it is not necessary that D intended to encourage or assist E to break the law; it is sufficient to prove that he intended to encourage or assist the doing of an act which would amount to the commission of that offence (s 47(2)).

Under s 45, D must *believe* both (i) that the offence would be committed and (ii) that his act would encourage or assist its commission. As with s 44, it is not necessary that D believed he was encouraging or assisting E to break the law. Instead, it is enough to prove that D believed (a) that an act would be done which would amount to the commission of that offence; and (b) that his act would encourage or assist the doing of that act (s 47(3)).

To illustrate the operation of these provisions, imagine that one night D drives E to a factory which E plans to burgle. Here, D's act (driving the car to the factory) is clearly 'capable' of assisting burglary, but is D liable under s 44 or s 45? This will depend on D's *mens rea* (if any). For example:

- If D and E and friends and have planned the whole thing in advance, then D is probably liable under s 44 – he *intends* to assist E.
- If D is sure that E is going to burgle the factory, perhaps because D knows that E has committed several burglaries before, but drives E to the factory anyway, then D is probably liable under s 45 – he believes that burglary (or rather, an act which would amount to the commission of burglary, i.e. entering a building as a trespasser) will be committed.
- If D is a taxi driver and does not think, or even suspect, that E plans a burglary then he has no *mens rea* and is not liable under either ss 44 or 45.

The *mens rea* of s 46 is that D *believes* that one or more of those offences will be committed (but has no belief as to which) and that his act will encourage or assist the commission of one or more of them. Under s 46, it is not necessary that D believed he was encouraging or assisting E to break the law. Instead, it is sufficient to prove that D believed (a) that one or more of a number of acts would be done which would amount to the commission of one or more of those offences; and (b) that his act would encourage or assist the doing of one or more of those acts (s 47(4)). An example of a situation where s 46 might apply is where D lends a knife to E believing that E will use it to commit either wounding or robbery (but D is unsure which).

Section 47(5)(a) applies to all three of the new offences. It states that, where the act(s) that D is assisting or encouraging E to commit requires some element of 'fault' in order for it to be a criminal offence (i.e. it is not a strict liability offence), then D must believe that (or be reckless whether) it would be done with that fault, were the act to actually be done by E. Thus, for example, if D assists E to commit burglary by providing him with a ladder, then D must believe that (or be reckless whether) E is going to enter a building as a trespasser with intent to steal, inflict GBH or do unlawful damage. It would be insufficient to prove that D believed that (or was reckless whether) E was going to enter the building for some other purpose as that would not constitute the 'fault' required.

Section 47(5)(b) further provides that if the offence is one requiring 'proof of particular circumstances or consequences (or both)', it must be proved that D believed that (or was reckless whether) it would be done in those circumstances or with those consequences, were the act to actually be done by E. Thus, for example, if D intentionally does an act capable of assisting E to stab V by providing E with a knife, D is liable for assisting wounding, but D is not liable for assisting murder (should V bleed to death) unless D believed that V would die or he had foreseen V's death (i.e. he would have been reckless as to that particular consequence).

'Doing of acts' (s 47(8))

Section 47(8) provides that:

SECTION

'Reference in this section to the doing of an act includes reference to –

(a) a failure to act;
(b) the continuation of an act that has already begun;
(c) an attempt to do an act (except an act amounting to the commission of the offence of attempting to commit another offence).'

The words 'in this section' are important, as it means that this subsection actually applies only to E's acts, not D's.

Section 47(8)(a) presumably only applies where E would be under a duty to act and D tries to encourage or assist E to breach that duty by failing to act. Thus, s 47(8) (a) might apply where D is watching a building that has caught fire when the fire brigade arrive, and D shouts encouragement to the firemen to stand back and let the fire burn. D could be convicted under s 44 of intentionally doing an act capable of encouraging a fireman, E, to fail to do an act which would amount to the commission of an offence (arson), E being under a contractual duty to take reasonable steps to put the fire out.

Section 47(8)(b) is more straightforward. If D sees E, a 14-year-old schoolboy, in the act of throwing rocks through the windows of a school building, and starts gathering more rocks for E to throw, this would seem to be a straightforward application of s 47(8) (b) – D has intentionally done an act which is capable of assisting E to continue an act (which E had already begun) and which would amount to the commission of an offence (criminal damage).

In the above two situations it would be irrelevant whether or not E took any notice of D's acts of encouragement or assistance or even whether or not E was aware of D's act – D is liable if his act is 'capable' of encouraging or assisting, not whether it actually does encourage or assist.

'Belief'

Sections 45 and 46 both refer to D's 'belief', but this word is not defined anywhere in the 2007 Act. D Ormerod and R Fortson, 'Serious Crime Act 2007: the Part 2 offences' [2009] Crim LR 389, suggest that belief 'constitutes a state of subjective awareness short of knowledge, but greater than mere suspicion'.

6.4.5 No requirement for substantive offence to be committed (s 49)

A key provision in the 2007 Act is s 49(1). This states that:

SECTION

'49(1) A person may commit an offence under this Part whether or not any offence capable of being encouraged or assisted by his act is committed.'

Thus, if D provides E with a gun to be used in a bank robbery then D is liable under ss 44 or 45, depending on D's *mens rea*, regardless of whether or not the robbery goes ahead. D commits the ss 44 or 45 offence as soon as he hands over the gun. Of course, if the robbery did go ahead, then D could also be convicted, under secondary liability principles, of aiding the offence (see Chapter 5). There is therefore considerable overlap between the Accessories and Abettors Act 1861 and the Serious Crime Act 2007.

6.4.6 Defence of 'acting reasonably' (s 50)

Section 50 provides a defence of 'acting reasonably' to anyone charged under ss 44–46. The section provides that:

SECTION

'50(1) A person is not guilty of an offence under this Part if he proves –

(a) that he knew certain circumstances existed; and
(b) that it was reasonable for him to act as he did in those circumstances.

(2) A person is not guilty of an offence under this Part if he proves –

(a) that he believed certain circumstances to exist;
(b) that his belief was reasonable; and
(c) that it was reasonable for him to act as he did in the circumstances as he believed them to be.

(3) Factors to be considered in determining whether it was reasonable for a person to act as he did include –

(a) the seriousness of the anticipated offence (or, in the case of an offence under s 46, the offences specified in the indictment);
(b) any purpose for which he claims to have been acting;
(c) any authority by which he claims to have been acting.'

Note that the burden of proof is on D, albeit on the balance of probabilities. Without the benefit of case law it is a matter of speculation when (if at all) these defences might operate. One possible scenario where s 50(2) might apply involves D, a shopkeeper, who sells tools to E, believing that E is going to use the tools to commit a burglary. D might face liability under s 45 unless he can prove that it was 'reasonable' to act as he did in the circumstances that he believed to exist.

6.4.7 Defence for victims (s 51)

Section 51 provides a defence, in certain circumstances, for victims:

SECTION

'51(1) In the case of protective offences, a person does not commit an offence under this Part by reference to such an offence if –

(a) he falls within the protected category; and

(b) he is the person in respect of whom the protective offence was committed or would have been if it had been committed.

(2) "Protective offence" means an offence that exists (wholly or in part) for the protection of a particular category of persons ("the protected category").'

If D is accused of intentionally doing an act capable of encouraging or assisting E to commit an offence, but that offence exists for 'the protection of a particular category of persons', and D falls within the 'protected category', then D has a defence. Thus, where D, a 13-year-old girl, sends a text message to E, an older man, suggesting that they have sex, D would appear not to be guilty under s 44 of intentionally doing an act which is capable of encouraging E to commit an offence (specifically, sexual activity with a child, contrary to s 9 of the Sexual Offences Act 2003). The 2003 Act is designed to protect people like D, so it would be paradoxical to convict her in those circumstances.

6.4.8 Impossibility

The SCA is silent on the question of impossibility. For example, if D is charged under s 44 with intentionally doing an act capable of encouraging or assisting E to murder V by selling a handgun to E, does it matter if V is (unknown to either of them) already dead, killed the previous day in a road traffic accident? A literal reading of s 44 would suggest that D is liable. He has intentionally done 'an act' (selling the gun) and that act is clearly 'capable of encouraging or assisting the commission of an offence'. The imposition of liability on D in such circumstances would also be consistent with the purpose of the Act, which is to criminalise those who assist or encourage others to commit crimes, whether or not those crimes are committed (as s 49(1) makes explicit). This would also bring the SCA provisions in line with attempts and conspiracy, where impossibility is not a defence. However, under the old law of incitement, impossibility was a defence (*Fitzmaurice* [1983] QB 1083) and the Act's silence on this point will allow defendants to at least try to argue that impossibility is a defence under the SCA.

6.4.9 Attempt liability

Prior to its abolition it was possible for D to be convicted of attempted incitement and it is perfectly possible for D to be charged (under s 1 of the Criminal Attempts Act 1981) with attempting to do an act that is capable of encouraging or assisting the commission of an offence. Thus, for example, in the scenario given earlier (where D drives E to a factory which E plans to burgle), it appears that D will be liable (for an attempt) even if on the way the car breaks down, or they are involved in a car crash, or simply get lost, so that they never reach their destination. In each situation, D has probably not done an act which is 'capable' of assisting E to commit burglary, but he has gone beyond the 'merely preparatory' stage and has therefore attempted to do so. Another example might be D trying to send an email or text to E encouraging E to commit an offence, but D mistypes the address or phone number and the message is sent but never received.

6.4.10 Evaluation of the Serious Crime Act 2007

The provisions described above have been heavily criticised by a number of leading academics. For example, D Ormerod and R Fortson, 'Serious Crime Act 2007: the Part 2 offences' [2009] Crim LR 389, describe the new legislation as 'complex', 'convoluted', 'tortuously difficult' and containing 'some of the worst criminal provisions to fall from Parliament in recent years … These are offences of breathtaking scope and complexity. They constitute both an interpretative nightmare and a prosecutor's dream.' J Spencer and G Virgo agree, describing the new provisions as 'complicated and unintelligible … over-detailed, convoluted and unreadable' ('Encouraging and assisting crime: legislate in haste, repent at leisure' (2008) 9 Arch News 7). Section 47 is singled out as an 'example of impenetrable drafting'; Spencer and Virgo admit that even they cannot 'make sense' of s 47(8)(c) and suggest that a prize be awarded to anyone who can!

In *Sadique and Hussain* [2011] EWCA Crim 2872; [2012] 1 WLR 1700, the Court of Appeal rejected an argument that s 46 was so vague and uncertain as to be contrary to art 7 of the European Convention on Human Rights (which provides that 'No one shall be held guilty of any criminal offence on account of any act or omission which did not constitute a criminal offence under national or international law at the time when it was committed'). Hooper LJ explained the operation of the allegedly vague provision as follows (emphasis in the original):

JUDGMENT

'Section 46 should only be used, and needs only to be used, when it may be that D, at the time of doing the act, believes that one or more of *either* offence X, *or* offence Y *or* offence Z will be committed, but has no belief as to which one or ones of the three will be committed. To take an example. D gives P a gun. Giving P a gun is, we shall assume, capable of encouraging or assisting the commission of offences X, Y and Z and the prosecution specify those three offences in the indictment. If it may be that D, at the time of giving the gun, believes that one or more of offences X, Y and Z will be committed but has no belief as to which will be committed, s 46 should be used.'

That much is clear enough. Unfortunately, certain other observations in *Sadique and Hussain* led to a second appeal, *Sadique (No 2)* [2013] EWCA Crim 1150; [2014] 1 WLR 986, which provided the Court of Appeal with another opportunity to clarify the operation of s 46. This time, the Lord Chief Justice gave the judgment of the appeal court. Lord Judge CJ said:

JUDGMENT

'Section 46 creates the offence of encouraging or assisting the commission of one or more offences. Its specific ingredients and the subsequent legislative provisions underline that an indictment charging a s 46 offence of encouraging one or more offences is permissible. This has the advantage of reflecting practical reality. A defendant may very well believe that his conduct will assist in the commission of one or more of a variety of different offences by another individual without knowing or being able to identify the precise offence or offences which the person to whom he offers encouragement or assistance intends to commit, or will actually commit.'

CASE EXAMPLE

Sadique (No 2) [2013] EWCA Crim 1150; [2014] 1 WLR 986

Omar Sadique (S) was charged under s 46 with doing acts capable of assisting one or more offences involving the supply of Class A and/or Class B controlled drugs. The Crown case was that S operated a national distribution business and in the course of it he had supplied chemical 'cutting agents' (benzocaine, lignocaine and other chemicals) to drug dealers. S was convicted but appealed, *inter alia*, on the basis that the trial judge's summing up on the *mens rea* of s 46 was incorrect. The appeal was rejected; the trial judge had directed the jury correctly.

The above-quoted academics all agree that the new offences were largely unnecessary. Whilst there were some problems with certain aspects of the old offence of incitement, it was simple, well established and understood. All that the law actually needed was an offence of 'facilitation'. This would cover the situation where, for example, D provides E with a gun intending for E to use it as part of a bank robbery. If E never uses the gun then D cannot be prosecuted under secondary liability (he has not aided, abetted or counselled the commission of an offence), nor can he be prosecuted for conspiracy unless there is evidence that D and E agreed that E would commit robbery. Finally, there would be no guarantee of an incitement conviction as the handing over of the gun would not necessarily amount to encouragement. The creation of a new facilitation offence might have been achieved with a simple provision; instead, we have the Serious Crime Act to deal with.

KEY FACTS

Inchoate offence	Impossibility a defence?	Authority
Attempt	No	Criminal Attempts Act 1981; *Shivpuri* (1987)
Conspiracy	No	Criminal Law Act 1977 (as amended)
Assisting or encouraging crime	Unknown	*Fitzmaurice* (1983) decided that impossibility was a defence to incitement but the Serious Crime Act 2007 is silent on the subject

ACTIVITY

Applying the law

1. D is an expert in bank security systems, now retired. E is a former racing driver. They are both in need of cash having lost heavily on the stock market and gambling, respectively. They agree to form a team to steal money from a bank: D will provide the knowledge required to get past the bank's security systems and into the safe; E will be the getaway driver in the event that a high-speed escape is required. D is reluctant to actually enter the bank himself and E must wait outside in the getaway car. They therefore 'advertise' their plan in underworld circles, and invite a third party to join them to do the physical task of entering the bank and stealing from the safe. F, who has recently been released from prison having served eight years for armed robbery, responds to their 'advertisement'. F believes that D and E plan to carry out an armed robbery in broad daylight; D and E actually intend to quietly break into the bank during the night.

   At this point, consider whether D and E, and F, have committed conspiracy and, if so, conspiracy to commit which offence(s)?

2. The police, who have been tipped off, think they know what D, E and F are plotting and set up observation of the bank. The police observe F walk up to a bank in the early hours of the morning. F, who is dressed all in black and carrying a black holdall, stops next to a rear window of the bank and is examining it when the police rush from their hiding place and arrest him. D and E are also arrested in a car parked nearby. Diagrams showing the position of security cameras and alarms for the bank are found in the car. D, E and F do not deny that they planned to burgle the bank but insist that they intended to carry out the burglary the next night and that F was simply making a reconnaissance trip.

   Consider whether D, E and F have committed attempted burglary. (If necessary, refer back to Chapter 5 for a reminder of the principles of secondary participation/joint enterprise.)
3. F was also found to have a loaded firearm hidden in an inside jacket pocket. He admits to police that he would have used this to shoot any security guard who might have been in the bank when the burglary went ahead.

   Consider whether D, E and F have committed conspiracy to murder.

Note: For the purposes of the above activities, theft is the dishonest appropriation of property belonging to another; burglary involves entering a building as a trespasser with intent to steal; robbery is theft with the use of or threat of force; murder is causing the death of another human being with intent to kill or cause serious harm.

SUMMARY

The law of attempts is set out in the Criminal Attempts Act 1981. D is guilty of an attempt if he does an act that is more than merely preparatory to the commission of an offence, with intent to commit it. The phrase 'more than merely preparatory' has proven difficult to define and apply consistently (see *Gullefer*, *Campbell*, *Jones* and *Geddes*), prompting the Law Commission to recommend reform, including the creation of a new offence of criminal preparation. Intention has been described as the 'principal ingredient of the crime' (*Whybrow*).

The law of statutory conspiracy is set out in the Criminal Law Act 1977. D will be guilty of conspiracy if he agrees with any other person or persons that a course of conduct shall be pursued which, if the agreement is carried out in accordance with their intentions, will necessarily amount to or involve the commission of any offence or offences by one or more of the parties to the agreement. The essence of the offence is the agreement (*Saik*). The Law Commission has recommended some reform of the 1977 Act, including the rewording of s 1(2) and the abolition of spousal immunity in s 2(2).

There are also two forms of common law conspiracy: conspiracy to corrupt public morals and conspiracy to defraud.

The Serious Crime Act 2007 (SCA) created three new offences of doing an act capable of encouraging or assisting the commission of an offence. The SCA also abolished the common law offence of incitement. The SCA has been heavily criticised for its breadth, complexity and convoluted structure.

Impossibility is not a defence under the Criminal Attempts Act 1981 (*Shivpuri*) nor is it a defence under the Criminal Law Act 1977. However, it was a defence under the common law of incitement (*Fitzmaurice*) and the SCA is silent on this issue. It is therefore a moot point as to whether or not impossibility provides a defence to anyone charged with encouraging or assisting an offence.

SAMPLE ESSAY QUESTION

In an offence of attempt 'the intent becomes the principal ingredient of the crime' (*Whybrow* (1951)). Critically consider the extent to which you agree with this statement.

Briefly explain the law of attempt:

- Define liability for attempts under s 1, Criminal Attempts Act 1981
- D must have intent
- D must do an act which is more than merely preparatory to the commission of the offence
- Liability may be imposed for an impossible attempt

Explain the meaning of 'more than merely preparatory' (note focus of the question is on the *mens rea* so this should be fairly brief):

- Refer to case law, e.g. *Boyle & Boyle* (1987), *Gullefer* (1990), *Jones* (1990), *Campbell* (1991), *A-G's Reference (No 1 of 1992), Geddes* (1996)
- Contrast with the tests used pre-1981 Act

Discuss the element of intention, and consider whether intent is the 'principal' ingredient, e.g.

- Note that Parliament and the courts regard the attempted offence as potentially as serious as the substantive offence. Presence of the intent means that D is just as 'morally culpable' (*Mohan* (1976))
- Note that intention to kill is essential for an attempted murder case (*White* (1910), *Whybrow* (1951)). In *Gotts* (1992), a duress case (see Chapter 8), the intent of an attempted murderer was said to be 'more evil' than that of a murderer
- Note that conditional intent may suffice (*Walkington* (1979), *A-G's Ref (Nos 1 and 2 of 1979)*)
- Note that oblique intent may suffice (*Walker and Hayles* (1990))
- Discuss how liability can be imposed for impossible attempts and the key role played here by D's intention (*Shivpuri* (1987), *Jones* (2007))
- Note that a lesser *mens rea* (recklessness) may suffice in relation to circumstances (*Khan and others* (1990), *A-G's Ref (No 3 of 1992)*)

Conclude

Further Reading

Books

Ormerod, D, *Smith and Hogan Criminal Law* (13th edn, Oxford University Press, 2011), Chapter 13.

Articles

Arenson, K, 'The pitfalls in the law of attempt: a new perspective' (2005) 69 JoCL 146.

Christie, S A, 'The relevance of harm as the criterion for the punishment of impossible attempts' (2009) 73 JoCL 153.

Horder, J, 'Reforming the auxiliary part of the criminal Law' (2007) 10 Arch News 6.

Jarvis, P and Bisgrove, M, 'The use and abuse of conspiracy' [2014] Crim LR 261.

Ormerod, D and Fortson, R, 'Serious Crime Act 2007: the Part 2 offences' [2009] Crim LR 389.

Rogers, J, 'The codification of attempts and the case for "preparation"' [2008] Crim LR 937.

Spencer, J and Virgo, G, 'Encouraging and assisting crime: legislate in haste, repent at leisure' (2008) 9 Arch News 7.

Sullivan, G R, 'Inchoate liability for assisting and encouraging crime' [2006] Crim LR 1047.

Virgo, G, 'Laundering conspiracy' (2006) 65 CLJ 482.

Internet links

Law Commission Consultation Paper, *Conspiracy and Attempts* (Paper No 183) (2007), available at www.lawcom.gov.uk.

7

Capacity

AIMS AND OBJECTIVES

After reading this chapter you should be able to:

- Understand the limitations on liability of children in criminal law
- Understand the effects a person's mental state may have on their criminal liability
- Understand the concept and basic principles of vicarious liability in the criminal law
- Analyse critically the concept of vicarious liability
- Understand the basic principles of corporate liability in the criminal law
- Analyse critically the need for corporate liability and the tests used in establishing it

There are some circumstances in which the law rules that a person is not capable of committing a crime. The main limitations are on:

- children under the age of ten;
- mentally ill persons;
- corporations.

On the other hand, there are some circumstances in which a person may be liable for the actions of another under the principle of vicarious liability.

Capacity to commit a crime is important, as one of the principles of justice is that only those who are blameworthy should be liable for their crimes. Without capacity to understand or be responsible for his actions, a person has no moral blame. For this reason English law recognises categories of those without capacity and they are generally not held to be criminally responsible for their actions. This means that if, for example, a five-year-old child takes some sweets from a counter in a shop, he cannot be guilty of theft. He has done the *actus reus* of theft (appropriation of property belonging to another), but the law automatically assumes that he is not capable of forming the necessary *mens rea*.

7.1 Children

7.1.1 Children under the age of ten

The age of criminal responsibility in England and Wales is ten. This age was set by the Children and Young Persons Act 1933, which states in s 50 that:

SECTION

> '50 It shall be conclusively presumed that no child under the age of ten years can be guilty of any offence.'

doli incapax
Incapable of wrong

This is known as the ***doli incapax*** presumption. Children under the age of ten cannot be criminally liable for their acts. This conclusive presumption that a child under ten cannot commit a crime means that those who use children to do the act of an offence are liable as principals, rather than as secondary participants in the offence. For example, if two teenage boys get a child aged eight to enter into a house through a small window and bring out to them money or other valuables, the eight-year-old cannot be guilty of burglary. Normally anyone who waited outside during a burglary would be a secondary participant in the offence, but in this case the teenagers are guilty as principal offenders.

Prior to the Children and Young Persons Act 1933 the age of criminal responsibility in England and Wales was eight. This was thought to be too low. The age of ten is now the lowest age of criminal responsibility in any Western European country, and many critics think that it should be increased to 12. In fact as long ago as 1960 the Ingelby Committee, Cmnd 1911 (1960) recommended that it should be increased to 12 in England and Wales.

Recently Heather Keeting has itemised criticism of the age made by major bodies in her article 'Reckless children' (2007) Crim LR 547:

QUOTATION

> 'The Government has increasingly come under fire both internationally and domestically in relation to this low age of criminal responsibility: the United Nations Committee on the Rights of the Child; the European Committee on Social Rights which stated in 2005 that the age of criminal responsibility "is manifestly too low and . . . not in conformity with Article 17 of the [Social] Charter" which assures the right of children to social and economic protection.'

She also points out that the low age of responsibility is in breach of human rights. In 2003 the Parliamentary Joint Committee on Human Rights criticised the age in their Tenth Report of Session 2002–03 HL1 17/High Court 81 at paras 35 to 38. Also, in 2006, the Council of Europe Commissioner for Human Rights commented on the low age in a speech, 'The Human Rights Dimension of Juvenile Justice'.

Interestingly, Scotland used to have an even lower age of criminal responsibility at eight years of age. However, in 2010 the Scottish Executive passed the Criminal Justice and Licensing (Scotland) Act in the Scottish Parliament which raised the age to 12 in Scotland.

Care orders

Children under ten who have committed criminal-type behaviour can be dealt with in other ways. The local authority can bring proceedings in the family court under s 31 of the Children Act 1989 asking for an order that the child be placed in the care of the local authority or for an order placing the child under the supervision of the local authority or a probation officer. Such an order will only be made if it is in the interests of the child's welfare and the court is satisfied under s 31(2) of the Children Act 1989:

SECTION

'31(2) (a) that the child concerned is suffering, or is likely to suffer, significant harm; and
(b) that harm, or the likelihood of harm, is attributable to –
(i) the care given to the child, or likely to be given to him if the order were not made, not being what it would be reasonable to expect a parent to give to him; or
(ii) the child's being beyond parental control.'

7.1.2 Child safety orders

The other area where the law allows orders to be made in respect of children under ten is in respect of child safety orders under s 11 of the Crime and Disorder Act 1998. This focuses on behavioural problems of the child and an order can be made if:

- the child has committed an act which, if he had been aged ten or over, would be an offence; or
- a child safety order is necessary to prevent the child committing an act which, if he had been aged ten or over, would be an offence.

The local authority has to apply to a Magistrates' Family Proceedings Court for an order. If it is granted the magistrates can place the child under the supervision of a social worker or a member of a youth offending team for a period of up to three months. This period can be extended to 12 months if the court is satisfied that the circumstances of the case are exceptional. The magistrates can also add on other conditions.

Child safety orders are aimed at preventing children from becoming criminal offenders when they are older.

7.1.3 Children aged ten and over

In the legal system there are different terms for different age groups. These are the following:

- Those aged ten but under 14 are known as 'children'.
- Those aged 14 but under 17 are known as 'young persons'.
- Those offenders aged 14 but under 21 are known as 'young offenders'.

Until 1998 there was a rebuttable presumption that those aged 10 to 13 inclusive were *doli incapax*. This meant that they were presumed not to be capable of committing an offence but the prosecution could rebut this presumption by bringing evidence that the child knew that what he did was seriously wrong. The need for such a presumption was challenged by the Queen's Bench Divisional Court in *C v DPP* [1995] 2 All ER 43.

CASE EXAMPLE

C v DPP [1995] 2 All ER 43

D, a boy aged 12, was seen tampering with a motorcycle and, when challenged, ran away. The prosecution relied on the fact that he had run away as evidence that he knew that what he was doing was seriously wrong. The Divisional Court held that this was insufficient to rebut the presumption of *doli incapax*, as it could show mere naughtiness rather than a realisation that what he was doing was seriously wrong.

However, the judges in the Divisional Court thought that the presumption was out of date and should no longer be part of our law. Mann LJ said:

JUDGMENT

'Whatever may have been the position in any earlier age, when there was no system of universal compulsory education and when perhaps children did not grow up as quickly as they do nowadays, this presumption at the present time is a serious disservice to our law . . . it is unreal and contrary to common sense.'

When the case was appealed to the House of Lords, they held that it was not the judges' role to abolish such a long-standing law. If the government thought it should be abolished, then the government could do so democratically through Parliament. The government did take action and s 34 Crime and Disorder Act 1998 abolished the rebuttable presumption that a child aged 10 to 13 is incapable of committing an offence.

Doubts were raised as to whether s 34 completely abolished the *doli incapax* rule or whether only the presumption had been abolished. Professor Walker in 'The end of an old song' (1999) 149 NLJ 64 put forward the view that all that had been abolished was the presumption that a child aged 10 to 13 did not know that his act was seriously wrong. The abolition of the presumption did not mean that the 'defence' of 'ignorance of serious wrong' had been abolished. In *DPP v P* [2007] EWHC 946 Admin, Smith LJ thought that it was possibly still open to a child defendant to prove that he did not know his act was seriously wrong.

However, the issue was finally settled by the House of Lords in *JTB* [2009] UKHL 20.

CASE EXAMPLE

JTB [2009] UKHL 20

D, aged 12 at the time of the offences, was charged under s 13(1) of the Sexual Offences Act 2003 with causing or inciting children under 13 to engage in sexual activity. When interviewed by police, D admitted the activity but said that he had not thought that what he was doing was wrong.

D wished to rely on the defence of *doli incapax*. The trial judge ruled that this defence was not available to him. On appeal, both the Court of Appeal and the House of Lords upheld D's conviction. In their judgment, the House of Lords looked at the wording and the background of s 34 of the Crime and Disorder Act 1998.

The Law Lords thought that it was not possible to decide from the wording of the Act whether both the presumption and the 'defence' of *doli incapax* had been abolished. They, therefore, looked at the legislative background to s 34. In the government's consultation paper, *Tackling Youth Crime* (1997), the government put forward alternative options for reform. These were (1) that the presumption could be abolished and (2) that the presumption could be reversed assuming that a child aged 10 to 13 was capable of forming criminal intent, but allowing him to prove that he did not know what he was doing was seriously wrong. The government stated that its preferred option was to abolish the defence.

Following consultation, a White Paper was issued, *No More Excuses: A New Approach to Tackling Youth Crime in England and Wales* (1997), which made it plain that the government intended to abolish the defence. The Crime and Disorder Bill was then introduced into Parliament. During the passage of this Bill through Parliament amendments were proposed to reverse the presumption rather than completely abolish it. These amendments were defeated.

The Law Lords held that this legislative background showed that Parliament had clearly intended the presumption to be completely abolished.

Not everyone agreed that the presumption should have been abolished. One view is that the abolition means that a child aged ten and over is considered to be 'as responsible for his actions as if he were 40'. This was particularly so for offences in which the concept of objective recklessness used to apply the standards of the reasonable adult and the fact that the defendant was a child was ignored. However, since *G and another* [2003] UKHL 50, in which the House of Lords effectively abolished the concept of objective recklessness at least as far as criminal damage is concerned, this objection is no longer valid.

In any case the normal burden of proof applies, so the prosecution has to prove the relevant *mens rea* for the offence charged and a child defendant, like any other defendant, will only be found guilty if he or she is proved to have had the necessary intent.

Rape cases

There also used to be an irrebuttable presumption that boys under the age of 14 were incapable of having sexual intercourse and therefore incapable of committing as principal the offence of rape or any other offence requiring proof of sexual penetration. This presumption was felt to be out of date due to the fact that physical development can be much earlier and it seemed unjust to have a rule which prevented prosecution for such serious offences. The presumption was eventually abolished by s 1 of the Sexual Offences Act 1993 and since then there have been a number of convictions for rape by boys between the ages of 10 and 13.

Trial

One way in which child defendants are dealt with differently from older offenders is that, for all but the most serious offences, children and young persons are tried in the Youth Court. The procedure here is more informal and in private. For some very serious offences, including murder, manslaughter and rape, a child defendant must be tried in the Crown Court. It is also possible for them to be sent for trial at the Crown Court where the offence would, if the defendant was an adult, carry a maximum penalty of 14 years' imprisonment. Where a child or young person is being tried in the Crown Court, special arrangements must be made to allow him to participate effectively in the trial. In *T v UK; V v UK* (1999) 7 EHRR 659 it was held that if this is not done, there may be a breach of art 6 of the European Convention on Human Rights.

There are also different sentencing powers for child offenders and young offenders compared to those for adults. Most sentences for children are aimed at reforming their behaviour. However, for serious offences or for repeat offenders, custodial sentences can be imposed.

KEY FACTS

Key facts on the liability of children for criminal offences

Age	Law	Comment
Under 10	They are *doli incapax*, that is deemed incapable of committing a crime (s 50 Children and Young Persons Act 1933).	Is 10 the right age? Should it be raised to 12?
	Liable to a child safety order (s 11 Crime and Disorder Act 1998).	Is the use of a child safety order merely a way round the *doli incapax* rule? Or does it serve a useful purpose in preventing young children from becoming criminal offenders when they are older?

10–13 inclusive	Now fully responsible for their actions (s 34 Crime and Disorder Act 1998 and *JTB* (2009)). Previously there was a rebuttable presumption that they were *doli incapax*.	Is it right that the level of responsibility for their actions be the same as for an adult? Should the rebuttable presumption have been abolished?
14–17 inclusive	Fully responsible for their actions.	Allowance for their age can be made in sentencing.

7.2 Mentally ill persons

The defendant's mental capacity is relevant at three different stages in the criminal justice process. These are:

- at the point of the commission of the offence;
- at the time of trial;
- when the defendant is sentenced.

There is also a special defence to murder of diminished responsibility, where the defendant's mental state may provide a partial defence so that the offence is reduced to manslaughter.

7.2.1 Unfitness to plead

Even before the trial, there are procedures for dealing with mentally ill defendants. Under the Mental Health Act 1983 it is possible for a defendant who has been refused bail to be detained in a mental hospital, instead of on remand in prison. This can only occur where the Home Secretary has reports from at least two medical practitioners and is satisfied that the defendant is suffering from mental illness or severe mental impairment. The Home Secretary will only exercise this power,

QUOTATION

> 'where the prisoner's condition is such that immediate removal to a mental hospital is necessary, that it would not be practicable to bring him before a court, or that the trial is likely to have an injurious effect on his mental state.'
>
> *Report of the Royal Commission on Capital Punishment*, Cmd 8932 (1953)

If the Home Secretary uses this power, then the defendant will still be brought to trial when he is well enough.

At the trial

When the defendant is brought up for trial the court may consider the question of whether he is fit to plead. This can occur whether or not the accused has been sent to a mental hospital under the power above.

The criteria for deciding whether D is unfit to plead originate from the case of *Pritchard* (1836) 7 C & P 303 in which the defendant was a deaf mute. The ruling was made when there was very limited knowledge about mental illness and the effect it might have on a defendant.

The criteria set by *Pritchard* were restated in *John M* [2003] EWCA Crim 3452. They set out that D must have sufficient ability in the following six matters:

- to understand the charges;
- to understand the plea;
- to challenge jurors;
- to instruct counsel and his solicitor;
- to understand the course of the trial;
- to give evidence if he so wishes.

Where he is unable to defend himself properly because of his mental state the Criminal Procedure (Insanity) Act 1964, as amended by the Criminal Procedure (Insanity and Unfitness to Plead) Act 1991 and the Domestic Violence, Crime and Victims Act 2004, allows him to be found unfit to plead.

The issue is decided by a judge without a jury. There must be evidence of at least two medical practitioners, at least one of whom is approved by the Home Office as having special experience in the field of mental disorder.

Burden of proof

If the defence raises the issue that the defendant is unfit to plead, then the burden of proof is on the defence, but it need only prove it to the civil standard of the balance of probabilities (see Chapter 1, section 1.8.2). If the prosecution raises the issue then it must prove it beyond reasonable doubt.

Finding of unfitness to plead

If the defendant is found unfit to plead then a jury must be sworn in to decide whether the defendant 'did the act or made the omission charged against him'. This provision is in the Criminal Procedure (Insanity) Act 1964 as amended. In *Antoine* [2000] 2 All ER 208 it was decided that the words 'did the act or made the omission' mean that the jury only have to consider the *actus reus* of the offence. It is not necessary for the jury to consider the mental element of the crime. If the jury find that the defendant did not do the *actus reus*, then the defendant cannot be held under any criminal law provision, though he may still be detained in a mental hospital if his condition warrants this under the Mental Health Act 1983.

When a defendant is found unfit to plead and the jury decide that he or she did do the relevant *actus reus*, the judge has the power to make one of the following orders:

- a hospital order (with or without a restriction order);
- a supervision order;
- an absolute discharge.

If the offence is one for which the sentence is fixed by law, for example murder, where there is a mandatory sentence of life imprisonment, and the court has the power to make a hospital order, then the judge must make a hospital order with a restriction order.

The defendant has a right to appeal to the Court of Appeal against a finding of unfitness to plead.

The Law Commission's proposals

In October 2010 the Law Commission issued a consultation paper, *Unfitness to Plead* (2010) CP 197. In this it pointed out the problems in the existing law. The main problem the Commission highlighted is that the *Pritchard* criteria were formulated in 1836 at a time when mental illness and its effects on a defendant's ability were not properly understood. As the Law Commission points out at para 2.47:

QUOTATION

> 'The *Pritchard* test really only addresses extreme cases of a particular type (usually bearing on cognitive deficiency) and . . . it continues to set a high threshold for finding an accused unfit to plead.'

The Law Commission's main proposal is to replace the *Pritchard* test with a new test based on whether the accused has decision-making capacity for the trial. The test should take into account all the requirements for meaningful participation in the criminal proceedings.

Where a defendant is found unfit to plead, the Law Commission proposes that on the trial of the facts, the prosecution should have to prove not only that D has done the act or made the omission charged but also that there are no grounds for an acquittal.

7.2.2 Insanity at time of offence

Where a person is fit to plead but is found to be insane at the time he committed the offence, a special verdict of 'Not guilty by reason of insanity' is given by the jury. The rules on insanity come from the *M'Naghten* Rules (see Chapter 8). Where the verdict is 'Not guilty by reason of insanity', the judge has the same powers of disposal under the Criminal Procedure (Insanity and Unfitness to Plead) Act 1991 as set out above in section 7.2.1.

7.2.3 Diminished responsibility

This is a partial defence which is only available on a charge of murder. It is set out in s 2 Homicide Act 1957 and operates where a person suffers from an abnormality of mental functioning, arising from a recognised medical condition which substantially impaired D's ability to:

- understand the nature of his conduct, or
- form a rational judgment, or
- exercise self-control,

and which provides an explanation for D's acts and omissions. (see Chapter 10 for full discussion of the defence). If the defence is successful the charge of murder is reduced to manslaughter.

7.2.4 Sentencing mentally ill offenders

As well as the normal range of custodial and community penalties there are also special powers available to the courts when dealing with mentally ill people who have been convicted of an offence. The aim is to provide treatment and help for such people while at the same time balancing the need for society to be protected from any danger posed by the person. The main additional powers available to the courts are:

- a community sentence with a treatment requirement;
- a hospital order;
- a restriction order under s 41 of the Mental Health Act 1983.

This last order can only be made in the Crown Court when the offender is considered to be a danger to the community. The order means that the offender is sent to a secure hospital for a set period or, where necessary, for an indefinite period.

ACTIVITY

Self-test questions

1. What is the *doli incapax* presumption and at what age does it cease to apply in England and Wales?
2. What other differences are there in the way children and young people are dealt with in the criminal justice system?
3. What is the purpose of the unfitness to plead procedure?
4. What safeguards are there for defendants when the unfitness to plead procedure is used?
5. Apart from the unfitness to plead procedure when is the mental health of the defendant a relevant matter in criminal proceedings?

7.3 Vicarious liability

There is a rule in the law of torts that one person can be liable for the torts committed by another. This is known as vicarious liability. It usually occurs in the employer/employee relationship where the employer is liable for any torts committed by an employee in the course of his employment. However, in criminal law the normal rule is that one person is not liable for crimes committed by another. This was illustrated nearly 300 years ago in *Huggins* (1730) 2 Strange 883, where the warden of Fleet prison was acquitted of the murder of a prisoner who had been placed in an unhealthy cell by one of the turnkeys (gaolers). The warden did not know that this had been done. Raymond CJ in this 1730 case pointed out the difference between civil and criminal law when he said:

JUDGMENT

'It is a point not to be disputed but that in criminal cases the principal is not answerable for the act of the deputy as he is in civil cases; they must each answer for their own acts and stand or fall by their own behaviour. All the authors that treat of criminal proceedings proceed on the foundation of this distinction; that to affect the superior by the act of the deputy there must be command of the superior which is not found in this case.'

However, there are some situations in criminal law where one person can be liable for the acts or omission of another. These are:

- common law crimes of public nuisance and criminal libel;
- statutory offences where a statute imposes vicarious liability.

At common law the principle expressed in *Huggins* nearly always applies. The only exceptions are the offences of public nuisance and criminal libel where the actions of an employee can make his employer vicariously liable. Causing a public nuisance on the highway can be disruptive to the general public and a reason for having vicarious liability for public nuisance is that it is likely to encourage employers to take steps to prevent their employees from creating the nuisance.

In statute law Parliament can make any offence it thinks appropriate one of vicarious liability by including such words as 'person, himself or by his servant or agent' in the offence. As well as having clear wording imposing vicarious liability it also imposed in two other ways. These are:

- through the extended meanings of words;
- under the principle of delegation.

Who can be vicariously liable?

The main categories of people who can be vicariously liable are:

- principals, including corporations, for acts of their agents;
- employers, including corporations, for acts of their employees;
- licensees for acts of others employed in the business for which the licensee holds the licence where they have delegated control of the business. This is so even though the licensee may himself be an employee of the brewer or other owner of the premises which are licensed.

Vicarious liability can make principals responsible for the actions of their agents. In *Duke of Leinster* [1924] 1 KB 311 the Duke was bankrupt. He was convicted of obtaining credit without disclosing his bankrupt status. In fact it was his agent who, contrary to the Duke's instructions, had obtained the credit without disclosing the facts. The Duke was guilty because he was vicariously liable for his agent's failure to disclose the bankruptcy.

The main area in which vicarious liability exists is where employers are liable for the actions of their employees.

7.3.1 Extended meaning of words

Words such as 'sell' and 'use' are usually taken to include the employer (or principal or licensee), even though the actual sale or use is by an employee. These are strict liability offences where there is no need to prove any mental element. In such a case the act of the employee (selling, using, etc.) is the act of the employer. However, vicarious liability can only occur where an employee is doing an act which he is employed or authorised to do. Where the employee is not authorised to carry out the act then the employer is not liable. In *Adams v Camfoni* [1929] 1 KB 95, D was a licensee who was charged with selling alcohol outside the hours permitted by the licence. The sale had been made by a messenger boy who had no authority to sell anything. D was held to be not guilty.

If the employee is carrying out an authorised act then the employer will be liable even though the employee does it in a way which has not been authorised. This was seen in *Coppen v Moore (No 2)* [1898] 2 QB 306 where a sales assistant sold ham which she wrongly described as 'Scotch ham' against instruction of the employer. The employer was liable because the assistant was authorised to sell the item.

Vicarious liability still exists even where the employer has taken steps to ensure that such an offence is not committed. In *Harrow LBC v Shah and Shah* [1999] 3 All ER 302 the Shahs were newsagents who were convicted of selling a lottery ticket to a boy under 16. They had instructed their staff not to sell tickets to underage children and also told the staff that if they were not sure, they should ask the Shahs to check that it was all right to sell a ticket. An employee sold a ticket to a boy whom he reasonably thought was 16 or over, when the boy was in fact under 16. One of the Shahs was on the premises, though not in the shop when the sale was made. Despite these facts the Shahs were still held to be vicariously liable for the sale.

7.3.2 Delegation principle

Where an offence requires proof of *mens rea* then vicarious liability can only exist if the principal has delegated responsibility. In such instances the acts and intention of the person to whom responsibility has been delegated are imputed to the principal. This was demonstrated in *Allen v Whitehead* [1930] 1 KB 211.

CASE EXAMPLE

Allen v Whitehead [1930] 1 KB 211

The defendant owned a cafe which was run by a manager. He was charged under s 44 of the Metropolitan Police Act 1839 with the offence of knowingly permitting or suffering prostitutes to meet together and remain in a place where refreshments are sold and consumed. D had been warned by the police that prostitutes were meeting in his cafe and had instructed his manager not to allow this. D also had a notice displayed on the wall of the cafe forbidding prostitutes to meet at the cafe. He visited the cafe once or twice a week and there was no evidence that there had been any breach of the 1839 Act while he was on the premises. However, the manager allowed prostitutes to stay at the cafe for several hours on eight consecutive days. D was charged and it was held by the Divisional Court that both the acts and knowledge of his manager were to be imputed to D. The fact that he did not know of the breach was not a defence. He had delegated the management of the cafe to the manager and this made D liable.

In *Linnett v Metropolitan Police commissioner* [1946] 1 All ER 380 the same principle was used to make a co-licensee liable for the acts of his fellow co-licensee. He had delegated the management of a refreshment house to his co-licensee and was absent from the premises but was still held guilty of 'knowingly permitting disorderly conduct', even though he personally had no knowledge of it.

There must be complete delegation for the principal to be vicariously liable, as seen in the case of *Vane v Yiannopoullos* [1964] 3 All ER 820.

CASE EXAMPLE

Vane v Yiannopoullos [1964] 3 All ER 820

D was the licensee of a restaurant. He had given instructions to the waitress in the restaurant not to serve alcoholic drinks to people unless they ordered a meal as well. While D was on another floor of the building a waitress served alcohol to two youths who did not order a meal. D was charged with the offence of 'knowingly selling intoxicating liquor to persons to whom he was not entitled to sell', contrary to s 22 of the Licensing Act 1961, but acquitted. The prosecution appealed against this but the Divisional Court dismissed the appeal. The prosecutor appealed to the House of Lords. The Lords dismissed the appeal, holding that there had not been sufficient delegation to make D vicariously liable for the employee's actions.

The House of Lords pointed out that the principle had never been extended to cover the case where the whole of the authority has not been transferred to another. In fact Lord Reid appeared to confine the principle to situations in which the licensee was not on the premises but had left someone else in charge. However, in *Howker v Robinson* [1972] 2 All ER 786 the Divisional Court found that the magistrates had correctly decided that a licensee was guilty when an illegal sale was made by a barman in the lounge, even though the licensee was present (and working) in the public bar of the business. This decision is contrary to the House of Lords' judgment in *Vane* and is unlikely to be followed in future cases. Indeed, in the later case of *Bradshaw v Ewart-Jones* [1983] 1 All ER 12, the Divisional Court did not apply the doctrine but held that the master of a ship was not liable for breach of statutory duty when he had delegated performance of the duty to his chief officer. The master was still on board the ship and in command, so the delegation was only partial.

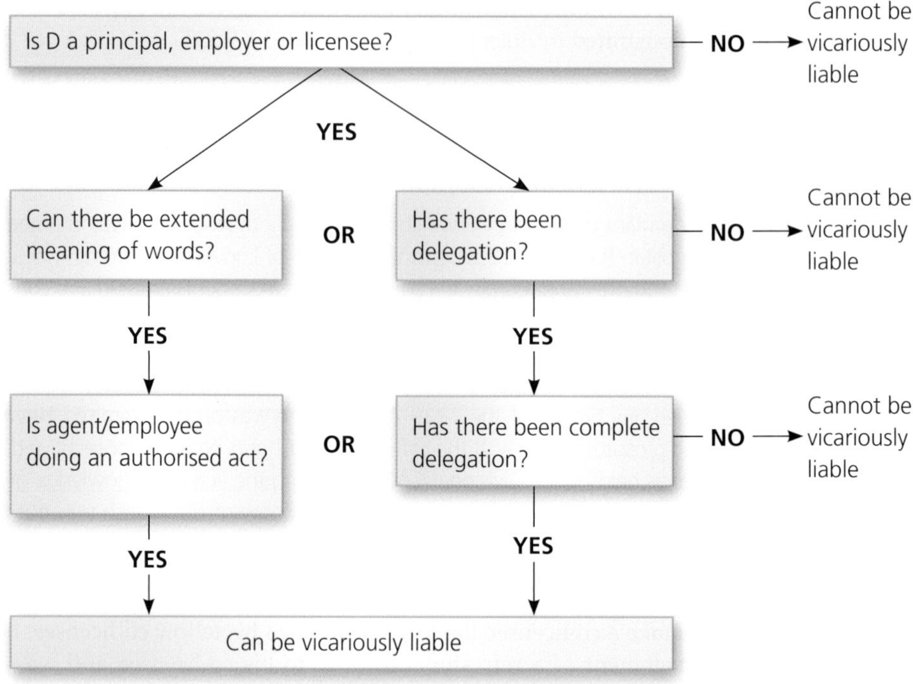

Figure 7.1 Flow chart on vicarious liability.

Should delegation impose liability?

In most of the offences where the delegation principle is used there is no provision for making the servant himself liable to prosecution. So, unless the licensee is made liable, it would be impossible to enforce the law adequately. The main problem comes where the particular offence includes the word 'knowingly'. If the licensee does not know the relevant facts, should the knowledge of the person to whom he has delegated control be imputed to him? In *Vane v Yiannopoullos* (1964) the House of Lords was unhappy about the use of the delegation principle where the offence charged included the word 'knowingly'. Lord Reid, who gave the leading judgment, pointed out that there had been only four cases in the 60 years before *Vane* in which the offence used the word 'knowingly'. Two of these were *Allen v Whitehead* (1930) and *Linnett v Metropolitan Police Commissioner* (1946), which are explained above. Lord Reid, in *Vane*, said:

JUDGMENT

'[T]he courts adopted a construction which on any view I find hard to justify. They drew a distinction between acts done by a servant without the knowledge of the licence holder while the licence holder was on the premises and giving general supervision to his business, and acts done without the knowledge of the licence holder but with the knowledge of a person whom the license holder had left in charge of the premises. In the latter case they held that the knowledge of the person left in charge must be imputed to the licence holder . . . If this were a new distinction recently introduced by the courts I would think it necessary to consider whether a provision that the licence holder shall not knowingly sell can ever make him vicariously liable by reason of the knowledge of some other person; but this distinction has now been recognised and acted on by the courts for over half a century. It may have been unwarranted in the first instance, but I would think it now too late to upset so long-standing a practice.'

7.3.3 Reasons for vicarious liability

The main reason for vicarious liability is that it makes it easier to enforce regulations about such matters as selling food and alcohol and using vehicles. Modern regulatory legislation in these areas is aimed at protecting consumers and promoting public health and safety and preventing pollution. If employers were not liable for the acts of their employees then it would be virtually impossible to enforce such legislation. It is fair and just that those who make the profits from a business should also pay for any breaches of standards in that business. Without the principle of vicarious liability, it would be difficult to convict those responsible for the business. By imposing liability on the principal, employer or licensee this will make him do all he can to prevent breaches of the legislation by his agents, servants or delegates. Employers are more likely to train and control staff properly and the principle of delegation makes a licensee retain proper control over his business even when he is not there.

KEY FACTS

Key facts on vicarious liability

	Law	Cases
Who can be vicariously liable?	Principals for acts of their agents. Employers for acts of their employees. Licensees for acts of those to whom they delegate responsibility.	*Duke of Leinster* (1924) *Coppen v Moore (No 2)* (1898) *Allen v Whitehead* (1930)
When does vicarious liability exist?	Common law offences of public nuisance and criminal libel. Extended meaning of words in statutory offences where an employee is acting within the scope of his employment. Delegation principle.	Very rare *Coppen v Moore (No 2)* (1898) – owner of business was liable for a sale made by employee *Allen v Whitehead* (1930)
The extended meanings of words	An employer is liable even though the employee is disobeying instructions. An employer is not liable if the employee is not acting within the scope of his employment.	*Coppen v Moore (No 2)* (1898) *Adams v Camfoni* (1929)
The delegation principle	A licensee is liable where there is full delegation. A licensee is not liable where there is partial delegation.	*Allen v Whitehead* (1930) *Vane v Yiannopoullos* (1964)

7.3.4 Criticisms of vicarious liability

The main criticism is that it is unjust to penalise someone for the actions of another. This is especially so where the principal has taken steps to ensure that no offence is committed. For example in *Coppen* (1898) the sales assistant had disobeyed the instructions of her employer and yet the employer was still liable. Also in *Duke of Leinster* (1924) the agent had acted contrary to the Duke's instructions when he obtained credit without disclosing the bankruptcy. Again in *Harrow LBC* (1999) the owners of the newsagent business had done all that was within their power to prevent the sale of lottery tickets to underage children yet were still convicted of the offence.

These criticisms would be avoided if a defence of 'due diligence' were available for all regulatory offences. Some statutes do contain this defence which can be used if the employer can show that he exercised all due diligence in the management of the business and that there was nothing more that could reasonably have been done to prevent a breach.

Where an offence requires *mens rea* it is even more unjust to convict someone who had no knowledge of the offence. This is the effect of the delegation principle as illustrated in the cases of *Allen* (1930) and *Linnett* (1946). In both those cases the licensee had no knowledge of the offence but was convicted of 'knowingly permitting' it. It should also be considered that the rules of vicarious liability have not been created by Parliament; they are judge-made. In some cases where Parliament has used the word 'knowingly' in an offence, the concept of vicarious liability appears to be contrary to the intentions of Parliament.

ACTIVITY

Self-test questions

1. Who can be held vicariously liable for a criminal offence?
2. Explain with examples the two ways in which vicarious liability may be imposed for statutory offences.
3. What problems have the courts identified with the use of the delegation principle in vicarious liability?
4. Why is vicarious liability used in criminal law?

7.4 Corporate liability

Corporation
A non-human body which has a separate legal personality from its human members

A **corporation** is a legal person. Corporations include limited companies, public corporations and local authorities. It was established in *Salomon v Salomon & Co Ltd* [1897] AC 22 that on incorporation, a company acquires a separate legal personality from its members.

As a corporation is a legal person, it can be criminally liable even though it has no physical existence. This ability to be liable for statutory offences is set out in the Interpretation Act 1978, which provides that in every Act, unless the contrary intention appears, 'person' includes a body of persons, corporate or unincorporate. This rule has existed for over 100 years as it existed in the previous Interpretation Act of 1889. In fact the interpretation is even wider than making corporations liable, as it also includes unincorporated bodies such as a partnership. As well as being liable for statutory offences the law also recognises that a corporation can be criminally liable for common law offences.

There are three different principles by which a corporation may be liable. These are:

- the principle of identification;
- vicarious liability;
- breach of statutory duty.

These are considered separately in sections 7.4.2–7.4.4.

7.4.1 Exceptions to the general rule of liability

There are two general exceptions to corporate liability for criminal offences. First, a corporation cannot be convicted of an offence where the only punishment available is physical, such as imprisonment or community service. Effectively the only offence that is currently eliminated by this rule is murder, which carries a mandatory sentence of life imprisonment. Corporations can be liable for any offence which has a discretionary maximum penalty of life imprisonment, since for these the judge can impose alternative penalties such as a fine.

Second, a corporation cannot be liable as a principal for crimes such as bigamy, rape, incest or perjury, which by their physical nature can only be committed by a real person. A corporation, however, may be liable as a secondary participant in such offences. J C Smith in *Criminal Law: Cases and Materials* (8th edn, Oxford University Press, 2002) puts forward the example that a corporation could be liable as a secondary participant for bigamy if the managing director of an incorporated marriage advisory bureau were to arrange a marriage which he knew to be bigamous.

In *Robert Millar (Contractors) Ltd* [1971] 1 All ER 577 a company was convicted of being a secondary participant to the offence of causing death by dangerous driving. The managing director of the company had sent a lorry on a long journey, knowing that it had a seriously defective tyre. The tyre burst and the lorry crashed causing six deaths. The driver was convicted as principal of six offences of causing death by dangerous driving and the managing director and the company were convicted of counselling and procuring those offences.

7.4.2 The principle of identification

Where an offence requires *mens rea* it is necessary to show that the corporation had the required *mens rea*. As a corporation has no body and no mind this causes problems in making corporations liable. In order to hold corporations liable the courts have sought to identify a person (or persons) within the company structure whose mind is the 'directing mind and will' of the corporation. This phrase was first used in *Lennard's Carrying Co Ltd v Asiatic Petroleum Co Ltd* [1915] AC 705, but the identification principle was really established by three cases in 1944. These were:

- *DPP v Kent and Sussex Contractors Ltd* [1944] KB 146;
- *ICR Haulage Ltd* [1944] KB 551;
- *Moore v I Bresler Ltd* [1944] 2 All ER 515.

In each case one or more senior members of the management of the company were identified as the directing mind and will, so that their intent was deemed to be the intent of the company. For example in *DPP v Kent and Sussex Contractors Ltd* (1944) the offence required an intent to deceive, and the courts held that the intent of the transport manager of the company was the intent of the company. It could, however, be argued that a transport manager is not sufficiently senior for his intent to be the intent of the company. In *ICR Haulage Ltd* (1944) the company was convicted of a common law conspiracy to defraud. The act and the intent of the managing director were held to be the act and intent of the company. In *Moore v I Bresler Ltd* (1944) the company was convicted of making false returns with intent to deceive, contrary to the Finance (No 2) Act 1940. The returns had been made by the company secretary and a branch sales manager. There is no doubt that a company secretary is an official whose acts and intent will be viewed as the company's acts and intent. However, this case can be criticised for including a branch sales manager in the category of the directing mind and will of the company.

As a corporation has no physical existence it is always necessary to identify those people within the corporation who can be considered as the directing mind and will of the company. In *H L Bolton (Engineering) Co. Ltd v TJ Graham & Sons Ltd* [1956] 3 All ER 624 Denning LJ pointed out that:

JUDGMENT

'A company may in many ways be likened to a human body. It has a brain and a nerve centre which controls what it does. It also has hands which hold the tools and act in accordance with directions from the centre. Some of the people in the company are mere servants and agents who are nothing more than hands to do the work and cannot be said to represent the mind or will. Others are directors and managers who represent the directing mind and will of the company and control what it does. The state of mind of these managers is the state of mind of the company and is treated by the law as such.'

This concept was used by the courts in subsequent cases, but in very large companies with several layers of management, there can be difficulties in deciding who exactly is the 'brain', in Lord Denning's analogy, as against those who are 'nothing more than hands to do the work'. For example, in *Tesco Supermarkets Ltd v Nattrass* [1972] AC 153 Tesco advertised packs of washing powder in the shop window of one of their stores at a reduced price. An employee failed to tell the store manager when all the packs were sold, so that the advertisement continued even though there were no reduced packs left. A shopper who tried to buy a reduced priced pack was told that the only packets left were full price. The shopper complained to the Inspector of Weights and Measures, and Tesco was prosecuted under s 11 of the Trade Descriptions Act 1968, which provides that:

SECTION

'11 If any person offering to supply any goods gives, by whatever means, any indication likely to be taken as an indication that the goods are being offered at a price less than that at which they are in fact being offered he shall . . . be guilty of an offence.'

Tesco accepted that this had happened, but claimed a defence under s 24(1) of the Trade Descriptions Act, that the fault was due to another person. As it was the fault of the manager for not adequately supervising the employee who had failed to check the packs, the question for the courts to decide was whether the store manager was identified as the company, or whether he was 'another person' for the purpose of s 24(1). Tesco was convicted and appealed. The Divisional Court held that the store manager was 'the embodiment of the company' and dismissed the appeal. The case was then appealed to the House of Lords, who ruled that a store manager was not sufficiently senior for his acts to be the acts of the company.

Lord Reid started his judgment by considering the nature of corporate personality. He said:

JUDGMENT

'A living person has a mind which can have knowledge or intention or be negligent and he has hands to carry out his intentions. A corporation has none of these; it must act through living persons, though not always one or the same person. Then the person who acts is not speaking or acting for the company. He is acting as the company and his mind which directs his acts is the mind of the company. There is no question of the company being vicariously liable. He is not acting as a servant, representative, agent or delegate. He is an embodiment of the company or, one could say, he hears and speaks through the persona of the company, within his appropriate sphere, and his mind is the mind of the company. If it is a guilty mind then that guilt is the guilt of the company.'

Lord Reid also referred to Lord Denning's comparison of a company to a human body in *H L Bolton (Engineering) Co Ltd* (1956). He pointed out that there had been attempts to apply Lord Denning's words to all servants of a company whose work was brainwork or who exercised some managerial discretion under the direction of superior officers of the company. Lord Reid felt that this was not what had been intended. Lord Denning had limited the category to those 'who represent the directing mind and will of the company and control what it does'. For this reason the manager of a local store could not be identified with the company and so, for the purposes of s 24(1) of the Trade Descriptions Act 1968, the manager was 'another person'. Effectively this case decided that only those in senior positions or those who have been given power to act as the company can be considered as the 'controlling mind' of a corporation.

Lord Reid thought that those who would be the embodiment of the company were:

JUDGMENT

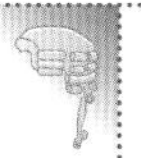

'the board of directors, the managing director and perhaps other superior officers of a company [who] carry out the functions of management and speak and act as the company.'

However, other judges in the House of Lords gave slightly different definitions. Viscount Dilhorne thought that it was a person:

JUDGMENT

'who is in actual control of the operations of a company or of part of them and who is not responsible to another person in the company for the manner in which he discharges his duties in the sense of being under orders.'

Lord Diplock thought that it was necessary to identify:

JUDGMENT

'those natural persons who by the memorandum and articles of association or as a result of action taken by the directors or by the company in general meeting pursuant to the articles are entrusted with the exercise of the powers of the company.'

Problems of the principle of identification

Apart from deciding who exactly can be identified as being the company, the principle of identification causes problems in the following three areas.

1. The bigger the company and the more layers of management, the less likely it is that a senior officer will have made a decision (or have the required *mens rea*) to make the company liable. This means that bigger companies are more likely to avoid prosecution.
2. The principle of identification does not work where several people have combined to create a dangerous situation, but individually they have not got the required *mens rea*. This was seen in *P & O European Ferries (Dover) Ltd* (1991) where there were several failures by different levels of staff which resulted in the cross-channel ferry, the *Herald of Free Enterprise*, leaving the port of Zeebrugge with her bow doors open. As a result the ship sank and 193 people were killed. The company was not criminally liable for the deaths as there was no individual whose negligence could be

identified as the negligence of the company. It can be argued that the faults of different people should be aggregated to prove the guilty mind of the company. The opposite view was put by Devlin J in *Armstrong v Strain* [1952] 1 All ER 139, when he said that:

JUDGMENT

'You cannot add an innocent state of mind to an innocent state of mind and get as a result a dishonest state of mind.'

3. The principle in *Tesco v Nattrass* (1972) could lead to companies being found not guilty of regulatory offences and this would make regulation ineffective against big companies. However, in *Tesco v Brent LBC* [1993] 2 All ER 718 this result was avoided by the Divisional Court. In this case Tesco was convicted of supplying a pre-recorded video with an 18 rating to someone under the age of 18, contrary to s 11(1) of the Video Recordings Act 1984. The Act allowed a defence if the defendant 'neither knew nor had reasonable grounds to believe that the person concerned had not attained that age'. Tesco argued that the directing minds of the company, in other words the board and managing director, would have no way of knowing the age of the purchaser. They would not be present at the store, but worked from the London headquarters of the company. The Divisional Court dismissed Tesco's appeal. They held it was impracticable to suppose that those who controlled a large company would have any knowledge or information about the age of a purchaser. The only person who could have that knowledge was the cashier who served the purchaser. As the magistrates had been satisfied that the cashier had reasonable grounds to believe that the purchaser was under 18, then that was enough to make the company liable. This can be viewed as an extension of the principle of vicarious liability where a company is responsible for the acts of its employees (see section 7.4.3).

In addition to the above problems, Lord Denning's analogy in *H L Bolton (Engineering)* (1956) has been criticised by the Privy Council in *Meridian Global Funds Management Asia Ltd v Securities Commission* [1995] 3 All ER 918.

CASE EXAMPLE

Meridian Global Funds Management Asia Ltd v Securities Commission [1995] 3 All ER 918

The chief investment officer and the senior portfolio manager of Meridian used funds managed by the company to acquire shares in a public issue. They did not give notice as required by s 20 of the New Zealand Securities Amendment Act 1988. The board of directors and managing director were not aware of the purchase or the failure to give notice. The trial judge found the company guilty of a breach of s 20 as he held that the knowledge of the chief investment officer and the senior portfolio manager was to be attributed to the company. On appeal to New Zealand's Court of Appeal the conviction was upheld on the basis that the chief investment officer was the directing mind and will of the company. The case was then appealed to the Privy Council.

In the Privy Council Lord Hoffmann pointed out that the phrase 'directing mind and will' had first been used by Viscount Haldane in *Lennard's Carrying Co Ltd* (1915) in a very specific circumstance. Lord Hoffmann said of Denning LJ's comments:

JUDGMENT

'But this ... by the very power of the image, distracts attention from the purpose for which Viscount Haldane said he was using the notion of the directing mind and will, namely to apply the attribution rule derived from s 502 [of the Merchant Shipping Act 1894] to the particular defendant in the case:

"For if Mr Lennard was the directing mind of the company, then his action must, unless a corporation is not to be liable at all, have been an action which was the action of the company itself within the meaning of section 502."'

Instead of using the identification principle, the Privy Council relied on the idea of the 'rules of attribution'. Lord Hoffmann explained what was meant when he said:

JUDGMENT

'Any proposition about a company necessarily involves a reference to a set of rules. A company exists because there is a rule (usually in a statute) which says that a *persona ficta* [fictional person] shall be deemed to exist and to have certain of the powers, rights and duties of a natural person. But there would be little sense in deeming such a *persona ficta* to exist unless there were also rules to tell one what acts were to count as acts of the company. It is therefore a necessary part of corporate personality that there should be rules by which acts are attributed to the company. These may be called "the rules of attribution". The company's primary rules of attribution will generally be found in its constitution, typically the articles of association, and will say things such as "for the purpose of appointing members of the board, a majority vote of shareholders shall be a decision of the company" or "the decisions of the board in managing the company's business shall be the decisions of the company" ...

The company's primary rules of attribution together with the general principles of agency, vicarious liability and so forth are usually sufficient to enable one to determine its rights and obligations.'

Lord Hoffmann did accept that there would be exceptional cases where these rules would not provide an answer. In these cases he thought that the normal rules of interpretation would provide the answer:

JUDGMENT

'Given that it was intended to apply to a company, how was it intended to apply? Whose act (or knowledge, or state of mind) was for this purpose intended to count as the act etc of the company? One finds the answer to this question by applying the usual canons of interpretation, taking into account the language of the rule (if it is a statute) and its contents and policy.'

The main problem with this is that it appears to ignore common law offences where there is no written version of the offence to be interpreted. A major area where very few prosecutions have succeeded against corporations is in the common law offence of involuntary manslaughter. In view of the difficulty of establishing liability for manslaughter, the Law Commission recommended a new offence of corporate killing where a management failure is the cause (or one of the causes) of death, and that failure constitutes conduct falling far below what can reasonably be expected (see section 7.5 for further discussion on corporate manslaughter).

7.4.3 Vicarious liability

As already seen in section 7.3 the law recognises situations where one person may be liable for offences committed by another under the principles of vicarious liability. The principles of vicarious liability apply equally to corporations. So corporations may be vicariously liable for the acts of their employees in the same way as a natural person may be liable for his employee or agent. Liability of corporations by way of vicarious liability was first recognised many years ago in *Great North of England Railway Co* (1846) 9 QB 315.

Corporations can be liable where a statute imposes vicarious liability or, in rare instances, under the common law, for example the offence of creating a public nuisance. Examples of corporations being vicariously liable include *Coppen v Moore (No 2)* (1898), where a sales assistant sold ham which she wrongly described as 'Scotch ham', against instruction of the employer. The employer was convicted of selling goods to which a false trade description applied because the assistant had sold the ham. The court pointed out that:

JUDGMENT

'It cannot be doubted that the appellant sold the ham in question, although the transaction was carried out by his servants. In other words he was the seller, although not the salesman.'

Another example is *National Rivers Authority v Alfred McAlpine Homes (East) Ltd* (1994) 158 JP 628, in which employees of the company were constructing a water feature on the site. In doing this they discharged wet cement into it. The company was convicted of polluting a river. The judge said:

JUDGMENT

'to make an offence an effective weapon in the defence of environmental protection, a company must, by necessary implication, be criminally liable for the acts and omissions of its servant or agents during activities being done for the company. I do not find that this affects our concept of a just or fair criminal justice system, having regard to the magnitude of environmental pollution.'

Distinction between the identification principle and vicarious liability

The liability of corporations under vicarious liability is quite different from the way in which liability arises under the identification principle. This was explained in *HM Coroner for East Kent, ex parte Spooner* (1989) 88 Cr App R 10 by Bingham LJ when he distinguished between the identification principle and a company being vicariously liable, saying:

JUDGMENT

'A company may be vicariously liable for the negligent acts and omissions of its servants and agents, but for a company to be criminally liable for manslaughter it is required that *mens rea* and *actus reus* should be established not against those who acted for or in the name of the company but against those who were to be identified with the embodiment of the company itself.'

So for liability by the principle of identification it is necessary to prove *mens rea* and *actus reus* in someone who can be considered the company, whereas under the principles of vicarious liability the acts and omissions of employees or agents can make the company liable.

7.4.4 Breach of statutory duty

A statute or regulation can make a corporation liable for offences. In particular this can happen where the statute (or regulation) makes the occupier liable. If the corporation is the occupier of premises then it is liable for offences committed in relation to those premises. Equally a law may make an employer liable. If the corporation is the employer then it is liable. An important statute is the Health and Safety at Work etc Act 1974. In *Attorney-General's Reference (No 2 of 1999)* [2000] 3 All ER 187, where a train crash killed seven people, the company was found not guilty of manslaughter. However, the company pleaded guilty to a breach of statutory duty under the Health and Safety at Work etc Act 1974 and was fined £1.5 million.

This rule of liability for statutory breach also applies to unincorporated bodies if they are the occupier or employer. This was seen in *Clerk to the Croydon Justices, ex parte Chief Constable of Kent* [1989] Crim LR 910, where the Queen's Bench Divisional Court held that if an unincorporated body was the 'registered keeper' of a vehicle then it was liable for fixed penalties for illegal parking under the Transport Act 1982.

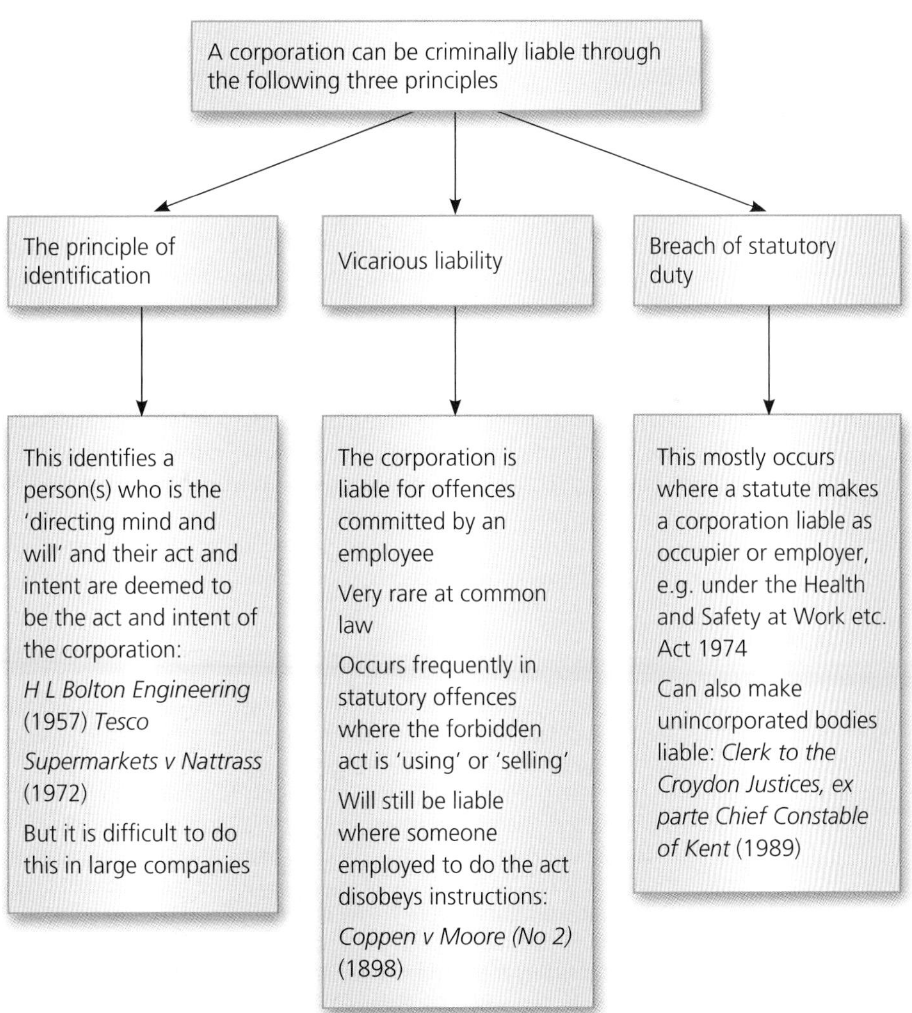

A corporation can be criminally liable through the following three principles
The principle of identification
Vicarious liability
Breach of statutory duty
This identifies a person(s) who is the 'directing mind and will' and their act and intent are deemed to be the act and intent of the corporation:
H L Bolton Engineering (1957) Tesco
Supermarkets v Nattrass (1972)
But it is difficult to do this in large companies
The corporation is liable for offences committed by an employee
Very rare at common law
Occurs frequently in statutory offences where the forbidden act is 'using' or 'selling'
Will still be liable where someone employed to do the act disobeys instructions:
Coppen v Moore (No 2) (1898)
This mostly occurs where a statute makes a corporation liable as occupier or employer, e.g. under the Health and Safety at Work etc. Act 1974
Can also make unincorporated bodies liable: Clerk to the Croydon Justices, ex parte Chief Constable of Kent (1989)

Figure 7.2 Corporate liability.

7.5 Corporate manslaughter

7.5.1 Previous law

During the last two decades of the twentieth century there were a number of high-profile disasters in which people died as a result of poor practice by a corporation. These included:

- the *Herald of Free Enterprise* disaster in 1987, in which 193 people died;
- the King's Cross fire in 1987, in which 31 people were killed;
- the Clapham rail crash in 1988 when 35 people died and nearly 500 others were injured;
- the Southall rail crash in 1997 when seven people were killed and 150 injured.

Initially it was thought that a corporation could not be liable for manslaughter. However, this was resolved in *P & O European Ferries (Dover) Ltd* (1990) when, following the *Herald of Free Enterprise* disaster, P & O (who had taken over Townsend Car Ferries Ltd, the operators of the ferry at the time of the disaster) was charged with manslaughter.

CASE EXAMPLE

P & O European Ferries (Dover) Ltd (1990) 93 Cr App R 72

The car ferry sailed from Zeebrugge harbour with its inner and outer bow doors (through which the cars were loaded) still open. The assistant bosun should have closed the doors but he failed to do so because he had overslept. The Chief Officer who was in charge of loading the car deck was responsible for checking that the doors were closed, but in practice he interpreted this as checking that the assistant bosun was at the controls. The Master of the day was responsible for the safety of the ship on that sailing, but he merely followed the system approved by the Senior Master who had overall responsibility for coordinating the practice of all crews and Masters who worked in the *Herald of Free Enterprise*. Shore management had not provided any instructions on this aspect of ship safety.

The causes of the disaster were investigated by the Sheen Inquiry. The investigation reached the conclusion that the immediate cause of the sinking was the Chief Officer's failure to ensure that the doors were closed. It also concluded that the Senior Master should have introduced a 'fail-safe system' so that the Master of the day knew when the doors were closed and it was safe to sail. However, the Sheen Report also found that the company's management had failed in their duties. The Report stated:

QUOTATION

'At first sight the faults which led to this disaster were the . . . errors of omission on the part of the Master, the Chief Officer and the assistant bosun, and also the failure by Captain Kirby [Senior Master] to issue and enforce clear orders. But a full investigation into the circumstances of the disaster leads inexorably to the conclusion that the underlying or cardinal faults lay higher up in the Company. The Board of Directors did not appreciate their responsibility for the safe management of their ships. They did not apply their minds to the question: What orders should be given for the safety of our ships? The directors did not have any proper comprehension what their duties were . . . All concerned in the management, from the members of the board down to junior superintendents, were guilty of fault in that all must be regarded as sharing responsibility for the failure of management. From the top to the bottom the body corporate was infected with the disease of sloppiness. The failure on the part of the shore management to give proper and clear directions was a contributory cause of the disaster.'

The Sheen Report (Department of Transport, Report of the Court No 8074, 1987), para 14.1

The Report went on to highlight three management failures. The first was that, although a proposal had been made by Masters that a warning light should be fitted on the bridge so that the Master on duty would know when the bow doors were shut, the management had failed to give this proposal serious consideration. Second, there had been five or six previous incidents when ferries had sailed with doors open but these incidents had not been documented and collated. If they had been then the management of the company would have been alerted to the risk of disaster. Third, there was a lack of any proper system within the company to ensure that their ships were operated in accordance with the highest standards of safety.

Ruling that a corporation could be charged with manslaughter

The company and seven individuals were charged with manslaughter. At the start of the trial the company submitted that the counts for manslaughter should be quashed for two reasons. First, that English law did not recognise the offence of corporate manslaughter, and, second, that manslaughter could only be committed by a natural person. The trial judge ruled that it was possible through the principle of identification for a corporation to be liable for manslaughter. He rejected the argument that manslaughter could only be committed by a natural person, pointing out that the old definitions of 'homicide' which use the words a killing by a *human being* were formulated when corporations did not exist. He held that where a corporation, through the controlling mind of one of its agents, did an act which fulfilled the definition of manslaughter, then the corporation could properly be indicted for the offence.

Although this case established that a corporation could be liable for manslaughter there has been only a very small number of prosecutions and even fewer convictions. This is because the way the principle of identification works makes it difficult to obtain a conviction against a corporation for manslaughter. For example, in the Clapham rail crash no prosecution was brought even though an inquiry into the matter criticised British Rail for allowing working practices which were 'positively dangerous'. Again, in the King's Cross fire no prosecution was brought because no one person had responsibility for fire precautions.

In the P & O case, although the company was prosecuted, the charge was eventually dismissed by the judge because it was not possible to identify one person who was the controlling mind and will of the company and who had been grossly negligent. The disaster had occurred because of errors by a number of people, some of whom were very junior. The judge dismissed the case against all the defendants except the bosun and the Chief Officer. The prosecution then withdrew the charges against these two.

Successful prosecutions for manslaughter prior to 2007 were nearly all of small companies where the managing director could easily be identified as the 'mind and will' of the company. The first successful prosecution was of OLL Ltd, *The Independent*, 9 December 1994. In this case four teenagers had died in a canoeing tragedy because of the risks taken by the leisure company who organised the activity. The company was a one-man outfit run by Kite. His gross negligence was attributed to the company and both he and the company were convicted of manslaughter.

Southall rail crash case

A prosecution was also brought in the Southall rail crash, where a high-speed train collided with a freight train, causing the deaths of seven people. There was evidence that two safety devices on the train which would have prevented the train from passing a signal at danger were switched off. The driver failed to see a sequence of signals (green, double yellow, yellow and red) until it was too late to avoid the collision. He gave evidence that he remembered seeing the green signal and the next signal he could recall was the red one. There was no second driver in the cab. The judge ruled that to establish a charge for gross negligence manslaughter it was necessary to prove a guilty mind. Where the defendant was a company it could only be convicted if a person with whom it was identified had the necessary guilty mind. As no such person could be identified (the train driver was too junior for his mind to embody the mind and will of the company), the judge dismissed the case against the company.

Following the judge's ruling, the Attorney-General referred two questions of law to the Court of Appeal (*Attorney-General's Reference (No 2 of 1999)* [2000] 3 All ER 187). These were:

JUDGMENT

'a. Can a defendant be properly convicted of manslaughter by gross negligence in the absence of evidence as to that defendant's state of mind?

b. Can a non-human defendant be convicted of the crime of manslaughter by gross negligence in the absence of evidence establishing the guilt of an identified human individual for the same crime?'

The Court of Appeal answered the first question 'yes' and the second question 'no'. There was considerable criticism of the decision on this second point. It created a further limitation on the possibility of convicting a corporation of manslaughter.

7.5.2 Reform of corporate manslaughter

The problems highlighted in the P & O (1991) case led to the Law Commission considering corporate manslaughter in a general review of the law on manslaughter. The Law Commission consulted on the problems before producing its report: *Legislating the Criminal Code: Involuntary Manslaughter* (Law Com No 237) (1996). It was noticeable that the Health and Safety Executive put in a response to the consultations and commented that death or personal injury resulting from a major disaster is rarely due to the negligence of a single individual. In the majority of cases the disaster is caused as a result of the failure of systems controlling the risk with the carelessness of individuals being a contributing factor.

The Law Commission's main proposals for corporate liability were that:

- There should be a special offence of corporate killing and this should broadly correspond to the Law Commission's proposal of a new offence of killing by gross carelessness.
- The offence would be committed only where the corporation's conduct in causing death fell far below what could reasonably be expected.
- A death should be regarded as having been caused by the conduct of the corporation if it is caused by a 'management failure'. A management failure is described as occurring if the way in which its activities are managed or organised fails to ensure the health and safety of persons employed in or affected by its activities.
- Such a failure would be regarded as a cause of a person's death even if the immediate cause is the act or omission of an individual.
- Individuals within a company could still be liable for offences of reckless killing and killing by gross carelessness (which the Law Commission had recommended should replace the current offence of manslaughter but has never done so) as well as the company being liable for the offence of corporate killing.

tutor tip

'Make sure you understand the Corporate Manslaughter and Corporate Homicide Act 2007.'

The Law Commission's report was published in 1996. In 2000 the government issued a consultation paper on the matter, *Reforming the Law on Involuntary Manslaughter: The Government's Proposals*. Finally in 2007, the Corporate Manslaughter and Corporate Homicide Act was passed by Parliament.

7.5.3 Corporate Manslaughter and Corporate Homicide Act 2007

The offence of corporate manslaughter is set out in s 1(1) of the Act which states:

SECTION

'1(1) An organisation to which this section applies is guilty of an offence if the way in which any of its activities are managed:

(a) causes a person's death, and

(b) amounts to gross breach of a relevant duty of care owed by the organisation to the deceased.'

...

1(3) An organisation is guilty of an offence under this section only if the way in which its activities are managed or organised by its senior management is a substantial element in the breach referred to in subsection (1).'

Who can be liable?

The Act makes 'organisations' liable. This is considerably wider than the previous common law where only corporations could be liable for manslaughter. The Act states that it applies to:

- corporations;
- government departments or other bodies listed in Schedule 1;
- police forces;
- partnerships, trade unions or employers' associations.

The government departments and bodies listed in Schedule 1 include such wide-ranging bodies as the Department for Transport, the Department for Work and Pensions, the Department of Health, the Ministry of Defence, the Crown Prosecution Service and the Office for National Statistics. There are 48 bodies listed in Schedule 1 and the list can be added to or amended by the Secretary of State if required, for example where a government department is reorganised or renamed or a new department created.

Liability on police forces was only included through a House of Lords amendment to the Bill when it was going through Parliament. The government was reluctant to agree to this, but did eventually allow the amendment. There is an exemption for the police where a death is caused in terrorist cases.

Partnerships, trade unions and employers' associations can now be prosecuted for corporate manslaughter. This was not possible under the previous law.

Individuals cannot be liable for corporate manslaughter.

How liability exists

The key factor is the way in which the organisation's activities are 'managed or organised' by its senior managers. No single individual has to be identified as having any *mens rea* for the offence. The senior management contribution need only be a 'substantial element' in the breach of duty leading to the death. Conduct of other 'non-senior' managers is also relevant and may be substantial provided it does not render the senior management involvement something less than substantial.

Senior management

Senior management is defined as being persons who play significant roles in:

- the making of decisions about how the whole or a substantial part of its activities are to be managed or organised; or
- the actual managing or organising of the whole or a substantial part of those activities.

This definition is an effort to prevent the problems that have arisen over identification of the 'brain' of a corporation. It covers a wider section of managers than that under the identification principle. However, it still restricts the range of people whose acts or omissions can make an organisation liable for corporate manslaughter. The Law Commission had proposed that individuals could also be liable for corporate manslaughter as secondary parties. However, the government decided not to implement this proposal. So, the Act does not provide for individual senior managers to be liable for corporate manslaughter.

Relevant duty of care

The relevant duty of care means any of the following duties owed under the law of negligence:

- a duty owed to employees or to other persons working for the organisation or performing services for it;
- a duty owed as occupier of premises;
- a duty owed in connection with:
  - (i) the supply by the organisation of goods and services (whether for consideration or not),
  - (ii) the carrying on by the organisation of any construction or maintenance operations,
  - (iii) the carrying on by the organisation of any other activity on a commercial basis, or
  - (iv) the use or keeping by the organisation of any plant, vehicle or other thing;
- a duty owed to those in detention.

ex turpi causa
From his own wrong act

volenti
Willingly (or consenting)

The duty of care is based on the civil law of negligence. However, the Act specifically excludes two rules that apply in civil negligence cases. These are the ***ex turpi causa*** rule and the ***volenti*** rule. The first is the common law rule whereby a duty of care is prevented from being owed by one person to another by reason of the fact that they are jointly engaged in unlawful conduct. The second is the common law rule that has the effect of preventing a duty of care from being owed to a person by reason of his acceptance of a risk of harm.

By excluding the defence that D and V were engaged jointly in criminal activity, the offence of corporate manslaughter is in line with the law on gross negligence manslaughter. It was ruled in *Wacker* [2003] EWCA Crim 1944 that the civil law defence of *ex turpi causa* did not apply to the criminal offence. (See section 10.4.2 for more details on the case of *Wacker*.)

The judge decides whether there is a relevant duty of care and the judge must make the findings of fact necessary to determine this question. This is contrasted with gross negligence manslaughter where the jury decide if a duty of care is owed.

Gross breach

Once a relevant duty of care has been established, then, under s 8(1)(b), the jury decide if there has been a gross breach.

Section 8 sets out matters that the jury *must* consider and those that they *may* consider.

SECTION

'8(2) The jury must consider whether the evidence shows that the organisation failed to comply with any health and safety legislation that relates to the alleged breach, and if so:

(a) how serious that failure was,

(b) how much of a risk of death it posed.

8(3) The jury may also:

(a) consider the extent to which the evidence shows that there were attitudes, policies, systems or accepted practices within the organisation that were likely to have encouraged any such failure as is mentioned in subsection (2), or to have produced tolerance of it,

(b) have regard to any health and safety guidance that relates to the alleged breach.'

The jury are not limited to considering only the matters in subclauses (2) and (3). In fact s 8(4) states that the section does not prevent the jury from having regard to any other matters they consider relevant.

The factors in s 8(3) are an attempt to cover situations such as the *Herald of Free Enterprise* case. (See *P & O European Ferries (Dover)* (1990) 93 Cr App R 72 at section 7.5.1.)

Penalties

The Act provides that organisations found guilty of corporate manslaughter can be fined an unlimited amount. In addition, it gives the court power to order the organisation to take specific steps to remedy the gross breach of a relevant duty of care or any other matter that appears to have resulted from that breach and been a cause of the death.

The Guidelines for sentencing say:

QUOTATION

'The offence of corporate manslaughter, because it requires gross breach at a senior level, will ordinarily involve a level of seriousness significantly greater than a health and safety offence. The appropriate fine will seldom be less than £500,000 and may be measured in millions of pounds.'

Sentencing Guidelines Council, Definitive Guideline: Corporate Manslaughter and Health and Safety Offences Causing Death (2010), para 24

7.5.4 Is the Act working?

There are several problems apparent in the working of the Corporate Manslaughter and Corporate Homicide Act. These include:

(a) is the Act being sufficiently used?

(b) the difficulty of prosecuting the corporate body under the Act and in the same trial prosecuting directors or managers for gross negligence manslaughter;

(c) plea bargaining;

(d) the level of fines.

The use of the Act

The Act came into force in 2008. Since then there has not been any significant increase in the number of prosecutions for corporate manslaughter. The government had stated in its Regulatory Impact Assessment, issued when the Act was being proposed, that it would be likely to result in 10 to 13 additional prosecutions for corporate manslaughter each year. In reality, in the first six years from the Act coming into force there have only been four prosecutions in total.

The first corporation to be convicted under the Act was Cotswold Geotechnical Holdings Ltd in 2011. The company appealed against both its conviction and sentence.

CASE EXAMPLE

Cotswold Geotechnical Holdings Ltd [2011] EWCA Crim 1337

A geologist went into a 'trial pit' which had been dug in order to obtain soil samples. The pit was at least 3.5 metres deep and the sides were not shored up. Pits over a depth of 1.2 metres should be shored up for safe working. The sides collapsed and the geologist was killed.

The company was small (only eight employees) and run by a Mr Eaton who had many years of experience with trial pits. The evidence was that Mr Eaton himself had entered the trial pit earlier the same day without any safety precautions. There had also been a previous incident in which a young employee had complained about being expected to go into unshored pits. The Health and Safety Executive had on that occasion reminded Mr Eaton of the need for shoring and he had given them assurances that in the future shoring would be used. The company was convicted of corporate manslaughter.

The other prosecutions to date have been:

(a) *JMW Farms Ltd* (unreported, 8 May 2012, Crown Court Belfast) where the company was convicted of corporate manslaughter under the provisions applying to Northern Ireland after an employee was killed in a forklift truck incident.

(b) *Lion Steel Equipment Ltd* (unreported, 20 July 2012, Manchester Crown Court) in which the company was convicted when a factory worker was killed falling through a roof. He had not been provided with walking boards or safety line and harness, nor had he been given any relevant training.

(c) *MNS Mining Ltd* (unreported, 19 June 2014, Swansea Crown Court) where the company was found not guilty of corporate manslaughter when four miners drowned following a controlled explosion underground in order to link two shafts and improve ventilation in the mine.

Although there have been very few prosecutions, the number of deaths at work is still high. The Fatal Accidents figures provided by the Health and Safety Executive show that, for 2012–2013, 148 people were killed in the course of their employment (49 of these were self-employed so corporate manslaughter would not be relevant). In the five years before that there was an average of 181 deaths per year (with an average of 52 being self-employed). In addition, for 2011–2013, 113 members of the public were fatally injured in accidents related to work and for the previous five years there had been an average of 67 members of the public killed in work-related incidents. These figures suggest that there are many more cases where prosecutions for corporate manslaughter might be brought.

Another noticeable feature is that none of the companies prosecuted were particularly large. This seems to undermine what was intended by the enactment of the Act.

The creation of the Act followed a series of high-profile cases where there had been unsuccessful prosecutions of large organisations under the common law of manslaughter (see section 7.5). It was hoped that it would make it easier to establish liability for deaths caused through bad management practice and result in more successful convictions.

Difficulty of prosecuting under two laws

The Act created a statutory offence whereby a corporation can be convicted of manslaughter. The Act did not create any corresponding liability for managers/directors. So while the corporate body is prosecuted under the Act, individuals have to be charged with the common law offence of gross negligence manslaughter. In the *Cotswold* case and the *Lion Steel Equipment Ltd* case (and also *MNS Mining Ltd*) the prosecutors charged directors of the companies with gross negligence manslaughter. In addition, it is usual for both the organisation and the directors to be charged with offences under the health and safety legislation. This means that a jury will have to consider and apply three different areas of law in a case.

In *Lion Steel Equipment Ltd*, as well as charging the company with corporate manslaughter, the prosecution sought the conviction of three directors for gross negligence manslaughter on the basis that each director owed every employee a duty to keep them safe. The judge rejected this argument stating that the office of director did not of itself create a duty, but that the evidence must be examined against each director individually. The judge also emphasised how high the threshold is for gross negligence manslaughter to be established. In addition, there were three further counts on the indictment under health and safety legislation. There was the extra complication in this case that there would be evidence on the gross negligence manslaughter and health and safety counts of events which occurred prior to the commencement of the 2007 Act. That evidence would not be admissible in relation to the corporate manslaughter charge. The judge took the view that a joint trial would have required directions to the jury of 'baffling complexity' and ordered that the corporate manslaughter count should be severed from the other counts. This meant that there would be a separate trial for the corporate manslaughter charge.

In the *Cotswold* case the manslaughter charge against the director was stayed because, by the time the trial took place, he was terminally ill. In the *MNS Mining* case the jury acquitted the director of gross negligence manslaughter.

Plea bargaining

The prosecution of directors also leads to the question of whether this puts pressure on them to enter a plea of guilty on behalf of the company. In *Lion Steel Equipment Ltd* (2012) three out of the company's four statutory directors were charged with gross negligence manslaughter and also under health and safety legislation. One of the directors was a financial director with no involvement in how the workforce operated. A second was in charge of a factory some 50 miles from where the accident had occurred. The judge found that there was no case to answer in respect of gross negligence manslaughter for the finance director and the director of the other factory. At the end of the prosecution case and before any defence evidence was called, the prosecution agreed not to pursue either the gross negligence manslaughter charge against the third director or the health and safety charges against all the directors. At the same time the company pleaded guilty to corporate manslaughter. Commentators have suggested that it is possible an informal bargain was struck between the prosecution and the defence, in order to secure a conviction against the company in return for the cases against the individuals being dropped.

Does this eagerness to charge directors even though they clearly are not involved in the day-to-day operations where the fatal accident took place suggest that pressure is being brought to bear on individuals (after all, manslaughter carries a maximum penalty of life imprisonment). Thus, as they are the decision-makers of the corporate body, they may decide on a guilty plea, in order that they as individuals are acquitted.

Level of fines

In 2010 the Sentencing Guidelines Council (now the Sentencing Council) issued guidelines on sentencing for corporate manslaughter. Paragraph 24 of the guidelines on sentencing for corporate manslaughter states:

QUOTATION

> 'The offence of corporate manslaughter, because it requires gross breach at a senior level, will ordinarily involve a level of seriousness significantly greater than a health and safety offence. The appropriate fine will seldom be less than £500,000 and may be measured in millions of pounds.'

However, the guidelines also allow the court to consider whether the fine would have the effect of putting the defendant out of business and whether that would be desirable. If the fine is so high that the business cannot continue to operate, then employees would lose their jobs.

In the cases to date the fines have not effectively been over £500,000. In the *Cotswold* case the fine was £385,000. This amount was two-and-a-half times the amount of the company's annual turnover, so in relation to the company's finance it was a large amount. The judge took into account the relatively small turnover of the company and the fact that it had financial problems. He allowed the fine to be paid off over a period of ten years. However, he recognised that the effect of the fine would probably be that the company would go into liquidation. That would be an unavoidable consequence. One of the reasons for the relatively high level of fine was that there had been a previous incident following which the director had promised that shoring would be used in future, but had not done this. The company appealed in respect of the level of the fine but the Court of Appeal upheld it.

Lion Steel Equipment Ltd was fined £480,000 to be paid in four instalments. The amount of the fine included a 20 per cent reduction for the company's guilty plea, so that the original starting point was £600,000. The company's annual profit was £1.5 million, so compared to the *Cotswold* case the fine was one which the company was able to pay. *JMW Farms Ltd* was fined £187,500 with six months to pay. In this case a 25 per cent reduction had been given for the guilty plea with the starting point being £250,000. The low level of fines in respect to the guidelines is partly accounted for by the fact that none of the companies were large organisations. Even so the levels can be criticised as being too low, particularly in respect of *JMW Farms Ltd* which had made a profit of £1.5 million in the previous financial year.

7.5.5 Why make organisations criminally liable for manslaughter?

It is sometimes argued that it is pointless making an organisation criminally liable. After all, the act and the intention are those of a human person within the organisation. Since that person can be prosecuted as an individual, why is it necessary to prosecute the organisation as well? For example, in *Kite and OLL Ltd* (1994) (unreported), the first successful prosecution of a corporation for manslaughter under the common law prior to the 2007 Act, the managing director was also convicted of manslaughter and given a prison sentence. The company was fined £60,000. Was it necessary or worthwhile to prosecute the company in addition to prosecuting the managing director? In that case, the company was very small and it did not have enough funds to pay the fine, so it was forced into liquidation. Fines on bigger companies are often too small to be effective. Imposing criminal liability on an organisation can be justified for three main reasons:

- Many of the recent disasters have not been caused by one individual. The poor practices throughout the company have contributed; in such circumstances it is just that the company should be liable.
- Many offences involve breaches of laws relating to health and safety; companies should be encouraged to take their responsibilities in these areas seriously and not to put profits before health and safety.
- The public perceive large companies and organisations as being above the law; when there has been a death through poor practice, relatives of victims want to see the company 'named and shamed'.

In addition, on a successful prosecution, the 2007 Act gives power to the court to order the organisation to take specific steps to remedy any matter that appears to the court to have caused the relevant breach and led to the death. This includes remedying any deficiency as regards health and safety matters in the organisation's policies, systems or practices which the breach appears to indicate.

ACTIVITY

Self-test questions

1. What exceptions are there to the general rule that a corporation can be criminally liable?
2. What difficulties are there in using the principle of identification to decide whether or not a corporation is criminally liable?
3. Apart from the principle of identification, in what other two ways can a corporation be criminally liable?
4. What has to be proved for the offence of corporate manslaughter to be established?
5. Why is it considered necessary to be able to make corporations liable for manslaughter?

ACTIVITY

Applying the law

In each of the following situations, explain whether the law will operate to impose criminal liability.

1. Crazy Golf Club is a members' club with a management committee of seven members. The club has a bar and employs a full-time steward and two part-time stewards to work there. The club has a licence to sell alcohol to members only. One of the part-time stewards sells an alcoholic drink to a non-member. Can the club be held criminally liable for the sale?
2. Getupandgo Ltd is a company which owns and operates leisure and activity centres. The company has a board of directors and a managing director. In addition, each centre has a manager. The board operates very tight financial controls over the amount to be spent at each centre on general maintenance, and centre managers who overspend know that they will face dismissal. Many of the activity centres have climbing walls. The board of directors

has never issued any directions about safety or the level of supervision for the use of these climbing walls. At one of the centres there have been no maintenance checks on the climbing wall and it has become unsafe. Safety helmets are provided for climbers but the centre manager has not instructed the staff to ensure that they are used. Harry, aged 14, climbs the wall without using a safety helmet. When he is near the top, part of the wall becomes detached, causing him to fall and be killed. The problem with the wall would have been discovered if there had been a maintenance check.

The company faces prosecution for:

a. manslaughter of Harry;
b. breach of safety legislation as the occupier of the building.

3. Den owns a newsagents' shop. He employs Ella as a sales assistant and Freddy as a cleaner. Cigarettes are sold in the shop and Den has told Ella that she must not sell these to anyone under the age of 16, and if she is not sure then she must ask for proof of age. Ella sells a packet to a boy who looks at least 18. She is so convinced that he is over 16 she does not ask him for proof of his age. Later in the day Ella cuts her finger and needs to leave the till. As she does not want to leave it unattended she asks Freddy to mind it for her. During the time that Ella is absent Freddy sells a packet of cigarettes to a girl aged 12.

   Will liability be imposed on Den for:

   a. the sale by Ella?
   b. the sale by Freddy?

SUMMARY

Children

Children under ten are presumed incapable of forming the *mens rea* for any offence – *doli incapax*.

- Civil law allows care proceedings to be taken or a 'child safety order' to be made where a child under ten has committed an act which would have been an offence had he been aged ten or over.
- Children aged ten and over are responsible for the crimes.
- Trial arrangements are different from those for adults – trial for all but most serious offences will be in the Youth Court. When a child is tried in the Crown Court then special arrangements must be made to ensure that the child can participate effectively.

Mentally ill offenders

Unfitness to plead

Where because of his mental state the defendant is unable to understand the charge against him so as to be able to make a proper defence, he may be found unfit to plead. If D is so found then a jury must then decide whether D 'did the act or made the omission charged against him'. If so the judge can then make:

- a hospital order (with or without a restriction order);
- a supervision and treatment order;
- an absolute discharge.

The Law Commission has consulted on reform of the law.

Insanity

Where a person is fit to plead but it is found that he was insane at the time of the offence D is found 'not guilty by reason of insanity'. The judge can make a hospital order, a supervision order or an absolute discharge.

Diminished responsibility
This only applies where D is charged with murder. If established it reduces the charge to manslaughter.

Vicarious liability
The normal rule is that one person cannot be liable for crimes of another.

- Exceptions are for common law offences of public nuisance and criminal libel and statutory offences through the extended meanings of words or under the principle of delegation.
- The main categories of people who can be vicariously liable are principals, employers and licensees.
- Vicarious liability helps enforce regulations about such matters as selling food and alcohol and using vehicles.
- It can be criticised where the person has taken all reasonable precautions to ensure that no offence is committed.

Corporate liability
A corporation has a legal personality. It can be criminally liable through:

- the principle of identification;
- vicarious liability;
- breach of statutory duty.

Identification is where senior managers can be identified as the 'directing mind and will' of the corporation. This can be difficult if there are many layers of management or where several people have contributed to the making of a dangerous situation.

Vicarious liability is where the acts or omissions of its employees can make the corporation liable.

Breach of statutory duty mostly occurs where a statute makes the corporation liable as occupier or employer.

Corporate manslaughter
Because of the difficulty of proving manslaughter against big corporations the government passed the Corporate Manslaughter and Corporate Homicide Act 2007.

- This makes a corporation guilty of manslaughter if the way in which any of its activities are managed or organised causes a death and amounts to gross breach of a relevant duty.
- A corporation will only be liable if the way in which its activities are managed or organised by its senior management is a substantial element in the breach.
- The jury must consider whether the evidence shows that the organisation failed to comply with any health and safety legislation that relates to the alleged breach, and if so –

  (a) how serious that failure was;

  (b) how much of a risk of death it posed.
- The jury may consider the extent to which the evidence shows that there were attitudes, policies, systems or accepted practices within the organisation that were likely to have encouraged or tolerated any such failure.

SAMPLE ESSAY QUESTION

To what extent has the Corporate Manslaughter and Corporate Homicide Act 2007 satisfactorily reformed the law on corporate manslaughter?

State the law before the 2007 Act:

- Offence of gross negligence at common law
- The principle of vicarious liability
- The need to identify the 'brain' of the corporation
- Expand identification principle with cases, e.g. *ICR Haulage Ltd* (1944), *Tesco v Nattrass* (1972), *P & O European Ferries (Dover)* (1991)

Explain difficulties of previous law especially:

- Problem where failures by a number of people in the corporation had led to the situation causing death
- The decision in *A-G's Ref (No 2 of 1999)* (2000) that there must be evidence of guilt of a human person before the corporation could be liable
- Very few successful prosecutions

State the law under the 2007 Act:

Definition of offence s 1(1)

Expand on elements:

- relies on way in which activities are managed
- gross breach of a duty of care
- way in which activities are managed or organised by senior management must be a substantial element in the breach

Discuss points such as:

- 2007 Act applies to organisations not just corporations
- Points jury must/may consider for gross breach
- Concept of management failure
- No longer need to identify a specific individual as 'mind and will'
- Senior management failure need only be a substantial element
- The power of the court to make a remedial order

Consider potential problems in new law – e.g.:

- Jury to decide if there is gross negligence – will this be consistent?
- Still need to identify senior management but wider than under identification principle
- Act does not provide for individuals to be liable, although Law Commission recommended this
- Will relatives of V be satisfied if no individual is charged?

Conclude

Further reading

Books

Ormerod, D, *Smith and Hogan Criminal Law* (13th edn, Oxford University Press, 2011), Chapter 10.

Articles

Forlin, G, 'A softly, softly approach' (2006) NLJ 907.

Griffin, S, 'Corporate manslaughter: a radical reform? (2007) 71 J Crim L 151.

Keeting, H, 'Reckless children' (2007) Crim LR 547.

Jefferson, M, 'Corporate liability in the 1990s' (2000) 64 J Crim L 106.

Mackay, R D, 'Unfitness to plead: some observations of the Law Commission's consultation paper' (2011) Crim LR 433.

Pace, P J, 'Delegation – A doctrine in search of a definition' (1982) Crim LR 627.

Slapper, G, 'Justice is mocked if an important law is unenforced' (2013) J Crim L 91.

Sullivan, R, 'Corporate killing: some government proposals' (2001) Crim LR 31.

Woodley, M, 'Bargaining over corporate manslaughter: what price a life? (2013) J Crim L 33.

Internet links

http://lawcommission.justice.gov.uk for Law Commission reports and consultation papers.

http://sentencingcouncil.judiciary.gov.uk for sentencing guidelines.

www.hse.gov.uk for statistics on fatal accidents at work.

8

General defences

AIMS AND OBJECTIVES

After reading this chapter you should be able to:

- Understand the law on duress and necessity
- Understand the law on mistake
- Understand the law on self-defence
- Understand the law on consent
- Analyse critically the scope and limitations of the general defences and the reform proposals for the general defences
- Apply the law to factual situations to determine whether liability can be avoided by invoking a defence

8.1 Duress

duress
General defence where D is forced by threats or circumstances to commit an offence

With this defence, D is admitting that he committed the *actus reus* of the offence, with *mens rea*, but is claiming that he did so because he was faced with threats of immediate serious injury or even death, either to himself or to others close to him, if he did not commit the offence. **Duress** is not a denial of *mens rea*, like intoxication (see Chapter 9), or a plea that D's act was justified, as is the case with self-defence (see below). Rather, D is seeking to be excused, because his actions were involuntary – not in the literal, physical sense of the word, but on the basis that D had no other choice. In *Lynch v DPP of Northern Ireland* [1975] AC 653, Lord Morris said:

JUDGMENT

'It is proper that any rational system of law should take fully into account the standards of honest and reasonable men … If then someone is really threatened with death or serious injury unless he does what he is told is the law to pay no heed to the miserable, agonising plight of such a person? For the law to understand not only how the timid but also the stalwart may in a moment of crisis behave is not to make the law weak but to make it just.'

8.1.1 Sources of the duress

Duress comes in two types:

- Duress by threats: here, D is threatened by another person to commit a criminal offence. For example, D is ordered at gunpoint to drive armed robbers away from the scene of a robbery or he will be shot.
- Duress of circumstances (sometimes referred to as 'necessity', but in this chapter necessity will be dealt with separately): here, the threat does not come from a person, but the circumstances in which D finds himself.

The principles applying are identical in either case of duress. The principles were originally established in duress by threat cases and subsequently applied to duress of circumstances.

8.1.2 The seriousness of the threat

The threats must be of death or serious personal injury (*Hudson and Taylor* [1971] 2 QB 202; *Hasan* [2005] UKHL 22; [2005] 2 AC 467). In *A* [2012] EWCA Crim 434; [2012] 2 Cr App R 8, Lord Judge CJ stated that duress 'involves pressure which arises in extreme circumstances, the threat of death or serious injury, which for the avoidance of any misunderstanding, we have no doubt would also include rape'. Strictly speaking, this comment was *obiter*, because the Court of Appeal rejected A's appeal against her conviction on the ground of lack of evidence that she had, in fact, been threatened with rape. However, it seems perfectly sensible to regard rape as an example of 'serious personal injury'. In *A*, the Court of Appeal emphasised that 'pressure' falling short of a threat of death or serious injury did not support a plea of duress. This was designed to prevent the floodgates being opened because, as Lord Judge stated, 'the circumstances in which different individuals are subject to pressures, or perceive that they are under pressure, are virtually infinite'.

A threat to damage or destroy property is therefore insufficient (*M'Growther* [1746] Fost 13). In *Lynch* (1975), Lord Simon said: 'The law must draw a line somewhere; and as a result of experience and human valuation, the law draws it between threats to property and threats to the person.' Similarly, threats to expose a secret sexual orientation are insufficient (*Singh* [1974] 1 All ER 26; *Valderrama-Vega* [1985] Crim LR 220). In *Baker and Wilkins* [1996] EWCA Crim 1126; [1997] Crim LR 497, a duress of circumstances case, the Court of Appeal refused to accept an argument that the scope of the defence should be extended to cases where D believed the act was immediately necessary to avoid serious psychological injury as well as death or serious physical injury. More recently, in *Dao, Mai and Nguyen* [2012] EWCA Crim 1717, the Court of Appeal was asked whether a threat of false imprisonment would support a plea of duress. The Court found it unnecessary to reach a firm decision on the point – there was insufficient evidence of the appellants having been threatened with imprisonment, as they claimed – but did express a 'provisional' view, namely, that 'we would have been strongly disinclined to accept that a threat of false imprisonment suffices for the defence of duress … In our judgment, even if only provisionally, policy considerations point strongly towards confining the defence of duress to threats of death or serious injury.'

Although there must be a threat of death or serious personal injury, it need not be the sole reason why D committed the offence with which he is charged. This was seen in *Valderrama-Vega*.

CASE EXAMPLE

Valderrama-Vega [1985] Crim LR 220

D claimed that he had imported cocaine because of death threats made by a Mafia-type organisation. But he also needed the money because he was heavily in debt to his bank. Furthermore, he had been threatened with having his homosexuality disclosed. His conviction was quashed by the Court of Appeal: the jury had been directed he only had a defence if the death threats were the sole reason for acting.

ACTIVITY

In the light of the House of Lords' decision in *Ireland, Burstow* [1998] AC 147 to extend the scope of the phrase 'bodily harm' in the context of s 20 and s 47 OAPA 1861 to include psychiatric harm, discuss whether the Court of Appeal's decision in *Baker and Wilkins* is justifiable.

8.1.3 Threats against whom?

At one time it seemed that, in cases of duress by threats, the threat had to be directed at D personally. However, in *Ortiz* (1986) 83 Cr App R 173, D had been forced into taking part in a cocaine-smuggling operation after he was told that, if he refused, his wife and children would 'disappear'. At his trial, D pleaded duress by threats, but the jury rejected the defence. The trial judge had directed them that 'duress is a defence if a man acts solely as a result of threats of death or serious injury to himself or another'. The Court of Appeal did not disapprove of the inclusion in the direction of 'threats ... to another'. The view that the threats could be directed at someone other than D was confirmed in the early duress of circumstances cases, *Conway* [1988] 3 All ER 1025 and *Martin* [1989] 1 All ER 652. In the former case, the defence was allowed when D's passenger in his car was threatened and in the latter case D's wife threatened to harm herself. It is now well established that the threats can be directed towards members of D's immediate family, or indeed to 'some other person, for whose safety D would reasonably regard himself as responsible', according to Kennedy LJ in *Wright* [2000] Crim LR 510.

CASE EXAMPLE

Wright [2000] Crim LR 510

D had been arrested at Gatwick Airport with four kilos of cocaine worth nearly £0.5 million hidden under her clothing, having just flown in from St Lucia. She was charged with trying to import unlawful drugs and pleaded duress. She claimed that she had flown to St Lucia in order to bring back the drugs under threat of violence from her drug dealer, to whom she was £3,000 in debt. In St Lucia, D was threatened with a gun and told that her boyfriend Darren (who had flown out to join her) would be killed if she did not go through with the trip; she was also told that Darren would only be allowed to return to the United Kingdom once she had reached Gatwick. This meant that when she was arrested at Gatwick, she was still fearful for Darren's life. However, she was convicted after the trial judge directed the jury that duress was only available if a threat was directed at D herself or at a 'member of her immediate family'. He reminded the jury that D did not live with Darren and was not married to him. D was convicted but the Court of Appeal allowed her appeal (although it ordered a retrial). Kennedy LJ said that 'it was both unnecessary and undesirable for the judge to trouble the jury with the question of Darren's proximity. Still less to suggest, as he did, that Darren was insufficiently proximate.' The question for the jury should simply have been whether D had good cause to fear that if she did not import the drugs, she or Darren would be killed or seriously injured.

ACTIVITY

Applying the law

1. D is accosted in his car by armed robbers who direct him to drive them away, or they will shoot randomly into a group of schoolchildren at a bus stop. Should D have a defence of duress if charged with aiding and abetting armed robbery?
2. This question was posed by Professor Sir John Smith in his commentary on *Wright* in the Criminal Law Review: could a fan of Manchester United be reasonably expected to resist a threat to kill the team's star player if he did not participate in a robbery?

8.1.4 Imminence of the threat, opportunities to escape and police protection

Imminence of the threat

The threat must have been operative on D, or other parties, at the moment he committed the offence. This was established in *Hudson and Taylor* [1971] 2 QB 202.

CASE EXAMPLE

Hudson and Taylor [1971] 2 QB 202

D, aged 17, and E, aged 19, were the principal prosecution witnesses at the trial of a man called Jimmy Wright. He had been charged with malicious wounding. Both D and E had been in the pub where the wounding was alleged to have occurred and gave statements to the police. At the trial, however, the girls failed to identify Wright, and, as a result, he was acquitted. In due course, the girls were charged with perjury (lying in court). D claimed that another man, F, who had a reputation for violence, had threatened her that if she 'told on Wright in court' she would be cut up. She passed this threat on to E, and the result was that they were too frightened to identify Wright (especially when they arrived in court and saw F in the public gallery). The trial judge withdrew the defence of duress from the jury because the threat of harm could not be immediately put into effect when they were testifying in the safety of the courtroom. Their convictions were quashed.

Lord Widgery CJ said:

JUDGMENT

'When … there is no opportunity for delaying tactics and the person threatened must make up his mind whether he is to commit the criminal act or not, the existence at that moment of threats sufficient to destroy his will ought to provide him with a defence even though the threatened injury may not follow instantly but after an interval.'

In *Abdul-Hussain and others* [1999] Crim LR 570, confirmed in *Safi and others* [2003] EWCA Crim 1809, the Court of Appeal decided that, for the defence of duress to be available, the threat to D (or other persons) had to be believed by D to be 'imminent' but not necessarily 'immediate'. This led the Court of Appeal to quash hijacking convictions in both cases because the trial judge had directed the jury to disregard the threat to the defendants unless the threat was believed by D to be 'immediate'. However, when the House of Lords came to examine this issue, in *Hasan* [2005] UKHL 22; [2005] 2 AC 467, that court decided that the correct test was that the threat had to be believed by D to be 'immediate' or 'almost immediate'. Giving the leading judgment, Lord Bingham said:

JUDGMENT

'It should be made clear to juries that if the retribution threatened against the defendant or his family or a person for whom he reasonably feels responsible is not such as he reasonably expects to follow immediately or almost immediately on his failure to comply with the threat, there may be little if any room for doubt that he could have taken evasive action, whether by going to the police or in some other way, to avoid committing the crime with which he is charged.'

The *Hasan* case will be examined in more detail below.

Opportunities to escape and police protection

D will be expected to take advantage of any reasonable opportunity that he has to escape from the duressor and/or contact the police. If he fails to take it, the defence may fail. This was illustrated in *Gill* [1963] 2 All ER 688. D claimed that he had been threatened with violence if he did not steal a lorry. The Court of Criminal Appeal expressed doubts whether the defence was open, as there was a period of time in which he could have raised the alarm and wrecked the whole enterprise. In *Pommell* [1995] 2 Cr App R 607, Kennedy LJ accepted that 'in some cases a delay, especially if unexplained, may be such as to make it clear that any duress must have ceased to operate, in which case the judge would be entitled to conclude that ... the defence was not open'.

CASE EXAMPLE

Pommell [1995] 2 Cr App R 607

Police found D at 8 a.m. lying in bed with a loaded gun in his hand. He claimed that, during the night, a man called Erroll had come to see him, intent on shooting some people who had killed Erroll's friend. D had persuaded Erroll to give him the gun, which he took upstairs. This was between 12.30 a.m. and 1.30 a.m. D claimed that he had intended to hand the gun over to the police the next day. D was convicted of possessing a prohibited weapon, contrary to the Firearms Act 1968, after the trial judge refused to allow the defence of duress to go to the jury. This was on the basis that, even if D had been forced to take the gun, he should have gone immediately to the police. The Court of Appeal allowed the appeal on the basis that this was too restrictive and ordered a retrial.

In *Hudson and Taylor* (1971), the Crown contended that D and E should have sought police protection. Lord Widgery CJ rejected this argument, which, he said 'would, in effect, restrict the defence ... to cases where the person threatened had been kept in custody by the maker of the threats, or where the time interval between the making of the threats and the commission of the offence had made recourse to the police impossible'. Although the defence had to be kept 'within reasonable grounds', the Crown's argument would impose too 'severe' a restriction. He concluded that 'in deciding whether [an escape] opportunity was reasonably open to the accused the jury should have regard to his age and circumstances and to any risks to him which may be involved in the course of action relied upon'.

8.1.5 Duress does not exist in the abstract

It is only a defence if the defendant commits some specific crime which was nominated by the person making the threat. This was seen in *Cole* [1994] Crim LR 582, where money-lenders were pressuring D for money. They had threatened him, as well as his girlfriend and child, and hit him with a baseball bat. Eventually, D robbed two building societies.

To a charge of robbery he pleaded duress, but the judge held that the defence was not available and withdrew it from the jury. D's conviction was upheld by the Court of Appeal: the defence was only available where the threats were directed to the commission of the particular offence charged. The duressors had not said 'Go and rob a building society or else … '.

This was also the outcome in a recent case in the Supreme Court of Canada, *Ryan* [2013] 1 SCR 14. D was charged with counselling murder. She had agreed to pay a hitman $25,000 to have her husband, V, who was violent and abusive, killed. In fact, the 'hitman' was an undercover police officer, and D was arrested. In her defence she pleaded duress on the basis that V had often made threats to kill her and their daughter. The trial judge accepted this and ordered an acquittal. The Crown appealed, and the Supreme Court allowed the appeal on the basis that the defence of duress by threats was only available when a person committed an offence whilst under compulsion of a threat made for the purpose of compelling him or her to commit a specific offence.

8.1.6 Voluntary exposure to risk of compulsion

D will be denied the defence if he voluntarily places himself in such a situation that he risks being threatened with violence to commit crime. This may be because he joins a criminal organisation. In *Fitzpatrick* [1977] NI 20, D pleaded duress to a catalogue of offences, including murder, even though he was a voluntary member of the IRA. The trial judge rejected the defence, stating that 'If a man chooses to expose himself and still more if he chooses to submit himself to illegal compulsion, it may not operate even in mitigation of punishment.' Any other conclusion he said 'would surely be monstrous'. The Northern Ireland Court of Appeal dismissed the appeal. In *Sharp* [1987] 3 All ER 103, the Court of Appeal confirmed that duress was not available where D had voluntarily joined a 'criminal organisation or gang'.

CASE EXAMPLE

Sharp [1987] 3 All ER 103

D and two other men had attempted an armed robbery of a sub-post office but were thwarted when the sub-postmaster pressed an alarm. As they made their escape, one of the others fired a shotgun in the air to deter pursuers. Three weeks later they carried out a second armed robbery, which resulted in the murder of the sub-postmaster. D claimed that he was only the 'bagman', that he was not armed and only took part in the second robbery because he had been threatened with having his head blown off by one of the others if he did not cooperate. The trial judge withdrew the defence, and D was convicted of manslaughter, robbery and attempted robbery. The Court of Appeal upheld the convictions. The Court treated it as significant that D knew of the others' violent and trigger-happy nature several weeks before he attempted to withdraw from the enterprise.

Lord Lane CJ said:

JUDGMENT

'Where a person has voluntarily, and with knowledge of its nature, joined a criminal organisation or gang which he knew might bring pressure on him to commit an offence and was an active member when he was put under such pressure, he cannot avail himself of the defence.'

This principle has been confirmed, and extended, in a number of subsequent cases. It is now firmly established that D does not necessarily have to have joined a criminal organisation (as in *Lynch* (1975) or *Sharp*). Voluntarily associating with persons with a propensity for violence (typically, by buying unlawful drugs from suppliers) may well be enough to deny the defence.

- *Ali* [1995] Crim LR 303 and *Baker and Ward* [1999] EWCA Crim 913; [1999] 2 Cr App R 335 both concerned drug users who pleaded duress to robbery, having become indebted to their supplier and having then been threatened with violence if they did not find the money. In each case the Court of Appeal confirmed the defence would be denied in situations where D voluntarily placed himself in a position where the threat of violence was likely.
- In *Heath* [1999] EWCA Crim 1526; [2000] Crim LR 109, D was a drug user who had become heavily indebted to a man with a reputation for violence and who had threatened D with violence if he did not deliver a consignment of 98 kilos of cannabis from Lincolnshire to Bristol. D was caught and charged with being in possession of cannabis. He pleaded duress, but the defence was denied and he was convicted. The Court of Appeal rejected his appeal. D had voluntarily associated himself with the drug world, knowing that in that world, debts are collected via intimidation and violence.
- *Harmer* [2001] EWCA Crim 2930; [2002] Crim LR 401 was factually very similar to *Heath*. D had been caught at Dover docks trying to smuggle cocaine, hidden inside a box of washing-up powder, into the United Kingdom. At his trial D pleaded duress on the basis that his supplier had forced him to do it or suffer violence. D admitted that he had knowingly involved himself with criminals (he was a drug addict and had to have a supplier to get drugs) and knew that his supplier might use or threaten violence. However, he said that he had not appreciated that his supplier would demand that he get involved in crime. The defence was denied, and D was convicted; the Court of Appeal upheld his conviction, following *Heath*. Voluntary exposure to unlawful violence was enough to exclude the defence.

Professor Sir John Smith was critical of the decision in *Harmer*. He wrote in the commentary to the case in the Criminal Law Review that 'the joiner may know that he may be subjected to compulsion, but compulsion to pay one's debts is one thing, compulsion to commit crime is quite another'. Given the judicial uncertainty and academic criticism of the law, it was perhaps inevitable that the House of Lords would eventually be asked to clarify the position regarding the availability of duress when D voluntarily associates himself with a criminal gang or organisation. In *Hasan* [2005] UKHL 22; [2005] 2 AC 467, the Court of Appeal had quashed D's conviction of aggravated burglary but certified a question for the consideration of the House of Lords, seeking to establish whether the defence of duress is excluded when, as a result of the accused's voluntary association with others

1. he foresaw (or possibly should have foreseen) the risk of being then and there subjected to *any compulsion* by threats of violence; or
2. only when he foresaw (or should have foreseen) the risk of being subjected to compulsion to *commit criminal offences*; and, if the latter
3. only if the offences foreseen (or which should have been foreseen) were of the same type (or possibly the same type and gravity) as that ultimately committed.

The Lords reinstated D's conviction after taking the view that option (1) above correctly stated the law. By a four to one majority, the Lords confirmed that it was sufficient if D should have foreseen the risk of being subjected to 'any compulsion'.

CASE EXAMPLE

Hasan [2005] UKHL 22; [2005] 2 AC 467

Z, a driver and minder for Y, a prostitute, had been threatened by Y's boyfriend, X, who had a reputation as a violent gangster and drug dealer, to carry out a burglary. Z attempted to burgle a house, armed with a gun, but was scared off by the householder. Z was charged with aggravated burglary and pleaded duress. The trial judge directed the jury that the defence was not available if Z had voluntarily placed himself in a position in which threats of violence were likely. Z was convicted, and although the Court of Appeal quashed his conviction, it was reinstated by the House of Lords.

Lord Bingham stated:

JUDGMENT

'The defence of duress is excluded when as a result of the accused's voluntary association with others engaged in criminal activity he foresaw or ought reasonably to have foreseen the risk of being subjected to any compulsion by threats of violence.'

Only Baroness Hale departed from the majority: she would have preferred to take option (2). None of the five judges chose option (3). The case of *Baker and Ward* [1999] EWCA Crim 913, in which the Court of Appeal had decided that D had to foresee that he would be compelled to commit offences of the type with which he was charged (i.e. option (3)), was therefore overruled. However, the judgments in the other Court of Appeal cases, including *Heath* and *Harmer*, have now been confirmed.

Hasan was applied in *Ali* [2008] EWCA Crim 716, where D was charged with robbery. He had taken a Golf Turbo car on a test drive but then forced the car salesman out of the car at knifepoint before driving off. At his trial, D claimed that he had been threatened with violence by a man called Hussein if he did not commit the robbery. However, his duress defence was rejected on the basis that he had been friends with Hussein, who had a violent reputation, for many years. In the words of the trial judge, D had chosen to join 'very bad company'. Dismissing D's appeal, Dyson LJ stated:

JUDGMENT

'The core question is whether [D] voluntarily put himself in the position in which he foresaw or ought reasonably to have foreseen the risk of being subjected to any compulsion by threats of violence. As a matter of fact, threats of violence will almost always be made by persons engaged in a criminal activity; but in our judgment it is the risk of being subjected to compulsion by threats of violence that must be foreseen or foreseeable that is relevant, rather than the nature of the activity in which the threatener is engaged.'

One case in which the defence of duress succeeded, despite D voluntarily associating himself with a criminal gang, is *Shepherd* [1987] Crim LR 686. The decision in *Hasan* confirms that this case, too, was correctly decided. In *Shepherd*, D had joined a gang of apparently non-violent shoplifters. When charged with theft, D had pleaded duress on the basis that when he tried to leave the gang, one of the other members had threatened him and his family with violence. The trial judge had refused to put the defence to the jury, and D was convicted. The Court of Appeal allowed his appeal. Mustill LJ said:

JUDGMENT

'Common sense must recognise that there are certain kinds of criminal enterprises the joining of which, in the absence of any knowledge of propensity to violence on the part of one member, would not lead another to suspect that a decision to think better of the whole affair might lead him into serious trouble. The logic which appears to underlie the law of duress would suggest that if trouble did unexpectedly materialise and if it put the defendant into a dilemma in which a reasonable man might have chosen to act as he did, the concession to human frailty should not be denied to him.'

8.1.7 Should D have resisted the threats?

The defence is not available just because D reacted to a threat; the threat must be one that the ordinary man would not have resisted. In *Graham* [1982] 1 All ER 801, Lord Lane CJ laid down the following test to be applied by juries in future cases whenever duress was pleaded:

JUDGMENT

'The correct approach on the facts of this case would have been as follows: (1) Was [D], or may he have been, impelled to act as he did because, as a result of what he reasonably believed [the duressor] had said or done, he had good cause to fear that if he did not so act [the duressor] would kill him or ... cause him serious physical injury? (2) If so, have the prosecution made the jury sure that a sober person of reasonable firmness, sharing the characteristics of [D], would not have responded to whatever he reasonably believed [the duressor] said or did by taking part in the killing?'

In *Howe and Bannister* [1987] AC 417, the House of Lords approved the *Graham* test. It is clear that the same test applies (with appropriate modification to the wording to indicate the source of the threats) to duress of circumstances. The test is carefully framed in such a way to ensure the burden of proof remains on the prosecution at all times (although D must raise evidence of duress). If the jury believe that D may have been threatened and that the reasonable man might have responded to it, then they should acquit.

The first question

The first question, relating to D's belief, is essentially (if not entirely) subjective. That is, if the jury are satisfied that D reasonably believed he faced a threat of death or serious injury and that the belief gave him 'good cause', then the first question is answered in D's favour. This issue was examined by the Court of Appeal in *Nethercott* [2001] EWCA Crim 2535; [2002] Crim LR 402. D had been convicted of attempting to dishonestly obtain jewellery in May 1999. At his trial he had pleaded duress, relying on evidence that his co-accused, E, had stabbed him (a separate offence for which E had been charged with attempted murder) and that he therefore reasonably believed that if he did not take part in the crime, he had good cause to fear death or serious injury. The only problem for D was that the stabbing took place in August 1999 – three months after the alleged attempt. The trial judge refused to admit this evidence, and D was convicted. However, the Court of Appeal quashed his conviction. Evidence that E had stabbed D in August was relevant to the question whether, in May, he reasonably believed that E might kill or seriously injure him. It must be emphasised that there is no requirement that what D feared actually existed. This point was made clear in *Cairns* [1999] EWCA Crim 468; [1999] 2 Cr App R 137, a duress of circumstances case.

CASE EXAMPLE

Cairns [1999] EWCA Crim 468; [1999] 2 Cr App R 137

V, who was inebriated, stepped out in front of D's car, forcing him to stop. V climbed on to the bonnet and spread-eagled himself on it. D drove off with V on the bonnet. A group of V's friends ran after the car, shouting and gesticulating (they claimed later that they just wanted to stop V, not do any harm to D). D had to brake in order to drive over a speed bump, V fell off in front of the car, and was run over, suffering serious injury. D was convicted of inflicting grievous bodily harm (GBH) with intent contrary to s 18 OAPA 1861, after the trial judge ruled that the defence of duress of circumstances was only available when 'actually necessary to avoid the evil in question'. However, the Court of Appeal quashed the conviction. It was not necessary that the threat (or, in the judge's words, 'evil in question') was, in fact, real.

The principle that it is D's *belief* in the existence of a threat, as opposed to its existence in fact, was confirmed in *Safi and others* (2003).

CASE EXAMPLE

Safi and others [2003] EWCA Crim 1809

The appellants in this case had hijacked a plane in Afghanistan and ordered it to be flown to the United Kingdom, in order to escape the perceived threat of death or injury at the hands of the Taliban. (The facts of the case occurred in February 2000, i.e. before the overthrow of the Taliban regime by American-led military forces in 2002.) At their trial for hijacking, false imprisonment (relating to the appellants' failure to release the other passengers after the plane's arrival in the United Kingdom until three days had elapsed) and other charges, the appellants pleaded duress of circumstances. This was disputed by the Crown, and the jury at the first trial failed to agree. At the retrial, the trial judge told the jury to examine whether the appellants were in imminent peril (as opposed to whether they reasonably believed that they were in imminent peril). The Court of Appeal allowed the appeal and quashed the convictions. Longmore LJ suggested that, if public policy demanded the existence of an actual threat, as opposed to a reasonably perceived one, it was for Parliament to change the law.

The subjective limb as defined in *Graham* (1982) and approved in *Howe and Bannister* (1987) does have two objective aspects. First, D's belief must have been reasonable. Thus, if D honestly (but unreasonably) believes that he is being threatened and commits an offence, the defence is not available. Hence, if D's belief was based purely on his own imagination, it would not be difficult for a jury to conclude that his (honest) belief was unreasonable. This may be contrasted with the position in self-defence. There, if D believes he is being attacked and reacts in self-defence, he is entitled to be judged as if the facts were as he (honestly) believed them to be (*Williams* [1987] 3 All ER 411). One rationale for this difference could be that self-defence is a justification, while duress is 'only' an excuse. After a period of doubt on this point, in *Hasan* [2005] UKHL 22; [2005] 2 AC 467, the House of Lords confirmed that D's belief must be reasonable. Giving the leading judgment, Lord Bingham said that 'It is of course essential that the defendant should genuinely, that is actually, believe in the efficacy of the threat by which he claims to have been compelled. But there is no warrant for relaxing the requirement that the belief must be reasonable as well as genuine.'

A recent case demonstrates that, if D's belief is genuine – but unreasonable – then it will not support a plea of duress.

CASE EXAMPLE

S [2012] EWCA Crim 389; [2012] 1 Cr App R 31

S was charged with abducting her own daughter, L, contrary to s 1 of the Child Abduction Act 1984. S was divorced from L's father, but both parents shared custody. Under the terms of the divorce, neither parent was allowed to take L out of the country without the prior permission of the other parent or the High Court. In fact, S took her daughter to Spain without permission. S was tracked down in Gibraltar and ordered to return L to the United Kingdom, which she did. At her trial, S pleaded duress (of circumstances), based on her belief that there was an imminent risk of serious physical harm to L from sexual abuse from L's father. This was rejected, and the Court of Appeal upheld the guilty verdict. Sir John Thomas said that 'there could be no reasonable belief that a threat was imminent nor could it be said that a person was acting reasonably and proportionately by removing the child from the jurisdiction in order to avoid the threat of serious injury'.

The second objective aspect is that D's belief must have given him 'good cause' to fear death or serious injury. Thus, even if D genuinely (and reasonably) believed that death or serious injury would be done to him but, objectively (i.e. in the opinion of the jury), death or serious injury was unlikely, then the defence fails.

The second question

This question is objective, although certain characteristics of D will be attributed to the reasonable person. In *Graham* (1982), Lord Lane CJ said:

JUDGMENT

'As a matter of public policy, it seems to us essential to limit the defence of duress by means of an objective criterion formulated in terms of reasonableness … The law [of provocation] requires a defendant to have the self-control reasonably to be expected of the ordinary citizen in his situation. It should likewise require him to have the steadfastness reasonably to be expected of the ordinary citizen in his situation.'

Thus, if the ordinary person, sharing the characteristics of D, would have resisted the threats, the defence is unavailable. The relevant characteristics will include age and sex and, potentially at least, other permanent physical and mental attributes which would affect the ability of D to resist pressure and threats. In *Hegarty* [1994] Crim LR 353, however, the Court of Appeal held that the trial judge had correctly refused to allow D's characteristic of being in a 'grossly elevated neurotic state', which made him vulnerable to threats, to be considered as relevant. Similarly, in *Horne* [1994] Crim LR 584, the Court of Appeal agreed that evidence that D was unusually pliable and vulnerable to pressure did not mean that these characteristics had to be attributed to the reasonable man. In *Bowen* [1996] Crim LR 577, the Court of Appeal said that the following characteristics were obviously relevant:

- Age, as a young person may not be so robust as a mature one.
- Pregnancy, where there was an added fear for the unborn child.
- Serious physical disability, as that might inhibit self-protection.
- Recognised mental illness or psychiatric condition, such as post-traumatic stress disorder leading to learned helplessness. Psychiatric evidence might be admissible to show that D was suffering from such condition, provided persons generally suffering

them might be more susceptible to pressure and threats. It was not admissible simply to show that in a doctor's opinion D, not suffering from such illness or condition, was especially timid, suggestible or vulnerable to pressure and threats.

Finally, D's gender might possibly be relevant, although the court thought that many women might consider that they had as much moral courage to resist pressure as men. The Court of Appeal dismissed D's appeal holding that a low IQ – falling short of mental impairment or mental defectiveness – could not be said to be a characteristic that made those who had it less courageous and less able to withstand threats and pressure. The decision in *Bowen* to allow evidence of post-traumatic stress disorder leading to learned helplessness as a characteristic is interesting, and not particularly easy to reconcile with the earlier decisions of *Hegarty* and *Horne*. A jury faced with the question, 'Would the ordinary person, displaying the firmness reasonably to be expected of a person of the defendant's age and sex suffering from learnt helplessness have yielded to the threat?' is almost certain to answer in the affirmative, except if the threat was very trivial indeed.

8.1.8 The scope of the defence

Duress (either by threats or circumstances or both) has been accepted as a defence to manslaughter (*Evans and Gardiner* [1976] VR 517, an Australian case), causing GBH with intent (*Cairns* (1999)), criminal damage (*Crutchley* (1831) 5 C & P 133), theft (*Gill* (1963)), handling stolen goods (*Attorney-General v Whelan* [1934] IR 518) and obtaining property by deception (*Bowen* (1996)). It has also been accepted as a defence to the following: perjury (*Hudson and Taylor* (1971)), drug offences (*Valderrama-Vega* (1985)), firearms offences (*Pommell* (1995)), driving offences (*Willer* (1986) 83 Cr App R 225; *Conway* (1988); *Martin* [1989] 1 All ER 652), hijacking (*Abdul-Hussain* (1999); *Safi and others* (2003)), kidnapping (*Safi and others*) and breach of the Official Secrets Act (*Shayler* [2001] EWCA Crim 1977; [2001] 1 WLR 2206: see below). Indeed, it seems that duress (both forms) will be accepted as a defence to any crime except murder and attempted murder (and possibly some forms of treason).

Murder

The case of *Dudley and Stephens* (1884) 14 QBD 273 is often cited as authority for the proposition that necessity is not a defence to murder (a view not accepted by the Court of Appeal (Civil Division) in *Re A (Children) (Conjoined Twins: Surgical Separation)* [2000] EWCA Civ 254; [2000] 4 All ER 961, a case which will be discussed in section 8.2). *Dudley and Stephens* was, however, relied upon by Lords Hailsham, Griffiths and Mackay in *Howe and Bannister* (1987) as authority for the proposition that the defence of duress by threats was also unavailable to those charged with murder.

CASE EXAMPLE

Dudley and Stephens (1884) 14 QBD 273

D and S had been shipwrecked in a boat with another man and a cabin boy. After several days without food or water, they decided to kill and eat the boy, who was the weakest of the four. Four days later they were rescued. On the murder trial, the jury returned a special verdict, finding that they would have died had they not eaten the boy (although there was no greater necessity for killing the boy than anyone else). Lord Coleridge CJ agreed with the last point, adding that as the mariners were adrift on the high sea, killing any one of them was not going to guarantee their safety, and thus it could be argued that it was not necessary to kill anyone. D and S were sentenced to hang, but this was commuted to six months' imprisonment after Queen Victoria intervened and exercised the Royal Prerogative.

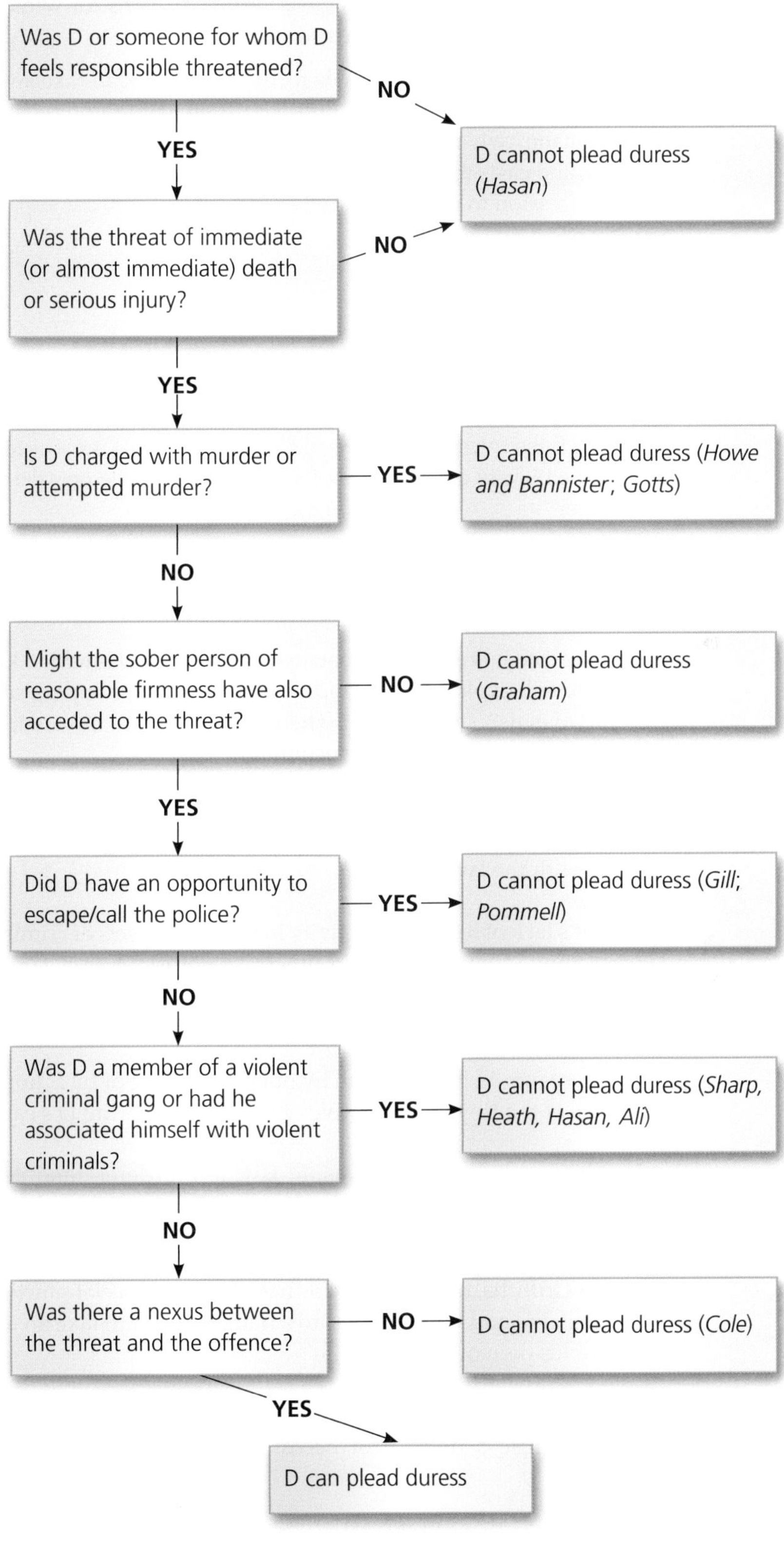

Figure 8.1 Can D plead duress?

In *Howe and Bannister*, the Lords gave various reasons for withdrawing the defence of duress by threats from those charged with murder.

- The ordinary man of reasonable fortitude, if asked to take an innocent life, might be expected to sacrifice his own. Lord Hailsham could not 'regard a law as either "just" or "humane" which withdraws the protection of the criminal law from the innocent victim, and casts the cloak of protection on the cowards and the poltroon in the name of a concession to human frailty'.

ACTIVITY

Self-test question

Discuss whether the law should require heroism. Refer back to Lord Lane's test in *Graham* (approved in *Howe and Bannister*) which sets a standard of the 'sober person of reasonable firmness'. If the reasonable man would have killed in the same circumstances, why should D be punished – with a life sentence for murder – when he only did what anyone else would have done?

- One who takes the life of an innocent cannot claim that he is choosing the lesser of two evils (per Lord Hailsham).

This may be true if D alone is threatened; but what if D is told to kill V and that if he does not, a bomb will explode in the middle of a crowded shopping centre? Surely that is the lesser of two evils? The situation where D's family are threatened with death if D does not kill a third party is far from uncommon.

- The Law Commission (LC) recommended in 1977 that duress be a defence to murder. That recommendation was not implemented; this suggested that Parliament was happy with the law as it was.

Parliament's lack of legislative activity in various aspects of criminal law, despite numerous promptings from the LC and others, is notorious (e.g. failure to reform non-fatal offences, discussed in Chapter 11). So its failure to adopt one LC proposal should not be taken to indicate Parliament's satisfaction instead of its intransigence.

- Hard cases could be dealt with by not prosecuting or by action of the Parole Board or exercise of the Royal Prerogative of Mercy in ordering D's early release.

But D still faces being branded as, in law, a 'murderer', and a morally innocent man should not have to rely on an administrative decision for his freedom.

- To recognise the defence would involve overruling *Dudley and Stephens*. According to Lord Griffiths, the decision was based on 'the special sanctity that the law attaches to human life and which denies to a man the right to take an innocent life even at the price of his own or another's life'.

The basis of the decision in *Dudley and Stephens* is in fact far from clear. It would be possible to recognise a defence of necessity to murder without overruling *Dudley and Stephens*.

- Lord Griffiths thought the defence should not be available because it was 'so easy to raise and may be difficult for the prosecution to disprove'.

This argument applies to most defences! It also ignores the fact that in *Howe and Bannister* itself, the jury had rejected the defence and convicted. Indeed, Lord Hailsham said that 'juries have been commendably robust' in rejecting the defence on other cases.

- Lord Bridge thought that it was for Parliament to decide the limits of the defence.

Why should this be? Duress is a common law defence, so the judges should decide its scope.

CASE EXAMPLE

Howe and Bannister [1987] AC 417

D, aged 19, and E, aged 20, together with two other men, one aged 19, and the other, Murray, aged 35, participated in the torture, assault and then strangling of two young male victims at a remote spot on the Derbyshire moors. At their trial on two counts of murder and one of conspiracy to murder, they pleaded duress, arguing that they feared for their lives if they did not do as Murray directed. He was not only much older than the others but had appeared in court several times before and had convictions for violence. D and E were convicted of all charges, and their appeals failed in the Court of Appeal and House of Lords.

Howe and Bannister was followed in *Wilson* [2007] EWCA Crim 1251; [2007] 2 Cr App R 31, where the Court of Appeal confirmed that duress was never a defence to murder, even though D was a 13-year-old boy. D and his father E murdered E's neighbour, V, using various weapons. At trial, D pleaded duress, on the basis that E had threatened him with violence if he did not participate. The defence was rejected. Lord Phillips CJ stated:

JUDGMENT

'There may be grounds for criticising a principle of law that does not afford a 13-year-old boy any defence to a charge of murder on the ground that he was complying with his father's instructions, which he was too frightened to refuse to disobey. But our criminal law holds that a 13-year-old boy is responsible for his actions and the rule that duress provides no defence to a charge of murder applies however susceptible D may be to the duress.'

The decision in *Wilson* reveals the arbitrary nature of the availability of duress, largely attributable to its common law development. Suppose that V had survived, and D had been charged with causing GBH with intent, instead of murder. D's conduct (he admitted hitting V, once, with a metal bar), and his *mens rea* at the time of doing so, would have been exactly the same. However, instead of facing indefinite detention for murder, there is a good chance that D would have been acquitted.

- First, duress would, in principle, have been available (*Cairns* (1999)).
- Second, the *Graham/Bowen* test would have applied. The jury would have been asked to decide (1) whether D may have been impelled to act as he did because, as a result of what he reasonably believed E had said or done, he had good cause to fear that if he did not so act E would kill or seriously injure him; (2) whether a sober 13-year-old boy of reasonable firmness might have taken part in the attack.

The failure of the judiciary to provide a defence to murder for those acting under duress was recently criticised by Arenson, 'The paradox of disallowing duress as a defence to murder' (2014) 78 J Crim L 65. He condemned their 'hypocrisy and sheer folly' in allowing provocation (originally a common law defence but now abolished and replaced by the statutory defence of loss of control – see Chapter 10) to provide a defence to murder but not allowing duress to do so. He contends that those who kill under duress are 'far less morally culpable' than those who kill having lost their self-control – yet it is the latter who have a defence, and not the former. There is undoubtedly strength in the argument that it is indeed paradoxical to excuse (albeit partially) those who kill having lost their self-control but not to excuse (even partially) those who kill having been forced by threats of death or serious injury to do so – especially when the person threatened with death or injury is not necessarily D but could be their spouse or child.

Arenson also flatly disagrees with Lord Hailsham's proposition in *Howe and others* that the law should expect D to sacrifice his own life rather than kill V if forced into choosing one or the other. It is difficult to disagree with the following proposition:

QUOTATION

'[It] requires nothing more than a rudimentary understanding of basic human instinct to appreciate that it is unrealistic to expect any person … to refuse to follow a direction to take an innocent life when the consequence of that refusal is all but certain to result in the loss of one's own life or that of a close friend or family member.'

Duress and attempted murder

In *Howe and Bannister*, Lord Griffiths said, *obiter*, that the defence of duress was not available to charges of attempted murder. This was confirmed in *Gotts* [1991] 2 All ER 1, where Lord Jauncey said that he could 'see no justification in logic, morality or law in affording to an attempted murderer the defence which is withheld from a murderer'.

CASE EXAMPLE

Gotts [1991] 2 All ER 1

D, aged 16, had been threatened with death by his father unless he tracked his mother down to a refuge and killed her. D did as directed but, although seriously injured, his mother survived. The trial judge withdrew the defence and D was convicted. The Court of Appeal and House of Lords upheld his conviction.

ACTIVITY

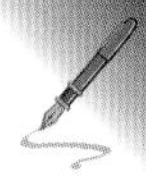

Self-test question

D1, with intent to do serious harm, attacks and kills V. He appears to be guilty of murder and would have no defence of duress to murder (*Howe and Bannister* (1987)) and would face life imprisonment. D2, with intent to do serious harm, attacks V and causes serious injury but not death. He could plead duress to a charge under s 18 OAPA 1861 (*Cairns* (1999)) and, if successful, would receive an acquittal. (D2 could not be convicted of attempted murder because this requires proof of intent to kill.) D1 and D2 have the same *mens rea*, but one is labelled a murderer and faces a long prison term; the other escapes with no punishment at all. Is this justifiable? Bear in mind that the difference between the two cases is simply whether V survives, which is subject to a number of variables (V's age and state of health, the quality of medical treatment available, etc.).

Reform

In its 2005 Consultation Paper, *A New Homicide Act?* the LC suggested that duress should be made available as a partial defence to murder. However, by the time of its 2006 Report, *Murder, Manslaughter and Infanticide*, the LC had changed its position and instead recommended that duress should be a full defence to both murder and attempted murder. This would entail abolishing the principles established by the House of Lords in *Howe and Bannister* (1987) and *Gotts* (1991). However, the Ministry of Justice Consultation Paper, *Murder, Manslaughter and Infanticide: Proposals for Reform of the Law* (July 2008), made no reference to these proposals, and since then there has been a change of government. It appears unlikely that Parliament will be invited to change the law on duress any time soon.

8.1.9 The development of duress of circumstances

Duress of circumstances has really only received official recognition from the appellate courts in the last 25 years. The first cases all, coincidentally, involved driving offences.

- *Willer* (1986). D was forced to drive his car on the pavement in order to escape a gang of youths who were intent on attacking him and his passenger. The Court of Appeal allowed D's appeal against a conviction for reckless driving, on the basis of duress of circumstances. Watkins LJ said that D was 'wholly driven by force of circumstance into doing what he did and did not drive the car otherwise than under that form of compulsion, ie under duress.'
- *Conway* (1988). D again successfully appealed against a conviction for reckless driving. He had driven his car at high speed to escape what he thought were two men intent on attacking his passenger (in fact they were police officers).
- *Martin* (1989). D's conviction for driving while disqualified was quashed. He had only driven his car after his wife became hysterical and threatened to kill herself if D did not drive his stepson to work.
- *DPP v Bell* [1992] Crim LR 176. D's conviction for driving with excess alcohol was quashed. He had only got into his car and driven it (a relatively short distance) in order to escape a gang who were pursuing him.
- *DPP v Davis; DPP v Pittaway* [1994] Crim LR 600. Both appellants had convictions for driving with excess alcohol quashed on the basis that they had only driven to escape perceived violence from other people.

In *Conway*, Woolf LJ (as he then was) spelled out the ingredients of the new defence as follows:

JUDGMENT

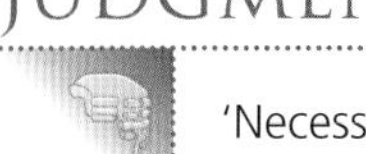

> 'Necessity can only be a defence … where the facts establish "duress of circumstances", that is, where [D] was constrained to act by circumstances to drive as he did to avoid death or serious bodily injury to himself or some other person … This approach does no more than recognise that duress is an example of necessity. Whether "duress of circumstances" is called "duress" or "necessity" does not matter. What is important is that it is subject to the same limitations as the "do this or else" species of duress.'

In *Martin* (1989), Simon Brown J said that English law did 'in extreme circumstances recognise a defence of necessity. Most commonly this defence arises as duress [by threats]. Equally, however, it can arise from other objective dangers threatening the accused or others. Arising thus it is conveniently called "duress of circumstances".' For a time there was a perception that duress of circumstances might be limited to driving offences, but in *Pommell* (1995), the Court of Appeal confirmed that the defence was of general application. It has subsequently been pleaded (not necessarily successfully) in cases of hijacking (*Abdul-Hussain* (1999); *Safi and others* (2003)) and breach of the Official Secrets Act 1989 (*Shayler* (2001)).

Duress of circumstances and necessity: are they the same thing?

You will have noted that in several of the above cases the courts have tended to describe duress of circumstances and necessity as the same thing. You are referred in particular to Lord Woolf's comments in *Conway* (1988) and *Shayler* (2001). In the latter case D, a former member of the British Security Service (MI5), was charged (and ultimately convicted of) disclosing confidential documents in breach of the Official Secrets Act 1989. Unusually, his defence (whether it is properly regarded as duress of circumstances or necessity is perhaps a moot point) was considered both by the Court of Appeal and by the House of Lords before the actual trial. Lord Woolf CJ, giving judgment in the Court of Appeal, gave a very strong indication that duress of circumstances and necessity were interchangeable. He stated:

JUDGMENT

The distinction between duress of circumstances and necessity has, correctly, been by and large ignored or blurred by the courts. Apart from some of the medical cases like *Re F* [1990] 2 AC 1, the law has tended to treat duress of circumstances and necessity as one and the same.

Another, more recent example, comes from the case of *Quayle and others* [2005] EWCA Crim 1415; [2005] 1 WLR 3642, discussed in section 8.2, where Mance LJ referred to a defence called 'necessity by circumstances', which seems to conflate 'duress of circumstances' and 'necessity' into a single defence. However, in this book they will be regarded as separate defences. There are two reasons for this.

- It is clear that duress, whether by threats or of circumstances, cannot be a defence to murder (or attempted murder). However, according to the case of *Re A (Children) (Conjoined Twins)* (2000), discussed in section 8.2, 'necessity' may be a defence to murder.
- Duress (again whether by threats or of circumstances) exists only where D or someone he is responsible for is in immediate danger of death or serious injury. This is not necessarily the case in necessity, a point for which *Re A* is again authority.

Academic support for the position adopted in this book comes from F Stark, 'Necessity and *Nicklinson*' [2013] Crim LR 949. Stark concedes that what he labels 'excusatory necessity' can be regarded as being synonymous with duress of circumstances, but contends that there is a separate defence which he labels 'justificatory necessity'. Stark's labels are significant as they indicate a deeper doctrinal distinction between the two defences:

- Excusatory necessity (also known as duress of circumstances) – this is categorisable as an *excuse*. In English law (and other common law jurisdictions) this signifies that D has committed a wrongful act or omission but, because of the prevailing circumstances at the time, D does not deserve to be blamed, either at all or at least not to the full extent of the law. Other examples of excuses are duress by threats (discussed above), automatism and insanity (discussed in Chapter 9) and diminished responsibility and loss of control (discussed in Chapter 10).

- Justificatory necessity – this is categorisable as a *justification*. This signifies that D has not committed a wrongful act at all. Other examples of justifications include self-defence (discussed below) and consent (discussed below).

It should be noted that (i) the categories of 'excuse' and 'justification' have been advanced by academics, rather than the courts, (ii) there is not necessarily a consensus amongst all academics about which crimes are excuses and which are justifications and (iii) the distinction between 'excuses' and 'justifications' itself is not accepted by all academics either.

KEY FACTS

Key facts on duress

Elements	Comment	Cases
Source of duress	By threats By circumstances	*Lynch* (1975) *Willer* (1986), *Conway* (1988), *Martin* (1989)
Degree of duress	Threat or danger posed must be of death or serious personal injury (including rape) This means physical injury not psychological injury Threat of exposure of secret sexual orientation insufficient	*Hasan* (2005), *A* (2012) *Baker and Wilkins* (1997) *Valderrama-Vega* (1985)
Duress against whom?	Usually D personally Also includes duress against family Even persons for whom defendant reasonably feels responsible	*Graham* (1982), *Cairns* (1999) *Ortiz* (1986), *Conway* (1988), *Martin* (1989) *Wright* (2000)
Imminence	Threat or danger must be believed to be immediate or almost immediate. Defendant should alert police as soon as possible; delay in doing so does not necessarily mean defence fails.	*Hasan* (2005) *Gill* (1963), *Pommell* (1995)
Association with crime	Voluntarily joining a violent criminal gang means defendant may not have the defence. Voluntary association with violent criminals has the same effect. But only if the defendant foresaw (or should have foreseen) that he may be subjected to duress.	*Fitzpatrick* (1977), *Sharp* (1987) *Ali* (1995), *Baker and Ward* (1999), *Heath* (2000) *Shepherd* (1987), *Hasan* (2005)
Reasonable man test	Defendant must have reasonably believed that a threat/danger existed. Defence fails if a sober person of reasonable firmness would have resisted the threats. The reasonable man shares some of D's characteristics, such as age and physical disability.	*Cairns* (1999), *Safi* (2003), *Hasan* (2005) *Graham* (1982), *Howe and Bannister* (1987) *Bowen* (1996)

Availability	Defence available to most crimes except murder … … and attempted murder.	*Howe and Bannister* (1987), *Wilson* (2007) *Gotts* (1991)
Burden of proof	It is for the prosecution to **disprove** beyond reasonable doubt.	
Effect of defence	Defendant is not guilty.	

8.2 Necessity

Ammunition for the proposition that 'necessity' is a separate defence comes from *Re A* (2000). There, Brooke LJ said, 'In cases of pure necessity the actor's mind is not irresistibly overborne by external pressures. The claim is that his or her conduct was not harmful because on a choice of two evils the choice of avoiding the greater harm was justified.' He went on to summarise the position as follows, by stating that 'there are three necessary requirements for the application of the doctrine of necessity':

- The act is needed to avoid inevitable and irreparable evil.
- No more should be done than is reasonably necessary for the purpose to be achieved.
- The evil inflicted must not be disproportionate to the evil avoided.

This definition is very different from that regarded as the classic test for duress of circumstances, which requires that D must have acted in order to avoid a perceived threat of immediate death or serious injury and with no reasonable opportunity for escaping from the threat or contacting the authorities.

CASE EXAMPLE

Re A (Conjoined Twins: Surgical Separation) [2000] EWCA Civ 254; [2000] 4 All ER 961

J and M were conjoined twin girls; that is, they were physically joined at the lower abdomen. J was capable of independent existence; M was not. An operation to separate the twins was deemed appropriate in order to give J a chance of a separate life. This operation would inevitably result in the death of M, who was alive only because of a common artery, through which J's stronger heart circulated enough oxygenated blood for both of them. Both girls would die, within six months at the outside, if the operation did not take place, because J's heart would eventually lack strength to pump blood around both bodies. However, the girls' parents, who were both Catholics, refused to give their consent. The hospital authorities therefore applied for a declaration that the proposed operation would be lawful. The Court of Appeal (Civil Division) found that the operation was a positive act and therefore had to be justified to prevent the surgeons from facing liability for murder. Justification came in the form of the necessity defence. The operation was carried out successfully, in that J survived (M died) and was released from hospital shortly afterwards.

Strictly speaking, as a matter of precedent, this case involved a decision of the Civil Division of the Court of Appeal and is only persuasive on criminal courts. In *Shayler* (2001), a decision of the Criminal Division of the Court of Appeal, Lord Woolf CJ gave a definition of the ingredients of 'necessity' in exactly the same terms as Brooke LJ in *Re A* (although, as noted above, he regarded necessity and duress of circumstances as interchangeable).

In *Quayle and others* [2005] EWCA Crim 1415; [2005] 1 WLR 3642, however, a defence of necessity was recognised, although the appeals were rejected, by the Court of Appeal (Criminal Division). The appellants had been charged with various offences relating to the 'cultivation, production, importation and possession' of cannabis. They were convicted and appealed, claiming that, because they used cannabis not as a recreational drug but for the purposes of relieving painful symptoms of conditions such as multiple sclerosis, a defence of necessity should be available. The Court of Appeal dismissed the appeals. Mance LJ said that whatever benefits there might be (real or perceived) for any individual patients, such benefits were regarded by Parliament as outweighed by disbenefits 'of sufficient strength to require a general prohibition in the national interest'. The suggested defence of 'necessitous medical use' on an individual basis was in conflict with the purpose of the legislation, for two reasons.

1. No such use was permitted under the legislation, even on doctor's prescription, except for medical research trials.
2. It would involve unqualified individuals prescribing cannabis to themselves as patients or assuming the role of unqualified doctors by obtaining, prescribing and supplying it to other individual 'patients'.

CASE EXAMPLE

Quayle and others [2005] EWCA Crim 1415; [2005] 1 WLR 3642

The case involved five appellants. Barry Quayle (a 38-year-old amputee who was still in considerable pain), Reay Wales (a 53-year-old man who suffered from various back injuries and illnesses which led to him becoming depressed and alcoholic and which in turn led to a condition called pancreatitis which left him in 'chronic' pain) and Graham Kenny (a 25-year-old man who had injured his back at work) had all been convicted of cultivating cannabis for their own use, contrary to the Misuse of Drugs Act 1971. Anthony Taylor, the manager of Tony's Holistic Clinic in London, a treatment centre for people with HIV and AIDS, had been stopped by customs officers at Luton Airport returning from Switzerland and Taylor was found to be carrying 20.5 kilos of cannabis worth £35,000, an offence under the Customs & Excise Management Act 1979. A month later, one of Taylor's employees, May Po Lee, was also caught at Luton Airport returning from Switzerland with just over five kilos of cannabis. At trial, the judge refused to allow any of the accused a defence of 'medical necessity' to be left to the jury and all were convicted. The Court of Appeal dismissed their appeals.

Mance LJ summarised the judgment as follows:

JUDGMENT

'The law has to draw a line at some point in the criteria which it accepts as sufficient to satisfy any defence of duress or necessity. Courts and juries have to work on evidence. If such defences were to be expanded in theory to cover every possible case in which it might be felt that it would be hard if the law treated the conduct in question as criminal, there would be likely to be arguments in considerable numbers of cases, where there was no clear objective basis by reference to which to test or determine such arguments. It is unlikely that this would lead overall to a more coherent result, or even necessarily to a more just disposition of any individual case. There is, on any view, a large element of subjectivity in the assessment of pain not directly associated with some current physical injury. The legal defences of duress by threats and necessity by circumstances should in our view be confined to cases where there is an imminent danger of physical injury.'

Quayle and others was followed in *Altham* [2006] EWCA Crim 7; [2006] 2 Cr App R 8.

CASE EXAMPLE

Altham [2006] EWCA Crim 7; [2006] 2 Cr App R 8

D had been involved in a road traffic accident some 15 years earlier which left him with both hips dislocated; subsequently, his left hip had to be surgically removed altogether leaving him 'in chronic pain in his lower limbs ever since'. After several pain-relieving strategies including acupuncture and prescribed antidepressants had failed, D turned to cannabis, which apparently provided the first form of pain relief since his accident. However, he was eventually prosecuted for and convicted of possessing a controlled drug.

The Court of Appeal upheld his conviction, relying heavily upon the judgment in *Quayle and others*. In addition, the Court held that a person who used cannabis for pain relief could not raise a defence of necessity by relying on art 3 of the European Convention on Human Rights (the prohibition of inhuman or degrading treatment or punishment). Baker LJ stated:

JUDGMENT

'In our judgment the state has done nothing to subject the appellant to either inhuman or degrading treatment and thereby engage the absolute prohibition in Article 3. If the true position is that, absent a defence of necessity, the appellant will either break the criminal law or continue to suffer degrading treatment, the state is not in breach of its Article 3 obligation ... We do not think that this is a case in which ... the state is properly to be regarded as responsible for the harm inflicted on the appellant. Nor do we think that Article 3 requires the state to take any steps to alleviate the appellant's condition.'

It is submitted that the cases of *Quayle and others* and *Altham* are authority for the proposition that 'necessity' exists as a defence in English law separate from 'duress of circumstances'. In his commentary in the Criminal Law Review on the former case, Professor David Ormerod argued that the case could be regarded as one of 'pure necessity' (*Quayle and others* [2006] Crim LR 149). He referred to the 'general principles of necessity' identified by Brooke LJ in *Re A* (2000) and added that:

QUOTATION

'Applying those criteria it would come as no surprise if a jury, having heard expert evidence of the genuine nature and severity of pain being avoided, regarded the action of breaking the law as justified. A plea of necessity avoids many of the restrictions which constrain duress of circumstances: there is no requirement of a threat of death or serious injury ... the defence is potentially available to all crimes, even murder, and there is no requirement of immediacy ... Clarification from the House of Lords as to the elements of the defence of necessity, its rationale, and its relationship with duress of circumstances is urgently needed. If necessity is to be subsumed within duress of circumstances it should, it is submitted, only be by express pronouncement of the House.'

(Note: Professor Ormerod's references to 'the House of Lords' should now be read as 'the Supreme Court'.) It follows that older cases which indicated that it did not exist should not now be relied upon. For example, in *Buckoke v GLC* [1975] Ch 655, Lord Denning stated, *obiter*, that the driver of a fire engine who crossed a red traffic light to rescue a man from a blazing building on the other side of the junction would commit an offence against the road traffic regulations.

ACTIVITY

Applying the law

If the circumstances described by Lord Denning in *Buckoke* (1975) did occur, discuss whether the driver would have a defence of necessity under the criteria laid down by Brooke LJ in *Re A* (2000).

Note: this particular issue is now a moot point, as reg 33(1)(b) of the Traffic Signs Regulations and General Directions (SI 1994 No 1519) 1994 provides that fire brigade, ambulance or police vehicles may cross red lights if stopping 'would be likely to hinder the use of that vehicle for the purpose for which it is being used'. However, the vehicle must not cross the red light 'in a manner or at a time likely to endanger any person' or cause another vehicle 'to change its speed or course in order to avoid an accident'.

In *Southwark LBC v Williams* [1971] Ch 734, a civil case, it was held that the defence of necessity did not apply to enable the homeless to enter and occupy empty houses owned by the local authority. Lord Denning MR justified the rule on the ground that:

JUDGMENT

'If hunger were once allowed to be an excuse for stealing, it would open a door through which all kinds of lawlessness and disorder would pass ... If homelessness were once admitted as a defence to trespass, no one's house could be safe. Necessity would open a door which no man could shut. It would not only be those in extreme need who would enter. There would be others who would imagine that they were in need, or would invent a need, so as to gain entry.'

ACTIVITY

Applying the law

Would homeless people seeking shelter in empty properties now be able to satisfy the criteria for necessity laid down by Brooke LJ in *Re A* (2000)? What other information might you wish to have in order to be able to answer this question?

Even assuming that necessity – as a distinct defence – does exist, questions remain as to its scope. In particular, the question whether it provides a potential defence to a charge of murder is a particularly complicated one, as it inevitably raises ethical, moral and religious issues as well as legal ones. This question was recently put to the Court of Appeal in *Nicklinson v Ministry of Justice* [2013] EWCA Civ 961; [2014] 2 All ER 32. The court decided that, apart from a case such as *Re A* (2000), the answer was 'no'. The Court explained that the question whether the law should be changed so as to allow a defence of necessity in murder cases was one that could only be answered (if at all) by Parliament.

CASE EXAMPLE

Nicklinson v Ministry of Justice [2013] EWCA Civ 961; [2014] 2 All ER 32

Tony Nicklinson, aged 57, suffered a stroke while on a business trip to Athens in 2005 which left him with 'locked-in' syndrome, almost completely paralysed – he was only able to communicate by blinking and with limited head movement, although his mental capacity was unimpaired. After seven years, he applied to the High Court for a declaration that it would not be unlawful, on the grounds of necessity, for a doctor to terminate or assist in the termination of his life. The Ministry of Justice responded that the law on murder was clear and settled and any change was a matter for Parliament. The High Court rejected his application and held that allowing a doctor to deliberately take Nicklinson's life would be murder. The Court distinguished the superficially similar case of *Re A* on the basis of its 'highly unusual' facts.

On hearing this news, Nicklinson effectively committed suicide by refusing all food and fluids. He died of pneumonia a week after the judgment. However, his widow, Jane, continued the legal fight on his behalf by appealing to the Court of Appeal (Civil Division). However, that court rejected her appeal, primarily on the basis that such a radical change in the law required the approval of Parliament. Lord Dyson MR and Lord Elias (with whom Lord Judge CJ agreed) stated:

JUDGMENT

[The appellant's] submission that the common law should recognise a defence of necessity to apply to certain cases of euthanasia is wholly unsustainable ... It is simply not appropriate for the court to fashion a defence of necessity in such a complex and controversial field; this is a matter for Parliament ... Parliament as the conscience of the nation is the appropriate constitutional forum, not judges who might be influenced by their own particular moral perspectives; the judicial process which has to focus on the particular facts and circumstances before the court is not one which is suited to enabling the judges to deal competently with the range of conflicting considerations and procedural requirements which a proper regulation of the field may require; and there is a danger that any particular judicial decision, influenced perhaps by particular sympathy for an individual claimant, may have unforeseen consequences, creating an unfortunate precedent binding in other contexts.

F Stark, 'Necessity and *Nicklinson*' [2013] Crim LR 949 suggests that an (implicit) reason for the Court of Appeal's rejection of necessity was the concern for setting too dangerous a precedent. He contends that, were the courts to allow Nicklinson's doctors a defence of necessity, it would open the floodgates to other cases involving patients with life-limiting or terminal conditions seeking the court's approval to be lawfully killed. He writes:

QUOTATION

'Lurking behind the refusal to engage in a discussion [about necessity in euthanasia cases] is the danger of repetition of the facts of *Nicklinson*. Justificatory necessity is a defence that can only really be endorsed in truly exceptional circumstances, lest the law's authority be undermined. The danger is that the law would find itself having to discuss arguments which were ... irresolvable, leading to inconsistency and instability.'

Jane Nicklinson was granted leave to appeal to the Supreme Court, but did not pursue the necessity argument before that court. Instead, the appeal was focused exclusively on whether the offence of assisted suicide, contrary to s 2 of the Suicide Act 1961, was compatible with the European Convention on Human Rights (in particular the right to privacy in art 8). The Supreme Court ruled that s 2 was not in breach of the ECHR (*Nicklinson v Ministry of Justice* [2014] UKSC 38; [2014] 3 WLR 200). For further discussion of the *Nicklinson* case, and the arguments for and against the legalisation of euthanasia and 'mercy killings', see Chapter 10 (section 10.2.4).

Support for a change in English law comes from across the Atlantic. In Canadian law, necessity has long been established, not just as a general defence in its own right but as a potential defence to murder. In the leading case, *Perka* [1984] 2 SCR 232, the Supreme Court of Canada explained that the defence only applied where three conditions were met. First, action had to have been taken to avoid a direct and immediate peril. Second, the act in question had to be inevitable, unavoidable and where no reasonable opportunity for an alternative course of action that did not involve a breach of the law was available. Finally, the harm inflicted by the violation of the law had to be less than the harm that the accused sought to avoid. These constraints mean that the defence is rarely successful, as the three leading Canadian Supreme Court decisions illustrate:

- *Perka*: a boat carrying a consignment of cannabis from Colombia to Alaska was forced to seek shelter in Canadian waters during bad weather, but ran aground. The smugglers unloaded drugs worth $6 million on to the shore to avoid it being washed away into the Pacific Ocean. They were caught and charged with trafficking cannabis into Canada, to which they pleaded necessity. Defence rejected on the facts: it was not necessary to smuggle the drugs.
- *Latimer* [2001] 1 SCR 3: D was charged with murdering his 12-year-old daughter, Tracy. She had a 'severe' form of cerebral palsy which meant that she had the mental capacity of a four-month-old baby, was completely dependent on others for her care and could communicate only by means of facial expressions, laughter and crying. She suffered five to six seizures daily, and it was thought that she experienced a great deal of pain. Eventually, on being told that an operation to insert a feeding tube into her stomach was required, D killed her by placing her in his truck with the engine running and a hose attached to the exhaust. Defence rejected on the facts: it was not necessary to kill Tracy.
- *Kerr* [2004] 2 SCR 371: D, an inmate in a maximum security jail, killed a fellow inmate with a weapon made from sharpened prison cutlery. D was charged with murder (to which he pleaded self-defence) and possession of a dangerous weapon (to which he pleaded necessity on the basis that the victim had made death threats against him). Both defences accepted.

Latimer is clearly the closest case, factually, to *Nicklinson*. The defence was rejected for several reasons: Tracy's medical condition did not pose an imminent threat to her life; D had at least one reasonable legal alternative to killing his daughter: he could have helped Tracy by minimising her pain as much as possible or by permitting an institution to do so; the harm inflicted (killing Tracy) was 'immeasurably' more serious than the harm avoided (relieving her perceived suffering). Whilst leaving open the question whether necessity could ever be available in homicide cases, the Supreme Court concluded that killing a person in order to relieve the suffering produced by a medically manageable physical or mental condition was *not* a proportionate response to the harm represented by the non-life-threatening suffering resulting from that condition.

All of this suggests that, even if the Supreme Court and/or Parliament in the UK explicitly endorse a defence of necessity in cases involving the deliberate ending of another person's life (i.e. murder) it is only going to be available in 'truly exceptional circumstances'.

8.3 Marital coercion

A defence of marital coercion was created in common law that provided a presumption that any crime committed by a married woman in the presence of her husband was done under 'coercion'. The presumption was abolished by Parliament in the Criminal Justice Act 1925, s 47, but the defence itself survived until 2014, when it was abolished by the Anti-social Behaviour, Crime and Policing Act 2014, s 177. The Law Commission had twice recommended its abolition (in 1977 and in 1993) on the basis that it was anachronistic to have a special defence for married women (but not for unmarried women, or men). Successive governments had ignored those recommendations and the law was only changed after an independent peer, Lord Pannick, introduced the clause that was to become s 177 as a Lords' amendment to the Bill that became the 2014 Act.

In March 2013, the defence was relied on, possibly for the last time, in the high-profile trial of Vicky Pryce, the former wife of ex-Liberal Democrat MP and Cabinet Minister Chris Hulme, for perverting the course of justice. During her trial, Ms Pryce claimed that Hulme, when the couple were still married, had forced her to claim that she was driving their car over the speed limit on the M11, whereas in fact he was the driver. This meant that she, and not he, had her driving licence endorsed with penalty points, which in turn allowed him to keep his licence (Huhne's licence already had nine points on it and an extra three might have meant a driving ban). The defence was rejected and Ms Pryce was sentenced to imprisonment.

With the defence abolished, married women are now placed in the same position as every other member of English and Welsh society who claims to have been forced to commit a crime: plead duress.

8.4 Mistake

8.4.1 Mistakes of fact

'Mistake of fact' is not really a 'defence' as such; it operates by preventing the prosecution from establishing that D possessed the relevant *mens rea* at the time of the offence. At one time only mistakes of fact that were reasonably made could operate to negate liability. However, that was changed by the leading case, *DPP v Morgan* [1976] AC 182, where it was held that mistakes of fact may negate liability provided they were honestly made. Lord Hailsham said:

JUDGMENT

'Either the prosecution proves that [D] had the requisite intent, or it does not. In the former case it succeeds, and in the latter it fails. Since honest belief clearly negatives intent, the reasonableness or otherwise of that belief can only be evidence for or against the view that the belief and therefore the intent was actually held.'

Morgan was a rape case, but the proposition of Lord Hailsham, above, extends to most criminal offences. It was followed in the indecent assault case of *Kimber* [1983]

3 All ER 316, a Court of Appeal judgment concerning D's mistaken belief that V was consenting. *Morgan* has now been overruled by Parliament's enactment of the Sexual Offences Act 2003, which restores a requirement that, in rape cases, D's belief as to whether or not V was consenting to sexual intercourse must be a reasonable one (see Chapter 12). However, the principle stated above remains applicable to other crimes and, therefore, D will have a good defence if he honestly believed in a mistaken set of facts such that he did not have the *mens rea*. A good example of the continuing legacy of *Morgan* is any case where D is charged with murder, manslaughter or some non-fatal offence and claims to have acted in self-defence, having used force in the mistaken belief about the need to use (a) any force, or (b) the amount of force he did in fact use. In *Williams* [1987] 3 All ER 411, the Court of Appeal held that D had a good defence provided his belief that he was under attack was honestly held. Lord Lane CJ said:

JUDGMENT

'The mental element necessary to constitute guilt is the intent to apply unlawful force to the victim. [The] question is, does it make any difference if the mistake of [D] was ... an unreasonable mistake? ... The reasonableness or unreasonableness of [D]'s belief is material to the question of whether the belief was held by [D] at all. If the belief was in fact held, its unreasonableness, so far as guilt or innocence is concerned, is neither here nor there. It is irrelevant.'

student mentor tip

'Look for the factors that link to other areas; you simply cannot pick and choose but have to understand the basic law in all areas and build up your knowledge from there.'
Pelena, University of Surrey

In *Beckford* [1988] AC 130, in which D was accused of murder but pleaded honest mistaken belief in the need to act in self-defence, the Privy Council approved both *Morgan* and *Williams*. Lord Griffiths said that 'If then a genuine belief, albeit without reasonable grounds, is a defence to rape because it negatives the necessary intention, so also must a genuine belief in facts which if true would justify self-defence be a defence to a crime of personal violence because the belief negates the intent to act unlawfully.' The cases of *Williams* and *Beckford* will be further discussed in section 8.5.

Intoxicated mistakes

An intoxicated defendant is often really pleading mistake. If this is the case, then the rules described above do not apply; instead the intoxication rules as set out in *DPP v Majewski* [1977] AC 443, apply instead (see Chapter 9, in particular the case of *Lipman* [1970] 1 QB 152).

8.4.2 Mistakes of law

It is no defence for D who causes the *actus reus* of an offence with *mens rea* to say that he did not know the *actus reus* was an offence, ignorance of the law being no excuse. Thus, in *Esop* (1836) 7 C & P 456, D, from Iraq, buggered a man on board a ship lying in an English port. Buggery was not illegal in Iraq and D assumed it was lawful in England. He was convicted. A similar decision was reached in *Lee* [2000] Crim LR 991.

CASE EXAMPLE

Lee [2000] Crim LR 991

D was convicted of two offences of assault with intent to resist arrest (contrary to s 38 OAPA 1861). He had given a roadside breathalyser test which the two police officers had said was positive. D said it was not clear that the crystals had changed colour beyond the red line. There was no doubt he had assaulted the officers; the question was whether he had the *mens rea*, the intent to resist arrest. The defence case was that, because he thought the test was negative, the officers had no power of arrest and therefore he could not have intended to resist arrest. However, under s 6(5) of the Road Traffic Act 1988, a power of arrest arises provided that the police officer, as a result of a breath test, 'has reasonable cause to suspect' that D was over the limit. He was convicted. On appeal it was submitted that the trial judge should have directed the jury to acquit unless sure that D had no honest belief that he had passed the breathalyser test. However, the Court of Appeal dismissed the appeal, distinguishing *Morgan*, *Williams* and *Beckford*. D's mistake was not one of fact but one of law, that is, the lawfulness of his arrest. Once the lawfulness of his arrest was established (and it was conceded on appeal that there was evidence on which the jury could conclude that the officers were acting lawfully), then the *mens rea* required was an intent to resist arrest with knowledge that the person was seeking to arrest him.

8.5 Self-defence and related defences

Causing injury or even death to other persons may be justified if the force was reasonably used in self-defence or to protect another person. The term 'self-defence' will be used in this section, although it should be remembered that D may use force to defend others (the term 'private defence' is sometimes used instead for this reason). Self-defence is a common law defence (although it has been 'clarified' by s 76 of the Criminal Justice and Immigration Act 2008 (as amended)). It overlaps to some extent with the prevention of crime defence, which is covered by s 3 of the Criminal Law Act 1967, which provides:

SECTION

'3(1) A person may use such force as is reasonable in the circumstances in the prevention of crime, or in effecting or assisting in the lawful arrest of offenders or suspected offenders or of persons unlawfully at large.'

Section 3(2) of the 1967 Act adds that s 3(1) 'shall replace the rules of common law on the question when force used for a purpose mentioned in the subsection is justified by that purpose'. Despite that, the courts have accepted that self-defence remains and that the two justifications operate in parallel (*Cousins* [1982] QB 526). Where there is evidence of self-defence, this must be left to the jury (*DPP v Bailey* [1995] 1 Cr App R 257). However, there must be evidence before the court on which a jury might think it was reasonably possible that D was acting in self-defence. If it was 'a mere fanciful and speculative matter', the judge could withdraw the defence (*Johnson* [1994] Crim LR 376). Self-defence or the s 3 defence are usually raised to charges of homicide or non-fatal offences against the person, but are not confined to them. Thus the s 3 defence was pleaded to a charge of reckless driving in *Renouf* [1986] 2 All ER 449 (D had driven his car at speed in attempting to prevent people who had assaulted him from escaping in another vehicle).

Self-defence was pleaded to a charge of dangerous driving in *Symonds* [1998] Crim LR 280 (D had driven away in his car at speed to escape from someone who he thought was trying to attack him).

The Criminal Justice and Immigration Act 2008, s 76

In an unusual move, Parliament has enacted most (but not all) of the common law principles on self-defence, but without amending them. The stated purpose of doing so is to 'clarify' the law. Section 76 of the Criminal Justice and Immigration Act 2008 (as amended by s 148 of the Legal Aid, Sentencing and Punishment of Offenders Act 2012 and by s 43 of the Crime and Courts Act 2013) should therefore be referred to alongside the case law.

In *McGrath; Keane* [2010] EWCA Crim 2514; [2011] Crim LR 393, the Court of Appeal offered some guidance as to the relationship between the common law defence of self-defence and s 76. Hughes LJ said:

JUDGMENT

'For the avoidance of doubt, it is perhaps helpful to say of s 76 three things: (a) it does not alter the law as it has been for many years; (b) it does not exhaustively state the law of self-defence but it does state the basic principles; (c) it does not require any summing-up to rehearse the whole of its contents just because they are now contained in statute. The fundamental rule of summing-up remains the same. The jury must be told the law which applies to the facts which it might find; it is not to be troubled by a disquisition on the parts of the law which do not affect the case.'

8.5.1 The necessity of force

The use of any force is not justified if it is not necessary, and this depends on whether D thought that the use of force was necessary. A good example of this principle is provided by *Hussain and others* [2010] EWCA Crim 94; [2010] Crim LR 428.

CASE EXAMPLE

Hussain and others [2010] EWCA Crim 94; [2010] Crim LR 428

One night, V and two others disguised themselves with balaclavas, armed themselves with knives and burgled D's home. D, his wife and son were ordered to lie on the floor and threatened that if they moved they would be killed. However, D and his son managed to overpower V, who ran off. V was chased by a group of men including D. He was caught and attacked using various weapons including a cricket bat and a pole. V suffered a fracture of the skull with consequent brain injury, and fractures to his ribs, jaw, elbow and a finger. D and another man were convicted of causing GBH with intent. They appealed, but their convictions were upheld. The Court of Appeal held that, when V was lying on the ground, none of his assailants were acting in self-defence or, in D's case, in defence of his wife, children, himself or his home. According to Lord Judge CJ, 'the burglary was over. No one was in any danger. The purpose of the appellants' violence was revenge.'

It does not matter if D wrongly imagined that a threat existed. Moreover, there is no requirement that D's mistaken belief be based on reasonable grounds. These principles were set out in *Williams* [1987] 3 All ER 411, a decision of the Court of Appeal.

CASE EXAMPLE

Williams [1987] 3 All ER 411

D was charged with an assault occasioning actual bodily harm (ABH) on a man called Mason. His defence was that he was preventing Mason from assaulting and torturing a black youth. D claimed that he had seen Mason dragging the youth along and repeatedly punching him. The youth was struggling and calling for help. D approached Mason to ask him what on earth he was doing; Mason replied that he was arresting the youth for mugging an old lady (which was true) and that he was a police officer (which was not true). D asked to see Mason's warrant card, which was of course not forthcoming, at which point a struggle broke out between them. As a result of this altercation, Mason sustained injuries to his face, loosened teeth and bleeding gums. D did not deny punching Mason but claimed that he did so in order to save the youth from further beatings and torture. The jury were directed that D only had a defence if he believed on reasonable grounds that Mason was acting unlawfully. The Court of Appeal quashed his conviction.

The decision in *Williams* was approved by the Privy Council in *Beckford* [1988] AC 130. Thus, if D is walking alone along a road late at night and sees what he thinks is a large man about to attack him with a club, but in reality, D had made a foolish mistake and the 'large man' was in fact an elderly woman and the 'club' was actually an umbrella, the defence is available. It therefore follows that D can use force to repel what is in fact perfectly lawful behaviour, provided D honestly thinks that force is necessary. This was made explicit in the case of *Re A (Children) (Conjoined Twins)* (2000), discussed above in the context of necessity. Ward LJ adopted a different approach from that of Brooke LJ, although he reached the same conclusion. Ward LJ equated M's dependence on blood from J's heart as, in effect, a potentially fatal attack upon J, which entitled doctors to intervene and use force to save her.

In *McGrath* [2010] EWCA Crim 2514; [2011] Crim LR 393, the Court of Appeal emphasised that it was wrong for a trial judge to direct a jury about the law on *mistaken belief* in the need to use self-defence in a case where D's defence was based on a *genuine* need. In the case, D had pleaded self-defence to a charge of murder after stabbing her boyfriend through the heart when he attacked her. She was convicted (of manslaughter), but only after the trial judge directed the jury with reference to a mistaken belief in self-defence. However, the Court of Appeal upheld the conviction. Although the introduction of the possibility of mistaken belief was an 'unnecessary complication which should not have been present', it was not sufficient to render D's conviction unsafe.

In *Rashford* [2005] EWCA Crim 3377; [2006] Crim LR 547, the Court of Appeal decided that – in principle at least – it was possible to plead self-defence to a charge of murder, even though D admitted that he had gone out looking for revenge. Dyson LJ stated that:

JUDGMENT

'The mere fact that a defendant goes somewhere in order to exact revenge from the victim does not of itself rule out the possibility that in any violence that ensues self-defence is necessarily not available as a defence. It must depend on the circumstances. It is common ground that a person only acts in self-defence if in all the circumstances he honestly believes that it is necessary for him to defend himself and if the amount of force that he uses is reasonable.'

In the event, the Court of Appeal upheld D's murder conviction on the basis that, according to his own testimony, he had not actually been placed in a position where it was necessary to use force at the time when he stabbed V through the heart.

Pre-emptive strike

It is not necessary for there to be an attack in progress; it is sufficient if D apprehends an attack. In *Beckford*, Lord Griffiths said, 'A man about to be attacked does not have to wait for his assailant to strike the first blow or fire the first shot; circumstances may justify a pre-emptive strike.' In *DPP v Bailey* [1995] 1 Cr App R 257, Lord Slynn said 'Self-defence as a concept embraces not only aggressive action such as a pre-emptive strike or aggressive reaction but applies equally to a wholly defensive posture.' It follows that it will be permissible for D to issue threats of force, even death, if that might prevent an attack upon himself or prevent a crime from taking place (*Cousins* (1982)).

Preparing for an attack

Where D apprehends an attack upon himself, may he make preparations to defend himself, even where that involves breaches of the law? In *Attorney-General's Reference (No 2 of 1983)* [1984] QB 456, the Court of Appeal answered this question in the affirmative.

CASE EXAMPLE

Attorney-General's Reference (No 2 of 1983) [1984] QB 456

D's shop had been attacked and damaged by rioters. Fearing further attacks, he made petrol bombs. D was charged with possessing an explosive substance in such circumstances as to give rise to a reasonable suspicion that he did not have it for a lawful object, contrary to s 4(1) of the Explosive Substances Act 1883. He pleaded self-defence and the jury acquitted. The Court of Appeal accepted that this was correct.

Lord Lane CJ stated:

JUDGMENT

'D is not left in the paradoxical position of being able to justify acts carried out in self-defence but not acts immediately preparatory to it. There is no warrant for the submission . . . that acts of self-defence will only avail [D] when they have been done spontaneously . . . [A person] may still arm himself for his own protection, if the exigency arises, although in doing so he may commit other offences.'

A duty to retreat?

At one time, it had been thought that the law required D to retreat as far as possible before resorting to violence (*Julien* [1969] 1 WLR 839). However, this is no longer the test. In *Bird* [1985] 2 All ER 513, D was convicted after the trial judge directed the jury that it was necessary for D to have demonstrated by her actions that she did not want to fight. The Court of Appeal, allowing the appeal, made it clear that this direction 'placed too great an obligation' on D. In particular, it was going too far to say that it was 'necessary' for her to demonstrate a reluctance to fight.

CASE EXAMPLE

Bird [1985] 2 All ER 513

D was at a house party when a former boyfriend of hers, V, arrived. An argument broke out between D and V which became heated; eventually V slapped D. At this D lunged forward with her hand, which held an empty glass. The glass broke in V's face and gouged his eye out. At D's trial for malicious wounding, the prosecution claimed that she knew she had a glass; the defence claimed that it was self-defence. D's conviction was quashed on appeal.

Lord Lane CJ said:

JUDGMENT

'If [D] is proved to have been attacking or retaliating or revenging himself, then he was not truly acting in self-defence. Evidence that [D] tried to retreat or tried to call off the fight may be a cast-iron method of casting doubt on the suggestion that he was the attacker or retaliator or the person trying to revenge himself. But it is not by any means the only method of doing that.'

Self-induced self-defence

In a recent case, the Court of Appeal considered the situation where D self-induces an attack on himself. There appear to be two situations where this might occur: (1) where D was the aggressor in a fight with V; and (2) where D provoked V into attacking him. In such situations, it appears that self-defence is still available to D but *only* in circumstances where 'the tables had been turned' or 'the roles were reversed'. In *Keane* [2010] EWCA Crim 2514; [2011] Crim LR 393, D had been charged with inflicting GBH. He had punched V once in the face, knocking him on to the ground where he hit his head, suffering serious injury. At trial, D relied on self-defence but was convicted after the trial judge directed the jury that self-defence was unavailable where D was 'the aggressor' or had 'successfully and deliberately provoked a fight'. D appealed, but the Court of Appeal dismissed his appeal. The Court ruled that where D deliberately provoked V into punching him, that did *not* provide D with a guaranteed plea of self-defence were he to punch V in return. However, the Court acknowledged that there may be situations where self-induced self-defence might be available. Hughes LJ stated:

JUDGMENT

'Self-defence may arise in the case of an original aggressor but only where the violence offered by [V] was so out of proportion to what the original aggressor did that in effect the roles were reversed … We need to say as clearly as we may that it is not the law that if [D] sets out to provoke another to punch him and succeeds, [D] is then entitled to punch the other person. What that would do would be to legalise the common coin of the bully who confronts [V] with taunts which are deliberately designed to provide an excuse to hit him. The reason why it is not the law is that underlying the law of self-defence is the commonsense morality that what is not unlawful is force which is reasonably necessary … On the contrary, it has been engineered entirely unreasonably by [D].'

Self-defence and third parties

The case of *Hichens* [2011] EWCA Crim 1626; [2011] Crim LR 873 raised the interesting question whether D may use force in self-defence against an entirely innocent third party. The Court of Appeal answered the question 'yes'.

CASE EXAMPLE

Hichens [2011] EWCA Crim 1626; [2011] Crim LR 873

D shared a flat with V. She had an on–off relationship with X, who objected to the fact that D and V were living together. One day, X called at the flat and V wished to let him in. D thought that if she did so, X would assault him, and so he slapped V across the face. D was charged with assault occasioning ABH, and pleaded self-defence, but the judge withdrew it from the jury. D was convicted of battery and appealed. The Court of Appeal dismissed his appeal on the basis that, in his particular case, it was unnecessary for D to have used force against V. However, the Court did state that, in some situations at least, it would be possible to plead self-defence and/or crime prevention in a case where force had been used against an innocent third party.

Gross LJ stated:

JUDGMENT

'Although we suspect that the facts capable realistically of giving rise to such a defence will only rarely be encountered, examples can be adduced and two will suffice: (1) A police constable bundles a passerby out of the way to get at a man he believes about to shoot with a firearm or detonate an explosive device. (2) Y seeks to give Z car keys with Z about to drive. X, believing Z to be unfit drive through drink, knocks the keys out of Y's hands and retains them.'

8.5.2 The reasonableness of force

This is a question for the jury. The general principle is that only such force may be used as is reasonable in the circumstances. However, as with the question of whether any force was necessary, it is critical that the jury put themselves in the circumstances which D perceived (whether reasonably or not) to exist. In *Palmer* [1971] AC 814, Lord Morris said:

JUDGMENT

'If there has been attack so that defence is reasonably necessary it will be recognised that a person defending himself cannot weigh to a nicety the exact measure of his necessary defensive action. If a jury thought that in a moment of unexpected anguish a person attacked had only done what he honestly and instinctively thought was necessary that would be most potent evidence that only reasonable defensive action had been taken.'

The Court of Appeal affirmed this proposition in *Shannon* [1980] Cr App R 192, where a conviction of murder was quashed after the trial judge told the jury simply to consider whether D had used more force than was necessary in the circumstances, neglecting to remind them to consider this from D's perception of events. Similarly, in *Whyte* [1987] 3 All ER 416, Lord Lane CJ held that 'where the issue is one of self-defence, it is necessary and desirable that the jury should be reminded that [D]'s state of mind, that is his view of the danger threatening him at the time of the incident, is material. The test of reasonableness is not … a purely objective test.'

In *Owino* [1996] 2 Cr App R 128, Collins LJ summarised the law as follows:

JUDGMENT

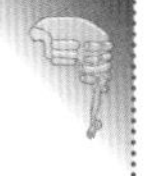

'The essential elements of self-defence are clear enough. The jury have to decide whether [D] honestly believed that the circumstances were such as required him to use force to defend himself from attack or threatened attack. In this respect [D] must be judged in accordance with his honest belief, even though that belief may have been mistaken. But the jury must then decide whether the force used was reasonable in the circumstances as he believed them to be.'

The principles established in cases such as *Palmer* (1971), *Bird* (1985), *Williams* (1987) and *Owino* (1996) have now been incorporated into legislation. Sections 76(3), (4), (6), (6A), (7) and (8) of the Criminal Justice and Immigration Act 2008 state as follows:

SECTION

'(3) The question whether the degree of force used by D was reasonable in the circumstances is to be decided by reference to the circumstances as D believed them to be, and subsections (4) to (8) also apply in connection with deciding that question.

(4) If D claims to have held a particular belief as regards the existence of any circumstances –

(a) the reasonableness or otherwise of that belief is relevant to the question whether D genuinely held it; but

(b) if it is determined that D did genuinely hold it, D is entitled to rely on it for the purposes of subsection (3), whether or not –

(i) it was mistaken, or

(ii) (if it was mistaken) the mistake was a reasonable one to have made.

(6) In a case other than a householder case, the degree of force used by D is not to be regarded as having been reasonable in the circumstances as D believed them to be if it was disproportionate in those circumstances.

(6A) In deciding the question mentioned in subsection (3), a possibility that D could have retreated is to be considered (so far as relevant) as a factor to be taken into account, rather than as giving rise to a duty to retreat.

(7) In deciding the question mentioned in subsection (3) the following considerations are to be taken into account (so far as relevant in the circumstances of the case) –

(a) that a person acting for a legitimate purpose may not be able to weigh to a nicety the exact measure of any necessary action; and

(b) that evidence of a person's having only done what the person honestly and instinctively thought was necessary for a legitimate purpose constitutes strong evidence that only reasonable action was taken by that person for that purpose.

(8) Subsections (6A) and (7) are not to be read as preventing other matters from being taken into account where they are relevant to deciding the question mentioned in subsection (3).'

QUESTION

Given that these legislative provisions simply restate the common law, without amending it, what was the point of s 76?

Relevance of D's characteristics

In *Martin* [2001] EWCA Crim 2245; [2002] 2 WLR 1, the Court of Appeal held that psychiatric evidence that caused D to perceive much greater danger than the average person was irrelevant to the question of whether D had used reasonable force. In a case of self-defence the question was whether the amount of force used was (objectively) reasonable, according to what D (subjectively) believed. Lord Woolf CJ said that the jury are entitled to take into account D's physical characteristics (this might have an impact on D's perception of events). However, he said that the Court did not accept that it was 'appropriate ... in deciding whether excessive force has been used to take into account whether [D] is suffering from some psychiatric condition'.

CASE EXAMPLE

Martin [2001] EWCA Crim 2245; [2002] 2 WLR 1

D lived alone at a remote farmhouse in Norfolk. One night two men, V and W, broke into D's farmhouse. D was awakened by the break-in and, armed with a pump-action shotgun, went downstairs to investigate. There was a dispute about exactly what happened next, but what is undisputed is that D fired the shotgun three times, hitting both men. V was wounded in the legs and W, who had been shot in the back, died shortly afterwards. D was convicted of murder and wounding after the jury rejected his plea of self-defence. On appeal, he argued (amongst other things) that psychiatric evidence had emerged after the trial showing that he suffered from a paranoid personality disorder with recurrent bouts of depression. This meant that he may have genuinely (but mistakenly) thought he was in an extremely dangerous situation on the night in question. The Court rejected his appeal on the basis of self-defence, for the reasons given above, but did quash the murder conviction (substituting one of manslaughter), on the basis that the evidence would instead have supported a plea of diminished responsibility at his trial.

In *Canns* [2005] EWCA Crim 2264, the Court of Appeal followed *Martin* in holding that, when deciding whether D had used reasonable force in self-defence, it was not appropriate to take into account whether D was suffering from some psychiatric condition (in the present case, paranoid schizophrenia, which may have produced delusional beliefs that he was about to be attacked), except in 'exceptional circumstances which would make the evidence especially probative'. The Court held that, generally speaking, it was for the jury, considering all the circumstances – but not evidence of D's psychiatric condition – to set the standards of reasonableness of force.

Martin and *Canns* were both followed in *Oye* [2013] EWCA Crim 1725; [2014] 1 All ER 902. D, who had been convicted of inflicting GBH and affray, appealed. He argued that, if a person reacted violently to a genuine, but insanely deluded, belief that he was being attacked or threatened, and used force that was reasonable in the circumstances as he believed them to be, he was entitled to an acquittal on the basis of self-defence. The Court of Appeal rejected his appeal, following *Martin* and *Canns*. Davis LJ said:

JUDGMENT

'[Accepting D's argument] could mean that the more insanely deluded a person may be in using violence in purported self-defence the more likely that an entire acquittal may result. It could mean that such an individual who for his own benefit and protection may require hospital treatment or supervision gets none. It could mean that the public is exposed to possible further violence from an individual with a propensity for suffering insane delusions, without any intervening preventative remedies being available to the courts in the form of hospital or supervision orders. Thus, whatever the purist force in the argument, there are strong policy objections to the approach advocated on behalf of the appellant. In our view it is not right ... An insane person cannot set the standards of reasonableness as to the degree of force used by reference to his own insanity.'

CASE EXAMPLE

Oye [2013] EWCA Crim 1725; [2014] 1 All ER 902

Seun Oye, a 29-year-old man of previous good character, had been discovered behaving oddly in a café in west London. The police were called. Oye hid in a void in the ceiling, giving non-sensical reasons for his refusal to come down, and throwing crockery at the police officers. He was arrested and detained but his disconcerting behaviour continued in the police station. At one point he tried to escape, knocking a male police officer to the ground and punching a female officer, fracturing her jaw. As other officers arrived, he fought violently, lashing out and shrieking. He was eventually hospitalised under the Mental Health Act. Oye was charged with inflicting GBH and affray, to which he pleaded self-defence and insanity. He claimed that the police officers had 'demonic faces' and to be the agents of 'evil spirits' against whom he needed to protect himself. Medical experts agreed that Oye had experienced a 'psychotic episode'. The jury rejected both of his defences and convicted. On appeal, the Court of Appeal agreed that Oye was not entitled to plead self-defence because of his psychotic delusions but did allow his appeal on the basis of insanity. The Court quashed his convictions and substituted a 'special verdict' of not guilty by reason of insanity (see Chapter 9 for a discussion of the implications of this).

In *Martin* (2001), Lord Woolf said that, although it was a general principle that evidence of psychiatric disorder could not be adduced to support a plea of self-defence, such evidence might nevertheless be admissible 'in exceptional circumstances which would make the evidence especially probative'. In *Oye*, D sought to distinguish *Martin* and *Canns* on the basis that his case involved 'exceptional circumstances'. This was rejected. The Court of Appeal acknowledged that what exactly Lord Woolf in *Martin* had meant by 'exceptional circumstances' was 'unexplained', but Davis LJ said that 'at all events if *Martin* was not considered an exceptional case then we do not see how or why the present case should be'.

QUESTIONS

(a) What 'exceptional circumstances' might trigger the admission of psychiatric disorder in self-defence cases?

(b) The principles set out in *Martin*, *Canns* and *Oye* remain purely common law and have not (yet) been incorporated into the Criminal Justice and Immigration Act 2008. Should Parliament amend s 76 again, perhaps along the following lines?

'Subsection (4)(b) does not enable D to rely on any mistaken belief induced by psychosis or any other psychiatric disorder, unless there are exceptional circumstances which would make the evidence especially probative.'

8.5.3 Intoxication, mistake and self-defence

It was seen, above, that D can plead self-defence even where there was no actual attack, provided that D genuinely believed that he was under attack, and the force used was reasonable in the circumstances that D genuinely believed to exist (*Williams*, *Beckford* and *Owino*). However, according to the Court of Appeal in *O'Grady* [1987] QB 995, a mistaken belief in the need to use force in self-defence is no defence if that mistake was caused by D's voluntary intoxication. Lord Lane CJ was concerned that, because self-defence is a full defence, if the principles described above were to be applied to intoxicated defendants, then dangerous criminals could go unpunished.

CASE EXAMPLE

O'Grady [1987] QB 995

D and his friend V had been drinking heavily when they fell asleep in the former's flat. D, who claimed that he awoke when V began hitting him with a piece of glass, picked up an ashtray and hit V with it, killing him. The judge's direction suggested that D would have a defence if his intoxication caused him to believe he was under attack; but not if his intoxication caused him to use unreasonable force. He was convicted of manslaughter. The Court of Appeal held that this direction in fact erred in favour of D. Instead, they concluded that where the jury are satisfied that D was mistaken either that any force or the force which he in fact used was necessary and, furthermore, that the mistake was caused by intoxication, the defence must fail.

Lord Lane CJ said:

JUDGMENT

'This brings us to the question of public order. There are two competing interests. On the one hand the defendant who has only acted according to what he believed to be necessary to protect himself, and on the other hand that of the public and the victim in particular who probably through no fault of his own, has been injured or perhaps killed because of the defendant's drunken mistake. Reason recoils from the conclusion that in such circumstances a defendant is entitled to leave the court without a stain on his character.'

Lord Lane's opinion in *O'Grady*, that a drunken mistake was no basis for a defence of self-defence, was applied by the Court of Appeal in *O'Connor* [1991] Crim LR 135 and *Hatton* [2005] EWCA Crim 2951; [2006] 1 Cr App R 16. In *Hatton*, D was charged with murder. The defence suggested that D, who was drunk, may have believed that V was attacking him with a sword. The trial judge, however, ruled that a mistaken belief in the need to use force in self-defence, where the mistake was due to intoxication, provided no defence – even to murder. The jury convicted D of murder and the Court of Appeal upheld his conviction.

CASE EXAMPLE

Hatton [2005] EWCA Crim 2951; [2006] 1 Cr App R 16

One night D battered V to death with a sledgehammer. The pair had only met that evening, at a nightclub, before returning to D's flat. During the evening V, who was a manic depressive, had been behaving 'strangely', falsely representing that he had been an SAS officer, striking martial art poses and exhibiting a hatred of homosexuals. After D's arrest he claimed to have no recollection of the killing because he had been drinking heavily beforehand (some 20 pints of beer according to his own evidence). However, he did claim to have a 'vague recollection of being involved in an altercation' with V and that he may have been acting in self-defence. A stick, which had been fashioned into the shape of a samurai sword, belonging to D was found under V's body and provided the basis for D's claim that he may have been attacked by V. D's murder conviction was upheld.

The *O'Grady/Hatton* principle has now been enacted. Section 76(5) of the Criminal Justice and Immigration Act 2008 states that s 76(4)(b) 'does not enable D to rely on any mistaken belief attributable to intoxication that was voluntarily induced'.

8.5.4 'Grossly disproportionate' force in 'householder' cases

Section 43 of the Crime and Courts Act 2013 inserted new provisions into s 76 of the Criminal Justice and Immigration Act 2008. Section 76(5A) of the 2008 Act now provides:

SECTION

'In a householder case, the degree of force used by D is not to be regarded as having been reasonable in the circumstances as D believed them to be if it was grossly disproportionate in those circumstances.'

The effect of this amendment is to allow a 'householder' to use 'disproportionate' force against an intruder and still be entitled to plead self-defence. Only if the 'householder' uses 'grossly disproportionate' force will the defence be rendered unavailable. The new legislation was designed to clarify the law in cases where homeowners use force, potentially lethal force, against burglars. The changes will undoubtedly attract popular support. In 2003, listeners to the BBC Radio 4 programme *Today* were invited to suggest new laws; the most popular suggestion involved this very issue (see M Jefferson, 'Householders and the use of force against intruders' (2005) 69 J Crim L 405). Nevertheless, to say that this is a controversial development is an understatement.

First, there are questions about whether the new law is right in principle. Is it right that the law should afford one, relatively small, category of potential defendant (i.e. the 'householder') a better chance of avoiding criminal liability than other categories? As one commentator has pointed out, the 2013 amendments place 'the "startled householder" in a better position than *every other defendant* in cases involving self-defence' (N Wake, 'Battered women, startled householders and psychological self-defence: Anglo-Australian perspectives' (2013) 77 J Crim L 433, emphasis added).

There is also an argument that the new law, ostensibly designed to protect homeowners, might actually have the opposite effect. This argument postulates that, once burglars become aware that homeowners can use 'disproportionate' force against them, some of those burglars might be more likely to arm themselves with weapons, creating more danger for homeowners.

There is also an argument that, by sanctioning the use of 'disproportionate' force, the state is encouraging a more dangerous, revenge-driven, vigilante culture. If a householder stabs a burglar to death with a kitchen knife using 'disproportionate' force in self-defence, this is lawful under s 76(5A). Does this mean that Parliament has effectively reintroduced the death penalty for burglary?

Second, there are numerous ambiguities in the legislation which raise questions about the practical application of the new law and which will inevitably attract litigation. Section 76(8A) of the 2008 Act (as amended by the 2013 Act) does provide some clarification of what is meant by 'a householder case':

SECTION

'For the purposes of this section "a householder case" is a case where –

(a) the defence concerned is the common law defence of self-defence,
(b) the force concerned is force used by D while in or partly in a building, or part of a building, that is a dwelling ...
(c) D is not a trespasser at the time the force is used, and
(d) at that time D believed V to be in, or entering, the building or part as a trespasser.'

Section 76(8D) provides that 'subsections (4) and (5) apply for the purposes of subsection (8A)(d) as they apply for the purposes of subsection (3)' and s 76(8F) adds that 'building' includes a 'vehicle or vessel'.

These provisions do help, to an extent, but do they go far enough? Some commentators think not. In particular, it has been pointed out that there is no explanation in the Act as to the difference between 'disproportionate' force (which is permitted in 'householder' cases) and 'grossly disproportionate' force (which is not). I Dobinson and E Elliott, 'A householder's right to kill or injure an intruder under the Crime & Courts Act 2013: an Australian comparison' (2014) 78 J Crim L 80, comment:

QUOTATION

> 'The amendments are not only vague in terms of "disproportionate" force, but also in terms of the circumstances of a so-called "householder case" ... There appears to be no requirement that the householder be attacked or threatened with violence.'

To similar effect, see S Miller, 'Grossly disproportionate: home owners' legal licence to kill' (2013) 77 J Crim L 299, who notes:

QUOTATION

> 'It is difficult to see how the amendments to s 76 of the Criminal Justice and Immigration Act 2008 will help clarify the law in this area. Widening the scope with regard to what homeowners can do to intruders only extends the permitted violence – it does not clarify the law any further. It is still within the court's discretion to judge what is "grossly disproportionate" rather than "reasonable".'

Notwithstanding this criticism, the following points should be noted about the scope of the 'householder case'.

(a) Need to be acting in 'self-defence'

Section 76(5A) only concerns 'the common law defence of self-defence'. At first glance, this appears to rule out cases where D was acting in defence of others, for example his or her children. However, this is not the case: s 76(10) of the 2008 Act states that 'references to self-defence include acting in defence of another person'. Thus, D is entitled to use 'disproportionate' force in protecting themselves and/or other people in a dwelling.

On the other hand, D cannot use 'disproportionate' force in order to defend property – only 'proportionate'/'reasonable' force may be used here.

(b) Need to be in – or partly in – a 'dwelling'

D must be in, or partly in, a 'building' which is also a 'dwelling'. Most obviously, this means that if D is in his or her own home, s 76(5A) will apply. However, there is no requirement that it be D's *own* dwelling. For example, if D is staying as a guest with friends or relatives in their home and uses 'disproportionate' force against a burglar, it will still be classed as a 'householder case'. Vehicles and vessels are included as 'buildings', which means that if D is in, or partly in, a caravan or houseboat, s 76(5A) will apply. But it would appear that D could not invoke s 76(5A) if they were in, or partly in, a tent, for example.

The concept of being 'partly in' a building is undefined in the Act and may well attract litigation. However, it is clearly designed to deal with cases where D uses 'disproportionate' force against a burglar (or attempted burglar) whilst stood in the doorway or other entrance of a dwelling – perhaps even whilst leaning out of a window. As long as D was at least 'partly' in a building which is also a 'dwelling', s 76(5A) will apply.

(c) Need to believe that V was trespassing

Although s 76(5A) is clearly designed to deal with householders who use force against burglars, there is no requirement that V actually was trespassing, or even that V was in the building, at the time. It is sufficient that D *believed* that V was in, or was entering, the building as a trespasser. To reiterate, s 76(8D) of the 2008 Act states that 'subsections (4) and (5) apply for the purposes of subsection (8A)(d) as they apply for the purposes of subsection (3)'. This means that:

- D's belief may be mistaken, even unreasonably mistaken; provided it is a genuinely held (and sober) belief, D can rely upon it.
- D cannot rely upon a mistaken belief if that belief was induced by voluntary intoxication.

It is useful to consider how s 76(5A) might apply to some of the pre-existing cases, discussed above, involving householders and burglars. In *Martin* (2001), D's plea of self-defence was rejected and he was convicted of murder (and wounding with intent) on the basis that he used excessive force in shooting at two burglars in his home, killing one of them and injuring the other. Under the new law, Tony Martin may well have been acquitted on the basis that the force used was not 'grossly disproportionate' according to the facts as he believed them to be. In *Hussain and another* (2010), however, the outcome would be exactly the same. In that case, the defendants chased a burglar down the street before attacking him with a cricket bat and other weapons, causing serious injury. Their self-defence plea failed and it is clear that s 76(5A) would not alter this verdict: at the time of the force being used, the defendants were not 'in or partly in a building'.

8.5.5 Should excessive force in homicide reduce murder to manslaughter?

In *Palmer*, Lord Morris said that if the prosecution proves that D had used excessive force in self-defence, then 'that issue is eliminated from the case'. He added that 'self-defence either succeeds so as to result in an acquittal or it is disproved in which case as a defence it is rejected'. That principle of law has the potential to produce harsh results, particularly in murder cases where the use of some force was necessary, but D has used more force than was reasonable. It has therefore been suggested that the use of excessive force in murder cases should result in a conviction of manslaughter (which would allow the judge to exercise sentencing discretion). The House of Lords in *Clegg* [1995] 1 AC 482 considered this question. On the facts of the case, the Lords found that, as the danger had passed, the issue of excessive force did not, strictly speaking, arise. The Lords nevertheless reviewed the authorities on the use of excessive force in self-defence. Their speeches, although *obiter*, are obviously very persuasive. According to Lord Lloyd, if excessive force is used in self-defence, this did not justify reducing liability from murder to manslaughter.

CASE EXAMPLE

Clegg [1995] 1 AC 482

D, a soldier of the Parachute Regiment, was on duty at a checkpoint in west Belfast one night. The purpose of the checkpoint was to catch joyriders, although this had not been explained to D. A car (which turned out to be stolen) approached D's section of patrol at speed with its headlights full on. Someone from a different section shouted to stop the car. All four members of D's section fired at the car. D fired three shots through the windscreen as the car approached and a fourth at the car as it passed. This last shot hit a female passenger in the back and killed her. Forensic evidence showed that the last shot was fired after the car had passed and would already have been ten yards away on the road to Belfast. On trial for murder of the passenger and the attempted murder of the driver, D pleaded self-defence of himself and a fellow soldier. He was convicted after the trial judge found that this last shot was fired with the intention of causing death or serious harm and that D could not have fired in self-defence because, once the car had passed, none of the soldiers were in any danger. The Northern Ireland Court of Appeal upheld the conviction, on the basis that the last shot was a 'grossly excessive and disproportionate' use of force. The House of Lords rejected D's appeal.

KEY FACTS

Key facts on self-defence

Elements	Comment	Case
Must be necessary to use some force	Purely subjective test, based on D's genuine belief. D may be mistaken but is still entitled to plead the defence.	*Williams* (1987), *Beckford* (1988)
	D may make a pre-emptive strike.	*Beckford*
	D may prepare for an attack. There is no 'duty' to retreat.	*A-G's Ref (No 2 of 1983)* (1984) *Bird* (1985), s 76(6A) Criminal Justice and Immigration Act 2008
Amount of force used must be reasonable	Objective test (decided by jury) but based on D's genuine perception of events, whether or not D was mistaken.	*Palmer* (1971), *Shannon* (1980), *Whyte* (1987), *Owino* (1996), s 76(3), (4) and (7) Criminal Justice and Immigration Act 2008
	D's psychological characteristics are not relevant.	*Martin* (2001), *Canns* (2005), *Oye* (2013)
	The use of 'disproportionate' force means that the defence fails.	S 76(6) Criminal Justice and Immigration Act 2008
	The use of excessive force cannot reduce murder to manslaughter.	*Clegg* (1995) (but see s 54 of the Coroners and Justice Act 2009)
Role of intoxication	If D pleads self-defence based on an intoxicated mistake, then the defence fails.	*O'Grady* (1987), *O'Connor* (1991), *Hatton* (2005), s 76(5) Criminal Justice and Immigration Act 2008
Special rules apply in 'householder cases'	'Disproportionate' force may be used against an intruder. Only 'grossly disproportionate' force negates the defence in 'householder' cases.	s 76(5A) Criminal Justice and Immigration Act 2008

However, Parliament has now provided a partial defence where D kills but used excessive force in doing so. The defence, found in s 54 of the Coroners and Justice Act 2009, will be discussed in more detail in Chapter 10. In essence it provides a defence where D lost self-control as the result of a 'fear of serious violence', provided that a person of D's age and sex, with a 'normal degree of tolerance and self-restraint', and in the circumstances of D, might have reacted in 'the same or in a similar way'. If these elements are satisfied (and the burden of proof is on the prosecution to disprove them), then D will be found not guilty of murder but guilty of manslaughter.

8.6 Consent

Consent is a defence to, in theory at least, all non-fatal offences and even homicides. The onus of proving lack of consent rests on the prosecution (*Donovan* [1934] 2 KB 498). Is consent a defence, or is lack of consent an element of the offence? In the leading House of Lords case, *Brown and others* [1994] 1 AC 212, the majority (Lords Templeman, Lowry and Jauncey) assumed that all physical contact is assault unless a specific defence (here consent) applied; the minority assumed that it is a prerequisite of assault that there is no consent.

8.6.1 Consent must be real

The fact that V apparently consents to D's act does not mean that the law will treat that consent as valid. If V is a child, or has learning difficulties, this apparent consent may not suffice (*Howard* [1965] 3 All ER 684). The question is whether V was able to comprehend the nature of the act. Thus, in *Burrell v Harmer* [1967] Crim LR 169, D was convicted of assault occasioning ABH after tattooing two boys aged 12 and 13, the result being that their arms became inflamed and painful. The court held there was no consent, as the boys did not understand the nature of the act. Presumably they understood what a tattoo was, but they would not have understood the level of pain involved.

8.6.2 Consent and fraud

Fraud does not necessarily negative consent. It only does so if it deceives V as to the identity of the person or the 'nature and quality' of the act. In *Clarence* (1888) 22 QBD 23, D had sexual intercourse with his wife (with her consent), having failed to reveal to her the fact that he was infected with gonorrhoea, a sexually transmittable disease. D was convicted of inflicting GBH and ABH, but, on appeal, these convictions were quashed. Stephen J said:

JUDGMENT

'Is the man's concealment of the fact that he was infected such a fraud as vitiated his wife's consent to his exercise of marital rights and converted the act of connection into an assault? It seems to me the proposition that fraud vitiates consent in criminal matters is not true if taken to apply in the fullest sense of the word and without qualification ... If we apply it ... to the present case, it is difficult to say that the prisoner was not guilty of rape, for the definition of rape is having connection with a woman without her consent; and if fraud vitiates consent, every case in which a man infects a woman ... is also a case of rape.'

On similar reasoning there was no offence committed in the following cases:

- *Bolduc and Bird* (1967) 63 DLR (2d) 82. D, a doctor, by falsely telling V that E was a medical student, obtained her consent to the latter's presence at a vaginal examination.

In fact E was a musician. The Supreme Court of Canada held that there was no assault because the fraud was not as to the 'nature and quality' of what was to be done.

- *Richardson* [1998] EWCA 1086; [1998] 2 Cr App R 200. D was a dentist until August 1996 when the General Dental Council suspended her from practice. However, she continued to treat patients. She was subsequently charged with six counts of ABH following treatment given to six patients in September 1996. She was convicted, but the Court of Appeal allowed the appeal. The Court held that, where the patients' consent to treatment was procured only by a failure to inform them that she was no longer qualified to practice, she could not be guilty of an assault. The Court confirmed that fraud only negatived consent to an assault if V was deceived as to the identity of the person concerned or the 'nature and quality' of the act performed. The concept of 'identity of the person', moreover, could not be extended to cover D's qualifications or other attributes.

However, in *Tabassum* [2000] 2 Cr App R 328, the Court of Appeal distinguished both *Clarence* (1888) and *Richardson* (1998). The Court of Appeal drew a distinction between consent to the 'nature' of a touching and consent as to its 'quality'. Rose LJ said that the victims were 'consenting to touching for medical purposes not to indecent behaviour, that is, there was consent to the nature of the act but not its quality'.

CASE EXAMPLE

Tabassum [2000] 2 Cr App R 328

D had a degree in chemistry and postgraduate qualifications on the use of IT in training doctors. However, he had no medical training or qualifications. Over a period of some months in 1997 he examined the breasts of three women, in two cases using his hands and on the third and final occasion with a stethoscope. He obtained their consent on the pretext that the examinations were part of a survey he was conducting, leading ultimately to the production of a computer software package for sale to doctors, to assist in the diagnosis of breast cancer. He did not actually tell them that he was medically qualified, although he did tell two of the women that he had worked at Christie's cancer hospital in Manchester and was a breast cancer specialist. When arrested he denied touching the women's breasts for sexual gratification but had done it in order to show them how to do it for themselves. He also denied acting or pretending to be a doctor. The prosecution case was that all three women would not have consented, had they known the truth about D. The defence case was that the women had all consented to D touching their breasts; he had touched their breasts; but he had done nothing for which he had not been given consent. He was convicted on three counts of indecent assault (an offence which has since been abolished by the Sexual Offences Act 2003; see Chapter 12), and the Court of Appeal upheld all three convictions. As the women were only consenting for medical purposes, they had been deceived as to the 'quality' of D's act, and hence there was no consent.

Support for the decision in *Tabassum* came from the Supreme Court of Canada. In *Cuerrier* [1998] 2 SCR 371, D had unprotected sex with two women, despite knowing that he had contracted HIV and despite having been warned by a nurse to always use a condom when having sexual intercourse. He obtained their consent, but did not tell either woman of his condition (he actually told one of the women that he was not HIV positive when she asked him). Both women testified in court that they would never have consented to unprotected sex with D had they known of his condition. By a majority, the court ruled that *Clarence* was distinguishable and that, on the facts, it was possible that

D had committed a form of aggravated assault. Justifying the decision, L'Heureux-Dube J said that 'those who know they are HIV-positive have a fundamental responsibility to advise their partners of their condition and to ensure that their sex is as safe as possible'.

The doctrine of informed consent

The decisions in *Cuerrier* and *Tabassum* suggested that the decision in *Clarence* was open to review. In *Dica* [2004] EWCA Crim 1103; [2004] QB 1257, the Court of Appeal confirmed that *Clarence* was, indeed, wrongly decided. In *Dica*, the facts of which are virtually identical to *Cuerrier*, D was convicted of two counts of inflicting 'biological' GBH contrary to s 20 OAPA 1861 and, although his convictions were quashed by the Court of Appeal because of a judicial misdirection, the Court took the opportunity to overrule *Clarence*.

CASE EXAMPLE

Dica [2004] EWCA Crim 1103; [2004] QB 1257

Mohammed Dica had been diagnosed with HIV in 1995. Despite this knowledge, he had unprotected sex on a number of occasions with two women, V and W, who had been willing to be sexual partners with D but were unaware of his condition at the time. V claimed that D insisted that they have unprotected sex because he had had a vasectomy. According to V, each time they had sex, D said 'Forgive me in the name of God'. After some time V noticed that her glands were swollen; she went to hospital and was diagnosed with HIV. W's story was similar. D was charged with two offences of inflicting GBH, contrary to s 20 OAPA 1861. He denied the offences contending that any sexual intercourse which had taken place had been consensual. The trial judge made two legal rulings (a) that it was open to the jury to convict D of the charges, notwithstanding the decision in *Clarence*, and (b) that any consent by V and W was irrelevant and provided no defence, because of the serious nature of the disease. D was convicted in October 2003. The Court of Appeal allowed D's appeal, but only on the basis that the trial judge had erred in withdrawing the issue of consent from the jury. If V and/or W had consented to the risk, that continued to provide a defence under s 20. However, the Court confirmed that *Clarence* was no longer good law. Finally, the Court ordered a retrial.

Judge LJ held as follows:

JUDGMENT

'The effect of this judgment . . . is to remove some of the outdated restrictions against the successful prosecution of those who, knowing that they are suffering HIV or some other serious sexual disease, recklessly transmit it through consensual sexual intercourse, and inflict GBH on a person from whom the risk is concealed and who is not consenting to it. In this context, *Clarence* has no continuing relevance. Moreover, to the extent that *Clarence* suggested that consensual sexual intercourse of itself was to be regarded as consent to the risk of consequent disease, again, it is no longer authoritative.'

At Dica's retrial in March 2005, he was again convicted of inflicting 'biological' GBH and sentenced to four-and-a-half years in prison. He then appealed against that conviction and sentence, unsuccessfully, to the Court of Appeal (*Dica* [2005] EWCA Crim 2304). The *Dica* (2004) ruling was relied on shortly afterwards in the similar case of *Konzani* [2005] EWCA Crim 706; [2005] 2 Cr App R 14.

Although *Cuerrier*, *Dica* and *Konzani* all involved HIV, the decisions in those cases could be applied to any life-threatening sexually transmitted disease.

In the first edition of this book, a question was posed whether the defendant in *Dica* could be guilty of rape, on the basis that the victims in that case had not consented to the 'quality' of the act in question, namely sex. That question has now been answered by the Court of Appeal. The answer is 'no'. In *B* [2006] EWCA Crim 2945; [2007] 1 WLR 1567, D – who had previously been diagnosed as HIV positive – was charged with rape contrary to s 1 of the Sexual Offences Act 2003 (see Chapter 12) after having sex with V without disclosing his medical condition. The prosecution's case was that D had subjected V to a prolonged assault; this was denied by D who claimed that V had consented to sex. The prosecution therefore pursued an alternative argument that, notwithstanding V's consent to the physical act of sex, she had not consented to the risk of contracting a potentially fatal disease. This lack of consent meant that D was guilty of rape. The trial judge allowed this argument to go to the jury, and D was convicted of rape, but the Court of Appeal allowed his appeal (although it confirmed that the facts could support a conviction of inflicting GBH contrary to s 20 OAPA 1861, following *Dica*, and ordered a retrial on that charge).

Latham LJ added that the question whether the facts of the *B* case could amount to rape was a matter requiring debate not in a court of law but as a matter of public and social policy, bearing in mind all the facts concerning, *inter alia*, 'questions of personal autonomy in delicate personal relationships'. In other words, that was a matter for Parliament to decide.

The cases of *Cuerrier*, *Dica*, *Konzani* and *B* all involved the situation where D had unprotected sex with V, knowing that he had a sexually transmittable disease beforehand. This knowledge appears to be essential in order for the prosecution to establish subjective recklessness, the minimum *mens rea* state for all non-fatal offences. It follows that, if D did not know (or even suspect) that he was HIV positive, no charge could be brought against him for assaulting V. Authority for this proposition comes from the Supreme Court of Canada case of *Williams* [2003] 2 SCR 134. Here, D had unprotected sex with V despite his knowledge that he was HIV positive. After she contracted the disease as well, D was prosecuted but his conviction of aggravated assault was quashed because the couple had been having unprotected sex for six months prior to D learning of his HIV status. Binnie J (with whom the rest of the Supreme Court of Canada agreed) said that, although D had shown a 'shocking level of recklessness and selfishness', the prosecution could not prove that D's conduct after he learned of his condition had harmed V, because at that point she was possibly, and even probably, already HIV positive herself. The Court accepted medical evidence that a single act of unprotected sex carried a 'significant risk' of HIV transmission. It was therefore at least doubtful that V was free of HIV infection on the date when D learned of his condition. However, the Court convicted D of an attempted aggravated assault (for the law on attempt in English law, see Chapter 6). It is therefore quite possible that, should a case on similar facts occur in England, the court would be required to distinguish *Dica* and *Konzani* but could follow *Williams* and convict D of attempted ABH, attempted GBH – or even attempted murder.

8.6.3 The scope of consent

There are limits to anyone's right to consent to the infliction of harm upon themselves. Consensual killing is still murder (or possibly manslaughter on the ground of diminished responsibility), or euthanasia as it is popularly known. According to Lord Mustill in *Brown and others* [1994] 1 AC 212, 'The maintenance of human life is "an overriding imperative".' However, V may consent to a high *risk* of injury, or even death, if justified by the purpose of D's act. This depends on the social utility of the act. Where the act has some social purpose, it is a question of balancing the degree of harm which will or may be caused, against the value of D's purpose. In *Attorney-General's Reference (No 6 of 1980)* [1981] 2 All ER 1057, two youths, aged 17 and 18, decided to settle an argument with a bare-knuckle fist fight. One had sustained a bloody nose and a bruised face. Following acquittals, the Court of Appeal held that the defence of consent was not available in this situation. Lord Lane CJ said:

JUDGMENT

'It is not in the public interest that people should try to cause or should cause each other actual bodily harm for no good reason ... Nothing we have said is intended to cast doubt on the accepted legality of properly conducted games and sports, lawful chastisement or correction, reasonable surgical interference, dangerous exhibitions etc. These apparent exceptions can be justified as involving the exercise of a legal right, in the case of chastisement or correction, or as needed in the public interest, in the other cases.'

In *Brown and others* [1994] 1 AC 212, the majority's view was that consent was a defence to a charge of common assault, but not to any offence under s 47, s 20 or s 18 OAPA 1861 unless a recognised exception applied. These, according to Lord Templeman, related to 'lawful activities' which carried a risk of harm. He listed the following examples:

- contact sports, including boxing
- surgery
- ritual circumcision
- tattooing
- ear-piercing.

The appellants argued for a different test altogether. They suggested that GBH should always be unlawful but that the infliction of wounds or ABH would not be unlawful, provided there was consent. The majority rejected the argument, holding that precedent drew the line below ABH. The majority seemed concerned that if the law was drawn too high, it might encourage more serious behaviour, with the attendant risk that even more serious harm might occur. Lord Jauncey said, 'An inflicter who is carried away by sexual excitement or by drink or drugs could very easily inflict pain and injury beyond the level to which the receiver had consented.'

Contact sports

No prosecutions have ever been brought in respect of boxing matches conducted within the Queensberry Rules. The high entertainment value and popularity of the sport is taken to justify V's consent to D trying to inflict serious injury potentially amounting to GBH. The enormously popular 'sport' of professional wrestling is regarded in the same light. However, fights conducted outside the scope of the Rules (sometimes referred to as 'prize fights') are not regarded as justifying V's consent. Any entertainment value they may have is far outweighed by the risk of injury to the fighters. Thus, in *Coney* (1882) 8 QBD 534, prosecutions were brought against various spectators at a bare-knuckle prize fight, for aiding and abetting the unlawful activities. One question for the court was whether the consent of the participants negated the unlawful element of assault. Cave J said:

JUDGMENT

> 'The true view is that a blow struck in anger, or which is likely or is intended to do corporal hurt, is an assault, but that a blow struck in sport, and not likely, nor intended to cause bodily harm, is not an assault, and that, an assault being a breach of the peace and unlawful, the consent of the person struck is immaterial. If this view is correct, a blow struck in a prize-fight is clearly an assault; but . . . wrestling [does] not involve an assault, nor does boxing with gloves in the ordinary way.'

More recently, in *Lee* [2006] 3 NZLR 42, Glazebrook J in the New Zealand Court of Appeal attempted to rationalise the distinction between (lawful) boxing matches and (unlawful) street-fighting or prize-fights. He said:

JUDGMENT

> 'In organised matches, opponents are usually properly matched by weight and skill level and the rules are designed to minimise the risk of GBH occurring. There is a referee to ensure that the rules are complied with and thus that the level of violence does not exceed that consented to by the protagonists. There seems minimal risk that those participating in organised bouts are not truly consenting . . . In addition, organised properly, such sports do not have a tendency to lead to a breach of the peace, one of the reasons given in *Coney* for outlawing prize fights. There also remains a significant portion of the community who consider that such fights are acceptable forms of entertainment and therefore (presumably) that they have some social utility.'

With other contact sports such as football, rugby and ice hockey, a clear distinction must be drawn between two situations. An off-the-ball incident is in principle no different to any other assault, involving as it does the deliberate use of unlawful force. There is no suggestion that players consent, impliedly or otherwise, to the use of force in such situations. This is shown by *Billinghurst* [1978] Crim LR 553.

CASE EXAMPLE

Billinghurst [1978] Crim LR 553

D punched V in an off-the-ball incident during a rugby union match, fracturing his jaw in two places. He was convicted of inflicting GBH. The only defence was consent. D gave evidence that on previous occasions he had been punched and had himself punched opponents on the rugby field. The trial judge directed the jury that rugby was a contact sport involving the use of force and that players are deemed to consent to force 'of a kind which could reasonably be expected to happen during a game'. He went on to direct them that a rugby player has no unlimited licence to use force and that 'there must obviously be cases which cross the line of that to which a player is deemed to consent'. A distinction that the jury might regard as decisive was that between force used in the course of play and force used outside the course of play. The jury convicted.

The commentary to *Billinghurst* (1978) gives another example, contrasting a batsman in cricket being accidentally hit on the head by a 'fast' delivery (no assault, regardless of the seriousness of the injury) and another batsman being hit on the head after the bowler picked up a 'dead' ball and deliberately threw it at his head (assault). Problems arise where the alleged assault occurs on-the-ball, during play. The players in modern contact sports impliedly consent to D doing what the rules of the particular game permit, and even to go *beyond* the rules – in other words, to commit fouls. Otherwise, every time a foul was committed in football or rugby it would constitute a criminal offence, which would rapidly turn contact sports into non-contact sports, completely defeating the object of having a contact sport in the first place.

The rules themselves, therefore, only provide a guide as to what has been consented to. In *Bradshaw* (1878) 14 Cox CC 83 and *Moore* (1898) 14 TLR 229, it was said that 'no rules or practice of any game whatever can make lawful that which is unlawful by the law of the land'. Therefore where an alleged criminal assault has occurred during play, this should be assessed independently of the rules. Lord Mustill in *Brown and others* (1994) referred to a series of Canadian decisions on ice hockey, including *Ciccarelli* (1989) 54 CCC (3d) 121. There the courts accept that all the players consent to a certain level of violence. Each particular case should be treated on its facts: could V be said to have tacitly accepted a risk of violence at the level that actually occurred? The Canadian courts have provided a helpful list of criteria to determine the scope of implied consent in sport, including:

- the nature of the game played, whether amateur or professional league and so on;
- the nature of the particular acts(s) and their surrounding circumstances;
- the degree of force employed;
- the degree of risk of injury;
- the state of mind of the accused.

Ice hockey is a particularly violent sport, and in one Canadian case, *Moloney* (1976) 28 CCC (2d) 323, the judge ruled that ice hockey players impliedly consented to 'body contacts, boardings [i.e. being shoved into the boards around the rink] and maybe even a fight if it is two players consenting to the fight with each other'. In another case, *Gray* (1981) 24 CR (3d) 109, the judge said that 'it might well be that it would be extremely difficult to convict any hockey player of a common assault for his play during a game'. The position is obviously different if the referee's whistle has been blown to stop play before the alleged assault occurred. In *Ciccarelli* (1989), D was a professional ice hockey player with the Minnesota North Stars. He was convicted of assaulting V, a player with the Toronto Maple Leafs, during a game. The whistle had blown for offside against D when V, who had been skating across to block D, was unable to stop and they collided. D retaliated, using his stick to hit V over the head three times. The officials intervened to separate the pair but D punched out at them too. D was convicted of assault and his appeal dismissed.

In *Barnes* [2004] EWCA Crim 3246; [2005] 1 WLR 910, the Court of Appeal held that prosecutions should only be brought against a player who injured another player in the course of a sporting event if his conduct was 'sufficiently grave to be properly categorised as criminal', where what had occurred had gone beyond what the injured player could reasonably be regarded as having accepted by taking part in the sport.

CASE EXAMPLE

Barnes [2004] EWCA Crim 3246; [2005] 1 WLR 910

Mark Barnes was convicted of inflicting GBH under s 20 OAPA 1861 following a tackle in the course of an amateur football match. The prosecution alleged that it was the result of a 'late, unnecessary, reckless and high crashing tackle'. D claimed that the tackle was a fair, if hard, challenge in the course of play and that any injury caused was accidental. The Court of Appeal allowed the appeal.

Lord Woolf CJ said that the starting point was the fact that most organised sports had their own disciplinary procedures for enforcing their particular rules and standards of conduct. There was also the possibility of an injured player obtaining damages in a civil action. A criminal prosecution should be reserved for situations where the conduct was sufficiently grave to be properly categorised as criminal. In all contact sports, the participants impliedly consent to the risk of certain levels of harm. However, according to Lord Woolf, what was implicitly accepted in one sport would not necessarily be covered by the defence in another sport. In highly competitive sports, such as rugby, football and ice hockey conduct outside the rules could be expected to occur in the 'heat of the moment' and, even if the conduct justified a warning or a sending off, it still might not reach the threshold level required for it to be criminal. That level was an objective one and did not depend on the views of individual players.

The type of sport, the level at which it was played, the nature of the act, the degree of force used, the extent of the risk of injury and D's state of mind were all likely to be relevant in determining whether D's actions went beyond the threshold. Whether conduct reached the required threshold to be criminal would therefore depend on all the circumstances. There would be cases that fell within a 'grey area' and then the tribunal of fact would have to make its own determination as to which side of the line the case fell. In such a situation the jury would need to ask themselves, among other questions, whether the contact was so 'obviously late and/or violent' that it could not be regarded as 'an instinctive reaction, error or misjudgment in the heat of the game'.

In *Attorney-General's Reference (No 6 of 1980)*, 'games and sports' were the first examples provided by the Court of Appeal of situations where there is a 'good reason' for people to consent to the risk of being injured, because it was in 'the public interest' to do so. But what, exactly, is that 'interest'? The Court of Appeal did not explain but commentators have attempted to do so instead. S Cooper and M James, 'Entertainment: the painful process of rethinking consent' [2012] Crim LR 188, for example, contend that 'Sport is socially beneficial because it promotes health, exercise and principles, such as teamwork and fair play, which are valued by society.'

Surgery

With 'reasonable surgical interference' there is really no issue of consent as a defence to bodily harm, given that no harm is caused or inflicted. But in surgery there is certainly a 'wounding', and the patient must consent to that. Consent to any recognised surgical procedure is effective; this includes sex-change operations (*Corbett v Corbett* [1971] P 83) and probably cosmetic surgery and organ transplants. In *Bravery v Bravery* [1954] 3 All ER 59, which concerned the legality of a sterilisation operation, Denning LJ stated:

JUDGMENT

> 'When it is done with the man's consent for a just cause, it is quite lawful, as, for instance, when it is done to prevent the transmission of an hereditary disease. But when it is done without just cause or excuse, it is unlawful, even though the man consents to it. Take a case where a sterilisation operation is done so as to enable a man to have the pleasure of sexual intercourse without shouldering the responsibilities attaching to it. The operation is then injurious to the public interest.'

The point was reversed by the National Health Service (Family Planning) Amendment Act 1972, but the view of the court and the influence of public policy are nevertheless interesting.

It is important to note that the Court of Appeal referred to 'reasonable surgical interference', the implication being that not all surgery is 'reasonable'. One example of 'unreasonable' surgery is female circumcision. This is undoubtedly 'surgical interference' but it is only lawful in certain specific circumstances, i.e. when necessary for a girl's 'physical or mental health' or for 'purposes connected with labour or birth'. Otherwise, female circumcision is a criminal offence (s 1(1), Female Genital Mutilation Act 2003).

Horseplay

Society accepts that community life, such as in the playground, may involve a mutual risk of deliberate physical contact and that the criminal law may distance itself. Honest belief, even if based on unreasonable grounds, that the others consent, will negative recklessness. In *Jones and others* [1987] Crim LR 123, some boys were injured having been tossed into the air by schoolmates. Despite not consenting to being thrown in the air at all, never mind the height at which they were thrown, the Court of Appeal held that there was no assault. A similar result was achieved in *Aitken and others* [1992] 1 WLR 1006.

CASE EXAMPLE

Aitken and others [1992] 1 WLR 1006

All those involved were RAF officers who attended a party where they all became drunk and engaged in an 'initiation ceremony' which involved setting fire to V's fire-resistant suit. The appellants overcame V's resistance and poured a large quantity of white spirit on to his suit before igniting it. He was severely burned. Nevertheless, the Courts-Martial Appeal Court quashed convictions of GBH on the basis that the question of whether or not the appellants genuinely believed V to be consenting had not been put to the court.

The presence of 'horseplay' on the list of 'good reasons' where consent to the risk of injury is valid is controversial. There is a school of thought which suggests that tolerating 'rough' physical activity presents bullies with an opportunity to use violence against other (typically, physically and/or psychologically weaker) people with legal impunity. C Stychin, 'Unmanly diversions' (1994) 32 Osgood Hall LJ 503, categorises the events in *Aitken and others* as involving a 'brutalization' of the victim. He contends that the Court of Appeal reduced the activity to 'mere' or 'friendly' horseplay, a term which 'conjures up innocent schoolboys'.

In a number of cases involving off-the-ball incidents in contact sports, the judiciary has observed that lawful activities such as rugby do not provide the participants with a 'licence for thuggery' (see e.g. Pill LJ in *Lloyd* (1989) 11 Cr App R (S) 36). One could argue that, whereas in sports like football and rugby where there are rules and a referee to at least try to ensure that the players do not cross the line between robust physical activity (lawful) and thuggery (unlawful), with 'rough horseplay' there are no such protections. As Stychin observes about *Aitken and others*, V's injuries were 'the result of a controlled activity that got out of hand. The rules of the game, *if they ever existed*, were transgressed as the thrill of victimization caused the limits to be crossed' (emphasis added).

So, what justification is there for tolerating horseplay? Cooper and James (2012) suggest that 'it appears that this category of activity is exempted because one must expect a bit of rough play in life and that this is a normal and healthy part of growing up, provided that the injury is not inflicted intentionally'.

Sexual activity

In *Boyea* [1992] Crim LR 574, D inserted his hand into V's vagina, and twisted it causing injuries consistent with the use of force. He was convicted of indecent assault and the Court of Appeal dismissed his appeal, which was based on his belief that V was consenting. The court held that V's consent to an assault was irrelevant if the jury were satisfied that the assault was intended to, or likely to, cause harm, provided the injury was not 'transient or trifling'. In *Slingsby* [1995] Crim LR 570, the question was whether D had committed an unlawful act for the purposes of constructive manslaughter (see Chapter 10). The answer was 'no', because V had given a valid consent in the context of sexual activity.

CASE EXAMPLE

Slingsby [1995] Crim LR 570

D had met the deceased, V, at a nightclub and later had vaginal and anal intercourse with her, with her consent. Subsequently, also with her consent, he had penetrated her vagina and rectum with his hand. V suffered internal cuts caused by a ring on D's hand. She was unaware how serious these were and, although she was eventually admitted to hospital, she died of septicaemia. The trial judge held that it was clearly established that the deliberate infliction of bodily harm on another without good reason was unlawful. Furthermore, the infliction of violence for the purposes of sexual gratification, whether that be the gratification of either party, is unlawful (relying on *Boyea* (1992) and *Brown and others* (1994)). However, in this case it was clear that all the activities were consented to by V; consequently, there was no assault, and therefore D was not guilty of manslaughter.

Tattooing and other forms of branding

Consent is a valid defence to tattooing. The majority of the Lords in *Brown and others* (1994) accepted that much. The Court of Appeal confirmed and extended this proposition in *Wilson* [1997] 3 WLR 125, saying that branding was no more hazardous than a tattoo.

CASE EXAMPLE

Wilson [1997] 3 WLR 125

D had branded his initials, 'A' and 'W', on to his wife's buttocks using a hot blade. She regarded the branding as 'a desirable personal adornment' and had apparently originally requested that the branding be on her breasts. It was D who persuaded her to have the branding on her buttocks instead. The matter only came to light when her doctor reported the incident to the police. D was convicted of assault occasioning ABH and appealed. The Court of Appeal allowed the appeal.

In *R v Barker* [2009] NZCA 186; [2010] 1 NZLR 235, a majority of the Court of Appeal of New Zealand held that consent was available in a case involving 'scarification' (the cutting of skin to produce scars). D was a 50-year-old man who had an interest in bondage, discipline and sadomasochism (BDSM), including scarification. There were two alleged victims. The first victim, A, was a 15-year-old girl who had gone to D's house and allowed herself to be tied up and whipped, and to have D cut a dragon symbol into her back using a scalpel. The second alleged victim, B, a 17-year-old girl, allowed D to cut at her breasts and wrists then place her against a mirror to create a 'blood angel'. Both A and B were left with scars. D was convicted of various non-fatal offences under New Zealand's Crimes Act 1961 after the trial judge withdrew consent as a defence, but successfully appealed. Hammond J emphasised the importance of 'personal autonomy' which, he said, outweighed the interest of the state in protecting members of society from harm (the 'ethical paternalistic objection'). Hammond J stated:

JUDGMENT

'Body ornamentation of one form or another – including scarification – appears to be remarkably commonplace today, including amongst young people. Undoubtedly, resort to these practices is seen in many instances as having distinct social utility, for a variety of reasons. The particular practice may be a form of communication, it may be a form of ornamentation, or it may be a cultural practice which may go as far as rites of initiation or personhood. Persons resorting to the practice of scarification are undoubtedly exercising their right to personal autonomy in having recourse to such practices.'

The majority of the New Zealand Court of Appeal in *Barker* followed an earlier decision of the same court, *R v Lee* [2006] 3 NZLR 42, in which Glazebrook J said:

JUDGMENT

'There is an ability to consent to the intentional infliction of harm short of death unless there are good public policy reasons to forbid it and those policy reasons outweigh the social utility of the activity and the value placed by our legal system on personal autonomy. A high value should be placed on personal autonomy.'

Sadomasochism is beyond acceptable limits

As seen above, the courts do accept that injury accidentally inflicted during the course of sexual activity between consenting adults does not amount to assault (even where one of the parties dies). However, the law does not tolerate the idea of consent being a defence to injuries inflicted for the sexual gratification of either party. This was shown by *Donovan* [1934] 2 KB 498.

CASE EXAMPLE

Donovan [1934] 2 KB 498

D had been convicted of common and indecent assault. He had, apparently for his own sexual gratification, beaten a 17-year-old prostitute on the buttocks with a cane 'in circumstances of indecency'. A doctor examined her two days later and concluded that she had had a 'fairly severe beating'. D's convictions were quashed but only because the trial judge had failed to direct the jury that the issue of disproving consent was on the Crown.

In *Brown and others*, when the case was still in the Court of Appeal, Lord Lane CJ said, 'It is not in the public interest that people should try to cause or should cause each other actual bodily harm for no good reason.' This was confirmed by a majority of the Law Lords when the case reached the House of Lords.

CASE EXAMPLE

Brown and others [1994] 1 AC 212

The appellants belonged to a group of sadomasochistic homosexuals who, over a ten-year period, willingly and enthusiastically participated in acts of violence against each other for sexual pleasure. Many of these acts took place in rooms designed as torture chambers. The activities included branding with wire or metal heated by a blowlamp, use of a cat o'nine tails and genital torture. All the activities were carried out in private with the consent of the passive partner or 'victim'. There were no complaints to the police, no medical attention was ever sought and no permanent injury suffered. The police discovered the activities by accident. All members were charged with various offences, including wounding contrary to s 20 and assaults contrary to s 47 OAPA 1861. They were convicted and their appeals dismissed by the Court of Appeal and House of Lords (albeit by a three to two majority).

Lord Templeman said:

JUDGMENT

'In my opinion sado-masochism is not only concerned with sex. Sado-masochism is also concerned with violence ... The violence of sado-masochistic encounters involves the indulgence of cruelty by sadists and the degradation of victims. Such violence is injurious to the participants and unpredictably dangerous.'

Justifying their decision, the majority referred to the risk of infection and the possible spread of AIDS. They did not comment about the role the criminal law should play in tackling the spread of AIDS; rather, no doubt, it was raised in order to make it even harder for the appellants to argue that their activities were a justifiable exception in the public interest. Lord Lowry commented that homosexual sadomasochism could not be regarded as a 'manly diversion', nor were they 'conducive to the enhancement of enjoyment of family life or conducive to the welfare of society'. For Lord Jauncey the corruption of young men was a real danger to be considered. This harks back to the 1957 Wolfenden Report (Committee on Homosexual Offences and Prostitution), which commented that the criminal law in relation to homosexual behaviour was designed 'to preserve public order and decency, to protect the citizen from what is offensive or injurious, and to provide sufficient safeguards against exploitation and corruption of others, particularly those who are especially vulnerable because they are young, weak in body or mind, inexperienced, or in a state of special, physical, official or economic dependence'.

ACTIVITY

Self-test question

Do you agree that the activities in *Brown and others* (1994) can be described as 'offensive or injurious'? Bear in mind everything took place in private. No one was induced or coerced into the activities; there was no evidence that anyone was 'exploited' or 'corrupted'.

The minority (Lords Mustill and Slynn), meanwhile, treated the question as whether the particular activities should be treated as included within the offences charged and concluded that they should not. Lord Mustill said, 'This is not a case about the criminal law of violence. In my opinion it should be about the criminal law of private sexual relations, if about anything at all.' After analysing the authorities, the minority found that there were none binding the House, which was therefore free to decide. Both Law Lords decided that a victim's consent to the infliction of GBH was ineffective but that consent was not necessarily ineffective to the occasioning of ABH. They were clear about what they were being asked to decide. Despite their disgust at the conduct, and their disapproval of it, the only issue was whether the activities were criminal. Lord Mustill identified the specific policy considerations that might point towards criminal liability.

- First, the risk of infection and septicaemia. This was, Lord Mustill said, greatly reduced by modern medicine.
- Second, contrary to what Lord Jauncey said about risks of more serious harm, Lord Mustill thought that the possibility that things might get out of hand with grave results was no reason for criminalising the appellants' conduct. If grave results did occur, however, then they would, of course, attract criminal sanctions.
- Third, the evidence adduced in the case did not support the risk of the spread of AIDS. Such evidence as there was suggested that consensual buggery was the main cause of transmission, and this was, of course, legal.
- Fourth, the possibility of corrupting the young was already provided for by existing legislation.

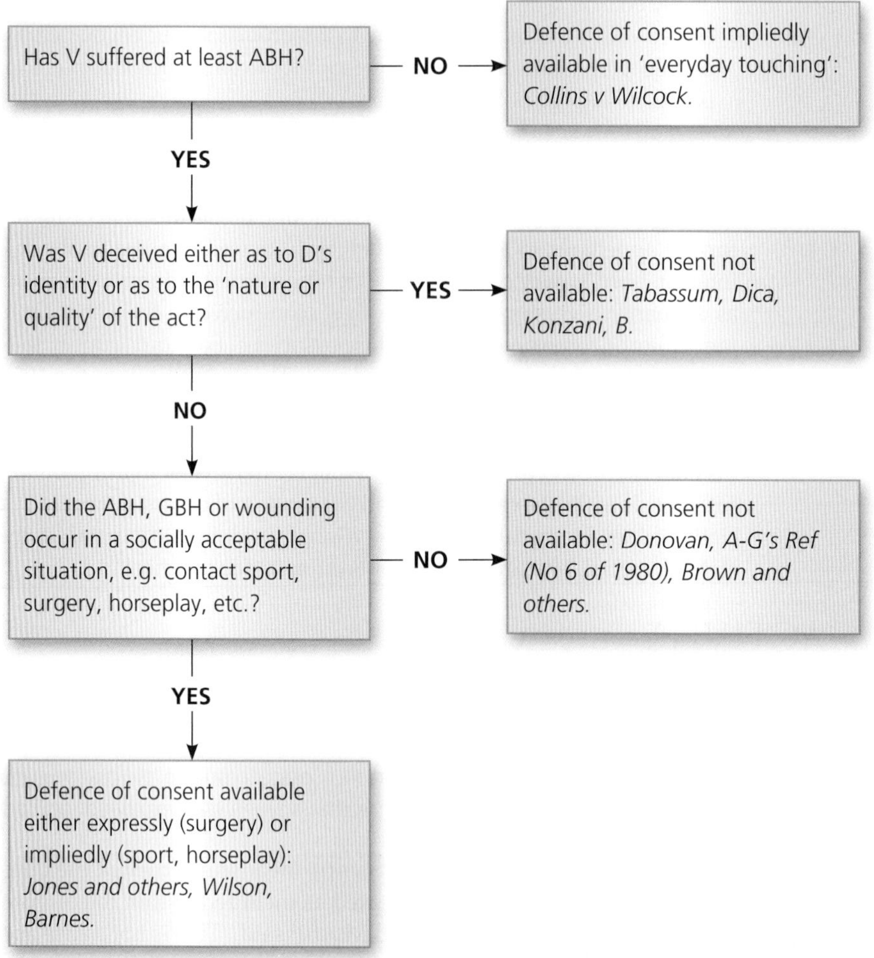

Figure 8.2 The defence of consent.

KEY FACTS

Key facts on consent

Elements	Comment	Cases
Scope of defence	There is implied consent available to all batteries.	*Collins v Wilcock* (1984)
	For ABH, GBH and wounding, consent is only available when there is a 'good reason'.	*Attorney-General's Reference (No 6 of 1980)*
	Consent may be a defence to manslaughter . . .	*Slingsby* (1995)
	. . . but not deliberate killing.	*Pretty* (2002) (see Chapter 2)
Good reasons	Sport (including boxing) is a good reason, but not if defendant is involved in 'off-the-ball' incident.	*Billinghurst* (1978), *Barnes* (2004)
	Horseplay is a good reason, whether involving children or adults.	*Jones and others* (1987), *Aitken and others* (1992)
	Surgery is a good reason, as is tattooing and branding.	*Wilson* (1997)
	Sexual contact is a good reason.	*Slingsby* (1995)
Reasons which are not good	Boxing is good but street fighting is not a good reason.	*Coney* (1882), *Attorney-General's Reference (No 6 of 1980)*
	Sadomasochistic behaviour is not a good reason.	*Donovan* (1934), *Brown and others* (1994), *Emmett* (1999)
Consent and fraud	Victim must have consented to the nature and quality of the defendant's act.	*Clarence* (1888), *Bolduc and Bird* (1967), *Richardson* (1998)
	'Nature' and 'quality' are separate elements and victim must have consented to both of them.	*Cuerrier* (1998), *Tabassum* (2000), *Dica* (2004), *Konzani* (2005)

Lord Slynn thought that the whole area was for Parliament to decide. In *Wilson* (1997), the Court of Appeal distinguished *Brown and others* on its facts but in *Emmett* [1999] EWCA Crim 1710, *The Times*, 15 October 1999, the Court of Appeal applied the House of Lords' judgment. D and his girlfriend, G, enjoyed sadomasochistic sex. On one occasion D had placed a plastic bag over G's head and tied it tightly around her neck. As a result of lack of oxygen, she nearly lost consciousness and suffered bruising to the neck and ruptured blood vessels in her eyes. On another occasion D poured lighter fluid over G's left breast and ignited it. As a result of that injury, D persuaded her to go to the doctor, who informed the police. D was charged with two counts of s 47 ABH. D was convicted and appealed. He sought to rely on *Jones and others* (1986), but the Court of Appeal dismissed the appeal. The acts in the present case could not be construed as 'rough and undisciplined love-play'.

8.6.4 The impact of the European Convention on Human Rights (1950) and the Human Rights Act 1998

In *Laskey v UK* (1997) 24 EHRR 39, the European Court of Human Rights in Strasbourg upheld the judgment of the majority in *Brown and others*. It had been argued before the

Strasbourg Court that the imposition of criminal punishment constituted a breach of art 8(1) of the European Convention, which provides that 'Everyone has the right to respect for his private and family life, his home and his correspondence.' However, the Strasbourg court applied art 8(2), which justifies interference by the State in the art 8(1) rights which 'is necessary in a democratic society ... for the protection of health or morals'. The court ruled that, once conduct had gone beyond a potential risk with a sufficient degree of seriousness, it could not possibly amount to a breach of art 8(1). The Court of Appeal in *Emmett* reached the same conclusion.

JUDGMENT

Extract adapted from the judgment in *R v Brown and others* [1994] 1 AC 212, House of Lords

Facts The appellants, a group of sadomasochists, willingly and enthusiastically participated in the commission of acts of violence against each other for the sexual pleasure it engendered in the giving and receiving of pain. They were charged with various offences under ss 20 and 47 of the Offences Against the Person Act 1861, relating to the infliction of wounds or actual bodily harm on genital and other areas of the body of the consenting victim. After the trial judge ruled that, in the particular circumstances, the prosecution did not have to prove lack of consent by the victim, the appellants changed their pleas to guilty, but appealed against conviction on the ground that the judge had erred in his rulings, in that the willing and enthusiastic consent of the victim to the acts on him prevented the prosecution from proving an essential element of the offence. The Court of Appeal (Criminal Division) dismissed the appeal. The appellants appealed to the House of Lords.	*The significant facts were:* *the appellants were sadomasochists* *they enjoyed giving and receiving pain,* *the trial judge ruled that consent was no defence in the circumstances,* *the appellants claimed that all the participants had given consent.*
Judgment LORD TEMPLEMAN: In some circumstances violence is not punishable under the criminal law. When no actual bodily harm is caused, the consent of the person affected precludes him from complaining. There can be no conviction for the summary offence of common assault if the victim has consented to the assault. Even when violence is intentionally inflicted and results in actual bodily harm, wounding or serious bodily harm the accused is entitled to be acquitted if the injury was a foreseeable incident of a lawful activity in which the person injured was participating. Surgery involves intentional violence resulting in actual or sometimes serious bodily harm but surgery is a lawful activity. Other activities carried on with consent by or on behalf of the injured person have been accepted as lawful notwithstanding that they involve actual bodily harm or may cause serious bodily harm. Ritual circumcision, tattooing, ear-piercing and violent sports including boxing are lawful activities. The question whether the defence of consent should be extended to the consequences of sado-masochistic encounters can only be decided by consideration of policy and public interest.	*Whether or not consent is a valid defence depends on policy and the public interest.*

In my opinion sado-masochism is not only concerned with sex. Sado-masochism is also concerned with violence. The evidence discloses that the practices of the appellants were unpredictably dangerous and degrading to body and mind and were developed with increasing barbarity and taught to persons whose consents were dubious or worthless.

Sadomasochism involves violence and is 'unpredictably dangerous'.

The charges against the appellants were based on genital torture and violence to the buttocks, anus, penis, testicles and nipples. The victims were degraded and humiliated sometimes beaten, sometimes wounded with instruments and sometimes branded. Bloodletting and the smearing of human blood produced excitement. There were obvious dangers of serious personal injury and blood infection.

The appellants' activities created a danger of physical injury and blood infection.

In principle there is a difference between violence which is incidental and violence which is inflicted for the indulgence of cruelty. The violence of sado-masochistic encounters involves the indulgence of cruelty by sadists and the degradation of victims. Such violence is injurious to the participants and unpredictably dangerous. I am not prepared to invent a defence of consent for sado-masochistic encounters which breed and glorify cruelty and result in offences under sections 47 and 20 of the Act of 1861.

Violence alone is insufficient reason to deny the consent defence, but when it is combined with 'the indulgence of cruelty' and the 'degradation' of victims, the defence of consent is invalid.

The appellants' counsel relied on article 8 of the European Convention for the Protection of Human Rights and Fundamental Freedoms (1953) (Cmd. 8969). It is not clear to me that the activities of the appellants were exercises of rights in respect of private and family life. But assuming that the appellants are claiming to exercise those rights I do not consider that article 8 invalidates a law which forbids violence which is intentionally harmful to body and mind. Society is entitled and bound to protect itself against a cult of violence. Pleasure derived from the infliction of pain is an evil thing. Cruelty is uncivilised. I would answer the certified question in the negative and dismiss the appeals of the appellants against conviction.

There was no breach of the appellants' human rights (the right to privacy).

Lord Templeman (along with Lord Jauncey and Lord Lowry) dismissed the appeals.

LORD SYLNN (dissenting):
In the present case there is no doubt that there was consent; indeed there was more than mere consent. Astonishing though it may seem, the persons involved positively wanted, asked for, the acts to be done to them, acts which it seems from the evidence some of them also did to themselves. All the accused were old enough to know what they were doing. The acts were done in private. Neither the applicants nor anyone else complained as to what was done. The matter came to the attention of the police 'coincidentally'; the police were previously unaware that the accused were involved in these practices though some of them had been involved for many years. The acts did not result in any permanent or serious injury or disability or any infection and no medical assistance was required even though there may have been some risk of infection, even injury.

My conclusion is thus that as the law stands, adults can consent to acts done in private which do not result in serious bodily harm, so that such acts do not constitute criminal assaults for the purposes of the Act of 1861.

Lord Slynn (along with Lord Mustill) would have allowed the appeals.

Key points from Brown and others

- Consent is generally available as a defence to common assault.
- When injuries are inflicted which amount to ABH, GBH or wounding, and charges are brought under ss 20 or 47 OAPA 1861, then consent is only available as a defence when it is in the context of a 'lawful' activity.
- Whether an activity is lawful depends on considerations of policy and the public interest.
- Recognised lawful activities include surgery, tattooing, ear-piercing and 'violent' sports including boxing.
- Sadomasochistic activities involve violence and are 'unpredictably' dangerous. There is a danger of physical injury and blood infection.
- The fact that violence is involved is not reason enough to rule out consent (otherwise boxing would be unlawful). However, it is a different situation when violence is combined with 'the indulgence of cruelty'.
- Sadomasochism is unpredictably dangerous and glorifies cruelty. Consent is therefore not available as a defence to charges under ss 20 or 47 OAPA 1861 when injuries are inflicted in that context.
- There is no breach of the European Convention on Human Rights, specifically art 8 (the right to respect for privacy), in bringing charges in such cases.

Apply the above principles in the following factual situations

(a) Gary, a boxer, punched Henrik in the head during a bout at their local gym. The punch caused a broken nose, which required hospital treatment.

(b) Jason and his girlfriend Kia enjoy sadomasochistic sex, including 'scarification' (the cutting of skin to produce scars). One evening, in the bedroom of their flat, Jason deliberately cut Kia's arms and breasts several times with a scalpel in order to produce scars.

(c) Tariq went to see a concert by a heavy metal band at the Student Union. During the show, the people on the dance floor enthusiastically and willingly shoved and pushed each other around. Tariq joined in with the crowds. He shoved Ulrich, who then slipped in a puddle of beer on the dance floor and fell over. Fortunately, Ulrich was not injured.

SUMMARY

- Duress (whether by threats or from circumstances) is a full defence. It requires a threat of immediate (or almost immediate) death or serious injury to D or to someone for whom D reasonably feels responsible (*Hasan*). The defence may fail if D joined a violent criminal gang or associated with a violent criminal (*Hasan*). It is no defence to murder (*Howe and Bannister*, *Wilson*) or attempted murder (*Gotts*). The jury have to test D's susceptibility to threats against the standards of a reasonable man sharing some (but not all) of D's characteristics (*Graham*, *Bowen*).
- Necessity is a full defence. It applies where D acted to avoid 'inevitable and irreparable evil' (*Re A: Conjoined Twins*). Apart from the 'unusual' case of *Re A*, it is not a defence to murder (*Nicklinson*).
- Mistake of fact is really not a 'defence' as such but rather a denial of *mens rea* (*DPP v Morgan*). It is often used in conjunction with self-defence – an honest, mistaken belief in the need to use force is a good defence (*Williams*), unless D's mistake was caused by intoxication, in which case the defence fails (*O'Grady*). Ignorance of the law is not a defence (*Esop*).

- Self-defence is a full defence. It must be necessary for D to use some force and the amount of force used must be 'reasonable' (*Palmer*). That is a jury question, although the jury must place themselves in the position that D honestly – and not necessarily reasonably – believed to exist (*Williams, Owino*). The law on the use of reasonable force was 'clarified' in s 76 of the Criminal Justice and Immigration Act 2008. Excessive force is, generally speaking, no defence, although (i) disproportionate force may be used in 'householder' cases and (ii) if D uses excessive force and kills, he may be able to rely on the loss of control defence in s 54 of the Coroners and Justice Act 2009.
- Consent is a full defence. It is impliedly available in all assault and battery cases. If the injuries caused amount to ABH (or worse), then consent is only available in socially acceptable situations such as contact sports (*Barnes*), surgery, 'vigorous' sexual activity (*Slingsby*), horseplay (*Jones and others*), tattooing and branding (*Wilson*), etc. It is not available as a defence to injuries inflicted in street or prize fights (*Coney*) or in sadomasochistic encounters (*Brown and others*). Fraud as to D's identity (*Richardson*) or as to the nature or quality of D's act will invalidate any consent from V (*Tabassum, Dica, Konzani*).
- There are a number of controversial aspects to the defences, for example the non-availability of duress as a defence to murder or attempted murder (prompting the LC in 2006 to propose reform); discrepancies in the defence of consent, for example its availability in boxing matches but not prize fights, and its availability in 'vigorous' sexual activities but not sadomasochistic encounters.

SAMPLE ESSAY QUESTION

The parameters of the consent defence are vague and lead to inconsistency in the courts – for example compare *Brown and others* (1994) with *Wilson* (1996) and compare *Richardson* (1998) with *Tabassum* (2000). Legislative action is required to bring clarity. Discuss.

Explain the law relating to consent:

- Implied consent available to all 'everyday' touchings (*Collins v Wilcock* (1984))
- For ABH, GBH and wounding, consent is only available in acceptable situations (*A-G's Reference (No 6 of 1980)*), which are determined by the courts
- The Sexual Offences Act 2003 introduces a definition of consent (s 74) but this does not apply to non-sexual offences

Explain situations when general defence is available:

- Contact sports (*Barnes* (2004)), but not 'off-the-ball' incidents
- Surgery
- Tattooing and branding (*Wilson* (1996))
- 'Horseplay' (*Jones and others* (1986); *Aitken and others* (1992))
- 'Vigorous' sexual activity (*Slingsby* (1995))
- This list is not closed

Explain situations when defence is not available:

- Sadomasochism (*Donovan* (1934); *Brown and others* (1993))
- Street fighting or prize fighting (*Coney* (1882))
- When V does not understand the nature of the act (*Burrell v Harmer* (1967))
- When V has been deceived as to D's identity and/or the nature or quality of D's act (*Tabassum* (2000); *Dica* (2004); *Konzani* (2005); *B* (2006)). See also s 76 of the Sexual Offences Act 2003
- Deception as to D's qualifications does not negate V's consent (*Richardson* (1998))

Discuss problems with the law, e.g.

- Is there a clear distinction between sadomasochistic practices (unlawful) and branding/'vigorous' sexual activity (both lawful)?
- Why should street fighting be illegal while boxing is lawful?
- Why should V's consent obtained by deception as to D's identity be negated but not when V is deceived as to D's qualifications?

Discuss possible reform options, e.g.

- The SOA 2003 defines consent (s 74) and introduces 'evidential presumptions' when consent is not available, e.g. where V or another person is threatened with violence, V is asleep or unconscious, V is unlawfully detained, V is unable to communicate because of physical disability, V is involuntarily intoxicated (s 75)
- Should these presumptions also apply to non-sexual offences?

Conclude

Further reading

Articles

Anderson, J, 'No licence for thuggery: violence, sport and the criminal law' [2008] Crim LR 751.

Arenson, K, 'The paradox of disallowing duress as a defence to murder' (2014) 78 J Crim L 65.

Cooper, S and James, M, 'Entertainment: the painful process of rethinking consent' [2012] Crim LR 188.

Dingwall, G, 'Intoxicated mistakes about the need for self-defence' (2007) 70 MLR 127.

Dobinson, I and Elliott, E, 'A householder's right to kill or injure an intruder under the Crime & Courts Act 2013: an Australian comparison' (2014) 78 J Crim L 80.

Elliott, T, 'Body dysmorphic disorder, radical surgery and the limits of consent' (2009) 17 Med L Rev 149.
Huxtable, R, 'Separation of conjoined twins: where next for English law?' [2002] Crim LR 459.
Miller, S, 'Grossly disproportionate: home owners' legal licence to kill' (2013) 77 J Crim L 299.
Ryan, S, 'Reckless transmission of HIV: knowledge and culpability' [2006] Crim LR 981.
Stark, F, 'Necessity and *Nicklinson*' [2013] Crim LR 949.
Tolmie, J, 'Consent to harmful assaults: the case for moving away from category based decision making' [2012] Crim LR 656.
Wake, N, 'Battered women, startled householders and psychological self-defence: Anglo-Australian perspectives' (2013) 77 J Crim L 433.
Weait, M, 'Criminal law and the sexual transmission of HIV: R v Dica' [2005] 68 MLR 121; 'Knowledge, autonomy and consent: R v Konzani' (2005) Crim LR 763.

9

Mental capacity defences

AIMS AND OBJECTIVES

After reading this chapter you should be able to:

- Understand the law on insanity and automatism
- Understand the law on intoxication
- Analyse critically the scope and limitations of the mental capacity defences and the reform proposals
- Apply the law to factual situations to determine whether liability can be avoided by invoking a defence

9.1 Insanity

insanity
General defence where D suffers a 'defect of reason' caused by a 'disease of the mind'

Although the **insanity** defence is rarely used and is therefore of little real practical significance, it nevertheless raises fundamental questions about criminal responsibility and the role of criminal law in dealing with violent people. Its importance had been much reduced, particularly in murder cases, by two developments:

- the introduction of the diminished responsibility defence in 1957 (see Chapter 10);
- the abolition of the death penalty in 1965.

It is a general defence and may be pleaded as a defence to any crime requiring *mens rea* (including murder), whether tried on indictment in the Crown Court or summarily in the magistrates' court (*Horseferry Road Magistrates' Court, ex parte K* [1996] 3 All ER 719). However, it is not, apparently, a defence to crimes of strict liability (see Chapter 4). In *DPP v H* [1997] 1 WLR 1406, the High Court held that insanity was no defence to a charge of driving with excess alcohol contrary to s 5 of the Road Traffic Act 1988. Medical evidence that D was suffering manic depressive psychosis with symptoms of distorted judgment and impaired sense of time and of morals at the time of the offence was, therefore, irrelevant.

9.1.1 Procedure

Often D does not specifically raise the defence of insanity but places the state of his mind in issue by raising another defence such as automatism. The question whether such a defence, or a denial of *mens rea*, really amounts to the defence of insanity is a question of law to be decided by the judge on the basis of medical evidence (*Dickie* [1984] 3 All ER 173). Whether D, or even his medical witnesses, would call it insanity or not is irrelevant. According to Lord Denning in *Bratty v Attorney-General of Northern Ireland* [1963] AC 386, in such cases the prosecution may – indeed must – raise the issue of insanity.

Importance of medical evidence

If the judge decides that the evidence does support the defence, then he should leave it to the jury to determine whether D was insane (*Walton* [1978] 1 All ER 542). In practice, the evidence of medical experts is critically important. Section 1 of the Criminal Procedure (Insanity and Unfitness to Plead) Act 1991 provides that a jury shall not return a special verdict (see below) except on the written or oral evidence of two or more registered medical practitioners, at least one of whom is approved as having special expertise in the field of medical disorder.

9.1.2 The special verdict

If D is found to have been insane at the time of committing the *actus reus*, then the jury should return a verdict of 'not guilty by reason of insanity' (s 1 Criminal Procedure (Insanity) Act 1964), otherwise referred to as the special verdict. Until quite recently this verdict obliged the judge to order D to be detained indefinitely in a mental hospital. In many cases the dual prospect of being labelled 'insane' and indefinite detention in a special hospital such as Broadmoor or Rampton discouraged defendants from putting their mental state in issue. In some cases it led to guilty pleas to offences of which defendants were probably innocent (*Quick* [1973] QB 910; *Sullivan* [1984] AC 156; *Hennessy* [1989] 1 WLR 287, all of which will be considered below).

The Criminal Procedure (Insanity and Unfitness to Plead) Act 1991

The position described above was modified by the 1991 Act. The Act made a number of changes but, most significantly, substituted a new s 5 into the Criminal Procedure (Insanity) Act 1964. The new section allowed the judge considerable discretion with regard to disposal on a special verdict being returned. That section has since been replaced by another version of s 5 following the enactment of the Domestic Violence, Crime and Victims Act 2004. Now, following a special verdict, the judge may make:

(a) a hospital order (with or without a restriction order);

(b) a supervision order; or

(c) an order for absolute discharge.

This is particularly useful where the offence is trivial and/or the offender does not require treatment. The new power was first utilised in *Bromley* (1992) 142 NLJ 116.

This new power does not, however, apply to murder cases when indefinite hospitalisation is unavoidable. However, as noted above, defendants charged with murder are far more likely to plead diminished responsibility under s 2 of the Homicide Act 1957 than insanity.

This much broader range of disposal options should make the insanity defence more attractive. Nevertheless, the 1991 Act does not tackle the definition of insanity, and so the stigma of being labelled 'insane' remains. This issue will be addressed below.

***M'Naghten* Rules**
The legal principles governing the insanity defence

9.1.3 The *M'Naghten* Rules

The law of insanity in England is contained in the ***M'Naghten* Rules**, the result of the deliberations of the judges of the House of Lords in 1843. Media and public outcry at one

Daniel M'Naghten's acquittal on a charge of murder led to the creation of rules to clarify the situation. Lord Tindal CJ answered on behalf of himself and 13 other judges, while Maule J gave a separate set. The Rules are not binding as a matter of strict precedent. Nevertheless, the Rules have been treated as authoritative of the law ever since (*Sullivan* (1984)). The Rules state as follows:

QUOTATION

'The jurors ought to be told in all cases that every man is presumed to be sane, and to possess a sufficient degree of reason to be responsible for his crimes, until the contrary be proved to their satisfaction; and that to establish a defence on the ground of insanity it must be clearly proved that, at the time of the committing of the act, the party accused was labouring under such a defect of reason, from disease of the mind, as not to know the nature and quality of the act he was doing, or, if he did know it, that he did not know he was doing what was wrong.'

The Rules can be broken down into three distinct elements, all of which must be established.

- defect of reason;
- disease of the mind;
- not knowing what D was doing or not knowing that it was 'wrong'.

Because of the presumption of sanity, the burden of proof is on the defence (albeit on the lower standard, the balance of probabilities).

Defect of reason

The phrase 'defect of reason' was explained in *Clarke* [1972] 1 All ER 219 by Ackner J, who said that it referred to people who were 'deprived of the power of reasoning'. It did not apply to those who 'retain the power of reasoning but who in moments of confusion or absent-mindedness fail to use their powers to the full'.

JUDGMENT

'The *M'Naghten* Rules relate to accused persons who by reason of a "disease of the mind" are deprived of the power of reasoning. They do not apply and never have applied to those who retain the power of reasoning but who in moments of confusion or absent-mindedness fail to use their powers to the full.'

CASE EXAMPLE

Clarke [1972] 1 All ER 219

D went into a supermarket. She placed various items, including a pound of butter, a jar of coffee and a jar of mincemeat into her own bag and left the supermarket without paying for them. At her trial for theft she claimed to have lacked the intention to permanently deprive on the basis of absent-mindedness caused by diabetes and depression. She claimed to have no recollection of putting the items into her bag. The trial judge ruled that this amounted to a plea of insanity, at which point D pleaded guilty. The Court of Appeal quashed her conviction. D was not insane; she was simply not guilty because of a lack of *mens rea*.

Disease of the mind

automatism
General defence where D lacks control of the muscles or is unconscious

'Disease of the mind' is a legal term, not a medical term. In *Kemp* [1957] 1 QB 399, D suffered from arteriosclerosis (hardening of the arteries) which restricted the flow of blood to the brain, causing blackouts. In this condition he committed the *actus reus* of grievous bodily harm (GBH) (he hit his wife with a hammer). The question arose whether arteriosclerosis supported the defence of **automatism** or insanity. Devlin J decided that it was a case of insanity. He stated:

JUDGMENT

'The law is not concerned with the brain but with the mind, in the sense that "mind" is ordinarily used, the mental faculties of reason, memory and understanding. If one read for "disease of the mind" "disease of the brain", it would follow that in many cases pleas of insanity would not be established because it could not be proved that the brain had been affected in any way, either by degeneration of the cells or in any other way. In my judgment the condition of the brain is irrelevant and so is the question whether the condition is curable or incurable, transitory or permanent.'

Thus, if D suffers from a condition (not necessarily a condition of the brain) which affects his 'mental faculties', then this amounts to the defence of insanity. The problem is, how to distinguish such cases from situations when D suffers some temporary condition (e.g. concussion following a blow to the head). In the latter situation, D loses his 'mental faculties', but the problem is extremely unlikely to repeat itself and so ordering hospitalisation or treatment would be pointless. Hence, in such cases the true defence is automatism (see below). In order to distinguish cases of insanity from cases of automatism, the courts have adopted a test based on whether the cause of D's 'defect of reason' was internal or external (such as the blow to the head example). In *Quick* (1973), Lawton LJ said:

JUDGMENT

'Our task has been to decide what the law now means by the words "disease of the mind". In our judgment the fundamental concept is of a malfunctioning of the mind caused by disease. A malfunctioning of the mind of transitory effect caused by the application to the body of some external factor such as violence, drugs, including anaesthetics, alcohol and hypnotic influences cannot fairly be said to be due to disease.'

The implications of this decision have been profound and not without criticism. In *Quick*, D was a diabetic who had taken prescribed insulin to control his blood sugar levels. However, he had forgotten to eat afterwards, with the result that he subsequently suffered a condition known medically as hypoglycaemia (low blood sugar). While in this condition he physically assaulted V and was charged accordingly. At his trial, he testified that he could not remember what he had done. However, the judge ruled that the evidence only supported a plea of insanity. At this point, D changed his plea to guilty and appealed. The Court of Appeal quashed his conviction. The cause of D's lack of awareness was not his diabetes, but his insulin overdose. This was an external factor, and so the proper defence was automatism.

This case should be contrasted with that of *Hennessy* (1989).

CASE EXAMPLE

Hennessy [1989] 1 WLR 287

D, a diabetic, had forgotten to take his insulin. He suffered what is known medically as hyperglycaemia (high blood sugar). In this condition he was seen by police officers driving a car that had been reported stolen. D was charged with two counts of taking a motor vehicle without consent and driving a motor vehicle while disqualified. D testified that he could not remember taking the car and driving it away. The trial judge declared that the evidence supported a defence of insanity. D changed his plea to guilty and appealed. However, distinguishing *Quick*, the Court of Appeal confirmed that hyperglycaemia was caused by an internal factor, namely diabetes, and was therefore a disease of the mind. The correct verdict was insanity.

Two criticisms may be made here.

- A relatively common medical condition (diabetes) is regarded by the criminal law as supporting a defence of insanity, with all the negative implications that that label conveys.
- This is only the case in certain situations, namely when D suffers hyperglycaemia.

According to the Diabetes UK website, over 3.2 million people in the United Kingdom have been diagnosed with diabetes (and another 630,000 people are estimated to have the condition without realising it). Does the decision in *Hennessy* mean that nearly four million people in the United Kingdom are legally insane? For more information refer to the 'Internet links' section at the end of this chapter. The problem associated with diabetes is not the only one created by the decision in *Quick*. According to the House of Lords, epileptics who suffer grand mal seizures and inadvertently assault someone nearby are also to be regarded as insane. This was seen in two cases: *Bratty* (1963) and *Sullivan* (1984).

CASE EXAMPLE

Sullivan [1984] AC 156

D had suffered from epilepsy since childhood. He occasionally suffered fits. One day he was sitting in a neighbour's flat with a friend, V. The next thing D remembered was standing by a window with V lying on the floor with head injuries. D was charged with assault. The trial judge ruled that the evidence that D had suffered a post-epileptic seizure amounted to a disease of the mind. To avoid hospitalisation, D pleaded guilty and appealed. Both the Court of Appeal and House of Lords upheld his conviction.

In *Sullivan*, Lord Diplock stated:

JUDGMENT

'It matters not whether the aetiology of the impairment is organic, as in epilepsy, or functional, or whether the impairment itself is permanent or is transient and intermittent, provided that it subsisted at the time of the commission of the act. The purpose of the ... defence of insanity ... has been to protect society against recurrence of the dangerous conduct. The duration of a temporary suspension of the mental faculties ... particularly if, as in Sullivan's case, it is recurrent, cannot ... be relevant to the application by the courts of the M'Naghten Rules.'

According to the Epilepsy Action website, 600,000 people in the United Kingdom have epilepsy (this corresponds to one in every 107 people). In the event that any one of these people commits the *actus reus* of a crime, are they to be regarded as legally insane too? For more information, refer to the 'Internet links' section at the end of this chapter. Thus, diabetics (sometimes) and epileptics are regarded as 'insane' by English criminal law. What about someone who carries out the *actus reus* of a crime, such as assault, while sleepwalking? This was a question for the Court of Appeal in *Burgess* [1991] 2 QB 92. There was a persuasive precedent for deciding that this amounted to automatism (*Tolson* (1889) 23 QBD 168), but the Court of Appeal held that, after *Quick* (1973) and *Sullivan*, it had to be regarded as insanity. Lord Lane CJ stated that sleepwalking was 'an abnormality or disorder, albeit transitory, due to an internal factor'.

CASE EXAMPLE

Burgess [1991] 2 QB 92

D and his friend, V, were in D's flat watching videos. They both fell asleep but, during the night, D attacked V while she slept, hitting her with a wine bottle and a video recorder. She suffered cuts to her scalp which required sutures. To a charge of unlawful wounding contrary to s 20 OAPA 1861, D pleaded automatism, but the trial judge ruled he was pleading insanity and the jury returned the special verdict. The Court of Appeal dismissed D's appeal.

According to a study carried out in Finland involving over 11,000 people, some 4 per cent of women and 3 per cent of men sleepwalk (C Hublin, J Kaprio, M Partinen, K Heikkila and M Koskenvuo, 'Prevalence and genetics of sleepwalking' (1997) 48 Neurology 177). With the UK population in excess of 64 million, this equates to more than two million sleepwalkers in the United Kingdom alone. It is useful to note at this point that in Canada (which also uses the *M'Naghten* Rules), the Supreme Court in Canada has diverged from English law on this point. In *Parks* (1992) 95 DLR (4d) 27, D had carried out a killing and an attempted killing whilst asleep. However, the Supreme Court found that his defence was automatism. During the trial the defence had called expert witnesses in sleep disorders, whose evidence was that sleepwalking was not regarded as a neurological, psychiatric or any other illness, but a sleep disorder, quite common in children but also found in 2–2.5 per cent of adults. Furthermore, aggression while sleepwalking was quite rare and repetition of violence almost unheard of. Using this evidence, the Canadian Chief Justice, Lamer CJC, said that 'Accepting the medical evidence, [D's] mind and its functioning must have been impaired at the relevant time but sleepwalking did not impair it. The cause was the natural condition, sleep.'

Another possible basis for an insanity plea is dissociation, most commonly referred to now as post-traumatic stress disorder. If D suffers this condition (which is triggered by experiencing and/or witnessing extremely traumatic events) and carries out the *actus reus* of a crime whilst in this state, does it amount to a plea of insanity or automatism? In *T* [1990] Crim LR 256, the Crown Court decided that it could support a plea of automatism.

CASE EXAMPLE

T [1990] Crim LR 256

D had been raped three days prior to carrying out a robbery and causing actual bodily harm. She was diagnosed as suffering post-traumatic stress disorder, such that at the time of the alleged offences she had entered a dissociative state. The trial judge allowed automatism to be left to the jury, noting that 'such an incident could have an appalling effect on any young woman, however well-balanced normally'.

In Canada, meanwhile, a plea of dissociation was regarded as one of insanity. The difference was that in that case, the traumatic events leading up to the alleged dissociative state were much less distressing. In *Rabey* (1980) 114 DLR (3d) 193, D had developed an attraction towards a girl. When he discovered that she regarded him as a 'nothing', he hit her over the head with a rock and began to choke her. He was charged with causing bodily harm with intent to wound, and pleaded automatism, based on the psychologically devastating blow of being rejected by the girl. The trial judge accepted that D had been in a complete dissociative state. The prosecution doubted that D was suffering from such a state (the reality being that he was in an extreme rage) but that if he were then his condition was properly regarded as a disease of the mind. The trial judge ordered an acquittal based on automatism, but the appeal court allowed the prosecution appeal. The Supreme Court of Canada upheld that decision – the defence was insanity.

To summarise the law on 'disease of the mind', the following conditions have been held to support a plea of insanity (in England):

- arteriosclerosis (*Kemp* (1957));
- epilepsy (*Sullivan* (1984));
- hyperglycaemia (high blood sugar: *Hennessy* (1989)) but not hypoglycaemia (low blood sugar: *Quick* (1973));
- sleepwalking (*Burgess* (1991)).

And in Canada, post-traumatic stress disorder caused by a relatively mundane event such as rejection by a prospective girlfriend (*Rabey* (1980)). In Australia, meanwhile, although the *M'Naghten* Rules have been adopted there, the internal/external factor test in *Quick* has not. In *Falconer* (1990) 171 CLR 30, Toohey J described the internal/external factor theory as 'artificial' and said that it failed to pay sufficient regard to 'the subtleties surrounding the notion of mental disease'. In Australia, therefore, the distinction between insanity and automatism is found by identifying whether D's mental state at the time of the *actus reus* was either:

- 'the reaction of an unsound mind to its own delusions, or to external stimuli, on the one hand', which is insanity; or
- 'the reaction of a sound mind to external stimuli including stress-producing factors on the other hand', which is automatism.

ACTIVITY

Applying the law

Applying the Australian sound/unsound mind test, as opposed to the English internal/external factor test, would the defendants in *Sullivan* (1984), *Hennessy* (1989) and *Burgess* (1991) have been found to be sane or insane?

Nature and quality of the act

It seems there will be a good defence provided that when D acted he was not aware of, or did not appreciate, what he was actually doing, or the circumstances in which he was acting, or the consequences of his act. D's lack of knowledge must be fundamental. Two famous old examples used to illustrate this point are

- D cuts a woman's throat but thinks (because of his 'defect of reason') that he is cutting a loaf of bread.
- D chops off a sleeping man's head because it would be amusing to see him looking for it when he wakes up.

Obviously, in both these situations D does not know what he is doing and is entitled to the special verdict. If, on the contrary, D kills a man whom he believes, because of a paranoid delusion, to be possessed by demons, then he is still criminally responsible and not insane – his delusion has not prevented him from understanding that he is committing murder.

The act was wrong

What is meant here by 'wrong'? Does it mean wrong as in 'contrary to the criminal law' or wrong as in 'morally unacceptable' – or perhaps both? In *M'Naghten* (1843) the Law Lords said that if D knew at the time of committing the *actus reus* of a crime that he 'was acting contrary to law; by which expression we understand your lordships to mean the law of the land', then he would not have the defence. This clearly suggested D will have the defence if he does not realise that he is committing a crime. The Court of Criminal Appeal in *Windle* [1952] 2 QB 826 confirmed this view of the word 'wrong'. D had poisoned his wife and, on giving himself up to the police, said, 'I suppose they will hang me for this?' Despite medical evidence for the defence that he was suffering from a medical condition known as *folie à deux*, this statement showed that D was aware of acting unlawfully. D was convicted of murder. Lord Goddard CJ said:

JUDGMENT

'Courts of law can only distinguish between that which is in accordance with law and that which is contrary to law ... The law cannot embark on the question and it would be an unfortunate thing if it were left to juries to consider whether some particular act was morally right or wrong. The test must be whether it is contrary to law ... [T]here is no doubt that in the M'Naghten Rules "wrong" means contrary to the law, and does not have some vague meaning which may vary according to the opinion of one man or of a number of people on the question of whether a particular act might or might not be justified.'

The position, therefore, is that if D knew his act was illegal, then he has no defence of insanity. This is the case even if he is suffering from delusions which cause him to believe that his act was morally right. This position has, however, been criticised. In 1975, the Royal Committee on Mentally Abnormal Offenders (Butler Committee) stated that the *Windle* definition of 'wrong' was 'a very narrow ground of exemption since even persons who are grossly disturbed generally know that murder and arson, for instance, are crimes'.

In *Johnson* [2007] EWCA Crim 1978, the Court of Appeal was invited to reconsider the decision in *Windle*. However, although the court agreed that the decision in *Windle* was 'strict', they felt unable to depart from it, believing that, if the law was to be changed, it should be done by Parliament.

CASE EXAMPLE

Johnson [2007] EWCA Crim 1978

D suffered from delusions and auditory hallucinations. One day, armed with a large kitchen knife, he forced his way into V's flat and stabbed him four times (fortunately, V recovered). Following his arrest, D was assessed by two psychiatrists who diagnosed him as suffering from paranoid schizophrenia. They agreed that D knew that his actions were against the law; however, one psychiatrist asserted that D did not consider what he had done to be 'wrong in the moral sense'. The trial judge declined to leave the insanity defence to the jury, and D was convicted of wounding with intent. He appealed, but the Court of Appeal upheld his conviction.

Latham LJ stated:

JUDGMENT

> 'The strict position at the moment remains as stated in *Windle* ... This area, however, is a notorious area for debate and quite rightly so. There is room for reconsideration of rules and, in particular, rules which have their genesis in the early years of the 19th century. But it does not seem to us that that debate is a debate which can properly take place before us at this level in this case.'

In *Stapleton* (1952) 86 CLR 358, the High Court of Australia refused to follow *Windle*. That Court decided that morality, and not legality, was the concept behind the use of 'wrong'. Thus in Australia the insanity defence is available if 'through the disordered condition of the mind [D] could not reason about the matter with a moderate degree of sense and composure'. The same is true in Canada. In *Chaulk* (1991) 62 CCC (3d) 193, D had been charged with murder. Medical evidence showed that he suffered paranoid delusions such that he believed he had power to rule the world and that the killing had been a necessary means to that end. D believed himself to be above the law (of Canada). Finally, he deemed V's death appropriate because he was a 'loser'. The Supreme Court stated that 'It is possible that a person may be aware that it is ordinarily wrong to commit a crime but, by reason of a disease of the mind, believes that it would be "right" according to the ordinary standards of society to commit the crime in a particular context. In this situation, [D] would be entitled to be acquitted by reason of insanity.'

9.1.4 Situations not covered by the Rules

Irresistible impulse

Until the early twentieth century, a plea of irresistible impulse was a good defence under the *M'Naghten* Rules. In *Fryer* (1843) 10 Cl & F, the jury were directed that if D was deprived of the capacity to control his actions, it was open for them to find him insane. By 1925, however, the fact that D was unable to resist an impulse to act was held to be irrelevant, if he was nonetheless aware that his act was wrong. In *Kopsch* (1925) 19 Cr App R 50, D confessed to strangling his aunt with a necktie, apparently at her request. Upholding his conviction, Lord Hewart CJ described the defence argument, that a person acting under an uncontrollable impulse was not criminally responsible as a 'fantastic theory', which if it were to become part of the law, 'would be merely subversive'. The reluctance of the courts to recognise a defence of irresistible impulse appears to be based on two grounds.

- The difficulty of distinguishing between an impulse caused by insanity, and one motivated by greed, jealousy or revenge.
- The view that the harder an impulse is to resist, the greater is the need for a deterrent.

In 1953 the Royal Commission on Capital Punishment suggested, as an alternative to replacing the Rules altogether, adding a third limb, i.e. that D should be considered insane if at the time of his act he 'was incapable of preventing himself from committing it'. This was not taken up. However, irresistible impulse may support a defence of diminished responsibility (*Byrne* [1960] 2 QB 396). Thus, if D is charged with murder and claims that he could not resist killing V he may avoid a murder conviction. But the same defendant who fails to kill V and is charged with attempted murder will have neither insanity nor diminished responsibility available.

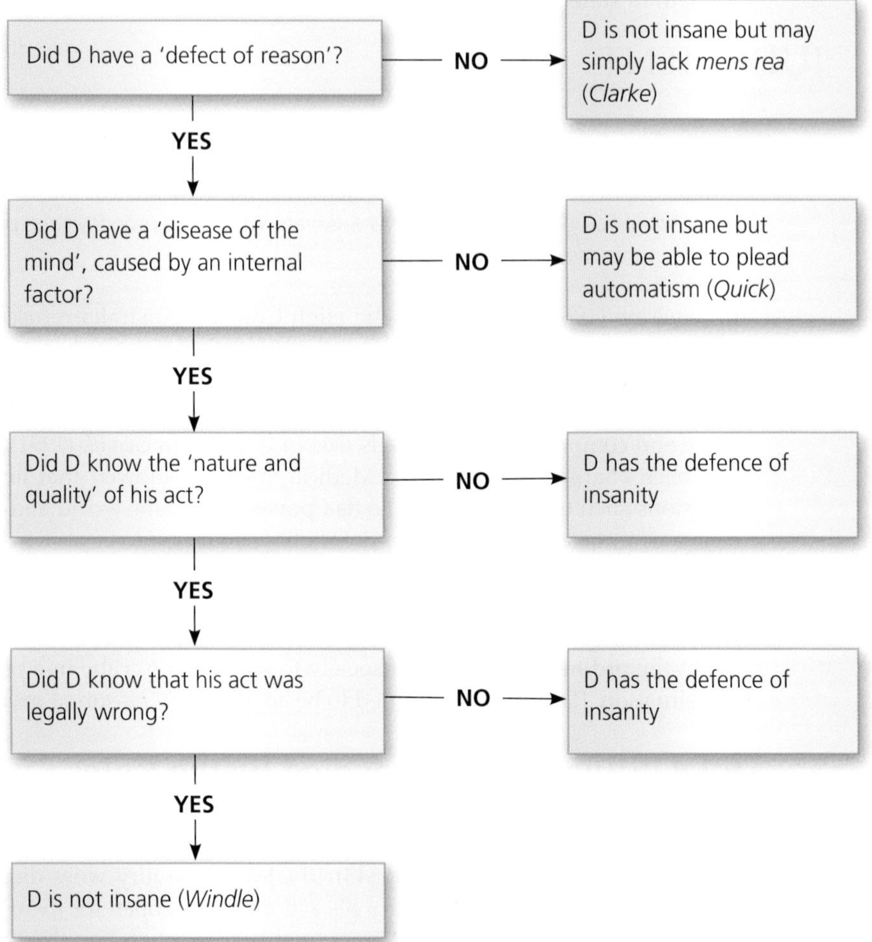

Figure 9.1 Insanity.

9.1.5 Criticism and reform proposals

Criticisms

Many criticisms have been made of the defence of insanity over the years. In their Discussion Paper, *Criminal Liability: Insanity and Automatism*, published in July 2013, the Law Commission (LC) observed that 'there are significant problems with the law when examined from a theoretical perspective', whilst conceding that there was 'less evidence that the defences cause significant difficulties in practice'. This section summarises the main criticisms that have been made about the insanity defence in English law.

Terminology

- The terminology used in the context of the insanity defence is, at best, old-fashioned; at worst, it is inappropriate and insulting. One of the reasons for reforming diminished responsibility in 2009 was to dispense with old-fashioned, offensive terminology in the 1957 Homicide Act, such as 'retarded development', and similar considerations continue to apply to insanity. In their 2013 Discussion Paper, the LC observed that:

QUOTATION

> 'The very name of the defence might be off-putting or even offensive to many people. Sometimes a label is itself so offensive that it deserves to be changed for that reason alone.'

- It is psychiatrically meaningless to refer to 'disease of the mind', 'defect of reason', etc. These are legal phrases, created by the House of Lords in the mid-nineteenth century, and have no direct correlation to twenty-first century psychiatry. The LC in their 2013 Discussion Paper said that 'the mismatch between the legal test and modern psychiatry is striking'. This is not just a theoretical issue: the 'mismatch' makes it more difficult for doctors and psychiatrists to provide their evidence during trials.

'Defect of Reason'

- The definition of 'defect of reason' given in *Clarke* (1972) is very narrow – D must be 'deprived of the power of reasoning'. What about D who is deprived of the power to control his actions? Why does insanity not allow a defence for 'irresistible impulse'?

'Disease of the Mind'

- The focus of the *M'Naghten* Rules is on the word 'mind'. According to *Kemp* (1957), 'the condition of the brain is irrelevant'. Is this sensible?
- The emphasis on the internal/external cause of D's condition leads to illogical outcomes. In *Hennessy* (1989), D, a diabetic, was classed as 'insane' having *failed to take* his insulin but, in *Quick* (1973), another diabetic was given the automatism defence because he had *taken too much* of his insulin. The High Court of Australia described the internal/external cause test as 'artificial' in *Falconer* (1990). In their 2012 Scoping Paper, which paved the way for the 2013 Discussion Paper, the LC described the outcome in the cases of *Hennessy* and *Quick* as 'odd'.
- The internal/external cause test has the potential to catch too many people in the insanity net, including people with diabetes (some of the time) or epilepsy, or those people who are predisposed to sleepwalking. In their 2012 Scoping Paper, the LC observed that:

QUOTATION

> 'The pool of individuals who would potentially fall within the scope of the defence is surprisingly wide.'

- The application of the *M'Naghten* Rules in practice is very inconsistent, particularly in sleep-walking cases. The LC in both its 2012 and 2013 papers has noted that whereas some trial courts are following *Burgess* (1991) and declaring that sleepwalkers are 'insane' (*Lowe* (2005) *The Times*, 19 March – D was given the special verdict), not all are doing so and instead allowing acquittals (*Bilton* (2005) *The Guardian*, 20 December; *Pooley* (2007) *The Daily Mail*, 12 January).

'The nature and quality of the act'

- This has been interpreted very narrowly, focusing purely on the physical, as opposed to moral, nature and quality of the act (*Codere* (1917)).

'Wrong'

- In *Johnson* (2007), the Court of Appeal described the decision in *Windle* (1952), that 'wrong' meant 'contrary to law' as 'strict' (and the whole defence as 'a notorious area for debate'). However, the court felt unable to do anything about it and left it for Parliament to change the law.
- In Australia or Canada, a defendant who believed (because of a disease of the mind) that his/her act was *morally right* (even if he or she knew that it was *legally wrong*), could plead insanity, whereas an equivalent defendant in England or Wales could not do so – even though all of these jurisdictions use the *M'Naghten* Rules as the basis for their insanity defence.

The Burden of Proof

- Under the *M'Naghten* Rules, everyone is presumed sane. The burden of proving insanity is therefore on the accused (albeit on the balance of probabilities). Does this breach art 6(2) of the European Convention on Human Rights (ECHR), the presumption of innocence?

The Special Verdict

- Following a successful plea, the trial judge has three options: (1) a hospital order (with or without a restriction order attached), (2) a supervision order or (3) an absolute discharge. This is an improvement compared with 25 years ago (when only option (1) existed), but the LC in 2012 described the three options as still being 'limited'.

Human Rights issues

- The narrowness of certain aspects of the insanity defence (described above) could lead to some defendants with genuine psychiatric disorders being unable to invoke the defence (e.g. because they understood the nature and quality of their act and that it was legally wrong) and being convicted and sentenced to a term of imprisonment, instead of receiving help in hospital or elsewhere. This could be regarded as a breach of their rights under the ECHR, including art 2 (the right to life), because of the increased risk of suicide, and/or art 3 (the right not to be subjected to inhuman and degrading treatment), because of the increased risk of self-harm. The lack of suitable healthcare facilities available in mainstream prisons means that some prisoners with psychiatric disorders and other mental health problems are not being helped prior to their release, which in turn poses a potential risk to society at large.

Reform proposals

The insanity defence has recently been reformed in Scotland. Section 51A of the Criminal Procedure (Scotland) Act 1995, as amended by the Criminal Justice and Licensing (Scotland) Act 2010, states:

SECTION

> 'A person is not criminally responsible for conduct constituting an offence, and is to be acquitted of the offence, if the person was at the time of the conduct unable by reason of mental disorder to appreciate the nature or wrongfulness of the conduct.'

At the very least, this dispenses with outdated terminology such as 'disease of the mind' and 'defect of reason'.

In their 2013 Discussion Paper, the LC set out the following proposals for reform of insanity in English law. The LC acknowledges that these proposals are 'radical' but insists that such reform is necessary.

- The abolition of the existing insanity defence.
- The creation of a new defence of 'not criminally responsible by reason of recognised medical condition' to replace it.
- Determining what constitutes a 'recognised medical condition' will be a question of law, not of medicine, to be decided by the court, not by doctors. Having said that, the condition would *first* have to be one that was recognised by medical professionals (in order to deter 'fake' defences) but a condition's acceptance by the medical community would not be conclusive. Ultimately, it will be for the courts to decide whether a condition supports the defence or not. There will be no definitive list of such 'conditions', but the appeal courts will be able to provide guidance over time. It will include, but will not be restricted to, 'mental' conditions: 'if a physical condition leads to a total loss of capacity' then the defence should be available. However, two conditions will be explicitly excluded:
  - Intoxication will *not* be classed as a 'recognised medical condition'. The defence of intoxication will continue to apply to those under the influence of alcohol and/or drugs at the time of the alleged wrongdoing.
  - Nor will the defence apply to a defendant with a 'personality disorder characterised solely or principally by abnormally aggressive or seriously irresponsible behaviour'.
- More generally, if D was at fault in bringing about the recognised medical condition, they will not be able to invoke the defence.
- The defendant will have an evidential burden only. The burden of proof will be reversed compared to the existing insanity defence, requiring the Crown to disprove the defence beyond reasonable doubt.
- The defendant will need to adduce evidence (from at least two experts) that at the time of the alleged offence they wholly lacked the capacity:
  (i) rationally to form a judgment about the relevant conduct or circumstances;
  (ii) to understand the wrongfulness of what he or she is charged with having done; or
  (iii) to control his or her physical acts in relation to the relevant conduct or circumstances as a result of a qualifying recognised medical condition.
- 'Wrongfulness' will *not* be limited to 'illegality'.
- The new defence would be founded on complete loss of 'capacity'. Impaired, or even substantially impaired, capacity would *not* be enough for the defence to succeed, let alone a difficulty in (for example) controlling physical acts. 'Capacity' will be 'issue and time-specific', meaning that the question for the court will be whether or not the accused lacked capacity 'in relation to the charge' that he or she was facing (and not in some general, abstract sense).
- A lack of capacity alone would *not* support the defence – there would have to be a 'recognised medical condition' as well. Where the accused lacked capacity for some other reason, this might allow for the automatism defence instead.
- The defence would be available in relation to any type of offence, not just those which require proof of *mens rea*, and it would be available in the magistrates' courts and the Crown Court.

- The range of disposals would be the same as that currently available following a verdict of not guilty by reason of insanity.

The 2012 Scoping Paper and the 2013 Discussion Paper are both available from the Law Commission's website, http://lawcommission.justice.gov.uk/areas/insanity.htm.

Commentary on the proposals

The proposals offer an improvement on the existing defence of insanity in several ways:

- The offensive and stigmatising label of 'insanity' will be consigned to history.
- The modern terminology will fit much better with twenty-first century psychiatry than the old-fashioned, psychiatrically meaningless phrases in the *M'Naghten* Rules.
- The internal/external cause test with its potential for erratic and illogical outcomes is removed.
- The concept of the 'irresistible impulse' test has finally been recognised.
- The new test for 'wrongfulness' removes one of the most stringent restrictions on the defence and insanity and brings English law into line with that in Australia and Canada.
- The reversal of the burden of proof provides a much better fit with the presumption of innocence.

KEY FACTS

Key facts on insanity as a defence

Elements	Comment	Cases
Defect of reason	To be deprived of the power of reasoning	*Clarke* (1972)
Disease of the mind	Not concerned with the brain but with the mind	*Kemp* (1957)
	Must derive from an internal source	*Quick* (1973)
Examples	Arteriosclerosis	*Kemp* (1957)
	Epilepsy	*Bratty* (1963), *Sullivan* (1984)
	Hyperglycaemia	*Hennessy* (1989)
	Sleepwalking	*Burgess* (1991)
Not knowing what D was doing or not knowing that it was 'wrong'	'Wrong' means legally wrong	*Windle* (1952), *Johnson* (2007)
Burden of proof	It is for the defence to prove on the balance of probabilities	
Effect of defence	Defendant is not guilty 'by reason of insanity' (the special verdict)	Unless charge was murder, judge has various disposal options: hospital order, supervision order, absolute discharge If charge was murder, judge must order indefinite hospitalisation in a special hospital

9.2 Automatism

9.2.1 What is automatism?

'Automatism' is a phrase that was introduced into the criminal law from the medical world. There, it has a very limited meaning, describing the state of unconsciousness suffered by certain epileptics. In law it seems to have two meanings. According to Lord Denning in *Bratty* (1963):

JUDGMENT

'Automatism ... means an act which is done by the muscles without any control by the mind such as a spasm, a reflex action or a convulsion; or an act done by a person who is not conscious of what he is doing such as an act done whilst suffering from concussion or whilst sleepwalking.'

Conscious but uncontrolled

Here D is fully aware of what is going on around him but is incapable of preventing his arms, legs or even his whole body from moving. In this sense, automatism is incompatible with *actus reus*: D is aware of what his body is doing but there is no voluntary act.

Impaired consciousness

In *Bratty*, Lord Denning arguably gave 'automatism' too narrow a definition in referring to D being 'not conscious'. While automatism certainly includes unconsciousness, it is suggested that is should also include states of 'altered', 'clouded' or 'impaired' consciousness. If correct, this analysis suggests that automatism is a defence because it is incompatible with *mens rea*: D is not aware (or not fully aware) of what he is doing.

In *Coley, McGhee and Harris* [2013] EWCA Crim 223, Hughes LJ offered this definition:

JUDGMENT

'Automatism, if it occurs, results in a complete acquittal on the grounds that the act was not that of D at all. The essence of it is that the movements or actions of D at the material time were wholly involuntary. The better expression is complete destruction of voluntary control.'

This definition certainly fits with the first of Lord Denning's two meanings given in *Bratty* but appears to overlook the second. It is submitted, however, that the second meaning still represents English law and that, if D fails to form *mens rea* because he is 'not conscious of what he is doing', then automatism should be available as a complete defence.

9.2.2 The need for an evidential foundation

If D wishes to plead automatism, it is necessary for him to place evidence in support of his plea before the court. The reasoning behind this rule was explained by Devlin J (as he then was) in *Hill v Baxter* [1958] 1 QB 277:

JUDGMENT

'It would be quite unreasonable to allow the defence to submit at the end of the prosecution's case that the Crown had not proved affirmatively and beyond a reasonable doubt that the accused was at the time of the crime sober, or not sleepwalking or not in a trance or black-out. I am satisfied that such matters ought not to be considered at all until the defence has provided at least prima facie evidence.'

More recently, in C [2007] EWCA Crim 1862, Moses LJ in the Court of Appeal said that 'It is a crucial principle in cases such as this that D cannot rely on the defence of automatism without providing some evidence of it.' The evidence of D himself will rarely be sufficient, unless it is supported by medical evidence, because otherwise there is a possibility of the jury being deceived by spurious or fraudulent claims. In *Bratty* (1963), Lord Denning stated that it would be insufficient for D to simply say 'I had a black-out' because that was 'one of the first refuges of a guilty conscience and a popular excuse'. He continued:

JUDGMENT

'When the cause assigned is concussion or sleep-walking, there should be some evidence from which it can reasonably be inferred before it should be left to the jury. If it is said to be due to concussion, there should be evidence of a severe blow shortly beforehand. If it is said to be sleep-walking, there should be some credible support for it. His mere assertion that he was asleep will not suffice.'

9.2.3 Extent of involuntariness required

Must D's control over his bodily movements be totally destroyed before automatism is available? How unconscious does D have to be before he can be said to be an automaton? It seems that the extent of involuntariness required to be established depends on the offence charged. There are two categories.

Crimes of strict liability

As we saw in Chapter 4, when D is charged with a strict liability offence, denial of *mens rea* is no defence, so a plea that D was unconscious would seem doomed to failure. D must therefore provide evidence that he was incapable of exercising control over his bodily movements. If, despite some lack of control, he was still able to appreciate what he was doing and operate his body to a degree, then the defence is not made out. The majority of cases in this area involve driving offences. In *Isitt* (1978) 67 Cr App R 44, Lawton LJ said:

JUDGMENT

'The mind does not always operate in top gear. There may be some difficulty in functioning. If the difficulty does not amount to either insanity or automatism, is the accused entitled to say, "I am not guilty because my mind was not working in top gear"? In our judgment he is not ... it is clear that the appellant's mind was working to some extent. The driving was purposeful driving, which was to get away from the scene of the accident. It may well be that, because of panic or stress or alcohol, the appellant's mind was shut to the moral inhibitions which control the lives of most of us. But the fact that his moral inhibitions were not working properly ... does not mean that the mind was not working at all.'

In *Isitt*, D was convicted of dangerous driving after he drove off following an accident, evading a police car and roadblock in the process. Medical evidence suggested that he was in a dissociative state. The Court of Appeal, however, held that this did not amount to a defence. Other cases with similar facts and legal outcomes include:

- *Hill v Baxter* [1958] 1 QB 277. Although D claimed to have become unconscious as a result of being overcome by a sudden illness, the High Court found that the facts showed that D was 'driving', in the sense of controlling the car and directing its movements, and D's plea of automatism was rejected.

- *Watmore v Jenkins* [1962] 2 QB 572. D, a diabetic, suffered a hypoglycaemic episode while driving. He was able to drive some five miles before crashing. He was charged with, *inter alia*, dangerous driving, but was acquitted on the basis of automatism. On appeal, this decision was reversed. There was not 'such a complete destruction of voluntary control as could constitute in law automatism'. There had to be some evidence to raise a reasonable doubt that D's bodily movements were 'wholly uncontrolled and uninitiated by any function of conscious will'.
- *Broome v Perkins* [1987] Crim LR 271. D, charged with driving without due care and attention, after he had been observed driving erratically for some miles, pleaded a loss of consciousness. The Court of Appeal, however, found that he was only intermittently an automaton: although he was not in full control, there was evidence that his mind was controlling his limbs enough to allow him to avoid crashing by veering away from other traffic or braking violently.

These decisions may be explained on the ground that the automatism must be of such a degree that D cannot be said to have performed the *actus reus* voluntarily. But they do seem harsh. The defendant who retains some control over his actions faces conviction. The LC, in its *Commentary to the Draft Criminal Code* (1989), stated, 'Finding it necessary to choose between the authorities, we propose a formula under which we expect (and indeed hope) that a person in the condition of the defendant in *Broome v Perkins* would be acquitted (subject to the question of prior fault).' The Commission therefore proposed that, for any crime, D should have an automatism defence when no longer in 'effective control' of his acts (see below).

Crimes of mens rea

In this category the degree of automatism is, or should be, much reduced. D will have a good defence provided he was prevented from forming *mens rea*. In a New Zealand case, *Burr* [1969] NZLR 736, North P said:

JUDGMENT

'I think it should be made plain that when Lord Denning [in *Bratty*] speaks of "an act which is done by the muscles without any control by the mind", he does not mean that the accused person must be absolutely unconscious because you cannot move a muscle without a direction given by the mind. What his Lordship in my opinion was saying is that all the deliberative functions of the mind must be absent so that the accused person acts automatically.'

student mentor tip

'Never forget the difference between automatism and insanity.'
Holly, University of Southampton

The leading case in England is *T* (1990). D was charged with robbery and assault occasioning actual bodily harm. These are crimes which require at least subjective recklessness. However, the prosecution claimed, *inter alia*, that D's opening of the blade of a pen-knife had required a 'controlled and positive action', that following *Broome v Perkins* (1987) and *Isitt* (1978) this was a case of partial loss of control only and that automatism was not, therefore, available. However, those cases were distinguished by the trial judge, who held that D was 'acting as though in a dream'.

However, comments made by the Court of Appeal in *Narbrough* [2004] EWCA Crim 1012 seriously undermine the value of *T* as a precedent.

CASE EXAMPLE

Narbrough [2004] EWCA Crim 1012

D had been convicted of wounding with intent to do GBH contrary to s 18 OAPA 1861 after stabbing V with a Stanley knife. On appeal, he argued that psychiatric evidence that he had been seriously sexually abused as an 8- to 12-year-old child had left him suffering post-traumatic stress disorder, with flashbacks, so that he sometimes confused the past and the present. He claimed that, during the attack on V, he had suffered such a flashback and had acted 'like a zombie'. In other words, the evidence supported a plea of automatism, but the trial judge had declared it to be inadmissible. The Court of Appeal, however, rejected the appeal.

Zucker J said that the defence psychiatrist had not referred

JUDGMENT

'to any authority or to any research which supports the conclusion that a post-traumatic stress disorder can so affect a person's normal mental processes that his mind is no longer in control of his actions or that he behaves as an automaton. We have no doubt that the evidence ... was rightly ruled by the judge to be inadmissible.'

9.2.4 Self-induced automatism

intoxication
General defence where D fails to form *mens rea* because of alcohol and/or drugs (see section 9.3 for full discussion)

Where the automatism was due to D's consumption of alcohol and/or drugs, then the rules of **intoxication** apply (*Lipman* [1970] 1 QB 152, approved in *DPP v Majewski* [1977] AC 443). These rules will be explained fully in the next section of this chapter, but, essentially, they state that D cannot rely on evidence that he was intoxicated in order to deny having appreciated the consequences of his actions.

This means that, while D may have a defence to a crime requiring intention, he could be convicted of an offence requiring some lower level of *mens rea*, such as recklessness. This principle should apply whenever automatism is self-induced. For example, a driver who feels drowsy but continues to drive, then falls asleep at the wheel, may still be held liable for a motoring offence should he cause an accident (*Kay v Butterworth* (1945) 173 LT 191). Likewise, a driver who suffers an epileptic fit or hypoglycaemic episode whilst driving and causes an accident may be held liable, despite being in an automatic state at the time of the accident, depending on whether he was aware in advance of the onset of the automatic state. In other words, he is liable if the automatic state can be regarded as self-induced.

This was the situation in two recent and very similar cases, *C* [2007] EWCA Crim 1862 and *Clarke* [2009] EWCA Crim 921. In both cases, D was a diabetic who suffered a hypoglycaemic episode whilst driving, lost control of his car, left the road and hit and killed a pedestrian. Both pleaded automatism to charges of causing death by dangerous driving. In *C* the trial judge accepted the plea and ruled that the driver had no case to answer but the Appeal Court disagreed and allowed the Crown's appeal against that ruling on the basis that there was evidence that D was aware of his deteriorating condition before the onset of the hypoglycaemic episode. In *Clarke*, D was convicted after the jury rejected his automatism plea on the basis that it was self-induced and the Court of Appeal upheld his conviction. In the *C* case, Moses LJ summarised the situation as follows:

JUDGMENT

'Automatism due to a hypoglycaemic attack will not be a defence if the attack might reasonably have been avoided. If the driver ought to have tested his blood glucose level before embarking on his journey, or appreciated the onset of symptoms during the journey, then the fact that he did suffer a hypoglycaemic attack, even if it caused a total loss of control over his limbs at the moment the car left the road, would be no defence.'

In *Coley, McGhee and Harris* [2013] EWCA Crim 223, the second defendant (McGhee) invoked the defence of automatism, in response to charges of actual bodily harm (ABH) and wounding with intent, on the basis that he had drunk himself into an involuntary state. This was rejected by the trial judge and the Court of Appeal upheld his convictions on the grounds that, even if he was in an automatic state, he had induced it 'through his voluntary fault'. The fact that he was also taking prescription medication – temazepam – to help him deal with tinnitus made no difference, because he was 'well aware of the dangers of taking them together'. This meant that his true defence was intoxication (discussed in section 9.3), not automatism. Hughes LJ stated:

JUDGMENT

'The defence of automatism is not available to a defendant who has induced an acute state of involuntary behaviour by his own fault . . . The voluntary consumption of intoxicants leading to an acute condition is the prime example of self-induced behaviour.'

CASE EXAMPLE

McGhee [2013] EWCA Crim 223

D suffered from a 'particularly gross' form of tinnitus (persistent and permanent internal ringing in the ears). He took a prescription tranquiliser, temazepam, to help him sleep, but also resorted to drinking alcohol, despite warnings that he should not drink after taking temazepam. One night, he took his usual dose of temazepam and also consumed alcohol. At about 4 a.m., he went to an off-licence to buy more alcohol. There, he became aggressive. He invited one of the shopkeepers, V, to a fight and then did start a fight with another customer, W, during which he pressed his fingers into W's eye, causing him pain and blurred vision for two days, which required medical treatment. D then left the shop, only to return a few minutes later armed with a kitchen knife and with a T-shirt wrapped around his head 'like a bizarre head-dress'. There, he stabbed V in the arm. At his trial, D pleaded guilty to ABH but denied that he had intended to do GBH to V on the basis of automatism. The trial judge ruled that there was no evidence to support that defence. D was convicted and appealed, unsuccessfully, to the Court of Appeal.

9.2.5 Reflex actions

In *Ryan v R* (1967) 40 ALJR 488, an Australian case, a defence of reflex action was advanced. D had shot and killed a petrol station attendant, V, during an armed robbery. D claimed that as he was tying V up the latter moved and, startled, D had pulled the trigger of the shotgun he was carrying. He was convicted of manslaughter and the High Court of Australia upheld the conviction. Windeyer J stated that, even assuming D's act was 'involuntary' in a dictionary sense, it was incapable of absolving him from criminal responsibility. The judge added that there were only two legally recognised categories of involuntary actor: those which were involuntary because 'by no exercise of the will could the actor refrain from doing it', such as convulsions or an epileptic seizure; and those which were involuntary 'because he knew not what he was doing', such as the sleepwalker or a person rendered unconscious for some other reason. However, reflex actions did not bear any true analogy to either category.

JUDGMENT

'Such phrases as "reflex action" and "automatic reaction" can, if used imprecisely and unscientifically, be, like "blackout", mere excuses. They seem to me to have no real application to the case of a fully conscious man who has put himself in a situation in which he has his finger on the trigger of a loaded rifle levelled at another man. If he then presses the trigger in immediate response to a sudden threat or apprehension of danger, as is said to have occurred in this case, his doing so is, it seems to me, a consequence probable and foreseeable of a conscious apprehension of danger, and in that sense a voluntary act.'

9.2.6 Reform

In their Discussion Paper, *Criminal Liability: Insanity and Automatism*, published in July 2013, the Law Commission (LC) suggests the following proposals for reform of the defence of automatism.

- The existing common law defence of automatism to be abolished.
- It would be replaced by a new defence of automatism, which would be available 'only where there is a total loss of capacity to control one's actions which is not caused by a recognised medical condition and for which the accused was not culpably responsible'.
- Those defendants whose lack of capacity was caused by a recognised medical condition (such as diabetes, epilepsy or a sleep disorder) would be required to plead the new 'recognised medical condition' defence described above (see section 9.1.5)
- The outcome (as with the exiting defence) would be a complete acquittal.
- The defence would continue to have an evidential burden; the legal burden would be on the Crown to disprove the defence beyond reasonable doubt if/when the evidential burden had been discharged.

Commentary on the proposals

These proposals are relatively modest compared to the LC's 'radical' proposals for reforming the defence of insanity. In many ways they simply confirm the existing automatism defence. In particular, the requirement that the accused 'was not culpably responsible' for his or her loss of capacity confirms the decisions in cases such as *Lipman* (1970), *C* (2007), *Clarke* (2009) and *McGhee* (2013). However, there would be some changes.

- The requirement for a 'total loss of capacity to control one's actions' would appear to preclude the automatism defence in a case such as *T* (1990). In their Discussion Paper, the LC considers that the defendant in *T* would in future be entitled to the new 'recognised medical condition' defence instead, on the basis of her post-traumatic stress disorder, but this appears to overlook the fact that, on the evidence, she had not suffered a 'total loss of capacity' and would therefore have neither defence available to her.
- The diabetic defendant in a case like *Quick* (1973) might no longer be able to claim an acquittal on the basis of automatism. In its Discussion Paper, the LC considers that the defendant in *Quick* would in future be entitled to the new 'recognised medical condition' defence on the basis of his diabetes (subject to arguments about whether

the accused was at fault for self-inducing his own medical condition). Should the accused in a case like *Quick* try to argue that the new automatism defence applied instead, on the basis that his 'loss of capacity' was *not* caused by a 'recognised medical condition' but, rather, by taking insulin, the Crown would presumably counter by seeking to prove that D was 'culpably responsible' for his own defence. This would entail both defences failing and the accused would be facing liability.

9.3 Intoxication

Intoxication as a defence in English law is a means of putting doubt into the minds of the magistrates or jury as to whether D formed the necessary *mens rea*. It is an area governed (for the time being at least) exclusively by case law. Although the majority of those cases involve alcohol, the defence potentially applies to any case where D has consumed a substance (or cocktail of substances) which is capable of affecting D's ability to intend or foresee the consequences of his or her actions. It follows that if, despite the intoxication, D forms the necessary *mens rea* required for the crime in question (whether it be intention or recklessness or some other state of mind such as dishonesty), then the defence is not available. Alcohol and many other drugs, most notably hallucinogenic drugs such as LSD and tranquilisers, are obviously capable of affecting a person's perception of their surroundings. But if D, having consumed several pints of lager, is still sufficiently aware of what is going on when he gets involved in a fight, his intoxication would provide no defence to any charges of actual bodily harm or malicious wounding that may result.

But does it also necessarily follow that if D, because of intoxication, failed to form *mens rea*, then he is automatically entitled to be acquitted, regardless of what he may have actually done whilst in the intoxicated condition? Logically, the answer is 'yes' and, indeed, courts in other common law jurisdictions such as Australia and New Zealand are content to leave the matter there. In the leading Australian case on intoxication, *O'Connor* [1980] ALR 449, the Australian High Court decided that if the prosecution is unable to prove that D formed *mens rea* because of intoxication, then D must be acquitted. This reflected the earlier decision of the New Zealand Court of Appeal in *Kamipeli* [1975] 2 NZLR 610. South African courts have reached the same conclusion (*Chretien* [1981] (1) SA 1097).

In England, however, the courts have decided that this logical conclusion would send out dangerous signals. As a matter of public policy, there is clearly a need to discourage antisocial behaviour caused by excessive drinking or drug consumption. In the leading English case, *DPP v Majewski* [1977] AC 443, Lord Simon expressed the concern that, without special rules on intoxication, the public would be 'legally unprotected from unprovoked violence where such violence was the consequence of drink or drugs having obliterated the capacity of the perpetrator to know what he was doing or what were its consequences'. The result in England has been an uneasy compromise between the logical conclusion reached in Australia and New Zealand (on the one hand) and the public policy demands of discouraging violent crime (on the other). The law in England can be summarised as follows:

- Intoxication is no defence if, despite the intoxication, D formed *mens rea*.
- Where D was involuntarily intoxicated and failed to form *mens rea*, D is entitled to be acquitted.
- Where D was voluntarily intoxicated and failed to form *mens rea*, D is entitled to be acquitted if the offence charged is one of 'specific intent'. If the offence charged is one of 'basic intent' then the jury must consider whether D would have formed *mens rea* had he been sober.

9.3.1 Intoxication is no defence if D still formed *mens rea*

According to the Court of Appeal in *Sheehan* [1975] 1 WLR 739, where D raises intoxication in an attempt to show lack of *mens rea*, the jury should be directed that:

JUDGMENT

'The mere fact that the defendant's mind was affected by drink so that he acted in a way in which he would not have done had he been sober does not assist him at all, provided that the necessary intention was there. A drunken intent is nevertheless an intent.'

The leading case on this point is now *Kingston* [1995] 2 AC 355. D had been convicted by a jury of indecent assault. The prosecution had satisfied the jury that D, despite being involuntarily intoxicated at the time, had enough appreciation of his surroundings to have formed *mens rea*. However, the Court of Appeal allowed D's appeal on the basis that D was not at fault in becoming intoxicated in the first place. Lord Taylor CJ said that, if a 'drink or a drug, surreptitiously administered, causes a person to lose his self-control and for that reason to form an intent which he would not otherwise have formed ... the law should exculpate him because the operative fault is not his'. The prosecution appealed against this ruling to the House of Lords, which allowed the appeal and reinstated D's conviction.

CASE EXAMPLE

Kingston [1995] 2 AC 355

D was a middle-aged businessman. He had admitted paedophiliac, homosexual tendencies, which he was able to control whilst sober. This presented an opportunity for former business associates of his to blackmail him. As part of the set-up, both D and a 15-year-old boy were lured, separately, to a flat and drugged. While the boy fell asleep, D was intoxicated but not unconscious. In this condition D was encouraged to abuse the boy, which he did, and was photographed and tape-recorded doing so. In the prosecution's view there was evidence that D, despite the effects of the drugs, intended to touch the boy in circumstances of indecency, and the jury agreed.

In *O'Connell* [1997] Crim LR 683, D appealed against his murder conviction on the basis that Halcion, a sleeping drug that he was taking, may have prevented him from forming the *mens rea* for murder. The appeal was dismissed, however, because of lack of any evidence that the drug had prevented D from forming the intent.

Another example of 'drunken intent' is *Heard* [2007] EWCA Crim 125; [2008] QB 43. D had been charged with sexual assault, contrary to s 3 of the Sexual Offences Act 2003 (see Chapter 12). This requires, among other things, that D touch V 'intentionally'. D did not deny touching V but argued that it was unintentional; he asked that evidence of intoxication be taken into account to support his argument. However, the trial judge ruled that D's behaviour demonstrated that the touching was intentional (despite evidence of D being intoxicated) and therefore D had no defence. The Court of Appeal agreed.

CASE EXAMPLE

Heard [2007] EWCA Crim 125; [2008] QB 43

The police had been called to D's house where he was found in an 'emotional state'. He was obviously drunk and had cut himself, and so the police took him to hospital. There, he became abusive and began singing and was taken outside to avoid disturbing others. Shortly afterwards, he 'began to dance suggestively' in front of one of the policemen. He then 'undid his trousers, took his penis in his hand and rubbed it up and down' the policeman's thigh. At that point he was arrested. The next day, after he had sobered up, he claimed to be unable to remember what had happened but did accept that when he was ill or drunk he sometimes might 'go silly and start stripping'. D was charged with and convicted of intentional sexual touching, and the Court of Appeal upheld his conviction. Hughes LJ said, 'On the evidence the appellant plainly did intend to touch the policeman with his penis.'

Most recently, in *Press and Thompson* [2013] EWCA Crim 1849, the two defendants were both charged with causing GBH with intent and attempting to cause GBH with intent, both specific intent offences. The Crown case was that the defendants had attacked two men who were waiting to be served at a burger van, causing serious injury to one of them and attempting to do so to the other. Despite the evidence that the pair of them were very drunk at the time of the attack, the jury convicted on all counts and the Court of Appeal upheld their convictions on the basis of 'drunken intent'. Pitchford LJ succinctly noted that the trial judge 'correctly informed the jury that even if [D's] intention was formed in drink it was nevertheless an intention'.

9.3.2 Involuntary intoxication

If D was involuntarily intoxicated such that the prosecution cannot prove *mens rea*, then D is entitled to an acquittal. Involuntary intoxication refers to any situation where D consumes alcohol or some other drug unintentionally. The following is a non-exhaustive examination of the circumstances where intoxication will be regarded as involuntary.

'Lacing'

Intoxication is involuntary when D's non-alcoholic drink has been drugged or 'laced' without his knowledge. The surreptitious drugging of D's coffee in *Kingston* (1995), above, is one example. It is, however, crucial that D thought he was consuming a non-alcoholic drink. The mere fact that D's alcoholic drink (or drug) has a stronger effect than he expected is not enough to render the intoxication involuntary. In *Allen* [1988] Crim LR 698, D had been given some home-made wine. Unknown to him it was particularly strong wine. As a result he became extremely drunk and in that state carried out a serious sexual assault. He was convicted of buggery and indecent assault and the Court of Appeal upheld the convictions. There was no evidence that D's drinking was anything other than voluntary. This is obviously correct. D knew he was drinking alcohol and therefore took the risk as to its strength. Moreover, it is common knowledge that home-made alcohol is often much stronger than the conventional pub strength, and D ought to have realised this. If intoxication through alcohol was deemed to be voluntary only if D knew exactly what he was drinking, including in terms of strength, that would severely undermine the public policy argument advanced in *Majewski* (1977) because it would enable D to escape liability simply because he had failed to appreciate the strength of his drinks.

In *Allen* (1988), D was drinking wine and knew he was drinking wine; it just happened to be stronger than he realised. But what about D who drinks alcohol surreptitiously laced with another (much stronger) drug? This may be regarded as involuntary intoxication. In *Eatch* [1980] Crim LR 650, D at a party had drunk from a can of beer to which another, stronger drug had been added without his knowledge. The judge directed the jury that it was up to them to decide whether D's condition was 'due solely to voluntary intoxication'. This seems correct: although D had taken one intoxicating substance voluntarily, he was unaware, through no fault of his own, of the additional substance. To similar effect are the cases of *Ross v HM Advocate* (1991) SLT 564 (Scotland) and *People v Cruz* 83 Cal App 3d 308 (1978) (California), in both of which intoxication caused by the surreptitious addition of LSD to beer was deemed to be involuntary. However, a different conclusion was reached in *People v Velez* 175 Cal App 3d 785 (1985) (California), where D had voluntarily smoked marijuana at a party, apparently unaware that PCP, a much stronger drug, had been added to it. D was held to be voluntarily intoxicated after the court pointed out that the effect of marijuana consumption was itself unpredictable.

What about the defendant who consumes a substance that he knows is an intoxicant, but does not know exactly what it is or how strong it is? There is no English case law on this point, but the public policy approach laid down in *Majewski* (1977) would dictate that such conduct be deemed voluntary intoxication. In *Hanks v State* 542 SW 2d 413 (1976) (Texas), where D knew that a drug had been placed in his drink but did not necessarily know what it was, this was nevertheless deemed to be voluntary intoxication.

Drugs taken under medical prescription

In *Majewski*, Lord Elwyn-Jones LC specifically included those who take 'drugs not on medical prescription' within the scope of voluntary intoxication; by implication, therefore, we can say that those who do take drugs under medical prescription will be deemed to be involuntarily intoxicated.

CASE EXAMPLE

Bailey [1983] 1 WLR 760

D had been charged with malicious wounding. His defence was that he was a diabetic and had taken insulin (which had been medically prescribed for him). However, because he had forgotten to eat afterwards, the insulin had triggered a hypoglycaemic episode, and this had prevented him from fully appreciating what he was doing.

The Court of Appeal held that a distinction should be drawn between intoxication arising from alcohol and 'certain sorts of drugs to excess', on the one hand, and the unexpected side effects of therapeutic substances, on the other. It was 'common knowledge' that those who took alcohol and certain drugs could become 'aggressive or do dangerous or unpredictable things'. Griffiths LJ stated:

JUDGMENT

'The question in each case will be whether the prosecution have proved the necessary element of recklessness. In cases of assault, if [D] knows that his actions or inaction are likely to make him aggressive, unpredictable or uncontrolled with the result that he may cause some injury to others and he persists in the action or takes no remedial action when he knows it is required, it will be open to the jury to find that he was reckless.'

In most cases D who takes prescribed medicines will be quite unaware of potential side effects. However, where D is aware of the effect of a prescribed drug and takes it anyway, then he is in the same position as D who drinks alcohol. The exception is likely to be rarely applicable to alcohol, though it might apply where brandy is administered to D after an accident. In *Johnson v Commonwealth* 135 Va 524 (1923) a court in Virginia held that D who drank whisky to relieve pain was doing so voluntarily because no medical advice was involved; the implication being that had medical advice been given to drink whisky, then his drinking could be classified as involuntary.

'Soporific or sedative' drugs

A third example of involuntary intoxication involves drugs that are said to have a soporific or sedative influence, as opposed to an inhibition-lowering or mind-expanding effect. In *Burns* (1974) 58 Cr App R 364, D had consumed, *inter alia*, morphine tablets (not medically prescribed) for a stomach complaint, before committing an offence. The Court of Appeal quashed his conviction. The jury should have been directed to acquit if they believed that Burns did not appreciate that morphine was likely to produce unawareness. The leading case is now *Hardie* [1985] 1 WLR 64, where D had taken Valium tablets (not medically prescribed) before committing acts of criminal damage.

CASE EXAMPLE

Hardie [1985] 1 WLR 64

D was depressed at having been asked to move out of the South London flat he had shared with his girlfriend, V, for some years. He reluctantly agreed to leave and packed. Before he left, however, he took one of V's prescription Valium tablets from her medicine cabinet. During the course of the day he took more of the pills, moved some of his possessions out and returned that evening. Shortly after, he started a fire in the wardrobe in the bedroom. His defence was that he did not know what he was doing because of the Valium. The jury convicted of arson after being directed to ignore the effects of the Valium. However, D's conviction was quashed.

Parker LJ said

JUDGMENT

'There was no evidence that it was known to [D] or even generally known that the taking of valium in the quantity taken would be liable to render a person aggressive or incapable of appreciating risks or have other side effects such that its self-administration would itself have an element of recklessness ... [T]he drug is ... wholly different in kind from drugs which are liable to cause unpredictability or aggressiveness ... if the effect of a drug is merely soporific or sedative the taking of it, even in some excessive quantity, cannot in the ordinary way raise a conclusive presumption against the admission of proof of intoxication ... such as would be the case with alcoholic intoxication or incapacity or automatism resulting from the self-administration of dangerous drugs ... [The jury] should have been directed that if they came to the conclusion that, as a result of the valium, [D] was, at the time, unable to appreciate the risks to property and persons from his actions they should consider whether the taking of the valium was itself reckless.'

Identifying 'soporific and sedative' drugs

One problem in this area is how to draw a distinction between 'dangerous' drugs on one hand, and 'soporific and sedative' drugs on the other, if indeed such a distinction is possible. Marijuana, depending on the circumstances, may be a sedative or a hallucinogen. Heroin is presumably a 'dangerous' drug, but it has undeniably 'soporific' effects. Much depends on several variables: the user himself; the amount taken; how much has been taken before; how the drug is taken (injecting generally produces more dramatic effects than smoking or eating); the surroundings in which the drug is taken; even what the user expects or hopes will happen. The same person may take the same drug at different times with markedly different consequences. Uncertainty in predicting the effect of taking a single drug becomes much more complicated when two or more drugs are taken at the same time, because of the likelihood of interaction. A common example is the enhancing effect of alcohol on the sedative qualities of tranquilisers. The courts in England have yet to address these questions, but you should recall the importance placed on public policy by the House of Lords in *Majewski* (1977). It is suggested that where there is doubt about whether a drug is 'dangerous' or 'soporific', such as heroin, the courts could deem it to be both, and therefore ingestion of it would be regarded as voluntary.

Intoxication under duress

Although there is no English case law on this point, there is American authority for the proposition that 'intoxication under duress' should be regarded as involuntary. In *Burrows v State* 38 Ariz 99, 297 (1931) (Arizona), where D, an 18-year-old boy, had killed his adult victim only after the latter had vehemently insisted the boy drink several bottles of beer and some whisky, the court held that it was possible for this to be regarded as involuntary.

9.3.3 Voluntary intoxication

In the leading English case, *Majewski* (1977), D was charged with, *inter alia*, assault occasioning actual bodily harm, a crime requiring subjective recklessness, that is awareness of risk. But this is a modest standard; even fleeting awareness will suffice for a conviction. It follows that D's intoxication must be extreme in order to remove altogether the ability to appreciate the risks created by his actions (a point acknowledged by the Court of Appeal in *Stubbs* (1989) 88 Cr App R 53). Moreover, the defence medical evidence in *Majewski* (1977) was to the effect that his intoxication was more likely to have produced amnesia afterwards, rather than inducing a state of intoxication during the assaults. In shouting 'You pigs, I'll kill you all', D was obviously aware that (a) he was assaulting someone, and (b) the people whom he was assaulting were police officers.

CASE EXAMPLE

Majewski [1977] AC 443

D had consumed a combination of barbiturates, amphetamines and alcohol, beginning on a Sunday morning and continuing until Monday night, when he was involved in a pub brawl and assaulted a customer, the manager and police officers sent to deal with him. He was charged with three offences of assault contrary to s 47 of the Offences Against the Person Act (OAPA) 1861 and three offences of assaulting a police officer in the execution of his duty. His defence was that he was suffering the effects of the alcohol and drugs at the time. He was convicted, after the trial judge directed the jury that they could ignore the effect of drink and drugs as being in any way a defence to assault. The Court of Appeal and House of Lords upheld his convictions.

Of course the public must be protected from violent drunkards; no one denies that. But it must surely be in very rare cases that D's capacity has been 'obliterated' such that he must be acquitted? So, were the matter simply to be left to the jury, the number of cases where D might escape conviction would be very few. This reasoning underpins the approach of the courts in the Australia, New Zealand and South Africa, as mentioned in the introduction to this section. The result of this approach, moreover, has not been a proliferation of acquittals (G Orchard, 'Surviving without *Majewski*: a view from down under' [1993] Crim LR 426). The English judiciary, however, does not possess such confidence in the jury's ability to reject intoxication in all but a handful of cases. In England, to reiterate this point, the law states that when intoxication is voluntary, and D has failed to form *mens rea*:

- D will have a defence if the offence charged is one of 'specific intent'.
- Where the offence charged is one of 'basic intent', the magistrates or jury must consider whether D would have formed *mens rea* had he been sober.

To understand this approach it is necessary to appreciate its historical origins. Until the mid-nineteenth century, voluntary intoxication was not regarded as any form of defence at all. Instead intoxicated defendants were treated as more culpable. But in the early twentieth century, the courts began to relax the strict approach. In *Meade* [1909] 1 KB 895, Lord Coleridge J said, 'if the mind at the time is so obscured by drink, if the reason is dethroned and the man is incapable of forming the intent, it justifies the reduction of the charge from murder to manslaughter'. This proposition of law (which is still true in the twenty-first century) was confirmed in *DPP v Beard* [1920] AC 479. Lord Birkenhead emphasised that intoxication was merely a means of demonstrating that D lacked, on a particular charge, the mental element necessary:

JUDGMENT

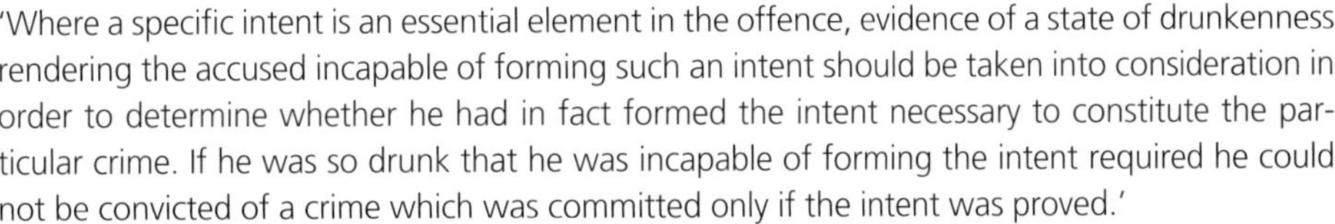
'Where a specific intent is an essential element in the offence, evidence of a state of drunkenness rendering the accused incapable of forming such an intent should be taken into consideration in order to determine whether he had in fact formed the intent necessary to constitute the particular crime. If he was so drunk that he was incapable of forming the intent required he could not be convicted of a crime which was committed only if the intent was proved.'

This principle has remained largely unchanged since, though it is now firmly accepted that D need not be incapable of forming intent; it is sufficient if he does not in fact do so (*Pordage* [1975] Crim LR 575; *Cole* [1993] Crim LR 300).

Basic and specific intent

It seems highly probable that in *Beard* Lord Birkenhead was using the word 'specific' to mean 'particular'. The rest of his speech shows that he was not proposing an exceptional rule for 'specific' intent crimes but was simply pointing out that where a particular crime required a particular intent to be proven, then the case was not made out until that was achieved: 'a person cannot be convicted of a crime unless the *mens* was *rea*'. At no point did Lord Birkenhead refer to anything called 'basic intent' (that concept seems to be attributed to Lord Simon in *DPP v Morgan* [1976] AC 182). Nevertheless, legal doctrine has developed over the last century to the present situation, according to which all crimes divide into two categories for the purposes of the voluntary intoxication defence. In *Bratty*, Lord Denning said:

JUDGMENT

'If the drunken man is so drunk that he does not know what he is doing, he has a defence to any charge, such as murder or wounding with intent, in which a specific intent is essential, but he is still liable to be convicted of manslaughter or unlawful wounding for which no specific intent is necessary, see *Beard's* case.'

Distinguishing basic and specific intent offences

The division of crimes into specific and basic intent is now well established in English criminal law (and has been adopted in most American states and Canada too). It is obviously crucial to demonstrate which offences belong in which category. Over the years there have been a number of attempts at an explanation:

- The 'purposive element' argument. A purposive element is some identifiable result desired by D. This possibility was suggested by Lord Simon in *Majewski* (1977) and has received support recently from the Court of Appeal in *Heard* [2007] EWCA Crim 125; [2008] QB 43 (see below).
- The 'fallback' argument. Specific intent crimes are those where D, were he to be acquitted because of intoxication, would only convict himself of some lesser offence of basic intent. Many specific intent offences do have this fallback, for example murder has a basic intent fallback (manslaughter), as does s 18 OAPA 1861 (s 20 OAPA 1861); however, some specific intent crimes have no fallback, for example theft.
- The 'ulterior intent' argument. This proposal received the support of Lord Elwyn-Jones LC in *Majewski* and was the first to gain broad acceptance. Ulterior intent crimes are those where the mental element goes beyond the *actus reus*. A good example is theft, where the *actus reus* is complete as soon as D appropriates property belonging to another. However, the *mens rea* goes beyond this in requiring that D have the intention to permanently deprive V of his property. However, murder is, as already noted, unquestionably a crime of specific intent, yet it is not a crime of ulterior intent. The *actus reus* is causing the death of a human being; the *mens rea* (malice aforethought) is intent to cause death (or even intent to cause serious harm).
- The recklessness argument. This theory holds that basic intent crimes are those offences that may be committed recklessly. This argument has now gained widespread acceptance. In *Caldwell* [1982] AC 341, Lord Diplock stated that *Majewski* is authority for the proposition that self-induced intoxication is no defence to a crime in which recklessness is enough to constitute the necessary *mens rea*. Certainly, there are numerous passages in *Majewski* which support this proposition. Most famously, Lord Elwyn-Jones LC stated that:

JUDGMENT

'If a man of his own volition takes a substance which causes him to cast off the restraints of reason and conscience, no wrong is done to him by holding him answerable criminally for any injury he may do while in that condition. His course of conduct in reducing himself by drugs and drink to that condition in my view supplies the evidence of *mens rea*, of guilty mind certainly sufficient for crimes of basic intent. It is a reckless course of conduct and recklessness is enough to constitute the necessary *mens rea* in assault cases. The drunkenness is itself an intrinsic, and integral part of the crime, the other part being the evidence of the unlawful use of force against the victim. Together they add up to criminal recklessness.'

The various definitions perhaps illustrate the need for statutory clarification. The lack of any definitive test poses potential problems for trial judges faced with a new crime (such as those introduced by Parliament in the Sexual Offences Act 2003). Nevertheless, the courts have now assigned most crimes to one category or another, as follows.

Crimes of specific intent:

- murder (*Beard* (1920); *Rowbotham* [2011] EWCA Crim 433);
- wounding or causing GBH with intent (*Bratty* (1963); *Pordage* (1975));
- theft (*Ruse v Read* [1949] 1 KB 377);
- robbery (*R v George* [1960] SCR 871, Supreme Court of Canada);
- burglary (*Rowbotham*);
- handling stolen goods (*Durante* [1972] 3 All ER 962);
- arson/criminal damage with intent to do so and/or with intent to endanger life; *Metropolitan Police Commissioner v Caldwell* (1982); *Bennett* [1995] Crim LR 877; *Rowbotham*); any attempt to commit one of these (*Coley* (2013), attempted murder; *Press and Thompson* (2013), attempted GBH with intent to do GBH).

Crimes of basic intent:

- manslaughter, in all its forms (*Beard*; *Lipman* (1970));
- rape (*Woods* (1981) 74 Cr App R 312; *Fotheringham* (1989) 88 Cr App R 206);
- sexual assault (*Heard* [2007] EWCA Crim 125);
- malicious wounding or infliction of GBH, s 20 OAPA 1861 (*Aitken and others* [1992] 1 WLR 1006);
- assault occasioning actual bodily harm (ABH), s 47 OAPA 1861 (*Majewski*);
- common assault;
- arson/criminal damage being reckless whether property would be damaged or destroyed (*Jaggard v Dickinson* [1980] 3 All ER 716);
- arson/criminal damage, being reckless whether property would be damaged or destroyed, and being reckless whether life would be endangered thereby (*Bennett* (1995); *Rowbotham*).

The Court of Appeal in *Heard* (2007) had to decide whether the offence of sexual assault, contrary to s 3 of the Sexual Offences Act 2003, was one of specific intent (as D argued) or basic intent (as the Crown argued). The offence requires, for its *mens rea*, proof that D intentionally touched V and did not reasonably believe that V was consenting. The requirement that D 'intentionally' touch V was seized on by D as an indicator that the offence could not be basic intent. In short, D's argument was that (1) basic intent crimes are those that can be committed recklessly, (2) sexual assault cannot be committed recklessly, (3) therefore sexual assault is not a crime of basic intent. However, as was noted above, the trial judge and the Court of Appeal agreed that, on the facts, there was evidence that D had formed intent anyway, notwithstanding his intoxication, so even if D's argument had been correct the appeal would still have failed. In the event, the Court of Appeal rejected D's argument regarding the status of sexual assault and held that it was one of basic intent. Hughes LJ stated that the 'first thing to say is that it should not be supposed that every offence can be categorised *simply* as either one of specific intent or of basic intent'. He went on:

JUDGMENT

> 'It is necessary to go back to *Majewski* in order to see the basis for the distinction there upheld between crimes of basic and of specific intent. It is to be found most clearly in the speech of Lord Simon. [His] analysis was that crimes of specific intent are those where the offence requires proof of purpose or consequence, which are not confined to, but amongst which are included, those where the purpose goes beyond the *actus reus*. We regard this as the best explanation of the sometimes elusive distinction between specific and basic intent ... By that test, element (a) (the touching) in sexual assault is an element requiring no more than basic intent. It follows that voluntary intoxication cannot be relied upon to negate that intent.'

It follows that the presence of 'recklessness' in the *mens rea* of an offence may indicate that it is a basic intent offence, but it is not essential. This decision has implications for other offences in the Sexual Offences Act 2003, in particular rape (s 1) and assault by penetration (s 2). The definition of rape prior to the 2003 Act included the word 'reckless' as part of its *mens rea* (s 1, Sexual Offences (Amendment) Act 1976), and so it was possible to apply the 'recklessness argument' to rape. Indeed, case law predating the 2003 Act had clearly established that rape was a crime of basic intent (see *Woods* (1981) and *Fotheringham* (1989)). The new definition of rape in s 1 of the 2003 Act does not include the word 'reckless' but instead requires proof that D 'intentionally' penetrated V with a lack of reasonable belief that V was consenting (and so 'recklessness' is no longer part of its *mens rea*). The 'recklessness argument', therefore, cannot apply to rape, but the decision in *Heard* clearly indicates that the redefinition of rape in the 2003 Act will not affect its basic intent status. This is because there is no requirement of any 'purpose' going beyond the 'penetration' element. The same argument applies to the offence of sexual penetration.

The Court of Appeal in *Heard* also explicitly acknowledged the importance of 'public policy' in determining whether an offence was one of specific or basic intent. Hughes LJ noted that rape had been categorised as basic intent prior to the SOA 2003, in *Woods* (1981), along with the now-abolished offence of indecent assault, in *C* [1992] Crim LR 642. He concluded that 'it is unlikely that it was the intention of Parliament in enacting the Sexual Offences Act 2003 to change the law by permitting reliance upon voluntary intoxication where previously it was not permitted'. The fact that the law surrounding the distinction between basic and specific intent remains unclear means that cases are still reaching the appeal courts involving arguments about whether a particular offence is 'specific'. For example, in *Carroll v DPP* [2009] EWHC 554 Admin, D tried to persuade the High Court that the offence of being drunk and disorderly in a public place, contrary to s 91 of the Criminal Justice Act 1967, was an offence of 'specific intent' and therefore intoxication would provide a good defence. This was on the basis that he was so drunk that he had not intended to be 'disorderly'. Unsurprisingly, the court rejected his argument, holding that there was no requirement of *mens rea* at all relating to disorderly behaviour (in other words, liability was strict).

Rowbotham [2011] EWCA Crim 433 involved the use of the intoxication defence in the context of three offences: murder, burglary (contrary to s 9(1)(a) of the Theft Act 1968) and aggravated arson with intent to endanger life (contrary to ss 1(2) and (3) of the Criminal Damage Act 1971).

CASE EXAMPLE

Rowbotham [2011] EWCA Crim 433

D had been out one night and was extremely drunk. He was seen by witnesses at around 1.30 a.m., already very drunk and drinking neat vodka. At around 2.30 a.m. he entered a house and demanded money and a computer. The householder threw him out. Shortly afterwards, D pushed three wheelie bins up against the porch of a nearby house and set them on fire. The fire spread into the house and one of the occupants, V, was trapped inside. Her husband was able to escape by jumping from a bedroom window, but V was unable to escape and was killed. At 2.53 a.m., D called the fire brigade on his mobile. He did not leave the area and was seen by witnesses stumbling around, obviously very drunk. He was still in the area some two-and-a-half hours after the fire was started. He was subsequently convicted of the murder of V, burglary and arson with intent to endanger life. This was despite evidence presented at the trial that D had an IQ that put him in the bottom 1 per cent of the population, in addition to his extreme drunkenness. He appealed, and the Court of Appeal quashed his convictions of on the basis of 'uncontradicted' expert evidence at D's trial that D's very low IQ combined with extreme intoxication from drinking neat vodka had prevented him from forming the requisite intent.

This appears to be the first occasion on which an appeal court in England has quashed a burglary conviction on the basis of evidence of intoxication; in other words, *Rowbotham* is the first case in this country to provide authority for the proposition that burglary (at least, the s 9(1)(a) version of that offence) is a crime of specific intent.

Intoxication and basic intent

If D is charged with, for example, murder, he may plead intoxication as a means of denying that he formed the intent to kill or cause GBH. But what if D is charged with a basic intent offence, such as manslaughter? Is there any point in pleading intoxication? There are suggestions by some of the Law Lords in *Majewski* that were D to do this he would, in effect, be pleading guilty. For example, refer back to the quotation from Lord Elwyn-Jones LC in *Majewski* (above).

According to *Majewski*, therefore, voluntary intoxication is to be regarded, in law, as a form of recklessness. This somewhat harsh view may not represent the law today. Another view which has been adopted in some cases is that, when faced with a defendant pleading intoxication to a basic intent offence, the magistrates or jury are required to consider whether D would have formed the requisite *mens rea* had he been sober. An early indication of the newer approach was seen in *Aitken and others* (1992), which was examined in Chapter 8 in the section on consent. The judge advocate (this was a court martial) had directed the jury that they had to be 'satisfied ... that each defendant, when he did the act, either foresaw that it might cause some injury ... or would have foreseen that the act might cause some injury, had he not been drinking'. The Court-Martial Appeal Court, although quashing the conviction on other grounds, confirmed that the judge advocate's direction was correct. *Aitken and others* was followed in *Richardson and Irwin* [1998] EWCA Crim 3269; [1999] 1 Cr App R 392.

CASE EXAMPLE

Richardson and Irwin [1998] EWCA Crim 3269; [1999] 1 Cr App R 392

The appellants and V were students at Surrey University. They had each consumed about five pints of lager before indulging in 'horseplay' – something they did regularly – during the course of which V was lifted over the edge of a balcony and dropped at least ten feet, suffering injury. D and E were charged with inflicting GBH contrary to s 20 OAPA 1861. The prosecution case was that they had both foreseen that dropping V from the balcony might cause him harm but, nevertheless, took that risk. Their defence was that V had consented to the horseplay and/or that his fall was an accident. On the question of *mens rea*, the jury were directed to consider each man's foresight of the consequences on the basis of what a reasonable, sober man would have foreseen. They were convicted, but the Court of Appeal quashed the conviction. The question was not what the reasonable, sober man would have foreseen, but what these particular men would have foreseen had they not been drinking. Clarke LJ memorably said that, 'the defendants were not hypothetical reasonable men, but University students'.

Obviously this poses a hypothetical question for the magistrates or jury. Nevertheless, if there is evidence of factors which might cast doubt on whether D would have formed *mens rea* had he been sober, such as fatigue or illness, then these must be taken into account. In *Majewski* (1977) one of the grounds of appeal was that the denial of intoxication as a defence in basic intent offences was irreconcilable with s 8 of the Criminal Justice Act 1967, which requires a jury to consider 'all the evidence' before deciding whether D intended or foresaw the result of his conduct. The view of Lord Elwyn-Jones LC was forthright:

JUDGMENT

'In referring to "all the evidence" [s 8] meant all the relevant evidence. But if there is a substantive rule of law that in crimes of basic intent, the factor of intoxication is irrelevant (and such I hold to be the substantive law), evidence with regard to it is irrelevant.'

The evidential burden

In all cases – whether specific or basic intent – D is required to adduce evidence of intoxication before the matter becomes a live issue. D's evidence must go to the degree of intoxication and not just to the fact of intoxication. The strength of evidence needed to discharge the evidential burden will differ from one situation to the next, depending on the nature of the crime and the circumstances. The mere assertion that D was drinking all day prior to the commission of the alleged offence will not, generally, suffice in itself. The question of whether D's intoxication is sufficient is a question of law for the judge. If the evidence is insufficient to raise a doubt that D possessed *mens rea*, the trial judge must remove the matter from the jury's consideration. This point was made clear in *Groark* [1999] EWCA Crim 207; [1999] Crim LR 669.

CASE EXAMPLE

Groark [1999] EWCA Crim 207; [1999] Crim LR 669

D had struck V whilst wearing a knuckleduster. He was charged with wounding under s 18 and s 20 OAPA 1861. At trial he gave evidence that he had drunk ten pints of beer but that he knew what he had done and that he had acted in self-defence. The judge did not direct the jury as to intoxication, and D was convicted of the s 18 offence. He appealed, arguing that there was a duty on the judge to direct the jury on intoxication. However, the Court of Appeal dismissed the appeal: there was no obligation on the judge to direct the jury.

9.3.4 'Dutch courage'

A special rule applies in the situation whereby D, having resolved to commit an offence requiring specific intent whilst sober, or at least when not intoxicated, then deliberately becomes intoxicated in order to provide himself with 'Dutch courage' before carrying out the offence. The situation remains theoretical, but it was discussed in *Attorney-General of Northern Ireland v Gallagher* [1963] AC 349.

CASE EXAMPLE

Gallagher [1963] AC 349

D, having decided to kill his wife, bought a knife and a bottle of whisky. He drank much of the whisky, then killed her with the knife. His defence was that he was either insane or too drunk to be able to form the intent at the time of the stabbing. He was convicted, but the NI Court of Appeal quashed his conviction, holding that the judge's directions to the jury required them to consider insanity at the time D started drinking, not when he killed his wife. The Lords agreed that this would have been a misdirection but found that the judge had directed the jury to consider D's state of mind at the time of the killing. The jury having found that D had *mens rea* at that time, there was no need to consider the question of intoxication. Lord Denning, however, ventured the opinion that even if D had been found to be lacking *mens rea* at the time of the killing, he would still have no defence even for murder.

Lord Denning said:

JUDGMENT

'If a man, whilst sane and sober, forms an intention to kill and makes preparation for it knowing it is a wrong thing to do, and then gets himself drunk so as to give himself Dutch courage to do the killing, and whilst drunk carries out his intention, he cannot rely on this self-induced drunkenness as a defence to murder, not even as reducing it to manslaughter. He cannot say he got himself into such a stupid state that he was incapable of an intent to kill ... The wickedness of his mind before he got drunk is enough to condemn him, coupled with the act which he intended to do and did do.'

9.3.5 Intoxication and insanity

Where intoxication produces a 'disease of the mind' as defined in the *M'Naghten* Rules, then those latter rules apply. In *Davis* (1881) 14 Cox CC 563, where D claimed that a history of alcohol abuse had caused delirium tremens and based his defence on insanity, Stephen J directed the jury that:

JUDGMENT

'Drunkenness is one thing and disease to which drunkenness leads are different things; and if a man by drunkenness brings on state of disease which causes such a degree of madness, even for a time, which would have relieved him from responsibility if it had been caused in any other way, then he would not be criminally responsible.'

However, a state of intoxication which does not lead to a 'disease of the mind' remains subject to the rules on intoxication, no matter how extreme the temporary effects of the intoxicants on D may have been. This point of law was decided in a recent Canadian case, *Bouchard-Lebrun* [2011] 3 SCR 575. Here, the Supreme Court of Canada had to decide whether a temporary state of 'toxic psychosis' induced by taking a type of ecstasy tablet could support a plea of insanity. D had been convicted of two counts of aggravated assault (the equivalent of inflicting GBH contrary to s 20 OAPA in English law) after his defence of voluntary intoxication had failed, the offences with which he was charged being of 'general' (basic) intent. He appealed, arguing that he should have been allowed the insanity defence instead. The Supreme Court unanimously rejected his appeal. Lebel J, giving judgment for the whole Court, said that a 'malfunctioning of the mind that results exclusively from self-induced intoxication cannot be considered a disease of the mind in the legal sense, since it is not a product of the individual's inherent psychological makeup … toxic psychosis seems to be nothing more than a symptom, albeit an extreme one, of the accused person's state of self-induced intoxication'.

Two years later, the Court of Appeal in England reached the same conclusion. In *Coley, McGhee and Harris* [2013] EWCA Crim 223, the first defendant (Coley) had been convicted of attempted murder after stabbing a neighbour several times with a knife during a 'brief psychotic episode' triggered by long-term cannabis use. The trial judge ruled that his only defence was intoxication, not insanity. On appeal, the Court of Appeal had to decide whether the evidence supported the defence of insanity. Hughes LJ held not. He stated:

JUDGMENT

'The law has to cope with the synthesising of the law of insanity with the law of voluntary intoxication. The first calls for a special verdict of acquittal and very particular means of disposal. The latter is generally no defence at all, but may be relevant to whether D formed a specific intention … The precise line between the law of voluntary intoxication and the law of insanity may be difficult to identify in some borderline cases. In order to engage the law of insanity, it is not enough that there is an effect on the mind, or, in the language of the *M'Naghten* rules, a "defect of reason". There must also be what the law classifies as a "disease of the mind". Direct acute effects on the mind of intoxicants, voluntarily taken, are not so classified. That is the distinction drawn by Stephen J in *Davis* and maintained ever since. Drugs or alcohol are an external factor. When voluntarily taken their acute effects are not treated by the law as a "disease of the mind" for the purposes of the *M'Naghten* rules. Such a case is governed by the law of voluntary intoxication.'

CASE EXAMPLE

Coley [2013] EWCA Crim 223

D was a heavy cannabis user. One evening, after having smoked cannabis all day before going to bed, he got up, dressed himself in dark clothing and a balaclava, left his home and entered the home of his next-door neighbour, V. There, he stood in the doorway of the bedroom where V and her partner, W, were asleep. V awoke and screamed; W got up and confronted D on the upstairs hallway. There, D stabbed W seven times with a nine-inch 'Rambo-style' knife that he had brought with him from his own personal collection. W was very badly injured and nearly died. At D's trial for attempted murder, he did not deny responsibility for W's injuries, but claimed to have 'blacked out' and to have no memory of the attack, and no idea why he did it. The psychiatric evidence was that D had committed the attack during a 'brief psychotic episode' triggered by cannabis. The trial judge ruled that D's case was one of voluntary intoxication, and refused to leave insanity to the jury. D was convicted and appealed, submitting that his was not a case of intoxication but rather had passed to a recognised condition of mental illness, namely a psychotic episode, albeit transient, and therefore the judge should have left insanity to the jury. The Court of Appeal disagreed and upheld his conviction.

9.3.6 Intoxication and automatism

An act done in a state of (non-insane) automatism will negative criminal liability except where the automotive state is self-induced. This is most obviously the case where the automotive state is due to intoxication, in which case the normal rules of intoxication apply. *Lipman* (1970) is the clearest example of this.

CASE EXAMPLE

Lipman [1970] 1 QB 152

D and his girlfriend had both taken LSD. During the subsequent 'trip', D believed that he had descended to the centre of the earth and the girl was a snake. He proceeded to kill the girl by stuffing eight inches of bed sheet down her throat. Although clearly lacking intent to kill the girl, and so not guilty of the specific intent crime of murder, D was convicted of the basic intent offence of manslaughter.

The latest example of this is *Coley, McGhee and Harris* [2013] EWCA Crim 223, discussed at section 9.2.4. Although the second defendant (McGhee) pleaded automatism, the trial judge rejected this and ruled that D's only defence was intoxication, on the basis that D's condition was self-induced by a combination of alcohol and prescription medication. In the event, D's intoxication defence also failed as the evidence showed that he had formed the intent despite being intoxicated.

In Canada, meanwhile, a new policy has emerged. Until recently, the law concerning intoxication in England and Canada was essentially identical. In *Bernard* [1988] 2 SCR 833, the Supreme Court confirmed that intoxication was no defence in cases of 'general' intent (equivalent to 'basic' intent in English law). However, in *Daviault* (1995) 118 DLR (4d) 469, the Supreme Court created a new rule, recognising a defence when a person charged with a general intent offence was so intoxicated that it produced a state of automatism. D bears the burden of proving, on the balance of probabilities, that his intoxication had reached this extreme level. However, the Canadian Parliament subsequently enacted legislation to restrict the scope of the *Daviault* rule to offences that do not involve 'an element an assault or any other interference or threat of interference by a person with the bodily integrity of another person'. Hence, if D is charged with a general intent offence such as sexual assault, intoxication will be no defence. But if D is charged with a general intent offence not involving assault, such as criminal damage, it will be open to him to try to prove, on the balance of probabilities, that he was so drunk as to have become an automaton.

9.3.7 Intoxicated mistakes

An intoxicated defendant is sometimes actually pleading mistake. As was seen in Chapter 8, when a (sober) defendant pleads the defence of mistake, he is entitled to be judged on the facts as he genuinely perceived them to be. However, when D is intoxicated, this changes and D is subjected to the normal *Majewski* rules. He will be assumed to be aware of any circumstances and consequences of which he would have been aware had he been sober. A good example is *Fotheringham* (1989). The Court of Appeal held that self-induced intoxication was no defence, whether the issue was intention, consent or mistake as to the identity of the victim.

CASE EXAMPLE

Fotheringham (1989) 88 Cr App R 206

D had been out with his wife one evening and had been drinking heavily. When they returned home, D climbed into the marital bed where the babysitter, V, was asleep. Under the mistaken impression that V was his wife, he had sex with her without her consent. At the time, the fact that D was married meant he could not be convicted of rape if he genuinely believed D was his wife. However, the judge directed the jury to disregard intoxication. He was convicted and the Court of Appeal upheld the conviction.

Statutory exceptions

Fotheringham represents the common law position. There is one significant statutory exception, found in s 5(2) of the Criminal Damage Act 1971. This provides that a person charged with criminal damage shall have a lawful excuse in two situations: belief in consent and belief in the need to damage property in order to protect other property. Section 5(3) provides that 'it is immaterial whether a belief is justified or not, provided it is honestly held'. In *Jaggard v Dickinson* (1980), Donaldson LJ in the High Court refused to allow the *Majewski* rule to override the express words of Parliament by introducing a qualification that 'the honesty of the belief is not attributable only to self-induced intoxication'.

CASE EXAMPLE

Jaggard v Dickinson [1980] 3 All ER 716

D's friend, H, had invited her to treat his house at no 67 as if it were her own. One night, when drunk, D ordered a taxi and asked to be taken to H's house. Instead, she was dropped off outside no 35, which looked identical. She assumed it was H's house and entered the garden. She was ordered to leave by the occupier, V. Rather than leaving, D broke in by breaking the window in the back door, damaging a net curtain in the process. Charged with criminal damage, D relied upon the statutory defence. She contended that, at the time she broke into no 35, she had a genuine belief she was breaking into no 67 and that her relationship with D was such that she had his consent to break into his house. Hence, s 5(2) afforded her a defence to the charge. The magistrates ruled that she was unable to rely upon the defence because of her self-induced intoxication, and she was convicted. On appeal, the High Court accepted that, although criminal damage is a basic intent offence, s 5(2) and (3) meant that D's intoxication had to be considered, resulting in her acquittal. Donaldson LJ said that her intoxication 'helped to explain what would otherwise have been inexplicable, and hence lent colour to her evidence about the state of her belief'.

9.3.8 Criticism and reform proposals

There are many criticisms that have been made about the intoxication defence. The following is a non-exhaustive list of some of them:

- There is no clear test for drawing a distinction between crimes of specific intent and those of basic intent (compare *Caldwell* (1981) with *Heard* (2007)).
- Some specific intent crimes have a basic intent fall-back (e.g. murder to manslaughter; s 18 OAPA 1861 to s 20 OAPA 1861), but many do not (e.g. theft, burglary).
- Attempts are specific intent (*Coley* (2013); *Press and Thompson* (2013)), but rape is basic intent (*Woods* (1982); *Fotheringham* (1989)). Thus, D could plead intoxication as a defence to attempted rape, but not rape itself, creating a legal paradox.

- There is uncertainty regarding the situation where D pleads intoxication to a basic intent offence. *Majewski* (1976) suggests D is automatically liable (because intoxication is itself a reckless course of conduct) but *Richardson and Irwin* (1999) suggests that there may be a defence if D would not have formed *mens rea* even when sober.
- Imposing liability on D based on his/her recklessness in getting intoxicated prior to committing the *actus reus* of a basic intent offence (arson, battery, etc.) involves a breach of the rule that the *actus reus* and *mens rea* of an offence must coincide at the same point in time.
- Recklessness in criminal law normally involves foresight of a particular risk (*Cunningham* (1957); *Savage* (1991); *R v G and another* (2003), etc.) but the *Majewski* form of recklessness does not.
- The *Richardson and Irwin* test avoids that problem but does require the jury to decide what D *would have* foreseen at the time of committing the *actus reus*, had he or she not been intoxicated. Other than by guessing, how does the jury decide that issue?
- The *Majewski* rules are simply unnecessary – they are not used in many other common law jurisdictions, including parts of Australia (the states of South Australia and Victoria (see in particular *O'Connor* [1980] HCA 17)) or New Zealand (see *Kamipeli* [1975] 2 NZLR 610; *R v Kirby* [2013] NZCA 451). In those jurisdictions, intoxication (whether voluntary or involuntary) can be used to deny proof of any *mens rea* state (including recklessness).
- It should, however, be noted that many common law jurisdictions have (essentially) the same rules as in England and Wales, including the Australian states of New South Wales, Queensland, Tasmania and Western Australia (see e.g. *Snow* [1962] Tas SR 271) and Canada (see e.g. *Bernard* [1988] 2 SCR 833; *Bouchard-Lebrun* [2011] 3 SCR 575).

In January 2009, the LC published a report entitled *Intoxication and Criminal Liability* (Law Com No 314) including a draft bill. In the report, the LC makes a number of recommendations for reform of the intoxication defence. The key recommendations can be summarised as follows.

General points

- References to 'specific intent' and 'basic intent' should be abolished.
- The distinction between voluntary and involuntary intoxication should be retained.
- Where D relies on the intoxication defence (whether voluntary or involuntary), there should be a presumption that D was *not* intoxicated. Hence, D would have to produce evidence that he or she was intoxicated. This essentially confirms the present law, as set out in *Groark* (1999).
- However, if D is taken to have been intoxicated, there should then be a second presumption that D was voluntarily intoxicated. Therefore, if D contends that he or she was involuntarily intoxicated, D would have to prove this (albeit on the balance of probabilities). This is a completely new set of legal principles.

Voluntary intoxication

- There should be a 'general rule' that would apply when D is charged with an offence the *mens rea* of which is 'not an integral fault element' – for example, if the *mens rea* 'merely requires proof of recklessness' – and D was voluntarily intoxicated at the time of allegedly committing it.
- The 'general rule' is that D should be treated as having been aware of anything which D would then have been aware of but for the intoxication. This is an attempt to place on a statutory basis the principle set out in *Richardson and Irwin* (1999).

- Certain *mens rea* states – which the LC refers to as 'integral fault elements' – should be excluded from the 'general rule'. These are intention, knowledge, belief (where that is equivalent to knowledge), fraud and dishonesty.
- Thus, the 'general rule' would not apply to murder, wounding or causing GBH with intent (s 18 OAPA), theft, robbery and burglary (all of which require intent). In such cases, 'the prosecution should have to prove that D acted with that relevant state of mind'. This essentially confirms the present law, as set out in cases like *Beard* (1920) and *Lipman* (1970).
- D should not be able to rely on a genuine mistake of fact arising from voluntary intoxication in support of a defence, unless D would have held the same belief had he not been intoxicated. This is consistent with the Court of Appeal's stance on intoxicated mistakes in the context of self-defence in *O'Grady* (1987), *O'Connor* (1991) and *Hatton* (2005), discussed in Chapter 8. But it would entail overruling the High Court's decision in *Jaggard v Dickinson*, above, involving intoxicated mistakes about whether the owner of property would consent to it being damaged.

Involuntary intoxication

- There should be 'a non-exhaustive list of situations which would count as involuntary intoxication'. The LC gives four examples, so that D would be involuntarily intoxicated if they could prove (on the balance of probabilities) that they took an intoxicant:
  1. without consent (such as the spiking of soft drinks with alcohol);
  2. under duress;
  3. which they 'reasonably believed was not an intoxicant';
  4. for a 'proper medical purpose'.
- Where D was involuntarily intoxicated, then D's intoxication should be taken into account in deciding whether D acted with the requisite *mens rea*. This essentially confirms the present law, as set out in *Kingston* (1995).
- D should also be able to rely on a genuine mistake of fact arising from involuntary intoxication in support of a defence.
- The distinction drawn between 'dangerous' and 'soporific' drugs should be abolished – thus, if D became intoxicated having taken 'soporific' drugs such as Valium (unless 'for a proper medical purpose'), then this would be classed as voluntary intoxication. This would entail overruling the Court of Appeal decision in *Hardie* (1985).

KEY FACTS

Key facts on intoxication

	Specific intent crimes	Basic intent crimes
Voluntary intoxication	If defendant has *mens rea*, he is guilty (*Sheehan* (1975)). If defendant has no *mens rea*, he is not guilty (*Beard* (1920)).	The defendant is probably guilty of the offence. Becoming intoxicated may be deemed to be a reckless course of conduct (*Majewski* (1977)). D will be deemed to have appreciated any risk he would have appreciated had he been sober (*Richardson and Irwin* (1999)).

Involuntary intoxication	If defendant has *mens rea*, he is guilty (*Kingston* (1995)). If defendant has no *mens rea*, he is not guilty (*Hardie* (1985)).	If defendant has *mens rea*, he is guilty (*Kingston* (1995)). The defendant has not been reckless in becoming intoxicated, so if he has no *mens rea*, he is not guilty (*Hardie* (1985)).
Drunken mistake	If the mistake negates *mens rea*, the defendant is not guilty (*Lipman* (1970)). If the mistake is about the need to defend oneself, it is not a defence. The defendant will be guilty (*O'Grady* (1987); *Hatton* (2005)).	This is a reckless course of conduct, so the defendant is guilty (*Fotheringham* (1989)). Unless the mistake concerns belief in owner's consent to criminal damage (*Jaggard v Dickinson* (1980)).

SUMMARY

The law on insanity is laid down in the *M'Naghten* Rules (1843). D must prove that he had a 'defect of reason', from a 'disease of the mind', so that he did not know the 'nature and quality' of his act or that it was 'wrong'. A 'disease of the mind' is a legal term and refers to any internal condition which is prone to recur. It includes conditions such as diabetes, epilepsy and sleepwalking (*Bratty*, *Sullivan*, *Hennessy*, *Burgess*). 'Wrong' means legally wrong (*Windle*). If the defence succeeds D receives the 'special verdict' which is a form of qualified acquittal – D may be hospitalised or made subject to other orders.

The defence of automatism is available if D lacks control or is unconscious (*Bratty*). The cause of the automatism must be external to D (*Quick*). The prosecution must disprove the defence once D has raised evidence of it (*Hill v Baxter*). If the defence succeeds, D receives an acquittal. If automatism is self-induced through drink or drugs, then the intoxication defence applies instead (*Lipman*, *McGhee*). If automatism is self-induced by other means, then D may be held liable, for offences not requiring proof of intent, based on his prior fault (*C*, *Clarke*).

There are two types of intoxication: voluntary and involuntary. With voluntary intoxication, D may have a defence to 'specific intent' crimes only, such as murder, theft and robbery, provided D lacks the necessary *mens rea* (*Lipman*), but D will not have a defence to crimes of 'basic intent', such as assault, ABH, GBH, rape and manslaughter (*Majewski*). Involuntary intoxication is potentially a defence to all crimes, but again only if D lacks *mens rea* (*Kingston*). A drunken intent is still an intent (*Sheehan*).

The insanity defence may be criticised on several grounds: its age (the *M'Naghten* Rules are over 160 years old); it is based on legal tests ('defect of reason' and 'disease of the mind') rather than psychiatric ones; the application of the internal/external factor test means that diabetics (sometimes), epileptics and sleepwalkers may be classed as 'insane'; the narrowness of the *Windle* interpretation of 'wrong'; the refusal to sanction an irresistible impulse defence; the retention of the stigmatising label 'insanity' as opposed to a more modern alternative such as 'mental disorder' or 'recognised medical condition'. This has prompted the LC to propose 'radical' reforms.

The intoxication defence may also be criticised on several grounds: for allowing policy considerations to take priority over legal logic; the categorisation of offences as 'specific' and 'basic', and the lack of a single clear explanation of the distinction between the two categories, creates confusion; and uncertainty as to when intoxication is regarded as voluntary or involuntary. This has prompted the LC to propose sweeping reforms.

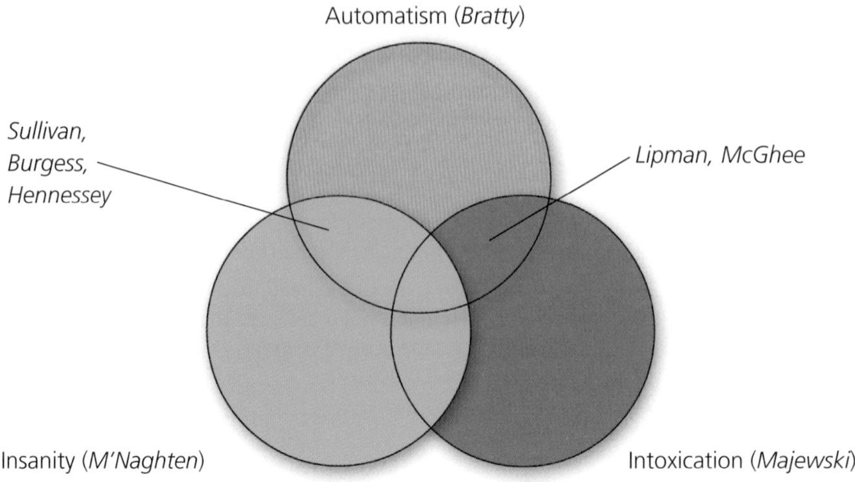

Figure 9.2 Venn diagram on mental capacity defences.

SAMPLE ESSAY QUESTION

The defence of voluntary intoxication represents an uneasy compromise between legal principle and public policy. But experience in Australia and New Zealand shows that these public policy considerations are overstated. The *Majewski* rules should be scrapped. Discuss.

Briefly explain the law relating to voluntary intoxication (the *Majewski* rules)

- Voluntary intoxication is never a defence to 'basic' intent offences
- It may be a defence to 'specific' intent offences
- D will still be liable if *mens rea* was formed – drunken intent is nevertheless intent (*Sheehan* (1975))
- D will also be liable if he drank for 'Dutch courage' (*Gallagher* (1963))

State problems with the *Majewski* rules:

- Distinction between 'basic' and 'specific' intent offences unclear – various tests have been proposed – none is definitive (*Caldwell* (1981); *Heard* (2007))
- The effect of pleading intoxication to a basic intent offence is unclear. *Majewski* suggests D is guilty as intoxication = recklessness. *Richardson & Irwin* (1999) asks whether D would have formed *mens rea* if sober
- Some 'specific' intent offences have a 'basic' intent fallback, some do not
- *Majewski* treats evidence of voluntary intoxication as irrelevant – this appears to breach s 8 of the Criminal Justice Act 1967
- Recklessness argument used in Majewski breaches the rule that *actus reus* and *mens rea* should coincide in time

Explain legal principles and policy:

- Legal principle suggests that if D fails to form *mens rea* then D is not guilty of both 'specific' and 'basic' intent offences
- Policy demands that those who commit offences whilst voluntarily intoxicated should be held responsible – hence the *Majewski* rules
- Courts in Australia and New Zealand do not separate crimes into 'specific' and 'basic' intent offences, apparently without proliferation of acquittals
- But similar approach to *Majewski* used in Canada

Consider reform proposals:

- LC report *Intoxication and Criminal Liability*, Law Com No 314 (2009) proposed scrapping distinction between 'specific' and 'basic' intent offences
- D would have a defence if an offence required an 'integral fault element' such as intention, belief, dishonesty, but otherwise not
- This would essentially incorporate the *Richardson & Irwin* rule into statute

Conclude

SAMPLE ESSAY QUESTION

The meaning and scope of the insanity defence is in urgent need of legislative overhaul. Discuss.

Give a brief outline of the present law:

- *M'Naghten* Rules (1843)
- Presumption of sanity
- 'Defect of reason'
- 'Disease of the mind'
- D must not know 'nature and quality' of act or, if so, D must not know that it is 'wrong'

State problems with the law, e.g.

- Presumption of sanity imposes reversed burden of proof on D
- The *M'Naghten* Rules are over 150 years old
- They are based on legal definitions rather than medical/psychiatric definitions
- 'Disease of the mind' too widely defined and produces illogical results. The external/internal factor test means that diabetics (sometimes), epileptics and sleepwalkers may be found insane (*Bratty* (1963); *Sullivan* (1984); *Hennessy* (1989); *Burgess* (1991))
- 'Wrong' defined narrowly as legally wrong only (*Windle* (1952))
- The terminology is old-fashioned and offensive (e.g. the Trial of Lunatics Act 1883 is still in force)
- Successful defence leads to label of 'insanity' and potentially indefinite hospitalisation (mandatory in murder cases)
- There is no irresistible impulse defence

Outline reforms that have taken place, e.g.

- Introduction of diminished responsibility defence (in murder cases) in s 2 of the Homicide Act 1957 (as amended)
- Trial judges were given a wider range of disposal options under the Criminal Procedure (Insanity and Unfitness to Plead) Act 1991, including hospital and supervision orders and absolute discharge – this should make the defence more attractive but the label of 'insanity' still remains

Discuss further reform options, e.g.

- Replacement of label 'insanity' with 'mental disorder'
- Burden of proof shifted to the prosecution
- Abolition of the legal tests of 'defect of reason' and 'disease of the mind', replaced with modern psychiatric definitions
- Possible redefinition of 'wrong' to include morally wrong, as in Australia and Canada

Conclude

Further reading

Articles

Child, J, 'Drink, drugs and law reform: a review of Law Commission Report No. 314' [2009] Crim LR 488.

Gough, S, 'Surviving without Majewski?' [2002] Crim LR 719.

Jones, T H, 'Insanity, automatism and the burden of proof on the accused' (1995) 111 LQR 475.

Loughnan, A, 'Manifest madness: towards a new understanding of the insanity defence' (2007) 70 MLR 379.

Mackay, R D, 'Epilepsy and the defence of insanity: time for change?' [2007] Crim LR 782.

Mackay, R D, 'Righting the wrong? Some observations on the second limb of the M'Naghten Rules' [2009] Crim LR 80.

Mackay, R D, Mitchell, B and Howe, L, 'Yet more facts about the insanity defence' [2006] Crim LR 399.

Williams, R, 'Voluntary intoxication: a lost cause?' (2013) 129 LQR 264.

Wilson, W, Ebrahim, I, Fenwick, P and Marks, R, 'Violence, sleepwalking and the criminal law: (2) the legal aspects' [2005] Crim LR 614.

Internet links

Diabetes UK: www.diabetes.org.uk.

Epilepsy Action: www.epilepsy.org.uk.

Law Commission Report, *Intoxication and Criminal Liability*, Law Com No 314, available at www.lawcom.gov.uk.

Law Commission Discussion Paper, *Criminal Liability: Insanity and Automatism*, available at www.lawcom.gov.uk.

Part II

Specific offences

10

Homicide

AIMS AND OBJECTIVES

After reading this chapter you should be able to:

- Understand the law of murder
- Understand the law of diminished responsibility
- Understand the law of loss of self-control
- Understand the law of involuntary manslaughter (constructive, gross negligence and reckless manslaughter)
- Understand the law on other homicide offences
- Analyse critically the law on homicide, including reform proposals
- Apply the law to factual situations to determine whether there is liability for murder or manslaughter

10.1 *Actus reus* of homicide

murder
The unlawful killing of a human being with malice aforethought

Murder is not defined in any legislation. According to the common law definition, it is the unlawful killing of another human being, within any county of the realm, under the King or Queen's Peace, with malice aforethought. The *actus reus* elements of **murder** are as follows:

- causing death of a human being;
- under the King or Queen's Peace;
- within any county of the realm.

The *actus reus* is fundamentally the same for manslaughter. Causation was dealt with in Chapter 2.

10.1.1 Human being: birth

A foetus that is killed in the womb cannot be a victim of homicide, although there are other (statutory) offences (see below). When does a foetus become a person in being? It appears that the child must be wholly expelled from the mother (*Poulton* (1832) 5 C & P 329) and have a separate existence from her (*Enoch* (1833) 5 C & P 539).

That requirement creates its own problems: for example, it is now accepted that a foetus in the womb has an independent circulation within two months of conception. Where a foetus has been born alive but dies afterwards from injuries inflicted whilst in the womb, this may be manslaughter but not murder (*Attorney-General's Reference (No 3 of 1994)* [1997] 3 WLR 421, considered in Chapter 3).

10.1.2 Human being: death

A person who is already dead cannot be the victim of homicide. But the legal definition of death has proved elusive. There is conventional death, when the heartbeat and breathing stop. But there is also brain death, when through artificial means the heart continues to beat and air circulates in the lungs. Brain death is recognised by the British Medical Association and is the point when life-support machinery will be switched off. In *Malcharek, Steel* [1981] 2 All ER 422 (the facts of which were discussed in Chapter 2), the Court of Appeal adverted to this test, although they did not have to decide the point. It is likely that if the question arose squarely, then the courts would adopt the brain death test (or strictly tests, as there are six of them). Thus, if D stabs V who has been certified brain dead but whose functions are being maintained on a ventilating machine, it is unlikely that the Court of Appeal would uphold a murder conviction.

In *Inglis* [2010] EWCA Crim 2637; [2011] 1 WLR 1110, which is discussed in detail in section 10.2.4, the Court of Appeal rejected an argument that the law of murder did not apply to the 'mercy' killing of a severely disabled man. Lord Judge CJ stated:

JUDGMENT

'The law does not recognise the concept implicit in the defence statement that [V] was "already dead in all but a small physical degree". The fact is that he was alive, a person in being. However brief the time left for him, that life could not lawfully be extinguished. Similarly, however disabled [V] might have been, a disabled life, even a life lived at the extremes of disability, is not one jot less precious than the life of an able-bodied person.'

10.1.3 Under the King or Queen's Peace

This serves to exclude from the scope of homicide enemy soldiers killed in the course of war. Outside the battlefield, soldiers and other military personnel are subject to the same rules of criminal law as everyone else, and soldiers do occasionally face prosecution for murder. For example, see *Smith* (*Thomas*) [1959] 2 QB 35 (discussed in Chapter 2) and *Clegg* [1995] 1 AC 482 (discussed in Chapter 8). More recently, in *Blackman* [2014] EWCA Crim 1029, a British soldier was convicted of murder after shooting dead a seriously injured and unarmed member of the Taliban insurgency in Afghanistan in September 2011.

10.1.4 Within any county of the realm

The limitations in this phrase have now all but disappeared. Murder (and manslaughter) committed by a British citizen outside the UK may be tried in England (ss 9 and 10, Offences Against the Person Act (OAPA) 1861; s 3, British Nationality Act 1948).

Section 4 of the Suppression of Terrorism Act 1978 allows for the prosecution, in the UK, of a number of criminal offences, including murder, committed in any of the 'convention countries' listed in the Act, either by a British or foreign national. In short, this statute allows for British courts to hear cases involving the prosecution of foreign nationals for committing crimes in foreign countries. The statute is rarely needed: for example, if a French national kills another French national in France then any resulting criminal trial would almost certainly take place in France and there would be no need for the

British courts to get involved. However, s 4 was recently invoked in *Venclovas* [2013] EWCA Crim 2182, in order to obtain the conviction of D, a Lithuanian national, for the murder of V, his Lithuanian ex-wife. V had last been seen alive in England and her body was discovered several weeks later in a remote Polish wood. The Crown alleged that D kidnapped and murdered V but could not prove exactly where the killing took place; it may have been in England, or Poland, or in any one of a number of other European countries in between, but the trial judge told the jury that it was 'immaterial' whether or not the victim was killed in England. The jury convicted and the Court of Appeal, applying s 4 of the 1978 Act, upheld the conviction.

Murder committed on a British aircraft may be tried in the UK (s 92, Civil Aviation Act 1982). Murder committed on a foreign aircraft coming to the UK may also be tried in England (s 1, Civil Aviation (Amendment) Act 1996).

10.1.5 The year and a day rule

Until 1996 there was a further element: that V had to die within a year and a day. This rule was originally justified because of the difficulty in establishing causation where there was a long interval between the original wound, injury etc., and V's death. The net result was that if D stabbed, shot, strangled or otherwise fatally injured V, but V was kept alive for at least 367 days on a life-support machine before death, D could not be guilty of homicide (see *Dyson* [1908] 2 KB 454). However, over time, medical science developed to such an extent that the original justification was no longer valid and it was abolished by Parliament in 1996. The main impetus for change was public perception of 'murderers' escaping conviction for murder because the victim had been kept alive for more than 366 days. In the case of gross negligence manslaughter, there was not even an alternative offence for which D might be held liable if V survived the 367 days.

SECTION

'Law Reform (Year and a Day Rule) Act 1996

1 The rule known as the "year and a day rule" (that is, the rule that, for the purposes of offences involving death and of suicide, an act or omission is conclusively presumed not to have caused a person's death if more than a year and a day have elapsed before he died) is abolished for all purposes.

2 (1) Proceedings to which this section applies may only be instituted by or with the consent of the Attorney-General.

(2) This section applies to proceedings against a person for a fatal offence if (a) the injury alleged to cause death was sustained more than three years before the death occurred, or (b) the person has previously been convicted of an offence committed in circumstances alleged to be connected with the death.

(3) In subsection (2) "fatal offence" means (a) murder, manslaughter, infanticide or any other offence of which one of the elements is causing a person's death, or (b) the offence of aiding, abetting, counselling or procuring a person's death.'

The consent of the Attorney-General is required in two circumstances. First, where several years had passed since the original incident, it was thought to be undesirable to have the history of the case trawled over again in a homicide trial. It would mean some defendants having to live for years with the threat of a murder charge hanging over them. Second, where D has already been convicted of a non-fatal offence, or attempt, on the same set of facts. This encourages the prosecution to bring assault or wounding charges earlier, while V is still alive, rather than wait for years to see whether V dies or not.

10.2 Murder

malice aforethought
The mental or fault element in murder

The *actus reus* elements of murder have been dealt with above. The only remaining element is that of *mens rea*, 'with **malice aforethought**'. This is a legal term – potentially very misleading – which requires neither ill will nor premeditation. A person who kills out of compassion to alleviate suffering (a so-called 'mercy killing') acts with malice aforethought – see *Inglis* (2010), discussed in detail below. Proof of malice aforethought means that a jury are satisfied that, at the time of killing V, D either (*Moloney* [1985] AC 905):

- intended to kill (express malice); or
- intended to cause grievous bodily harm (implied malice).

Thus, it is possible for D to be convicted of murder when he intends some serious injury but does not contemplate that V's life be endangered. This has generated some controversy and calls for reform (see below).

10.2.1 Intention

All of the leading cases on the meaning and scope of intention have involved murder. You should refer back to the discussion of these cases – especially *Woollin* [1998] 3 WLR 382 – in Chapter 2, for a reminder of the principles.

10.2.2 Grievous bodily harm

The meaning of the phrase 'grievous bodily harm' is the same as when the phrase is used in the context of ss 18 and 20 OAPA 1861 (see Chapter 11). In *DPP v Smith* [1961] AC 290, a murder case, Viscount Kilmuir, with whom the rest of the Lords agreed, held that there was no reason to give the words any special meaning. Thus, he said, bodily harm 'needs no explanation' while 'grievous' means no more and no less than 'really serious'. Subsequently, in the context of s 20 OAPA 1861, the Court of Appeal held that the omission of the word 'really' when a judge was directing a jury were not significant (*Saunders* [1985] Crim LR 230). This was confirmed in the context of murder in *Janjua and Choudury* [1998] EWCA Crim 1419; [1998] Crim LR 675. The Court of Appeal dismissed the defendants' argument on appeal that the word 'really' had to be used in every single murder case.

10.2.3 Procedure in murder trials

In *Coutts* [2006] UKHL 39; [2006] 1 WLR 2154, the House of Lords allowed an appeal against a murder conviction on the basis that the jury were not allowed to consider manslaughter as an alternative verdict. D had pleaded not guilty, his defence being that V's death was a tragic accident, but the jury rejected that version of events and therefore convicted him of murder. Lord Rodger explained as follows:

JUDGMENT

'The jury were told that they had to choose between convicting the appellant of murder and acquitting him on the ground that the victim had died as a result of an accident. On that basis they chose to convict of murder. But the jury should also have been told that, depending on their view of the facts, they could convict him of manslaughter ... The reality is that, in the course of their deliberations, a jury might well look at the overall picture, even if they eventually had to separate out the issues of murder, manslaughter and accident. So, introducing the possibility of convicting for manslaughter could have changed the way the jury went about considering their verdict.'

Reform

The Draft Criminal Code (1989), cl 54(1), defines murder as follows: 'A person is guilty of murder if he causes the death of another (a) intending to cause death; or (b) intending to cause serious personal harm and being aware that he may cause death.' This would narrow the *mens rea* of murder from its present common law definition. See also the discussion in section 10.9.

ACTIVITY

Self-test questions

1. Should the definition of murder be amended so as to impose a requirement that, if D did not intend to cause death but did intend to cause serious injury, he also had an awareness that death may be caused?
2. Consider the following scenario. D is a 'loan shark'. One of his clients, V, is in considerable debt to D but cannot afford to repay it. D decides to physically punish V in such a way that D's other clients will be left in no doubt as to the consequences if they fail to repay their debts. D specifically wants V to survive the punishment, to provide a long-term reminder of the implications of failing to repay D's loans. One night D ambushes V and shoots him in the leg with a handgun. The idea is to leave V with a permanent limp. However, the bullet hits an artery and, within minutes, V bleeds to death. Is D guilty of murder:
   (a) Under the present common law definition?
   (b) Under the Draft Criminal Code?

10.2.4 Mercy killings and euthanasia

The courts have recently been confronted with difficult questions regarding the scope of murder, specifically whether 'mercy killing' and/or euthanasia should be treated differently from other deliberate killings. Mercy killing can be defined as the situation where D kills V in order to alleviate V's suffering. Euthanasia is the situation where V consents to his or her own death, typically because V is suffering from an incurable condition.

The law of 'mercy killing' was examined in *Inglis* [2010] EWCA Crim 2637; [2011] 1 WLR 1110. The Court of Appeal ruled that, as far as the criminal law was concerned, there was no special defence available for those who kill out of compassion: 'mercy killing' is murder.

CASE EXAMPLE

Inglis [2010] EWCA Crim 2637; [2011] 1 WLR 1110

D was charged with the murder of her own son, V, 22, by injecting him with a fatal overdose of heroin. At the time, V was in a 'desperate state of disability'. Some 18 months earlier, V had suffered serious head injuries after falling from an ambulance and had been in a deep coma on a life-support machine ever since. Two operations had been carried out after the accident, which involved removing part of the front of his skull to relieve pressure on the brain, which left V with a 'severe disfigurement'. D found all of this extremely depressing and distressing. She regarded the operations as 'evil' and wished that V had been allowed to die a natural death; she was convinced that he was in pain and that it was her duty as his mother to release him from his suffering. She became further obsessed with the notion that she had to kill V, quickly and peacefully, to prevent what she regarded as a 'prolonged and lingering' death. At D's murder trial, she relied on provocation but was convicted after the trial judge ruled that there was no evidence of a loss of self-control to support that defence. She appealed, arguing that her case was not murder but a 'mercy killing'; alternatively, V was so severely disabled as to no longer be a 'human being'. The Court of Appeal rejected those arguments and upheld her murder conviction, holding that mercy killing was murder, and that V was still a 'human being'.

Lord Judge CJ stated (emphasis added):

JUDGMENT

'The law of murder does *not* distinguish between murder committed for malevolent reasons and murder motivated by familial love. Subject to well established partial defences, *mercy killing is murder*. Whether or not he might have died within a few months anyway, [V's] life was protected by the law, and no one, not even his mother, could lawfully step in and bring it to a premature conclusion.'

The Court of Appeal added that, if 'mercy killings' were to be treated differently from other deliberate killings, then that was a matter for Parliament to decide, not the courts. Subsequently, in *Nicklinson and others v Ministry of Justice* [2013] EWCA Civ 961; [2014] 2 All ER 32 (discussed in Chapter 8), the Court of Appeal reached a very similar decision with respect to euthanasia. In reaching that decision, the Court of Appeal followed both *Inglis* and *Bland* [1993] AC 789 (discussed in Chapter 2). In *Bland*, the House of Lords had accepted that, whilst the withdrawal of feeding from a patient in a 'persistent vegetative state' was lawful, the deliberate 'ending of life by active means' was murder. This was because 'the interest of the state in preserving life overrides the otherwise all-powerful interests of patient autonomy' (per Lord Mustill). In *Nicklinson and others*, Lord Dyson MR and Elias LJ (with whom Lord Judge CJ agreed) said:

JUDGMENT

'Euthanasia involves not merely assisting another to commit suicide, but actually bringing about the death of that other ... At common law *euthanasia is the offence of murder*.'

In a subsequent appeal to the Supreme Court, the arguments about whether or not the courts had the power to create a defence to murder in euthanasia cases were not pursued. Instead, the focus shifted to whether or not the offence of assisted suicide under s 2 of the Suicide Act 1961 infringed the human rights of people such as Tony Nicklinson who were prevented from taking their own lives because of a disability and who would therefore need third party assistance in order to commit suicide. The Supreme Court held not (*Nicklinson and others v Ministry of Justice* [2014] UKSC 38).

Therefore, until such time (if ever) that Parliament deems it appropriate to amend the law by enacting legislation, the law remains as follows:

- Mercy killing is murder: *Inglis* (2010).
- Euthanasia (the deliberate ending of life by active means) is murder: *Bland* (1993); *Nicklinson and others* (2013).

ACTIVITY

Self-test questions

- Should 'mercy killing' and/or euthanasia be treated differently from other killings, perhaps as an alternative offence or as a defence to murder?
- If a defence, should it be a full defence (leading to an acquittal) or a partial defence (leading to a conviction of manslaughter)?

10.3 Voluntary manslaughter

If D is charged with murder there are three 'special' and 'partial' defences which may be pleaded. They are called 'special' as they are only available to those charged with murder, and 'partial' because, if successful, D must be convicted of voluntary manslaughter instead. This allows the trial judge more discretion when it comes to sentencing; it also means that D avoids the label of 'murderer'. With these defences, D is not denying killing V, or denying malice aforethought, but is asking to be excused from full liability. There are three such defences:

- diminished responsibility;
- loss of control;
- suicide pact.

diminished responsibility
Special and partial defence to murder

10.3.1 Diminished responsibility

The defence of **diminished responsibility** (DR) evolved at common law in the courts of Scotland and was introduced into English law by s 2 of the Homicide Act 1957. That section was amended by s 52 of the Coroners and Justice Act 2009, and it now provides that:

SECTION

'2(1) A person ("D") who kills or is a party to the killing of another is not to be convicted of murder if D was suffering from an abnormality of mental functioning which –

(a) arose from a recognised medical condition,
(b) substantially impaired D's ability to do one or more of the things mentioned in subsection (1A), and
(c) provides an explanation for D's acts and omissions in doing or being a party to the killing.

(1A) Those things are –

(a) to understand the nature of D's conduct;
(b) to form a rational judgment;
(c) to exercise self-control.

(1B) For the purposes of subsection (1)(c), an abnormality of mental functioning provides an explanation for D's conduct if it causes, or is a significant contributory factor in causing, D to carry out that conduct.'

student mentor tip

'Understand the Homicide Act of 1957.'
Anthony, London South Bank University

The background to the reform of DR lies with the Law Commission (LC), who had been advocating modernisation of the definition for several years. For example, in its report, *Murder, Manslaughter and Infanticide*, published in November 2006, the LC observed that the 'definition of diminished responsibility is now badly out of date'. Key amendments made by the 2009 Act are as follows:

- 'Abnormality of mental functioning' replaces the original phrase 'abnormality of mind'.
- 'Recognised medical condition' replaces the original list of causes: 'condition of arrested or retarded development of mind', 'any inherent cause' or 'induced by disease or injury'.
- 'Substantially impaired' ability to 'understand the nature of D's conduct', 'form a rational judgment' or 'exercise self-control' replaces the original phrase 'substantially impaired mental responsibility'.

- The requirement that D's abnormality of mental functioning 'provides an explanation' for D's involvement in killing V is a new element of the offence.

Notwithstanding these amendments, much of the case law that built up around the original s 2 will continue to be relevant.

DR is a 'special' defence in that it is purely a defence to murder. This allows the trial judge more discretion in terms of sentencing than he would have were D to be convicted of murder, because of the mandatory life sentence. In *Campbell* [1997] Crim LR 495, the Court of Appeal rejected the argument that DR should be allowed as a defence to attempted murder. This decision must be correct, because the trial judge already has discretion when it comes to sentencing those convicted of attempted murder, and so the defence is simply unnecessary in attempted murder trials. Had it been accepted (and successfully pleaded), moreover, then it would have introduced a new crime into English law: attempted manslaughter.

In *Antoine* [2000] UKHL 20; [2001] 1 AC 340, the House of Lords held that evidence of DR is not relevant when a jury are deciding whether or not D is fit to stand trial on a charge of murder.

CASE EXAMPLE

Antoine [2000] UKHL 20; [2001] 1 AC 340

D had been charged with the 'brutal' murder of a 15-year-old boy, apparently as a human sacrifice to the devil. He was found unfit to plead under the Criminal Procedure (Insanity) Act 1964, on the basis of paranoid schizophrenia, and another jury were brought in to determine whether he had done 'the act … charged against him'. He sought to rely upon DR but the judge ruled that it was unavailable. The jury duly found that he had done the act charged, and the judge ordered indefinite hospitalisation. The Court of Appeal and House of Lords dismissed D's appeals.

Procedure

D bears the burden of proving DR (Homicide Act 1957, s 2(2)) on the balance of probabilities (*Dunbar* [1958] 1 QB 1). In *Foye* [2013] EWCA Crim 475, the Court of Appeal rejected an appeal in which D sought to argue that the reversed burden of proof in s 2(2) of the 1957 Act was incompatible with the presumption of innocence protected by article 6(2) of the European Convention of Human Rights. Hughes LJ said:

JUDGMENT

'The very clear justification for s 2(2) lies in the following factors.

(i) Diminished responsibility is an exceptional defence available in an appropriate case with a view to avoiding the mandatory sentence which would otherwise apply, so that a discretionary sentence can be imposed, tailored to the circumstances of the individual case.

(ii) Diminished responsibility depends on the highly personal condition of the defendant himself, indeed on the internal functioning of his mental processes.

(iii) A wholly impractical position would arise if the Crown had to bear the onus of disproving diminished responsibility whenever it was raised on the evidence; that would lead not to a fair, but to a potentially unfair trial.'

A successful defence results in a verdict of not guilty to murder but guilty of manslaughter (Homicide Act 1957, s 2(3)). This allows the judge full discretion on sentencing. Some defendants may receive an absolute discharge, others probationary or suspended sentences, while in appropriate circumstances some will receive hospital or guardianship orders under s 37(1) of the Mental Health Act 1983. Others may still face imprisonment, with some receiving life sentences for manslaughter (about 15 per cent of cases). If D raises the defence, and the prosecution has evidence that he is insane then, under s 6 Criminal Procedure (Insanity) Act 1964, evidence may be adduced to prove this. Here, the burden remains on the prosecution to prove insanity. The converse situation is also allowed by s 6, that is, if D raises insanity, then the prosecution may argue it is really a case of DR. Where this happens, the burden is on the prosecution to prove DR beyond reasonable doubt (*Grant* [1960] Crim LR 424).

Pleading guilty to manslaughter on grounds of DR

Originally, the courts took the view that DR had to be proved to the jury in every case and could not be accepted by a trial judge. However, it is now accepted that D may plead guilty to a charge of manslaughter on the ground of DR. Such a plea would be proper 'where the medical evidence available, in the possession of the prosecution as well as the defence, showed perfectly plainly that the plea' was one that could properly be accepted (*Cox* [1968] 1 WLR 308). In *Vinagre* (1979) 69 Cr App R 104 the Court of Appeal said that pleas of guilty to manslaughter on the ground of DR should only be accepted where there was 'clear evidence' of mental imbalance. The plea was refused in the following cases.

- *Din* [1962] 1 WLR 680. D attacked and killed a man whom he believed was having an affair with his wife, stabbing him several times and almost severing V's head. After death, D cut off V's penis. D pleaded DR, based on paranoia induced by an unreasonable belief in his wife's infidelity. Two medical experts supported the plea; the prosecution was prepared to accept it. However, the judge insisted on leaving the defence to the jury, which returned a verdict of guilty of murder. D's appeal was dismissed. Lord Parker CJ said that the case was 'a very good illustration of what for long has been apparent', namely, that the prosecution were 'only too ready to fall in with and to support' a defence of DR.
- *Walton* (1978) 66 Cr App R 25. D shot and killed a random stranger, a 16-year-old girl. Charged with murder, he pleaded DR. Two defence medical experts described D as 'retarded in certain respects', suffering from 'an extremely immature personality' and 'having an inadequate personality enhanced by emotional immaturity and low tolerance level'. The jury, however, rejected the defence. The Privy Council rejected D's appeal. Lord Keith said that the jury were entitled to regard the medical evidence as 'not entirely convincing'.

Where D pleads DR but it is rejected by the jury, the Court of Appeal may, if it believes the murder conviction to be unsupported by the evidence, quash it and substitute one of manslaughter. This happened in the following cases.

- *Matheson* [1958] 2 All ER 87. D killed a 15-year-old boy. The medical experts agreed that D was suffering a mental abnormality but the jury rejected the defence. D's murder conviction was quashed on appeal. Lord Goddard CJ said that where there was 'unchallenged' evidence of medical abnormality and 'no facts or circumstances appear that can displace or throw doubt on that evidence' then the Court was 'bound' to say that the conviction was unsafe.
- *Bailey* [1961] Crim LR 828. D battered V, a 16-year-old girl, to death with an iron bar. Three medical experts agreed that D suffered from epilepsy, that he had

suffered a fit at the time of the killing, and that it had substantially impaired his mental responsibility at that time. The jury rejected the defence. D appealed and his murder conviction was quashed.

According to research (S Dell, 'Diminished responsibility reconsidered' (1982) Crim LR 809) in practice 80 per cent of pleas of guilty to manslaughter on grounds of DR are accepted. Where the case does go to trial (usually because the prosecution disputes the defence), there is about a 60 per cent chance of conviction for murder. Thus the overall failure rate of the defence is quite small, around 10 per cent.

Importance of medical evidence

Medical evidence is crucial to the success of the defence. In *Byrne* [1960] 2 QB 396 it was said that, while there is no statutory requirement that a plea be supported by medical evidence, the 'aetiology of the abnormality … does, however, seem to be a matter to be determined on expert evidence'. Thus, where D was suffering a condition that was not, at the time of the trial, regarded by psychiatrists as a mental condition the defence will be unavailable but, if the condition subsequently becomes so regarded, a conviction may be quashed. This was the outcome in *Hobson* [1998] 1 Cr App R 31.

The Court of Appeal in *Dix* (1982) 74 Crim LR 302 declared that medical evidence was a 'practical necessity if the defence is to begin to run at all'. The jury were not, however, bound to accept that evidence if there was other material, which, in their opinion, conflicted with and outweighed the medical evidence. Occasionally, the jury may be faced with conflicting medical evidence. They are then required to weigh up and choose between the different opinions.

The principle established in *Dix* (1982), that medical evidence was a 'practical necessity' if DR was to run as a defence, was followed in the post-2009 Act case of *Bunch* [2013] EWCA Crim 2498. D had invoked DR during his murder trial on the basis of his alcohol dependence syndrome, but this was rejected because of a lack of medical evidence. The Court of Appeal agreed and upheld his murder conviction.

Operation of the defence

Section 2(1) breaks down into four components:

- There must be an 'abnormality of mental functioning'.
- It must arise from a 'recognised medical condition'.
- D must have a 'substantially impaired' ability to understand the nature of their conduct, or form a rational judgement, or exercise self-control.
- The abnormality must provide an 'explanation' for D's acts and omissions in doing or being a party to the killing.

There are no further requirements or exceptions. In *Matheson* (1958) it was accepted that the fact that a killing was premeditated did not destroy a plea of DR and this remains the position today (Brennan [2014] EWCA Crim 2387).

'Abnormality of mental functioning'

This is a new phrase, introduced by the 2009 amendment, to replace 'abnormality of mind'. The reason for the change was explained by the Law Commission (LC) in its report, *Murder, Manslaughter and Infanticide* (November 2006), at para 5.111. The LC stated that the original definition in s 2(1) had not been 'drafted with the needs and practices of medical experts in mind, even though their evidence is crucial to the legal viability' of any DR defence. The phrase 'abnormality of mind' was 'not a psychiatric term', and it received no further definition in the statute. As the LC pointed out, 'its meaning has had to be developed by the courts from case to case'. As it happens, the courts had interpreted the phrase very widely, most famously in *Byrne* [1960] 2 QB 396, where Lord Parker CJ described it as 'a state of mind so different from that of ordinary human beings that the reasonable man would term it abnormal'. It will be interesting to see if the courts in the future interpret the new phrase as widely. Note that there is nothing in the legislation to indicate that the 'abnormality of mental functioning' has to have any degree of permanence. Nor is there any requirement that the mental abnormality should have existed since birth (*Gomez* (1964) 48 Cr App R 310). It should suffice that it existed at the time of the killing.

A 'recognised medical condition'

This is another of the 2009 amendments. The original s 2(1) required the 'abnormality of mind' to arise from a 'condition of arrested or retarded development of mind' or 'any inherent cause' or be 'induced by disease or injury'. That list has now been consolidated into the single, simpler, but potentially wider, requirement of a 'recognised medical condition'. The Law Commission explained the thinking behind the redefinition in its 2006 report by pointing out that 'diagnostic practice' in DR cases 'has long since developed beyond identification of the narrow range of permissible causes' stipulated in s 2(1). Moreover, the LC observed that 'the stipulated permissible causes never had an agreed psychiatric meaning'. A further improvement is the long-overdue removal of the obsolete – and insulting – reference to retardation as a means of supporting a plea of DR.

The government agreed, claiming that the redefinition will bring 'the existing terminology up-to-date' whilst allowing for 'future developments in diagnostic practice' and encouraging defences to 'be grounded in a valid medical diagnosis linked to the accepted classificatory systems which together encompass the recognised physical, psychiatric and psychological conditions' (Ministry of Justice Consultation Paper, *Murder, Manslaughter and Infanticide* (July 2008), para 49).

No further definition of 'recognised medical condition' is provided in the Act so it will be interesting to see how the courts apply this new criterion. However, it is not unreasonable to expect that the courts will, in the future, be prepared to accept the following conditions, all of which fell within the scope of the original s 2(1):

- adjustment disorder (*Dietschmann* [2003] UKHL 10; [2003] 1 AC 1209; *Brown* [2011] EWCA Crim 2796; [2012] Crim LR 223);
- alcohol dependence syndrome (discussed below);
- Asperger's syndrome (*Jama* [2004] EWCA Crim 960);
- battered woman syndrome (*Hobson* (1998));
- depression (*Gittens* [1984] 3 All ER 252; *Seers* (1984) 79 Cr App R 261; *Ahluwalia* (1992) 4 All ER 869; *Swan* [2006] EWCA Crim 3378);
- epilepsy (*Bailey* (1961); *Campbell* [1997] 1 Cr App R 199);
- Othello syndrome, a form of extreme jealousy (*Vinagre* (1979) 69 Cr App R 104);
- paranoia (*Simcox* [1964] Crim LR 402);
- premenstrual tension and postnatal depression (*Reynolds* [1988] Crim LR 679);
- psychopathy (*Byrne* (1960); *Hendy* [2006] EWCA Crim 819);
- schizophrenia (*Moyle* [2008] EWCA Crim 3059; *Erskine* [2009] EWCA Crim 1425, [2009] 2 Cr App R 29; *Khan* [2009] EWCA Crim 1569).

It is possible that there will be more than one cause of D's 'abnormality of mental functioning'. If both causes are medical conditions (as in *Reynolds* (1988)), then if anything D's defence is strengthened. However, if one of the causes is a medical condition but the other is not, the latter must be discounted. This situation has been raised before the courts a number of times where D pleaded DR and was also intoxicated. These cases will be examined below.

The Law Commission had suggested that 'developmental immaturity in a defendant under the age of 18' should be able to support a plea of DR, separately from a 'recognised medical condition'. However, the government rejected this. In its Consultation Paper, *Murder, Manslaughter and Infanticide* (July 2008), the Ministry of Justice asserted that the term 'recognised medical condition' would cover conditions 'such as learning disabilities and autistic spectrum disorders which can be particularly relevant in the context of juveniles'. There was therefore no need to have a separate category alongside 'recognised medical condition'.

'Substantially impaired ability to understand the nature of conduct, or form a rational judgment, or exercise self-control'

This is another amendment, replacing the original expression used in s 2(1), 'substantially impaired mental responsibility'. The amendment was brought about after the government accepted the Law Commission's criticism in its 2006 report that the phrase 'mental responsibility' was too vague. The LC had argued (at para 5.110) that the 'implication' was that D's mental abnormality 'must significantly reduce the offender's culpability' but without saying, precisely, how or in what way it did so. The redefinition makes explicit what was, at best, implicit in the original version of the Act. Now D must prove that his abnormality of mental functioning impaired his 'ability to understand the nature of [his or her] conduct' and/or 'form a rational judgment' and/or 'exercise self-control'.

In *Byrne* (1960), the Court of Criminal Appeal said that the question of whether D's impairment could be described as 'substantial' was a question of degree and, hence, although medical evidence was not irrelevant, one for the jury. This was confirmed in *Eifinger* [2001] EWCA Crim 1855, the Court of Appeal describing this question as 'the jury's function'. More recently, in *Khan* [2009] EWCA Crim 1569, the Court of Appeal acknowledged that 'scientific understanding of how the mind works and the extent to which states of mind and physical responses to them have physical or chemical causes have undoubtedly advanced considerably' since the time when *Byrne* was decided. However, despite those advances, the Court said that 'even today, it is impossible to provide any accurate scientific measurement of the extent to which a particular person' might be able to 'understand or control his physical impulses on a particular occasion'. In short, there was no 'scientific test' for measuring this aspect of the DR defence. It remained a question for the jury. It seems reasonable to assume that this will continue to be the case under the amended statute.

As to what is meant by 'substantial', in *Lloyd* [1967] 1 QB 175, the trial judge, Ashworth J, directed the jury as follows:

JUDGMENT

'Substantial does not mean total, that is to say, the mental responsibility need not be totally impaired, so to speak, destroyed altogether. At the other end of the scale substantial does not mean trivial or minimal. It is something in between and Parliament has left it to you and other juries to say on the evidence, was the mental responsibility impaired and if so, was it substantially impaired?'

The direction from *Lloyd* was confirmed as still representing the law under the reformed defence in *Brown* (2011). However, in *Golds* [2014] EWCA Crim 748, the Court of Appeal formulated a 'more rigorous' definition of the scope of 'substantial' impairment than that adopted in *Lloyd* and approved in *Brown*. In *Golds*, the Court said that the word 'substantial' had two possible meanings: (1) more than trivial or minimal (the *Lloyd/Brown* formulation); (2) significant or appreciable. The Court held that the latter definition, which it described as both 'more rigorous' and 'more appropriate', should be adopted in preference to the former definition. Elias LJ explained that whilst a jury could potentially find that an impairment had 'some modest impact, and to that extent will be more than merely minimal or trivial' that was not necessarily enough for it to 'properly be described as substantial'. Hence, the law now requires the jury to be satisfied that D's impairment was 'significant or appreciable'.

Notwithstanding the adoption of the 'more rigorous' definition in *Golds*, this aspect of the DR defence clearly gives juries a wide discretion. Sympathy/empathy for the defendant is crucial. On the one hand, it is not uncommon for manslaughter verdicts to be returned in cases with little evidence of abnormality but where D has reacted to situations of extreme grief or stress. Thus mercy killers, or killings committed by the severely depressed, may receive convictions for manslaughter instead of murder. Conversely, murder convictions have been returned in cases when the psychiatrists all agreed that D was suffering severe mental abnormality but whose actions evoked little or no jury sympathy. The classic example is the Yorkshire Ripper, Peter Sutcliffe, who in 1981 was charged with murdering 13 women. Despite medical evidence from four psychiatrists that he was suffering from paranoid schizophrenia, the case went to trial. The jury rejected his DR plea and he was convicted of murder.

The abnormality must provide 'an explanation' for D's acts and omissions in doing or being a party to the killing

This requirement, in s 2(1)(c), is an entirely new legal principle, introduced by the 2009 amendment. The Law Commission proposed that this amendment be made and the government agreed. Section 2(1B) further provides that 'an abnormality of mental functioning provides an explanation for D's conduct if it causes, or is a significant contributory factor in causing, D to carry out that conduct'. It essentially means that there must now be some causal connection between D's mental abnormality and the killing.

However, notice the use of the word 'an', as opposed to 'the', before the word 'explanation' in s 2(1)(c). This means that, although the 'abnormality' must at least be 'a significant contributory factor' for D killing, it need not necessarily be the *only* reason for doing so. The government agreed with the LC that it would be 'impractical' to require mental abnormality to be the 'sole' explanation for D's killing of V, on the basis that 'it is rare that a person's actions will be driven solely from within to such an extent that they would not otherwise have committed the offence, regardless of the influence of external circumstances, and a strict causation requirement of this kind would limit the availability of the partial defence too much' (Ministry of Justice Consultation Paper, *Murder, Manslaughter and Infanticide* (July 2008), para 49).

Diminished responsibility and intoxication

It is now well established that a state of intoxication (falling short of the level of intoxication at which D fails to form *mens rea*) on its own cannot be used to support a plea of DR. In *Fenton* (1975) 61 Cr App R 261, Lord Widgery CJ said that 'We do not see how self-induced intoxication can of itself produce an abnormality of mind.' This has been confirmed as still representing the law under the reformed defence. In *Dowds* [2012] EWCA Crim 281; [2012] 3 All ER 154, it was argued that, because 'Acute Intoxication' appears in the World Health Organization's International Statistical Classification of Diseases and Related Health Problems (ICD), where it is defined as 'a condition that follows the administration of a psychoactive substance resulting in disturbances in level of consciousness, cognition, perception, affect or behaviour, or other physiological functions or responses', it was therefore a 'recognised medical condition' for the purposes of s 2. The Court of Appeal rejected this argument, stating that, if Parliament had meant to alter the law as decided in *Fenton*, it would have made its intention explicit. Hughes LJ pointed out that a variety of conditions appeared in the ICD and/or the American Medical Association's Diagnostic & Statistical Manual that would not support a plea of DR, such as 'unhappiness', 'irritability and anger', 'suspiciousness and marked evasiveness', 'pyromania', 'paedophilia', 'sado-masochism', 'kleptomania', 'exhibitionism' and 'sexual sadism'. Hughes LJ stated:

JUDGMENT

'It is quite clear that the re-formulation of the statutory conditions for [DR] was *not* intended to reverse the well-established rule that voluntary acute intoxication is not capable of being relied upon to found [DR]. That remains the law. The presence of a "recognised medical condition" is a necessary, but not always a sufficient, condition to raise the issue of [DR] ... Voluntary acute intoxication, whether from alcohol or other substance, is not capable of founding [DR].'

CASE EXAMPLE

Dowds [2012] EWCA Crim 281; [2012] 3 All ER 154

D and his girlfriend, V, were both 'habitual, heavy binge drinkers'. One night, D stabbed V 60 times, mostly in the neck, severing the carotid artery causing her to bleed to death. At the time, both had drunk a lot of vodka. At his murder trial, D did not deny being the killer but pleaded lack of intent due to intoxication and/or loss of control. The jury rejected both of these and he was convicted of murder. D appealed, arguing that DR, based on a state of 'acute intoxication', should have been left to the jury. The Court of Appeal disagreed and upheld his murder conviction.

The decision in *Dowds* was confirmed in *Bunch* [2013] EWCA Crim 2498. Holroyde LJ stated that 'the law draws an important distinction between voluntary intoxication and alcohol dependency. The former *cannot* found a defence of diminished responsibility' (emphasis added).

However, what is the situation where D suffers from an underlying abnormality of mental functioning (e.g. depression) and kills whilst intoxicated? This issue has arisen on several occasions, and the courts have taken a consistent line: a plea of DR may not be supported with evidence of voluntary intoxication. The trial judge should direct the jury to ignore the effects of the intoxication and consider whether the medical condition on its own would have been enough to amount to an abnormality of mental functioning. This was the decision in *Gittens* [1984] 3 All ER 252.

CASE EXAMPLE

Gittens [1984] 3 All ER 252

D was suffering depression and had, on the night in question, consumed a large amount of drink and antidepressant pills. In this state he clubbed his wife to death with a hammer and then raped and strangled his 15-year-old stepdaughter. He was convicted of murder but the Court of Appeal allowed his appeal, on the basis that the underlying depression may on its own have amounted to an 'abnormality of mind'. The Court did stress, however, that the jury should be directed to disregard the effect (if any) on D of any alcohol or drugs consumption.

This decision was confirmed by the Court of Appeal in *Egan* (1992) 4 All ER 470, where it was said that 'the vital question' for the jury in such cases is to ask, 'was the appellant's abnormality of mind such that he would have been under diminished responsibility, drink or no drink?' In *Dietschmann* (2003), it was further held that it was wrong to ask a jury whether D would still have killed V, even if he had not been intoxicated. The question was whether or not D would have had an 'abnormality of mind', even if he had not been drinking.

CASE EXAMPLE

Dietschmann [2003] UKHL 10; [2003] 1 AC 1209

D killed V by punching him and kicking him in the head in a savage attack. At the time of the killing, D was heavily intoxicated, in addition to suffering from an 'adjustment disorder', a 'depressed grief reaction' to the recent death of his girlfriend. At his trial for murder D relied on DR. The expert evidence for D was that, as well as the adjustment disorder, he had suffered a 'transient psychotic episode' at the time of the incident so that, even if he had been sober, he would still probably have killed V. The Crown's case was that the alcohol had been a significant factor as a disinhibitor and that, if D had been sober, he would probably have exercised self-control. The judge directed the jury that the question was whether D would still have killed V had he not been drinking, and the jury convicted. D appealed and although the Court of Appeal dismissed the appeal, he was successful in the House of Lords. The jury had been misdirected.

Lord Hutton suggested the following model direction for future juries:

JUDGMENT

'Assuming that the defence have established that [D] was suffering from mental abnormality as described in s 2, the important question is: did that abnormality substantially impair his mental responsibility for his acts in doing the killing? . . . Drink cannot be taken into account as something which contributed to his mental abnormality and to any impairment of mental responsibility arising from that abnormality. But you may take the view that both [D]'s mental abnormality and drink played a part in impairing his mental responsibility for the killing and that he might not have killed if he had not taken drink. If you take that view, then the question for you to decide is this: has [D] satisfied you that, despite the drink, his mental abnormality substantially impaired his mental responsibility for his fatal acts, or has he failed to satisfy you of that? If he has satisfied you of that, you will find him not guilty of murder but you may find him guilty of manslaughter. If he has not satisfied you of that, the defence of diminished responsibility is not available to him.'

Dietschmann has been followed by the Court of Appeal in a number of DR cases:

- *Hendy* [2006] EWCA Crim 819; [2006] 2 Cr App R 33 – D admitted killing V while intoxicated on alcohol, but there was evidence of an underlying brain damage and a psychopathic disorder.
- *Robson* [2006] EWCA Crim 2749 – D was heavily intoxicated, but also suffering from an 'acute stress disorder', when he killed V.
- *Swan* [2006] EWCA Crim 3378 – intoxication on top of underlying depression.

In each case, the jury had been directed that a defence of DR required proof that D would still have killed had they been sober. In each case the Court of Appeal, following

Dietschmann, quashed the resulting murder convictions and substituted convictions of manslaughter. However, the rule of law laid down in *Dietschmann* and applied in *Hendy*, *Robson* and *Swan* now has to be read in the light of the amended s 2(1), specifically the requirement that D's abnormality of mental functioning provide 'an explanation' for the killing. Thus, in future cases involving a combination of underlying abnormality plus intoxication, as in *Gittens*, *Egan*, *Dietschmann* and so on, the jury should be directed to:

(a) ignore the effect of D's drinking and/or drug-taking;

(b) decide whether D's underlying abnormality arose from a 'recognised medical condition';

(c) decide whether this underlying abnormality substantially impaired D's ability to understand their conduct, form a rational judgement and/or exercise self-control;

(d) decide whether the underlying abnormality caused, or was a 'significant contributory factor', in D's killing of V.

In short, whilst the courts had held that it was wrong for the trial judge in such cases to ask juries to decide whether D *would* have killed had he been sober, Parliament has decided that juries should, in future, be asked to decide whether D *might* have done so. This is because, if D definitely would not have killed V (or anyone else) had he remained sober, then there cannot be any causal connection between the underlying condition and the killing, as required by s 2(1)(c), and D would be liable for murder.

Diminished responsibility and alcoholism

Different rules apply where it is suggested that D's 'abnormality of mental functioning' was itself caused by long-term alcohol and/or drug abuse, and that D has developed a medical condition, sometimes known as alcohol dependence syndrome (ADS). In *Fenton* (1975), Lord Widgery CJ in the Court of Appeal envisaged the possibility that a craving for drink or drugs could produce an 'abnormality of mind'. However, until recently the leading case in this area was *Tandy* [1989] 1 WLR 350, in which Watkins LJ added a very important caveat, holding that alcoholism on its own would not suffice for a plea of DR. Instead, it would have to be proved (by the defence) that either D's alcoholism 'had reached the level at which her brain had been injured by the repeated insult from intoxicants so that there was gross impairment of ... judgment and emotional responses' or, if not, that D's 'drinking had become involuntary, that is to say she was no longer able to resist the impulse to drink'.

The decision in *Tandy* was criticised on the basis that it unduly limited the scope of the defence. One commentator argued that 'very few, if any, alcoholics will be permanently in a condition where the immediate consumption of alcohol is required to prevent or assuage the symptoms of withdrawal from alcohol' (G R Sullivan, 'Intoxicants and diminished responsibility' (1994) Crim LR 156). Another commentator criticised the rule in *Tandy* that D's drinking must be 'involuntary' before alcoholism can be used to support a DR defence. Goodliffe pointed out that, under *Tandy*, 'the symptoms of the disease are seen in isolation from the disease itself, leaving the idea of "disease" devoid of meaning' (J Goodliffe '*Tandy* and the concept of alcoholism as a disease' (1990) 53 MLR 809). Despite this criticism, in *Inseal* [1992] Crim LR 35, the Court of Appeal followed *Tandy*. In that case D, an alcoholic, had killed his girlfriend whilst in a drunken stupor. He claimed that he was either too drunk to have the intent to kill (the intoxication defence; see Chapter 9) or, if he did have the intent, his alcoholism was an 'abnormality of mind'. The jury convicted and the Court of Appeal dismissed the appeal. The jury must have been satisfied that D could have resisted the temptation to drink and that 'accordingly' any 'abnormality of mind' was not induced by ADS.

However, in two recent decisions, the Court of Appeal has shown more sympathy for defendants who kill whilst suffering from ADS. In the first case, *Wood* [2008] EWCA Crim 1305; [2009] 1 WLR 496, the court held that the 'rigid' principles established in *Tandy* (1989) had to be 're-assessed' in the light of the House of Lords' decision in *Dietschmann* (2003). The court laid down the following principles.

- Alcohol dependence syndrome (ADS) is a condition which may amount to an 'abnormality of mind'. Whether it does or not is a matter for the jury to decide.
- It is not essential that brain damage has occurred – although if it has, that can only help D to prove the defence.
- If D's syndrome does amount to an 'abnormality of mind', then the jury must then consider whether D's mental responsibility was substantially impaired.
- In deciding that question the jury should focus 'exclusively' on the effect of alcohol consumed by D as a 'direct result' of D's condition but the jury should 'ignore the effect of any alcohol consumed voluntarily'.

CASE EXAMPLE

Wood [2008] EWCA Crim 1305

After a day's heavy drinking, Clive Wood killed V in a frenzied attack with a meat cleaver. At Wood's murder trial, four psychiatrists agreed that Wood suffered from alcohol dependence syndrome, but the trial judge told the jury that a verdict of manslaughter based on DR was only open to them if D's consumption of alcohol was truly involuntary, and that simply giving into a craving for alcohol was not involuntary drinking. D was convicted of murder but the Court of Appeal quashed his conviction and substituted a verdict of manslaughter.

Sir Igor Judge stated:

JUDGMENT

'The sharp effect of the distinction drawn in *Tandy* between cases where brain damage has occurred as a result of alcohol dependency syndrome and those where it has not is no longer appropriate.'

Commenting on *Wood* in the Criminal Law Review, Professor Andrew Ashworth states:

QUOTATION

'If there is no proof of brain damage it is still open to the jury to decide that the alcohol dependency syndrome amounted to an "abnormality of mind" within s.2. If they do so, then the next question is whether that abnormality "substantially impaired" D's responsibility, discounting any effects of alcohol consumed voluntarily. So the jury are left to determine how much of D's drinking derived from his alcohol dependency and how much was "voluntary". This is a fearsomely difficult question to ask.'

Partly as a result of this criticism, *Wood* was followed – and clarified – in *Stewart* [2009] EWCA Crim 593. Here, the Court of Appeal quashed D's murder conviction (but ordered a retrial) because the jury had been directed in accordance with the 'rigid' directions laid down in *Tandy*. At D's retrial, the jury would be directed in accordance with the new, more flexible, principles laid down in *Wood*. To provide further clarification, Lord Judge CJ in *Stewart* established the following three-step test.

1. Was D suffering from an 'abnormality of mind'? The mere fact that D has ADS will not automatically amount to such an 'abnormality of mind', because the jury need to assess 'the nature and extent of the syndrome'.
2. Was D's 'abnormality of mind' caused by the ADS? If the answer to question (1) was yes, then this is likely to be straightforward.
3. Was D's 'mental responsibility' 'substantially impaired'? Here, the jury should be directed to consider all the evidence, including any medical evidence. The issues likely to arise would include (a) the extent and seriousness of D's dependency, (b) the extent to which his ability to control his drinking or to choose whether or not to drink was reduced, (c) whether he was capable of abstinence from alcohol and, if so, (d) for how long and (e) whether he was choosing for some particular reason, such as a birthday celebration, to get drunk, or to drink more than usual. D's pattern of drinking in the days leading up to the killing and his ability to make 'apparently sensible and rational decisions' about ordinary day-to-day matters at the relevant time might all bear on the jury's decision.

KEY FACTS

Key facts on diminished responsibility

	Law	Section/Case
Definition	• abnormality of mental functioning; • arising from a recognised medical condition; • which substantially impairs D's ability to understand the nature of D's conduct, form a rational judgement or exercise self-control; • and which provides an explanation for D's conduct.	ss 2(1) and (1A) Homicide Act 1957 (as amended by s 52 Coroners and Justice Act 2009)
Abnormality of mental functioning	A new expression, introduced by the 2009 Act.	None yet
Recognised medical condition	A new expression, introduced by the 2009 Act, to replace the list of causes in the original 1957 Act. However, the pre-reform cases provide examples of likely 'conditions': • alcoholism • battered woman syndrome • depression • epilepsy • psychopathy • schizophrenia.	 *Wood* (2008) *Hobson* (1998) *Seers* (1984) *Bailey* (1961) *Byrne* (1960) *Moyle* (2008), *Erskine* (2009)
Substantially impaired	A question for the jury to decide. 'Substantial' means 'significant or appreciable'.	*Byrne* (1960), *Khan* (2009) *Golds* (2014)

Effect of intoxication	Intoxication must be ignored. Where D has an underlying mental disorder, the question is whether this disorder on its own amounts to an abnormality of mental functioning.	*Fenton* (1975), *Dowds* (2012), *Bunch* (2013) *Gittens* (1984), *Dietschmann* (2003), *Hendy* (2006)
Effect of alcoholism	Alcohol dependence syndrome (ADS) may amount to an abnormality of mental functioning. It is not necessary to prove either brain damage or that all of D's drinking was involuntary. Whether it substantially impairs D's ability to understand his or her conduct/form a rational judgement/exercise self-control is to be decided by a jury, ignoring the effect of any alcohol consumed voluntarily.	*Wood* (2008), *Stewart* (2009)
Burden of proof	It is for the defence to prove, on the balance of probabilities.	s 2(2) Homicide Act 1957, *Dunbar* (1958), *Foye* (2013)
Effect of defence	The charge of murder is reduced to manslaughter.	s 2(3) Homicide Act 1957

10.3.2 Loss of self-control

Loss of self-control is a relatively new, special and partial defence to murder, introduced by ss 54 and 55 of the Coroners and Justice Act 2009. It replaces the ancient common law defence of 'provocation', which was abolished by s 56(1) of the 2009 Act.

loss of self-control
Special and partial defence to murder

Background to the reform

The Law Commission (LC) had been advocating reform of the provocation defence for several years. In its report, *Murder, Manslaughter and Infanticide* (November 2006), it stated that the 'defence of provocation is a confusing mixture of judge-made law and legislative provision'. The government agreed. The Ministry of Justice Consultation Paper, *Murder, Manslaughter and Infanticide: Proposals for Reform of the Law* (July 2008), states (para 34):

QUOTATION

'We want to provide a partial defence which has a much more limited application than the current partial defence of provocation. We propose to do this ... by abolishing the existing partial defence of provocation and the term "provocation" itself which carries negative connotations.'

The common law provocation defence had already been modified by Parliament, in s 3 of the Homicide Act 1957, which has been repealed by s 56(2) of the 2009 Act. For the purposes of comparison, s 3 is set out here:

SECTION

'Where on a charge of murder there is evidence on which the jury can find that the person charged was provoked (whether by things done or by things said or by both together) to lose his self-control, the question whether the provocation was enough to make a reasonable man do as he did shall be left to be determined by the jury; and in determining that question the jury shall take into account everything both done and said according to the effect which, in their opinion, it would have on a reasonable man.'

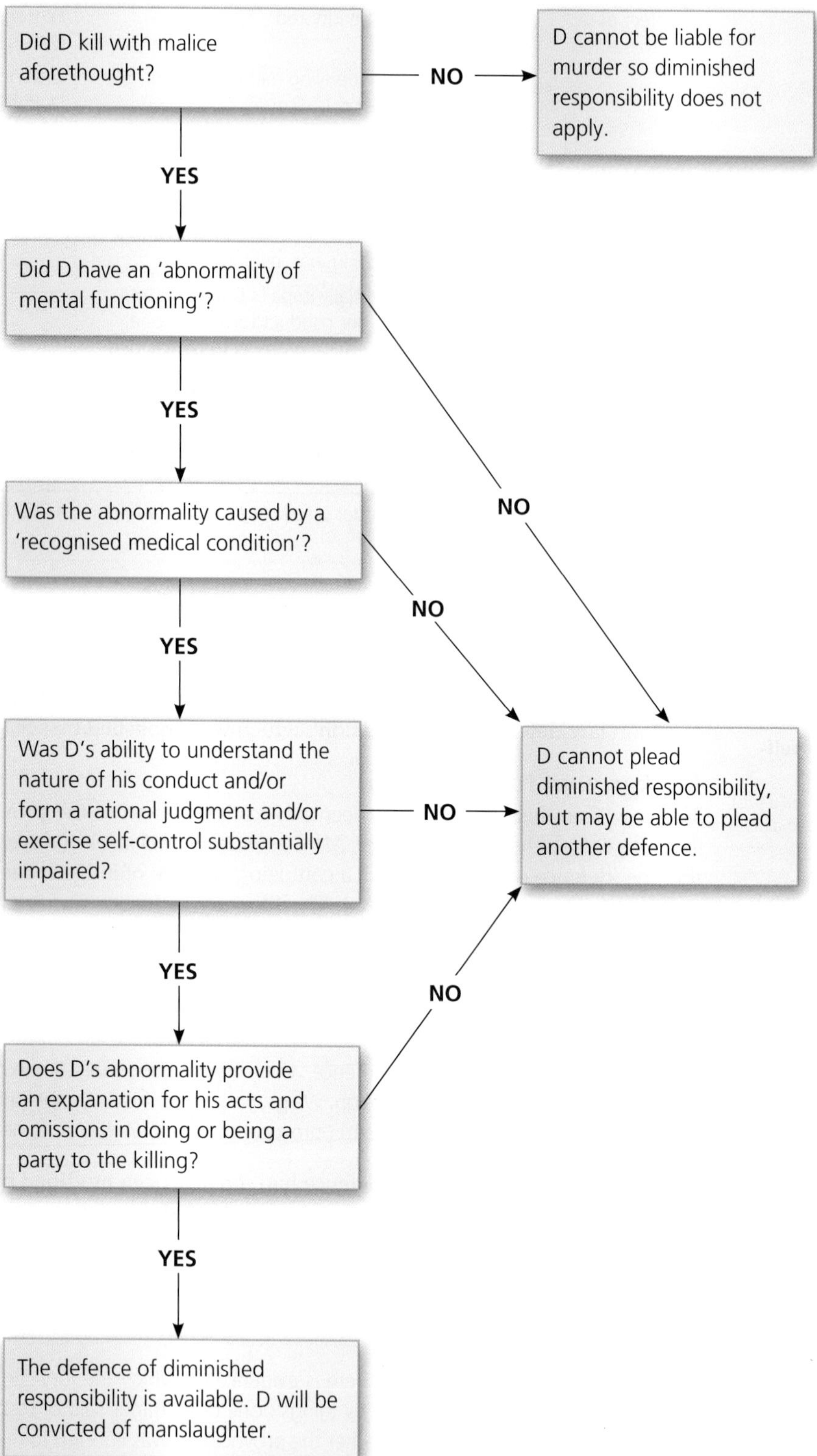

Figure 10.1 Diminished responsibility.

The new defence

The 2009 Act provides as follows.

SECTION

'54 (1) Where a person ("D") kills or is a party to the killing of another ("V"), D is not to be convicted of murder if –

(a) D's acts and omissions in doing or being a party to the killing resulted from D's loss of self-control,

(b) the loss of self-control had a qualifying trigger, and

(c) a person of D's sex and age, with a normal degree of tolerance and self-restraint and in the circumstances of D, might have reacted in the same or in a similar way to D.

(2) For the purposes of subsection (1)(a), it does not matter whether or not the loss of control was sudden.

(3) In subsection (1)(c) the reference to "the circumstances of D" is a reference to all of D's circumstances other than those whose only relevance to D's conduct is that they bear on D's general capacity for tolerance or self-restraint.

(4) Subsection (1) does not apply if, in doing or being a party to the killing, D acted in a considered desire for revenge.

(5) On a charge of murder, if sufficient evidence is adduced to raise an issue with respect to the defence under subsection (1), the jury must assume that the defence is satisfied unless the prosecution proves beyond reasonable doubt that it is not.

(6) For the purposes of subsection (5), sufficient evidence is adduced to raise an issue with respect to the defence if evidence is adduced on which, in the opinion of the trial judge, a jury, properly directed, could reasonably conclude that the defence might apply.

(7) A person who, but for this section, would be liable to be convicted of murder is liable instead to be convicted of manslaughter.

(8) The fact that one party to a killing is by virtue of this section not liable to be convicted of murder does not affect the question whether the killing amounted to murder in the case of any other party to it.

55 (1) This section applies for the purposes of s 54.

(2) A loss of self-control had a qualifying trigger if subsection (3), (4) or (5) applies.

(3) This subsection applies if D's loss of self-control was attributable to D's fear of serious violence from V against D or another identified person.

(4) This subsection applies if D's loss of self-control was attributable to a thing or things done or said (or both) which-

(a) constituted circumstances of an extremely grave character, and

(b) caused D to have a justifiable sense of being seriously wronged.

(5) This subsection applies if D's loss of self-control was attributable to a combination of the matters mentioned in subsections (3) and (4).

(6) In determining whether a loss of self-control had a qualifying trigger –

(a) D's fear of serious violence is to be disregarded to the extent that it was caused by a thing which D incited to be done or said for the purpose of providing an excuse to use violence;

(b) a sense of being seriously wronged by a thing done or said is not justifiable if D incited the thing to be done or said for the purpose of providing an excuse to use violence;

(c) the fact that a thing done or said constituted sexual infidelity is to be disregarded.

(7) In this section references to 'D' and 'V' are to be construed in accordance with s 54.

56 (1) The common law defence of provocation is abolished and replaced by sections 54 and 55.'

Procedure

Like diminished responsibility (and the old provocation defence), the loss of self-control defence is only a partial defence to murder. The references in s 54(1) to 'kills' and 'killing' means that the defence will not be available to a charge of attempted murder. If the defence is successful, D will be found guilty of manslaughter instead of murder (s 54(7)).

If D wishes to rely on the loss of self-control defence, they must provide 'sufficient evidence' of it. The onus is then on the prosecution to disprove it, beyond reasonable doubt (s 54(5)). The 2009 Act states that the evidence must be 'sufficient', meaning that the trial judge must be satisfied that a jury, properly directed, could 'reasonably conclude that the defence might apply' (s 54(6)). In the first case under the 2009 Act to reach the Court of Appeal – *Clinton* [2012] EWCA Crim 2; [2012] 2 All ER 947 – Lord Judge CJ explained the procedure as follows:

JUDGMENT

'The statutory provision is clear. If there is evidence on which the jury could reasonably conclude that the loss of control defence might apply, it must be left to the jury: if there is no such evidence, then it must be withdrawn. Thereafter in accordance with the judge's directions the jury will consider and return its verdict.'

In *Jewell* [2014] EWCA Crim 414, D's loss of control defence was withdrawn by the trial judge on the basis that there was insufficient evidence to support it, and the Court of Appeal upheld D's resulting murder conviction. D had driven to V's house, ostensibly to pick him up for work, and shot him at point blank range, twice, with a shotgun. Rafferty LJ said that the killing 'bore every hallmark of a pre-planned, cold-blooded execution... the evidence that this was a planned execution is best described as overwhelming'. In *Workman* [2014] EWCA Crim 575, the Court of Appeal rejected D's appeal against his conviction for murdering his ex-wife. D contended that the trial judge should have directed the jury on loss of control but the appeal court held that, although it was incumbent on a trial judge to direct the jury on loss of control if there was 'sufficient evidence' of it (whether it was positively relied upon by the defence or not), in this case there was simply no evidence.

A loss of self-control

The central issue to the defence is a 'loss of self-control' (s 54(1)(a)), which was also key to the provocation defence. Whether or not D has had a loss of self-control will be a question for the jury. Unlike the provocation defence, the 2009 Act explicitly states that the loss of control does not need to be 'sudden' (s 54(2)). This point was reiterated by the Court of Appeal in *Dawes* [2013] EWCA Crim 322; [2014] 1 WLR 947. Lord Judge CJ said that:

JUDGMENT

'Provided there was a loss of control, it does not matter whether the loss was sudden or not. A reaction to circumstances of extreme gravity may be delayed. Different individuals in different situations do not react identically, nor respond immediately.'

The new defence should, therefore, be available in some factual situations where provocation would not have succeeded. If so, this appears to contradict the government's stated intention of replacing provocation with a new defence of 'much more limited application'. However, it is submitted that this change in the law is unlikely to make that much difference in practice. In many of the old cases where provocation failed, there was simply no, or insufficient, evidence of any loss of self-control, 'sudden' or otherwise. The new defence will obviously not be available in such situations either. Three provocation cases illustrate this point:

- *Ibrams and Gregory* (1981) 74 Cr App R 154. D and E had been 'provoked' by V and carried out a pre-planned killing which involved luring V into a trap and then jointly attacking him with various weapons.
- *Thornton (No 1)* [1992] 1 All ER 306. D had been 'provoked' by her husband, V, and stabbed him to death. However, prior to the stabbing, she had gone into another room to sharpen a knife before killing V.
- *Ahluwalia* (1992). D had been 'provoked' by her husband, V, and killed him by pouring petrol on him as he slept and setting it on fire.

In all three cases, the defendants pleaded provocation but were convicted of murder (despite the evidence of provocation) because there was no 'loss of self-control' (although both Thornton and Ahluwalia later succeeded in having their convictions quashed because of evidence of DR). Would any of these cases be decided differently under the 2009 Act? It would seem not.

The courts had already accepted, in the context of the provocation defence, that 'sudden' did not mean 'immediate' and that a time delay – a so-called 'slow-burn' reaction – between the last provocative incident and D's eventual loss of control was not necessarily fatal to the defence, although it did weaken it (*Ahluwalia* (1992)). By omitting the word 'sudden' from the new defence it does mean that whether or not there is a time delay is irrelevant: the defence of loss of self-control will not be weakened as a result. As a result, women who find themselves trapped in abusive relationships and eventually (but not necessarily suddenly) lose self-control and kill their partners should find it easier to plead the new defence than they did provocation. (It has been argued that a 'sudden' loss of self-control involving an explosive outburst of anger and violence is a more typical male reaction, whereas women tend not to react 'suddenly'.)

However, the retention of the 'loss of self-control' element means that an opportunity to provide a viable defence for women in abusive relationships who kill (but without losing self-control) has been missed. After all, both Thornton and Ahluwalia were in such a relationship and killed their respective husbands only after enduring years of physical and psychological abuse. Yet, the evidence of provocation (which was particularly severe in Ahluwalia's case) did not help either woman to plead that defence because they did not suffer a loss of self-control – 'sudden' or otherwise. Under the 2009 Act, the outcome in cases like *Thornton* and *Ahluwalia* would be exactly the same.

The Law Commission had proposed removing the loss of self-control criterion entirely, in order to provide a defence to women in abusive relationships who killed their partners from 'a combination of anger, fear, frustration and a sense of desperation' (*Murder, Manslaughter and Infanticide* (2006), para 5.18). The government, however, disagreed, because of concerns that 'there is a risk of the partial defence being used inappropriately, for example in cold-blooded, gang-related or "honour" killings'. Even in abusive relationship cases, the government concluded that there was a 'fundamental problem about providing a partial defence in situations where a defendant has killed while basically in full possession of his or her senses, even if he or she is frightened, other than in a situation which is complete self-defence' (*Murder, Manslaughter and Infanticide: Proposals for Reform of the Law* (2008), paras 35–36). For a detailed analysis of both sides of the 'loss of control' debate, see Anna Carline, 'Reforming provocation: perspectives from the Law Commission and the government' (2009) 2 Web JCLI.

Section 54(4) adds that s 54(1) does not apply if 'D acted in a considered desire for revenge'. This appears to add nothing of substance – after all, unless D has lost self-control (as required by s 54(1)(a)), the defence cannot run at all. The use of the word 'considered' implies the polar opposite of a killing committed having lost control, so s 54(4) appears just to be there for emphasis.

The 'qualifying triggers'

D's loss of control must be based on one (or both) of two 'qualifying triggers' (s 54(1)(b)): a 'fear of serious violence from V against D or another identified person' (s 55(3)) or 'a thing or things done or said (or both) which constituted circumstances of an extremely grave character and caused D to have a justifiable sense of being seriously wronged' (s 55(4)).

Trigger 1: a 'fear of serious violence' (s 55(3))

When will this trigger apply? Two situations present themselves.

- Those who would be unable to plead self-defence because there was an anticipated attack, but no immediate threat, and hence no necessity to use force. This trigger could be used in domestic violence cases, such as *Ahluwalia* and *Thornton* (discussed above). Another possible example of a case involving this trigger is provided by the facts of *Ibrams and Gregory* (1982), also discussed above. In that case, although their provocation defence failed, the Court of Appeal acknowledged that the defendants were subjected to 'gross bullying and terrorising' from V.
- Those who would be unable to plead self-defence because, although they were (or believed themselves to be) under attack, they had used excessive force. An example given in the Law Commission's report (2006) is a householder who reacts spontaneously but with unreasonable force when confronted by an intruder (para 4.18). Under the common law, the use of excessive force in self-defence is no defence at all to murder as a result of the House of Lords' decision in *Clegg* [1995] 1 AC 482 – see Chapter 8.

There are two important limitations on this trigger. First, D must fear violence from V, as opposed to from some third party. Second, D must fear that the violence will be used against D or 'another identified person' – a phrase not defined in the Act. The case of *Ward* [2012] EWCA Crim 3139 illustrates the application of this trigger. D, his brother E and V had spent the day drinking and taking cocaine. This continued at E's house where spontaneous violence erupted, which started when V head-butted E. D went to his brother's defence, picked up a pick-axe handle and struck V with it. V suffered 'multiple heavy and sustained blows, mainly to the head area, which caused catastrophic injuries: multiple skull fractures, fractures of the left cheekbone, fractures to both eye sockets and the base of the skull' from which he later died. The Crown accepted D's plea of not guilty to murder on the basis of loss of control.

Trigger 2: a thing or things done or said (or both) (s 55(4))

This trigger covers roughly the same terrain as the old provocation defence, which also required things to be said or done. However, the new defence is much narrower than provocation because s 3 of the Homicide Act 1957 imposed no further requirements whereas s 55(4) has two:

- circumstances of an extremely grave character;
- a justifiable sense of being seriously wronged.

That certainly seems to be the view of the Court of Appeal. In *Clinton* (2012), Lord Judge CJ stated (emphasis in original):

JUDGMENT

'Sections 55(3) and (4) define the circumstances in which a qualifying trigger may be present. The statutory language is not bland. In s 55(3) it is not enough that [D] is fearful of violence. He must fear *serious* violence. In subsection (4)(a) the circumstances must not merely be grave, but *extremely* so. In subsection (4)(b) it is not enough that [D] has been caused by the circumstances to feel a sense of grievance. It must arise from a *justifiable* sense not merely that he has been wronged, but that he has been *seriously* wronged. By contrast with the former law of provocation, these provisions have raised the bar.'

The Lord Chief Justice reiterated this view in *Dawes* [2013] EWCA Crim 322; [2014] 1 WLR 947 when he said that the 'circumstances in which the qualifying triggers will arise is much more limited than the equivalent provisions in the former provocation defence ... some of the more absurd trivia which nevertheless required the judge to leave the provocation defence to the jury will no longer fall within the ambit of the qualifying triggers defined in the new defence'.

The combined effect of these conditions means that it would surely be impossible for the new defence to work in a case such as *Doughty* (1986) 83 Cr App R 319. D had killed his 17-day-old son after the child would not stop crying. Although he was convicted of murder, the Court of Appeal allowed his appeal (substituting a manslaughter conviction) on the basis that there was evidence of provocation by 'things done'. To illustrate how the 2009 Act has 'raised the bar', consider the case of *Zebedee* [2012] EWCA Crim 1428. Here, a jury rejected a loss of control defence based on trigger 2, and the Court of Appeal upheld D's murder conviction. The Court held that the jury 'must have concluded that whatever it was that triggered [D's] violence did not constitute "circumstances of an extremely grave character" sufficient to satisfy the statutory test for a qualifying trigger'. Had the provocation defence still been in force, then D may have been entitled to a manslaughter conviction instead on the basis of 'things done'.

CASE EXAMPLE

Zebedee [2012] EWCA Crim 1428

D was charged with the murder of V, his 94-year-old father, who had Alzheimer's and was doubly incontinent. V lived with D's sister, but D would often stay at her house to help out. One night, D punched and strangled V to death. D did not deny the killing but pleaded loss of control. He claimed that V had soiled himself during the night, after which D had cleaned him up, only for V to soil himself again only 20 minutes later, which had triggered D's loss of self-control. The defence was rejected and D was convicted of murder. The Court of Appeal upheld the conviction.

A good example of an old provocation case where trigger 2 almost certainly would be satisfied is *DPP v Camplin* [1978] AC 705, where D was raped by V and then laughed at afterwards. Being raped would surely amount to 'circumstances of an extremely grave character' and D would no doubt feel 'a justifiable sense of being seriously wronged', not just by the physical violation of the rape itself but also the psychological humiliation of being laughed at afterwards. Another possible example of trigger 2 is *Humphreys* [1995] 4 All ER 1008, discussed below.

The phrases 'constituted circumstances of an extremely grave character' and 'a justifiable sense of being seriously wronged' are undefined in the 2009 Act, so there will almost inevitably be appeals in the years to come to clarify their precise meaning and scope. Some guidance was offered in *Clinton* (2012). Lord Judge CJ stated:

JUDGMENT

> 'The defendant himself must have a sense of having been seriously wronged. However even if he has, that is not the end of it. In short, [D] cannot invite the jury to acquit him of murder on the ground of loss of control because he personally sensed that he had been seriously wronged in circumstances which he personally regarded as extremely grave. The questions whether the circumstances were extremely grave, and whether [D's] sense of grievance was justifiable, indeed all the requirements of s.55(4)(a) and (b), require objective evaluation.'

This principle was confirmed in *Dawes* (2013). Lord Judge CJ also explained the reason for adopting an objective test:

JUDGMENT

> 'If it were otherwise it would mean that a qualifying trigger would be present if D were to give an account to the effect that, "the circumstances were extremely grave to me and caused me to have what I believed was a justifiable sense that I had been seriously wronged". If so, when it is clear that the availability of a defence based on the loss of control has been significantly narrowed, one would have to question the purpose of s 55(3), (4) and (5).'

Under the common law, a doctrine known as 'cumulative provocation' had developed, whereby the jury could take into account anything that had been said and/or done to D, possibly over an extended period of time, in deciding whether D had lost their self-control. The case of *Humphreys* (1995), discussed below, is the best-known example of 'cumulative provocation' where the Court of Appeal referred to D and V having a 'tempestuous relationship ... a complex story with several distinct and cumulative strands of potentially provocative conduct building up until the final encounter'. The 2009 Act makes no explicit reference to this doctrine but it does not rule it out, either. In *Dawes* (2013), one of the questions for the Court of Appeal was whether the concept of 'cumulative provocation' applied in the context of the new defence. Lord Judge CJ answered in the affirmative:

JUDGMENT

> 'The loss of control may follow from the cumulative impact of earlier events ... the response to what used to be described as "cumulative provocation" requires consideration in the same way as it does in relation to cases in which the loss of control is said to have arisen suddenly. Given the changed description of this defence, perhaps "cumulative impact" is the better phrase to describe this particular feature.'

The fact that 'cumulative provocation' (now 'cumulative impact') has survived the abolition of provocation itself should not come as a surprise; after all, s 55(4) of the 2009 Act explicitly refers to 'things' done or said.

A combination of triggers (s 55(5))

A loss of self-control triggered by a combination of both 'fear of serious violence' and 'things done or said' will also suffice (s 55(5)). The provocation case of *Humphreys* (1995) provides an example where both 'qualifying triggers' may have been present. D believed that V (her violent boyfriend/pimp) and his friends were going to gang-rape her and hence she probably had a 'fear of serious violence'; she also claimed that V had mocked her failed suicide attempt – this is a 'thing said' which could constitute 'circumstances of an extremely grave character' and give D a 'justifiable sense of being seriously wronged'.

In *Dawes* (2013), Lord Judge CJ observed that, where trigger 2 is relied upon, it was very likely that the evidence would tend to support trigger 1 as well:

JUDGMENT

'There are unlikely to be many cases where the only feature of the evidence relating to the qualifying trigger in the context of fear of violence will arise in total isolation from things done or said. In most cases the qualifying trigger based on a fear of violence will almost inevitably to include consideration of things said and done, in short, a combination of the features identified in s 55(3) and (4).'

Self-inflicted triggers may not be relied upon (s 55(6)(a) and (b))

Even if D has a 'fear of serious violence' or a 'sense of being seriously wronged by a thing done or said' and has a loss of self-control resulting in V's death, he will not be able to rely on the new defence if the trigger was self-inflicted, that is, if D 'incited' something to be done or said 'for the purpose of providing an excuse to use violence'. This partly overrules an established common law doctrine that provocation could be self-induced, although the presence of the words 'incited' and 'purpose' in s 55(6) clearly mean that D will still be able to rely on either or both triggers if the violence that he fears or the things said and/or done were inadvertently self-induced.

In *Dawes* (2013), Lord Judge CJ offered the following guidance on the circumstances in which s 55(6)) might (and might not) apply:

JUDGMENT

'One may wonder (and the judge would have to consider) how often D who is out to incite violence could be said to "fear" serious violence; often he may be welcoming it. Similarly, one may wonder how D may have a justifiable sense of being seriously wronged if he successfully incites someone else to use violence towards him. Those are legitimate issues for consideration, but as a matter of statutory construction, the mere fact that in some general way D was behaving badly and looking for and provoking trouble does not of itself lead to the disapplication of the qualifying triggers unless his actions were intended to provide him with the excuse or opportunity to use violence.'

CASE EXAMPLE

Dawes [2013] EWCA Crim 322; [2014] 1 WLR 947

Carlo Dawes (D) had come home to his Brighton flat to find V asleep on the sofa with D's estranged wife, K. Both were fully clothed. The Crown case was that D flew into a jealous rage, grabbed a kitchen knife and stabbed V in the neck, killing him. The defence case was that V had woken up and then attacked D, who had acted in self-defence. As an alternative, defence counsel suggested that the trial judge should direct the jury on loss of self-control. However, the judge decided that D did not qualify for that defence because he had incited the violence offered to him by V, so that no qualifying trigger was available because of s 55(6). The jury convicted of murder and the Court of Appeal upheld the conviction.

'Sexual infidelity' ruled out (s 55(6)(c))

One situation is singled out in the 2009 Act. Section 55(6)(c) states that 'the fact that a thing done or said constituted sexual infidelity is to be disregarded'. This is designed to overrule cases like *Davies* [1975] QB 691, where D shot and killed his wife after being 'provoked' by seeing her lover. This may appear surprising, particularly bearing in mind that the provocation defence developed hundreds of years ago through cases of sexual infidelity. However, the government was adamant. The Ministry of Justice's Consultation Paper (2008) states (para 32):

QUOTATION

'It is quite unacceptable for [D] who has killed an unfaithful partner to seek to blame [V] for what occurred. We want to make it absolutely clear that sexual infidelity on the part of [V] can never justify reducing a murder charge to manslaughter. This should be the case even if sexual infidelity is present in combination with a range of other trivial and commonplace factors.'

Section 55(6)(c) was therefore designed by the government to ensure that men who intentionally kill their wives or other female relatives who have allegedly been unfaithful in order to preserve or restore the family 'honour' will not be able to plead loss of control, and nor will excessively jealous husbands or boyfriends who kill their wives or girlfriends on discovering that they have been having an affair.

However, despite the apparently clear wording of s 55(6)(c), the Court of Appeal in *Clinton* (2012) managed to interpret the 2009 Act in such a way as to allow evidence of 'sexual infidelity' to support a loss of control defence after all. Lord Judge CJ stated:

JUDGMENT

'On the face of the statutory language, however grave the betrayal, however humiliating, indeed however provocative in the ordinary sense of the word it may be, "sexual infidelity" is to be disregarded as a qualifying trigger ... The question, however, is whether it is a consequence of the legislation that sexual infidelity is similarly excluded when it may arise for consideration in the context of another or a number of other features of the case which are said to constitute an appropriate permissible qualifying trigger ... To seek to compartmentalise sexual infidelity and exclude it when it is integral to the facts as a whole is not only much more difficult, but is unrealistic and carries with it the potential for injustice ... We do not see how any sensible evaluation of the gravity of the circumstances or their impact on [D] could be made if the jury, having, in accordance with the legislation, heard the evidence, were then to be directed to excise from their evaluation of the qualifying trigger the matters said to constitute sexual infidelity, and to put them into distinct compartments to be disregarded. In our judgment, where sexual infidelity is integral to and forms an essential part of the context in which to make a just evaluation whether a qualifying trigger properly falls within the ambit of ss 55(3) and (4), the prohibition in s 55(6)(c) does not operate to exclude it.'

In other words, if the *only* 'trigger' for D's loss of control is sexual infidelity, then that is to be disregarded and D will be convicted of murder (unless an alternative defence is available). However, if sexual infidelity is 'integral to and forms an essential part of the context' of D's defence, alongside other evidence which is admissible in support of a qualifying trigger, then it would be wrong to 'compartmentalise' the evidence.

CASE EXAMPLE

Clinton [2012] EWCA Crim 2; [2012] All ER 947

D had bludgeoned and strangled his wife, V, to death. The day before her death, V told D that she was having an affair. On the day of her death, D and V had begun to argue. According to D, V had told him about her sexual activities in detail. V was also aware that D had been looking at suicide websites on his computer and had taunted him about this; she had suggested that D did not have the courage to commit suicide and that it would have been better for everyone if he had. Finally, V told D that he could have their children. It was at this point that D had grabbed a piece of wood and beat V about the head with it before strangling her to death. At his trial for murder, D did not deny the killing but pleaded DR and/or loss of control. However, he was convicted of murder after the trial judge ruled that the loss of control defence should not be left to the jury because the loss of self-control had been triggered by V's sexual infidelity. D appealed on the grounds that the defence of loss of control should have been left to the jury. The Court of Appeal agreed, holding that what V said about her sexual infidelity could not 'of itself' amount to a qualifying trigger. However, it did not have to be disregarded: 'The totality of matters relied on as a qualifying trigger, evaluated in the context of the evidence relating to [V's] sexual infidelity, and examined as a cohesive whole, were of sufficient weight to leave to the jury.'

The 'normal' person test

The 2009 Act requires that, whichever trigger is relied upon, a 'person of D's sex and age, with a normal degree of tolerance and self-restraint and in the circumstances of D, might have reacted in the same or in a similar way to D' (s 54(1)(c)).

A 'person of D's sex and age, with a normal degree of tolerance and self-restraint'

This confirms the common law principles established in the context of provocation. In *DPP v Camplin* [1978] AC 705, Lord Diplock said that D's reaction should be tested against a 'person having the power of self-control to be expected of an ordinary person of the sex and age' of D.

The reference to a 'normal degree of tolerance' means that any irrational prejudices such as racism and homophobia are excluded, while the reference to a 'normal degree of self-restraint' means that characteristics such as bad temper and pugnacity are excluded from the 'normal person' test. The government explained this aspect of the 'normal person' test as follows (Consultation Paper (2008), para 22):

QUOTATION

'Factors, such as alcoholism or a mental condition, which affect the defendant's general capacity for self-control, would not be relevant to this partial defence (though they might be to diminished responsibility). Characteristics (eg intoxication, irritability, excessive jealousy) which do not arise from a medical condition and do not satisfy the test for diminished responsibility should be disregarded altogether.'

The proposition that intoxication should be 'disregarded' when the jury apply the normal person test was confirmed by the Court of Appeal in *Asmelash* [2013] EWCA Crim 157; [2014] QB 103. D, who was very drunk at the time of killing his flatmate, unsuccessfully invoked the loss of control defence. In upholding his murder conviction, Lord Judge CJ said:

JUDGMENT

'The only relevance of the drunkenness was that it affected [D's] self-restraint, and caused him to act in a way in which he would not have acted if sober. Such drunkenness was an irrelevant consideration. It may have had some relevance to his general capacity for tolerance or self-restraint: but no more.'

CASE EXAMPLE

Asmelash [2013] EWCA Crim 157; [2014] QB 103

D and V lived in the same house in Middlesbrough. They were friends and often used to drink together. One night, however, they began arguing and eventually D stabbed V twice, once in the back and once in the chest, the latter penetrating his heart and lung. Both men were drunk at the time. At his trial for murder, D pleaded loss of control. He claimed that V had been aggressive and physically abusive towards him on the day of the murder, and he (D) had swung out at V with a knife because he was frightened. The trial judge directed the jury to consider whether they were sure that a person of D's sex and age with a normal degree of tolerance and self-restraint and in the same circumstances, but unaffected by alcohol, would not have reacted in the same or similar way. D was convicted of murder and appealed, arguing that the fact that he was drunk at the time of the stabbing was a relevant 'circumstance'. The Court of Appeal disagreed and upheld his murder conviction.

'In the circumstances of D'

However, the 'normal person' must be placed in 'the circumstances' of D. This reflects the common law development in the provocation defence that in certain cases D's characteristics may be taken into account in determining the reaction to provocation of the 'reasonable man'. Placing the 'normal person' in D's circumstances is likely to be applicable more to trigger 2, specifically the requirement that the things said and/or done constituted circumstances 'of an extremely grave character'. Case law may be needed to determine what exactly is meant by 'circumstances', although s 54(3) states that 'all of D's circumstances' are potentially relevant, 'other than those whose only relevance to D's conduct is that they bear on D's general capacity for tolerance or self-restraint'.

In *Clinton* (2012), Lord Judge CJ pointed out that the exclusion of 'sexual infidelity' in s 55(6)(c) was limited to the assessment of whether D had a qualifying trigger. However, when it came to the normal person test, 'the circumstances' were 'not constrained or limited'. It followed that, 'notwithstanding s 55(6)(c), account may, and in an appropriate case, should be taken of sexual infidelity'. He went on to consider the implications of this:

JUDGMENT

'We must reflect briefly on the directions to be given by the judge to the jury. On one view they would require the jury to disregard any evidence relating to sexual infidelity when they are considering the second component of the defence, yet, notwithstanding this prohibition, would also require the same evidence to be addressed if the third component arises for consideration. In short, there will be occasions when the jury would be both disregarding and considering the same evidence. That is, to put it neutrally, counter intuitive.'

'Might have reacted in the same or in a similar way to D'

This requirement confirms case law in the context of the provocation defence that it is not enough for the jury to be satisfied that the 'reasonable man' might have lost self-control – they had to be satisfied that the reasonable man might have gone on to kill V in the same way that D did. Under the 2009 Act, the jury will have to consider whether the 'normal person' might have 'reacted' in the same or in a similar way to D.

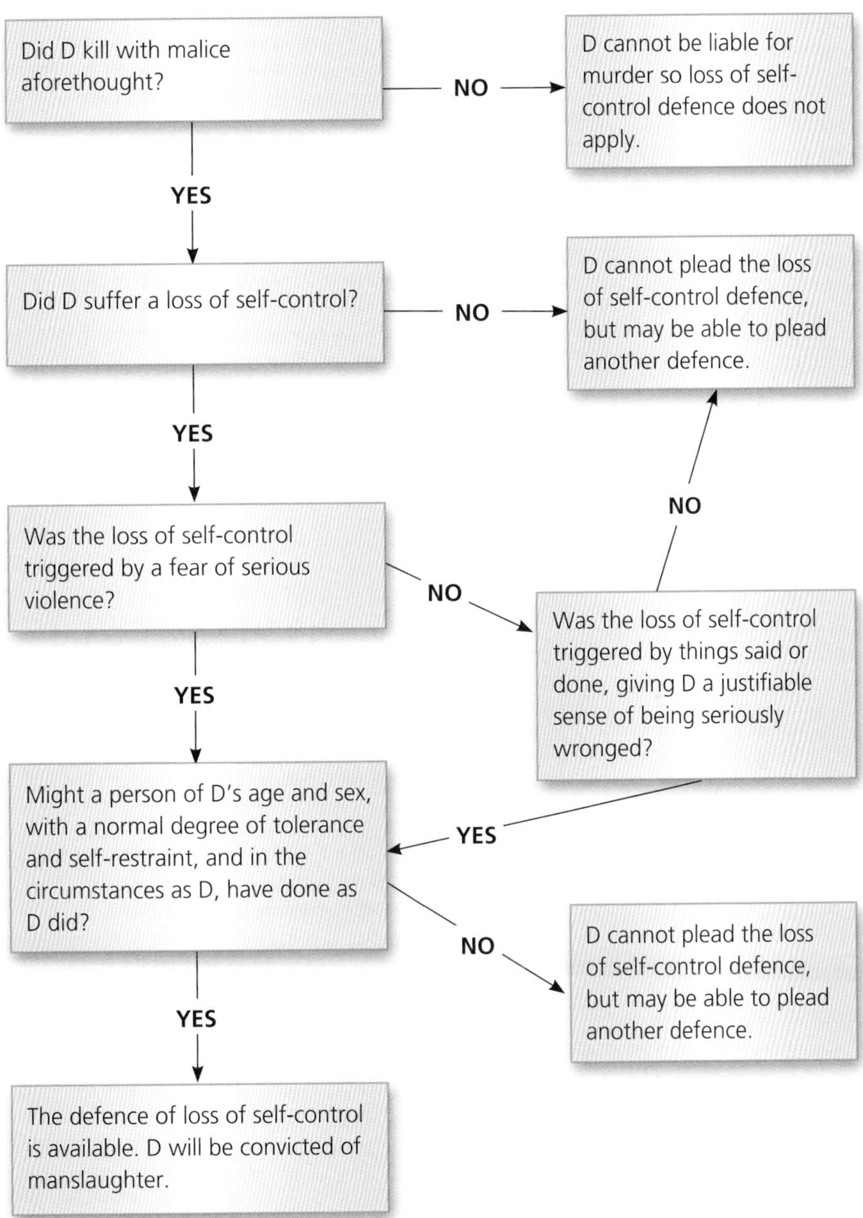

Figure 10.2 Loss of self-control.

KEY FACTS

Key facts on loss of self-control

	Law	Section/case
Definition	• a loss of self-control • a qualifying trigger • a normal person of D's sex and age might have reacted in the same or a similar way	s 54(1) Coroners and Justice Act 2009
Loss of selfcontrol	• no requirement that it be sudden • loss of self-control is not sudden if D acted in 'considered desire' for revenge	s 54(2) and (4)
'Qualifying trigger' 1	A 'fear of serious violence' from V against D or 'another identified person'.	s 55 (3)
'Qualifying trigger' 2	A thing or things done or said or both, 'constituting circumstances of an extremely grave character' and causing D to have a 'justifiable sense of being seriously wronged'.	s 55 (4)
Both triggers	Both triggers may apply simultaneously.	s 55(5)
Self-induced triggers	Neither trigger applies if D 'incited' a thing to be done or said for the 'purpose of providing an excuse to use violence'.	s 55(6)(a) and (b)
Sexual infidelity	Must be disregarded … … except where it forms 'part of the context'.	s 55(6)(c) *Clinton* (2012)
The 'normal person' test	• D's age and sex • a 'normal degree of tolerance and self-restraint' • in the 'circumstances' of D • all of D's circumstances are relevant, other than those whose 'only' relevance is that they bear on D's 'general capacity for tolerance or self-restraint'	s 54(1)(c) and (3)
Evidence	There must be 'sufficient' evidence – a question of law for the judge – enabling a properly directed jury to 'reasonably conclude that the defence might apply'.	s 54(5) and (6)
Burden of proof	The prosecution must disprove the defence beyond reasonable doubt.	s 54(5)
Effect of defence	D is not guilty of murder but guilty of manslaughter instead.	s 54(7)

10.3.3 Suicide pacts

suicide pact
Special and partial defence to murder

Section 4(1) of the Homicide Act 1957 provides that the survivor of a **suicide pact** (where the other party to the pact is killed by D) is not guilty of murder but guilty of voluntary manslaughter. Section 4(3) defines a 'suicide pact' as 'a common agreement between two or more persons having for its object the death of all of them'. The burden of proof is on D on the balance of probabilities.

10.4 Involuntary manslaughter

Involuntary manslaughter describes any form of unlawful killing where there is no proof of malice aforethought. There are three forms of involuntary manslaughter:

- constructive manslaughter
- gross negligence manslaughter
- reckless manslaughter.

10.4.1 Constructive manslaughter

constructive manslaughter
Where V is killed by an unlawful and dangerous act

D will be guilty of **constructive manslaughter** if he kills by an unlawful and dangerous act. The following elements must be proven to exist:

- D must commit an unlawful act (in the sense of a crime).
- The act must be 'dangerous'.
- D must have intended to commit the unlawful act.
- That act must have caused death.

The requirement of an unlawful act

At one time it was thought that it was sufficient if D committed a civil wrong (a tort), such as in *Fenton* [1830] 1 Lew CC 179, where D was convicted of manslaughter on the basis that he had committed the unlawful act of trespass to property. This approach quickly changed and the law now requires that D commit a criminal offence. In *Franklin* (1883) 15 Cox CC 163, the court stated that 'The mere fact of a civil wrong committed by one person against another ought not to be used as an incident which is a necessary step in a criminal case.' If there is no criminal offence, then there is no possibility of a manslaughter conviction (regardless of how 'dangerous' D's acts may have been). The leading case is *Lamb* [1967] 2 QB 981.

CASE EXAMPLE

Lamb [1967] 2 QB 981

D shot his best friend, V, with a Smith & Wesson revolver. The shooting was accidental; neither D nor V foresaw any risk of the gun firing when D pulled the trigger. Although the gun was loaded, in that there were two bullets in the five-chamber cylinder, there were no bullets in the chamber opposite the barrel. Critically, neither man appreciated that the cylinder revolved before the hammer struck the back of the mechanism. Consequently, V did not apprehend any possibility of injury being caused to himself, and therefore the *actus reus* of assault had not been performed. The Court of Appeal quashed D's conviction. Sachs LJ said that D's act was not 'unlawful in the criminal sense of the word'.

Similarly, in *Jennings* [1990] Crim LR 588, where D had been convicted of manslaughter on the basis that his act of carrying an uncovered knife in the street was unlawful, the Court of Appeal quashed his conviction. Because there was no proof that he had any intent to cause injury (which would have amounted to a crime under s 1 of the Prevention of Crime Act 1953), simply walking along with the knife was 'not a criminal offence which could constitute the unlawful act for this purpose'. The criminal act could, for example, be any of the following:

- assault (*Larkin* [1943] 1 All ER 217; *Lamb* [1967] 2 QB 981; *Mallet* [1972] Crim LR 260);
- battery (*Church* [1965] 2 All ER 72; *Mitchell* [1983] QB 741);

- criminal damage (*DPP v Newbury and Jones* [1977] AC 500);
- arson (*Goodfellow* [1986] Crim LR 468; *Willoughby* [2004] EWCA Crim 3365; [2005] 1 WLR 1880);
- theft (*Willett* [2010] EWCA Crim 1620; [2011] Crim LR 65);
- robbery (*Dawson* (1985) 81 Cr App R 150);
- burglary (*Watson* [1989] 2 All ER 865; *Bristow and others* [2013] EWCA Crim 1540, [2014] Crim LR 457);
- administering a noxious substance, contrary to s 23 OAPA 1861 (*Cato* [1976] 1 All ER 260);
- affray, contrary to s 3 of the Public Order Act 1986 (*Carey and others* [2006] EWCA Crim 17; *M & M* [2012] EWCA Crim 2293, [2013] 1 WLR 1083);
- cruelty to a person under 16, contrary to s 1 Children and Young Persons Act 1933 (*Gay* [2006] EWCA Crim 820);
- endangering road users, contrary to s 22A(1)(b) of the Road Traffic Act 1988 (*Meeking* [2012] EWCA Crim 641).

You may note that, although the 'unlawful act' must be a criminal offence, it need not be a crime against the person – offences against property, such as theft, burglary and criminal damage, will suffice. Also, it is not necessary that the 'unlawful act' be a particularly serious crime: assault and battery are both summary offences which on their own carry maximum sentences of only six months' imprisonment. However, it is important to remember that there are other elements to the crime of constructive manslaughter, in particular the element of 'dangerousness' (discussed below).

Omissions as unlawful 'acts'

Given that constructive manslaughter requires an unlawful and dangerous 'act', it follows that if D simply omits to act, he cannot be guilty of this form of manslaughter. In *Lowe* [1973] QB 702, Phillimore J said:

JUDGMENT

'If I strike a child in a manner likely to cause harm it is right that if the child dies I may be charged with manslaughter. If, however, I omit to do something, with the result that it suffers injury to its health which results in its death, we think that a charge of manslaughter should not be an inevitable consequence even if the omission is deliberate.'

CASE EXAMPLE

Lowe [1973] QB 702

D was convicted of both neglecting his child so as to cause it unnecessary suffering or injury to its health contrary to s 1(1) of the Children and Young Persons Act 1933 and constructive manslaughter. The trial judge had directed the jury that if they found D guilty of the s 1 offence they had to find him also guilty of manslaughter. The Court of Appeal quashed his manslaughter conviction.

The mental element of the unlawful act

While an unlawful act is essential in constructive manslaughter cases, D must also possess the mental element which combines with the unlawful act to constitute a criminal offence. Hence, another ground for allowing D's appeal in *Lamb* (1967), above, was the fact that D (as well as V) did not appreciate that the chamber of the revolver would rotate prior to firing. Therefore, D did not appreciate any risk of the gun firing and, hence, did not possess the mental element of assault (intention or subjective recklessness as to causing immediate violence to be apprehended by V). It appears that this requirement only applies if there is a mental element required for the underlying criminal offence. In *Andrews* [2002] EWCA Crim 3021; [2003] Crim LR 477, the Court of Appeal upheld a manslaughter conviction based on s 58(2)(b) of the Medicines Act 1968, which states that 'no person shall administer any [specified] medicinal product unless he is an appropriate practitioner or a person acting in accordance with the directions of an appropriate practitioner'. This is a strict liability offence; that is, there is no requirement that D be proven to have formed any particular mental element with respect to the elements of the *actus reus*. D had given V, and others, insulin injections to give them a 'rush'. V, who was undernourished and had been drinking, died. D's appeal was based on the fact that V had consented, but this was dismissed. (You will recall from reading cases such as *Brown and others* [1994] AC 212 in Chapter 8 that, for public policy reasons, consent is restricted in all situations where V runs the risk of suffering at least actual bodily harm, as in this case.)

Dangerousness

In *Church* (1965) (the facts of which appeared in Chapter 3 in the context of the requirement of coincidence of *actus reus* and *mens rea*), the Court of Criminal Appeal laid down a requirement that D's act had to be dangerous (this is in addition to the acts being unlawful). Edmund Davies J, giving judgment for the court, imposed an objective standard for assessing dangerousness:

JUDGMENT

'An unlawful act causing the death of another cannot, simply because it is an unlawful act, render a manslaughter verdict inevitable. For such a verdict inexorably to follow, the unlawful act must be such as all sober and reasonable people would inevitably recognise must subject the other person to, at least, the risk of some harm resulting therefrom, albeit not serious harm.'

The courts approach this test by asking whether a hypothetical 'sober and reasonable' bystander, who happened to be watching the unlawful act, would regard the act as dangerous. The fact that this is an objective test was emphasised by the Court of Appeal in *Ball* [1989] Crim LR 730.

CASE EXAMPLE

Ball [1989] Crim LR 730

D, who had been involved in a dispute with his neighbour, V, grabbed a handful of cartridges which he loaded into his shotgun and fired at her. V was killed and D was charged with murder. He was acquitted as the jury accepted that he honestly thought the cartridges were blanks. However, his conviction of manslaughter was upheld. The bystander would have regarded D's act of firing a loaded shotgun at V as dangerous. Moreover, the 'sober and reasonable' bystander would not have made D's mistake of thinking the cartridges were blanks.

The jury are entitled to ascribe to the bystander D's pre-existing knowledge about V (if any), including any knowledge which D acquires during the commission of the unlawful act. This is illustrated by the case of *Watson* (1989).

CASE EXAMPLE

Watson [1989] 2 All ER 865

D burgled the house of an 87-year-old man, V. A brick was thrown through a window to gain access and this alerted V, who came down to investigate. There was a confrontation between D and V during which V was verbally abused. D left without stealing anything but V died of a heart attack 90 minutes later. D pleaded guilty to burglary but was also convicted of manslaughter. The Court of Appeal allowed D's appeal against the latter conviction (on causation grounds) but was satisfied that the jury were entitled to find that the burglary was dangerous.

Lord Lane CJ stated:

JUDGMENT

'The judge clearly took the view that the jury were entitled to ascribe to the bystander the knowledge which [D] gained during the whole of his stay in the house and so directed them. Was this a misdirection? In our judgment it was not. The unlawful act in the present circumstances comprised the whole of the burglarious intrusion … That being so, D (and therefore the bystander) during the course of the unlawful act must have become aware of [V]'s frailty and approximate age, and the judge's directions were accordingly correct.'

Similar reasoning was adopted in *Bristow and others* [2013] EWCA Crim 1540; [2014] Crim LR 457. Treacy LJ said that 'whilst burglary of itself is not a dangerous crime, a particular burglary may be dangerous because of the circumstances surrounding its commission'.

CASE EXAMPLE

Bristow and others [2013] EWCA Crim 1540; [2014] Crim LR 457

In October 2010, six men burgled V's off-road vehicle repair business located on a secluded site in east Sussex. To access the workshops (where numerous vehicles, tyres and valuable tools were located), the burglars had to drive down a single-track road past V's home in a converted barn. During the burglary, the defendants were disturbed by V, who was then killed by being hit and/or run over by one or possibly two vehicles used by the burglars as they attempted to escape. In due course, four of the six burglars were charged with manslaughter. The trial judge held that there was sufficient evidence for the jury to find that the burglary (i) could be regarded as an ongoing offence at the time of V's appearance on the scene, and (ii) was dangerous, on the basis that a reasonable bystander would recognise the risk of some harm being caused to a person intervening at night, in the dark, in a relatively confined space, where powerful vehicles were involved, and there was only one route of escape from the workshops (i.e. down the single-track road past V's home). The jury convicted and the Court of Appeal upheld their convictions.

The decision in *Watson* (1989) should be contrasted with that in *Dawson* (1985). D and another man carried out an armed robbery of a petrol station while masked and armed with pickaxe handles and replica guns. The attendant, V, was 60 years old. He also had a heart condition and died of a heart attack. The Court of Appeal held this was not manslaughter – neither D nor the 'sober and reasonable' bystander would have been aware of this condition.

ACTIVITY

Self-test question

Do you agree that the convictions in *Dawson* (1985) should have been quashed? How does the approach of the Court of Appeal in this case compare with the decision of the same Court in *Blaue* [1975] 3 All ER 446 (considered in Chapter 2), that D must take their victim as they find them?

A similar outcome to that in *Watson* was achieved in *Carey and others* [2006] EWCA Crim 17.

CASE EXAMPLE

Carey and others [2006] EWCA Crim 17

V, a 15-year-old girl, had run away from the three defendants after being punched and threatened with further violence, but had collapsed after running about 100 metres and died of an undiagnosed heart complaint aggravated by the running. The defendants were convicted of affray and constructive manslaughter but their manslaughter convictions were quashed on appeal. The Court of Appeal held that the count of constructive manslaughter should have been withdrawn from the jury as the only physical harm to V (a single punch) did not cause her death. Although there were other threats of violence in the course of the affray they were not dangerous, inasmuch as a reasonable person would not have foreseen their causing any physical harm to V.

'Harm'

According to the *Church* (1965) test, V must be subjected to 'the risk of some harm'. In *Reid* (1975) 62 Cr App R 109, Lawton LJ thought that 'the very least kind of harm is causing fright by threats', but the court thought that as D was armed, the act was likely to cause death or serious injury and therefore was dangerous. In *Dawson* (1985), Watkins LJ said that 'a proper direction would have been that the requisite harm is caused if the unlawful act so shocks the victim as to cause him physical injury'. Thus, merely frightening or shocking V is insufficient; the trauma must pose a risk of some physical injury.

In *M and M* [2012] EWCA Crim 2293, [2013] 1 WLR 1083, the Court of Appeal emphasised that the *Church* test simply required the jury to decide whether D's unlawful act exposed V to the risk of 'some' harm. There was no requirement that the 'sober and reasonable' bystander had to have foreseen the 'sort' or 'type' of harm to which V was, in fact, exposed.

CASE EXAMPLE

M and M [2012] EWCA Crim 2293; [2013] 1 WLR 1083

Two brothers faced manslaughter charges following the death of V, a nightclub bouncer. The Crown case was that the brothers had been involved in an affray in the club which eventually caused V to suffer a ruptured aneurysm in his heart, as a result of a surge in blood pressure, from which he died. In a pre-trial hearing, the trial judge ruled that the Crown would not be able to prove that a 'sober and reasonable' bystander would have foreseen that V would suffer this 'sort' of harm. The Crown appealed and the Appeal Court allowed the appeal. The trial judge had elevated the requisite risk from an appreciation that 'some' harm would occur into foresight of the type of harm which actually ensued.

Mens rea *of manslaughter*

In *DPP v Newbury and Jones* (1977), the House of Lords explained the *mens rea* requirement for constructive manslaughter. It was held that, although it must be proved that D intended to commit the unlawful act, there was no requirement that D foresaw that his act may cause death or even harm.

D's unlawful act must cause V's death

The final element in a constructive manslaughter case is proof that D's 'unlawful act' caused V's death. Here, the normal rules of causation apply (see Chapter 2). In *Mitchell* (1983), which was considered in Chapter 2, Staughton LJ said that, 'Although there was no direct contact between [D] and [V], she was injured as a direct and immediate result of his act ... The only question was one of causation: whether her death was caused by [D]'s acts. It was open to the jury to conclude that it was so caused.' The Court of Appeal in that case upheld D's conviction because it was reasonably foreseeable that pushing an elderly man in a crowded post office could cause him to fall and knock over someone else, and hence there was no break in the chain of causation. Similarly, in *Goodfellow* (1986), where D set fire to his council house (hoping to be rehoused) and ended up killing his wife, two-year-old son and another woman, all of whom were in the house at the time, the Court of Appeal upheld his conviction. The deaths were reasonably foreseeable.

However, there have been problems in some constructive manslaughter cases, specifically, those involving deaths allegedly 'caused' by drug dealers or suppliers providing drug addicts with heroin, leading to a fatal drug overdose. In the earliest case, *Cato* (1976), D injected V with a mixture of heroin and water. V overdosed and died and D was convicted of manslaughter. The Court of Appeal upheld the conviction on the basis that D's 'unlawful act' of administering a noxious substance (heroin) contrary to s 23 OAPA 1861, actually caused V's death.

In hindsight, the fact that D actually performed the injection was crucial to the guilty verdict in *Cato*. Subsequent cases have decided that the same result does not follow if D gives the drug to V, who then takes it himself (and overdoses and dies). In *Dalby* [1982] 1 All ER 916, the Court of Appeal held that in this situation D has not caused V's death. D gave some of his prescribed Diconal tablets (a form of heroin substitute) to V, who took them but overdosed and died. The Court of Appeal quashed D's manslaughter conviction on the basis that V's self-administration of the tablets broke the chain of causation.

This line of thinking was confirmed in the similar case of *Dias* [2001] EWCA Crim 2986; [2002] 2 Cr App R 5, where the Court of Appeal stated that V's self-injection of heroin 'probably' broke the chain of causation (D's appeal in *Dias* was allowed on a different point). The leading case is now *Kennedy* [2007] UKHL 38; [2008] 1 AC 269, a decision of the House of Lords, the facts of which were given in Chapter 2. The House of Lords, approving both *Dalby* and *Dias*, quashed D's conviction of constructive manslaughter on the basis that V's self-injection of the heroin which D had given to him broke the chain of causation.

Thus, the situation involving drug dealers is that

- where D actually injects V with a drug, and V dies, then D may face liability for constructive manslaughter (*Cato*); but
- where D hands over the drugs and V self-administers (and dies), then D is not liable for constructive manslaughter (*Dalby*, *Dias*, *Kennedy*).

KEY FACTS

Key facts on unlawful act manslaughter

Elements	Comment	Cases
Unlawful act	Must be a crime. A civil wrong is not enough. It must be an act; an omission is not sufficient.	*Lamb* (1967) *Franklin* (1883) *Lowe* (1973)
Examples of unlawful acts	• Assault, • battery, • criminal damage, • arson, • robbery, • burglary, • administering noxious substance (heroin).	*Larkin* (1943), *Lamb* (1967) *Church* (1965), *Mitchell* (1983) *Newbury and Jones* (1977) *Goodfellow* (1986) *Dawson* (1985) *Watson* (1989), *Bristow & Others* (2013) *Cato* (1976), *Dalby* (1982), *Dias* (2002), *Kennedy* (2007)
Dangerous act	The test for this is objective – would a sober and reasonable person realise the risk of some harm? The risk need only be of some harm – not serious harm. An act aimed at property can still be such that a sober and reasonable person would realise the risk of some harm. There must be a risk of physical harm; mere fear is not enough.	*Church* (1965) *Larkin* (1943) *Goodfellow* (1986) *Dawson* (1985)
Causes death	Normal rules of causation apply; the act must be the factual and legal cause of death. An intervening act such as the victim self-injecting a drug breaks the chain of causation.	*Goodfellow* (1986) *Dalby* (1982), *Dias* (2001), *Kennedy* (2007)
Mens rea	D must have *mens rea* for the unlawful act but it is not necessary to prove that D foresaw any harm from his act.	*Newbury and Jones* (1977)

gross negligence manslaughter
Causing death by breaching a duty of care in circumstances of gross negligence

10.4.2 Gross negligence manslaughter

The leading case is the House of Lords' decision in *Adomako* [1995] 1 AC 171. The elements of this form of involuntary manslaughter are:

- the existence of a duty of care;
- breach of that duty causing death;
- gross negligence which the jury consider justifies criminal conviction.

Where manslaughter by gross negligence is raised, it is incumbent upon the judge to direct the jury in accordance with the passage of Lord Mackay's speech in *Adomako* at 187 (*Watts* [1998] Crim LR 833).

Duty of care

The concept of a duty of care is well known in civil law, but less so in criminal law. The criminal law recognises certain duty situations, as seen in Chapter 2; for example, a doctor owes his patient a duty of care by virtue of his contractual obligations. *Adomako* itself involved a breach of duty owed by a hospital anaesthetist towards a patient. Similarly, in *Adomako*, the House of Lords approved *Stone and Dobinson* [1977] QB 354 (the facts of which appear in Chapter 2) who were found to have undertaken a duty of care. So the ambit of the offence could be limited to those who, for whatever reason, have either undertaken or had a duty imposed upon them. However, Lord Mackay in *Adomako* said that 'ordinary principles of law of negligence apply to ascertain whether or not D has been in breach of a duty of care towards the victim'. That being so, it logically follows that those same principles should apply in determining those persons to whom a duty is owed. These principles are to be found in *Donoghue v Stevenson* [1932] AC 562, where Lord Atkin in the House of Lords said:

JUDGMENT

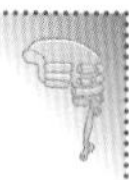

'You must take reasonable care to avoid acts or omissions which you can reasonably foresee would be likely to injure your neighbour. Who then is my neighbour? The answer seems to be – persons who are so closely and directly affected by my act that I ought reasonably to have them in contemplation as being so affected when I am directing my mind to the acts or omissions which are called into question.'

This clearly goes much further than the traditional duty situations in criminal law, giving this form of manslaughter a very wide scope indeed. The following cases illustrate the development of the duty concept.

CASE EXAMPLE

Litchfield [1998] Crim LR 507; [1997] EWCA Crim 3290

D was the master of the *Maria Asumpta*, a sailing ship, which ran aground off the north Cornish coast and broke up, killing three of her 14 crew. D was charged with manslaughter, on the basis that, in sailing on – when he knew that the engines might fail through fuel contamination – he had been in breach of duty serious enough to amount to gross negligence. The jury convicted. On appeal, the Court of Appeal, applying *Adomako* (1995), held that the question had been appropriately left for the jury to decide.

CASE EXAMPLE

Wacker [2003] EWCA Crim 1944; [2003] 4 All ER 295

D was convicted of 58 counts of manslaughter. He was the driver of a lorry found at Dover docks to contain 60 illegal Chinese immigrants – all bar two of them dead. At about 7 p.m., while the lorry was waiting at Zeebrugge to board the North Sea ferry, D had closed the only ventilation into the lorry; it could not be opened from the inside. (Presumably this closure was not done with the intent to cause GBH or death, otherwise D would have faced 58 counts of murder.) The journey had taken some five hours, by which time, as Kay LJ described it, 'the dreadful loss of life was discovered'. The Court dismissed D's appeal, which had been based on the premise that, as he and the 60 Chinese immigrants had been jointly engaged on an illegal operation, he did not owe them a duty of care. The Court, following *Adomako* (1995), confirmed that the issue whether a duty of care was owed for the purposes of gross negligence manslaughter was determined by 'the same legal criteria as governed whether there was a duty of care in the law of negligence'. However, this did not include the tortious principle of *ex turpi causa* (according to which the participants in a criminal enterprise did not owe a duty of care to each other).

In *Willoughby* [2005] 1 WLR 1880; [2004] EWCA Crim 3365, the Court of Appeal followed and confirmed *Wacker*. D, the owner of The Old Locomotive, a disused pub in Canterbury, had hired V to help him burn down the pub (there were financial reasons for doing so). One night the pair of them spread petrol around the pub and started a fire. However, there was an explosion and the building collapsed, killing V. D was charged with gross negligence manslaughter. The prosecution convinced the jury that D had breached his duty of care to V in a grossly negligent way and D was convicted. On appeal, the Court of Appeal accepted that it was possible for the same set of circumstances to give rise to liability for both constructive and gross negligence manslaughter, and that D was almost certainly guilty of constructive manslaughter (based on the unlawful and dangerous act of arson). In terms of gross negligence manslaughter, however, the prosecution had to prove that D breached a duty of care to V. On this point, Rose LJ stated:

JUDGMENT

'We accept that there could not be a duty in law to look after [V]'s health and welfare arising merely from the fact that [D] was the owner of the premises. But the fact that [D] was the owner, that his public house was to be destroyed for his financial benefit, that he enlisted [V] to take part in this enterprise, and that [V]'s role was to spread petrol inside were, in conjunction, factors which were capable, in law, of giving rise to a duty to the deceased on the part of [D].'

In *Evans* [2009] EWCA Crim 650 (discussed in Chapter 2), the Court of Appeal applied the principle developed in the case of *Miller* [1983] 2 AC 161 (also discussed in Chapter 2) that a duty of care may be imposed on those who create a dangerous situation. In *Evans*, a duty was imposed on D because she had obtained heroin for her 16-year-old sister which the latter then took but shortly afterwards lapsed into unconsciousness and died. D was found to be in breach of her duty to her sister (by failing to contact the emergency services after her sister was obviously in need of medical attention) and was convicted of gross negligence manslaughter. The Court of Appeal dismissed her appeal.

Evans therefore provides a potential solution to the problem created by the House of Lords' ruling in *Kennedy* (2007), above, that a drug dealer's unlawful act in supplying V with drugs which V self-administers (with fatal consequences) does not cause the death and thus D cannot be convicted of constructive manslaughter. Instead, using *Evans*, drug dealers can now be prosecuted for gross negligence manslaughter if they fail to take adequate steps to assist a customer who has overdosed on drugs supplied by the dealer.

Breach of duty

The next issue is at what point D breaches that duty. In civil law, D is judged against the standard of the reasonably competent person performing the activity involved. Hence:

- If D is driving a car, he must reach the standard of the reasonably competent driver (*Andrews v DPP* [1937] AC 576, discussed below).

- If D is sailing a boat, he must reach the standard of the reasonably competent sailor (*Litchfield* (1998)).
- If D is a doctor, he is judged against the standard of the reasonably competent doctor (*Bateman* (1925) 19 Cr App R 8).
- If D is an anaesthetist, he is judged against the standard of the reasonably competent anaesthetist (*Adomako* (1995)).

ACTIVITY

Essay writing

Against what benchmark should the defendants in, respectively, *Stone and Dobinson* and *Wacker* be judged?

In the civil law, no concession is made for inexperience. Thus, a learner driver is judged against the standard of the reasonably competent driver (*Nettleship v Weston* [1971] 3 All ER 581); and a junior doctor is judged against the standard of the reasonably competent doctor (*Wilsher v Essex Area Health Authority* [1986] 3 All ER 801). Should the same policy apply in the criminal law?

'Gross negligence'

Simply proving that D has been in breach of a duty owed to another person will not lead inevitably to criminal liability, even though D has been responsible for that person's death. Something more is required to justify imposing punishment. In *Adomako* (1995), the House of Lords confirmed that the correct test for this extra element was 'gross negligence'. This confirmed a line of case law dating back to the nineteenth century (albeit a line which had been temporarily broken by the appearance of objective recklessness in the early 1980s). In one of the early cases, *Doherty* (1887) 16 Cox CC 306, the judge said that 'the kind of forgetfulness which is common to everybody' or 'a slight want of skill' might give rise to civil damages, but for criminal liability there had to 'be culpable negligence of a grave kind'. In *Bateman* (1925), which involved negligent treatment by a doctor which caused the patient to die, Lord Hewart CJ explained the gross negligence test as follows:

JUDGMENT

'In explaining to juries the test which they should apply to determine whether the negligence, in the particular case, amounted to or did not amount to a crime, judges have used many epithets such as "culpable", "criminal", "gross", "wicked", "clear", "complete". But whatever epithet be used or not, in order to establish criminal liability the facts must be such that, in the opinion of the jury, the negligence of the accused went beyond a mere matter of compensation between subjects and showed such disregard for the life and safety of others as to amount to a crime against the state and conduct deserving punishment.'

This test received approval from the House of Lords in *Andrews v DPP* (1937), which involved manslaughter through negligent driving. Lord Atkin said that 'Simple lack of care as will constitute civil liability is not enough. For purposes of the criminal law there are degrees of negligence, and a very high degree of negligence is required to be proved.' Lord Atkin excluded from the scope of gross negligence manslaughter 'mere inadvertence'. For inadvertence to amount to criminal behaviour, D must have had 'criminal disregard' for others' safety, or 'the grossest ignorance or the most criminal inattention'. In *Stone and Dobinson* (1977), Lane LJ offered the following guidance:

JUDGMENT

'What the prosecution have to prove is a breach of ... duty in such circumstances that the jury feel convinced that [D]'s conduct can properly be described as reckless, that is to say a reckless disregard of danger to the health and welfare of the infirm person. Mere inadvertence is not enough. [D] must be proved to have been indifferent to an obvious risk of injury to health, or actually to have foreseen the risk but to have determined nevertheless to run it.'

In *Adomako*, however, Lord Mackay stated that the test for the jury to consider was 'whether the extent to which [D]'s conduct departed from the proper standard of care incumbent on him, involving as it must have done a risk of death ... was such that it should be judged criminal'. But is a 'risk of death' essential? Lane LJ set the standard much lower, with indifference to 'an obvious risk to health' being enough for liability. This issue has now been clarified by the Court of Appeal in *Misra and Srivastava* (2004), discussed below. The test for 'gross negligence' may also be criticised for circularity: it tells the jury to convict if they think D was guilty of a crime. However, in *Adomako*, Lord Mackay said:

JUDGMENT

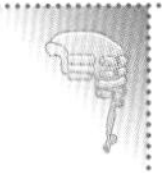

'It is true that to a certain extent this involves an element of circularity, but in this branch of law I do not believe that it is fatal to its being correct as a test of how far conduct must depart from accepted standards to be characterised as criminal. This is necessarily a question of degree and an attempt to specify that degree more closely is I think likely to achieve only a spurious precision. The essence of the matter, which is supremely a jury question, is whether, having regard to the risk of death involved, the conduct of the defendant was so bad in all the circumstances as to amount in their judgment to a criminal act or omission.'

CASE EXAMPLE

Adomako [1995] 1 AC 171

D was employed as an anaesthetist. One day he was supposed to be supervising the breathing equipment during surgery to repair V's detached retina. During the operation, an essential breathing tube became disconnected. However, D failed to notice anything wrong, until after V went into cardiac arrest nine minutes later, by which time it was too late (V lapsed into a coma and eventually died six months later of hypoxia). The prosecution called two witnesses who described D's failure to notice the problem as 'abysmal' and said that a competent anaesthetist would have recognised the problem 'within 15 seconds'. The jury convicted and D's conviction was upheld by the Court of Appeal and House of Lords.

In *Misra and Srivastava* [2004] EWCA Crim 2375; [2005] 1 Cr App R 21, the Court of Appeal held that the ingredients of gross negligence manslaughter involved no uncertainty which offended against art 7 of the European Convention on Human Rights. It had been argued that the implementation of the ECHR into British law via the Human Rights Act 1998 meant that the principles set out in *Adomako* were no longer good law. Judge LJ disagreed with that argument. He said (emphasis added):

JUDGMENT

'The question for the jury was not whether D's negligence was gross and whether, *additionally*, it was a crime, but whether his behaviour was grossly negligent and *consequently* criminal. This was not a question of law, but one of fact, for decision in the individual case ... [Gross negligence manslaughter] involves an element of uncertainty about the outcome of the decision-making process, but not unacceptable uncertainty about the offence itself. In our judgment the law is clear. The ingredients of the offence have been clearly defined, and the principles decided in the House of Lords in *Adomako*. They involve no uncertainty.'

Another point which arose in *Misra* was whether a risk of death was essential in gross negligence manslaughter cases. On this point, Judge LJ said:

JUDGMENT

'In our judgment, where the issue of risk is engaged, *Adomako* demonstrates, and it is now clearly established, that it relates to the risk of death, and is not satisfied by the risk of bodily injury or injury to health. In short, the offence requires gross negligence in circumstances where what is at risk is the life of an individual to whom the defendant owes a duty of care. As such it serves to protect his or her right to life.'

CASE EXAMPLE

Misra and Srivastava [2004] EWCA Crim 2375; [2005] 1 Cr App R 21

D and E were senior house officers at Southampton General Hospital responsible for the post-operative care of a young man, V, who had undergone surgery to repair his patella tendon on 23 June 2000. He became infected with *Staphylococcus aureus* but the condition was untreated and he died on 27 June 2000. It was alleged that V died as a result of D and E's gross negligence in failing to identify and treat the severe infection from which he died. The Court of Appeal dismissed their appeals.

KEY FACTS

Key facts on gross negligence manslaughter

Elements	Comment	Cases
Duty of care	D must owe V a duty of care. The civil concept of negligence applies. The fact that V was party to an illegal act is not relevant.	*Adomako* (1995) *Donoghue v Stevenson* (1932) *Wacker* (2003), *Willoughby* (2004)
Examples of duty situations	• Duty under contract. • Voluntary assumption of care. • Duty of landlord to tenant. • Driver of motor vehicle to road users and own passengers. • Captain of ship to crew.	*Pittwood* (1902), *Adomako* (1995) *Stone and Dobinson* (1977) *Singh* (1999) *Andrews* (1937), *Wacker* (2003) *Litchfield* (1998)

Breach of duty	This can be by an act or an omission. Involves falling below the standard of the reasonable person.	*Adomako* (1995)
Gross negligence	Going beyond a matter of mere compensation ... showing such disregard for the life and safety of others as to amount to a crime.	*Bateman* (1925)
	A very high degree of negligence.	*Andrews* (1937)
	Conduct so bad in all the circumstances as to amount to a criminal act or omission.	*Adomako* (1995)
	Gross negligence relates to nothing less than a risk of death.	*Misra* (2004)

ACTIVITY

Applying the law

In *Holloway* [1994] QB 302, D was a professional electrician who was prosecuted for manslaughter after wrongly connecting wiring in a new house, with the result that one of the householders was fatally electrocuted. His conviction was quashed by the Court of Appeal because of a misdirection (the trial judge had used the objective recklessness test instead of gross negligence). Imagine you were the presiding judge in a case involving these facts. How would you direct the jury on the meaning of the following?

(a) duty of care
(b) breach of duty
(c) gross negligence.

10.4.3 Reckless manslaughter

Until recently it was unclear whether this form of manslaughter still existed after *Adomako* (1995). However, in *Lidar* [2000] (unreported), the Court of Appeal dismissed an appeal which was based on an alleged misdirection, the trial judge having referred to recklessness (and not gross negligence) as the criterion for liability. Evans LJ said that 'the judge was correct in his view that this was a case of "reckless" manslaughter and to direct the jury accordingly ... the recklessness direction in fact given made the gross negligence direction superfluous and unnecessary'. As to the meaning of 'reckless' manslaughter, Evans LJ said that the question was whether D 'was aware of the necessary degree of risk of serious injury to the victim and nevertheless chose to disregard it, or was indifferent to it'.

CASE EXAMPLE

Lidar [2000] (unreported)

D was part of a group that had been asked to leave a public house in Leicester. The group got into a Range Rover with D in the driving seat. D's brother, who was in the front passenger seat, then shouted something at V, a doorman at the pub, who approached the vehicle and put his arms through the open passenger window. At that point, D started to drive off, with V now half-in and half-out of the window. The Range Rover left the car park and 'sped up the road'. After about 225 metres, V was dragged under the rear wheel and suffered fatal injuries. D's manslaughter conviction was upheld on appeal.

10.4.4 Reform

In its paper *A New Homicide Act for England & Wales?* (Consultation Paper No 177), published in December 2005, the Law Commission proposed that reckless manslaughter (defined as occurring where D acted with 'reckless indifference' to causing death) should be upgraded to 'second-degree murder' (see further section 10.9 on this point).

The Commission also proposed that the remaining two forms of involuntary manslaughter should be retained, albeit with some changes from the present law. The Commission proposed that D should be guilty of manslaughter when:

- D committed a criminal act, intending to cause physical harm or with foresight that there was a risk of causing physical harm. This would redefine constructive manslaughter. The main difference is that the proposal requires foresight by D of at least a risk of causing harm (a subjective test). The present *Church* test of dangerousness is based on whether 'all sober and reasonable people' would recognise the risk (an objective test).
- Death occurred as a result of D's conduct falling far below what could reasonably be expected in the circumstances, where there was a risk that D's conduct would cause death and this risk would have been obvious to a reasonable person in D's position. D must have had the capacity to appreciate the risk. This essentially describes what is presently gross negligence manslaughter.

The Commission essentially repeated these proposals in its Final Report, *Murder, Manslaughter and Infanticide* (Law Com No 304), published in November 2006, although there are differences in terms of the details. One is that 'second-degree murder' would include killings where D

- was aware that their conduct posed a serious risk of death; and
- had intent to cause either some injury, a fear of injury, or a risk of injury.

The 2006 definition of constructive manslaughter is also slightly different – it is defined as occurring where death was caused by a criminal act

- intended to cause injury, or
- where there was an awareness that the act involved a serious risk of causing injury.

10.5 Causing or allowing the death or serious physical harm of a child or vulnerable adult

Section 5(1) of the Domestic Violence, Crime and Victims Act 2004 (as amended by the Domestic Violence, Crime and Victims (Amendment) Act 2012) provides that it is an offence to cause or allow the death or serious physical harm of a child or vulnerable adult. It was enacted to deal with situations where a child or vulnerable adult lives with at least two other people in the same household and dies as the result of an unlawful act committed by one of them, but where it might be difficult to prove who exactly was responsible, especially if the other people all blame each other. Section 5(1) provides as follows:

SECTION

'A person ("D") is guilty of an offence if –

(a) a child or vulnerable adult ("V") dies or suffers serious physical harm as a result of the unlawful act of a person who –
  (i) was a member of the same household as V, and
  (ii) had frequent contact with him,
(b) D was such a person at the time of that act,
(c) at that time there was a significant risk of serious physical harm being caused to V by the unlawful act of such a person, and
(d) either D was the person whose act caused V's death or serious physical harm or
  (i) D was, or ought to have been, aware of the risk mentioned in paragraph (c),
  (ii) D failed to take such steps as he could reasonably have been expected to take to protect V from the risk, and
  (iii) the act occurred in circumstances of the kind that D foresaw or ought to have foreseen.'

A 'child' is defined in s 5(6) as a person under the age of 16, while a 'vulnerable adult' means a 'person aged 16 or over whose ability to protect himself from violence, abuse or neglect is significantly impaired through physical or mental disability or illness, through old age or otherwise'.

The case of *Ikram and Parveen* [2008] EWCA Crim 586; [2008] 4 All ER 253 perfectly illustrates the situation for which the new offence was created.

CASE EXAMPLE

Ikram and Parveen [2008] EWCA Crim 586; (2008) 4 All ER 253

D and E lived together along with D's 16-month-old son from a previous relationship. One morning, V was found dead in his cot. The post-mortem revealed that V had died of a 'fat embolism' (when fat enters the blood stream) caused by a broken leg, plus several other injuries, including three fractured ribs and bruises and abrasions to various parts of his body. Both D and E, who were the only adults in the house in the hours leading up to V's death, denied any knowledge as to how the broken leg was caused. Although charges of murder were brought against both D and E, these were eventually dropped given the difficulty in proving which one had caused V's broken leg. Instead, they were both convicted under s 5 of causing or allowing the death of V, and the Court of Appeal upheld their convictions.

However, the s 5 offence can be committed in other ways. In *Mujuru* [2007] EWCA Crim 2810; [2007] 2 Cr App R 26, D had gone to work leaving her live-in partner, Jerry Stephens, alone with her four-month-old daughter, V, despite knowledge of his history of violence. On a previous occasion, Stephens had broken V's arm. On the fateful day, Stephens killed V either by striking her head with an instrument or by slamming her head into a hard surface. Stephens was convicted of murder and D was convicted under s 5. The Court of Appeal dismissed her appeal, holding that the jury had been entitled to conclude that, by going to work and leaving V in Stephens' care, knowing that he had broken her arm on a previous occasion, D had 'failed to take such steps as she could reasonably have been expected to take to protect' V from the 'significant risk of serious physical harm' posed by Stephens.

Khan and others [2009] EWCA Crim 2; [2009] 1 Cr App R 28 involved the death of a 'vulnerable adult'. V, aged 19, was murdered by her husband. His two sisters and brother-in-law, who all lived in the same house, were convicted under s 5 of allowing V's death. Medical evidence revealed that V had suffered numerous injuries to her head and neck, and 15 rib fractures, 'sustained over an extended period of time in the course of three distinct attacks'. The Court of Appeal dismissed the appeals, holding that V was potentially 'vulnerable' after the first attack on her, this being a question of fact for the jury.

The Court of Appeal went on to provide some important guidance on when an adult might be classed as 'vulnerable'. The Court refused to 'rule out the possibility that an adult who is utterly dependent on others, even if physically young and apparently fit, may fall within the protective ambit of the Act'. The Court also held that 'the state of vulnerability envisaged by the Act does not need to be long-standing. It may be short, or temporary. A fit adult may become vulnerable as a result of accident, or injury, or illness. The anticipation of a full recovery may not diminish the individual's temporary vulnerability.'

10.6 Causing death by dangerous driving

Section 1 of the Road Traffic Act (RTA) 1988 (as substituted by s 1 of the RTA 1991) provides that 'A person who causes the death of another person by driving a mechanically propelled vehicle dangerously on a road or other public place is guilty of an offence.' This replaced the previous offence of causing death by reckless driving. The meaning of 'dangerous driving' is set out in s 2A.

SECTION

'2A(1) For the purposes of section 1 ... above a person is to be regarded as driving dangerously if (and subject to subsection (2) below, only if):

(a) the way he drives falls far below what would be expected of a competent and careful driver, and

(b) it would be obvious to a competent and careful driver that driving in that way would be dangerous.

(2) A person is also to be regarded as driving dangerously ... if it would be obvious to a competent and careful driver that driving the vehicle in its current state would be dangerous.

(3) In subsections (1) and (2) above dangerous refers to danger either of injury to any person or of serious damage to property; and in determining for the purposes of those subsections what would be expected of or obvious to a competent and careful driver in a particular case, regard shall be had not only to the circumstances of which he could be expected to be aware but also to any circumstances shown to have been within the knowledge of the accused.

(4) In determining for the purposes of subsection (2) above the state of a vehicle regard may be had to anything attached to or carried on or in it and to the manner in which it is attached or carried.'

The manner of the driving must be dangerous, or the condition of the vehicle (whether from lack of maintenance or positive alteration) must make it dangerous. It is not enough that the inherent design of the vehicle makes it dangerous to be on a public road, if authorisation has been granted under road traffic regulations. This was vividly demonstrated in *Marchant and Muntz* [2003] EWCA Crim 2099; [2004] 1 WLR 442, involving the use of an agricultural vehicle on public roads.

CASE EXAMPLE

Marchant and Muntz [2003] EWCA Crim 2099; [2004] 1 WLR 442

E, a Warwickshire farmer, owned a Matbro TR250 loading machine, an agricultural vehicle with a grab attached at the front for lifting and moving large round hay bales. The grab consisted of nine spikes each one metre in length. E gave instructions to an employee, D, to take the vehicle on to a public road to deliver some hay bales. D was stopped, waiting to make a turn on to a farm track when V, a motorcyclist, approached at high speed (estimated at 80 m.p.h.) from the opposite direction, collided with the vehicle and was impaled on one of the spikes. He suffered injuries described as 'catastrophic' and died. D and E were convicted, respectively, of causing death by dangerous driving and procuring the offence. The Court of Appeal quashed the convictions. The machine was authorised for use on public roads by virtue of the Motor Vehicles (Authorisation of Special Types) General Order (SI 1979 No 1198) 1979 and the Court of Appeal held there was nothing dangerous in the way D had driven it. Grigson J said that 'where the state of a vehicle is inherent and the vehicle is authorised for use on the road and is being used in a rural area in which agricultural machinery is frequently driven along country roads, we consider that some reference to these facts should be made to the jury'.

Section 2B of the 1988 Act creates a new offence of causing death by careless, or inconsiderate, driving. Section 2B was inserted by the Road Safety Act 2006. It provides

SECTION

'2B A person who causes the death of another person by driving a mechanically propelled vehicle on a road or other public place without due care and attention, or without reasonable consideration for other persons using the road or place, is guilty of an offence.'

Section 3A of the 1988 Act (as inserted by the 1991 Act) creates offences of causing death 'by driving a mechanically propelled vehicle on a road or other public place without due care and attention, or without reasonable consideration for other persons', provided one of three aggravating factors are present:

- D was unfit to drive through drink or drugs.
- D was over the prescribed alcohol limit.
- D fails to provide a specimen within 18 hours without reasonable excuse.

10.7 Infanticide

Section 1(1) of the Infanticide Act 1938 (as amended by s 57 of the Coroners and Justice Act 2009) provides as follows:

SECTION

'1(1) Where a woman by any wilful act or omission causes the death of her child being a child under the age of 12 months, but at the time of the act or omission the balance of her mind was disturbed by reason of her not having fully recovered from the effect of giving birth to the child or by reason of the effect of lactation consequent upon the birth of the child, then, if the circumstances were such that but for this Act the offence would have amounted to murder or manslaughter, she shall be guilty of [an offence], to wit of infanticide, and may for such offence be dealt with and punished as if she had been guilty of the offence of manslaughter of the child.'

infanticide
Defence/offence where a woman kills her own child under 12 months

Infanticide is both a partial defence to murder and an offence in its own right. The purpose of the defence/offence is to avoid the mandatory life sentence for murder and allow the judge discretion in sentencing. On a charge of murder, there is an evidential burden on D to produce some evidence that 'the balance of her mind was disturbed'; it is then for the prosecution to disprove this. Where the prosecution charges infanticide, then it bears the burden of proving that the balance of the mother's mind was disturbed.

Section 1(1) was amended by the Coroners and Justice Act 2009 in response to the Court of Appeal's ruling in *Gore* [2007] EWCA Crim 2789, to the effect that the only *mens rea* requirement for infanticide was that D acted (or omitted to do so) 'wilfully'.

The Court of Appeal specifically rejected the suggestion that malice aforethought had to be proven in infanticide cases. The Court stated that Parliament, in enacting the 1938 Act, intended the offence of infanticide to be broader than murder, and to allow for infanticide convictions without having to force a mother who had killed her own child to have to deal with allegations that she had intended to kill or seriously injure the child. The purpose of the offence, therefore, was to show compassion to women who had killed their own baby.

However, the government realised that the judgment in *Gore* meant that convictions of infanticide could be obtained in cases that would not otherwise amount to manslaughter, never mind murder, purely on the basis that D had acted (or omitted to act) 'wilfully'. Hence, the wording of s 1(1) has been amended to make clear that infanticide can only be proven 'if the circumstances were such that but for this Act the offence would have amounted to murder or manslaughter'.

Another problem was identified in an earlier Court of Appeal case, *Kai-Whitewind* [2005] EWCA Crim 1092; [2005] Cr App R 31.

CASE EXAMPLE

Kai-Whitewind [2005] EWCA Crim 1092; [2005] Cr App R 31

D had been convicted of murdering her three-month-old son after refusing to give evidence at her own trial, instead maintaining that his death was the result of unexplained, but natural, causes. All the expert evidence presented at trial, however, indicated that the baby had been deliberately starved of oxygen. Although there was evidence that D had suffered a form of postnatal depression, this had not been presented during the trial, and the Court of Appeal upheld D's murder conviction. Lord Judge LJ pointed out that in some cases where infanticide might be available (the clear implication being that the present case was one of them) the defence was not pleaded because the mother's mind was still 'disturbed' and this meant that she was unable to admit the killing. Lord Judge suggested that there were several possible reasons for this: D might still be too unwell, or 'too emotionally disturbed by what she has in fact done, or too deeply troubled by the consequences of an admission of guilt on her ability to care for any surviving children'.

In its 2008 Consultation Paper, the government refers to this exact situation, but describes it as 'a theoretical problem', and does not suggest any proposals to deal with it.

10.8 Offences against a foetus

10.8.1 Child destruction

The offence of child destruction, under s 1(1) of the Infant Life (Preservation) Act 1929, makes it a criminal offence for a person to cause a child to die 'before it has an existence independent of its mother'. Section 1(2) adds that 'evidence that a woman had ... been pregnant for a period of 28 weeks or more shall be prima facie proof that she was at that time pregnant [with] a child capable of being born alive'. Section 1(1) imposes a mental element: D must have had 'intent to destroy the life of a child capable of being born alive'. A defence is provided in s 1(1), if the act which causes the death of the child was 'done in good faith for the purpose only of preserving the life of the mother'. This can be regarded as a specific example of the necessity defence (see Chapter 8).

10.8.2 Procuring a miscarriage

The crime of procuring a miscarriage is contained in s 58 OAPA 1861. This provides that a pregnant woman who 'with intent to procure her own miscarriage' administers to herself 'any poison or other noxious thing' or uses 'any instrument or other means whatsoever' to carry out that intent commits the offence. Section 58 adds that any person with the same intent who administers poison or uses an instrument to a woman – whether she is in fact pregnant or not – is also guilty of an offence. The offence is now subject to a defence available in s 1 of the Abortion Act 1967 (as amended by s 37 of the Human Fertilisation and Embryology Act 1990). The 1967 Act allows for abortions to be carried out by a registered medical practitioner, subject to various safeguards.

ACTIVITY

Applying the law

1. D has been married for 15 years. Over the last two years he has become increasingly convinced that his wife, V, has been having an affair and this has made him anxious and depressed. For this his doctor has prescribed mildly sedative drugs. D has also taken to drinking, often on his own in pubs after work and at home when V is out, ostensibly working late or with friends. This has led him to put on weight. D and V have argued about the amount of time she spends out of the house. One night they have a particularly heated row, during which V says that if D wasn't such a 'miserable bastard' she wouldn't feel the need to go out so much. She then leaves the room and goes upstairs. D goes into the kitchen to pour himself a whisky. As he drinks he broods on V's behaviour and her comment about him. Eventually he goes upstairs to the bedroom, where V is already in bed reading, and begins to undress. As he does so V looks up and points at D's paunch: 'Not exactly Brad Pitt, are we?' she says. At this, D feels his temper rising. He picks up a pair of scissors from the dressing table and waves them in V's face. 'What the hell are you doing that for?' she cries and tries to grab the scissors. There is a brief struggle during which the scissors end up embedded in V's neck. At D's trial for murder, he pleads the following defences:
   (a) Lack of intent to kill or cause grievous bodily harm. He admits waving the scissors in V's face but says this was purely out of a desire to frighten his wife and stop her taunting him.
   (b) Loss of self-control.
   (c) Diminished responsibility.

Consider D's liability.

2. Consider whether the Law Commission's proposals to reform involuntary manslaughter should be adopted.
3. D, a 16-year-old schoolboy, has a predilection for playing with matches. One evening he deliberately sets fire to a pile of newspapers that has been left at the back of a newsagent's shop. The fire quickly spreads and, within minutes, the shop itself is in flames. D runs off.

A passer-by calls the fire brigade, who arrive soon afterwards and begin to tackle the fire, which has now spread to neighbouring shops. One of the firemen goes inside one of the shops to check for signs of anyone being inside. Tragically, while he is inside the roof collapses and the fireman is killed.

Consider D's liability for:

(a) constructive manslaughter
(b) gross negligence manslaughter
(c) reckless manslaughter.

10.9 Reform of the law of homicide

In December 2005, the Law Commission published a Paper entitled *A New Homicide Act for England and Wales?* (Consultation Paper No 177). This proposed a sweeping reform of murder, and voluntary and involuntary manslaughter – most interestingly, they proposed a new idea of a three-tier structure for homicide offences. Unsurprisingly, the Paper attracted considerable academic attention, which was broadly supportive of the new three-tier structure although there were disagreements about the details. Victor Tadros, in 'The homicide ladder' (2006) 69 MLR 601, was not untypical of the commentators. He said:

QUOTATION

'Overall, the Commission's proposals are impressive, imaginative and detailed. The range of issues considered is broad, and the technicalities in the area are addressed with vigour. However, there are also some weaknesses both in the offence definitions and the role of defences ... The law at present is, in a sense, the worst of both worlds. Some morally significant elements such as common *mens rea* concepts are picked out, but poorly defined. A narrow range of partial defences does some work to avoid the worst consequences of that, but not nearly enough to result in a system that is even broadly fair ... The Commission's proposals would remedy some of these defects significantly ... However, some defects still remain ... the range of partial defences would still, in my view, be too narrow ... more importantly, extant partial defences would only operate in relation to first degree murder ... A consequence is that the category difference between second degree murder and manslaughter would reflect moral differences between cases only in the crudest manner.'

After 11 months of consultation, and no doubt cognisant of the academic analysis, the Commission published its Final Report, entitled *Murder, Manslaughter and Infanticide* (Law Com No 304) in November 2006. In it, they retain the idea of a three-tier structure and endorse most of their 2005 proposals. However, there are some differences.

10.9.1 The structure of homicide offences

The Law Commission proposes a new three-point structure (penalties on conviction in brackets):

- first-degree murder (mandatory life);
- second-degree murder (discretionary life);
- manslaughter (fixed term maximum).

10.9.2 First-degree murder

This would cover all unlawful killings where D was proved to have

- intent to kill; or

- intent to do serious injury and where D was also aware that his or her conduct posed a serious risk of death;

unless D could plead a partial defence, of which there would be three (diminished responsibility, provocation – now abolished and replaced by the 'loss of self-control' defence – and suicide pact). If one of the partial defences was pleaded successfully, it would reduce D's liability to second-degree murder (not voluntary manslaughter – this category of homicide would cease to exist). In 2005, the Law Commission had proposed a narrower definition of first-degree murder where D had intent to kill only. However, that idea was later dropped on the basis that the offence would be too narrow and difficult to prove.

10.9.3 Second-degree murder

This would include all unlawful killings where:

- D had the intent required for first-degree murder but pleaded one of the partial defences.
- D had intent to do serious injury but was not aware of a serious risk of death.
- D was aware that their conduct posed a serious risk of death and had intent to cause
    - some injury, or
    - a fear of injury, or
    - a risk of injury.

This third category essentially describes what is presently reckless manslaughter, and hence that offence would be upgraded from involuntary manslaughter to murder under the Law Commission's latest proposals.

The Commission did consider the creation of another category of murder, which could be described as 'aggravated murder'. This could include, for example, serial killers (those who kill on more than one occasion) and/or those who kill using torture. Alternatively, it could include those whose killings cause fear amongst a group within society, for example killings with a racist motive. However, the Commission eventually decided that, instead of recommending the creation of a new offence, such killings would remain as murder (whether first or second degree) and their aggravating features would be 'best reflected though an uncompromising approach to the length of the minimum custodial sentence imposed'.

The government's response to these proposals was less than enthusiastic. Paragraph 9 of the Ministry of Justice's Consultation Paper *Murder, Manslaughter and Infanticide: Proposals for Reform of the Law*, published in July 2008, noted that the Law Commission's recommendations for reform of voluntary manslaughter (mostly now implemented in the Coroners and Justice Act 2009) were 'predicated on their proposed new offence structure' and then stated that 'The wider recommendations in the Law Commission's report may be considered at a later stage of the review.'

10.9.4 Manslaughter

The Law Commission's proposals to reform involuntary manslaughter have already been examined in detail earlier in this chapter. It should also be noted that, as a consequence of the Commission's proposal to abolish voluntary manslaughter, there would be no need to refer to 'involuntary' manslaughter either. The third tier of homicide would simply be called 'manslaughter'.

10.9.5 Intention

The 2005 Paper proposed two models. First, there could be a definition of intention, as follows: 'D acts intentionally with respect to a consequence if he acts (i) to bring it about or (ii) knowing that it will be virtually certain to occur.' This would finally equate foresight of a virtually certain consequence with intention, as opposed to it being merely evidence of intention. Second, codification of *Woollin*: this would mean that foresight of a virtually certain consequence would remain as evidence of intention, allowing juries to 'find' it. In 2006, the Commission recommended adopting the second model, that is, codification of *Woollin*.

10.9.6 Duress

In 2005, the Law Commission recommended that duress should become a new partial defence to first-degree murder – available where D was threatened with 'death or life-threatening harm'. By 2006, however, the Commission's position had changed and it now recommends that duress should be a full defence to murder and attempted murder. In other words, the House of Lords' decisions in *Howe* [1986] QB 626 and *Gotts* [1992] 2 AC 412 (discussed in Chapter 8) would be overruled. The government's response to the Law Commission's proposals (published in July 2008) did not address either of these proposals.

10.9.7 A single offence of criminal homicide?

Back in 2005, the Law Commission rejected this idea on the basis that it was too wide, as it would include everyone from a hired contract killer to a battered wife to a negligent doctor. The Commission pointed out that the labels of 'murder' and 'manslaughter' serve a function and reflect different levels of culpability.

ACTIVITY

Self-test questions

Discuss whether the Law Commission's 2006 proposals resolve all of the existing defects and problems within the law of homicide. In particular, consider the following:

- Should murder be split into first and second degrees? If so, how should the different offences be defined?
- Is it right that the partial defences should be available to charges of first-degree murder only?
- Should duress be (a) a full defence to murder; (b) a partial defence to murder; (c) no defence to murder at all?
- Should reckless manslaughter be upgraded to second-degree murder?

SUMMARY

- Murder is the unlawful killing of another human being under the King or Queen's Peace with malice aforethought (an intention to kill or do grievous bodily harm).
- There are three special and partial defences capable of reducing D's liability from murder to voluntary manslaughter: diminished responsibility (s 2, Homicide Act 1957, as amended), loss of self-control (ss 54 and 55, Coroners and Justice Act 2009) and suicide pact (s 4, Homicide Act 1957).
- There are three forms of involuntary manslaughter (where D unlawfully kills but without malice aforethought): constructive manslaughter (killing as the result of an

unlawful and dangerous act), gross negligence manslaughter (killing as the result of a grossly negligent breach of a duty of care involving a risk of death) and reckless manslaughter (killing with foresight of an unjustifiable risk of death or serious harm).

- There are other homicide offences: causing or allowing the death of a child or vulnerable adult, under s 5 of the Domestic Violence, Crime and Victims Act 2004; causing death by dangerous driving under s 1 of the Road Traffic Act 1988 (as amended); infanticide, under s 1 of the Infanticide Act 1938 (as amended).
- The law of voluntary manslaughter has recently been completely overhauled by Parliament in the Coroners and Justice Act 2009, so the focus of attention may now shift to reform of involuntary manslaughter. The Law Commission has made reform proposals here. The Law Commission has also proposed reclassifying homicide by introducing 'degrees' of murder.

LEGAL PROBLEM SOLVING

Consider the following situation:

Ronnie is a drug dealer. One day, he is visited by one of his regular clients, Marco, a heroin addict. Marco complains that his withdrawal symptoms are much worse than usual and demands twice his usual amount of heroin. Ronnie knows that giving a heroin addict more than their usual amount can often be fatal and he tells Marco this. However, Marco is insistent and gives Ronnie the extra money. Ronnie prepares the syringe. Marco's hands are shaking with withdrawal symptoms so he asks Ronnie to perform the injection. Ronnie does so. Within five minutes, however, it is obvious that Marco is suffering a very bad reaction to the drugs. Ronnie takes Marco outside to a bus shelter and calls for an ambulance on his mobile phone. He tells the emergency operator that there is a 'druggie' in the bus shelter.

The ambulance arrives ten minutes later and Marco is taken to hospital. He is very pale and shaking. The doctor on the accident and emergency ward, Doctor Hastie, gives Marco a quick examination. He concludes that Marco is actually suffering from a bad flu. He prescribes some antibiotics and discharges him. Marco staggers off but collapses and dies in the street 20 minutes later from heart failure brought on by a heroin overdose.

Answering the question

Identifying the facts

The main facts are:

1. Marco is a 'regular client' of Ronnie's.
2. Marco injects Ronnie with heroin.
3. Marco suffers an 'obvious' bad reaction.
4. Ronnie leaves Marco at a bus shelter.
5. Doctor Hastie gives Marco a 'quick' examination.
6. Marco dies from a heroin overdose.

From these, now identify the areas of law involved.

1. This suggests that Ronnie lacks direct intent to kill or seriously injure Marco.
2. This is the administration of a noxious substance, contrary to s 23 OAPA 1861. It is also an unlawful and dangerous act for the purposes of constructive manslaughter.

3. This may impose a duty of care on Ronnie sufficient to establish gross negligence manslaughter.
4. The issues here are (a) whether Ronnie has breached any duty of care that he may have owed to Marco; (b) if so, whether the negligence is 'gross'.
5. There are three issues here: (a) whether Doctor Hastie has breached his duty of care to Marco; (b) if so, whether the negligence is 'gross'; (c) whether Doctor Hastie's negligence breaks the chain of causation between the heroin injection performed by Ronnie and Marco's death.
6. Death has been caused, so we need to consider homicide.

Having identified the areas of law, you must now explain them in more detail, especially where there is some doubt on the point. So, now look at the relevant law in detail and apply it.

1. Murder

Explain

The definition of murder is causing the unlawful death of another human being under the Queen's Peace with malice aforethought. There is no doubt that Marco is a human being and that the events occur under the Queen's Peace, so there is no need to elaborate on those issues.

Causation requires proof that D caused V's death both in fact and law. Factual causation involves the 'but for' test (*White* [1910] 2 KB 124) whereas legal causation involves establishing that the original injury remains the 'operating' and 'substantial' cause (*Smith* [1959] 2 QB 35). According to *Pagett* (1983) 76 Cr App R 279, D's acts need not be the sole or even the main cause of death provided that they make a 'significant' contribution to V's death. When medical negligence occurs, only negligence which is both 'independent' and 'potent' such that D's contribution can be regarded as insignificant breaks the causal chain (*Cheshire* [1991] 1 WLR 844).

'Malice aforethought' means an intention to kill or cause grievous bodily harm (*Cunningham* [1982] AC 566; *Attorney-General's Reference (No. 3 of 1994)* [1998] AC 245). Grievous bodily harm means 'really serious injury' (*DPP v Smith* [1961] AC 290). Intention can be direct (D's aim, purpose or desire) or oblique (where intention can be 'found' by a jury if there is evidence that D foresaw death or GBH as a virtual certainty (*Woollin* [1999] 1 AC 82).

Apply

Ronnie is potentially liable for murder if causation and malice aforethought can be proven.

Presumably, Marco would not have died in exactly the same way had Ronnie not injected so much heroin into him, so factual causation can be proven. Does Dr Hastie break the causal chain? Probably not. The heroin overdose remains the 'operating' and 'substantial' cause (*Smith*); Dr Hastie's negligence is probably not so 'independent' and 'potent' that Ronnie's contribution can be regarded as insignificant (*Cheshire*). The fact that Ronnie is not the sole cause of death (arguably, he is not even the main cause) does not exonerate him, provided that the jury are sure that he made a 'significant' contribution (*Pagett*).

Presumably, Ronnie does not desire the death of Marco, one of his regular clients (and an income source), but a jury would be entitled to 'find' that Ronnie intended to kill (or do at least GBH) on the evidence that he foresaw Marco's death (or serious injury) as a virtual certainty. This is because Ronnie 'knows that giving a heroin addict more than their usual amount can often be fatal'.

2. Constructive manslaughter

Explain

Constructive manslaughter is defined as causing V's death by an unlawful, dangerous act. The act (but not the death) must be intentional (*DPP v Newbury and Jones* [1977] AC 500). There must be an act, as opposed to an omission (*Lowe* [1973] QB 702). The act must be 'unlawful' – this means in the criminal, as opposed to civil, sense of the word (*Franklin* (1883) 15 Cox CC 163). The act must also be 'dangerous', which means an 'act which is likely to injure another person' (*Larkin* [1943] KB 174); one which all sober and reasonable men would recognise as posing a risk of 'some harm' (*Church* [1966] 1 QB 59). 'Harm' means physical harm (*Dawson and others* (1985) 81 Cr App R 150). The unlawful, dangerous act must cause death (*Dalby* [1982] 1 All ER 916).

Apply to Ronnie

Ronnie may be liable for constructive manslaughter based on the administration of a noxious substance, as in *Cato* [1976] 1 All ER 260. This is an unlawful act, contrary to s 23 OAPA 1861. It is dangerous, applying the *Larkin/Church* test, as it subjects Marco to the risk of some physical harm. The injection is clearly an act and it was performed intentionally. Causation has already been dealt with in the context of murder, above.

Apply to Doctor Hastie

Doctor Hastie's cursory examination of Marco may well be negligent but he has not committed an unlawful (in the criminal sense of the word) act and so cannot be convicted of constructive manslaughter.

3. Gross negligence manslaughter

Explain

Gross negligence manslaughter can be defined as causing V's death through the 'grossly negligent' breach of a duty of care. A duty of care is essentially a civil concept. In the context of gross negligence manslaughter can be imposed via a sufficiently close relationship, through the assumption of responsibility (*Stone and Dobinson* [1977] QB 354; *Ruffell* [2003] EWCA Crim 122), through an employment relationship, through a doctor/ patient relationship (*Bateman* (1927) 19 Cr App R 8; *Adomako* [1995] 1 AC 171; *Misra and Srivastava* [2004] EWCA Crim 2375), through the creation of a dangerous situation (*Miller*; *Evans* [2009] 1 WLR 1999) and in many other ways.

A breach of duty occurs when D falls below a reasonable standard of care and competence (*Bateman*). Gross negligence implies 'a very high degree of negligence' (*Andrews v DPP* [1937] AC 576) that D's conduct was 'so bad in all the circumstances' as to amount to a criminal act or omission (*Adomako*). The breach of duty must cause death.

Apply to Ronnie

Ronnie probably does not owe Marco a duty of care based purely on their drug dealer/ drug addict relationship (*Khan and Khan* [1998] Crim LR 830). However, Ronnie may owe Marco a duty of care based on the assumption of responsibility for him (as in *Ruffell*) or based on the creation of a dangerous situation (as in *Evans*). Ronnie's efforts in taking Marco to the bus stop and leaving him there, albeit after phoning for an ambulance, may or may not breach Ronnie's duty of care. Ultimately a jury would need to decide this. A jury would also need to decide whether or not any breach of duty that had occurred was so sufficiently 'bad' as to amount to gross negligence. Causation has already been dealt with in the context of murder, above.

Apply to Doctor Hastie

Doctor Hastie owes Marco a duty of care based on the doctor/patient relationship. Doctor Hastie's 'quick' examination may or may not breach Ronnie's duty of care. Ultimately a jury would need to decide this. A jury would also need to decide whether or not any breach of duty that had occurred was so sufficiently 'bad' as to amount to gross negligence. Causation has already been dealt with in the context of murder, above.

Conclusion

Ronnie may be liable for the manslaughter of Marco, based on constructive manslaughter or gross negligence. Doctor Hastie's negligence is unlikely to break the causal chain. Ronnie may even be liable for the murder of Marco, but proving malice aforethought would be difficult.

Doctor Hastie may also be liable for the manslaughter of Marco, based on gross negligence.

SAMPLE ESSAY QUESTION

In enacting the Coroners and Justice Act 2009, Parliament has done an admirable job in updating the defence of diminished responsibility. Discuss.

Give brief outline of the old law (s 2, Homicide Act 1957):

- Defence which may reduce murder liability to manslaughter
- Burden of proof on D, on the balance of probabilities
- An 'abnormality of the mind'
- Caused by a 'condition of arrested or retarded development of mind' or 'any inherent causes' or 'induced by disease or injury'
- D's mental responsibility must have been 'substantially impaired' This meant more than trivial but not necessarily total impairment (*Lloyd* (1967))

Identify examples of conditions giving rise to the defence, e.g.

- Pychopathic states (*Byrne* (1960))
- Schizophrenia (*Terry* (1961))
- Depression (*Seers* (1984); *Gittens* (1984); *Ahluwalia* (1992))
- Battered woman syndrome (*Hobson* (1998))
- Alcohol dependence syndrome (*Wood* (2008); *Stewart* (2009))
- Does not include intoxication (*Fenton* (1975); confirmed in *Dowds* (2012)). Where D had some underlying condition and was intoxicated as well, the question is whether the underlying condition on its own amounted to an abnormality of mind (*Gittens, Dietschmann* (2003); *Hendy* (2006))

Discuss why the law needed to be updated:

- Definitions (such as 'retarded development') were out of date
- Definitions (such as 'abnormality of mind' and 'mental responsibility') were too vague

Discuss changes made by the Coroners and Justice Act 2009, e.g.

- 'Abnormality of mind' changed to 'abnormality of mental functioning'
- List of causes in s 2 – replaced by 'recognised medical condition'
- D's abnormality must 'substantially impair' D's ability to (i) understand the nature of his conduct, (ii) form a rational judgment or (iii) exercise self-control (replaces 'mental responsibility')
- The abnormality must provide an 'explanation' for the killing (a new criterion)

Consider whether the reform achieves its objective:

- New definitions are clearer and more specific than the old, vague definitions
- Some uncertainty remained, e.g. the relationship between alcoholism and intoxication – more case law inevitable
- Burden of proof is still on D rather than prosecution – should this have been reversed?

Conclude

SAMPLE ESSAY QUESTION

Constructive manslaughter should be abolished. It is fundamentally unfair to convict anyone of a homicide offence based on a different and far less serious offence, such as battery or criminal damage. Discuss.

Give a brief outline of the law:

- Constructive manslaughter occurs when D intentionally commits an unlawful, dangerous act which causes death (*Mitchell* (1983))
- There is no need for D to have foreseen the consequence of the act (*DPP v Newbury & Jones* (1977))

Explain the 'unlawful act' element with examples, e.g.

- There must be an act not a mere omission (*Lowe* (1973))
- The unlawful act must be a criminal offence (*Franklin* (1883))
- The criminal offence could be, e.g. assault/battery/ABH (*Mitchell, Pagett* (1984)); theft (*Willett* (2010)); robbery (*Dawson* (1985)); burglary (*Watson* (1989)); criminal damage (*Newbury & Jones*); arson (*Goodfellow* (1986); *Willoughby* (2004)); administering a noxious substance (*Cato* (1976)); affray (*Carey* (2006)); endangering road users (*Meeking* (2012))

Explain the 'dangerousness' element:

- The act must be 'dangerous' (*Larkin* (1943))
- This is tested objectively (*Church* (1965)) – foresight by reasonable people of the risk of 'some harm'
- This means some physical harm (*Dawson, Carey*)

Explain the causation element:

- The unlawful act must cause death
- Ordinary rules of causation apply (*Pagett*)
- Where D administers an unlawful drug to V who overdoses and dies, D faces liability (*Cato*). But where D provides V with a drug and V self-injects, the chain of causation is broken (*Kennedy* (2007))

Discuss areas of doubt/uncertainty, e.g.

- Question why an omission does not suffice
- Discuss whether *Church* sets too low a threshold for manslaughter liability. Should the test not require the risk of serious harm, at least?
- Discuss whether the *Church* test should be subjective, instead of objective
- Consider whether *Dawson/Carey* contradict the 'thin skull' rule
- Consider whether there is a clear distinction between the situations in *Cato* and *Kennedy*

Discuss implications of abolition, e.g.

- Constructive manslaughter cases would be charged as either gross negligence or reckless manslaughter instead
- The former requires a duty of care to be established while the latter is based on subjective awareness of a risk of death/serious injury
- Note that there is overlap already (*Willoughby*)

Conclude

Further reading

Articles

Baker, D and Zhao, L, 'Contributory qualifying and non-qualifying triggers in the loss of control defence: a wrong turn on sexual infidelity' (2012) 76 J Crim L 254.

Coe, P, 'Justifying reverse burdens of proof: a tale of diminished responsibility and a tangled knot of authorities' (2013) 77 J Crim L 360.

Gibson, M, 'Intoxicants and diminished responsibility: the impact of the Coroners and Justice Act 2009' [2011] Crim LR 909.

Herring, J, 'Familial homicide, failure to protect and domestic violence: who's the victim?' [2007] Crim LR 923.

Hirst, M, 'Murder under the Queen's Peace' [2008] Crim LR 541.

Keating, H and Bridgeman, J, 'Compassionate killings: the case for a partial defence' (2012) 75 MLR 697.

Kennefick, L, 'Introducing a new diminished responsibility defence in England and Wales' (2011) 74 MLR 750.

Williams, G, 'Gross negligence manslaughter and duty of care in "drugs" cases: R v Evans' [2009] Crim LR 631.

Withey, C, 'Loss of control, loss of opportunity?' [2011] Crim LR 263.

11

Non-fatal offences against the person

AIMS AND OBJECTIVES

student mentor tip

'Reflecting on the *actus reus* and *mens rea* aspect of all new areas of criminal law you study will ensure you grasp the basics of criminal law thoroughly.'
Gayatri, University of Leicester

After reading this chapter you should be able to:

- Understand the *actus reus* and *mens rea* of common assault
- Understand the *actus reus* and *mens rea* of occasioning actual bodily harm (s 47)
- Understand the *actus reus* and *mens rea* of malicious wounding/inflicting grievous bodily harm (s 20)
- Understand the *actus reus* and *mens rea* of wounding or causing grievous bodily harm with intent (s 18)
- Understand factors which may aggravate an assault
- Analyse critically the law on non-fatal offences against the person
- Apply the law to factual situations to determine whether there is liability for non-fatal offences against the person

The main offences are set out in the Offences Against the Person Act 1861 (OAPA). This Act merely tidied up the then existing law by putting all of the offences into one Act. It did not try to create a coherent set of offences, and as a result, there have been many problems in the law. There have been many proposals for reform. In 1980, the Criminal Law Revision Committee made recommendations in its 14th Report, *Offences Against the Person*, Cmnd 7844 (1980). The Law Commission adopted these ideas, first in its Draft Criminal Code (1989) and then in 1993 in its report *Legislating the Criminal Code: Offences against the Person and General Principles*. In February 1998 the Home Office issued a Consultation Document, *Violence: Reforming the Offences Against the Person Act 1861*. This pointed out that the 1861 Act 'was itself not a coherent statement of the law but a consolidation of much older law. It is therefore not surprising that the law has been widely criticised as archaic and unclear and that it is now in urgent need of reform.' The consultation document included a draft Bill (see section 11.5). Despite all of this, Parliament, as yet, has not reformed the law.

The main offences are based on whether the victim was injured; if there were injuries, their level of seriousness; and the intention of the defendant. The main offences, in ascending order of seriousness, are:

- assault – contrary to s 39 of the Criminal Justice Act 1988;
- battery – contrary to s 39 of the Criminal Justice Act 1988;
- assault occasioning actual bodily harm – contrary to s 47 OAPA;
- malicious wounding or inflicting grievous bodily harm – contrary to s 20 OAPA;
- wounding or causing grievous bodily harm with intent – contrary to s 18 OAPA.

11.1 Common assault

There are two ways of committing this:

- assault
- battery.

Assault and battery are common law offences. There is no statutory definition for either assault or battery. However, statute law recognises their existence, as both of these offences are charged under s 39 Criminal Justice Act 1988 which states:

SECTION

'39 Common assault and battery shall be summary offences and a person guilty of either of them shall be liable to a fine not exceeding level 5 on the standard scale, to imprisonment for a term not exceeding six months, or to both.'

The definitions of both assault and battery, therefore, come from case law. In *Collins v Wilcock* [1984] 3 All ER 374, Goff LJ gave the standard definitions:

JUDGMENT

'The law draws a distinction … between an assault and a battery. An assault is an act which causes another person to apprehend the infliction of immediate, unlawful, force on his person; a battery is the actual infliction of unlawful force on another person.'

As can be seen, the act involved is different for assault and battery. For assault there is no touching, only the fear of immediate, unlawful, force. For battery there must be actual force. There are often situations in which both occur. For example, where the defendant approaches the victim shouting that he is going to 'get him', then punches the victim in the face. The approaching and shouting are an assault, while the punch is the battery. As the act is different for each, it is easier to consider assault and battery separately.

11.1.1 *Actus reus* of assault

An assault is also known as a technical assault or a psychic assault. There must be

- an act
- which causes the victim to apprehend the infliction of immediate, unlawful force.

Act

An assault requires some act or words. In *Fagan v Metropolitan Police Commissioner* [1968] 3 All ER 442, where the defendant failed to remove his car from a police officer's foot, the court thought that an omission was not sufficient to constitute an assault. However, they decided that there was a continuing act in this case (see section 11.1.2). In *Lodgon v DPP*

[1976] Crim LR 121, D opened a drawer in his office to show another person that there was a gun in it, which D said was loaded. In fact the gun was a fake. The actions of D were held to amount to an assault.

Words are sufficient for an assault. These can be verbal or written. In *Constanza* [1997] Crim LR 576, the Court of Appeal held that letters could be an assault. D had written 800 letters and made a number of phone calls to the victim. The victim interpreted the last two letters as clear threats. The Court of Appeal said that there was an assault, as there was a 'fear of violence at some time, not excluding the immediate future'. In *Ireland* (1997) 4 All ER 225, it was held that even silent telephone calls can be an assault. It depends on the facts of the case.

Apprehend immediate unlawful force

The important point is that the act or words must cause the victim to apprehend that immediate force is going to be used against them. There is no assault if the situation is such that it is obvious that the defendant cannot actually use force. For example, where the defendant shouts threats from a passing train, there is no possibility that he can carry out the threats in the immediate future. It was decided in *Lamb* [1967] 2 All ER 1282 that pointing an unloaded gun at someone who knows that it is unloaded cannot be an assault. This is because the other person does not fear immediate force. However, if the other person thought the gun was loaded, then this could be an assault.

Fear of immediate force is necessary; immediate does not mean instantaneous, but 'imminent', so an assault can be through a closed window, as in *Smith v Chief Superintendent of Woking Police Station* [1983] Crim LR 323.

CASE EXAMPLE

Smith v Chief Superintendent of Woking Police Station [1983] Crim LR 323

D got into a garden and looked through the victim's bedroom window on the ground floor at about 11 p.m. The victim was terrified and thought that he was about to enter the room. Although D was outside the house and no attack could be made at that immediate moment, the court held that the victim was frightened by his conduct. The basis of the fear was that she did not know what D was going to do next but that it was likely to be of a violent nature. Fear of what he might do next was sufficiently immediate for the purposes of the offence.

The same line of reasoning was taken in *Ireland* (1997) regarding the fear that a telephone call might generate. Lord Steyn in the House of Lords said:

JUDGMENT

'It involves questions of fact within the province of the jury. After all, there is no reason why a telephone caller who says to a woman in a menacing way "I will be at your door in a minute or two" may not be guilty of an assault if it causes his victim to apprehend immediate personal violence. Take now the case of the silent caller. He intends by his silence to cause fear and he is so understood. The victim is assailed by uncertainty about his intentions. Fear may dominate her emotions, and it may be the fear that the caller's arrival at her door may be imminent. She may fear the possibility of immediate personal violence. As a matter of law the caller may be guilty of an assault: whether he is or not will depend on the circumstance and in particular on the impact of the caller's potentially menacing call or calls on the victim.'

Words indicating there will be no violence may prevent an act from being an assault. This is a principle which comes from the old case of *Tuberville v Savage* (1669) 1 Mod Rep 3, where D placed one hand on his sword and said, 'If it were not assize time, I would not take such language from you.' This was held not to be an assault, but there are other cases where words have not negatived the assault. For example in *Light* (1857) D & B 332, the defendant raised a sword above his wife's head and said, 'Were it not for the bloody policeman outside, I would split your head open.' It was held that this was an assault. These cases are difficult to reconcile, but it could be argued that in *Tuberville* (1669) D did not even draw his sword, while in *Light* D had raised the sword above his wife's head, giving her clear cause to apprehend that immediate unlawful force would be used.

Fear of any unwanted touching is sufficient: the force or unlawful personal violence which is feared need not be serious.

There are many examples of assault, for example

- raising a fist as though about to hit the victim;
- throwing a stone at the victim which just misses;
- pointing a loaded gun at someone within range;
- making a threat by saying 'I am going to hit you'.

Unlawfulness of the force

The force which is threatened must be unlawful. If it is lawful, there is no offence of common assault. When force is lawful or unlawful is discussed in detail under battery at section 11.1.2.

11.1.2 *Actus reus* of battery

The *actus reus* of battery is the actual infliction of unlawful force on another person. Force is a slightly misleading word as it can include the slightest touching, as shown by the case of *Collins v Wilcock* (1984).

CASE EXAMPLE

Collins v Wilcock [1984] 3 All ER 374

Two police officers saw two women apparently soliciting for the purposes of prostitution. The appellant was asked to get into the police car for questioning but she refused and walked away. As she was not known to the police, one of the officers walked after her to try to find out her identity. She refused to speak to the officer and again walked away. The officer then took hold of her by the arm to prevent her leaving. She became abusive and scratched the officer's arm. She was convicted of assaulting a police officer in the execution of his duty. She appealed against that conviction on the basis that the officer was not acting in the execution of his duty but was acting unlawfully by holding the defendant's arm as the officer was not arresting her. The court held that the officer had committed a battery and the defendant was entitled to free herself.

Goff LJ said in his judgment:

JUDGMENT

'The fundamental principle, plain and incontestable, is that every person's body is inviolate. It has long been established that any touching of another person, however slight, may amount to battery . . . As Blackstone wrote in his Commentaries, "the law cannot draw the line between different degrees of violence, and therefore totally prohibits the first and lowest stage of it; every man's person being sacred, and no other having a right to meddle with it, in any the slightest manner." The effect is that everybody is protected not only against physical injury but against any form of physical molestation.'

Goff LJ also pointed out that touching a person to get his attention was acceptable, provided that no greater degree of physical contact was used than was necessary but that while touching might be acceptable, physical restraint was not. He also said that 'persistent touching to gain attention in the face of obvious disregard may transcend the norms of acceptable behaviour'.

Even touching the victim's clothing can be sufficient to form a battery. In *Thomas* (1985) 81 Cr App Rep 331, D touched the bottom of a woman's skirt and rubbed it. The Court of Appeal said, *obiter*, 'There could be no dispute that if you touch a person's clothes while he is wearing them that is equivalent to touching him.'

Hostility

There are conflicting case decisions on whether there needs to be any element of hostility in a battery. In *Faulkner v Talbot* [1981] 3 All ER 468, Lord Lane CJ said that a battery 'need not necessarily be hostile'. However in *Wilson v Pringle* [1986] 2 All ER 440, a civil case, in which one schoolboy sued another for injuries caused when they were fooling around in the corridor at school, it was suggested that the touching must be 'hostile'. Croome-Johnson LJ in the Court of Appeal said:

JUDGMENT

'In our view the authorities lead to the conclusion that in a battery there must be an intentional touching or contact in one form or another of the plaintiff by the defendant. That touching must be proved to be a hostile touching. That still leaves unanswered the question, when is a touching to be called hostile? Hostility cannot be equated with ill-will or malevolence. It cannot be governed by the obvious intention shown in acts like punching, stabbing or shooting. It cannot be solely governed by an expressed intention, although that may be strong evidence. But the element of hostility, in the sense in which it is now to be considered, must be a question of fact for the tribunal of fact.'

In a later civil case, *F v West Berkshire Health Authority* [1989] 2 All ER 545, Lord Goff doubted whether there was a requirement that the touching need be hostile. Yet in *Brown* [1993] 2 All ER 75, a case on sadomasochism (see section 11.2.3), Lord Jauncey in the House of Lords approved the judgment of Croome-Johnson LJ in *Wilson v Pringle* (1986). However, he added that if the defendant's actions are unlawful, they are necessarily hostile. This appears to remove any real meaning from 'hostility' in relation to battery as the key element of a battery is the application of unlawful force.

Continuing act

A battery may be committed through a continuing act, as in *Fagan v Metropolitan Police Commander* (1969).

CASE EXAMPLE

Fagan v Metropolitan Police Commander [1969] 1 QB 439; [1968] 3 All ER 442

D parked his car with one of the tyres on a police officer's foot. When he parked he was unaware that he had done this, but when the police officer asked him to remove it, he refused to do so for several minutes. The court described this as 'an act constituting a battery which at its inception was not criminal because there was no element of intention, but which became criminal from the moment the intention was formed to produce the apprehension which was flowing from the continuing act'.

Indirect act

A battery can also be through an indirect act such as use of a booby trap. In this situation the defendant causes force to be applied, even though he does not personally touch the victim. This occurred in *Martin* (1881) 8 QBD 54, where the defendant placed an iron bar across the doorway of a theatre. He then switched off the lights. In the panic which followed, several of the audience were injured when they were trapped and unable to open the door. Martin was convicted of an offence under s 20 of the OAPA 1861. A more modern example is seen in *DPP v K* [1990] 1 All ER 331.

CASE EXAMPLE

DPP v K [1990] 1 All ER 331

D, a 15-year-old schoolboy, without permission took sulphuric acid from his science lesson to try its reaction on some toilet paper. While he was in the toilet he heard footsteps in the corridor, panicked and put the acid into a hot air hand drier to hide it. He returned to his class intending to remove the acid later. Before he could do so another pupil used the drier and was sprayed by the acid. The defendant was charged with assault occasioning actual bodily harm (s 47). The magistrates acquitted him because he said he had not intended to hurt anyone (see section 11.2.2 for the *mens rea* of s 47).

The prosecution appealed by way of case stated to the Queen's Bench Divisional Court. On the point of whether a common assault (remember this includes both an assault and a battery) could be committed by an indirect act, Parker LJ said:

JUDGMENT

'The position was correctly and simply stated by Stephen J in *R v Clarence* (1888) 22 QBD 23 where he said: "If man laid a trap for another into which he fell after an interval, the man who laid the trap would during the interval be guilty of an attempt to assault, and of an actual assault as soon as the man fell in."

In the same way a defendant who pours a dangerous substance into a machine just as truly assaults the next user of the machine as if he had himself switched the machine on.'

Another example of indirect force occurred in *Haystead v Chief Constable of Derbyshire* [2000] Crim LR 758, where the defendant caused a small child to fall to the floor by punching the woman holding the child. The defendant was found guilty because he was reckless as to whether his acts would injure the child. It is worth noting that, in this case, the conviction could also be justified by the principle of transferred malice.

Omissions

Criminal liability can arise by way of an omission, but only if the defendant is under a duty to act. Such a duty can arise out of a contract or a relationship, from the assumption of care for another or from the creation of a dangerous situation (see Chapter 2, section 2.3). As the *actus reus* of battery is the application of unlawful force, it is difficult to think how examples could arise under these duty situations, but there has been one reported case, *DPP v Santana-Bermudez* [2003] EWHC 2908 where it appears possible that the Divisional Court accepted an omission as sufficient.

CASE EXAMPLE

DPP v Santana-Bermudez [2003] EWHC 2908

In this case a policewoman, before searching the defendant's pockets, asked him whether he had any needles or other sharp objects on him. The defendant said 'no', but when the police officer put her hand in his pocket she was injured by a needle which caused bleeding. The Divisional Court held that the defendant's failure to tell her of the needle could amount to the *actus reus* for the purposes of an assault causing actual bodily harm.

Kay J said:

JUDGMENT

'where someone (by an act or word or a combination of the two) creates a danger and thereby exposes another to a reasonable foreseeable risk of injury which materialises, there is an evidential basis for the *actus reus* of an assault occasioning actual bodily harm. It remains necessary for the prosecution to prove an intention to assault or appropriate recklessness.'

This appears to rely on the principle set in *Miller* [1983] 1 All ER 978 where D accidentally set fire to his mattress but failed to do anything to prevent damage to the building in which he was sleeping.

Another scenario which could make a defendant liable by way of omission under *Miller* is if there had been other people asleep in the room and D had not awakened them to warn them of the danger, and one of them had been hit by plaster which fell from the ceiling as a result of the fire, then there appears no reason why D could not have been charged with battery of that person. It is noticeable that in the draft Bill in 1998 (see section 11.5), it was proposed that only intentionally causing serious injury could be committed by omission; the equivalent of battery would not be able to be committed by omission.

Consent

Where the other person consents to the touching, then there is no battery as there is no unlawful force. This was illustrated by *Slingsby* [1995] Crim LR 570, which was a charge of involuntary manslaughter by an unlawful act.

CASE EXAMPLE

Slingsby [1995] Crim LR 570

The defendant and the victim had taken part in sexual activity which was described as 'vigorous' but which had taken place with the victim's consent. During this a signet ring which the defendant was wearing caused an injury to the victim, and this led to blood poisoning from which she died. The victim's consent meant that there was no battery or other form of assault, and so the defendant was held to be not guilty of manslaughter as there was no unlawful act.

There must, however, be true consent. In *Tabassum* [2000] Crim LR 686, D had persuaded women to allow him to measure their breasts for the purpose of preparing a database for sale to doctors. The women were fully aware of the nature of the acts he proposed to do, but they said they consented only because they thought that D had either medical qualifications or medical training. The Court of Appeal approved the trial judge's direction when he said: 'I should prefer myself to say that consent in such cases does not exist at all, because the act consented to is not the act done. Consent to a surgical operation or examination is not consent to sexual connection or indecent behaviour.'

Implied consent

There are also situations in which the courts imply consent to minor touchings. These are the everyday situations in which there is a crowd of people and it is impossible not to have some contact. In *Wilson v Pringle* (1986) it was held that the ordinary 'jostlings' of everyday life were not battery. This was also said in *Collins v Wilcock* (1984):

JUDGMENT

'Although we are all entitled to protection from physical molestation, we live in a crowded world in which people must be considered as taking on themselves some risk of injury (where it occurs) from the acts of others which are not in themselves unlawful.

Generally speaking, consent is a defence to a battery; and most of the physical contacts of ordinary life are not actionable because they are impliedly consented to by all who move in society and so expose themselves to the risk of bodily contact. So nobody can complain of the jostling which is inevitable from his presence in, for example, a supermarket, an underground station or a busy street; nor can a person who attends a party complain if his hand is seized in friendship, or even if his back is (within reason) slapped.'

This also applies to contact sports. When a person takes part in sports such as rugby or judo, he is agreeing to the contact which is part of that sport. However, if the contact goes beyond what is reasonable, then it is possible for an offence to be committed. For example, a rugby player consents to a tackle within the rules of the game, but he does not consent to an opposition player stamping on his head. See Chapter 8, section 8.6, for a fuller discussion on consent as a defence.

Unlawful force

For a battery to be committed, the force must be unlawful. As seen above, the force may be lawful if the victim gives a genuine consent to it. Force may also be lawful where it is used in self-defence or prevention of crime (see Chapter 8, section 8.5). If the force used is reasonable in the situation, then the person using the force is not guilty of a battery. The police can use reasonable force to arrest a person, but if they are not arresting the person, then it is unlawful to use force, however slight. This was shown by *Wood (Fraser) v DPP* [2008] EWHC 1056 (Admin).

CASE EXAMPLE

Wood (Fraser) v DPP [2008] EWHC 1056 (Admin)

The police had received a report that a man named Fraser had thrown an ashtray at another person in a public house. The ashtray had missed the person but had been smashed. Three police officers went to the scene. They saw a man (the appellant, W) who fit the description of 'Fraser' coming out of the public house. One of the police officers took hold of W by the arm and asked if he was Fraser. W denied this and struggled, trying to pull away. At that point another officer took hold of W's other arm. W was charged with assaulting two of the police officers while they were acting in the execution of their duty.

The police officer who had first caught hold of W's arm said that he had done this in order to detain W, but was not at that point arresting him. It was held that as the officer had not arrested W, then there was a technical assault (battery) by the police officers. This meant that W was entitled to struggle and was not guilty of any offence of assault against the police.

Battery without an assault

It is possible for there to be a battery even though there is no assault. This can occur where the victim is unaware that unlawful force is about to be used on him, such as where the attacker comes up unseen behind the victim's back. The first thing the victim knows is when he is struck; there has been a battery but no assault.

11.1.3 *Mens rea* of assault and battery

The *mens rea* for an assault is either an intention to cause another to fear immediate unlawful personal violence, or recklessness as to whether such fear is caused. The *mens rea* for battery is either an intention to apply unlawful physical force to another, or recklessness as to whether unlawful force is applied. So intention or recklessness is sufficient for both assault and battery.

In *Venna* [1975] 3 All ER 788, the Court of Appeal rejected arguments that only intention would suffice for the mental element of all assault-based offences:

JUDGMENT

'We see no reason in logic or in law why a person who recklessly applies physical force to the person of another should be outside the criminal law of assault. In many cases the dividing line between intention and recklessness is barely distinguishable.'

The test for recklessness is subjective. For an assault, the defendant must realise there is a risk that his acts/words could cause another to fear unlawful personal violence. For a battery the defendant must realise there is a risk that his act (or omission) could cause unlawful force to be applied to another.

Assault and battery are classed as offences of basic intent. This means that if the defendant is intoxicated when he does the relevant *actus reus* he is reckless. This was considered by the House of Lords in *DPP v Majewski* [1976] 2 All ER 142, where D had consumed large quantities of alcohol and drugs and then attacked people in a public house and also the police officers who tried to arrest him. Lord Elwyn-Jones said:

JUDGMENT

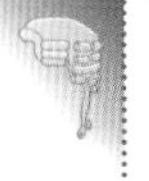

'If a man of his own volition takes a substance which causes him to cast off the restraints of reason and conscience, no wrong is done to him by holding him answerable criminally for any injury he may do while in that condition. His course of conduct in reducing himself by drink and drugs to that condition in my view supplies the evidence of *mens rea*, of guilty mind certainly sufficient for crime of basic intent. It is a reckless course of conduct and recklessness is enough to constitute the necessary *mens rea* in assault cases.'

This ruling can be criticised, as the point at which the drink or drugs is taken is a quite separate time to the point when the *actus reus* for the offence is committed. It is difficult to see how there is coincidence of the two. It is reasonable to say that the defendant is reckless when he takes drink or other intoxicating substances, but this does not necessarily mean that when he commits an assault or battery three or four hours later, he is reckless for the purposes of the offence. The decision can be viewed as a public policy decision.

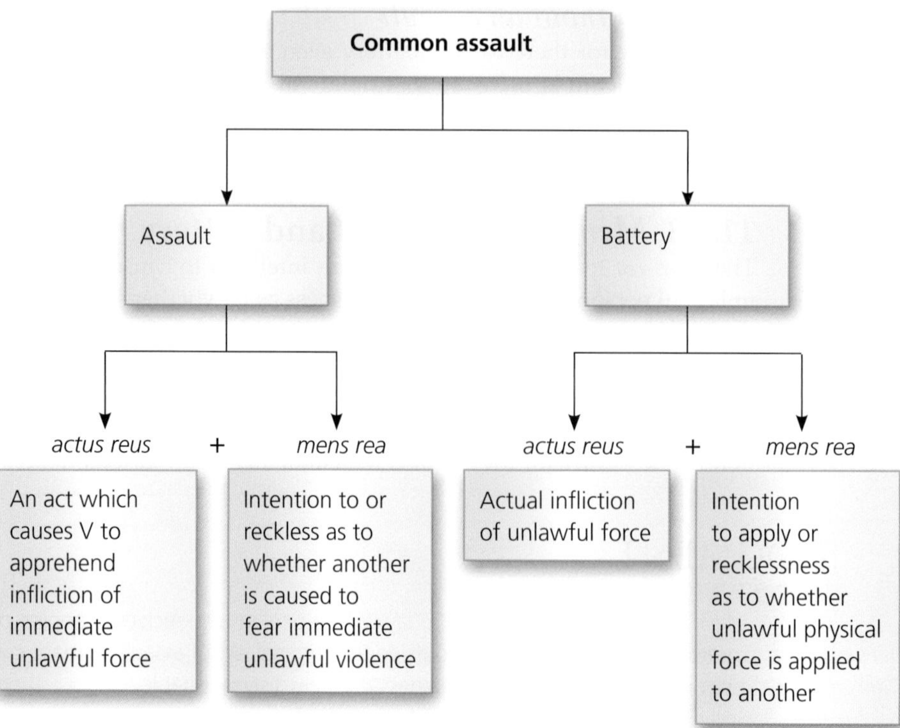

Figure 11.1 Assault and battery.

ACTIVITY

Applying the law

Explain whether there is an assault and/or battery in the following situations.

1. Rick and Sue are having an argument. During the argument, Rick says 'If you don't shut up I'll thump you.' Sue is so annoyed at this that she gets out a penknife and waves it in front of Rick's face.
2. At a party Tanya sneaks up behind William and slaps him on the back.
3. Vince throws a stone at Una, but misses. He picks up another stone, and this time hits the loose end of Una's scarf.
4. Grant turns round quickly without realising that Harry is standing just behind him and bumps into Harry. Harry shouts at him, 'If you were not wearing glasses, I would hit you in the face.'

11.2 Section 47

We now look at assaults where an injury is caused. The lowest level of injury is referred to as 'actual bodily harm', and it is an offence under s 47 of the OAPA 1861, which states:

SECTION

'47 Whosoever shall be convicted of any assault occasioning actual bodily harm shall be liable . . . to imprisonment for five years.'

The offence is triable either way.

As can be seen from this very brief section, there is no definition of 'assault' or 'actual bodily harm'. Nor is there any reference to the level of *mens rea* required. For all these points it is necessary to look at case law.

11.2.1 *Actus reus* of s 47

This requires

- a technical assault or a battery, which must
- occasion (i.e. cause)
- actual bodily harm.

Actual bodily harm

actual bodily harm
Any physical or mental harm

In *Donovan* [1934] 2KB 498 the court said that the ordinary meaning of *'actual bodily harm'* was: 'any hurt or injury calculated to interfere with the health or comfort of the [victim]. Such hurt or injury need not be permanent, but must, no doubt, be more than merely transient and trifling.'

In *R(T) v DPP* [2003] Crim LR 622, the assault caused the victim to lose consciousness briefly. The court held that although the harm might be transient it was not trifling. Loss of consciousness, even momentarily, was held to be actual bodily harm.

So s 47 can be charged where there is any injury. Bruising, grazes and scratches all come within this.

In *DPP v Smith (Michael)* [2006] 2 All ER 16; [2006] 2 Cr App R 1, it was decided that even cutting the victim's hair can amount to actual bodily harm.

CASE EXAMPLE

DPP v Smith (Michael) [2006] 2 All ER 16; [2006] 2 Cr App R 1

D had had an argument with his girlfriend. He cut off her ponytail and some hair from the top of her head without her consent. He was charged with an offence under s 47 of the OAPA 1861. The magistrates found that there was no case to answer as cutting hair could not amount to actual bodily harm. The Divisional Court allowed the prosecution's appeal by way of case stated, holding that cutting off a substantial amount of hair could amount to actual bodily harm. They remitted the case to the justices for the case to continue.

In the judgment, Sir Igor Judge (P) held that physical pain was not a necessary ingredient of actual bodily harm. He said:

JUDGMENT

'In my judgment, whether it is alive beneath the surface of the skin or dead tissue above the surface of the skin, the hair is an attribute and part of the human body. It is intrinsic to each individual and to the identity of each individual ... Even if, medically and scientifically speaking, the hair above the surface of the scalp is no more than dead tissue, it remains part of the body and is attached to it. While it is so attached, in my judgment it falls within the meaning of "bodily" in the phrase "actual bodily harm".'

One area which was less certain was whether psychiatric injury could be classed as 'actual bodily harm'. This was resolved in *Chan Fook* [1994] 2 All ER 552, where the Court of Appeal ruled that psychiatric injury is capable of amounting to actual bodily harm.

JUDGMENT

'The first question on the present appeal is whether the inclusion of the word "bodily" in the phrase "actual bodily harm" limits harm to harm to the skin, flesh and bones of the victim … The body of the victim includes all parts of his body, including his organs, his nervous system and his brain. Bodily injury therefore may include injury to any of those parts of his body responsible for his mental and other faculties.'

However, the court stated that actual bodily harm does not include 'mere emotions such as fear, distress or panic', nor does it include 'states of mind that are not themselves evidence of some identifiable clinical condition'.

This decision was approved by the House of Lords in *Burstow* (1997) 4 All ER 225, where Lord Steyn said that 'bodily harm' in s 18, s 20 and s 47 must be interpreted so as to include recognisable psychiatric illness.

The matter was considered again by the Court of Appeal in *Dhaliwal* [2006] EWCA Crim 1139; [2006] All ER (D) 236. D was charged with manslaughter of his wife when she committed suicide. The prosecution relied on unlawful act manslaughter (see section 9.1.4). They, therefore, had to prove that D had committed an unlawful act. They tried to prove that D had inflicted psychological harm on his wife over a number of years. However, the prosecution failed because they were unable to prove that V had suffered any recognisable psychiatric illness. This meant that there was no offence under s 47, s 20 or s 18 of the OAPA 1861 and so no unlawful act for the purpose of proving manslaughter.

11.2.2 *Mens rea* of s 47

Section 47 makes no reference to *mens rea* but, as the essential element is a common assault, the courts have held that the *mens rea* for a common assault is sufficient for the *mens rea* of a s 47 offence. So the defendant must intend or be subjectively reckless as to whether the victim fears or is subjected to unlawful force. This is the same *mens rea* as for an assault or a battery, and there is no need for the defendant to intend or be reckless as to whether actual bodily harm is caused. In *Roberts* [1971] Crim LR 27 the defendant, who was driving a car, made advances to the girl in the passenger seat and tried to take her coat off. She feared that he was going to commit a more serious assault and jumped from the car while it was travelling at about 30 miles per hour. As a result of this she was slightly injured. He was found guilty of assault occasioning actual bodily harm, even though he had not intended any injury nor realised there was a risk of injury. He had intended to apply unlawful force when he touched her as he tried to take her coat off. This satisfied the *mens rea* for a common assault and so he was guilty of an offence under s 47.

This was confirmed by the House of Lords in the combined appeals of *Savage and Parmenter* (1991) 4 All ER 698.

CASE EXAMPLE

Savage (1991) 4 All ER 698

A woman in a pub threw beer over another woman. In doing this the glass slipped from the defendant's hand and the glass cut the victim's hand. The defendant said that she had only intended to throw beer over the woman. She had not intended her to be injured, nor had she realised that there was a risk of injury. She was convicted of a s 20 offence but the Court of Appeal quashed that and substituted a conviction under s 47 (assault occasioning actual bodily harm). She appealed against this to the House of Lords. The Law Lords dismissed her appeal.

The fact she intended to throw the beer over the other woman meant she had the intent to apply unlawful force, and this was sufficient for the *mens rea* of the s 47 offence. Lord Ackner said:

JUDGMENT

'The verdict of assault occasioning actual bodily harm may be returned upon proof of an assault together with proof of the fact that actual bodily harm was occasioned by the assault. The prosecution are not obliged to prove that the defendant intended to cause some actual bodily harm or was reckless as to whether such harm would be caused.'

11.2.3 Consent and s 47

There have been arguments as to whether consent could be a defence to a s 47 offence. Originally it was thought that it could be a defence where the injuries were not serious. However, in some cases, such as *Donovan* [1934] 2 KB 498, it was held that an unlawful act 'cannot be rendered lawful because the person to whose detriment it is done consents to it. No person can license another to commit a crime.' This is an area where the courts are prepared to limit the defence on the basis of public policy grounds. It is now accepted that consent is not a defence to a s 47 offence, unless it is one of the exceptions which have been recognised by the courts. Lord Jauncey in *Brown* (1993) pointed out that consent could be a defence to a common assault but not to another more serious assault where there was some injury, even if not serious:

JUDGMENT

'[T]he line properly falls to be drawn between assault at common law and the offence of assault occasioning actual bodily harm created by section 47 of the Offences Against the Person Act 1861, with the result that consent of the victim is no answer to anyone charged with the latter offence or with a contravention of section 20 unless the circumstances fall within one of the well-known exceptions such as organised sporting contests and games, parental chastisement or reasonable surgery. There is nothing in sections 20 and 47 to suggest that consent is either an essential ingredient of the offences or a defence thereto.'

This confirmed the decision by the Court of Appeal in *Attorney-General's Reference (No 6 of 1980)* [1981] 2 All ER 1057, where two young men agreed to fight in the street to settle their differences following a quarrel. The Court of Appeal held that consent could not be a defence to such an action as it was not in the public interest. Lord Lane CJ said:

JUDGMENT

'It is not in the public interest that people should try to cause, or should cause, each other bodily harm for no good reason. Minor struggles are another matter. So, in our judgment, it is immaterial whether the act occurs in private or public; it is an assault if actual bodily harm is intended and/or caused. This means that most fights will be unlawful regardless of consent.'

Lord Lane recognised that there were exceptions where consent might still be a defence, as he went on to say:

JUDGMENT

> 'Nothing which we have said is intended to cast doubt upon the accepted legality of properly conducted games and sports, lawful chastisement or correction, reasonable surgical interference, dangerous exhibitions, etc. These apparent exceptions can be justified as involving the exercise of a legal right, in the case of lawful chastisement or correction, or as needed in the public interest, in other cases.'

In deciding what was in the public interest, the courts have come to decisions which are difficult to reconcile. In *Brown* (1993) the House of Lords held that consent was not a defence to sadomasochistic acts done by homosexuals, even though all the participants were adult and the injuries inflicted were transitory and trifling. But in *Wilson* [1996] Crim LR 573, the Court of Appeal held that where a defendant branded his initials on his wife's buttocks with a hot knife at her request, this was not an unlawful act, even though she had to seek medical attention for the burns which were caused. It held it was not in the public interest that such consensual behaviour should be criminalised.

It is also odd that acts which have caused 'transitory and trifling' injuries are regarded as criminal, whereas very serious injuries can be deliberately inflicted in boxing because it is a recognised sport. This could be seen as showing the bias of the elderly white males, who make up the great majority of judges in our appeal courts. They approve of what they term 'manly sports'.

Consent in organised sport

In *Barnes* [2005] 2 All ER 113, D made a late tackle on V during an amateur football match. V suffered a serious leg injury. D was convicted of an offence contrary to s 20 of the OAPA 1861. On appeal, the Court of Appeal quashed his conviction. They held that criminal prosecutions should be reserved for those situations where the conduct was sufficiently grave to be properly categorised as criminal.

The Court of Appeal set out the following points:

- Consent is not normally available as a defence where there is bodily harm, but sporting activities are one of the exceptions to this rule.
- The exceptions are based on public policy.
- In contact sports, conduct which goes beyond what a player can reasonably be regarded as having accepted by taking part is not covered by the defence of consent.
- However, in a sport in which bodily contact is a commonplace part of the game, the players consent to such contact, even though an unfortunate accident or serious injury may result.

In deciding whether conduct in the course of a sport is criminal, the following factors should be considered:

- Intentional infliction of injury will always be criminal.
- For reckless infliction of injury – did the injury occur during actual play, or in a moment of temper or overexcitement when play has ceased?
- 'Off the ball' injuries are more likely to be criminal.
- The fact that the play is within the rules and practice of the game and does not go beyond it will be a firm indication that what has happened is not criminal.

Mistaken belief in consent

Where the defendant genuinely, but mistakenly, believes that the victim is consenting, then there is a defence to an assault. In this area the decisions of the courts are even more difficult to reconcile with the general principle that 'it is not in the public interest that people should try to cause, or should cause, each other bodily harm for no good reason'. In *Jones* (1986) 83 Cr App R 375, two schoolboys aged 14 and 15 were tossed into the air by older boys. One victim suffered a broken arm and the other a ruptured spleen. The defendants claimed they believed that the two victims consented to the activity. The Court of Appeal quashed their convictions for offences under s 20 of the OAPA 1861 because the judge had not allowed the issue of mistaken belief in consent to go to the jury. The Court held that a genuine mistaken belief in consent to 'rough and undisciplined horseplay' could be a defence, even if that belief was unreasonable. A similar decision was reached in *Aitken and others* [1992] 1 WLR 1006, where RAF officers poured white spirit over a colleague who was wearing a fire-resistant flying suit, but who was asleep and drunk at the time this was done. He suffered 35 per cent burns. Their convictions under s 20 were quashed, as the mistaken belief in the victim's consent should have been left to the jury.

In *Richardson and Irwin* [1999] Crim LR 494, it was even held that a drunken mistake that the victim was consenting to horseplay could be a defence to a charge under s 20. However, this decision is doubtful, as it is inconsistent with decisions that a drunken mistaken belief that a victim is consenting to sexual intercourse is not a defence to rape. For further discussion, see consent as a defence in Chapter 8, section 8.6.

11.3 Section 20

The next offence in seriousness is commonly known as 'malicious wounding'. It is an offence under s 20 of the OAPA 1861:

SECTION

'20 Whosoever shall unlawfully and maliciously wound or inflict any grievous bodily harm upon any other person, either with or without a weapon or instrument, shall be guilty of an offence and shall be liable ... to imprisonment for not more than five years.'

The offence is triable either way and the maximum sentence is five years. This is the same as for a s 47 offence, although s 20 is seen as a more serious offence and requires a higher degree of injury and *mens rea* as to an injury. For the offence to be proved, it must be shown that the defendant

- wounded or
- inflicted grievous bodily harm,

and that he did this

- intending some injury to be caused or
- being reckless as to whether some injury would be inflicted.

11.3.1 *Actus reus* of s 20

The *actus reus* can be committed by

- wounding or
- inflicting grievous bodily harm.

Wounding

wound
A cut of all the layers of skin

For this the defendant must have caused a **wound** to the victim. Originally it was thought that the wound had to be caused by an assault or a battery. However, in *Beasley* (1981) 73 Cr App R 44, the Court of Appeal held that the narrow view of assault given by the trial judge was not a necessary ingredient of the offence of unlawful wounding under s 20. The trial judge had defined assault as an act which causes the victim to apprehend the infliction of immediate unlawful force. The Court of Appeal held that unlawful wounding can be committed without the victim being frightened or aware of what is going on.

'Wound' means a cut or a break in the continuity of the whole skin. A cut of internal skin, such as in the cheek, is sufficient, but internal bleeding where there is no cut of the skin is not sufficient. In *ICC v Eisenhower* [1983] 3 All ER 230, the victim was hit in the eye by a shotgun pellet. This did not penetrate the eye but did cause severe bleeding under the surface. As there was no cut, it was held that this was not a wound. The cut must be of the whole skin, so that a scratch is not considered a wound. Even a broken bone is not considered a wound, unless the skin is broken as well. In the old case of *Wood* [1830] 1 Mood CC 278, the victim's collarbone was broken but, as the skin was intact, it was held there was no wound.

Inflicting grievous bodily harm

Section 20 uses the word 'inflict'. Originally this was taken as meaning that there had to be a technical assault or battery. Even so it allowed the section to be interpreted quite widely, as shown in *Lewis* [1974] Crim LR 647 where D shouted threats at his wife through a closed door in a second-floor flat and tried to break his way through the door. The wife was so frightened that she jumped from the window and broke both her legs. Lewis was convicted of a s 20 offence. The threats could be considered as a technical assault. However, it was thought there had to be an assault for s 20 to be committed. The issue was again considered in *Metropolitan Police Commissioner v Wilson* [1984] AC 242 where the House of Lords, following the Australian case of *Salisbury* [1976] VR 452, decided that 'inflict' does not imply an assault.

However, this left a problem because a contrast was drawn between this section and s 18, where the word 'cause' is used. It was thought that the word 'cause' was wider than 'inflict'. It was held that for 'cause', it was only necessary to prove that the defendant's act was a substantial cause of the wound or grievous bodily harm, whereas 'inflict' suggests a direct application of force. However, in *Mandair* [1994] 2 All ER 715, Lord Mackay said there was 'no radical divergence between the meaning of the two words'. In *Burstow* (1997) it was decided that 'inflict' does not require a technical assault or a battery. These decisions mean that there now appears to be little, if any, difference in the *actus reus* of the offences under s 20 and s 18. In *Burstow* (1997) Lord Hope said that for all practical purposes there was no difference between the words, and approved Lord Mackay's judgment in *Mandair* (1994). However, he went on to say:

JUDGMENT

'But I would add that there is this difference, the word "inflict" implies that the consequence of the act is something which the victim is likely to find unpleasant or harmful. The relationship between cause and effect, when the word "cause" is used, is neutral. It may embrace pleasure as well as pain. The relationship when the word "inflict" is used is more precise, because it invariably implies detriment to the victim of some kind.'

Grievous bodily harm

grievous bodily harm
Serious physical or mental harm

It was held in *DPP v Smith* [1961] AC 290 that **grievous bodily harm** means 'really serious harm'; but this does not have to be life threatening. In *Saunders* [1985] Crim LR 230 it was held that a direction to the jury which referred only to 'serious harm' was not a misdirection.

In *Bollom* [2003] EWCA Crim 2846; [2004] 2 Cr App R 6, the Court of Appeal held that the age, health or other factors relating to the victim could be taken into consideration when considering what constituted grievous bodily harm.

CASE EXAMPLE

Bollom [2003] EWCA Crim 2846; [2004] 2 Cr App R 6

V, a 17-month-old baby, suffered bruising and abrasions to her body, arms and legs. D, the partner of the baby's mother, was found guilty of an offence contrary to s 18 of the OAPA 1861. He appealed against this conviction on several grounds, one of which that the severity of injuries had to be assessed without considering the age, health or other factors relating to V. The Court of Appeal held that the effect of the harm on the particular individual had to be taken into consideration in determining whether the injuries amounted to grievous bodily harm. However, the conviction was quashed on other grounds, and a conviction under s 47 OAPA 1861 substituted.

In *Burstow* (1997), where the victim of a stalker suffered a severe depressive illness, it was decided that serious psychiatric injury can be grievous bodily harm. In October 2003, in *Dica*, there was the first ever conviction for causing 'biological' harm where the defendant had infected two women with HIV when he had unprotected sex with them without telling them he was HIV positive. On appeal in *Dica* [2004] EWCA Crim 1103, the Court of Appeal sent the case back for retrial on the issue of consent but accepted that biological harm came within the meaning of grievous bodily harm. Since this decision there have been about 20 convictions for 'causing' a sexually transmittable disease. One of these in 2008 was the first conviction for infecting a victim with hepatitis B.

In *Golding* [2014] EWCA Crim 889 the defendant was convicted after pleading guilty to inflicting grievous bodily harm contrary to s 20 when he had infected his girlfriend with genital herpes (HSV-2). He knew that he suffered from herpes and that it was a sexually transmitted disease. He had not told his girlfriend that he had the disease. The defendant challenged the conviction on the basis that the Crown Prosecution Service guidelines in force at the time had not been properly followed. Also he had felt pressurised to plead guilty when the judge at the Goodyear hearing had said that he considered s 20 rather than a plea to s 47 was the appropriate one.

The Court of Appeal held that the evidence of the painful nature of the symptoms of herpes, their recurrence and the fact that they could recur indefinitely without any effective cure available were sufficient to amount to really serious bodily harm.

11.3.2 *Mens rea* of s 20

The defendant must intend to cause another person some harm or be subjectively reckless as to whether he suffers some harm. The word used in the section is 'maliciously'. In *Cunningham* [1957] 2 All ER 412, it was held that 'maliciously' did not require any ill will towards the person injured. It simply meant either:

1. an intention to do the particular kind of harm that was in fact done; or
2. recklessness as to whether such harm should occur or not (i.e. the accused has foreseen that the particular kind of harm might be done, and yet gone on to take the risk of it).

CASE EXAMPLE

Cunningham [1957] 2 All ER 412

D tore a gas meter from the wall of an empty house in order to steal the money in it. This caused gas to seep into the house next door, where a woman was affected by it. Cunningham was not guilty of an offence against s 23 of the OAPA 1861 of maliciously administering a noxious thing, as he did not appreciate the risk of gas escaping into the next-door house. He had not intended to cause the harm, nor had he been subjectively reckless about it.

The joined cases of *Savage and Parmenter* (1992) confirmed that *Cunningham* (1957) recklessness applies to all offences in which the statutory definition uses the word 'maliciously'.

This left another point which the courts had to resolve. What was meant by the particular kind of harm? Did the defendant need to realise the risk of a wound or grievous bodily harm? It has been decided that, although the *actus reus* of s 20 requires a wound or grievous bodily harm, there is no need for the defendant to foresee this level of serious injury. In *Parmenter* (1992) the defendant injured his three-month-old baby when he threw the child in the air and caught him. Parmenter said that he had often done this with slightly older children and did not realise that there was risk of any injury. He was convicted of an offence under s 20. The House of Lords quashed this conviction but substituted a conviction for assault occasioning actual bodily harm under s 47. Lord Ackner cited the judgment in *Mowatt* [1967] 3 All ER 47, where Lord Diplock said:

JUDGMENT

'In the offence under s 20 … for … which [no] specific intent is required – the word "maliciously" does import … an awareness that his act may have the consequence of causing some physical harm to some other person … It is quite unnecessary that the accused should have foreseen that his unlawful act might cause physical harm of the gravity described in the section, ie a wound or serious injury.'

This decision means that, although there are four offences which appear to be on a ladder in terms of seriousness, there is overlap in terms of the *mens rea*.

KEY FACTS

Key facts: Different levels of *mens rea* and injury

Offence	*Mens rea*	Injury
s 18	Specific intent to cause GBH or resist arrest etc.	Wound or grievous bodily harm
s 20	Intention or recklessness as to some harm	
s 47	Intention or recklessness as to putting V in fear of unlawful force or applying unlawful force	Actual bodily harm
Common assault		No injury

11.4 Section 18

This offence under s 18 of the OAPA 1861 is often referred to as 'wounding with intent'. In fact it covers a much wider range than this implies. It is considered a much more serious offence than s 20, as can be seen from the difference in the maximum punishments.

Section 20 has a maximum of five years' imprisonment, whereas the maximum for s 18 is life imprisonment. Also s 20 is triable either way but s 18 must be tried on indictment at the Crown Court. The definition in the Act states:

SECTION

'18 Whosoever shall unlawfully and maliciously by any means whatsoever wound or cause any grievous bodily harm to any person, with intent to do some grievous bodily harm to any person, or with intent to resist or prevent the lawful apprehension or detainer of any person, shall be guilty of . . . an offence.'

From this it can be seen that the elements to be proved are that the defendant

- wounded or
- caused grievous bodily harm and that he did this
- intending to do some grievous bodily harm or
- intending to resist or prevent the lawful apprehension or detention of either himself or another person and being reckless as to whether this caused injury.

11.4.1 *Actus reus* of s 18

This can be committed in two ways:

- wounding
- causing grievous bodily harm.

The meanings of 'wound' and 'grievous bodily harm' are the same as for s 20.

The word 'cause' is very wide, so that it is only necessary to prove that the defendant's act was a substantial cause of the wound or grievous bodily harm.

11.4.2 *Mens rea* of s 18

This is a specific intent offence. The defendant must be proved to have intended to

- do some grievous bodily harm; or
- resist or prevent the lawful apprehension or detainer of any person.

Intent to do some grievous bodily harm

Although the word 'maliciously' appears in s 18, it was held in *Mowatt* (1967) that this adds nothing to the *mens rea* of this section where grievous bodily harm is intended. For this the important point is that s 18 is a specific intent crime. Intention must be proved; recklessness is not enough for the *mens rea* of s 18. Intention has the same meaning as shown in the leading cases on murder. So, as decided in *Moloney* [1985] 1 All ER 1025, foresight of consequences is not intention; it is only evidence from which intention can be inferred or found. And following the cases of *Nedrick* [1986] 3 All ER 1 and *Woollin* [1998] 4 All ER 103, intention cannot be found unless the harm caused was a virtual certainty as a result of the defendant's actions and the defendant realised that this was so. (See Chapter 3, section 3.2, for a fuller discussion on the meaning of intention.)

Intent to resist lawful arrest etc.

Where the charge is wounding or causing grievous bodily harm with intent to resist or prevent the lawful apprehension or detainer of any person, then the prosecution have to prove two things for the *mens rea* of the offence. The first is that the defendant had specific intention to resist or prevent lawful arrest or detention. If the arrest or detainer was unlawful then the defendant has not committed any offence. The second point is that the defendant acted 'maliciously' in respect to the wounding or grievous bodily harm. This point was considered in *Morrison* (1989) 89 Cr App R 17, where a police officer seized hold of D and told him that she was arresting him. He dived through a window dragging her with him as far as the window so that her face was badly cut by the glass. The trial judge directed the jury that D would be guilty of a s 18 offence if he intended to resist arrest and was *Caldwell* (1982) reckless (i.e. D either saw the risk or it would have been obvious to an ordinary prudent person) as to whether he caused the officer harm. The Court of Appeal held that this was wrong and that maliciously has the same meaning as in *Cunningham* (1957). This means that the prosecution must prove that the defendant realised there was a risk of injury and took that risk. There is still one point unresolved: that is, what degree of harm does the defendant need to foresee? Does he need to foresee that serious harm or a wound will be caused or does he only need to foresee that some harm will be caused? Under s 20 the test is that the defendant should foresee that some physical harm will be caused. For consistency it seems reasonable that the same test should apply to s 18. However, there has been no decision on this point.

ACTIVITY

Applying the law

Explain in each of the situations below what type of offence may have been committed.

1. In a football match Victor kicks Danny. This causes bruising to Danny's leg. Danny is annoyed at this and punches Victor in the face causing a cut to his lip.
2. Anish is walking along a canal bank. Kim, who is in a hurry, pushes past him, knocking him into the canal. Anish hits his head on the side and suffers a fractured skull.
3. Karl waves a knife at Emma, saying, 'I am going to cut that silly smile off.' Emma is very frightened and faints. She falls against Nita, who is knocked to the ground and suffers bruising.

NOTE: see Appendix 2 for an example of how to apply the law of non-fatal offences to a problem/scenario type question.

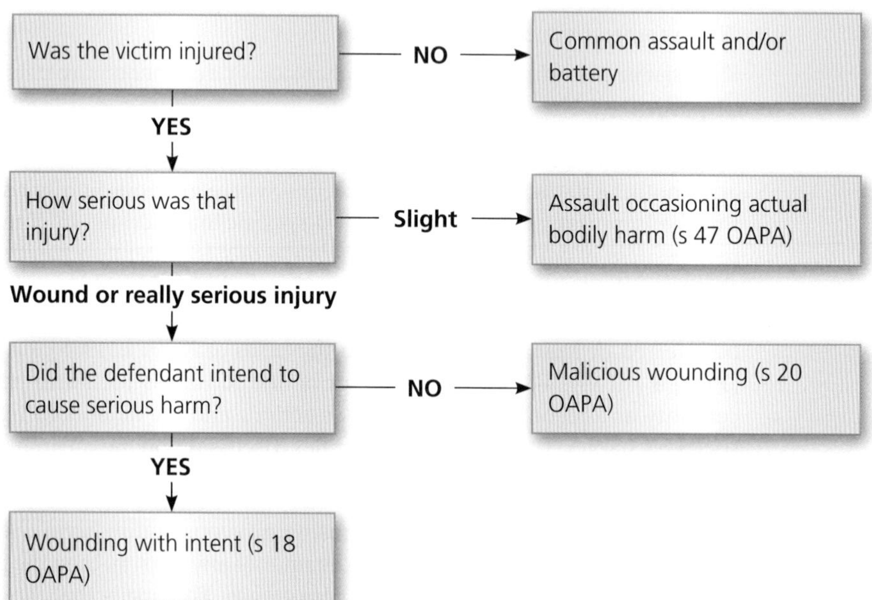

Figure 11.2 Flow chart on non-fatal offences against the person.

11.5 Reform

This area of the law is in need of reform, and as stated in the opening paragraph of this chapter, recommendations were made as long ago as 1980 by the Criminal Law Revision Committee in its 14th Report, *Offences against the Person*, Cmnd 7844 (1980). This was then adopted in the Law Commission Draft Criminal Code and, as no action had been taken, put forward again by the Law Commission in a modified form in its report, *Legislating the Criminal Code: Offences Against the Person and General Principles* (Law Com No 218) (1993). In 1998 the Home Office issued a Consultation Document, *Violence: Reforming the Offences Against the Person Act 1861*, and attached a draft Bill to this document.

The draft Bill published by the Home Office in 1998 proposed the following offences:

CLAUSE

'Intentional serious injury

1(1) A person is guilty of an offence if he intentionally causes serious injury to another.

(2) A person is guilty of an offence if he omits to do an act which he has a duty to do at common law, the omission results in serious injury to another, and he intends the omission to have that effect.

(3) An offence under this section is committed notwithstanding that the injury occurs outside England and Wales if the act causing that injury is done in England and Wales or the omission resulting in the injury is made there.

(4) A person guilty of an offence under this section is liable on conviction on indictment to imprisonment for life.

Reckless serious injury

2(1) A person is guilty of an offence if he recklessly causes serious injury to another.

(2) An offence under this section is committed notwithstanding that the injury occurs outside England and Wales if the act causing that injury is done in England and Wales.

(3) A person guilty of an offence under this section is liable –

(a) on conviction on indictment, to imprisonment for a term not exceeding 7 years;

(b) on summary conviction, to imprisonment for a term not exceeding 6 months or a fine not exceeding the statutory maximum or both.

Intentional or reckless injury

3(1) A person is guilty of an offence if he intentionally or recklessly causes injury to another.

(2) An offence under this section is committed notwithstanding that the injury occurs outside England and Wales if the act causing that injury is done in England and Wales.

(3) A person guilty of an offence under this section is liable –

(a) on conviction on indictment, to imprisonment for a term not exceeding 5 years;

(b) on summary conviction, to imprisonment for a term not exceeding 6 months or a fine not exceeding the statutory maximum or both.

Assault

4(1) A person is guilty of an offence if –

(a) he intentionally or recklessly applies force to or causes an impact on the body of another, or

(b) he intentionally or recklessly causes the other to believe that any such force or impact is imminent.

(2) No offence is committed if the force or impact, not being intended or likely to cause injury, is in the circumstances such as is generally acceptable in the ordinary conduct of daily life and the defendant does not know or believe that it is in fact unacceptable to the other person.

(3) A person guilty of an offence under this section is liable on summary conviction, to imprisonment for a term not exceeding 6 months or a fine not exceeding the statutory maximum or both.

Assault on a constable

5(1) A person is guilty of an offence if he assaults

(a) a constable acting in the execution of his duty, or
(b) a person assisting a constable acting in the execution of his duty.

(2) For the purposes of this section a person assaults if he commits the offence under section 4.

Causing serious injury to resist arrest etc.

6(1) A person is guilty of an offence if he causes serious injury to another intending to resist, prevent or terminate the lawful arrest or detention of himself or a third person.

(2) The question of whether the defendant believes the arrest or detention is lawful must be determined according to circumstances as he believes them to be.

(3) A person guilty of an offence under this section is liable on conviction on indictment to imprisonment for life.

Assault to resist arrest etc.

7(1) A person is guilty of an offence if he assaults another intending to resist, prevent or terminate the lawful arrest or detention of himself or a third person.

(2) The question of whether the defendant believes the arrest or detention is lawful must be determined according to circumstances as he believes them to be.

(3) For the purposes of this section a person assaults if he commits the offence under section 4.

(4) A person guilty of an offence under this section is liable –

(a) on conviction on indictment, to imprisonment for a term not exceeding 2 years;
(b) on summary conviction, to imprisonment for a term not exceeding 6 months or a fine not exceeding the statutory maximum or both . . .

Meaning of fault terms

14(1) A person acts intentionally with respect to a result if –

(a) it is his purpose to cause it, or
(b) although it is not his purpose to cause it, he knows that it would occur in the ordinary course of events if he were to succeed in his purpose of causing some other result.

(2) A person acts recklessly with respect to a result if he is aware of a risk that it will occur and it is unreasonable to take that risk having regard to the circumstances as he knows or believes them to be.

Meaning of injury

15(1) In this Act "injury" means –

(a) physical injury
(b) mental injury.

(2) Physical injury does not include anything caused by disease but (subject to that) it includes pain, unconsciousness and any other impairment of a person's physical condition.

(3) Mental injury does not include anything caused by disease but (subject to that) it includes any impairment of a person's mental health.

(4) In its application to section 1 this section applies without the exception relating to things caused by disease.'

This Bill would have tidied up the law and resolved many of the points which have been unclear in case decisions. In particular the *mens rea* of each section is specified. It is also clear that only cl 1 offences could be caused by omission. The more serious offences nominate serious injury rather than wound or grievous bodily harm. A serious wound would be treated as a serious injury while a minor wound would be merely an injury. The difficulty over mental health injury is also tackled with 'any impairment of a person's mental health' being sufficient to prove offences requiring injury, though for cl 1 and 2 this would have to be serious. It also makes it clear that it would be possible to convict a defendant of a cl 1 offence by infecting a person with HIV. However, an injury through disease was not included for the purposes of any other clause. Although it was sent out for consultation in 1998, the Bill was never placed before Parliament.

Recent developments

The Law Commission (LC) in its eleventh programme stated that it would look again at the law on non-fatal offences against the person. The Ministry of Justice asked the LC first to produce a scoping paper. Originally the LC stated that it would start the work in the winter of 2012 and publish the paper in autumn 2013. However, it put this date back and had not started work on the project by the summer of 2014. In its online statement regarding the project the LC states that: 'The Offences Against the Person Act 1861 is widely recognized as being outdated. It uses archaic language and follows a Victorian approach . . . The structure of the Act is also unsatisfactory; there is no clear hierarchy of offences and the differences between section 18, 20 and 47 are not clearly spelt out.'

11.6 Racially or religiously aggravated assaults

Under s 29 Crime and Disorder Act 1998, a common assault or an offence under s 47 or s 20 of the OAPA 1861 becomes a racially or religiously aggravated assault if either:

- At the time of committing the offence, or immediately before or after doing so, the offender demonstrates towards the victim of the offence hostility based on the victim's membership (or presumed membership) of a racial or religious group.
- The offence is motivated (wholly or partly) by hostility towards members of a racial or religious group based on their membership of that group.

Where an offence is racially aggravated in this way, the maximum penalty is increased from six months to two years for common assault and from five years to seven years for both s 47 and s 20.

Membership in relation to a racial or religious group includes association with members of that group. 'Racial group' is widely defined in the Act, as it includes a group of persons defined by reference to race, colour, nationality (including citizenship) or ethnic or national origins. In *DPP v Pal* [2000] Crim LR 756, it was held that an Asian defendant was not demonstrating racial hostility because of membership of a racial group when he assaulted a caretaker at a community centre who was of Asian appearance and whom he called a 'white man's arse licker' and a 'brown Englishman'. The Queen's Bench Divisional Court held that the insults were related to the victim's attitude to English people, rather than because he was Asian.

'Religious group' means a group of persons defined by reference to religious belief or lack of religious belief.

11.7 Administering poison

The OAPA 1861 creates two offences under ss 23 and 24:

SECTION

'23 Whosoever shall unlawfully and maliciously administer to or cause to be administered to or taken by any other person any poison or other destructive or noxious thing, so as to endanger the life of such person, or so as thereby to inflict upon such person any grievous bodily harm, shall be guilty of an offence ...

24 Whosoever shall unlawfully and maliciously administer to or cause to be administered to or taken by any other person any poison or other destructive or noxious thing, with intent to injure, aggrieve, or annoy such person shall be guilty of an offence.'

The maximum penalty for s 23 is ten years' imprisonment and the maximum for s 24 is five years' imprisonment.

For both offences it has to be proved that the defendant

- unlawfully and maliciously
- administered to or caused to be administered to or taken by any other person
- any poison or other destructive or noxious thing.

The differences are that for s 23 it must be shown that it endangered life or inflicted grievous bodily harm, while for s 24 there is no need to show that it had any effect on the victim, but it must be done with intent to injure, aggrieve or annoy the victim.

11.7.1 Administer

In *Gillard* [1998] Crim LR 53, the Court of Appeal held that 'administer' includes 'conduct which not being the direct application of force to the victim nevertheless brings the noxious thing into contact with his body'. In that case the defendant was convicted of conspiring to commit an offence under s 23 when he agreed to spray CS gas into the faces of others.

The sections also make it an offence where the defendant causes the substance to be administered to or taken by the victim. This allows for a conviction where there is no direct administration of the poison or other destructive or noxious thing. An example of causing the administration of a noxious thing is seen in *Cunningham* (1957), where the ripping out of a gas meter caused gas to seep into the next-door house and be inhaled by the victim. In *Kennedy* [1999] Crim LR 65, the Court of Appeal thought that there was an offence under s 23 where the defendant had filled a syringe with heroin and then handed it to the victim who had injected himself. However, in *Dias* [2001] EWCA Crim 2986, where the facts were similar to *Kennedy* (1999), the Court of Appeal left open the question as to whether there might be a conviction in the future for manslaughter on the basis that there was an unlawful act of administering a noxious substance under s 23 of the OAPA 1861.

11.7.2 Noxious thing

The 1861 Act specifically mentions 'poison or other destructive thing', but it also includes any 'noxious thing'. This allows the offences to be wider ranging than merely administering poison. In *Cato* [1976] 1 All ER 260, the defendant injected another man with heroin. The other had consented to it and was a regular user of heroin. The victim died and Cato was convicted of unlawful act manslaughter and of an offence under s 23. The Court of Appeal considered whether heroin should come within the meaning of 'noxious thing'. Lord Widgery CJ said:

JUDGMENT

'The authorities show that an article is not to be described as noxious for present purposes merely because it has a potentiality for harm if taken in an overdose. There are many articles of value in common use which may be harmful in overdose, and ... one cannot describe an article as noxious merely because it has that aptitude. On the other hand, if an article is liable to injure in common use, not when an overdose in the sense of accidental excess is used but is liable to cause an injury in common use, should it then not be regarded as a noxious thing for present purposes?

When one has regard to the potentiality of heroin in the circumstances which we read about and hear about in our courts today we have no hesitation in saying that heroin is a noxious thing.'

For s 24 a harmless substance, such as a sedative or a laxative, may become 'noxious' if administered in large quantities. In *Marcus* [1981] 2 All ER 833 a woman put eight sedative and sleeping pills into a neighbour's bottle of milk. The defence relied on the decision in *Cato* (1976) and argued that these could not be a 'noxious thing' because they were harmless in themselves. The Court of Appeal held that for s 24, the quantity could be taken into account in light of the necessary intent to injure, aggrieve or annoy.

11.7.3 Maliciously

The word 'maliciously' in both sections has the meaning given to it in *Cunningham* (1957). This means that the defendant must intend or be subjectively reckless about the administration of the substance. For s 23 there is no need to prove that the defendant intended or was reckless in respect of endangering life or inflicting grievous bodily harm. Section 24 has an additional requirement for *mens rea* of intent to injure, aggrieve or annoy. In *Hill* (1985) 81 Cr App R 206 the defendant was a homosexual who gave slimming tablets to two boys intending that it would keep them awake and disinhibit them so they would be more likely to accept his sexual advances. It was held that this was sufficient for an intent to injure.

ACTIVITY

Self-test questions

1. Explain when
   (a) words can be sufficient for a technical assault;
   (b) words will negate an assault.
2. Explain what is necessary for the *actus reus* of a battery.
3. What are the problems in deciding whether consent will be a defence to a battery of a s 47 offence?
4. Explain the difficulties in s 20 using the word 'inflict', while s 18 uses the word 'cause'.
5. Explain the different levels of *mens rea* required for s 47, s 20 and s 18.

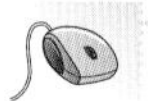

SUMMARY

- Common assault can be either an assault or a battery.
- An *assault* is an act which intentionally or recklessly causes another to fear immediate and unlawful violence. There must be some act or words; an omission is not enough. A silent phone call has been held to be sufficient.
- *Battery* is the application, intentionally or recklessly, of unlawful force to another person. This can be by an act or omission when D is under a duty to act.

Assault occasioning actual bodily harm, s 47 OAPA

- An assault or battery which causes actual bodily harm. It must 'occasion' (cause) actual bodily harm.
- Actual bodily harm is 'any hurt or injury calculated to interfere with the health or comfort' of the victim. It includes psychiatric injury.

Section 20 OAPA offence

- Unlawfully and maliciously wounding or inflicting grievous bodily harm upon another person.
- Grievous bodily harm means 'really serious harm', but this does not have to be life threatening.
- Wound means a cut or a break in the continuity of the whole skin. Internal bleeding where there is no cut of the skin is not sufficient.
- D must intend to cause another person some harm or be subjectively reckless as to whether he suffers some harm. There is no need for the defendant to foresee serious injury.

Section 18 OAPA offence

- Wounding or causing grievous bodily harm with intent to do so.
- The meanings of 'wound' and 'grievous bodily harm' are the same as for s 20.
- It is a specific intent offence. D must be proved to have intended to:
  - do some grievous bodily harm; or
  - resist or prevent the lawful apprehension or detainer of any person.
- Where D intends to resist or prevent lawful apprehension or detainer, there is no need for him to intend to cause grievous bodily harm. Recklessness as to injury is sufficient.

Reform

- A draft Bill was published in 1998 but never enacted.
- The Law Commission is going to look at the area of law again.

Racially and religiously aggravated assaults

- Section 29 of the Crime and Disorder Act 1998 creates aggravated offences where:
  - D demonstrates hostility based on race and/or religion;
  - the offence is motivated by racial/religious hostility.

Administering poison

- Section 23 OAPA 1861 where administering poison or a 'noxious substance' endangers life.
- Section 24 OAPA 1861 where there is no need to show any effect on V.

SAMPLE ESSAY QUESTION

The law on non-fatal offences against the person is in need of a complete reform. Discuss.

Briefly state the law on the main non-fatal offences:

Common assault: assault/battery

- s 47 Offences Against the Person Act 1861 (OAPA 1861)
- s 20 OAPA 1861
- s 18 OAPA 1861

Explain problems in the law, e.g.

- 1861 Act uses complicated, obscure and old-fashioned language
- No coherent structure to the offences
- No statutory definition of common assault
- Need to extend 'harm' to mental harm
- Problems with the word 'inflict' in s 20
- Failure to distinguish between serious and minor wounds
- Where D is resisting arrest etc., recklessness as to injury is sufficient for the *mens rea*: s 18 Expand these with case examples

Point out the number of proposals for reform:

- Criminal Law Revision Committee 14th Report 1980
- Law Commission's Report No 218 1993
- Home Office Consultation Document *Violence: Reforming the Offences against the Person Act 1861* (1998)

Discuss the proposals for reform:

- Especially the draft Bill in the Home Office consultation document
- Consider whether these proposals would have adequately reformed the problems in the current law

Conclude

Further reading

Books

Clarkson, C M V, Keating, H M and Cunningham, S R, *Criminal Law: Text and Materials* (7th edn, Sweet & Maxwell, 2010), Chapter 7, Part I.

Articles

Bell, B and Harrison, K, 'R v Savage, DPP v Parmenter and the law of assault' (1993) 56 MLR 83.

Burney, E, 'Using the law on racially aggravated offences' (2003) Crim LR 28.

Cherkassy, L, 'Being informed: the complexities of knowledge, deception and consent when transmitting HIV' (2010) J Crim L 242.

Horder, J, 'Reconsidering psychic assault' (1994) Crim LR 176.

Jefferson, M, 'Offences against the person: into the 21st century' (2012) J Crim L 472.

Smith, J C, 'Offences against the person; the Home Office Consultation Paper' (1998) Crim LR 317.

Weait, M, 'Criminal liablity for sexually transmitted diseases' (2009) 173 CL&J 45.

12

Sexual offences

AIMS AND OBJECTIVES

After reading this chapter you should be able to:

- Understand the law of rape
- Understand the law of assault by penetration, sexual assault, incest and other sexual offences
- Analyse critically the law on sexual offences
- Apply the law to factual situations to determine whether there is liability for rape or for another sexual offence

The law of sexual offences in England and Wales has undergone radical reform in the last fifteen years. The reform process can be traced back to the then Home Secretary's announcement in January 1999 that a major review of the law governing sex offenders was to take place. An independent review body was set up and its findings, contained in a document entitled *Setting the Boundaries: Reforming the Law on Sex Offenders*, were published in July 2000. The opening paragraphs of the document explain why the review was necessary:

QUOTATION

'Why did the law need reviewing? It is a patchwork quilt of provisions ancient and modern that works because people make it do so, not because there is a coherence and structure. Some is quite new – the definition of rape for example was last changed in 1994. But much is old, dating from nineteenth century laws that codified the common law of the time, and reflected the social attitudes and roles of men and women of the time. With the advent of a new century and the incorporation of the European Convention of Human Rights into our law, the time was right to take a fresh look at the law to see that it meets the need of the country today.'

At the time of the review, 'rape' was defined as penetration of the vagina or anus of another person without consent (s 1(1) of the Sexual Offences Act 1956 (as amended by the Criminal Justice and Public Order Act 1994)). Other forms of non-consensual sexual contact were dealt with under an offence called 'indecent assault' (contrary to ss 14 and 15 of the Sexual Offences Act 1956). The *actus reus* of the latter crime covered a very wide range of activities:

- oral sex (*McAllister* [1997] Crim LR 233);
- penetration of the vagina with D's hand (*Boyea* [1992] Crim LR 574);
- spanking (*Court* [1989] AC 28);
- stroking a woman's breasts (*Tabassum* [2000] 2 Cr App R 328);
- stroking a woman's lower leg (*Price* [2003] EWCA Crim 2405; *The Times*, 20 August 2003).

rape
Non-consensual vaginal, anal or oral sex

sexual assault
Non-consensual sexual touching

In addition to the width of the offence, there was also sometimes difficulty in establishing that an assault had been 'indecent'. According to Lord Ackner in *Court* (1989), it was a matter for the jury to decide whether 'right-minded persons would consider the conduct indecent or not'. *Setting the Boundaries: Reforming the Law on Sex Offenders* sets out the review body's position on the law of sexual offences as follows (para 0.9):

> 'In looking at the law on **rape** and **sexual assault** we recommend that these offences should be redefined in the following way:
>
> - that rape be redefined to include penetration of the mouth, anus or female genitalia by a penis;
> - a new offence of sexual assault by penetration to deal with all other forms of penetration of the anus and genitalia;
> - rape and sexual assault by penetration should be seen as equally serious, and both should carry a maximum sentence of life imprisonment;
> - a new offence of sexual assault to replace other non-penetrative sexual touching now contained in the offence of sexual assault.'

After a consultation period culminating in March 2001, in November 2002 the government published a White Paper called *Protecting the Public: Strengthening Protection against Sex Offenders and Reforming the Law on Sexual Offences* setting out its proposals for reform. The government clearly endorsed the findings of the independent review body, as this extract shows (Overview, paragraphs 8–9):

> 'The law on sex offences, as it stands, is archaic, incoherent and discriminatory. Much of it is contained in the Sexual Offences Act 1956, and most of that was simply a consolidation of 19th century law. It does not reflect the changes in society and social attitudes that have taken place since the Act became law, and it is widely considered to be inadequate and out of date. While some piecemeal reform has taken place over the years, we have now undertaken a comprehensive review of the law so that it can meet the needs of today's society.'

The proposed reforms were put to Parliament and in due course the Sexual Offences Act 2003 was passed, the main provisions of which entered into force on 1 May 2004.

12.1 Rape

Section 1(1) of the Sexual Offences Act 2003 defines 'rape' in the following terms.

SECTION

> '1(1) A person (A) commits an offence if –
> (a) he intentionally penetrates the vagina, anus or mouth of another person (B) with his penis,
> (b) B does not consent to the penetration, and
> (c) A does not reasonably believe that B consents.'

Section 1(2) provides that 'whether a belief is reasonable is to be determined having regard to all the circumstances, including any steps A has taken to ascertain whether B consents'.

Actus reus *elements*

- Penetration of the vagina, anus or mouth of another person, V, with the penis.
- Lack of consent by V.

Mens rea *elements*

- Intent to penetrate V's vagina, anus or mouth.
- Lack of reasonable belief in V's consent.

Summary of changes

- Penetration of the mouth becomes rape.
- Genuine belief that V was consenting is no longer a good defence. The belief must be reasonable.

12.1.1 Penetration of the vagina, anus or mouth of another person, with the penis

Prior to the Criminal Justice and Public Order Act 1994, rape could only be committed by penetration of V's vagina (it followed that only women could be the victims of rape). The definition of 'rape' was expanded in 1994 to include penetration of the anus, which meant that prosecution for male rape was possible for the first time (prior to 1994, the non-consensual anal penetration of either a man or woman would have been charged as buggery). Following the 2003 Act, the non-consensual penetration of either the vagina, anus or mouth amounts to the *actus reus* of rape. The one constant feature over this time has been the requirement that the penetration be by D's penis. The non-consensual penetration of V's vagina or anus by some other body part, or anything else, may now be charged under s 2 of the 2003 Act, as 'assault by penetration' (see section 12.2). Section 79(3) of the 2003 Act states that 'references to a part of the body include references to a part surgically constructed (in particular, through gender reassignment surgery)'. This would allow:

- a post-operative female-to-male transsexual to commit rape using an artificially created penis;
- a post-operative male-to-female transsexual to be the victim of rape if her artificially created vagina were to be penetrated by D's penis.

One of the first cases under s 1 to reach the Court of Appeal under the 2003 Act involved the extended definition of rape, that is, penetration of V's mouth with D's penis. In the case, *Ismail* [2005] EWCA Crim 397, Lord Woolf CJ noted that 'the fact that this was oral rape does not mean that it is any less serious than vaginal or anal rape'.

CASE EXAMPLE

Ismail [2005] EWCA Crim 397

D, aged 18, approached V, aged 16 and a virgin, who was standing near a phone box in Sheffield. V decided to walk to her friend's house and D accompanied her. When they reached a deserted path through grass verges D suddenly grabbed V from behind and pulled her on to the verge. He touched her vagina (which led to a separate conviction of sexual assault under s 3, see below) and then forced V to suck on his penis. He threatened to stab her if she did not comply and slapped and punched her about the face until he ejaculated into her mouth. Afterwards he stroked her hair and apologised. After D was arrested and charged he claimed consent but V had recorded the whole incident on her mobile phone. D changed his plea to guilty and his appeal (against sentence) was dismissed.

Penetration

Section 79(2) of the Sexual Offences Act 2003 states that 'penetration is a continuing act from entry to withdrawal'. This gives statutory effect to the Privy Council ruling in *Kaitamaki* [1984] 2 All ER 435, where the Court held that D commits rape if, having penetrated with consent, or believing he has consent, D declines to withdraw on consent being revoked, or on realising that V does not consent. This was confirmed by the Court of Appeal in *Cooper and Schaub* [1994] Crim LR 531. V had allegedly been raped by the two defendants, whom she had met in a pub and later had sex with. After retiring to consider a verdict, the jury asked the judge: 'If we find that initially there was consent to intercourse and this was subsequently withdrawn and intercourse continued, does this by law constitute rape?' The judge answered in the affirmative and the jury convicted. Although the convictions were quashed on appeal, the Court of Appeal confirmed the correctness of the judge's direction on the point of law.

The offence of rape is committed as soon as the non-consensual penile penetration of V's vagina, anus or mouth occurs. There are no further *actus reus* elements, a point which was stressed by the High Court in *Assange v Sweden* [2011] EWHC 2849. Sir John Thomas P stated that 'ejaculation is irrelevant to this definition: so is pregnancy. If ejaculation occurs it may be an aggravating feature relevant to sentence: it is irrelevant to proof of the offence itself.'

12.1.2 The absence of consent

An essential element in rape is the absence of consent to penetration. As rape is an indictable offence, this is a matter for the jury to decide. Early authorities emphasised the use of force that the penetration had to be against V's will. However, it is now clear that the lack of consent may exist with or without force being used. In *Olugboja* [1982] QB 320, D contended that rape required the submission of the victim, induced by force or the threat of force. He had been convicted of raping a 16-year-old girl who had not offered resistance or cried for help, because she was too frightened. The Court of Appeal dismissed the appeal. Dunn LJ said:

JUDGMENT

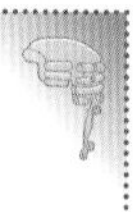

'It is not necessary for the prosecution to prove that what might otherwise appear to have been consent was in reality merely submission induced by force, fear or fraud, although one or more of these factors will no doubt be present in the majority of cases of rape ... [The jury] should be directed that consent, or the absence of it, is to be given its ordinary meaning and if need be, by way of example, that there is a difference between consent and submission.'

Further guidance on the distinction between 'consent' and 'submission' was provided in *Doyle* [2010] EWCA Crim 119.

CASE EXAMPLE

Doyle [2010] EWCA Crim 119

D had been convicted of raping his 17-year-old girlfriend, V, after she said that they were no longer in a relationship and that she did not want to have sex with him. V's testimony at trial was that D had forced her to have sex. Initially she had protested 'but once he had succeeded in penetrating her she ceased to resist because she thought it would only get worse if she did'. D appealed against his conviction, arguing that the trial judge had failed to explain to the jury the distinction between 'submission' and consent freely given by choice. The Court of Appeal disagreed and upheld the conviction.

However, Pitchford LJ acknowledged that there may be cases where the line between consent and submission would be more difficult to draw. He said:

JUDGMENT

'There are circumstances in which the jury may well require assistance as to the distinction to be drawn between reluctant but free exercise of choice on the one hand, especially in the context of a long-term and loving relationship, and unwilling submission to demand in fear of more adverse consequences from refusal on the other.'

Similar observations were made in *B* [2013] EWCA Crim 3; [2014] Crim LR 312. Hughes LJ observed that 'the line between reluctant consent and submission despite lack of consent is often a fine one, especially in cases of an existing sexual relationship'. To summarise:

- Consent and submission are not the same thing. Where V 'merely' or 'unwillingly' submits to penetration, he or she is not consenting.
- It is a question for the jury whether V gave consent or 'merely' submitted.
- In some (but not necessarily all) cases, especially those involving an existing relationship, the jury may require assistance from the judge as to where the line between consent and submission is to be drawn.

Pitchford LJ's reference to the 'free exercise of choice' being the key defining characteristic of consensual sex is based on the statutory definition of 'consent' found in the SOA 2003 (see below). The point is that V may appear to be consenting – perhaps through fear that physical resistance, struggling, screaming or shouting for help may provoke D into violence – and yet not actually be doing so. This was demonstrated vividly in *McFall* [1994] Crim LR 226. D kidnapped his former girlfriend, V, at gunpoint and had driven her from Leeds to a hotel in Hull, where they had sex. V faked orgasms throughout the intercourse, so that it may have appeared that she was consenting. However, D's rape conviction was upheld. Taking into account the fact that D had kidnapped V with a gun (although in fact an imitation, it looked real, and he had told her that it was loaded), there was sufficient evidence that V's apparent consent was not genuine in order for the jury to convict.

In *AC* [2012] EWCA Crim 2034, the Court of Appeal confirmed that there is a distinction to be drawn between 'apparent' consent to sexual activity and 'real' consent.

If D has sex with V whose consent is only 'apparent' then the *actus reus* of rape has been committed.

CASE EXAMPLE

AC [2012] EWCA Crim 2034

D was charged with 18 sexual offences against his stepdaughter, V, who was 18 years younger. The charges related to incidents over a period of 20 years, starting when V was aged around five and ending when she was around 25. At trial, D's case was that there had been no sexual activity between them until V was 16 and that thereafter they were in a consensual sexual relationship. The prosecution, however, argued that D, having abused and sexually controlled V when she was a child, continued to abuse, dominate and control her after her sixteenth birthday. The jury convicted and the Court of Appeal upheld the convictions.

Lord Judge CJ stated:

JUDGMENT

'Once the jury were satisfied that the sexual activity of the type alleged had occurred when [V] was a child, and that it impacted on and reflected [D's] dominance and control over [V], it was open to them to conclude that the evidence of apparent consent when [V] was no longer a child was indeed apparent, not real, and that [D] was well aware that in reality she was not consenting.'

The statutory definition of consent

Prior to the enactment of the SOA 2003, the law of consent was entirely found in the case law. However, Parliament has now provided the first statutory definition of consent. Section 74 SOA states that a person 'consents if he agrees by choice, and has the freedom and capacity to make that choice'. The meaning and scope of s 74 was first examined by the Court of Appeal in *Jheeta* [2007] EWCA Crim 1699; [2008] 1 WLR 2582.

CASE EXAMPLE

Jheeta [2007] EWCA Crim 1699; [2008] 1 WLR 2582

D and V had been in a sexual relationship but, when V indicated that she wished to end it, D sent her a series of anonymous threatening text messages. These messages were in fact sent by D but V was unaware of this fact. Instead, V was so distressed that she sought protection against those making the threats from D. This allowed him to prolong their sexual relationship for far longer than would otherwise have been the case (several years, in fact). Eventually the whole 'complicated and unpleasant scheme', in the words of Sir Igor Judge, was discovered and D was charged with and convicted of several rapes. The Court of Appeal upheld the convictions, pointing out that V's apparent consent 'was not a free choice, or consent for the purposes of the Act'.

Section 74 was invoked in *Assange v Sweden* [2011] EWHC 2849, in which it was alleged that V had only agreed to have penetrative sex with D on the understanding that he would use a condom, but when intercourse took place, D was either not using a condom at all, or had removed it or torn it without V realising. The High Court held that these facts would constitute the *actus reus* of rape. Sir John Thomas P said:

JUDGMENT

'The allegation is clear ... It not an allegation that the condom came off accidentally or was damaged accidentally ... It would plainly be open to a jury to hold that, if [V] had made clear that she would only consent to sexual intercourse if [D] used a condom, then there would be no consent if, without her consent, he did not use a condom, or removed or tore the condom without her consent. His conduct in having sexual intercourse without a condom in circumstances where [V] had made clear she would only have sexual intercourse if [D] used a condom would therefore amount to an offence under the SOA 2003.'

CASE EXAMPLE

Assange v Sweden [2011] EWHC 2849

In August 2010, Julian Assange, the Australian journalist and founder of the Wikileaks website, visited Sweden to give a lecture. Whilst there, he had sexual relations with two women, both of whom later complained to the police. Assange was interviewed by the police, but left Sweden prior to a Swedish court issuing an arrest warrant. In November 2010, the Swedish prosecuting authority issued a European Arrest Warrant alleging *inter alia* 'sexual molestation' under Swedish law. The specific allegation was that he had unprotected sex with a woman who had agreed to sex on the express condition that he used a condom. By this time, Assange was living in the UK. A district judge ordered his extradition to Sweden on the basis that the alleged facts would constitute rape under English law. Assange appealed but, in November 2011, the High Court dismissed his appeal. (Before he could be extradited to Sweden, Assange was granted political asylum by the government of Ecuador, and he took up residence at their embassy in London where (at the time of writing) he remains.)

Section 74 was invoked again in *F v DPP* [2013] EWHC 945; [2014] 2 WLR 190, in which it was held that if V only agreed to have unprotected sex with D on the basis that he would withdraw prior to ejaculating, but D secretly intended to ejaculate inside V despite V's wishes to the contrary, then the *actus reus* of rape had been committed. Lord Judge CJ stated:

JUDGMENT

'The evidence relating to "choice" and the "freedom" to make any particular choice must be approached in a broad commonsense way. If before penetration began, [D] had made up his mind that he would penetrate and ejaculate within [V's] vagina, or even that he would not withdraw at all, just because he deemed [V] subservient to his control, [V] was deprived of "choice" relating to the crucial feature on which her original consent to sexual intercourse was based. Accordingly her consent was negated. Contrary to her wishes, and knowing that she would not have consented, and did not consent to penetration or the continuation of penetration if she had any inkling of his intention, [D] deliberately ejaculated within her vagina. In law, this combination of circumstances falls within the statutory definition of rape.'

CASE EXAMPLE

F v DPP [2013] EWHC 945; [2014] 2 WLR 190

The High Court was asked to judicially review the DPP's decision not to prosecute V's husband (D) for rape. V had complained to the police, alleging that she had only agreed to have penetrative sex with D on the understanding that D would either use a condom or withdraw prior to ejaculation. (V did not want to become pregnant and could not use contraceptive pills for medical reasons.) However, on one occasion when they were having unprotected sex, D said that he would not withdraw prior to ejaculation 'because you are my wife and I'll do it if I want'. V subsequently found out that she was pregnant. The High Court ruled in V's favour and instructed the CPS to review its decision not to prosecute D.

Lord Judge CJ's recommendation that the courts should adopt a 'broad commonsense' approach to consent (or the lack thereof) was accepted by the Court of Appeal in *McNally* [2013] EWCA Crim 1051; [2014] 2 WLR 200. The case involved allegations that the female defendant (D) had penetrated V's vagina with her fingers and tongue without V's consent. The Crown alleged a lack of consent on V's behalf on the basis that, at the relevant time, V had been induced into believing that D was, in fact, male. At her trial, D pleaded guilty to six counts of assault by penetration (contrary to s 2 SOA; see section 12.2 below), but subsequently appealed, arguing that deception as to gender did not vitiate consent. This was rejected. Leveson LJ in the Court of Appeal said:

JUDGMENT

'In reality, some deceptions (such as, for example, in relation to wealth) will obviously not be sufficient to vitiate consent. [However] while, in a physical sense, the acts of assault by penetration of the vagina are the same whether perpetrated by a male or a female, the sexual nature of the acts is, on any common sense view, different where [V] is deliberately deceived by [D] into believing that the latter is a male. [V] chose to have sexual encounters with a boy and her preference (her freedom to choose whether or not to have a sexual encounter with a girl) was removed by [D's] deception. It follows from the foregoing analysis that we conclude that, depending on the circumstances, deception as to gender can vitiate consent.'

CASE EXAMPLE

McNally [2013] EWCA Crim 1051; [2014] 2 WLR 200

Justine McNally (D) forged a relationship with V, a teenage girl, over the internet. When they first 'met' on the social networking website Habbo, D was aged 13 and lived in Scotland; V was a year younger and lived in London. D used a male avatar with the name 'Scott' and V believed that she was communicating with a boy called 'Scott Hill' from Glasgow. Over the following three-and-a-half years they communicated, initially via MSN and later via telephone calls. Throughout this time, D maintained her 'Scott' persona. Shortly after V's sixteenth birthday, D travelled down to London to meet her. D was dressed in black 'gothic' clothing and 'presented' herself as a teenage boy. Over the next few months, D travelled to London to visit V on a number of occasions and they engaged in sexual activity involving D penetrating V's vagina with her fingers and tongue. The room was always dark and D kept her clothes on, so that V remained oblivious as to the fact that D was not actually 'Scott'. It was V's mother who became suspicious and eventually confronted D. The Court of Appeal upheld D's convictions for assault by penetration on the basis that D's deception as to gender had vitiated V's consent.

McNally was discussed by J Rogers, 'Further developments under the Sexual Offences Act' (2013) 7 Arch Rev 7. He agreed with the Court of Appeal that V's 'misunderstanding' about D's gender could vitiate V's consent, arguing that since V 'wished to experience a heterosexual encounter, the nature of the acts done by [D] were thereby different ... [V] was used for the sexual gratification of another in a manner which in no way accorded with her own sexual preferences, and it is right that she be regarded as the victim of a non-consensual sexual offence'.

Do you agree with Rogers that 'the acts' done by D were 'different' from those which V had agreed would be done? V agreed to have her vagina penetrated by Justine McNally and that is exactly what happened. Should it matter that V thought (wrongly) that Justine was 'Scott'?

A Sharpe, 'Criminalising sexual intimacy: transgender defendants and the legal construction of non-consent' [2014] Crim LR 207 questions the rationale for the decision in *McNally*, i.e. Leveson LJ's assertion that V had been 'deliberately deceived' into thinking that D was male. Sharpe points out that 'Justine now apparently identifies as female, a gender position consistent with her birth designated sex. At the time of the alleged offences, however, she appears to have identified and lived as a young man and made reference to her desire for gender reassignment surgery.' She had also 'expressed some confusion about her gender'. Sharpe argues that 'at the time of conviction and appeal there was sufficient information available to conclude that McNally identified as male prior to and at the time of the alleged offences, and therefore that [V's] apparent consent was valid consent and that McNally was not deceptive'.

Informed consent?

You will recall that in the cases of *Dica* [2004] EWCA Crim 1103 and *Konzani* [2005] EWCA Crim 706, examined in Chapter 8, the Court of Appeal imported a doctrine of 'informed consent' into the law of non-fatal offences. The result of these cases is that, if D knows that he is HIV positive, has unprotected penetrative sex with V without informing them of his condition, and transmits the virus, this can lead to a conviction under s 20 of the Offences Against the Person Act 1861 (inflicting grievous bodily harm (GBH)). The justification for this is that V's consent to have sex with D does not extend to consent to the risk of contracting a potentially fatal illness. The reason for repeating these principles here is that the Court of Appeal was asked, in *B* [2006] EWCA Crim 2945; [2007] 1 WLR 1567, whether such facts could lead to a conviction of rape. The Court answered 'no'.

CASE EXAMPLE

B [2006] EWCA Crim 2945

In the early hours of the morning, D and V had sex in the street outside a nightclub where they had just met. Subsequently, V made a complaint of rape. D was arrested and informed the custody officer that he was HIV positive, a fact which he had not disclosed to V prior to their having sex. He was charged with and convicted of rape. He appealed, submitting that the judge was wrong in directing the jury that his HIV status was relevant to whether V had the 'freedom and capacity' to consent to sex in the absence of that knowledge. The Court of Appeal quashed the conviction.

Latham LJ stated:

JUDGMENT

> 'Where one party to sexual activity has a sexually transmissible disease which is not disclosed to the other party, any consent that may have been given to that activity by the other party is not thereby vitiated. The act remains a consensual act. However, the party suffering from the sexually transmissible disease will not have any defence to any charge which may result from harm created by that sexual activity, merely by virtue of that consent, because such consent did not include consent to infection by the disease.'

Before moving on to consider ss 75 and 76 SOA, it may be useful to summarise some of the leading cases on s 74 and to consider the extent to which they have applied the law consistently:

- *B* (2006): D had sex with V without informing her that he was HIV positive. Held: V's consent valid.
- *Assange* (2011): D (allegedly) had sex with V either without using a condom or using a torn condom, contrary to their agreement to have sex with a condom. Held: V's consent vitiated.
- *F v DPP* (2013): D had sex with V and ejaculated inside her, contrary to their agreement that he would withdraw beforehand. Held: V's consent vitiated.
- *McNally* (2013): D induced V into believing that D was a boy called 'Scott' before penetrating her vagina with D's fingers and tongue. Held: V's consent vitiated.

Do you agree with these decisions? J Rogers, 'The effect of deception in the Sexual Offences Act 2003' (2013) 4 Arch Rev 7, argues that there is an inconsistency here:

QUOTATION

> 'If a man with HIV is charged for communicating it through sexual intercourse, having deceived his partner about his status, he faces a maximum penalty under s 20 of the OAPA. But following *Assange* a man who is sexually healthy and does not wear the condom which he is asked to wear can be charged for the more serious and stigmatic offence of rape.'

His solution to the problem is to say that 'conduct involving risks or perceived risks about health should be the subject of separate legislation'. Do you agree that a new crime is required? There is an argument that, were a man to actually 'deceive' his partner about his HIV status prior to them having unprotected penetrative sex, this could be rape. In *B* (2006) there was no actual deception, so that case could be distinguished and *Assange*, *F* and *McNally* followed instead.

Presumptions about consent

Sections 75 and 76 of the Sexual Offences Act 2003 apply to the offences in s 1 (rape), s 2 (assault by penetration), s 3 (sexual assault) and s 4 (causing a person to engage in sexual activity without consent).

Evidential presumptions

Section 75 of the 2003 Act is headed 'Evidential presumptions about consent'.

SECTION

'75(1) If in proceedings for an offence to which this section applies it is proved –

(a) that [D] did the relevant act,
(b) that any of the circumstances specified in subsection (2) existed, and
(c) that [D] knew that those circumstances existed,

[V] is to be taken not to have consented to the relevant act unless sufficient evidence is adduced to raise an issue as to whether he consented, and [D] is to be taken not to have reasonably believed that [V] consented unless sufficient evidence is adduced to raise an issue as to whether he reasonably believed it.

(2) The circumstances are that –

(a) any person was, at the time of the relevant act or immediately before it began, using violence against [V] or causing [V] to fear that immediate violence would be used against him;
(b) any person was, at the time of the relevant act or immediately before it began, causing [V] to fear that violence was being used, or that immediate violence would be used, against another person;
(c) [V] was, and [D] was not, unlawfully detained at the time of the relevant act;
(d) [V] was asleep or otherwise unconscious at the time of the relevant act;
(e) because of [V]'s physical disability, [V] would not have been able at the time of the relevant act to communicate to [D] whether [V] consented;
(f) any person had administered to or caused to be taken by [V], without [V]'s consent, a substance which, having regard to when it was administered or taken, was capable of causing or enabling [V] to be stupefied or overpowered at the time of the relevant act.'

One of the evidential presumptions in s 75 is the situation where V is 'unlawfully detained' (s 75(2)(c)), although the Court of Appeal did not need to refer to that section in *B* [2006] EWCA Crim 400. In the words of Swift J, D forced V to 'put her wrists into some dog leads, which he secured to the bedposts. He tied her ankles with a belt and forced open her legs. He pulled down her pyjama bottoms and her thong to her ankles. He then took off his own clothes and said, "You have a choice, either up the front or up the back". He turned her over and committed an act of anal rape.' Section 75(2)(d) refers to the situation in cases such as *Larter and Castleton* [1995] Crim LR 75. There, D had sexual intercourse with V, a 14-year-old girl, who was asleep at the time. He was charged with rape and argued that it had to be proved that V had demonstrated lack of consent. The Court of Appeal upheld D's conviction, confirming that it is not necessary to prove a positive dissent by V. It is enough that he/she did not assent. On these facts, there would now be an 'evidential presumption' that V was not consenting, requiring D to rebut the presumption.

Section 75(2)(d) was invoked in *Ciccarelli* [2011] EWCA Crim 2665; [2012] 1 Cr App R 15, a case involving sexual assault, contrary to s 3 SOA 2003 (for detailed explanation of this offence see section 12.3).

CASE EXAMPLE

Ciccarelli [2011] EWCA Crim 2665; [2012] 1 Cr App R 15

D was at a party with several people including his girlfriend and V, who was very drunk. At one point, V fell asleep and D, the girlfriend and V took a taxi back to D's flat, where V was to spend the night in the spare room. During the night, D got up and went into the room where

V was asleep. There, he lay down next to her, kissed her on the face, and rubbed his penis against her bottom. He then tried to get on top of her at which point she woke up and shouted at him to get off, which he did. D was charged with sexual assault.

The trial judge told the jury that the evidential presumption in s 75(2)(d) had been created by the fact that V was asleep at the time of the touching, D knew that V was asleep and D had committed the relevant act of touching V in a sexual way. This meant that it was rebuttably presumed both that V was not consenting and that D had no reasonable belief in V's consent. Furthermore, the trial judge ruled that there was no evidence to rebut the presumption. At that point D changed his plea to guilty and appealed. He contended that he reasonably believed that V was consenting to the touching, despite the fact that she was asleep. The Court of Appeal dismissed his appeal, holding that once one of the evidential presumptions was raised, it could only be rebutted by evidence. On the facts there was no evidence, other than D's own testimony.

In a recent Canadian case, it was held that, where D engages in sexual activity with V who is asleep, then the activity is non-consensual – even where D and V are partners. In *JA* [2011] 2 SCR 440, the appellant (JA) placed his hands around the throat of his long-term partner (KD) and choked her until she was unconscious. When she regained consciousness about three minutes later, she was on her knees at the edge of the bed with her hands tied behind her back, and JA was inserting a dildo into her anus. They then had vaginal intercourse. When they finished, JA cut KD's hands loose. Two months later, KD made a complaint to the police, stating that while she had consented to the choking, she had not consented to the sexual activity that had occurred whilst she was unconscious. JA was convicted of sexual assault and appealed, successfully, to the Court of Appeal in Ontario. The Crown then appealed, and the Supreme Court of Canada restored the conviction, holding that consent in Canadian law required ongoing, conscious consent to ensure that women and men were not the victims of sexual exploitation, and to ensure that individuals engaging in sexual activity were capable of asking their partners to stop at any point.

If the facts of this case had occurred in England, then the Crown would presumably have relied upon s 75(2)(d) in order to create presumptions that the alleged victim was not consenting and that the appellant lacked reasonable belief in her consent, but the appellant would have been able to counter that by introducing evidence (most obviously, the fact that he and his partner were in a long-term relationship) in order to try to rebut the presumptions.

Section 75(2)(f) refers to the situation in cases such as *Camplin* [1845] 1 Den 89, where D was convicted of rape after rendering a woman insensible by plying her with alcohol before having intercourse. On these facts, there would now be an 'evidential presumption' that V was not consenting, requiring D to rebut the presumption. This situation is all too familiar in the twenty-first century, with incidents involving the use of 'date rape' drugs. Powerful sedatives designed to alleviate sleeping disorders are available in tablet form and can be easily crushed and dissolved in liquid. Because they are usually tasteless and odourless, they can be slipped into V's drinks in a bar or nightclub without her knowledge, in order to render her unconscious or semi-conscious during sex.

The evidential presumption does not apply where V has become drunk or drugged or otherwise intoxicated of his/her own free will, as opposed to through use of force or some subterfuge on the part of D. Nevertheless, if D takes advantage of V whilst he/she is in this condition, this could still be rape as demonstrated in the pre-2003 Act case of *Malone* [1998] EWCA Crim 1462; [1998] 2 Cr App R 447.

CASE EXAMPLE

Malone [1998] EWCA Crim 1462; [1998] 2 Cr App R 447

V, a 16-year-old girl, got so drunk when out with friends that she was incapable of walking and had to be given a lift home. D, a neighbour, was asked to help carry her into her house where her friends undressed her and put her to bed. Thereafter D stayed, ostensibly to make sure she did not vomit and choke. However, V claimed that he then climbed on top of her and had intercourse before she could kick him off. D was convicted of rape and appealed on the ground that, in this sort of case involving neither force nor fraud, a lack of consent had to be demonstrated either by speech or physical conduct. The Court of Appeal disagreed and dismissed the appeal.

The leading case on this area of law, where D is alleged to have raped V whilst the latter was voluntarily intoxicated, is *Bree* [2007] EWCA Crim 804; [2008] QB 131. The Court of Appeal quashed D's rape conviction because the jury had not been adequately directed on the issue of V's consent. The facts indicated that V, although very drunk, had retained the capacity to consent (and hence s 75(2)(d) did not apply) and V had become intoxicated voluntarily (and hence neither did s 75(2)(f)). The case therefore hinged on whether the Crown had proved that V was not consenting at the time of the alleged rape. The Court found that this had not been proven, given the inadequacy of the trial judge's directions, and therefore the conviction was unsafe.

CASE EXAMPLE

Bree [2007] EWCA Crim 804; [2008] QB 131

D, aged 25, had gone to stay at his brother's student flat at Bournemouth University. One of the brother's flatmates, V, agreed to go out with D, his brother and the latter's girlfriend. Over the course of the evening the four of them consumed large quantities of alcohol before returning to the flat. Back in the flat, D initiated sex with V. At this point D's version of events and V's version differ. D claimed that V – although still drunk – was conscious throughout, was capable of consenting, and did so. V's version was that she was drunk and kept passing out, she either could not or did not consent and hence had been raped. At trial, D was convicted of rape but the Court of Appeal quashed his conviction. The Court of Appeal took the opportunity to clarify the law of rape in cases where V's capacity to consent may have been affected by voluntary intoxication. Sir Igor Judge stated:

JUDGMENT

'A "drunken consent is still consent". In the context of consent to intercourse, the phrase lacks delicacy, but, properly understood, it provides a useful shorthand accurately encapsulating the legal position . . . If, through drink (or for any other reason) [V] has temporarily lost her capacity to choose whether to have intercourse on the relevant occasion, she is not consenting, and subject to questions about [D's] state of mind, if intercourse takes place, this would be rape. However, where [V] has voluntarily consumed even substantial quantities of alcohol, but nevertheless remains capable of choosing whether or not to have intercourse, and in drink agrees to do so, this would not be rape.'

It is open for debate whether the Court of Appeal in *Bree* has provided sufficient clarity in the law. There is an argument that s 75(2) of the SOA 2003 should be amended and that 'extreme intoxication' (or words to that effect) should be added as a further circumstance. This would mean that, if it could be proved that V was in a state of extreme intoxication (albeit voluntary) at the time of the alleged rape, and that D had knowledge of V's intoxication, it would create an evidential presumption that V was not consenting. After all, the involuntarily intoxicated V is protected by s 75(2)(f), so why not the voluntarily intoxicated V?

Conclusive presumptions

Section 76 of the Act is headed 'Conclusive presumptions about consent'.

SECTION

'76(1) If in proceedings for an offence to which this section applies it is proved that [D] did the relevant act and that any of the circumstances specified in subsection (2) existed, it is to be conclusively presumed –

(a) that [V] did not consent to the relevant act, and
(b) that [D] did not believe that [V] consented to the relevant act.

(2) The circumstances are that –

(a) [D] intentionally deceived [V] as to the nature or purpose of the relevant act;
(b) [D] intentionally induced [V] to consent to the relevant act by impersonating a person known personally to [V].'

Rape through fraud and deception

Where D deceives V as to the very nature of the act which he is performing, there is now a 'conclusive' presumption that V did not consent and that D did not believe that V was consenting (s 76(2)(a)). The new presumption would, presumably, apply to the situations which arose in the following cases:

- *Flattery* [1877] 2 QBD 410. V had sex with D – although she was under the impression that he was performing a surgical operation which would cure her fits.
- *Williams* [1923] 1 KB 340. V (a 16-year-old choirgirl) had sex with D (the choirmaster) – although she was under the impression that he was performing exercises to help her breathing (she did not, apparently, even realise she was actually having sex).

However, the presumption will not apply in cases such as arose in *Linekar* [1995] 3 All ER 69, where D's deception does not go to the 'nature or purpose' of the act. For example, misrepresentations by D as to his wealth or professional status would not render sex obtained thereby rape. In *Linekar* (1995), Morland J stated: 'An essential ingredient in the law of rape is the proof that the woman did not consent to [the act of penetration] with the particular man who penetrated her.'

CASE EXAMPLE

Linekar [1995] 3 All ER 69

V, a prostitute, agreed to have sex with D in return for £25 after he approached her outside the Odeon cinema in Streatham. They duly had sex on the balcony of a block of flats. Afterwards D made off without paying. V complained that she had been raped. D was convicted of rape on the basis that he had never had any intention of paying and hence V's consent was vitiated by his fraud. The Court of Appeal quashed the conviction. It was the absence of consent, not the presence of fraud, which made otherwise lawful sexual intercourse rape.

The Court of Appeal in *Linekar* (1995) approved an Australian case, *Papadimitropoulos* (1958) 98 CLR 249, in which V was deceived into thinking that she was married to D. In fact the marriage was a sham. The High Court of Australia held that this consent was a defence to rape. A very similar case to that of *Linekar* (1995) is the British Columbia Court of Appeal judgment in *Petrozzi* (1987) 35 CCC (3d) 528. D had agreed to pay V $100 for sexual services but did not intend to make that payment. The Court held that this type of deception could not be said to relate to the nature and quality of the act and was insufficient to vitiate V's consent. The first case to be decided by the Court of Appeal involving s 76 was *Jheeta* (2007), the facts of which were given above. Although the Court of Appeal upheld D's rape convictions, this was on the basis of s 74, not s 76. The Court decided that, although V had been deceived by D into thinking that her life was in danger, and in turn to seek protection from D which allowed him to artificially prolong their sexual relationship, this deception did not trigger s 76. The Court acknowledged that D had 'created a bizarre and fictitious fantasy which, because it was real enough... pressurised [V] to have intercourse with [D] more frequently than she otherwise would have done'. However, s 76 did not apply because V was not deceived as to the 'nature or purpose' of their sexual relationship; rather, she had been deceived 'as to the situation in which she found herself'. Sir Igor Judge in the Court of Appeal summarised the scope of s 76 as follows:

JUDGMENT

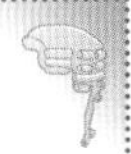

'The ambit of s 76 is limited to the "act" to which it is said to apply. In rape cases the "act" is vaginal, anal or oral intercourse ... it will be seen that s 76(2)(a) is relevant only to the comparatively rare cases where [D] deliberately deceives [V] about the nature or purpose of one or other form of intercourse. No conclusive presumptions arise merely because [V] was deceived in some way or other by disingenuous blandishments of or common or garden lies by [D]. These may well be deceptive and persuasive, but they will rarely go to the nature or purpose of intercourse.'

ACTIVITY

Self-test question

Can you think of some 'disingenuous blandishments' or 'common or garden lies' which a defendant might use to persuade V to have sex, which would not trigger s 76?

Section 76(2)(a) was used to secure a conviction in *Devonald* [2008] EWCA Crim 527.

CASE EXAMPLE

Devonald [2008] EWCA Crim 527.

D's 16-year-old daughter had been in a relationship with V, a 16-year-old boy. After that relationship broke down, much to the distress of the girl, D assumed the identity of a 20-year-old woman, 'Cassey', and began corresponding with V online. Their conversations 'quickly turned to sex' and eventually, D persuaded V to masturbate in front of a webcam while D watched. D was later charged with causing another person to engage in sexual activity without consent (contrary to s 4 SOA; and see section 12.4). D said that his motivation was to teach V a lesson for mistreating D's daughter by embarrassing him. D was convicted and appealed, contending that, although he had intentionally caused V to engage in sexual activity (masturbation), V had consented. The Court of Appeal dismissed the appeal, applying s 76(2)(a): D *had* deceived V as to the 'purpose' of his act. V's purpose in masturbating was to please a 20-year-old woman called 'Cassey'; he would never have done so had he known that the 37-year-old father of his former girlfriend was watching him instead.

The meaning and scope of s 76 – in particular the word 'purpose' in s 76(2)(a) – was considered again by the Court of Appeal in *Bingham* [2013] EWCA Crim 823; [2013] 2 Cr App R 29. Hallett LJ said that s 76 had to be 'strictly construed' and would only apply in 'rare' cases:

JUDGMENT

'There is no definition of the word "purpose" in the Act. It is a perfectly ordinary English word and one might have hoped it would not be necessary to provide a definition. It has been left to the courts and academics to struggle with its meaning in the context of a sexual act. We say "struggle" advisedly because it may not be straightforward to ascertain the "purpose" of a sexual act. Those engaging in a sexual act may have a number of reasons or objectives and each party may have a different objective or reason. The Act does not specify whose "purpose" is under consideration. There is, therefore, a great danger in attempting any definition of the word "purpose" and in defining it too widely. A wide definition could bring within the remit of s 76 situations never contemplated by Parliament. We shall, therefore, simply apply the normal rules of statutory construction and echo what was said in *Jheeta*. Where, as here, a statutory provision effectively removes from an accused his only line of defence to a serious criminal charge it must be strictly construed . . . Thus, it will be a rare case in which s 76 should be applied.'

CASE EXAMPLE

Bingham [2013] EWCA Crim 823; [2013] 2 Cr App R 29

Darrell Bingham (DB) had been in a relationship with his girlfriend, C, for several years. One day, he contacted her via Facebook purporting to be someone called 'Grant'. He persuaded her to send him topless photos of herself. The next month, he threatened to email these photos to C's employer unless she performed sexual acts over a web link. C complied with these threats and duly penetrated her vagina with her fingers and a hairbrush while DB watched via the web link. Later, DB repeated the deception but this time in the guise of 'Chad', ostensibly a friend of Grant's. Again, C complied with the threats and again performed sexual acts via a web link while DB watched. Eventually, C contacted the police, who arrested DB and charged him with causing another person to engage in sexual activity without consent (contrary to s 4 SOA; and see section 12.4). He admitted that he had assumed the false identities but said he reasonably believed that C was consenting. The trial judge directed the jury that, if they found that C had been deceived as to the purpose of the act, then the conclusive presumption under s 76 applied, removing DB's defence that he had a reasonable belief that C was consenting. DB was convicted and appealed. He submitted that C had never been asked at trial what she believed DB's purpose was but that, if she had been asked, she would have said sexual gratification, in which case C had not been misled. Further, he argued that, if the trial judge was satisfied that s 76 was triggered, he should have directed the jury on the meaning of the word 'purpose' in s 76(2)(a). The Court of Appeal allowed the appeal (although a retrial was ordered). Hallett LJ described DB's conduct as 'not unlike' that in *Jheeta*. She said that DB 'undoubtedly deceived his girlfriend in a cruel and despicable way' but doubted whether there was 'deception as to purpose so as to trigger the operation of s 76'. She explained that while DB's purpose was 'far from clear', the 'most likely' explanation was 'some kind of perverted sexual gratification'; meanwhile, C's understanding of what she was being asked to do (and did in fact do) was to perform sexual acts in front of a camera for the sexual gratification of whoever was watching.

In *Bingham*, the Court of Appeal cast doubt on *Devonald*. Hallett LJ said that 'If there is any conflict between the decisions in *Jheeta* and *Devonald*, we would unhesitatingly follow *Jheeta*.' Nevertheless, *Devonald* has not been overruled and it remains an authority for the proposition that a sexual activity such as masturbation could have more than one purpose (sexual gratification on one hand, embarrassment and humiliation on the other) and if D deceives V about which purpose is applicable, s 76(2)(a) applies.

Commenting on *Bingham*, K Laird, 'Rapist or rogue? Deception, consent and the Sexual Offences Act 2003' [2014] Crim LR 492, suggests that 'the applicability of s 76 has been reduced to vanishing point' and that this development 'is to be welcomed'. He contends that, in future, cases such as *Jheeta* and *Bingham* are more likely to be argued on the basis of s 74, rather than s 76. This, he suggests, will help both the prosecution and the defence. It will help the prosecution because, whereas s 76 only applies in cases of intentional deception, s 74 'does not contain the same restriction'. And reliance on s 74 instead of s 76 'at least permits [D] to mount a defence and so avoids the issue of whether any subsequent conviction violates the presumption of innocence' in art 6 of the European Convention of Human Rights.

Rape through impersonation

Where D impersonates V's husband, fiancé or boyfriend (or some other person known to V), then again the conclusive presumption applies (s 76(2)(b)). This would apply to the type of situation that arose in *Elbekkay* [1995] Crim LR 163.

CASE EXAMPLE

Elbekkay [1995] Crim LR 163

D had deceived V into thinking that he was her boyfriend. He was convicted of rape after the trial judge directed the jury that there was no difference between impersonating a husband and impersonating a boyfriend or fiancé: both cases amount to rape. The Court of Appeal upheld the conviction.

12.1.3 Intent to penetrate

The meaning of 'intention' is the same throughout the criminal law. Refer to Chapter 3 for discussion.

12.1.4 Lack of reasonable belief

It must be proved that, at the time of the penetration, D did not reasonably believe that V was consenting. It will no longer be a defence to plead that D honestly (but unreasonably) believed that V was consenting, even where D was sober. The House of Lords' judgment in *DPP v Morgan and others* [1976] AC 182 has therefore been overruled in so far as it concerns offences in the Sexual Offences Act 2003. If D's belief that V was consenting was mistaken, and this mistake was due to alcohol or other intoxicants, then it would seem to follow that such belief would be regarded almost automatically as unreasonable (unless there are other factors to explain D's mistake). The defendant in *Woods* (1981) 74 Cr App R 312 committed the *actus reus* of rape but pleaded in his defence that he mistakenly thought the victim was consenting (the mistake being caused by intoxication). He was convicted after the jury were directed that evidence of intoxication was irrelevant. Following the 2003 Act, the jury would be directed to consider whether D's belief was reasonable. It is submitted that they would convict.

In *Fotheringham* (1989) 88 Cr App R 206, D had been out with his wife and had been drinking heavily (seven to eight pints of lager). When they returned home, he climbed into the marital bed where the babysitter, V, was asleep. Under the mistaken impression that V was his wife, he had sex with her without her consent. D pleaded not guilty to rape on the basis that he genuinely believed V was his wife. However, the judge directed the jury to ignore the effects of drink in considering whether there were reasonable grounds for his belief that he was having lawful intercourse: 'The reasonable grounds are grounds which would be reasonable to a sober man.' He was convicted and the Court of Appeal upheld the conviction. Watkins LJ said that: 'in rape self-induced intoxication is no defence, whether the issue be intention, consent or, as here, mistake as to the identity of the victim'. This decision would certainly be the same today.

In *Taran* [2006] EWCA Crim 1498, the Court of Appeal considered the provision in s 1 that D is not guilty if he reasonably believed that V was consenting. In the case D had been convicted of raping a girl in his car; her version of events was that throughout the incident she had been struggling to escape. Hughes LJ stated (emphasis added):

JUDGMENT

'A direction upon absence of reasonable belief clearly falls to be given when, but only when, there is material on which a jury might come to the conclusion that (a) the complainant did not in fact consent, but (b) the defendant thought that she was consenting. Such a direction does not fall to be given unless there is such material . . . we are, in the circumstances, unaltered in our conclusion that a misunderstanding as to whether or not the complainant consented was simply not a realistic possibility on the evidence before this jury.'

Although it is now settled that D's honest (but unreasonable) belief in V's consent will not provide D with any defence to a charge of rape (or other sexual offence under the SOA 2003), there is little in the way of further explanation as to what exactly is meant by 'reasonable belief'. In *MM* [2011] EWCA Crim 1291, Pitchford LJ stated that there is 'an interesting argument to be addressed as to whether there is a material difference between (1) an honest belief held by [D] which may have been reasonable in the circumstances and (2) a belief which a reasonable man, placed in [D's] circumstances, may have held'. However, the Court did not find it necessary to explore that argument further and the position remains slightly unclear.

Further guidance has been provided by the Court of Appeal in *B* [2013] EWCA Crim 3; [2014] Crim LR 312, at least in cases where D's mental health is in question. The appellant (D) was seeking to challenge his conviction for raping his partner (V) on the basis that he lacked *mens rea*. There was evidence that D was suffering from a mental disorder and had delusional beliefs that he possessed 'sexual healing powers' which may have affected his belief as to whether or not V was consenting. Hughes LJ said:

JUDGMENT

'We take the clear view that delusional beliefs cannot in law render reasonable a belief that his partner was consenting when in fact she was not . . . The Act does not ask whether it was reasonable (in the sense of being understandable or not his fault) for [D] to suffer from the mental condition which he did . . . The Act asks a different question: whether the belief in consent was a reasonable one. A delusional belief in consent, if entertained, would be by definition irrational and thus unreasonable, not reasonable. If such delusional beliefs were capable of being described as reasonable, then the more irrational the belief of [D] the better would be its prospects of being held reasonable ... Unless and until the state of mind amounts to insanity in law, then under the rule enacted in the Sexual Offences Act beliefs in consent arising from conditions such as delusional psychotic illness or personality disorders must be judged by objective standards of reasonableness and not by taking into account a mental disorder which induced a belief which could not reasonably arise without it.'

CASE EXAMPLE

B [2013] EWCA Crim 3; [2014] Crim LR 312

D was charged with, *inter alia*, two counts of raping his partner, V. There was expert medical evidence that D had been suffering from a mental disorder, probably paranoid schizophrenia, or possibly schizo-affective disorder, at the time of the alleged offences. The medical expert said that the acts of intercourse might have been motivated by D's delusional beliefs that he had 'sexual healing powers', but that any such delusions did not extend to a belief that V had consented. The trial judge directed the jury that they should ignore D's mental illness when asking whether any belief that D might have had in V's consent had been reasonable. D was convicted and appealed. He argued that the judge ought to have directed the jury that his mental illness was a factor that they should consider when deciding whether any belief in consent was reasonable. The Court of Appeal dismissed his appeal.

Hughes LJ added that there may be cases 'in which the personality or abilities of the defendant may be relevant to whether his positive belief in consent was reasonable'. He said that there may be cases 'in which the reasonableness of such belief depends on the reading by the defendant of subtle social signals, and in which his impaired ability to do so is relevant to the reasonableness of his belief'. The Court refused to 'attempt exhaustively to foresee the circumstances' in which such a belief might be held to be reasonable; this was a decision which depended 'on their particular facts'. However, he stressed that 'once a belief could be judged reasonable only by a process which labelled a plainly irrational belief as reasonable, it is clear that it cannot be open to the jury so to determine without stepping outside the Act'.

12.1.5 The marital exception to rape

At common law, it was formerly the case that rape did not apply to married couples. The rule that a man could not rape his wife survived until the later years of the twentieth century (*Jones* [1973] Crim LR 710). This rule was finally removed by the Lords in *R* [1992] 1 AC 599.

12.1.6 Women as defendants

Before the 2003 Act, it was explicit that only a man could commit rape. Although the 2003 Act changes the wording of the offence from 'man' to 'person', it then makes clear that only a man can commit rape because there has to be penetration by a penis. Thus, that aspect of the law is unchanged. However, despite the fact that only a man may commit rape as a principal, a woman may be convicted of rape as a secondary party (refer back to Chapter 5, section 5.3, if necessary, for a reminder of these terms). This was demonstrated in *DPP v K and C* [1997] Crim LR 121, when two girls were convicted of procuring the rape of a girl by an unknown youth (the girls had ordered V to remove her clothing and have sex). This is surely right: without the girls' actions the rape might never have taken place; and in terms of liability as a secondary party, the girls' gender was irrelevant to their liability.

12.2 Assault by penetration

This is a new offence created by the Sexual Offences Act 2003. Section 2(1) of the Act states:

SECTION

'2(1) A person (A) commits an offence if (a) he intentionally penetrates the vagina or anus of another person (B) with a part of his body or anything else; (b) the penetration is sexual; (c) B does not consent to the penetration; and (d) A does not reasonably believe that B consents.'

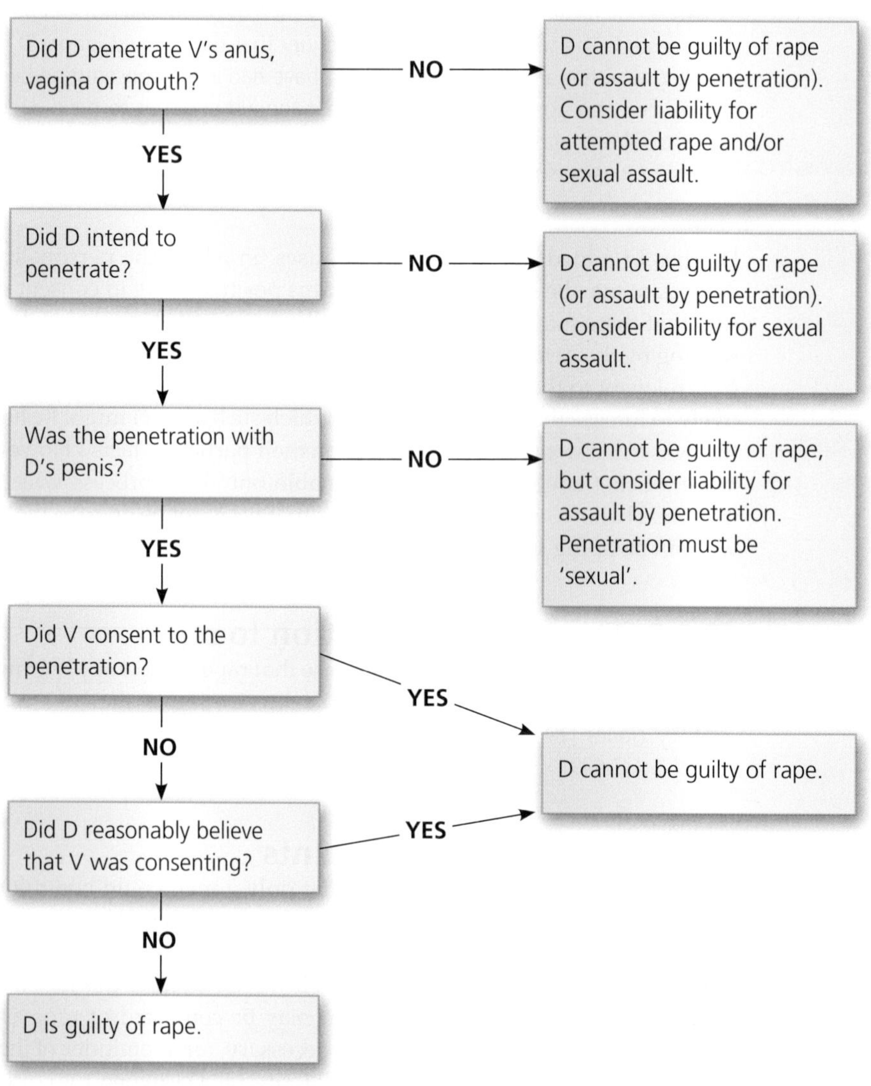

Figure 12.1 Rape.

Section 2(2) repeats the wording of s 1(2). (See section 12.1.)

Actus reus *elements*

- Penetration of the vagina or anus of another person, V.
- With a body part or anything else.
- Penetration must be 'sexual'.
- V does not consent.

Mens rea *elements*

- Intent to penetrate V's vagina or anus.
- Lack of reasonable belief in V's consent.

'Sexual'

This word is defined in s 78 of the Sexual Offences Act 2003 as follows.

SECTION

> '78 Penetration, touching or any other activity is sexual if a reasonable person would consider that (a) whatever its circumstances or any person's purpose in relation to it, it is because of its nature sexual, or (b) because of its nature it may be sexual and because of its circumstances or the purpose of any person in relation to it (or both) it is sexual.'

An early case involving s 2 is *Coomber* [2005] EWCA Crim 1113. D had penetrated the anus of V, a sleeping boy (D had drugged V with sleeping tablets) with his finger. D was convicted after footage which D had taken himself using his own digital camera was seized. In *Cunliffe* [2006] EWCA Crim 1706, D was convicted of a s 2 assault after attacking a 14-year-old girl on a deserted field and inserting one or more of his fingers into her anus. In both of these cases it is clear that D's penetration was sexual 'because of its nature'.

The relationship between s 1 and s 2 of the 2003 Act was considered in *Lyddaman* [2006] EWCA Crim 383. Openshaw J noted that on the evidence 'plainly there had been some sexual interference and indeed penetration. The question for the jury was whether it was penile penetration to make the appellant guilty of rape … or *digital* penetration to render him guilty of sexual assault by penetration' (emphasis added). Upholding the conviction, the Court of Appeal noted that the jury had convicted D under s 2, which was described as 'the lesser offence'.

12.3 Sexual assault

This is another new offence created by the Sexual Offences Act 2003, although it clearly replaces that of indecent assault. This development was described by A P Simester and G R Sullivan, in the second edition of their book *Criminal Law Theory and Doctrine* (Hart Publishing, 2003) as 'very welcome'. They criticised the old offence as 'an anachronism', the emphasis on 'indecency' being 'beside the point in a modern law focused on sexual violence'. Section 3(1) of the Act states that:

SECTION

> '3(1) A person (A) commits an offence if (a) he intentionally touches another person (B), (b) the touching is sexual, (c) B does not consent to the touching, and (d) A does not reasonably believe that B consents.'

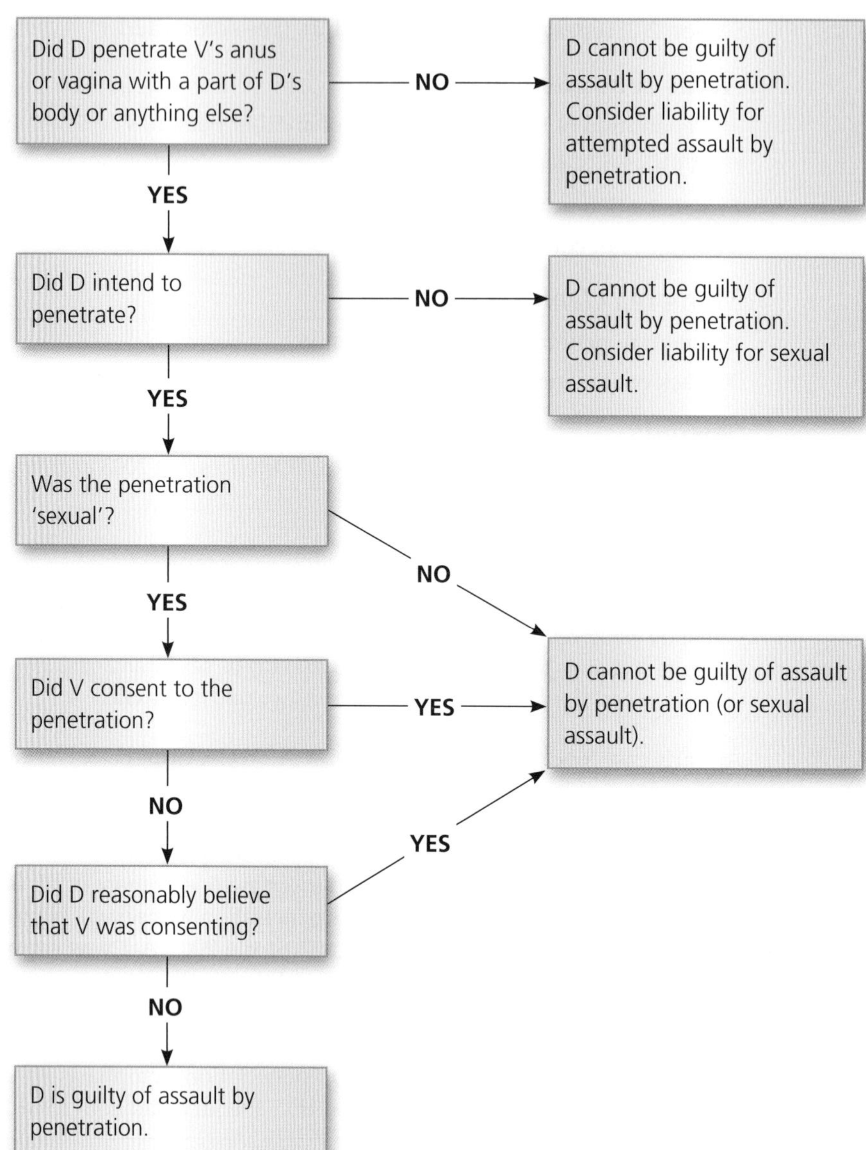

Figure 12.2 Assault by penetration.

Section 3(2) repeats the wording of s 1(2). (See section 12.1.)

Actus reus *elements*

- Touching of another person, V.
- Touching is 'sexual' (see the definition in s 78 above).
- V does not consent to the touching.

'Touching'/'sexual touching'

This is a new concept for English criminal law. Previously, it was necessary to establish an 'assault'. Clearly any physical contact between D and V will suffice, but is not necessary. Section 79(8) provides a definition of what is included in the concept of 'touching'

– in other words, this is not an exhaustive but an illustrative definition. It states that 'touching' includes touching (a) with any part of the body, (b) with anything else, (c) through anything. Finally, 'touching amounting to penetration' is included 'in particular'. This means that there is deliberate overlap between the offences in ss 2(1) and 3(1). Under the definition of 'sexual' in s 78, certain 'touchings' are automatically 'sexual' (para (a)), whereas other touchings are ambiguous and whether they are 'sexual' or not depends on the circumstances and/or D's purpose (para (b)). Since the 2003 Act entered into force in May 2004 the Court of Appeal has dealt with several cases under s 3, mostly appeals against sentence. Nevertheless these cases illustrate the wide range of circumstances in which the offence may be committed (as you read through this list consider which of these touchings are automatically sexual because of their 'nature' and which are only sexual because of the circumstances and/or D's purpose):

- touching V's breasts (*Bamonadio* [2005] EWCA Crim 3355; *Burns* [2006] EWCA Crim 1451; *Ralston* [2005] EWCA Crim 3279);
- touching V's private parts (*Elvidge* [2005] EWCA Crim 1194; *Forrester* [2006] EWCA Crim 1748);
- kissing V's private parts (*Turner* [2005] EWCA Crim 3436);
- kissing V's face (*W* [2005] EWCA Crim 3138);
- pressing D's body against V's buttocks (*Nika* [2005] EWCA Crim 3255);
- rubbing D's penis against V's body (*Osmani* [2006] EWCA Crim 816);
- sniffing V's hair while stroking her arm (*Deal* [2006] EWCA Crim 684);
- ejaculating on to V's clothes while dancing close together (*Bounekhla* [2006] EWCA Crim 1217);

Section 3(1) requires that D 'touches another person', although s 79(8)(c) provides that it can be 'through anything'. This was considered in *R v H* [2005] EWCA Crim 732; [2005] 1 WLR 2005, where the Court of Appeal held that the touching of V's clothing was sufficient to amount to 'touching' for the purposes of an offence under s 3(1).

Mens rea *elements*

- Intent to touch another person.
- Lack of reasonable belief in V's consent.

You will note that it is not essential that D has any *mens rea* with respect to whether or not the touching is 'sexual'. It has been argued that it is potentially unfair that D may be convicted under s 3 with no *mens rea* except the intent to touch and the lack of reasonable belief in V's consent (I Bantekas, 'Can touching always be sexual when there is no sexual intent?' (2008) 73 JoCL 251). However, if a touching is 'sexual' because a reasonable person would consider it to be so 'because of its nature' under s 78(a), then it is irrelevant whether or not D even realised that the touching might be 'sexual'. As Lord Woolf CJ in the Court of Appeal described it in *R v H* (2005), some touchings are 'inevitably sexual'. Moreover, when a case involves a more ambiguous touching, it can still be found to be 'sexual' by reference to 'its circumstances', under s 78(b), again with no requirement that D even realise that the touching might be regarded as 'sexual'.

12.4 Causing a person to engage in sexual activity

This is yet another new offence created by the SOA 2003. Section 4(1) of the Act states:

SECTION

'A person (A) commits an offence if (a) he intentionally causes another person (B) to engage in an activity, (b) the activity is sexual, (c) B does not consent to engaging in the activity, and, (d) A does not reasonably believe that B consents.'

In *Devonald* [2008] EWCA Crim 527, D was convicted under s 4 after tricking V into masturbating in front of a webcam, and in *Ayeva* [2009] EWCA Crim 2640, D was convicted under s 4 after he grabbed V and physically forced her to masturbate him. More recently, in *Bingham* [2013] EWCA Crim 823; [2013] 2 Cr App R 29, D was convicted under s 4 after persuading V to perform sexual acts while D watched via a web link (although as noted above, the convictions were quashed on the basis that V had not been deceived as to D's purpose and hence her consent was not vitiated).

12.5 Other crimes under the Sexual Offences Act 2003

Space precludes giving detailed coverage to all the offences contained in the 2003 Act. The following table provides a summary of a selection of the other crimes.

KEY FACTS

Offence	Definition
Administering a substance with intent (s 61)	Intentionally administering a 'substance' to V, knowing that V does not consent, with the intention of 'stupefying or overpowering' V, so as to enable any person to engage in a sexual activity that involves V. In *Spall* [2007] EWCA Crim 1623, D was convicted under s 61 after slipping sedatives into V's wine glass.
Committing an offence with intent to commit a sexual offence (s 62)	In *Wisniewski* [2004] EWCA Crim 3361 D was convicted of two counts of battery with intent to rape.
Trespass with intent to commit a sexual offence (s 63)	Trespassing 'on any premises' with intent to 'commit a relevant sexual offence on the premises'. D must know or be reckless as to the trespass. This replaces the offence in s 9(1)(a) of the Theft Act 1968, whereby D is guilty of burglary if he enters a building (or part of a building) with intent to rape anyone therein. The s 63 offence is wider in two respects: (1) D need not necessarily intend to commit rape (sexual assault, for example, would suffice); (2) 'premises' is a more flexible concept than 'building'.
Exposure (s 66)	Intentionally exposing D's genitals with intent that 'someone will see them and be caused alarm or distress'.

Voyeurism (s 67)	Observing, for the purposes of obtaining sexual gratification, 'another person doing a private act' if D knows that the other person, V, does not consent to being observed. A 'private act' is one done in a place which 'would reasonably be expected to provide privacy' and where (a) V's 'genitals, buttocks or breasts are exposed or covered only with underwear'; or (b) V is using a lavatory; or (c) V is 'doing a sexual act that is not of a kind ordinarily done in public' (s 68(1)). In *Bassett* [2008] EWCA Crim 1174; [2009] 1 WLR 1032, D's conviction under s 67 for secretly filming a man, in his trunks, in a swimming pool showers was quashed. The word 'breasts' referred only to female breasts and not the exposed male chest.
Intercourse with an animal (s 69)	Intentionally 'performing an act of penetration' with D's penis into the vagina or anus, or 'any similar part', of 'a living animal'. D must know or be reckless as to whether that is what is being penetrated.
Sexual penetration of a corpse (s 70)	Intentionally 'performing an act of penetration' with a part of D's body or anything else into 'a part of the body of a dead person'. D must know or be reckless as to whether that is what is being penetrated. The penetration must be sexual (liability is strict in this respect).

SUMMARY

- All sexual offences are contained in the Sexual Offences Act 2003.
- *Rape (s 1)*. The intentional penetration of V's vagina, anus or mouth, with D's penis and without V's consent. D must intend to penetrate and have no reasonable belief in V's consent. Consent and submission are not the same thing (*Olugboja*, *Doyle*). Consent must be 'real and not just 'apparent' (*AC*). V must have the 'freedom and capacity' to choose whether to consent (s 74). In certain circumstances there is a rebuttable presumption that V is not consenting (s 75) and in other circumstances a conclusive presumption applies (s 76). Where s 75 applies, evidence other than D's own testimony is required to rebut the presumption (*Ciccarelli*). Where V is voluntarily intoxicated there may still be consent (*Bree*).
- *Assault by penetration (s 2)*. The intentional penetration of V's vagina or anus with a part of D's body or anything else without V's consent.
- *Sexual assault (s 3)*. The 'touching' of V's body or clothing without V's consent. Penetration or touching must be 'sexual', either because of their nature or because of the circumstances or D's purpose. D must intend to penetrate/touch and have no reasonable belief in V's consent.
- *Causing another person to engage in sexual activity (s 4)*. Intentionally causing V to engage in a sexual activity (e.g. masturbation) without V's consent
- *Analysis*. Redefinition of rape and creation of new offences in ss 2, 3 and 4 (replacing 'indecent assault') designed to modernise and clarify the law. Requirement that D has no reasonable belief in V's consent designed to improve conviction rates (previously an honest belief in consent was a good defence).
- *Present debate*. Should the law on consent in rape cases be clearer, especially in cases like *Bree* where V is voluntarily intoxicated? Should the offences under ss 2 and 3 require D to have some *mens rea* as to the 'sexual' element?

SAMPLE ESSAY QUESTION

The Sexual Offences Act 2003 was designed to bring 'coherence and structure' to the law. Consider the extent to which it has succeeded in achieving this purpose.

Give a brief outline of the old law:

Sexual Offences Act 1956, as amended

State problems with the old law, e.g.

- Narrow definition of rape
- Very wide scope of indecent assault
- Ambiguity about meaning of 'indecency'
- D's honest (but unreasonable) belief that V was consenting was a good defence (*Morgan* (1976))
- Marital exception had already been abolished in *R* (1992)

Use comments from:

- *Setting the Boundaries*, Independent review (2000)
- *Protecting the Public*, White Paper (2002)

Set out the main offences in the SOA 2003:

S 1 rape

S 2 assault by penetration

S 3 sexual assault

S 4 causing V to engage in sexual activity

Outline good points of the SOA 2003, e.g.

- Wider definition of rape, e.g. oral rape now included
- Honest but unreasonable belief in consent no longer a defence (*Morgan* overruled)
- Introduction of statutory defintion of 'consent' (s 74) and presumptions about consent (ss 75 and 76) are designed to clarify the law and facilitate more successful prosecutions
- Replacement of 'indecent' with 'sexual' designed to clarify the law. Abolition of 'indecent assault' and replacement with new offences in s 2 (penetration) and s 3 (touching) means that clear distinctions may be drawn between different factual situations

State problems with the SOA 2003, e.g.

- The decision in *Bree* (2007) that 'drunken consent is still consent' will make convictions more difficult
- The decision in *G* (2008) that the s 5 offence (rape of a child) is strict liability is arguably harsh

Conclude

Further reading

Books

Loveless, J, *Criminal Law Text, Cases, and Materials* (4th edn, Oxford University Press, 2014), Chapter 11.

Articles

Ashworth, A and Temkin, J, 'The Sexual Offences Act 2003: rape, sexual assault and the problems of consent' [2004] Crim LR 328.

Finch, E and Munro, V E, 'Intoxicated consent and the boundaries of drug-assisted rape' [2003] Crim LR 773.

Firth, G, 'Not an invitation to rape: the Sexual Offences Act 2003, consent and the case of the "drunken" victim' (2011) 62 NILQ 99.

Herring, J, 'Mistaken sex' [2005] Crim LR 511.

Rumney, P and Fenton, R, 'Intoxicated consent in rape: Bree and juror decision-making' (2008) 71 MLR 279.

Tadros, V, 'Rape without consent' (2006) 26 OJLS 515.

Wallerstein, S, '"A drunken consent is still consent" – or is it? A critical analysis of the law on a drunken consent to sex following Bree' (2009) 73 JoCL 318.

Internet links

Independent Review, *Setting the Boundaries – Reforming the Law on Sex Offenders* (2000) and Home Office, *Protecting the Public: Strengthening Protection against Sex Offenders and Reforming the Law on Sexual Offences* White Paper (2002), both at: http://webarchive.nationalarchives.gov.uk/.

Sexual Offences Act 2003: www.legislation.gov.uk.

13

Theft

AIMS AND OBJECTIVES

After reading this chapter you should be able to:

- Understand the basic origins and character of theft
- Understand the *actus reus* and *mens rea* of theft
- Be able to analyse critically the concept of appropriation in the definition of theft
- Understand the meaning of 'property' in the definition of theft and when that property is regarded as belonging to another
- Understand the concept of dishonesty in the law of theft
- Understand the importance of an intention to permanently deprive in the offence of theft
- Be able to analyse critically all the elements of the theft
- Be able to apply the law to factual situations to determine whether an offence of theft has been committed

13.1 Background

The law relating to theft, robbery, burglary and other connected offences against property (see Chapters 14 and 15) is contained in three Acts:

- Theft Act 1968
- Theft Act 1978 (s 3 only)
- Fraud Act 2006.

The Theft Act 1968 was an attempt to write a new and simple code for the law of theft and related offences. It made sweeping and fundamental changes to the law that had developed prior to 1968. The Act was based on the Eighth Report of the Criminal Law Revision Committee, *Theft and Related Offences*, Cmnd 2977 (1966).

Previous Acts were repealed and the 1968 Act was meant to provide a complete code of the law in this area.

The Act is intended to be

JUDGMENT

'expressed in simple language, as used and understood by ordinary literate men and women. It avoids as far as possible those terms of art which have acquired a special meaning understood only by lawyers in which many of the penal enactments were couched.'

Lord Diplock in *Treacy v DPP* [1971] 1 All ER 110

Despite this, the wording of the Theft Act 1968 has led to a number of cases going to the appeal courts. The decisions in some of these cases are not always easy to understand. In particular there have been complex decisions on the meaning of the word 'appropriates'. Another problem is that, as the wording uses ordinary English, the precise meaning is often left to the jury to decide. This can lead to inconsistency in decisions. As Professor Sir John Smith pointed out:

QUOTATION

'Even such ordinary words in the Theft Act as "dishonesty", "force", "building" etc. may involve definitional problems on which a jury require guidance if like is to be treated as like.'

D Ormerod, *Smith and Hogan Criminal Law* (13th edn, Butterworths, 2011), p. 779

Amendments to the Theft Act 1968

It soon became apparent that the law was defective in the area of obtaining by deception and, following the Thirteenth Report by the Criminal Law Revision Committee, Cmnd 6733 (1977), the Theft Act 1978 was passed. This repealed part of s 16 of the 1968 Act and instead created four new offences. The 1978 Act also added another offence, of making off without payment, to fill a gap in the law.

Despite this amendment, it was held in the case of *Preddy* [1996] 3 All ER 481 that the law still did not cover certain deception frauds in obtaining mortgages and money transfers. The Law Commission was asked to research this area of law, and following its report *Offences of Dishonesty: Money Transfers*, Law Com No 243, the Theft (Amendment) Act 1996 was passed to fill these gaps. This Act made amendments to both the Theft Act 1968 and the Theft Act 1978. However, the offences of deception were still not satisfactory and all deception offences were repealed and replaced by offences under the Fraud Act 2006.

Trial

Until 2014 all offences of theft were triable either way, and thus defendants could opt for trial at the Crown Court. However, under the Anti-social Behaviour, Crime and Policing Act 2014, low-value shoplifting cases under £200 are now summary only and so must be tried in the magistrates' court.

13.1.1 Theft

Theft is defined in s 1 of the Theft Act 1968 which states that:

SECTION

'1 A person is guilty of theft if he dishonestly appropriates property belonging to another with the intention of permanently depriving the other of it.'

tutor tip

'Learn all parts of the definition of theft thoroughly.'

The Act then goes on in the next five sections to give some help with the meaning of the words or phrases in the definition. This is done in the order that the words or phrases appear in the definition, making it easy to remember the section numbers. They are:

- s 2 – 'dishonestly';
- s 3 – 'appropriates';
- s 4 – 'property';
- s 5 – 'belonging to another';
- s 6 – 'with the intention of permanently depriving the other of it'.

Remember that the offence is in s 1. A person charged with theft is always charged with stealing 'contrary to section 1 of the Theft Act 1968'. Sections 2 to 6 are definition sections explaining s 1. They do not themselves create any offence.

13.1.2 The elements of theft

The *actus reus* of theft is made up of the three elements in the phrase 'appropriates property belonging to another'. So to prove the *actus reus* it has to be shown that there was appropriation by the defendant of something which is property within the definition of the Act and which, at the time of the appropriation, belonged to another. All these seem straightforward words, but the effect of the definitions in the Act together with case decisions means that there can be some surprises. For example, although the wording 'belonging to another' seems very clear, it is possible for a defendant to be found guilty of stealing his own property. (See section 13.4.1.)

There are two elements which must be proved for the *mens rea* of theft. These are that the appropriation of the property must be done 'dishonestly', and there must be the intention of permanently depriving the other person of it.

We will now go on to consider each of the elements of theft in depth.

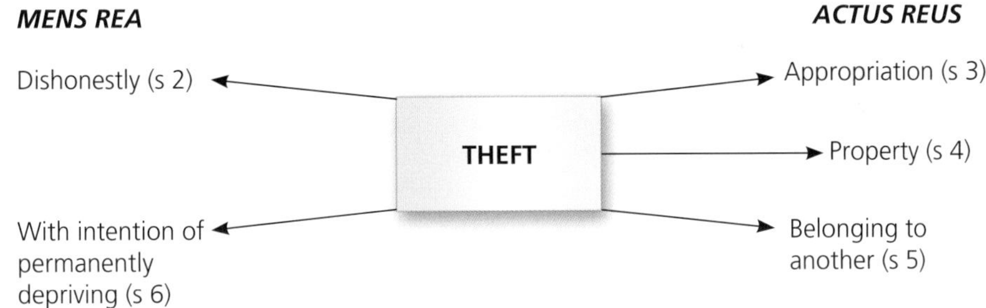

Figure 13.1 The elements of theft.

13.2 Appropriation

The more obvious situations of theft involve a physical taking, for example a pickpocket taking a wallet from someone's pocket. But appropriation is much wider than this.

Section 3(1) states that:

SECTION

'3(1) Any assumption by a person of the rights of an owner amounts to an appropriation, and this includes, where he has come by the property (innocently or not) without stealing it, any later assumption of a right to it by keeping or dealing with it as owner.'

13.2.1 Assumption of the rights of an owner

The first part to be considered is the statement that 'any assumption by a person of the rights of an owner amounts to appropriation'. The rights of the owner include selling the property or destroying it as well as such things as possessing it, consuming it, using it, lending it or hiring it out.

In *Pitham v Hehl* [1977] Crim LR 285, CA, D had sold furniture belonging to another person. This was held to be an appropriation. The offer to sell was an assumption of the rights of an owner and the appropriation took place at that point. It did not matter whether the furniture was removed from the house or not. Even if the owner was never deprived of the property, the defendant had still appropriated it by assuming the rights of the owner to offer the furniture for sale.

In *Corcoran v Anderton* (1980) Cr App 104, two youths tried to pull a woman's handbag from her grasp, causing it to fall to the floor. The seizing of the handbag was enough for an appropriation (the youths were found guilty of robbery which has to have a theft as one of its elements), even though they did not take the bag away.

The wording in s 3(1) is '*any* assumption by a person of the rights of an owner'. One question which the courts have had to deal with is whether the assumption has to be of *all* of the rights or whether it can just be of *any* of the rights. This was considered in *Morris* [1983] 3 All ER 288.

CASE EXAMPLE

Morris [1983] 3 All ER 288

D had switched the price labels of two items on the shelf in a supermarket. He had then put one of the items, which now had a lower price on it, into a basket provided by the store for shoppers and taken the item to the check-out, but had not gone through the check-out when he was arrested. He was convicted of theft. The House of Lords upheld his conviction on the basis that D had appropriated the items when he switched the labels.

Lord Roskill in the House of Lords stated that:

JUDGMENT

'It is enough for the prosecution if they have proved … the assumption of any of the rights of the owner of the goods in question.'

So there does not have to be an assumption of all the rights. This is a sensible decision since in many cases the defendant will not have assumed all of the rights. Quite often only one right will have been assumed, usually the right of possession.

Later assumption of a right

Section 3(1) also includes within the meaning of appropriation situations where a defendant has come by the property without stealing it, but has later assumed a right to it by keeping it or dealing with it as owner. This covers situations where the defendant has picked up someone else's property, e.g. a coat or a briefcase, thinking that it was his own. On getting home the defendant then realises that it is not his. If he then decides to keep the property, this is a later assumption of a right and is an appropriation for the purposes of the Theft Act 1968.

However, under s 3(1) if the person has stolen the item originally, then any later keeping or dealing is not an appropriation. This was important in *Atakpu and Abrahams*

[1994] Crim LR 693. The defendants had hired cars in Germany and Belgium using false driving licences and passports. They were arrested at Dover and charged with theft. The Court of Appeal quashed their convictions because the moment of appropriation under the law in *Gomez* (1993) (see section 13.2.3) was when they obtained the cars. So the theft had occurred outside the jurisdiction of the English courts. As they had already stolen the cars, keeping and driving them could not be an appropriation. This meant that the theft was completed in the country where they hired the cars, and there was no theft in this country.

13.2.2 Consent to the appropriation

Can a defendant appropriate an item when it has been given to them by the owner? This is an area which has caused major problems. Nowhere in the Theft Act does it say that the appropriation has to be without the consent of the owner. So, what is the position where the owner has allowed the defendant to take something because the owner thought that the defendant was paying for it with a genuine cheque? Or where the item was hired (as in *Atakpu and Abrahams*), but unknown to the owner the defendant intended to take it permanently? This point was addressed in *Lawrence* [1972] AC 626; [1971] Cr App R 64.

CASE EXAMPLE

Lawrence [1972] AC 626; [1971] Cr App Rep 64

An Italian student, who spoke very little English, arrived at Victoria Station and showed an address to Lawrence who was a taxi driver. The journey should have cost 50p, but Lawrence told him it was expensive. The student got out a £1 note and offered it to the driver. Lawrence said it was not enough and so the student opened his wallet and allowed Lawrence to help himself to another £6. Lawrence put forward the argument that he had not appropriated the money, as the student had consented to him taking it. Both the Court of Appeal and the House of Lords rejected this argument and held that there was appropriation in this situation.

Viscount Dilhorne said:

JUDGMENT

'I see no ground for concluding that the omission of the words "without the consent of the owner" was inadvertent and not deliberate, and to read the subsection as if they were included is, in my opinion, wholly unwarranted. Parliament by the omission of these words has relieved the prosecution of the burden of establishing that the taking was without the owner's consent. That is no longer an ingredient of the offence.'

This view of Viscount Dilhorne is supported by the fact that under the old law in the Larceny Act 1916, the prosecution had to prove that the property had been taken without the consent of the owner.

However, in *Morris* (1983) the House of Lords did not take the same view. This was the case where the defendant had switched labels on goods in a supermarket. Lord Roskill said 'the concept of appropriation involves not an act expressly or impliedly authorised by the owner but an act by way of adverse interference with or usurpation of [the rights of an owner]'.

In fact this part of the judgment in *Morris* (1983) was *obiter*, since the switching of the labels was clearly an unauthorised act. But the judgment in *Morris* (1983) caused confusion since it contradicted *Lawrence* without the Law Lords saying whether *Lawrence* (1972) was overruled or merely distinguished.

In subsequent cases, matters became even more complicated. In *Dobson v General Accident Fire and Life Insurance Corp* [1990] 1 QB 354, a civil case, Dobson made a claim on his insurance policy for theft of some jewellery after he had agreed to sell the jewellery to X, who gave as payment a building society cheque which unknown to Dobson was stolen. The insurance company refused to pay on the basis that, although there had been an offence of obtaining property by deception (s 15 Theft Act 1968), there was no theft and the policy only covered theft. The Court of Appeal held that there had been a theft, on the basis that the property was not intended to pass to X except in exchange for a valid cheque, so the property still belonged to Dobson and X had appropriated it at the moment he took delivery of it.

Parker LJ pointed out that in *Lawrence* (1972) the student had merely allowed or permitted the taxi driver to take the extra money. This was consistent with the concept of consent but differed from situations where the owner had authorised the taking as in *Skipp* [1975] Crim LR 114 and *Fritschy* [1985] Crim LR 745. In *Skipp* (1975), a lorry driver posing as a haulage contractor was given three loads of oranges and onions to take from London to Leicester. Before reaching the place for delivery he drove off with the loads. The Court of Appeal held that the collecting of the loads was done with the consent of the owner and that the appropriation had only happened at the moment he diverted from his authorised route.

Parker LJ considered this case in his judgment in *Dobson* (1990) and pointed out that at the time of loading the goods on to the lorry there was more than consent: there was express authority. The same had happened in *Fritschy* (1985) where D, the agent of a Dutch company dealing in coins was asked by the company to collect some krugerrands (foreign coins) from England and take them to Switzerland. He collected them and went to Switzerland but then went off with them. The Court of Appeal quashed his conviction for theft because all that he did in England was consistent with the authority given to him. There was no act of appropriation within the jurisdiction: this only occurred after Fritschy had got to Switzerland.

13.2.3 The decision in *Gomez*

The point as to whether the appropriation had to be without the consent of the owner was considered again by the House of Lords in *Gomez* [1993] 1 All ER 1.

CASE EXAMPLE

Gomez [1993] 1 All ER 1

Gomez was the assistant manager of a shop. He persuaded the manager to sell electrical goods worth over £17,000 to an accomplice and to accept payment by two cheques, telling the manager they were as good as cash. The cheques were stolen and had no value. Gomez was charged and convicted of theft of the goods.

The Court of Appeal quashed the conviction, relying on the judgment in *Morris* (1983) that there had to be 'adverse interference' for there to be appropriation. They decided that the manager's consent to and authorisation of the transaction meant there was no appropriation at the moment of taking the goods. The case was appealed to the House of Lords with the Court of Appeal certifying, as a point of law of general public importance, the following question:

> 'When theft is alleged and that which is alleged to be stolen passes to the defendant with the consent of the owner, but that has been obtained by a false representation, has (a) an appropriation within the meaning of section 1(1) of the Theft Act 1968 taken place, or (b) must such a passing of property necessarily involve an element of adverse interference with or usurpation of some right of the owner?'

The House of Lords decided, by a majority of four to one, in answer to (a) 'yes' an appropriation had taken place and in answer to (b) 'no' there was no need for adverse interference with or usurpation of some right of the owner. Lord Keith giving the majority decision referred back to the case of *Lawrence* (1972), pointing out the effect of judgment in that case:

JUDGMENT

'While it is correct to say that appropriation for purposes of section 3(1) includes the latter sort of act [adverse interference or usurpation], it does not necessarily follow that no other act can amount to an appropriation and, in particular, that no act expressly or impliedly authorised by the owner can in any circumstances do so. Indeed *Lawrence v Commissioner of Metropolitan Police* is a clear decision to the contrary since it laid down unequivocally that an act may be an appropriation notwithstanding that it is done with the consent of the owner.'

Lord Keith also stated that no sensible distinction could be made between consent and authorisation. Lord Browne-Wilkinson who agreed with Lord Keith put the point on consent even more clearly when he said:

JUDGMENT

'I regard the word "appropriate" in isolation as being an objective description of the act done irrespective of the mental state of the owner or the accused. It is impossible to reconcile the decision in *Lawrence* (that the question of consent is irrelevant in considering whether this has been an appropriation) with the views expressed in *Morris* which latter views, in my judgment, were incorrect.'

This judgment in *Gomez* (1993) resolved the conflicts of the earlier cases as the judgment in *Lawrence* was approved while the dictum of Lord Roskill in *Morris* (1983) was disapproved. The cases of *Skipp* (1975) and *Fritschy* (1985) were overruled.

The decision widened the scope of theft but it can be argued that it is now too wide. It made s 15 of the Theft Act 1968 (obtaining property by deception – now repealed and replaced by offences under the Fraud Act 2006) virtually unnecessary as situations of obtaining by deception could be charged as theft. The facts in *Gomez* (1993) were clearly obtained by deception as he persuaded the manager to hand over the goods by telling him the cheques were as good as cash when he knew they were worthless.

This factor was one of the reasons for Lord Lowry dissenting from the decision of the majority in *Gomez* (1993). He also thought that extending the meaning of appropriation in this way was contrary to the intentions of the Criminal Law Revision Committee in their Eighth Report. Lord Lowry thought that the Law Lords should have looked at that report in deciding the meaning of appropriation. However, the majority accepted Lord Keith's view that it served no useful purpose to do so.

It can be argued that the effect of the decision in *Gomez* (1993) has been to redefine theft. This point of view was put by a leading academic, Professor Sir John Smith, who wrote:

QUOTATION

'Anyone doing anything whatever to property belonging to another, with or without his consent, appropriates it; and, if he does so dishonestly and with intent by that, or any subsequent act, to permanently deprive, he commits theft.'

D Ormerod, *Smith and Hogan Criminal Law* (13th edn, Oxford University Press, 2011), p. 787

ACTIVITY

Looking at judgments

The following are two extracts from the decision in the House of Lords in the case of *Gomez* [1993] 1 All ER 1. The first is from the judgment of Lord Keith of Kinkel. The second is from the dissenting judgment by Lord Lowry.

Read the extracts and answer the questions on the next page.

Lord Keith of Kinkle The actual decision in *Morris* was correct, but it was erroneous, in addition to being unnecessary for the decision, to indicate that an act expressly or impliedly authorised by the owner could never amount to an appropriation. There is no material distinction between the facts in *Dobson* and those in the present case. In each case the owner of the goods was induced by fraud to part with them to the rogue. *Lawrence* makes it clear that consent to or authorisation by the owner of the taking by the rogue is irrelevant. The taking amounted to an appropriation within the meaning of section 1(1) of the Theft Act.	*Discussion of earlier case decisions*
The decision in *Lawrence* was a clear decision of this House upon the construction of the word 'appropriate' in section 1(1) of the Act, which had stood for twelve years when doubt was thrown upon it by obiter dicta in *Morris*. *Lawrence* must be regarded as authoritative and correct, and there is no question of it now being right to depart from it.	*Upholding the decision in* Lawrence
Lord Lowry To be guilty of theft the offender, as I shall call him, must act dishonestly and must have the intention of permanently depriving the owner of property. Section 1(3) shows that in order to interpret the word 'appropriates' (and thereby to define theft), sections 1 to 6 must be read together. The ordinary and natural meaning of 'appropriate' is to take for oneself, or to treat as one's own, property which belongs to someone else. The primary dictionary meaning is 'take possession of, take to oneself, especially without authority', and that is in my opinion the meaning which the word bears in section 1(1). The act of appropriating property is a one-sided act, done without the consent or authority of the owner. And, if the owner consents to transfer property to the offender or to a third party, the offender does not appropriate the property, even if the owner's consent has been obtained by fraud. This statement represents the old doctrine in regard to obtaining property by false pretences, to which I shall advert presently.	*Dissenting judgment* *Definition of theft* *Dictionary meaning of 'appropriate'* *Effect if owner consents*

Coming now to section 3, the *primary* meaning of 'assumption' is 'taking on oneself', again a unilateral act, and this meaning is consistent with subsections (1) and (2). To use the word in its secondary, neutral sense would neutralise the word 'appropriation', to which assumption is here equated, and would lead to a number of strange results. Incidentally, I can see no magic in the words 'an owner' in subsection (1). Every case in real life must involve *the* owner or *the* person described in section 5(1); 'the rights' may mean 'all the rights', which would be the normal grammatical meaning, or (less probably, in my opinion) 'any rights': see *R. v. Morris* (1984) A.C. at p. 332H. For present purposes it does not appear to matter; the word 'appropriate' does not on either interpretation acquire the meaning contended for by the Crown.

Meaning of 'assumption' in s 3 Theft Act 1968

Disagrees on meaning of appropriate

QUESTIONS

1. This decision was by the House of Lords. (Remember, this was the final court of appeal at the time – the Supreme Court has since replaced the House of Lords.) What effect do judgments of the House of Lords have on courts below them in the court hierarchy?
2. In his judgment Lord Keith refers to the cases of *Morris* [1983] 3 All ER 288, *Dobson v General Accident and Fire Insurance Corp* [1990] 1 QB 354 and *Lawrence* (1972) AC 626. Explain briefly the facts and decisions in these three cases.
3. According to Lord Keith, what did the case of *Lawrence* make clear?
4. In the penultimate sentence of the extract from Lord Keith's judgment, he refers to *obiter dicta*. Explain what is meant by *obiter dicta*.
5. Lord Lowry gave a dissenting judgment. What is meant by a 'dissenting judgment'?
6. What meaning did Lord Lowry state that 'appropriates' has?
7. Why did Lord Lowry disagree with the other judges in the House of Lords?

KEY FACTS

Key facts on appropriation

Law on appropriation	Section/case	Comment
Definition is 'any assumption of the rights of an owner'.	s 3(1) Theft Act 1968	Includes a later assumption where D has come by the property without stealing it.
No need to touch property for an appropriation.	*Pitham v Hehl* (1977)	An offer to sell property was appropriation of the rights of the owner.
No need for the assumption of all of the rights of an owner.	*Morris* (1983)	An assumption of any of the rights is sufficient (label swapping on goods in supermarket).
There can be an assumption even though there is apparent consent.	*Lawrence* (1972)	Irrelevant whether owner consents to appropriation or not.

Where consent is obtained by fraud there can still be appropriation.	*Gomez* (1993)	An assumption of any of the rights is sufficient. No need for adverse interference with or usurpation of some right of the owner.
There can still be appropriation even though the owner truly consents to it.	*Hinks* (2000)	Appropriation is a neutral word. No differentiation between cases of consent induced by fraud and consent given in any other circumstances. All are appropriation, even gifts.
Where property is transferred for value to a person acting in good faith, no later assumption of rights can be theft.	s 3(2) Theft Act 1968, *Wheeler* (1990)	When sale is complete before the seller knows the items are stolen, the later completion of the sale when the facts are known does not make it theft.

13.2.4 Consent without deception

So does the decision in *Gomez* (1993) extend to situations where a person has given property to another without any deception being made? This was the problem raised in the case of *Hinks* (2000) 4 All ER 833.

CASE EXAMPLE

Hinks (2000) 4 All ER 833

Hinks was a 38-year-old woman who had befriended a man who had a low IQ and was very naive. He was, however, mentally capable of understanding the concept of ownership and of making a valid gift. Over a period of about eight months Hinks accompanied the man on numerous occasions to his building society where he withdrew money. The total was about £60,000 and this money was deposited in Hinks' account. The man also gave Hinks a television set. She was convicted of theft of the money and the TV set. The judge directed the jury to consider whether the man was so mentally incapable that the defendant herself realised that ordinary and decent people would regard it as dishonest to accept a gift from him.

On appeal it was argued that, if the gift was valid, the acceptance of it could not be theft. The Court of Appeal dismissed the appeal and the following question was certified for the House of Lords to consider: 'Whether the acquisition of an indefeasible title to property is capable of amounting to an appropriation of property belonging to another for the purposes of section 1(1) of the Theft Act 1968?' In the House of Lords the appeal was dismissed on a majority of three judges to two with four of them giving the answer 'yes' to the question. Lord Hobhouse dissented and answered the question in the negative. Lord Hutton, although agreeing with the majority on the point of law, dissented on whether the conduct showed dishonesty.

Lord Steyn gave the leading judgment. He pointed out that in the case of *Gomez* (1993), the House of Lords had already made it clear that any act may be an appropriation regardless of whether it was done with or without the consent of the owner. They had also rejected a submission that there could be no appropriation where the entire proprietary interest in property passed. Lord Steyn summarised the law in *Gomez* (1993) as follows.

JUDGMENT

> 'it is immaterial whether the act was done with the owner's consent or authority. It is true of course that the certified question in *R v Gomez* referred to the situation where consent had been obtained by fraud. But the majority judgments do not differentiate between cases of consent induced by fraud and consent given in any other circumstances. The ratio involves a proposition of general application. *R v Gomez* therefore gives effect to s 3(1) of the 1968 Act by treating "appropriation" as a neutral word comprehending "any assumption by a person of the rights of an owner".'

A major argument against the ruling in *Hinks* (2000) is that in civil law the gift was valid and the £60,000 and the TV set belonged to the defendant. Lord Steyn accepted that this was the situation, but he considered that this was irrelevant to the decision.

JUDGMENT

> 'The purposes of the civil law and the criminal law are somewhat different. In theory the two systems should be in perfect harmony. In a practical world there will sometimes be some disharmony between the two systems. In any event it would be wrong to assume on *a priori* grounds that the criminal law rather than the civil law is defective. Given the jury's conclusions, one is entitled to observe that the appellant's conduct should constitute theft, the only charge available. The tension which exists between the civil and the criminal law is therefore not in my view a factor which justifies a departure from the law as stated in *Lawrence*'s case and *R v Gomez*.'

Lord Hobhouse dissented for three main reasons:

- That the law on gifts involves conduct by the owner in transferring the gift, and once this was done, the gift was the property of the donee. It was not even necessary that the donee should know of the gift, for example, money could be transferred to the donee's bank account without the donee's knowledge. In view of this it was impossible to say, as the Court of Appeal had, that a gift may be clear evidence of appropriation.
- That, as a gift transfers the ownership in the goods to the donee at the moment the owner completes the transfer, the property ceased to be 'property belonging to another' unless it could be brought within the situations identified in s 5 of the Theft Act 1968 (see section 13.4.2).
- If the acceptance of a gift is treated as an appropriation, this creates difficulties under s 2(1)(a) of the Act which states that a person is not dishonest if he appropriated property in the belief that he had in law a right to deprive the other person of it. The donee does indeed have a right to deprive the donor of the property.

He also pointed out that there were further difficulties under the Theft Act 1968, as under s 6 (which defines intention to permanently deprive – see section 13.6) the donee would not be acting regardless of the donor's rights as the donor has already surrendered his rights. Further it was difficult to say that under s 3 the donee was 'assuming the rights of an owner' when she already had those rights under the law on gifts.

Despite these arguments put forward by Lord Hobhouse, the majority ruling means that even where there is a valid gift the defendant is considered to have appropriated the property. The critical question is whether what the defendant did was dishonest.

13.2.5 Appropriation of credit balances

Another area which has created difficulty for the courts is deciding when appropriation takes place where the object of the theft is a credit balance in a bank or building society account. In such cases the thief may be in a different place (or even country) from the account. In *Tomsett* [1985] Crim LR 369, $7 million was being transferred by one bank to another in New York in order to earn overnight interest. The defendant, an employee of the first bank in London, sent a telex diverting the $7 million plus interest to another bank in New York for the benefit of an account in Geneva. The Court of Appeal accepted, without hearing any argument on the point, that the theft could only occur where the property was. This meant that D was not guilty of theft under English law, as the theft was either in New York or Geneva. The money had never been in an account in England. So even though D's act occurred in London, the matter was outside the jurisdiction of the English courts.

This does not seem a very satisfactory decision, and in fact it was not followed by the Divisional Court in *Governor of Pentonville Prison, ex parte Osman* [1989] 3 All ER 701 when deciding whether Osman could be deported to stand trial for theft in Hong Kong. Osman had sent a telex from Hong Kong to a bank in New York instructing payment from one company's account to another company's account. If *Tomsett* (1985) had been followed, then the theft would have been deemed to have occurred in New York. However, the Divisional Court held that the sending of the telex was itself the appropriation, and so the theft took place in Hong Kong.

JUDGMENT

'In *R v Morris* . . . the House of Lords made it clear that it is not necessary for an appropriation that the defendant assume all rights of an owner. It is enough that he should assume any of the owner's rights . . . If so, then one of the plainest rights possessed by the owner of the chose in action in the present case must surely have been the right to draw on the account in question . . . So far as the customer is concerned, he has a right as against the bank to have his cheques met. It is that right which the defendant assumes by presenting a cheque, or by sending a telex instruction without authority. The act of sending the telex instruction is therefore the act of theft itself.'

The most surprising point about this decision is that two of the judges (Lloyd LJ and French J) had also decided the case of *Tomsett* (1985) but then refused to follow their own decision.

In the judgment in *Osman* (1989) the court had mentioned presenting a cheque as one of the rights of an owner, and this was the situation which occurred in *Ngan* [1998] 1 Cr App R 331.

CASE EXAMPLE

Ngan [1998] 1 Cr App Rep 331

D had opened a bank account in England and been given an account number which had previously belonged to a debt collection agency. Over £77,000 intended for the agency was then paid into D's bank account. Because of s 5(4) of the Theft Act 1968 (see section 13.4.4) this money was regarded as belonging to the agency. D realised there was a mistake but signed and sent blank cheques to her sister (who also knew of the circumstances) in Scotland. Two cheques were presented in Scotland and one in England.

The Court of Appeal applied the principle in *Osman* (1989) that the presentation of a cheque was the point at which the assumption of a right of the owner took place. They quashed D's conviction for theft in respect of the two cheques presented in Scotland, as they were outside the jurisdiction of the English courts, but upheld her conviction for theft in respect of the cheque presented in England. They took the view that signing blank cheques and sending them to her sister were preparatory acts to the theft and not the actual theft.

However, it should be noted that in *Osman* (1989) the court had also stated that appropriation took place when the defendant dishonestly issued a cheque. So, it could be argued that the decision in *Ngan* was wrong as sending the cheques to her sister was 'issuing' them.

The problems of when and where appropriation takes place in banking cases has become even more difficult with the use of computer banking. In *Governor of Brixton Prison, ex parte Levin* [1997] 3 All ER 289, the Divisional Court distinguished the use of a computer from the sending of a telex or the presentation of a cheque. D had used a computer in St Petersburg, Russia to gain unauthorised access to a bank in Parsipenny, America and divert money into false accounts. The court ruled that appropriation took place where the effect of the keyboard instructions took place.

JUDGMENT

'We see no reason why the appropriation of the client's right to give instructions should not be regarded as having taken place in the computer [in America]. Lloyd LJ [in *Osman*] did not rule out the possibility of the place where the telex was received also being counted as the place where the appropriation occurred if the courts ever adopted the view that a crime could have a dual location ... [T]he operation of the keyboard by a computer operator produces a virtually instantaneous result on the magnetic disc of the computer even though it may be 10,000 miles away. It seems to us artificial to regard the act as having been done in one rather than the other place. But, in the position of having to choose ... we would opt for Parsipenny. The fact that the applicant was physically in St Petersburg is of far less significance than the fact that he was looking at and operating on magnetic discs located in Parsipenny. The essence of what he was doing was there. Until the instruction is recorded on the disc there is in fact no appropriation.'

KEY FACTS

Key facts on the law on appropriation of credit balances

Type of transaction	Case	Where does the appropriation take place?		
		Place where thief does act	Place where instructions are received	Place where transfer is complete
Cheque	*Ngan* (1998)	No. Signing cheque and sending it to sister not appropriation.	Yes. The point of presenting cheque at bank.	n.a.
Telex	*Tomsett* (1985)	No.	Either here.	Or here.
Telex	*Osman* (1989)	Yes.	No. Unless it could occur at two places.	No.
Computer	*Levin* (1997)	No. Unless it could occur at two places.	Yes. As the operation of the keyboard produced a 'virtually instantaneous' result.	–

These cases leave the law on where and when appropriation takes places in banking cases a little uncertain, but the principles appear to be:

- telex instructions – appropriation at place and point of sending telex;
- presenting a cheque – appropriation at place and point of presentation;
- computer instructions – appropriation at place and point of receipt of instructions.

13.2.6 Protection of innocent purchasers

As appropriation has been ruled to be a 'neutral word comprehending any assumption by a person of the rights of an owner', it is important to protect people who innocently acquire a right in property for value from a charge of theft. This is done by s 3(2) of the Theft Act 1968:

SECTION

'3(2) Where property or a right or interest in property is or purports to be transferred for value to a person acting in good faith, no later assumption by him of rights which he believed himself to be acquiring shall, by reason of any defect in the transferor's title, amount to theft of the property.'

This section was included by the Criminal Law Revision Committee because without it a purchaser who bought goods for the market value not knowing they were stolen, but who later discovered they were stolen, would be guilty of theft if he then decided to keep the goods. The CLRC thought that, while there might be a case for making such conduct criminal, 'on the whole it seems to us that, whatever view is taken of the buyer's moral duty, the law would be too strict if it made him guilty of theft'.

Under s 3(2), not only is the original acquisition not theft, but also any later dealing in the property by the innocent purchaser cannot be theft. This was illustrated in *Wheeler* (1990) 92 Cr App Rep 279.

CASE EXAMPLE

Wheeler (1990) 92 Cr App Rep 279

D purchased some military antiques which, unknown to him, were stolen. Before he knew they were stolen he agreed a sale of some of the items to another person. The arrangement was that the items would be left with D while the new purchaser arranged for payment. By the time the new purchaser returned to collect and pay for the items, D had been told by the police that they were stolen. D could not be guilty of theft by keeping them for himself or by selling them.

ACTIVITY

Applying the law

Discuss whether there has been an appropriation in each of the following situations.

1. Jasper has an argument with his neighbour. When his neighbour is out, Jasper holds an auction of the neighbour's garden tools and patio furniture. The neighbour returns before any of the furniture is taken away.
2. Poppy goes shopping at the local supermarket and takes her three-year-old daughter, Selina, with her. While at the check-out, Selina takes some bars of chocolate and puts

them in the pocket of her pushchair. Poppy does not realise Selina has done this until she finds the chocolate when they get home. Poppy decides that she will not take the chocolate back to the supermarket.

3. The owner of a shop asks Carry, who is a lorry driver, to pick up a load of DVD equipment and take it to a warehouse. Carry agrees to do this, but after collecting the equipment decides that she will not take it to the warehouse but will instead sell it.
4. Brendan, aged 19, is infatuated with Hannah, a married woman aged 30. Brendan uses his student loan to buy expensive presents for Hannah. She knows he is a student and has very little money but she accepts the gifts from him.
5. Adam buys some motorcycle parts from a small garage. Three days later he is told by one of his friends that the garage has just been raided by the police and much of their stock of spare parts has been identified as stolen goods. Adam decides to keep the parts he has and not to say anything about them.
6. Mike, who lives in England, goes on holiday to Poland. While there he uses a computer to get unauthorised access to his company's English bank accounts and arranges for money to be transferred to an account he has in Switzerland. While in Poland he is asked by a colleague to drive a car to Switzerland. Mike agrees to do this although he has already decided to take the car to England and sell it.

13.3 Property

For there to be theft, the defendant must have appropriated 'property'. Section 4 gives a very comprehensive definition of property which means that almost anything can be stolen. The definition is in s 4(1) of the Theft Act 1968:

SECTION

'4(1) "Property" includes money and all other property real or personal, including things in action and other intangible property.'

This section lists five types of items which are included in the definition of 'property'. These are:

- money
- real property
- personal property
- things in action
- other intangible property.

personal property
All moveable property

In this list, money is self-explanatory. It means coins and banknotes of any currency.

Personal property is also straightforward as it covers all moveable items. Books, CDs, jewellery, clothes and cars are obvious examples, but it also includes very large items such as aeroplanes or tanks and very small trivial items such as a sheet of paper. It has even been held in *Kelly and Lindsay* [1998] 3 All ER 741 that body parts from dead bodies can be personal property, for the purposes of theft.

CASE EXAMPLE

Kelly and Lindsay [1998] 3 All ER 741

Kelly was a sculptor who asked Lindsay to take body parts from the Royal College of Surgeons where he worked as a laboratory assistant. Kelly then made casts of the parts. They were convicted of theft and appealed on the point of law that body parts were not property. The Court of Appeal held that, though a dead body was not normally property within the definition of the Theft Act, the body parts were property as they had acquired 'different attributes by virtue of the application of skill, such as dissection or preservation techniques, for exhibition or teaching purposes'.

13.3.1 Things which cannot be stolen

However, there are some exceptions which cannot be stolen. These are set out in s 4(3) and s 4(4) of the Theft Act 1968. The first of these concerns plants and fungi growing wild.

SECTION

'4(3) A person who picks mushrooms growing wild on any land, or who picks flowers, fruit or foliage from a plant growing wild on any land, does not (although not in possession of the land) steal what he picks, unless he does it for reward or sale or other commercial purpose.

For the purposes of this subsection "mushroom" includes any fungus, and "plant" includes any shrub or tree.'

This only applies to plants etc. growing wild, so it is possible to steal cultivated plants. Taking apples from trees in a farmer's orchard would be theft, but picking blackberries growing wild in the hedgerow around the field would not be theft unless it was done for sale or reward or other commercial purpose. Similarly, picking roses from someone's garden would be theft, but picking wild flowers in a field would not (unless for sale or reward). However, it should be noted that it is an offence to pick, uproot or destroy certain wild plants under the Wildlife and Countryside Act 1981.

Where picking fungi, flowers, fruit or foliage is done with the intention of selling them or for reward or any commercial purpose, then they are considered property which can be stolen. An example of this would be picking holly to sell at Christmas time.

The other exception of personal property which is not 'property' for the purpose of theft concerns wild creatures.

SECTION

'4(4) Wild creatures, tamed or untamed, shall be regarded as property; but a person cannot steal a wild creature not tamed nor ordinarily kept in captivity, or the carcase of any such creature, unless it has been reduced into possession by or on behalf of another person and possession of it has not since been lost or abandoned, or another person is in course of reducing it into possession.'

The effect of this subsection is that it is not theft if a wild creature such as a deer is taken from the grounds of a large estate (though there is an offence of poaching) but it is theft if a deer is taken from a zoo, as in this case it is ordinarily kept in captivity. In *Cresswell v DPP* [2006] EWHC 3379 (Admin), a case on criminal damage, it was held that wild badgers were not property (see section 16.1.5). The definition of wild creatures as 'property' in the Criminal Damage Act 1971 is similar (though not identical) to the definition in the Theft Act 1968.

real property
Land and buildings

13.3.2 Real property

Real property is the legal term for land and buildings. Under s 4(1), land can be stolen, but s 4(2) states that this can only be done in three circumstances:

SECTION

'4(2) A person cannot steal land, or things forming part of land and severed from it by him or by his directions, except in the following cases, that is to say –

(a) when he is a trustee or personal representative, or is authorised by power of attorney, or as liquidator of a company, or otherwise, to sell or dispose of land belonging to another, and he appropriates the land or anything forming part of it by dealing with it in breach of the confidence reposed in him: or

(b) when he is not in possession of the land and appropriates anything forming part of the land by severing it or causing it to be severed or after it has been severed; or

(c) when, being in possession of the land under a tenancy, he appropriates the whole or any part of any fixture or structure let to be used with the land.'

So there is only one category of person who can be charged with stealing any land itself. These are trustees etc., who act in breach of confidence. The second circumstance only applies where something has been severed from the land. This makes it theft to dig up turfs from someone's lawn or to dismantle a wall and take the bricks. In 1972, a man was prosecuted for stealing Cleckheaton railway station by dismantling it and removing it. He was in fact acquitted by the jury as he said he was acting under a claim of right, but there was no doubt that the station could be property under the Theft Act definition. Section 4(2)(b) also covers situations where the owner of the land has legitimately severed something, such as stone from a quarry, but another person then appropriates the stone. This person will be guilty under s 4(2)(b).

The final part of s 4(2)(c) applies only to tenants of land, who can be guilty of theft if they appropriate fixtures or structures from the land. As tenants they are in possession of the land and so cannot be guilty under s 4(2)(b). However, if a tenant appropriates an item such as a door handle or a washbasin, then this can be theft. This subsection only requires appropriation; it does not require the item to be severed from the land. As appropriation means 'any assumption of the rights of an owner', this could include a situation where the tenant sold a fireplace to a dealer on the basis that the dealer would dismantle it later. The act of selling is an assumption of the rights of an owner so the theft occurs even if the dealer never does dismantle the fireplace.

13.3.3 Things in action

thing in action
A right which can be enforced against another person

A **thing in action** is a right which can be enforced against another person by an action in law. The right itself is property under the definition in s 4. An example is a bank account. The bank does not keep coins or banknotes for each customer's account in a separate box! Instead the customer has a right to the payment of the amount in his account. Even an overdraft facility is a thing in action as the customer who has the facility has a right to withdraw money from the bank up to the limit of the overdraft.

So if D causes the bank to debit another person's account, he has appropriated a thing in action. If he does this dishonestly and with the intention permanently to deprive the other of it, then D is guilty of theft.

CASE EXAMPLE

Kohn (1979) 69 Cr App R 395

Kohn was an accountant authorised by a company to draw cheques on the company's account to pay the company's debts. The company had an overdraft facility and was sometimes overdrawn. When Kohn drew cheques on the company's account to meet his own personal liabilities he was guilty of theft, as the bank account was a thing in action. This was so whether it was a credit balance or the overdraft facility.

A cheque itself is a thing in action, but it is also a piece of paper which is property that can be stolen, and it is a 'valuable security' which can also be stolen under the definition of 'property'.

13.3.4 Other intangible property

This refers to other rights which have no physical presence but can be stolen under the Theft Act. In *Attorney-General of Hong Kong v Chan Nai-Keung* [1987] 1 WLR 1339, an export quota for textiles was intangible property which could be stolen. A patent is also intangible property which can be stolen.

However, there are some types of intangible property which have been held not to be property within the Theft Act definition. In *Oxford v Moss* [1979] Crim LR 119, knowledge of the questions on an examination paper was held not to be property. Electricity is another sort of intangible property which cannot be stolen, but there is a separate offence under s 13 of the Theft Act 1968 of dishonestly using electricity without due authority, or dishonestly causing it to be wasted or diverted. Figure 13.2 summarises what property can be or cannot be stolen under the Theft Act 1978.

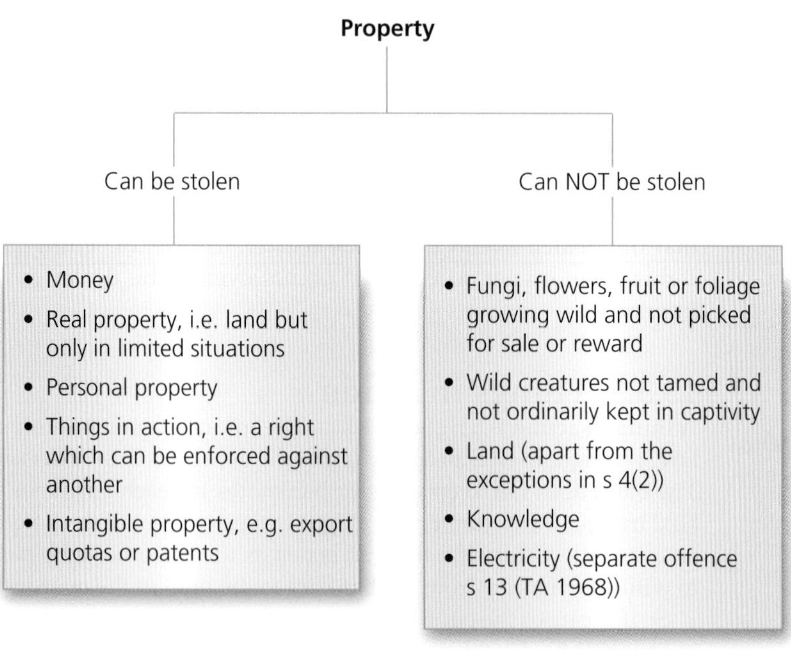

Figure 13.2 Property in the law of theft.

ACTIVITY

Applying the law

Explain whether the items in each of the following situations would be property for the purposes of theft.

1. Arnie runs a market stall selling flowers. Just before Christmas he picks a lot of holly from a wood, intending to sell it on his stall. He then digs up a small fir tree for his own use. On his way home he sees some late flowering roses in a garden and picks them to give to his girlfriend.
2. Della finds the examination papers she is to sit next week in the next-door office. She writes out the questions from the first paper on to a notepad of her own. The second paper is very long, so she uses the office photocopier to take a copy, using paper already in the machine.
3. Gareth and Harry go out poaching pheasants. Gareth successfully shoots one pheasant and picks up the dead bird. Harry fails to hit any. As they are going home Harry sees an unattended Land Rover. He looks inside it and sees that in the back are two dead pheasants. He takes them.

13.4 Belonging to another

For the purposes of theft, the property must belong to another. However, s 5(1) of the Theft Act 1968 gives a very wide definition of what is meant by 'belonging to another'.

SECTION

'5(1) Property shall be regarded as belonging to any person having possession or control of it, or having in it any proprietary right or interest (not being an equitable interest arising only from an agreement to transfer or grant an interest).'

From this it can be seen that possession or control of the property or any proprietary interest in it is sufficient. One reason for making it wide is so that the prosecution does not have to prove who is the legal owner.

13.4.1 Possession or control

Obviously, the owner of property normally has possession and control of it, but there are many other situations in which a person can have either possession or control of property. Someone who hires a car has both possession and control during the period of hire. If the car is stolen during this time, then the thief can be charged with stealing it from the hirer. Equally, as the car hire firm still own the car (a proprietary right), the thief could be charged with stealing it from them.

The possession or control of the item does not have to be lawful. Where B has stolen jewellery from A and subsequently C steals it from B, B is in possession or control of that jewellery and C can be charged with stealing it from B. This is useful where it is not known who the original owner is, as C can still be guilty of theft. This wide definition of 'belonging to' has led to the situation in which an owner was convicted of stealing his own car.

CASE EXAMPLE

Turner (No 2) [1971] 2 All ER 441

Turner left his car at a garage for repairs. It was agreed that he would pay for the repairs when he collected the car after the repairs had been completed. When the repairs were almost finished the garage left the car parked on the roadway outside their premises. Turner used a spare key to take the car during the night without paying for the repairs. The Court of Appeal held that the garage was in possession or control of the car and so Turner could be guilty of stealing his own car.

lien
A right to retain an article in one's possession

The decision in this case has been criticised. The garage clearly had a **lien** (a legal right to retain the car until payment was made), and it could have been held that this gave the garage control of the car. However, the judge had directed the jury to ignore any question of a lien. On appeal to the Court of Appeal the judges simply based their decision to uphold the conviction on the fact that the garage had possession and control. In fact, if the question of lien is ignored, the garage were bailees of the car, and under the law of bailment, Turner had the right to end the bailment at any time and take the car back. The point also involved whether Turner was acting dishonestly and this is discussed at section 13.6.1.

In a subsequent case, *Meredith* [1973] Crim LR 253, a Crown Court judge directed a jury differently. In this case D's car had been impounded by the police because it was causing an obstruction. D removed it without the police knowing and without paying the charge to get it out of the pound. It was held that D could not be convicted of theft even though the car was apparently in the possession and control of the police. Although the police had a right to enforce the charge for its removal, they had no right to keep the car.

The decision in *Turner* that the words 'possession or control' were not qualified in any way was followed in *Smith and others* [2011] EWCA Crim 66.

CASE EXAMPLE

Smith and others [2011] EWCA Crim 66

Ds arranged to meet V, who was a drug dealer, to buy some heroin from him. When they met, Ds used force on V so that he handed over the heroin without any payment. Ds were convicted of robbing V of the drugs. On appeal Smith argued that there was no theft (an essential element of robbery) as V was unlawfully in possession of the drugs. The Court of Appeal quoted from the judgment in *Turner* in which Lord Parker CJ said:

JUDGMENT

'This Court is quite satisfied that there is no ground whatever for qualifying the words "possession or control" in any way. It is sufficient if it is found that the person from whom the property is … appropriated was at the time in fact in possession or control. At the trial there was a long argument as to whether that possession or control must be lawful … The only question was: was [V] in fact in possession or control?'

If the argument in *Smith and others* that there could be no theft where possession was unlawful had succeeded, it would have led to chaos. It would allow all those who misuse drugs to take them from each other with impunity. This could scarcely be in the public interest.

It is possible for someone to be in possession or control of property even though they do not know it is there. In *Woodman* [1974] 2 All ER 955, a company, English China Clays, had sold all the scrap metal on its site to another company which arranged for it to be removed. Unknown to English China Clays, a small amount had been left on the site. There was no doubt that they were in control of the site itself as they had put a barbed wire fence round it and had notices warning trespassers to keep out. D took the remaining scrap metal. He was convicted of theft and the Court of Appeal upheld the conviction.

13.4.2 Proprietary right or interest

Clearly, legal ownership comes within this, but a proprietary right or interest is much wider than just ownership. There are also equitable rights to property, for example the trustees of a trust fund have the legal ownership of the fund, but the beneficiaries have the equitable interest.

Co-owners

If there are co-owners of property, then each can be guilty of stealing from the other, as each has a proprietary interest in the property. This happened in *Bonner* [1970] 2 All ER 97, where D was a partner who was found guilty of stealing partnership property. In partnership law each partner is joint owner of all the partnership property, but he can be guilty of theft if he appropriates the property intending to permanently deprive the other partners of their rights in the property.

Lost or abandoned property

Where property has been lost, the owner still has a proprietary right in it. It is only if the property has been completely abandoned that it is ownerless and so does not belong to another for the purposes of theft. However, the courts are reluctant to reach the conclusion that property has been abandoned, or may decide that ownership has passed to the owner of the land on which it was abandoned. For example, where a golfer hits a golf ball into a lake and decides to leave it there, he has abandoned it, but it becomes the property of the owner of the golf course.

The property will only be considered abandoned if the owner is completely indifferent as to what happens to the property. If a householder puts out rubbish to be collected by the local refuse operators, he has not abandoned it. He intends the ownership to go to the refuse operators. If anyone else takes the rubbish, then this is theft. This was seen in the case of *R (on the application of Ricketts) v Basildon Magistrates' Court* [2010] EWHC 2358 (Admin).

CASE EXAMPLE

R (on the application of Ricketts) v Basildon Magistrates' Court [2010] EWHC 2358 (Admin)

D was charged with two offences of theft, and Basildon magistrates committed the case for trial at the Crown Court. D applied for judicial review of the decision to commit the case for trial on the basis that there was no evidence the property belonged to anyone.

In the first offence D had taken bags containing items of property from outside a charity shop. He argued that the original owner had abandoned the property and, therefore, it did not belong to another. The High Court held that the magistrates had been entitled to infer that the goods had been left with the intention of giving them to the charity. They were also entitled to infer that the goods had been not been abandoned: the giver had attempted to deliver them to the charity and delivery would only be complete when the charity took possession. Until then the goods remained the property of the giver.

In the second offence, D had taken bags of goods from a bin at the rear of another charity shop. The High Court held that these bags were in the possession of the charity at the time they were appropriated by D.

Special situations

Section 5 goes on to make it clear that in certain situations a defendant can be guilty of theft even though the property may not 'belong to another'. These are situations in which the defendant is acting dishonestly and has caused a loss to another or has made a gain. These are:

- trust property;
- property received under an obligation;
- property received by another's mistake.

Trust property

Normally both trustees and beneficiaries have proprietary rights or interests in the trust property. So if a trustee takes the trust property for his own, he can be charged with theft as it also belongs to the beneficiaries. But to make sure that any dishonest appropriation of trust property by a trustee could be theft, s 5(2) sets out:

SECTION

'5(2) Where property is subject to a trust, the persons to whom it belongs shall be regarded as any person having a right to enforce the trust and an intention to defeat the trust shall be regarded accordingly as an intention to deprive of the property any person having that right.'

In particular this avoids problems with theft by a trustee from a charitable trust as there are no specific beneficiaries with a right to enforce the trust. However, charitable trusts are enforceable by the Attorney-General, making him a 'person having a right to enforce the trust' for the purposes of this subsection.

13.4.3 Property received under an obligation

There are many situations in which property (usually money) is handed over to D on the basis that D will keep it for the owner or will deal with it in a particular way. Section 5(3) tries to make sure that such property is still considered as 'belonging to the other' for the purposes of the law of theft.

SECTION

'5(3) Where a person receives property from or on account of another, and is under an obligation to the other to retain and deal with that property or its proceeds in a particular way, the property shall be regarded (as against him) as belonging to the other.'

Under this subsection there must be an obligation to retain and deal with the property in a particular way. So, where money is paid as a deposit to a business, the prosecution must prove that there was an obligation to retain and deal with those deposits in a particular way. If the person paying the deposit only expects it to be paid into a bank account of the business, then if that is what happens there cannot be theft, even if all the money from the account is used for other business expenses and the client does not get the goods or service for which he paid the deposit. This is what happened in *Hall* [1972] 2 All ER 1009.

CASE EXAMPLE

Hall [1972] 2 All ER 1009

Hall was a travel agent who received deposits from clients for air trips to America. D paid these deposits into the firm's general account, but never organised any tickets and was unable to return the money. He was convicted of theft, but on appeal, his conviction was quashed because when D received the deposits he was not under an obligation to deal with them in a particular way. The Court of Appeal did stress that each case depended on its facts.

In *Klineberg and Marsden* [1999] Crim LR 419, there was a clear obligation to deal with deposits in a particular way. The two defendants operated a company which sold time-share apartments in Lanzarote to customers in England. Each purchaser paid the purchase price on the understanding that the money would be held by an independent trust company until the apartment was ready for the purchaser to occupy. Over £500,000 was paid to the defendants' company, but only £233 was actually paid into the trust company's account. The defendants were guilty of theft as it was clear that they were under an obligation to the purchasers 'to retain and deal with that property or its proceeds in a particular way' and that they had not done this.

There can be an obligation in less formal situations. This was the case in *Davidge v Bunnett* [1984] Crim LR 297.

CASE EXAMPLE

Davidge v Bunnett [1984] Crim LR 297

D was guilty of theft when she was given money by her flatmates to pay the gas bill but instead used it to buy Christmas presents. There was a legal obligation in this situation, as there was an intention to create legal relations under contract law. It is not clear whether there would be a legal obligation (and so theft) if the situation happened between members of the same family or whether this would be a domestic arrangement without the intention to create legal relations.

Another problem area can occur when D collects money from sponsors for charity but then does not pay the money over. In *Lewis v Lethbridge* [1987] Crim LR 59, D was sponsored to run the London Marathon for charity. His sponsors paid the money to him but he did not hand it over to the charity. The Queen's Bench Divisional Court quashed the conviction since the magistrates had not found that there was any rule of the charity which required him to hand the actual cash over or to set up a separate fund for it. This meant that as against the charity he was not under an obligation 'to retain and deal with that property' in a particular way. He was merely a creditor of the charity. This decision was criticised by Professor Sir John Smith and this criticism was adopted by the Court of Appeal in *Wain* [1995] 2 Cr App R 660 when it disapproved of the decision in *Lewis v Lethbridge* (1987).

CASE EXAMPLE

Wain [1995] 2 Cr App R 660

D had organised various events to raise money for The Telethon Trust, a charity created by Yorkshire Television Company. He paid the money, totalling £2,833.25, into a special bank account, but then, with permission of a representative of the TV company, transferred the money to his personal bank account. He then spent the money from his own account and was unable to pay any money to the charity.

The Court of Appeal considered the point of whether the defendant was obliged to hand over the actual coins and notes or whether there was a more general principle that he was under an obligation to hand over an amount equal to the money he had raised. It quoted from Professor Sir John Smith in its judgment when it said:

JUDGMENT

'Professor Smith … in his *Law of Theft* (6th ed.) at p. 39 [states] "… In *Lewis v Lethbridge* … no consideration was given to the question whether any obligation was imposed by the sponsors. Sponsors surely do not give the collector (whether he has a box or not) the money to do as he likes with. Is there not an overwhelming inference … that the sponsors intend to give the money to the charity, imposing an obligation in the nature of a trust on the collector?"

It seems to us that the approach of the court in the Lethbridge case was a very narrow one based, apparently, on the finding by the justices that there was no requirement of the charity that the appellant hand over the same notes and coins … it seems to us that by virtue of section 5(3), the appellant was plainly under an obligation to retain, if not the actual note and coins, at least their proceeds, that is to say the money credited in the bank account which he opened for the trust with the actual property.'

This decision is preferable to that in *Lewis v Lethbridge* (1987). Any person giving money to a person collecting for charity, whether it is by sponsoring him or by some other donation, is only doing this because they want to support the charity. They intend that amount to be paid to the charity.

13.4.4 Property got by a mistake

The final subsection of s 5 deals with situations where property has been handed over to D by another's mistake and so has become D's property. If there were no special provision in the Act, then this could not be 'property belonging to another' for the purposes of the law of theft.

SECTION

'5(4) Where a person gets property by another's mistake, and is under an obligation to make restoration (in whole or in part) of the property or its proceeds or of the value thereof, then to the extent of that obligation the property or proceeds shall be regarded (as against him) as belonging to the person entitled to restoration, and an intention not to make restoration shall be regarded accordingly as an intention to deprive that person of the property or proceeds.'

In *Attorney-General's Reference (No 1 of 1983)* [1985] 3 All ER 369, the facts were that D's salary was paid into her bank account by transfer. On one occasion her employers mistakenly overpaid her by £74.74. She was acquitted by the jury of theft, but the prosecution sought a ruling on a point of law, namely, assuming that she dishonestly decided not to repay the £74.74, would she have been guilty of theft? The Court of Appeal held that s 5(4) clearly provided for exactly this type of situation. She was under an 'obligation to make restoration', and if there was an intention not to make restoration, then the elements of theft were present.

There must be a legal obligation to restore the property. In *Gilks* [1972] 3 All ER 280, D had placed a bet on a horse race. The bookmaker made a mistake about which horse D had backed and overpaid D on the bets he had placed. D realised the error and decided not to return the money. The ownership of the money had passed to D, so the only way he could be guilty of theft was if s 5(4) applied. It was held that as betting transactions are not enforceable at law, s 5(4) did not apply and D was not guilty.

KEY FACTS

Key facts on 'belonging to another'

Theft Act 1968	Rule	Comment/case(s)
s 5(1)	Property is regarded as belonging to any person having possession or control or having any proprietary right.	Not limited to owner – *Turner (No 2)* (1971) stole own car. One co-owner can steal from another – *Bonner* (1970).
s 5(2)	Trust property 'belongs' to any person having right to enforce the trust.	–
s 5(3)	Property belongs to the other where it is received under an obligation to retain and deal with it in a particular way.	Must have to deal with it in a specific way. *Hall* (1972) not guilty because no specific way. *Klineberg and Marsden* (1999) guilty because should have been placed in special account.
s 5(4)	Where D gets property by another's mistake, then it 'belongs' to the other. But there must be a legal obligation to make restoration.	*Attorney-General's Reference (No 1 of 1983)* (1985). *Gilks* (1972).

13.5 Dishonestly

There are two points which need to be proved for the *mens rea* of theft. These are:

- dishonesty
- intention permanently to deprive.

Apart from these the Act also states in s 1(1) that it is immaterial whether the appropriation is made with a view to gain, or is made for the thief's own benefit. In other words, if all the elements of theft are present, the motive of D is not relevant. So a modern-day Robin Hood stealing to give to the poor could be guilty of theft. D does not have to gain anything from the theft, so destroying property belonging to another can be theft, although it is also, of course, criminal damage. Theft can also be charged where D does not destroy the other's property but throws it away. For example, if D threw a waterproof watch belonging to another into the sea, this could be theft.

13.5.1 Dishonesty

The 1968 Theft Act does not define 'dishonesty', though it does give three situations in which D's behaviour is not considered dishonest. These are in s 2 of the 1968 Act.

SECTION

'2(1) A person's appropriation of property belonging to another is not to be regarded as dishonest –

(a) if he appropriates the property in the belief that he has in law the right to deprive the other of it, on behalf of himself or of a third person; or

(b) if he appropriates the property in the belief that he would have the other's consent if the other knew of the appropriation and the circumstances of it; or

(c) (except where the property came to him as trustee or personal representative) if he appropriates the property in the belief that the person to whom the property belongs cannot be discovered by taking reasonable steps.'

All three situations depend on D's belief. It does not matter whether it is a correct belief or even whether it is a reasonable belief. If D has a genuine belief in one of these three, then he is not guilty of theft.

Belief in a right at law

Section 2(1)(a) was considered in the case of *Turner (No 2)* (1971) (see section 13.4.1). Turner claimed that he believed he had the right to take back his car from the garage. The Court of Appeal pointed out that the judge had dealt fully and correctly with the law on this point, saying:

JUDGMENT

'[The judge] went on to give [the jury] a classic direction in regard to claim of right, emphasising that it is immaterial that there exists no basis in law for such belief. He reminded the jury that the appellant had said categorically in evidence: "I believe that I was entitled in law to do what I did." At the same time he directed the jury to look at the surrounding circumstances. He said this: "The Prosecution say that the whole thing reeks of dishonesty, and if you believe Mr Brown that the [appellant] drove the car away from Carlyle Road, using a duplicate key, and having told Brown that he would come back tomorrow and pay, you may think the Prosecution right."

The whole test of dishonesty is the mental element of belief.'

Belief of owner's consent

Section 2(1)(b) covers situations where D does not have the chance to get permission from the person to whom the property belongs, but D believes he would have been given permission. For example, if you are babysitting at a friend's house and while there you cut your finger, you take a plaster from your friend's first aid box believing that they would consent if they knew about it.

Belief that owner cannot be found

This appears to be aimed at situations where D finds property such as money or other personal items in the street. If D genuinely believes that he cannot find out who the owner is by taking what he thinks are reasonable steps, then D's appropriation of the property is not dishonest and he cannot be guilty of theft. D's belief does not have to be reasonable. However, the more unreasonable it is, then the more likely a jury will not accept that he actually held that belief.

In *Small* [1987] Crim LR 777, D took a car. He said he believed it was abandoned. It had been parked in the same place without being moved for two weeks. Also it appeared abandoned because the doors were unlocked, the keys were in the ignition, there was no petrol in the tank, the battery was flat, one of the tyres was flat and the windscreen wipers did not work. D put petrol in the tank and managed to start it. When he was driving it he suddenly saw police flashing their lights at him. At that point he panicked and ran off, but he claimed that until he saw the police he had never thought that it might be a stolen car. He was convicted, but the Court of Appeal quashed the conviction because the question was whether D had (or might have had) an honest belief that the owner could not be found and there was evidence that he might have believed the car was abandoned.

Willing to pay

In some situations D may say that he is willing to pay for the property or may, on taking property, leave money to pay for it. This does not prevent D's conduct from being dishonest, as s 2(2) states that:

SECTION

'2(2) A person's appropriation of property belonging to another may be dishonest notwithstanding that he is willing to pay for the property.'

At first this may seem severe, but it prevents D taking what he likes, regardless of the owner's wishes. For example, D likes a painting which is hanging in a friend's home. He asks the friend how much it is worth and is told that it is only a copy, worth less than £100, but it was painted by the friend's grandmother and is of sentimental value. A few days later D takes the painting without the friend's consent but leaves £200 in cash to pay for it. D's taking of the painting may be considered dishonest, even though he left more than the cash value of it.

13.5.2 The *Ghosh* test

As can be seen, s 2 only applies in specific circumstances. It does not create a general rule or definition about dishonesty. In its Eighth Report, the Criminal Law Revision Committee stated that it had used the word 'dishonestly' in preference to the word 'fraudulently' because:

QUOTATION

'The question "Was this dishonest?" is easier for a jury to answer than the question "Was this fraudulent?" Dishonesty is something which laymen can recognise when they see it, whereas "fraud" may seem to involve technicalities which have to be explained by a lawyer.'

It appears that, since they took the view that dishonesty was something laymen could recognise, there was no need for a definition. Not surprisingly, the early cases on the Theft Act took the view that whether the defendant's state of mind was dishonest was a matter for the jury to decide. In *Brutus v Cozens* [1972] 2 All ER 1297, the House of Lords held that the meaning of an ordinary word such as dishonestly was not a question of law for the judge, but one of fact for the jury.

In *Feely* [1973] 1 All ER 341, the Court of Appeal did at least give a standard of dishonesty to be applied by the jury. Feely was the manager at a branch of bookmakers. The firm notified all branches that the practice of borrowing from the till was to stop. D knew this, but still 'borrowed' £30. When it was realised there was a shortfall in the till, D immediately said what he had done and offered an IOU. In addition, he was owed more than twice the amount by the firm. At his trial the judge directed the jury that what Feely had done was dishonest and he was convicted of theft. He appealed on the ground that the question of dishonesty should have been left to the jury. The Court of Appeal allowed the appeal, stating:

JUDGMENT

'Jurors, when deciding whether an appropriation was dishonest can reasonably be expected to, and should, apply the current standards of ordinary decent people. In their own lives they have to decide what is and what is not dishonest. We can see no reason why, when in a jury box, they should require the help of a judge to tell them what amounts to dishonesty.'

This does give a guideline to the jury of the 'current standards of ordinary decent people'. However, a criticism of this is that different juries might well have different standards, even though they are notionally applying the 'current standards of ordinary decent people'. Another criticism is that it is too objective. It does not take into account whether the defendant believed he was being honest. In *Boggeln v Williams* [1978] 2 All ER 1061, a subjective test was used of the defendant's belief as to his own honesty. The defendant's electricity had been cut off, but he had reconnected it without authorisation. He notified the electricity board that he was doing this, and he believed that he would be able to pay the bill. The court decided that his belief was the most important factor.

This left a conflict of whether the test should be objective (standards of ordinary decent people) or subjective (whether the defendant believed that what he was doing was honest). This was finally resolved in *Ghosh* [1982] 2 All ER 689, which is now the leading case on the matter.

CASE EXAMPLE

Ghosh [1982] 2 All ER 689

Ghosh was a doctor acting as a locum consultant in a hospital. He claimed fees for an operation he had not carried out. He said that he was not dishonest as he was owed the same amount for consultation fees. The trial judge directed the jury that they must apply their own standards to decide if what he did was dishonest. He was convicted and appealed against the conviction.

The Court of Appeal considered all the previous cases on the matter and decided that the test for dishonesty should have both objective and subjective elements. It put it in this way:

JUDGMENT

'In determining whether the prosecution has proved that the defendant was acting dishonestly, a jury must first of all decide whether according to the ordinary standards of reasonable and honest people what was done was dishonest. If it was not dishonest by those standards, that is the end of the matter and the prosecution fails. If it was dishonest by those standards, then the jury must consider whether the defendant himself must have realised that what he was doing was by those standards dishonest.'

So this means that the jury have to start with an objective test. Was what was done dishonest by the ordinary standards of reasonable and honest people? If it was not the defendant is not guilty. However, if the jury decide that it was dishonest by those standards, then they must consider the more subjective test of whether the defendant knew it was dishonest by those standards.

This second test is not totally subjective as the defendant is judged by what he realised ordinary standards were. This prevents a defendant from saying that, although he knew that ordinary people would regard his actions as dishonest, he did not think that those standards applied to him. This was made clear in the judgment in *Ghosh* [1982] 2 All ER 689.

JUDGMENT

'It is dishonest for a defendant to act in a way which he knows ordinary people consider to be dishonest, even if he asserts or genuinely believes that he was morally justified in acting as he did. For example, Robin Hood or those ardent anti-vivisectionists who remove animals from vivisection laboratories are acting dishonestly, even though they may consider themselves to be morally justified in doing what they do, because they know that ordinary people would consider these actions to be dishonest.'

In *DPP v Gohill and another* [2007] EWHC 239 (Admin), it was stressed that the *Ghosh* test had to be dealt with in two parts.

CASE EXAMPLE

DPP v Gohill and another [2007] EWHC 239 (Admin)

The defendants were manager and assistant manager of an outlet hiring plant and equipment to customers. Ds had allowed some customers to borrow equipment for periods of less than two hours without charge. These hirings were recorded by Ds on the computer. However, when the customer returned the item within two hours, Ds had either recorded that it had been returned as faulty or incorrectly chosen (for which no charge was made under the company's rules) or altered the computer records to show that the item had only been reserved and not actually borrowed.

Ds stated that they regarded this as good customer service which kept customers who frequently hired happy. It was not done for personal gain and they did not ask for any money for doing this. Sometimes the customer would tip them £5 or £10 and at other times they were not given any money by the customer.

The magistrates acquitted Ds of theft and false accounting on the basis that they 'were not satisfied beyond reasonable doubt that by the ordinary standards of reasonable and honest people the [Ds] had acted dishonestly'.

The Divisional Court allowed the prosecution appeal against the acquittal. They held that the behaviour of the Ds was dishonest by the ordinary standards of reasonable and honest people and they remitted the case for retrial by a new bench of magistrates as the two parts of the *Ghosh* test had to be considered.

When remitting the case for retrial, Levenson LJ said:

JUDGMENT

'In my judgment the question posed by the justices must be split into two. Were they entitled to conclude that by the ordinary standards of reasonable and honest people the [Ds] had not been proved to have acted dishonestly must be answered in the negative. The second question is whether the [Ds] themselves must have realised that what they were doing was by those standards dishonest.'

13.5.3 Problems with the *Ghosh* test

The case of *Gohill* emphasises one of the main problems with the *Ghosh* test, that is that different people may have different standards of dishonesty. The main criticism is that it leaves too much to the jury (or lay magistrates as in *Gohill*), so that there is a risk of inconsistent decisions with different juries coming to different decisions in similar situations. It has been argued that it would be better for the judge to rule on whether there was dishonesty as a point of law rather than leave it as a matter of fact for the jury. However, this overlooks the fact that the jury still need to decide whether they believe what the defendant says.

Another criticism of the test is that it places too much emphasis on objective views of what is dishonest rather than the defendant's intentions. The first stage of the test requires the jury to consider whether what was done is dishonest according to the ordinary standards of reasonable and honest people. This has the odd effect that if the jury think it is not dishonest, then the defendant will be found not guilty even though he may have thought he was being (and intended to be) dishonest.

The points above were emphasised by Professor Griew in an article he wrote in 1985, 'Dishonesty: the objections to *Feely* and *Ghosh*' (1985) Crim LR 341. He put forward several problems with the definition of theft following the decision in *Ghosh*. As well as the points above he also pointed out:

- The *Ghosh* test leads to longer and more difficult trials.
- The idea of standards of ordinary reasonable and honest people is a fiction.
- The *Ghosh* test is unsuitable in specialised cases.
- It allows for a 'Robin Hood' defence.

Longer trials

The complicated nature of the *Ghosh* test means that trials take longer. The jury have first to decide whether the defendant's behaviour was dishonest according to the ordinary standards of reasonable and honest people. This is not always a straightforward matter. Then they have to decide if the defendant realised that what he was doing was dishonest by those standards. This is another difficult point as evidence of a state of mind is not easy to prove. Griew also thought that the nature of the test meant that more defendants might decide to plead not guilty in the hope that a jury would decide their behaviour was not dishonest.

Fiction of community standards

Griew points out that using a test of ordinary standards of reasonable and honest people assumes that there is a common standard. In fact society is very diverse and different sections of the community may well have slightly varying standards. Griew's view is supported by the Law Commission in its report on the law of fraud in 2002 when it said: 'There is some evidence that people's moral standards are surprisingly varied.'

This creates problems when the jury have to decide on the ordinary standards. The jurors are likely to come from different backgrounds with different experiences of life. They can also vary in age from 18 to 70. All these factors may mean that the jury disagree on what the ordinary standards are. The *Ghosh* test may backfire in the case of a jury composed of 'ordinary dishonest jurors' whose own standards may be regarded as dishonest. In 2009 online research by Finch and Fafinsky of Brunel University involving 15,000 people found that people's views on what is dishonest do indeed vary quite widely.

The case of *Gohill* demonstrates that even magistrates and judges may have differing standards of what is dishonest. In that case the magistrates trying the case decided they were not satisfied beyond reasonable doubt that D was dishonest by the standards of reasonable and honest people. However the Divisional Court took the opposite point of view with Leveson LJ saying:

JUDGMENT

'In my judgment, it is quite impossible to justify the proposition that the ordinary standards of reasonable and honest people would not find dishonest the deliberate falsification of a company record to permit a customer, however valued, to borrow equipment without charge in a business that exists solely to hire such equipment for payment, particularly where the procedures of the company did not permit such alteration to the record in any event.'

Specialised cases

It is even more difficult to apply ordinary standards where the offence involves a specialised area such a futures trading or other complex financial dealing. The first part of the *Ghosh* test is even more unsuitable in such cases. Ordinary people have no experience of such financial dealing, so how can they say what is 'honest' or 'not honest' in such cases?

'Robin Hood' defence

Griew points out that the *Ghosh* test enables a 'Robin Hood defence' where the defendant believes that, as a result of the conviction of his own moral or political beliefs, that 'ordinary people' will think he is acting correctly. So, in this situation, the defendant will be acquitted.

Other problems

The reverse situation of 'Robin Hood' can occur where the defendant believes that he is being dishonest, but the jury find that by the first part of the test, he is not dishonest according to the ordinary standards of reasonable and honest people. As Andrew Halpin wrote in 'The test for dishonesty' (1996) Crim LR 283:

QUOTATION

'If the point of the test is to prevent a defendant escaping liability in a case that is generally regarded as involving wrongdoing by using his own personal morality, then it is only when the defendant's failure to perceive that his behaviour would ordinarily be regarded as dishonest is itself considered to be excusable by ordinary standards that he should be acquitted.'

Finally, whether the defendant is being dishonest has become much more important in view of the ruling in *Hinks* (2000) that appropriation is a neutral word. This means that whether a theft has occurred or not is dependent on whether the appropriation was dishonest. The whole of the illegality of the act is based on the *mens rea* of the defendant. This makes it even more unsatisfactory that the *Ghosh* test can be subjected to so many criticisms.

ACTIVITY

Self-test questions on dishonesty in theft

1. Explain the three situations in s 2(1) of the Theft Act 1968 in which D is not regarded as dishonest.
2. Explain why D may be dishonest even though he is willing to pay for the goods he appropriates.
3. The Theft Act 1968 does not define 'dishonesty'. What different approaches have the courts used in deciding what is meant by 'dishonesty'?
4. Explain the *Ghosh* (1982) test.
5. Is it necessary to have an objective element in deciding whether D's conduct was dishonest?

13.6 With intention to permanently deprive

The final element which has to be proved for theft is that the defendant had the intention to permanently deprive the other of the property. In many situations there is no doubt that the defendant had such an intention. For example, where an item is taken and sold to another person, or where cash is taken and spent by the defendant. This last example is true even when D intends to replace the money later, as was shown in *Velumyl* [1989] Crim LR 299 where D, a company manager, took £1,050 from the office safe. He said that he was owed money by a friend and he was going to replace the money when that friend repaid him. The Court of Appeal upheld his conviction for theft as he had the intention of permanently depriving the company of the banknotes which he had taken from the safe, even if he intended to replace them with other banknotes to the same value later.

Another situation where there is a clear intention to permanently deprive is where the defendant destroys property belonging to another. This can be charged as theft, although it is also criminal damage. There are, however, situations where it is not so clear and to help in these s 6 of the Theft Act 1968 explains and expands the meaning of the phrase.

SECTION

'6(1) A person appropriating property belonging to another without meaning the other permanently to lose the thing itself is nevertheless to be regarded as having the intention to permanently deprive the other of it if his intention is to treat the thing as his own to dispose of regardless of the other's rights; and a borrowing or lending of it may amount to so treating it, if, but only if, the borrowing or lending is for a period and in circumstances making it equivalent to an outright taking or disposal.'

Intention is to treat the thing as his own

So the basic rule is that there must be an intention to treat the thing as his own to dispose of regardless of the other's rights. One problem for the courts has been the meaning of 'dispose of' and what, if anything, it adds to 'treat the thing as his own'. In *Cahill* [1993] Crim LR 141, the Court of Appeal accepted that the meaning of 'dispose of' should be that given by the *Shorter Oxford Dictionary*: this was 'To deal with definitely; to get rid of; to get done with, finish. To make over by way of sale or bargain, sell.' However, in *DPP v Lavender* [1994] Crim LR 297, the Divisional Court did not refer to *Cahill* (1993) but ruled that the dictionary definition of 'dispose of' was too narrow as a disposal could include 'dealing with' property.

CASE EXAMPLE

DPP v Lavender [1994] Crim LR 297

D took doors from a council property which was being repaired and used them to replace damaged doors in his girlfriend's council flat. The doors were still in the possession of the council but had been transferred without permission from one council property to another. The Divisional Court held that the question was whether D intended to treat the doors as his own, regardless of the rights of the council. The answer to this was yes, so D was guilty of theft.

A similar decision was reached in *Marshall* [1998] 2 Cr App R 282, where the defendants obtained day tickets to travel on the London Underground (LU) from travellers who had finished with them, and the defendants then sold the tickets to other travellers. They were convicted but appealed on the ground that, as each ticket would be returned to (LU) when they had been used by the second traveller, there was no intention to permanently deprive LU of the tickets. The Court of Appeal upheld their convictions on the basis that the men were treating the tickets as their own to dispose of, regardless of LU's rights. It was not relevant that the tickets would eventually be returned to LU.

In *R v Raphael and another* [2008] EWCA Crim 1014, the Court of Appeal held that taking V's car and demanding money to return it was treating the car as their own 'to dispose of regardless of the other's rights'.

CASE EXAMPLE

R v Raphael and another [2008] EWCA Crim 1014

V arranged to sell his car to D1. They arranged that D2 would inspect it. When D2 was doing this (D1 not being present) V was attacked by three other people and his car driven away. V informed the police. After this he received a phone call telling him that if he wanted his car back it would cost him £500. D2 was traced by the police and he then phoned V telling V that he had not intended to set him up and he would try to get the car back but it would cost V £300. V's car was eventually found parked in a street and locked. D1 and D2 were convicted of conspiracy to rob. On appeal, they argued that they had no intention permanently to deprive V of the car. The Court of Appeal dismissed the appeals and upheld their convictions on the basis that they had treated the car as their own to dispose of regardless of V's rights.

On this point of treating the car as their own to dispose of Judge J said:

JUDGMENT

'The express language of section 6 specifies that the subjective element necessary to establish the *mens rea* for theft includes an intention on the part of the taker "to treat the thing as his own to dispose of regardless of the other's rights". In our judgment it is hard to find a better example of such an intention than an offer, not to return V's car to him in exactly the same condition it was when it was removed from his possession and control, but to sell his own property back to him, and to make its return subject to a condition or conditions inconsistent with his right to possession of his own property.'

The Court of Appeal also considered whether the abandoning of the car in a street meant that there was no intention permanently to deprive for the offence of theft, but instead an offence of taking and driving away under s 12 of the Theft Act. On this point Judge J said:

JUDGMENT

'This is not a case in which the vehicle was taken for what is sometimes inaccurately described as a "joy ride". Section 12 of the Theft Act has no application to it. It was only "abandoned" after the purpose of the robbery had been frustrated and its possible usefulness to the robbers dissipated.'

13.6.1 Borrowing or lending

Another difficulty with s 6 is the point at which 'borrowing or lending' comes within the definition. Normally borrowing would not be an intention to permanently deprive. Take the situation of a student taking a textbook from a fellow student's bag in order to read one small section and then replace the book. This is clearly outside the scope of s 6 and cannot be considered as an intention to permanently deprive. But what if that student also took a photocopying card, which had a limit placed on its use, used it, then returned it? The photocopy card has been returned, but it is no longer as valuable as it was. So is there an intention to permanently deprive so far as the card is concerned?

Section 6 states that borrowing is not theft unless it is for a period and in circumstances making it equivalent to an outright taking or disposal. In *Lloyd* [1985] 2 All ER 661 it was held that this meant borrowing the property and keeping it until 'the goodness, the virtue, the practical value … has gone out of the article'. In this case a film had been taken for a short time and copied, then the original film replaced undamaged. This was not sufficient for an intention to permanently deprive. Lord Lane CJ said:

JUDGMENT

'[s 6(1)] is intended to make clear that a mere borrowing is never enough to constitute the guilty mind unless the intention is to return the thing in such a changed state that it can truly be said that all its goodness or virtue has gone.'

From this it appears that in the example of the photocopy card, there would be an intention to permanently deprive if all the value of the card had been used up, but if it still had value, then there is no intention to permanently deprive.

Another difficulty is where D picks up property to see if there is anything worth stealing. What is the position if he decides it is not worth stealing and returns it? This is what happened in *Easom* [1971] 2 All ER 945. D picked up a handbag in a cinema, rummaged through the contents and then replaced the handbag without having taken anything. He was convicted of theft of the handbag and its contents, but the Court of Appeal quashed this conviction. They held that even though he may have had a conditional intention to deprive, this was not enough. Note that he could now probably be charged with attempted theft under the Criminal Attempts Act 1981. (See Chapter 6, section 6.4.)

13.6.2 Conditional disposition

The final part of s 6 covers situations where D parts with property, taking the risk that he may not be able to get it back.

SECTION

'6(2) Without prejudice to the generality of subsection (1) above, where a person, having possession or control (lawfully or not) of property belonging to another, parts with the property under a condition as to its return which he may not be able to perform, this (if done for purposes of his own and without the other's authority) amounts to treating the property as his own to dispose of regardless of the other's rights.'

The first point to note is that this subsection applies even if D is lawfully in possession or control of the property. The second point is that the act must be done for D's own purpose and without the other's authority. The common example given to illustrate this is where D has been lent an item and then pawns it, but hopes he will have enough money to redeem it before he is due to give it back to the owner. This is a condition as to its return which he may not be able to perform and so he is treating it as his own to dispose of regardless of the other's rights.

NOTE: see Appendix 2 for an example of how to apply the law of theft to a problem/scenario type question.

KEY FACTS

Key facts on theft

Section of Theft Act 1968	Definition	Comment/cases
s 1	A person is guilty of theft if he dishonestly appropriates property belonging to another with the intention of permanently depriving the other of it.	Full definition of theft. D is charged under this section.
s 2	(1) Not dishonest if believes: • has right in law; • would have the other's consent; • owner cannot be discovered. (2) Can be dishonest even if intends paying for property.	No definition of dishonesty in the Act. *Ghosh* two-part test: • Is it dishonest by ordinary standards? • If so, did D know it was dishonest by those standards?
s 3	Appropriation (1) 'Any assumption of the rights of an owner.' (2) *Bona fide* purchaser has not appropriated.	Held to be assumption of any of the rights of an owner – *Gomez* (1993). Given 'neutral' meaning, so consent irrelevant – *Lawrence* (1971) *Hinks* (2000).

s4	(1) 'Property' includes money and all other property real or personal, including things in action and other intangible property. (2) Land cannot be stolen except by trustee or tenant or by severing property from land. (3) Wild mushrooms, fruit, flowers and foliage cannot be stolen unless done for commercial purpose. (4) Wild animals cannot be stolen unless tamed or in captivity.	
s5	(1) Property is regarded as belonging to any person having possession or control or any proprietary right. (2) Trust property belongs to any person having a right to enforce the trust. (3) Property belongs to the other where it is received under an obligation to retain and deal with it in a particular way. (4) Property received by a mistake where there is a legal obligation to make restoration belongs to the other.	Not limited to owner – *Turner (No 2)* (1971). Must be a particular way – *Hall* (1972), *Klineberg and Marsden* (1999). *Attorney-General's Reference (No 1 of 1983)* (1985). Must be a legal obligation – *Gilks* (1972).
s6	(1) Intention to permanently deprive includes to treat the thing as his own to dispose of regardless of the other's rights and includes a borrowing or lending for a period and in circumstances making it equivalent to an outright taking or disposal. (2) Includes disposing of property under a condition as to its return which he may not be able to perform.	Conflicting views on 'dispose of' – *Cahill* (1993), *Lavender* (1994). The 'goodness or practical value must have gone from the property' – *Lloyd* (1985).

ACTIVITY

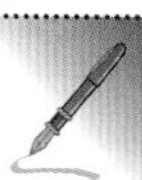

Applying the law

In each of the following situations, explain whether the elements of theft are satisfied.

1. Denise comes from a country where property placed outside a shop is meant for people to take free of charge. She sees a rack of clothes on the pavement outside a shop and takes a pair of jeans from it.
2. Katya is given a Christmas cash bonus in a sealed envelope. She has been told by her boss that the bonus would be £50. When she gets home and opens the envelope she finds there is £60 in it. She thinks her employer decided to be more generous and so keeps the money. Would your answer be different if (a) Katya realised there had been a mistake but did not return the money or (b) the amount in the envelope was £200?
3. Engelbert is given permission by his employer to borrow some decorative lights for use at a party. Engelbert also takes some candles without asking permission. When putting up the lights Engelbert smashes one of them. He lights two of the candles so that by the end of the evening they are partly burned down. One of the guests admires the remaining lights and asks if he can have them to use at a disco at the weekend. Engelbert agrees to let him take the lights.

SUMMARY

Definition of theft

Dishonestly appropriating property belonging to another with the intention of permanently depriving the other of it.

Appropriation

- Any assumption of the rights of an owner.
- It includes a later assumption where D has come by the property without stealing it.
- There is an appropriation even though the owner has consented.
- *Property* includes money and all other property real or personal, including things in action and other intangible property.
- Things which *cannot* be stolen are:
  - land or thing forming part of land (unless taken by a trustee, or when D is not in possession of the land and takes a severed item or a tenant who takes any fixture or fitting);
  - plants and fungi growing wild and which are not picked for reward, sale or other commercial purpose;
  - wild creatures which are not in the possession of any person.

Belonging to another

- Property shall be regarded as belonging to any person having possession or control of it, or having in it any proprietary right or interest.
- Where property is received under an obligation to deal with it in a particular way the property is regarded as 'belonging' to the other.
- Where a person gets property by another's mistake, and is under a legal obligation to make restoration it is regarded as 'belonging' to the other.

Dishonesty

- It is immaterial whether the appropriation is made with a view to gain or is made for the thief's own benefit.
- The Act does not define dishonesty. The courts have developed the *Ghosh* test for dishonesty. This is a two-part test, so D is dishonest only if:
  - what was done was dishonest according to the ordinary standards of reasonable and honest people; and
  - D realised that what he was doing was dishonest by those standards.
- Section 2(1) Theft Act 1968 states that D is not dishonest if he believes:
  - he has in law the right to deprive the other of it, on behalf of himself or of a third person; or
  - he would have the other's consent if the other knew of the appropriation and the circumstances of it; or
  - the person to whom the property belongs cannot be discovered by taking reasonable steps.

Intention to permanently deprive

- D is regarded as having the intention to permanently deprive the other of it if his intention is to treat the thing as his own to dispose of regardless of the other's rights.
- Borrowing is not theft unless it is for a period and in circumstances making it equivalent to an outright taking or disposal. This is keeping it until 'the goodness, the virtue, the practical value ... has gone out of the article'.

SAMPLE ESSAY QUESTION

The key elements in the crime of theft are 'appropriation' and 'dishonesty'. Neither element was satisfactorily defined in the Theft Act 1968, but the courts have resolved the problems through case law. Discuss.

State definition of theft s 1(1) of Theft Act 1986:

- Identify appropriation and dishonesty as elements in the definition
- Give definition of appropriation in s 3(1) TA 1968
- Point out there is no definition of dishonesty in Act

Expand on the definition of appropriation:

- 'Any assumption' of the 'rights of an owner'
- Explain how this has been interpreted by the courts in cases, e.g. *Pitham v Hehl* (1977), *Corcoran v Anderton* (1980), *Lawrence* (1972), *Morris* (1983), *Gomez* (1993)

Discuss the problems with the definition of appropriation, e.g.

- Is it right that the wording of s 3(1) should be read as 'the assumption of any of the rights of the owner'? *Morris*
- Is it right that there need be no adverse interference? *Gomez*
- Should it cover gifts? *Hinks* (2000)
- Width of meaning places greater emphasis on 'dishonesty' in deciding guilt or innocence

Expand on 'dishonesty':

- Although no definition in Act, s 2(1) gives three situations where D is not dishonest
- Section 2(2) states may be dishonest even if willing to pay test
- Courts have developed *Ghosh* two-part test

Discuss problems of Ghosh test, e.g.

- The idea of standards of ordinary reasonable and honest people is a fiction
- It leaves too much to the jury
- Different juries (or magistrates) may have different standards (*Gohill* (2007))
- The test may lead to longer and more complicated trials

Conclude

Further reading

Books

Ormerod, D and Williams, D, *Smith's Law of Theft* (9th edn, Oxford University Press, 2007).

Articles

Beatson, J and Simester, A P, 'Stealing one's own property' (1999) 115 LQR 372.
Gardner, S, 'Property and theft' (1998) Crim LR 35.
Griew, E, 'Dishonesty: the objections to *Feely* and *Ghosh*' (1985) Crim LR 341.
Halpin, A, 'The Test for Dishonesty' (1996) Crim LR 283.
Meissaris, E, 'The concept of appropriation and the law of theft' (2007) MLR 581.
Shute, S, 'Appropriation and the law of theft' (2002) Crim LR 445.
Smith, A T H, 'Gifts and the law of theft' (1999) CLJ 10.

14

Robbery, burglary and other offences in the Theft Acts

AIMS AND OBJECTIVES

student mentor tip

'Learn the definitions of each crime off by heart.'
Andrie, University of Dundee

After reading this chapter you should be able to:

- Understand the *actus reus* and *mens rea* of robbery
- Understand the *actus reus* and *mens rea* of burglary and related offences
- Understand the *actus reus* and *mens rea* of taking a conveyance
- Understand the *actus reus* and *mens rea* of blackmail
- Understand the *actus reus* and *mens rea* of handling stolen goods
- Understand the *actus reus* and *mens rea* of making off without payment
- Analyse critically all the above offences
- Apply the law to factual situations to determine whether robbery, burglary or other offences under the Theft Acts have been committed

In the last chapter we focused on the offence of theft. This chapter discusses other offences contained in the Theft Act 1968, together with one offence from the Theft Act 1978. Some of these have theft as an essential element, such as robbery. Others are connected to theft, such as going equipped for theft or handling stolen goods.

14.1 Robbery

Robbery is an offence under s 8 of the Theft Act 1968 and is, in effect, theft aggravated by the use or threat of force.

SECTION

'8 A person is guilty of robbery if he steals, and immediately before or at the time of doing so, and in order to do so, he uses force on any person or puts or seeks to put any person in fear of being then and there subjected to force.'

14.1.1 The *actus reus* of robbery

The elements which must be proved for the *actus reus* of robbery are:

- theft
- force or putting or seeking to put any person in fear of force.

In addition there are two conditions on the force, and these are that it

- must be immediately before or at the time of the theft; and
- must be in order to steal.

14.1.2 Theft as an element of robbery

There must be a completed theft for a robbery to have been committed. This means that all the elements of theft have to be present. If any one of them is missing then, just as there would be no theft, there is no robbery. So there is no theft in the situation where D takes a car, drives it a mile and abandons it because D has no intention permanently to deprive. Equally there is no robbery where D uses force to take that car. There is no offence of theft, so using force cannot make it into robbery. This was illustrated by the case of *Zerei* [2012] EWCA Crim 1114.

CASE EXAMPLE

Zerei [2012] EWCA Crim 1114

D and another man in a car park approached V, whom they knew, and told him they were going to take his car. D then punched V and pulled out a knife, while the co-defendant held V, and took V's car keys. They then drove off in the car. The car was found soon afterwards, abandoned about one kilometre away. D was convicted of robbery but the conviction was quashed on appeal.

The Court of Appeal held that the trial judge had misdirected the jury on the issue of intention to permanently deprive. The judge had given the jury the impression that a forcible taking was enough to show an intention to permanently deprive. This was not the law. The judge had also failed to deal with the relevance of the car being abandoned by D after a short time.

D was also convicted of assault occasioning actual bodily harm and that conviction was upheld.

Another example is where D has a belief that he has a right in law to take the property. This would mean he was not dishonest and one of the elements of theft would be missing, as seen in *Robinson* [1977] Crim LR 173.

CASE EXAMPLE

Robinson [1977] Crim LR 173

D ran a clothing club and was owed £7 by I's wife. D approached the man and threatened him. During a struggle the man dropped a £5 note and D took it claiming he was still owed £2. The judge directed the jury that D had honestly to believe he was entitled to get the money in that way. This was not the test. The jury should have been directed to consider whether he had a belief that he had a right in law to the money which would have made his actions not dishonest under s 2(1)(a) of the Theft Act. The Court of Appeal quashed the conviction for robbery.

Where force is used to steal, then the moment the theft is complete, there is a robbery. This is shown by *Corcoran v Anderton* [1980] Crim LR 385.

CASE EXAMPLE

Corcoran v Anderton [1980] Crim LR 385

One defendant hit a woman in the back and tugged at her bag. She let go of it and it fell to the ground. The defendants ran off without it (because the woman was screaming and attracting attention). It was held that the theft was complete so the defendants were guilty of robbery.

However, if the theft is not completed, for instance if the woman in the case of *Corcoran v Anderton* had not let go of the bag, then there is an attempted theft and D could be charged with attempted robbery.

14.1.3 Force or threat of force

Whether D's actions amount to force is something to be left to the jury. The amount of force can be small. In *Dawson and James* (1976) 64 Cr App R 170, one of the defendants pushed the victim, causing him to lose his balance, which enabled the other defendant to take his wallet. The Court of Appeal held that 'force' was an ordinary word and it was for the jury to decide if there had been force.

It was originally thought that the force had to be directed at the person and that force used on an item of property would not be sufficient for robbery. In fact this was the intention of the Criminal Law Revision Committee when it put forward its draft Bill. It said in its report that it would

QUOTATION

'not regard mere snatching of property, such as a handbag, from an unresisting owner as using force for the purpose of the definition [of robbery], though it might be so if the owner resisted.'

This point was considered in *Clouden* [1987] Crim LR 56.

CASE EXAMPLE

Clouden [1987] Crim LR 56

The Court of Appeal held that D was guilty of robbery when he had wrenched a shopping basket from the victim's hand. The Court of Appeal held that the trial judge was right to leave to the jury the question of whether D had used force on a person.

It can be argued that using force on the bag was effectively using force on the victim, as the bag was wrenched from her hand. However, if a thief pulls a shoulder bag so that it slides off the victim's shoulder, would this be considered force? Probably not. And it would certainly not be force if a thief snatched a bag which was resting (not being held) on the lap of someone sitting on a park bench.

This view is supported by *P v DPP* (2012) in which D snatched a cigarette from V's hand without touching V in any way. It was held that as there had been no direct contact between D and V it could not be said that force had been used 'on a person'. Therefore D was not guilty of robbery. The situation was analogous to pickpocketing where D is unaware of any contact. However, where the pickpocket (or accomplice) jostles V to distract him while the theft is taking place, there is force which could support a charge of robbery.

Fear of force

The definition of 'robbery' makes clear that robbery is committed if D puts or seeks to put a person in fear of force. It is not necessary that the force be applied. Putting V 'in fear of being there and then subjected to force' is sufficient for robbery. This covers threatening words, such as 'I have a knife and I'll use it unless you give me your wallet', and threatening gestures, such as holding a knife in front of V.

CASE EXAMPLE

Bentham [2005] UKHL 18

D put his fingers into his jacket pocket to give the appearance that he had a gun in there. He then demanded money and jewellery. He was charged with robbery and pleaded guilty. He was also charged with having in his possession an imitation firearm during the course of the robbery contrary to s 17(2) of the Firearms Act 1968. His conviction for this was quashed by the House of Lords.

It was clear that D was guilty of robbery as he had sought to put V in fear of being then and there subjected to force. The fact that it was only his fingers did not matter for the offence of robbery. However, for the offence of possessing an imitation firearm there had to be some item and not just a part of D's body. This was because what had to be possessed had to be a 'thing' and that meant something which was separate and distinct from oneself. Fingers were therefore not a 'thing'. In addition, the House of Lords pointed out that if fingers were regarded as property for the purposes of s 143 of the Powers of Criminal Courts (Sentencing) Act 2000 then this created the nonsense that a court could theoretically make an order depriving D of his rights in them! Robbery is also committed even if the victim is not actually frightened by D's actions or words. If D seeks to put V in fear of being then and there subjected to force, this element of robbery is present. So if V is a plain clothes policeman put there to trap D and is not frightened, the fact that D sought to put V in fear is enough. This was shown by *B and R v DPP* [2007] EWHC 739 (Admin).

CASE EXAMPLE

B and R v DPP [2007] EWHC 739 (Admin)

V, a schoolboy aged 16, was stopped by five other schoolboys. They asked for his mobile phone and money. As this was happening, another five or six boys joined the first five and surrounded the victim. No serious violence was used against the victim, but he was pushed and his arms were held while he was searched. The defendants took his mobile phone, £5 from his wallet, his watch and a travel card. The victim said that he did not feel particularly threatened or scared but that he was bit shocked.

The defendants appealed against their convictions for robbery on the basis that no force had been used and the victim had not felt threatened. The Divisional Court upheld the convictions for robbery on the grounds that:

- There was no need to show that the victim felt threatened; s 8 of the Theft Act 1968 states that robbery can be committed if the defendant 'seeks to put any person in fear of being then and there subjected to force'.
- There could be an implied threat of force; in this case the surrounding of the victim by so many created an implied threat.
- In any event, there was some limited force used by holding the victim's arms and pushing him.

On any person

This means that the person threatened does not have to be the person from whom the theft occurs. An obvious example is an armed robber who enters a bank, seizes a customer and threatens to shoot that customer unless a bank official gets money out of the safe. This is putting a person in fear of being then and there subjected to force. The fact that it is not the customer's property which is being stolen does not matter.

14.1.4 Force immediately before or at the time of the theft

The force must be immediately before or at the time of stealing. This raises two problems. First, how 'immediate' does 'immediately before' have to be? What about the situation where a bank official is attacked at his home by a gang in order to get keys and security codes from him? The gang then drive to the bank and steal money. The theft has taken place an hour after the use of force. Is this 'immediately before'? It would seem right that the gang should be convicted of robbery. But what if the time delay were longer, as could happen if the attack on the manager was on Saturday evening and the theft of the money not until 24 hours later? Does this still come within 'immediately before'? There have been no decided cases on this point. The second problem is deciding the point at which a theft is completed, so that the force is no longer 'at the time of stealing'.

CASE EXAMPLE

Hale [1979] Crim LR 596

Two defendants knocked on the door of a house. When a woman opened the door they forced their way into the house and one defendant put his hand over her mouth to stop her screaming while the other defendant went upstairs to see what he could find to take. He took a jewellery box. Before they left the house they tied up the householder and gagged her.

They argued on appeal that the theft was complete as soon as the second defendant picked up the jewellery box, so the use of force in tying up the householder was not at the time of stealing. However, the Court of Appeal upheld their convictions. The Court of Appeal thought that the jury could have come to the decision that there was force immediately before the theft when one of the defendants put his hand over the householder's mouth. In addition, the Court of Appeal thought that the tying up of the householder could also be force for the purpose of robbery as it held that the theft was still ongoing.

JUDGMENT

'We also think that [the jury] were also entitled to rely upon the act of tying her up provided they were satisfied (and it is difficult to see how they could not be satisfied) that the force so used was to enable them to steal. If they were still engaged in the act of stealing the force was clearly used to enable them to continue to assume the rights the owner and permanently to deprive Mrs Carrett of her box, which is what they began to do when they first seized it . . .

To say that the conduct is over and done with as soon as he laid hands on the property . . . is contrary to common-sense and to the natural meaning of words . . . the act of appropriation does not suddenly cease. It is a continuous act and it is a matter for the jury to decide whether or not the act of appropriation has finished.'

So, in this case for robbery, appropriation is viewed as a continuing act or a course of conduct. However, *Hale* (1979) was decided before *Gomez* (1993), which is the leading case on appropriation in theft. *Gomez* (1993) rules that the point of appropriation is when D first does an act assuming a right of the owner. This point was argued in *Lockley* [1995] Crim LR 656. D was caught shoplifting cans of beer from an off-licence, and used force on the shopkeeper who was trying to stop him from escaping.

He appealed on the basis that *Gomez* (1993) had impliedly overruled *Hale* (1979). However, the Court of Appeal rejected this argument and confirmed that the principle in *Hale* (1979) still applied in robbery.

But there must be a point when the theft is complete and so any force used after this point does not make it robbery. What if in *Lockley* (1995) D had left the shop and was running down the road when a passer-by (alerted by the shouts of the shopkeeper) tried to stop him? D uses force on the passer-by to escape. Surely the theft is completed before this use of force? The force used is a separate act to the theft and does not make the theft a robbery. The force would, of course, be a separate offence of assault.

The point that force must be used 'immediately before or at the time of stealing' was the critical issue in *Vinall* [2011] EWCA Crim 6252.

CASE EXAMPLE

Vinall [2011] EWCA Crim 6252

Ds punched V causing him to fall off his bicycle. One of the defendants said to V, 'Don't try anything stupid, I've got a knife.' V fled on foot chased by Ds. Ds gave up the chase and went back to the bicycle and walked off with it. They abandoned it by a bus shelter about 50 yards from where V had left it.

The trial judge directed the jury that the intention to permanently deprive V of the bicycle could have been formed either at the point in time when the bicycle was first taken or when it was abandoned as this would amount to a fresh appropriation. The jury convicted Ds of robbery. On appeal the Court of Appeal quashed their convictions.

They pointed out that robbery requires proof that D stole and used (or threatened) force either 'immediately before or at the time of' stealing and that the force was used in order to steal. It was not possible to know whether the jury had decided that the intention to permanently deprive was formed at the time when the bicycle was first taken or when it was left at the bus stop. If the jury had found that the intention for theft was only formed at the time of abandonment, then there was no robbery. So the convictions were unsafe.

Finally it should be noted that the threat of force in the future cannot constitute robbery, although it may be blackmail.

14.1.5 Force in order to steal

The force must be used in order to steal. So if the force was not used for this purpose, then any later theft will not make it into robbery. Take the situation where D has an argument with V and punches him, knocking him out. D then sees that some money has fallen out of V's pocket and decides to take it. The force was not used for the purpose of that theft and D is not guilty of robbery, but guilty of two separate offences: an assault and theft.

14.1.6 *Mens rea* for robbery

D must have the *mens rea* for theft, that is, he must be dishonest and he must intend to permanently deprive the other of the property. He must also intend to use force to steal.

14.1.7 Possible reform of law of robbery

Robbery is a combination of two offences: theft and an assault of some level. The amount of force required is very small. Andrew Ashworth in 'Robbery reassessed' (2002) Crim LR 851 points out that non-fatal offences against the person reflect the amount of force used and suggests that robbery should have at least two levels with different degrees of force. Ashworth also questions whether it is necessary for the offence to exist. Instead of charging robbery it would be possible to charge D with separate offences of theft and the relevant assault.

QUOTATION

'A more radical proposal would be to abolish the offence of robbery. It would then be left to prosecutors to charge the components of theft and violence separately, which would focus the court's attention on those two elements, separately and then (for sentencing purposes) in combination. The principal difficulty with this is the absence from English law of an offence of threatening injury: between the summary offence of assault by posing a threat of force, and the serious offence of making a threat to kill, there is no intermediate crime. This gap ought to be closed, and, if it were, there would be a strong argument that the crime of robbery would be unnecessary.'

KEY FACTS

Key facts on robbery

Element	Law	Case
Theft	There must be a completed theft; if any element is missing there is no theft and therefore no robbery.	*Robinson* (1977)
	The moment the theft is completed (with the relevant force) there is robbery.	*Corcoran v Anderton* (1980)
Force or threat of force	The jury decide whether the acts were force, using the ordinary meaning of the word.	*Dawson and James* (1976)
	It includes wrenching a bag from V's hand.	*Clouden* (1987)
	It does not include snatching a cigarette from V's fingers	*P v DPP* (2012)
Immediately before or at the time of the theft	For robbery, theft has been held to be a continuing act.	*Hale* (1979)
	Using force to escape can still be at the time of the theft.	*Lockley* (1995)
In order to steal	The force must be in order to steal.	–
	Force used for another purpose does not become robbery if D later decides to steal.	
On any person	The force can be against any person.	–
	It does not have to be against the victim of the theft.	

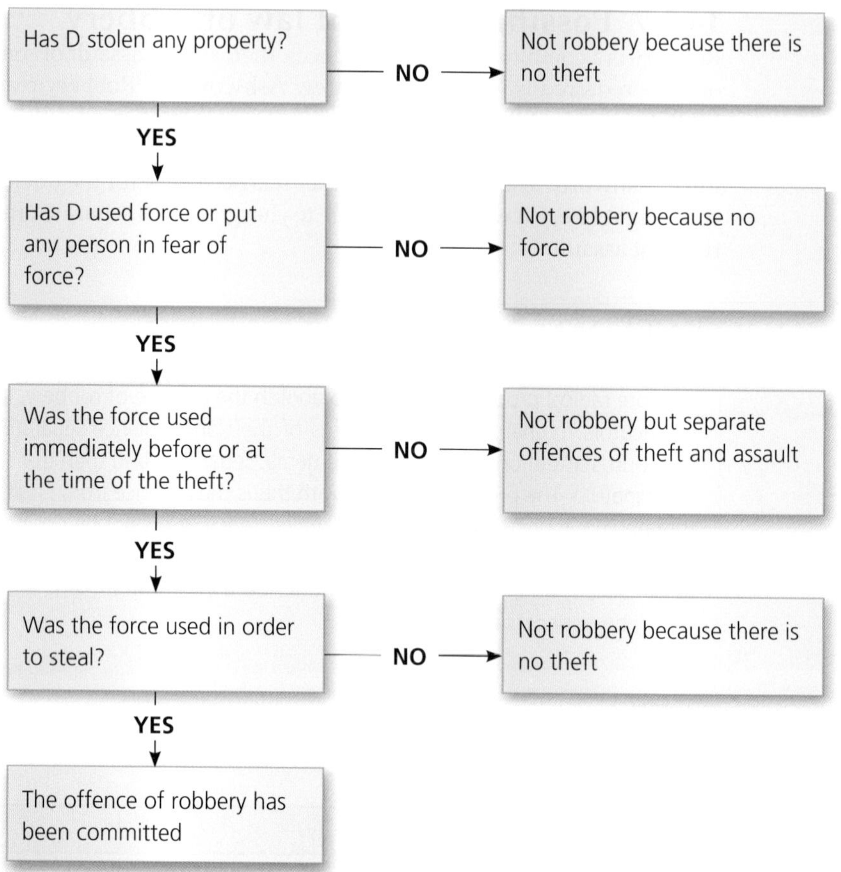

Figure 14.1 Flow chart on robbery.

ACTIVITY

Applying the law

Explain whether or not a robbery has occurred in each of the following situations.

1. Arnie holds a knife to the throat of a one-month-old baby and orders the baby's mother to hand over her purse or he will 'slit the baby's throat'. The mother hands over her purse.
2. Brendan threatens staff in a post office with an imitation gun. He demands that they hand over the money in the till. One of the staff presses a security button and a grill comes down in front of the counter so that the staff are safe and Brendan cannot reach the till. He leaves without taking anything.
3. Carla snatches a handbag from Delia. Delia is so surprised that she lets go of the bag and Carla runs off with it.
4. Egbert breaks into a car in a car park and takes a briefcase out of it. As he is walking away from the car, the owner arrives, realises what has happened and starts to chase after Egbert. The owner catches hold of Egbert, but Egbert pushes him over and makes his escape.
5. Fenella tells Gerry to hand over his Rolex watch and, that if he does not, Fenella will send her boyfriend round to beat Gerry up. Gerry hands over the watch.

NOTE: see Appendix 2 for an example of how to apply the law of robbery in a problem/scenario type question.

14.2 Burglary

This is an offence under s 9 of the Theft Act 1968.

SECTION

'9(1) A person is guilty of burglary if –

(a) he enters any building or part of a building as a trespasser and with intent to commit any such offence as is mentioned in subsection (2) below; or

(b) having entered a building or part of a building as a trespasser he steals or attempts to steal anything in the building or that part of it or inflicts or attempts to inflict on any person therein any grievous bodily harm.

(2) The offences referred to in subsection (1)(a) above are offences of stealing anything in the building or part of a building in question, of inflicting on any person therein any grievous bodily harm, and of doing unlawful damage to the building or anything therein.'

As can be seen by reading these subsections, burglary can be committed in a number of ways and the following chart shows this.

KEY FACTS

Key facts on different ways of committing burglary

Burglary	
Section 9(1)(a)	**Section 9(1)(b)**
Enters a building or part of a building as a trespasser.	Having entered a building or part of a building as a trespasser.
With intent to: • steal • inflict grievous bodily harm • do unlawful damage. N.B. used to include intention to rape but this is now covered by s 63 Sexual Offences Act 2003.	• steals or attempts to steal; or • inflicts or attempts to inflict grievous bodily harm.

14.2.1 The *actus reus* of burglary

To prove the *actus reus* of burglary under s 9(1)(a) the prosecution must show that D entered a building or part of a building as a trespasser. For the *actus reus* of burglary under s 9(1)(b) it has to be proved that D had entered a building or part of a building as a trespasser and then stolen or attempted to steal or inflicted or attempted to inflict grievous bodily harm.

Although ss 9(1)(a) and 9(1)(b) create different ways of committing burglary, they do have common elements. These are that there must be:

- entry
- of a building or part of a building
- as a trespasser.

The distinguishing feature between the subsections is the intention at the time of entry. For s 9(1)(a) the defendant must intend to do one of the three listed offences (known as ulterior offences) at the time of entering. However, there is no need for the ulterior offence to take place or even be attempted. For s 9(1)(b), what the defendant intended on entry is irrelevant, but the prosecution must prove that he actually committed or attempted to commit theft or grievous bodily harm.

14.2.2 Entry

'Entry' is not defined in the 1968 Act. Prior to the Act, common law rules had developed on what constituted entry. The main rules were that the entry of any part of the body (even a finger) into the building was sufficient and also that there was an entry if D did not physically enter but inserted an instrument for the purpose of theft (for example, where D used a fishing net to try to pick up items). Initially when the courts had to interpret the word 'enters' in the Theft Act 1968, they took a very different line from the old common law rules.

The first main case on this point was *Collins* [1972] 2 All ER 1105 (see section 14.2.4 for the facts of *Collins*). In this case the Court of Appeal said that the jury had to be satisfied that D had made 'an effective and substantial entry'. However, in *Brown* [1985] Crim LR 167, this concept of 'an effective and substantial entry' was modified to 'effective entry'.

CASE EXAMPLE

Brown [1985] Crim LR 167

D was standing on the ground outside but leaning in through a shop window rummaging through goods. The Court of Appeal said that the word 'substantial' did not materially assist the definition of entry and his conviction for burglary was upheld as clearly in this situation his entry was effective.

However, in *Ryan* [1996] Crim LR 320, the concept of 'effective' entry does not appear to have been followed.

CASE EXAMPLE

Ryan [1996] Crim LR 320

D was trapped when trying to get through a window into a house at 2.30 a.m. His head and right arm were inside the house but the rest of his body was outside. The fire brigade had to be called to release him. This could scarcely be said to be an 'effective' entry. However, the Court of Appeal upheld his conviction for burglary, saying that there was evidence on which the jury could find that D had entered.

14.2.3 Building or part of a building

The Theft Act 1968 does not define building but does give an extended meaning to it to include inhabited places such as houseboats or caravans, which would otherwise not be included in the offence. This is set out in s 9(4).

SECTION

'9(4) References … to a building shall apply also to an inhabited vehicle or vessel, and shall apply to any such vehicle or vessel at times when the person having a habitation is not there as well as at times when he is.'

The main problems for the courts have come where a structure such as a portacabin has been used for storage or office work. In a very old case decided well before the Theft Act 1968, *Stevens v Gourley* (1859) 7 CB NS 99, it was said that a building must be 'intended to be permanent, or at least to endure for a considerable time'.

This means that the facts of each case must be considered. There are two cases on whether a large storage container is a building. In these cases the court came to different decisions after looking at the facts.

- In *B and S v Leathley* [1979] Crim LR 314 a 25-foot-long freezer container which had been in a farmyard for over two years was used as a storage facility. It rested on sleepers, had doors with locks and was connected to the electricity supply. This was held to be a building.
- In *Norfolk Constabulary v Seekings and Gould* [1986] Crim LR 167 a lorry trailer with wheels which had been used for over a year for storage, had steps that provided access and was connected to the electricity supply was held not to be a building. The fact that it had wheels meant that it remained a vehicle.

Part of a building

The phrase 'part of building' is used to cover situations in which the defendant may have permission to be in one part of the building (and therefore is not a trespasser in that part) but does not have permission to be in another part. A case example to demonstrate this is *Walkington* [1979] 2 All ER 716. D went into the counter area in a shop and opened a till. He was guilty of burglary under s 9(1)(a) because he had entered part of a building (the counter area) as a trespasser with the intention of stealing. Other examples include storerooms in shops where shoppers would not have permission to enter or where one student entered another student's room in a hall of residence without permission.

14.2.4 As a trespasser

In order for D to commit burglary he must enter as a trespasser. If a person has permission to enter he is not a trespasser. This was illustrated by the unusual case of *Collins* (1972). N.B. Since May 2004, Collins would be charged with an offence under s 63, Sexual Offences Act 2003.

CASE EXAMPLE

Collins [1972] 2 All ER 1105

D, having had quite a lot to drink, decided he wanted to have sexual intercourse. He saw an open window and climbed a ladder to look in. He saw there was a naked girl asleep in bed. He then went down the ladder, took off all his clothes except for his socks and climbed back up the ladder to the girl's bedroom. As he was on the window sill outside the room, she woke up, thought he was her boyfriend and helped him into the room where they had sex. He was convicted of burglary under s 9(1)(a), i.e. that he had entered as a trespasser with intent to rape. (He could not be charged with rape, as the girl accepted that she had consented to sex.) He appealed on the basis that that he was not a trespasser as he had been invited in. The Court of Appeal quashed his conviction, pointing out:

JUDGMENT

'there cannot be a conviction for entering premises "as a trespasser" within the meaning of s 9 of the Theft Act 1968 unless the person entering does so knowing he is a trespasser and nevertheless deliberately enters, or, at the very least, is reckless whether or not he is entering the premises of another without the other party's consent.'

So to succeed on a charge of burglary, the prosecution must prove that the defendant knew, or was subjectively reckless, as to whether he was trespassing.

Going beyond permission

However, where the defendant goes beyond the permission given, he may be considered a trespasser. In *Smith and Jones* [1976] 3 All ER 54, Smith and his friend went to Smith's father's house in the middle of the night and took two television sets without the father's knowledge or permission. The father stated that his son would not be a trespasser in the house; he had a general permission to enter. The Court of Appeal referred back to the judgment in *Collins* (1972) and added this principle.

JUDGMENT

'It is our view that a person is a trespasser for the purpose of s 9(1)(b) of the Theft Act 1968 if he enters premises of another knowing that he is entering in excess of the permission that has been given to him to enter, or being reckless whether he is entering in excess of [that] permission.'

This meant that Smith was guilty of burglary. This decision was in line with the Australian case of *Barker v R* (1983) 7 ALJR 426, where one person who was going away asked D, who was a neighbour, to keep an eye on the house and told D where a key was hidden should he need to enter. D used the key to enter and steal property. He was found guilty of burglary. The Australian court said:

JUDGMENT

'If a person enters for a purpose outside the scope of his authority then he stands on no better position than a person who enters with no authority at all.'

Professor Sir John Smith argued that this would mean that a person who enters a shop with the intention of stealing would be guilty of burglary as he only has permission to enter for the purpose of shopping. However, it would be difficult in most cases to prove that the intention to shoplift was there at the point of entering the shop.

There are many situations where a person has permission to enter for a limited purpose. For example, someone buys a ticket to attend a concert in a concert hall or to look round an historic building or an art collection. The ticket is a licence (or permission) to be in the building for a very specific reason and/or time. If D buys a ticket intending to steal one of the paintings from the art collection, this line of reasoning would suggest that he is guilty of burglary. However, in *Byrne v Kinematograph Renters Society Ltd* [1958] 2 All ER 579, a civil case, it was held that it was not trespass to gain entry to a cinema by buying a ticket with the purpose of counting the number in the audience, not with the purpose of seeing the film. This case was distinguished in *Smith and Jones* (1976) on the basis that the permission to enter a cinema was in general terms and not limited to viewing the film and was very different from the situation where D enters with the intention to steal (or cause grievous bodily harm or criminal damage).

If a person has been banned from entering a shop (or other place), then there is no problem. When they enter they are entering as a trespasser. This means that a known shoplifter who is banned from entering a local supermarket would be guilty of burglary if he or she entered intending to steal goods (s 9(1)(a)) or if, having entered, he then stole goods (s 9(1)(b)).

The law is also clear where D gains entry through fraud, such as where he claims to be a gas meter reader. There is no genuine permission to enter and D is a trespasser.

14.2.5 *Mens rea* of burglary

There are two parts to the mental element in burglary. These are in respect of:

- entering as a trespasser;
- the ulterior offence.

First, as stated above, the defendant must know, or be subjectively reckless, as to whether he is trespassing. In addition, for s 9(1)(a) the defendant must have the intention to commit one of the offences at the time of entering the building. Where D is entering intending to steal anything he can find which is worth taking, then this is called a conditional intent. This is sufficient for D to be guilty under s 9(1)(a). This was decided in *Attorney-General's References Nos 1 and 2 of 1979* [1979] 3 All ER 143.

For s 9(1)(b), the defendant must have the *mens rea* for theft or grievous bodily harm when committing (or attempting to commit) the *actus reus* of these offences.

14.2.6 Burglary of a dwelling

This carries a higher maximum sentence than burglary of other types of building as a result of an amendment to the Theft Act 1968 by the Criminal Justice Act 1991. Section 9(3) now reads:

SECTION

'9(3) A person guilty of burglary shall on conviction on indictment be liable to imprisonment for a term not exceeding –

(a) where the offence was committed in respect of a building or part of a building which is a dwelling, fourteen years;

(b) in any other case, ten years.'

This reflects the public view that burglary of someone's home is more serious (and more frightening for the victim) than burglary of another type of building such as a shed or an office or a warehouse. The word 'dwelling' includes an inhabited vehicle or vessel.

KEY FACTS

Key facts on burglary

Elements	Comment	Case/section
Entry	This has changed from • 'effective and substantial' entry to • 'effective' entry to • evidence for the jury to find D had entered.	 *Collins* (1972) *Brown* (1985) *Ryan* (1996)
Building or part of a building	Must have some permanence. Includes inhabited vehicle or vessel. Can be entry of part of a building.	*B and S v Leathley* (1979) *Norfolk Constabulary v Seekings and Gould* (1986) s 9(4) Theft Act 1968 *Walkington* (1979)

As a trespasser	If has permission is not a trespasser. If goes beyond permission then can be a trespasser.	*Collins* (1972) *Smith and Jones* (1976)
Mens rea	Must know or be subjectively reckless as to whether he is a trespasser PLUS EITHER intention at point of entry to commit • theft or • grievous bodily harm or • criminal damage OR *mens rea* for theft or grievous bodily harm at point of committing or attempting to commit these offences in a building.	s 9(1)(a) Theft Act 1968 s 9(1)(b) Theft Act 1968

ACTIVITY

Applying the law

In each of the following, explain whether or not a burglary has occurred, and if so whether it would be an offence under s 9(1)(a) or s 9(1)(b).

1. Jonny has been banned from a local pub. One evening he goes there for a drink with a friend. While he is waiting for the friend to get the drinks at the bar, Jonny sees a handbag under one of the chairs. He picks it up and takes a £10 note from it. He then puts the handbag back under the chair.
2. Ken and his partner, Lola, have split up and Ken has moved out of the flat he shared with Lola, taking most of his belongings with him. One evening he goes back there to collect the rest of his belongings. Lola is out so Ken asks the neighbour to let him have the spare key which the neighbour keeps for emergencies. While Ken is packing his clothes, Lola returns. They have an argument and Ken beats up Lola causing her serious injuries.
3. Mike works as a shelf-filler in a DIY store. One day when he is putting packs of batteries out on to a shelf, he slips one in his pocket. He does not intend to pay for it. Later in the day he sees the manager leave her office. Mike goes in and takes money from the desk. The door to the office has a notice saying 'Private'.
4. Nigella, who is a pupil at the local comprehensive, goes to the school buildings late in the evening after school. She intends to damage the science lab as she hates the teacher. She gets in through a window but is caught by the caretaker before she does any damage.

NOTE: see Appendix 2 for an example of how to apply the law of burglary to a problem/scenario type question.

14.3 Aggravated burglary

This is where a burglary is made more serious by the carrying of an article which could be used to inflict injury. The Criminal Law Revision Committee in its Eighth Report pointed out that 'burglary when in possession of the articles mentioned [in s 10] is so serious that it should in our opinion be punishable with imprisonment for life. The offence is comparable with robbery … It must be extremely frightening to those in the building, and it might well lead to loss of life.'

The offence is set out by s 10 of the Theft Act 1968:

SECTION

'10 A person is guilty of aggravated burglary if he commits any burglary and at the time has with him any firearm or imitation firearm, any weapon of offence, or any explosive, and for this purpose –

(a) "firearm" includes an airgun or air pistol and "imitation firearm" means anything which has the appearance of being a firearm, whether capable of being discharged or not; and

(b) "weapon of offence" means any article made or adapted for use for causing injury to or incapacitating a person, or intended by the person having it with him for such use; and

(c) "explosive" means any article manufactured for the purpose of producing a practical effect by explosion, or intended by the person having it with him for that purpose.'

These articles cover a wide range of things, especially 'weapon of offence', which is much wider than the definition of 'offensive weapon' in the Prevention of Crime Act 1953. In s 10 it includes any article intended by D to cause injury or to incapacitate a person. This appears to include such items as rope or masking tape which D intends to use to tie up the householder.

14.3.1 Has with him

A key part of the offence of aggravated burglary is that D has the article with him at the time of the burglary. So for a s 9(1)(a) burglary, he must have it at the moment of entry, but for a s 9(1)(b) burglary he must have it at the point when he commits or attempts to commit the ulterior offence. These points are illustrated by the case of *Francis* [1982] Crim LR 363.

CASE EXAMPLE

Francis [1982] Crim LR 363

The defendants, who were armed with sticks, demanded entry. Having been allowed to enter, they then put down the sticks. Later they stole items from the house. Their convictions for aggravated burglary were quashed because although they had the weapons with them on entry, there was no evidence that they intended to steal at that point. Then, when they did actually steal, they did not have the weapons with them, so the condition for s 9(1)(b) was not satisfied.

Conversely the fact that D has no weapon when he enters does not prevent him from being guilty of aggravated burglary if he picks up an article in the house and has it with him when he then steals or causes grievous bodily harm. This was the position in *O'Leary* (1986) 82 Cr App R 341. D did not have a weapon when he entered a house as a trespasser, but while in the house he picked up a knife from the kitchen. He then went upstairs and threatened the occupants with the knife so that they gave him property. He had the knife with him when he stole and, as this was the point at which he committed a s 9(1)(b) burglary, he was guilty of aggravated burglary. It is also worth noting that, as D had the knife with him at the point at which the burglary was committed, he would have been guilty of aggravated burglary even if he had not used the knife.

Joint burglars

Where there are two or more offenders participating in the burglary, but only one of them has a weapon, all of them may be guilty of aggravated burglary. The key fact is that those without a weapon must know that one of the others has a weapon. However, in *Klass* [1998] 1 Cr App R 453, it was decided that if the accomplice with one of the aggravating articles remains outside the building, then the person entering will not have committed aggravated burglary.

14.4 Removal of items from a place open to the public

This offence was included in the Theft Act 1968 to cover situations where an item is removed from a museum, art gallery or historic house etc., but where it might not be possible to prove an intention to deprive permanently for a charge of theft. The offence is set out in s 11 of the Theft Act 1968:

SECTION

'11(1) ... where the public have access to a building in order to view the building or any part of it, or a collection or part of a collection housed in it, any person who without lawful authority removes from the building or its grounds the whole or part of any article displayed or kept for display to the public in the building or that part of it shall be guilty of an offence. For this purpose "collection" includes a collection got together for a temporary purpose, but references in this section to a collection do not apply to a collection made or exhibited for the purpose of effecting sales or other commercial dealings.'

14.4.1 *Actus reus* of removal of items from a public place

It has to be proved that an article was taken in the following circumstances:

- It must be from a place where the public have access; this can be a building or part of a building or its grounds.
- The article must be displayed or kept for display; so this includes items which are not at the time on display, e.g. those in a storeroom or upon which restoration work is being carried out.
- The display must not be for a commercial purpose.

Section 11(2) makes it clear that where there is a permanent display, such as in a museum or art gallery, then, even if the taking is on a day when the public do not have access to the building, this offence is committed. However, where the display is temporary the taking must be on a day when the public have access.

ACTIVITY

Self-test questions

1. Explain the amount of force needed to prove robbery.
2. How does the ruling in *Lockley* (1995) appear to conflict with the ruling in *Gomez* (1993) on appropriation?
3. Explain the different tests the courts have used for 'entry' in burglary.
4. How do the courts define trespasser for the purposes of burglary?
5. Why is it necessary to have an offence of removal of items from a public place (s 11 Theft Act 1968) when there are offences of theft and burglary?

14.5 Taking a conveyance without consent

This is another offence which does not require proof of an intention permanently to deprive. There are instances where the taking of a vehicle is theft and can be charged as that; for example, where an expensive car is stolen and then sold to an innocent third party. This section is not intended for that type of situation. It is meant to cover situations which are commonly referred to as 'joyriding'; in other words, where D temporarily takes or drives a vehicle and then abandons it.

The rationale for the offence is to cover temporary use of a conveyance, since it is often difficult to prove that there was the intention permanently to deprive which is necessary for proving theft.

The basic offence is set out in s 12(1) of the Theft Act 1968.

SECTION

'12(1) Subject to subsections (5) and (6) below, a person shall be guilty of an offence if, without having the consent of the owner or other lawful authority, he takes any conveyance for his own or another's use or, knowing that any conveyance has been taken without such authority, drives it or allows himself to be carried in or on it.'

Subsection (5) states that s 12(1) does not apply to pedal cycles, but instead it creates a separate offence of taking a pedal cycle.

Subsection (6) goes to D's *mens rea* and states that 'a person does not commit an offence under this section by anything done in the belief that he has lawful authority to do it or that he would have the owner's consent if the owner knew of his doing it and the circumstances of it'.

14.5.1 *Actus reus* of taking a conveyance

There are three ways in which the *actus reus* of this offence can be committed:

- taking for his own or another's use;
- driving;
- allowing oneself to be carried.

Each of these needs to be further explained.

Taking for his own or another's use

There have been several cases on what is meant by taking. In *Bogacki* [1973] 2 All ER 864 the three defendants had got onto a bus in a depot and tried, unsuccessfully, to start it. The Court of Appeal quashed their conviction because there was no 'taking'. They explained the decision by saying:

JUDGMENT

'[It must] be shown that he took the vehicle, that is to say, that there was an unauthorised taking possession or control of the vehicle by him adverse to the rights of the true owner, coupled with some movement, however small ... of that vehicle following such unauthorised taking.'

In *Bogacki* (1973) the defendants could have been guilty of attempting to take the bus, but not of the completed offence under s 12. In *Bow* [1977] Crim LR 176 D, his brother and father were stopped by a gamekeeper, who suspected they were poaching. The gamekeeper parked his Land Rover blocking the way so that they could not drive off in their own car. D got into the Land Rover, released the handbrake and sat in it while it rolled about 200 yards, so that their escape route was no longer blocked. He did not start the engine.

It was accepted that if D had not been in the vehicle while it rolled down the road, then he would not have been guilty of an offence, as he had not taken it for his own or another's use. The Court of Appeal referred to J C Smith and B Hogan, *Smith and Hogan's Criminal Law* (3rd edn, Oxford University Press, 1973) and quoted the following passage:

QUOTATION

'But subject to the requirement of taking, the offence does seem, in essence, to consist in stealing a ride. This seems implicit in the requirement that the taking be for "his own or another's use". Thus if D releases the handbrake of a car so that it runs down an incline, or releases a boat from its moorings so that it is carried off by the tide this would not as such be an offence within the section. The taking must be for D's use or the use of another and if he intends to make no use of the car or the boat there would be no offence under section 12. But it would be enough if D were to release the boat from its moorings so that he would be carried downstream in the boat.'

The taking does not need to involve driving or being in the conveyance, provided it is intended for use later. This was shown in *Pearce* [1973] Crim LR 321 where D took a boat away on a trailer.

Drive or allow himself to be carried

Where a person did not 'take' the conveyance, he can still be guilty under this section, if he

- drove it knowing that it had been taken without consent; or
- allowed himself to be carried in it knowing that it had been taken without consent.

14.5.2 Without consent

The usual situation in cases charged under this section is where D has taken a car from the street or a car park. In this type of situation there is no question that D did not have the consent of the owner. However, there are cases where the owner has given consent for some use of the conveyance but D has gone beyond the permission given. In these cases it is still possible for D to be guilty.

An example is *McGill* (1970) 54 Cr App R 300.

CASE EXAMPLE

McGill (1970) 54 Cr App Rep 300

D was given permission to use a car to drive another person to the station, on the condition that D then returned the car immediately. D drove to the train station but then continued to use the car and did not return it for some days. It was held that he was guilty under s 12. The taking without permission occurred from the moment he used the car for his own purpose after leaving the station.

This situation can also happen where an employee has permission to drive a company vehicle for work. If he uses it for his own purposes, then that is a taking without consent of the owner. In *McKnight v Davies* [1974] RTR 4 the Queen's Bench Divisional Court upheld the conviction of a lorry driver who had not returned a lorry at the end of his working day but had used it for his own purposes, only returning it in the early hours of the following morning.

In both these cases there was a clear limit on the permission given to D and when D went beyond that permission he was guilty under s 12. However, in *Peart* [1970] 2 All ER 823 it was held that D was not guilty of an offence under s 12 when he obtained the use of a van by pretending that he had an urgent appointment in Alnwick and would return the van by 7.30 p.m. In fact, he drove to Burnley and was found there with the van by the police at 9 p.m. The Court of Appeal took the view that the owner had merely been deceived as to the purpose for which the van was to be used and this did not vitiate the owner's consent to the taking of the van at the start of the journey. The Court of Appeal could not consider whether there was a taking at a later point (either when D diverted from the route to Alnwick or when he continued to use the van after 7.30 p.m.), because this point had not been left to the jury.

In *Whittaker v Campbell* [1983] 3 All ER 582 the Queen's Bench Divisional Court came to the decision that D was not guilty of a s 12 offence where D, who did not hold a driving licence, hired a van using a driving licence belonging to another person. The fraud went only to the hiring of the van and not its use. The actual use that D made of the van was within the terms of the hiring.

14.5.3 Conveyance

What can be taken? The word used is 'conveyance' and this is defined very widely in s 12(7)(a):

SECTION

'12(7)(a) "Conveyance" means any conveyance constructed or adapted for the carriage of a person or persons whether by land, water or air, except that it does not include a conveyance constructed or adapted for use only under the control of a person not carried in or on it, and "drive" shall be construed accordingly.'

So this does not cover just road vehicles: it also includes trains, boats and aircraft. There are only two conditions placed on this wide definition. The first is that the conveyance must have been constructed or adapted for carrying people. The second is that the operator (or person in control) must also be carried in it or on it. This excludes radio-operated vehicles.

14.5.4 *Mens rea* of taking a conveyance

The *mens rea* of this offence differs according to whether D has taken, driven or allowed himself to be carried.

Where D has taken the conveyance, the taking must be intended. D must also know that he does not have the consent of the owner or any other lawful authority for the taking. Under s 12(6) D does not commit an offence if he believes he has the owner's consent or has lawful authority for the taking. The test for this appears to be subjective. Provided D has a genuine belief that the owner would have consented, it does not matter that the owner did not in fact consent.

Where D is not the original taker, but drives or allows himself to be carried in the conveyance, then the prosecution must prove that D knew the conveyance had been taken without the owner's consent or other lawful authority. 'Wilful blindness' as to this probably suffices for the *mens rea*.

NOTE: see Appendix 2 for an example of how to apply the law of taking a conveyance in a problem/scenario type question.

14.6 Aggravated vehicle-taking

This offence was added to the Theft Act 1968 by the Aggravated Vehicle-Taking Act 1992 because of the number of cases under s 12 where cars, having been taken, were driven dangerously, causing injury or damage. It was clear that a higher penalty was needed for such cases. The new section states:

SECTION

'12A(1) Subject to subsection (3) below, a person is guilty of aggravated taking of a vehicle if –

(a) he commits an offence under section 12(1) above (in this section referred to as a 'basic offence') in relation to a mechanically propelled vehicle; and

(b) it is proved that, at any time after the vehicle was unlawfully taken (whether by him or another) and before it was recovered, the vehicle was driven, or injury or damage caused in one or more of the circumstances set out in paragraphs (a) to (d) of subsection (2) below.

(2) The circumstances referred to in subsection (1)(b) above are –

(a) that the vehicle was driven dangerously on a road or other public place;

(b) that, owing to the driving of the vehicle, an accident occurred by which injury was caused to any person;

(c) that, owing to the driving of the vehicle, an accident occurred by which damage was caused to any property, other than the vehicle;

(d) that damage was caused to the vehicle.'

So in order to prove this offence the prosecution must show that

1. the basic offence was committed; and
2. that this was in relation to a mechanically propelled vehicle; and
3. one of the following:
   - dangerous driving;
   - injury owing to the driving;
   - damage to other property owing to the driving;
   - damage to the vehicle.

14.6.1 Dangerous driving

There is a two-part test for dangerous driving set out in s 12A(7). First, the way D drives must fall 'far below what would be expected of a competent and careful driver', and second, 'it would be obvious to a competent and careful driver that driving the vehicle in that way would be dangerous'. This imposes an objective standard on D.

14.6.2 Injury or damage

For the three situations set out in ss 12A(2)(b), 12A(2)(c) and 12A(2)(d), it is not necessary to prove any fault in the driving of the defendant. The prosecution need only show that D committed the basic offence and that one of the three things then occurred. This was shown in the case of *Marsh* [1997] Crim LR 205, where a pedestrian ran out in front of the car and was slightly injured. The Court of Appeal held that D was guilty even though there was no fault in his driving.

Section 12A(3) allows for a person to be not guilty in two situations. These are:

- if the driving, accident or damage occurred before the basic offence was committed;
- if he was not in or on the vehicle or in the immediate vicinity when the driving, accident or damage occurred.

NOTE: see Appendix 2 for an example of how to apply the law of aggravated vehicle-taking in a problem/scenario type question.

14.7 Abstracting electricity

It is necessary to have a separate offence for this, since electricity does not come within the definition of property for the purposes of theft.

Section 13 of the Theft Act 1968 makes it an offence where a person 'dishonestly uses without due authority, or dishonestly causes to be wasted or diverted, any electricity'.

The concept of dishonesty is that in the *Ghosh* [1982] 2 All ER 689 test (see Chapter 13, section 12.5.2) so the first question is, was what was done dishonest by the ordinary standards of reasonable and honest people? If it was not the defendant is not guilty. However, if the jury decide that it was dishonest by those standards, then they must consider the more subjective test of whether the defendant knew it was dishonest by those standards.

14.8 Blackmail

This is an offence under s 21 Theft Act 1968 which states:

SECTION

'21(1) A person is guilty of blackmail if, with a view to gain for himself or another or with intent to cause loss to another, he makes any unwarranted demand with menaces; and for this purpose a demand with menaces is unwarranted unless the person making it does so in the belief –

(a) that he has reasonable grounds for making the demand; and
(b) that the use of the menaces is a proper means of reinforcing the demand.

(2) The nature of the act or omission demanded is immaterial, and it is also immaterial whether the menaces relate to action to be taken by the person making the demand.'

So, from this it can be seen that there are four elements to be proved:

- a demand
- which is unwarranted; and
- made with menaces
- with a view to gain or loss.

For the *actus reus* D must make an unwarranted demand with menaces. For the *mens rea* D must act with a view to gain or loss and must also intend to make an unwarranted demand with menaces.

14.8.1 Demand

There must be a demand, but that demand may take any form, for example it may be by words, conduct, in writing or by e-mail. It need not even be made explicitly to the victim. In *Collister and Warhurst* (1955) 39 Cr App R 100 two police officers discussed the chances of them dropping a charge against the defendant in return for payment. They did this in circumstances where the defendant could easily overhear them and they meant him to overhear them. Even though they did not make a direct demand, this was held to be a demand for the purpose of blackmail. This case established that the demand need not be made in an aggressive or forceful manner. It was followed in *Lambert* [2009] EWCA Crim 2860.

CASE EXAMPLE

Lambert [2009] EWCA Crim 2860

A owed D money, so D phoned A's grandmother pretending to be A. He said 'Nana this is [A]. They've got me tied up. They want £5,000, Nana.' The grandmother believed the caller was A but said she did not have the money. A second demand was also unsuccessful. D was convicted of blackmail. It was held that the phone call of D was clearly a demand.

Making the demand is the *actus reus* of the offence. It does not have to be received by the victim. So, if a demand is sent through the post then the demand is considered made at the point the letter is posted. This was decided by the House of Lords in *Treacy* [1971] 1 All ER 110, when D posted a letter containing a demand with menaces posted in England to someone in Germany. The offence of blackmail was therefore committed in England. However, Lord Diplock thought that the demand continues until it reaches the victim. So, if the reverse had happened, i.e. a letter posted in Germany to someone in England, the demand can also be considered as occurring at the point when the victim reads it and, again, the offence would have been committed in England.

In *Lambert* (2009) the Court of Appeal also pointed out that a demand was still a demand even if it was impossible to carry it out.

14.8.2 Unwarranted demand

Section 21 explains that any demand made with menaces is unwarranted unless the two tests set out in s 21(1)(a) and s 21(1)(b) are fulfilled. This means that D has to show that he believed:

- he had reasonable grounds for making the demand;
- the use of the menaces was a proper means of reinforcing the demand.

These tests focus on D's belief and so give a subjective element to what is an unwarranted demand. They also mean that where D has a genuine claim, he can still be guilty of blackmail if he does not believe that the use of the menaces was a proper means of reinforcing the demand. This was clearly the intention of the Criminal Law Revision Committee, which wrote in its Eighth Report:

QUOTATION

'The essential feature of the offence will be that the accused demands something with menaces when he knows either that he has no right to make the demand or that the use of the menaces is improper. This, we believe, will limit the offence to what would ordinarily be thought to be included in blackmail. The true blackmailer will know that he has no reasonable grounds for demanding money as the price of his victim's secret: the person with a genuine claim will be guilty unless he believes that it is proper to use the menaces to enforce his claim.'

The report also explained that the word 'proper' was chosen because 'it directs the mind to the consideration of what is morally and socially acceptable'.

The fact that menaces were *not* a proper means of reinforcing a demand was essential in *Harvey* (1981) 72 Cr App R 139.

CASE EXAMPLE

Harvey (1981) 72 Cr App R 139

D and others had paid the victim £20,000 for what was claimed to be cannabis. In fact it was, as D put it, 'a load of rubbish'. The defendants wanted their money back as they felt they had been 'ripped off' to the tune of £20,000. In fact, as the deal was an illegal contract, there was no right in law to recover the money. However, it could be accepted that the defendants believed they had 'reasonable grounds for making the demand'. But the defendants reinforced their demand by kidnapping the victim, his wife and child, and threatened to cause them serious physical injury if the money was not repaid. They were guilty.

The same point was made in *Lambert* [2009] EWCA Crim 2860 where D was owed money by A. D attempted to get the money paid by A's grandmother by pretending to be A and stating that he was being held for ransom. D argued that as he was owed the money the demand was not unwarranted. His conviction was upheld as threatening A's grandmother was not a proper means of enforcing his demand. Menacing the grandmother in the way he did is unlikely to be a 'morally and socially acceptable' way of enforcing a debt.

14.8.3 Menaces

The demand must be made with menaces. Menaces have been held to be a serious threat, but are wider than just a threat. In *Thorne v Motor Trade Association* [1937] 3 All ER 157, Lord Wright said:

JUDGMENT

'I think the word "menace" is to be liberally construed and not as limited to threats of violence but as including threats of any action detrimental to or unpleasant to the person addressed. It may also include a warning that in certain events such action is intended.'

In *Clear* [1968] 1 All ER 74 it was said that the menace must either be 'of such a nature and extent that the mind of an ordinary person of normal stability and courage might be influenced or made apprehensive by it so as to unwillingly accede to it'. It is not necessary to prove that the victim was actually intimidated. So if the menaces would affect an ordinary person, this is sufficient, but if they would not, then blackmail cannot usually be proved. However, in *Garwood* [1987] 1 All ER 1032 the Court of Appeal said that where a threat is made which would not affect a normal person, this can still be menaces if the defendant was aware of the likely effect on the victim.

CASE EXAMPLE

Harry [1974] Crim LR 32

D, who was the treasurer of a college rag committee, sent letters to 115 local shopkeepers asking them to buy a poster, with the money to go to charity. The poster contained the words 'These premises are immune from all Rag 73 activities whatever they may be'. The letter sent out indicated that paying for a poster would avoid 'any rag activity which could in any way cause you inconvenience'. Of the 115 shopkeepers who received that letter, only about five complained. The trial judge pointed out that as a group, the shopkeepers who had received the letter were unconcerned about the supposed 'threat'. He, therefore, ruled that according to the definition given in *Clear* (1968), blackmail was not proved. There had not been any 'threat' which influenced or made them apprehensive so as to unwillingly accede to the demand.

It is irrelevant that D is not in a position to effect the menaces. In *Lambert* [2009] EWCA Crim 2860, D pretended to be A and claimed that he was tied up and money was being demanded for his release. As A was not tied up by anyone, the menaces could not be carried out. The Court of Appeal referred to s 21(2) of the Theft Act 1968 which states that it is immaterial whether the menaces relate to action to be taken by the person making the demand.

14.8.4 View to gain or loss

The *mens rea* of blackmail is that D must be acting with a view to gain for himself or another or with intent to cause loss to another. The interpretation section in the Theft Act 1968, s 34(2)(a) defines 'gain' and 'loss'. This states that:

SECTION

'34(2) For the purposes of this Act –

(a) "gain" and "loss" are to be construed as extending only to gain or loss in money or other property, but as extending to any such gain or loss whether temporary or permanent; and –

(i) "gain" includes a gain by keeping what one has, as well as a gain by getting what one has not; and

(ii) "loss" includes a loss by not getting what one might get, as well as a loss by parting with what one has.'

So the gain or loss must involve money or other property, but need not be permanent; it can be temporary.

An unusual case on view to a gain or a loss was *Bevans* [1988] Crim LR 236 where D, who was suffering from severe osteoarthritis, pointed a gun at his doctor and demanded a morphine injection for pain relief. The doctor gave him the injection. It was held that the morphine was property and, also, that it was both a gain for the defendant and a loss to the doctor from whom it was demanded.

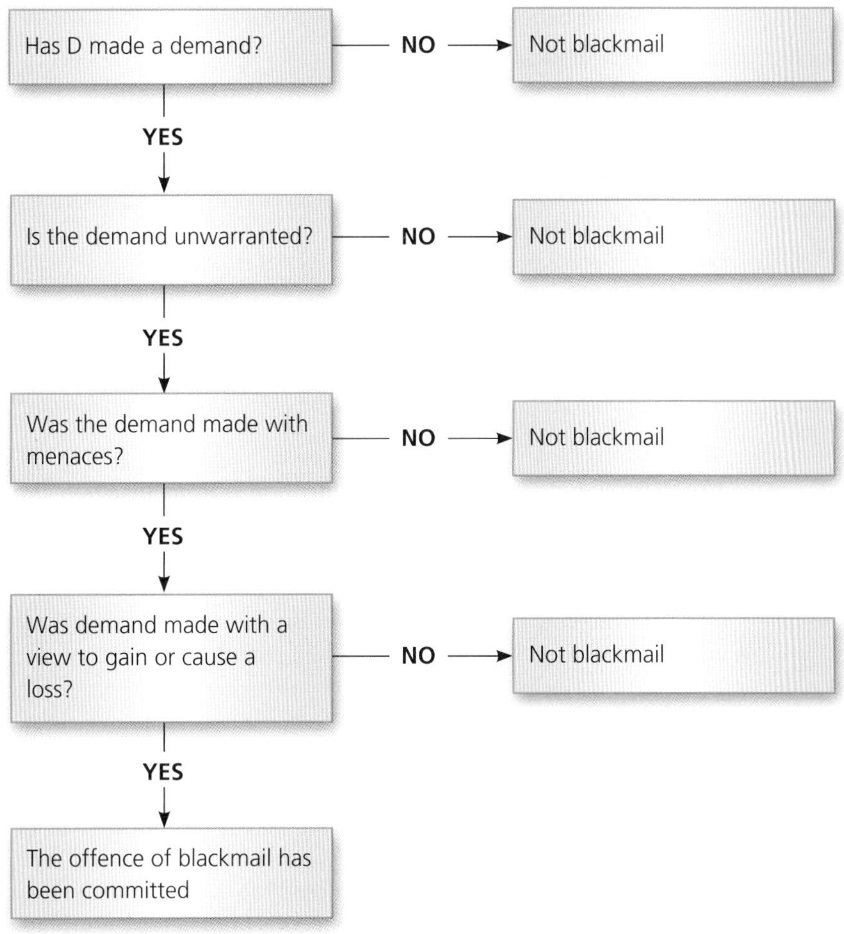

Figure 14.2 Flow chart on blackmail.

14.9 Handling stolen goods

This is an offence under s 22 Theft Act 1968, which states that:

SECTION

> '22 A person handles stolen goods if (otherwise than in the course of stealing) knowing or believing them to be stolen goods he dishonestly receives the goods, or dishonestly undertakes or assists in their retention, removal, disposal or realisation by or for the benefit of another person or he arranges to do so.'

So to prove a charge of handling the following must be shown:

- The property comes within the definition of 'goods' in s 34(2)(b).
- Those goods were stolen at the time of the handling.
- The handler received or undertook or assisted in their retention, removal, disposal or realisation.
- Where the allegation is that D undertook or assisted in their retention, removal, disposal or realisation, this must be by another person or for another person's benefit.

- D knew or believed the goods to be stolen.
- D was dishonest.

The first four points are the *actus reus* of the offence, and the last two points are the *mens rea*.

14.9.1 Goods

The definition of goods set out by s 34(2)(b) is:

SECTION

'34(2)(b) "goods" ... includes money and every other description of property except land, and includes things severed from the land by stealing.'

This definition does not specifically mention 'a thing in action' but the Court of Appeal, in *Attorney-General's Reference (No 4 of 1979)* [1981] 1 All ER 1193, was prepared to take the view that it could be included in the wide definition of 'every other description of property'. The only exception to what can be handled is land. Things which have been severed from land can be handled but the land itself (even though it is possible to steal land in some circumstances) cannot be handled.

14.9.2 Stolen

The goods must be stolen for the full offence of handling to be committed, but where the defendant believes the goods are stolen there can be an attempt to handle them, even though they are not stolen. This was decided in *Shivpuri* [1986] 2 All ER 334 which, although not a case on handling, overruled *Anderton v Ryan* [1985] 2 All ER 355 on the point of attempting to commit the impossible (see Chapter 6, section 6.4).

Section 24(4) states that as well as goods obtained by theft (and remember that theft is an element of robbery and can also be an element of burglary), stolen goods for the purposes of the Theft Act 1968 include those obtained by deception under s 15(1) and those obtained by blackmail.

Section 24(2) extends the definition of stolen goods to include other goods which represent the stolen goods:

SECTION

'24(2) ... references to stolen goods shall include, in addition to the goods originally stolen and any parts of them (whether in their original state or not) –

(a) any other goods which directly or indirectly represent the stolen goods in the hands of the thief as being the proceeds of any disposal or realisation of the whole or part of the stolen goods or of goods representing the stolen goods; and

(b) any other goods which directly or indirectly represent or have at any time represented the stolen goods in the hands of a handler of the stolen goods or any part of them as being the proceeds of any disposal or realisation of the whole or part of the stolen goods handled by him or of goods so representing them.'

This means that if the original goods are sold for cash, the money obtained for them is proceeds, and is also regarded as stolen. This was accepted by the Court of Appeal in *Attorney-General's Reference (No 4 of 1979)*, where it was stated that:

JUDGMENT

'where ... a person obtains cheques by deception and pays them into her bank account, the balance in that account may, to the value of the tainted cheque, be goods which "directly ... represent ... the stolen goods in the hands of the thief as being the proceeds of any disposal or realisation of the ... goods stolen" ... within the meaning of section 24(2)(a).'

Also note that it is sufficient if D handles part of the goods. This could apply where a car is stolen and broken up to be used in other cars. If D buys one of these cars (knowing or believing that it or part of it is stolen), then he is guilty of handling.

A thief cannot be charged with handling for anything done in the course of the theft. The correct charge against him is theft. However, if he steals, passes the goods on to an accomplice and then later receives them back, at this point he can be guilty of handling those goods, even though he stole them originally.

Goods ceasing to be stolen

Section 24(3) states that, where stolen goods have been restored to the person they were stolen from, or to other lawful possession or custody, they are not considered stolen goods for the purposes of handling. This has been important in cases where it is discovered that goods have been stolen and a plan has been made to trap the handler as, if the plan involves the goods returning into lawful possession, they will no longer be stolen goods and D will not be guilty of handling. If the owner or person from whom they were stolen (or the police) merely follows the thief to catch the handler, then the goods have not been 'restored to the person they were stolen from or to other lawful possession or custody'. For example, in *Greater London Metropolitan Police Commissioner v Streeter* (1980) 71 Cr App R 113, the goods were marked in order to trap the handler, but they were still considered to be stolen goods. It was made clear in *Attorney-General's Reference (No 1 of 1974)* [1974] 2 All ER 899 that the facts of each case have to be carefully considered.

CASE EXAMPLE

Attorney-General's Reference (No 1 of 1974) [1974] 2 All ER 899

A police officer suspected that goods in the back of a parked car were stolen, so he removed the rotor arm of the car to prevent it being driven away and kept watch. When D returned to the car the officer questioned him about the goods and arrested him because he could not give a satisfactory account. The jury acquitted the defendant and the Attorney-General referred the point of law to the Court of Appeal. The Court held that the jury should have been asked to consider the officer's intention. If he had not made up his mind to take possession of the goods before questioning D, then the goods would have remained stolen goods. If he had already decided to take possession of the goods, then, by removing the rotor arm he had reduced them into his possession. The police officer's state of mind was something which should have been left to the jury to find as a fact.

14.9.3 Handling

Section 24 creates a number of ways in which the *actus reus* of handling may be committed. These are:

- receiving or arranging to receive stolen goods;

- undertaking or assisting or arranging their
  - retention
  - removal
  - disposal
  - realisation.

These last four must be by another person or for the benefit of another person.

Each word used in s 24 to describe handling has a separate meaning. Receiving means taking possession or control. As arranging to receive is sufficient for guilt, D does not have to be in possession or control if he has arranged to be so in the future.

'Retention' means 'keep possession of, not lose, continue to have'. This was demonstrated by the case of *Pitchley* [1972] Crim LR 705.

CASE EXAMPLE

Pitchley [1972] Crim LR 705

D was given £150 in cash by his son who asked him to take care of it for him. D put the money into his Post Office savings account. At the time of receiving the money D was not aware that it was stolen. His son said he had won it betting on horse races. Two days later D found out that it was stolen, but did nothing, leaving the money in the account. He was convicted of handling. By leaving the money in the account he had retained it on behalf of another person.

'Removal' is literally moving goods from one place to another. So this covers carrying the goods from one house to the next-door house, up to arranging for the goods to be flown out of the country. 'Disposal' is getting rid of them. This can be by destroying the goods, giving them away or doing another act such as melting down silver items. 'Realisation' means selling.

As already stated, the retention, removal, disposal and realisation must be done for the benefit of another. In *Bloxham* [1982] 1 All ER 582 D purchased a car which he later came to believe was stolen. He sold the car very cheaply to another person and was charged with handling on the basis that he had disposed of or realised the car for another's benefit, the prosecution alleging that this was for the benefit of the purchaser. The House of Lords held that he had been wrongly convicted. The disposal was for his own benefit. It was the purchase which benefited the purchaser; and a purchase was not a disposal or realisation of the car by the purchaser.

14.9.4 Undertaking or assisting

To be an offence the undertaking or assisting must be done in relation to retention, removal, disposal or realisation of the goods. To be considered as assistance, something must be done by the offender towards one of those four things. Knowing that stolen items are being kept in your neighbour's garage is not enough. Even using them does not come within the offence. This was decided in *Sander* [1982] Cr App R 84, where D used a stolen heater and battery charger in his father's garage. By using them he had not assisted in retaining or removing them (nor, of course, had he assisted in disposing of or realising them). If he had allowed the items to be stored in his own garage, then that would have been assisting in retaining them.

Although the undertaking or assistance is often by a physical act, for example, helping to carry goods, it can also take the form of verbal or written representations. In addition, the assistance need not be successful in achieving the retaining, removal, disposal or realisation of the goods. Both these points were illustrated in *Kanwar* (1982) 75 2 All ER 528.

CASE EXAMPLE

Kanwar [1982] 2 All ER 528

D's husband had used stolen goods to furnish their home. D was aware that the items were stolen. When the police called and made inquiries about them, she gave answers which were lies. The Court of Appeal in their judgment gave two specific examples. These were first that in relation to a painting which was hanging on their living room, she said that she had purchased it at a shop and had a receipt for it. She was unable to produce any receipt and tacitly admitted that no such receipt existed. The second example was when she told the police that she had bought a mirror in the market. Again this answer was a lie. Her conviction for handling stolen goods was upheld on the basis that her lies were aimed at assisting the retention of the stolen goods.

The Court of Appeal explained the offence in this way:

JUDGMENT

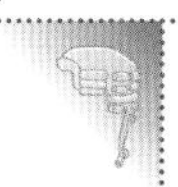

'To constitute the offence, something must be done by the offender, and done intentionally and dishonestly, for the purpose of enabling the goods to be retained. Examples of such conduct are concealing or helping to conceal the goods, or doing something to make them more difficult to find or identify. Such conduct must be done knowing or believing the goods to be stolen and done dishonestly and for the benefit of another.

We see no reason why the requisite assistance should be restricted to physical acts. Verbal representations, whether oral or in writing, for the purpose of concealing the identity of stolen goods may, if made dishonestly and for the benefit of another, amount to handling stolen goods by assisting in their retention ... The requisite assistance need not be successful in its object.'

The court went on to explain that if the assistance had to be successful, it would lead to the absurd situation that D would be not guilty of assisting in the retention of goods when caught in the act of doing something such as hiding them. D could argue that, as the police had recovered the goods, his effort at hiding them had not succeeded and he should be not guilty.

14.9.5 *Mens rea* of handling

The defendant must know or believe the goods to be stolen at the time he does the act of handling. In *Pitchley* (1972) D was not guilty when he received the money from his son because at that time he did not know or believe it to be stolen. He only became guilty when he knew the money was stolen and he then assisted by keeping the money. This was why the charge related to the 'retention of' the money, as D did retain the money after he had the knowledge that the money was stolen.

The test is subjective. It is what D knows or believes, and not what he ought to have known or realised. 'Know' is where D has first-hand information about the fact the goods are stolen, e.g. he has been told by the thief that this is so. 'Believe' is the state of mind where D says to himself, 'I cannot say I know for certain that these goods are stolen, but there can be no other reasonable conclusion in the light of all the circumstances.' This definition of 'believe' was given in *Hall* [1985] Crim LR 377. The Court of Appeal went on to say that 'What is not enough, of course, is mere suspicion.' This part of the judgment was held later in *Forsyth* [1997] Crim LR 581 to be confusing because of the use of the word 'mere'. This might lead juries to consider that although 'mere' suspicion was not enough, 'great' suspicion was enough to convict, when in fact suspicion is never enough to convict.

Professor Sir John Smith puts forward the theory that the Criminal Law Revision Committee thought 'believe' would in fact cover a high level of suspicion. The Committee pointed out in its Eighth Report that there was a 'serious defect' in the law prior to the 1968 Act, as the prosecution had to prove actual knowledge that the goods were stolen and this was often impossible. It said:

QUOTATION

'In many cases indeed guilty knowledge does not exist, although the circumstances of the transaction are such that the receiver ought to be guilty of an offence. The man who buys goods at a ridiculously low price from an unknown seller whom he meets in a public house may not know that the goods are stolen, and he may take the precaution of asking no questions. Yet it may be clear on the evidence that he believes that the goods were stolen.'

Cmnd 2977 (1966), para 64

Professor Sir John Smith said that this showed they intended to include what is known as 'wilful blindness', which has been held in some offences to be included in the word 'knowing'. In other words, D could be guilty of handling where he had great suspicion that the goods were stolen, and chose to shut his eyes to the fact. However, the decision in *Forsyth* (1997) means that even a very high level of suspicion does not come within the definition of 'believe'.

Dishonestly

The handling must be done dishonestly. The test for dishonesty is the same *Ghosh* (1982) test as for theft. Was what was done dishonest by the ordinary standards of reasonable and honest people? If it was not, the defendant is not guilty. However, if the jury decide that it was dishonest by those standards, then they must consider the more subjective test of whether the defendant knew it was dishonest by those standards.

14.10 Going equipped for stealing

This is an offence under s 25(1) Theft Act 1968, which states:

SECTION

'25(1) A person shall be guilty of an offence if, when not at his place of abode, he has with him any article for use in the course of or in connection with any burglary, theft or cheat.'

For the purposes of this section, 'theft' includes taking a conveyance under s 12(1) of the Theft Act 1968 and 'cheat' refers to any offence under s 15.

14.10.1 *Actus reus* of going equipped

From s 25, it can be seen that the requirements for the *actus reus* of this offence are:

- D has with him
- any article
- for use in the course of or in connection with any burglary, theft or cheat; and
- D must not be at his place of abode.

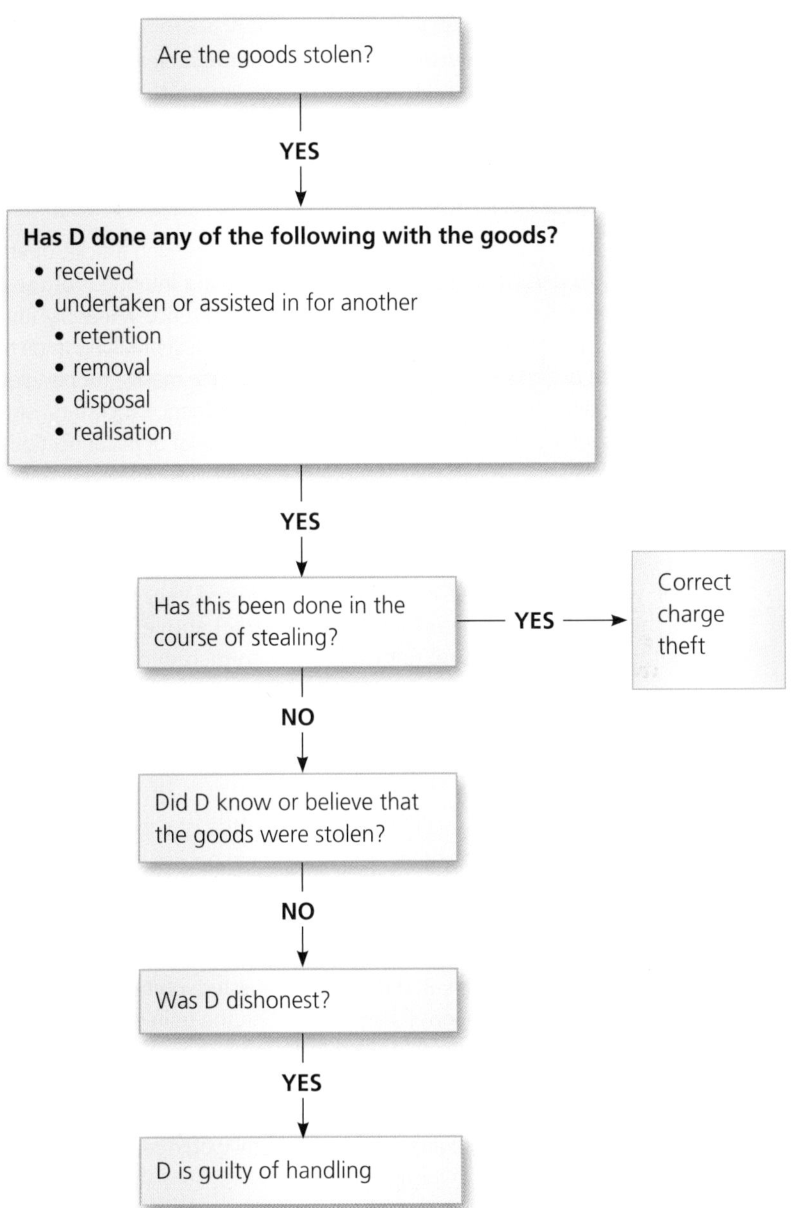

Figure 14.3 Flow chart on handling stolen goods.

Has with him

This, of course, includes items which D physically has on his person, such as car keys which are in his pocket or gloves which he is wearing. But it also includes situations where D can be thought of as being in possession or control of an article, such as a car he has parked down the street. The items do not need to belong to him. It can be something which he has just picked up. This point of view is supported by *Minor v DPP* [1988] Crim LR 55, where D and another man were seen getting ready to siphon petrol from a car. They had two empty petrol cans and a tube with them. There was no evidence that they had brought these from their homes, but they clearly had them with them when the police stopped them, and this was enough to make them guilty under s 25.

Any article

The Criminal Law Revision Committee made it clear that any article could come within this section if it was intended for use in committing a burglary, theft or obtaining by deception. In its Eighth Report it said:

QUOTATION

'[T]he offence under the [section] applies to possessing articles of any kind. There is no reason for listing particular kinds of articles ... anything intended for use in committing any of the offences referred to should be included. The offence will apply for example, to firearms and other offensive weapons, imitation firearms, housebreaking implements, any articles for the purpose of concealing identity (for example, face masks, rubber gloves and false car number-plates) and ... [a variety of] car keys and confidence tricksters' outfits. The reference to the offender having the article for use "in the course of or in connection with" any of the offences mentioned will secure that the offence under the clause will apply to having an article (for example a motor car) for getting to the place of the crime.'

Cmnd 2799 (1966), para 148

The word 'article' has indeed been interpreted very widely by the courts, so that as well as the type of items mentioned in the extract above, such articles as bottles of wine and clothing with fake brand names have been included.

CASE EXAMPLE

Doukas [1978] 1 All ER 1061

D was a wine waiter in a hotel. He took bottles of wine into the hotel, intending to sell them to people dining at the hotel, so that he could pocket the money. There was no doubt that the bottles of wine were articles for the purpose of s 25. The main point on appeal was whether they were for use in a s 15 offence of obtaining money by deception. In the earlier case of *Rashid* [1977] 2 All ER 237, where a British Rail waiter had taken his own tomato sandwiches to sell on board a train, Bridge LJ had suggested, *obiter*, that there would be no obtaining by deception. It was thought that customers on the train would be indifferent as to whether their sandwiches were 'genuine' British Rail sandwiches or from another source, so the deception would not have any effect on their actions.

The Court of Appeal in *Doukas* (1978) disagreed with the *obiter dicta* statements in *Rashid* (1977). It thought that any diner in the hotel would refuse to have the wine if they knew that it was brought in by D for his own profit.

For use

In *Minor v DPP* (1988) it was held that it did not matter when D had come into possession of the cans and tube. The important point was that the 'having with' must be before the theft or other offence. This was also seen in *Ellames* [1974] 3 All ER 130 where D was stopped and he had with him articles which had been used in a robbery (masks, guns, gloves) and which he was trying to get rid of. He was not guilty of having with him these articles 'for use', as the robbery was in the past. The court did, however, say that D could commit the offence if he had the items for future use by another person.

Under s 25(3) Theft Act 1968, proof that a person had with him any article made or adapted for use in committing a burglary, theft or cheat shall be evidence that he had it with him for such use. Where the item has an innocent use, such as a pair of gloves, then it is for the prosecution to prove that the defendant intended to use it for a burglary, theft or cheat.

Not at his place of abode

In *Bundy* [1977] 2 All ER 382 D argued that he used his car as his 'place of abode', as he had nowhere to live. However, when he was arrested he had been driving the car and was not at the site where he usually parked it to sleep. It was accepted that a car could be a 'place of abode', but in the circumstances he was not there and so was guilty under s 25.

14.10.2 *Mens rea* of going equipped

The prosecution must prove that D

- knew he had the article; and
- intended to use it in the course of or in connection with one of the listed crimes.

The intention to use must be for a future crime. See *Ellames* above.

14.11 Making off without payment

This offence was created as it became obvious that the Theft Act 1968 left gaps in the law where D was not guilty of any offence, even though his conduct would be seen as 'criminal' by most people. The Criminal Law Revision Committee in its Thirteenth Report, *Section 16 of the Theft Act 1968*, Cmnd 6733 (1977) recommended a new Act to fill those gaps. This was done by the Theft Act 1978.

One of the gaps had become apparent in *Greenburg* [1972] Crim LR 331, where D had filled his car up at a garage and then driven off without paying. He was not guilty of theft because at the moment he appropriated the petrol it belonged to him. This is because the civil law rules on the transfer of ownership in a sale of goods state that the goods become D's the moment that the petrol is put into the tank of his car. It was also not possible to prove an offence of obtaining the petrol by false pretences because he claimed he had gone into the garage intending to pay, and so made no deception about his conduct. He only decided not to pay when he had filled up the tank.

This situation is now covered by s 3(1) of the Theft Act 1978 (remember this is a different Act from the Theft Act 1968), which makes it an offence, stating:

SECTION

'3(1) Subject to subsection 3 below, a person who, knowing that payment on the spot for any goods supplied or service done is required or expected from him, dishonestly makes off without having paid as required or expected and with intent to avoid payment of the amount due shall be guilty of an offence.

14.11.1 *Actus reus* of making off without payment

The points that have to be proved for the *actus reus* are the following:

- Goods have been supplied or a service done.
- Payment is required on the spot.
- D has made off.
- D has not paid as required.

Goods supplied or service done

The goods supplied or service done must be lawful. If the supply of goods is unlawful (e.g. cigarettes to someone under 16) or the service is not legally enforceable (e.g. prostitution), then under s 3(3) no offence has been committed.

If the service is not complete then there is no offence. This is shown by the case of *Troughton v Metropolitan Police* [1987] Crim LR 138.

CASE EXAMPLE

Troughton v Metropolitan Police [1987] Crim LR 138

D, who was drunk, hired a taxi to take him home but did not give the driver his exact address. The driver stopped to get directions from D and there was an argument in which D accused the driver of taking an unnecessary diversion. As the taxi driver could not get the exact address from D, he drove to the nearest police station to see if someone could help. When the taxi stopped D ran off.

The magistrates convicted D but, on appeal to the Divisional Court, the conviction was quashed. This was because the journey had not been completed. That meant there was a breach of contract by the taxi driver and so D was not required to pay the fare.

The offence covers a wide range of situations which include making off without paying for a haircut or a taxi ride. It can also apply to customers in restaurants who leave without paying for their meal or hotel guests who leave the hotel without paying for their room.

Payment required on the spot

It has to be proved that payment on the spot was required or expected. In *Vincent* [2001] Crim LR 488 D had stayed at two hotels and not paid his bills. He said that he had arranged with the proprietors of each to pay when he could, so payment on the spot was not required or expected. At his trial the judge directed the jury that D could not rely on a dishonestly obtained agreement to avoid payment. His conviction was quashed, as s 3 merely states that payment on the spot must be required or expected. If there had been an agreement not to expect payment on the spot, it was irrelevant for the purposes of s 3 that that agreement had been dishonestly obtained. In fact D could have been charged with an entirely different offence under s 2(1)(b) of the Theft Act 1978.

Makes off

A key ingredient of the offence is that D 'makes off'. In other words, he leaves the scene where payment was expected. In *McDavitt* [1981] Crim LR 843 D had an argument with the manager of a restaurant and refused to pay his bill for a meal. He got up and started to walk out, but was advised not to leave as the police had been called. He then went into the toilet and stayed there until the police came. The judge directed the jury to acquit D at the end of the prosecution case, as he had not 'made off'.

D has not paid

This is a question of fact. The payment must be of the amount due.

14.11.2 *Mens rea* of making off without payment

The *mens rea* of the offence involves:

- dishonesty (this is the same test as for theft; see Chapter 3, section 3.1.5);
- knowledge that payment on the spot is required;
- an intention to avoid payment.

The Act only states 'with intent to avoid payment of the amount due', but in *Allen* [1985] 2 All ER 641 the House of Lords held that there must be an intent permanently to avoid payment. D owed £1,286 for his stay at a hotel. He left without paying, but his defence was that he genuinely intended to pay in the near future, as he was expecting to receive sufficient money to cover the bill. The House of Lords agreed with the decision of the Court of Appeal, who had said:

JUDGMENT

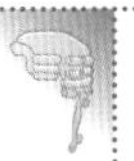

'[T]he phrase "and with intent to avoid payment of the amount due" adds a further ingredient: an intention to do more than delay or defer, an intention to evade payment altogether.'

It has been argued that this decision in *Allen* (1985) allows defendants to put forward fictitious defences of what they hoped to be able to do about payment in the future. But there have been no further cases on this point, so presumably the law is working satisfactorily.

ACTIVITY

Applying the law

The following scenarios involve offences covered in this chapter. In each situation, explain what offences have or may have been committed.

1. Aziz rides his own bicycle to college and leaves it in the cycle park available for students. When he leaves to go home he takes Ben's bicycle, which is the same model, by mistake. The next morning he realises his mistake but he decides to keep the bicycle for a few days. Two days later he abandons the bicycle near the college.
2. Cate takes several skeleton keys out with her as she intends to break into a house to steal money. She goes round to the back of one house and manages to open the back door. In the house she finds a wallet which she takes. She then hears the front door being opened and realises that the householder, who is an elderly woman, has come home. Cate is unable to leave without being seen, so she punches the woman and knocks her out, causing her a serious head injury. Cate then leaves the house.
3. Dylan, who is a known shoplifter, has been banned from entering his local supermarket. He is very annoyed about this and persuades Errol to come to the shop with him in order to cause damage to the displays. On entering the shop Dylan goes to the magazine stand and sprays paint over the magazines on it. Errol goes through a door marked 'staff only' and takes a bottle of whisky he finds in the room there. He is caught in there by Frankie. Frankie tells Errol that he will call the manager unless Errol gives him all the money he has on him.
4. Gina knows that her boyfriend has stolen some television sets from a warehouse. Two weeks later he brings a set round to her house and asks her if he can leave it there. Gina is suspicious that it may be one of the ones he stole, and tells him she will not have it in the house but he can put it in the garage.

SUMMARY

Robbery

- Section 8 Theft Act 1968 (TA 68) – stealing, and immediately before or at the time of doing so, using force or putting someone in fear of being subjected to force.
- There must be a completed theft.
- D must use force or put or seek to put any person in fear of force: the amount of force can be small.

- The force must be immediately before or at the time of the theft *and* it must used be in order to steal.
- Theft has been held to be ongoing so that the force is still at the time of the theft.
- D must intend to steal and intend to use force to steal.

Burglary

- Section 9(l)a TA 68 – entering a building or part of a building as a trespasser
  - intending to steal, inflict grievous bodily harm or
  - do unlawful damage.
- Or s 9(l)b TA 68 – having entered a building or part of a building as a trespasser, steals or attempts to steal or inflicts or attempts to inflict grievous bodily harm.
- Being a trespasser includes where D has gone beyond the permission to enter.
- Building includes inhabited vehicles and boats.

Aggravated burglary

- Section 10 TA 68 – a burglary where D has with him any firearm, imitation firearm, any weapon of offence or any explosive.

Removal of items from a place open to the public

- Section 11 TA 68 – where the public have access to a building in order to view the building or a collection and D removes an article displayed or kept for display to the public.

Taking a conveyance without consent

- Section 12 TA 68 – D, without having the consent of the owner or other lawful authority, takes any conveyance for his own or another's use or, knowing that any conveyance has been taken without such authority, drives it or allows himself to be carried in or on it.

Aggravated vehicle-taking

- An offence (under s 12 TA 68) of taking a mechanically propelled conveyance and which involves one of the following:
  - dangerous driving;
  - injury owing to the driving;
  - damage to other property owing to the driving;
  - damage to the vehicle.

Blackmail

- Section 21 TA 68 – D, with a view to gain for himself or another or with intent to cause loss to another, makes any unwarranted demand with menaces.
- The demand can be in any form or even implicit.
- A demand is unwarranted unless D can show that he believed:
  - he had reasonable grounds for making the demand;
  - the use of the menaces was a proper means of reinforcing the demand.
- The gain or loss must involve money or other property, but need not be permanent.
- Menaces means a serious threat that either the menace be such that an 'ordinary person of normal stability and courage might be influenced or made apprehensive by it so as to unwillingly accede to it' or one that would affect the V.

Handling stolen goods

- Section 22 TA 68 – D knowing or believing goods to be stolen goods dishonestly receives them, or dishonestly undertakes or assists in their retention, removal, disposal or realisation by or for the benefit of another person or arranges to do so.

Going equipped to steal

- Section 25 TA 68 – D, when not at his place of abode, has with him any article for use in the course of or in connection with any burglary, theft or cheat.

Making off without payment

- Section 3 Theft Act 1978 – D, knowing that payment on the spot for any goods supplied or service done is required or expected from him, dishonestly makes off without having paid as required or expected and with intent to avoid payment.

SAMPLE ESSAY QUESTION

To what extent is the offence of burglary adequately defined in the Theft Act 1968?

State the definition of burglary:

- S 9(1)(a) and 9(1)(b) TA 1968
- Identify the key elements of 'entry', trespasser', 'building or part of a building'
- Note that the only definition in the Act is for building, s 9(4)

Expand on the element of 'entry':

- No definition in Act
- Discuss difficulties and changing definitions that have emerged in cases:
  - *Collins* (1972)
  - *Brown* (1985)
  - *Ryan* (1996)

Expand on the element of 'trespasser':

- No definition in Act
- Assumed that civil definition of trespass would apply
- The addition of 'knowing he was a trespasser or intended to trespass' *Collins* (1972)
- Discuss the extension of 'trespasser' to those who go beyond the permission to enter *Smith and Jones* (1976)
- Should shoppers who steal be liable for burglary?

Expand on the element of 'building or part of a building':

- Give definition of 'building'
- Discuss problems in cases such as *B and S v Leathley* (1979) and *Norfolk Constabulary v Seeking and Gould* (1986) which leave it to the facts of each case
- Discuss the problems of 'part of a building' and the case of *Walkington* (1979) – should this have been burglary?

Conclude

Further reading

Books

Ormerod, D and Laird, K, *Smith and Hogan Criminal Law: Cases and Materials* (11th edn, Oxford University Press, 2014), Chapters 23–25, 27–29.

Articles

Ashworth, A, 'Robbery reassessed' (2002) Crim LR 851.

Pace, P J, 'Burglarious trespass' (1985) Crim LR 716.

Reed, A, 'Case comment: robbery: the use of force and s 8 of the Theft Act 1968' (2012) J Crim L 282.

Spencer, J, 'Handling, theft and the mala fide purchaser' (1985) Crim LR 92 and 440.

Spencer, J, 'The Aggravated Vehicle-Taking Act 1992' (1992) Crim LR 699.

Williams, G, 'Temporary appropriations should be theft' (1981) Crim LR 129.

15

Fraud

AIMS AND OBJECTIVES

After reading this chapter you should be able to:

- Understand the reasons for the enactment of the Fraud Act 2006
- Understand the offences of fraud created by the Fraud Act 2006
- Understand the offence of obtaining services by fraud
- Analyse critically all the above offences
- Apply the law to factual situations to determine whether an offence of fraud has been committed

15.1 Background to the Fraud Act 2006

Prior to the Fraud Act 2006 there had been various attempts at creating laws to cover situations of fraud. There had been a major reform of the law with the Theft Act 1968 which abolished all earlier offences involving deception or fraud. This Act created an offence of obtaining property by deception (s 15) and an offence of obtaining a pecuniary advantage by deception (s 16). This latter offence originally could be committed in one of three ways, but part (a) of s 16 quickly proved to be unsatisfactory and it was repealed by the Theft Act 1978. This second Theft Act created offences of obtaining services by deception (s 1) and securing remission of a liability (s 2). Section 2 of the Theft Act 1978 was complex as it included three ways in which the offence could be committed. These were:

- remission of a liability;
- inducing a creditor to wait for or forgo payment;
- obtaining an exemption from or an abatement of a liability.

Even these reforms did not cover all the gaps in the law and, in addition, there was confusion due to the overlapping of the offences.

One gap in the law was highlighted in the case of *Preddy* [1996] 3 All ER 481 where the defendants made false representations in order to obtain a number of mortgage advances from building societies to purchase houses. They intended to repay the mortgages when they sold the houses, as they hoped, at a profit. The mortgage advances were in the form of money transfers. The House of Lords quashed Ds' convictions on the basis that no property belonging to another had been obtained. As a result of this decision a further amendment was made to the Theft Act 1968 by the Theft (Amendment) Act 1996. This inserted an extra section (s 15A) into the Theft Act 1968 creating the offence of obtaining a money transfer by deception.

15.2 The need for reform

All the reforms to the Theft Act 1968 left the law very fragmented and difficult to apply. The Law Commission in its report *Fraud* (Law Com No 276 (2002)) stated that:

QUOTATION

'3.11 Arguably, the law of fraud is suffering from an "undue particularisation of closely allied crimes". Over-particularisation or "untidiness" is undesirable in itself, but it also has undesirable consequences.

3.12 First, it allows technical arguments to prosper. When the original Theft Act deception offences were first proposed by the CLRC in their Eighth Report, this problem was foreseen by a minority of the committee members: To list and define the different objects which persons who practise deception aim at achieving is unsatisfactory and dangerous, because it is impossible to be certain that any list would be complete . . .

3.20 The second difficulty that arises from over-particularisation is that a defendant may face the wrong charge, or too many charges.'

Various cases had highlighted areas where the law was difficult to apply. One problem that arose was whether silence could be a deception. In *DPP v Ray* [1973] 3 All ER 131 D had ordered a meal and then run off without paying for it. At that time (1973) there was no offence of making off without payment (see section 14.11), so D was charged with obtaining property by deception. The Court of Appeal quashed his conviction, but the House of Lords reinstated the conviction, taking the view that 'where a new customer orders a meal in a restaurant, he must be held to make an implied representation that he can and will pay for it before he leaves'. They also thought that this was an ongoing representation.

Another problem was that the prosecution had to prove the deception caused the obtaining. V must have acted because of D's deception. This meant that if V knew D was lying, and still handed over property, then the offence of obtaining property by deception had not been committed (although there would have been an attempt). It also created problems where V stated that the deception had not been relevant to the handing over of property. For example, in *Laverty* [1970] 3 All ER 432 D changed the registration number plates and the chassis number on a car and sold the car to V. The changing of the numbers was a representation that the car was the original car to which these numbers had been allocated. However, D's conviction was quashed as there was no evidence that the deception regarding the number plates had influenced V to buy the car, so there was no proof that D had obtained the purchase money from V as a result of that deception.

This showed a gap in the law, although in later cases the courts became inventive in finding that V had acted as the result of the particular deception. This was seen in *Lambie* [1981] 2 All ER 776.

CASE EXAMPLE

Lambie [1981] 2 All ER 776

D had a credit card (Barclaycard) with a £200 limit. She exceeded this limit and the bank which had issued the card wrote asking her to return the card. She agreed that she would return the card, but she did not do so. She then purchased goods in a Mothercare shop with the card. She was convicted of obtaining a pecuniary advantage by deception, contrary to s 16(1) of the Theft Act 1968. The departmental manager in Mothercare made it plain that she made no assumption about the defendant's credit standing at the bank. Provided the signature matched that on the card and the card was not on a 'stop list' the manager would hand over the goods.

Because of this the Court of Appeal allowed her appeal as the deception had not been the cause of the obtaining, but the House of Lords reinstated the conviction. The Law Lords held that it was not necessary to have direct evidence of the reliance on a particular deception if the facts were such that 'it is patent that there was only one reason which anybody could suggest for the person alleged to have been defrauded parting with his money'. They thought that in the case of credit cards it would make the law unworkable if there had to be direct evidence that the deception induced the obtaining in every case.

Another problem arose where the deception was made to a machine so that no human person had been deceived. The Law Commission in its report *Fraud* (Law Com No 276 (2002)) explained this problem:

QUOTATION

'3.34 A machine has no mind, so it cannot believe a proposition to be true or false, and therefore cannot be deceived. A person who dishonestly obtains a benefit by giving false information to a computer or machine is not guilty of any deception offence. Where the benefit obtained is property, he or she will normally be guilty of theft, but where it is something other than property (such as a service), there may be no offence at all.'

This was becoming an increasingly important gap in the law as the Law Commission went on to point out in the next paragraph of the report:

QUOTATION

'3.35 This has only become a problem in recent years, as businesses make more use of machines as an interface with their customers. There are now many services available to the public which will usually be paid for via a machine. For example, one would usually pay an internet service provider by entering one's credit card details on its website. Using card details to pay for such a service without the requisite authority would not currently constitute an offence. As the use of the internet and automated call centres expands, this gap in the law will be increasingly indefensible.'

15.2.1 Proposals for reform

In 1999 the Law Commission published a Consultation Paper No 155, *Legislating the Criminal Code: Fraud and Deception*. It followed this by publishing a report, *Fraud* (Law Com No 276) which had a draft Bill attached to it. In 2004 the government consulted on the report and this led to the passing of the Fraud Act in 2006.

15.3 Fraud Act 2006

tutor tip

'Make sure you understand how the Fraud Act 2006 has reformed the law.'

The Fraud Act 2006 repealed ss 15, 15A, 15B, 16 and 20(2) of the Theft Act 1968 and also ss 1 and 2 of the Theft Act 1978. The previous offences are replaced by four new offences under the Fraud Act 2006. These are:

- fraud by false representation (s 2);
- fraud by failing to disclose information (s 3);
- fraud by abuse of position (s 4);
- obtaining services dishonestly (s 11).

The 2006 Act also creates other offences connected to fraud. The main ones are:

- possession etc. of articles for use in frauds (s 6);
- making or supplying articles for use in frauds (s 7).

15.4 Fraud by false representation

Under s 2 of the Fraud Act 2006, the offence of fraud by false representation is committed if D:

SECTION

'2(1) (a) dishonestly makes a false representation, and
(b) intends, by making the representation –
(i) to make a gain for himself or another, or
(ii) to cause loss to another or to expose another to the risk of loss.'

The *actus reus* of the offence is that the defendant must make a representation which is false. The *mens rea* has three parts to it. The defendant must be dishonest, he must know the representation is or might be untrue or misleading and he must have an intention to make a gain or cause a loss.

15.4.1 False representation

Section 2 of the Act defines false representation.

SECTION

'2(2) A representation is false if –
(a) it is untrue or misleading, and
(b) the person making it knows that it is, or might be, untrue or misleading.

2(3) 'Representation' means any representation as to fact or law, including a representation as to the state of mind of
(a) the person making the representation, or
(b) any other person.

2(4) A representation may be express or implied.'

From this, it can be seen that 'representation' covers a wide area. A representation as to fact clearly covers situations where someone uses a false identity or states that they own property when they do not. It also covers situations such as someone stating that a car has only done 22,000 miles when they know it has done double that amount.

A representation as to state of mind covers such matters as a customer saying they will pay their bill when they have no intention of doing so.

Express representations

The Act also states that a representation may be express or implied (s 2(4)). For an express representation, the Explanatory Notes to the Act make it clear that there is no limit on the way in which the representation must be expressed. The notes point out that it could, for example, be written or spoken or posted on a website.

The Explanatory Notes to the Act also point out that the offence can be committed by 'phishing' on the Internet. That is where a person sends out an email to a large number of people falsely representing that the email has been sent by a legitimate bank. The email asks the receiver to provide information such as credit card and bank numbers so that the 'phisher' can gain access to others' assets.

There have been no cases appealed on substantial points of law, but there have been appeals on sentencing in cases charged under the Fraud Act. These cases give examples of the type of conduct charged under s 2 and two examples are given below.

CASE EXAMPLE

Hamilton [2008] EWCA Crim 2518

V's son had bought some new fence panels for V's garden, but as they had turned out to be the wrong size he left them leaning up against the side of the house until such time as he was able to replace them. D and his brother called at V's house claiming that they had come to collect payment for the panels. In fact, the victim's son had already paid for them in full. D told V that once that sum was paid they would arrange for replacement panels to be delivered. V paid them £60.

This is clearly an express representation as D told V the panels had not been paid for when they had. Another case where there was an express representation was *Cleps* (2009).

CASE EXAMPLE

Cleps [2009] EWCA Crim 894

D went to a building society and falsely claimed to be George Roper. He opened a Liquid Gold account in the name of George Roper. Two days later D returned to the same branch. He produced a passport in the name of George Roper and the passbook for the Liquid Gold account as identification. He asked to close a Guarantee Reserve account (held by the real George Roper) and had the £181,950 in that account transferred into the Liquid Gold account. He then obtained a banker's draft for that amount.

The representation that he was George Roper was an express representation.

Implied representations

There are many ways in which it is possible to make an implied representation through one's conduct. This was shown by the old case of *Barnard* (1837) 7 C & P 784.

CASE EXAMPLE

Barnard (1837) 7 C & P 784

D went into a shop in Oxford wearing the cap and gown of a fellow commoner of the university. He also said he was a fellow commoner and as a result the shopkeeper agreed to sell him goods on credit. The court said, *obiter*, that he would have been guilty even if he had said nothing. The wearing of the cap and gown was itself a false pretence.

In fact the case of *Barnard* demonstrates both an implied representation and an express representation. The wearing of the cap and gown was an implied representation while the statement that he was a fellow commoner was an express representation.

A more modern example of an implied representation would be standing on a street corner with a collecting box labelled 'Guide Dogs for the Blind'. This is implying that D is collecting on behalf of the charity. If D intends to pocket the money then he is guilty of an offence under s 2 of the Fraud Act 2006.

Although there is no definition of what is meant by implied false representation by conduct in the Fraud Act, the Explanatory Notes to the Act state that:

QUOTATION

'An example of a representation by conduct is where a person dishonestly misuses a credit card to pay for items. By tendering the card, he is falsely representing that he has the authority to use it.'

This example is the same situation as occurred in the case of *Lambie* (1981) under the old law on deception (see section 15.2). It is likely that the courts will still look back to decisions under the old law on the point of whether D's acts are an implied representation, though, of course, the courts do not have to do so.

Under the old law several other situations of implied representation were identified. These included the following:

- Ordering and eating a meal in a restaurant: this is a representation that the meal will be paid for.
- Paying by cheque: this is a representation that the bank will honour the cheque.
- Use of a cheque guarantee card: this represents that the bank will meet any cheque up to the limit on the card.

All these situations were considered in cases under the law prior to the Fraud Act.

Ordering and eating a meal in a restaurant

CASE EXAMPLE

DPP v Ray [1973] 3 All ER 131

D went to a restaurant with three friends. He did not have enough money to pay for a meal but one of his friends agreed to lend him enough to pay for the meal. After eating the meal they all decided not to pay for it. Ten minutes later when the waiter went into the kitchen all four ran out of the restaurant without paying. The Court of Appeal had quashed the defendant's conviction for obtaining a pecuniary advantage under s 16(2)(a) of the Theft Act 1968 (this section has now been repealed). The House of Lords reinstated the conviction. The problem was whether the defendant could be guilty when his original representation that he would pay was genuine. Did the change of mind produce a deception? The House of Lords held that it did.

Paying by cheque

CASE EXAMPLE

Gilmartin [1983] 1 All ER 829

D, a stationer, paid for supplies with post-dated cheques which he knew would not be met. This was held to be a deception. By drawing the cheques he was representing that there would be funds in the account to meet the cheques on the dates they were due to be presented.

Use of a cheque guarantee card

CASE EXAMPLE

Metropolitan Police Commander v Charles [1976] 3 All ER 112

D had a bank account with an overdraft facility of £100. The bank had issued him a cheque card which guaranteed that any cheques he wrote up to £30 would be honoured by the bank. D wrote out 25 cheques for £30 in order to buy gaming chips and backed each cheque with the cheque card. He knew that the bank would have to pay the gambling club the money so there was no deception in respect of the fact that the cheques would be honoured. However, he knew that he did not have enough money in his account to meet the cheques and also that the amount would exceed his overdraft limit. He had also been told by the bank manager that he should not use the card to cash more than one cheque of £30 a day.

The House of Lords held that there was a false representation that he had the bank's authority to use the card in the way he did and upheld his conviction under s 16 of the 1968 Act of obtaining a pecuniary advantage by deception.

Representations to machines

The representation can be made to a person or to a machine. Section 2(5) of the Fraud Act 2006 specifically covers representations made to any system or device. It states:

SECTION

'2(5) A representation may be regarded as made if it (or anything implying it) submitted in any form to any system or device designed to receive, convey or respond to communications (with or without human intervention).'

This is designed to cover the many situations in the modern world where it is possible to obtain property via a machine or the Internet or other automated system such as cash dispensers or automated telephone services. The provision in the Act is wide enough to cover putting a false coin into a machine to obtain sweets or other goods or submitting a claim on the Internet. The Explanatory Notes to the Act make this clear. They state:

QUOTATION

'The main purpose of this provision is to ensure that fraud can be committed where a person makes a representation to a machine and a response can be produced without any need for human involvement. (An example is where a person enters a number into a "CHIP and PIN" machine.)'

The Explanatory Notes also state:

QUOTATION

'This offence would also be committed by someone who engages in "phishing": i.e. where a person disseminates an email to large groups of people falsely representing that the email has been sent by a legitimate financial institution. The email prompts the reader to provide information such as credit card and bank account numbers so that the "phisher" can gain access to others' assets.'

15.4.2 False

For the purposes of the Fraud Act a representation is false if

(a) it is untrue or misleading, and

(b) the person making it knows that it is, or might be, untrue or misleading.

So making a false representation means representing what one knows is untrue or might be untrue or what one knows is misleading or might be misleading. It does not matter whether anyone believes the representation.

It is a matter of fact whether something is true or not. The difficult word in the phrase is 'misleading'. It is not defined in the Act, but the government in its paper, *Fraud Law: Government Response to Consultation* (2004) stated that a representation was misleading if it was:

QUOTATION

'less than wholly true and capable of interpretation to the detriment of the victim.'

A statement can be misleading even if it is true. For example, if a salesperson says of a car 'I have never had anyone complain about this model' but in actual fact the salesperson has never sold anyone this particular model before. This statement is literally true, but it is clearly misleading.

Another problem area is the scenario where the statement is true when D makes it, but it later becomes untrue and D knows this. If D is under a legal duty to disclose information, then he can be charged under s 3 of the Fraud Act 2006 (see section 15.5). However, if D is not under a legal duty to disclose information, can he be guilty under s 2? The likelihood is that the courts will follow the case of *DPP v Ray* (1973) (see section 15.4.1) and hold that D, by staying silent when he knew the circumstances had changed, made an implied representation.

Yet another area in which difficulties may arise is that of quotations for work to be done. If D quotes a very much higher price than the job is worth has he made a false or misleading statement? Prior to the Fraud Act 2006, in *Silverman* [1987] Crim LR 574, D gave an excessive quotation to two elderly sisters for work to be done on their flat. He had done work for them previously and had built up a situation of mutual trust. Although the Court of Appeal quashed his conviction because of an inadequate summing-up to the jury, they held that by giving an exorbitant quotation he was deceiving them as to the true cost of the repairs and the amount of profit he was making.

caveat emptor
Let the buyer beware

This case had special circumstances through the previous dealings of the parties, but will excessive quotations in any circumstances now be caught by the new Act? Or should such situations be ones of ***caveat emptor***? As C M V Clarkson and H M Keating point out:

QUOTATION

> 'In a free market economy it is regarded as acceptable to maximise one's profits – in short, to make as big a profit as possible. Those making grossly inflated quotations had, in the past, only to contend with the risk of their quotations being rejected. Since this case [*Silverman*] the risk of criminal prosecution is a possibility. Again we are dealing with dubious business practice being criminalised.'
>
> *Clarkson and Keating Criminal Law: Text and Materials* (6th edn, Sweet & Maxwell, 2007)

This will make the element of dishonesty (see section 15.4.4) important in distinguishing between quotations where there should be criminal liability and those where there should not.

15.4.3 Gain or loss

The offence requires that D intends to make a gain for himself or another, or to cause loss to another or to expose another to the risk of loss. The definition of 'gain' and 'loss' is given in s 5 of the Act and is the same for all three fraud offences.

SECTION

> '5(2) "Gain" and "loss" –
>
> (a) extend only to gain or loss in money or other property;
>
> (b) include any such gain or loss whether temporary or permanent; and "property" means any property whether real or personal (including things in action and other intangible property).
>
> 5(3) "Gain" includes a gain by keeping what one has, as well as a gain by getting what one does not have.
>
> 5(4) "Loss" includes a loss by not getting what one might get, as well as a loss by parting with what one has.'

The definitions of gain and loss are essentially the same as in s 34(2) of the Theft Act 1968 (see blackmail at section 14.8). An important point is that the gain or loss does not actually have to take place. The offence is complete if D intends to make a gain or cause a loss. This is different from the previous law of obtaining by deception where it had to be proved that something had been obtained.

The gain or loss can be permanent or temporary. For example, D asks his neighbour (V) if he can borrow V's lawnmower as D's is not working. After using the mower for an hour, D returns it to the neighbour. The gain to D of the use of the lawnmower (and the loss of it to V) is a temporary one. If D had lied about the fact that his mower was not working in order to persuade his neighbour to let him borrow the neighbour's mower, then D has committed an offence under s 2 of the Fraud Act. He has made a false representation with the intention of making a gain or causing loss, even though these are only temporary and the mower is returned in perfect condition to the neighbour.

Property for the purposes of 'gain or loss' is defined as 'any property whether real or personal including things in action and other intangible property'. Note that this also is very similar to the definition of property in s 4(1) of the Theft Act 1968.

Obvious examples of 'gain' and 'loss' are shown in the case of *Kapitene* [2010] EWCA Crim 2061 where D appealed against sentence.

CASE EXAMPLE

Kapitene [2010] EWCA Crim 2061

D, who was an illegal immigrant, applied for a job at ISS Cleaning Services Ltd. He signed a declaration stating that he was legally entitled to remain in the United Kingdom and showed them a Congolese passport containing his details, his photograph and an immigration stamp indicating that he had "indefinite leave" to remain in the United Kingdom. He began work as a cleaner. D's 'gain' was the wages he was paid by ISS Cleaning Services. V's 'loss' was the wages paid out.

15.4.4 *Mens rea* of s 2

As already stated in the opening section of this chapter, the *mens rea* of the offence of fraud by false representation has three parts to it. The defendant must

- be dishonest;
- know that the representation is, or might be, untrue or misleading;
- have an intention to make a gain or cause a loss.

Dishonesty

There is no definition of dishonesty in the Act. The Law Commission in its report proposed that the *Ghosh* test for dishonesty used in theft cases (see section 13.5.2) should apply to fraud. The government in the Explanatory Notes issued with the Act makes it clear that this proposal has been accepted. Also, during the debates on the Bill in Parliament, the Attorney General confirmed that the *Ghosh* test should apply (Hansard, House of Lords Debates, 19 July 2005, col 1424).

Ghosh sets out a two-stage test. The first question is whether a defendant's behaviour would be regarded as dishonest by the ordinary standards of reasonable and honest people. If the answer to that question is 'yes', then the second question is whether the defendant was aware that his conduct was dishonest and would be regarded as dishonest by reasonable and honest people. See section 13.5.2 for a fuller discussion of the test.

The difference from the meaning of 'dishonesty' in theft is that there is no equivalent to s 2(1) of the Theft Act 1968 which states that D is not dishonest if he believed he had in law the right to deprive the other of it. The Law Commission explained why it had not included a 'claim of right' defence in the draft Bill:

QUOTATION

'7.66 We do not therefore recommend that a "claim of right" should be a complete defence to the offence of fraud, nor do we recommend that "belief in a claim of right" should be a complete defence. However, we believe that in the vast majority of such cases the requirements of *Ghosh* dishonesty will suffice to ensure that justice is done, and that the civil and criminal law are kept closely in line with each other.

7.67 The first limb of the *Ghosh* test requires the jury to consider, on an objective basis, whether the defendant's actions were dishonest. If the defendant may have believed that she had a legal right to act as she did, it will usually follow that the jury will be unable to conclude that they are sure that she was dishonest, on an objective basis. In appropriate cases we believe it would be proper for a judge to direct the jury to the effect that if that is the case then an acquittal should follow, without their having to consider the second limb of the *Ghosh* test.'

Know the representation is or might be untrue or misleading

To be guilty the defendant must know that the representation he is making is, or might be, untrue or misleading. This is a subjective test. The focus is on what the defendant knew.

Knowledge is a strict form of *mens rea*. The House of Lords pointed this out in *Saik* [2006] UKHL 18 when they said:

JUDGMENT

'the word "know" should be interpreted strictly and not watered down ... knowledge means true belief.'

However, in the Fraud Act, the knowledge required from D is at the lowest level only that he knew the representation might be misleading. This is a very different level from that of knowing that a representation is untrue. Does this low level put salespeople who make ambitious claims for the product they are selling at risk of being found guilty of fraud? For such situations the need for dishonesty is very important in protecting people from the risk of being prosecuted for fraud.

Intention to make a gain or cause a loss

'Intention' has the same meaning as throughout the criminal law (see Chapter 3). So it will include foresight of a virtual certainty. If D makes a false representation realising that it is virtually certain that this will cause V a loss, then D will be guilty, even though he may hope that V will not suffer a loss.

An example of where D could be held to have intended to expose V to the risk of loss is where D makes a false representation on a health insurance form stating that he does not smoke when, in fact, he does. D does not want to become ill and hopes that he will not need the insurance. However, he intends the insurance company to be exposed to the risk of loss by paying out if he is ill.

The wording of the offence means that it is not necessary for the fraud to succeed. It is only necessary for the defendant to intend to make a gain or cause a loss.

Under the old law the prosecution had to prove that the deception had caused the obtaining of property. This led to problems in many cases, for example, *Laverty* (1970) where D changed the registration number plates and the chassis number on a car and sold the car to V. Under the old law it was held that no offence had been committed because V did not rely on the false representation made by changing the number plates. However, under the offence of fraud by false representation it is not necessary to show that V was influenced to buy the car because of its new number plates and D would be guilty. All the prosecution has to prove is that D intended to make a gain or cause a loss through this act.

It does not matter that the victim becomes suspicious, does not hand over any property and reports the matter to the police. The defendant has still committed the completed offence as he intended to make a gain or cause a loss.

KEY FACTS

Key facts on fraud by false representation

Definition of offence	D dishonestly makes a false representation, and intends, by making the representation • to make a gain for himself or another, or • to cause loss to another or to expose another to the risk of loss.	s2(1) Fraud Act 2006.

Actus reus	• Make a representation.	Can be any representation as to fact or law, including making a representation as to state of mind, s 2(3) Fraud Act 2006. Representation can be express or implied, s 2(4) Fraud Act 2006.
	• Representation must be false.	It is false if it is untrue or misleading, s 2(2) Fraud Act 2006.
Mens rea	• Dishonestly	*Ghosh* two-part test is intended to apply.
	• knows or believes representation to be untrue or misleading	Explanatory Notes
	• intends to make a gain or cause a loss.	Gain/loss must be of money or property, s 5 Fraud Act 2006.
Representations made to machines or automated services	A representation is regarded as being made when it is submitted to any form of system or device.	s 2(5) Fraud Act 2006.

15.5 Fraud by failing to disclose information

Under s 3 of the Fraud Act 2006 the offence of fraud by failing to disclose information will be committed where a person

SECTION

'3 (a) dishonestly fails to disclose information to another person which he is under a legal duty to disclose; and
(b) intends by failing to disclose the information:
(i) to make a gain for himself or another, or
(ii) to cause loss to another or to expose another to the risk of loss.'

Originally the Law Commission in its draft Bill, as well as including fraud where there was a legal duty to disclose, had also included any situation where:

- The information is the kind that V trusts D to disclose.
- D knows this.
- Any reasonable person would disclose the information.

After consultation, the government omitted this type of failure to disclose from the Bill that went before Parliament. The omission of this means that the prosecution will have to prove there was a legal obligation on D. Will this cover the situation in *Rai* [2000] Crim LR 192?

CASE EXAMPLE

Rai [2000] Crim LR 192

D applied for a grant from the local council towards installing a downstairs bathroom for his elderly mother. A grant of £9,500 was approved by the council, but two days later his mother died. D carried on with the improvement and did not tell the local council of his mother's death. The Court of Appeal upheld his conviction for obtaining property by deception under s 15 of the 1968 Act.

Under the Law Commission's additional duty to disclose this would clearly have been covered. But is there a legal duty to disclose the fact that his mother had died after the application had been approved?

15.5.1 Legal duty

Arlidge and Parry on Fraud (3rd edn, Sweet and Maxwell, 2007) states that there are two situations where a person may be under a legal duty to disclose information. First, he is literally under a legal obligation. Second, where he is precluded from enforcing a transaction or retaining the benefit of it on the ground that he had failed to disclose relevant information to another party before the other party entered into the transaction.

The Fraud Act does not define legal duty but it seems it intends to cover both kinds of duty. The Explanatory Notes published with the Act make it clear that the Law Commission's definition of 'legal duty' is relevant as it quotes from the Law Commission's report on *Fraud* (Law Com No 276 Cm 5560 (2002)) where it stated:

QUOTATION

> '7.28 Such a duty may derive from statute (such as the provisions governing company prospectuses), from the fact that the transaction in question is one of the utmost good faith (such as a contract of insurance), from the express or implied terms of a contract, from the custom of a particular trade or market, or from the existence of a fiduciary relationship between the parties (such as that of agent and principal).
>
> 7.29 For this purpose there is a legal duty to disclose information not only if the defendant's failure to disclose it gives the victim a cause of action for damages, but also if the law gives the victim a right to set aside any change in his or her legal position to which he or she may consent as a result of the non-disclosure. For example, a person entering into a contract with his or her beneficiary, in the sense that a failure to make such disclosure will entitle the beneficiary to rescind the contract and to reclaim any property transferred under it.'

Also, when the Bill was before Parliament, the Attorney General echoed para 7.28 when he said:

QUOTATION

> 'There are many occasions in the law where there is a duty of disclosure: under certain market customs or certain contractual arrangements.'

So it appears that s 3 is intended to apply to non-disclosure in the course of negotiations towards a transaction rather than being intended to apply to a breach of duty to disclose in the strict sense. This raises the question of whether the section is too wide and will catch situations where the civil law provides an adequate remedy.

15.5.2 *Mens rea* of s 3

There are two parts to this. D must

- be dishonest; and
- intend to make a gain or cause a loss.

However, it must be noted there is no requirement set out in that Act that D has to be aware of the circumstances that generate the duty of disclosure. The Law Commission's draft Bill did explicitly include the requirement that D must either know that the circumstances exist which give rise to the duty to disclose or be aware that they might exist. The Fraud Act does not include this, but unawareness of a duty to disclose is likely to mean that D is not dishonest.

The Explanatory Notes give two examples of situations which would be covered by s 3. These are (1) the failure of a solicitor to share vital information with a client within the context of their work relationship, in order to perpetrate a fraud upon that client and (2) where a person intentionally failed to disclose information relating to his heart condition when making an application for life insurance.

15.6 Fraud by abuse of position

Under s 4 of the Fraud Act 2006 the offence of fraud by abuse of position will be committed where a person

SECTION

> '4(1) (a) occupies a position in which he is expected to safeguard, or not to act against, the financial interests of another person;
> (b) dishonestly abuses that position, and
> (c) intends by means of abuse of that position:
> (i) to make a gain for himself or another, or
> (ii) to cause loss to another or to expose another to the risk of loss.'

Subsection 4(2) states that this offence can be committed by an omission as well as by an act.

The original Law Commission draft included the word 'secretly' so that it read in (b) 'dishonestly and secretly abuses that position'. As the Act does not include the word 'secretly', s 4 will apparently cover situations where V knows what is going on. This may be intended to cover situations such as *Hinks* [2000] 4 All ER 833 (see section 13.2.4) where D accepted gifts of large sums of money from a vulnerable person whom she had befriended and was found guilty of theft. A charge of fraud by abuse of position seems more appropriate in such circumstances.

15.6.1 Occupies a position

The position must be one where D is expected to safeguard or not act against the financial interests of another person. The Explanatory Notes to the Fraud Act quote from the Law Commission's Report to demonstrate the types of 'position' the Act is meant to cover:

QUOTATION

> '7.38 The necessary relationship will be present between trustee and beneficiary, director and company, professional person and client, agent and principal, employee and employer, or between partners. It may arise otherwise, for example within a family, or in the context of voluntary work, or in any context where the parties are not at arm's length. In nearly all cases where it arises, it will be recognised by the civil law as importing fiduciary duties, and any relationship that is so recognised will suffice. We see no reason, however, why the existence of such duties should be essential. This does not of course mean that it would be entirely a matter for the fact-finders whether the necessary relationship exists. The question whether the particular facts alleged can properly be described as giving rise to that relationship will be an issue capable of being ruled upon by the judge and, if the case goes to the jury, of being the subject of directions.'

So the Law Commission expects the judge to rule on whether the particular facts of the case are capable of giving rise to the necessary relationship and direct the jury accordingly. The jury will then have to decide if there has been an abuse of that position.

The words 'expected to safeguard, or not act against, the financial interests of another person' are not defined. *Arlidge and Parry on Fraud* (3rd edn, Sweet & Maxwell, 2007) suggests that they are 'impenetrable'.

The Solicitor General in the course of debates on the Bill in the Standing Committee indicated that an obligation arising from a 'position' can extend beyond the actual time of employment etc. He stated:

QUOTATION

> 'A person can occupy a position where they owe a duty that goes beyond the performance of a job. A contract that is entered into that obliges a person to have duties of confidentiality, perhaps, can go well beyond the time when that employment ceases. The duty may, however, still arise. The person entered into the duty at the beginning of the employment and it exists indefinitely. Therefore a person may still occupy a position in which there is a legitimate expectation.'

This suggestion that a duty can be owed indefinitely goes beyond the normal expectation in employment contracts. Where there is a clause in the contract protecting the employer from competition when an employee leaves his post, that clause is usually limited to a relatively short period of time. If it is too wide it may be held to be void under contract law. It seems unlikely that that criminal liability would extend beyond the period thought suitable for civil liability.

15.6.2 Abuse of position

The Explanatory Notes state that the term 'abuse' is not limited by a definition, because it is intended to cover a wide range of conduct. The Notes give examples of 'abuse'. These are:

- an employee who fails to take up the chance of a crucial contract in order that an associate or rival company can take it up instead at the expense of the employer;
- an employee of a software company who uses his position to clone software products with the intention of selling the products on;
- where a person who is employed to care for an elderly or disabled person has access to that person's bank account and abuses his position by transferring funds to invest in a high-risk business venture of his own.

It would also cover the situation in the case of *Doukas* [1978] 1 All ER 1061 where D was a wine waiter in a hotel. He took bottles of wine into the hotel, intending to sell them to people dining at the hotel, so that he could pocket the money (see section 14.10.1). D was clearly in a position where he was expected not to act against the financial interests of his employer and, by selling his own wine instead of the hotel's wine, he was abusing that position.

An example charged under s 4 of the Fraud Act is the case of *Marshall* [2009] EWCA Crim 2076.

CASE EXAMPLE

Marshall [2009] EWCA Crim 2076

D was the joint manager of a residential care home. V was a resident in the home and had severe learning difficulties. V had a bank account which she could not exercise any proper control over herself. She was dependent on others to do so on her behalf. There were strict rules governing withdrawals from her account. They should only have been done in V's presence and, of course, the money withdrawn should have been used entirely for her benefit. D made several withdrawals and used the money for her own benefit. She pleaded guilty to offences under s 4 of the Fraud Act and was sentenced to 12 months' imprisonment.

This is an obvious type of situation which s 4 was enacted to cover. Another more unusual case under s 4 is *Gale* [2008] EWCA Crim 1344.

CASE EXAMPLE

Gale [2008] EWCA Crim 1344

D was an office manager for one of DHL's divisions at Heathrow Airport. He used that position to send a large crate from Heathrow to New York. He certified the crate as 'known cargo'. Because of this and the paperwork he provided stating that the crate contained empty plastic pots and the fact that he, himself, took the crate to the airline's goods reception agents, it was passed through without the usual X-ray screening. In fact the crate contained 500 kilos of khat, a drug that is not illegal in England but is illegal in America. He pleaded guilty to fraud by abuse of position.

15.6.3 *Mens rea* of s 4

As with ss 2 and 3 D has to be dishonest and intend to make a gain or cause a loss. There is no specific requirement that D is aware that he is in a position where he is expected to safeguard V's financial interests. However, if D was unaware of this then it would presumably go to the issue of dishonesty.

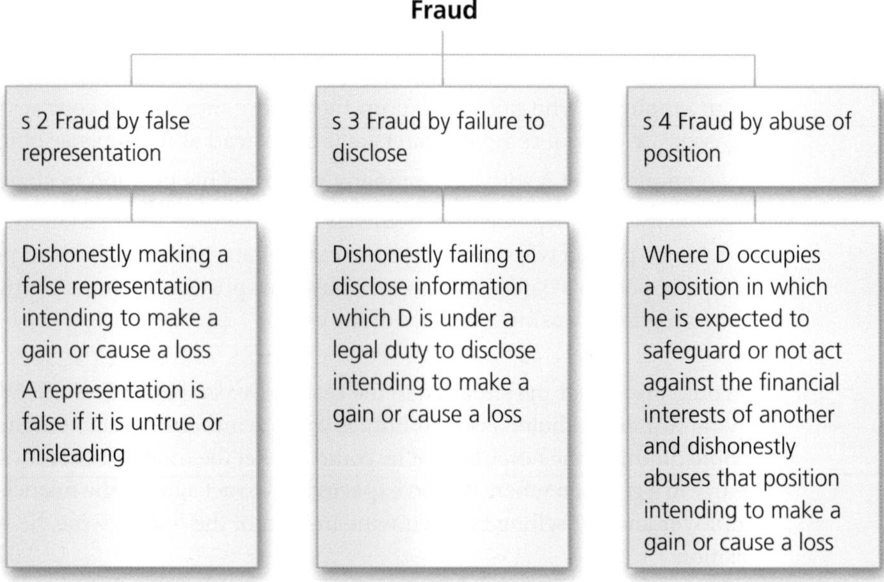

Figure 15.1 The offences of fraud in the Fraud Act 2006.

ACTIVITY

Applying the law

Discuss whether there are breaches of ss 2, 3 or 4 of the Fraud Act 2006 in the following situations:

1. Anna has discovered that fake coins provided with one of her child's toys fit into a slot machine selling sweets and drinks. She uses one of the fake coins to obtain a packet of chocolate from the machine.
2. Barack, who smokes occasionally, does not mention this fact on his application form for health insurance.
3. Chantelle, who owns a shop, puts a collecting box on the counter with a label 'Cancer Research' on it. Customers often put coins in it. Chantelle keeps all the money which customers put in the box.
4. Dmitri applies for a credit card. On the form he states that he is self-employed as a taxi driver. In fact, he is unemployed. Dmitri is given the card and he uses it to buy goods, but has always paid the money back to the credit card company.
5. Ellis applies for car insurance. He has had points on his licence for driving offences, but they expired ten years ago. Ellis does not mention this in his application as he believes the offences are not relevant as they were so long ago.
6. Ferdinand works for a cinema operating the digital projector for the films. He takes the most popular films home and makes copies of them which he sells.

15.7 Possession of articles for use in fraud

Section 6 Fraud Act 2006 states:

SECTION

'(1) A person is guilty of an offence if he has in his possession or under his control any article for use in the course of or in connection with any fraud.'

In the Act it is made clear that 'article' includes any program or data held in electronic form.

The wording of this section draws on that of the existing law in s 25 of the Theft Act 1968 (going equipped for stealing etc.; see section 14.10). There is a difference between this section and s 25 of the Theft Act 1968 in that a s 6 offence can be committed anywhere, including at D's home. Section 25 specifically states that the offence must be committed when D is not at his place of abode.

This difference is because articles for use in fraud are quite likely to be used at home. For example, a computer program or electronic data could be used in the course of or in connection with any fraud. There is no requirement that that article is specifically designed for fraud. A computer program such as a spreadsheet can be used legitimately, but if it is intended to be used to produce a false set of accounts for the purpose of fraud, then this is an article for use in the course of or in connection with any fraud.

15.7.1 *Mens rea* of s 6

The Explanatory Notes to the Act state that the intention is to attract the case law on s 25, which has established that proof is required that the defendant had the article for the purpose or with the intention that it be used in the course of or in connection with the offence. For this offence under the Fraud Act a general intention to commit fraud will suffice.

The Notes quote from *R v Ellames* [1974] 3 All ER 130, where the court said that:

JUDGMENT

'In our view, to establish an offence under s 25(1) the prosecution must prove that the defendant was in possession of the article, and intended the article to be used in the course of or in connection with some future burglary, theft or cheat. But it is not necessary to prove that he intended it to be used in the course of or in connection with any specific burglary, theft or cheat; it is enough to prove a general intention to use it for some burglary, theft or cheat; we think that this view is supported by the use of the word 'any' in s 25(1). Nor, in our view, is it necessary to prove that the defendant intended to use it himself; it will be enough to prove that he had it with him with the intention that it should be used by someone else.'

For this offence under the Fraud Act a general intention to commit fraud will suffice.

15.8 Making or supplying articles for use in frauds

This is an offence under s 7 of the Fraud Act 2006.

SECTION

'7(1) A person is guilty of an offence if he makes, adapts, supplies or offers to supply any article –

(a) knowing that it is designed or adapted for use in the course of or in connection with any fraud, or

(b) intending it to be used to commit, or assist in the commission of, fraud.'

As with s 6 the word 'article' includes any program or data held in electronic form. The wording of s 7 means there are a number of ways that the *actus reus* can be committed. These are by:

- making an article;
- adapting an article;
- supplying an article;
- offering to supply an article.

The Explanatory Notes give as an example the person who makes devices which, when attached to electricity meters, cause the meter to malfunction. The actual amount of electricity used is concealed from the provider, who thus makes a loss.

15.8.1 *Mens rea* of s 7

The *mens rea* can be shown in two distinct ways. These are

- knowledge that the article is designed or adapted for use in the course of or in connection with any fraud; or
- intention that it will be used to commit, or assist in the commission of, fraud.

The person making, adapting, supplying or offering to supply the article does not have to intend to use it personally. It is enough that it is intended to be used at sometime by someone for the purpose of a fraud.

15.9 Obtaining services dishonestly

This offence was created to replace s 1 of the Theft Act 1978. The offence is set out in s 11 of the Fraud Act 2006 which states:

SECTION

'11(1) A person is guilty of an offence under this section if he obtains services for himself or another –

(a) by a dishonest act, and
(b) in breach of subsection (2).

(2) A person obtains services in breach of this subsection if –

(a) they are made available on the basis that payment has been or will be made for or in respect of them;
(b) he obtains them without any payment having been made for or in respect of them or without payment having been made in full, and –
(c) when he obtains them he knows –

(i) that they are being made available on the basis described in paragraph (a), or
(ii) that they might be,

but intends that payment will not be made, or will not be made in full.'

The *actus reus* of this offence has several parts to it. These are:

- obtains
- services
- not paid for or not paid in full.

Note that there must be an act; the offence cannot be committed by omission. The *mens rea* consists of three parts:

- dishonesty;
- knowing that the services are or might be being made available on the basis that payment has been or will be made for them;
- intention not to pay or not to pay in full.

We will now go on to look at the *actus reus* and *mens rea* in more detail.

15.9.1 *Actus reus* of obtaining services dishonestly

Obtains

The offence requires that the services are actually obtained. This is unlike the offence of fraud by false representation which we considered in section 15.4. For that offence it was not necessary for anything to be obtained. The making of the false representation intending to make a gain or cause a loss was sufficient.

Services

These are not defined by the Act, but the Explanatory Notes to the Act give examples of situations where services are obtained. These include:

- using false credit card details to obtain services on the Internet;
- climbing over a wall and watching a football match without paying the entrance fee.

The Explanatory Notes also give an example of the situation where a person attaches a decoder to her television to enable viewing access to cable/satellite television channels for which she has no intention of paying.

There are many other situations which would be offences under this section. These could include:

- using a false bus pass to get a free or reduced price journey;
- claiming falsely to be under 14 in order to have cheaper admission to see a film in a cinema;
- using a stolen decoder card to receive satellite television programmes.

Not paid for

The offence is only committed if the defendant does not pay anything or does not pay in full for the service. Even if the defendant has made a false statement, but pays full price for the service, then he has not committed the offence of obtaining services dishonestly.

15.9.2 *Mens rea* of obtaining services dishonestly

Dishonesty

This is not defined in the act, nor is any mention made of it in the Explanatory Notes to the Act. This is different from fraud by false representation where the Explanatory Notes say that it is intended the *Ghosh* two-part test should apply.

This makes it difficult to know whether the *Ghosh* two-part test will be applied by the courts. However, it seems likely that it will. If so the first question will be whether a defendant's behaviour would be regarded as dishonest by the ordinary standards of reasonable and honest people. If the answer to that question is 'yes', then the second question will be whether the defendant was aware that his conduct was dishonest and would be regarded as dishonest by reasonable and honest people.

Intention not to pay

The prosecution must prove that the defendant intended not to pay or not to pay in full for the services. If the defendant thought that someone else had already paid, then he would not be guilty of this offence.

ACTIVITY

Applying the law

Discuss the criminal liability, if any, in each of the following situations.

1. Kadeem goes to a local cinema. He pays for entry, but is late and finds he has missed the first 20 minutes of the film. When the film is finished, he decides to stay and see the next performance.
2. Lauren stays at a health spa for two nights. While there she uses the leisure facilities and has a beauty treatment. She also has meals in the restaurant. When she checks out at the end of her stay she uses a stolen credit card to pay for everything.
3. Miah works in a sandwich bar. Each day she makes up sandwiches at home from ingredients she has bought. She then takes these sandwiches to work and sells them, pocketing any money she makes on them. Her employers do not know she does this.
4. Nic advertises an electronic device for sale that he knows can be used to make electricity meters give lower readings.

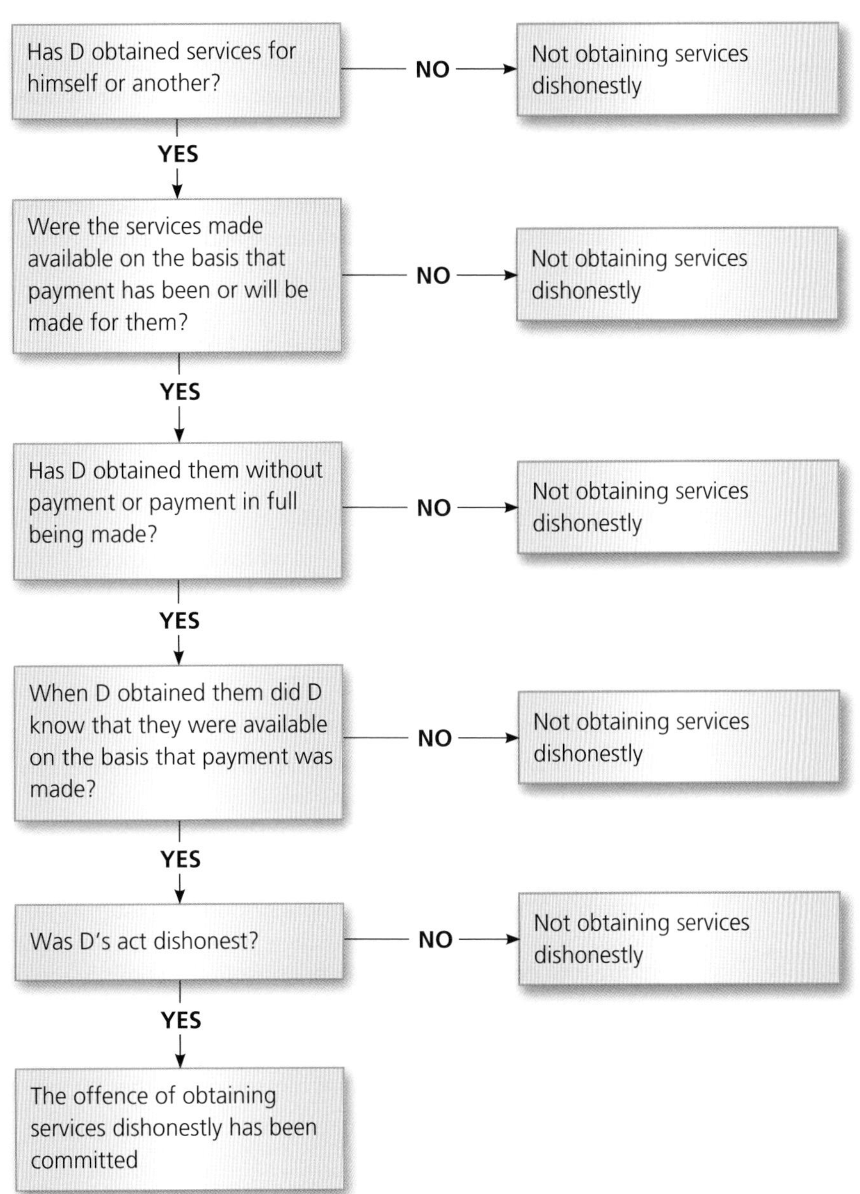

Figure 15.2 Flow chart for obtaining services dishonestly.

SUMMARY

Reasons for the enactment of the Fraud Act 2006

- Previous law on deception under the Theft Acts was very fragmented and difficult to apply.
- Over-particularisation of the law meant that a defendant could face the wrong charge or too many charges.
- Obtaining from a machine or by electronic means was not covered by the old law on deception.

Fraud by false representation (s 2 FA 2006)

- Committed if D dishonestly makes a false representation, and intends, by making the representation to make a gain for himself or another, or to cause loss to another or to expose another to the risk of loss.
- The *actus reus* of the offence is that D must make a representation which is false.
- The *mens rea* has three parts to it. D must be dishonest, he must know or believe the representation to be untrue or misleading and must have an intention to make a gain or cause a loss.

Fraud by failing to disclose information (s 3 FA 2006)

- Committed if D dishonestly fails to disclose information to another person which he is under a legal duty to disclose, intending to make a gain for himself or another, or to cause loss to another or to expose another to the risk of loss.

Fraud by abuse of position (s 4 FA 2006)

- Committed if D occupies a position in which he is expected to safeguard, or not to act against, the financial interests of another person and D dishonestly abuses that position intending to make a gain for himself or another, or to cause loss to another or to expose another to the risk of loss.

Possession of articles for use in fraud (s 6 FA 2006)

- Committed if D has in his possession or under his control any article for use in the course of or in connection with any fraud.

Making or supplying articles for use in frauds (s 7 FA 2006)

- Committed if D makes, adapts, supplies or offers to supply any article knowing that it is designed or adapted for use in the course of or in connection with any fraud, or intending it to be used to commit, or assist in the commission of, fraud.

Obtaining services dishonestly (s 11 FA 2006)

- Committed if D obtains services for himself or another by a dishonest act.
- The services must be made available on the basis that payment has been or will be made for or in respect of them.
- D must obtain them without any payment or payment in full having been made for or in respect of them.
- D must know that they are being made available on the basis described in s 11(2)(a) or that they might be and D must intend that payment or payment in full will not be made.

SAMPLE ESSAY QUESTION

To what extent has the Fraud Act 2006 satisfactorily reformed the law on fraud and deception?

Give a brief outline of old law:

- ss 15, 15A and 16 of Theft Act 1968
- ss 1 and 2 of Theft Act 1978
- The fact that the 1968 Act and the 1978 Act had to be amended because of problems

Discuss problems with the old law, e.g.

- Need to prove that a person was deceived
- Was silence deception?
- The need to prove obtaining of property (s 15 TA 1968)
- Overlap and difficulty of subsections of s 2 TA 1978
- Expand all these with case examples

Expand with comments from:

- Law Commission Consultation Paper: *Legislating the Criminal Code, Fraud and Deception* No 155 (1999)
- Law Commission Report: *Fraud* No 276 (2002)
- Home Office: *Fraud Law Reform: Consultation on Proposals for Legislation* (2004)

Set out the main offences in the Fraud Act 2006:

- s 2 fraud by false representation
- s 3 fraud by failing to disclose information
- s 4 fraud by abuse of position
- s 11 obtaining services dishonestly

Discuss problems of Fraud Act 2006:

The fact not all the Law Com's proposals used, e.g.

- What is meant by legal duty?
- Should s 3 extend to situations where there is no legal duty to disclose?
- Should s 4 include a secrecy element?

FA has created inchoate offences

Discuss good points of Fraud Act 2006, e.g.

- Consistency of definition across offences
- No need to prove a person was deceived
- No need to prove obtaining (except for s 11)
- False representation is a more sensible way of covering misuse of credit cards
- Covers representations as to state of mind

Conclude

Further reading

Books

Arlidge, A, Milne, A and Sprenger, P J, *Arlidge and Parry on Fraud* (4th edn, Sweet & Maxwell, 2013), Chapters 5, 6 and 10.

Ormerod, D and Williams, D, *Smith's Law of Theft* (9th edn, Oxford University Press, 2007), Chapter 3.

Articles

Collins, J, 'Fraud by abuse of position: theorising s 4 of the Fraud Act 2006' (2011) Crim LR 513.

Ormerod, D, 'The Fraud Act 2006: criminalising lying?' (2007) Crim LR 193.

Withey, C, 'The Fraud Act 2006' (2007) 71 J Crim L 220.

Yeo, N, 'Bull's-eye' (2007) NLJ, Part 1 at 212 and part 2 at 418.

16

Criminal damage

AIMS AND OBJECTIVES

After reading this chapter you should be able to:

- Understand the *actus reus* and *mens rea* of the basic offence of criminal damage
- Understand the *actus reus* and *mens rea* of the offence of endangering life when committing criminal damage
- Understand the *actus reus* and *mens rea* of arson
- Understand other offences related to criminal damage
- Analyse critically all offences in the Criminal Damage Act 1971
- Apply the law to factual situations to determine whether there is criminal liability for an offence under the Criminal Damage Act 1971

The law on criminal damage is contained in the Criminal Damage Act 1971. This created a complete code for this area of the law, just as the Theft Act 1968 did for the law on theft. The Criminal Damage Act was the result of a report by the Law Commission, *Offences of Damage to Property* (1970) Law Com No 29. As well as codifying the law on criminal damage, one of the aims of the Law Commission was to bring the law in line with the law on theft, so far as was practicable. For this reason some of the words used in the Act are the same as the words used in the Theft Act 1968.

The Criminal Damage Act creates four offences which are:

- the basic offence of criminal damage;
- aggravated criminal damage;
- arson;
- aggravated arson.

16.1 The basic offence

The basic offence is set out in s 1(1) of the Criminal Damage Act 1971:

SECTION

'1(1) A person who without lawful excuse destroys or damages any property belonging to another intending to destroy or damage any such property or being reckless as to whether any such property would be destroyed or damaged shall be guilty of an offence.'

The *actus reus* is made up of three elements. These are that D must

- destroy or damage
- property
- belonging to another.

16.1.1 Destroy or damage

This phrase is not defined in the 1971 Act. However, the same phrase was used in the law prior to 1971 (the Malicious Damage Act 1861), and old cases ruled that even slight damage was sufficient to prove damage. For example, in *Gayford v Chouler* [1898] 1 QB 316, trampling down grass was held to be damage. The cases prior to the Criminal Damage Act 1971 are, of course, no longer binding, but they may still be used as persuasive precedent.

Destroy

'Destroy' is a much stronger word than 'damage', but it includes where the property has been made useless even though it is not completely destroyed.

Damage

Damage covers a wide range, and in *Roe v Kingerlee* [1986] Crim LR 735, the Divisional Court said that whether property has been damaged was a 'matter of fact and degree and it is for the justices to decide whether what occurred was damage or not'. In that case D had smeared mud on the walls of a police cell. It had cost £7 to have it cleaned off and it was held that this could be damage even though it was not permanent.

In an Australian case, *Samuels v Stubbs* [1972] SASR 200 it was stated that:

JUDGMENT

'[I]t is difficult to lay down any very general rule and, at the same time, precise and absolute rule as to what constitutes "damage". One must be guided in a great degree by the circumstances of each case, the nature of the article and the mode in which it is affected or treated ... [T]he word is sufficiently wide in its meaning to embrace injury, mischief or harm done to property, and that to constitute "damage" it is unnecessary to establish such definite or actual damage as renders property useless, or prevents it from serving its normal function.'

In *Samuels v Stubbs* (1972) D had jumped on a policeman's cap, denting it. There was no evidence that it was not possible to return the cap to its original shape without any cost or real trouble. Even so the judge ruled that there was damage, as there was a 'temporary functional derangement' of the cap.

In English cases under the Criminal Damage Act 1971, although it has been held that non-permanent damage can come within the definition of 'damage', the courts' approach seems to be based on whether it will cost money, time and/or effort to remove the damage. If so, then an offence has been committed, but if not then there is no offence. This is illustrated in the following case.

CASE EXAMPLE

Hardman v Chief Constable of Avon and Somerset Constabulary [1986] Crim LR 330 CND

Protesters, to mark the fortieth anniversary of the dropping of the atomic bomb on Hiroshima, painted silhouettes on the pavement with water-soluble paint. The local council had the paintings removed with water jets. The defendants argued that the damage was only temporary and the paintings would have quickly been erased by the weather and by people walking on them and there was no need for the local council to go to the expense of having the paintings removed by high-pressure water jets. The court held that this was damage.

Similar decisions were made in *Blake v DPP* [1993] Crim LR 586. D wrote a biblical quotation on a concrete pillar. This needed to be cleaned off and so was held to be criminal damage. The same decision was reached in *Roe v Kingerlee* (1986) where it cost £7 to remove mud from a cell wall.

The 'temporary impairment of value or usefulness' was the key factor in *Fiak* [2005] EWCA Crim 2381.

CASE EXAMPLE

Fiak [2005] EWCA Crim 2381

D was arrested on suspicion of being in charge of a vehicle when he was over the limit for alcohol and for assault on a police officer. He was taken to a police station and placed in a cell. He put a blanket in the toilet in the cell and flushed the toilet several times. This caused water to overflow and flood the cell and two adjoining cells. The blanket was not visibly soiled but it had to be cleaned and dried before it could be used again. The cells had to be cleaned. This was held to be criminal damage.

However, in *A (a Juvenile) v R* [1978] Crim LR 689, spit which landed on a policeman's uniform was not damage as it could be wiped off with a wet cloth with very little effort. But what if the spit had landed on a light coloured T-shirt and left a stain, so that the T-shirt needed washing or dry cleaning? It seems that could be enough to constitute damage.

A debatable decision is that in *Fancy* [1980] Crim LR 171 where D was charged under s 3 of the Criminal Damage Act 1971 with possessing an article with intent to damage property. D was found in possession of a bucket of paint and a roller. He admitted that he had painted over National Front slogans on walls. The judge at the Crown Court ruled that there was no case to answer. The judge said he was not satisfied that applying white paint over 'mindless National Front graffiti could constitute damage to a wall per se'. This decision was criticised by the editors of *Smith and Hogan Criminal Law* in the following way:

QUOTATION

'The defendant's opinion that what he did was not damage is irrelevant if damage is caused in law and fact. V's wall is damaged by D's graffiti irrespective of whether D regards it as an improvement.'

Smith and Hogan Criminal Law (13th edn, Oxford University Press, 2011) p. 1015

So, even though the application of white paint was to cover a previous layer of graffiti, the white paint should still have been classified as damage. Indeed it would cost money to have the paint removed. The only possible argument might be where the white paint did no new damage to the wall. That would have to mean that it exactly covered the graffiti without doing any further damage to the wall. So there would be no extra cost of cleaning. Even so, it is probable that having to clean two layers of paint off would take more effort than removing just the original.

The type and purpose of the property may be relevant, as in *Morphitis v Salmon* [1990] Crim LR 48 DC, where it was held that a scratch on a scaffolding pole was not damage. Scaffolding poles are likely to get quite scratched in the ordinary course of use and it does not affect their usefulness or integrity. However, a scratch on a car would almost certainly be considered damage.

Computer disks and programs

Altering computer programs was held to be within the definition of criminal damage in *Whiteley* (1991) 93 Cr App R 25, when a computer hacker had altered and deleted files and changed some passwords. It was held that there was damage to the magnetic particles on the hard disk which made the computer inoperable. However, it was recognised that there were problems in proving damage in some cases of computer hacking, and the Computer Misuse Act 1990 was passed to clarify the law. This Act creates an offence of 'unauthorised modification of computer material'. It also makes it clear that the Criminal Damage Act no longer applies as s 3(6) provides that '[F]or the purposes of the Criminal Damage Act 1971 a modification of the contents of a computer shall not be regarded as damaging any computer or computer storage medium unless its effect on that computer or computer storage medium impairs its physical condition'.

ACTIVITY

Applying the law

Explain whether there is 'damage' within the meaning of the Criminal Damage Act 1971 in each of the following situations.

1. Aisha throws a bucket of clean water over Bess. The water thoroughly wets Bess's jacket and skirt. Would it make any difference to your answer if the water was muddy?
2. Conrad writes on the brick wall of the local town hall with white chalk.
3. Dan is working on a construction site. He throws a spanner down. It hits a wall which is being constructed and causes a small piece of brick to chip off. The spanner also hits a scaffolding post and causes a small dent in it.

16.1.2 Property

'Property' is defined in s 10(1) of the Criminal Damage Act 1971:

SECTION

'10(1) In this Act "property" means property of a tangible nature, whether real or personal, including money and –

(a) including wild creatures which have been tamed or are ordinarily kept in captivity, and any other wild creatures or their carcasses if, but only if, they have been reduced into possession which has not been lost or abandoned or are in the course of being reduced into possession; but

(b) not including mushrooms growing wild on any land or flowers, fruit or foliage of a plant growing wild on any land.'

The wording of this is similar to the Theft Act 1968 but there are two main differences. First, land is property which can be damaged although it cannot normally be stolen and, second, intangible rights cannot be damaged, though they may be stolen.

16.1.3 Belonging to another

Again, the definition of 'belonging to another' set out in s 10(2) is similar to the definition which is used for the purposes of theft.

SECTION

'10(2) Property shall be treated for the purposes of this Act as belonging to any person –

(a) having the custody or control of it;

(b) having in it any proprietary right or interest (not being an equitable interest arising only from an agreement to transfer or grant an interest); or

(c) having a charge on it.

(3) Where property is subject to a trust, the person to whom it belongs shall be so treated as including any person having a right to enforce the trust.'

This gives the same wide definition of 'belonging to' as in theft. It is not restricted to the owner. In fact a co-owner can be guilty of criminal damage as the other co-owner has a proprietary right in the property, as shown in *Smith* [1974] 1 All ER 632.

CASE EXAMPLE

Smith [1974] 1 All ER 632

D removed some electrical wiring, which he had earlier fitted in the flat which he rented. In doing this he damaged some of the fixtures he had put in. In civil law these fixtures belong to the landlord and this was property 'belonging to another'. However, D was found not guilty because he lacked the necessary *mens rea* (see section 16.1.4).

It is important to note that for the purposes of the basic offence the property affected must belong to another. A person cannot be guilty of the basic offence if the property he destroys or damages is his own. But for the aggravated offence a person can be guilty even though it is his own property (see section 16.2).

16.1.4 *Mens rea* of the basic offence

The defendant must do the damage or destruction either intentionally or recklessly. For the meanings of intention and recklessness, the Law Commission meant the previous principles of *mens rea* used in criminal damage cases to apply. So far as intention is concerned the courts have done this, but the meaning of the word 'reckless' has caused problems and debate.

Prior to the passing of the Criminal Damage Act 1971 the law on criminal damage was contained in the Malicious Damage Act 1861 and amending Acts. These used the phrase 'unlawfully and maliciously'. Maliciously was taken to have the meaning of either intending the damage or knowing there was a risk of damage and taking that risk. This type of risk taking is known as subjective recklessness. When the Law Commission recommended reform of the law it identified the essential mental element in the malicious damage offences as 'intent to do the forbidden act or recklessness in relation to its foreseen consequences'. It suggested replacing the old-fashioned word of maliciously with the phrase 'intending or being reckless'. This was meant to have the same meaning as the courts had given to the word 'maliciously'.

Intention

D must intend to destroy or damage property belonging to another. As Professor Sir John Smith pointed out:

QUOTATION

'It is not enough that D intended to do the act which caused the damage unless he intended to cause the damage; proof that D intended to throw a stone is not proof that he intended to break a window. Nor is it enough that D intends to damage property if he does not intend to damage property of another.'

Smith and Hogan Criminal Law (13th edn, Oxford University Press, 2011), p. 1019

The first point made by Professor Sir John Smith that proving the act is not enough, there must be intention to do the damage, was seen in the old case of *Pembliton* [1874–80] All ER Rep 1163 where D threw a stone at some men whom he had been fighting with. The stone missed them but hit and broke a window. D was not guilty of causing damage to the window as he had no intention to damage the window (or any other property), even though he intended to throw the stone. (But note that under the Criminal Damage Act 1971 he may have been reckless if he aimed at a person standing in front of a window.)

The second point on the need to intend to damage property belonging to another was illustrated in *Smith* [1974] 1 All ER 632. Smith mistakenly believed that the property he was damaging was his own. His conviction was quashed by the Court of Appeal, who said:

JUDGMENT

'The element of *mens rea* relates to all the circumstances of the criminal act. The criminal act in the offence is causing damage to or destruction of "property belonging to another" and the element of *mens rea*, therefore, must relate to "property belonging to another". Honest belief, whether justifiable or not, that the property is the defendant's own negatives the element of *mens rea*.'

Where D intends to do what is caused then, if this is damage, D has the *mens rea* for the offence. This was seen in *Seray-White* [2012] EWHC 208 Admin.

CASE EXAMPLE

Seray-White [2012] EWHC 208 Admin

Dr Seray-White wrote with a black marker pen on two parking notices, which had been placed by the management company in the estate where D lived. He said he did not intend to cause damage nor was he reckless as to whether damage was caused. He was convicted and appealed first to the Crown Court and from there to the Divisional Court.

The Crown Court had found the writing to be damage and this was confirmed by the Court of Appeal. As D had intended to do the writing the Court of Appeal held that he had intention to cause criminal damage. They held that no question of recklessness arose as the case concerned an act with an intended result.

The decision in *Seray-White* can be contrasted with that in *Pembliton* (1874). In *Pembliton* D had thrown a stone with the intention of hitting the men with whom he had been fighting. The damage (the broken window) was not an intended result. In *Seray-White*, D intended to write on the parking notices. As that writing was found to be damage within the meaning of s 1 of the Criminal Damage Act 1971, then D intend to do the damage.

Reckless

This word has caused problems. In *Stephenson* [1979] 2 All ER 1198, D was a tramp who sheltered in a hollow in a haystack and, because he was cold, lit a fire there. The haystack caught fire and was destroyed. The Court of Appeal quashed D's conviction on the grounds that, although an ordinary person would realise the risk of the haystack catching fire, he did not as he suffered from schizophrenia and this point should have been left to the jury to decide. The Court of Appeal was using the subjective test for reckless.

However, in *Caldwell* [1981] 1 All ER 961, the House of Lords stated that a person is reckless if he did an act which in fact created an obvious risk that property will be destroyed, and when he did the act he either:

- had not given any thought to the possibility of there being any risk (objective); or
- had recognised that there was some risk involved and had nonetheless gone on to take it (subjective).

tutor tip

'Case examples are important as there are many fine distinctions on areas such as what constitutes damage.'

This became known as *Caldwell* (1981) recklessness and, as can be seen, it included both subjective and objective recklessness. The objective test considered whether the risk was obvious to an ordinary prudent person. If so, then the fact that the defendant did not give any thought to the possibility of there being any risk was enough to make the defendant guilty.

This objective test was harsh in its application, particularly where the defendant was young or mentally backward. This was seen in *Elliott v C* [1983] 2 All ER 1005, where the defendant was incapable of appreciating the risk but was still guilty under this test. D was a 14-year-old girl with severe learning difficulties who had been out all night without food or sleep. She got into a garden shed and in an effort to get warm, poured white spirit on to the carpet and set light to it. The magistrates found that she had given no thought to the possibility that the shed might be destroyed. They also found that in the circumstances the risk would not have been obvious to her and they acquitted her. The prosecution appealed by way of case stated to the Queen's Bench Divisional Court which ruled that as the risk would have been obvious to a reasonably prudent man, the magistrates had to convict the girl. A similar decision was reached by the Court of Appeal in *Gemmell and Richards* [2002] EWCA Crim 192, but was later reversed by the House of Lords (*G and another* [2003] UKHL 50).

CASE EXAMPLE

G and another [2003] UKHL 50

The defendants were two boys aged 11 and 12 years. During a night out camping, they went into the yard of a shop and set fire to some bundles of newspapers which they threw under a large wheelie bin. They then left the yard. They expected that as there was a concrete floor under the wheelie bin the fire would extinguish itself. In fact the bin caught fire and this spread to the shop and other buildings, causing about £1 million damage. The boys were convicted under both s 1 and s 3 of the Criminal Damage Act 1971. The Court of Appeal upheld their convictions but the House of Lords quashed the convictions overruling the case of *Caldwell* (1981).

The trial judge directed the jury that whether there was an obvious risk of the shop and other buildings being damaged should be decided by reference to the reasonable man, i.e. the reasonable adult. He said: 'the ordinary reasonable bystander is an adult ... He has got in mind that stock of everyday information which one acquires in the process of growing up' and 'no allowance is made by the law for the youth of these boys or their lack of maturity or their own inability, if you find it to be, to assess what was going on'. The Court of Appeal held that this direction was in line with the law in *Caldwell* (1981) and dismissed the appeal on the basis that *Caldwell* (1981) was binding on it.

However, it certified the following point of law of general public importance:

QUOTATION

'Can a defendant properly be convicted under section 1 of the Criminal Damage Act 1971 on the basis that he was reckless as to whether property was destroyed or damaged when he gave no thought to the risk but, by reason of his age and/or personal characteristics the risk would not have been obvious to him, even if he had thought about it?'

The House of Lords ruled that a defendant could not be guilty unless he had realised the risk and decided to take it. It overruled the decision in *Caldwell* (1981), holding that in that case the Law Lords had 'adopted an interpretation of section 1 of the 1971 Act which was beyond the range of feasible meanings'. It emphasised the meaning that the Law Commission had intended and which Parliament must also have intended. Lord Bingham said:

JUDGMENT

'[S]ection 1 as enacted followed, subject to an immaterial addition, the draft proposed by the Law Commission. It cannot be supposed that by "reckless" Parliament meant anything different from the Law Commission. The Law Commission's meaning was made plain both in its Report (Law Com No 29) and in Working Paper No 23 which preceded it. These materials (not, it would seem, placed before the House in *R v Caldwell*) reveal a very plain intention to replace the old expression "maliciously" by the more familiar expression "reckless" but to give the latter expression the meaning which *R v Cunningham* [1957] 2 QB 396 had given to the former ... . No relevant change in the *mens rea* necessary for the proof of the offence was intended, and in holding otherwise the majority misconstrued section 1 of the Act.'

Lord Bingham also quoted from the Law Commission's Draft Criminal Code when he said that he would answer the certified question. He gave cl 18(c) of the Draft Bill for the Criminal Code (1989) Law Com No 177, as his answer:

CLAUSE

'18(c) A person acts recklessly within the meaning of section 1 of the Criminal Damage Act 1971 with respect to –

(i) a circumstance when he is aware of a risk that it exists or will exist;

(ii) a result when he is aware of a risk that it will occur; and it is in the circumstances known to him, unreasonable to take the risk.'

This judgment by the House of Lords in *G and another* (2003) affects the meaning of reckless for all the offences created by s 1.

In *Seray-White* (2012), although the Divisional Court ruled that D intended the damage and so his conviction under s 1 of the Criminal Damage Act was safe on that basis, the court also commented on the question of recklessness. D had argued on appeal that the Crown Court had applied an objective test with respect to recklessness. The Divisional Court pointed out that the Crown Court concluded that they were sure D appreciated that damage was likely to result from his writing on parking notices (see section 16.1.1 for full facts of the case). This was a subjective state of mind and complied with the ruling in *G* (2003) that only a subjective test should be used to decide if D was reckless. Lloyd Jones J giving judgment in the Divisional Court said:

JUDGMENT

'I am entirely satisfied that there is ample evidence from which the Crown Court could infer that [D] foresaw a risk of damaging the signs by writing on them. Not only was this an obvious risk in itself, but [D], having done the same thing before, was aware that the cleaning up operation on that earlier occasion had failed to erase all traces of the pen.'

16.1.5 Without lawful excuse

The Act defines two lawful excuses in s 5. These are available only for the basic offence.

SECTION

'5(2) A person charged with an offence to which this section applies shall whether or not he would be treated for the purposes of this Act as having a lawful excuse apart from this subsection, be treated as having a lawful excuse –

(a) if at the time of the act or acts alleged to constitute the offence he believed that the person or persons whom he believed to be entitled to consent to the destruction of or damage to the property in question had so consented, or would have so consented to it if he or they had known of the destruction or damage and its circumstances; or

(b) if he destroyed or damaged or threatened to destroy or damage the property in question ... in order to protect property belonging to himself or another or a right or interest in property which was or which he believed was vested in himself or another, and at the time of the act or acts alleged to constitute the offence he believed –

(i) that the property was in need of immediate protection; and

(ii) that the means of protection adopted or proposed to be adopted were or would be reasonable in all the circumstances.

(3) For the purposes of this section it is immaterial whether a belief is justified or not if it is honestly held.'

There is therefore a defence under s 5 in two circumstances. D must honestly believe either that

- the owner (or another person with rights in the property) would have consented to the damage; or
- other property was at risk and in need of immediate protection and what he did was reasonable in all the circumstances.

Belief in consent

In *Denton* [1982] 1 All ER 65, D, who worked in a cotton mill, thought that his employer had encouraged him to set fire to the mill so that the employer could make an insurance claim. The Court of Appeal quashed his conviction as he had a defence under s 5(2)(a).

The combination of s 5(2)(a) and s 5(3) allows a defence of mistake to be used, even where the defendant makes the mistake because they are intoxicated as seen in *Jaggard v Dickinson* [1980] 3 All ER 716.

CASE EXAMPLE

Jaggard v Dickinson [1980] 3 All ER 716

D, who was drunk, went to what she thought was a friend's house. There was no one in and so she broke a window to get in as she believed (accurately) her friend would consent to this. Unfortunately in her drunken state she had mistaken the house and had actually broken into the house of another person. The Divisional Court quashed her conviction, holding that she could rely on her intoxicated belief as Parliament had 'specifically required the court to consider the defendant's actual state of belief, not the state of belief which ought to have existed'.

The Divisional Court in *Jaggard* pointed out that a belief may be honestly held whether it is caused by intoxication, stupidity, forgetfulness or inattention.

Belief that other property was in immediate need of protection

Under s 5(2)(b) there is a defence where D believes the destruction or damage of property is needed for the immediate protection of other property. This could give a defence in situations where trees are cut down or a building demolished to prevent the spread of fire. A case in which the defence was successfully pleaded in a jury trial was in April 2000 when Lord Melchett and several other members of Greenpeace damaged genetically modified (GM) crops in order to prevent non-GM crops in neighbouring fields being contaminated with pollen from the GM crops. The judge allowed the defence to go to the jury, but they were unable to agree on a verdict. A retrial was ordered and this time the jury acquitted the defendants.

If D has another purpose in doing the damage, then the court may rule that the defence is not available to him. Also there is an objective test to decide whether the act that the defendant did was done for the immediate protection of other property. This was stressed in *Hunt* (1977) 66 Cr App R 105.

CASE EXAMPLE

Hunt (1977) 66 Cr App R 105

D helped his wife in her post as deputy warden of a block of old people's flats. He set fire to some bedding in order, as he claimed, to draw attention to the fact that the fire alarm was not in working order. The judge refused to allow a defence under s 5(2)(b) to go to the jury as his act was not done in order to protect property which was in immediate need of protection. The Court of Appeal upheld his conviction, despite the very subjective wording of s 5(2)(b). They held that the question whether or not a particular act of destruction or damage or threat of destruction or damage was in order to protect property belonging to another must be, on the true construction of the statute, an objective test. In this case the damage was done in order to draw attention to the defective fire alarm.

Hunt was followed in the cases of *R v Hill: R v Hall* (1988) 89 Cr App R 74.

CASE EXAMPLE

R v Hill: R v Hall (1988) 89 Cr App R 74

Both Ds were convicted of possessing articles with intent to damage. They had gone to a US naval base in south Wales with hacksaws and the intention of damaging the perimeter fence. They believed the naval base was an obvious target for a nuclear attack and that, as a result, surrounding homes were in need of protection. They wanted the naval base to be removed. The Court of Appeal upheld their convictions. The court held that the correct approach was whether it could be said as a matter of law, on the facts believed by Ds, cutting the perimeter fence could amount to something done to protect their homes. This was an objective test and the proposed act was too remote from the eventual aim.

In *Jones (Margaret) and another* [2004] EWCA Crim 1981; (2004) 4 All ER 955, the question of whether the damage D is seeking to prevent has to be unlawful damage was addressed. The defendants entered an airbase and caused damage to three refuelling trucks, two munitions trailers and their tractor units. It was their intention to prevent the United States and the United Kingdom from using the base to support the war in Iraq. The Court of Appeal pointed out that the defence was not limited to lawful damage by the Act. Latham LJ said:

JUDGMENT

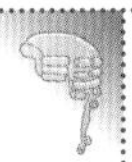

'Whilst there are clearly strong policy arguments for imposing such a further restriction on the availability of the defence, the fact is that the statute does not so provide.'

The Court of Appeal dismissed Ds' appeals against conviction on other grounds. The case was appealed to the House of Lords but the point on whether the damage has to be unlawful to come within the s 5 defence was not taken there. In the case of *Blake v DPP* [1993] Crim LR 586, the defendant put forward defences under both s 5(2)(a) and s 5(2)(b).

CASE EXAMPLE

Blake v DPP [1993] Crim LR 586

D was a vicar who believed that the government should not use military force in Kuwait and Iraq in the Gulf War. He wrote a biblical quotation with a marker pen on a concrete post outside the Houses of Parliament. He claimed that

- he was carrying out the instructions of God and this gave him a defence under s 5(2)(a), as God was entitled to consent to the damage of property; and
- the damage he did was in order to protect the property of civilians in Kuwait and Iraq and so he had a defence under s 5(2)(b).

He was convicted and appealed, but both the claims were rejected. The court held that God could not consent to damage and that what the vicar had done was not capable of protecting property in the Gulf judged objectively, again despite the apparent subjective wording of both s 5(2)(a) and (b).

Property

Property is defined in s 10 of the Criminal Damage Act and the same definition applies to property that a defendant is trying to protect. This was important in *Cresswell and Currie v DPP* [2006] EWHC 3379 (Admin).

CASE EXAMPLE

Cresswell and Currie v DPP [2006] EWHC 3379 (Admin)

Ds had destroyed four badger traps that had been placed by officers of the Department for Environment, Food and Rural Affairs (DEFRA) in the course of a cull on farmland in Cornwall where there were badger setts. They argued that they had acted with lawful excuse under s 5(2) because they had destroyed the traps in order to protect badgers and that badgers were property as they were 'in the course of being reduced into possession'. Ds were convicted and the Court of Appeal upheld their convictions. It was held that wild badgers were not property within the definition in s 10. They were not in the course of being reduced into the possession of DEFRA.

Keene LJ also pointed out that DEFRA owned the badger traps which Ds damaged and so, if the badgers had become the property of DEFRA, it could not be a lawful excuse to seek to protect them against actions by those who own them. He said:

JUDGMENT

'It is not the purpose of s 5(2), as I see it, to prevent the owner of property from destroying it or damaging it if he wishes to do so, unless that in itself is an unlawful act (in which case another defence will arise) or someone in addition has some interest in the property in question.'

The other judge, Walker LJ was not convinced that this was a correct interpretation of the law. He thought that there might be circumstances where it could be possible to use s 5 as a defence even though both the property being damaged and the property being protected belonged to the same person. He gave as an example the situation where the owner of a valuable piece of antique furniture was drunkenly swinging at it with an axe, where it might be desirable that a bystander should be entitled to act so as to protect the property. However, he declined to give a ruling on this point as it had not been argued before the court.

No defence to protect a person

Oddly enough the Act does not provide a defence where D believes he is acting to protect a person from harm. In *Baker and Wilkins* [1997] Crim LR 497, the two defendants believed that Baker's daughter was being held in a house. They tried to enter the house, causing damage to the door. They were convicted and their conviction was upheld on appeal as s 5(2)(b) only provides a defence where other property is in immediate need of protection.

The Law Commission in its report, *Legislating the Criminal Code: Offences against the Person and General Principles* (1993) Law Com No 218 at para 37.6 acknowledged that it is anomalous that no defence is available for protection of people when there is a defence for protection of property. It recommended that s 5 should be brought into line with self-defence and a defence allowed when the act is for the immediate protection of a person.

16.2 Endangering life

This is an aggravated offence of criminal damage under s 1(2) Criminal Damage Act 1971, which states:

SECTION

'1(2) A person who without lawful excuse destroys or damages any property, whether belonging to himself or another –

(a) intending to destroy or damage any property or being reckless as to whether any property would be destroyed or damaged; and

(b) intending by the destruction or damage to endanger the life of another or being reckless as to whether the life of another would be thereby endangered; shall be guilty of an offence.'

This offence is regarded as much more serious than the basic offence and it carries a maximum sentence of life imprisonment.

16.2.1 Danger to life

The danger to life must come from the destruction or damage, not from another source in which damage was caused. In *Steer* [1987] 2 All ER 833, D fired three shots at the home of his former business partner, causing damage to the house. The Court of Appeal quashed his conviction as it held the danger came from the shots, not from any damage done to the house through those shots. It certified the following question to go to the House of Lords:

QUOTATION

'Whether, upon a true construction of s 1(2)(b) of the Criminal Damage Act 1971, the prosecution are required to prove that the danger to life resulted from the destruction of or damage to the property, or whether it is sufficient for the prosecution to prove that it resulted from the act of the defendant which caused the destruction or damage.'

The House of Lords ruled that as the Act used the phrase 'by the destruction or damage', it could not be extended to mean 'by the damage or by the act which caused the damage'. It also pointed out that if it did include the act (as opposed to the damage), then there would be an anomaly which Parliament could not have intended, which it illustrated in the following way.

JUDGMENT

'If A and B both discharge firearms in a public place, being reckless whether life would be endangered, it would be absurd that A, who incidentally causes some trifling damage to the property, should be guilty of an offence punishable with life imprisonment, but that B, who causes no damage, should be guilty of no offence. In the same circumstances, if A is merely reckless but B actually intends to endanger life, it is scarcely less absurd that A should be guilty of the graver offence under s 1(2)(b) of the 1971 Act, B of the lesser offence under s 16 of the Firearms Act 1968.'

In the later conjoined cases of *Webster and Warwick* [1995] 2 All ER 168, the Court of Appeal strained to distinguish the decision in *Steer* (1987). In *Webster* (1995) three defendants pushed a large stone from a bridge on to a train underneath. The stone hit the roof of one coach and caused debris to shower the passengers in that coach, although the stone itself did not fall into the carriage. In *Warwick* (1995), D rammed a police car and threw bricks at it causing the rear window to smash and shower the officers with broken glass. The Court of Appeal quashed the conviction in *Webster* (1995) because the judge had misdirected the jury that an intention to endanger life by the stone falling was sufficient for guilt, but it substituted a conviction based on recklessness. In *Warwick* (1995) it upheld the conviction. Lord Taylor CJ stated:

JUDGMENT

'[I]f a defendant throws a brick at a windscreen of a moving vehicle, given that he causes some damage to the vehicle, whether he is guilty under s 1(2) does not depend on whether the brick hits or misses the windscreen, but whether he intended to hit it and intended that the damage therefrom should endanger life or whether he was reckless as to that outcome. As to the dropping of stones from bridges, the effect of the statute may be thought strange. If the defendant's intention is that the stone itself should crash through the roof of a train ... and thereby directly injure a passenger or if whether he was reckless only as to that outcome, the section would not bite ... If, however, the defendant intended or was reckless that the stone would smash the roof of the train or vehicle so that metal or wood struts from the roof would or obviously might descend upon a passenger, endangering life, he would surely be guilty. This may seem a dismal distinction.'

It is of interest to note that the Court of Appeal's decision in these cases is contrary to *obiter* statements in the judgment in *Steer* (1987), where Lord Bridge specifically considered this type of situation:

JUDGMENT

'Counsel for the Crown put forward other examples of cases which he suggested ought to be liable to prosecution under s 1(2) of the 1971 Act, including that of the angry mob of striking miners who throw a hail of bricks through the window of a cottage occupied by the working miner and that of people who drop missiles from motorway bridges on passing vehicles. I believe that the criminal law provides adequate sanctions for these cases without the need to resort to s 1(2) of the 1971 Act. But, if my belief is mistaken, this would still be no reason to distort the plain meaning of that subsection.'

16.2.2 Life not actually endangered

Life does not actually have to be endangered. In *Sangha* [1988] 2 All ER 385, D set fire to a mattress and two chairs in a neighbour's flat. The flat was empty at the time and, because of the design of the building, people in adjoining flats were not at risk. The Court of Appeal applied the now discredited test from *Caldwell* (1982) when it said that:

JUDGMENT

'The test to be applied is this: is it proved that an ordinary prudent bystander would have perceived an obvious risk that property would be damaged and that life would thereby be endangered? The ordinary prudent bystander is not deemed to be invested with expert knowledge relating to the construction of the property, nor to have the benefit of hindsight. The time at which the perception is relevant is the time when the fire started.'

This decision took the objective test to a ridiculous degree. It meant that if D was an expert and knows there is no risk of endangering life by his actions, he would not have been judged by that but by whether an uninformed ordinary prudent bystander would think there was a risk. This objective interpretation must now be taken to be superseded by the use of subjective recklessness in *G and another* (2003). So, the test is whether the defendant realised that life might be endangered. If he did then he would be guilty even if there was no actual risk.

16.2.3 Own property

Section 1(2) applies where the property damaged is the defendant's own. This can be justified in most situations, as the aim of the section is to make D guilty where he has intended or been reckless as to whether life is endangered by the damage he does. It does not matter whether the damage is to his property or someone else's. However, the case of *Merrick* [1995] Crim LR 802 shows how the section can be extended to absurd lengths.

In *Merrick* (1995), D was employed by a householder to remove some old television cable. While doing this D left the live cable exposed for about six minutes. The Court of Appeal upheld his conviction under s 1(2) of the 1971 Act. In this case the householder was using *Merrick* (1995) as an agent, but if the householder had done the work personally it seems that he would equally have been guilty. The other anomaly shown by this case is that *Merrick* (1995) was guilty only because he was removing old cable and 'damaging' it by this process. If he had been installing new wiring and left that exposed for six minutes it would have been difficult to argue that there was any damage and so he would have been not guilty. Yet the action and the danger in both situations are the same.

16.2.4 *Mens rea*

There are two points which the prosecution must prove. These are:

1. intention or recklessness as to destroying or damaging any property;
2. intention or recklessness as to whether life is endangered by the destruction or damage.

Intention and recklessness have the same meaning as for the basic offence (see section 16.1.4). This means that the *Caldwell* (1982) test for recklessness has been overruled and the prosecution must prove that the defendant was aware both that there was a risk the property would be destroyed or damaged and that life would be endangered.

The decision in *R (Stephen Malcolm)* (1984) 79 Cr App R 334, where the Court of Appeal followed the decision in *Elliott v C* (1983), even though they were reluctant to do so, must be taken as overruled. In that case the defendant was a 15-year-old boy who, with two friends, had thrown milk bottles filled with petrol at the outside wall of a neighbour's ground-floor flat. These had caused sheets of flame which flashed across the window of the flat, endangering the lives of the occupants. D argued that he had not realised the risk, but the Court of Appeal held that the test was whether an ordinary prudent man would have appreciated the risk that life might be endangered. The decision following *G and another* (2003) would be whether the defendant had realised the risk.

This was confirmed in *Cooper* [2004] EWCA Crim 1382 and *Castle* [2004] EWCA Crim 2758.

CASE EXAMPLE

Cooper [2004] EWCA Crim 1382

D, who lived in a hostel for people needing support for mental illness, set fire to his mattress and bedding. There was no serious damage. When asked by the police if it had crossed his mind that people might have been hurt, he replied 'I don't think, it did cross my mind a bit but nobody would have got hurt.' He was charged with arson being reckless as to whether life would be endangered. The trial judge directed the jury in accordance with *Caldwell*. D was convicted but the conviction was quashed as the Court of Appeal held that the *Caldwell* test was no longer appropriate. The test for recklessness was subjective.

Rose LJ made it clear that *G and R* (2003) had affected the law in respect of the level of recklessness required for all criminal damage offences when he said:

JUDGMENT

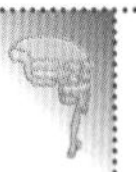

'In the light of the House of Lords speeches in *G and R*, the *Caldwell* direction was a misdirection. It is now, in the light *G and R*, incumbent on a trial judge to direct a jury, in a case of this kind, that the risk of danger to life was obvious and significant to the defendant. In other words, a subjective element is essential before the jury can convict of this offence.'

A similar decision was reached in *Castle* [2004] EWCA Crim 2758 where D broke into some offices at night to burgle them. On leaving he set fire to the premises. There were two flats above the offices but neither of the occupants was at home. These flats suffered

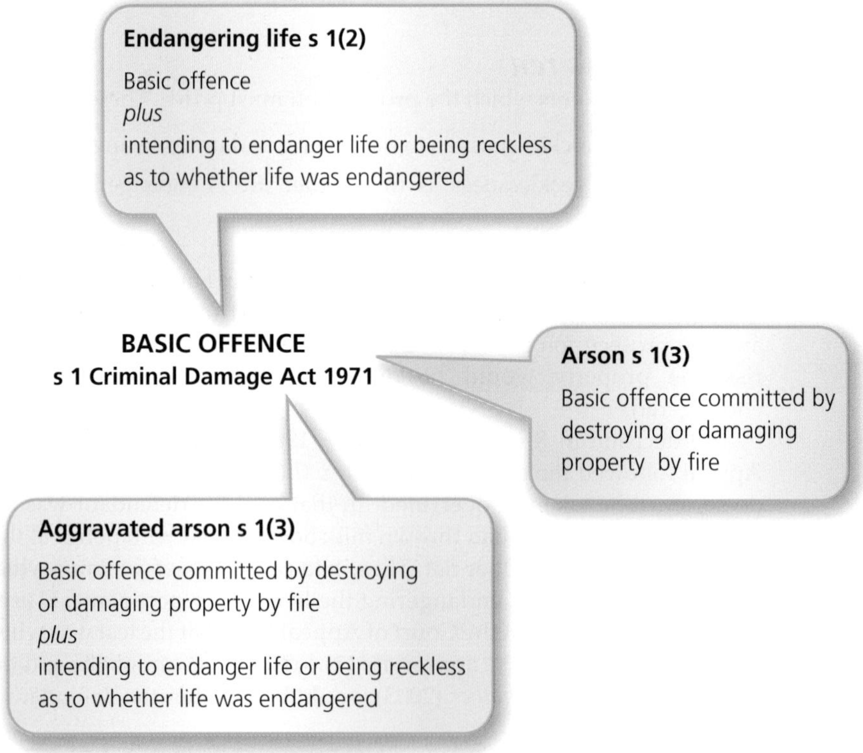

Endangering life s 1(2)

Basic offence
plus
intending to endanger life or being reckless as to whether life was endangered

BASIC OFFENCE
s 1 Criminal Damage Act 1971

Arson s 1(3)

Basic offence committed by destroying or damaging property by fire

Aggravated arson s 1(3)

Basic offence committed by destroying or damaging property by fire
plus
intending to endanger life or being reckless as to whether life was endangered

Figure 16.1 Offences of criminal damage.

smoke and soot damage from the fire. The trial judge directed the jury in accordance with *Caldwell*. As in *Cooper* the Court of Appeal quashed D's conviction stating that the *Caldwell* test was no longer appropriate. The test for recklessness was subjective.

16.3 Arson

Under s 1(3) Criminal Damage Act 1971, where an offence under s 1 Criminal Damage Act 1971 is committed by destroying or damaging property by fire, the offence becomes arson. The maximum penalty is life imprisonment.

The basic offence of criminal damage must be destruction or damage by fire. All the other ingredients of the offence are the same as for the basic offence. Where aggravated arson is charged then it is necessary for the prosecution to prove that the defendant intended or was reckless as to whether life was endangered by the damage or destruction by fire.

In *Miller* [1983] 1 All ER 978, the House of Lords held that arson could be committed by an omission where the defendant accidentally started a fire and failed to do anything to prevent damage from that fire.

KEY FACTS

Key facts on criminal damage

Criminal Damage Act 1971	*Actus reus*	Comment/case	*Mens rea*	Comment/case
s 1(1) Basic offence	Destroy or damage property belonging to another.	Damage need only be slight and non-permanent *Roe v Kingerlee* (1986) but must need some effort to remove it *A (a Juvenile)* (1978). Any tangible property including land can be damaged. Having a proprietary right.	Intending or being reckless as to destruction or damage.	Normal principles of intention apply. *Cunningham* (1957) recklessness applies. *G and another* (2003).
s 1(2) Endangering life	Basic offence and intending or being reckless as to whether life was endangered.	Danger must come from destruction or damage (*Steer* (1987); *Webster and Warwick* (1995)). Can commit offence by damaging own property.	*Mens rea* for basic offence and intention or recklessness as to whether life was endangered.	Intention and recklessness have the same meaning as for the basic offence (*Castle* (2004)).
s 1(3) Arson	Committed by fire. Aggravated offence committed by fire.	Can be committed by omission (*Miller* (1983)).	The intending or being reckless as to destruction or damage must be by fire.	–

16.4 Threats to destroy or damage property

This is an offence against s 2 of the Criminal Damage Act 1971:

SECTION

'2 A person who without lawful excuse makes to another a threat, intending that that other would fear it would be carried out –

(a) to destroy or damage any property belonging to that other or a third person; or
(b) to destroy or damage his own property in a way which he knows is likely to endanger the life of that other or a third person; shall be guilty of an offence.'

The threat is, therefore, of conduct which would be an offence under s 1 of the Act. However, there is a key difference in that the defendant must intend that the other would fear the threat would be carried out. Section 2 does not give any alternative of being reckless as to whether the other would fear the threat would be carried out. In *Cakman and others*, [2002] Crim LR 581, the defendants had occupied two of the 'pods' of the London Eye, demonstrating against human rights abuses in Turkey. They used an intercom to contact the operator of the wheel. They threatened to set fire to themselves if any attempt was made to storm the pods. Some of the protesters were seen to pour liquid over themselves. They were convicted of an offence under s 2(b).

The Court of Appeal quashed the convictions as they held that it was not enough to prove that the threatener was reckless as to whether the person threatened feared that the threats would be carried out. It had to be proved that the person making the threat intended that the person threatened would fear that the threat would be carried out. There is no mention of 'recklessly' in s 2, whereas in s 1, for the basic offence, 'recklessly' is expressly included. The Court of Appeal also pointed out that the nature of the threat of damage to the property had to be considered objectively. It does not matter what the person threatened thought.

16.5 Possessing anything with intent to destroy or damage property

Section 3 of the Criminal Damage Act 1971 sets out:

SECTION

'3 A person who has anything in his custody or under his control intending without lawful excuse to use it or cause or permit another to use it –

(a) to destroy or damage any property belonging to some other person; or
(b) to destroy or damage his own property in a way which he knows is likely to endanger the life of some other person; shall be guilty of an offence.'

The *actus reus* is having the item in one's custody or control. The possession must be for the purpose of committing an offence under s 1. There is no time limit on when the offence will be committed, so there is no need to prove that it was imminent. The *mens rea* is the intention of using the item to commit a s 1 offence. This can be a conditional intention where the defendant only intends to use the item if he has to or in a certain event.

16.6 Racially aggravated criminal damage

This is an offence under s 30(1) of the Crime and Disorder Act 1998. An offence under s 1(1) of the Criminal Damage Act 1971 must have been committed together with the special circumstances set out in s 28 of the Crime and Disorder Act 1998. These are that

- at the time of committing the offence, or immediately before or after doing so, the offender demonstrates towards the victim of the offence hostility based on the victim's membership (or presumed membership) of a racial group; or
- the offence is motivated (wholly or partly) by hostility towards members of a racial group based on their membership of that group.

The meaning of s 28 is the same as for racially or religiously aggravated assaults (see section 11.6). However, as the offence is aimed at property and not a person, s 30(3) of the Crime and Disorder Act 1998 states that s 28(1) of the Act shall have effect as if the person to whom the property belongs or is treated as belonging were the victim of the offence.

Note that only the basic offence of criminal damage under s 1(1) of the Criminal Damage Act 1971 can become a racially or religiously aggravated offence. There is no provision for the offence of arson to be a racially or religiously aggravated offence. This is because the purpose of making an offence a racially or religiously aggravated one is to increase the maximum penalty. As arson has a maximum term of imprisonment of life, it is impossible for the maximum to be increased.

The penalty for racially or religiously aggravated criminal damage is 14 years as compared to ten years for the straightforward basic offence.

SUMMARY

Basic offence

D destroys or damages any property belonging to another intending to destroy or damage any such property or being reckless as to whether any such property would be destroyed or damaged and without lawful excuse.

Section 5 defences

D has a lawful excuse for the damage or destruction in the following circumstances:

- Section 5(2)(a) if at the time of the act or acts alleged to constitute the offence, D believed that the person(s) entitled to consent to the destruction of or damage to the property had consented, or would have so consented to it if he had known of the destruction or damage and its circumstances.
- Section 5(2)(b) if D destroyed or damaged the property in question in order to protect property belonging to himself or another, and at the time of the act or acts alleged to constitute the offence he believed –
  - (i) that the property was in need of immediate protection; and
  - (ii) that the means of protection adopted or proposed to be adopted were or would be reasonable in all the circumstances.

For s 5(2)(a) D has a defence even if he made a mistake through intoxication.

Endangering life

- This is where D commits the basic offence and intends by the destruction or damage to endanger the life of another or is reckless as to whether the life of another would be endangered.

- Life does not actually have to be endangered.
- The offence can be committed even though the property damaged is the defendant's own.

Arson

- Where the basic offence of criminal damage is destruction or damage by fire.

Aggravated arson

- Life was endangered and D intended or was reckless as to whether life was endangered by the damage or destruction by fire.

Threats to destroy or damage property

Where, without lawful excuse, D makes a threat to another, intending that that other would fear it would be carried out:

- to destroy or damage any property belonging to that other or a third person; or
- to destroy or damage D's own property in a way which he knows is likely to endanger the life of that other or a third person.

Possessing anything with intent to destroy or damage property

Where D has anything in his custody or under his control intending without lawful excuse to use it or cause or permit another to use it:

- to destroy or damage any property belonging to some other person; or
- to destroy or damage his own property in a way which he knows is likely to endanger the life of some other person.

Racially aggravated criminal damage

Where D commits an offence under s 1 and at the time of the offence, or immediately before or after doing so, demonstrates towards V hostility based on V's membership (or presumed membership) of a racial group or is motivated by hostility towards members of a racial group.

ACTIVITY

Applying the Law

Discuss what offences, if any, have been committed in the following situations.

1. Anwal, aged ten, stands at the side of a country road and throws stones at passing cars. One stone hits the door of a car and causes a slight mark on the door. Another stone hits the side window of the car causing it to smash, showering the driver with glass. The driver swerves but manages to stop the car safely. Would your answer be different if Anwal was aged 20 and throwing stones on to cars from a bridge across a busy motorway?
2. Charlene has had an argument with her flatmate, Louisa. Charlene decides to teach Louisa a lesson by setting fire to some of her clothes. Charlene hangs an expensive dress out of the window and sets it alight. She then goes out. The flames from the dress set the window curtains alight and the fire spreads to the rest of the flat.
3. Donovan writes racially abusive words in chalk on the pavement outside a neighbour's house. The next day it rains and the chalk is washed away.

4. Errol and Fred are demolition workers for a local council. They are given instructions to demolish houses owned by the council in Green Street. The house numbers they are given are 1, 3, 5, 7, 9 and 11. When they arrive at Green Street they find that the houses are semi-detached in pairs, 1 and 3, 5 and 7, 9 and 11. They start by demolishing the pair of numbers 1 and 3. They then use heavy machinery to knock down the side wall of number 5. At this point Hannah comes out from number 7 and tells them to stop as she owns number 7 and if they continue to demolish number 5 it will damage her house. Errol and Fred insist they have the right to demolish both number 5 and number 7. While Hannah is arguing with them, her son, Ian, aged 14, removes some wiring from the engine of their demolition machinery. This means they are unable to do any more work. However, they have so weakened the structure of number 5 that it collapses and causes damage to number 7.

SAMPLE ESSAY QUESTION

Critically discuss whether the defences under s 5 of the Criminal Damage Act 1971 should be reformed.

State the defences under s 5:

- s 5(2)(a) believed would have consent of person whose property was damaged
- s 5(2)(b) damage done in order to protect property
- s 5(3) immaterial whether a belief is justified or not if it is honestly held

Defences only available to basic offence

Explain the effect of s 5(2)(a):

Consider decisions such as:

- *Denton* (1982)
- *Jaggard v Dickinson* (1980)

Explain the effect of s 5(2)(b):

Consider decisions such as:

- *Hunt* (1977)
- *R v Hill; R v Hall* (1988)
- *Jones (Margaret) and another* (2004)
- *Cresswell and Currie v DPP* (2006)

Discuss points such as:

- Defence under s 5(2)(b) not available for protection of people *Baker and Wilkins* (1997)
- Law Commission recommendations regarding a defence for protection of people
- Should protection of property be limited to where the risk is from unlawful damage?
- Should the defence be allowed where the damage is caused due to a drunken mistake as in *Jaggard v Dickinson*?

Compare the defences under s 5 with defences available for assaults especially:

- Drunken mistake cannot be relied on in defence of self-defence to assault although it is allowed for criminal damage

Conclude

Further reading

Books

Ormerod, D and Laird, K, *Smith and Hogan Criminal Law: Cases and Materials* (11th edn, Oxford University Press, 2014), Chapter 30.

Articles

Elliott, D W, 'Endangering life by destroying or damaging property' (1997) Crim LR 382.

Haralambous, N, 'Retreating from Caldwell: restoring subjectivism' (2003) NLJ 1712.

Law Commission, *Criminal Law: Report on Offences of Damage to Property* (1970) (Law Com No 29).

17

Public order offences

AIMS AND OBJECTIVES

After reading this chapter you should be able to:

- Understand the *actus reus* and *mens rea* of the offences of riot, violent disorder and affray
- Understand the *actus reus* and *mens rea* of other offences created by the Public Order Act 1986
- Analyse critically offences under the Public Order Act 1986
- Apply the law to factual situations to determine whether there is criminal liability for an offence under the Public Order Act 1986

The main public order offences are now contained in the Public Order Act 1986 as amended by the Crime and Courts Act 2013, though there are other offences, for example wearing a uniform for a political purpose under the Public Order Act 1936, and aggravated trespass under s 68 of the Criminal Justice and Public Order Act 1994.

The Public Order Act 1986 abolished the old common law offences of riot, rout, unlawful assembly and affray and created three new offences in their place. These are riot, violent disorder and affray. The law has been made more coherent, with common themes of using or threatening unlawful violence, and conduct which would cause a person of reasonable firmness present at the scene to fear for his personal safety.

Although these offences are aimed at maintaining public order, the Act states that all three offences can be committed in private as well as in a public place.

17.1 Riot

This is an offence under s 1 of the Public Order Act 1986:

SECTION

'1(1) Where twelve or more persons who are present together use or threaten unlawful violence for a common purpose and the conduct of them (taken together) is such as would cause a person of reasonable firmness present at the scene to fear for his personal safety, each of the persons using unlawful violence for the common purpose is guilty of riot.

(2) It is immaterial whether or not the twelve or more use or threaten unlawful violence simultaneously.

(3) The common purpose may be inferred from conduct.

(4) No person of reasonable firmness need actually be, or likely to be, present at the scene.

(5) Riot may be committed in private as well as public places.'

17.1.1 The *actus reus* of riot

This has several elements. It requires:

- at least 12 people to be present together with a common purpose;
- violence to be used or threatened by them;
- so that the conduct would cause a person of reasonable firmness present at the scene to fear for his personal safety.

The 12 or more people need not have agreed to have assembled together; the fact that they are there together is the key point. The common purpose need not have been previously agreed. As s 1(3) states, the common purpose can be inferred from the conduct of the 12 or more people. This covers situations where a number of people come to the scene (whether together or one by one) and then because of an incident involving one person (perhaps being arrested by the police), 12 or more of the people there start threatening the police. All those threatening or using violence will then be guilty of riot.

The offence of riot can be committed even if the common purpose is lawful, for example employees want to discuss redundancies with their employer. But if 12 or more of them use or threaten unlawful violence they may be guilty of riot.

Violence

The meaning of 'violence' is explained in s 8 of the Act:

SECTION

'8 ... (i) except in the context of affray, it includes violent conduct towards property as well as violent conduct towards persons, and

(ii) it is not restricted to conduct causing or intended to cause injury or damage but includes any other violent conduct (for example, throwing at or towards a person a missile of a kind capable of causing injury which does not hit or falls short).'

Only unlawful violence can create riot. If the violence is lawful, for example in prevention of crime, or self-defence, then there is no offence.

17.1.2 *Mens rea* of riot

Section 6(1) states the mental element required for the offence:

SECTION

'6(1) A person is guilty of riot only if he intends to use violence or is aware that his conduct may be violent.'

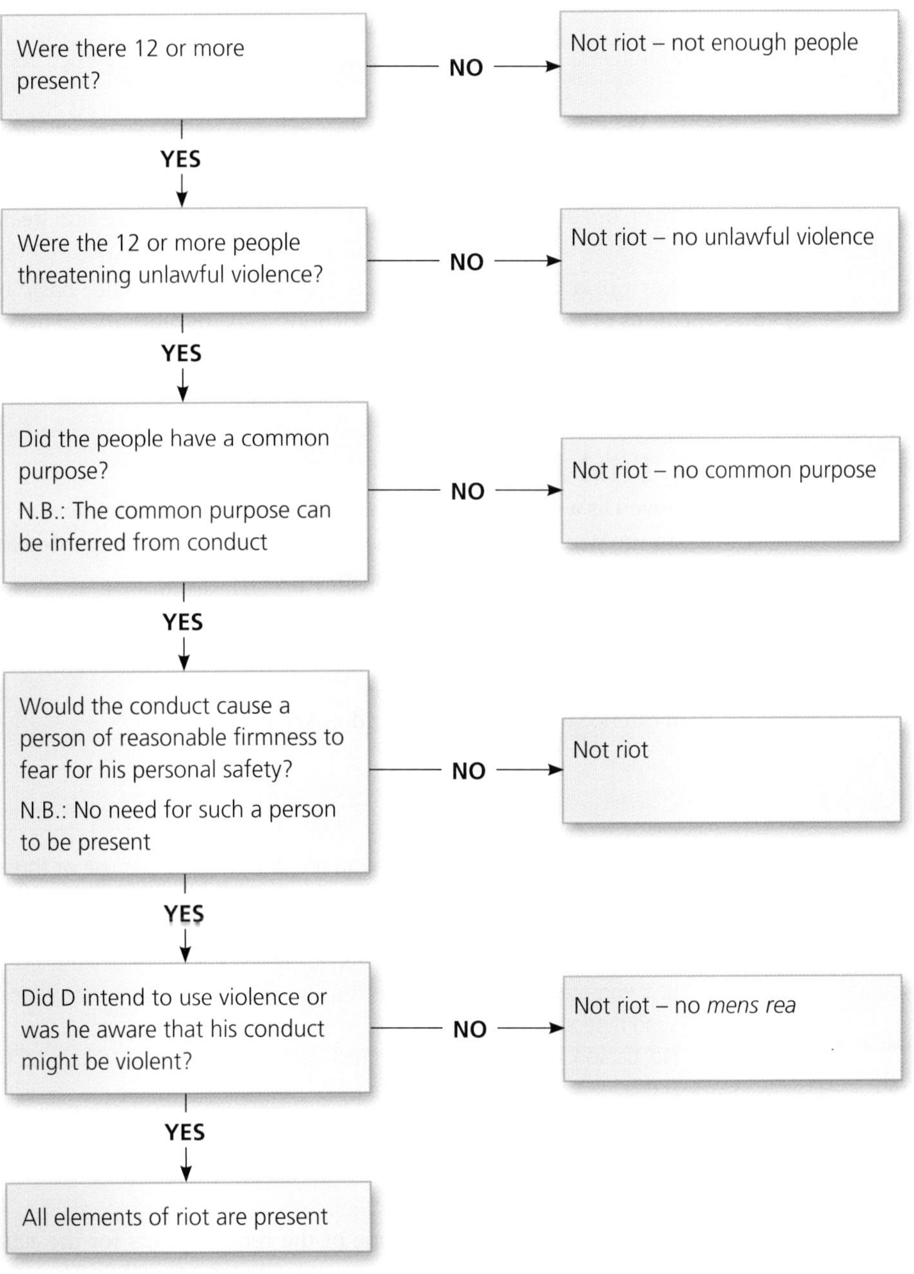

Were there 12 or more present?
NO
Not riot – not enough people
YES
Were the 12 or more people threatening unlawful violence?
NO
Not riot – no unlawful violence
YES
Did the people have a common purpose?
N.B.: The common purpose can be inferred from conduct
NO
Not riot – no common purpose
YES
Would the conduct cause a person of reasonable firmness to fear for his personal safety?
N.B.: No need for such a person to be present
NO
Not riot
YES
Did D intend to use violence or was he aware that his conduct might be violent?
NO
Not riot – no *mens rea*
YES
All elements of riot are present

Figure 17.1 Flow chart on riot.

So from this it can be seen that intention or 'awareness' is the mental element. Intention has the normal meaning in criminal law. However, awareness is a new concept. It has some similarity to *Cunningham* (1957) recklessness (see Chapter 3, section 3.3) as it is a partly subjective test: the defendant must be aware that his conduct may be violent. But it is not fully subjective as it does not require the defendant to be aware that it is unreasonable to take the risk that his conduct may be considered violent or threatening.

Section 6 also has a subsection specifically on the effect of intoxication on a defendant's *mens rea*. Section 6(5) states that:

SECTION

'6(5) For the purposes of this section a person whose awareness is impaired by intoxication shall be taken to be aware of that which he would be aware if not intoxicated, unless he shows either that his intoxication was not self-induced or that it was caused solely by the taking or administration of a substance in the course of medical treatment.'

This makes riot a basic intent offence. However, unlike other basic intent offences, it puts the onus of proving that the intoxication was involuntary on the defendant.

Intoxication is defined in s 6(6) as 'any intoxication, whether caused by drink, drugs or other means, or by a combination of means'.

17.1.3 Trial and penalty

Riot is viewed as a serious offence and has to be tried on indictment at the Crown Court. The maximum penalty is imprisonment for ten years. Riot is regarded as serious because there is criminal behaviour by a large group of persons.

17.2 Violent disorder

This is an offence under s 2 Public Order Act 1986:

SECTION

'2(1) Where three or more persons who are present together use or threaten unlawful violence and the conduct of them (taken together) is such as would cause a person of reasonable firmness present at the scene to fear for his personal safety, each of the persons using or threatening unlawful violence is guilty of violent disorder.

(2) It is immaterial whether or not the three or more use or threaten unlawful violence simultaneously.

(3) No person of reasonable firmness need actually be, or likely to be, present at the scene.

(4) Violent disorder may be committed in private as well as public places.'

17.2.1 Present together

As can be seen from s 2(1) above, one of the requirements for the *actus reus* of violent disorder is that three or more persons must be present together. The meaning of 'present together' was considered in *NW* [2010] EWCA Crim 404.

CASE EXAMPLE

NW [2010] EWCA Crim 404

A friend of NW dropped litter and was asked to pick it up by a police officer. The friend did pick it up but then dropped it again. The police officer asked her to pick it up again and when she failed to do so, the police officer took hold of her arm. NW intervened and held on to her friend's jacket. The incident escalated into violence with NW using violence towards the police, and a crowd gathering some of whom also threatened or used violence towards the police. The defendant and two others were charged with violent disorder and convicted.

On appeal, the defence argued that although there did not need to be a common purpose, there must be some degree of conscious participation or cooperation with others or at least some foresight that more widespread disorder might result from his or her actions. The Court of Appeal rejected this argument and held that the offence was committed when three persons were present threatening or using violence. The expression 'present together' meant no more than being in the same place at the same time. They pointed out that three or more people threatening or using violence in the same place at the same time is a daunting prospect for other people who may be there. It makes no difference whether the threat or use of violence is for the same purpose or a different purpose. The court also pointed out that ss 1 (riot), 2 (violent disorder) and 3 (affray) in the Public Order Act 1986 were all aimed at public disorder of a kind which would cause ordinary people at the scene to fear for their safety.

The decision in *NW* (2010) stresses the fact that no common purpose is needed for the offence of violent disorder.

17.2.2 *Mens rea* of violent disorder

Under s 6(2) of the Public Order Act 1986, the *mens rea* required is that D intends to use or threaten violence or be aware that his conduct may be violent or threaten violence. The same rule on intoxication under s 6(5) of the Act that applies to riot also applies to violent disorder. So violent disorder is a basic intent offence. If D claims that the intoxication was involuntary, then the burden of proving this is on the defendant.

17.2.3 Comparison with riot

tutor tip

'Make sure that you understand the difference between riot, violent disorder and affray.'

Most of the elements are the same as for riot. The similarities are the following:

- The people must be present together.
- They must use or threaten unlawful violence so that their conduct would cause a person of reasonable firmness present at the scene to fear for his personal safety.
- The violence can be to a person or to property.
- It can be in either a public or a private place.
- There must be intention to use violence or awareness by D that his conduct may be violent. This is specifically stated in s 6(2) of the Act.
- Section 6(5) applies to both riot and violent disorder, so violent disorder is also a basic intent offence and D has to prove that any intoxication was involuntary.

The differences are:

- There need only be three people involved (although it can be charged where there is a greater number of persons involved – even where there are 12 or more).
- There is no need for a common purpose.

17.2.4 Trial and penalty

Violent disorder is regarded as less serious than riot. It is intended to be used where fewer people are involved or for less serious happenings of public disorder. This can be seen by the fact that it is triable either way (though in most cases it is tried on indictment). Where it is tried on indictment, the maximum penalty is imprisonment for five years.

17.3 Affray

This is an offence under s 3 Public Order Act 1986:

SECTION

'3(1) A person is guilty of affray if he uses or threatens unlawful violence towards another and his conduct is such as would cause a person of reasonable firmness present at the scene to fear for his personal safety.

(2) If two or more persons use or threaten unlawful violence, it is the conduct of them taken together that must be considered for the purposes of subsection (1).

(3) For the purposes of this section a threat cannot be made by the use of words alone.

(4) No person of reasonable firmness need actually be, or likely to be, present at the scene.

(5) Affray may be committed in private as well as public places.'

17.3.1 *Actus reus* of affray

For this offence there has to be:

- use or threat of violence towards another person; and
- conduct which would cause a reasonable person present at the scene to fear for his safety.

Use or threat of violence towards another person

There must be someone present at the scene, as the use or threat of unlawful violence must be against a person. (This is different from riot and violent disorder.) The point was decided in *I, M and H v DPP* [2001] UKHL 10.

CASE EXAMPLE

I, M and H v DPP [2001] UKHL 10

All three Ds were members of a gang. They had armed themselves with petrol bombs which they intended to use against a rival gang. Before the rival gang came on the scene, the police arrived, and the group (including the three Ds) threw away their petrol bombs and dispersed. The stipendiary magistrate found that there was no one present apart from the police. There was no threat to the police because the moment they arrived, the gang dispersed. The House of Lords quashed their conviction, as affray can only be committed where the threat was directed towards another person or persons actually present at the scene.

Lord Hutton in his judgment pointed out that the defendants should have been charged under s 1 of the Prevention of Crime Act 1953 or s 4 of the Explosive Substances Act 1883.

Conduct

The threat cannot be made by words alone, even if the words are very threatening and the tone of voice aggressive. There must be some conduct. In *Dixon* [1993] Crim LR 579, the Court of Appeal upheld D's conviction for affray where the police had been called to a domestic incident. When they got there D ran away, accompanied by his Alsatian-type dog. The police officers cornered him and he encouraged the dog to attack them. Two officers were bitten before extra police arrived, and D was arrested. Encouraging the dog to attack was held to be conduct.

Person of reasonable firmness

Section 3(4) states that it is not necessary for a person of reasonable firmness to have been at the scene. This point was illustrated in *Davison* [1992] Crim LR 31, where the police were called to a domestic incident. D waved an eight-inch knife at a police officer saying, 'I'll have you.' The Court of Appeal upheld his conviction for affray. It was not a question of whether the police officer feared for his personal safety. The test was whether a hypothetical person of reasonable firmness who was present at the scene would have feared for his personal safety.

The offence of affray is a public disorder offence designed for the protection of the bystander. In *R (on the application of Leeson) v DPP* [2010] EWHC 994 Admin, the court had to consider a purely domestic incident.

CASE EXAMPLE

R (on the application of Leeson) v DPP [2010] EWHC 994 Admin

D, who had a history of irrational behaviour, lived with V. D, while holding a knife, walked into the bathroom of their home where V was taking a bath. She was very calm and said 'I am going to kill you.' V did not believe that she would use the knife and easily disarmed her. The magistrates convicted D of affray on the basis that, although the chance of anyone arriving at the house while D was holding the knife was small, it could not be discounted. The Divisional Court allowed D's appeal as on the evidence they did not think that any bystander would have feared for his own safety.

In her judgment Rafferty J reviewed earlier cases, in particular the case of *Sanchez* [1996] Crim LR 527 where D had tried to attack her former boyfriend with a knife outside a block of flats. V deflected the blow and ran. The Court of Appeal quashed her conviction for affray as the violence was merely between the two individuals, and as it was outdoors in an open space, there was ample opportunity for any bystander to distance himself from the violence. Thus, there was no real possibility that any bystander would fear for his personal safety.

17.3.2 *Mens rea* of affray

The defendant is only guilty if he intends to use or threaten violence or is aware that his conduct may be violent or threaten violence. This is the same rule as for violent disorder (s 6(2) of the Act). Like riot and violent disorder, affray is also a basic intent offence, and the same rule also applies of the onus being on the defendant to prove that any intoxication was involuntary (s 6(5)).

17.3.3 Trial and penalty

Affray is triable either way, but it is usually tried summarily at a magistrates' court. If it is tried on indictment then the maximum penalty is three years' imprisonment.

KEY FACTS

Key facts on riot, violent disorder and affray

	Riot	Violent disorder	Affray
Public Order Act 1986	s 1	s 2	s 3
Number needed	12	3	1
Use or threaten alone (s 3(3))	Yes	Yes	Yes, but not words, unlawful violence
Common purpose required	Yes Can be inferred from conduct (s 1(3))	No	No
Can be in public place or in private	Yes (s 1(5))	Yes (s 2(4))	Yes (s 3(5))
Can include violent conduct towards property	Yes (s 8(a))	Yes (s 8(a))	No
Must intend violence or be aware conduct might be violent	Yes (s 6(1))	Yes (s 6(2))	Yes (s 6(2))

17.4 Fear or provocation of violence

Section 4 of the 1986 Act states:

SECTION

'4(1) A person is guilty of an offence if he:

(a) uses towards another person threatening, abusive or insulting words or behaviour, or

(b) distributes or displays to another person any writing, sign or other visible representation which is threatening, abusive or insulting, with intent to cause that person to believe that immediate unlawful violence will be used against him or another by any person, or to provoke the immediate use of unlawful violence by that person or another, or whereby that person is likely to believe that such violence will be used or it is likely that such violence will be provoked.

(2) An offence under this section may be committed in a public or private place, except that no offence is committed where the words or behaviour are used, or the writing, sign or other visible representation is distributed or displayed, by a person inside a dwelling and the other person is also inside that or another dwelling.'

This is a summary offence, triable only in a magistrates' court and carrying a maximum sentence of six months' imprisonment.

17.4.1 *Actus reus* of a s 4 offence

This offence can be committed in four different ways:

- using threatening, abusive or insulting words towards another person;

- using threatening, abusive or insulting behaviour towards another person;
- distributing to another person any writing, sign or other visible representation which is threatening, abusive or insulting;
- displaying to another person any writing, sign or other visible representation which is threatening, abusive or insulting.

The offence can be committed in a public or private place, but s 1(2) specifically excludes events that occur within a dwelling. In *Atkin v DPP* [1989] Crim LR 581, D used threatening words while in his own home. This could not be an offence under s 4 of the Act.

17.4.2 Threatening, abusive or insulting

The common element of the four ways of committing this offence is the phrase 'threatening, abusive or insulting'. These words are not defined in the Act, but they were previously used in the Public Order Act 1936. Cases on that Act held that these words should be given their ordinary meaning. In *Brutus v Cozens* [1972] 2 All ER 1297, it was even stated that it was not helpful to try to explain them by the use of synonyms or dictionary definitions, because 'an ordinary sensible man knows an insult when he sees or hears it'. In this case the House of Lords held that whether something was 'threatening, abusive or insulting' was a question of fact.

CASE EXAMPLE

Brutus v Cozens [1972] 2 All ER 1297

D made a protest about apartheid in South Africa by running onto the court during a tennis match at Wimbledon and blowing a whistle and distributing leaflets. The protest lasted about two or three minutes. The magistrates acquitted him of an offence under s 5 of the Public Order Act 1936 (since repealed) and found as a fact that his behaviour was not insulting. The House of Lords held that this finding of fact was not unreasonable and the acquittal could not therefore be challenged.

Although it was said that 'an ordinary sensible man knows an insult when he sees or hears it', there have been some convictions under s 4 which appear strange. In *Masterson v Holden* [1986] 3 All ER 39, intimate cuddling by two homosexual men in Oxford Street at 1:55 a.m. in the presence of two young men and two young women was held capable of being insulting.

17.4.3 Towards another person

Section 4(1)(a) provides that the threatening, abusive or insulting words must be towards another person. In *Atkin v DPP* (1989) it was held that this means 'in the presence of and in the direction of another person directly'. In *Atkin* (1989), D knew that a bailiff was in a car outside his house. He told customs officers who entered his house that if the bailiff came in, he was 'a dead un'. The bailiff was informed of this and felt threatened. However, because he was not present and the words were not used at him, D was not guilty.

17.4.4 *Mens rea* of s 4

Section 6(3) states:

SECTION

'6(3) A person is guilty of an offence under section 4 only if he intends his words or behaviour, or the writing sign or other visible representation, to be threatening, abusive or insulting, or is aware that it may be threatening, abusive or insulting.'

The first point is that D must intend, or be aware, that his words or behaviour towards the other person might be threatening, abusive or insulting. Then, for an offence under this section to be proved, it must also be shown that:

- D intends that the other person will believe that immediate unlawful violence will be used against him; or
- D intends to provoke the immediate use of unlawful violence by the other person; or
- the other person is likely to believe that immediate unlawful violence will be used against him; or
- it is likely to provoke the immediate use of unlawful violence.

If D carries out an attack, but does not intend V to be aware that D is about to use unlawful violence on V, then D cannot be guilty under s 4. This was the situation in *Hughes v DPP* [2012] EWHC 606 (Admin).

CASE EXAMPLE

Hughes v DPP [2012] EWHC 606 (Admin)

D approached V from V's right side and from slightly behind V. D struck V a violent blow to the side of V's head. V immediately fell down, unconscious. D's conviction for a s 4 offence was quashed as there was no evidence that D intended V to believe that immediate unlawful violence would be used against him. The way D approached V from slightly behind and the fact that D hit V without warning suggested that D's intention was to hit V before V knew what was happening. This did not show that D had the necessary *mens rea* for s 4.

17.5 Intentionally causing harassment, alarm or distress

Section 4A was added to the Public Order Act 1986 by the Criminal Justice and Public Order Act 1994. It creates a more serious version of the offence in s 5 of the 1986 Act, as D must act intending to cause harassment, alarm or distress. There are also similarities with s 4, as there must be:

- threatening, abusive or insulting words or behaviour or distribution or display of writing, sign or other visible representation which is threatening, abusive or insulting (although there can also be a charge where there is disorderly behaviour);
- this can be in a public or private place, but not a dwelling.

Section 4A states:

SECTION

'4A(1) A person is guilty of an offence if, with intent to cause a person harassment, alarm or distress, he

(a) uses threatening, abusive or insulting words or behaviour, or disorderly behaviour, or

(b) displays any writing, sign or other visible representation which is threatening, abusive or insulting, thereby causing that or another person harassment, alarm or distress.'

Like s 4, this is a summary offence triable only in a magistrates' court.

It must be proved both that D intended to cause a person harassment, alarm or distress and that D's behaviour did in fact cause someone harassment, alarm or distress. This was shown by *R v DPP* [2006] EWHC 1375 (Admin).

CASE EXAMPLE

R v DPP [2006] EWHC 1375 (Admin)

D, aged 12, was with his sister when she was arrested for criminal damage. D made masturbatory gestures towards the police and called them 'wankers'. One police officer, who was over six feet in height and weighed over 17 stones, arrested D, and he was charged with an offence contrary to s 4A. The officer gave evidence that he was not personally annoyed by D's behaviour but that he found it distressing that a boy of D's age was acting in such a manner. The Divisional Court quashed D's conviction as there was no evidence that D intended to cause real emotional disturbance or upset to the police officer. Also the Youth Court could not properly have concluded on the evidence of the police officer that he was distressed by D's behaviour.

In the consideration of the word 'distress' Toulson J stated:

JUDGMENT

'The word "distress" in section 4A takes its colour from its context. It is part of a trio of words: harassment, alarm or distress. They are expressed as alternatives, but in combination they give a sense of the mischief which the section is aimed at preventing. They are relatively strong words befitting an offence which may carry imprisonment or a substantial fine. I would hold that the word "distress" in this context requires emotional disturbance or upset. The statute does not attempt to define the degree required. It does not have to be grave but nor should the requirement be trivialised. There has to be something which amounts to real emotional disturbance or upset.'

In *Dehal v DPP* [2005] EWHC 2154 (Admin), it was held that there should be a threat to public order for a prosecution to be the method of dealing with behaviour. If not, then there could be a breach of the right to freedom of speech under art 10 of the European Convention on Human Rights.

CASE EXAMPLE

Dehal v DPP [2005] EWHC 2154 (Admin)

D entered a temple and placed a notice stating that the preacher at the temple was 'a hypocrite'. D was convicted of an offence under s 4A of the Public Order Act 1986. D argued that his right to freedom of expression was infringed by being prosecuted for his action. The Divisional Court quashed his conviction. They held that the criminal law should not be invoked unless the conduct amounted to such a threat to public order that it required the use of the criminal law and not merely the civil law.

Mens rea

For the *mens rea* of s 4A, D must intend to cause another person harassment, alarm or distress.

17.5.1 Defences

Section 4A(3) provides a specific defence to a charge under s 4A. This states that:

SECTION

'4A(3) It is a defence for the accused person to prove –

(a) that he was inside a dwelling and had no reason to believe that the words or behaviour used, or the writing, sign or other visible representation displayed would be heard or seen by a person outside that or any other dwelling, or

(b) that his conduct was reasonable.'

Note that the burden of proof is on the defendant.

The first point is that D must be in a 'dwelling'. Dwelling is defined in s 8 of the Act as 'any structure or part of a structure occupied as a person's home or as other living accommodation'. The dwelling can be separate or shared with others. In *R v Francis* (2007) *The Times*, 17 January 2007, D was charged with racially aggravated harassment under s 31(1)(b) of the Crime and Disorder Act 1998. For this offence it has to be shown that there has been a s 4A offence committed. The offence had taken place in a police cell, and the defence argued that there was no s 4A offence as a police cell was a 'dwelling' within the definition in s 8. The trial judge accepted this argument and ruled that the offence under s 4A had not been made out. The prosecution appealed against this ruling to the Court of Appeal. The Court of Appeal held that a police cell was not a home or living accommodation, and the judge had been wrong in his ruling.

Another case on the meaning of dwelling is *Le Vine v DPP* [2010] EWHC 1129 (Admin) where the incident took place in the communal laundry of a block of flats.

CASE EXAMPLE

Le Vine v DPP [2010] EWHC 1129 (Admin)

D and V were residents in separate self-contained flats in sheltered accommodation. All residents had the use of a communal lounge and a communal laundry room. A friend of D was using the washing machine when V entered the laundry room. V told D that she would come back to use the machine after it had finished its cycle. When V returned to the room she found it empty and the washing machine finished but the washing still in the machine. She removed that load of washing and put her own in. D came into the room and shouted at V saying she would knock her block off.

D was convicted of a s 4 offence. He appealed on the basis that the laundry room was part of a dwelling, and he therefore had a defence under s 4A(3).

The High Court upheld the conviction on the ground that the communal laundry was not occupied as part of D's home even though it had a domestic function.

In his judgment Elias LJ stated:

JUDGMENT

'In my judgment [the laundry] is a communal room shared by those who live in a number of homes within the building, but cannot be properly described as part of the structure of any individual home in this building ... The communal room is open to a number of persons. It is true it is limited to those who are in the flats or those connected with people in the flats, and to that extent it is only a small section of the public, but in my judgment the interpretation of the section I have given is compatible with a principle which is seeking to exclude disputes in people's homes, but not otherwise.'

For the defence to succeed, the defendant also has to prove that he had no reason to believe that his behaviour or words would be seen or heard by anyone outside the dwelling.

Alternatively, the defendant has to prove that his conduct was reasonable. It could be argued that this last requirement is difficult to fulfil as behaviour which is intended to cause harassment, alarm or distress is not likely to be reasonable.

17.6 Harassment, alarm or distress

Section 5 of the 1986 Act as amended by s 57 Crime and Courts Act 2013 provides that:

SECTION

'5(1) A person is guilty of an offence if he –

(a) uses threatening or abusive words or behaviour, or disorderly behaviour, or

(b) displays any writing, sign or other visible representation which is threatening or abusive, within the hearing or sight of a person likely to be caused harassment, alarm or distress thereby.'

The person who is likely to be caused harassment, alarm or distress can include a police officer who is called to deal with a domestic incident. This was shown in the case of *DPP v Orum* [1988] 3 All ER 449.

CASE EXAMPLE

DPP v Orum [1988] 3 All ER 449

D had an offensive and public argument with his girlfriend. The police intervened, and he was abusive to them. They arrested him for breach of the peace. When he was put in the back of a police van, he assaulted a police officer. He was charged with and found guilty of an offence under s 5 and assaulting a police officer in the execution of his duty.

The Divisional Court held that a police officer may be a person who is likely to be harassed, alarmed or distressed for the purpose of s 5(1).

In this case, the use of a public order offence seems inappropriate. There were other offences the defendant could have been charged with. Indeed, he was also charged, far more appropriately, with assaulting a police office in the execution of his duty.

In *Taylor v DPP* [2006] EWHC 1202 (Admin), it was held that proving there was someone near enough to hear the words was sufficient. It was not necessary to prove that any person actually heard. In *Taylor v DPP*, a police officer gave evidence that D had shouted, screamed and sworn using racist language. There were a number of people on the scene near enough to hear the abusive language. The Divisional Court held that this was sufficient to uphold D's conviction.

The words 'harassment, alarm or distress' are the same as in s 4A of the Public Order Act 1986. The Divisional Court considered the meaning of these words in *Southard v DPP* [2006] EWHC 3449 (Admin).

CASE EXAMPLE

Southard v DPP [2006] EWHC 3449 (Admin)

D and his brother were cycling with poor lighting at about midnight. They were stopped by the police. While his brother was being searched by one of the officers, D approached the officer twice and swore at him, interfering with the search process. D also took photos of the search on his phone saying, 'Don't fucking touch me, you can't touch him.' D was convicted of an offence under s 5 of the Public Order Act 1986.

On appeal the defence put forward several arguments. These included that the conduct had not occurred in the presence of a person 'likely' to be caused harassment by it as D's behaviour was of the sort which police often encountered and they were not likely to be caused harassment, alarm or distress by it. The defence also referred to the judgment in *R v DPP* [2006] EWHC 1375 (Admin) (see section 17.5) and pointed out that the court in that case had ruled that there had to be 'real emotional disturbance or upset' and that swearing at a police officer was unlikely to cause this. The police's reaction to such behaviour would be more likely to be 'mere irritation or annoyance'. The defence also argued that using the word 'fucking' twice could not amount to threatening, abusive or insulting words.

The Divisional Court rejected all these submissions and upheld the conviction.

Note: when this case was heard, in respect of the wording of s 4, the behaviour and/or words had to be 'threatening, abusive or insulting'. The word 'insulting' was removed by the Crime and Courts Act 2013.

When considering whether D's behaviour was 'likely to cause harassment', the court pointed out that the three words, 'harassment, alarm or distress' do not have the same meaning as each other. So, although the court agreed with Toulson J's analysis of what was required for distress (see *R v DPP* (2006) in section 17.5), it was not relevant in Southard's case as the allegation was that his behaviour had caused harassment. Fulford J said:

JUDGMENT

'Whilst I respectfully agreed with Toulson J's analysis of what is required in this regard for distress, I do not consider that the same applies to harassment. Distress by its very nature involves an element of real emotional disturbance or upset but the same is not necessarily true of harassment. You can be harassed, indeed seriously harassed, without experiencing emotional disturbance or upset at all. That said, although the harassment does not have to be grave, it should also not be trivial.'

In relation to the defence's submission that words such as 'fuck you' or 'fuck off' were not threatening, abusive or insulting, the Court stated that 'frequently though they may be used these days, we have not yet reached the stage where a court is required to conclude that those words are of such little significance that they no longer constitute abuse'.

This decision appears to make the offence very wide. Although the conduct was in the open, it was midnight and there were only the police and the two brothers present. D did not touch the officer, and, indeed, the other officer said that after D had sworn the first time he (the officer) had called him back. D had come back straightaway without causing any problem, and the officer then warned him about his language. A little later D had again gone towards the officer searching his brother and sworn at him the second time, and this was when he was arrested. Did this behaviour really go beyond 'trivial' harassment?

It is possible that the amendment of the act to remove the word 'insulting' may cause any future case to be viewed differently. However, as the judgment referred to 'abuse' rather than 'insulting', the decision may still stand.

The case of *Harvey* (2012) 176 JP 265 also involved D using swear words when speaking to the police, but in this case the High Court held that there was no evidence of the language causing harassment, alarm or distress.

CASE EXAMPLE

Harvey (2012) 176 JP 265

Two police officers stopped and searched a group of people including D, whom they suspected were in possession of cannabis. D objected to the search, saying, 'Fuck this man, I ain't been smoking nothing.' The officer warned him about his language stating that he would charge him with a s 5 offence if he continued. No drugs were found on D, whereupon he said, 'Told you, you won't find fuck all.' D was again warned about his swearing. The officer carried out a name search and asked D for his middle name. D replied 'No, I have already fucking told you so.' D was charged with a s 5 offence and found guilty at the magistrates' court. The High Court allowed his appeal as no evidence had been given that the officers had been caused harassment, alarm or distress.

The difference between the cases of *Southard* and *Harvey* is purely on the evidence given. In *Southard* the police stated that D's language and behaviour had caused them harassment, while in *Harvey* no evidence on this point was given at the trial. Swearing is not a crime in itself, but if the language causes harassment, alarm or distress, then a s 5 offence is committed.

In *Harvey* only the police and the rest of D's group were present and the judge pointed out that it was highly unlikely that the young people in the vicinity had experienced harassment, alarm or distress by hearing such commonplace swear words. Had there been evidence that other members of the public were within earshot, then there might have been a possible basis for inferring harassment, alarm or distress.

17.6.1 Defences

As with a s 4A offence, there are special defences. For this section these (set out in s 5(3)) are that:

(a) D had no reason to believe that there was any person within sight who was likely to be caused harassment, alarm or distress; or

(b) he was inside a dwelling and had no reason to believe that the words or behaviour used, or the writing, sign or other visible representation displayed would be heard or seen by a person outside that or any other dwelling; or

(c) his conduct was reasonable.

The defences at (a) and (c) were considered in the case of *Gough v DPP* [2013] EWHC 3267 (Admin).

CASE EXAMPLE

Gough v DPP [2013] EWHC 3267 (Admin)

For some ten years D had walked naked (wearing only socks, walking boots and a hat) throughout many places in the United Kingdom. On this occasion he walked naked through the town centre of Halifax. His attitude was that being naked was a natural state and being naked was not indecent. He was charged and found guilty of an offence under s 5(1) of the Public Order Act 1986. Among the issues on appeal were (1) whether he had a defence to the charge as he had no reason to believe that there was any person within sight who was likely to be caused harassment, alarm or distress and/or (2) that his conduct was reasonable. The appeal was rejected as D knew from previous occasions that many members of the public would be both alarmed and distressed by the sight of his naked body.

D also raised the issue that, under art 10 of the European Convention on Human Rights, he had the right to freedom of expression and that going about naked was a form of that expression. The court held that, although he had the right to freedom of expression, the restriction of this right imposed by s 5 corresponded to social need. As s 5 was only a level 3 summary offence with a maximum fine of £1,000 the restriction was proportionate.

17.6.2 *Mens rea* of a s 5 offence

Under s 6(4) of the Act, D can only be guilty if he intends his words or behaviour, or the writing, sign or other visible representation, to be threatening or abusive, or is aware that it may be threatening or abusive or (as the case may be) he intends his behaviour to be or is aware that it may be disorderly.

Figure 17.2 summarises the offences under ss 4, 4A and 5.

17.7 Racially aggravated public order offences

Section 31 of the Crime and Disorder Act 1998 created racially aggravated versions of the offences under s 4, s 4A and s 5 of the Public Order Act 1986.

These involve the offences above committed in the special circumstances set out in s 28 of the Crime and Disorder Act 1998. These are that

- at the time of committing the offence, or immediately before or after doing so, the offender demonstrates towards the victim of the offence hostility based on the victim's membership (or presumed membership) of a racial group; or
- the offence is motivated (wholly or in part) by hostility towards members of a racial group based on their membership of that group.

It is clear that if a defendant uses words identifying specific nationalities or races, then this can make the offence an aggravated one within the definition of s 28. It has also been held that more general words such as 'foreigners' or 'immigrants' come within the scope of s 28.

Public Order Act s 4, s 4A and s 5

s 4 Fear or provocation of violence	s 4A Intentional harassment, alarm or distress	s 5 Harassment, alarm or distress
(a) uses threatening, abusive or insulting words or behaviour *or* (b) distributes or displays anything threatening, abusive or insulting *and* with intent to cause fear of violence or to provoke violence	a) uses threatening, abusive or insulting words or behaviour or disorderly behaviour *or* (b) distributes or displays anything threatening, abusive or insulting *and* intends to cause a person harassment, alarm or distress	a) uses threatening or abusive words or behaviour or disorderly behaviour *or* (b) distributes or displays anything threatening or abusive *and* within the hearing or sight of a person likely to be caused harassment, alarm or distress

Figure 17.2 Sections 4, 4A and 5 of the Public Order Act 1986.

CASE EXAMPLE

Rogers (Philip) [2007] UKHL 8

D encountered three Spanish women. D, who was using a mobility scooter, called them 'bloody foreigners' and told them to go back to their own country. He then pursued them to a kebab house in an aggressive manner. He was convicted of using racially aggravated abusive or insulting words contrary to s 31(1)(a) of the Crime and Disorder Act 1998. He appealed on the basis that his words were not capable of demonstrating hostility based on membership of a racial group. 'Foreigners' did not constitute a racial group as defined in s 28(4) of the Act. The Court of Appeal certified the question 'Do those who are not of British origin constitute a racial group within s 28(4) of the Crime and Disorder Act 1998?'.

The House of Lords answered this question 'Yes' and upheld his conviction. They held that a racial group within the definition of s 28(4) did not have to be distinguished by particular racial characteristics. The definition was sufficiently wide to embrace within a single racial group all those who were 'foreign'.

The House of Lords referred to the judgment of the Divisional Court in *DPP v M (minor)* [2004] EWHC 1453 (Admin); [2004] 1 WLR 2758 where D had used the same phrase 'bloody foreigners' and the Divisional Court had decided that this was capable of describing a racial group. They also referred to the decision in *Attorney-General's Reference (No 4 of 2004)* [2005] EWCA Crim 889; [2005] 2 Cr App R 26 where the Court of Appeal held that using the words 'an immigrant doctor' was capable of demonstrating hostility based on the doctor's membership of a racial group.

Wholly or in part

The offence can be motivated wholly or in part by hostility based on race or religion. In *DPP v Johnson* [2008] All ER (D) 371 (Feb), the fact that the offence was motivated only in part by the racial origin of V was held to be sufficient for D to be guilty of an offence.

CASE EXAMPLE

DPP v Johnson [2008] All ER (D) 371 (Feb)

D walked towards two parking attendants who were checking on cars. He said to them 'leave us alone, you're always picking on us up here'. He then went on to say 'why don't you get up ... with your white uncles and aunties'. He was convicted of an offence contrary to s 5 Public Order Act and the conviction upheld by the Divisional Court. They held it did not matter that D's conduct was also motivated partly by the fact that Vs were parking attendants. The hostility was partly based on membership or presumed membership of a racial group and that was sufficient for D to be guilty of the offence.

SUMMARY

Riot (s 1 POA 1986) is where 12 or more persons present together use or threaten unlawful violence for a common purpose. The conduct must be such as would cause a person of reasonable firmness to fear for his personal safety, but no such person need actually be present. D has to intend to use violence or be aware that his conduct may be violent.

Violent Disorder (s 2 POA 1986) is where three or more persons present together use or threaten unlawful violence. The conduct must be such as would cause a person of reasonable firmness to fear for his personal safety, but no such person need actually be present. D has to intend to use or threaten violence or be aware that his conduct may be violent or threaten violence.

Affray (s 3 POA 1986) is where a person sues or threatens unlawful violence, and this conduct would cause a person of reasonable firmness to fear for his personal safety, but no such person need actually be present, although there must be some other person at the scene. D has to intend to use or threaten violence, or be aware that his conduct may be violent or threaten violence.

Fear or provocation of violence (s 4 POA 1986)
For the *actus reus* D must:

- use threatening, abusive or insulting words towards another person; or
- use threatening, abusive or insulting behaviour towards another person; or
- distribute to another person any writing, sign or other visible representation which is threatening, abusive or insulting; or
- display to another person any writing, sign or other visible representation which is threatening, abusive or insulting.

For the *mens rea* D must intend his words or behaviour, or the writing sign or other visible representation, to be threatening, abusive or insulting, or be aware that it may be threatening, abusive or insulting.

Intentionally causing harassment, alarm or distress (s 4A POA 1986)
For the *actus reus* D must:

- use threatening, abusive or insulting words or behaviour, or disorderly behaviour; or

- display any writing, sign or other visible representation which is threatening, abusive or insulting;
- thereby causing that or another person harassment, alarm or distress.

For the *mens rea* D must intend to cause another person harassment, alarm or distress. There is a special defence that D was inside a dwelling and had no reason to believe that his words or act would be seen or heard by anyone else or that his conduct was reasonable.

Harassment, alarm or distress (s 5 POA 1986)
For the *actus reus* D must:

- use threatening or abusive words or behaviour, or disorderly behaviour; or
- display any writing, sign or other visible representation which is threatening or abusive;
- within the hearing or sight of a person likely to be caused harassment, alarm or distress thereby.

For the *mens rea* D must intend his words or behaviour, or the writing, sign or other visible representation, to be threatening or abusive, or is aware that it may be threatening or abusive or disorderly.

Special defences are that D:

- had no reason to believe that there was any person within sight who was likely to be caused harassment, alarm or distress; or
- that he was inside a dwelling and had no reason to believe that the words or behaviour used, or the writing, sign or other visible representation displayed would be heard or seen by a person outside that or any other dwelling; or
- that his conduct was reasonable.

Racially aggravated public order offences
Section 31 of the Crime and Disorder Act 1998 creates racially aggravated versions of the offences under s 4, s 4A and s 5 of the Public Order Act 1986. An offence is racially aggravated if:

- at the time of committing the offence, or immediately before or after doing so, the offender demonstrates towards the victim of the offence hostility based on the victim's membership (or presumed membership) of a racial group; or
- the offence is motivated (wholly or in part) by hostility towards members of a racial group based on their membership of that group.

ACTIVITY

Self-test questions

1. Explain the differences between riot and violent disorder.
2. What is unusual about the effect of s 6(5) of the Public Order Act 1986?
3. Explain the rules on what has to be proved about the presence and/or effect on a person of reasonable firmness in the offence of affray.
4. Is the fact that riot, violent disorder and affray can be committed in private satisfactory?
5. Why is the offence under s 4A of the Public Order Act 1986 regarded as more serious than the offence under s 4 of the same Act?

ACTIVITY

Applying the law

Explain what offences, if any, have been committed in the following situation.

Sonya and Tex are against the use of animals for testing drugs. They agree to demonstrate outside a local drugs company who use animals for this purpose. They have a banner which reads 'Death to those who do tests on animals'. They stand outside the entrance to the company holding up this banner and shouting. Wilbur and Zoe, who have been drinking, see them and think that it will be amusing to join the protest. They stand opposite Sonya and Tex, shouting and making it difficult for workers to get past them on their way into work.

SAMPLE ESSAY QUESTION

Public order offences must maintain a balance between maintaining public order while protecting human rights. Discuss.

Briefly set out the main public order offences (POA 1986):

s 1 Riot
s 2 Violent disorder
s 3 Affray
s 4 Fear or provocation of violence
s 5 Intentionally causing harassment, alarm or distress
s 6 Harassment, alarm or distress

Discuss how such offences are important in maintaining public order and include such points as:

- Violent behaviour whether by a group or an individual must be discouraged
- Unlawful violence is justifiably criminalised
- Innocent people need to be protected from threatening behaviour

Explain key human rights which can be affected by public order offences:

- Right to liberty
- Freedom of association
- Freedom of expression

Discuss how public order offences may interfere with such rights: include points such as:

- Arrest for an alleged offence interferes with liberty
- The offences carry a potential custodial sentence
- Freedom of association is curtailed by s 1 and s 2, though only if there is unlawful violence
- Freedom of expression is curtailed by s 4, s 5 and s 6

Consider and discuss whether a balance between public order and human rights exists:

Refer to cases such as
I, M and H v DPP (2001)
R v DPP (2006)
Dehal v DPP (2005)
Taylor v DPP (2006)
Southard v DPP (2006)

Conclude

Further reading

Articles

Hare, I, 'Legislating against hate: the legal response to bias crimes' (1997) 17 OJLS 415.

Newman, C J, 'Racially aggravated public order offence: motivation of racial remark an absence of a victim' (2009) 173 JP 88.

Thompson, K and Parpworth, N, 'Flag desecration: an offence under s 5 of the Public Order Act 1986?' (2002) 166 JPN 220.

Appendix 1

Problem-solving questions

The following scenarios require you to apply the law from different areas:

1. Annika and Britney are the directors of a small company, Bustit Ltd, which is unable to pay its debts. Annika and Britney decide to spend the weekend in a luxury hotel to discuss the financial problems. The hotel reservations are made by the company secretary. After reviewing the company accounts, Annika and Britney leave the hotel without paying the bill.

Consider the criminal liability, if any, of Annika, Britney and Bustit Ltd.

2. Craig and Del are next-door neighbours and workmates. Some of Craig's work tools, including a powerdrill, have gone missing and he suspects that Del has taken them. One evening, when Del is out, Craig enters Del's garden and goes into a garden shed to look for his possessions. He finds two screwdrivers which he mistakenly believes are his and takes them. He also finds a powerdrill which he suspects is his. He decides to teach Del a lesson and he alters the wiring in the drill so that it will give Del an electric shock when he next uses it. In fact the two screwdrivers and the powerdrill are Del's own.

   The next day Del lends the powerdrill to a friend, Elmer. When Elmer switches the drill on, he gets a massive electric shock which kills him.

Discuss the criminal liability, if any, of Craig.

3. Fiona meets a friend, Grant. Fiona knows that Grant is a drug dealer and has convictions for violence. Grant threatens Fiona that he will 'mark' her two-year-old son unless Fiona agrees to take some crack cocaine to another friend, Hayley and bring back £200 which Hayley owes Grant. Fiona reluctantly agrees to do this. She goes to Hayley's house and tells her she has the cocaine for her, but that she must have the £200 before she will hand it over. Hayley refuses to give her the money, so Fiona grabs Hayley's purse from her hand. Hayley tries to stop her and Fiona pushes her hard, causing her to fall and cut her head.

Discuss the criminal liability, if any, of Fiona.

4. Ian's car has broken down on a country road. He finds that he has left his mobile phone at home, so he decides to walk to a cottage which he had passed a mile back down the road to get help. When he gets to the cottage he knocks on the door, but no one answers. Ian can see that there is a telephone in the hallway and so he uses a penknife to open a window catch and climbs into the house. He phones a local garage who say they cannot come out for at least an hour. As it is cold, Ian decides to wait in the house and make himself a cup of tea. When he is sitting in the kitchen, the householder, Jamal, returns. Jamal sees Ian's penknife with the blade open on the table and, thinking Ian will attack him, Jamal seizes the knife. Ian tries to stop him and both Ian and Jamal suffer cuts to their hands. Ian then pushes Jamal away from him, causing Jamal to hit his head on a shelf. Jamal falls to the floor, unconscious. Ian runs out of the house, leaving Jamal there. Jamal suffers bleeding to the brain. He is not discovered for two days and dies as a result.

Discuss the criminal liability, if any, of Ian.

5. Kate and her friend, Lennox, decide to demonstrate against the visit of a foreign politician from a country in which there are human rights abuses. They stand silently outside a hotel where he is staying. After half an hour Malcolm, who has been watching them, starts shouting abuse at them. Kate and Lennox ignore this to start with but when Malcolm starts making racist remarks about Lennox, Kate rushes at him and threatens to hit him. Two women who are walking past are afraid that there will be a fight.

Discuss the criminal liability, if any, of Kate, Lennox and Malcolm.

6. Naomi, Olga and Peter are drug addicts. At Olga's flat Naomi fills a syringe with heroin and gives it first to Olga who injects herself. Naomi then injects herself and then hands the empty syringe to Peter who refills it and injects himself. Naomi is HIV positive but does not tell Peter, nor warn him not to use the needle she has just used. All three lapse into unconsciousness after taking the heroin. When Naomi and Peter come round they realise that Olga's breathing is very bad and they cannot rouse her. They both leave the flat, leaving Olga still unconscious. Olga is found dead the next day. Some weeks later, Peter discovers that he is HIV positive.

Discuss what offences, if any, have been committed by Naomi.

7. Robert belongs to a teenage gang. One day they all decide to 'see off' a rival gang. Fourteen of them arm themselves with sticks and drive to a street where they know the other gang often meet. They park their vehicles and join up at the end of the street. Before they can start walking down the road, they see a police car coming towards them. They all drop their sticks and run away.

Discuss what criminal offences, if any, have been committed.

Appendix 2

How to answer questions

When studying law you will be expected to write essays and you will also have to apply the law in legal problems based on scenarios. This appendix gives some hints on the skills you need for both of these.

Legal problem solving

There are four essential ingredients to answering problem questions. You need to:

1. Identify the important facts in the questions and from these identify the area of law you need to apply.
2. Define the area of law.
3. Expand your definition including relevant sections and cases to show that you know and understand the area of law thoroughly.
4. Apply the law to the problem and reach a conclusion.

The initial letters of this list give IDEA: a simple idea to remember!

Consider the following situation.

Ella and Gary agree to steal electrical goods from a local shop. Ella takes a car belonging to her next-door neighbour without the owner's permission, so that the number plate cannot be traced to either Ella or Gary. She drives Gary to the shop and waits around the corner in the car while he goes in.

In the shop Gary takes a basket and selects several expensive small items, placing them in the basket. He notices that only two check-outs are staffed and he goes to one of the empty check-outs at the far end of the line. He leans into the cashier's area and tries to open the till, but is unable to do so. Unknown to him, the till has just been emptied. As he is doing this, a store attendant notices him and walks over to the till. Gary runs out of the shop and is chased by the store attendant, who catches him. Gary punches the man hard in the face, breaking his jaw. Gary then runs round the corner and jumps into the car. He shouts at Ella to drive off fast. Ella does this but a mile down the road she loses control of the car and it crashes into a barrier. Gary and Ella get out of the car and run off.

Answering the question

Identifying the facts

The tutor or examiner who sets the question will make sure that most of the facts are relevant. So work your way through, looking at what both Ella and Gary do. Where there are two or more people involved in the criminal activity it is often easier to tackle one person at a time. So, starting with Gary, the main facts are:

1. an agreement to steal;
2. being a passenger in a car which has been taken without the owner's consent;
3. places items in a basket provided by the store and eventually leaves the store without paying for these;
4. leans into the cashier's area and tries to open a till;
5. assaults the store attendant who is chasing him;
6. encourages Ella to drive fast.

From these, now identify the areas of law involved. Some of them are very clear from writing down these facts.

1. Wherever there is an agreement to do a criminal act, the law on conspiracy is relevant.
2. Being a passenger in a car which has been taken without the owner's consent brings s 12 of the Theft Act 1968 into play.
3. For the goods in the shop the offence of theft (s 1 Theft Act 1968) is relevant.
4. Trying to open the till makes the law on attempt relevant. Also, as he has leaned into the cashier's area, consider burglary as a possibility.
5. The assault is an offence against the person, but it is also linked to the theft so robbery must also be considered.
6. Is there participation by encouraging dangerous driving?

Having identified the areas of law you must now explain them in more detail, especially where there is some doubt on the point. So now look at the relevant law in detail and apply it.

1. Conspiracy

The definition of 'conspiracy' is in s 1 of the Criminal Law Act 1977: agreeing a course of conduct which will necessarily amount to or involve the commission of an offence by one or more of the parties to the agreement. The agreement to commit theft is clearly within this definition of 'conspiracy'.

2. Section 12

Under s 12 of the Theft Act 1968 it is an offence to allow oneself to be carried in a conveyance knowing that it has been taken without the consent of the owner. The scenario does not state whether Gary knew that Ella had taken the car without her neighbour's consent. If he does (and this includes where he wilfully shuts his eyes to the obvious), he is guilty of this offence. If he does not then he is not guilty of the offence.

3. Theft

The definition of 'theft' is in s 1 of the Theft Act 1968: dishonestly appropriating property belonging to another with the intention of permanently depriving that other of it. The only point for discussion in this scenario is exactly when the appropriation took place. This is at the point when Gary puts the goods in the basket: *Morris* [1983] 3 All ER 288, *Gomez* [1993] 1 All ER 1.

4. (a) Attempted theft

The Criminal Attempts Act 1981 s 1(1) defines an attempt as where 'with intent to commit an offence a person does an act which is more than merely preparatory to the commission of the offence'. As Gary has tried to open the till, this is clearly more than merely preparatory. However, there is nothing in the till so the law on attempting the impossible must be considered. Under s 1(2) of the Criminal Attempts Act 1981 a person may be guilty of attempting to commit an offence even though the facts are such that the commission of the offence is impossible. This subsection makes Gary guilty of attempted theft even though there is nothing in the till to steal.

(b) Burglary

Under s 9(1)a of the Theft Act 1968 one of the ways of committing burglary is where the defendant enters as a trespasser with intent to commit theft. Has Gary entered as a trespasser? He intends to steal, so is going beyond the purpose for which he is permitted to enter: *Smith and Jones* [1976] 3 All ER 54. He therefore enters as a trespasser. Also, he has leaned into a private area of the shop where shoppers do not have permission to go. In *Walkington* [1979] 2 All ER 716 the defendant was held guilty of burglary where he walked behind the counter in a shop and opened the till. To be a trespasser there must be effective entry. Is leaning in an effective entry? *Brown* [1994] 1 AC 212 was guilty of burglary by leaning through a window, so by analogy Gary is likely to be guilty.

5. (a) Assault

Under s 47 of the Offences Against the Person Act 1861 it is an offence to occasion actual bodily harm; under s 20 it is an offence to inflict grievous bodily harm; under s 18 it is an offence to cause grievous bodily harm with intent to do so. Applying this to the punch by which Gary breaks the store attendant's jaw, at the least Gary is guilty of s 47. The points for discussion are: is a broken jaw capable of being grievous bodily harm and, if so, has Gary the necessary *mens rea* for s 18?

(b) Robbery

Section 8 of the Theft Act 1968 says that robbery is committed where a person steals, and immediately before or at the time of doing so, and in order to do so, he uses force on any person or puts or seeks to put any person in fear of being then and there subjected to force. The points which need exploring are whether the force was 'at the time' of the theft and was it used 'in order to' steal. In *Hale* [1979] Crim LR 596 it was held that the act of appropriation can be a continuing one, so that any force used in order to steal while the appropriation is continuing would make this robbery. This contrasts with *Gomez* (1993) where it was decided that the point of appropriation in theft is when D first does an act assuming a right of the owner. So which decision should be applied to Gary? A similar situation to Gary's occurred in *Lockley* [1995] Crim LR 656 where D was caught shoplifting cans of beer from an off-licence and used force on the shopkeeper who was trying to stop him from escaping. In that case the Court of Appeal rejected an argument that *Gomez* (1993) had impliedly overruled *Hale* and confirmed that the principle in *Hale* (1979) still applied in robbery. As Gary has left the shop before he uses force the *Hale* principle is not likely to apply.

6. Participation

To be a secondary party the defendant must 'aid, abet', counsel or procure' the commission of an offence (s 8 Accessories and Abettors Act 1861). Abetting has been held to be any conduct which instigates, incites or encourages the commission of the offence, including shouting encouragement or paying for a ticket for an illegal performance as in *Wilcox v Jeffrey* [1951] 1 All ER 464. As Gary shouts encouragement, this could make him liable as a secondary party for any offence of dangerous driving committed by Ella as principal.

Now move on to consider Ella. The relevant facts for Ella are:

1. an agreement to steal;
2. takes a car without consent of the owner;
3. getaway driver for Gary;
4. drives too fast, crashes car.

The first point on conspiracy has already been identified and dealt with under Gary. The same law will apply to Ella. For the other points the areas of law which need to be identified are s 12 taking a conveyance without consent (and possibly theft of the car), secondary participation in the theft from the shop, the burglary, assault and robbery and, finally, aggravated vehicle-taking through the possibility of dangerous driving and/or the damage to the car.

1. Section 12 Theft Act 1968

Section 12 makes a person guilty of an offence if, without having the consent of the owner or other lawful authority, he takes any conveyance for his own or another's use. The only possible point for discussion is whether Ella believed she would have her neighbour's consent, giving a defence under s 12(6) which states that 'a person does not commit an offence under this section by anything done in the belief that he has lawful authority to do it or that he would have the owner's consent if the owner knew of his doing it and the circumstances of it'. However, it is highly unlikely that consent would be given to use the car to commit a crime.

2. Theft of car

Theft requires that there is an intention permanently to deprive the owner. Applying this to the scenario, it is unlikely that Ella has committed theft.

3. Secondary participation

As already stated in relation to Gary, to be a secondary party it is necessary to prove that D aided, abetted, counselled or procured the commission of an offence (s 8 Accessories and Abettors Act 1861). Aiding is giving help, support or assistance. This can be before the offence or during the time it is being committed, for example acting as look-out, as in *Betts and Ridley* (1930) 22 Cr App R 148. By driving Gary to the shop and waiting outside as getaway driver, Ella is a secondary participant in the theft of the goods in the shop. The point which needs more detailed examination is whether she is also a secondary participant in the burglary, the assault or the robbery.

In *Chan Wing-Siu* [1985] 1 AC 168 and also in *Powell* [1999] AC 1; (1997) 4 All ER 545; [1997] UKHL 45 it was held that contemplation or foresight that the principal might commit a certain type of offence is sufficient to a make a secondary party liable for the offence committed by the principal offender. Ella knows that Gary is going to steal so clearly she is a secondary party to that. Is burglary sufficiently close to be within the range of possible offences, as in *Maxwell v DPP of Northern Ireland* [1978] 1 WLR 1350? Almost certainly. However, the plan did not involve any violence. Ella can only be liable as a secondary party for these if she contemplated or foresaw that Gary might use violence if he was challenged by anyone in the shop. So, if she knows he has used violence in such situations in the past she may be a secondary party to both the assault and robbery.

4. Aggravated vehicle-taking

Finally, Ella crashed the car, bringing in aggravated vehicle-taking (s 12A Theft Act 1968). Under s 12A the basic offence must be committed plus an aggravating factor. Two of these factors are that the vehicle was driven dangerously on a road or other public place, or that damage was caused to the vehicle. The test for 'dangerous' is objective, in that 'the driving must fall far below what would be expected of a competent and careful driver' and that 'it would be obvious to a competent and careful driver that driving the vehicle in that way would be dangerous'. Discuss Ella losing control of the car because of excessive speed in the light of these tests.

General hints

Where the potential defendant is involved in more than one situation, make a list of the relevant facts. Where there is more than one person's criminal liability involved, always make a list of the facts relevant to each one separately. Doing this will help to identify the different aspects of law relevant to the scenario.

Legal essay writing

Consider the following essay title:

> 'Critically discuss the way in which the courts have interpreted the meaning of "appropriation" in the definition of theft.'

Answering the question

There are nearly always two key elements in answering essays in law. These are:

1. setting out certain factual information on a particular area of law with supporting statutes and cases;
2. answering the actual question set which usually takes the form of some sort of critical element. This may be discussing development of law or analysing case decisions or comment on an area of law or evaluating the contribution of a case or the need for reform of an area, etc.

The first element is the easiest to do, but you must be careful to explain only relevant areas of law. Usually the question will be quite specific on the area required. In the question above the area is limited to 'appropriation' in the definition of theft. This means that there is no requirement to set out the law on the other elements of theft.

The second part involving analysis, criticism, evaluation, etc., is more demanding, but needs to be based on the law you have set out. Arguments must be supported with reference to relevant decisions. Where the judges have given different reasons for a decision or where there is a dissenting judgment then the differences need to be explored and commented on.

Putting this into practice

When explaining the law for the above title, start with the definition of appropriation in s 3(1) of the Theft Act 1968 which states 'any assumption by a person of the rights of an owner amounts to an appropriation, and this includes, where he has come by the property (innocently or not) without stealing it, any later assumption of a right to it by keeping or dealing with it as owner'. Then it is necessary to cover the following points:

1. Discuss what is meant by 'the rights' in particular, whether the assumption has to be of all of the rights or whether it can just be of any of the rights: *Morris* (1983).
2. Explain what the courts have decided where the defendant has taken the item with the consent of the owner: *Lawrence* [1972] AC 626; *Gomez* (1993).
3. Explain the decision in *Hinks* (2000) 4 All ER 833 on there being appropriation even though the consent was genuine and the goods were gifts.
4. Explain the problem of when appropriation takes place in appropriation of credit balances: *Tomsett* [1985] Crim LR 369; *Governor of Pentonville Prison, ex parte Osman* [1989] 3 All ER 701; *Governor of Brixton Prison, ex parte Levin* [1997] 3 All ER 289.
5. Explain the decisions in cases of robbery that appropriation is a continuing act: *Hale* (1979); *Lockley* (1995).

Remember that simply writing out the decisions is not enough. The question demands that you critically discuss these various decisions. There is plenty of material for discussion and comment. The points which can be raised include:

1. The fact that if appropriation had to be of all the rights of an owner, then there would be far fewer successful prosecutions for theft. The decision in *Morris* (1983) can be regarded as sensible and pragmatic.
2. The fact that cases where consent is obtained by fraud could be charged under s 15 Theft Act 1968 as obtaining by deception and the problem the judges faced when this charge had not been brought in the cases of *Lawrence* (1972) and *Gomez* (1993). The decisions can be criticised as an endeavour to ensure that the convictions for theft were upheld, because the actions of the defendants were 'criminal'.
3. Is the extension of this principle in *Hinks* (2000) to a situation where the victim had genuinely consented pushing the definition of 'appropriation' beyond what was meant in the Theft Act? The comments by Lord Hobhouse in his dissenting judgment can be usefully explored on this point.
4. The conflicting decisions in *Tomsett* (1985) and *Governor of Pentonville Prison, ex parte Osman* (1989) on when appropriation took place. Is it necessary that appropriation takes place in only one location?
5. Are decisions in the two robbery cases in conflict with the decision in *Gomez* (1993)? Can the judgment of the Court of Appeal in *Lockley* (1995) that *Gomez* (1993) had not impliedly overruled *Hale* (1979) be justified?

Conclusion

Having discussed all your points, you must then end with a conclusion in which you briefly summarise your arguments, showing where decisions are justified and where a decision is open to criticism.

Glossary of legal terminology

absolute liability
an offence where no *mens rea* is required and where *actus reus* need not be voluntary – very rare

actual bodily harm
any physical or mental harm

actus reus
the physical element of an offence (see Chapter 2 for full discussion)

aiding and abetting
providing help or encouragement to another person to commit a crime

attempt
trying to commit an offence, with intent to do so

automatism
general defence where D lacks control of the muscles or is unconscious (see Chapter 9 for full discussion)

coincidence
principle that the *actus reus* and *mens rea* elements of an offence must occur at the same time

bankruptcy
a declaration by a court that a person's liabilities exceed his assets

caveat emptor
let the buyer beware

conspiracy
an agreement to commit a criminal offence

constructive manslaughter
where V is killed by an unlawful and dangerous act (see Chapter 10 for full discussion)

contemplation principle
mental or fault element in joint enterprise cases

contempt of court
interfering with course of justice especially in relation to court proceedings

corporation
a non-human body which has a separate legal personality from its human members

counselling
advising or persuading another person to commit a crime

doli incapax
incapable of wrong

diminished responsibility
special and partial defence to murder (see Chapter 10 for full discussion)

direct intent
mental or fault element involving aim, purpose or desire

due diligence
where D has taken all possible care not to do the forbidden act or omission

duress
general defence where D is forced by threats or circumstances to commit an offence (see Chapter 8 for full discussion)

ex turpi causa
from his own wrong act

grievous bodily harm
serious physical or mental harm

gross negligence manslaughter
causing death by breaching a duty of care in circumstances of gross negligence

infanticide defence
offence where a woman kills her own child under 12 months

indictable offence
an offence that can only be tried in the Crown Court

insanity
general defence where D suffers a 'defect of reason' caused by a 'disease of the mind' (see Chapter 9 for full discussion)

intoxication
general defence where D fails to form *mens rea* because of alcohol and/or drugs (see Chapter 9 for full discussion)

joint enterprise
where two or more people commit an offence together (see Chapter 5 for full discussion)

lien
a right to retain an article in one's possession

loss of control
special and partial defence to murder (see Chapter 10 for full discussion)

M'Naghten rules
the legal principles governing the insanity defence

malice aforethought
the mental or fault element in murder

maliciously
mental or fault element meaning either intentionally or recklessly

mens rea
the mental or fault element of an offence (see chapter 3 for full discussion)

murder
the unlawful killing of a human being with malice aforethought

nolle prosequi
an order halting the prosecution of case

novus actus interveniens
a new intervening act – something which breaks the chain of causation

oblique intention
where D has foreseen a consequence as virtually certain

personal property
all moveable property

procuring
taking steps to cause another person to commit a crime

rape
non-consensual vaginal, anal or oral sex

real property
land and buildings

recklessness
foresight by D of an unjustifiable risk (see Chapter 3 for full discussion)

sexual assault
non-consensual sexual touching

suicide pact
special and partial defence to murder (see Chapter 10 for full discussion)

summary offence
an offence that can only be tried in a magistrates' court

thing in action
a right which can be enforced against another person

transferred malice
situation where the mental or fault element for an offence is transferred from one victim to another

triable either way offence
an offence which can be tried in either the magistrates' court or the Crown Court

volenti
willingly (or consenting)

wound
a cut of all the layers of skin

Index

Page numbers in *italics* denote tables, those in **bold** denote figures.